MW00810155

THE LENSMAN

Super Pack
(Positronic Super Pack Series #54)

Hardcover ISBN 13: 978-1-5154-6085-5
Trade Paperback ISBN 13: 978-1-5154-6086-2
E-book ISBN 13: 978-1-5154-6087-9

THE LENSMAN
Super Pack

ACKNOWLEDGMENTS

Triplanetary was originally published in *Amazing Stories*, January 1934, *Amazing Stories*, February 1934, *Amazing Stories*, March 1934, and *Amazing Stories*, April 1934.

First Lensman was originally published in 1950.

Galactic Patrol was originally published in *Astounding Stories*, September 1937, *Astounding Stories*, October 1937, *Astounding Stories*, November 1937, *Astounding Stories*, December 1937, *Astounding Stories*, January 1938, and *Astounding Stories*, February 1938.

Gray Lensman was originally published in *Astounding Science-Fiction*, October 1939, *Astounding Science-Fiction*, November 1939, *Astounding Science Fiction*, December 1939, and *Astounding Science-Fiction*, January 1940.

Second Stage Lensmen was originally published in *Astounding Science-Fiction*, November 1941, *Astounding Science-Fiction*, December 1941, *Astounding Science-Fiction*, January 1942, and *Astounding Science-Fiction*, February 1942.

Children of the Lens was originally published in *Astounding Science Fiction*, November 1947, *Astounding Science Fiction*, December 1947, *Astounding Science Fiction*, January 1948, *Astounding Science Fiction*, February 1948.

The Vortex Blaster was originally published in 1960.

TABLE OF CONTENTS

TRIPLANETARY

TO ROD

BOOK ONE
DAWN

ARISIA AND EDDORE

Two thousand million or so years ago two galaxies were colliding; or, rather, were passing through each other. A couple of hundreds of millions of years either way do not matter, since at least that much time was required for the inter-passage. At about that same time—within the same plus-or-minus ten percent margin of error, it is believed—practically all of the suns of both those galaxies became possessed of planets.

There is much evidence to support the belief that it was not merely a coincidence that so many planets came into being at about the same time as the galactic inter-passage. Another school of thought holds that it was pure coincidence; that all suns have planets as naturally and as inevitably as cats have kittens.

Be that as it may, Arisian records are clear upon the point that before the two galaxies began to coalesce, there were never more than three solar systems present in either; and usually only one. Thus, when the sun of the planet upon which their race originated grew old and cool, the Arisians were hard put to it to preserve their culture, since they had to work against time in solving the engineering problems associated with moving a planet from an older to a younger sun.

Since nothing material was destroyed when the Eddorians were forced into the next plane of existence, their historical records also have become available. Those records—folios and tapes and playable discs of platinum alloy, resistant indefinitely even to Eddore's noxious atmosphere—agree with those of the Arisians upon this point. Immediately before the Coalescence began there was one, and only one, planetary solar system in the Second Galaxy; and, until the advent of Eddore, the Second Galaxy was entirely devoid of intelligent life.

Thus for millions upon untold millions of years the two races, each the sole intelligent life of a galaxy, perhaps of an entire space-time continuum, remained completely in ignorance of each other. Both were already ancient at the time of the Coalescence. The only other respect in which the two were similar, however, was in the possession of minds of power.

Since Arisia was Earth-like in composition, atmosphere, and climate, the Arisians were at that time distinctly humanoid. The Eddorians were not. Eddore was and is large and dense; its liquid a poisonous, sludgy syrup; its atmosphere a foul and corrosive fog. Eddore was and is unique; so different from any other world of either galaxy that its very existence was inexplicable until its own records revealed the fact that it did not originate in normal space-time at all, but came to our universe from some alien and horribly different other.

As differed the planets, so differed the peoples. The Arisians went through the usual stages of savagery and barbarism on the way to Civilization. The Age of Stone. The Ages of Bronze, of Iron, of Steel, and of Electricity. Indeed, it is probable that it is because the Arisians went through these various stages that all subsequent Civilizations have done so, since the spores which burgeoned into life upon the cooling surfaces of all the planets of the commingling galaxies were Arisian, not Eddorian, in origin. Eddorian spores, while undoubtedly present, must have been so alien that they could not develop in any one of the environments, widely variant although they are, existing naturally or coming naturally into being in normal space and time.

The Arisians—especially after atomic energy freed them from physical labor—devoted themselves more and ever more intensively to the exploration of the limitless possibilities of the mind.

Even before the Coalescence, then, the Arisians had need neither of space-ships nor of telescopes. By power of mind alone they watched the lenticular aggregation of stars which was much later to be known to Tellurian astronomers as Lundmark's Nebula approach their own galaxy. They observed attentively and minutely and with high elation the occurrence of mathematical impossibility; for the chance of two galaxies ever meeting in direct, central, equatorial-plane impact and of passing completely through each other is an infinitesimal of such a high order as to be, even mathematically, practically indistinguishable from zero.

They observed the birth of numberless planets, recording minutely in their perfect memories every detail of everything that happened; in the hope that, as ages passed, either they or their descendants would be able to develop a symbology and a methodology capable of explaining the then inexplicable phenomenon. Carefree, busy, absorbedly intent, the Arisian mentalities roamed throughout space—until one of them struck an Eddorian mind.

*

While any Eddorian could, if it chose, assume the form of a man, they were in no sense man-like. Nor, since the term implies a softness and a lack of organization, can they be described as being amoeboid. They were both versatile and variant. Each Eddorian changed, not only its shape, but also its texture, in accordance with the requirements of the moment. Each produced—extruded—members whenever and wherever it needed them; members uniquely appropriate to the task then in work. If hardness was indicated, the members were hard; if softness, they were soft. Small or large, rigid or flexible; joined or tentacular—all one. Filaments or cables; fingers or feet; needles or mauls—equally simple. One thought and the body fitted the job.

They were asexual: sexless to a degree unapproached by any form of Tellurian life higher than the yeasts. They were not merely hermaphroditic, nor androgynous, nor parthenogenetic. They were completely without sex. They were also, to all intents and purposes and except for death by violence, immortal. For each Eddorian, as its mind approached the stagnation of saturation after a lifetime of millions of years, simply divided into two new-old beings. New in capacity and in zest; old in ability and in power, since each of the two "children" possessed in toto the knowledges and the memories of their one "parent."

And if it is difficult to describe in words the physical aspects of the Eddorians, it is virtually impossible to write or to draw, in any symbology of Civilization, a true picture of an Eddorian's—*any* Eddorian's—mind. They were intolerant, domineering, rapacious, insatiable, cold, callous, and brutal. They were keen, capable, persevering, analytical, and efficient. They had no trace of any of the softer emotions or sensibilities possessed by races adherent to Civilization. No Eddorian ever had anything even remotely resembling a sense of humor.

While not essentially bloodthirsty—that is, not loving bloodshed for its own sweet sake—they were no more averse to blood-letting than they were in favor of it. Any amount of killing which would or which might advance an Eddorian toward his goal was commendable; useless slaughter was frowned upon, not because it was slaughter, but because it was useless—and hence inefficient.

And, instead of the multiplicity of goals sought by the various entities of any race of Civilization, each and every Eddorian had only one. The same one: power. *Power!* P-O-W-E-R!!

Since Eddore was peopled originally by various races, perhaps as similar to each other as are the various human races of Earth, it is understandable that the early history of the planet—while it was still in its own space, that is—was one of continuous and ages-long war. And, since war always was and probably always will be linked solidly to technological advancement, the race now known simply as "The Eddorians" became technologists supreme. All other races disappeared. So did all other forms of life, however lowly, which interfered in any way with the Masters of the Planet.

Then, all racial opposition liquidated and overmastering lust as unquenched as ever, the surviving Eddorians fought among themselves: "push-button" wars employing engines of destruction against which the only possible defense was a fantastic thickness of planetary bedrock.

Finally, unable either to kill or to enslave each other, the comparatively few survivors made a peace of sorts. Since their own space was practically barren of planetary systems, they would move their planet from space to space until they found one which so teemed with planets that each living Eddorian could become the sole Master of an ever increasing number of worlds. This was a program very much worthwhile, promising as it did an outlet for even the recognizedly insatiable Eddorian craving for power. Therefore the Eddorians, for the first time in their prodigiously long history of fanatical non-cooperation, decided to pool their resources of mind and of material and to work as a group.

Union of a sort was accomplished eventually; neither peaceably nor without highly lethal friction. They knew that a democracy, by its very nature, was inefficient; hence a democratic form of government was not even considered. An efficient government must of necessity be dictatorial. Nor were they all exactly alike or of exactly equal ability; perfect identity of any two such complex structures was in fact impossible, and any difference, however slight, was ample justification for stratification in such a society as theirs.

Thus one of them, fractionally more powerful and more ruthless than the rest, became the All-Highest—His Ultimate Supremacy—and a group of about a dozen others, only infinitesimally weaker, became his Council; a cabinet which was later to become known as the Innermost Circle. The tally of this cabinet varied somewhat from age to age; increasing by one when a member divided, decreasing by one when a jealous fellow or an envious underling managed to perpetrate a successful assassination.

And thus, at long last, the Eddorians began really to work together. There resulted, among other things, the hyper-spatial tube and the fully inertialess drive—the drive which was, millions of years later, to be given to Civilization by an Arisian operating under the name of Bergenholm. Another result, which occured shortly after the galactic inter-passage had begun, was the eruption into normal space of the planet Eddore.

"I must now decide whether to make this space our permanent headquarters or to search farther," the All-Highest radiated harshly to his Council. "On the one hand, it will take some time for even those planets which have already formed to cool. Still more will be required for life to develop sufficiently to form a part of the empire which we have planned or to occupy our abilities to any great degree. On the other, we have already spent millions of years in surveying hundreds of millions of continua, without having found anywhere such a profusion of planets as will, in all probability, soon fill both of these galaxies. There may also be certain advantages inherent in the fact that these planets are not yet populated. As life develops, we can mold it as we please. Krongenes, what are your findings in regard to the planetary possibilities of other spaces?"

The term "Krongenes" was not, in the accepted sense, a name. Or, rather, it was more than a name. It was a key-thought, in mental shorthand; a condensation and abbreviation of the life-pattern or ego of that particular Eddorian.

"Not at all promising, Your Supremacy," Krongenes replied promptly. "No space within reach of my instruments has more than a small fraction of the inhabitable worlds which will presently exist in this one."

"Very well. Have any of you others any valid objections to the establishment of our empire here in this space? If so, give me your thought now."

No objecting thoughts appeared, since none of the monsters then knew anything of Arisia or of the Arisians. Indeed, even if they had known, it is highly improbable that any objection would have been raised. First, because no Eddorian, from the All-Highest down, could conceive or would under any circumstances admit that any race, anywhere, had ever approached or ever would approach the Eddorians in any quality whatever; and second, because, as is routine in all dictatorships, disagreement with the All-Highest did not operate to lengthen the span of life.

"Very well. We will now confer as to . . . but hold! That thought is not one of ours! Who are you, stranger, to dare to intrude thus upon a conference of the Innermost Circle?"

"I am Enphilistor, a younger student, of the planet Arisia." This name, too, was a symbol. Nor was the young Arisian yet a Watchman, as he and so many of his fellows were so soon to become, for before Eddore's arrival Arisia had had no need of Watchmen. "I am not intruding, as you know. I have not touched any one of your minds; have not read any one of your thoughts. I have been waiting for you to notice my presence, so that we could become acquainted with each other. A surprising development, truly—we have thought for many cycles of time that we were the only highly advanced life in this universe . . . ."

"Be silent, worm, in the presence of the Masters. Land your ship and surrender, and your planet will be allowed to serve us. Refuse, or even hesitate, and every individual of your race shall die."

"Worm? Masters? Land my ship?" The young Arisian's thought was pure curiosity, with no tinge of fear, dismay, or awe. "Surrender? Serve you? I seem to be receiving your thought without ambiguity, but your meaning is entirely . . . ."

"Address me as 'Your Supremacy'," the All-Highest directed, coldly. "Land now or die now—this is your last warning."

"Your Supremacy? Certainly, if that is the customary form. But as to landing—and warning—and dying—surely you do not think that I am present in the flesh? And can it be possible that you are actually so aberrant as to believe that you can kill me—or even the youngest Arisian infant? What a peculiar—what an *extraordinary*—psychology!"

"Die, then, worm, if you must have it so!" the All-Highest snarled, and launched a mental bolt whose energies were calculated to slay any living thing.

Enphilistor, however, parried the vicious attack without apparent effort. His manner did not change. He did not strike back.

The Eddorian then drove in with an analyzing probe, only to be surprised again—the Arisian's thought could not be traced! And Enphilistor, while warding off the raging Eddorian, directed a quiet thought as though he were addressing someone close by his side:

"Come in, please, one or more of the Elders. There is a situation here which I am not qualified to handle."

"We, the Elders of Arisia in fusion, are here." A grave, deeply resonant pseudo-voice filled the Eddorians' minds; each perceived in three-dimensional fidelity an aged, white-bearded human face. "You of Eddore have been expected. The course of action which we must take has been determined long since. You will forget this incident completely. For cycles upon cycles of time to come no Eddorian shall know that we Arisians exist."

Even before the thought was issued the fused Elders had gone quietly and smoothly to work. The Eddorians forgot utterly the incident which had just happened. Not one of them retained in his conscious mind any inkling that Eddore did not possess the only intelligent life in space.

*

And upon distant Arisia a full meeting of minds was held.

"But why didn't you simply kill them?" Enphilistor asked. "Such action would be distasteful in the extreme, of course—almost impossible—but even I can perceive . . . ." He paused, overcome by his thought.

"That which you perceive, youth, is but a very small fraction of the whole. We did not attempt to slay them because we could not have done so. Not because of squeamishness, as you intimate, but from sheer inability. The Eddorian tenacity of life is a thing far beyond your present understanding; to have attempted to kill them would have rendered it impossible to make them forget us. We must have time . . . cycles and cycles of time." The fusion broke off, pondered for minutes, then addressed the group as a whole:

"We, the Elder Thinkers, have not shared fully with you our visualization of the Cosmic All, because until the Eddorians actually appeared there was always the possibility that our findings might have been in error. Now, however, there is no doubt. The Civilization which has been pictured as developing peacefully upon all the teeming planets of two galaxies will not now of itself come into being. We of Arisia should be able to bring it eventually to full fruition, but the task will be long and difficult.

"The Eddorians' minds are of tremendous latent power. Were they to know of us now, it is practically certain that they would be able to develop powers and mechanisms by the use of which they would negate our every effort—they would hurl us out of this, our native space and time. We must have time . . . given time, we shall succeed. There shall be Lenses . . . and entities of Civilization worthy in every respect to wear them. But we of Arisia alone will never be able to conquer the Eddorians. Indeed, while this is not yet certain, the probability is exceedingly great that despite our utmost efforts at self-development our descendants will have to breed, from some people to evolve upon a planet not yet in existence, an entirely new race—a race tremendously more capable than ours—to succeed us as Guardians of Civilization."

*

Centuries passed. Millenia. Cosmic and geologic ages. Planets cooled to solidity and stability. Life formed and grew and developed. And as life evolved it was subjected to, and strongly if subtly affected by, the diametrically opposed forces of Arisia and Eddore.

*

THE FALL OF ATLANTIS
1. EDDORE

"Members of the Innermost Circle, wherever you are and whatever you may be doing, tune in!" the All-Highest broadcast. "Analysis of the data furnished by the survey just completed shows that in general the Great Plan is progressing satisfactorily. There seem to be only four planets which our delegates have not been or may not be able to control properly: Sol III, Rigel IV, Velantia III, and Palain VII. All four, you will observe, are in the other galaxy. No trouble whatever has developed in our own.

"Of these four, the first requires drastic and immediate personal attention. Its people, in the brief interval since our previous general survey, have developed nuclear energy and have fallen into a cultural pattern which does not conform in any respect to the basic principles laid down by us long since. Our deputies there, thinking erroneously that they could handle matters without reporting fully to or calling for help upon the next higher operating echelon, must be disciplined sharply. Failure, from whatever cause, can not be tolerated.

"Gharlane, as Master Number Two, you will assume control of Sol III immediately. This Circle now authorizes and instructs you to take whatever steps may prove necessary to restore order upon that planet. Examine carefully this data concerning the other three worlds which may very shortly become troublesome. Is it your thought that one or more others of this Circle should be assigned to work with you, to be sure that these untoward developments are suppressed?"

"It is not, Your Supremacy," that worthy decided, after a time of study. "Since the peoples in question are as yet of low intelligence; since one form of flesh at a time is all that will have to be energized; and since the techniques will be essentially similar; I can handle all four more efficiently alone than with the help or cooperation of others. If I read this data correctly, there will be need of only the most elementary precaution in the employment of mental force, since of the four races, only the Velantians have even a rudimentary knowledge of its uses. Right?"

"We so read the data." Surprisingly enough, the Innermost Circle agreed unanimously.

"Go, then. When finished, report in full."

"I go, All-Highest. I shall render a complete and conclusive report."

2. ARISIA

"We, the Elder Thinkers in fusion, are spreading in public view, for study and full discussion, a visualization of the relationships existing and to exist between Civilization and its irreconcilable and implacable foe. Several of our younger members, particularly Eukonidor, who has just attained Watchmanship, have requested instruction in this matter. Being as yet immature, their visualizations do not show clearly why Nedanillor, Kriedigan, Drounli, and Brolenteen, either singly or in fusion, have in the past performed certain acts and have not performed certain others; or that the future actions of those Moulders of Civilization will be similarly constrained.

"This visualization, while more complex, more complete, and more detailed than the one set up by our forefathers at the time of the Coalescence, agrees with it in every essential. The five basics remain unchanged. First: the Eddorians can be overcome only by mental force. Second: the magnitude of the required force is such that its only possible generator is such an organization as the Galactic Patrol toward which we have been and are working. Third: since no Arisian or any fusion of Arisians will ever be able to spearhead that force, it was and is necessary to develop a race of mentality sufficient to perform that task. Fourth: this new race, having been instrumental in removing the menace of Eddore, will as a matter of course displace the Arisians as Guardians of Civilization. Fifth: the Eddorians must not become informed of us until such a time as it will be physically, mathematically impossible for them to construct any effective counter-devices."

"A cheerless outlook, truly," came a somber thought.

"Not so, daughter. A little reflection will show you that your present thinking is loose and turbid. When that time comes, every Arisian will be ready for the change. We know the way. We do not know to what that way leads; but the Arisian purpose in this phase of existence—this space-time continuum—will have been fulfilled and we will go eagerly and joyfully on to the next. Are there any more questions?"

13

There were none.

"Study this material, then, each of you, with exceeding care. It may be that some one of you, even a child, will perceive some facet of the truth which we have missed or have not examined fully; some fact or implication which may be made to operate to shorten the time of conflict or to lessen the number of budding Civilizations whose destruction seems to us at present to be sheerly unavoidable."

Hours passed. Days. No criticisms or suggestions were offered.

"We take it, then, that this visualization is the fullest and most accurate one possible for the massed intellect of Arisia to construct from the information available at the moment. The Moulders therefore, after describing briefly what they have already done, will inform us as to what they deem it necessary to do in the near future."

"We have observed, and at times have guided, the evolution of intelligent life upon many planets," the fusion began. "We have, to the best of our ability, directed the energies of these entities into the channels of Civilization; we have adhered consistently to the policy of steering as many different races as possible toward the intellectual level necessary for the effective use of the Lens, without which the proposed Galactic Patrol cannot come into being.

"For many cycles of time we have been working as individuals with the four strongest races, from one of which will be developed the people who will one day replace us as Guardians of Civilization. Blood lines have been established. We have encouraged matings which concentrate traits of strength and dissipate those of weakness. While no very great departure from the norm, either physically or mentally, will take place until after the penultimates have been allowed to meet and to mate, a definite general improvement of each race has been unavoidable.

"Thus the Eddorians have already interested themselves in our budding Civilization upon the planet Tellus, and it is inevitable that they will very shortly interfere with our work upon the other three. These four young Civilizations must be allowed to fall. It is to warn every Arisian against well-meant but inconsidered action that this conference was called. We ourselves will operate through forms of flesh of no higher intelligence than, and indistinguishable from, the natives of the planets affected. No traceable connection will exist between those forms and us. No other Arisians will operate within extreme range of any one of those four planets; they will from now on be given the same status as has been so long accorded Eddore itself. The Eddorians must not learn of us until after it is too late for them to act effectively upon that knowledge. Any chance bit of information obtained by any Eddorian must be obliterated at once. It is to guard against and to negate such accidental disclosures that our Watchmen have been trained."

"But if all of our Civilizations go down . . . ." Eukonidor began to protest.

"Study will show you, youth, that the general level of mind, and hence of strength, is rising," the fused Elders interrupted. "The trend is ever upward; each peak and valley being higher than its predecessor. When the indicated level has been reached—the level at which the efficient use of the Lens will become possible—we will not only allow ourselves to become known to them; we will engage them at every point."

"One factor remains obscure." A Thinker broke the ensuing silence. "In this visualization I do not perceive anything to preclude the possibility that the Eddorians may at any time visualize us. Granted that the Elders of long ago did not merely visualize the Eddorians, but perceived them in time-space surveys; that they and subsequent Elders were able to maintain the status quo; and that the Eddorian way of thought is essentially mechanistic, rather than philosophic, in nature. There is still a possibility that the enemy may be able to deduce us by processes of logic alone. This thought is particularly disturbing to me at the present time because a rigid statistical analysis of the occurrences upon those four planets shows that they cannot possibly have been due to chance. With such an analysis as a starting point, a mind of even moderate ability could visualize us practically in toto. I assume, however, that this possibility has been taken into consideration, and suggest that the membership be informed."

"The point is well taken. The possibility exists. While the probability is very great that such an analysis will not be made until after we have declared ourselves, it is not a certainty. Immediately upon deducing our existence, however, the Eddorians would begin to build against us, upon the four planets and elsewhere. Since there is only one effective counter-structure possible, and since we Elders have long been alert to detect the first indications of that particular activity, we know that the situation remains unchanged. If it changes, we will call at once another full meeting of minds. Are there any other matters of moment . . . ? If not, this conference will dissolve."

3. ATLANTIS

Ariponides, recently elected Faros of Atlantis for his third five-year term, stood at a window of his office atop the towering Farostery. His hands were clasped loosely behind his back. He did not really see the tremendous expanse of quiet ocean, nor the bustling harbor, nor the metropolis spread out so magnificently and so busily beneath him. He stood there, motionless, until a subtle vibration warned him that visitors were approaching his door.

"Come in, gentlemen . . . . Please be seated." He sat down at one end of a table molded of transparent plastic. "Psychologist Talmonides, Statesman Cleto, Minister Philamon, Minister Marxes and Officer Artomenes, I have asked you to come here personally because I have every reason to believe that the shielding of this room is proof against eavesdroppers; a thing which can no longer be said of our supposedly private television channels. We must discuss, and if possible come to some decision concerning, the state in which our nation now finds itself.

"Each of us knows within himself exactly what he is. Of our own powers, we cannot surely know each others' inward selves. The tools and techniques of psychology, however, are potent and exact; and Talmonides, after exhaustive and rigorous examination of each one of us, has certified that no taint of disloyalty exists among us."

"Which certification is not worth a damn," the burly Officer declared. "What assurance do we have that Talmonides himself is not one of the ringleaders? Mind you, I have no reason to believe that he is not completely loyal. In fact, since he has been one of my best friends for over twenty years, I believe implicitly that he is. Nevertheless the plain fact is, Ariponides, that all the precautions you have taken, and any you can take, are and will be useless insofar as definite knowledge is concerned. The real truth is and will remain unknown."

"You are right," the Psychologist conceded. "And, such being the case, perhaps I should withdraw from the meeting."

"That wouldn't help, either." Artomenes shook his head. "Any competent plotter would be prepared for this, as for any other contingency. One of us others would be the real operator."

"And the fact that our Officer is the one who is splitting hairs so finely could be taken to indicate which one of us the real operator could be," Marxes pointed out, cuttingly.

"Gentlemen! Gentlemen!" Ariponides protested. "While absolute certainty is of course impossible to any finite mind, you all know how Talmonides was tested; you know that in his case there is no reasonable doubt. Such chance as exists, however, must be taken, for if we do not trust each other fully in this undertaking, failure is inevitable. With this word of warning I will get on with my report.

"This worldwide frenzy of unrest followed closely upon the controlled liberation of atomic energy and may be—probably is—traceable to it. It is in no part due to imperialistic aims or acts on the part of Atlantis. This fact cannot be stressed too strongly. We never have been and are not now interested in Empire. It is true that the other nations began as Atlantean colonies, but no attempt was ever made to hold any one of them in colonial status against the wish of its electorate. All nations were and are sister states. We gain or lose together. Atlantis, the parent, was and is a clearing-house, a co-ordinator of effort, but has never claimed or sought authority to rule; all decisions being based upon free debate and free and secret ballot.

"But now! Parties and factions everywhere, even in old Atlantis. Every nation is torn by internal dissensions and strife. Nor is this all. Uighar as a nation is insensately jealous of the Islands of the South, who in turn are jealous of Maya. Maya of Bantu, Bantu of Ekopt, Ekopt of Norheim, and Norheim of Uighar. A vicious circle, worsened by other jealousies and hatreds intercrossing everywhere. Each fears that some other is about to try to seize control of the entire world; and there seems to be spreading rapidly the utterly baseless belief that Atlantis itself is about to reduce all other nations of Earth to vassalage.

"This is a bald statement of the present condition of the world as I see it. Since I can see no other course possible within the constituted framework of our democratic government, I recommend that we continue our present activities, such as the international treaties and agreements upon which we are now at work, intensifying our effort wherever possible. We will now hear from Statesman Cleto."

"You have outlined the situation clearly enough, Faros. My thought, however, is that the principal cause of the trouble is the coming into being of this multiplicity of political parties, particularly those composed principally of crackpots and extremists. The connection with atomic energy is clear: since the atomic bomb gives a small group of people the power to destroy the world, they reason that it thereby confers upon them the authority to dictate to the world. My recommendation is merely a special case of yours;

that every effort be made to influence the electorates of Norheim and of Uighar into supporting an effective international control of atomic energy."

"You have your data tabulated in symbolics?" asked Talmonides, from his seat at the keyboard of a calculating machine.

"Yes. Here they are."

"Thanks."

"Minister Philamon," the Faros announced.

"As I see it—as any intelligent man should be able to see it—the principal contribution of atomic energy to this worldwide chaos was the complete demoralization of labor," the gray-haired Minister of Trade stated, flatly. "Output per man-hour should have gone up at least twenty percent, in which case prices would automatically have come down. Instead, short-sighted guilds imposed drastic curbs on production, and now seem to be surprised that as production falls and hourly wages rise, prices also rise and real income drops. Only one course is possible, gentlemen; labor *must* be made to listen to reason. This feather-bedding, this protected loafing, this . . . ."

"I protest!" Marxes, Minister of Work, leaped to his feet. "The blame lies squarely with the capitalists. Their greed, their rapacity, their exploitation of . . . ."

"One moment, please!" Ariponides rapped the table sharply. "It is highly significant of the deplorable condition of the times that two Ministers of State should speak as you two have just spoken. I take it that neither of you has anything new to contribute to this symposium?"

Both claimed the floor, but both were refused it by vote.

"Hand your tabulated data to Talmonides," the Faros directed. "Officer Artomenes?"

"You, our Faros, have more than intimated that our defense program, for which I am primarily responsible, has been largely to blame for what has happened," the grizzled warrior began. "In part, perhaps it was—one must be blind indeed not to see the connection, and biased indeed not to admit it. But what should I have done, knowing that there is no practical defense against the atomic bomb? Every nation has them, and is manufacturing more and more. Every nation is infested with the agents of every other. Should I have tried to keep Atlantis toothless in a world bristling with fangs? And could I—or anyone else—have succeeded in doing so?"

"Probably not. No criticism was intended; we must deal with the situation as it actually exists. Your recommendations, please?"

"I have thought this thing over day and night, and can see no solution which can be made acceptable to our—or to any real—democracy. Nevertheless, I have one recommendation to make. We all know that Norheim and Uighar are the sore spots—particularly Norheim. We have more bombs as of now than both of them together. We know that Uighar's super-sonic jobs are ready. We don't know exactly what Norheim has, since they cut my Intelligence line a while back, but I'm sending over another operative—my best man, too—tonight. If he finds out that we have enough advantage in speed, and I'm pretty sure that we have, I say hit both Norheim and Uighar right then, while we can, before they hit us. And hit them hard—pulverize them. Then set up a world government strong enough to knock out any nation—including Atlantis—that will not cooperate with it. This course of action is flagrantly against all international law and all the principles of democracy, I know; and even it might not work. It is, however, as far as I can see, the only course which *can* work."

"You—we all—perceive its weaknesses." The Faros thought for minutes. "You cannot be sure that your Intelligence has located all of the danger points, and many of them must be so far underground as to be safe from even our heaviest missiles. We all, including you, believe that the Psychologist is right in holding that the reaction of the other nations to such action would be both unfavorable and violent. Your report, please, Talmonides."

"I have already put my data into the integrator." The Psychologist punched a button and the mechanism began to whir and to click. "I have only one new fact of any importance; the name of one of the higher-ups and its corollary implication that there may be some degree of cooperation between Norheim and Uighar . . . ."

He broke off as the machine stopped clicking and ejected its report.

"Look at that graph—up ten points in seven days!" Talmonides pointed a finger. "The situation is deteriorating faster and faster. The conclusion is unavoidable—you can see yourselves that this summation line is fast approaching unity—that the outbreaks will become uncontrollable in approximately eight days. With one slight exception—here—you will notice that the lines of organization and purpose are as random as ever. In spite of this conclusive integration I would be tempted to believe that this seeming lack of coherence was due to insufficient data—that back of this whole movement there is a carefully-set-up and completely-integrated plan—except for the fact that the factions and the nations are so evenly matched. But the data are sufficient. It is shown conclusively that no one of the other nations can possibly win, even by totally destroying Atlantis. They would merely destroy each other and our entire Civilization. According to this forecast, in arriving at which the data furnished by our Officer were prime determinants, that will surely be the outcome unless remedial measures be taken at once. You are of course sure of your facts, Artomenes?"

"I am sure. But you said you had a name, and that it indicated a Norheim-Uighar hookup. What is that name?"

"An old friend of yours . . . ."

"Lo Sung!" The words as spoken were a curse of fury.

"None other. And, unfortunately, there is as yet no course of action indicated which is at all promising of success."

"Use mine, then!" Artomenes jumped up and banged the table with his fist. "Let me send two flights of rockets over right now that will blow Uigharstoy and Norgrad into radioactive dust and make a thousand square miles around each of them uninhabitable for ten thousand years! If that's the only way they can learn anything, let them learn!"

"Sit down, Officer," Ariponides directed, quietly. "That course, as you have already pointed out, is indefensible. It violates every Prime Basic of our Civilization. Moreover, it would be entirely futile, since this resultant makes it clear that every nation on Earth would be destroyed within the day."

"What, then?" Artomenes demanded, bitterly. "Sit still here and let them annihilate us?"

18

"Not necessarily. It is to formulate plans that we are here. Talmonides will by now have decided, upon the basis of our pooled knowledge, what must be done."

"The outlook is not good: not good at all," the Psychologist announced, gloomily. "The only course of action which carries any promise whatever of success—and its probability is only point one eight—is the one recommended by the Faros, modified slightly to include Artomenes' suggestion of sending his best operative on the indicated mission. For highest morale, by the way, the Faros should also interview this agent before he sets out. Ordinarily I would not advocate a course of action having so little likelihood of success; but since it is simply a continuation and intensification of what we are already doing, I do not see how we can adopt any other."

"Are we agreed?" Ariponides asked, after a short silence.

They were agreed. Four of the conferees filed out and a brisk young man strode in. Although he did not look at the Faros his eyes asked questions.

"Reporting for orders, sir." He saluted the Officer punctiliously.

"At ease, sir." Artomenes returned the salute. "You were called here for a word from the Faros. Sir, I present Captain Phryges."

"Not orders, son . . . no." Ariponides' right hand rested in greeting upon the captain's left shoulder, wise old eyes probed deeply into gold-flecked, tawny eyes of youth; the Faros saw, without really noticing, a flaming thatch of red-bronze-auburn hair. "I asked you here to wish you well; not only for myself, but for all our nation and perhaps for our entire race. While everything in my being rebels against an unprovoked and unannounced assault, we may be compelled to choose between our Officer's plan of campaign and the destruction of Civilization. Since you already know the vital importance of your mission, I need not enlarge upon it. But I want you to know fully, Captain Phryges, that all Atlantis flies with you this night."

"Th . . . thank you, sir." Phryges gulped twice to steady his voice. "I'll do my best, sir."

And later, in a wingless craft flying toward the airfield, young Phryges broke a long silence. "So *that* is the Faros . . . I like him, Officer . . . I have never seen him close up before . . . there's something about him . . . . He isn't like my father, much, but it seems as though I have known him for a thousand years!"

"Hm . . . m . . . m. Peculiar. You two are a lot alike, at that, even though you don't look anything like each other. . . . Can't put a finger on exactly what it is, but it's there." Although Artomenes nor any other of his time could place it, the resemblance was indeed there. It was in and back of the eyes; it was the "look of eagles" which was long later to become associated with the wearers of Arisia's Lens. "But here we are, and your ship's ready. Luck, son."

"Thanks, sir. But one more thing. If it should—if I don't get back—will you see that my wife and the baby are . . . ?"

"I will, son. They will leave for North Maya tomorrow morning. They will live, whether you and I do or not. Anything else?"

"No, sir. Thanks. Goodbye."

The ship was a tremendous flying wing. A standard commercial job. Empty—passengers, even crewmen, were never subjected to the brutal accelerations regularly used by unmanned carriers. Phryges scanned the panel. Tiny motors were pulling tapes through the controllers. Every light showed green. Everything was set. Donning a water-proof coverall, he slid through a flexible valve into his acceleration-tank and waited.

A siren yelled briefly. Black night turned blinding white as the harnessed energies of the atom were released. For five and six-tenths seconds the sharp, hard, beryllium-bronze leading edge of the back-sweeping V sliced its way through ever-thinning air.

The vessel seemed to pause momentarily; paused and bucked viciously. She shuddered and shivered, tried to tear herself into shreds and chunks; but Phryges in his tank was unconcerned. Earlier, weaker ships went to pieces against the solid-seeming wall of atmospheric incompressibility at the velocity of sound; but this one was built solidly enough, and powered to hit that wall hard enough, to go through unharmed.

The hellish vibration ceased; the fantastic violence of the drive subsided to a mere shove; Phryges knew that the vessel had leveled off at its cruising speed of two thousand miles per hour. He emerged, spilling the least possible amount of water upon the polished steel floor. He took off his coverall and stuffed it back through the valve into the tank. He mopped and polished the floor with towels, which likewise went into the tank.

He drew on a pair of soft gloves and, by manual control, jettisoned the acceleration tank and all the apparatus which had made that unloading possible. This junk would fall into the ocean; would sink; would never be found. He examined the compartment and the hatch minutely. No scratches, no scars, no mars; no tell-tale marks or prints of any kind. Let the Norskies search. So far, so good.

Back toward the trailing edge then, to a small escape-hatch beside which was fastened a dull black ball. The anchoring devices went out first. He gasped as the air rushed out into near-vacuum, but he had been trained to take sudden and violent fluctuations in pressure. He rolled the ball out upon the hatch, where he opened it; two hinged hemispheres, each heavily padded with molded composition resembling sponge rubber. It seemed incredible that a man as big as Phryges, especially when wearing a parachute, could be crammed into a space so small; but that lining had been molded to fit.

This ball *had* to be small. The ship, even though it was on a regularly-scheduled commercial flight, would be scanned intensively and continuously from the moment of entering Norheiman radar range. Since the ball would be invisible on any radar screen, no suspicion would be aroused; particularly since—as far as Atlantean Intelligence had been able to discover—the Norheimans had not yet succeeded in perfecting any device by the use of which a living man could bail out of a super-sonic plane.

Phryges waited—and waited—until the second hand of his watch marked the arrival of zero time. He curled up into one half of the ball; the other half closed over him and locked. The hatch opened. Ball and closely-prisoned man plummeted downward; slowing abruptly, with a horrible deceleration, to terminal velocity. Had the air been any trifle thicker the Atlantean captain would have died then and there; but that, too, had been computed accurately and Phryges lived.

And as the ball bulleted downward on a screaming slant, it *shrank!*

This, too, the Atlanteans hoped, was new—a synthetic which air-friction would erode away, molecule by molecule, so rapidly that no perceptible fragment of it would reach ground.

The casing disappeared, and the yielding porous lining. And Phryges, still at an altitude of over thirty thousand feet, kicked away the remaining fragments of his cocoon and, by judicious planning, turned himself so that he could see the ground, now dimly visible in the first dull gray of dawn. There was the highway, paralleling his line of flight; he wouldn't miss it more than a hundred yards.

He fought down an almost overwhelming urge to pull his rip-cord too soon. He had to wait—wait until the last possible second—because parachutes were big and Norheiman radar practically swept the ground.

Low enough at last, he pulled the ring. Z-r-r-e-e-k—WHAP! The chute banged open; his harness tightened with a savage jerk, mere seconds before his hard-sprung knees took the shock of landing.

That was close—too close! He was white and shaking, but unhurt, as he gathered in the billowing, fighting sheet and rolled it, together with his harness, into a wad. He broke open a tiny ampoule, and as the drops of liquid touched it the stout fabric began to disappear. It did not burn; it simply disintegrated and vanished. In less than a minute there remained only a few steel snaps and rings, which the Atlantean buried under a meticulously-replaced circle of sod.

He was still on schedule. In less than three minutes the signals would be on the air and he would know where he was—unless the Norsks had succeeded in finding and eliminating the whole Atlantean under-cover group. He pressed a stud on a small instrument; held it down. A line burned green across the dial—flared red—vanished.

"Damn!" he breathed, explosively. The strength of the signal told him that he was within a mile or so of the hide-out—first-class computation—but the red flash warned him to keep away. Kinnexa—*it had better be Kinnexa!*—would come to him.

How? By air? Along the road? Through the woods on foot? He had no way of knowing—talking, even on a tight beam, was out of the question. He made his way to the highway and crouched behind a tree. Here she could come at him by any route of the three. Again he waited, pressing infrequently a stud of his sender.

A long, low-slung ground-car swung around the curve and Phryges' binoculars were at his eyes. It was Kinnexa—or a duplicate. At the thought he dropped his glasses and pulled his guns—blaster in right hand, air-pistol in left. But no, that wouldn't do. She'd be suspicious, too—she'd have to be—and that car probably mounted heavy stuff. If he stepped out ready for business she'd fry him, and quick. Maybe not—she might have protection—but he couldn't take the chance.

The car slowed; stopped. The girl got out, examined a front tire, straightened up, and looked down the road, straight at Phryges' hiding place. This time the binoculars brought her up to little more than arm's length. Tall, blonde, beautifully built; the slightly crooked left eyebrow. The thread-line of gold betraying a one-tooth bridge and the tiny scar on her upper lip, for both of which he had been responsible—she always did insist on playing cops-and-robbers with boys older and bigger than herself—it *was* Kinnexa! Not even Norheim's science could imitate so perfectly every personalizing characteristic of a girl he had known ever since she was knee-high to a duck!

The girl slid back into her seat and the heavy car began to move. Open-handed, Phryges stepped out into its way. The car stopped.

"Turn around. Back up to me, hands behind you," she directed, crisply.

The man, although surprised, obeyed. Not until he felt a finger exploring the short hair at the back of his neck did he realize what she was seeking—the almost imperceptible scar marking the place where she bit him when she was seven years old!

"Oh, Fry! It *is* you! *Really* you! Thank the gods! I've been ashamed of that all my life, but now . . . ."

He whirled and caught her as she slumped, but she did not quite faint.

"Quick! Get in . . . drive on . . . not too fast!" she cautioned, sharply, as the tires began to scream. "The speed limit along here is seventy, and we can't be picked up."

"Easy it is, Kinny. But *give*! What's the score? Where's Kolanides? Or rather, what happened to him?"

"Dead. So are the others, I think. They put him on a psycho-bench and turned him inside out."

"But the blocks?"

"Didn't hold—over here they add such trimmings as skinning and salt to the regular psycho routine. But none of them knew anything about me, nor about how their reports were picked up, or I'd have been dead, too. But it doesn't make any difference, Fry—we're just one week too late."

"What do you mean, too late? Speed it up!" His tone was rough, but the hand he placed on her arm was gentleness itself.

"I'm telling you as fast as I can. I picked up his last report day before yesterday. They have missiles just as big and just as fast as ours—maybe more so—and they are going to fire one at Atlantis tonight at exactly seven o'clock."

"Tonight! Holy gods!" The man's mind raced.

"Yes." Kinnexa's voice was low, uninflected. "And there was nothing in the world that I could do about it. If I approached any one of our places, or tried to use a beam strong enough to reach anywhere, I would simply have got picked up, too. I've thought and thought, but could figure out only one thing that might possibly be of any use, and I couldn't do that alone. But two of us, perhaps . . . ."

"Go on. Brief me. Nobody ever accused you of not having a brain, and you know this whole country like the palm of your hand."

"Steal a ship. Be over the ramp at exactly Seven Pay Emma. When the lid opens, go into a full-power dive, beam Artomenes—if I had a second before they blanketed my wave—and meet their rocket head-on in their own launching-tube."

This was stark stuff, but so tense was the moment and so highly keyed up were the two that neither of them saw anything out of the ordinary in it.

"Not bad, if we can't figure out anything better. The joker being, of course, that you didn't see how you could steal a ship?"

"Exactly. I can't carry blasters. No woman in Norheim is wearing a coat or a cloak now, so I can't either. And just look at this dress! Do you see any place where I could hide even one?"

He looked, appreciatively, and she had the grace to blush.

"Can't say that I do," he admitted. "But I'd rather have one of our own ships, if we could make the approach. Could both of us make it, do you suppose?"

"Not a chance. They'd keep at least one man inside all the time. Even if we killed everybody outside, the ship would take off before we could get close enough to open the port with the outside controls."

"Probably. Go on. But first, are you sure that you're in the clear?"

"Positive." She grinned mirthlessly. "The fact that I am still alive is conclusive evidence that they didn't find out anything about me. But I don't want you to work on that idea if you can think of a better one. I've got passports and so on for you to be anything you want to be, from a tube-man up to an Ekoptian banker. Ditto for me, and for us both, as Mr. and Mrs."

"Smart girl." He thought for minutes, then shook his head. "No possible way out that I can see. The sneak-boat isn't due for a week, and from what you've said it probably won't get here. But you might make it, at that. I'll drop you somewhere . . . ."

"You will not," she interrupted, quietly but definitely. "Which would *you* rather—go out in a blast like that one will be, beside a good Atlantean, or, after deserting him, be psychoed, skinned, salted, and—still alive—drawn and quartered?"

"Together, then, all the way," he assented. "Man and wife. Tourists—newlyweds—from some town not too far away. Pretty well fixed, to match what we're riding in. Can do?"

"Very simple." She opened a compartment and selected one of a stack of documents. "I can fix this one up in ten minutes. We'll have to dispose of the rest of these, and a lot of other stuff, too. And you had better get out of that leather and into a suit that matches this passport photo."

"Right. Straight road for miles, and nothing in sight either way. Give me the suit and I'll change now. Keep on going or stop?"

"Better stop, I think," the girl decided. "Quicker, and we'll have to find a place to hide or bury this evidence."

While the man changed clothes, Kinnexa collected the contraband, wrapping it up in the discarded jacket. She looked up just as Phryges was adjusting his coat. She glanced at his armpits, then stared.

"Where are your blasters?" she demanded. "They ought to show, at least a little, and even I can't see a sign of them."

He showed her.

"But they're so tiny! I never saw blasters like that!"

"I've got a blaster, but it's in the tail pocket. These aren't. They're air-guns. Poisoned needles. Not worth a damn beyond a hundred feet, but deadly close up. One touch anywhere and the guy dies right then. Two seconds max."

"Nice!" She was no shrinking violet this young Atlantean spy. "You have spares, of course, and I can hide two of them easily enough in leg-holsters. Gimme, and show me how they work."

"Standard controls, pretty much like blasters. Like so." He demonstrated, and as he drove sedately down the highway the girl sewed industriously.

The day wore on, nor was it uneventful. One incident, in fact—the detailing of which would serve no useful purpose here—was of such a nature that at its end:

"Better pin-point me, don't you think, on that ramp?" Phryges asked, quietly. "Just in case you get scragged in one of these brawls and I don't?"

"Oh! Of course! Forgive me, Fry—it slipped my mind completely that you didn't know where it was. Area six; pin-point four seven three dash six oh five."

"Got it." He repeated the figures.

But neither of the Atlanteans was "scragged", and at six P.M. an allegedly honeymooning couple parked their big roadster in the garage at Norgrad Field and went through the gates. Their papers, tickets included, were in perfect order; they were as inconspicuous and as undemonstrative as newlyweds are wont to be. No more so, and no less.

Strolling idly, gazing eagerly at each new thing, they made their circuitous way toward a certain small hangar. As the girl had said, this field boasted hundreds of super-sonic fighters, so many that servicing was a round-the-clock routine. In that hangar was a sharp-nosed, stubby-V'd flyer, one of Norheim's fastest. It was serviced and ready.

It was too much to hope, of course, that the visitors could actually get into the building unchallenged. Nor did they.

"Back, you!" A guard waved them away. "Get back to the Concourse, where you belong—no visitors allowed out here!"

F-f-t! F-f-t! Phryges' air-gun broke into soft but deadly coughing. Kinnexa whirled—hands flashing down, skirt flying up-and ran. Guards tried to head her off; tried to bring their own weapons to bear. Tried—failed—died.

Phryges, too, ran; ran backward. His blaster was out now and flaming, for no living enemy remained within needle range. A rifle bullet w-h-i-n-g-e-d past his head, making him duck involuntarily and uselessly. Rifles were bad; but their hazard, too, had been considered and had been accepted.

Kinnexa reached the fighter's port, opened it, sprang in. He jumped. She fell against him. He tossed her clear, slammed and dogged the door. He looked at her then, and swore bitterly. A small, round hole marred the bridge of her nose: the back of her head was gone.

He leaped to the controls and the fleet little ship screamed skyward. He cut in transmitter and receiver, keyed and twiddled briefly. No soap. He had been afraid of that. They were already blanketing every frequency he could employ; using power through which he could not drive even a tight beam a hundred miles.

But he could still crash that missile in its tube. Or—could he? He was not afraid of other Norheiman fighters; he had a long lead and he rode one of their very fastest. But since they were already so suspicious, wouldn't they launch the bomb *before* seven o'clock? He tried vainly to coax another knot out of his wide-open engines.

With all his speed, he neared the pin-point just in time to see a trail of super-heated vapor extending up into and disappearing beyond the stratosphere. He nosed his flyer upward, locked the missile into his sights, and leveled off. Although his ship did not have the giant rocket's acceleration, he could catch it before it got to Atlantis, since he did not need its altitude and since most of its journey would be made without power. What he could do about it after he caught it he did not know, but he'd do *something*.

He caught it; and, by a feat of piloting to be appreciated only by those who have handled planes at super-sonic speeds, he matched its course and velocity. Then, from a distance of barely a hundred feet, he poured his heaviest shells into the missile's war-head. He *couldn't* be missing! It was worse than shooting sitting ducks—it was like dynamiting fish in a bucket! Nevertheless, nothing happened. The thing wasn't fuzed for impact, then, but for time; and the activating mechanism would be shell-and shock-proof.

But there was still a way. He didn't need to call Artomenes now, even if he could get through the interference which the fast-approaching pursuers were still sending out. Atlantean observers would have lined this stuff up long since; the Officer would know exactly what was going on.

Driving ahead and downward, at maximum power, Phryges swung his ship slowly into a right-angle collision course. The fighter's needle nose struck the war-head within a foot of the Atlantean's point of aim, and as he died Phryges knew that he had accomplished his mission. Norheim's missile would not strike Atlantis, but would fall at least ten miles short, and the water there was very deep. Very, *very* deep. Atlantis would not be harmed.

It might have been better, however, if Phryges had died with Kinnexa on Norgrad Field; in which case the continent would probably have endured. As it was, while that one missile did not reach the city, its frightful atomic charge exploded under six hundred fathoms of water, ten scant miles from Atlantis' harbor, and very close to an ancient geological fault.

Artomenes, as Phryges had surmised, had had time in which to act, and he knew much more than Phryges did about what was coming toward Atlantis. Too late, he knew that not one missile, but seven, had been launched from Norheim, and at least five from Uighar. The retaliatory rockets which were to wipe out Norgrad, Uigharstoy, and thousands of square miles of environs were on their way long before either bomb or earthquake destroyed all of the Atlantean launching ramps.

But when equilibrium was at last restored, the ocean rolled serenely where a minor continent had been.

THE FALL OF ROME
1. EDDORE

Like two high executives of a Tellurian corporation discussing business affairs during a chance meeting at one of their clubs, Eddore's All Highest and Gharlane, his second in command, were having the Eddorian equivalent of an after-business-hours chat.

"You did a nice job on Tellus," the All-Highest commended. "On the other three, too, of course, but Tellus was so far and away the worst of the lot that the excellence of the work stands out. When the Atlantean nations destroyed each other so thoroughly I thought that this thing called 'democracy' was done away with forever, but it seems to be mighty hard to kill. However, I take it that you have this Rome situation entirely under control?"

"Definitely. Mithradates of Pontus was mine. So were both Sulla and Marius. Through them and others I killed practically all of the brains and ability of Rome, and reduced that so-called 'democracy' to a howling, aimless mob. My Nero will end it. Rome will go on by momentum—outwardly, will even appear to grow—for a few generations, but what Nero will do can never be undone."

"Good. A difficult task, truly."

"Not difficult, exactly . . . but it's so damned *steady*." Gharlane's thought was bitter. "But that's the hell of working with such short-lived races. Since each creature lives only a minute or so, they change so fast that a man can't take his mind off of them for a second. I've been wanting to take a little vacation trip back to our old time-space, but it doesn't look as though I'll be able to do it until after they get some age and settle down."

"That won't be too long. Life-spans lengthen, you know, as races approach their norms."

"Yes. But none of the others is having half the trouble that I am. Most of them, in fact, have things coming along just about the way they want them. My four planets are raising more hell than all the rest of both galaxies put together, and I know that it isn't me—next to you, I'm the most efficient operator we've got. What I'm wondering about is why I happen to be the goat."

"Precisely because you *are* our most efficient operator." If an Eddorian can be said to smile, the All-Highest smiled. "You know, as well as I do, the findings of the Integrator."

"Yes, but I am wondering more and more as to whether to believe them unreservedly or not. Spores from an extinct life-form—suitable environments—operation of the laws of chance—Tommyrot! I am beginning to suspect that chance is being strained beyond its elastic limit, for my particular benefit, and as soon as I can find out who is doing that straining there will be one empty place in the Innermost Circle."

"Have a care, Gharlane!" All levity, all casualness disappeared. "Whom do you suspect? Whom do you accuse?"

"Nobody, as yet. The true angle never occurred to me until just now, while I have been discussing the thing with you. Nor shall I either suspect or accuse, ever. I shall determine, then I shall act."

"In defiance of *me*? Of my orders?" the All-Highest demanded, his short temper flaring.

"Say, rather, in support," the lieutenant shot back, unabashed. "If some one is working on me through my job, what position are you probably already in, without knowing it? Assume that I am right, that these four planets of mine got the way they are because of monkey business inside the Circle. Who would be next? And how sure are you that there isn't something similar, but not so far advanced, already aimed at you? It seems to me that serious thought is in order."

"Perhaps so . . . . You may be right . . . . There have been a few nonconformable items. Taken separately, they did not seem to be of any importance; but together, and considered in this new light . . . ."

Thus was borne out the conclusion of the Arisian Elders that the Eddorians would not at that time deduce Arisia; and thus Eddore lost its chance to begin in time the forging of a weapon with which to oppose effectively Arisia's—Civilization's—Galactic Patrol, so soon to come into being.

If either of the two had been less suspicious, less jealous, less arrogant and domineering—in other words, had not been Eddorians—this History of Civilization might never have been written; or written very differently and by another hand.

Both were, however, Eddorians.

2. ARISIA

In the brief interval between the fall of Atlantis and the rise of Rome to the summit of her power, Eukonidor of Arisia had aged scarcely at all. He was still a youth. He was, and would be for many centuries to come, a Watchman. Although his mind was powerful enough to understand the Elders' visualization of the course of Civilization—in fact, he had already made significant progress in his own visualization of the Cosmic All—he was not sufficiently mature to contemplate unmoved the events which, according to all Arisian visualizations, were bound to occur.

"Your feeling is but natural, Eukonidor." Drounli, the Moulder principally concerned with the planet Tellus, meshed his mind smoothly with that of the young Watchman. "We do not enjoy it ourselves, as you know. It is, however, *necessary*. In no other way can the ultimate triumph of Civilization be assured."

"But can nothing be done to alleviate . . . ?" Eukonidor paused.

Drounli waited. "Have you any suggestions to offer?"

"None," the younger Arisian confessed. "But I thought . . . you, or the Elders, so much older and stronger . . . could . . . ."

"We can not. Rome will fall. It must be allowed to fall."

"It will be Nero, then? And we can do nothing?"

"Nero. We can do little enough. Our forms of flesh—Petronius, Acte, and the others—will do whatever they can; but their powers will be exactly the same as those of other human beings of their time. They must be and will be constrained, since any show of unusual powers, either mental or physical, would be detected instantly and would be far too revealing. On the other hand, Nero—that is, Gharlane of Eddore—will be operating much more freely."

"Very much so. Practically unhampered, except in purely physical matters. But, if nothing can be done to stop it . . . . If Nero must be allowed to sow his seeds of ruin . . . ."

And upon that cheerless note the conference ended.

3. ROME

THE LENSMAN

"But what have you, Livius, or any of us, for that matter, got to live for?" demanded Patroclus the gladiator of his cell-mate. "We are well fed, well kept, well exercised; like horses. But, like horses, we are lower than slaves. Slaves have some freedom of action; most of us have none. We fight—fight whoever or whatever our cursed owners send us against. Those of us who live fight again; but the end is certain and comes soon. I had a wife and children once. So did you. Is there any chance, however slight, that either of us will ever know them again; or learn even whether they live or die? None. At this price, is your life worth living? Mine is not."

Livius the Bithynian, who had been staring out past the bars of the cubicle and over the smooth sand of the arena toward Nero's garlanded and purple-bannered throne, turned and studied his fellow gladiator from toe to crown. The heavily-muscled legs, the narrow waist, the sharply-tapering torso, the enormous shoulders. The leonine head, surmounted by an unkempt shock of red-bronze-auburn hair. And, lastly, the eyes—gold-flecked, tawny eyes—hard and cold now with a ferocity and a purpose not to be concealed.

"I have been more or less expecting something of this sort," Livius said then, quietly. "Nothing overt—you have builded well, Patroclus—but to one who knows gladiators as I know them there has been something in the wind for weeks past. I take it that someone swore his life for me and that I should not ask who that friend might be."

"One did. You should not."

"So be it. To my unknown sponsor, then, and to the gods, I give thanks, for I am wholly with you. Not that I have any hope. Although your tribe breeds men—from your build and hair and eyes you descend from Spartacus himself—you know that even he did not succeed. Things now are worse, infinitely worse, than they were in his day. No one who has ever plotted against Nero has had any measure of success; not even his scheming slut of a mother. All have died, in what fashions you know. Nero is vile, the basest of the base. Nevertheless, his spies are the most efficient that the world has ever known. In spite of that, I feel as you do. If I can take with me two or three of the Praetorians, I die content. But by your look, your plan is not what I thought, to storm vainly Nero's podium yonder. Have you, by any chance, some trace of hope of success?"

"More than a trace; much more." The Thracian's teeth bared in a wolfish grin. "His spies are, as you say, very good. But, this time, so are we. Just as hard and just as ruthless. Many of his spies among us have died; most, if not all, of the rest are known. They, too, shall die. Glatius, for instance. Once in a while, by the luck of the gods, a man kills a better man than he is; but Glatius has done it six times in a row, without getting a scratch. But the next time he fights, in spite of Nero's protection, Glatius dies. Word has gone out, and there are gladiators' tricks that Nero never heard of."

"Quite true. One question, and I too may begin to hope. This is not the first time that gladiators have plotted against Ahenobarbus. Before the plotters could accomplish anything, however, they found themselves matched against each other and the signal was always for death, never for mercy. Has this . . . ?" Livius paused.

"It has not. It is that which gives me the hope I have. Nor are we gladiators alone in this. We have powerful friends at court; one of whom has for days been carrying a knife sharpened especially to slip between Nero's ribs. That he still carries that knife and that we still live are proofs enough for me that Ahenobarbus, the matricide and incendiary, has no suspicion whatever of what is going on."

(At this point Nero on his throne burst into a roar of laughter, his gross body shaking with a merriment which Petronius and Tigellinus ascribed to the death-throes of a Christian woman in the arena.)

"Is there any small thing which I should be told in order to be of greatest use?" Livius asked.

"Several. The prisons and the pits are so crowded with Christians that they die and stink, and a pestilence threatens. To mend matters, some scores of hundreds of them are to be crucified here tomorrow."

"Why not? Everyone knows that they are poisoners of wells and murderers of children, and practitioners of magic. Wizards and witches."

"True enough." Patroclus shrugged his massive shoulders. "But to get on, tomorrow night, at full dark, the remaining hundreds who have not been crucified are to be—have you ever seen sarmentitii and semaxii?"

"Once only. A gorgeous spectacle, truly, almost as thrilling as to feel a man die on your sword. Men and women, wrapped in oil-soaked garments smeared with pitch and chained to posts, make splendid torches indeed. You mean, then, that . . . ?"

"Aye. In Caesar's own garden. When the light is brightest Nero will ride in parade. When his chariot passes the tenth torch our ally swings his knife. The Praetorians will rush around, but there will be a few moments of confusion during which we will go into action and the guards will die. At the same time others of our party will take the palace and kill every man, woman, and child adherent to Nero."

"Very nice—in theory." The Bithynian was frankly skeptical. "But just how are we going to get there? A few gladiators—such champions as Patroclus of Thrace—are at times allowed to do pretty much as they please in their free time, and hence could possibly be on hand to take part in such a brawl, but most of us will be under lock and guard."

"That too, has been arranged. Our allies near the throne and certain other nobles and citizens of Rome, who have been winning large sums by our victories, have prevailed upon our masters to give a grand banquet to *all* gladiators tomorrow night, immediately following the mass crucifixion. It is going to be held in the Claudian Grove, just across from Caesar's Gardens."

"Ah!" Livius breathed deep; his eyes flashed. "By Baal and Bacchus! By the round, high breasts of Isis! For the first time in years I begin to live! Our masters die first, then there . . . but hold—weapons?"

"Will be provided. Bystanders will have them, and armor and shields, under their cloaks. Our owners first, yes; and then the Praetorians. But note, Livius, that Tigellinus, the Commander of the Guard, is mine—mine alone. I, personally, am going to cut his heart out."

"Granted. I heard that he had your wife for a time. But you seem quite confident that you will still be alive tomorrow night. By Baal and Ishtar, I wish I could feel so! With something to live for at last, I can feel my guts turning to water—I can hear Charon's oars. Like as not, now, some toe-dancing stripling of a retiarius will entangle me in his net this very afternoon, and no mercy signal has been or will be given this day. Such is the crowd's temper, from Caesar down, that even you will get 'Pollice verso' if you fall."

"True enough. But you had better get over that feeling, if you want to live. As for me, I'm safe enough. I have made a vow to Jupiter, and he who has protected me so long will not desert me now. Any man or any thing who faces me during these games, dies."

"I hope so, sin . . . but listen! The horns . . . and someone is coming!"

The door behind them swung open. A lanista, or master of gladiators, laden with arms and armor, entered. The door swung to and was locked from the outside. The visitor was obviously excited, but stared wordlessly at Patroclus for seconds.

"Well, Iron-heart," he burst out finally, "aren't you even curious about what you have got to do today?"

"Not particularly," Patroclus replied, indifferently. "Except to dress to fit. Why? Something special?"

"*Extra* special. The sensation of the year. Fermius himself. Unlimited. Free choice of weapons and armor."

"Fermius!" Livius exclaimed. "Fermius the Gaul? May Athene cover you with her shield!"

"You can say that for me, too," the lanista agreed, callously. "Before I knew who was entered, like a fool, I bet a hundred sesterces on Patroclus here, at odds of only one to two, against the field. But listen, Bronze-head. If you get the best of Fermius, I'll give you a full third of my winnings."

"Thanks. You'll collect. A good man, Fermius, and smart. I've heard a lot about him, but never saw him work. He has seen me, which isn't so good. Both heavy and fast—somewhat lighter than I am, and a bit faster. He knows that I always fight Thracian, and that I'd be a fool to try anything else against him. He fights either Thracian or Samnite depending upon the opposition. Against me his best bet would be to go Samnite. Do you know?"

"No. They didn't say. He may not decide until the last moment."

"Unlimited, against me, he'll go Samnite. He'll have to. These unlimiteds are tough, but it gives me a chance to use a new trick I've been working on. I'll take that sword there—no scabbard—and two daggers, besides my gladius. Get me a mace; the lightest real mace they've got in their armory."

"A *mace*! Fighting *Thracian*, against a *Samnite*?"

"Exactly. A mace. Am I going to fight Fermius, or do you want to do it yourself?"

The mace was brought and Patroclus banged it, with a two-handed roundhouse swing, against a stone of the wall. The head remained solid upon the shaft. Good. They waited.

Trumpets blared; the roar of the vast assemblage subsided almost to silence.

"Grand Champion Fermius versus Grand Champion Patroclus," came the raucous announcement. "Single combat. Any weapons that either chooses to use, used in any way possible. No rest, no intermission. Enter!"

Two armored figures strode toward the center of the arena. Patroclus' armor, from towering helmet down, and including the shield, was of dully-gleaming steel, completely bare of ornament. Each piece was marred and scarred; very plainly that armor was for use and had been used. On the other hand, the Samnite half-armor of the Gaul was resplendent with the decorations affected by his race. Fermius' helmet sported three brilliantly-colored plumes, his shield and cuirass, enameled in half the colors of the spectrum, looked as though they were being worn for the first time.

Five yards apart, the gladiators stopped and wheeled to face the podium upon which Nero lolled. The buzz of conversation—the mace had excited no little comment and speculation—ceased. Patroclus heaved his ponderous weapon into the air; the Gaul whirled up his long, sharp sword. They chanted in unison:

> "Ave, Caesar Imperator!
> Morituri te salutant!"

The starting-flag flashed downward; and at its first sight, long before it struck the ground, both men moved. Fermius whirled and leaped; but, fast as he was, he was not quite fast enough. That mace, which had seemed so heavy in the Thracian's hands a moment before, had become miraculously maneuverable—it was hurtling through the air directly toward the middle of his body! It did not strike its goal—Patroclus hoped that he was the only one there who suspected that he had not expected it to touch his opponent—but in order to dodge the missile Fermius had to break his stride; lost momentarily the fine co-ordination of his attack. And in that moment Patroclus struck. Struck, and struck again.

But, as has been said, Fermius was both strong and fast. The first blow, aimed backhand at his bare right leg, struck his shield instead. The left-handed stab, shield-encumbered as the left arm was, ditto. So did the next trial, a vicious forehand cut. The third of the mad flurry of swordcuts, only partially deflected by the sword which Fermius could only then get into play, sheared down and a red, a green, and a white plume floated toward the ground. The two fighters sprang apart and studied each other briefly.

From the gladiators' standpoint, this had been the veriest preliminary skirmishing. That the Gaul had lost his plumes and that his armor showed great streaks of missing enamel meant no more to either than that the Thracian's supposedly surprise attack had failed. Each knew that he faced the deadliest fighter of his world; but if that knowledge affected either man, the other could not perceive it.

But the crowd went wild. Nothing like that first terrific passage-at-arms had ever before been seen. Death, sudden and violent, had been in the air. The arena was saturated with it. Hearts had been ecstatically in throats. Each person there, man or woman, had felt the indescribable thrill of death—vicariously, safely—and every fiber of their lusts demanded more. More! Each spectator knew that one of those men would die that afternoon. None wanted, or would permit them both to live. This was to the death, and death there would be.

Women, their faces blotched and purple with emotion, shrieked and screamed. Men, stamping their feet and waving their arms, yelled and swore. And many, men and women alike, laid wagers.

"Five hundred sesterces on Fermius!" one shouted, tablet and stylus in air.

"Taken!" came an answering yell. "The Gaul is done—Patroclus all but had him there!"

"One thousand, you!" came another challenge. "Patroclus missed his chance and will never get another—a thousand on Fermius!"

"Two thousand!"

"Five thousand!"

"Ten!"

The fighters closed—swung—stabbed. Shields clanged vibrantly under the impact of fended strokes, swords whined and snarled. Back and forth—circling—giving and taking ground—for minute after endless minute that desperately furious exhibition of skill, of speed and of power and of endurance went on. And as it went on, longer and longer past the time expected by even the most optimistic, tension mounted higher and higher.

Blood flowed crimson down the Gaul's bare leg and the crowd screamed its approval. Blood trickled out of the joints of the Thracian's armor and it became a frenzied mob.

No human body could stand that pace for long. Both men were tiring fast, and slowing. With the drive of his weight and armor, Patroclus forced the Gaul to go where he wanted him to go. Then, apparently gathering his every resource for a final effort, the Thracian took one short, choppy step forward and swung straight down, with all his strength.

The blood-smeared hilt turned in his hands; the blade struck flat and broke, its length whining viciously away. Fermius, although staggered by the sheer brute force of the abortive stroke, recovered almost instantly; dropping his sword and snatching at his gladius to take advantage of the wonderful opportunity thus given him.

But that breaking had not been accidental; Patroclus made no attempt to recover his balance. Instead, he ducked past the surprised and shaken Gaul. Still stooping, he seized the mace, which everyone except he had forgotten, and swung; swung with all the totalized and synchronized power of hands, wrists, arms, shoulders, and magnificent body.

The iron head of the ponderous weapon struck the center of the Gaul's cuirass, which crunched inward like so much cardboard. Fermius seemed to leave the ground and, folded around the mace, to fly briefly through the air. As he struck the ground, Patroclus was upon him. The Gaul was probably already dead—that blow would have killed an elephant—but that made no difference. If that mob knew that Fermius was dead, they might start yelling for his life, too. Hence, by lifting his head and poising his dirk high in air, he asked of Caesar his Imperial will.

The crowd, already frantic, had gone stark mad at the blow. No thought of mercy could or did exist in that insanely bloodthirsty throng; no thought of clemency for the man who had fought such a magnificent fight. In cooler moments they would have wanted him to live, to thrill them again and yet again; but now, for almost half an hour, they had been loving the hot, the suffocating thrill of death in their throats. Now they wanted, and would have, the ultimate thrill.

"Death!" The solid structure rocked to the crescendo roar of the demand. "*Death!* DEATH!"

Nero's right thumb pressed horizontally against his chest. Every vestal was making the same sign. Pollice verso. Death. The strained and strident yelling of the mob grew even louder.

Patroclus lowered his dagger and delivered the unnecessary and unfelt thrust; and—

"Peractum est!" arose one deafening yell.

*

Thus the red-haired Thracian lived; and also, somewhat to his own surprise, did Livius.

"I'm glad to see you, Bronze-heart, by the white thighs of Ceres, I am!" that worthy exclaimed, when the two met, the following day. Patroclus had never seen the Bithynian so buoyant. "Pallas Athene covered you, like I asked her to. But by the red beak of Thoth and the sacred Zaimph of Tanit, it gave me the horrors when you made that throw so quick and missed it, and I went as crazy as the rest of them when you pulled the real coup. But now, curse it, I suppose that we'll all have to be on the lookout for it—or no, unlimiteds aren't common, thank Ninib the Smiter and his scarlet spears!"

"I hear you didn't do so badly, yourself," Patroclus interrupted his friend's loquacity. "I missed your first two, but I saw you take Kalendios. He's a high-rater—one of the best of the locals—and I was afraid he might snare you, but from the looks of you, you got only a couple of stabs. Nice work."

"Prayer, my boy. Prayer is the stuff. I prayed to 'em in order, and hit the jackpot with Shamash. My guts curled up again, like they belong, and I knew that the portents were all in my favor. Besides, when you were walking out to meet Fermius, did you notice that red-headed Greek posturer making passes at you?"

"Huh? Don't be a fool. I had other things to think of."

"So I figured. So did she, probably, because after a while she came around behind with a lanista and made eyes at me. I must have the next best shape to you here, I guess. What a wench! Anyway, I felt better and better, and before she left I knew that no damn retiarius that ever waved a trident could put a net past my guard. And they couldn't either. A couple more like that and I'll be a Grand Champion myself. But they're digging holes for the crosses and there's the horn that the feast is ready. This show is going to be really good."

They ate, hugely and with unmarred appetite, of the heaped food which Nero had provided. They returned to their assigned places to see crosses, standing as close together as they could be placed and each bearing a suffering Christian, filling the whole vast expanse of the arena.

And, if the truth must be told, those two men enjoyed thoroughly every moment of that long and sickeningly horrible afternoon. They were the hardest products of the hardest school the world has ever known: trained rigorously to deal out death mercilessly at command; to accept death unflinchingly at need. They should not and can not be judged by the higher, finer standards of a softer, gentler day.

The afternoon passed; evening approached. All the gladiators then in Rome assembled in the Claudian Grove, around tables creaking under their loads of food and wine. Women, too, were there in profusion; women for the taking and yearning to be taken; and the tide of revelry ran open, wide, and high. Although all ate and apparently drank

33

with abandon, most of the wine was in fact wasted. And as the sky darkened, most of the gladiators, one by one, began to get rid of their female companions upon one pretext or another and to drift toward the road which separated the festivities from the cloaked and curious throng of lookers-on.

At full dark, a red glare flared into the sky from Caesar's garden and the gladiators, deployed now along the highway, dashed across it and seemed to wrestle briefly with cloaked figures. Then armed, more-or-less-armored men ran back to the scene of their reveling. Swords, daggers, and gladii thrust, stabbed, and cut. Tables and benches ran red; ground and grass grew slippery with blood.

The conspirators turned then and rushed toward the Emperor's brilliantly torch-lit garden. Patroclus, however, was not in the van. He had had trouble in finding a cuirass big enough for him to get into. He had been delayed further by the fact that he had had to kill three strange lanistae before he could get at his owner, the man he really wanted to slay. He was therefore some little distance behind the other gladiators when Petronius rushed up to him and seized him by the arm.

White and trembling, the noble was not now the exquisite Arbiter Elegantiae; nor the imperturbable Augustian.

"Patroclus! In the name of Bacchus, Patroclus, why do the men go there now? No signal was given—I could not get to Nero!"

"What?" the Thracian blazed. "Vulcan and his fiends! It *was* given—I heard it myself! What went wrong?"

"Everything." Petronius licked his lips. "I was standing right beside him. No one else was near enough to interfere. It was—should have been—easy. But after I got my knife out I couldn't move. It was his *eyes*, Patroclus—I swear it, by the white breasts of Venus! He has the evil eye—I couldn't move a muscle, I tell you! Then, although I didn't want to, I turned and ran!"

"How did you find *me* so quick?"

"I—I—I—don't know," the frantic Arbiter stuttered. "I ran and ran, and there you were. But what are we—you—going to do?"

Patroclus' mind raced. He believed implicitly that Jupiter guarded him personally. He believed in the other gods and goddesses of Rome. He more than half believed in the multitudinous deities of Greece, of Egypt, and even of Babylon. The other world was real and close; the evil eye only one of the many inexplicable facts of every-day life. Nevertheless, in spite of his credulity—or perhaps in part because of it—he also believed firmly in himself; in his own powers. Wherefore he soon came to a decision.

"Jupiter, ward from me Ahenobarbus' evil eye!" he called aloud, and turned.

"Where are you going?" Petronius, still shaking, demanded.

"To do the job *you* swore to do, of course—to kill that bloated toad. And then to give Tigellinus what I have owed him so long."

At full run, he soon overtook his fellows, and waded resistlessly into the fray. He was Grand Champion Patroclus, working at his trade; the hard-learned trade which he knew so well. No Praetorian or ordinary soldier could stand before him save momentarily. He did not have all of his Thracian armor, but he had enough. Man after man faced him, and man after man died.

And Nero, sitting at ease with a beautiful boy at his right and a beautiful harlot at his left, gazed appreciatively through his emerald lens at the flaming torches; the while, with a very small fraction of his Eddorian mind, he mused upon the matter of Patroclus and Tigellinus.

Should he let the Thracian kill the Commander of his Guard? Or not? It didn't really matter, one way or the other. In fact, nothing about this whole foul planet—this ultra-microscopic, if offensive, speck of cosmic dust in the Eddorian Scheme of Things—really mattered at all. It would be mildly amusing to watch the gladiator consummate his vengeance by carving the Roman to bits: But, on the other hand, there was such a thing as pride of workmanship. Viewed in that light, the Thracian could not kill Tigellinus, because that bit of corruption had a few more jobs to do. He must descend lower and lower into unspeakable depravity, finally to cut his own throat with a razor. Although Patroclus would not know it—it was better technique not to let him know it—the Thracian's proposed vengeance would have been futility itself compared with that which the luckless Roman was to wreak on himself.

Wherefore a shrewdly-placed blow knocked the helmet from Patroclus' head and a mace crashed down, spattering his brains abroad.

*

Thus ended the last significant attempt to save the civilization of Rome; in a fiasco so complete that even such meticulous historians as Tacitus and Suetonius mention it merely as a minor disturbance of Nero's garden party.

*

The planet Tellus circled its sun some twenty hundred times. Sixty-odd generations of men were born and died, but that was not enough. The Arisian program of genetics required more. Therefore the Elders, after due deliberation, agreed that that Civilization, too, must be allowed to fall. And Gharlane of Eddore, recalled to duty from the middle of a much-too-short vacation, found things in very bad shape indeed and went busily to work setting them to rights. He had slain one fellow-member of the Innermost Circle, but there might very well have been more than one Master involved.

BOOK TWO
THE WORLD WAR

1918

Sobbing furiously, Captain Ralph Kinnison wrenched at his stick—with half of his control surfaces shot away the crate was hellishly logy. He could step out, of course, the while saluting the victorious Jerries, but he wasn't on fire—yet—and hadn't been hit—yet. He ducked and flinched sidewise as another burst of bullets stitched another seam along his riddled fuselage and whanged against his dead engine. Afire? Not yet—good! Maybe he could land the heap, after all!

Slowly—oh, *so* sluggishly—the Spad began to level off, toward the edge of the wheatfield and that friendly, inviting ditch. If the krauts didn't get him with their next pass . . . .

He heard a chattering beneath him—Brownings, by God!—and the expected burst did not come. He knew that he had been just about over the front when they conked his engine; it was a toss-up whether he would come down in enemy territory or not. But now, for the first time in ages, it seemed, there were machine-guns going that were not aimed at him!

His landing-gear swished against stubble and he fought with all his strength of body and of will to keep the Spad's tail down. He almost succeeded; his speed was almost spent when he began to nose over. He leaped, then, and as he struck ground he curled up and rolled—he had been a motorcycle racer for years—feeling as he did so a wash of heat: a tracer had found his gas-tank at last! Bullets were thudding into the ground; one shrieked past his head as, stooping over, folded into the smallest possible target, he galloped awkwardly toward the ditch.

The Brownings still yammered, filling the sky with cupro-nickeled lead; and while Kinnison was flinging himself full length into the protecting water and mud, he heard a tremendous crash. One of those Huns had been too intent on murder; had stayed a few seconds too long; had come a few meters too close.

The clamor of the guns stopped abruptly.

"We got one! We got one!" a yell of exultation.

"Stay down! Keep low, you boneheads!" roared a voice of authority, quite evidently a sergeant's. "Wanna get your blocks shot off? Take down them guns; we gotta get to hell out of here. Hey, you flyer! Are you O.K., or wounded, or maybe dead?"

Kinnison spat out mud until he could talk. "O.K.!" he shouted, and started to lift an eye above the low bank. He stopped, however, as whistling metal, sheeting in from the north, told him that such action would be decidedly unsafe. "But I ain't leaving this ditch right now—sounds mighty hot out there!"

"You said it, brother. It's hotter than the hinges of hell, from behind that ridge over there. But ooze down that ditch a piece, around the first bend. It's pretty well in the clear there, and besides, you'll find a ledge of rocks running straight across the flat. Cross over there and climb the hill—join us by that dead snag up there. We got to get out of here. That sausage over there must have seen this shindig and they'll blow this whole damn area off the map. Snap it up! And you, you goldbricks, get the lead out of your pants!"

Kinnison followed directions. He found the ledge and emerged, scraping thick and sticky mud from his uniform. He crawled across the little plain. An occasional bullet whined through the air, far above him; but, as the sergeant had said, this bit of terrain was "in the clear." He climbed the hill, approached the gaunt, bare tree-trunk. He heard men moving, and cautiously announced himself.

"OK., fella," came the sergeant's deep bass. "Yeah, it's us. Shake a leg!"

"That's easy!" Kinnison laughed for the first time that day. "I'm shaking already, like a hula-hula dancer's empennage. What outfit is this, and where are we?"

"BRROOM!" The earth trembled, the air vibrated. Below and to the north, almost exactly where the machine-guns had been, an awe-inspiring cloud billowed majestically into the air; a cloud composed of smoke, vapor, pulverized earth, chunks of rock, and debris of what had been trees. Nor was it alone.

"Crack! Bang! Tweet! Boom! Wham!" Shells of all calibers, high explosive and gas, came down in droves. The landscape disappeared. The little company of Americans, in complete silence and with one mind, devoted themselves to accumulating distance. Finally, when they had to stop for breath:

"Section B, attached to the 76th Field Artillery," the sergeant answered the question as though it had just been asked. "As to where we are, somewhere between Berlin and Paris is about all I can tell you. We got hell knocked out of us yesterday, and have been running around lost ever since. They shot off a rally signal on top of this here hill, though, and we was just going to shove off when we seen the krauts chasing you."

"Thanks. I'd better rally with you, I guess—find out where we are, and what's the chance of getting back to my own outfit."

"Damn slim, I'd say. Boches are all around us here, thicker than fleas on a dog."

They approached the summit, were challenged, were accepted. They saw a gray-haired man—an old man, for such a location—seated calmly upon a rock, smoking a cigarette. His smartly-tailored uniform, which fitted perfectly his not-so-slender figure, was muddy and tattered. One leg of his breeches was torn half away, revealing a blood-soaked bandage. Although he was very evidently an officer, no insignia were visible. As Kinnison and the gunners approached, a first lieutenant—practically spic-and-span—spoke to the man on the rock.

"First thing to do is to settle the matter of rank," he announced, crisply. "I'm First Lieutenant Randolph, of . . . ."

"Rank, eh?" The seated one grinned and spat out the butt of his cigarette. "But then, it was important to me, too, when I was a first lieutenant—about the time that you were born. Slayton, Major-General."

"Oh . . . excuse me, sir . . . ."

"Skip it. How many men you got, and what are they?"

"Seven, sir. We brought in a wire from Inf . . . ."

"A *wire*! Hellanddamnation, why haven't you got it with you, then? Get it!"

The crestfallen officer disappeared; the general turned to Kinnison and the sergeant.

"Have you got any ammunition, sergeant?"

"Yes, sir. About thirty belts."

"Thank God! We can use it, and you. As for you, Captain, I don't know . . . ."

The wire came up. The general seized the instrument and cranked.

"Get me Spearmint . . . Spearmint? Slayton—give me Weatherby . . . . This is Slayton . . . yes, but . . . No, but I want . . . Hellanddamnation, Weatherby, shut up and let me talk—don't you know that this wire's apt to be cut any second? We're on top of Hill Fo-wer, Ni-yun, Sev-en—that's right—about two hundred men; maybe three. Composite—somebody, apparently, from half the outfits in France. Too fast and too far—both flanks wide open—cut off . . . Hello! Hello! Hello!" He dropped the instrument and turned to Kinnison. "You want to go back, Captain, and I need a runner—bad. Want to try to get through?"

"Yes, sir."

"First phone you come to, get Spearmint—General Weatherby. Tell him Slayton says that we're cut off, but the Germans aren't in much force nor in good position, and for God's sake to get some air and tanks in here to keep them from consolidating. Just a minute. Sergeant, what's your name?" He studied the burly non-com minutely.

"Wells, sir."

"What would you say ought to be done with the machine-guns?"

"Cover that ravine, there, first. Then set up to enfilade if they try to come up over there. Then, if I could find any more guns, I'd . . . ."

"Enough. Second Lieutenant Wells, from now. GHQ will confirm. Take charge of all the guns we have. Report when you have made disposition. Now, Kinnison, listen. I can probably hold out until tonight. The enemy doesn't know yet that we're here, but we are due for some action pretty quick now, and when they locate us—if there aren't too many of their own units here, too—they'll flatten this hill like a table. So tell Weatherby to throw a column in here as soon as it gets dark, and to advance Eight and Sixty, so as to consolidate this whole area. Got it?"

"Yes, sir."

"Got a compass?"

"Yes, sir."

"Pick up a tin hat and get going. A hair north of due west, about a kilometer and a half. Keep cover, because the going will be tough. Then you'll come to a road. It's a mess, but it's ours—or was, at last accounts—so the worst of it will be over. On that road, which goes south-west, about two kilometers further, you'll find a Post—you'll know it by the motorcycles and such. Phone from there. Luck!"

Bullets began to whine and the general dropped to the ground and crawled toward a coppice, bellowing orders as he went. Kinnison crawled, too, straight west, availing himself of all possible cover, until he encountered a sergeant-major reclining against the south side of a great tree.

"Cigarette, buddy?" that wight demanded.

"Sure. Take the pack. I've got another that'll last me—maybe more. But what the hell goes on here? Who ever heard of a major general getting far enough up front to get shot in the leg, and he talks as though he were figuring on licking the whole German army. Is the old bird nuts, or what?"

"Not so you would notice it. Didn'cha ever hear of 'Hellandamnation' Slayton? You will, buddy, you will. If Pershing doesn't give him three stars after this, he's crazier than hell. He ain't supposed to be on combat at all—he's from GHQ and can make or break anybody in the AEF. Out here on a look-see trip and couldn't get back. But you got to hand it to him—he's getting things organized in great shape. I came in with him—I'm about all that's left of them that did—just waiting for this breeze to die down, but its getting worse. We'd better duck—over there!"

Bullets whistled and stormed, breaking more twigs and branches from the already shattered, practically denuded trees. The two slid precipitately into the indicated shell-hole, into stinking mud. Wells' guns burst into action.

"Damn! I hated to do this," the sergeant grumbled, "On accounta I just got half dry."

"Wise me up," Kinnison directed. "The more I know about things, the more apt I am to get through."

"This is what is left of two battalions, and a lot of casuals. They made objective, but it turns out the outfits on their right and left couldn't, leaving their flanks right out in the open air. Orders come in by blinker to rectify the line by falling back, but by then it couldn't be done. Under observation."

Kinnison nodded. He knew what a barrage would have done to a force trying to cross such open ground in daylight.

"One man could prob'ly make it, though, if he was careful and kept his eyes wide open," the sergeant-major continued. "But you ain't got no binoculars, have you?"

"No."

"Get a pair easy enough. You saw them boots without any hobnails in 'em, sticking out from under some blankets?"

"Yes. I get you." Kinnison knew that combat officers did not wear hobnails, and usually carried binoculars. "How come so many at once?"

"Just about all the officers that got this far. Conniving, my guess is, behind old Slayton's back. Anyway, a kraut aviator spots 'em and dives. Our machine-guns got him, but not until after he heaved a bomb. Dead center. Christ, what a mess! But there's six-seven good glasses in there. I'd grab one myself, but the general would see it—he can see right through the lid of a mess-kit. Well, the boys have shut those krauts up, so I'll hunt the old man up and tell him what I found out. *Damn* this mud!"

Kinnison emerged sinuously and snaked his way to a row of blanket covered forms. He lifted a blanket and gasped: then vomited up everything, it seemed, that he had eaten for days. But he *had* to have the binoculars.

He got them.

Then, still retching, white and shaken, he crept westward; availing himself of every possible item of cover.

For some time, from a point somewhere north of his route, a machine-gun had been intermittently at work. It was close; but the very loudness of its noise, confused as it was by resounding echoes, made it impossible to locate at all exactly the weapon's position. Kinnison crept forward inchwise; scanning every foot of visible terrain through his powerful glass. He knew by the sound that it was German. More, since what he did not know about machine-guns could have been printed in bill-poster type upon the back of his hand, he knew that it was a Maxim, Model 1907—a mean, mean gun. He deduced that it was doing plenty of damage to his fellows back on the hill, and that they had not been able to do much of anything about it. And it was beautifully hidden; even he, close as he must be, couldn't see it. But damn it, there *had* to be a . . . .

Minute after minute, unmoving save for the traverse of his binoculars, he searched, and finally he found. A tiny plume—the veriest wisp—of vapor, rising from the surface of the brook. Steam! Steam from the cooling jacket of that Maxim 1907! And there was the tube!

Cautiously he moved around until he could trace that tube to its business end—the carefully-hidden emplacement. There it was! He couldn't maintain his westward course without them spotting him; nor could he go around far enough. And besides . . . and besides that, there would be at least a patrol, if it hadn't gone up the hill already. And there were grenades available, right close . . . .

He crept up to one of the gruesome objects he had been avoiding, and when he crept away he half-carried, half-dragged three grenades in a canvas bag. He wormed his way to a certain boulder. He straightened up, pulled three pins, swung his arm three times.

Bang! Bam! Pow! The camouflage disappeared; so did the shrubbery for yards around. Kinnison had ducked behind the rock, but he ducked still deeper as a chunk of something, its force pretty well spent, clanged against his steel helmet. Another object thudded beside him—a leg, gray-clad and wearing a heavy field boot!

Kinnison wanted to be sick again, but he had neither the time nor the contents.

And damn! What *lousy* throwing! He had never been any good at baseball, but he supposed that he could hit a thing as big as that gun-pit—but not one of his grenades had gone in. The crew would probably be dead—from concussion, if nothing else—but the gun probably wasn't even hurt. He would have to go over there and cripple it himself.

He went—not exactly boldly—forty-five in hand. The Germans looked dead. One of them sprawled on the parapet, right in his way. He gave the body a shove, watched it roll down the slope. As it rolled, however, it came to life and yelled; and at that yell there occurred a thing at which young Kinnison's hair stood straight up inside his iron helmet. On the gray of the blasted hillside hitherto unseen gray forms moved; moved toward their howling comrade. And Kinnison, blessing for the first time in his life his inept throwing arm, hoped fervently that the Maxim was still in good working order.

A few seconds of inspection showed him that it was. The gun had practically a full belt and there was plenty more. He placed a box—he would have no Number Two to help him here—took hold of the grips, shoved off the safety, and squeezed the trip. The gun roared—what a gorgeous, what a heavenly racket that Maxim made! He traversed until he could see where the bullets were striking: then swung the stream of metal to and fro. One belt and the Germans were completely disorganized; two belts and he could see no signs of life.

He pulled the Maxim's block and threw it away; shot the water-jacket full of holes. That gun was done. Nor had he increased his own hazard. Unless more Germans came very soon, nobody would ever know who had done what, or to whom.

He slithered away; resumed earnestly his westward course: going as fast as—sometimes a trifle faster than—caution would permit. But there were no more alarms. He crossed the dangerously open ground; sulked rapidly through the frightfully shattered wood. He reached the road, strode along it around the first bend, and stopped, appalled. He had heard of such things, but he had never seen one; and mere description has always been and always will be completely inadequate. Now he was walking right into it—the thing he was to see in nightmare for all the rest of his ninety-six years of life.

SUPER PACK

Actually, there was very little to see. The road ended abruptly. What had been a road, what had been wheatfields and farms, what had been woods, were practically indistinguishable, one from the other; were fantastically and impossibly the same. The entire area had been churned. Worse—it was as though the ground and its every surface object had been run through a gargantuan mill and spewed abroad. Splinters of wood, riven chunks of metal, a few scraps of bloody flesh. Kinnison screamed, then, and ran; ran back and around that blasted acreage. And as he ran, his mind built up pictures; pictures which became only the more vivid because of his frantic efforts to wipe them out.

That road, the night before, had been one of the world's most heavily traveled highways. Motorcycles, trucks, bicycles. Ambulances. Kitchens. Staff-cars and other automobiles. Guns; from seventy-fives up to the big boys, whose tremendous weight drove their wide caterpillar treads inches deep into solid ground. Horses. Mules. And people—*especially* people—like himself. Solid columns of men, marching as fast as they could step—there weren't trucks enough to haul them all. That road had been crowded—jammed. Like State and Madison at noon, only more so. Over-jammed with all the personnel, all the instrumentation and incidentalia, all the weaponry, of war.

And upon that teeming, seething highway there had descended a rain of steel-encased high explosive. Possibly some gas, but probably not. The German High Command had given orders to pulverize that particular area at that particular time; and hundreds, or perhaps thousands, of German guns, in a micrometrically-synchronized symphony of firepower, had pulverized it. Just that. Literally. Precisely. No road remained; no farm, no field, no building, no tree or shrub. The bits of flesh might have come from horse or man or mule; few indeed were the scraps of metal which retained enough of their original shape to show what they had once been.

Kinnison ran—or staggered—around that obscene blot and struggled back to the road. It was shell-pocked, but passable. He hoped that the shell-holes would decrease in number as he went along, but they did not. The enemy had put this whole road out of service. And that farm, the P.C., ought to be around the next bend.

It was, but it was no longer a Post of Command. Either by directed fire—star-shell illumination—or by uncannily accurate chart-work, they had put some heavy shell exactly where they would do the most damage. The buildings were gone; the cellar in which the P.C. had been was now a gaping crater. Parts of motorcycles and of staff cars littered the ground. Stark tree trunks—all bare of leaves, some riven of all except the largest branches, a few stripped even of bark—stood gauntly. In a crotch of one, Kinnison saw with rising horror, hung the limp and shattered naked torso of a man; blown completely out of his clothes.

Shells were—had been, right along—coming over occasionally. Big ones, but high; headed for targets well to the west. Nothing close enough to worry about. Two ambulances, a couple of hundred meters apart, were coming; working their way along the road, between the holes. The first one slowed . . . stopped.

"Seen anybody—Look out! Duck!"

Kinnison had already heard that unmistakable, unforgettable screech, was already diving headlong into the nearest hole. There was a crash as though the world were falling apart. Something smote him; seemed to drive him bodily into the ground. His light went out. When he recovered consciousness he was lying upon a stretcher; two men were bending over him.

"What hit me?" he gasped. "Am I . . . ?" He stopped. He was afraid to ask: afraid even to try to move, lest he should find that he didn't have any arms or legs.

"A wheel, and maybe some of the axle, of the other ambulance, is all," one of the men assured him. "Nothing much; you're practically as good as ever. Shoulder and arm bunged up a little and something—maybe shrapnel, though—poked you in the guts. But we've got you all fixed up, so take it easy and . . . ."

"What we want to know is," his partner interrupted, "Is there anybody else alive up here?"

"Uh-huh," Kinnison shook his head.

"O.K. Just wanted to be sure. Lots of business back there, and it won't do any harm to have a doctor look at you."

"Get me to a 'phone, as fast as you can," Kinnison directed, in a voice which he thought was strong and full of authority, but which in fact was neither. "I've got an important message for General Weatherby, at Spearmint."

"Better tell us what it is, hadn't you?" The ambulance was now jolting along what had been the road. "They've got phones at the hospital where we're going, but you might faint or something before we get there."

Kinnison told, but fought to retain what consciousness he had. Throughout that long, rough ride he fought. He won. He himself spoke to General Weatherby—the doctors, knowing him to be a Captain of Aviation and realizing that his message should go direct, helped him telephone. He himself received the General's sizzlingly sulphurous assurance that relief would be sent and that that quadruply-qualified line would be rectified that night.

Then someone jabbed him with a needle and he lapsed into a dizzy, fuzzy coma, from which he did not emerge completely for weeks. He had lucid intervals at times, but he did not, at the time or ever, know surely what was real and what was fantasy.

There were doctors, doctors, doctors; operations, operations, operations. There were hospital tents, into which quiet men were carried; from which still quieter men were removed. There was a larger hospital, built of wood. There was a machine that buzzed and white-clad men who studied films and papers. There were scraps of conversation.

"Belly wounds are bad," Kinnison thought—he was never sure—that he heard one of them say. "And such contusions and multiple and compound fractures as those don't help a bit. Prognosis unfavorable—distinctly so—but we'll soon see what we can do. Interesting case . . . fascinating. What would you do, Doctor, if you were doing it?"

"I'd let it alone!" A younger, stronger voice declared, fervently. "Multiple perforations, infection, extravasation, oedema—uh-uh! I am watching, Doctor, and learning!"

Another interlude, and another. Another. And others. Until finally, orders were given which Kinnison did not hear at all.

"Adrenalin! Massage! Massage hell out of him!"

Kinnison again came to—partially to, rather—anguished in every fiber of his being. Somebody was sticking barbed arrows into every square inch of his skin; somebody else was pounding and mauling him all over, taking particular pains to pummel and to wrench at all the places where he hurt the worst. He yelled at the top of his voice; yelled and swore bitterly: "QUIT IT!" being the expurgated gist of his luridly profane protests. He did not make nearly as much noise as he supposed, but he made enough.

"Thank God!" Kinnison heard a lighter, softer voice. Surprised, he stopped swearing and tried to stare. He couldn't see very well, either, but he was pretty sure that there was a middle-aged woman there. There was, and her eyes were not dry. "He is going to live, after all!"

As the days passed, he began really to sleep, naturally and deeply.

He grew hungrier and hungrier, and they would not give him enough to eat. He was by turns sullen, angry, and morose.

In short, he was convalescent.

For Captain Ralph K. Kinnison, THE WAR was over.

1941

Chubby, brownette Eunice Kinnison sat in a rocker, reading the Sunday papers and listening to her radio. Her husband Ralph lay sprawled upon the davenport, smoking a cigarette and reading the current issue of EXTRAORDINARY STORIES against an unheard background of music. Mentally, he was far from Tellus, flitting in his super-dreadnaught through parsec after parsec of vacuous space.

The music broke off without warning and there blared out an announcement which yanked Ralph Kinnison back to Earth with a violence almost physical. He jumped up, jammed his hands into his pockets.

"Pearl Harbor!" he blurted. "How in . . . . How could they have let them get *that* far?"

"But *Frank!*" the woman gasped. She had not worried much about her husband; but Frank, her son . . . . "He'll have to go . . . ." Her voice died away.

"Not a chance in the world." Kinnison did not speak to soothe, but as though from sure knowledge. "Designing Engineer for Lockwood? He'll want to, all right, but anyone who was ever even exposed to a course in aeronautical engineering will sit this war out."

"But they say it can't last very long. It can't, can it?"

"I'll say it can. Loose talk. Five years minimum is my guess—not that my guess is any better than anybody else's."

He prowled around the room. His somber expression did not lighten.

"I knew it," the woman said at length. "You, too—even after the last one . . . . You haven't said anything, so I thought, perhaps . . . ."

"I know I didn't. There was always the chance that we wouldn't get drawn into it. If you say so, though, I'll stay home."

"Am I apt to? I let you go when you were really in danger . . . ."

"What do you mean by *that* crack?" he interrupted.

"Regulations. One year too old—Thank Heaven!"

"So what? They'll need technical experts, bad. They'll make exceptions."

"Possibly. Desk jobs. Desk officers don't get killed in action—or even wounded. Why, perhaps, with the children all grown up and married, we won't even have to be separated."

"Another angle—financial."

"Pooh! Who cares about that? Besides, for a man out of a job . . . ."

"From you, I'll let that one pass. Thanks, Eunie—you're an ace. I'll shoot 'em a wire."

The telegram was sent. The Kinnisons waited. And waited. Until, about the middle of January, beautifully-phrased and beautifully-mimeographed letters began to arrive.

"The War Department recognizes the value of your previous military experience and appreciates your willingness once again to take up arms in defense of the country . . . Veteran Officer's Questionnaire . . . please fill out completely . . . Form 191A . . . Form 170 in duplicate . . . Form 315 . . . . Impossible to forecast the extent to which the War Department may ultimately utilize the services which you and thousands of others have so generously offered . . . Form . . . Form . . . . Not to be construed as meaning that you have been permanently rejected . . . Form . . . Advise you that while at the present time the War Department is unable to use you . . . ."

"Wouldn't that fry you to a crisp?" Kinnison demanded. "What in hell have they got in their heads—sawdust? They think that because I'm fifty one years old I've got one foot in the grave—I'll bet four dollars that I'm in better shape than that cursed Major General and his whole damned staff!"

"I don't doubt it, dear." Eunice's smile was, however, mostly of relief. "But here's an ad—it's been running for a week."

"CHEMICAL ENGINEERS . . . shell loading plant . . . within seventy-five miles of Townville . . . over five years experience . . . organic chemistry . . . technology . . . explosives . . . ."

"They want *you*," Eunice declared, soberly.

"Well, I'm a Ph.D. in Organic. I've had more than five years experience in both organic chemistry and technology. If I don't know something about explosives I did a smart job of fooling Dean Montrose, back at Gosh Whatta University. I'll write 'em a letter."

He wrote. He filled out a form. The telephone rang.

"Kinnison speaking . . . yes . . . Dr. Sumner? Oh, yes, Chief Chemist . . . . That's it—one year over age, so I thought . . . . Oh, that's a minor matter. We won't starve. If you can't pay a hundred and fifty I'll come for a hundred, or seventy five, or fifty . . . . That's all right, too. I'm well enough known in my own field so that a title of Junior Chemical Engineer wouldn't hurt me a bit . . . O.K., I'll see you about one o'clock . . . Stoner and Black, Inc., Operators, Entwhistle Ordnance Plant, Entwhistle, Missikota . . . . What! Well, maybe I could, at that . . . . Goodbye."

He turned to his wife. "You know what? They want me to come down right away and go to work. Hot Dog! Am I glad that I told that louse Hendricks exactly where he could stick that job of mine!"

"He must have known that you wouldn't sign a straight-salary contract after getting a share of the profits so long. Maybe he believed what you always say just before or just after kicking somebody's teeth down their throats; that you're so meek and mild—a regular Milquetoast. Do you really think that they'll want you back, after the war?" It was clear that Eunice was somewhat concerned concerning Kinnison's joblessness; but Kinnison was not.

"Probably. That's the gossip. And I'll come back—when hell freezes over." His square jaw tightened. "I've heard of outfits stupid enough to let their technical brains go because they could sell—for a while—anything they produced, but I didn't know that I was working for one. Maybe I'm not exactly a Timid Soul, but you'll have to admit that I never kicked anybody's teeth out unless they tried to kick mine out first."

*

Entwhistle Ordnance Plant covered twenty-odd square miles of more or less level land. Ninety-nine percent of its area was "Inside the fence." Most of the buildings within that restricted area, while in reality enormous, were dwarfed by the vast spaces separating them; for safety-distances are not small when TNT and tetryl by the ton are involved. Those structures were built of concrete, steel, glass, transite, and tile.

"Outside the Fence" was different. This was the Administration Area. Its buildings were tremendous wooden barracks, relatively close together, packed with the executive, clerical, and professional personnel appropriate to an organization employing over twenty thousand men and women.

Well inside the fence, but a safety-distance short of the One Line—Loading Line Number One—was a long, low building, quite inadequately named the Chemical Laboratory. "Inadequately" in that the Chief Chemist, a highly capable—if more than a little cantankerous—Explosives Engineer, had already gathered into his Chemical Section most of Development, most of Engineering, and all of Physics, Weights and Measures, and Weather.

One room of the Chemical Laboratory—in the corner most distant from Administration—was separated from the rest of the building by a sixteen-inch wall of concrete and steel extending from foundation to roof without a door, window, or other opening. This was the laboratory of the Chemical Engineers, the boys who played with explosives high and low; any explosion occurring therein could not affect the Chemical Laboratory proper or its personnel.

Entwhistle's main roads were paved; but in February of 1942, such minor items as sidewalks existed only on the blue-prints. Entwhistle's soil contained much clay, and at that time the mud was approximately six inches deep. Hence, since there were neither inside doors nor sidewalks, it was only natural that the technologists did not visit at all frequently the polished-tile cleanliness of the Laboratory. It was also natural enough for the far larger group to refer to the segregated ones as exiles and outcasts; and that some witty chemist applied to that isolated place the name "Siberia."

The name stuck. More, the Engineers seized it and acclaimed it. They were Siberians, and proud of it, and Siberians they remained; long after Entwhistle's mud turned into dust. And within the year the Siberians were to become well and favorably known in every ordnance plant in the country, to many high executives who had no idea of how the name originated.

Kinnison became a Siberian as enthusiastically as the youngest man there. The term "youngest" is used in its exact sense, for not one of them was a recent graduate. Each had had at least five years of responsible experience, and "Cappy" Sumner kept on building. He hired extravagantly and fired ruthlessly—to the minds of some, senselessly. But he knew what he was doing. He knew explosives, and he knew men. He was not liked, but he was respected. His building was good.

Being one of the only two "old" men there—and the other did not stay long—Kinnison, as a Junior Chemical Engineer, was not at first accepted without reserve. Apparently he did not notice that fact, but went quietly about his assigned duties. He was meticulously careful with, but very evidently not in any fear of, the materials with which he worked. He pelleted and tested tracer, igniter, and incendiary compositions; he took his turn at burning out rejects. Whenever asked, he went out on the lines with any one of them.

His experimental tetryls always "miked" to size, his TNT melt-pours—introductory to loading forty-millimeter on the Three Line—came out solid, free from checks and cavitations. It became evident to those young but keen minds that he, alone of them all, was on familiar ground. They began to discuss their problems with him. Out of his years of technological experience, and by bringing everyone present into the discussion, he either helped them directly or helped them to help themselves. His stature grew.

Black-haired, black-eyed "Tug" Tugwell, two hundred pounds of ex-football-player in charge of tracer on the Seven Line, called him "Uncle" Ralph, and the habit spread. And in a couple of weeks—at about the same time that "Injun" Abernathy was slightly injured by being blown through a door by a minor explosion of his igniter on the Eight line—he was promoted to full Chemical Engineer; a promotion which went unnoticed, since it involved only changes in title and salary.

Three weeks later, however, he was made Senior Chemical Engineer, in charge of Melt-Pour. At this there was a celebration, led by "Blondie" Wanacek, a sulphuric-acid expert handling tetryl on the Two. Kinnison searched minutely for signs of jealousy or antagonism, but could find none. He went blithely to work on the Six line, where they wanted to start pouring twenty-pound fragmentation bombs, ably assisted by Tug and by two new men. One of these was "Doc" or "Bart" Barton, who, the grapevine said, had been hired by Cappy to be his Assistant. His motto, like that of Rikki-Tikki-Tavi, was to run and find out, and he did so with glee and abandon. He was a good egg. So was the other newcomer, "Charley" Charlevoix, a prematurely gray paint-and-lacquer expert who had also made the Siberian grade.

A few months later, Sumner called Kinnison into the office. The latter went, wondering what the old hard-shell was going to cry about now; for to be called into that office meant only one thing—censure.

"Kinnison, I like your work," the Chief Chemist began, gruffly, and Kinnison's mouth almost dropped open. "Anybody who ever got a Ph.D. under Montrose would have to know explosives, and the F.B.I. report on you showed that you had brains, ability, and guts. But none of that explains how you can get along so well with those damned

Siberians. I want to make you Assistant Chief and put you in charge of Siberia. Formally, I mean—actually, you have been for months."

"Why, no . . . I didn't . . . . Besides, how about Barton? He's too good a man to kick in the teeth that way."

"Admitted." This *did* surprise Kinnison. He had never thought that the irascible and tempestuous Chief would ever confess to a mistake. This was a Cappy he had never known. "I discussed it with him yesterday. He's a damned good man—but it's decidedly questionable whether he has got whatever it is that made Tugwell, Wanacek and Charlevoix work straight through for seventy two hours, napping now and then on benches and grabbing coffee and sandwiches when they could, until they got that frag bomb straightened out."

Sumner did not mention the fact that Kinnison had worked straight through, too. That was taken for granted.

"Well, I don't know." Kinnison's head was spinning. "I'd like to check with Barton first. O.K.?"

"I expected that. O.K."

Kinnison found Barton and led him out behind the testing shed.

"Bart, Cappy tells me that he figures on kicking you in the face by making me Assistant and that you O.K.'d it. One word and I'll tell the old buzzard just where to stick the job and exactly where to go to do it."

"Reaction, perfect. Yield, one hundred percent." Barton stuck out his hand. "Otherwise, I would tell him all that myself and more. As it is, Uncle Ralph, smooth out the ruffled plumage. They'd go to hell for you, wading in standing straight up—they might do the same with me in the driver's seat, and they might not. Why take a chance? You're IT. Some things about the deal I don't like, of course—but at that, it makes me about the only man working for Stoner and Black who can get a release any time a good permanent job breaks. I'll stick until then. O.K.?" It was unnecessary for Barton to add that as long as he was there he would really work.

"I'll say it's O.K.!" and Kinnison reported to Sumner.

"All right, Chief, I'll try it—if you can square it with the Siberians."

"That will not be too difficult."

Nor was it. The Siberians' reaction brought a lump to Kinnison's throat.

"Ralph the First, Czar of Siberia!" they yelled. "Long live the Czar! Kowtow, serfs and vassals, to Czar Ralph the First!"

Kinnison was still glowing when he got home that night, to the Government Housing Project and to the three-room "mansionette" in which he and Eunice lived. He would never forget the events of that day.

"What a gang! *What* a gang! But listen, ace—they work under their own power—you couldn't *keep* those kids from working. Why should I get the credit for what they do?"

"I haven't the foggiest." Eunice wrinkled her forehead—and her nose—but the corners of her mouth quirked up. "Are you quite sure that you haven't had *anything* to do with it? But supper is ready—let's eat."

More months passed. Work went on. Absorbing work, and highly varied; the details of which are of no importance here. Paul Jones, a big, hard, top-drawer chicle technologist, set up the Four line to pour demolition blocks. Frederick Hinton came in, qualified as a Siberian, and went to work on Anti-Personnel mines.

Kinnison was promoted again: to Chief Chemist. He and Sumner had never been friendly; he made no effort to find out why Cappy had quit, or had been terminated, whichever it was. This promotion made no difference. Barton, now Assistant, ran the whole Chemical Section save for one unit—Siberia—and did a superlative job. The Chief Chemist's secretary worked for Barton, not for Kinnison. Kinnison was the Czar of Siberia.

The Anti-Personnel mines had been giving trouble. Too many men were being killed by prematures, and nobody could find out why. The problem was handed to Siberia. Hinton tackled it, missed, and called for help. The Siberians rallied round. Kinnison loaded and tested mines. So did Paul and Tug and Blondie. Kinnison was testing, out in the Firing Area, when he was called to Administration to attend a Staff Meeting. Hinton relieved him. He had not reached the gate, however, when a guard car flagged him down.

"Sorry, sir, but there has been an accident at Pit Five and you are needed out there."

"Accident! Fred Hinton! Is he . . . ?"

"I'm afraid so, sir."

It is a harrowing thing to have to help gather up what fragments can be found of one of your best friends. Kinnison was white and sick as he got back to the firing station, just in time to hear the Chief Safety Officer say:

"Must have been carelessness—rank carelessness. I warned this man Hinton myself, on one occasion."

"Carelessness, hell!" Kinnison blazed. "You had the guts to warn *me* once, too, and I've forgotten more about safety in explosives than you ever will know. Fred Hinton was *not* careless—if I hadn't been called in, that would have been me."

"What is it, then?"

"I don't know—yet. I tell you now, though, Major Moulton, that I *will* know, and the minute I find out I'll talk to you again."

He went back to Siberia, where he found Tug and Paul, faces still tear-streaked, staring at something that looked like a small piece of wire.

"This is it, Uncle Ralph," Tug said, brokenly. "Don't see how it could be, but it is."

"What is what?" Kinnison demanded.

"Firing pin. Brittle. When you pull the safety, the force of the spring must break it off at this constricted section here."

"But damn it, Tug, it doesn't make sense. It's tension . . . but wait—there'd be some horizontal component, at that. But they'd have to be brittle as glass."

"I know it. It doesn't seem to make much sense. But we were there, you know—and I assembled every one of those God damned mines myself. Nothing else could possibly have made that mine go off just when it did."

"O.K., Tug. We'll test 'em. Call Bart in—he can have the scale-lab boys rig us up a gadget by the time we can get some more of those pins in off the line."

They tested a hundred, under the normal tension of the spring, and three of them broke. They tested another hundred. Five broke. They stared at each other.

"That's it." Kinnison declared. "But this will stink to high Heaven—have Inspection break out a new lot and we'll test a thousand."

Of that thousand pins, thirty two broke.

"Bart, will you dictate a one-page preliminary report to Vera and rush it over to Building One as fast as you can? I'll go over and tell Moulton a few things."

Major Moulton was, as usual, "in conference," but Kinnison was in no mood to wait.

"Tell him," he instructed the Major's private secretary, who had barred his way, "that either he will talk to me right now or I will call District Safety over his head. I'll give him sixty seconds to decide which."

Moulton decided to see him. "I'm very busy, Doctor Kinnison, but . . . ."

"I don't give a swivel-eyed tinker's damn how busy you are. I told you that the minute I found out what was the matter with the M2 mine I'd talk to you again. Here I am. Brittle firing pins. Three and two-tenths percent defective. So I'm . . . ."

"Very irregular, Doctor. The matter will have to go through channels . . . ."

"Not this one. The formal report is going through channels, but as I started to tell you, this is an emergency report to you as Chief of Safety. Since the defect is not covered by specs, neither Process nor Ordnance can reject except by test, and whoever does the testing will very probably be killed. Therefore, as every employee of Stoner and Black is not only authorized but positively instructed to do upon discovering an unsafe condition, I am reporting it direct to Safety. Since my whiskers are a trifle longer than an operator's, I am reporting it direct to the Head of the Safety Division; and I am telling you that if you don't do something about it damned quick—stop production and slap a HOLD order on all the M2AP's you can reach—I'll call District and make you personally responsible for every premature that occurs from now on."

Since any safety man, anywhere, would much rather stop a process than authorize one, and since this particular safety man loved to throw his weight around, Kinnison was surprised that Moulton did not act instantly. The fact that he did not so act should have, but did not, give the naive Kinnison much information as to conditions existing Outside the Fence.

"But they need those mines very badly; they are an item of very heavy production. If we stop them . . . how long? Have you any suggestions?"

"Yes. Call District and have them rush through a change of spec—include heat-treat and a modified Charpy test. In the meantime, we can get back into full production tomorrow if you have District slap a hundred-per-cent inspection onto those pins."

"Excellent! We can do that—very fine work, Doctor! Miss Morgan, get District at once!"

This, too, should have warned Kinnison, but it did not. He went back to the Laboratory.

Tempus fugited.

Orders came to get ready to load M67 H.E., A.T. (105 m/m High Explosive, Armor Tearing) shell on the Nine, and the Siberians went joyously to work upon the new load.

The explosive was to be a mixture of TNT and a polysyllabic compound, everything about which was highly confidential and restricted.

"But what the hell's so hush-hush about *that* stuff?" demanded Blondie, who, with five or six others, was crowding around the Czar's desk. Unlike the days of Cappy Sumner, the private office of the Chief Chemist was now as much Siberia as Siberia itself. "The Germans developed it originally, didn't they?"

"Yes, and the Italians used it against the Ethiopians—which was why their bombs were so effective. But it says 'hush-hush,' so that's the way it will be. And if you talk in your sleep, Blondie, tell Betty not to listen."

The Siberians worked. The M67 was put into production. It was such a success that orders for it came in faster than they could be filled. Production was speeded up. Small cavitations began to appear. Nothing serious, since they passed Inspection. Nevertheless, Kinnison protested, in a formal report, receipt of which was formally acknowledged.

General Somebody-or-other, Entwhistle's Commanding Officer, whom none of the Siberians had ever met, was transferred to more active duty, and a colonel—Snodgrass or some such name—took his place. Ordnance got a new Chief Inspector.

An M67, Entwhistle loaded, prematured in a gun-barrel, killing twenty seven men. Kinnison protested again, verbally this time, at a staff meeting. He was assured—verbally—that a formal and thorough investigation was being made. Later he was informed—verbally and without witnesses—that the investigation had been completed and that the loading was not at fault. A new Commanding Officer—Lieutenant-Colonel Franklin—appeared.

The Siberians, too busy to do more than glance at newspapers, paid very little attention to a glider-crash in which several notables were killed. They heard that an investigation was being made, but even the Czar did not know until later that Washington had for once acted fast in correcting a bad situation; that Inspection, which had been under Production, was summarily divorced therefrom. And gossip spread abroad that Stillman, then Head of the Inspection Division, was not a big enough man for the job. Thus it was an entirely unsuspecting Kinnison who was called into the innermost private office of Thomas Keller, the Superintendent of Production.

"Kinnison, how in hell do you handle those Siberians? I never saw anything like them before in my life."

"No, and you never will again. Nothing on Earth except a war could get them together or hold them together. I don't 'handle' them—they can't be 'handled'. I give them a job to do and let them do it. I back them up. That's all."

"Umngpf." Keller grunted. "That's a hell of a formula—if I want anything done right I've got to do it myself. But whatever your system is, it works. But what I wanted to talk to you about is, how'd you like to be Head of the Inspection Division, which would be enlarged to include your present Chemical Section?"

"Huh?" Kinnison demanded, dumbfounded.

"At a salary well up on the confidential scale." Keller wrote a figure upon a piece of paper, showed it to his visitor, then burned it in an ash-tray.

Kinnison whistled. "I'd like it—for more reasons than that. But I didn't know that you—or have you already checked with the General and Mr. Black?"

"Naturally," came the smooth reply. "In fact, I suggested it to them and have their approval. Perhaps you are curious to know why?"

"I certainly am."

"For two reasons. First, because you have developed a crew of technical experts that is the envy of every technical man in the country. Second, you and your Siberians have done every job I ever asked you to, and done it fast. As a Division Head, you will no longer be under me, but I am right, I think, in assuming that you will work with me just as efficiently as you do now?"

"I can't think of any reason why I wouldn't." This reply was made in all honesty; but later, when he came to understand what Keller had meant, how bitterly Kinnison was to regret its making!

He moved into Stillman's office, and found there what he thought was ample reason for his predecessor's failure to make good. To his way of thinking it was tremendously over-staffed, particularly with Assistant Chief Inspectors. Delegation of authority, so widely preached throughout Entwhistle Ordnance Plant, had not been given even lip service here. Stillman had not made a habit of visiting the lines; nor did the Chief Line Inspectors, the boys who really knew what was going on, ever visit him. They reported to the Assistants, who reported to Stillman, who handed down his Jovian pronouncements.

Kinnison set out, deliberately this time, to mold his key Chief Line Inspectors into just such a group as the Siberians already were. He released the Assistants to more productive work; retaining of Stillman's office staff only a few clerks and his private secretary, one Celeste de St. Aubin, a dynamic, vivacious—at times explosive—brunette. He gave the boys on the Lines full authority; the few who could not handle the load he replaced with men who could. At first the Chief Line Inspectors simply could not believe; but after the affair of the forty millimeter, in which Kinnison rammed the decision of his subordinate past Keller, past the General, past Stoner and Black, and clear up to the Commanding Officer before he made it stick, they were his to a man.

Others of his Section Heads, however, remained aloof. Pettler, whose Technical Section was now part of Inspection, and Wilson, of Gages, were two of those who talked largely and glowingly, but acted obstructively if they acted at all. As weeks went on, Kinnison became wiser and wiser, but made no sign. One day, during a lull, his secretary hung out the "In Conference" sign and went into Kinnison's private office.

"There isn't a reference to any such Investigation anywhere in Central Files." She paused, as if to add something, then turned to leave.

"As you were, Celeste. Sit down. I expected that. Suppressed—if made at all. You're a smart girl, Celeste, and you know the ropes. You know that you can talk to me, don't you?"

"Yes, but this is . . . well, the word is going around that they are going to break you, just as they have broken every other good man on the Reservation."

"I expected that, too." The words were quiet enough, but the man's jaw tightened. "Also, I know how they are going to do it."

"How?"

"This speed-up on the Nine. They know that I won't stand still for the kind of casts that Keller's new procedure, which goes into effect tonight, is going to produce . . . and this new C.O. probably will."

Silence fell, broken by the secretary.

"General Sanford, our first C.O., was a soldier, and a good one," she declared finally. "So was Colonel Snodgrass. Lieutenant Colonel Franklin wasn't; but he was too much of a man to do the dir . . . "

"Dirty work," dryly. "Exactly. Go on."

"And Stoner, the New York half—ninety five percent, really—of Stoner and Black, Inc., is a Big Time Operator. So we get this damned nincompoop of a major, who doesn't know a f-u-s-e from a f-u-z-e, direct from a Wall Street desk."

"So what?" One must have heard Ralph Kinnison say those two words to realize how much meaning they can be made to carry.

"So what!" the girl blazed, wringing her hands. "Ever since you have been over here I have been expecting you to blow up—to smash something—in spite of the dozens of times you have told me a fighter can not slug effectively, Celeste, until he gets both feet firmly planted.' When—*when*—are you going to get your feet planted?"

"Never, I'm afraid," he said glumly, and she stared. "So I'll have to start slugging with at least one foot in the air."

That startled her. "Explain, please?"

"I wanted *proof*. Stuff that I could take to the District—that I could use to tack some hides out flat on a barn door with. Do I get it? I do not. Not a shred. Neither can you. What chance do you think there is of ever getting any real proof?"

"Very little," Celeste admitted. "But you can at least smash Pettler, Wilson, and that crowd. *How* I hate those slimy snakes! I wish that you could smash Tom Keller, the poisonous moron!"

"Not so much moron—although he acts like one at times—as an ignorant puppet with a head swelled three sizes too big for his hat. But you can quit yapping about slugging—fireworks are due to start at two o'clock tomorrow afternoon, when Drake is going to reject tonight's run of shell."

"Really? But I don't see how either Pettler or Wilson come in."

"They don't. A fight with those small fry—even smashing them—wouldn't make enough noise. Keller."

"Keller!" Celeste squealed. "But you'll . . . ."

"I know I'll get fired. So what? By tackling him I can raise enough hell so that the Big Shots will have to cut out at least some of the rough stuff. You'll probably get fired too, you know—you've been too close to me for your own good."

"Not me." She shook her head vigorously. "The minute they terminate you, I quit. Poof! Who cares? Besides, I can get a better job in Townville."

"Without leaving the Project. That's what I figured. It's the boys I'm worried about. I've been getting them ready for this for weeks."

"But they will quit, too. Your Siberians—your Inspectors—of a surety they will quit, every one!"

"They won't release them; and what Stoner and Black will do to them, even after the war, if they quit without releases, shouldn't be done to a dog. They won't quit, either—at least if they don't try to push them around too much. Keller's mouth is watering to get hold of Siberia, but he'll never make it, nor any one of his stooges . . . . I'd better dictate a memorandum to Black on that now, while I'm calm and collected; telling him what he'll have to do to keep my boys from tearing Entwhistle apart."

"But do you think he will pay any attention to it?"

"I'll say he will!" Kinnison snorted. "Don't kid yourself about Black, Celeste. He's a smart man, and before this is done he'll know that he'll have to keep his nose clean."

"But you—how can you do it?" Celeste marveled. "Me, I would urge them on. Few would have the patriotism . . . ."

"Patriotism, hell! If that were all, I would have stirred up a revolution long ago. It's for the boys, in years to come. They've got to keep *their* noses clean, too. Get your notebook, please, and take this down. Rough draft—I'm going to polish it up until it has teeth and claws in every line."

And that evening, after supper, he informed Eunice of all the new developments.

"Is it still O.K. with you," he concluded, "for me to get myself fired off of this high-salaried job of mine?"

"Certainly. Being you, how can you do anything else? Oh, how I wish I could wring their necks!" That conversation went on and on, but additional details are not necessary here.

Shortly after two o'clock of the following afternoon, Celeste took a call; and listened shamelessly.

"Kinnison speaking."

"Tug, Uncle Ralph. The casts sectioned just like we thought they would. Dead ringers for Plate D. So Drake hung a red ticket on every tray. Piddy was right there, waiting, and started to raise hell. So I chipped in, and he beat it so fast that I looked to see his coat-tail catch fire. Drake didn't quite like to call you, so I did. If Piddy keeps on going at the rate he left here, he'll be in Keller's office in nothing flat."

"O.K., Tug. Tell Drake that the shell he rejected are going to stay rejected, and to come in right now with his report. Would you like to come along?"

"*Would* I!" Tugwell hung up and:

"But do you want *him* here, Doc?" Celeste asked, anxiously, without considering whether or not her boss would approve of her eavesdropping.

"I certainly do. If I can keep Tug from blowing his top, the rest of the boys will stay in line."

A few minutes later Tugwell strode in, bringing with him Drake, the Chief Line Inspector of the Nine Line. Shortly thereafter the office door was wrenched open. Keller had come to Kinnison, accompanied by the Superintendent whom the Siberians referred to, somewhat contemptuously, as "Piddy."

"Damn your soul, Kinnison, come out here—I want to talk to you!" Keller roared, and doors snapped open up and down the long corridor.

"Shut up, you God damned louse!" This from Tugwell, who, black eyes almost emitting sparks, was striding purposefully forward. "I'll sock you so damned hard that . . . ."

"Pipe down, Tug, I'll handle this." Kinnison's voice was not loud, but it had then a peculiarly carrying and immensely authoritative quality. "Verbally or physically; however he wants to have it."

He turned to Keller, who had jumped backward into the hall to avoid the young Siberian.

"As for you, Keller, if you had the brains that God gave bastard geese in Ireland, you would have had this conference in private. Since you started it in public, however, I'll finish it in public. How you came to pick *me* for a yes-man I'll never know—just one more measure of your stupidity, I suppose."

"Those shell are perfect!" Keller shouted. "Tell Drake here to pass them, right now. If you don't, by God I'll . . . ."

"Shut up!" Kinnison's voice cut. "I'll do the talking—you listen. The spec says quote shall be free from objectionable cavitation unquote. The Line Inspectors, who know their stuff, say that those cavitations are objectionable. So do the Chemical Engineers. Therefore, as far as I am concerned, they are objectionable. Those shell are rejected, and they will *stay* rejected."

"That's what *you* think," Keller raged. "But there'll be a new Head of Inspection, who will pass them, tomorrow morning!"

"In that you may be half right. When you get done licking Black's boots, tell him that I am in my office."

Kinnison re-entered his suite. Keller, swearing, strode away with Piddy. Doors clicked shut.

"I *am* going to quit, Uncle Ralph, law or no law!" Tugwell stormed. "They'll run that bunch of crap through, and then . . . ."

"Will you promise not to quit until they do?" Kinnison asked, quietly.

"Huh?" "What?" Tugwell's eyes—and Celeste's—were pools of astonishment. Celeste, being on the inside, understood first.

"Oh—to keep his nose clean—I see!" she exclaimed.

"Exactly. Those shell will not be accepted, nor any like them. On the surface, we got licked. I will get fired. You will find, however, that we won this particular battle. And if you boys stay here and hang together and keep on slugging you can win a lot more."

"Maybe, if we raise enough hell, we can make them fire us, too?" Drake suggested.

"I doubt it. But unless I'm wrong, you can just about write your own ticket from now on, if you play it straight." Kinnison grinned to himself, at something which the young people could not see.

"You told me what Stoner and Black would do to us," Tugwell said, intensely. "What I'm afraid of is that they'll do it to you."

"They can't. Not a chance in the world," Kinnison assured him. "You fellows are young—not established. But I'm well-enough known in my own field so that if they tried to black-ball me they'd just get themselves laughed at, and they know it. So beat it back to the Nine, you kids, and hang red tickets on everything that doesn't cross-section up to standard. Tell the gang goodbye for me—I'll keep you posted."

In less than an hour Kinnison was called into the Office of the President. He was completely at ease; Black was not.

"It has been decided to . . . uh . . . ask for your resignation," the President announced at last.

"Save your breath," Kinnison advised. "I came down here to do a job, and the only way you can keep me from doing that job is to fire me."

"That was not . . . uh . . . entirely unexpected. A difficulty arose, however, in deciding what reason to put on your termination papers."

"I can well believe that. You can put down anything you like," Kinnison shrugged, "with one exception. Any implication of incompetence and you'll have to prove it in court."

"Incompatibility, say?"

"O.K."

"Miss Briggs—'Incompatibility with the highest echelon of Stoner and Black, Inc.,' please. You may as well wait, Dr. Kinnison; it will take only a moment."

"Fine. I've got a couple of things to say. First, I know as well as you do that you're between Scylla and Charybdis—damned if you do and damned if you don't."

"Certainly not! Ridiculous!" Black blustered, but his eyes wavered. "Where did you get such a preposterous idea? What do you mean?"

"If you ram those sub-standard H.E.A.T. shell through, you are going to have some more prematures. Not many—the stuff is actually almost good enough—one in ten thousand, say: perhaps one in fifty thousand. But you know damned well that you can't afford *any*. What my Siberians and Inspectors know about you and Keller and Piddy and the Nine Line would be enough; but to cap the climax that brainless jackal of yours let the cat completely out of the bag this afternoon, and everybody in Building One was listening. One more premature would blow Entwhistle wide open—would start something that not all the politicians in Washington could stop. On the other hand, if you scrap those lots and go back to pouring good loads, your Mr. Stoner, of New York and Washington, will be very unhappy and will scream bloody murder. I'm sure, however, that you won't offer any Plate D loads to Ordnance—in view of the temper of my boys and girls, and the number of people who heard your dumb stooge give you away, you won't dare to. In fact, I told some of my people that you wouldn't; that you are a smart enough operator to keep your nose clean."

"You *told* them!" Black shouted, in anger and dismay.

"Yes? Why not?" The words were innocent enough, but Kinnison's expression was full of meaning. "I don't want to seem trite, but you are just beginning to find out that honesty and loyalty are a hell of a hard team to beat."

"Get out! Take these termination papers and GET OUT!"

And Doctor Ralph K. Kinnison, head high, strode out of President Black's office and out of Entwhistle Ordnance Plant.

THE LENSMAN

"Theodore K. Kinnison!" a crisp, clear voice snapped from the speaker of an apparently cold, ordinary-enough-looking radio-television set.

A burly young man caught his breath sharply as he leaped to the instrument and pressed an inconspicuous button.

"Theodore K. Kinnison acknowledging!" The plate remained dark, but he knew that he was being scanned.

"Operation Bullfinch!" the speaker blatted.

Kinnison gulped. "Operation Bullfinch—Off!" he managed to say.

"Off!"

He pushed the button again and turned to face the tall, trim honey-blonde who stood tensely poised in the archway. Her eyes were wide and protesting; both hands clutched at her throat.

"Uh-huh, sweets, they're coming—over the Pole," he gritted. "Two hours, more or less."

"Oh, Ted!" She threw herself into his arms. They kissed, then broke away.

The man picked up two large suitcases, already packed—everything else, including food and water, had been in the car for weeks—and made strides. The girl rushed after him, not bothering even to close the door of the apartment, scooping up *en passant* a leggy boy of four and a chubby, curly-haired girl of two or thereabouts. They ran across the lawn toward a big, low-slung sedan.

"Sure you got your caffeine tablets?" he demanded as they ran.

"Uh-huh."

"You'll need 'em. Drive like the devil—*stay ahead!* You can—this heap has got the legs of a centipede and you've got plenty of gas and oil. Eleven hundred miles from anywhere and a population of one-tenth per square mile—you'll be safe there if anybody is."

"It isn't us I'm worried about—it's you!" she panted. "Technos' wives get a few minutes' notice ahead of the H-blast—I'll be ahead of the rush and I'll stay ahead. It's you, Ted—*you!*"

"Don't worry, keed. That popcycle of mine has got legs, too, and there won't be so much traffic, the way I'm going."

"Oh, blast! I didn't mean that, and you know it!"

They were at the car. While he jammed the two bags into an exactly-fitting space, she tossed the children into the front seat, slid lithely under the wheel, and started the engine.

"I know you didn't, sweetheart. I'll be back." He kissed her and the little girl, the while shaking hands with his son. "Kidlets, you and mother are going out to visit Grand-dad Kinnison, like we told you all about. Lots of fun. I'll be along later. Now, Lady Lead-Foot, scram—and shovel on the coal!"

The heavy vehicle backed and swung; gravel flew as the accelerator-pedal hit the floor.

Kinnison galloped across the alley and opened the door of a small garage, revealing a long, squat motorcycle. Two deft passes of his hands and two of his three spotlights were no longer white—one flashed a brilliant purple, the other a searing blue. He dropped a perforated metal box into a hanger and flipped a switch—a peculiarly-toned siren began its ululating shriek. He took the alley turn at an angle of forty-five degrees; burned the pavement toward Diversey.

The light was red. No matter—everybody had stopped—that siren could be heard for miles. He barreled into the intersection; his step-plate ground the concrete as he made a screaming left turn.

A siren—creeping up from behind. City tone. Two red spots—city cop—so soon—good! He cut his gun a trifle, the other bike came alongside.

"Is this IT?" the uniformed rider yelled, over the coughing thunder of the competing exhausts.

"Yes!" Kinnison yelled back. "Clear Diversey to the Outer Drive, and the Drive south to Gary and north to Waukegan. Snap it up!"

The white-and-black motorcycle slowed; shot over toward the curb. The officer reached for his microphone.

Kinnison sped on. At Cicero Avenue, although he had a green light, traffic was so heavy that he had to slow down; at Pulaski two policemen waved him through a red. Beyond Sacramento nothing moved on wheels.

Seventy . . . seventy five . . . he took the bridge at eighty, both wheels in air for forty feet. Eighty five . . . ninety . . . that was about all he could do and keep the heap on so rough a road. Also, he did not have Diversey all to himself any more; blue-and-purple-flashing bikes were coming in from every side-street. He slowed to a conservative fifty and went into close formation with the other riders.

The H-blast—the city-wide warning for the planned and supposedly orderly evacuation of all Chicago—sounded, but Kinnison did not hear it.

Across the Park, edging over to the left so that the boys going south would have room to make the turn—even such riders as those need *some* room to make a turn at fifty miles per hour!

Under the viaduct—biting brakes and squealing tires at that sharp, narrow, right-angle left turn—north on the wide, smooth Drive!

That highway was made for speed. So were those machines. Each rider, as he got into the flat, lay down along his tank, tucked his chin behind the cross-bar, and twisted both throttles out against their stops. They were in a hurry. They had a long way to go; and if they did not get there in time to stop those trans-polar atomic missiles, all hell would be out for noon.

Why was all this necessary? This organization, this haste, this split-second timing, this city-wide exhibition of insane hippodrome riding? Why were not all these motorcycle-racers stationed permanently at their posts, so as to be ready for any emergency? Because America, being a democracy, could not strike first, but had to wait—wait in instant readiness—until she was actually attacked. Because every good Techno in America had his assigned place in some American Defense Plan; of which Operation Bullfinch was only one. Because, without the presence of those Technos at their every-day jobs, all ordinary technological work in America would perforce have stopped.

THE LENSMAN

A branch road curved away to the right. Scarcely slowing down, Kinnison bulleted into the turn and through an open, heavily-guarded gate. Here his mount and his lights were passwords enough: the real test would come later. He approached a towering structure of alloy—jammed on his brakes—stopped beside a soldier who, as soon as Kinnison jumped off, mounted the motorcycle and drove it away.

Kinnison dashed up to an apparently blank wall, turned his back upon four commissioned officers holding cocked forty-fives at the ready, and fitted his right eye into a cup. Unlike fingerprints, retinal patterns cannot be imitated, duplicated, or altered; any imposter would have died instantly, without arrest or question. For every man who belonged aboard that rocket had been checked and tested—*how* he had been checked and tested!—since one spy, in any one of those Technos' chairs, could wreak damage untellable.

The port snapped open. Kinnison climbed a ladder into the large, but crowded, Operations Room.

"Hi, Teddy!" a yell arose.

"Hi, Walt! Hi-ya, Red! What-ho, Baldy!" and so on. These men were friends of old.

"Where are they?" he demanded. "Is our stuff getting away? Lemme take a peek at the Ball!"

"I'll say it is! O.K., Ted, squeeze in here!"

He squeezed in. It was not a ball, but a hemisphere, slightly oblate and centered approximately by the North Pole. A multitude of red dots moved slowly—a hundred miles upon that map was a small distance—northward over Canada; a closer-packed, less numerous group of yellowish-greens, already on the American side of the Pole, was coming south.

As had been expected, the Americans had more missiles than did the enemy. The other belief, that America had more adequate defenses and better-trained, more highly skilled defenders, would soon be put to test.

A string of blue lights blazed across the continent, from Nome through Skagway and Wallaston and Churchill and Kaniapiskau to Belle Isle; America's First Line of Defense. Regulars all. Ambers almost blanketed those blues; their combat rockets were already grabbing altitude. The Second Line, from Portland, Seattle, and Vancouver across to Halifax, also showed solid green, with some flashes of amber. Part Regulars; part National Guard.

Chicago was in the Third Line, all National Guard, extending from San Francisco to New York. Green—alert and operating. So were the Fourth, the Fifth, and the Sixth. Operation Bullfinch was clicking; on schedule to the second.

A bell clanged; the men sprang to their stations and strapped down. Every chair was occupied. Combat Rocket Number One Oh Six Eight Five, full-powered by the disintegrating nuclei of unstable isotopes, took off with a whooshing roar which even her thick walls could not mute.

The Technos, crushed down into their form-fitting cushions by three G's of acceleration, clenched their teeth and took it.

Higher! Faster! The rocket shivered and trembled as it hit the wall at the velocity of sound, but it did not pause.

Higher! Faster! Higher! Fifty miles high. One hundred . . . five hundred . . . a thousand . . . fifteen hundred . . . two thousand! Half a radius—the designated altitude at which the Chicago Contingent would go into action.

Acceleration was cut to zero. The Technos, breathing deeply in relief, donned peculiarly-goggled helmets and set up their panels.

Kinnison stared into his plate with everything he could put into his optic nerve. This was not like the Ball, in which the lights were electronically placed, automatically controlled, clear, sharp, and steady. This was radar. A radar considerably different from that of 1948, of course, and greatly improved, but still pitifully inadequate in dealing with objects separated by hundreds of miles and traveling at velocities of thousands of miles per hour!

Nor was this like the practice cruises, in which the targets had been harmless barrels or equally harmless dirigible rockets. This was the real thing; the targets today would be lethal objects indeed. Practice gunnery, with only a place in the Proficiency List at stake, had been exciting enough: this was too exciting—*much* too exciting—for the keenness of brain and the quickness and steadiness of eye and of hand so soon to be required.

A target? Or was it? Yes—three or four of them!

"Target One—Zone Ten," a quiet voice spoke into Kinnison's ear and one of the white specks upon his plate turned yellowish green. The same words, the same lights, were heard and seen by the eleven other Technos of Sector A, of which Kinnison, by virtue of standing at the top of his Combat Rocket's Proficiency List, was Sector Chief. He knew that the voice was that of Sector A's Fire Control Officer, whose duty it was to determine, from courses, velocities, and all other data to be had from ground and lofty observers, the order in which his Sector's targets should be eliminated. And Sector A, an imaginary but sharply-defined cone, was in normal maneuvering the hottest part of the sky. Fire Control's "Zone Ten" had informed him that the object was at extreme range and hence there would be plenty of time. Nevertheless:

"Lawrence—two! Doyle—one! Drummond—stand by with three!" he snapped, at the first word.

In the instant of hearing his name each Techno stabbed down a series of studs and there flowed into his ears a rapid stream of figures—the up-to-the-second data from every point of observation as to every element of motion of his target. He punched the figures into his calculator, which would correct automatically for the motion of his own vessel—glanced once at the printed solution of the problem—tramped down upon a pedal once, twice, or three times, depending upon the number of projectiles he had been directed to handle.

Kinnison had ordered Lawrence, a better shot than Doyle, to launch two torpedoes; neither of which, at such long range, was expected to strike its mark. His second, however, should come close; so close that the instantaneous data sent back to both screens—and to Kinnison's—by the torpedo itself would make the target a sitting duck for Doyle, the less proficient follower.

Drummond, Kinnison's Number Three, would not launch his missiles unless Doyle missed. Nor could both Drummond and Harper, Kinnison's Number Two, be "out" at once. One of the two had to be "in" at all times, to take Kinnison's place in charge of the Sector if the Chief were ordered out. For while Kinnison could order either Harper or Drummond on target, he could not send himself. He could go out only when ordered to do so by Fire Control: Sector Chiefs were reserved for emergency use only.

"Target Two—Zone Nine," Fire Control said.

"Carney, two. French, one. Day, stand by with three!" Kinnison ordered.

"Damn it—missed!" This from Doyle. "Buck fever—no end."

"O.K., boy—that's why we're starting so soon. I'm shaking like a vibrator myself. We'll get over it . . . ."

The point of light which represented Target One bulged slightly and went out. Drummond had connected and was back "in".

"Target Three—Zone Eight. Four—eight," Fire Control remarked.

"Target Three—Higgins and Green; Harper stand by. Four—Case and Santos: Lawrence."

After a minute or two of actual combat the Technos of Sector A began to steady down. Stand-by men were no longer required and were no longer assigned.

"Target Forty-one—six," said Fire Control; and:

"Lawrence, two. Doyle, two," ordered Kinnison. This was routine enough, but in a moment:

"Ted!" Lawrence snapped. "Missed—wide—both barrels. Forty-one's dodging—manned or directed—coming like hell—watch it, Doyle—WATCH IT!"

"Kinnison, take it!" Fire Control barked, voice now neither low nor steady, and without waiting to see whether Doyle would hit or miss. "It's in Zone Three already—collision course!"

"Harper! Take over!"

Kinnison got the data, solved the equations, launched five torpedoes at fifty gravities of acceleration. One . . . two—three-four-five; the last three as close together as they could fly without setting off their proximity fuzes.

Communications and mathematics and the electronic brains of calculating machines had done all that they could do; the rest was up to human skill, to the perfection of co-ordination and the speed of reaction of human mind, nerve, and muscle.

Kinnison's glance darted from plate to panel to computer-tape to meter to galvanometer and back to plate; his left hand moved in tiny arcs the knobs whose rotation varied the intensities of two mutually perpendicular components of his torpedoes' drives. He listened attentively to the reports of triangulating observers, now giving him data covering his own missiles, as well as the target object. The fingers of his right hand punched almost constantly the keys of his computer; he corrected almost constantly his torpedoes' course.

"Up a hair," he decided. "Left about a point."

The target moved away from its predicted path.

Down two—left three—down a hair—*Right!* The thing was almost through Zone Two; was blasting into Zone One.

He thought for a second that his first torp was going to connect. It almost did—only a last-instant, full-powered side thrust enabled the target to evade it. Two numbers flashed white upon his plate; his actual error, exact to the foot of distance and to the degree on the clock, measured and transmitted back to his board by instruments in his torpedo.

Working with instantaneous and exact data, and because the enemy had so little time in which to act, Kinnison's second projectile made a very near miss indeed. His third was a graze; so close that its proximity fuze functioned, detonating the cyclonite-packed warhead. Kinnison knew that his third went off, because the error-figures vanished, almost in the instant of their coming into being, as its detecting and transmitting instruments were destroyed. That one detonation might have been enough; but Kinnison had had one glimpse of his error—how small it was!—and had a fraction of a second of time. Hence Four and Five slammed home; dead center. Whatever that target had been, it was no longer a threat.

"Kinnison, in," he reported briefly to Fire Control, and took over from Harper the direction of the activities of Sector A.

The battle went on. Kinnison sent Harper and Drummond out time after time. He himself was given three more targets. The first wave of the enemy—what was left of it—passed. Sector A went into action, again at extreme range, upon the second. Its remains, too, plunged downward and onward toward the distant ground.

The third wave was really tough. Not that it was actually any worse than the first two had been, but the CR10685 was no longer getting the data which her Technos ought to have to do a good job; and every man aboard her knew why. Some enemy stuff had got through, of course; and the observatories, both on the ground and above it—the eye of the whole American Defense—had suffered heavily.

Nevertheless, Kinnison and his fellows were not too perturbed. Such a condition was not entirely unexpected. They were now veterans; they had been tried and had not been found wanting. They had come unscathed through a bath of fire the like of which the world had never before known. Give them any kind of computation at all—or no computation at all except old CR10685's own radar and their own torps, of which they still had plenty—and they could and would take care of anything that could be thrown at them.

The third wave passed. Targets became fewer and fewer. Action slowed down . . . stopped.

The Technos, even the Sector Chiefs, knew nothing whatever of the progress of the battle as a whole. They did not know where their rocket was, or whether it was going north, east, south, or west. They knew when it was going up or down only by the "seats of their pants." They did not even know the nature of the targets they destroyed, since upon their plates all targets looked alike—small, bright, greenish-yellow spots. Hence:

"Give us the dope, Pete, if we've got a minute to spare," Kinnison begged of his Fire Control Officer. "You know more than we do—give!"

THE LENSMAN

"It's coming in now," came the prompt reply. "Six of those targets that did such fancy dodging were atomics, aimed at the Lines. Five were dirigibles, with our number on 'em. You fellows did a swell job. Very little of their stuff got through—not enough, they say, to do much damage to a country as big as the U.S.A. On the other hand, they stopped scarcely any of ours—they apparently didn't have anything to compare with you Technos.

"But all hell seems to be busting loose, all over the world. Our east and west coasts are both being attacked, they say; but are holding. Operation Daisy and Operation Fairfield are clicking, just like we did. Europe, they say, is going to hell—everybody is taking pot-shots at everybody else. One report says that the South American nations are bombing each other . . . Asia, too . . . nothing definite; as straight dope comes in I'll relay it to you.

"We came through in very good shape, considering . . . losses less than anticipated, only seven percent. The First Line—as you know already—took a God-awful shellacking; in fact, the Churchill-Belcher section was practically wiped out, which was what lost us about all of our Observation . . . . We are now just about over the southern end of Hudson Bay, heading down and south to join in making a vertical Fleet Formation . . . no more waves coming, but they say to expect attacks from low-flying combat rockets—there goes the alert! On your toes, fellows—but there isn't a thing on Sector A's screen . . . ."

There wasn't. Since the CR10685 was diving downward and southward, there wouldn't be. Nevertheless, some observer aboard that rocket saw that atomic missile coming. Some Fire Control Officer yelled orders; some Technos did their best—and failed.

And such is the violence of nuclear fission; so utterly incomprehensible is its speed, that Theodore K. Kinnison died without realizing that anything whatever was happening to his ship or to him.

*

Gharlane of Eddore looked upon ruined Earth, his handiwork, and found it good. Knowing that it would be many of hundreds of Tellurian years before that planet would again require his personal attention, he went elsewhere; to Rigel Four, to Palain Seven, and to the solar system of Velantia, where he found that his creatures the Overlords were not progressing according to schedule. He spent quite a little time there, then searched minutely and fruitlessly for evidence of inimical activity within the Innermost Circle.

And upon far Arisia a momentous decision was made: the time had come to curb sharply the hitherto unhampered Eddorians.

"We are ready, then, to war openly upon them?" Eukonidor asked, somewhat doubtfully. "Again to cleanse the planet Tellus of dangerous radioactives and of too-noxious forms of life is of course a simple matter. From our protected areas in North America a strong but democratic government can spread to cover the world. That government can be extended easily enough to include Mars and Venus. But Gharlane, who is to operate as Roger, who has already planted, in the Adepts of North Polar Jupiter, the seeds of the Jovian Wars . . . ."

"Your visualization is sound, youth. Think on."

"Those interplanetary wars are of course inevitable, and will serve to strengthen and to unify the government of the Inner Planets . . . provided that Gharlane does not interfere . . . . Oh, I see.

Gharlane will not at first know; since a zone of compulsion will be held upon him. When he or some Eddorian fusion perceives that compulsion and breaks it—at some such time of high stress as the Nevian incident—it will be too late. Our fusions will be operating. Roger will be allowed to perform only such acts as will be for Civilization's eventual good. Nevia was selected as Prime Operator because of its location in a small region of the galaxy which is almost devoid of solid iron and because of its watery nature; its aquatic forms of life being precisely those in which the Eddorians are least interested. They will be given partial neutralization of inertia; they will be able to attain velocities a few times greater than that of light. That covers the situation, I think?"

"Very good, Eukonidor," the Elders approved. "A concise and accurate summation."

Hundreds of Tellurian years passed. The aftermath. Reconstruction. Advancement. One world—two worlds—three worlds—united, harmonious, friendly. The Jovian Wars. A solid, unshakeable union.

Nor did any Eddorian know that such fantastically rapid progress was being made. Indeed, Gharlane knew, as he drove his immense ship of space toward Sol, that he would find Tellus inhabited by peoples little above savagery.

And it should be noted in passing that not once, throughout all those centuries, did a man named Kinnison marry a girl with red-bronze-auburn hair and gold-flecked, tawny eyes.

BOOK THREE
TRIPLANETARY

PIRATES OF SPACE

Apparently motionless to her passengers and crew, the Interplanetary liner *Hyperion* bored serenely onward through space at normal acceleration. In the railed-off sanctum in one corner of the control room a bell tinkled, a smothered whirr was heard, and Captain Bradley frowned as he studied the brief message upon the tape of the recorder—a message flashed to his desk from the operator's panel. He beckoned, and the second officer, whose watch it now was, read aloud:

"Reports of scout patrols still negative."

"Still negative." The officer scowled in thought. "They've already searched beyond the widest possible location of wreckage, too. Two unexplained disappearances inside a month—first the *Dione*, then the *Rhea*—and not a plate nor a lifeboat recovered. Looks bad, sir. One might be an accident; two might possibly be a coincidence . . . ." His voice died away.

"But at three it would get to be a habit," the captain finished the thought. "And whatever happened, happened quick. Neither of them had time to say a word—their location recorders simply went dead. But of course they didn't have our detector screens nor our armament. According to the observatories we're in clear ether, but I wouldn't trust them from Tellus to Luna. You have given the new orders, of course?"

"Yes, sir. Detectors full out, all three courses of defensive screen on the trips, projectors manned, suits on the hooks. Every object detected to be investigated immediately—if vessels, they are to be warned to stay beyond extreme range. Anything entering the fourth zone is to be rayed."

"Right—we are going through!"

"But no known type of vessel could have made away with them without detection," the second officer argued. "I wonder if there isn't something in those wild rumors we've been hearing lately?"

"Bah! Of course not!" snorted the captain. "Pirates in ships faster than light—sub-ethereal rays—nullification of gravity mass without inertia—ridiculous! Proved impossible, over and over again. No, sir, if pirates are operating in space—and it looks very much like it—they won't get far against a good big battery full of kilowatt-hours behind three courses of heavy screen, and good gunners behind multiplex projectors. They're good enough for anybody. Pirates, Neptunians, angels, or devils—in ships or on broomsticks—if they tackle the *Hyperion* we'll burn them out of the ether!"

Leaving the captain's desk, the watch officer resumed his tour of duty. The six great lookout plates into which the alert observers peered were blank, their far-flung ultra-sensitive detector screens encountering no obstacle—the ether was empty for thousands upon thousands of kilometers. The signal lamps upon the pilot's panel were dark, its warning bells were silent. A brilliant point of white light in the center of the pilot's closely ruled micrometer grating, exactly upon the cross-hairs of his directors, showed that the immense vessel was precisely upon the calculated course, as laid down by the automatic integrating course plotters. Everything was quiet and in order.

"All's well, sir," he reported briefly to Captain Bradley—but all was not well.

Danger—more serious by far in that it was not external—was even then, all unsuspected, gnawing at the great ship's vitals. In a locked and shielded compartment, deep down in the interior of the liner, was the great air purifier. Now a man leaned against the primary duct—the aorta through which flowed the stream of pure air supplying the entire vessel. This man, grotesque in full panoply of space armor, leaned against the duct, and as he leaned a drill bit deeper and deeper into the steel wall of the pipe. Soon it broke through, and the slight rush of air was stopped by the insertion of a tightly fitting rubber tube. The tube terminated in a heavy rubber balloon, which surrounded a frail glass bulb. The man stood tense, one hand holding before his silica-and-steel-helmeted head a large pocket chronometer, the other lightly grasping the balloon. A sneering grin was upon his face as he waited the exact second of action—the carefully predetermined instant when his right hand, closing, would shatter the fragile flask and force its contents into the primary air stream of the *Hyperion*!

*

Far above, in the main saloon, the regular evening dance was in full swing. The ship's orchestra crashed into silence, there was a patter of applause, and Clio Marsden, radiant belle of the voyage, led her partner out onto the promenade and up to one of the observation plates.

"Oh, we can't see the Earth any more!" she exclaimed. "Which way do you turn this, Mr. Costigan?"

"Like this," and Conway Costigan, burly young First Officer of the liner, turned the dials. "There—this plate is looking back, or down, at Tellus; this other one is looking ahead."

Earth was a brilliantly shining crescent far beneath the flying vessel. Above her, ruddy Mars and silvery Jupiter blazed in splendor ineffable against a background of utterly indescribable blackness—a background thickly besprinkled with dimensionless points of dazzling brilliance which were the stars.

"Oh, isn't it wonderful!" breathed the girl, awed. "Of course, I suppose that it's old stuff to you, but I'm a ground-gripper, you know, and I could look at it forever, I think. That's why I want to come out here after every dance. You know, I . . . . "

Her voice broke off suddenly, with a queer, rasping catch, as she seized his arm in a frantic clutch and as quickly went limp. He stared at her sharply, and understood instantly the message written in her eyes—eyes now enlarged, staring, hard, brilliant, and full of soul-searing terror as she slumped down, helpless but for his support. In the act of exhaling as he was, lungs almost entirely empty, yet he held his breath until he had seized the microphone from his belt and had snapped the lever to "emergency."

"Control room!" he gasped then, and every speaker throughout the great cruiser of the void blared out the warning as he forced his already evacuated lungs to absolute emptiness. "Vee-Two Gas! Get tight!"

Writhing and twisting in his fierce struggle to keep his lungs from gulping in a draft of that noxious atmosphere, and with the unconscious form of the girl draped limply over his left arm, Costigan leaped toward the portal of the nearest lifeboat. Orchestra instruments crashed to the floor and dancing couples fell and sprawled inertly while the tortured First Officer swung the door of the lifeboat open and dashed across the tiny room to the air-valves. Throwing them wide open, he put his mouth to the orifice and let his laboring lungs gasp their eager fill of the cold blast roaring from the tanks. Then, air-hunger partially assuaged, he again held his breath, broke open the emergency locker, donned one of the space-suits always kept there, and opened its valves wide in order to flush out of his uniform any lingering trace of the lethal gas.

He then leaped back to his companion. Shutting off the air, he released a stream of pure oxygen, held her face in it, and made shift to force some of it into her lungs by compressing and releasing her chest against his own body. Soon she drew a spasmodic breath, choking and coughing, and he again changed the gaseous stream to one of pure air, speaking urgently as she showed signs of returning consciousness.

"Stand up!" he snapped. "Hang onto this brace and keep your face in this air-stream until I get a suit around you! Got me?"

She nodded weakly, and, assured that she could hold herself at the valve, it was the work of only a minute to encase her in one of the protective coverings. Then, as she sat upon a bench, recovering her strength, he flipped on the lifeboat's visiphone projector and shot its invisible beam up into the control room, where he saw space-armored figures furiously busy at the panels.

"Dirty work at the cross-roads!" he blazed to his captain, man to man—formality disregarded, as it so often was in the Triplanetary service. "There's skulduggery afoot somewhere in our primary air! Maybe that's the way they got those other two ships—pirates! Might have been a timed bomb—don't see how anybody could have stowed away down there through the inspections, and nobody but Franklin can neutralize the shield of the air room—but I'm going to look around, anyway. Then I'll join you fellows up there."

"What was it?" the shaken girl asked. "I think that I remember your saying 'Vee-Two gas.' That's forbidden! Anyway, I owe you my life, Conway, and I'll never forget it—never. Thanks—but the others—how about all the rest of us?"

"It was Vee-Two, and it is forbidden," Costigan replied grimly, eyes fast upon the flashing plate, whose point of projection was now deep in the bowels of the vessel. "The penalty for using it or having it is death on sight. Gangsters and pirates use it, since they have nothing to lose, being on the death list already. As for your life, I haven't saved it yet—you may wish I'd let it ride before we get done. The others are too far gone for oxygen—couldn't have brought even you around in a few more seconds, quick as I got to you. But there's a sure antidote—we all carry it in a lock-box in our armor—and we all know how to use it, because crooks all use Vee-Two and so we're always expecting it. But since the air will be pure again in half an hour we'll be able to revive the others easily enough if we can get by with whatever is going to happen next. There's the bird that did it, right in the air-room. It's the Chief Engineer's suit, but that isn't Franklin that's in it. Some passenger—disguised—slugged the Chief—took his suit and projectors—hole in duct—p-s-s-t! All washed out! Maybe that's all he was scheduled to do to us in this performance, but he'll do nothing else in his life!"

"Don't go down there!" protested the girl. "His armor is so much better than that emergency suit you are wearing, and he's got Mr. Franklin's Lewiston, besides!"

"Don't be an idiot!" he snapped. "We can't have a live pirate aboard—we're going to be altogether too busy with outsiders directly. Don't worry, I'm not going to give him a break. I'll take a Standish—I'll rub him out like a blot. Stay right here until I come back after you," he commanded, and the heavy door of the lifeboat clanged shut behind him as he leaped out into the promenade.

Straight across the saloon he made his way, paying no attention to the inert forms scattered here and there. Going up to a blank wall, he manipulated an almost invisible dial set flush with its surface, swung a heavy door aside, and lifted out the Standish—a fearsome weapon. Squat, huge, and heavy, it resembled somewhat an overgrown machine rifle, but one possessing a thick, short telescope, with several opaque condensing lenses and parabolic reflectors. Laboring under the weight of the thing, he strode along corridors and clambered heavily down short stairways. Finally he came to the purifier room, and grinned savagely as he saw the greenish haze of light obscuring the door and walls—the shield was still in place; the pirate was still inside, still flooding with the terrible Vee Two the *Hyperion's* primary air.

He set his peculiar weapon down, unfolded its three massive legs, crouched down behind it, and threw in a switch. Dull red beams of frightful intensity shot from the reflectors and sparks, almost of lightning proportions, leaped from the shielding screen under their impact. Roaring and snapping, the conflict went on for seconds, then, under the superior force of the Standish, the greenish radiance gave way. Behind it the metal of the door ran the gamut of color—red, yellow, blinding white—then literally exploded; molten, vaporized, burned away. Through the aperture thus made Costigan could plainly see the pirate in the space-armor of the chief engineer—an armor which was proof against rifle fire and which could reflect and neutralize for some little time even the terrific beam Costigan was employing. Nor was the pirate unarmed—a vicious flare of incandescence leaped from his Lewiston, to spend its force in spitting, crackling pyrotechnics against the ether-wall of the squat and monstrous Standish. But Costigan's infernal engine did not rely only upon vibratory destruction. At almost the first flash of the pirate's weapon the officer touched a trigger, there was a double report, ear-shattering in that narrowly confined space, and the pirate's body literally flew into mist as a half-kilogram shell tore through his armor and exploded. Costigan shut off his beam, and with not the slightest softening of one hard lineament stared around the air-room; making sure that no serious damage had been done to the vital machinery of the air-purifier—the very lungs of the great space-ship.

Dismounting the Standish, he lugged it back up to the main saloon, replaced it in its safe, and again set the combination lock. Thence to the lifeboat, where Clio cried out in relief as she saw that he was unhurt.

"Oh, Conway, I've been so afraid something would happen to you!" she exclaimed, as he led her rapidly upward toward the control room. "Of course you . . . " she paused.

"Sure," he replied, laconically. "Nothing to it. How do you feel—about back to normal?"

"All right, I think, except for being scared to death and just about out of control. I don't suppose that I'll be good for anything, but whatever I can do, count me in on."

"Fine—you may be needed, at that. Everybody's out, apparently, except those like me, who had a warning and could hold their breath until they got to their suits."

"But how did you know what it was? You can't see it, nor smell it, nor anything."

"You inhaled a second before I did, and I saw your eyes. I've been in it before—and when you see a man get a jolt of that stuff just once, you never forget it. The engineers down below got it first, of course—it must have wiped them out. Then we got it in the saloon. Your passing out warned me, and luckily I had enough breath left to give the word. Quite a few of the fellows up above should have had time to get away—we'll see 'em all in the control room."

"I suppose that was why you revived me—in payment for so kindly warning you of the gas attack?" The girl laughed; shaky, but game.

"Something like that, probably," he answered, lightly. "Here we are—now we'll soon find out what's going to happen next."

In the control room they saw at least a dozen armored figures; not now rushing about, but seated at their instruments, tense and ready. Fortunate it was that Costigan—veteran of space as he was, though young in years—had been down in the saloon; fortunate that he had been familiar with that horrible outlawed gas; fortunate that he had had presence of mind enough and sheer physical stamina enough to send his warning without allowing one paralyzing trace to enter his own lungs. Captain Bradley, the men on watch, and several other officers in their quarters or in the wardrooms—space-hardened veterans all—had obeyed instantly and without question the amplifiers' gasped command to "get tight". Exhaling or inhaling, their air-passages had snapped shut as that dread "Vee-Two" was heard, and they had literally jumped into their armored suits of space—flushing them out with volume after volume of unquestionable air; holding their breath to the last possible second, until their straining lungs could endure no more.

Costigan waved the girl to a vacant bench, cautiously changing into his own armor from the emergency suit he had been wearing, and approached the captain.

"Anything in sight, sir?" he asked, saluting. "They should have started something before this."

"They've started, but we can't locate them. We tried to send out a general sector alarm, but had hardly started when they blanketed our wave. Look at that!"

Following the captain's eyes, Costigan stared at the high powered set of the ship's operator. Upon the plate, instead of a moving, living, three-dimensional picture, there was a flashing glare of blinding white light; from the speaker, instead of intelligible speech, was issuing a roaring, crackling stream of noise.

"It's impossible!" Bradley burst out, violently. "There's not a gram of metal inside the fourth zone—within a hundred thousand kilometers—and yet they must be close to send such a wave as that. But the Second thinks not—what do you think, Costigan?" The bluff commander, reactionary and of the old school as was his breed, was furious—baffled, raging inwardly to come to grips with the invisible and indetectable foe. Face to face with the inexplicable, however, he listened to the younger men with unusual tolerance.

"It's not only possible; it's quite evident that they've got something we haven't." Costigan's voice was bitter. "But why shouldn't they have? Service ships never get anything until it's been experimented with for years, but pirates and such always get the new stuff as soon as it's discovered. The only good thing I can see is that we got part of a message away, and the scouts can trace that interference out there. But the pirates know that, too—it won't be long now," he concluded, grimly.

He spoke truly. Before another word was said the outer screen flared white under a beam of terrific power, and simultaneously there appeared upon one of the lookout plates a vivid picture of the pirate vessel—a huge, black torpedo of steel, now emitting flaring offensive beams of force.

Instantly the powerful weapons of the *Hyperion* were brought to bear, and in the blast of full-driven beams the stranger's screens flamed incandescent. Heavy guns, under the recoil of whose fierce salvos the frame of the giant globe trembled and shuddered, shot out their tons of high-explosive shell. But the pirate commander had known accurately the strength of the liner, and knew that her armament was impotent against the forces at his command. His screens were invulnerable, the giant shells were exploded harmlessly in mid-space, miles from their objective. And suddenly a frightful pencil of flame stabbed brilliantly from the black hulk of the enemy. Through the empty ether it tore, through the mighty defensive screens, through the tough metal of the outer and inner walls. Every ether-defense of the *Hyperion* vanished, and her acceleration dropped to a quarter of its normal value.

"Right through the battery room!" Bradley groaned. "We're on the emergency drive now. Our rays are done for, and we can't seem to put a shell anywhere near her with our guns!"

But ineffective as the guns were, they were silenced forever as a frightful beam of destruction stabbed relentlessly through the control room, whiffing out of existence the pilot, gunnery, and lookout panels and the men before them. The air rushed into space, and the suits of the three survivors bulged out into drum-head tightness as the pressure in the room decreased.

Costigan pushed the captain lightly toward a wall, then seized the girl and leaped in the same direction.

"Let's get out of here, quick!" he cried, the miniature radio instruments of the helmets automatically taking up the duty of transmitting speech as the sound disks refused to function. "They can't see us—our ether wall is still up and their spy-rays can't get through it from the outside, you know. They're working from blue-prints, and they'll probably take your desk next," and even as they bounded toward the door, now become the outer seal of an airlock, the pirates' beam tore through the space which they had just quitted.

Through the airlock, down through several levels of passengers' quarters they hurried, and into a lifeboat, whose one doorway commanded the full length of the third lounge—an ideal spot, either for defense or for escape outward by means of the miniature cruiser. As they entered their retreat they felt their weight begin to increase. More and more force was applied to the helpless liner, until it was moving at normal acceleration.

"What do you make of that, Costigan?" asked the captain. "Tractor beams?"

"Apparently. They've got something, all right. They're taking us somewhere, fast. I'll go get a couple of Standishes, and another suit of armor—we'd better dig in," and soon the small room became a veritable fortress, housing as it did those two formidable engines of destruction. Then the first officer made another and longer trip, returning with a complete suit of Triplanetary space armor, exactly like those worn by the two men, but considerably smaller.

"Just as an added factor of safety, you'd better put this on, Clio—those emergency suits aren't good for much in a battle. I don't suppose that you ever fired a Standish, did you?"

"No, but I can soon learn how to do it," she replied pluckily.

"Two is all that can work here at once, but you should know how to take hold in case one of us goes out. And while you're changing suits you'd better put on some stuff I've got here—Service Special phones and detectors. Stick this little disk onto your chest with this bit of tape; low down, out of sight. Just under your wishbone is the best place. Take off your wrist-watch and wear this one *continuously*—never take it off for a second. Put on these pearls, and wear them all the time, too. Take this capsule and hide it against your skin, some place where it can't be found except by the most rigid search. Swallow it in an emergency—it goes down easily and works just as well inside as outside. It is the most important thing of all—you can get along with it alone if you lose everything else, but without that capsule the whole system's shot to pieces. With that outfit, if we should get separated, you can talk to us—we're both wearing 'em, although in somewhat different forms. You don't need to talk loud—just a mutter will be enough. They're handy little outfits—almost impossible to find, and capable of a lot of things."

"Thanks, Conway—I'll remember that, too," Clio replied, as she turned toward the tiny locker to follow his instructions. "But won't the scouts and patrols be catching us pretty quick? The operator sent a warning."

"Afraid the ether's empty, as far as we're concerned."

Captain Bradley had stood by in silent astonishment during this conversation. His eyes had bulged slightly at Costigan's "we're both wearing 'em," but he had held his peace and as the girl disappeared a look of dawning comprehension came over his face.

"Oh, I see, sir," he said, respectfully—far more respectfully than he had ever before addressed a mere first officer. "Meaning that we both *will be* wearing them shortly, I assume. 'Service Specials'—but you didn't specify exactly *what* Service, did you?"

"Now that you mention it, I don't believe that I did," Costigan grinned.

"That explains several things about you—particularly your recognition of Vee-Two and your uncanny control and speed of reaction. But aren't you . . . ."

"No," Costigan interrupted. "This situation is apt to get altogether too serious to overlook any bets. If we get away, I'll take them away from her and she'll never know that they aren't routine equipment. As for you, I know that you can and do keep your mouth shut. That's why I'm hanging this junk on you—I had a lot of stuff in my kit, but I flashed it all with the Standish except what I brought in here for us three. Whether you think so or not, we're in a real jam—our chance of getting away is mighty close to zero . . . ."

He broke off as the girl came back, now to all appearances a small Triplanetary officer, and the three settled down to a long and eventless wait. Hour after hour they flew through the ether, but finally there was a lurching swing and an abrupt increase in their acceleration. After a short consultation Captain Bradley turned on the visiray set and, with the beam at its minimum power, peered cautiously downward, in the direction opposite to that in which he knew the pirate vessel must be. All three stared into the plate, seeing only an infinity of emptiness, marked only by the infinitely remote and coldly brilliant stars. While they stared into space a vast area of the heavens was blotted out and they saw, faintly illuminated by a peculiar blue luminescence, a vast ball—a sphere so large and so close that they seemed to be dropping downward toward it as though it were a world! They came to a stop—paused, weightless—a vast door slid smoothly aside—they were drawn *upward* through an airlock and floated quietly in the air above a small, but brightly-lighted and orderly city of metallic buildings! Gently the *Hyperion* was lowered, to come to rest in the embracing arms of a regulation landing cradle.

"Well, wherever it is, we're here," remarked Captain Bradley, grimly, and:

"And now the fireworks start," assented Costigan, with a questioning glance at the girl.

"Don't mind me," she answered his unspoken question. "I don't believe in surrendering, either."

"Right," and both men squatted down behind the ether-walls of their terrific weapons; the girl prone behind them.

They had not long to wait. A group of human beings—men and to all appearances Americans—appeared unarmed in the little lounge. As soon as they were well inside the room, Bradley and Costigan released upon them without compunction the full power of their frightful projectors. From the reflectors, through the doorway, there tore a concentrated double beam of pure destruction—but that beam did not reach its goal. Yards from the men it met a screen of impenetrable density. Instantly the gunners pressed their triggers and a stream of high-explosive shells issued from the roaring weapons. But shells, also, were futile. They struck the shield and vanished—vanished without exploding and without leaving a trace to show that they had ever existed.

Costigan sprang to his feet, but before he could launch his intended attack a vast tunnel appeared beside him—something had gone through the entire width of the liner, cutting effortlessly a smooth cylinder of emptiness. Air rushed in to fill the vacuum, and the three visitors felt themselves seized by invisible forces and drawn into the tunnel. Through it they floated, up to and over buildings, finally slanting downward toward the door of a great high-towered structure. Doors opened before them and closed behind them, until at last they stood upright in a room which was evidently the office of a busy executive. They faced a desk which, in addition to the usual equipment of the business man, carried also a bewilderingly complete switchboard and instrument panel.

Seated impassively at the desk there was a gray man. Not only was he dressed entirely in gray, but his heavy hair was gray, his eyes were gray, and even his tanned skin seemed to give the impression of grayness in disguise. His overwhelming personality radiated an aura of grayness—not the gentle gray of the dove, but the resistless, driving gray of the super-dreadnought; the hard, inflexible, brittle gray of the fracture of high-carbon steel.

"Captain Bradley, First Officer Costigan, Miss Marsden," the man spoke quietly, but crisply. "I had not intended you two men to live so long. That is a detail, however, which we will pass by for the moment. You may remove your suits."

Neither officer moved, but both stared back at the speaker, unflinchingly.

"I am not accustomed to repeating instructions," the man at the desk continued; voice still low and level, but instinct with deadly menace. "You may choose between removing those suits and dying in them, here and now."

Costigan moved over to Clio and slowly took off her armor. Then, after a flashing exchange of glances and a muttered word, the two officers threw off their suits simultaneously and fired at the same instant; Bradley with his Lewiston, Costigan with a heavy automatic pistol whose bullets were explosive shells of tremendous power. But the man in gray, surrounded by an impenetrable wall of force, only smiled at the fusillade, tolerantly and maddeningly. Costigan leaped fiercely, only to be hurled backward as he struck that unyielding, invisible wall. A vicious beam snapped him back into place, the weapons were snatched away, and all three captives were held to their former positions.

"I permitted that, as a demonstration of futility," the gray man said, his hard voice becoming harder, "but I will permit no more foolishness. Now I will introduce myself. I am known as Roger. You probably have heard nothing of me: very few Tellurians have, or ever will. Whether or not you two live depends solely upon yourselves. Being something of a student of men, I fear that you will both die shortly. Able and resourceful as you have just shown yourselves to be, you could be valuable to me, but you probably will not—in which case you shall, of course, cease to exist. That, however, in its proper time—you shall be of some slight service to me in the process of being eliminated. In your case, Miss Marsden, I find myself undecided between two courses of action; each highly desirable, but unfortunately mutually exclusive. Your father will be glad to ransom you at an exceedingly high figure, but in spite of that fact I may decide to use you in a research upon sex."

"Yes?" Clio rose magnificently to the occasion. Fear forgotten, her courageous spirit flashed from her clear young eyes and emanated from her taut young body, erect in defiance. "You may think that you can do anything with me that you please, but you can't!"

"Peculiar—highly perplexing—why should that one stimulus, in the case of young females, produce such an entirely disproportionate reaction?" Roger's eyes bored into Clio's; the girl shivered and looked away. "But sex itself, primal and basic, the most widespread concomitant of life in this continuum, is completely illogical and paradoxical. Most baffling—decidedly, this research on sex must go on."

Roger pressed a button and a tall, comely woman appeared—a woman of indefinite age and of uncertain nationality.

"Show Miss Marsden to her apartment," he directed, and as the two women went out a man came in.

"The cargo is unloaded, sir," the newcomer reported. "The two men and the five women indicated have been taken to the hospital."

"Very well, dispose of the others in the usual fashion." The minion went out, and Roger continued, emotionlessly:

"Collectively, the other passengers may be worth a million or so, but it would not be worthwhile to waste time upon them."

"What are you, anyway?" blazed Costigan, helpless but enraged beyond caution. "I have heard of mad scientists who tried to destroy the Earth, and of equally mad geniuses who thought themselves Napoleons capable of conquering even the Solar System. Whichever you are, you should know that you can't get away with it."

"I am neither. I am, however, a scientist, and I direct many other scientists. I am not mad. You have undoubtedly noticed several peculiar features of this place?"

"Yes, particularly the artificial gravity and those screens. An ordinary ether-wall is opaque in one direction, and doesn't bar matter—yours are transparent both ways and something more than impenetrable to matter. How do you do it?"

"You could not understand them if I explained them to you, and they are merely two of our smaller developments. I do not intend to destroy your planet Earth; I have no desire to rule over masses of futile and brainless men. I have, however, certain ends of my own in view. To accomplish my plans I require hundreds of millions in gold and other hundreds of millions in uranium, thorium, and radium; all of which I shall take from the planets of this Solar System before I leave it. I shall take them in spite of the puerile efforts of the fleets of your Triplanetary League.

"This structure was designed by me and built under my direction. It is protected from meteorites by forces of my devising. It is indetectable and invisible—ether waves are bent around it without loss or distortion. I am discussing these points at such length so that you may realize exactly your position. As I have intimated, you can be of assistance to me if you will."

"Now just what could you offer any *man* to make him join your outfit?" demanded Costigan, venomously.

"Many things," Roger's cold tone betrayed no emotion, no recognition of Costigan's open and bitter contempt. "I have under me many men, bound to me by many ties. Needs, wants, longings, and desires differ from man to man, and I can satisfy practically any of them. Many men take delight in the society of young and beautiful women, but there are other urges which I have found quite efficient. Greed, thirst for fame, longing for power, and so on, including many qualities usually regarded as 'noble.' And what I promise, I deliver. I demand only loyalty to me, and that only in certain things and for a relatively short period. In all else, my men do as they please. In conclusion, I can use you two conveniently, but I do not need you. Therefore you may choose now between my service and—the alternative."

"Exactly what is the alternative?"

"We will not go into that. Suffice it to say that it has to do with a minor research, which is not progressing satisfactorily. It will result in your extinction, and perhaps I should mention that extinction will not be particularly pleasant."

"I say NO, you . . . . ." Bradley roared. He intended to give an unexpurgated classification, but was rudely interrupted.

"Hold on a minute!" snapped Costigan. "How about Miss Marsden?"

"She has nothing to do with this discussion," returned Roger, icily. "I do not bargain—in fact, I believe that I shall keep her for a time. She has it in mind to destroy herself if I do not allow her to be ransomed, but she will find that door closed to her until I permit it to open."

"In that case, I string along with the Chief—take what he started to say about you and run it clear across the board for me!" barked Costigan.

"Very well. That decision was to be expected from men of your type." The gray man touched two buttons and two of his creatures entered the room. "Put these men into two separate cells on the second level," he ordered. "Search them; all their weapons may not have been in their armor. Seal the doors and mount special guards, tuned to me here."

Imprisoned they were, and carefully searched; but they bore no arms, and nothing had been said concerning communicators. Even if such instruments could be concealed, Roger would detect their use instantly. At least, so ran his thought. But Roger's men had no inkling of the possibility of Costigan's "Service Special" phones, detectors, and spy-ray—instruments of minute size and of infinitesimal power, but yet instruments which, working as they were below the level of the ether, were effective at great distances and caused no vibrations in the ether by which their use could be detected. And what could be more innocent than the regulation personal equipment of every officer of space? The heavy goggles, the wrist-watch and its supplementary pocket chronometer, the flash-lamp, the automatic lighter, the sender, the money-belt?

All these items of equipment were examined with due care; but the cleverest minds of the Triplanetary Service had designed those communicators to pass any ordinary search, however careful, and when Costigan and Bradley were finally locked into the designated cells they still possessed their ultra-instruments.

IN ROGER'S PLANETOID

In the hall Clio glanced around her wildly, seeking even the narrowest avenue of escape. Before she could act, however, her body was clamped as though in a vise, and she struggled, motionless.

"It is useless to attempt to escape, or to do anything except what Roger wishes," the guide informed her somberly, snapping off the instrument in her hand and thus restoring to the thoroughly cowed girl her freedom of motion.

"His lightest wish is law," she continued as they walked down a long corridor. "The sooner you realize that you must do exactly as he pleases, in all things, the easier your life will be."

"But I wouldn't *want* to keep on living!" Clio declared, with a flash of spirit. "And I can *always* die, you know."

"You will find that you cannot," the passionless creature returned, monotonously. "If you do not yield, you will long and pray for death, but you will not die unless Roger wills it. Look at me: I cannot die. Here is your apartment. You will stay here until Roger gives further orders concerning you."

The living automaton opened a door and stood silent and impassive while Clio, staring at her in horror, shrank past her and into the sumptuously furnished suite. The door closed soundlessly and utter silence descended as a pall. Not an ordinary silence, but the indescribable perfection of the absolute silence, complete absence of all sound. In that silence Clio stood motionless. Tense and rigid, hopeless, despairing, she stood there in that magnificent room, fighting an almost overwhelming impulse to scream. Suddenly she heard the cold voice of Roger, speaking from the empty air.

"You are over-wrought, Miss Marsden. You can be of no use to yourself or to me in that condition. I command you to rest; and, to insure that rest, you may pull that cord, which will establish about this room an ether wall: a wall to cut off even this my voice . . . ."

The voice ceased as she pulled the cord savagely and threw herself upon a divan in a torrent of gasping, strangling, but rebellious sobs. Then again came a voice, but not to her ears. Deep within her, pervading every bone and muscle, it made itself felt rather than heard.

"Clio?" it asked. "Don't talk yet . . . ."

"Conway!" she gasped in relief, every fiber of her being thrilled into new hope at the deep, well-remembered voice of Conway Costigan.

"Keep still!" he snapped. "Don't act so happy! He may have a spy-ray on you. He can't hear me, but he may be able to hear you. When he was talking to you you must have noticed a sort of rough, sandpapery feeling under that necklace I gave you? Since he's got an ether-wall around you the beads are dead now. If you feel anything like that under the wrist-watch, breathe deeply, twice. If you don't feel anything there, it's safe for you to talk, as loud as you please."

"I don't feel anything, Conway!" she rejoiced. Tears forgotten, she was her old, buoyant self again. "So that wall *is* real, after all? I only about half believed it."

"Don't trust it too much, because he can cut it off from the outside any time he wants to. Remember what I told you: that necklace will warn you of any spy-ray in the ether, and the watch will detect anything below the level of the ether. It's dead now, of course, since our three phones are direct-connected; I'm in touch with Bradley, too. Don't be too scared; we've got a lot better chance than I thought we had."

"What? You don't mean it!"

"Absolutely. I'm beginning to think that maybe we've got something he doesn't know exists—our ultra-wave. Of course I wasn't surprised when his searchers failed to find our instruments, but it never occurred to me that I might have a clear field to use them in! I can't quite believe it yet, but I haven't been able to find any indication that he can even detect the bands we are using. I'm going to look around over there with my spy-ray . . . I'm looking at you now—feel it?"

"Yes, the watch feels that way, now."

"Fine! Not a sign of interference over here, either. I can't find a trace of ultra-wave—anything below ether-level, you know—anywhere in the whole place. He's got so much stuff that we've never heard of that I supposed of course he'd have ultra-wave, too; but if he hasn't, that gives us the edge. Well, Bradley and I've got a lot of work to do . . . . Wait a minute, I just had a thought. I'll be back in about a second."

There was a brief pause, then the soundless, but clear voice went on:

"Good hunting! That woman that gave you the blue willies isn't alive—she's full of the prettiest machinery and circuits you ever saw!"

"Oh, Conway!" and the girl's voice broke in an engulfing wave of thanksgiving and relief. "It was so unutterably horrible, thinking of what must have happened to her and to others like her!"

"He's running a colossal bluff, I think. He's good, all right, but he lacks quite a lot of being omnipotent. But don't get too cocky, either. Plenty has happened to plenty of women here, and men too—and plenty may happen to us unless we put out a few jets. Keep a stiff upper lip, and if you want us, yell. 'Bye!"

The silent voice ceased, the watch upon Clio's wrist again became an unobtrusive timepiece, and Costigan, in his solitary cell far below her tower room, turned his peculiarly goggled eyes toward other scenes. His hands, apparently idle in his pockets, manipulated tiny controls; his keen, highly-trained eyes studied every concealed detail of mechanism of the great globe. Finally, he took off the goggles and spoke in a low voice to Bradley, confined in another windowless room across the hall.

"I think I've got dope enough, Captain. I've found out where he put our armor and guns, and I've located all the main leads, controls, and generators. There are no ether-walls around us here, but every door is shielded, and there are guards outside our doors—one to each of us. They're robots, not men. That makes it harder, since they're undoubtedly connected direct to Roger's desk and will give an alarm at the first hint of abnormal performance. We can't do a thing until he leaves his desk. See that black panel, a little below the cord-switch to the right of your door? That's the conduit cover. When I give you the word, tear that off and you'll see one red wire in the cable. It feeds the shield-generator of your door. Break that wire and join me out in the hall. Sorry I had only one of these ultra-wave spies, but once we're together it won't be so bad. Here's what I thought we could do," and he went over in detail the only course of action which his survey had shown to be possible.

"There, he's left his desk!" Costigan exclaimed after the conversation had continued for almost an hour. "Now as soon as we find out where he's going, we'll start something . . . he's going to see Clio, the swine! This changes things, Bradley!" His hard voice was a curse.

"Somewhat!" blazed the captain. "I know how you two have been getting on all during the cruise. I'm with you, but what can we do?"

"We'll do something," Costigan declared grimly. "If he makes a pass at her I'll get him if I have to blow this whole sphere out of space, with us in it!"

"Don't do that, Conway," Clio's low voice, trembling but determined, was felt by both men. "If there's a chance for you to get away and do anything about fighting him, don't mind me. Maybe he only wants to talk about the ransom, anyway."

"He wouldn't talk ransom to you—he's going to talk something else entirely," Costigan gritted, then his voice changed suddenly. "But say, maybe it's just as well this way. They didn't find our specials when they searched us, you know, and we're going to do plenty of damage right soon now. Roger probably isn't a fast worker—more the cat-and-mouse type, I'd say—and after we get started he'll have something on his mind besides you. Think you can stall him off and keep him interested for about fifteen minutes?"

"I'm sure I can—I'll do *anything* to help us, or you, get away from this horrible . . . ." Her voice ceased as Roger broke the ether-wall of her apartment and walked toward the divan, upon which she crouched in wide-eyed, helpless, trembling terror.

"Get ready, Bradley!" Costigan directed tersely. "He left Clio's ether-wall off, so that any abnormal signals would be relayed to him from his desk—he knows that there's no chance of anyone disturbing him in that room. But I'm holding a beam on that switch, so that the wall is on, full strength. No matter what we do now, he can't get a warning. I'll have to hold the beam exactly in place, though, so you'll have to do the dirty work. Tear out that red wire and kill those two guards. You know how to kill a robot, don't you?"

"Yes—break his eye-lenses and his ear-drums and he'll stop whatever he's doing and send out distress calls . . . . Got 'em both. Now what?"

"Open my door—the shield switch is to the right."

Costigan's door flew open and the Triplanetary captain leaped into the room.

"Now for our armor!" he cried.

"Not yet!" snapped Costigan. He was standing rigid, goggled eyes staring immovably at a spot on the ceiling. "I can't move a millimeter until you've closed Clio's ether-wall switch. If I take this ray off it for a second we're sunk. Five floors up, straight ahead down a corridor—fourth door on right. When you're at the switch you'll feel my ray on your watch. Snap it up!"

"Right," and the captain leaped away at a pace to be equalled by few men of half his years.

Soon he was back, and after Costigan had tested the ether-wall of the "bridal suite" to make sure that no warning signal from his desk or his servants could reach Roger within it, the two officers hurried away toward the room in which their space-armor was.

"Too bad they don't wear uniforms," panted Bradley, short of breath from the many flights of stairs. "Might have helped some as disguise."

"I doubt it—with so many robots around, they've probably got signals that we couldn't understand anyway. If we meet anybody it'll mean a battle. Hold it!" Peering through walls with his spy-ray, Costigan had seen two men approaching, blocking an intersecting corridor into which they must turn. "Two of 'em, a man and a robot—the robot's on your side. We'll wait here, right at the corner—when they round it take 'em!" and Costigan put away his goggles in readiness for strife.

All unsuspecting, the two pirates came into view, and as they appeared the two officers struck. Costigan, on the inside, drove a short, hard right low into the human pirate's abdomen. The fiercely-driven fist sank to the wrist into the soft tissues and the stricken man collapsed. But even as the blow landed Costigan had seen that there was a third enemy, following close behind the two he had been watching, a pirate who was even then training a ray projector upon him. Reacting automatically, Costigan swung his unconscious opponent around in front of him, so that it was into an enemy's body that the vicious ray tore, and not into his own. Crouching down into the smallest possible compass, he straightened out with the lashing force of a mighty steel spring, hurling the corpse straight at the flaming mouth of the projector. The weapon crashed to the floor and dead pirate and living went down in a heap. Upon that heap Costigan hurled himself, feeling for the pirate's throat. But the fellow had wriggled clear, and countered with a gouging thrust that would have torn out the eyes of a slower man, following it up instantly with a savage kick for the groin. No automaton this, geared and set to perform certain fixed duties with mechanical precision, but a lithe, strong man in hard training, fighting with every foul trick known to his murderous ilk.

But Costigan was no tyro in the art of dirty fighting. Few indeed were the maiming tricks of foul combat unknown to even the rank and file of the highly efficient under-cover branch of the Triplanetary Service; and Costigan, a Sector Chief, knew them all. Not for pleasure, sportsmanship, nor million-dollar purses did those secret agents use Nature's weapons. They came to grips only when it could not possibly be avoided, but when they were forced to fight in that fashion they went in with but one grim purpose—to kill, and to kill in the shortest possible space of time. Thus it was that Costigan's opening soon came. The pirate launched a vicious *coup de sabot*, which Costigan avoided by a lightning shift. It was a slight shift, barely enough to make the kicker miss, and two powerful hands closed upon that flying foot in midair like the sprung jaws of a bear-trap. Closed and twisted viciously, in the same fleeting instant.

There was a shriek, smothered as a heavy boot crashed to its carefully predetermined mark—the pirate was out, definitely and permanently.

The struggle had lasted scarcely ten seconds, coming to its close just as Bradley finished blinding and deafening the robot. Costigan picked up the projector, again donned his spy-ray goggles, and the two hurried on.

"Nice work, Chief—it must be a gift to rough-house the way you do," Bradley exclaimed. "That's why you took the live one?"

"Practice helps some, too—I've been in brawls before, and I'm a lot younger and maybe a bit faster than you are," Costigan explained briefly, penetrant gaze rigidly to the fore as they ran along one corridor after another.

Several more guards, both living and mechanical, were encountered on the way, but they were not permitted to offer any opposition. Costigan saw them first. In the furious beam of the projector of the dead pirate they were riven into nothingness, and the two officers sped on to the room which Costigan had located from afar. The three suits of Triplanetary space armor had been locked up in a cabinet; a cabinet whose doors Costigan literally blew off with a blast of force rather than consume time in tracing the power leads.

"I feel like something now!" Costigan, once more encased in his own armor, heaved a great sigh of relief. "Rough-and-tumble's all right with one or two, but that generator room is full of grief, and we won't have any too much stuff as it is. We've got to take Clio's suit along—we'll carry it down to the door of the power room, drop it there, and pick it up on the way back."

Contemptuous now of possible guards, the armored pair strode toward the power plant—the very heart of the immense fortress of space. Guards were encountered, and captains—officers who signaled frantically to their chief, since he alone could unleash the frightful forces at his command, and who profanely wondered at his unwonted silence—but the enemy beams were impotent against the ether walls of that armor; and the pirates, without armor in the security of their own planetoid as they were, vanished utterly in the ravening beams of the twin Lewistons. As they paused before the door of the power room, both men felt Clio's voice raised in her first and last appeal, an appeal wrung from her against her will by the extremity of her position.

"Conway! Hurry! His eyes—they're tearing me apart! Hurry, dear!" In the horror-filled tones both men read clearly—however inaccurately—the girl's dire extremity. Each saw plainly a happy, carefree young Earth-girl, upon her first trip into space, locked inside an ether-wall with an over-brained, under-conscienced human machine—a super-intelligent, but lecherous and unmoral mechanism of flesh and blood, acknowledging no authority, ruled by nothing save his own scientific drivings and the almost equally powerful urges of his desires and passions! She must have fought with every resource at her command. She must have wept and pleaded, stormed and raged, feigned submission and played for time—and her torment had not touched in the slightest degree the merciless and gloating brain of the being who called himself Roger. Now his tantalizing, ruthless cat-play would be done, the horrible gray-brown face would be close to hers—she wailed her final despairing message to Costigan and attacked that hideous face with the fury of a tigress.

Costigan bit off a bitter imprecation. "Hold him just a second longer, sweetheart!" he cried, and the power room door vanished.

Through the great room the two Lewistons swept at full aperture and at maximum power, two rapidly-opening fans of death and destruction. Here and there a guard, more rapid than his fellows, trained a futile projector—a projector whose magazine exploded at the touch of that frightful field of force, liberating instantaneously its thousands upon thousands of kilowatt-hours of-stored-up energy. Through the delicately adjusted, complex mechanisms the destroying beams tore. At their touch armatures burned out, high-tension leads volatilized in crashing, high-voltage arcs, masses of metal smoked and burned in the path of vast forces now seeking the easiest path to neutralization, delicate instruments blew up, copper ran in streams. As the last machine subsided into a semi-molten mass of metal the two wreckers, each grasping a brace, felt themselves become weightless and knew that they had accomplished the first part of their program.

Costigan leaped for the outer door. His the task to go to Clio's aid—Bradley would follow more slowly, bringing the girl's armor and taking care of any possible pursuit. As he sailed through the air he spoke.

"Coming, Clio! All right, girl?" Questioningly, half fearfully.

"All right, Conway." Her voice was almost unrecognizable, broken in retching agony. "When everything went crazy he . . . found out that the ether-wall was up and . . . forgot all about me. He shut it off . . . and seemed to go crazy too . . . he is floundering around like a wild man now . . . I'm trying to keep . . . him from . . . going downstairs."

"Good girl—keep him busy one minute more—he's getting all the warnings at once and wants to get back to his board. But what's the matter with you? Did he . . . hurt you, after all?"

"Oh, no, not that—he didn't do anything but look at me—but that was bad enough—but I'm sick—horribly sick. I'm falling . . . I'm so dizzy that I can scarcely see . . . my head is breaking up into little pieces . . . I just *know* I'm going to die, Conway! Oh . . . oh!"

"Oh, is *that* all!" In his sheer relief that they had been in time, Costigan did not think of sympathizing with Clio's very real present distress of mind and body. "I forgot that you're a ground-gripper—that's just a little touch of space-sickness. It'll wear off directly . . . . All right, I'm coming! Let go of him and get as far away from him as you can!"

He was now in the street. Perhaps two hundred feet distant and a hundred feet above him was the tower room in which were Clio and Roger. He sprang directly toward its large window, and as he floated "upward" he corrected his course and accelerated his pace by firing backward at various angles with his heavy service pistol, uncaring that at the point of impact of each of those shells a small blast of destruction erupted. He missed the window a trifle, but that did not matter—his flaming Lewiston opened a way for him, partly through the window, partly through the wall. As he soared through the opening he trained projector and pistol upon Roger, now almost to the door, noticing as he did so that Clio was clinging convulsively to a lamp-bracket upon the wall. Door and wall vanished in the Lewiston's terrific beam, but the pirate stood unharmed. Neither ravening ray nor explosive shell could harm him—he had snapped on the protective shield whose generator was always upon his person.

*

When Clio reported that Roger seemed to go crazy and was floundering around like a wild man, she had no idea of how she was understanding the actual situation; for Gharlane of Eddore, then energizing the form of flesh that was Roger, had for the first time in his prodigiously long life met in direct conflict with an overwhelming superior force.

Roger had been sublimely confident that he could detect the use, anywhere in or around his planetoid, of ultra-wave. He had been equally sure that he could control directly and absolutely the physical activities of any number of these semi-intelligent "human beings".

But four Arisians in fusion—Drounli, Brolenteen, Nedanillor, and Kriedigan—had been on guard for weeks. When the time came to act, they acted.

Roger's first thought, upon discovering what tremendous and inexplicable damage had already been done, was to destroy instantly the two men who were doing it. He could not touch them. His second was to blast out of existence this supposedly human female, but no more could he touch her. His fiercest mental bolts spent themselves harmlessly three millimeters away from her skin; she gazed into his eyes completely unaware of the torrents of energy pouring from them. He could not even aim a weapon at her! His third was to call for help to Eddore. He could not. The sub-ether was closed; nor could he either discover the manner of its closing or trace the power which was keeping it closed!

His Eddorian body, even if he could recreate it here, could not withstand the environment—this Roger-thing would have to do whatever it could, unaided by Gharlane's mental powers. And, physically, it was a very capable body indeed. Also, it was armed and armored with mechanisms of Gharlane's own devising; and Eddore's second-in-command was in no sense a coward.

But Roger, while not exactly a ground-gripper, did not know how to handle himself without weight; whereas Costigan, given six walls against which to push, was even more efficient in weightless combat than when handicapped by the force of gravitation. Keeping his projector upon the pirate, he seized the first club to hand—a long, slender pedestal of metal—launched himself past the pirate chief. With all the momentum of his mass and velocity and all the power of his good right arm he swung the bar at the pirate's head. That fiercely-driven mass of metal should have taken head from shoulders, but it did not. Roger's shield of force was utterly rigid and impenetrable; the only effect of the frightful blow was to set him spinning, end over end, like the flying baton of an acrobatic drum-major. As the spinning form crashed against the opposite wall of the room Bradley floated in, carrying Clio's armor. Without a word the captain loosened the helpless girl's grip upon the bracket and encased her in the suit. Then, supporting her at the window, he held his Lewiston upon the captive's head while Costigan propelled him toward the opening. Both men knew that Roger's shield of force must be threatened every instant—that if he were allowed to release it he probably would bring to bear a hand-weapon even superior to their own.

Braced against the wall, Costigan sighted along Roger's body toward the most distant point of the lofty dome of the artificial planet and gave him a gentle push. Then, each grasping Clio by an arm, the two officers shoved mightily with their feet and the three armored forms darted away toward their only hope of escape—an emergency boat which could be launched through the shell of the great globe. To attempt to reach the *Hyperion* and to escape in one of her lifeboats would have been useless; they could not have forced the great gates of the main airlocks and no other exits existed. As they sailed onward through the air, Costigan keeping the slowly-floating form of Roger enveloped in his beam, Clio began to recover.

"Suppose they get their gravity fixed?" she asked, apprehensively. "And they're raying us and shooting at us!"

"They may have it fixed already. They undoubtedly have spare parts and duplicate generators, but if they turn it on the fall will kill Roger too, and he wouldn't like that. They'll have to get him down with a helicopter or something, and they know that we'll get them as fast as they come up. They can't hurt us with hand-weapons, and before they can bring up any heavy stuff they'll be afraid to use it, because well be too close to their shell.

"I wish we could have brought Roger along," he continued, savagely, to Bradley. "But you were right, of course—it'd be altogether too much like a rabbit capturing a wildcat. My Lewiston's about done right now, and there can't be much left of yours—what he'd do to us would be a sin and a shame."

Now at the great wall, the two men heaved mightily upon a lever, the gate of the emergency port swung slowly open, and they entered the miniature cruiser of the void. Costigan, familiar with the mechanism of the craft from careful study from his prison cell, manipulated the controls. Through gate after massive gate they went, until finally they were out in open space, shooting toward distant Tellus at the maximum acceleration of which their small craft was capable.

Costigan cut the other two phones out of circuit and spoke, his attention fixed upon some extremely distant point.

"Samms!" he called sharply. "Costigan. We're out . . . all right . . . yes . . . sure . . . absolutely . . . you tell'em, Sammy, I've got company here."

Through the sound-disks of their helmets the girl and the captain had heard Costigan's share of the conversation. Bradley stared at his erstwhile first officer in amazement, and even Clio had often heard that mighty, half-mythical name. Surely that bewildering young man must rank high, to speak so familiarly to Virgil Samms, the all-powerful head of the space-pervading Service of the Triplanetary League!

"You've turned in a general call-out," Bradley stated, rather than asked.

"Long ago—I've been in touch right along," Costigan answered. "Now that they know what to look for and know that ether-wave detectors are useless, they can find it. Every vessel in seven sectors, clear down to the scout patrols, is concentrating on this point, and the call is out for all battleships and cruisers afloat. There are enough operatives out there with ultra-waves to locate that globe, and once they spot it they'll point it out to all the other vessels."

81

"But how about the other prisoners?" asked the girl. "They'll be killed, won't they?"

"Hard telling," Costigan shrugged. "Depends on how things turn out. We lack a lot of being safe ourselves yet."

"What's worrying me mostly is our own chance," Bradley assented. "They will chase us, of course."

"Sure, and they'll have more speed than we have. Depends on how far away the nearest Triplanetary vessels are. But we've done everything we can do, for now."

Silence fell, and Costigan cut in Clio's phone and came over to the seat upon which she was reclining, white and stricken—worn out by the horrible and terrifying ordeals of the last few hours. As he seated himself beside her she blushed vividly, but her deep blue eyes met his gray ones steadily.

"Clio, I . . . we . . . you . . . that is," he flushed hotly and stopped. This secret agent, whose clear, keen brain no physical danger could cloud; who had proved over and over again that he was never at a loss in any emergency, however desperate—this quick-witted officer floundered in embarrassment like any schoolboy; but continued, doggedly: "I'm afraid that I gave myself away back there, but . . . ."

"We gave ourselves away, you mean," she filled in the pause. "I did my share, but I won't hold you to it if you don't want—but I *know* that you love me, Conway!"

"*Love* you!" the man groaned, his face lined and hard, his whole body rigid. "That doesn't half tell it, Clio. You don't need to hold me—I'm held for life. There never was a woman who meant anything to me before, and there never will be another. You're the only woman that ever existed. It isn't that. Can't you see that it's impossible?"

"Of course I can't—it isn't impossible, at all." She released her shields, four hands met and tightly clasped, and her low voice thrilled with feeling as she went on: "You love me and I love you. That is all that matters."

"I wish it were," Costigan returned bitterly, "but you don't know what you'd be letting yourself in for. It's who and what you are and who and what I am that's griping me. You, Clio Marsden, Curtis Marsden's daughter. Nineteen years old. You think you've been places and done things. You haven't. You haven't seen or done anything—you don't know what it's all about. And whom am I to love a girl like you? A homeless spacehound who hasn't been on any planet three weeks in three years. A hard-boiled egg. A trouble-shooter and a brawler by instinct and training. A sp . . . " he bit off the word and went on quickly: "Why, you don't know me at all, and there's a lot of me that you never *will* know—that I can't let you know! You'd better lay off me, girl, while you can. It'll be best for you, believe me."

"But I can't, Conway, and neither can you," the girl answered softly, a glorious light in her eyes. "It's too late for that. On the ship it was just another of those things, but since then we've come really to know each other, and we're sunk. The situation is out of control, and we both know it—and neither of us would change it if we could, and you know that, too. I don't know very much, I admit, but I do know what you thought you'd have to keep from me, and I admire you all the more for it. We all honor the Service, Conway dearest—it is only you men who have made and are keeping the Three Planets fit places to live in—and I know that any one of Virgil Samms' assistants would have to be a man in a thousand million . . . ."

"What makes you think that?" he demanded sharply.

"You told me so yourself, indirectly. Who else in the three worlds could possibly call him 'Sammy?' You are hard, of course, but you must be so—and I never did like soft men, anyway. And you brawl in a good cause. You are very much a *man*, my Conway; a real, *real* man, and I love you! Now, if they catch us, all right—we'll die together, at least!" she finished, intensely.

"You're right, sweetheart, of course," he admitted. "I don't believe that I *could* really let you let me go, even though I know you ought to," and their hands locked together even more firmly than before. "If we ever get out of this jam I'm going to kiss you, but this is no time to be taking off your helmet. In fact, I'm taking too many chances with you in keeping your shields off. Snap 'em on again—they ought to be getting fairly close by this time."

Hands released and armor again tight, Costigan went over to join Bradley at the control board.

"How are they coming, Captain?" he asked.

"Not so good. Quite a ways off yet. At least an hour, I'd say, before a cruiser can get within range."

"I'll see if I can locate any of the pirates chasing us. If I do it'll be by accident; this little spy-ray isn't good for much except close work. I'm afraid the first warning we'll have will be when they take hold of us with a tractor or spear us with a needle. Probably a beam, though; this is one of their emergency lifeboats and they wouldn't want to destroy it unless they have to. Also, I imagine that Roger wants us alive pretty badly. He has unfinished business with all three of us, and I can well believe that his 'not particularly pleasant extinction' will be even less so after the way we rooked him."

"I want you to do me a favor, Conway." Clio's face was white with horror at the thought of facing again that unspeakable creature of gray. "Give me a gun or something, please. I don't want him ever to look at me that way again, to say nothing of what else he might do, while I'm alive."

"He won't," Costigan assured her, narrow of eye and grim of jaw. He was, as she had said, hard. "But you don't want a gun. You might get nervous and use it too soon. I'll take care of you at the last possible moment, because if he gets hold of us we won't stand a chance of getting away again."

For minutes there was silence, Costigan surveying the ether in all directions with his ultra-wave device. Suddenly he laughed, and the others stared at him in surprise.

"No, I'm not crazy," he told them. "This is really funny; it had never occurred to me that the ether-walls of all these ships make them invisible. I can see them, of course, with this sub-ether spy, but they can't see us! I knew that they should have overtaken us before this. I've finally found them. They've passed us, and are now tacking around, waiting for us to do something so that they can see us! They're heading right into the Fleet—they think they're safe, of course, but what a surprise they've got coming to them!"

But it was not only the pirates who were to be surprised. Long before the pirate ship had come within extreme visibility range of the Triplanetary Fleet it lost its invisibility and was starkly outlined upon the lookout plates of the three fugitives. For a few seconds the pirate craft seemed unchanged, then it began to glow redly, with a red that seemed to become darker as it grew stronger. Then the sharp outlines blurred, puffs of air burst outward, and the metal of the hull became a viscous, fluid-like something, flowing away in a long, red streamer into seemingly empty space. Costigan turned his ultra-gaze into that space and saw that it was actually far from empty. There lay a vast something, formless and indefinite even to his sub-etheral vision; a something into which the viscid stream of transformed metal plunged. Plunged and vanished.

Powerful interference blanketed his ultra-wave and howled throughout his body; but in the hope that some parts of his message might get through he called Samms, and calmly and clearly he narrated everything that had just happened. He continued his crisp report, neglecting not the smallest detail, while their tiny craft was drawn inexorably toward a redly impermeable veil; continued it until their lifeboat, still intact, shot through that veil and he found himself unable to move. He was conscious, he was breathing normally, his heart was beating; but not a voluntary muscle would obey his will!

FLEET AGAINST PLANETOID

One of the newest and fleetest of the patrol vessels of the Triplanetary League, the heavy cruiser *Chicago* of the North American Division of the Tellurian Contingent, plunged stolidly through interplanetary vacuum. For five long weeks she had patrolled her allotted volume of space. In another week she would report back to the city whose name she bore, where her space-weary crew, worn by their long "tour" in the awesomely oppressive depths of the limitless void, would enjoy to the full their fortnight of refreshing planetary leave.

She was performing certain routine tasks—charting meteorites, watching for derelicts and other obstructions to navigation, checking in constantly with all scheduled space-ships in case of need, and so on—but primarily she was a warship. She was a mighty engine of destruction, hunting for the unauthorized vessels of whatever power or planet it was that had not only defied the Triplanetary League, but was evidently attempting to overthrow it; attempting to plunge the Three Planets back into the ghastly sink of bloodshed and destruction from which they had so recently emerged. Every space-ship within range of her powerful detectors was represented by two brilliant, slowly-moving points of light; one upon a greater micrometer screen, the other in the "tank," the immense, three-dimensional, minutely cubed model of the entire Solar System.

A brilliantly intense red light flared upon a panel and a bell clanged brazenly the furious signals of the sector alarm. Simultaneously a speaker roared forth its message of a ship in dire peril.

"Sector alarm! N.A.T. *Hyperion* gassed with Vee-Two. Nothing detectable in space, but . . . ."

The half-uttered message was drowned out in a crackling roar of meaningless noise, the orderly signals of the bell became a hideous clamor, and the two points of light which had marked the location of the liner disappeared in widely spreading flashes of the same high-powered interference. Observers, navigators, and control officers were alike dumbfounded. Even the captain, in the shell-proof, shock-proof, and doubly ray-proof retreat of his conning compartment, was equally at a loss. No ship or thing could *possibly* be close enough to be sending out interfering waves of such tremendous power—yet there they were!

"Maximum acceleration, straight for the point where the *Hyperion* was when her tracers went out," the captain ordered, and through the fringe of that widespread interference he drove a solid beam, reporting concisely to GHQ. Almost instantly the emergency call-out came roaring in—every vessel of the Sector, of whatever class or tonnage, was to concentrate upon the point in space where the ill-fated liner had last been known to be.

Hour after hour the great globe drove on at maximum acceleration, captain and every control officer alert and at high tension. But in Quartermasters' Department, deep down below the generator rooms, no thought was given to such minor matters as the disappearance of a *Hyperion*. The inventory did not balance, and two Q.M. privates were trying, profanely and without success, to find the discrepancy.

"Charged calls for Mark Twelve Lewistons, none requisitioned, on hand eighteen thous . . . ." The droning voice broke off short in the middle of a word and the private stood rigid, in the act of reaching for another slip, every faculty concentrated upon something imperceptible to his companion.

"Come on, Cleve—snap it up!" the second commanded, but was silenced by a vicious wave of the listener's hand.

"What!" the rigid one exclaimed. "Reveal ourselves! Why, it's . . . . Oh, all right . . . . Oh, that's it . . . uh-huh . . . I see . . . yes, I've got it solid. So long!"

The inventory sheets fell unheeded from his hand, and his fellow private stared after him in amazement as he strode over to the desk of the officer in charge. That officer also stared as the hitherto easy-going and gold-bricking Cleve saluted crisply, showed him something flat in the palm of his left hand, and spoke.

"I've just got some of the funniest orders ever put out, lieutenant, but they came from 'way, 'way up. I'm to join the brass hats in the Center. You'll know all about it directly, I imagine. Cover me up as much as you can, will you?" and he was gone.

Unchallenged he made his way to the control room, and his curt "urgent report for the Captain" admitted him there without question. But when he approached the sacred precincts of the captain's own and inviolate room, he was stopped in no uncertain fashion by no less a personage than the Officer of the Day.

" . . . and report yourself under arrest immediately!" the O.D. concluded his brief but pointed speech.

"You were right in stopping me, of course," the intruder conceded, unmoved. "I wanted to get in there without giving everything away, if possible, but it seems that I can't. Well, I've been ordered by Virgil Samms to report to the Captain, at once. See this? Touch it!" He held out a flat, insulated disk, cover thrown back to reveal a tiny golden meteor, at the sight of which the officer's truculent manner altered markedly.

"I've heard of them, of course, but I never saw one before," and the officer touched the shining symbol lightly with his finger, jerking backward as there shot through his whole body a thrilling surge of power, shouting into his very bones an unpronounceable syllable—the password of the Triplanetary Service. "Genuine or not, it gets you to the Captain. He'll know, and if it's a fake you'll be breathing space in five minutes."

Projector at the ready, the Officer of the Day followed Cleve into the Holy of Holies. There the grizzled four-striper touched the golden meteor lightly, then drove his piercing gaze deep into the unflinching eyes of the younger man. But that captain had won his high rank neither by accident nor by "pull"—he understood at once.

"It *must* be an emergency," he growled, half-audibly, still staring at his lowly Q-M clerk, "to make Samms uncover this way." He turned and curtly dismissed the wondering O.D. Then: "All right! Out with it!"

"Serious enough so that every one of us afloat has just received orders to reveal himself to his commanding officer and to anyone else, if necessary to reach that officer at once—orders never before issued. The enemy have been located. They have built a base, and have ships better than our best. Base and ships cannot be seen or detected by any ether wave. However, the Service has been experimenting for years with a new type of communicator beam; and, while pretty crude yet, it was given to us when the *Dione* went out without leaving a trace. One of our men was in the *Hyperion*, managed to stay alive, and has been sending data. I am instructed to attach my new phone set to one of the universal plates in your conning room, and to see what I can find."

"Go to it!" The captain waved his hand and the operative bent to his task.

"Commanders of all vessels of the Fleet!" The Headquarters speaker, receiver sealed upon the wave-length of the Admiral of the Fleet, broke the long silence. "All vessels in sectors L to R, inclusive, will interlock location signals. Some of you have received, or will receive shortly, certain communications from sources which need not be mentioned. Those commanders will at once send out red K4 screens. Vessels so marked will act as temporary flagships. Unmarked vessels will proceed at maximum to the nearest flagship, grouping about it in the regulation squadron cone in order of arrival. Squadrons most distant from objective point designated by flagship observers will proceed toward it at maximum; squadrons nearest it will decelerate or reverse velocity—that point must not be approached until full Fleet formation has been accomplished. Heavy and light cruisers of all other sectors inside the orbit of Mars . . . ." The orders went on, directing the mobilization of the stupendous forces of the League, so that they would be in readiness in the highly improbable event of the failure of the massed power of seven sectors to reduce the pirate base.

In those seven sectors perhaps a dozen vessels threw out enormous spherical screens of intense red light, and as they did so their tracer points upon all the interlocked lookout plates also became ringed about with red. Toward those crimson markers the pilots of the unmarked vessels directed their courses at their utmost power; and while the white lights upon the lookout plates moved slowly toward and clustered about the red ones the ultra-instruments of the Service operatives were probing into space, sweeping the neighborhood of the computed position of the pirate's stronghold.

But the object sought was so far away that the small spy-ray sets of the Service men, intended as they were for close range work, were unable to make contact with the invisible planetoid for which they were seeking. In the captain's sanctum of the *Chicago*, the operative studied his plate for only a minute or two, then shut off his power and fell into a brown study, from which he was rudely aroused.

"Aren't you even going to *try* to find them?" demanded the captain.

"No," Cleve returned shortly. "No use—not half enough power or control. I'm trying to think . . . maybe . . . say, Captain, will you please have the Chief Electrician and a couple of radio men come in here?"

They came, and for hours, while the other ultra-wave men searched the apparently empty ether with their ineffective beams, the three technical experts and the erstwhile Quartermaster's clerk labored upon a huge and complex ultra-wave projector—the three blindly and with doubtful questions; the one with sure knowledge at least of what he was trying to do. Finally the thing was done, the crude, but efficient graduated circles were set, and the tubes glowed redly as their massed output drove into a tight beam of ultra-vibration.

"There it is, sir," Cleve reported, after some ten minutes of manipulation, and the vast structure of the miniature world flashed into being upon his plate. "You may notify the fleet—coordinates H 11.62, RA 124-31-16, and Dx about 173.2."

The report made and the assistants out of the room, the captain turned to the observer and saluted gravely.

"We have always known, sir, that the Service had *men*; but I had no idea that any one man could possibly do, on the spur of the moment, what you have just done—unless that man happened to be Lyman Cleveland."

"Oh, it doesn't . . . ." the observer began, but broke off, muttering unintelligibly at intervals; then swung the visiray beam toward the Earth. Soon a face appeared upon the plate; the keen, but careworn face of Virgil Samms!

"Hello, Lyman," his voice came clearly from the speaker, and the Captain gasped—his ultra-wave observer and sometime clerk was Lyman Cleveland himself, probably the greatest living expert in beam transmission! "I knew that you'd do something, if it could be done. How about it—can the others install similar sets on their ships? I'm betting that they can't."

"Probably not," Cleveland frowned in thought. "This is a patchwork affair, made of gunny sacks and hay-wire. I'm holding it together by main strength and awkwardness, and even at that, it's apt to go to pieces any minute."

"Can you rig it up for photography?"

"I think so. Just a minute—yes, I can. Why?"

"Because there's something going on out there that neither we nor apparently the pirates know anything about. The Admiralty seems to think that it's the Jovians again, but we don't see how it can be—if it is, they have developed a lot of stuff that none of our agents has even suspected," and he recounted briefly what Costigan had reported to him, concluding: "Then there was a burst of interference—on the *ultra-band*, mind you—and I've heard nothing from him since. Therefore I want you to stay out of the battle entirely.

Stay as far away from it as you can and still get good pictures of everything that happens. I will see that orders are issued to the *Chicago* to that effect."

"But listen . . . ."

"Those are orders!" snapped Samms. "It is of the utmost importance that we know every detail of what is going to happen. The answer is pictures. The only possibility of obtaining pictures is that machine you have just developed. If the fleet wins, nothing will be lost. If the fleet loses—and I am not half as confident of success as the Admiral is—the *Chicago* doesn't carry enough power to decide the issue, and we will have the pictures to study, which is all-important. Besides, we have probably lost Conway Costigan today, and we don't want to lose *you*, too."

Cleveland remained silent, pondering this startling news, but the grizzled Captain, veteran of the Fourth Jovian War that he was, was not convinced.

"We'll blow them out of space, Mr. Samms!" he declared.

"You just think you will, Captain. I have suggested, as forcibly as possible, that the general attack be withheld until after a thorough investigation is made, but the Admiralty will not listen. They see the advisability of withdrawing a camera ship, but that is as far as they will go."

"And that's plenty far enough!" growled the *Chicago's* commander, as the beam snapped off. "Mr. Cleveland, I don't like the idea of running away under fire, and I won't do it without direct orders from the Admiral."

"Of course you won't—that's why you are going . . . ."

He was interrupted by a voice from the Headquarters speaker. The captain stepped up to the plate and, upon being recognized, he received the exact orders which had been requested by the Chief of the Triplanetary Service.

Thus it was that the *Chicago* reversed her acceleration, cut off her red screen, and fell rapidly behind, while the vessels following her shot away toward another crimson-flaring loader. Farther and farther back she dropped, back to the limiting range of the mechanism upon which Cleveland and his highly-trained assistants were hard at work. And during all this time the forces of the seven sectors had been concentrating. The pilot vessels, with their flaming red screens, each followed by a cone of space-ships, drew closer and closer together, approaching the *Fearless*—the British super-dreadnought which was to be the flagship of the Fleet—the mightiest and heaviest space-ship which had yet lifted her stupendous mass into the ether.

Now, systematically and precisely, the great Cone of Battle was coming into being; a formation developed during the Jovian Wars while the forces of the Three Planets were fighting in space for their very civilizations' existence, and one never used since the last space-fleets of Jupiter's murderous hordes had been wiped out.

The mouth of that enormous hollow cone was a ring of scout patrols, the smallest and most agile vessels of the fleet. Behind them came a somewhat smaller ring of light cruisers, then rings of heavy cruisers and of light battleships, and finally of heavy battleships. At the apex of the cone, protected by all the other vessels of the formation and in best position to direct the battle, was the flagship. In this formation every vessel was free to use her every weapon, with a minimum of danger to her sister ships; and yet, when the gigantic main projectors were operated along the axis of the formation, from the entire vast circle of the cone's mouth there flamed a cylindrical field of force of such intolerable intensity that in it no conceivable substance could endure for a moment!

The artificial planet of metal was now close enough so that it was visible to the ultra-vision of the Service men, so plainly visible that the cigar-shaped warships of the pirates were seen issuing from the enormous airlocks. As each vessel shot out into space it sped straight for the approaching fleet without waiting to go into any formation—gray Roger believed his structures invisible to Triplanetary eyes, thought that the presence of the fleet was the result of mathematical calculations, and was convinced that his mighty vessels of the void would destroy even that vast fleet without themselves becoming known. He was wrong. The foremost vessels were allowed actually to enter the mouth of that conical trap before an offensive move was made. Then the vice-admiral in command of the fleet touched a button, and simultaneously every generator in every Triplanetary vessel burst into furious activity. Instantly the hollow volume of the immense cone became a coruscating hell of resistless energy, an inferno which with the velocity of light extended itself into a far-reaching cylinder of rapacious destruction. Ether-waves they were, it is true, but vibrations driven with such fierce intensity that the screens of deflection surrounding the pirate vessels could not handle even a fraction of their awful power. Invisibility lost, their defensive screens flared briefly; but even the enormous force backing Roger's inventions, far greater than that of any single Triplanetary vessel, could not hold off the incredible violence of the massed attack of the hundreds of mighty vessels composing the Fleet. Their defensive screens flared briefly, then went down; their great hulls first glowing red, then shining white, then in a brief moment exploding into flying masses of red hot, molten, and gaseous metal.

A full two-thirds of Roger's force was caught in that raging, incandescent beam; caught and obliterated: but the remainder did not retreat to the planetoid. Darting out around the edge of the cone at a stupendous acceleration, they attacked its flanks and the engagement became general. But now, since enough beams were kept upon each ship of the enemy so that invisibility could not be restored, each Triplanetary war vessel could attack with full efficiency. Magnesium flares and star-shells illuminated space for a thousand miles, and from every unit of both fleets was being hurled every item of solid, explosive and vibratory destruction known to the warfare of that age. Offensive beams, rods and daggers of frightful power struck and were neutralized by defensive screens equally capable; the long range and furious dodging made ordinary solid, or even atomic-explosive projectiles useless; and both sides were filling all space with such a volume of blanketing frequencies that such radio-dirigible atomics as were launched could not be controlled, but darted madly and erratically hither and thither, finally to be exploded or volatilized harmlessly in mid-space by the touch of some fiercely insistant, probing beam of force.

Individually, however, the pirate vessels were far more powerful than those of the fleet, and that superiority soon began to make itself felt. The power of the smaller ships began to fail as their accumulators became discharged under the awful drain of the battle, and vessel after vessel of the Triplanetary fleet was hurled into nothingness by the concentrated blasts of the pirates' rays. But the Triplanetary forces had one great advantage. In furious haste the Service men had been altering the controls of the dirigible atomic torpedoes, so that they would respond to ultra-wave control; and, few in number though they were, each was highly effective.

A hard-eyed observer, face almost against his plate and both hands and both feet manipulating controls, hurled the first torpedo. Propelling rockets viciously aflame, it twisted and looped around the incandescent rods of destruction so thickly and starkly outlined, under perfect control; unaffected by the hideous distortion of all ether-borne signals. Through a pirate screen it went, and under the terrific blast of its detonation the entire midsection of the stricken battleship vanished. It should have been out, cold—but to the amazement of the observers, both ends kept on fighting with scarcely lessened power! Two more of the frightful bombs had to be launched—each remaining section had to be blown to bits—before those terrible beams went out! Not a man in that great fleet had even an inkling of the truth; that those great vessels, those awful engines of destruction, did not contain a single living creature: that they were manned and fought by automatons; robots controlled by keen-eyed, space-hardened veterans inside the pirates' planetoid!

But they were to receive an inkling of it. As ship after ship of the pirate fleet was destroyed, Roger realized that his navy was beaten, and forthwith all his surviving vessels darted toward the apex of the cone, where the heaviest battleships were stationed. There each hurled itself upon a Triplanetary warship, crashing to its own destruction, but in that destruction insuring the loss of one of the heaviest vessels of the enemy. Thus passed the *Fearless*, and twenty of the finest space-ships of the fleet as well. But the ranking officer assumed command, the war-cone was re-formed, and, yawning maw to the fore, the great formation shot toward the pirate stronghold, now near at hand. It again launched its stupendous cylinder of annihilation, but even as the mighty defensive screens of the planetoid flared into incandescently furious defense, the battle was interrupted and pirates and Triplanetarians learned alike that they were not alone in the ether.

Space became suffused with a redly impenetrable opacity, and through that indescribable pall there came reaching huge arms of force incredible; writhing, coruscating beams of power which glowed a baleful, although almost imperceptible, red. A vessel of unheard-of armament and power, hailing from the then unknown solar system of Nevia, had come to rest in that space. For months her commander had been searching for one ultra-precious substance. Now his detectors had found it; and, feeling neither fear of Triplanetarian weapons nor reluctance to sacrifice those thousands of Triplanetarian lives, he was about to take it!

WITHIN THE RED VEIL

Nevia, the home planet of the marauding space-ship, would have appeared peculiar indeed to Terrestrial senses. High in the deep red heavens a fervent blue sun poured down its flood of brilliant purplish light upon a world of water. Not a cloud was to be seen in that flaming sky, and through that dustless atmosphere the eye could see the horizon—a horizon three times as distant as the one to which we are accustomed—with a distinctness and clarity impossible in our Terra's dust-filled air. As that mighty sun dropped below the horizon the sky would fill suddenly with clouds and rain would fall violently and steadily until midnight. Then the clouds would vanish as suddenly as they had come into being, the torrential downpour would cease, and through that huge world's wonderfully transparent gaseous envelope the full glory of the firmament would be revealed. Not the firmament as we know it—for that hot blue sun and Nevia, her one planet-child, were light-years distant from Old Sol and his numerous brood—but a strange and glorious firmament containing few constellations familiar to Earthly eyes.

Out of the vacuum of space a fish-shaped vessel of the void—the vessel that was to attack so boldly both the massed fleet of Triplanetary and Roger's planetoid—plunged into the rarefied outer atmosphere, and crimson beams of force tore shriekingly through the thin air as it braked its terrific speed. A third of the circumference of Nevia's mighty globe was traversed before the velocity of the craft could be reduced sufficiently to make a landing possible. Then, approaching the twilight zone, the vessel dived vertically downward, and it became evident that Nevia was neither entirely aqueous nor devoid of intelligent life. For the blunt nose of the space-ship was pointing toward what was evidently a half-submerged city, a city whose buildings were flat-topped, hexagonal towers, exactly alike in size, shape, color, and material. These buildings were arranged as the cells of a honeycomb would be if each cell were separated from its neighbors by a relatively narrow channel of water, and all were built of the same white metal. Many bridges and more tubes extended through the air from building to building, and the watery "streets" teemed with swimmers, with surface craft, and with submarines.

The pilot, stationed immediately below the conical prow of the space-ship, peered intently through thick windows which afforded unobstructed vision in every direction. His four huge and contractile eyes were active, each operating independently in sending its own message to his peculiar but capable brain. One was watching the instruments, the others scanned narrowly the immense, swelling curve of the ship's belly, the water upon which his vessel was to land, and the floating dock to which it was to be moored. Four hands—if hands they could be called—manipulated levers and wheels with infinite delicacy of touch, and with scarcely a splash the immense mass of the Nevian vessel struck the water and glided to a stop within a foot of its exact berth.

Four mooring bars dropped neatly into their sockets and the captain-pilot, after locking his controls in neutral, released his safety straps and leaped lightly from his padded bench to the floor. Scuttling across the floor and down a runway upon his four short, powerful, heavily scaled legs, he slipped smoothly into the water and flashed away, far below the surface. For Nevians are true amphibians. Their blood is cold; they use with equal comfort and efficiency gills and lungs for breathing; their scaly bodies are equally at home in the water or in the air; their broad, flat feet serve equally well for running about upon a solid surface or for driving their streamlined bodies through the water at a pace few fishes can equal.

Through the water the Nevian commander darted along, steering his course accurately by means of his short, vaned tail. Through an opening in a wall he sped and along a submarine hallway, emerging upon a broad ramp. He scurried up the incline and into an elevator which lifted him to the top of the hexagon, directly into the office of the Secretary of Commerce of all Nevia.

"Welcome, Captain Nerado!" The Secretary waved a tentacular arm and the visitor sprang lightly upon a softly cushioned bench, where he lay at ease, facing the official across his low, flat "desk." "We congratulate you upon the success of your final trial flight. We received all your reports, even while you were traveling at ten times the velocity of light. With the last difficulties overcome, you are now ready to start?"

"We are ready," the captain-scientist replied, soberly. "Mechanically, the ship is as nearly perfect as our finest minds can make her. She is stocked for two years. All the iron-bearing suns within reach have been plotted. Everything is ready except the iron. Of course the Council refused to allow us any of the national supply—how much were you able to purchase for us in the market?"

"Nearly ten pounds . . . ."

"Ten pounds! Why, the securities we left with you could not have bought two pounds, even at the price then prevailing!"

"No, but you have friends. Many of us believe in you, and have dipped into our own resources. You and your fellow scientists of the expedition have each contributed his entire personal fortune; why should not some of the rest of us also contribute, as private citizens?"

"Wonderful—we thank you. Ten pounds!" The captain's great triangular eyes glowed with an intense violet light. "At least a year of cruising. But . . . what if, after all, we should be wrong?"

"In that case you shall have consumed ten pounds of irreplaceable metal." The Secretary was unmoved. "That is the viewpoint of the Council and of almost everyone else. It is not the waste of treasure they object to; it is the fact that ten pounds of iron will be forever lost."

"A high price, truly," the Columbus of Nevia assented. "And after all, I may be wrong."

"You probably are wrong," his host made startling answer. "It is practically certain—it is almost a demonstrable mathematical fact—that no other sun within hundreds of thousands of light-years of our own has a planet. In all probability Nevia is the only planet in the entire Universe. We are very probably the only intelligent life in the Universe. There is only one chance in numberless millions that anywhere within the cruising range of your newly perfected space-ship there may be an iron-bearing planet upon which you can effect a landing. There is a larger chance, however, that you may be able to find a small, cold, iron-bearing cosmic body—small enough so that you can capture it. Although there are no mathematics by which to evaluate the probability of such an occurrence, it is upon that larger chance that some of us are staking a portion of our wealth. We expect no return whatever, but if you *should* by some miracle happen to succeed, what then? Deep seas being made shallow, civilization extending itself over the globe, science advancing by leaps and bounds, Nevia becoming populated as she should be peopled—that, my friend, is a chance well worth taking!"

SUPER PACK

The Secretary called in a group of guards, who escorted the small package of priceless metal to the space-ship. Before the massive door was sealed the friends bade each other farewell.

" . . . I will keep in touch with you on the ultra-wave," the Captain concluded. "After all, I do not blame the Council for refusing to allow the other ship to go out. Ten pounds of iron will be a fearful loss to the world. If we *should* find iron, however, see to it that she loses no time in following us."

"No fear of that! If you find iron she will set out at once, and all space will soon be full of vessels. Goodbye."

The last opening was sealed and Nerado shot the great vessel into the air. Up and up, out beyond the last tenuous trace of atmosphere, on and on through space it flew with ever-increasing velocity until Nevia's gigantic blue sun had been left so far behind that it became a splendid blue-white star. Then, projectors cut off to save the precious iron whose disintegration furnished them power, for week after week Captain Nerado and his venturesome crew of scientists drifted idly through the illimitable void.

There is no need to describe in detail Nerado's tremendous voyage. Suffice it to say that he found a G-type dwarf star possessing planets—not one planet only, but six . . . seven . . . eight . . . yes, at least nine! And most of those worlds were themselves centers of attraction around which were circling one or more worldlets! Nerado thrilled with joy as he applied a full retarding force, and every creature aboard that great vessel had to peer into a plate or through a telescope before he could believe that planets other than Nevia did in reality exist!

Velocity checked to the merest crawl, as space-speeds go, and with electro-magnetic detector screens full out, the Nevian vessel crept toward our sun. Finally the detectors encountered an obstacle, a conductive substance which the patterns showed conclusively to be practically pure iron. Iron—an enormous mass of it—floating alone out in space! Without waiting to investigate the nature, appearance, or structure of the precious mass, Nerado ordered power into the converters and drove an enormous softening field of force upon the object—a force of such a nature that it would condense the metallic iron into an allotropic modification of much smaller bulk; a red, viscous, extremely dense and heavy liquid which could be stored conveniently in his tanks.

No sooner had the precious fluid been stored away than the detectors again broke into an uproar. In one direction was an enormous mass of iron, scarcely detectable; in another a great number of smaller masses; in a third an isolated mass, comparatively small in size. Space seemed to be full of iron, and Nerado drove his most powerful beam toward distant Nevia and sent an exultant message.

"We have found iron—easily obtained and in unthinkable quantity—not in fractions of milligrams, but in millions upon unmeasured millions of tons! Send our sister ship here at once!"

"Nerado!" The captain was called to one of the observation plates as soon as he had opened his key. "I have been investigating the mass of iron now nearest us, the small one. It is an artificial structure, a small space-boat, and there are three creatures in it—monstrosities certainly, but they must possess some intelligence or they could not be navigating space."

"What? Impossible!" exclaimed the chief explorer. "Probably, then, the other was—but no matter, we had to have the iron. Bring the boat in without converting it, so that we may study at our leisure both the beings and their mechanisms," and Nerado swung his own visiray beam into the emergency boat, seeing there the armored figures of Clio Marsden and the two Triplanetary officers.

"They are indeed intelligent," Nerado commented, as he detected and silenced Costigan's ultra-beam communicator. "Not, however, as intelligent as I had supposed," he went on, after studying the peculiar creatures and their tiny space-ship more in detail. "They have immense stores of iron, yet use it for nothing other than building material. They make little and inefficient use of atomic energy. They apparently have a rudimentary knowledge of ultra-waves, but do not use them intelligently—they cannot neutralize even these ordinary forces we are now employing. They are of course more intelligent than the lower ganoids, or even than some of the higher fishes, but by no stretch of the imagination can they be compared to us. I am quite relieved—I was afraid that in my haste I might have slain members of a highly developed race."

The helpless boat, all her forces neutralized, was brought up close to the immense flying fish. There flaming knives of force sliced her neatly into sections and the three rigid armored figures, after being bereft of their external weapons, were brought through the airlocks and into the control room, while the pieces of their boat were stored away for future study. The Nevian scientists first analyzed the air inside the space-suits of the Terrestrials, then carefully removed the protective coverings of the captives.

Costigan—fully conscious through it all and now able to move a little, since the peculiar temporary paralysis was wearing off—braced himself for he knew not what shock, but it was needless; their grotesque captors were not torturers. The air, while somewhat more dense than Earth's and of a peculiar odor, was eminently breathable, and even though the vessel was motionless in space an almost-normal gravitation gave them a large fraction of their usual weight.

After the three had been relieved of their pistols and other articles which the Nevians thought might prove to be weapons, the strange paralysis was lifted entirely. The Earthly clothing puzzled the captors immensely, but so strenuous were the objections raised to its removal that they did not press the point, but fell back to study their find in detail.

Then faced each other the representatives of the civilizations of two widely separated solar systems. The Nevians studied the human beings with interest and curiosity blended largely with loathing and repulsion; the three Terrestrials regarded the unmoving, expressionless "faces"—if those coned heads could be said to possess such thing—with horror and disgust, as well as with other emotions, each according to his type and training. For to human eyes the Nevian is a fearful thing. Even today there are few Terrestrials—or Solarians, for that matter—who can look at a Nevian, eye to eye, without feeling a creeping of the skin and experiencing a "gone" sensation in the pit of the stomach. The horny, wrinkled, drought-resisting Martian, whom we all know and rather like, is a hideous being indeed. The bat-eyed, colorless, hairless, practically skinless

Venerian is worse. But they both are, after all, remote cousins of Terra's humanity, and we get along with them quite well whenever we are compelled to visit Mars or Venus. But the Nevians—

The horizontal, flat, fish-like body is not so bad, even supported as it is by four short, powerful, scaly, flat-footed legs; and terminating as it does in the weird, four-vaned tail. The neck, even, is endurable, although it is long and flexible, heavily scaled, and is carried in whatever eye-wringing loops or curves the owner considers most convenient or ornamental at the time. Even the smell of a Nevian—a malodorous reek of over-ripe fish—does in time become tolerable, especially if sufficiently disguised with creosote, which purely Terrestrial chemical is the most highly prized perfume of Nevia. But the head! It is that member that makes the Nevian so appalling to Earthly eyes, for it is a thing utterly foreign to all Solarian history or experience. As most Tellurians already know, it is fundamentally a massive cone, covered with scales, based spearhead-like upon the neck. Four great sea-green, triangular eyes are spaced equidistant from each other about half way up the cone. The pupils are contractile at will, like the eyes of the cat, permitting the Nevian to see equally well in any ordinary extreme of light or darkness. Immediately below each eye springs out a long, jointless, boneless, tentacular arm; an arm which at its extremity divides into eight delicate and sensitive, but very strong, "fingers." Below each arm is a mouth: a beaked, needle-tusked orifice of dire potentialities. Finally, under the overhanging edge of the cone-shaped head are the delicately-frilled organs which serve either as gills or as nostrils and lungs, as may be desired. To other Nevians the eyes and other features are highly expressive, but to us they appear utterly cold and unmoving. Terrestrial senses can detect no changes of expression in a Nevian's "face." Such were the frightful beings at whom the three prisoners stared with sinking hearts.

But if we human beings have always considered Nevians grotesque and repulsive, the feeling has always been mutual. For those "monstrous" beings are a highly intelligent and extremely sensitive race, and our—to us—trim and graceful human forms seem to them the very quintessence of malformation and hideousness.

"Good Heavens, Conway!" Clio exclaimed, shrinking against Costigan as his left arm flashed around her. "What horrible monstrosities! And they can't talk—not one of them has made a sound—suppose they can be deaf and dumb?"

But at the same time Nerado was addressing his fellows.

"What hideous, deformed creatures they are! Truly a low form of life, even though they do possess some intelligence. They cannot talk, and have made no signs of having heard our words to them—do you suppose that they communicate by sight? That those weird contortions of their peculiarly placed organs serve as speech?"

Thus both sides, neither realizing that the other had spoken. For the Nevian voice is pitched so high that the lowest note audible to them is far above our limit of hearing. The shrillest note of a Terrestrial piccolo is to them so profoundly low that it cannot be heard.

"We have much to do." Nerado turned away from the captives. "We must postpone further study of the specimens until we have taken aboard a full cargo of the iron which is so plentiful here."

"What shall we do with them, sir?" asked one of the Nevian officers. "Lock them in one of the storage rooms?"

"Oh, no! They might die there, and we must by all means keep them in good condition, to be studied most carefully by the fellows of the College of Science. What a commotion there will be when we bring in this group of strange creatures, living proof that there are other suns possessing planets; planets which are supporting organic and intelligent life! You may put them in three communicating rooms, say in the fourth section—they will undoubtedly require light and exercise. Lock all the exits, of course, but it would be best to leave the doors between the rooms unlocked, so that they can be together or apart, as they choose. Since the smallest one, the female, stays so close to the larger male, it may be that they are mates. But since we know nothing of their habits or customs, it will be best to give them all possible freedom compatible with safety."

Nerado turned back to his instruments and three of the frightful crew came up to the human beings. One walked away, waving a couple of arms in an unmistakable signal that the prisoners were to follow him. The three obediently set out after him, the other two guards falling behind.

"Now's our best chance!" Costigan muttered, as they passed through a low doorway and entered a narrow corridor. "Watch that one ahead of you, Clio—hold him for a second if you can. Bradley, you and I will take the two behind us—now!"

Costigan stooped and whirled. Seizing a cable-like arm, he pulled the outlandish head down, the while the full power of his mighty right leg drove a heavy service boot into the place where scaly neck and head joined. The Nevian fell, and instantly Costigan leaped at the leader, ahead of the girl. Leaped; but dropped to the floor, again paralyzed. For the Nevian leader had been alert, his four eyes covering the entire circle of vision, and he had acted rapidly. Not in time to stop Costigan's first berserk attack—the First Officer's reactions were practically instantaneous and he moved fast—but in time to retain command of the situation. Another Nevian appeared, and while the stricken guard was recovering, all four arms wrapped tightly around his convulsively looping, writhing neck, the three helpless Terrestrials were lifted into the air and carried bodily into the quarters to which Nerado had assigned them. Not until they had been placed upon cushions in the middle room and the heavy metal doors had been locked upon them did they again find themselves able to use arms or legs.

"Well, that's another round we lose," Costigan commented, cheerfully. "A guy can't mix it very well when he can neither kick, strike, nor bite. I expected those lizards to rough me up then, but they didn't."

"They don't want to hurt us. They want to take us home with them, wherever that is, as curiosities, like wild animals or something," decided the girl, shrewdly. "They're pretty bad, of course, but I like them a lot better than I do Roger and his robots, anyway."

"I think you have the right idea, Miss Marsden," Bradley rumbled. "That's it, exactly. I feel like a bear in a cage. I should think you'd feel worse than ever. What chance has an animal of escaping from a menagerie?"

"These animals, lots. I'm feeling better and better all the time," Clio declared, and her serene bearing bore out her words. "You two got us out of that horrible place of Roger's, and I'm pretty sure that you will get us away from here, somehow or other. They may think we're stupid animals, but before you two and the Triplanetary Patrol and the Service get done with them they'll have another think coming."

"That's the old fight, Clio!" cheered Costigan. "I haven't got it figured out as close as you have, but I get about the same answer. These four-legged fish carry considerably heavier stuff than Roger did, I'm thinking; but they'll be up against something themselves pretty quick that is *no* light-weight, believe me!"

"Do you know something, or are you just whistling in the dark?" Bradley demanded.

"I know a little; not much. Engineering and Research have been working on a new ship for a long time; a ship to travel so much faster than light that it can go anywhere in the Galaxy and back in a month or so. New sub-ether drive, new atomic power, new armament, new everything. Only bad thing about it is that it doesn't work so good yet—it's fuller of bugs than a Venerian's kitchen. It has blown up five times that I know of, and has killed twenty-nine men. But when they get it licked they'll *have something!*"

"When, or if?" asked Bradley, pessimistically.

"I said *when!*" snapped Costigan, his voice cutting. "When the Service goes after anything they get it, and when they get it it *stays* . . . ." He broke off abruptly and his voice lost its edge. "Sorry. Didn't mean to get high, but I think we'll have help, if we can keep our heads up a while. And it looks good—these are first-class cages they've given us. All the comforts of home, even to lookout plates. Let's see what's going on, shall we?"

After some experimenting with the unfamiliar controls Costigan learned how to operate the Nevian visiray, and upon the plate they saw the Cone of Battle hurling itself toward Roger's planetoid. They saw the pirate fleet rush out to do battle with Triplanetary's massed forces, and with bated breath they watched every maneuver of that epic battle to its savagely sacrificial end. And that same battle was being watched, also with the most intense interest, by the Nevians in their control room.

"It is indeed a bloodthirsty combat," mused Nerado at his observation plate. "And it is peculiar—or rather, probably only to be expected from a race of such a low stage of development—that they employ only ether-borne forces. Warfare seems universal among primitive types—indeed, it is not so long ago that our own cities, few in number though they are, ceased fighting each other and combined against the semicivilized fishes of the greater deeps."

He fell silent, and for many minutes watched the furious battle between the two navies of the void. That conflict ended, he watched the Triplanetary fleet reform its battle cone and rush upon the planetoid.

"Destruction, always destruction," he sighed, adjusting his power switches. "Since they are bent upon mutual destruction I can see no purpose in refraining from destroying all of them. We need the iron, and they are a useless race."

He launched his softening, converting field of dull red energy. Vast as that field was, it could not encompass the whole fleet, but half of the lip of the gigantic cone soon disappeared, its component vessels subsiding into a sluggishly flowing stream of allotropic iron. The fleet, abandoning its attack upon the planetoid, swung its cone around, to bring the flame-erupting axis to bear upon the formless something dimly perceptible to the ultra-vision of Samms' observers. Furiously the gigantic composite beam of the massed fleet was hurled, nor was it alone.

For Gharlane had known, ever since the easy escape of his human prisoners, that something was occurring which was completely beyond his experience, although not beyond his theoretical knowledge. He had found the sub-ether closed; he had been unable to make his sub-ethereal weapons operative against either the three captives or the war-vessels of the Triplanetary Patrol. Now, however, he could work in the sub-ethereal murk of the newcomers; a light trial showed him that if he so wished he could use sub-ethereal offenses against them. What was the real meaning of those facts?

He had become convinced that those three persons were no more human than was Roger himself. Who or what was activating them? It was definitely not Eddorian workmanship; no Eddorian would have developed those particular techniques, nor could possibly have developed them without his knowledge. What, then? To do what had been done necessitated the existence of a race as old and as capable as the Eddorians, but of an entirely different nature; and, according to Eddore's vast Information Center, no such race existed or ever had existed.

Those visitors, possessing mechanisms supposedly known only to the science of Eddore, would also be expected to possess the mental powers which had been exhibited. Were they recent arrivals from some other space-time continuum? Probably not—Eddorian surveys had found no trace of any such life in any reachable plenum. Since it would be utterly fantastic to postulate the unheralded appearance of two such races at practically the same moment, the conclusion seemed unavoidable that these as yet unknown beings were the protectors—the activators, rather—of the two Triplanetary officers and the woman. This view was supported by the fact that while the strangers had attacked Triplanetary's fleet and had killed thousands of Triplanetary's men, they had actually rescued those three supposedly human beings. The planetoid, then would be attacked next. Very well, he would join Triplanetary in attacking them—with weapons no more dangerous to them than Triplanetary's own—the while preparing his real attack, which would come later. Roger issued orders; and waited; and thought more and more intensely upon one point which remained obscure—why, when the strangers themselves destroyed Triplanetary's fleet, had Roger been unable to use his most potent weapons against that fleet?

Thus, then, for the first time in Triplanetary's history, the forces of law and order joined hands with those of piracy and banditry against a common foe. Rods, beams, planes, and stilettos of unbearable energy the doomed fleet launched, in addition to its terrifically destructive main beam: Roger hurled every material weapon at his command. But bombs, high-explosive shells, even the ultra-deadly atomic torpedoes, alike were ineffective; alike simply vanished in the redly murky veil of nothingness. And the fleet was being melted. In quick succession the vessels flamed red, shrank together, gave out their air, and merged their component iron into the intensely crimson, sullenly viscous stream which was flowing through the impenetrable veil against which both Triplanetarians and pirates were directing their terrific offense.

SUPER PACK

The last vessel of the attacking cone having been converted and the resulting metal stored away, the Nevians—as Roger had anticipated—turned their attention toward the planetoid. But that structure was no feeble warship. It had been designed by, and built under the personal supervision of, Gharlane of Eddore. It was powered, equipped, and armed to meet any emergency which Gharlane's tremendous mind had been able to envision. Its entire bulk was protected by the shield whose qualities had so surprised Costigan; a shield far more effective than any Tellurian scientist or engineer would have believed possible.

The voracious converting beam of the Nevians, below the level of the ether though it was, struck that shield and rebounded; defeated and futile. Struck again, again rebounded; then struck and clung hungrily, licking out over that impermeable surface in darting tongues of flame as the surprised Nerado doubled and then quadrupled his power. Fiercer and fiercer the Nevian flood of force drove in. The whole immense globe of the planetoid became one scintillant ball of raw, red energy; but still the pirates' shield remained intact.

Gray Roger sat coldly motionless at his great desk, the top of which was now swung up to become a panel of massed and tiered instruments and controls. He could carry this load forever—but unless he was very wrong, this load would change shortly. What then? The essence that was Gharlane could not be killed—could not even be hurt—by any physical, chemical, or nuclear force. Should he stay with the planetoid to its end, and thus perforce return to Eddore with no material evidence whatever? He would not. Too much remained undone. Any report based upon his present information could be neither complete nor conclusive, and reports submitted by Gharlane of Eddore to the coldly cynical and ruthlessly analytical innermost Circle had always been and always would be both.

It was a fact that there existed at least one non-Eddorian mind which was the equal of his own. If one, there would be a race of such minds. The thought was galling; but to deny the existence of a fact would be the essence of stupidity. Since power of mind was a function of time, that race must be of approximately the same age as his own. Therefore the Eddorian Information Center, which by the inference of its completeness denied the existence of such a race, was wrong. It was not complete.

Why was it not complete? The only possible reason for two such races remaining unaware of the existence of each other would be the deliberate intent of one of them. Therefore, at some time in the past, the two races had been in contact for at least an instant of time. All Eddorian knowledge of that meeting had been suppressed and no more contacts had been allowed to occur.

The conclusion reached by Gharlane was a disturbing thing indeed; but, being an Eddorian, he faced it squarely. He did not have to wonder how such a suppression could have been accomplished—he knew. He also knew that his own mind contained everything known to his every ancestor since the first Eddorian was: the probability was exceedingly great that if any such contact had ever been made his mind would still contain at least some information concerning it, however carefully suppressed that knowledge had been.

He thought. Back . . . back . . . farther back . . . farther still . . . .

And as he thought, an interfering force began to pluck at him; as though palpable tongs were pulling out of line the mental probe with which he was exploring the hitherto unplumbed recesses of his mind.

"Ah . . . so you do not want me to remember?" Roger asked aloud, with no change in any lineament of his hard, gray face. "I wonder . . . do you really believe that you can keep me from remembering? I must abandon this search for the moment, but rest assured that I shall finish it very shortly."

*

"Here is the analysis of his screen, sir." A Nevian computer handed his chief a sheet of metal, bearing rows of symbols.

"Ah, a polycyclic . . . complete coverage . . . a screen of that type was scarcely to have been expected from such a low form of life," Nerado commented, and began to adjust dials and controls.

As he did so the character of the clinging mantle of force changed. From red it flamed quickly through the spectrum, became unbearably violet, then disappeared; and as it disappeared the shielding wall began to give way. It did not cave in abruptly, but softened locally, sagging into a peculiar grouping of valleys and ridges—contesting stubbornly every inch of position lost.

Roger experimented briefly with inertialessness. No use. As he had expected, they were prepared for that. He summoned a few of the ablest of his scientist-slaves and issued instructions. For minutes a host of robots toiled mightily, then a portion of the shield bulged out and became a tube extending beyond the attacking layers of force; a tube from which there erupted a beam of violence incredible. A beam behind which was every erg of energy that the gigantic mechanisms of the planetoid could yield. A beam that tore a hole through the redly impenetrable Nevian field and hurled itself upon the inner screen of the fish-shaped cruiser in frenzied incandescence. And was there, or was there not, a lesser eruption upon the other side—an almost imperceptible flash, as though something had shot from the doomed planetoid out into space?

Nerado's neck writhed convulsively as his tortured drivers whined and shrieked at the terrific overload; but Roger's effort was far too intense to be long maintained. Generator after generator burned out, the defensive screen collapsed, and the red converter beam attacked voraciously the unresisting metal of those prodigious walls. Soon there was a terrific explosion as the pent-up air of the planetoid broke through its weakening container, and the sluggish river of allotropic iron flowed in an ever larger stream, ever faster.

"It is well that we had an unlimited supply of iron." Nerado almost tied a knot in his neck as he spoke in huge relief. "With but the seven pounds remaining of our original supply, I fear that it would have been difficult to parry that last thrust."

"Difficult?" asked the second in command. "We would now be free atoms in space. But what shall I do with this iron? Our reservoirs will not hold more than half of it. And how about that one ship which remains untouched?"

"Jettison enough supplies from the lower holds to make room for this lot. As for that one ship, let it go. We will be overloaded as it is, and it is of the utmost importance that we get back to Nevia as soon as possible."

This, if Gharlane could have heard it, would have answered his question. All Arisia knew that it was *necessary* for the camera-ship to survive. The Nevians were interested only in iron; but the Eddorian, being a perfectionist, would not have been satisfied with anything less than the complete destruction of every vessel of Triplanetary's fleet.

The Nevian space-ship moved away, sluggishly now because of its prodigious load. In their quarters in the fourth section the three Terrestrials, who had watched with strained attention the downfall and absorption of the planetoid, stared at each other with drawn faces. Clio broke the silence.

"Oh, Conway, this is ghastly! It's . . . it's just simply too damned perfectly horrible!" she gasped, then recovered a measure of her customary spirit as she stared in surprise at Costigan's face. For it was thoughtful, his eyes were bright and keen—no trace of fear or disorganization was visible in any line of his hard young face.

"It's not so good," he admitted frankly. "I wish I wasn't such a dumb cluck—if Lyman Cleveland or Fred Rodebush were here they could help a lot, but I don't know enough about any of their stuff to flag a hand-car. I can't even interpret that funny flash—if it really was a flash—that we saw."

"Why bother about one little flash, after all that really did happen?" asked Clio, curiously.

"You think Roger launched something? He couldn't have—I didn't see a thing," Bradley argued.

"I don't know what to think. I've never seen anything material sent out so fast that I couldn't trace it with an ultra-wave—but on the other hand, Roger's got a lot of stuff that I never saw anywhere else. However, I don't see that it has anything to do with the fix we're in right now—but at that, we might be worse off. We're still breathing air, you notice, and if they don't blanket my wave I can still talk."

He put both hands into his pockets and spoke.

"Samms? Costigan. Put me on a recorder, quick—I probably haven't got much time," and for ten minutes he talked, concisely and as rapidly as he could utter words, reporting clearly and exactly everything that had transpired. Suddenly he broke off, writhing in agony. Frantically he tore his shirt open and hurled a tiny object across the room.

"Wow!" he exclaimed. "They may be deaf, but they can certainly detect an ultra-wave, and what an interference they can set up on it! No, I'm not hurt," he reassured the anxious girl, now at his side, "but it's a good thing I had you out of circuit—it would have jolted you loose from six or seven of your back teeth."

"Have you any idea where they're taking us?" she asked soberly.

"No," he answered flatly, looking deep into her steadfast eyes. "No use lying to you—if I know you at all you'd rather take it standing up. That talk of Jovians or Neptunians is the bunk—nothing like that ever grew in our Solarian system. All the signs say that we're going for a long ride."

THE LENSMAN

NEVIAN STRIFE

The Nevian space-ship was hurtling upon its way. Space-navigators both, the two Terrestrial officers soon discovered that it was even then moving with a velocity far above that of light and that it must be accelerating at a high rate, even though to them it seemed stationary—they could feel only a gravitational force somewhat less than that of their native Earth.

Bradley, seasoned old campaigner that he was, had retired promptly as soon as he had completed a series of observations, and was sleeping soundly upon a pile of cushions in the first of the three inter-connecting rooms. In the middle room, which was to be Clio's, Costigan was standing very close to the girl, but was not touching her. His body was rigid, his face was tense and drawn.

"You are wrong, Conway; all wrong," Clio was saying, very seriously. "I know how you feel, but it's false chivalry."

"That isn't it, at all," he insisted, stubbornly. "It isn't only that I've got you out here in space, in danger and alone, that's stopping me. I know you and I know myself well enough to know that what we start now we'll go through with for life. It doesn't make any difference, that way, whether I start making love to you now or whether I wait until we're back on Tellus; but I'm telling you that for your own good you'd better pass me up entirely. I've got enough horsepower to keep away from you if you tell me to—not otherwise."

"I know it, both ways, dear, but . . . ."

"But nothing!" he interrupted. "Can't you get it into your skull what you'll be letting yourself in for if you marry me? Assume that we get back, which isn't sure, by any means. But even if we do, some day—and maybe soon, too, you can't tell—somebody is going to collect fifty grams of radium for my head."

"Fifty grams—and everybody knows that Samms himself is rated at only sixty? I *knew* that you were somebody, Conway!" Clio exclaimed, undeterred. "But at that, something tells me that any pirate will earn even that much reward several times over before he collects it. Don't be silly, my dear—goodnight."

She tipped her head back, holding up to him her red, sweetly curved, smiling lips, and his arms swept around her. Her arms went up around his neck and they stood, clasped together in the motionless ecstasy of love's first embrace.

"Girl, girl, how I love you!" Costigan's voice was husky, his usually hard eyes were glowing with a tender light. "That settles that. I'll really *live* now, anyway, while . . . ."

"Stop it!" she commanded, sharply. "You're going to live until you die of old age—see if you don't. You'll simply *have* to, Conway!"

"That's so, too—no percentage in dying now. All the pirates between Tellus and Andromeda couldn't take me after this—I've got too much to live for. Well, goodnight, sweetheart, I'd better beat it—you need some sleep."

The lovers' parting was not as simple and straightforward a procedure as Costigan's speech would indicate, but finally he did seek his own room and relaxed upon a pile of cushions, his stern visage transformed. Instead of the low metal ceiling he saw a beautiful, oval, tanned young face, framed in a golden-blonde corona of hair. His gaze sank into the depths of loyal, honest, dark blue eyes; and looking deeper and deeper into those blue wells he fell asleep. Upon his face, too set and grim by far for a man of his years—the lives of Sector Chiefs of the Triplanetary Service were not easy, nor as a rule were they long—there lingered as he slept that newly-acquired softness of expression, the reflection of his transcendent happiness.

For eight hours he slept soundly, as was his wont, then, also according to his habit and training he came wide awake, with no intermediate stage of napping.

"Clio?" he whispered. "Awake, girl?"

"Awake!" her voice come through the ultra phone, relief in every syllable. "Good heavens, I thought you were going to sleep until we got to wherever it is that we're going! Come on in, you two—I don't see how you can possibly sleep, just as though you were home in bed."

"You've got to learn to sleep anywhere if you expect to keep in . . . ." Costigan broke off as he opened the door and saw Clio's wan face. She had evidently spent a sleepless and wracking eight hours. "Good Lord, Clio, why didn't you call me?"

"Oh, I'm all right, except for being a little jittery. No need of asking how you feel, is there?"

"No—I feel hungry," he answered cheerfully. "I'm going to see what we can do about it—or say, guess I'll see whether they're still interfering on Samms' wave."

He took out the small, insulated case and touched the contact stud lightly with his finger. His arm jerked away powerfully.

"Still at it," he gave the unnecessary explanation. "They don't seem to want us to talk outside, but his interference is as good as my talking—they can trace it, of course. Now I'll see what I can find out about our breakfast."

He stepped over to the plate and shot its projector beam forward into the control room, where he saw Nerado lying, doglike, at his instrument panel. As Costigan's beam entered the room a blue light flashed on and the Nevian turned an eye and an arm toward his own small observation plate. Knowing that they were now in visual communication, Costigan beckoned an invitation and pointed to his mouth in what he hoped was the universal sign of hunger. The Nevian waved an arm and fingered controls, and as he did so a wide section of the floor of Clio's room slid aside. The opening thus made revealed a table which rose upon its low pedestal, a table equipped with three softly-cushioned benches and spread with a glittering array of silver and glassware.

Bowls and platters of a dazzlingly white metal, narrow-waisted goblets of sheerest crystal; all were hexagonal, beautifully and intricately carved or etched in apparently conventional marine designs. And the table utensils of this strange race were peculiar indeed. There were tearing forceps of sixteen needle-sharp curved teeth; there were flexible spatulas; there were deep and shallow ladles with flexible edges; there were many other peculiarly-curved instruments at whose uses the Terrestrials could not even guess; all having delicately-fashioned handles to fit the long slender fingers of the Nevians.

But if the table and its appointments were surprising to the Terrestrials, revealing as they did a degree of culture which none of them had expected to find in a race of beings so monstrous, the food was even more surprising, although in another sense. For the wonderful crystal goblets were filled with a grayish-green slime of a nauseous and overpowering odor, the smaller bowls were full of living sea spiders and other such delicacies; and each large platter contained a fish fully a foot long, raw and whole, garnished tastefully with red, purple, and green strands of seaweed!

Clio looked once, then gasped, shutting her eyes and turning away from the table, but Costigan flipped the three fish into a platter and set it aside before he turned back to the visiplate.

"They'll go good fried," he remarked to Bradley, signaling vigorously to Nerado that the meal was not acceptable and that he wanted to talk to him, *in person*. Finally he made himself clear, the table sank down out of sight, and the Nevian commander cautiously entered the room.

At Costigan's insistence, he came up to the visiplate, leaving near the door three alert and fully-armed guards. The man then shot the beam into the galley of the pirate's lifeboat, suggesting that they should be allowed to live there. For some time the argument of arms and fingers raged—though not exactly fluent conversation, both sides managed to convey their meanings quite clearly. Nerado would not allow the Terrestrials to visit their own ship—he was taking no chances—but after a thorough ultra-ray inspection he did finally order some of his men to bring into the middle room the electric range and a supply of Terrestrial food. Soon the Nevian fish were sizzling in a pan and the appetizing odors of coffee and browning biscuit permeated the room. But at the first appearance of those odors the Nevians departed hastily, content to watch the remainder of the curious and repulsive procedure in their visiray plates.

Breakfast over and everything made tidy and ship-shape, Costigan turned to Clio.

"Look here, girl; you've got to learn how to sleep. You're all in. Your eyes look like you've been on a Martian picnic and you didn't eat half enough breakfast. You've got to sleep and eat to keep fit. We don't want you passing out on us, so I'll put out this light, and you'll lie down here and sleep until noon."

"Oh, no, don't bother. I'll sleep tonight. I'm quite . . . ."

"You'll sleep now," he informed her, levelly. "I never thought of you being nervous, with Bradley and me on each side of you. We're both right here now, though, and we'll stay here. We'll watch over you like a couple of old hens with one chick between them. Come on; lie down and go bye-bye."

Clio laughed at the simile, but lay down obediently. Costigan sat upon the edge of the great divan holding her hand, and they chatted idly. The silences grew longer, Clio's remarks became fewer, and soon her long-lashed eyelids fell and her deep, regular breathing showed that she was sound asleep. The man stared at her, his very heart in his eyes. So young, so beautiful, so lovely—and *how* he did love her! He was not formally religious, but his every thought was a prayer. If he could only get her out of this mess . . . he wasn't fit to live on the same planet with her, but . . . just give him one chance, God . . . just one!

But Costigan had been laboring for days under a terrific strain, and had been going very short on sleep. Half hypnotized by his own mixed emotions and by his staring at the smooth curves of Clio's cheek, his own eyes closed and, still holding her hand, he sank down into the soft cushions beside her and into oblivion.

Thus sleeping hand in hand like two children Bradley found them, and a tender, fatherly expression came over his face as he looked down at them.

"Nice little girl, Clio," he mused, "and when they made Costigan they broke the mold. They'll do—about as fine a couple of kids as old Tellus ever produced. I could do with some more sleep myself." He yawned prodigiously, lay down at Clio's left, and in minutes was himself asleep.

Hours later, both men were awakened by a merry peal of laughter. Clio was sitting up, regarding them with sparkling eyes. She was refreshed, buoyant, ravenously hungry and highly amused. Costigan was amazed and annoyed at what he considered a failure in a self-appointed task; Bradley was calm and matter-of-fact.

"Thanks for being such a nice body-guard, you two." Clio laughed again, but sobered quickly. "I slept wonderfully well, but I wonder if I can sleep tonight without making you hold my hand all night?"

"Oh, he doesn't mind doing that," Bradley commented.

"Mind it!" Costigan exclaimed, and his eyes and his tone spoke volumes.

They prepared and ate another meal, one to which Clio did full justice. Rested and refreshed, they had begun to discuss possibilities of escape when Nerado and his three armed guards entered the room. The Nevian scientist placed a box upon a table and began to make adjustments upon its panels, eyeing the Terrestrials attentively after each setting. After a time a staccato burst of articulate speech issued from the box, and Costigan saw a great light.

"You've got it—hold it!" he exclaimed, waving his arms excitedly. "You see, Clio, their voices are pitched either higher or lower than ours—probably higher—and they've built an audio-frequency changer. He's nobody's fool, that lizard!"

Nerado heard Costigan's voice, there was no doubt of that. His long neck looped and twisted in Nevian gratification; and although neither side could understand the other, both knew that intelligent speech and hearing were attributes common to the two races. This fact altered markedly the relations between captors and captives. The Nevians admitted among themselves that the strange bipeds might be quite intelligent, after all; and the Terrestrials at once became more hopeful.

"It isn't so bad, if they can talk," Costigan summed up the situation. "We might as well take it easy and make the best of it, particularly since we haven't been able to figure out any possible way of getting away from them. They can talk and hear, and we can learn their language in time. Maybe we can make some kind of a deal with them to take us back to our own system, if we can't make a break."

The Nevians being as eager as the Terrestrials to establish communication, Nerado kept the newly devised frequency changer in constant use. There is no need of describing at length the details of that interchange of languages. Suffice it to say that starting at the very bottom they learned as babies learn, but with the great advantage over babies of possessing fully developed and capable brains. And while the human beings were learning the tongue of Nevia, several of the amphibians (and incidentally Clio Marsden) were learning Triplanetarian; the two officers knowing well that it would be much easier for the Nevians to learn the logically-built common language of the Three Planets than to master the senseless intricacies of English.

In a short time the two parties were able to understand each other after a fashion, by using a weird mixture of both languages. As soon as a few ideas had been exchanged, the Nevian scientists built transformers small enough to be worn collar-like by the Terrestrials, and the captives were allowed to roam at will throughout the great vessel; only the compartment in which was stored the dismembered pirate lifeboat being sealed to them. Thus it was that they were not left long in doubt when another fish-shaped cruiser of the void was revealed upon their lookout plates in the awful emptiness of interstellar space.

"This is our sister-ship going to your Solarian system for a cargo of the iron which is so plentiful there," Nerado explained to his involuntary guests.

"I hope the gang has got the bugs worked out of our super-ship!" Costigan muttered savagely to his companions as Nerado turned away. "If they have, that outfit will get something more than a load of iron when they get there!"

More time passed, during which a blue-white star separated itself from the infinitely distant firmament and began to show a perceptible disk. Larger and larger it grew, becoming bluer and bluer as the flying space-ship approached it, until finally Nevia could be seen, apparently close beside her parent orb.

Heavily laden though the vessel was, such was her power that she was soon dropping vertically downward toward a large lagoon in the middle of the Nevian city. That bit of open water was devoid of life, for this was to be no ordinary landing. Under the terrific power of the beams braking the descent of that unimaginable load of allotropic iron the water seethed and boiled; and instead of floating gracefully upon the surface of the sea, this time the huge ship of space sank like a plummet to the bottom. Having accomplished the delicate feat of docking the vessel safely in the immense cradle prepared for her, Nerado turned to the Tellurians, who, now under guard, had been brought before him.

"While our cargo of iron is being discharged, I am to take you three specimens to the College of Science, where you are to undergo a thorough physical and psychological examination. Follow me."

"Wait a minute!" protested Costigan, with a quick and furtive wink at his companions. "Do you expect us to go through *water*, and at this frightful depth?"

"Certainly," replied the Nevian, in surprise. "You are air-breathers, of course, but you must be able to swim a little, and this slight depth—but little more than thirty of your meters—will not trouble you."

"You are wrong, twice," declared the Terrestrial, convincingly. "If by 'swimming' you mean propelling yourself in or through the water, we know nothing of it. In water over our heads we drown helplessly in a minute or two, and the pressure at this depth would kill us instantly."

"Well, I could take a lifeboat, of course, but that . . . " the Nevian Captain began, doubtfully, but broke off at the sound of a staccato call from his signal panel.

"Captain Nerado, attention!"

"Nerado," he acknowledged into a microphone.

"The Third City is being attacked by the fishes of the greater deeps. They have developed new and powerful mobile fortresses mounting unheard-of weapons and the city reports that it cannot long withstand their attack. They are asking for all possible help. Your vessel not only has vast stores of iron, but also mounts weapons of power. You are requested to proceed to their aid at the earliest possible moment."

Nerado snapped out orders and the liquid iron fell in streams from wide-open ports, forming a vast, red pool in the bottom of the dock. In a short time the great vessel was in equilibrium with the water she displaced, and as soon as she had attained a slight buoyancy the ports snapped shut and Nerado threw on the power.

"Go back to your own quarters and stay there until I send for you," the Nevian directed, and as the Terrestrials obeyed the curt orders the cruiser tore herself from the water and flashed up into the crimson sky.

"What a barefaced liar!" Bradley exclaimed. The three, transformers cut off, were back in the middle room of their suite. "You can outswim an otter, and I happen to know that you came up out of the old DZ83 from a depth of . . . ."

"Maybe I did exaggerate a trifle," Costigan interrupted, "but the more helpless he thinks we are the better for us. And we want to stay out of any of their cities as long as we can, because they may be hard places to get out of. I've got a couple of ideas, but they aren't ripe enough to pick yet . . . . Wow! How this bird's been traveling! We're there already! If he hits the water going like this, he'll split himself, sure!"

With undiminished velocity they were flashing downward in a long slant toward the beleaguered Third City, and from the flying vessel there was launched toward the city's central lagoon a torpedo. No missile this, but a capsule containing a full ton of allotropic iron, which would be of more use to the Nevian defenders than millions of men. For the Third City was sore pressed indeed. Around it was one unbroken ring of boiling, exploding water—water billowing upward in searing, blinding bursts of super-heated steam, or being hurled bodily in all directions in solid masses by the cataclysmic forces being released by the embattled fishes of the greater deeps. Her outer defenses were already down, and even as the Terrestrials stared in amazement another of the immense hexagonal buildings burst into fragments; its upper structure flying wildly into scrap metal, its lower half subsiding drunkenly below the surface of the boiling sea.

The three Earth-people seized whatever supports were at hand as the Nevian space-ship struck the water with undiminished speed, but the precaution was needless—Nerado knew thoroughly his vessel, its strength and its capabilities. There was a mighty splash, but that was all. The artificial gravity was unchanged by the impact; to the passengers the vessel was still motionless and on even keel as, now a submarine, she snapped around like a very fish and attacked the rear of the nearest fortress.

For fortresses they were; vast structures of green metal, plowing forward implacably upon immense caterpillar treads. And as they crawled they destroyed, and Costigan, exploring the strange submarine with his visiray beam, watched and marveled. For the fortresses were full of water; water artificially cooled and aerated, entirely separate from the boiling flood through which they moved. They were manned by fish some five feet in length. Fish with huge, goggling eyes; fish plentifully equipped with long, armlike tentacles; fish poised before control panels or darting about intent upon their various duties. Fish with brains, waging war!

Nor was their warfare ineffectual. Their heat-rays boiled the water for hundreds of yards before them and their torpedoes were exploding against the Nevian defenses in one appallingly continuous concussion. But most potent of all was a weapon unknown to Triplanetary warfare. From a fortress there would shoot out, with the speed of a meteor, a long, jointed, telescopic rod; tipped with a tiny, brilliantly-shining ball. Whenever that glowing tip encountered any obstacle, that obstacle disappeared in an explosion world-wracking in its intensity. Then what was left of the rod, dark now, would be retracted into the fortress-only to emerge again in a moment with a tip once more shining and potent.

Nerado, apparently as unfamiliar with the peculiar weapon as were the Terrestrials, attacked cautiously; sending out far to the fore his murkily impenetrable screens of red. But the submarine was entirely non-ferrous, and its officers were apparently quite familiar with Nevian beams which licked at and clung to the green walls in impotent fury. Through the red veil came stabbing ball after ball, and only the most frantic dodging saved the space-ship from destruction in those first few furious seconds. And now the Nevian defenders of the Third City had secured and were employing the vast store of allotropic iron so opportunely delivered by Nerado.

From the city there pushed out immense nets of metal, extending from the surface of the ocean to its bottom; nets radiating such terrific forces that the very water itself was beaten back and stood motionless in vertical, glassy walls. Torpedoes were futile against that wall of energy. The most fiercely driven rays of the fishes flamed incandescent against it, in vain. Even the incredible violence of a concentration of every available force-ball against one point could not break through. At that unimaginable explosion water was hurled for miles. The bed of the ocean was not only exposed, but in it there was blown a crater at whose dimensions the Terrestrials dared not even guess. The crawling fortresses themselves were thrown backward violently and the very world was rocked to its core by the concussion, but that iron-driven wall held. The massive nets swayed and gave back, and tidal waves hurled their mountainously destructive masses through the Third City, but the mighty barrier remained intact. And Nerado, still attacking two of the powerful tanks with his every weapon, was still dodging those flashing balls charged with the quintessence of destruction. The fishes could not see through the sub-ethereal veil, but all the gunners of the two fortresses were combing it thoroughly with ever-lengthening, ever-thrusting rods, in a desperate attempt to wipe out the new and apparently all-powerful Nevian submarine whose sheer power was slowly but inexorably crushing even their gigantic walls.

"Well, I think that right now's the best chance we'll ever have of doing something for ourselves." Costigan turned away from the absorbing scenes pictured upon the visiplate and faced his two companions.

"But what can we possibly do?" asked Clio.

"Whatever it is, we'll try it!" Bradley exclaimed.

"Anything's better than staying here and letting them analyze us—no telling what they'd do to us," Costigan went on.

"I know a lot more about things than they think I do. They never did catch me using my spy-ray—it's on an awfully narrow beam, you know, and uses almost no power at all—so I've been able to dope out quite a lot of stuff. I can open most of their locks, and I know how to run their small boats. This battle, fantastic as it is, is deadly stuff, and it isn't one-sided, by any means, either, so that every one of them, from Nerado down, seems to be on emergency duty. There are no guards watching us, or stationed where we want to go—our way out is open. And once out, this battle is giving us our best possible chance to get away from them. There's so much emission out there already that they probably couldn't detect the driving force of the lifeboat, and they'll be too busy to chase us, anyway."

"Once out, then what?" asked Bradley.

"We'll have to decide that before we start, of course. I'd say make a break back for Earth. We know the direction and we'll have plenty of power."

"But good Heavens, Conway, it's so far!" exclaimed Clio. "How about food, water, and air—would we ever get there?"

"You know as much about that as I do. I think so, but of course anything might happen. This ship is none too big, is considerably slower than the big space-ship, and we're a long ways from home. Another bad thing is the food question. The boat is well stocked according to Nevian ideas, but it's pretty foul stuff for us to eat. However, it's nourishing, and we'll have to eat it, since we can't carry enough of our own supplies to the boat to last long. Even so, we may have to go on short rations, but I think that we'll be able to make it. On the other hand, what happens if we stay here? They will find us sooner or later, and we don't know any too much about these ultra-weapons. We are land-dwellers, and there is little if any land on this planet. Then, too, we don't know where to look for what land there may be, and even if we could find it, we know that it is all over-run with amphibians already. There's a lot of things that might be better, but they might be a lot worse, too. How about it? Do we try or do we stay here?"

"We try it!" exclaimed Clio and Bradley, as one.

"All right. I'd better not waste any more time talking—let's go!"

Stepping up to the locked and shielded door, he took out a peculiarly built torch and pointed it at the Nevian lock. There was no light, no noise, but the massive portal swung smoothly open. They stepped out and Costigan relocked and reshielded the entrance.

"How . . . what . . . ." Clio demanded.

"I've been going to school for the last few weeks," Costigan grinned, "and I've picked up quite a few things here and there—literally, as well as figuratively. Snap it up, guys! Our armor is stored with the pieces of the pirates' lifeboat, and I'll feel a lot better when we've got it on and have hold of a few Lewistons."

They hurried down corridors, up ramps, and along hallways, with Costigan's spy-ray investigating the course ahead for chance Nevians. Bradley and Clio were unarmed, but the operative had found a piece of flat metal and had ground it to a razor edge.

"I think I can throw this thing straight enough and fast enough to chop off a Nevian's head before he can put a paralyzing ray on us," he explained grimly, but he was not called upon to show his skill with the improvised cleaver.

As he had concluded from his careful survey, every Nevian was at some control or weapon, doing his part in that frightful combat with the denizens of the greater deeps. Their path was open; they were neither molested nor detected as they ran toward the compartment within which was sealed all their belongings. The door of that room opened, as had the other, to Costigan's knowing beam; and all three set hastily to work. They made up packs of food, filled their capacious pockets with emergency rations, buckled on Lewistons and automatics, donned their armor, and clamped into their external holsters a full complement of additional weapons.

"Now comes the ticklish part of the business," Costigan informed the others. His helmet was slowly turning this way and that, and the others knew that through his spy-ray goggles he was studying their route. "There's only one boat we stand a chance of reaching, and somebody's mighty apt to see us. There's a lot of detectors up there, and we'll have to cross a corridor full of communicator beams. There, that line's off—scoot!"

At his word they dashed out into the hall and hurried along for minutes, dodging sharply to right or left as the leader snapped out orders. Finally he stopped.

"Here's those beams I told you about. We'll have to roll under'em. They're less than waist high—right there's the lowest one. Watch me do it, and when I give you the word, one at a time, you do the same. *Keep low*—don't let an arm or a leg get up into a ray or they may see us."

He threw himself flat, rolled upon the floor a yard or so, and scrambled to his feet. He gazed intently at the blank wall for a space.

"Bradley—now!" he snapped, and the captain duplicated his performance.

But Clio, unused to the heavy and cumbersome space-armor she was wearing, could not roll in it with any degree of success. When Costigan barked his order she tried, but stopped, floundering almost directly below the network of invisible beams. As she struggled one mailed arm went up, and Costigan saw in his ultra-goggles the faint flash as the beam encountered the interfering field. But already he had acted. Crouching low, he struck down the arm, seized it, and dragged the girl out of the zone of visibility. Then in furious haste he opened a nearby door and all three sprang into a tiny compartment.

"Shut off all the fields of your suits, so that they can't interfere!" he hissed into the utter darkness. "Not that I'd mind killing a few of them, but if they start an organized search we're sunk. But even if they did get a warning by touching your glove, Clio, they probably won't suspect us. Our rooms are still shielded, and the chances are that they're too busy to bother much about us, anyway."

He was right. A few beams darted here and there, but the Nevians saw nothing amiss and ascribed the interference to the falling into the beam of some chance bit of charged metal. With no further misadventures the fugitives gained entrance to the Nevian lifeboat, where Costigan's first act was to disconnect one steel boot from his armor of space. With a sigh of relief he pulled his foot out of it, and from it carefully poured into the small power-tank of the craft fully thirty pounds of allotropic iron!

"I pinched it off them," he explained, in answer to amazed and inquiring looks, "and maybe you don't think it's a relief to get it out of that boot! I couldn't steal a flask to carry it in, so this was the only place I could put it. These lifeboats are equipped with only a couple of grams of iron apiece, you know, and we couldn't get half-way back to Tellus on that, even with smooth going; and we may have to fight. With this much to go on, though, we could go to Andromeda, fighting all the way. Well, we'd better break away."

Costigan watched his plate closely; and, when the maneuvering of the great vessel brought his exit port as far away as possible from the Third City and the warring tanks, he shot the little cruiser out and away. Straight out into the ocean it sped, through the murky red veil, and darted upward toward the surface. The three wanderers sat tense, hardly daring to breathe, staring into the plates—Clio and Bradley pushing at mental levers and stepping down hard upon mental brakes in unconscious efforts to help Costigan dodge the beams and rods of death flashing so appallingly close upon all sides. Out of the water and into the air the darting, dodging lifeboat flashed in safety; but in the air, supposedly free from menace, came disaster. There was a crunching, grating shock and the vessel was thrown into a dizzy spiral, from which Costigan finally leveled it into headlong flight away from the scene of battle. Watching the pyrometers which recorded the temperature of the outer shell, he drove the lifeboat ahead at the highest safe atmospheric speed while Bradley went to inspect the damage.

"Pretty bad, but better than I thought," the captain reported. "Outer and inner plates broken away on a seam. We wouldn't hold cotton waste, let alone air. Any tools aboard?"

"Some—and what we haven't got we'll make," Costigan declared. "We'll put a lot of distance behind us, then we'll fix her up and get away from here."

"What are those fish, anyway, Conway?" Clio asked, as the lifeboat tore along. "The Nevians are bad enough, Heaven knows, but the very idea of intelligent and educated *fish* is enough to drive one mad!"

"You know Nerado mentioned several times the 'semicivilized fishes of the greater deeps'?" he reminded her. "I gather that there are at least three intelligent races here. We know two—the Nevians, who are amphibians, and the fishes of the greater deeps. The fishes of the lesser deeps are also intelligent. As I get it, the Nevian cities were originally built in very shallow water, or perhaps were upon islands. The development of machinery and tools gave them a big edge on the fish; and those living in the shallow seas, nearest the Islands, gradually became tributary nations, if not actually slaves. Those fish not only serve as food, but work in the mines, hatcheries, and plantations, and do all kinds of work for the Nevians. Those so-called 'lesser deeps' were conquered first, of course, and all their races of fish are docile enough now. But the deep-sea breeds, who live in water so deep that the Nevians can hardly stand the pressure down there, were more intelligent to start with, and more stubborn besides. But the most valuable metals here are deep down—this planet is very light for its size, you know—so the Nevians kept at it until they conquered some of the deep-sea fish, too, and put 'em to work. But those high-pressure boys were nobody's fools. They realized that as time went on the amphibians would get further and further ahead of them in development, so they let themselves be conquered, learned how to use the Nevians' tools and everything else they could get hold of, developed a lot of new stuff of their own, and now they're out to wipe the amphibians off the map completely, before they get too far ahead of them to handle."

"And the Nevians are afraid of them, and want to kill them all, as fast as they possibly can," guessed Clio.

"That would be the logical thing, of course," commented Bradley. "Got pretty nearly enough distance now, Costigan?"

"There isn't enough distance on the planet to suit me," Costigan replied. "We'll need all we can get. A full diameter away from that crew of amphibians is too close for comfort—their detectors are keen."

"Then they can detect us?" Clio asked. "Oh, I wish they hadn't hit us—we'd have been away from here long ago."

"So do I," Costigan agreed, feelingly. "But they did—no use squawking. We can rivet and weld those seams, and things could be a lot worse—we are still breathing air!"

In silence the lifeboat flashed onward, and half of Nevia's mighty globe was traversed before it was brought to a halt. Then in furious haste the two officers set to work, again to make their small craft sound and spaceworthy.

WORM, SUBMARINE, AND FREEDOM

Since both Costigan and Bradley had often watched their captors at work during the long voyage from the Solar System to Nevia, they were quite familiar with the machine tools of the amphibians. Their stolen lifeboat, being an emergency craft, of course carried full repair equipment; and to such good purpose did the two officers labor that even before their air-tanks were fully charged, all the damage had been repaired.

The lifeboat lay motionless upon the mirror-smooth surface of the ocean. Captain Bradley had opened the upper port and the three stood in the opening, gazing in silence toward the incredibly distant horizon, while powerful pumps were forcing the last possible ounces of air into the storage cylinders. Mile upon strangely flat mile stretched that waveless, unbroken expanse of water, merging finally into the violent redness of the Nevian sky. The sun was setting; a vast ball of purple flame dropping rapidly toward the horizon. Darkness came suddenly as that seething ball disappeared, and the air became bitterly cold, in sharp contrast to the pleasant warmth of a moment before. And as suddenly clouds appeared in blackly banked masses and a cold, driving rain began to beat down.

"Br-r-r, it's cold! Let's go in—Oh! *Shut the door!*" Clio shrieked, and leaped wildly down into the compartment below, out of Costigan's way, for he and Bradley had also seen slithering toward them the frightful arm of the Thing.

Almost before the girl had spoken Costigan had leaped to the controls, and not an instant too soon; for the tip of that horrible tentacle flashed into the rapidly narrowing crack just before the door clanged shut. As the powerful toggles forced the heavy wedges into engagement and drove the massive disk home, that grisly tip fell severed to the floor of the compartment and lay there, twitching and writhing with a loathesome and unearthly vigor. Two feet long the piece was, and larger than a strong man's leg. It was armed with spiked and jointed metallic scales, and instead of sucking disks it was equipped with a series of *mouths*—mouths filled with sharp metallic teeth which gnashed and ground together furiously, even though sundered from the horrible organism which they were designed to feed.

The little submarine shuddered in every plate and member as monstrous coils encircled her and tightened inexorably in terrific, rippling surges eloquent of mastodonic power; and a strident vibration smote sickeningly upon Terrestrial ear-drums as the metal spikes of the monstrosity crunched and ground upon the outer plating of their small vessel. Costigan stood unmoved at the plate, watching intently; hands ready upon the controls. Due to the artificial gravity of the lifeboat it seemed perfectly stationary to its occupants. Only the weird gyrations of the pictures upon the lookout screens showed that the craft was being shaken and thrown about like a rat in the jaws of a terrier; only the gauges revealed that they were almost a mile below the surface of the ocean already, and were still going downward at an appalling rate. Finally Clio could stand no more.

"Aren't you going to do something, Conway?" she cried.

"Not unless I have to," he replied, composedly. "I don't believe that he can really hurt us, and if I use force of any kind I'm afraid that it will kick up enough disturbance to bring Nerado down on us like a hawk onto a chicken. However, if he takes us much deeper I'll have to go to work on him. We're getting down pretty close to our limit, and the bottom's a long ways down yet."

Deeper and deeper the lifeboat was dragged by its dreadful opponent, whose spiked teeth still tore savagely at the tough outer plating of the craft, until Costigan reluctantly threw in his power switches. Against the full propellant thrust the monster could draw them no lower, but neither could the lifeboat make any headway toward the surface. The pilot then turned on his beams, but found that they were ineffective. So closely was the creature wrapped around the submarine that his weapons could not be brought to bear upon it.

"What can it possibly be, anyway, and what can we do about it?" Clio asked.

"I thought at first it was something like a devilfish, or possibly an overgrown starfish, but it isn't," Costigan made answer. "It must be a kind of flat worm. That doesn't sound reasonable—the thing must be all of a hundred meters long—but there it is. The only thing left to do that I can think of is to try to boil him alive."

He closed other circuits, diffusing a terrific beam of pure heat, and the water all about them burst into furious clouds of steam. The boat leaped upward as the metallic fins of the gigantic worm fanned vapor instead of water, but the creature neither released its hold nor ceased its relentlessly grinding attack. Minute after minute went by, but finally the worm dropped limply away—cooked through and through; vanquished only by death.

"Now we've put our foot in it, clear to the neck!" Costigan exclaimed, as he shot the lifeboat upward at its maximum power. "Look at that! I knew that Nerado could trace us, but I didn't have any idea that *they* could!"

Staring with Costigan into the plate, Bradley and the girl saw, not the Nevian sky-rover they had expected, but a fast submarine cruiser, manned by the frightful fishes of the greater deeps. It was coming directly toward the lifeboat, and even as Costigan hurled the little vessel off at an angle and then sped upward into the air, one of the deadly offensive

113

rods, tipped with its glowing ball of pure destruction, flashed through the spot where they would have been had they held their former course.

But powerful as were the propellant forces of the lifeboat and fiercely though Costigan applied them, the denizens of the deep clamped a tractor beam upon the flying vessel before it had gained a mile of altitude. Costigan aligned his every driving projector as his vessel came to an abrupt halt in the invisible grip of the beam, then experimented with various dials.

"There ought to be some way of cutting that beam," he pondered audibly, "but I don't know enough about their system to do it, and I'm afraid to monkey around with things too much, because I might accidentally release the screens we've already got out, and they're stopping altogether too much stuff for us to do without them right now."

He frowned as he studied the flaring defensive screens, now radiating an incandescent violet under the concentration of forces being hurled against them by the warlike fishes, then stiffened suddenly.

"I thought so—they *can* shoot'em!" he exclaimed, throwing the lifeboat into a furious corkscrew turn, and the very air blazed into flaming splendor as a dazzlingly scintillating ball of energy sped past them and high into the air beyond.

Then for minutes a spectacular battle raged. The twisting, turning, leaping airship, small as she was and agile, kept on eluding the explosive projectiles of the fishes, and her screens neutralized and re-radiated the full power of the attacking beams. More—since Costigan did not need to think of sparing his iron, the ocean around the great submarine began furiously to boil under the full-driven offensive beams of the tiny Nevian ship. But escape Costigan could not. He could not cut that tractor beam and the utmost power of his drivers could not wrest the lifeboat from its tenacious clutch. And slowly but inexorably the ship of space was being drawn downward toward the ship of ocean's depths. Downward, in spite of the utmost possible effort of every projector and generator; and Clio and Bradley, sick at heart, looked once at each other. Then they looked at Costigan, who, jaw hard set and eyes unflinchingly upon his plate, was concentrating his attack upon one turret of the green monster as they settled lower and lower.

"If this is . . . if our number is going up, Conway," Clio began, unsteadily.

"Not yet, it isn't!" he snapped. "Keep a stiff upper lip, girl. We're still breathing air, and the battle's not over yet!"

Nor was it; but it was not Costigan's efforts, mighty though they were, that ended the attack of the fishes of the greater deeps. The tractor beams snapped without warning, and so prodigious were the forces being exerted by the lifeboat that as it hurled itself away the three passengers were thrown violently to the floor, in spite of the powerful gravity controls. Scrambling up on hands and knees, bracing himself as best he could against the terrific forces, Costigan managed finally to force a hand up to his panel. He was barely in time; for even as he cut the driving power to its normal value the outer shell of the lifeboat was blazing at white heat from the friction of the atmosphere through which it had been tearing with such an insane acceleration!

"Oh, I see—Nerado to the rescue," Costigan commented, after a glance into the plate. "I hope that those fish blow him clear out of the Galaxy!"

"Why?" demanded Clio. "I should think that you'd . . . ."

"Think again," he advised her. "The worse Nerado gets licked the better for us. I don't really expect that, but if they can keep him busy long enough, we can get far enough away so that he won't bother about us any more."

As the lifeboat tore upward through the air at the highest permissible atmospheric velocity Bradley and Clio peered over Costigan's shoulders into the plate, watching in fascinated interest the scene which was being kept in focus upon it. The Nevian ship of space was plunging downward in a long, slanting dive, her terrific beams of force screaming out ahead of her. The beams of the little lifeboat had boiled the waters of the ocean; those of the parent craft seemed literally to blast them out of existence. All about the green submarine there had been volumes of furiously-boiling water and dense clouds of vapor; now water and fog alike disappeared, converted into transparent super-heated steam by the blasts of Nevian energy. Through that tenuous gas the enormous mass of the submarine fell like a plummet, her defensive screens flaming an almost invisible violet, her every offensive weapon vomiting forth solid and vibratory destruction toward the Nevian cruiser so high in the angry, scarlet heavens.

For miles the submarine dropped, until the frightful pressure of the depth drove water into Nerado's beam faster than his forces could volatilize it. Then in that seething funnel there was waged a starkly fantastic conflict. At its wildly turbulent bottom lay the submarine, now apparently trying to escape, but held fast by the tractors of the space-ship; at its top, smothered almost to the point of invisibility by billowing masses of steam, hung poised the Nevian cruiser.

As the atmosphere had grown thinner and thinner with increasing altitude Costigan had regulated his velocity accordingly, keeping the outer shell of the vessel at the highest temperature consistent with safety. Now beyond measurable atmospheric pressure, the shell cooled rapidly and he applied full touring acceleration. At an appalling and constantly increasing speed the miniature space-ship shot away from the strange, red planet; and smaller and smaller upon the plate became its picture. The great vessel of the void had long since plunged beneath the surface of the sea, to come more closely to grips with the vessel of the fishes; for a long time nothing of the battle had been visible save immense clouds of steam, blanketing hundreds of square miles of the ocean's surface. But just before the picture became too small to reveal details a few tiny dark spots appeared above the banks of cloud, now brilliantly illuminated by the rays of the rising sun—dots which might have been fragments of either vessel, blown bodily from the depths of the ocean and, riven asunder, hurled high into the air by the incredible forces at the command of the other.

Nevia a tiny moon and the fierce blue sun rapidly growing smaller in the distance, Costigan swung his visiray beam into the line of travel and turned to his companions.

"Well, we're off," he said, scowling. "I hope it was Nerado that got blown up back there, but I'm afraid it wasn't. He whipped two of those submarines that we know of, and probably half their fleet besides. There's no particular reason why that one should be able to take him, so it's my idea that we should get ready for great gobs of trouble. They'll chase us, of course; and I'm afraid that with their power, they'll catch us."

"But what can we do, Conway?" asked Clio.

"Several things," he grinned. "I managed to get quite a lot of dope on that paralyzing ray and some of their other stuff, and we can install the necessary equipment in our suits easily enough."

They removed their armor, and Costigan explained in detail the changes which must be made in the Triplanetary field generators. All three set vigorously to work—the two officers deftly and surely; Clio uncertainly and with many questions, but with undaunted spirit. Finally, having done everything they could do to strengthen their position, they settled down to the watchful routine of the flight, with every possible instrument set to detect any sign of the pursuit they so feared.

THE HILL

The heavy cruiser Chicago hung motionless in space, thousands of miles distant from the warring fleets of space-ships so viciously attacking and so stubbornly defending Roger's planetoid. In the captain's sanctum Lyman Cleveland crouched tensely above his ultracameras, his sensitive fingers touching lightly their micrometric dials. His body was rigid, his face was set and drawn. Only his eyes moved; flashing back and forth between his instruments and the smoothly-running strands of spring-steel wire upon which were being recorded the frightful scenes of carnage and destruction.

Silent and bitterly absorbed, though surrounded by staring officers whose fervent, almost unconscious cursing was prayerful in its intensity, the visiray expert kept his ultra-instruments upon that awful struggle to its dire conclusion. Flawlessly those instruments noted every detail of the destruction of Roger's fleet, of the transformation of the armada of Triplanetary into an unknown fluid, and finally of the dissolution of the gigantic planetoid itself. Then furiously Cleveland drove his beam against the crimsonly opaque obscurity into which the peculiar, viscous stream of substance was disappearing. Time after time he applied his every watt of power, with no result. A vast volume of space, roughly ellipsoidal in shape, was closed to him by forces entirely beyond his experience or comprehension. But suddenly, while his rays were still trying to pierce that impenetrable murk, it disappeared instantly and without warning: the illimitable infinity of space once more lay revealed upon his plates and his beams flashed unimpeded through the void.

"Back to Tellus, sir?" The Chicago's captain broke the strained silence.

"I wouldn't say so, if I had the say." Cleveland, baffled and frustrated, straightened up and shut off his cameras. "We should report back as soon as possible, of course, but there seems to be a lot of wreckage out there yet that we can't photograph in detail at this distance. A close study of it might help us a lot in understanding what they did and how they did it. I'd say that we should get close-ups of whatever is left, and do it right away, before it gets scattered all over space; but of course I can't give you orders."

"You can, though," the captain made surprising answer. "My orders are that you are in command of this vessel."

"In that case we will proceed at full emergency acceleration to investigate the wreckage," Cleveland replied, and the cruiser—sole survivor of Triplanetary's supposedly invincible force—shot away with every projector delivering its maximum blast.

As the scene of the disaster was approached there was revealed upon the plates a confused mass of debris; a mass whose individual units were apparently moving at random, yet which was as a whole still following the orbit of Roger's planetoid. Space was full of machine parts, structural members, furniture, flotsam of all kinds; and everywhere were the bodies of men. Some were encased in space-suits, and it was to these that the rescuers turned first—space-hardened veterans though the men of the *Chicago* were, they did not care even to look at the others. Strangely enough, however, not one of the floating figures spoke or moved, and space-line men were hurriedly sent out to investigate.

"All dead." Quickly the dread report came back. "Been dead a long time. The armor is all stripped off the suits, and all the generators and other apparatus are all shot. Something funny about it, too—none of them seem to have been touched, but the machinery of the suits seems to be about half missing."

"I've got it all on the reels, sir." Cleveland, his close-up survey of the wreckage finished, turned to the captain. "What they've just reported checks up with what I have photographed everywhere. I've got an idea of what might have happened, but it's so new that I'll have to have some evidence before I'll believe it myself. You might have them bring in a few of the armored bodies, a couple of those switchboards and panels floating around out there, and half a dozen miscellaneous pieces of junk—the nearest things they get hold of, whatever they happen to be."

"Then back to Tellus at maximum?"

"Right—back to Tellus, as fast as we can possibly get there."

While the *Chicago* hurtled through space at full power, Cleveland and the ranking officers of the vessel grouped themselves about the salvaged wreckage. Familiar with space-wrecks as were they all, none of them had ever seen anything like the material before them. For every part and instrument was weirdly and meaninglessly disintegrated. There were no breaks, no marks of violence, and yet nothing was intact. Bolt-holes stared empty, cores, shielding cases and needles had disappeared, the vital parts of every instrument hung awry, disorganization reigned rampant and supreme.

"I never imagined such a mess," the captain said, after a long and silent study of the objects. "If you have a theory to cover *that*, Cleveland, I would like to hear it!"

"I want you to notice something first," the expert replied. "But don't look for what's there—look for what *isn't* there."

"Well, the armor is gone. So are the shielding cases, shafts, spindles, the housings and stems . . . " the captain's voice died away as his eyes raced over the collection. "Why everything that was made of wood, bakelite, copper, aluminum, silver, bronze, or anything but steel hasn't been touched, and every bit of that is gone. But that doesn't make sense—what does it mean?"

"I don't know—yet," Cleveland replied, slowly. "But I'm afraid that there's more, and worse." He opened a space-suit reverently, revealing the face; a face calm and peaceful, but utterly, sickeningly white. Still reverently, he made a deep incision in the brawny neck, severing the jugular vein, then went on, soberly:

"You never imagined such a thing as *white* blood, either, but it all checks up. Someway, somehow, every atom of free or combined iron in this whole volume of space was made off with."

"Huh? How come? And above all, *why?*" from the amazed and staring officers.

"You know as much as I do," grimly, ponderingly. "If it were not for the fact that there are solid asteroids of iron out beyond Mars, I would say that somebody wanted iron badly enough to wipe out the fleet and the planetoid to get it. But anyway, whoever they were, they carried enough power so that our armament didn't bother them at all. They simply took the metal they wanted and went away with it—so fast that I couldn't trace them with an ultra-beam. There's only one thing plain; but that's so plain that it scares me stiff. This whole affair spells intelligence, with a capital 'I', and that intelligence is anything but friendly. I want to put Fred Rodebush at work on this just as fast as I can get him."

He stepped over to his ultra-projector and put in a call for Virgil Samms, whose face soon appeared upon his screen.

"We got it all, Virgil," he reported. "It's something extraordinary—bigger, wider, and deeper than any of us dreamed. It may be urgent, too, so I think I had better shoot the stuff in on an ultra-beam and save some time. Fred has a telemagneto recorder there that he can synchronize with this outfit easily enough. Right?"

"Right. Good work, Lyman—thanks," came back terse approval and appreciation, and soon the steel wires were again flashing from reel to reel. This time, however, their varying magnetic charges were so modulating ultra-waves that every detail of that calamitous battle of the void was being screened and recorded in the innermost private laboratory of the Triplanetary Service.

Eager though he naturally was to join his fellow-scientists, Cleveland was not impatient during the long, but uneventful journey back to Earth. There was much to study, many improvements to be made in his comparatively crude first ultra-camera. Then, too, there were long conferences with Samms, and particularly with Rodebush, the nuclear physicist, who would have to do much of the work involved in solving the riddles of the energies and weapons of the Nevians. Thus it did not seem long before green Terra grew large beneath the flying sphere of the *Chicago*.

"Going to have to circle it once, aren't you?" Cleveland asked the chief pilot. He had been watching that officer closely for minutes, admiring the delicacy and precision with which the great vessel was being maneuvered preliminary to entering the Earth's atmosphere.

"Yes," the pilot replied. "We had to come in in the shortest possible time, and that meant a velocity here that we can't check without a spiral. However, even at that we saved a lot of time. You can save quite a bit more, though, by having a rocket-plane come out to meet us somewhere around fifteen or twenty thousand kilometers, depending upon where you want to land. With their drives they can match our velocity and still make the drop direct."

"Guess I'll do that—thanks," and the operative called his chief, only to learn that his suggestion had already been acted upon.

SUPER PACK

"We beat you to it, Lyman," Samms smiled. "The *Silver Sliver* is out there now, looping to match your course, acceleraction, and velocity at twenty two thousand kilometers. You'll be ready to transfer?"

"I'll be ready," and the Quartermaster's ex-clerk went to his quarters and packed his dunnage-bag.

In due time the long, slender body of the rocket-plane came into view, creeping "down" upon the space-ship from "above," and Cleveland bade his friends goodbye. Donning a space-suit, he stationed himself in the starboard airlock. Its atmosphere was withdrawn, the outer door opened, and he glanced across a bare hundred feet of space at the rocket-plane which, keel ports fiercely aflame, was braking her terrific speed to match the slower pace of the gigantic sphere of war. Shaped like a toothpick, needle-pointed fore and aft, with ultra-stubby wings and vanes, with flush-set rocket ports everywhere, built of a lustrous, silvery alloy of noble and almost infusible metals—such was the private speedboat of Triplanetary's head man. The fastest thing known, whether in planetary air, the stratosphere, or the vacuous depth of interplanetary space, her first flashing trial spins had won her the nickname of the *Silver Sliver*. She had had a more formal name, but that title had long since been buried in the Departmental files.

Lower and lower dropped the speedboat, her rockets flaming ever brighter, until her slender length lay level with the airlock door. Then her blasting discharges subsided to the power necessary to match exactly the *Chicago's* acceleration.

"Ready to cut, *Chicago*! Give me a three-second call!" snapped from the pilot room of the *Sliver*.

"Ready to cut!" the pilot of the *Chicago* replied. "Seconds! Three! Two! One! CUT!"

At the last word the power of both vessels was instantly cut off and everything in them became weightless. In the tiny airlock of the slender plane crouched a space-line man with coiled cable in readiness, but he was not needed. As the flaring exhausts ceased Cleveland swung out his heavy bag and stepped lightly off into space, and in a right line he floated directly into the open port of the rocket-plane. The door clanged shut behind him and in a matter of moments he stood in the control room of the racer, divested of his armor and shaking hands with his friend and co-laborer, Frederick Rodebush.

"Well, Fritz, what do you know?" Cleveland asked, as soon as greetings had been exchanged. "How do the various reports dovetail together? I know that you couldn't tell me anything on the wave, but there's no danger of eavesdroppers *here*."

"You can't tell," Rodebush soberly replied. "We're just beginning to wake up to the fact that there are a lot of things we don't know anything about. Better wait until we're back at the Hill. We have a full set of ultra screens around there now. There's a couple of other good reasons, too—it would be better for both of us to go over the whole thing with Virgil, from the ground up; and we can't do any more talking, anyway. Our orders are to get back there at maximum, and you know what that means aboard the *Sliver*. Strap yourself solid in that shock-absorber there, and here's a pair of ear-plugs."

THE LENSMAN

"When the *Sliver* really cuts loose it means a rough party, all right," Cleveland assented, snapping about his body the heavy spring-straps of his deeply cushioned seat, "but I'm just as anxious to get back to the Hill as anybody can be to get me there. All set."

Rodebush waved his hand at the pilot and the purring whisper of the exhausts changed instantly to a deafening, continuous explosion. The men were pressed deeply into their shock-absorbing chairs as the *Silver Sliver* spun around her longitudinal axis and darted away from the *Chicago* with such a tremendous acceleration that the spherical warship seemed to be standing still in space. In due time the calculated midpoint was reached, the slim space-plane rolled over again, and, mad acceleration now reversed, rushed on toward the Earth, but with constantly diminishing speed. Finally a measurable atmospheric pressure was encountered, the needle prow dipped downward, and the *Silver Sliver* shot forward upon her tiny wings and vanes, nose-rockets now drumming in staccato thunder. Her metal grew hot; dull red, bright red, yellow, blinding white; but it neither melted nor burned. The pilot's calculations had been sound, and though the limiting point of safety of temperature was reached and steadily held, it was not exceeded. As the density of the air increased so decreased the velocity of the man-made meteorite. So it was that a dazzling lance of fire sped high over Seattle, lower over Spokane, and hurled itself eastward, a furiously flaming arrow; slanting downward in a long, screaming dive toward the heart of the Rockies. As the now rapidly cooling greyhound of the skies passed over the western ranges of the Bitter Roots it became apparent that her goal was a vast, flat-topped, conical mountain, shrouded in violet light; a mountain whose height awed even its stupendous neighbors.

While not artificial, the Hill had been altered markedly by the engineers who had built into it the headquarters of the Triplanetary Service. Its mile-wide top was a jointless expanse of gray armor steel; the steep, smooth surface of the truncated cone was a continuation of the same immensely thick sheet of metal. No known vehicle could climb that smooth, hard, forbidding slope of steel; no known projectile could mar that armor; no known craft could even approach the Hill without detection. Could not approach it at all, in fact, for it was constantly inclosed in a vast hemisphere of lambent violet flame through which neither material substance nor destructive ray could pass.

As the *Silver Sliver*, crawling along at a bare five hundred miles an hour, approached that transparent, brilliantly violet wall of destruction, a light of the same color filled her control room and as suddenly went out; flashing on and off again and again.

"Giving us the once-over, eh?" Cleveland asked. "That's something new, isn't it?"

"Yes, it's a high-powered ultra-wave spy," Rodebush returned. "The light is simply a warning, which can be carried if desired. It can also carry voice and vision . . . ."

"Like this," Samms' voice interrupted from a speaker upon the pilot's panel and his clear-cut face appeared upon the television screen. "I don't suppose Fred thought to mention it, but this is one of his inventions of the last few days. We are just trying it out on you. It doesn't mean a thing though, as far as the *Sliver* is concerned. Come ahead!"

A circular opening appeared on the wall of force, an opening which disappeared as soon as the plane had darted through it; and at the same time her landing-cradle rose into the air through a great trap-door. Slowly and gracefully the space-plane settled downward into that cushioned embrace. Then cradle and nestled *Sliver* sank from view and, turning smoothly upon mighty trunnions, the plug of armor drove solidly back into its place in the metal pavement of the mountain's lofty summit. The cradle-elevator dropped rapidly, coming to rest many levels down in the heart of the Hill, and Cleveland and Rodebush leaped lightly out of their transport, through her still hot outer walls. A door opened before them and they found themselves in a large room of unshadowed daylight illumination; the office of the Chief of the Triplanetary Service. Calmly efficient executives sat at their desks, concentrating upon problems or at ease, according to the demands of the moment; agents, secretaries, and clerks, men and women, went about their wonted tasks; televisotypes and recorders flashed busily but silently—each person and machine an integral part of the Service which for so many years had been carrying an ever-increasing share of the load of governing the three planets.

"Right of way, Norma?" Rodebush paused before the desk of Virgil Samms' private secretary. She pressed a button and the door behind her swung wide.

"You two do not need to be announced," the attractive young woman smiled. "Go right in."

Samms met them at the door eagerly, shaking hands particularly vigorously with Cleveland.

"Congratulations on that camera, Lyman!" he exclaimed. "You did a wonderful piece of work on that. Help yourselves to smokes and sit down—there are a lot of things we want to talk over. Your pictures carried most of the story, but they would have left us pretty much at sea without Costigan's reports. But as it was, Fred here and his crew worked out most of the answers from the dope the two of you got; and what few they haven't got yet they soon will have."

"Nothing new on Conway?" Cleveland was almost afraid to ask the question.

"No." A shadow came over Samms' face. "I'm afraid . . . but I'm hoping it's only that those creatures, whatever they are, have taken him so far away he can't reach us."

"They certainly are so far away that we can't reach them," Rodebush volunteered. "We can't even get their ultra-wave interference any more."

"Yes, that's a hopeful sign," Samms went on. "I hate to think of Conway Costigan checking out. There, fellows, was a real observer. He was the only man I have ever known who combined the two qualities of the perfect witness. He could actually see everything he looked at, and could report it truly, to the last, least detail. Take all this stuff, for instance; especially their ability to transform iron into a fluid allotrope, and in that form to use its atomic—nuclear?—energy as power. Something brand new, and yet he described their converters and projectors so minutely that Fred was able to work out the underlying theory in three days, and to tie it in with our own super-ship. My first thought was that we'd have to rebuild it iron-free, but Fred showed me my error—you found it first yourself, of course."

"It wouldn't do any good to make the ship non-ferrous unless you could so change our blood chemistry that we could get along without hemoglobin, and that would be quite a feat," Cleveland agreed. "Then, too, our most vital electrical machinery is built around iron cores. We'll also have to develop a screen for those forces—screens, rather, so powerful that they can't drive anything through them."

"We've been working along those lines ever since you reported," Rodebush said, "and we're beginning to see light. And in that same connection it's no wonder that we couldn't handle our super-ship. We had some good ideas, but they were wrongly applied. However, things look quite promising now. We have the transformation of iron all worked out in theory, and as soon as we get a generator going we can straighten out everything else in short order. And think what that unlimited power means! All the power we want—power enough even to try out such hitherto purely theoretical possibilities as the neutralization of the inertia of matter!"

"Hold on!" protested Samms. "You certainly can't do *that*! Inertia is—*must* be—a basic attribute of matter, and surely cannot be done away with without destroying the matter itself. Don't start anything like that, Fred—I don't want to lose you and Lyman, too."

"Don't worry about us, Chief," Rodebush replied with a smile. "If you will tell me what matter is, fundamentally, I may agree with you . . . . No? Well, then, don't be surprised at anything that happens. We are going to do a lot of things that nobody on the Three Planets ever thought of doing before."

Thus for a long time the argument and discussion went on, to be interrupted by the voice of the secretary.

"Sorry to disturb you, Mr. Samms, but some things have come up that you will have to handle. Knobos is calling from Mars. He has caught the *Endymion*, and has killed about half her crew doing it. Milton has finally reported from Venus, after being out of touch for five days. He trailed the Wintons into Thalleron swamp. They crashed him there, and he won out and has what he went after. And just now I got a flash from Fletcher, in the asteroid belt. I think that he has finally traced that dope line. But Knobos is on now—what do you want him to do about the *Endymion*?"

"Tell him to—no, put him on here, I'd better tell him myself," Samms directed, and his face hardened in ruthless decision as the horny, misshapen face of the Martian lieutenant appeared upon the screen. "What do you think, Knobos? Shall they come to trial or not?"

"Not."

"I don't think so, either. It is better that a few gangsters should disappear in space than that the Patrol should have to put down another uprising. See to it."

"Right." The screen darkened and Samms spoke to his secretary. "Put Milton and Fletcher on whenever they come in." He turned to his guests. "We've covered the ground quite thoroughly. Goodbye—I wish I could go with you, but I'll be pretty well tied up for the next week or two."

"'Tied up' doesn't half express it," Rodebush remarked as the two scientists walked along a corridor toward an elevator. "He probably is the busiest man on three planets."

"As well as the most powerful," Cleveland supplemented. "And very few men could use his power as fairly—but he's welcome to it, as far as I'm concerned. I'd have the pink fantods for a month if I had to do only once what he's just done—and to him it's just part of a day's work."

"You mean the *Endymion*? What else could he do?"

"Nothing—that's the hell of it. It had to be done, since bringing them to trial would mean killing half the people of Morseca; but at the same time it's a ghastly thing to order a job of deliberate, cold-blooded, and illegal murder."

"You're right, of course, but you would . . . " he broke off, unable to put his thoughts into words. For while inarticulate, man-like, concerning their deepest emotions, in both men was ingrained the code of the organization; both knew that to every man chosen for it THE SERVICE was everything, himself nothing.

"But enough of that, we'll have plenty of grief of our own right here." Rodebush changed the subject abruptly as they stepped into a vast room, almost filled by the immense bulk of the *Boise*—the sinister space-ship which, although never flown, had already lined with black so many pages of Triplanetary's roster. She was now, however, the center of a furious activity. Men swarmed over her and through her, in the orderly confusion of a fiercely driven but carefully planned program of reconstruction.

"I hope your dope is right, Fritz!" Cleveland called, as the two scientists separated to go to their respective laboratories. "If it is, we'll make a perfect lady out of this unmanageable man-killer yet!"

THE SUPER-SHIP IS LAUNCHED

After weeks of ceaseless work, during which was lavished upon her every resource of mind and material afforded by three planets, the *Boise* was ready for her maiden flight. As nearly ready, that is, as the thought and labor of man could make her. Rodebush and Cleveland had finished their last rigid inspection of the aircraft and, standing beside the center door of the main airlock, were talking with their chief.

"You say that you think that it's safe, and yet you won't take a crew," Samms argued. "In that case it isn't safe enough for you two, either. We need you too badly to permit you to take such chances."

"You've *got* to let us go, because we are the only ones who are at all familiar with her theory," Rodebush insisted. "I said, and I still say, that I *think* it is safe. I can't prove it, however, even mathematically; because she's altogether too full of too many new and untried mechanisms, too many extrapolations beyond all existing or possible data. Theoretically, she is sound, but you know that theory can go only so far, and that mathematically negligible factors may become operative at those velocities. We do not need a crew for a short trip. We can take care of any minor mishaps, and if our fundamental theories are wrong, all the crews between here and Jupiter wouldn't do any good. Therefore we two are going—alone."

"Well, be very careful, anyway. I wish that you could start out slow and take it easy."

"In a way, so do I, but she wasn't designed to neutralize half of gravity, nor half of the inertia of matter—it's got to be everything or nothing, as soon as the neutralizers go on. We could start out on the projectors, of course, instead of on the neutralizers, but that wouldn't prove anything and would only prolong the agony."

"Well, then, be as careful as you can."

"We'll do that, Chief," Cleveland put in. "We think as much of us as anybody else does—maybe more—and we aren't committing suicide if we can help it. And remember about everybody staying inside when we take off—it's barely possible that we'll take up a lot of room. Goodbye!"

"Goodbye, fellows!"

The massive insulating doors were shut, the metal side of the mountain opened, and huge, squat caterpillar tractors came roaring and clanking into the room. Chains and cables were made fast and, mighty steel rails groaning under the load, the space-ship upon her rolling ways was dragged out of the Hill and far out upon the level floor of the valley before the tractors cast off and returned to the fortress.

"Everybody is under cover," Samms informed Rodebush. The Chief was staring intently into his plate, upon which was revealed the control room of the untried super-ship. He heard Rodebush speak to Cleveland; heard the observer's brief reply; saw the navigator push the switch-button—then the communicator plate went blank. Not the ordinary blankness of a cut-off, but a peculiarly disquieting fading out into darkness. And where the great space-ship had rested there was for an instant nothing. Exactly nothing—a vacuum. Vessel, falsework, rollers, trucks, the enormous steel I-beams of the tracks, even the deep-set concrete piers and foundations and a vast hemisphere of the solid ground; all disappeared utterly and instantaneously. But almost as suddenly as it had been formed the vacuum was filled by a cyclonic rush of air. There was a detonation as of a hundred vicious thunderclaps made one, and through the howling, shrieking blasts of wind there rained down upon valley, plain, and metaled mountain a veritable avalanche of debris; bent, twisted, and broken rails and beams, splintered timbers, masses of concrete, and thousands of cubic yards of soil and rock. For the atomic-powered "Rodebush-Cleveland" neutralizers were more powerful by far, and had a vastly greater radius of action, than the calculations of their designers had shown; and for a moment everything within a hundred yards or so of the *Boise* behaved as though it were an integral part of the vessel. Then, left behind immediately by the super-ship's almost infinite velocity, all this material had again become subject to all of Nature's every-day laws and had crashed back to the ground.

"Could you hold your beam, Randolph?" Samms' voice cut sharply through the daze of stupefaction which held spellbound most of the denizens of the Hill. But all were not so held—no conceivable emergency could take the attention of the chief ultra-wave operator from his instruments.

"No, sir," Radio Center shot back. "It faded out and I couldn't recover it. I put everything I've got behind a tracer on that beam, but haven't been able to lift a single needle off the pin."

"And no wreckage of the vessel itself," Samms went on, half audibly. "Either they have succeeded far beyond their wildest hopes or else . . . more probably . . . ." He fell silent and switched off the plate. Were his two friends, those intrepid scientists, alive and triumphant, or had they gone to lengthen the list of victims of that man-killing space-ship? Reason told him that they were gone. They *must* be gone, or else the ultra-beams—energies of such unthinkable velocity of propagation that man's most sensitive instruments had never been able even to estimate it—would have held the ship's transmitter in spite of any velocity attainable by matter under any conceivable conditions.

The ship must have been disintegrated as soon as Rodebush released his forces. And yet, had not the physicist dimly foreseen the possibility of such an actual velocity—or had he? However, individuals could come and go, but the Service went on. Samms squared his shoulders unconsciously; and slowly, grimly, made his way back to his private office.

"Mr. Fairchild would like to have a moment as soon as possible, sir," his secretary informed him even before he sat down. "Senator Morgan has been here all day, you know, and he insists on seeing you personally."

"Oh, that kind, eh? All right, I'll see him. Get Fairchild, please . . . Dick? Can you talk, or is he there listening?"

"No, he's heckling Saunders at the moment. He's been here long enough. Can you take a minute and throw him out?"

"Of course, if you say so, but why not throw the hooks into him yourself, as usual?"

"He wants to lay down the law to you, personally. He's a Big Shot, you know, and his group is kicking up quite a row, so it might be better to have it come straight from the top. Besides, you've got a unique knack—when you throw a harpoon, the harpoonee doesn't forget it."

"All right. He's the uplifter and leveler-off. Down with Triplanetary, up with National Sovereignty. We're power-mad dictators—iron-heel-on-the- necks-of-the-people, and so on. But what's he like, personally? Thick-skinned, of course—got a brain?"

"Rhinoceros. He's got a brain, but it's definitely weaseloid. Bear down—sink it in full length, and then twist it."

"O.K. You've got a harpoon, of course?"

"Three of'em!" Fairchild, Head of Triplanetary's Public Relations, grinned with relish. "Boss Jim Towne owns him in fee simple. The number of his hot lock box is N469T414. His subbest sub-rosa girl-friend is Fi-Chi le Bay . . . yes, everything that the name implies. She got a super-deluxe fur coat—Martian tekkyl, no less—out of that Mackenzie River power deal. Triple play, you might say—Clander to Morgan to le Bay."

"Nice. Bring him in."

"Senator Morgan, Mr. Samms," Fairchild made the introduction and the two men sized each other up in lightning glances. Samms saw a big man, florid, somewhat inclined toward corpulence, with the surface geniality—and the shrewd calculating eyes—of the successful politician. The senator saw a tall, hard-trained man in his forties; a lean, keen, smooth-shaven face; a shock of red-bronze-auburn hair a couple of weeks overdue for a cutting; a pair of gold-flecked tawny eyes too penetrant for comfort.

"I trust, Senator, that Fairchild has taken care of you satisfactorily?"

"With one or two exceptions, yes." Since Samms did not ask what the exceptions could be, Morgan was forced to continue. "I am here, as you know, in my official capacity as Chairman of the Pernicious Activities Committee of the North American Senate. It has been observed for years that the published reports of your organization have left much unsaid. It is common knowledge that high-handed outrages have been perpetrated; if not by your men themselves, in such circumstances that your agents could not have been ignorant of them. Therefore it has been decided to make a first-hand and comprehensive investigation, in which matter your Mr. Fairchild has not been at all cooperative."

"Who decided to make this investigation?"

"Why, the North American Senate, of course, through its Pernicious Activities . . . ."

"I thought so." Samms interrupted. "Don't you know, Senator, that the Hill is not a part of the North American Continent? That the Triplanetary Service is responsible only to the Triplanetary Council?"

"Quibbling, sir, and outmoded! This, sir, is a democracy!" the Senator began to orate. "All that will be changed very shortly, and if you are as smart as you are believed to be, I need only say that you and those of your staff who cooperate . . . ."

"You need say nothing at all." Samms' voice cut. "It has not been changed yet. The Government of North America rules its continent, as do the other Continental Governments. The combined Continental Governments of the Three Planets form the Triplanetary Council, which is a non-political body, the members of which hold office for life and which is the supreme authority in any matter, small or large, affecting more than one Continental Government. The Council has two principal operating agencies; the Triplanetary Patrol, which enforces its decisions, rules, and regulations, and the Triplanetary Service, which performs such other tasks as the Council directs. We have no interest in the purely internal affairs of North America. Have you any information to the contrary?"

"More quibbling!" the Senator thundered. "This is not the first time in history that a ruthless dictatorship has operated in the disguise of a democracy. Sir, I *demand* full access to your files, so that I can spread before the North American Senate the full facts of the various matters which I mentioned to Fairchild—one of which was the affair of the *Pelarion*. In a democracy, sir, facts should not be hidden; the people must and shall be kept completely informed upon any matter which affects their welfare or their political lives!"

"Is that so? If I should ask, then, for the purpose of keeping the Triplanetary Council, and through it your constituents, fully informed as to the political situation in North America, you would undoubtedly give me the key to safe-deposit box N469T414? For it is common knowledge, in the Council at least, that there is a certain amount of—shall we say turbidity?—in the supposedly pellucid reaches of North American politics."

"What? Preposterous!" Morgan made a heroic effort, but could not quite maintain his poise. "Private papers only, sir!"

"Perhaps. Certain of the Councillors believe, however mistakenly, that there are several things of interest there: such as the record of certain transactions involving one James F. Towne; references to and details concerning dealings—not to say deals—with Mackenzie Power, specifically with Mackenzie Power's Mr. Clander; and perhaps a juicy bit or two concerning a person known as le Bay and a tekkyl coat. Of interest no end, don't you think, to the dear people of North America?"

As Samms drove the harpoon in and twisted it, the big man suffered visibly. Nevertheless:

"You refuse to cooperate, eh?" he blustered. "Very well, I will go—but you have not heard the last of me, Samms!"

"No? Probably not. But remember, before you do any more rabble-rousing, that this lock-box thing is merely a sample. We of the Service know a lot of things that we do not mention to anybody—except in self-defense."

"I am holding Fletcher, Mr. Samms. Shall I put him on now?" Norma asked, as the completely deflated Morgan went out.

"Yes, please . . . . Hello, Sid; mighty glad to see you—we were scared for a while. How did you make out, and what was it?"

"Hi, Chief! Mostly hadive. Some heroin, and quite a bit of Martian ladolian. Lousy job, though—three of the gang got away, and took about a quarter of the loot with them. That was what I want to talk to you about in such a hurry—fake meteors; the first I ever saw."

Samms straightened up in his chair.

"Just a second. Norma, put Redmond on here with us . . . . Listen, Harry. Now, Fletcher, did you see that fake meteor yourself? Touch it?"

"Both. In fact, I've still got it. One of the runners, pretending to be a Service man, flashed it on me. It's really good, too, Chief. Even now, I can't tell it from my own except that mine is in my pocket. Shall I send it in?"

"By all means; to Dr. H.D. Redmond, Head of Research. Keep on slugging, Sid—goodbye. Now, Harry, what do you think? It *could* be one of our own, you know."

"Could be, but probably isn't. We'll know as soon as we get it in the lab. Chances are, though, that they have caught up with us again. After all, that was to be expected—anything that science can synthesize, science can analyze; and whatever the morals and ethics of the pirates may be, they have got brains."

"And you haven't been able to devise anything better?"

"Variations only, which wouldn't take much time to solve. Fundamentally, the present meteor is the best we know."

"Got anybody you would like to put on it, immediately?"

"Of course. One of the new boys will be perfect for the job, I think. Name of Bergenholm. Quite a character. Brilliant, erratic, flashes of sheer genius that he can't explain, even to us. I'll put him on it right away."

"Thanks a lot. And now, Norma, please keep everybody off my neck that you can. I want to think."

And think he did; keen eyes clouded, staring unseeingly at the papers littering his desk. Triplanetary needed a symbol—a something—which would identify a Service man anywhere, at any time, under any circumstances, without doubt or question . . . something that could not be counterfeited or imitated, to say nothing of being duplicated . . . something that no scientist not of Triplanetary Service could *possibly* imitate . . . better yet, something that no one not of Triplanetary could even wear . . . .

Samms grinned fleetingly at that thought. A tall order one calling for a *deus ex machina* with a vengeance . . . . But damn it, there ought to be *some* way to . . . .

"Excuse me, sir." His secretary's voice, usually so calm and cool, trembled as she broke in on his thinking. "Commissioner Kinnison is calling. Something terrible is going on again, out toward Orion. Here he is," and there appeared upon Samms' screen the face of the Commissioner of Public Safety, the commander-in-chief of Triplanetary's every armed force; whether of land or of water, of air or of empty space.

"They've come back, Virgil!" The Commissioner rapped out without preliminary or greeting. "Four vessels gone—a freighter and a passenger liner, with her escort of two heavy cruisers. All in Sector M, Dx about 151. I have ordered all traffic out of space for the duration of the emergency, and since even our warships seem useless, every ship is making for the nearest dock at maximum. How about that new flyer of yours—got anything that will do us any good?" No one beyond the "Hill's" shielding screens knew that the *Boise* had already been launched.

"I don't know. We don't even know whether we have a super-ship or not," and Samms described briefly the beginning—and very probably the ending—of the trial flight, concluding: "It looks bad, but if there was any possible way of handling her, Rodebush and Cleveland did it. All our tracers are negative yet, so nothing definite has . . . ."

He broke off as a frantic call came in from the Pittsburgh station for the Commissioner; a call which Samms both heard and saw.

"The city is being attacked!" came the urgent message. "We need all the reenforcements you can send us!" and a picture of the beleaguered city appeared in ghastly detail upon the screens of the observers; a view being recorded from the air. It required only seconds for the commissioner to order every available man and engine of war to the seat of conflict; then, having done everything they could do, Kinnison and Samms stared in helpless, fascinated horror into their plates, watching the scenes of carnage and destruction depicted there.

The Nevian vessel—the sister-ship, the craft which Costigan had seen in mid-space as it hurtled Earthward in response to Nerado's summons—hung poised in full visibility high above the metropolis. Scornful of the pitiful weapons wielded by man, she hung there, her sinister beauty of line sharply defined against the cloudless sky. From her shining hull there reached down a tenuous but rigid rod of crimson energy; a rod which slowly swept hither and thither as the Nevians searched out the richest deposits of the precious metal for which they had come so far. Iron, once solid, now a viscous red liquid, was sluggishly flowing in an ever-thickening stream up that intangible crimson duct and into the capacious storage tanks of the Nevian raider; and wherever that flaming beam went there went also ruin, destruction and death. Office buildings, skyscrapers towering majestically in their architectural symmetry and beauty, collapsed into heaps of debris as their steel skeletons were abstracted. Deep into the ground the beam bored; flood, fire, and explosion following in its wake as the mazes of underground piping disappeared. And the humanity of the buildings died: instantaneously and painlessly, never knowing what struck them, as the life-bearing iron of their bodies went to swell the Nevian stream.

Pittsburgh's defenses had been feeble indeed. A few antiquated railway rifles had hurled their shells upward in futile defiance, and had been quietly absorbed. The district planes of Triplanetary, newly armed with iron-driven ultra-beams, had assembled hurriedly and had attacked the invader in formation, with but little more success. Under the impact of their beams, the stranger's screens had flared white, then poised ship and flying squadron had alike been lost to view in a murkily opaque shroud of crimson flame.

The cloud had soon dissolved, and from the place where the planes had been there floated or crashed down a litter of non-ferrous wreckage. And now the cone of space-ships from the Buffalo base of Triplanetary was approaching Pittsburgh hurling itself toward the Nevian plunderer and toward known, gruesome, and hopeless defeat.

"Stop them, Rod!" Samms cried. "It's sheer slaughter! They haven't got a thing—they aren't even equipped yet with the iron drive!"

"I know it," the commissioner groaned, "and Admiral Barnes knows it as well as we do, but it can't be helped—wait a minute! The Washington cone is reporting. They're as close as the other, and they have the new armament. Philadelphia is close behind, and so is New York. Now perhaps we can do something!"

The Buffalo flotilla slowed and stopped, and in a matter of minutes the detachments from the other bases arrived. The cone was formed and, iron-driven vessels in the van, the old-type craft far in the rear, it bore down upon the Nevian, vomiting from its hollow front a solid cylinder of annihilation. Once more the screens of the Nevian flared into brilliance, once more the red cloud of destruction was flung abroad. But these vessels were not entirely defenseless. Their iron-driven ultra-generators threw out screens of the Nevians' own formulae, screens of prodigious power to which the energies of the amphibians clung and at which they clawed and tore in baffled, wildly coruscant displays of power unthinkable. For minutes the furious conflict raged, while the inconceivable energy being dissipated by those straining screens hurled itself in terribly destructive bolts of lightning upon the city far beneath.

No battle of such incredible violence could long endure. Triplanetary's ships were already exerting their utmost power, while the Nevians, contemptuous of Solarian science, had not yet uncovered their full strength. Thus the last desperate effort of mankind was proved futile as the invaders forced their beams deeper and deeper into the overloaded defensive screens of the war-vessels; and one by one the supposedly invincible space-ships of humanity dropped in horribly dismembered ruin upon the ruins of what had once been Pittsburgh.

SPECIMENS

Only too well founded was Costigan's conviction that the submarine of the deep-sea fishes had not been able to prevail against Nerado's formidable engines of destruction. For days the Nevian lifeboat with its three Terrestrial passengers hurtled through the interstellar void without incident, but finally the operative's fears were realized—his far flung detector screens reacted; upon his observation plate they could see Nerado's mammoth space-ship, in full pursuit of its fleeing lifeboat!

"On your toes, folks—it won't be long now!" Costigan called, and Bradley and Clio hurried into the tiny control room.

Armor donned and tested, the three Terrestrials stared into the observation plates, watching the rapidly-enlarging picture of the Nevian space-ship. Nerado had traced them and was following them, and such was the power of the great vessel that the now inconceivable velocity of the lifeboat was the veriest crawl in comparison to that of the pursuing cruiser.

"And we've hardly started to cover the distance back to Tellus. Of course you couldn't get in touch with anybody yet?" Bradley stated, rather than asked.

"I kept trying, of course, until they blanketed my wave, but all negative. Thousands of times too far for my transmitter. Our only hope of reaching anybody was the mighty slim chance that our super-ship might be prowling around out here already, but it isn't, of course. Here they are!"

Reaching out to the control panel, Costigan viciously shot out against the great vessel wave after wave of lethal vibrations, under whose fiercely clinging impacts the Nevian defensive screens flared white; but, strangely enough, their own screens did not radiate. As if contemptuous of any weapons the lifeboat might wield, the mother ship simply defended herself from the attacking beams, in much the same fashion as a wildcat mother wards off the claws and teeth of her spitting, snarling kitten who is resenting a touch of needed maternal discipline.

"They probably wouldn't fight us, at that," Clio first understood the situation. "This is their own lifeboat, and they want us alive, you know."

"There's one more thing we can try—hang on!" Costigan snapped, as he released his screens and threw all his power into one enormous pressor beam.

The three were thrown to the floor and held there by an awful weight as the lifeboat darted away at the stupendous acceleration of the beam's reaction against the unimaginable mass of the Nevian sky-rover; but the flight was of short duration. Along that pressor beam there crept a dull red rod of energy, which surrounded the fugitive shell and brought it slowly to a halt. Furiously then Costigan set and reset his controls, launching his every driving force and his every weapon, but no beam could penetrate that red murk, and the lifeboat remained motionless in space. No, not motionless—the red rod was shortening, drawing the truant craft back toward the launching port from which she had so hopefully emerged a few days before. Back and back it was drawn; Costigan's utmost efforts futile to affect by a hair's breadth its line of motion. Through the open port the boat slipped neatly, and as it came to a halt in its original position within the multi-layered skin of the monster, the prisoners heard the heavy doors clang shut behind them, one after another.

And then sheets of blue fire snapped and crackled about the three suits of Triplanetary armor—the two large human figures and the small ones were outlined starkly in blinding blue flame.

"That's the first thing that has come off according to schedule." Costigan laughed, a short, fierce bark. "That is their paralyzing ray, we've got it stopped cold, and we've each got enough iron to hold it forever."

"But it looks as though the best we can do is a stalemate," Bradley argued. "Even if they can't paralyze us, we can't hurt them, and we are heading back for Nevia."

"I think Nerado will come in for a conference, and we'll be able to make terms of some kind. He must know what these Lewistons will do, and he knows that we'll get a chance to use them, some way or other, before he gets to us again," Costigan asserted, confidently—but again he was wrong.

The door opened, and through it there waddled, rolled, or crawled a metal-clad monstrosity—a thing with wheels, legs and writhing tentacles of jointed bronze; a thing possessed of defensive screens sufficiently powerful to absorb the full blast of the Triplanetary projectors without effort. Three brazen tentacles reached out through the ravening beams of the Lewistons, smashed them to bits, and wrapped themselves in unbreakable shackles about the armored forms of the three human beings. Through the door the machine or creature carried its helpless load, and out into and along a main corridor. And soon the three Terrestrials, without arms, without armor, and almost without clothing, were standing in the control room, again facing the calm and unmoved Nerado. To the surprise of the impetuous Costigan, the Nevian commander was entirely without rancor.

"The desire for freedom is perhaps common to all forms of animate life," he commented, through the transformer. "As I told you before, however, you are specimens to be studied by the College of Science, and you shall be so studied in spite of anything you may do. Resign yourselves to that."

"Well, say that we don't try to make any more trouble; that we cooperate in the examination and give you whatever information we can," Costigan suggested. "Then you will probably be willing to give us a ship and let us go back to our own world?"

"You will not be allowed to cause any more trouble," the amphibian declared, coldly. "Your cooperation will not be required. We will take from you whatever knowledge and information we wish. In all probability you will never be allowed to return to your own system, because as specimens you are too unique to lose. But enough of this idle chatter—take them back to their quarters!"

Back to their three inter-communicating rooms the prisoners were led under heavy guard; and, true to his word, Nerado made certain that they had no more opportunities to escape. To Nevia the space-ship sped without incident, and in manacles the Terrestrials were taken to the College of Science, there to undergo the physical and psychical examinations which Nerado had promised them.

Nor had the Nevian scientist-captain erred in stating that their cooperation was neither needed nor desired. Furious but impotent, the human beings were studied in laboratory after laboratory by the coldly analytical, unfeeling scientists of Nevia, to whom they were nothing more or less than specimens; and in full measure they came to know what it meant to play the part of an unknown, lowly organism in a biological research. They were photographed, externally and internally. Every bone, muscle, organ, vessel, and nerve was studied and charted. Every reflex and reaction was noted and discussed. Meters registered every impulse and recorders filmed every thought, every idea, and every sensation. Endlessly, day after day, the nerve-wracking torture went on, until the frantic subjects could bear no more. White-faced and shaking, Clio finally screamed wildly, hysterically, as she was being strapped down upon a laboratory bench; and at the sound Costigan's nerves, already at the breaking point, gave way in an outburst of berserk fury.

The man's struggles and the girl's shrieks were alike futile, but the surprised Nevians, after a consultation, decided to give the specimens a vacation. To that end they were installed, together with their Earthly belongings, in a three-roomed structure of transparent metal, floating in the large central lagoon of the city. There they were left undisturbed for a time—undisturbed, that is, except by the continuous gaze of the crowd of hundreds of amphibians which constantly surrounded the floating cottage.

"First we're bugs under a microscope," Bradley growled, "then we're goldfish in a bowl. I don't know that . . . ."

He broke off as two of their jailers entered the room. Without a word into the transformers they seized Bradley and Clio. As those tentacular arms stretched out toward the girl, Costigan leaped. A vain attempt. In midair the paralyzing beam of the Nevians touched him and he crashed heavily to the crystal floor; and from that floor he looked on in helpless, raging fury while his sweetheart and his captain were carried out of their prison and into a waiting submarine.

SUPER-SHIP IN ACTION

Doctor Frederick Rodebush sat at the control panel of Triplanetary's newly reconstructed super-ship; one finger poised over a small black button. Facing the unknown though the physicist was, yet he grinned whimsically at his friend.

"Something, whatever it is, is about to occur. The *Boise* is about to take off. Ready, Cleve?"

"Shoot!" laconically. Cleveland also was constitutionally unable to voice his deeper sentiments in time of stress.

Rodebush drove his finger down, and instantly over both men there came a sensation akin to a tremendously intensified vertigo; but a vertigo as far beyond the space-sickness of weightlessness as that horrible sensation is beyond mere Earthly dizziness. The pilot reached weakly toward the board, but his leaden hands refused utterly to obey the dictates of his reeling mind. His brain was a writhing, convulsive mass of torment indescribable; expanding, exploding, swelling out with an unendurable pressure against its confining skull. Fiery spirals, laced with streaming, darting lances of black and green, flamed inside his bursting eyeballs. The Universe spun and whirled in mad gyrations about him as he reeled drunkenly to his feet, staggering and sprawling. He fell. He realized that he was falling, yet he could not fall! Thrashing wildly, grotesquely in agony, he struggled madly and blindly across the room, directly toward the thick steel wall. The tip of one hair of his unruly thatch touched the wall, and the slim length of that single hair did not even bend as its slight strength brought to an instant halt the hundred-and-eighty-odd pounds of mass—mass now entirely without inertia—that was his body.

But finally the sheer brain power of the man began to triumph over his physical torture. By force of will he compelled his grasping hands to seize a life-line, almost meaningless to his dazed intelligence; and through that nightmare incarnate of hellish torture he fought his way back to the control board. Hooking one leg around a standard, he made a seemingly enormous effort and depressed a red button; then fell flat upon the floor, weakly but in a wave of relief and thankfulness, as his racked body felt again the wonted phenomena of weight and of inertia. White, trembling, frankly and openly sick, the two men stared at each other in half-amazed joy.

"It worked," Cleveland smiled wanly as he recovered sufficiently to speak, then leaped to his feet. "Snap it up, Fred! We must be falling fast—we'll be wrecked when we hit!"

"We're not falling anywhere." Rodebush, foreboding in his eyes, walked over to the main observation plate and scanned the heavens. "However, it's not as bad as I was afraid it might be. I can still recognize a few of the constellations, even though they are all pretty badly distorted. That means that we can't be more than a couple of light-years or so away from the Solar System. Of course, since we had so little thrust on, practically all of our energy and time was taken up in getting out of the atmosphere. Even at that, though, it's a good thing that space isn't a perfect vacuum, or we would have been clear out of the Universe by this time."

"Huh? What are you talking about? Impossible! Where are we, anyway? Then we must be making mil . . . . Oh, I see!" Cleveland exclaimed, somewhat incoherently, as he also stared into the plate.

"Right. We aren't traveling at all—*now*." Rodebush replied. "We are perfectly stationary relative to Tellus, since we made that hop without inertia. We must have attained one hundred percent neutralization—one hundred point oh oh oh oh oh—which we didn't quite expect. Therefore we must have stopped instantaneously when our inertia was restored. Incidentally, that original, pre-inertialess velocity 'intrinsic' velocity, suppose we could call it?—is going to introduce plenty of complications, but we don't have to worry about them right now. Also, it isn't *where* we are that is worrying me—we can get fixes on enough recognizable stars to find that out in short order—it's *when*."

"That's right, too. Say we're two light years away from home. You think maybe that we're two years older now than we were ten minutes ago? Interesting no end—and distinctly possible. Maybe even probable—I wouldn't know—there's been a lot of discussion on that theory, and as far as I know we're the first ones who ever had a chance to prove or disprove it absolutely. Let's snap back to Tellus and find out, right now."

"We'll do that, after a little more experimenting. You see, I had no intention of giving us such a long push. I was going to throw the switches in and out, but you know what happened. However, there's one good thing about it—it's worth two years of anybody's life to settle that relativity-time thing definitely, one way or the other."

"I'll say it is. But say, we've got a lot of power on our ultra-wave; enough to reach Tellus, I think. Let's locate the sun and get in touch with Samms."

"Let's work on these controls a little first, so we'll have something to report. Out here's a fine place to try the ship out—nothing in the way."

"All right with me. But I *would* like to find out whether I'm two years older than I think I am, or not!"

Then for four hours they put the great super-ship through her paces, just as test-pilots check up on every detail of performance of an airplane of new and radical design. They found that the horrible vertigo could be endured, perhaps in time even conquered as space-sickness could be conquered, by a strong will in a sound body; and that their new conveyance had possibilities of which even Rodebush had never dreamed. Finally, their most pressing questions answered, they turned their most powerful ultra-beam communicator toward the yellowish star which they knew to be Old Sol.

"Samms . . . Samms." Cleveland spoke slowly and distinctly. "Rodebush and Cleveland reporting from the 'Space-Eating Wampus', now directly in line with Beta Ursae Minoris from the sun, distance about two point two light years. It will take six bands of tubes on your tightest beam, LSV3, to reach us. Barring a touch of an unusually severe type of space-sickness, everything worked beautifully; even better than either of us dared to believe. There's something we want to know right away—have we been gone four hours and some odd minutes, or better than two years?"

He turned to Rodebush and went on:

"Nobody knows how fast this ultra-wave travels, but if it goes as fast as we did coming out it's no creeper. I'll give him about thirty minutes, then shoot in another . . . ."

But, interrupting Cleveland's remark, the care-ravaged face of Virgil Samms appeared sharp and clear upon the plate and his voice snapped curtly from the speaker.

"Thank God you're alive, and twice that that the ship works!" he exclaimed. "You've been gone four hours, eleven minutes, and forty one seconds, but never mind about abstract theorizing. Get back here, to Pittsburgh, as fast as you can drive. That Nevian vessel or another one like her is mopping up the city, and has destroyed half the Fleet already!"

"We'll be back there in nine minutes!" Rodebush snapped into the transmitter. "Two to get from here to atmosphere, four from Atmosphere down to the Hill, and three to cool off. Notify the full four-shift crew—everybody we've picked out. Don't need anybody else. Ship, equipment, and armament are *ready!*"

"Two minutes to atmosphere? Think you can do it?" Cleveland asked, as Rodebush flipped off the power and leaped to the control panel. "You might, though, at that."

"We could do it in less than that if we had to. We used scarcely any power at all coming out, and I'm going to use quite a lot going back," the physicist explained rapidly, as he set the dials which would determine their flashing course.

The master switches were thrown and the pangs of inertialessness again assailed them—but weaker far this time than ever before—and upon their lookout plates they beheld a spectacle never before seen by eye of man. For the ultra-beam, with its heterodyned vision, is not distorted by any velocity yet attained, as are the ether-borne rays of light. Converted into light only at the plate, it showed their progress as truly as though they had been traveling at a pace to be expressed in the ordinary terms of miles per hour. The yellow star that was the sun detached itself from the firmament and leaped toward them, swelling visibly, momently, into a blinding monster of incandescence. And toward them also flung the Earth, enlarging with such indescribable rapidity that Cleveland protested involuntarily, in spite of his knowledge of the peculiar mechanics of the vessel in which they were.

"Hold it, Fred, hold it! Way 'nuff!" he exclaimed.

"I'm using only a few thousand kilograms of thrust, and I'll cut that as soon as we touch atmosphere, long before she can even begin to heat," Rodebush explained. "Looks bad, but we'll stop without a jar."

"What would you call this kind of flight, Fritz?" Cleveland asked. "What's the opposite of 'inert'?"

"Damned if I know. Isn't any, I guess. Light? No . . . how would 'free' be?"

"Not bad. 'Free' and 'Inert' maneuvering, eh? O.K."

Flying "free", then, the super-ship came from her practically infinite velocity to an almost instantaneous halt in the outermost, most tenuous layer of the Earth's atmosphere. Her halt was but momentary. Inertia restored, she dropped at a sharp angle downward. More than dropped; she was forced downward by one full battery of projectors; projectors driven by iron-powered generators. Soon they were over the Hill, whose violet screens went down at a word.

Flaming a dazzling white from the friction of the atmosphere through which she had torn her way, the *Boise* slowed abruptly as she neared the ground, plunging toward the surface of the small but deep artificial lake below the Hill's steel apron. Into the cold waters the space-ship dove, and even before they could close over her, furious geysers of steam and boiling water erupted as the stubborn alloy gave up its heat to the cooling liquid. Endlessly the three necessary minutes dragged their slow way into time, but finally the water ceased boiling and Rodebush tore the ship from the lake and hurled her into the gaping doorway of her dock. The massive doors of the airlocks opened, and while the full crew of picked men hurried aboard with their personal equipment, Samms talked earnestly to the two scientists in the control room.

" . . . and about half the fleet is still in the air. They aren't attacking; they are just trying to keep her from doing much more damage until you can get there. How about your take-off? We can't launch you again—the tracks are gone—but you handled her easily enough coming in?"

"That was all my fault," Rodebush admitted. "I had no idea that the fields would extend beyond the hull. We'll take her out on the projectors this time, though, the same as we brought her in—she handles like a bicycle. The projector blast tears things up a little, but nothing serious. Have you got that Pittsburgh beam for me yet? We're about ready to go."

"Here it is, Doctor Rodebush," came Norma's voice, and upon the screen there flashed into being the view of the events transpiring above that doomed city. "The dock is empty and sealed against your blast."

"Goodbye, and power to your tubes!" came Samms' ringing voice.

As the words were being spoken mighty blasts of power raved from the driving projectors, and the immense mass of the super-ship shot out through the portals and upward into the stratosphere. Through the tenuous atmosphere the huge globe rushed with ever-mounting speed, and while the hope of Triplanetary drove eastward Rodebush studied the ever-changing scene of battle upon his plate and issued detailed instructions to the highly trained specialists manning every offensive and defensive weapon.

But the Nevians did not wait to join battle until the newcomers arrived. Their detectors were sensitive—operative over untold thousands of miles—and the ultra-screen of the Hill had already been noted by the invaders as the Earth's only possible source of trouble. Thus the departure of the *Boise* had not gone unnoticed, and the fact that not even with his most penetrant rays could he see into her interior had already given the Nevian commander some slight concern. Therefore as soon as it was determined that the great globe was being directed toward Pittsburgh the fish-shaped cruiser of the void went into action.

High in the stratosphere, speeding eastward, the immense mass of the *Boise* slowed abruptly, although no projector had slackened its effort. Cleveland, eyes upon interferometer grating and spectrophotometer charts, fingers flying over calculator keys, grinned as he turned toward Rodebush.

"Just as you thought, Skipper; an ultra-band pusher. C4V63L29. Shall I give him a little pull?"

"Not yet; let's feel him out a little before we force a close-up. We've got plenty of mass. See what he does when I put full push on the projectors."

As the full power of the Tellurian vessel was applied the Nevian was forced backward, away from the threatened city, against the full drive of her every projector. Soon, however, the advance was again checked, and both scientists read the reason upon their plates. The enemy had put down reenforcing rods of tremendous power. Three compression members spread out fanwise behind her, bracing her against a low mountainside, while one huge tractor beam was thrust directly downward, holding in an unbreakable grip a cylinder of earth extending deep down into bedrock.

"Two can play at that game!" and Rodebush drove down similar beams, and forward-reaching tractors as well. "Strap yourselves in solid, everybody!" he sounded in general warning. "Something is going to give way somewhere soon, and when it does we'll get a jolt!"

And the promised jolt did indeed come soon. Prodigiously massive and powerful as the Nevian was, the *Boise* was even more massive and more powerful; and as the already enormous energy feeding the tractors, pushers, and projectors was raised to its inconceivable maximum, the vessel of the enemy was hurled upward, backward; and that of Earth shot ahead with a bounding leap that threatened to strain even her mighty members. The Nevian anchor rods had not broken; they had simply pulled up the vast cylinders of solid rock that had formed their anchorages.

"Grab him now!" Rodebush yelled, and even while an avalanche of falling rock was burying the countryside Cleveland snapped a tractor ray upon the flying fish and pulled tentatively.

Nor did the Nevian now seem averse to coming to grips. The two warring super-dreadnoughts darted toward each other, and from the invader there flooded out the dread crimson opacity which had theretofore meant the doom of all things Solarian. Flooded out and engulfed the immense globe of humanity's hope in its spreading cloud of redly impenetrable murk. But not for long. Triplanetary's super-ship boasted no ordinary Terrestrial defense, but was sheathed in screen after screen of ultra-vibrations: imponderable walls, it is true, but barriers impenetrable to any unfriendly wave. To the outer screen the red veil of the Nevians clung tenaciously, licking greedily at every square inch of the shielding sphere of force, but unable to find an opening through which to feed upon the steel of the *Boise's* armor.

"Get back—'way back! Go back and help Pittsburgh!" Rodebush drove an ultra communicator beam through the murk to the instruments of the Terrestrial admiral; for the surviving warships of the fleet—its most powerful units—were hurling themselves forward, to plunge into that red destruction. "None of you will last a second in this red field. And watch out for a violet field pretty soon—it'll be worse than this. We can handle them alone, I think; but if we can't, there's nothing in the System that can help us!"

And now the hitherto passive screen of the super-ship became active. At first invisible, it began to glow in fierce violet light, and as the glow brightened to unbearable intensity the entire spherical shield began to increase in size. Driven outward from the super-ship as a center, its advancing surface of seething energy consumed the crimson murk as a billow of blast-furnace heat consumes the cloud of snowflakes in the air above its cupola. Nor was the red death-mist all that was consumed. Between that ravening surface and the armor skin of the *Boise* there was nothing. No debris, no atmosphere, no vapor, no single atom of material substance—the first time in Terrestrial experience that an absolute vacuum had ever been attained!

Stubbornly contesting every foot of way lost, the Nevian fog retreated before the violet sphere of nothingness. Back and back it fell, disappearing altogether from all space as the violet tide engulfed the enemy vessel; but the flying fish did not disappear. Her triple screens flashed into furiously incandescent splendor and she entered unscathed that vacuous sphere, which collapsed instantly into an enormously elongated ellipsoid, at each focus a madly warring ship of space.

Then in that tube of vacuum was waged a spectacular duel of ultra-weapons—weapons impotent in air, but deadly in empty space. Beams, rays, and rods of Titanic power smote cracklingly against ultra-screens equally capable. Time after time each contestant ran the gamut of the spectrum with his every available ultra-force, only to find all channels closed. For minutes the terrible struggle went on, then:

"Cooper, Adlington, Spencer, Dutton!" Rodebush called into his transmitter. "Ready? Can't touch him on the ultra, so I'm going onto the macro-bands. Give him everything you have as soon as I collapse the violet. Go!"

At the word the violet barrier went down, and with a crash as of a disrupting Universe the atmosphere rushed into the void. And through the hurricane there shot out the deadliest material weapons of Triplanetary. Torpedoes—non-ferrous, ultra-screened, beam-dirigible torpedoes charged with the most effective forms of material destruction known to man. Cooper hurled his canisters of penetrating gas, Adlington his allotropic-iron atomic bombs, Spencer his indestructible armor-piercing projectiles, and Dutton his shatterable flasks of the quintessence of corrosion—a sticky, tacky liquid of such dire potency that only one rare Solarian element could contain it. Ten, twenty, fifty, a hundred were thrown as fast as the automatic machinery could launch them; and the Nevians found them adversaries not to be despised. Size for size, their screens were quite as capable as those of the *Boise*. The Nevians' destructive rays glanced harmlessly from their shields, and the Nevians' elaborate screens, neutralized at impact by those of the torpedoes, were impotent to impede their progress. Each projectile must needs be caught and crushed individually by beams of the most prodigious power; and while one was being annihilated dozens more were rushing to the attack. Then while the twisting, dodging invader was busiest with the tiny but relentless destroyers, Rodebush launched his heaviest weapon.

The macro-beams! Prodigious streamers of bluish-green flame which tore savagely through course after course of Nevian screen! Malevolent fangs, driven with such power and velocity that they were biting into the very walls of the enemy vessel before the amphibians knew that their defensive shells of force had been punctured! And the emergency screens of the invaders were equally futile. Course after course was sent out, only to flare viciously through the spectrum and to go black.

Outfought at every turn, the now frantically dodging Nevian leaped away in headlong flight, only to be brought to a staggering, crashing halt as Cleveland nailed her with a tractor beam. But the Tellurians were to learn that the Nevians held in reserve a means of retreat. The tractor snapped—sheared off squarely by a sizzling plane of force—and the fish-shaped cruiser faded from Cleveland's sight, just as the *Boise* had disappeared from the communicator plates of Radio Center, back in the Hill, when she was launched. But though the plates in the control room could not hold the Nevian, she did not vanish beyond the ken of Randolph, now Communications Officer in the super-ship. For, warned and humiliated by his losing one speeding vessel from his plates in Radio Center, he was now ready for any emergency. Therefore as the Nevian fled Randolph's spy-ray held her, automatically behind it as there was the full output of twelve special banks of iron-driven power tubes; and thus it was that the vengeful Earthmen flashed immediately along the Nevians' line of flight. Inertialess now, pausing briefly from time to time to enable the crew to accustom themselves to the new sensations, Triplanetary's super-ship pursued the invader; hurtling through the void with a velocity unthinkable.

"He was easier to take than I thought he would be," Cleveland grunted, staring into the plate.

"I thought he had more stuff, too," Rodebush assented, "but I guess Costigan got almost everything they had. If so, with all our own stuff and most of theirs besides, we should be able to take them. Conway's data indicated that they have only partial neutralization of inertia—if it's one hundred percent we'll never catch them—but it isn't—there they are!"

"And this time I'm going to hold her or burn out all our generators trying," Cleveland declared, grimly. "Are you fellows down there able to handle yourselves yet? Fine! Start throwing out your cans!"

Space-hardened veterans, all, the other Tellurian officers had fought off the horrible nausea of inertialessness, just as Rodebush and Cleveland had done. Again the ravening green macro-beams tore at the flying cruiser, again the mighty frames of the two space-ships shuddered sickeningly as Cleveland clamped on his tractor rod, again the highly dirigible torpedoes dashed out with their freights of death and destruction. And again the Nevian shear-plane of force slashed at the *Boise's* tractor beam; but this time the mighty puller did not give way. Sparkling and spitting high-tension sparks, the plane bit deeply into the stubborn rod of energy. Brighter, thicker, and longer grew the discharges as the gnawing plane drew more and more power; but in direct ratio to that power the rod grew larger, denser, and ever harder to cut. More and more vivid became the pyrotechnic display, until suddenly the entire tractor rod disappeared. At the same instant a blast of intolerable flame erupted from the *Boise's* flank and the whole enormous fabric of her shook and quivered under the force of a terrific detonation.

"Randolph! I don't see them! Are they attacking or running?" Rodebush demanded. He was the first to realize what had happened.

"Running—fast!"

"Just as well, perhaps, but get their line. Adlington!"

"Here!"

"Good! Was afraid you were gone—that was one of your bombs, wasn't it?"

"Yes. Well launched, just inside the screens. Don't see how it could have detonated unless something hot and hard struck it in the tube; it would need about that much time to explode. Good thing it didn't go off any sooner, or none of us would have been here. As it is, Area Six is pretty well done in, but the bulkheads held the damage to Six. What happened?"

"We don't know, exactly. Both generators on the tractor beam went out. At first, I thought that was all, but my neutralizers are dead and I don't know what else. When the G-4's went out the fusion must have shorted the neutralizers. They would make a mess; it must have burned a hole down into number six tube. Cleveland and I will come down, and we'll all look around."

Donning space-suits, the scientists let themselves into the damaged compartment through the emergency airlocks, and what a sight they saw! Both outer and inner walls of alloy armor had been blown away by the awful force of the explosion. Jagged plates hung awry; bent, twisted and broken. The great torpedo tube, with all its intricate automatic machinery, had been driven violently backward and lay piled in hideous confusion against the backing bulkheads. Practically nothing remained whole in the entire compartment.

"Nothing much we can do here," Rodebush said finally, through his transmitter. "Let's go see what number four generator looks like."

That room, although not affected by the explosion from without, had been quite as effectively wrecked from within. It was still stiflingly hot; its air was still reeking with the stench of burning lubricant, insulation, and metal; its floor was half covered by a semi-molten mass of what had once been vital machinery. For with the burning out of the generator bars the energy of the disintegrating allotropic iron had had no outlet, and had built up until it had broken through its insulation and in an irresistible flood of power had torn through all obstacles in its path to neutralization.

"Hm . . . m . . . m. Should have had an automatic shut-off—one detail we overlooked," Rodebush mused. "The electricians can rebuild this stuff here, though—that hole in the hull is something else again."

"I'll say it's something else," the grizzled Chief Engineer agreed. "She's lost all her spherical strength—anchoring a tractor with this ship now would turn her inside out. Back to the nearest Triplanetary shop for us, I would say."

"Come again, Chief!" Cleveland advised the engineer. "None of us would live long enough to get there. We can't travel inertialess until the repairs are made, so if they can't be made without very much traveling, it's just too bad."

"I don't see how we could support our jacks . . ." the engineer paused, then went on: "If you can't give me Mars or Tellus, how about some other planet? I don't care about atmosphere, or about anything but mass. I can stiffen her up in three or four days if I can sit down on something heavy enough to hold our jacks and presses; but if we have to rig up space-cradles around the ship herself it'll take a long time—months, probably. Haven't got a spare planet on hand, have you?"

"We might have, at that," Rodebush made surprising answer. "A couple of seconds before we engaged we were heading toward a sun with at least two planets. I was just getting ready to dodge them when we cut the neutralizers, so they should be fairly close somewhere—yes, there's the sun, right over there. Rather pale and small; but it's close, comparatively speaking. We'll go back up into the control room and find out about the planets."

The strange sun was found to have three large and easily located children, and observation showed that the crippled space-ship could reach the nearest of these in about five days. Power was therefore fed to the driving projectors, and each scientist, electrician, and mechanic bent to the task of repairing the ruined generators; rebuilding them to handle any load which the converters could possibly put upon them. For two days the *Boise* drove on, then her acceleration was reversed, and finally a landing was effected upon the forbidding, rocky soil of the strange world.

It was larger than the Earth, and of a somewhat stronger gravitation. Although its climate was bitterly cold, even in its short daytime, it supported a luxuriant but outlandish vegetation. Its atmosphere, while rich enough in oxygen and not really poisonous, was so rank with indescribably fetid vapors as to be scarcely breatheable. But these things bothered the engineers not at all. Paying no attention to temperature or to scenery and without waiting for chemical analysis of the air, the space-suited mechanics leaped to their tasks; and in only a little more time than had been mentioned by the chief engineer the hull and giant frame of the super-ship were as staunch as of yore.

"All right, Skipper!" came finally the welcome word. "You might try her out with a fast hop around this world before you shove off in earnest."

Under the fierce blast of her projectors the vessel leaped ahead, and time after time, as Rodebush hurled her mass upon tractor beam or pressor, the engineers sought in vain for any sign of weakness. The strange planet half girdled and the severest tests passed flawlessly, Rodebush reached for his neutralizer switches. Reached and paused, dumbfounded, for a brilliant purple light had sprung into being upon his panel and a bell rang out insistently.

"What the hell!" Rodebush shot out an exploring beam along the detector line and gasped. He stared, mouth open, then yelled:

"*Roger* is here, rebuilding his planetoid! STATIONS ALL!"

ROGER CARRIES ON

As has been intimated, gray Roger did not perish in the floods of Nevian energy which destroyed his planetoid. While those terrific streamers of force emanating from the crimson obscurity surrounding the amphibians' space-ship were driving into his defensive screens he sat impassive and immobile at his desk, his hard gray eyes moving methodically over his instruments and recorders.

When the clinging mantle of force changed from deep red into shorter and even shorter wave-lengths, however:

"Baxter, Hartkopf, Chatelier, Anandrusung, Penrose, Nishimura, Mirsky . . . " he called off a list of names. "Report to me here at once!"

"The planetoid is lost," he informed his select group of scientists when they had assembled, "and we must abandon it in exactly fifteen minutes, which will be the time required for the robots to fill this first section with our most necessary machinery and instruments. Pack each of you one box of the things he most wishes to take with him, and report back here in not more than thirteen minutes. Say nothing to anyone else."

They filed out calmly, and as they passed out into the hall Baxter, perhaps a trifle less case-hardened than his fellows, at least voiced a thought for those they were so brutally deserting.

"I say, it seems a bit thick to dash off this way and leave the rest of them; but still, I suppose . . . ."

"You suppose correctly." Bland and heartless Nishimura filled in the pause. "A small part of the planetoid may be able to escape; which, to me at least, is pleasantly surprising news. It cannot carry all our men and mechanisms, therefore only the most important of both are saved. What would you? For the rest it is simply what you call 'the fortune of war,' no?"

"But the beautiful . . . " began the amorous Chatelier.

"Hush, fool!" snorted Hartkopf. "One word of that to the ear of Roger and you too left behind are. Of such non-essentials the Universe full is, to be collected in times of ease, but in times hard to be disregarded. Und this is a time of *schrecklichkeit* indeed!"

The group broke up, each man going to his own quarters; to meet again in the First Section a minute or so before the zero time. Roger's "office" was now packed so tightly with machinery and supplies that but little room was left for the scientists. The gray monstrosity still sat unmoved behind his dials.

"But of what use is it, Roger?" the Russian physicist demanded. "Those waves are of some ultra-band, of a frequency immensely higher than anything heretofore known. Our screens should not have stopped them for an instant. It is a mystery that they have held so long, and certainly this single section will not be permitted to leave the planetoid without being destroyed."

"There are many things you do not know, Mirsky," came the cold and level answer. "Our screens, which you think are of your own devising, have several improvements of my own in the formulae, and would hold forever had I the power to drive them. The screens of this section, being smaller, can be held as long as will be found necessary."

"Power!" the dumbfounded Russian exclaimed. "Why, we have almost infinite power—unlimited—sufficient for a lifetime of high expenditure!"

But Roger made no reply, for the time of departure was at hand. He pressed down a tiny lever, and a mechanism in the power room threw in the gigantic plunger switches which launched against the Nevians the stupendous beam which so upset the complacence of Nerado the amphibian—the beam into which was poured recklessly every resource of power afforded by the planetoid, careless alike of burnout and of exhaustion. Then, while all of the attention of the Nevians and practically all of their maximum possible power output was being devoted to the neutralization of that last desperate thrust, the metal wall of the planetoid opened and the First Section shot out into space. Full-driven as they were, Roger's screens flared white as he drove through the temporarily lessened attack of the Nevians; but in their preoccupation the amphibians did not notice the additional disturbance and the section tore on, unobserved and undetected.

Far out in space, Roger raised his eyes from the instrument panel and continued the conversation as though it had not been interrupted.

"Everything is relative, Mirsky, and you have misused gravely the term 'unlimited.' Our power was, and is, very definitely limited. True, it then seemed ample for our needs, and is far superior to that possessed by the inhabitants of any solar system with which I am familiar; but the beings behind that red screen, whoever they are, have sources of power as far above ours as ours are above those of the Solarians."

"How do you know?"

"That power, what is it?"

"We have, then, the analyses of those fields recorded!" came simultaneous questions and exclamations.

"Their source of power is the intra-atomic energy of iron. Complete; not the partial liberation incidental to the nuclear fission of such unstable isotopes as those of thorium, uranium, plutonium, and so on. Therefore much remains to be done before I can proceed with my plan—I must have the most powerful structure in the macrocosmic universe."

Roger thought for minutes, nor did any one of his minions break the silence. Gharlane of Eddore did not have to wonder why such incredible advancement could have been made without his knowledge: after the fact, he knew. He had been and was still being hampered by a mind of power; a mind with which, in due time, he would come to grips.

"I now know what to do," he went on presently. "In the light of what I have learned, the losses of time, life, and treasure—even the loss of the planetoid—are completely insignificant."

"But what can you do about it?" growled the Russian.

"Many things. From the charts of the recorders we can compute their fields of force, and from that point it is only a step to their method of liberating the energy. We shall build robots. They shall build other robots, who shall in turn construct another planetoid; one this time that, wielding the theoretical maximum of power, will be suited to my needs."

"And where will you build it? We are marked. Invisibility now is useless. Triplanetary will find us, even if we take up an orbit beyond that of Pluto!"

"We have already left your Solarian system far behind. We are going to another system; one far enough removed so that the spy-rays of Triplanetary will never find us, and yet one that we can reach in a reasonable length of time with the energies at our command. Some five days will be required for the journey, however, and our quarters are cramped. Therefore make places for yourselves wherever you can, and lessen the tedium of those days by working upon whatever problems are most pressing in your respective researches."

The gray monster fell silent, immersed in what thoughts no one knew, and the scientists set out to obey his orders. Baxter, the British chemist, followed Penrose, the lantern-jawed, saturnine American engineer and inventor, as he made his way to the furthermost cubicle of the section.

"I say, Penrose, I'd like to ask you a couple of questions, if you don't mind?"

"Go ahead. Ordinarily it's dangerous to be a cackling hen anywhere around *him*, but I don't imagine that he can hear anything here now. His system must be pretty well shot to pieces. You want to know all I know about Roger?"

"Exactly so. You have been with him so much longer than I have, you know. In some ways he impresses one as being scarcely human, if you know what I mean. Ridiculous, of course, but of late I have been wondering whether he really *is* human. He knows too much, about too many things. He seems to be acquainted with many solar systems, to visit which would require lifetimes. Then, too, he has dropped remarks which would imply that he actually saw things that happened long before any living man could possibly have been born. Finally, he looks—well, peculiar—and certainly does not act human. I have been wondering, and have been able to learn nothing about him; as you have said, such talk as this aboard the planetoid was not advisable."

"You needn't worry about being paid your price; that's one thing. If we live—and that was part of the agreement, you know—we will get what we sold out for. You will become a belted earl. I have already made millions, and shall make many more. Similarly, Chatelier has had and will have his women, Anandrusung and Nishimura their cherished revenges, Hartkopf his power, and so on." He eyed the other speculatively, then went on:

"I might as well spill it all, since I'll never have a better chance and since you should know as much as the rest of us do. You're in the same boat with us and tarred with the same brush. There's a lot of gossip, that may or may not be true, but I know one very startling fact. Here it is. My great-great-grandfather left some notes which, taken in connection with certain things I myself saw on the planetoid, prove beyond question that our Roger went to Harvard University at the same time he did. Roger was a grown man then, and the elder Penrose noted that he was marked, like this," and the American sketched a cabalistic design.

"What!" Baxter exclaimed. "An adept of North Polar Jupiter—*then?*"

"Yes. That was before the First Jovian War, you know, and it was those medicine-men—really high-caliber scientists—that prolonged that war so . . . ."

"But I say, Penrose, that's really a bit thick. When they were wiped out it was proved a lot of hocus-pocus . . . ."

"*If* they were wiped out," Penrose interrupted in turn. "Some of it may have been hocus-pocus, but most of it certainly was not. I'm not asking you to believe anything except that one fact; I'm just telling you the rest of it. But it is also a fact that those adepts knew things and did things that take a lot of explaining. Now for the gossip, none of which is guaranteed. Roger is supposed to be of Tellurian parentage, and the story is that his father was a moon-pirate, his mother a Greek adventuress. When the pirates were chased off the moon they went to Ganymede, you know, and some of them were captured by the Jovians. It seems that Roger was born at an instant of time sacred to the adepts, so they took him on. He worked his way up through the Forbidden Society as all adepts did, by various kinds of murder and job lots of assorted deviltries, until he got clear to the top—the seventy-seventh mystery . . . ."

"The secret of eternal youth!" gasped Baxter, awed in spite of himself.

"Right, and he stayed Chief Devil, in spite of all the efforts of all his ambitious sub-devils to kill him, until the turning-point of the First Jovian War. He cut away then in a space-ship, and ever since then he has been working—and working hard—on some stupendous plan of his own that nobody else has ever got even an inkling of. That's the story. True or not, it explains a lot of things that no other theory can touch. And now I think you'd better shuffle along; enough of this is a great plenty!"

Baxter went to his own cubby, and each man of gray Roger's cold-blooded crew methodically took up his task. True to prediction, in five days a planet loomed beneath them and their vessel settled through a reeking atmosphere toward a rocky and forbidding plain. Then for hours they plunged along, a few thousand feet above the surface of that strange world, while Roger with his analytical detectors sought the most favorable location from which to wrest the materials necessary for his program of construction.

It was a world of cold; its sun was distant, pale, and wan. It had monstrous forms of vegetation, of which each branch and member writhed and fought with a grotesque and horrible individual activity. Ever and anon a struggling part broke from its parent plant and darted away in independent existence; leaping upon and consuming or being consumed by a fellow creature equally monstrous. This flora was of a uniform color, a lurid, sickly yellow. In form some of it was fern-like, some cactus-like, some vaguely tree-like; but it was all outrageous, inherently repulsive to all Solarian senses. And no less hideous were the animal-like forms of life which slithered and slunk rapaciously through that fantastic pseudo-vegetation. Snake-like, reptile-like, bat-like, the creatures squirmed, crawled, and flew; each covered with a dankly oozing yellow hide and each motivated by twin common impulses—to kill and insatiably and indiscriminately to devour. Over this reeking wilderness Roger drove his vessel, untouched by its disgusting, its appalling ferocity and horror.

"There should be intelligence, of a kind," he mused, and swept the surface of the planet with an exploring beam. "Ah, yes, there is a city, of sorts," and in a few minutes the outlaws were looking down upon a metal-walled city of roundly conical buildings.

Inside these structures and between and around them there scuttled formless blobs of matter, one of which Roger brought up into his vessel by means of a tractor. Held immovable by the beam it lay upon the floor, a strangely extensile, amoeba-like, metal-studded mass of leathery substance. Of eyes, ears, limbs, or organs it apparently had none, yet it radiated an intensely hostile aura; a mental effluvium concentrated of rage and of hatred.

"Apparently the ruling intelligence of the planet," Roger commented. "Such creatures are useless to us; we can build machines in half the time that would be required for their subjugation and training. Still, it should not be permitted to carry back what it may have learned of us." As he spoke the adept threw the peculiar being out into the air and dispassionately rayed it out of existence.

"That thing reminds me of a man I used to know, back in Penobscot." Penrose was as coldly callous as his unfeeling master. "The evenest-tempered man in town—mad all the time!"

Eventually Roger found a location which satisfied his requirements of raw materials, and made a landing upon that unfriendly soil. Sweeping beams denuded a great circle of life, and into that circle leaped robots. Robots requiring neither rest nor food, but only lubricants and power; robots insensible alike to that bitter cold and to that noxious atmosphere.

But the outlaws were not to win a foothold upon that inimical planet easily, nor were they to hold it without effort. Through the weird vegetation of the circle's bare edge there scuttled and poured along a horde of the metal-studded men—if "men" they might be called—who, ferocity incarnate, rushed the robot line. Mowed down by hundreds, still they came on; willing, it seemed to spend any number of lives in order that one living creature might once touch a robot with one outthrust metallic stud. Whenever that happened there was a flash of lightning, the heavy smoke of burning insulation, grease, and metal, and the robot went down out of control. Recalling his remaining automatons, Roger sent out a shielding screen, against which the defenders of their planet raged in impotent fury. For days they hurled themselves and their every force against that impenetrable barrier, then withdrew: temporarily stopped, but by no means acknowledging defeat.

Then while Roger and his cohorts directed affairs from within their comfortable and now sufficiently roomy vessel, there came into being around it an industrial city of metal peopled by metallic and insensate mechanisms. Mines were sunk, furnaces were blown in, smelters belched forth into the already unbearable air their sulphurous fumes, rolling mills and machine shops were built and were equipped; and as fast as new enterprises were completed additional robots were ready to man them. In record time the heavy work of girders, members, and plates was well under way; and shortly thereafter light, deft, multi-fingered mechanisms began to build and to install the prodigious amount of precise machinery required by the vastness of the structure.

As soon as he was sure that he would be completely free for a sufficient length of time, Roger-Gharlane assembled, boiled down and concentrated, his every mental force. He probed then, very gently, for whatever it was that had been and was still blocking him. He found it—synchronized with it—and in the instant hurled against it the fiercest thrust possible for his Eddorian mind to generate: a bolt whose twin had slain more than one member of Eddore's Innermost Circle; a bolt whose energies, he had previously felt sure, would slay any living thing save only His Ultimate Supremacy, the All-Highest of Eddore.

Now, however, and not completely to his surprise, that blast of force was ineffective; and the instantaneous riposte was of such intensity as to require for its parrying everything that Gharlane had. He parried it, however barely, and directed a thought at his unknown opponent.

"You, whoever you may be, have found out that you cannot kill me. No more can I kill you. So be it. Do you still believe that you can keep me from remembering whatever it was that my ancestor was compelled to forget?"

"Now that you have obtained a focal point we cannot prevent you from remembering; and merely to hinder you would be pointless. You may remember in peace."

Back and back went Gharlane's mind. Centuries . . . millenia . . . cycles . . . eons. The trace grew dim, almost imperceptible, deeply buried beneath layer upon layer of accretions of knowledge, experience, and sensation which no one of many hundreds of his ancestors had even so much as disturbed. But every iota of knowledge that any of his progenitors had ever had was still his. However dim, however deeply buried, however suppressed and camouflaged by inimical force, he could now find it.

He found it, and in the instant of its finding it was as though Enphilistor the Arisian spoke directly to him; as though the fused Elders of Arisia tried—vainly now—to erase from his own mind all knowledge of Arisia's existence. The fact that such a race as the Arisians had existed so long ago was bad enough. That the Arisians had been aware throughout all those ages of the Eddorians, and had been able to keep their own existence secret, was worse. The crowning fact that the Arisians had had all this time in which to work unopposed against his own race made even Gharlane's indomitable ego quail.

This was *important*. Such minor matters as the wiping out of non-conforming cultures—the extraordinarily rapid growth of which was now explained—must wait. Eddore must revise its thinking completely; the pooled and integrated mind of the Innermost Circle must scrutinize every fact, every implication and connotation, of this new-old knowledge. Should he flash back to Eddore, or should he wait and take the planetoid, with its highly varied and extremely valuable contents? He would wait; a few moments more would be a completely negligible addition to the eons of time which had already elapsed since action should have been begun.

The rebuilding of the planetoid, then, went on. Roger had no reason to suspect that there was anything physically dangerous within hundreds of millions of miles. Nevertheless, since he knew that he could no longer depend upon his own mental powers to keep him informed as to all that was going on around him, it was his custom to scan, from time to time, all nearby space by means of ether-borne detectors. Thus it came about that one day, as he sent out his beam, his hard gray eyes grew even harder.

"Mirsky! Nishimura! Penrose! Come here!" he ordered, and showed them upon his plate an enormous sphere of steel, its offensive beams flaming viciously. "Is there any doubt whatever in your minds as to the System to which that ship belongs?"

"None at all—Solarian," replied the Russian. "To narrow it still further, Triplanetarian. While larger than any I have ever seen before, its construction is unmistakable. They managed to trace us, and are testing out their weapons before attacking. Do we attack or do we run away?"

"If Triplanetarian, and it surely is, we attack," coldly. "This one section is armed and powered to defeat Triplanetary's entire navy. We shall take that ship, and shall add its slight resources to our own. And it may even be that they have picked up the three who escaped me . . . I have never been balked for long. Yes, we shall take that vessel. And those three sooner or later. Except for the fact that their escape from me is a matter which should be corrected, I care nothing whatever about either Bradley or the woman. Costigan, however, is in a different category . . . Costigan *handled* me . . . ." Diamond-hard eyes glared balefully at the urge of thoughts to a clean and normal mind unthinkable.

"To your posts," he ordered. "The machines will continue to function under their automatic controls during the short time it will require to abate this nuisance."

"One moment!" A strange voice roared from the speakers. "Consider yourselves under arrest, by order of the Triplanetary Council! Surrender and you shall receive impartial hearing; fight us and you shall never come to trial. From what we have learned of Roger, we do not expect him to surrender, but if any of you other men wish to avoid immediate death, leave your vessel at once. We will come back for you later."

"Any of you wishing to leave this vessel have my full permission to do so," Roger announced, disdaining any reply to the challenge of the *Boise*. "Any such, however, will not be allowed inside the planetoid area after the rest of us return from wiping out that patrol. We attack in one minute."

"Would not one do better by stopping on?" Baxter, in the quarters of the American, was in doubt as to the most profitable course to pursue. "I should leave immediately if I thought that that ship could win; but I do not fancy that it can, do you?"

"That ship? *One* Triplanetary ship against *us?*" Penrose laughed raucously. "Do as you please. I'd go in a minute if I thought that there was any chance of us losing; but there isn't, so I'm staying. I know which side my bread's buttered on. Those cops are bluffing, that's all. Not bluffing exactly, either, because they'll go through with it as long as they last. Foolish, but it's a way they have—they'll die trying every time instead of running away, even when they know they're licked before they start. They don't use good judgment."

"None of you are leaving? Very well, you each know what to do," came Roger's emotionless voice. The stipulated minute having elapsed, he advanced a lever and the outlaw cruiser slid quietly into the air.

Toward the poised *Boise* Roger steered. Within range, he flung out a weapon new-learned and supposedly irresistible to any ferrous thing or creature, the red converter-field of the Nevians. For Roger's analytical detector had stood him in good stead during those frightful minutes in the course of which the planetoid had borne the brunt of Nerado's super-human attack; in such good stead that from the records of those ingenious instruments he and his scientists had been able to reconstruct not only the generators of the attacking forces, but also the screens employed by the amphibians in the neutralization of similar beams. With a vastly inferior armament the smallest of Roger's vessels had defeated the most powerful battleships of Triplanetary; what had he to fear in such a heavy craft as the one he now was driving, one so superlatively armed and powered? It was just as well for his peace of mind that he had no inkling that the harmless-looking sphere he was so blithely attacking was in reality the much-discussed, half-mythical super-ship upon which the Triplanetary Service had been at work so long; nor that its already unprecedented armament had been reenforced, thanks to that hated Costigan, with Roger's own every worthwhile idea, as well as with every weapon and defense known to that arch-Nevian, Nerado!

Unknowing and contemptuous, Roger launched his converter field, and instantly found himself fighting for his very life. For from Rodebush at the controls down, the men of the *Boise* countered with wave after wave and with salvo after salvo of vibratory and material destruction. No thought of mercy for the men of the pirate ship could enter their minds. The outlaws had each been given a chance to surrender, and each had refused it. Refusing, they knew, as the Triplanetarians knew and as all modern readers know, meant that they were staking their lives upon victory. For with modern armaments few indeed are the men who live through the defeat in battle of a war-vessel of space.

Roger launched his field of red opacity, but it did not reach even the *Boise's* screens. All space seemed to explode into violet splendor as Rodebush neutralized it, drove it back with his obliterating zone of force; but even that all-devouring zone could not touch Roger's peculiarly efficient screen. The outlaw vessel stood out, unharmed. Ultra-violet, infra-red, pure heat, infra-sound, solid beams of high-tension, high-frequency stuff in whose paths the most stubborn metals would be volatilized instantly, all iron-driven; every deadly and torturing vibration known was hurled against that screen: but it, too, was iron-driven, and it held. Even the awful force of the macro-beam was dissipated by it—reflected, hurled away on all sides in coruscating torrents of blinding, dazzling energy. Cooper, Adlington, Spencer, and Dutton hurled against it their bombs and torpedoes—and still it held. But Roger's fiercest blasts and heaviest projectiles were equally impotent against the force-shields of the super-ship. The adept, having no liking for a battle upon equal terms, then sought safety in flight, only to be brought to a crashing, stunning halt by a massive tractor beam.

"That must be that polycyclic screen that Conway reported on." Cleveland frowned in thought. "I've been doing a lot of work on that, and I think I've calculated an opener for it, Fred, but I'll have to have number ten projector and the whole output of number ten power room. Can you let me play with that much juice for a while? All right, Blake, tune her up to fifty-five thousand—there, hold it! Now, you other fellows, listen! I'm going to try to drill a hole through that screen with a hollow, quasi-solid beam; like a diamond drill cutting out a core. You won't be able to shove anything into the hole from outside the beam, so you'll have to steer your cans out through the central orifice of number ten projector—that'll be cold, since I'm going to use only the outer ring. I don't know how long I'll be able to hold the hole open, though, so shoot them along as fast as you can. Ready? Here goes!"

He pressed a series of contacts. Far below, in number ten converter room, massive switches drove home and the enormous mass of the vessel quivered under the terrific reaction of the newly-calculated, semi-material beam of energy that was hurled out, backed by the mightiest of all the mighty converters and generators of Triplanetary's super-dreadnaught. That beam, a pipe-like hollow cylinder of intolerable energy, flashed out, and there was a rending, tearing crash as it struck Roger's hitherto impenetrable wall. Struck and clung, grinding, boring in, while from the raging inferno that marked the circle of contact of cylinder and shield the pirate's screen radiated scintillating torrents of crackling, streaming sparks, lightning like in length and in intensity.

Deeper and deeper the gigantic drill was driven. It was through! Pierced Roger's polycyclic screen; exposed the bare metal of Roger's walls! And now, concentrated upon one point, flamed out in seemingly redoubled fury Triplanetary's raging beams—in vain. For even as they could not penetrate the screen, neither could they penetrate the wall of Cleveland's drill, but rebounded from it in the cascaded brilliance of thwarted lightning.

"Oh, what a dumb-bell I am!" groaned Cleveland. "Why, oh *why* didn't I have somebody rig up a secondary SX7 beam on Ten's inner rings? Hop to it, will you, Blake, so that we'll have it in case they are able to stop the cans?"

But the pirates could not stop all of Triplanetary's projectiles, now hurrying along inside the pipe as fast as they could be driven. In fact, for a few minutes gray Roger, knowing that he faced the first real defeat of his long life, paid no attention to them at all, nor to any of his useless offensive weapons: he struggled only to break away from the savage grip of the *Boise's* tractor rod. Futile. He could neither cut nor stretch that inexorably anchoring beam. Then he devoted his every resource to the closing of that unbelievable breach in his shield. Equally futile. His most desperate efforts resulted only in more frenzied displays of incandescence along the curved surface of contact of that penetrant cylinder. And through that terrific conduit came speeding package after package of destruction. Bombs, armor-piercing shells, gas shells of poisonous and corrosive fluids followed each other in close succession. The surviving scientists of the planetoid, expert gunners and ray-men all, destroyed many of the projectiles, but it was not humanly possible to cope with them all. And the breach could not be forced shut against the all but irresistible force of Cleveland's "opener". And with all his power Roger could not shift his vessel's position in the grip of Triplanetary's tractors sufficiently to bring a projector to bear upon the super-ship along the now unprotected axis of that narrow, but deadly tube.

Thus it was that the end came soon. A war-head touched steel plating and there ensued a space-wracking explosion of atomic iron. Gaping wide, helpless, with all defenses down, other torpedoes entered the stricken hulk and completed its destruction even before they could be recalled. Atomic bombs literally volatilized most of the pirate vessel; vials of pure corrosion began to dissolve the solid fragments of her substance into dripping corruption. Reeking gasses filled every cranny of circumambient space as what was left of

Roger's battle cruiser began the long plunge to the ground. The super-ship followed the wreckage down, and Rodebush sent out an exploring spy-ray.

" . . . resistance was such that it was necessary to employ corrosive, and ship and contents were completely disintegrated," he dictated, a little later, into his vessel's log. "While there were of course no remains recognizable as human, it is certain that Roger and his last eleven men died; since it is clear that the circumstances and conditions were such that no life could possibly have survived."

*

It is true that the form of flesh which had been known as Roger was destroyed. The solids and liquids of its substance were resolved into their component molecules or atoms. That which had energized that form of flesh, however, could not be harmed by any physical force, however applied. Therefore that which made Roger what he was; the essence which was Gharlane of Eddore; was actually back upon his native planet even before Rodebush completed his study of what was left of the pirates' vessel.

The Innermost Circle met, and for a space of time which would have been very long indeed for any Earthly mind those monstrous being considered as one multi-ply intelligence every newly-exposed phase and facet of the truth. At the end, they knew the Arisians as well as the Arisians knew them. The All-Highest then called a meeting of all the minds of Eddore.

" . . . hence it is clear that these Arisians, while possessing minds of tremendous latent capability, are basically soft, and therefore inefficient," he concluded. "Not weak, mind you, but scrupulous and unrealistic; and it is by taking advantage of these characteristics that we shall ultimately triumph."

"A few details, All-Highest, if Your Ultimate Supremacy would deign," a lesser Eddorian requested. "Some of us have not been able to perceive at all clearly the optimum lines of action."

"While detailed plans of campaign have not yet been worked out, there will be several main lines of attack. A purely military undertaking will of course be one, but it will not be the most important. Political action, by means of subversive elements and obstructive minorities, will prove much more useful. Most productive of all, however, will be the operations of relatively small but highly organized groups whose functions will be to negate, to tear down and destroy, every bulwark of what the weak and spineless adherents of Civilization consider the finest things in life—love, truth, honor, loyalty, purity, altruism, decency, and so on."

"Ah, love . . . extremely interesting. Supremacy, this thing they call sex," Gharlane offered. "What a silly, what a meaningless thing it is! I have studied it intensively, but am not yet fully enough informed to submit a complete and conclusive report. I do know, however, that we can and will use it. In our hands, vice will become a potent weapon indeed. Vice . . . drugs . . . greed . . . gambling . . . extortion . . . blackmail . . . lust . . . abduction . . . assassination . . . ah-h-h!"

"Exactly. There will be room, and need, for the fullest powers of every Eddorian. Let me caution you all, however, that little or none of this work is to be done by any of us in person. We must work through echelon upon echelon of higher and lower executives and supervisors if we are to control efficiently the activities of the thousands of billions of operators which we must and will have at work. Each echelon of control will be vastly greater in number than the one immediately above it, but correspondingly lower in the individual power of its component personnel. The sphere of activity of each supervisor, however small or great, will be clearly and sharply defined. Rank, from the operators at planetary-population levels up to and including the Eddorian Directorate, will be a linear function of ability. Absolute authority will be delegated. Full responsibility will be assumed. Those who succeed will receive advancement and satisfaction of desire; those who fail will die.

"Since the personnel of the lower echelons will be of small value and easy of replacement, it is of little moment whether or not they become involved in reverses affecting the still lower echelons whose activities they direct. The echelon immediately below us of Eddore, however—and incidentally, it is my thought that the Ploorans will best serve as our immediate underlings—must never, under any conditions, allow any hint of any of its real business to become known either to any member of any lower echelon or to any adherent of Civilization. This point is vital; everyone here must realize that only in that way can our own safety remain assured, and must take pains to see to it that any violator of this rule is put instantly to death.

"Those of you who are engineers will design ever more powerful mechanisms to use against the Arisians. Psychologists will devise and put into practice new methods and techniques, both to use against the able minds of the Arisians and to control the activities of mentally weaker entities. Each Eddorian, whatever his field or his ability, will be given the task he is best fitted to perform. That is all."

*

And upon Arisia, too, while there was no surprise, a general conference was held. While some of the young Watchmen may have been glad that the open conflict for which they had been preparing so long was now about to break, Arisia as a whole was neither glad nor sorry. In the Great Scheme of Things which was the Cosmic All, this whole affair was an infinitesimal incident. It had been foreseen. It had come. Each Arisian would do to the fullest extent of his ability that which the very fact of his being an Arisian would compel him to do. It would pass.

"In effect, then, our situation has not really changed," Eukonidor stated, rather than asked, after the Elders had again spread their Visualization for public inspection and discussion. "This killing, it seems, must go on. This stumbling, falling, and rising; this blind groping; this futility; this frustration; this welter of crime, disaster, and bloodshed. Why? It seems to me that it would be much better—cleaner, simpler, faster, more efficient, and involving infinitely less bloodshed and suffering—for us to take now a direct and active part, as the Eddorians have done and will continue to do."

"Cleaner, youth, yes; and simpler. Easier; less bloody. It would not, however, be better; or even good; because no end-point would ever be attained. Young civilizations advance only by overcoming obstacles. Each obstacle surmounted, each step of progress made, carries its suffering as well as its reward. We could negate the efforts of any echelon below the Eddorians themselves, it is true. We could so protect and shield each one of our protege races that not a war would be waged and not a law would be broken. But to what end? Further contemplation will show you immature thinkers that in such a case not one of our races would develop into what the presence of the Eddorians has made it necessary for them to become.

"From this it follows that we would never be able to overcome Eddore; nor would our conflict with that race remain indefinitely at stalemate. Given sufficient time during which to work against us, they will be able to win. However, if every Arisian follows his line of action as it is laid out in this Visualization, all will be well. Are there any more questions?"

"None. The blanks which you may have left can be filled in by a mind of very moderate power."

*

"Look here, Fred." Cleveland called attention to the plate, upon which was pictured a horde of the peculiar inhabitants of that ghastly planet, wreaking their frenzied electrical wrath upon everything within the circle bared of native life by Roger's destructive beams. "I was just going to suggest that we clean up the planetoid that Roger started to build, but I see that the local boys and girls are attending to it."

"Just as well, perhaps. I would like to stay and study these people a little while, but we must get back onto the trail of the Nevians," and the *Boise* leaped away into space, toward the line of flight of the amphibians.

They reached that line and along it they traveled at full normal blast. As they traveled their detecting receivers and amplifiers were reaching out with their utmost power; ultra-instruments capable of rendering audible any signal originating within many light-years of them, upon any possible communications band. And constantly at least two men, with every sense concentrated in their ears, were listening to those instruments.

Listening—straining to distinguish in the deafening roar of background noise from the over-driven tubes any sign of voice or of signal:

Listening—while, millions upon millions of miles beyond even the prodigious reach of those ultra-instruments, three human beings were even then sending out into empty space an almost hopeless appeal for the help so desperately needed!

THE SPECIMENS ESCAPE

Knowing well that conversation with its fellows is one of the greatest needs of any intelligent being, the Nevians had permitted the Terrestrial specimens to retain possession of their ultra-beam communicators. Thus it was that Costigan had been able to keep in touch with his sweetheart and with Bradley. He learned that each had been placed upon exhibition in a different Nevian city; that the three had been separated in response to an insistent popular demand for such a distribution of the peculiar, but highly interesting creatures from a distant solar system. They had not been harmed. In fact, each was visited daily by a specialist, who made sure that his charge was being kept in the pink of condition.

As soon as he became aware of this condition of things Costigan became morose. He sat still, drooped, and pined away visibly. He refused to eat, and of the worried specialist he demanded liberty. Then, failing in that as he knew he would fail, he demanded something to *do*. They pointed out to him, reasonably enough, that in such a civilization as theirs there was nothing he could do. They assured him that they would do anything they could to alleviate his mental suffering, but that since he was a museum piece he must see, himself, that he must be kept on display for a short time. Wouldn't he please behave himself and eat, as a reasoning being should? Costigan sulked a little longer, then wavered. Finally he agreed to compromise. He would eat and exercise if they would fit up a laboratory in his apartment, so that he could continue the studies he had begun upon his own native planet. To this they agreed, and thus it came about that one day the following conversation was held:

"Clio? Bradley? I've got something to tell you this time. Haven't said anything before, for fear things might not work out, but they did. I went on a hunger strike and made them give me a complete laboratory. As a chemist I'm a damn good electrician; but luckily, with the sea-water they've got here, it's a very simple thing to make . . . ."

"Hold on!" snapped Bradley. "Somebody may be listening in on us!"

"They aren't. They can't, without my knowing it, and I'll cut off the second anybody tries to synchronize with my beam. To resume—making Vee-Two is a very simple process, and I've got everything around here that's hollow clear full of it . . . ."

"How come they let you?" asked Clio.

"Oh, they don't know what I'm doing. They watched me for a few days, and all I did was make up and bottle the weirdest messes imaginable. Then I finally managed to separate oxygen and nitrogen, after trying hard all of one day; and when they saw that I didn't know anything about either one of them or what to do with them after I had them, they gave me up in disgust as a plain dumb ape and haven't paid any attention to me since. So I've got me plenty of kilograms of liquid Vee-Two, all ready to touch off. I'm getting out of here in about three minutes and a half, and I'm coming over after you folks, in a new, iron-powered space-speedster that they don't know I know anything about. They've just given it its final tests, and it's the slickest thing you ever saw."

"But Conway, dearest, you can't possibly rescue me," Clio's voice broke. "Why, there are thousands of them, all around here. If you can get away, go, dear, but don't . . . ."

"I said I was coming after you, and if I get away I'll be there. A good whiff of this stuff will lay out a thousand of them just as easily as it will one. Here's the idea. I've made a gas mask for myself, since I'll be in it where it's thick, but you two won't need any. It's soluble enough in water so that three or four thicknesses of wet cloth over your noses will be enough. I'll tell you when to wet down. We're going to break away or go out trying—there aren't enough amphibians between here and Andromeda to keep us humans cooped up like menagerie animals forever! But here comes my specialist with the keys to the city; time for the overture to start. See you later!"

The Nevian physician directed his key tube upon the transparent wall of the chamber and an opening appeared, an opening which vanished as soon as he had stepped through it; Costigan kicked a valve open; and from various innocent tubes there belched forth into the water of the central lagoon and into the air over it a flood of deadly vapor. As the Nevian turned toward the prisoner there was an almost inaudible hiss and a tiny jet of the frightful, outlawed stuff struck his open gills, just below his huge, conical head. He tensed momentarily, twitched convulsively just once, and fell motionless to the floor. And outside, the streams of avidly soluble liquefied gas rushed out into air and into water. It spread, dissolved, and diffused with the extreme mobility which is one of its characteristics; and as it diffused and was borne outward the Nevians in their massed hundreds died. Died not knowing what killed them, not knowing even that they died. Costigan, bitterly resentful of the inhuman treatment accorded the three and fiercely anxious for the success of his plan of escape, held his breath and, grimly alert, watched the amphibians die. When he could see no more motion anywhere he donned his gas-mask, strapped upon his back a large canister of the poison—his capacious pockets were already full of smaller containers—and two savagely exultant sentences escaped him.

"I am a poor, ignorant specimen of ape that can be let play with apparatus, am I?" he rasped, as he picked up the key tube of the specialist and opened the door of his prison. "They'll learn now that it ain't safe to judge by the looks of a flea how far he can jump!"

He stepped out through the opening into the water, and, burdened as he was, made shift to swim to the nearest ramp. Up it he ran, toward a main corridor. But ahead of him there was wafted a breath of dread Vee-Two, and where that breath went, went also unconsciousness—an unconsciousness which would deepen gradually into permanent oblivion save for the prompt intervention of one who possessed, not only the necessary antidote, but the equally important knowledge of exactly how to use it. Upon the floor of that corridor were strewn Nevians, who had dropped in their tracks. Past or over their bodies Costigan strode, pausing only to direct a jet of lethal vapor into whatever branching corridor or open door caught his eye. He was going to the intake of the city's ventilation plant, and no unmasked creature dependent for life upon oxygen could bar his path. He reached the intake, tore the canister from his back, and released its full, vast volume of horrid contents into the primary air stream of the entire city.

And all throughout that doomed city Nevians dropped; quietly and without a struggle, unknowing. Busy executives dropped upon their cushioned, flat-topped desks; hurrying travelers and messengers dropped upon the floors of the corridors or relaxed in the noxious waters of the ways; lookouts and observers dropped before their flashing screens; central operators of communications dropped under the winking lights of their panels. Observers and centrals in the outlying sections of the city wondered briefly at the unwonted universal motionlessness and stagnation; then the racing taint in water and in air reached them, too, and they ceased wondering—forever.

Then through those quiet halls Costigan stalked to a certain storage room, where with all due precaution he donned his own suit of Triplanetary armor. Making an ungainly bundle of the other Solarian equipment stored there, he dragged it along behind him as he clanked back toward his prison, until he neared the dock at which was moored the Nevian space-speedster which he was determined to take. Here, he knew, was the first of many critical points. The crew of the vessel was aboard, and, with its independent air-supply, unharmed. They had weapons, were undoubtedly alarmed, and were very probably highly suspicious. They, too, had ultra-beams and might see him, but his very closeness to them would tend to protect him from ultra-beam observation. Therefore he crouched tensely behind a buttress, staring through his spy-ray goggles, waiting for a moment when none of the Nevians would be near the entrance, but grimly resolved to act instantly should he feel any touch of a spying ultra-beam.

"Here's where the pinch comes," he growled to himself. "I know the combinations, but if they're suspicious enough and act quick enough they can seal that door on me before I can get it open, and then rub me out like a blot; but . . . ah!"

The moment had arrived, before the touch of any revealing ray. He trained the key-tube, the entrance opened, and through that opening in the instant of its appearance there shot a brittle bulb of glass, whose breaking meant death. It crashed into fragments against a metallic wall and Costigan, entering the vessel, consigned its erstwhile crew one by one to the already crowded waters of the lagoon. He then leaped to the controls and drove the captured speedster through the air, to plunge it down upon the surface of the lagoon beside the door of the isolated structure which had for so long been his prison. Carefully he transferred to the vessel the motley assortment of containers of Vee-Two, and after a quick check-up to make sure that he had overlooked nothing, he shot his craft straight up into the air. Then only did he close his ultra-wave circuits and speak.

"Clio, Bradley—I got away clean, without a bit of trouble. Now I'm coming after you, Clio."

"Oh, it's wonderful that you got away, Conway!" the girl exclaimed. "But hadn't you better get Captain Bradley first? Then, if anything should happen, he would be of some use, while I . . . ."

"I'll knock him into an outside loop if he does!" the captain snorted, and Costigan went on:

"You won't need to. You come first, Clio, of course. But you're too far away for me to see you with my spy, and I don't want to use the high-powered beam of this boat for fear of detection; so you'd better keep on talking, so that I can trace you."

"That's one thing I *am* good at!" Clio laughed in sheer relief. "If talking were music, I'd be a full brass band!" and she kept up a flow of inconsequential chatter until Costigan told her that it was no longer necessary; that he had established the line.

"Any excitement around there yet?" he asked her then.

"Nothing unusual that I can see," she replied. "Why? Should there be some?"

"I hope not, but when I made my getaway I couldn't kill them all, of course, and I thought maybe they might connect things up with my jail-break and tell the other cities to take steps about you two. But I guess they're pretty well disorganized back there yet, since they can't know who hit them, or what with, or why. I must have got about everybody that wasn't sealed up somewhere, and it doesn't stand to reason that those who are left can check up very closely for a while yet. But they're nobody's fools—they'll certainly get conscious when I snatch you, maybe before . . . there, I see your city, I think."

"What are you going to do?"

"Same as I did back there, if I can. Poison their primary air and all the water I can reach . . . ."

"Oh, Conway!" Her voice rose to a scream. "They must know—they're all getting out of the water and are rushing inside the buildings as fast as they possibly can!"

"I see they are," grimly. "I'm right over you now, 'way up. Been locating their primary intake. They've got a dozen ships around it, and have guards posted all along the corridors leading to it; and *those guards are wearing masks!* They're clever birds, all right, those amphibians—they know what they got back there and how they got it. That changes things, girl! If we use gas here we won't stand a chance in the world of getting old Bradley. Stand by to jump when I open that door!"

"Hurry, dear! They are coming out here after me!"

"Sure they are." Costigan had already seen the two Nevians swimming out toward Clio's cage, and had hurled his vessel downward in a screaming power dive. "You're too valuable a specimen for them to let you be gassed, but if they can get there before I do they're traveling fools!"

He miscalculated slightly, so that instead of coming to a halt at the surface of the liquid medium the speedster struck with a crash that hurled solid masses of water for hundreds of yards. But no ordinary crash could harm that vessel's structure, her gravity controls were not overloaded, and she shot back to the surface; gallant ship and reckless pilot alike unharmed. Costigan trained his key-tube upon the doorway of Clio's cell, then tossed it aside.

"Different combination over here!" he barked. "Got to cut you out—lie down in that far corner!"

His hands flashed over the panel, and as Clio fell prone without hesitation or question a heavy beam literally blasted away a large portion of the roof of the structure. The speedster shot into the air and dropped down until she rested upon the tops of opposite walls; walls still glowing, semi-molten. The girl piled a stool upon the table and stood upon it, reached upward and seized the mailed hands extended downward toward her. Costigan heaved her up into the vessel with a powerful jerk, slammed the door shut, leaped to the controls, and the speedster darted away.

"Your armor's in that bundle there. Better put it on, and check your Lewistons and pistols—no telling what kind of jams we'll get into," he snapped, without turning. "Bradley, start talking . . . all right, I've got your line. Better get your wet rags ready and get organized generally—every second will count by the time we get there. We're coming so fast that our outer plating's white hot, but it may not be fast enough, at that."

"It isn't fast enough, quite," Bradley announced, calmly. "They're coming out after me now."

"Don't fight them and probably they won't paralyze you. Keep on talking, so that I can find out where they take you."

"No good, Costigan." The voice of the old spacehound did not reveal a sign of emotion as he made his dread announcement. "They have it all figured out. They're not taking any chances at all—they're going to paral . . . ." His voice broke off in the middle of the word.

With a bitter imprecation Costigan flashed on the powerful ultra-beam projector of the speedster and focused the plate upon Bradley's prison; careless now of detection, since the Nevians were already warned. Upon that plate he watched the Nevians carry the helpless body of the captain into a small boat, and continued to watch as they bore it into one of the largest buildings of the city. Up a series of ramps they took the still form, placing it finally upon a soft couch in an enormous and heavily guarded central hall. Costigan turned to his companion, and even through the helmets she could see plainly the white agony of his expression. He moistened his lips and tried twice to speak—tried and failed; but he made no move either to cut off their power or to change their direction.

"Of course," she approved steadily. "We are going through. I know that you *want* to run with me, but if you actually did it I would never want to see you or hear of you again, and you would hate me forever."

"Hardly that." The anguish did not leave his eyes and his voice was hoarse and strained, but his hands did not vary the course of the speedster by so much as a hair's breadth. "You're the finest little fellow that ever waved a plume, and I would love you no matter what happened. I'd trade my immortal soul to the devil if it would get you out of this mess, but we're both in it up to our necks and we can't back out now. If they kill him we beat it—he and I both knew that it was on the chance of that happening that I took you first—but as long as all three of us are alive it's all three or none."

"Of course," she said again, as steadily, thrilled this time to the depths of her being by the sheer manhood of him who had thus simply voiced his Code; a man of such fiber that neither love of life nor his infinitely greater love for her could make him lower its high standard. "We are going through. Forget that I am a woman. We are three human beings, fighting a world full of monsters. I am simply one of us three. I will steer your ship, fire your projectors, or throw your bombs. What can I do best?"

"Throw bombs," he directed, briefly. He knew what must be done were they to have even the slightest chance of winning clear. "I'm going to blast a hole down into that auditorium, and when I do you stand by that port and start dropping bottles of perfume. Throw a couple of big ones right down the shaft I make, and the rest of them most anywhere, after I cut the wall open. They'll do good wherever they hit, land or water."

"But Captain Bradley—he'll be gassed, too." Her fine eyes were troubled.

"Can't be helped. I've got the antidote, and it'll work any time under an hour. That'll be lots of time—if we aren't gone in less than ten minutes we'll be staying here. They're bringing in platoons of militia in full armor, and if we don't beat those boys to it we're in for plenty of grief. All right—start throwing!"

The speedster had come to a halt directly over the imposing edifice within which Bradley was incarcerated, and a mighty beam had flared downward, digging a fiery well through floor after floor of stubborn metal. The ceiling of the amphitheater was pierced. The beam expired. Down into that assembly hall there dropped two canisters of Vee-Two, to crash and to fill its atmosphere with imperceptible death. Then the beam flashed on again, this time at maximum power, and with it Costigan burned away half of the entire building. Burned it away until room above room gaped open, shelf-like, to outer atmosphere; the great hall now resembling an over-size pigeon-hole surrounded by smaller ones. Into that largest pigeon-hole the speedster darted, and cushioned desks and benches crashed down; crushed flat under its enormous weight as it came to rest upon the floor.

Every available guard had been thrown into that room, regardless of customary occupation or of equipment. Most of them had been ordinary watchmen, not even wearing masks, and all such were already down. Many, however, were masked, and a few were dressed in full armor. But no portable armor could mount defenses of sufficient power to withstand the awful force of the speedster's weapons, and one flashing swing of a projector swept the hall almost clear of life.

"Can't shoot very close to Bradley with this big beam, but I'll mop up on the rest of them by hand. Stay here and cover me, Clio!" Costigan ordered, and went to open the port.

"I can't—I won't!" Clio replied instantly. "I don't know the controls well enough. I'd kill you or Captain Bradley, sure; but I *can* shoot, and I'm going to!" and she leaped out, close upon his heels.

Thus, flaming Lewiston in one hand and barking automatic in the other, the two mailed figures advanced toward Bradley, now doubly helpless; paralyzed by his enemies and gassed by his friends. For a time the Nevians melted away before them, but as they approached more nearly the couch upon which the captain was they encountered six figures encased in armor fully as capable as their own. The beams of the Lewistons rebounded from that armor in futile pyrotechnics, the bullets of the automatics spattered and exploded impotently against it. And behind that single line of armored guards were massed perhaps twenty unarmored, but masked, soldiers; and scuttling up the ramps leading into the hall were coming the platoons of heavily armored figures which Costigan had previously seen.

Decision instantly made, Costigan ran back toward the speedster, but he was not deserting his companions.

"Keep the good work up!" he instructed the girl as he ran. "I'll pick those jaspers off with a pencil and then stand off the bunch that's coming while you rub out the rest of that crew there and drag Bradley back here."

Back at the control panel, he trained a narrow, but intensely dense beam—quasi-solid lightning—and one by one the six armored figures fell. Then, knowing that Clio could handle the remaining opposition, he devoted his attention to the reenforcements so rapidly approaching from the sides. Again and again the heavy beam lashed out, now upon this side, now upon that, and in its flaming path Nevians disappeared. And not only Nevians—in the incredible energy of that beam's blast floor, walls, ramps, and every material thing vanished in clouds of thick and brilliant vapor. The room temporarily clear of foes, he sprang again to Clio's assistance, but her task was nearly done. She had "rubbed out" all opposition and, tugging lustily at Bradley's feet, had already dragged him almost to the side of the speedster.

"At-a-girl, Clio!" cheered Costigan, as he picked up the burly captain and tossed him through the doorway. "Highly useful, girl of my dreams, as well as ornamental. In with you, and we'll go places!"

But getting the speedster out of the now completely ruined hall proved to be much more of a task than driving it in had been, for scarcely had Costigan closed his locks than a section of the building collapsed behind them, cutting off their retreat. Nevian submarines and airships were beginning to arrive upon the scene, and were beaming the building viciously in an attempt to entrap or to crush the foreigners in its ruins. Costigan managed finally to blast his way out, but the Nevians had had time to assemble in force and he was met by a concentrated storm of beams and of metal from every inimical weapon within range.

But not for nothing had Conway Costigan selected for his dash for liberty the craft which, save only for the two immense interstellar cruisers, was the most powerful vessel ever built upon red Nevia. And not for nothing had he studied minutely and to the last, least detail every item of its controls and of its armament during wearily long days and nights of solitary imprisonment. He had studied it under test, in action, and at rest; studied it until he knew thoroughly its every possibility—and what a ship it was! The atomic-powered generators of his shielding screens handled with ease the terrific load of the Nevians' assault, his polycyclic screens were proof against any material projectile, and the machines supplying his offensive weapons with power were more than equal to their tasks. Driven now at full rating those frightful beams lashed out against the Nevians blocking the way, and under their impacts her screens flared brilliantly through the spectrum and went down. And in the instant of their failure the enemy vessel was literally blown into nothingness—no unprotected metal, however resistant, could exist for a moment in the pathway of those iron-driven tornadoes of pure energy.

Ship after ship of the Nevians plunged toward the speedster in desperately suicidal attempts to ram her down, but each met the same flaming fate before it could reach its target. Then from the grouped submarines far below there reached up red rods of force, which seized the space-ship and began relentlessly to draw her down.

"What are they doing that for, Conway? *They* can't fight us!"

"They don't want to fight us. They want to hold us, but I know what to do about that, too," and the powerful tractor rods snapped as a plane of pure force knifed through them. Upward now at the highest permissible velocity the speedster leaped, and past the few ships remaining above her she dodged; nothing now between her and the freedom of boundless space.

"You did it, Conway; you did it!" Clio exulted. "Oh, Conway, you're just simply wonderful!"

"I haven't done it yet," Costigan cautioned her. "The worst is yet to come. Nerado. He's why they wanted to hold us back, and why I was in such a hurry to get away. That boat of his is bad medicine, girl, and we want to put plenty of kilometers behind us before he gets started."

"But do you think he will chase us?"

"*Think* so? I *know* so! The mere facts that we are rare specimens and that he told us that we were going to stay there all the rest of our lives would make him chase us clear to Lundmark's Nebula. Besides that, we stepped on their toes pretty heavily before we left. We know altogether too much now to be let get back to Tellus; and finally, they'd all die of acute enlargement of the spleen if we get away with this prize ship of theirs. I hope to tell you they'll chase us!"

He fell silent, devoting his whole attention to his piloting, driving his craft onward at such velocity that its outer plating held steadily at the highest point of temperature compatible with safety. Soon they were out in open space, hurtling toward the sun under the drive of every possible watt of power, and Costigan took off his armor and turned toward the helpless body of the captain.

"He looks so . . . so . . . so *dead*, Conway! Are you really sure that you can bring him to?"

"Absolutely. Lots of time yet. Just three simple squirts in the right places will do the trick." He took from a locked compartment of his armor a small steel box, which housed a surgeon's hypodermic and three vials. One, two, three, he injected small, but precisely measured amounts of the fluids into the three vital localities, then placed the inert form upon a deeply cushioned couch.

"There! That'll take care of the gas in five or six hours. The paralysis will wear off long before that, so he'll be all right when he wakes up; and we're going away from here with everything we can put out. I've done everything I know how to do, for the present."

Then only did Costigan turn and look down, directly into Clio's eyes. Wide, eloquent blue eyes that gazed back up into his, tender and unafraid; eyes freighted with the oldest message of woman to chosen man. His hard young face softened wonderfully as he stared at her; there were two quick steps and they were in each other's arms. Lips upon eager lips, blue eyes to gray, motionless they stood clasped in ecstasy; thinking nothing of the dreadful past, nothing of the fearful future, conscious only of the glorious, wonderful present.

"Clio mine . . . darling . . . girl, girl, how I love you!" Costigan's deep voice was husky with emotion. "I haven't kissed you for seven thousand years! I don't rate you, by a million steps; but if I can just get you out of this mess, I swear by all the gods of interplanetary space . . . ."

"You needn't, lover. Rate *me*? Good Heavens, Conway! It's just the other way . . . ."

"Stop it!" he commanded in her ear. "I'm still dizzy at the idea of your loving me at all, to say nothing of loving me *this* way! But you do, and that's all I ask, here or hereafter."

"Love you? *Love* you!" Their mutual embrace tightened and her low voice thrilled brokenly as she went on: "Conway dearest . . . I can't say a thing, but you know . . . . Oh, Conway!"

After a time Clio drew a long and tremulous, but supremely happy breath as the realities of their predicament once more obtruded themselves upon her consciousness. She released herself gently from Costigan's arms.

"Do you really think that there is a chance of us getting back to the Earth, so that we can be together . . . always?"

"A chance, yes. A probability, no," he replied, unequivocally. "It depends upon two things. First, how much of a start we got on Nerado. His ship is the biggest and fastest thing I ever saw, and if he strips her down and drives her—which he will—he'll catch us long before we can make Tellus. On the other hand, I gave Rodebush a lot of data, and if he and Lyman Cleveland can add it to their own stuff and get that super-ship of ours rebuilt in time, they'll be out here on the prowl; and they'll have what it takes to give even Nerado plenty of argument. No use worrying about it, anyway. We won't know anything until we can detect one or the other of them, and then will be the time to do something about it."

"If Nerado catches us, will you . . . ." She paused.

"Rub you out? I will not. Even if he does catch us, and takes us back to Nevia, I won't. There's lots more time coming onto the clock. Nerado won't hurt either of us badly enough to leave scars, either physical, mental, or moral. I'd kill you in a second if it were Roger; he's dirty. He's mean—he's thoroughly bad. But Nerado's a good enough old scout, in his way. He's big and he's clean. You know, I could really like that fish if I could meet him on terms of equality sometime?"

"I couldn't!" she declared vigorously. "He's crawly and scaly and snaky; and he smells so . . . so . . . ."

"So rank and fishy?" Costigan laughed deeply. "Details, girl; mere details. I've seen people who looked like money in the bank and who smelled like a bouquet of violets that you couldn't trust half the length of Nerado's neck."

"But look what he did to us!" she protested. "And they weren't trying to recapture us back there; they were trying to kill us."

"That was perfectly all right, what he did and what they did—what else could they have done?" he wanted to know. "And while you're looking, look at what we did to them—plenty, I'd say. But we all had it to do, and neither side will blame the other for doing it. He's a square shooter, I tell you."

"Well, maybe, but I don't like him a bit, and let's not talk about him any more. Let's talk about us. Remember what you said once, when you advised me to 'let you lay,' or whatever it was?" Woman-like, she wished to dip again lightly into the waters of pure emotion, even though she had such a short time before led the man out of their profoundest depths. But Costigan, into whose hard life love of woman had never before entered, had not yet recovered sufficiently from his soul-shaking plunge to follow her lead. Inarticulate, distrusting his newly found supreme happiness, he must needs stay out of those enchanted waters or plunge again. And he was afraid to plunge—diffident, still deeming himself unworthy of the miracle of this wonder-girl's love—even though every fiber of his being shrieked its demand to feel again that slender body in his arms. He did not consciously think those thoughts. He acted them without thinking; they were prime basics in that which made Conway Costigan what he was.

"I do remember, and I still think it's a sound idea, even though I am too far gone now to let you put it into effect," he assured her, half seriously. He kissed her, tenderly and reverently, then studied her carefully. "But you look as though you'd been on a Martian picnic. When did you eat last?"

"I don't remember, exactly. This morning, I think."

"Or maybe last night, or yesterday morning? I thought so! Bradley and I can eat anything that's chewable, and drink anything that will pour, but you can't. I'll scout around and see if I can't fix up something that you'll be able to eat."

He rummaged through the store-rooms, emerging with sundry viands from which he prepared a highly satisfactory meal.

"Think you can sleep now, sweetheart?" After supper, once more within the circle of Costigan's arms, Clio nodded her head against his shoulder.

"Of course I can, dear. Now that you are with me, out here alone, I'm not a bit afraid any more. You will get us back to Earth some way, sometime; I just know that you will. Good-night, Conway."

"Good-night, Clio . . . little sweetheart," he whispered, and went back to Bradley's side.

In due time the captain recovered consciousness, and slept. Then for days the speedster flashed on toward our distant solar system; days during which her wide-flung detector screens remained cold.

"I don't know whether I'm afraid they'll hit something or afraid that they won't," Costigan remarked more than once, but finally those tenuous sentinels did in fact encounter an interfering vibration. Along the detector line a visibeam sped, and Costigan's face hardened as he saw the unmistakable outline of Nerado's interstellar cruiser, far behind them.

"Well, a stern chase always was a long one," Costigan said finally. "He can't catch us for plenty of days yet . . . now what?" for the alarms of the detectors had broken out anew. There was still another point of interference to be investigated. Costigan traced it, and there, almost dead ahead of them, between them and their sun, nearing them at the incomprehensible rate of the sum of the two vessels' velocities, came another cruiser of the Nevians!

"Must be the sister-ship, coming back from our System with a load of iron," Costigan deduced. "Heavily loaded as she is, we may be able to dodge her; and she's coming so fast that if we can stay out of her range we'll be all right—he won't be able to stop for probably three or four days. But if our super-ship is anywhere in these parts, now's the time for her to rally 'round!"

He gave the speedster all the side-thrust she would take; then, putting every available communicator tube behind a tight beam, he aimed it at Sol and began sending out a long-continued call to his fellows of the Triplanetary Service.

Nearer and nearer the Nevian flashed, trying with all her power to intercept the speedster; and it soon became evident that, heavily laden though she was, she could make enough sideway to bring her within range at the time of meeting.

"Of course, they've got partial neutralization of inertia, the same as we have," Costigan cogitated, "and by the way he's coming I'd say that he had orders to blow us out of the ether—he knows as well as we do that he can't capture us alive at anything like the relative velocities we've got now. I can't give her any more side thrust without overloading the gravity controls, so overloaded they've got to be. Strap down, you two, because they may go out entirely!"

"Do you think that you can pull away from them, Conway?" Clio was staring in horrified fascination into the plate, watching the pictured vessel increase in size, moment by moment.

"I don't know whether I can or not, but I'm going to try. Just in case we don't, though, I'm going to keep on yelling for help. In solid? All right, boat, DO YOUR STUFF!"

SUPER PACK

GIANTS MEET

"Check your blast, Fred, I think that I hear something trying to come through!" Cleveland called out, sharply. For days the *Boise* had torn through the illimitable reaches of empty space, and now the long vigil of the keen-eared listeners was to be ended. Rodebush cut off his power, and through the crackling roar of tube noise an almost inaudible voice made itself heard.

" . . . all the help you can give us. Samms—Cleveland—Rodebush—anybody of Triplanetary who can hear me, listen! This is Costigan, with Miss Marsden and Captain Bradley, heading for where we think the sun is, from right ascension about six hours, declination about plus fourteen degrees. Distance unknown, but probably a good many light-years. Trace my call. One Nevian ship is overhauling us slowly, another is coming toward us from the sun. We may or may not be able to dodge it, but we need all the help you can give us. Samms—Rodebush—Cleveland—anybody of Triplanetary . . . ."

Endlessly the faint, faint voice went on, but Rodebush and Cleveland were no longer listening. Sensitive ultra-loops had been swung, and along the indicated line shot Triplanetary's super-ship at a velocity which she had never before even approached; the utterly incomprehensible, almost incalculable velocity attained by inertialess matter driven through an almost perfect vacuum by the *Boise's* maximum projector blasts—a blast which would lift her stupendous normal tonnage against a gravity five times that of Earth. At the full frightful measure of that velocity the super-ship literally annihilated distance, while ahead of her the furiously driven spy-ray beam fanned out in quest of the three Triplanetarians who were calling for help.

"Got any idea how fast we're going?" Rodebush demanded, glancing up for an instant from the observation plate. "We should be able to see him, since we could hear him, and our range is certainly as great as anything he can have."

"No. Can't figure velocity without any reliable data on how many atoms of matter exist per cubic meter out here." Cleveland was staring at the calculator. "It's constant, of course, at the value at which the friction of the medium is equal to our thrust. Incidentally, we can't hold it too long. We're running a temperature, which shows that we're stepping along faster than anybody ever computed before. Also, it points out the necessity for something that none of us ever anticipated needing in an open-space drive—refrigerators or radiating wall-shields or repellers or something of the sort. But to get back to our velocity—taking Throckmorton's estimates it figures somewhere near the order of magnitude of ten to the twenty-seventh. Fast enough, anyway, so that you'd better bend an eye on that plate. Even after you see them you won't know where they really are, because we don't know any of the velocities involved—our own, theirs, or that of the beam—and we may be right on top of them."

"Or, if we happen to be outrunning the beam, we won't see them at all. That makes it nice piloting."

"How are you going to handle things when we get there?"

"Lock to them and take them aboard, if we're in time. If not, if they are fighting already—*there they are!*"

The picture of the speedster's control room flashed upon the speaker.

"Hi, Fritz! Hi, Cleve! Welcome to our city! Where are you?"

"We don't know," Cleveland snapped back, "and we don't know where you are, either. Can't figure anything without data. I see you're still breathing air. Where are the Nevians? How much time have we got yet?"

"Not enough, I'm afraid. By the looks of things they will be within range of us in a couple of hours, and you haven't even touched our detector screen yet."

"A couple of *hours!*" In his relief Cleveland shouted the words. "That's time to burn—we can be just about out of the Galaxy in that . . . ." He broke off at a yell from Rodebush.

"Broadcast, Spud, BROADCAST!" the physicist had cried, as Costigan's image had disappeared utterly from his plate.

He cut off the *Boise's* power, stopping her instantaneously in mid-space, but the connection had been broken. Costigan could not possibly have heard the orders to change his beam signal to a broadcast, so that they could pick it up; nor would it have done any good if he had heard and had obeyed. So immeasurably great had been their velocity that they had flashed past the speedster and were now unknown thousands—or millions—of miles beyond the fugitives they had come so far to help; far beyond the range of any possible broadcast. But Cleveland understood instantly what had happened. He now had a little data upon which to work, and his hands flew over the keys of the calculator.

"Back blast, at maximum, seventeen seconds!" he directed crisply. "Not exact, of course, but that will put us close enough so that we can find 'em with our detectors."

For the calculated seventeen seconds the super-ship retraced her path, at the same awful speed with which she had come so far. The blast expired and there, plainly limned upon the observation plates, was the Nevian speedster.

"As a computer, you're good, Cleve," Rodebush applauded. "So close that we can't use the neutralizers to catch him. If we use one dyne of drive we'll overshoot a million kilometers before I could snap the switch."

"And yet he's so far away and going so fast that if we keep our inertia on it'll take all day at full blast to overtake—no, wait a minute—we could *never* catch him." Cleveland was puzzled. "What to do? Shunt in a potentiometer?"

"No, we don't need it." Rodebush turned to the transmitter. "Costigan! We are going to take hold of you with a very light tractor—a tracer, really—and whatever you do, DON'T CUT IT, or we can't reach you in time. It may look like a collision, but it won't be—we'll just touch you, without even a jar."

"A tractor—inertialess?" Cleveland wondered.

"Sure. Why not?" Rodebush set up the beam at its absolute minimum of power and threw in the switch.

While hundreds of thousands of miles separated the two vessels and the attractor was exerting the least effort of which it was capable, yet the super-ship leaped toward the smaller craft at a pace which covered the intervening distance in almost no time at all. So rapidly were the objectives enlarging upon the plates that the automatic focusing devices could scarcely function rapidly enough to keep them in place. Cleveland flinched involuntarily and seized his arm-rests in a spasmodic clutch as he watched this, the first inertialess space-approach; and even Rodebush, who knew better than anyone else what to expect, held his breath and swallowed hard at the unbelievable rate at which the two vessels were rushing together.

And if these two, who had rebuilt the super-ship, could hardly control themselves, what of the three in the speedster, who knew nothing whatever of the wonder-craft's potentialities? Clio, staring into the plate with Costigan, uttered one piercing shriek as she sank her fingers into his shoulders. Bradley swore a mighty deep-space oath and braced himself against certain annihilation. Costigan stared for an instant, unable to believe his eyes; then, in spite of the warning, his hand darted toward the studs which would cut the beam. Too late. Before his flying fingers could reach the buttons the *Boise* was upon them; had struck the speedster in direct central impact. Moving at the full measure of her unthinkable velocity though the super-ship was in the instant of impact, yet the most delicate recording instruments of the speedster could not detect the slightest shock as the enormous globe struck the comparatively tiny torpedo and clung to it; accommodating instantaneously and effortlessly her own terrific pace to that of the smaller and infinitely slower craft. Clio sobbed in relief and Costigan, one arm around her, sighed hugely.

"Hey, you spacelugs!" he cried. "Glad to see you, and all that, but you might as well kill a man outright as scare him to death! So *that's* the super-ship, huh? *Some* ship!"

"Hi-ya, Murf! Hi, Spud!" came from the speaker.

"Murf? Spud? How come?" Clio, practically recovered now, glanced upward questioningly. It was plain that she did not quite know whether or not to like the nicknames which the rescuers were calling her Conway.

"My middle name is Murphy, so they've called me things like that ever since I was so high." Costigan indicated a length of approximately twelve inches. "And now you'll probably live long enough—I hope—to hear me called a lot worse stuff than that."

"Don't *talk* that way—we're safe now, Con . . . Spud? It's nice that they like you so much—but they would, of course." She snuggled even closer, and both listened to what Rodebush was saying.

" . . . realize myself that it would look so bad; it scared me as much as it did anybody. Yes, this is IT. She really works—thanks more than somewhat to Conway Costigan, by the way. But you had better transfer. If you'll get your things . . . ."

"'Things' is good!" Costigan laughed, and Clio giggled sunnily.

"We've made so many transfers already that what you see is all we've got," Bradley explained. "We'll bring ourselves, and we'll hurry. That Nevian is coming up fast."

"Is there anything on this ship you fellows want?" Costigan asked.

"There may be, but we haven't any locks big enough to let her inside and we haven't time to study her now. You might leave her controls in neutral, so that we can calculate her position if we should want her later on."

"All right." The three armor-clad figures stepped into the *Boise's* open lock, the tractor beam was cut off, and the speedster flashed away from the now stationary super-ship.

"Better let formalities go for a while," Captain Bradley interrupted the general introductions taking place. "I was scared out of nine years' growth when I saw you coming at us, and maybe I've still got the humps; but that Nevian is coming up fast, and if you don't already know it I can tell you that she's *no light cruiser.*"

"That's so, too," Costigan agreed. "Have you fellows got enough stuff so that you think you can take him? You've got the legs on him, anyway—you can certainly run if you want to!"

"Run?" Cleveland laughed. "We have a bone of our own to pick with that ship. We licked her to a standstill once, until we burned out a set of generators, and since we got them fixed we've been chasing her all over space. We were chasing her when we picked up your call. See there? She's doing the running."

The Nevian was running, in truth. Her commander had seen and had recognized the great vessel which had flashed out of nowhere to the rescue of the three fugitives from Nevia; and, having once been at grips with that vengeful super-dreadnaught, he had little stomach for another encounter. Therefore his side-thrust was now being exerted in the opposite direction; he was frankly trying to put as much distance as possible between himself and Triplanetary's formidable warship. In vain. A light tractor was clamped on and the *Boise* flashed up to close range before Rodebush restored her inertia and Cleveland brought the two vessels relatively to rest by increasing gradually his tractor's pull. And this time the Nevian could not cut the tractor. Again that shearing plane of force bit into it and tore at it, but it neither yielded nor broke. The rebuilt generators of Number Four were designed to carry the load, and they carried it. And again Triplanetary's every mighty weapon was brought into play.

The "cans" were thrown, ultra-and infra-beams were driven, the furious macro-beam gnawed hungrily at the Nevian's defenses; and one by one those defenses went down. In desperation the enemy commander threw his every generator behind a polycyclic screen; only to see Cleveland's even more powerful drill bore relentlessly through it. After that puncturing, the end came soon. A secondary SX7 beam was now in place on mighty Ten's inner rings, and one fierce blast blew a hole completely through the Nevian cruiser. Into that hole entered Adlington's terrific bombs and their gruesome fellows, and where they entered, life departed. All defenses vanished, and under the blasts of the *Boise's* batteries, now unopposed, the metal of the Nevian vessel exploded into a widely spreading cloud of vapor. Sparkling vapor, with perhaps here and there a droplet or two of material which had been only liquefied.

So passed the sister-ship, and Rodebush turned his plates upon the vessel of Nerado. But that highly intelligent amphibian had seen all that had occurred. He had long since given over the pursuit of the speedster, and he did not rush in to do hopeless battle beside his fellow Nevians against the Tellurians. His analytical detectors had written down each detail of every weapon and of every screen employed; and even while prodigious streamers of force were raving out from his vessel, braking her terrific progress and swinging her around in an immense circle back toward far Nevia, his scientists and mechanics were doubling and redoubling the power of his already Titanic installations, to match and if possible to overmatch those of Triplanetary's super-dreadnaught.

"Do we kill him now or do we let him suffer a while longer?" Costigan demanded.

"I don't think so, yet," Rodebush replied. "Would you, Cleve?"

"Not yet," said Cleveland, grimly, reading the other's thought and agreeing with it. "Let him pilot us to Nevia; we might not be able to find it without a guide. While we're at it we want to so pulverize that crowd that if they never come near the Solarian system again they'll think it's twenty minutes too soon."

Thus it was that the *Boise*, increasing her few dynes of driving force at a rate just sufficient to match her quarry's acceleration, pursued the Nevian ship. Apparently exerting every effort, she never came quite within range of the fleeing raider; yet never was she so far behind that the Nevian space-ship was not in clear register upon her observation plates.

Nor was Nerado alone in strengthening his vessel. Costigan knew well and respected highly the Nevian scientist-captain, and at his suggestion much time was spent in reenforcing the super-ship's armament to the iron-driven limit of theoretical and mechanical possibility.

In mid-space, however, the Nevian slowed down.

"What gives?" Rodebush demanded of the group at large. "Not turn-over time already, is it?"

"No." Cleveland shook his head. "Not for at least a day yet."

"Cooking up something on Nevia, is my guess," Costigan put in. "If I know that lizard at all, he wired ahead—specifications for the welcoming committee. We're getting there too fast, so he's stalling. Check?"

"Check." Rodebush agreed. "But there's no use of us waiting, if you're sure you know which one of those stars up ahead is Nevia. Do you, Cleve?"

"Definitely."

"The only other thing is, then, shall we blow them out of the ether first?"

"You might try," Costigan remarked. "That is, if you're damned sure that you can run if you have to."

"Huh? *Run?*" demanded Rodebush.

"Just that. It's spelled R-U-N, run. I know those freaks better than you do. Believe me, Fritz, they've got what it takes."

"Could be, at that," Rodebush admitted. "We'll play it safe."

The *Boise* leaped upon the Nevian, every weapon aflame. But, as Costigan had expected, Nerado's vessel was completely ready for any emergency. And, unlike her sister-ship, she was manned by scientists well versed in the fundamental theory of the weapons with which they fought. Beams, rods, and lances of energy flamed and flared; planes and pencils cut, slashed, and stabbed; defensive screens glowed redly or flashed suddenly into intensely brilliant, coruscating incandescence. Crimson opacity struggled sullenly against violet curtain of annihilation. Material projectiles and torpedoes were launched under full beam control; only to be exploded harmlessly in mid-space, to be blasted into nothingness, or to disappear innocuously against impenetrable polycyclic screens. Even Cleveland's drill was ineffective. Both vessels were equipped completely with iron-driven mechanisms; both were manned by scientists capable of wringing the highest possible measure of power from their installations. Neither could harm the other.

The *Boise* flashed away; reached Nevia in minutes. Down into the crimson atmosphere she dropped, down toward the city which Costigan knew was Nerado's home port.

"Hold up a bit!" Costigan cautioned, sharply. "There's something down there that I don't like!"

As he spoke there shot upward from the city a multitude of flashing balls. The Nevians had mastered the secret of the explosive of the fishes of the greater deeps, and were launching it in a veritable storm against the Tellurian visitor.

"Those?" asked Rodebush, calmly. The detonating balls of destruction were literally annihilating even the atmosphere beyond the polycyclic screen, but that barrier was scarcely affected.

"No. That." Costigan pointed out a hemispherical dome which, redly translucent, surrounded a group of buildings towering high above their neighbors. "Neither those high towers nor those screens were there the last time I was in this town. Nerado *was* stalling for time, and that's what they're doing down there—that's all those fire-balls are for. Good sign, too—they aren't ready for us yet. We'd better take'em while the taking's good. If they *were* ready for us, our play would be to get out of here while we're all in one piece."

Nerado had been in touch with the scientists of his city; he had been instructing them in the construction of converters and generators of such weight and power that they could crush even the defenses of the super-ship. The mechanisms were not, however, ready; the entirely unsuspected possibilities of speed inherent in absolute inertialessness had not entered into Nerado's calculations.

"Better drop a few cans down onto that dome, fellows," Rodebush suggested to his gunners.

"We can't," came Adlington's instant reply. "No use trying it—that's a polycyclic screen. Can you drill it? If you can, I've got a real bomb here—that special we built—that will do the trick if you can protect it from them until it gets down into the water."

"I'll try it," Cleveland answered, at a nod from the physicist. "I couldn't drill Nerado's polycyclics, but I couldn't use any momentum on him. Couldn't ram him—he fell back with my thrust. But that screen down there can't back away from us, so maybe I can work on it. Get your special ready. Hang on, everybody!"

The *Boise* looped upward, and from an altitude of miles dove straight down through a storm of force-balls, beams, and shells; a dive checked abruptly as the hollow tube of energy which was Cleveland's drill snarled savagely down ahead of her and struck the shielding hemisphere with a grinding, lightning-spitting shock. As it struck, backed by all the enormous momentum of the plunging space-ship and driven by the full power of her prodigious generators it bored in, clawing and gouging viciously through the tissues of that rigid and unyielding barrier of pure energy. Then, mighty drill and plunging mass against iron-driven wall, eye-tearing and furiously spectacular warfare was waged.

Well it was for Triplanetary that day that its super-ship carried ample supplies of allotropic iron; well it was that her originally Gargantuan converters and generators had been doubled and quadrupled in power on the long Nevian way! For that ocean-girdled fortress was powered to withstand any conceivable assault—but the *Boise's* power and momentum were now inconceivable; and every watt and every dyne was solidly behind that hellishly flaming, that voraciously tearing, that irresistibly ravening cylinder of energy incredible!

Through the Nevian shield that cylinder gnawed its frightful way, and down its protecting length there drove Adlington's "Special" bomb. "Special" it was indeed; so great of girth that it could barely pass through the central orifice of Ten's mighty projector, so heavily charged with sensitized atomic iron that its detonation upon any planet would not have been considered for an instant if that planet's integrity meant anything to its attackers. Down the shielding pipe of force the "Special" screamed under full propulsion, and beneath the surface of Nevia's ocean it plunged.

"Cut!" yelled Adlington, and as the scintillating drill expired the bomber pressed his detonating switch.

For moments the effect of the explosion seemed unimportant. A dull, low rumble was all that was to be heard of a concussion that jarred red Nevia to her very center; and all that could be seen was a slow heaving of the water. But that heaving did not cease. Slowly, *so* slowly it seemed to the observers now high in the heavens, the waters rose up and parted; revealing a vast chasm blown deep into the ocean's rocky bed. Higher and higher the lazy mountains of water reared; effortlessly to pick up, to smash, to grind into fragments, and finally to toss aside every building, every structure, every scrap of material substance pertaining to the whole Nevian city.

Flattened out, driven backward for miles, the buffeted waters were pressed, leaving exposed bare ground and broken rock where once had been the ocean's busy floor. Tremendous blasts of incandescent gas raved upward, jarring even the enormous mass of the super-ship poised so high above the site of the explosion. Then the displaced millions of tons of water rushed to make even more complete the already total destruction of the city. The raging torrents poured into that yawning cavern, filled it, and piled mountainously above it; receding and piling up, again and again; causing tidal waves which swept a full half of Nevia's mighty, watery globe. That city was silenced—forever.

"MY . . . GOD!" Cleveland was the first to break the awed, the stunned, silence. He licked his lips. "But we had it to do . . . and at that, it's not as bad as what they did to Pittsburgh—they would have evacuated all except military personnel."

"Of course . . . what next?" asked Rodebush. "Look around, I suppose, to see if they have any more . . . ."

"Oh, no, Conway—no! Don't let them!" Clio was sobbing openly. "I'm going to my room and crawl under the bed—I'll see that sight all the rest of my life!"

"Steady, Clio." Costigan's arm tightened around her. "We'll have to look, but we won't find any more. One—if they could have finished it—would have been enough."

Again and again the *Boise* circled the world. No more super-powered installations were being built. And, surprisingly enough, the Nevians made no demonstration of hostility.

"I wonder why?" Rodebush mused. "Of course, we aren't attacking them, either, but you'd think . . . do you suppose that they are waiting for Nerado?"

"Probably." Costigan paused in thought. "We'd better wait for him, too. We can't leave things this way."

"But if we can't force engagement . . . a stalemate . . . ." Cleveland's voice was troubled.

"We'll do *something*!" Costigan declared. "This thing has got to be settled, some way or other, before we leave here. First, try talking. I've got an idea that . . . anyway, it can't do any harm, and I know that he can hear and understand you."

Nerado arrived. Instead of attacking, his ship hung quietly poised, a mile or two away from the equally undemonstrative *Boise*. Rodebush directed a beam.

"Captain Nerado, I am Rodebush of Triplanetary. What do you wish to do about this situation?"

"I wish to talk to you." The Nevian's voice came clearly from the speaker. "You are, I now perceive, a much higher form of life than any of us had thought possible; a form perhaps as high in evolution as our own. It is a pity that we did not take the time for a full meeting of minds when we first neared your planet, so that much life, both Tellurian and Nevian, might have been spared. But what is past cannot be recalled. As reasoning beings, however, you will see the futility of continuing a combat in which neither is capable of winning victory over the other. You may, of course, destroy more of our Nevian cities, in which case I should be compelled to go and destroy similarly upon your Earth; but, to reasoning minds, such a course would be sheerest stupidity."

Rodebush cut the communicator beam.

"Does he mean it?" he demanded of Costigan. "It sounds perfectly reasonable, but . . . ."

"But fishy!" Cleveland broke in. "Altogether too reasonable to be true!"

"He means it. He means every word of it," Costigan assured his fellows. "I had an idea that he would take it that way. That's the way they are. Reasonable; passionless. Funny—they lack a lot of things that we have; but they've got stuff that I wish more of us Tellurians had, too. Give me the plate—I'll talk for Triplanetary," and the beam was restored.

"Captain Nerado," he greeted the Nevian commander. "Having been with you and among your people, I know that you mean what you say and that you speak for your race. Similarly, I believe that I can speak for the Triplanetary Council—the governing body of three of the planets of our solar system—in saying that there is no need for any more conflict between our peoples. I also was compelled by circumstances to do certain things which I now wish could be undone; but as you have said, the past is past. Our two races have much to gain from each other by friendly exchanges of materials and of ideas, while we can expect nothing except mutual extermination if we elect to continue this warfare. I offer you the friendship of Triplanetary. Will you release your screens and come aboard to sign a treaty?"

"My screens are down. I will come." Rodebush likewise cut off his power, although somewhat apprehensively, and a Nevian lifeboat entered the main airlock of the *Boise*.

Then, at a table in the control room of Triplanetary's first super-ship, there was written the first Inter-Systemic Treaty. Upon one side were the three Nevians; amphibious, cone-headed, loop-necked, scaly, four-legged things to us monstrosities: upon the other were human beings; air-breathing, round-headed, short-necked, smooth-bodied, two-legged creatures equally monstrous to the fastidious Nevians. Yet each of these representatives of two races so different felt respect for the other race increase within him minute by minute as the conversation went on.

The Nevians had destroyed Pittsburgh, but Adlington's bomb had blown an important Nevian city completely out of existence. One Nevian vessel had wiped out a Triplanetarian fleet; but Costigan had depopulated one Nevian city, had seriously damaged another, and had beamed down many Nevian ships. Therefore loss of life and material damage could be balanced off. The Solarian System was rich in iron, to which the Nevians were welcome; red Nevia possessed abundant stores of substances which upon Earth were either rare or of vital importance, or both. Therefore commerce was to be encouraged. The Nevians had knowledges and skills unknown to Earthly science, but were entirely ignorant of many things commonplace to us. Therefore interchange of students and of books was highly desirable. And so on.

Thus was signed the Triplanetario-Nevian Treaty of Eternal Peace. Nerado and his two companions were escorted ceremoniously to their vessel, and the *Boise* took off inertialess for Earth, bearing the good news that the Nevian menace was no more.

Clio, now a hardened spacehound, immune even to the horrible nausea of inertialessness, wriggled lithely in the curve of Costigan's arm and laughed up at him.

"You can talk all you want to, Conway Murphy Spud Costigan, but I don't like them the least little bit. They give me goose-bumps all over. I suppose that they are really estimable folks; talented, cultured, and everything; but just the same I'll bet that it will be a long, long time before anybody on Earth will really, truly *like* them!"

FIRST LENSMAN

CHAPTER 1

The visitor, making his way unobserved through the crowded main laboratory of The Hill, stepped up to within six feet of the back of a big Norwegian seated at an electrono-optical bench. Drawing an automatic pistol, he shot the apparently unsuspecting scientist seven times, as fast as he could pull the trigger; twice through the brain, five times, closely spaced, through the spine.

"Ah, Gharlane of Eddore, I have been expecting you to look me up. Sit down." Blonde, blue-eyed Dr. Nels Bergenholm, completely undisturbed by the passage of the stream of bullets through his head and body, turned and waved one huge hand at a stool beside his own.

"But those were not ordinary projectiles!" the visitor protested. Neither person—or rather, entity—was in the least surprised that no one else had paid any attention to what had happened, but it was clear that the one was taken aback by the failure of his murderous attack. "They should have volatilized that form of flesh—should at least have blown you back to Arisia, where you belong."

"Ordinary or extraordinary, what matter? As you, in the guise of Gray Roger, told Conway Costigan a short time since, 'I permitted that, as a demonstration of futility.' Know, Gharlane, once and for all, that you will no longer be allowed to act directly against any adherent of Civilization, wherever situate. We of Arisia will not interfere in person with your proposed conquest of the two galaxies as you have planned it, since the stresses and conflicts involved are necessary—and, I may add, sufficient—to produce the Civilization which must and shall come into being. Therefore, neither will you, or any other Eddorian, so interfere. You will go back to Eddore and you will stay there."

"Think you so?" Gharlane sneered. "You, who have been so afraid of us for over two thousand million Tellurian years that you dared not let us even learn of you? So afraid of us that you dared not take any action to avert the destruction of any one of your budding Civilizations upon any one of the worlds of either galaxy? So afraid that you dare not, even now, meet me mind to mind, but insist upon the use of this slow and unsatisfactory oral communication between us?"

"Either your thinking is loose, confused, and turbid, which I do not believe to be the case, or you are trying to lull me into believing that you are stupid." Bergenholm's voice was calm, unmoved. "I do not *think* that you will go back to Eddore; I know it. You, too, as soon as you have become informed upon certain matters, will know it. You protest against the use of spoken language because it is, as you know, the easiest, simplest, and surest way of preventing you from securing any iota of the knowledge for which you are so desperately searching. As to a meeting of our two minds, they met fully just before you, operating as Gray Roger, remembered that which your entire race forgot long ago. As a consequence of that meeting I so learned every line and vibration of your life pattern as to be able to greet you by your symbol, Gharlane of Eddore, whereas you know nothing of me save that I am an Arisian, a fact which has been obvious from the first."

In an attempt to create a diversion, Gharlane released the zone of compulsion which he had been holding; but the Arisian took it over so smoothly that no human being within range was conscious of any change.

"It is true that for many cycles of time we concealed our existence from you," Bergenholm went on without a break. "Since the reason for that concealment will still further confuse you, I will tell you what it was. Had you Eddorians learned of us sooner you might have been able to forge a weapon of power sufficient to prevent the accomplishment of an end which is now certain.

"It is true that your operations as Lo Sung of Uighar were not constrained. As Mithridates of Pontus—as Sulla, Marius, and Nero of Rome—as Hannibal of Carthage—as those self-effacing wights Alcixerxes of Greece and Menocoptes of Egypt—as Genghis Khan and Attila and the Kaiser and Mussolini and Hitler and the Tyrant of Asia—you were allowed to do as you pleased. Similar activities upon Rigel Four, Velantia, Palain Seven, and elsewhere were also allowed to proceed without effective opposition. With the appearance of Virgil Samms, however, the time arrived to put an end to your customary pernicious, obstructive, and destructive activities. I therefore interposed a barrier between you and those who would otherwise be completely defenseless against you."

"But why now? Why not thousands of cycles ago? And why Virgil Samms?"

"To answer those questions would be to give you valuable data. You may—too late—be able to answer them yourself. But to continue: you accuse me, and all Arisia, of cowardice; an evidently muddy and inept thought. Reflect, please, upon the completeness of your failure in the affair of Roger's planetoid; upon the fact that you have accomplished nothing whatever since that time; upon the situation in which you now find yourself.

"Even though the trend of thought of your race is basically materialistic and mechanistic, and you belittle ours as being 'philosophic' and 'impractical', you found—much to your surprise—that your most destructive physical agencies are not able to affect even this form of flesh which I am now energizing, to say nothing of affecting the reality which is I.

"If this episode is the result of the customary thinking of the second-in-command of Eddore's Innermost Circle . . . but no, my visualization cannot be that badly at fault. Overconfidence—the tyrant's innate proclivity to underestimate an opponent—these things have put you into a false position; but I greatly fear that they will not operate to do so in any really important future affair."

"Rest assured that they will not!" Gharlane snarled. "It may not be—exactly—cowardice. It is, however, something closely akin. If you could have acted effectively against us at any time in the past, you would have done so. If you could act effectively against us now, you would be acting, not talking. That is elementary—self-evidently true. So true that you have not tried to deny it—nor would you expect me to believe you if you did." Cold black eyes stared level into icy eyes of Norwegian blue.

"Deny it? No. I am glad, however, that you used the word 'effectively' instead of 'openly'; for we have been acting effectively against you ever since these newly-formed planets cooled sufficiently to permit of the development of intelligent life."

"What? You have? How?"

"That, too, you may learn—too late. I have now said all I intend to say. I will give you no more information. Since you already know that there are more adult Arisians than there are Eddorians, so that at least one of us can devote his full attention to blocking the direct effort of any one of you, it is clear to you that it makes no difference to me whether you elect to go or to stay. I can and I will remain here as long as you do; I can and I will accompany you whenever you venture out of the volume of space protected by Eddorian screen, wherever you go. The election is yours."

Gharlane disappeared. So did the Arisian—instantaneously. Dr. Nels Bergenholm, however, remained. Turning, he resumed his work where he had left off, knowing exactly what he had been doing and exactly what he was going to do to finish it. He released the zone of compulsion, which he had been holding upon every human being within sight or hearing, so dexterously that no one suspected, then or ever, that anything out of the ordinary had happened. He knew these things and did these things in spite of the fact that the form of flesh which his fellows of the Triplanetary Service knew as Nels Bergenholm was then being energized, not by the stupendously powerful mind of Drounli the Molder, but by an Arisian child too young to be of any use in that which was about to occur.

Arisia was ready. Every Arisian mind capable of adult, or of even near-adult thinking was poised to act when the moment of action should come. They were not, however, tense. While not in any sense routine, that which they were about to do had been foreseen for many cycles of time. They knew exactly what they were going to do, and exactly how to do it. They waited.

"My visualization is not entirely clear concerning the succession of events stemming from the fact that the fusion of which Drounli is a part did not destroy Gharlane of Eddore while he was energizing Gray Roger," a young Watchman, Eukonidor by symbol, thought into the assembled mind. "May I take a moment of this idle time in which to spread my visualization, for enlargement and instruction?"

"You may, youth." The Elders of Arisia—the mightiest intellects of that tremendously powerful race—fused their several minds into one mind and gave approval. "That will be time well spent. Think on."

"Separated from the other Eddorians by inter-galactic distance as he then was, Gharlane could have been isolated and could have been destroyed," the youth pointed out, as he somewhat diffidently spread his visualization in the public mind. "Since it is axiomatic that his destruction would have weakened Eddore somewhat and to that extent would have helped us, it is evident that some greater advantage will accrue from allowing him to live. Some points are clear enough: that Gharlane and his fellows will believe that the Arisian fusion could not kill him, since it did not; that the Eddorians, contemptuous of our powers and thinking us vastly their inferiors, will not be driven to develop such things as atomic-energy-powered mechanical screens against third-level thought until such a time as it will be too late for even those devices to save their race from extinction; that they will, in all probability, never even suspect that the Galactic Patrol which is so soon to come into being will in fact be the prime operator in that extinction. It is not clear, however, in view of the above facts, why it has now become necessary for us to slay one Eddorian upon Eddore. Nor can I formulate or visualize with any clarity the techniques to be employed in the final wiping out of the race; I lack certain fundamental data concerning events which occurred and conditions which obtained many, many cycles before my birth. I am unable to believe that my perception and memory could have been so imperfect—can it be that none of that basic data is, or ever has been available?"

"That, youth, is the fact. While your visualization of the future is of course not as detailed nor as accurate as it will be after more cycles of labor, your background of knowledge is as complete as that of any other of our number."

"I see." Eukonidor gave the mental equivalent of a nod of complete understanding. "It is necessary, and the death of a lesser Eddorian—a Watchman—will be sufficient. Nor will it be either surprising or alarming to Eddore's Innermost Circle that the integrated total mind of Arisia should be able to kill such a relatively feeble entity. I see."

Then silence; and waiting. Minutes? Or days? Or weeks? Who can tell? What does time mean to any Arisian?

Then Drounli arrived; arrived in the instant of his leaving The Hill—what matters even inter-galactic distance to the speed of thought? He fused his mind with those of the three other Molders of Civilization. The massed and united mind of Arisia, poised and ready, awaiting only his coming, launched itself through space. That tremendous, that theretofore unknown concentration of mental force arrived at Eddore's outer screen in practically the same instant as did the entity that was Gharlane. The Eddorian, however, went through without opposition; the Arisians did not.

*

Some two thousand million years ago, when the Coalescence occurred—the event which was to make each of the two interpassing galaxies teem with planets—the Arisians were already an ancient race; so ancient that they were even then independent of the chance formation of planets. The Eddorians, it is believed, were older still. The Arisians were native to this, our normal space-time continuum; the Eddorians were not.

Eddore was—and is—huge, dense, and hot. Its atmosphere is not air, as we of small, green Terra, know air, but is a noxious mixture of gaseous substances known to mankind only in chemical laboratories. Its hydrosphere, while it does contain some water, is a poisonous, stinking, foully corrosive, slimy and sludgy liquid.

And the Eddorians were as different from any people we know as Eddore is different from the planets indigenous to our space and time. They were, to our senses, utterly monstrous; almost incomprehensible. They were amorphous, amoeboid, sexless. Not androgynous or parthenogenetic, but absolutely sexless; with a sexlessness unknown in any Earthly form of life higher than the yeasts. Thus they were, to all intents and purposes and except for death by violence, immortal; for each one, after having lived for hundreds of thousands of Tellurian years and having reached its capacity to live and to learn, simply divided into two new individuals, each of which, in addition to possessing in full its parent's mind and memories and knowledges, had also a brand-new zest and a greatly increased capacity.

And, since life was, there had been competition. Competition for power. Knowledge was worth while only insofar as it contributed to power. Warfare began, and aged, and continued; the appallingly efficient warfare possible only to such entities as those. Their minds, already immensely powerful, grew stronger and stronger under the stresses of internecine struggle.

But peace was not even thought of. Strife continued, at higher and even higher levels of violence, until two facts became apparent. First, that every Eddorian who could be killed by physical violence had already died; that the survivors had developed such tremendous powers of mind, such complete mastery of things physical as well as mental, that they could not be slain by physical force. Second, that during the ages through which they had been devoting their every effort to mutual extermination, their sun had begun markedly to cool; that their planet would very soon become so cold that it would be impossible for them ever again to live their normal physical lives.

Thus there came about an armistice. The Eddorians worked together—not without friction—in the development of mechanisms by the use of which they moved their planet across light-years of space to a younger, hotter sun. Then, Eddore once more at its hot and reeking norm, battle was resumed. Mental battle, this time, that went on for more than a hundred thousand Eddorian years; during the last ten thousand of which not a single Eddorian died.

Realizing the futility of such unproductive endeavor, the relatively few survivors made a peace of sorts. Since each had an utterly insatiable lust for power, and since it had become clear that they could neither conquer nor kill each other, they would combine forces and conquer enough planets—enough galaxies—so that each Eddorian could have as much power and authority as he could possibly handle.

What matter that there were not that many planets in their native space? There were other spaces, an infinite number of them; some of which, it was mathematically certain, would contain millions upon millions of planets instead of only two or three. By mind and by machine they surveyed the neighboring continua; they developed the hyper-spatial tube and the inertialess drive; they drove their planet, space-ship-wise, through space after space after space.

And thus, shortly after the Coalescence began, Eddore came into our space-time; and here, because of the multitudes of planets already existing and the untold millions more about to come into existence, it stayed. Here was what they had wanted since their beginnings; here were planets enough, here were fields enough for the exercise of power, to sate even the insatiable. There was no longer any need for them to fight each other; they could now cooperate whole-heartedly—as long as each was getting more—and *more* and MORE!

Enphilisor, a young Arisian, his mind roaming eagerly abroad as was its wont, made first contact with the Eddorians in this space. Inoffensive, naive, innocent, he was surprised beyond measure at their reception of his friendly greeting; but in the instant before closing his mind to their vicious attacks, he learned the foregoing facts concerning them.

The fused mind of the Elders of Arisia, however, was not surprised. The Arisians, while not as mechanistic as their opponents, and innately peaceful as well, were far ahead of them in the pure science of the mind. The Elders had long known of the Eddorians and of their lustful wanderings through plenum after plenum. Their Visualizations of the Cosmic All had long since forecast, with dreadful certainty, the invasion which had now occurred. They had long known what they would have to do. They did it. So insidiously as to set up no opposition they entered the Eddorians' minds and sealed off all knowledge of Arisia. They withdrew, tracelessly.

They did not have much data, it is true; but no more could be obtained at that time. If any one of those touchy suspicious minds had been given any cause for alarm, any focal point of doubt, they would have had time in which to develop mechanisms able to force the Arisians out of this space before a weapon to destroy the Eddorians—the as yet incompletely designed Galactic Patrol—could be forged. The Arisians could, even then, have slain by mental force alone all the Eddorians except the All-Highest and his Innermost Circle, safe within their then impenetrable shield; but as long as they could not make a clean sweep they could not attack—then.

Be it observed that the Arisians were not fighting for themselves. As individuals or as a race they had nothing to fear. Even less than the Eddorians could they be killed by any possible application of physical force. Past masters of mental science, they knew that no possible concentration of Eddorian mental force could kill any one of them. And if they were to be forced out of normal space, what matter? To such mentalities as theirs, any given space would serve as well as any other.

No, they were fighting for an ideal; for the peaceful, harmonious, liberty-loving Civilization which they had envisaged as developing throughout, and eventually entirely covering the myriads of planets of, two tremendous Island Universes. Also, they felt a heavy weight of responsibility. Since all these races, existing and yet to appear, had sprung from and would spring from the Arisian life-spores which permeated this particular space, they all were and would be, at bottom, Arisian. It was starkly unthinkable that Arisia would leave them to the eternal dominance of such a rapacious, such a tyrannical, such a hellishly insatiable breed of monsters.

Therefore the Arisians fought; efficiently if insidiously. They did not—they could not—interfere openly with Eddore's ruthless conquest of world after world; with Eddore's ruthless smashing of Civilization after Civilization. They did, however, see to it, by selective matings and the establishment of blood-lines upon numberless planets, that the trend of the level of intelligence was definitely and steadily upward.

Four Molders of Civilization—Drounli, Kriedigan, Nedanillor, and Brolenteen, who, in fusion, formed the "Mentor of Arisia" who was to become known to every wearer of Civilization's Lens—were individually responsible for the Arisian program of development upon the four planets of Tellus, Rigel IV, Velantia, and Palain VII. Drounli established upon Tellus two principal lines of blood. In unbroken male line of descent the Kinnisons went back to long before the dawn of even mythical Tellurian history. Kinnexa of Atlantis, daughter of one Kinnison and sister of another, is the first of the blood to be named in these annals; but the line was then already old. So was the other line;

characterized throughout its tremendous length, male and female, by peculiarly spectacular red-bronze-auburn hair and equally striking gold-flecked, tawny eyes.

Nor did these strains mix. Drounli had made it psychologically impossible for them to mix until the penultimate stage of development should have been reached.

While that stage was still in the future Virgil Samms appeared, and all Arisia knew that the time had come to engage the Eddorians openly, mind to mind. Gharlane-Roger was curbed, savagely and sharply. Every Eddorian, wherever he was working, found his every line of endeavor solidly blocked.

Gharlane, as has been intimated, constructed a supposedly irresistible weapon and attacked his Arisian blocker, with results already told. At that failure Gharlane knew that there was something terribly amiss; that it had been amiss for over two thousand million Tellurian years. Really alarmed for the first time in his long life, he flashed back to Eddore; to warn his fellows and to take counsel with them as to what should be done. And the massed and integrated force of all Arisia was only an instant behind him.

*

Arisia struck Eddore's outermost screen, and in the instant of impact that screen went down. And then, instantaneously and all unperceived by the planet's defenders, the Arisian forces split. The Elders, including all the Molders, seized the Eddorian who had been handling that screen—threw around him an impenetrable net of force—yanked him out into inter-galactic space.

Then, driving in resistlessly, they turned the luckless wight inside out. And before the victim died under their poignant probings, the Elders of Arisia learned everything that the Eddorian and all of his ancestors had ever known. They then withdrew to Arisia, leaving their younger, weaker, partially-developed fellows to do whatever they could against mighty Eddore.

Whether the attack of these lesser forces would be stopped at the second, the third, the fourth, or the innermost screen; whether they would reach the planet itself and perhaps do some actual damage before being driven off; was immaterial. Eddore must be allowed and would be allowed to repel that invasion with ease. For cycles to come the Eddorians must and would believe that they had nothing really to fear from Arisia.

The real battle, however, had been won. The Arisian visualizations could now be extended to portray every essential element of the climactic conflict which was eventually to come. It was no cheerful conclusion at which the Arisians arrived, since their visualizations all agreed in showing that the only possible method of wiping out the Eddorians would also of necessity end their own usefulness as Guardians of Civilization.

Such an outcome having been shown necessary, however, the Arisians accepted it, and worked toward it, unhesitatingly.

CHAPTER 2

As has been said, The Hill, which had been built to be the Tellurian headquarters of the Triplanetary Service and which was now the headquarters of the half-organized Solarian Patrol, was—and is—a truncated, alloy-sheathed, honey-combed mountain. But, since human beings do not like to live eternally underground, no matter how beautifully lighted or how carefully and comfortably air-conditioned the dungeon may be, the Reservation spread far beyond the foot of that gray, forbidding, mirror-smooth cone of metal. Well outside that farflung Reservation there was a small city; there were hundreds of highly productive farms; and, particularly upon this bright May afternoon, there was a Recreation Park, containing, among other things, dozens of tennis courts.

One of these courts was three-quarters enclosed by stands, from which a couple of hundred people were watching a match which seemed to be of some little local importance. Two men sat in a box which had seats for twenty, and watched admiringly the pair who seemed in a fair way to win in straight sets the mixed-doubles championship of the Hill.

"Fine-looking couple, Rod, if I do say so myself, as well as being smooth performers." Solarian Councillor Virgil Samms spoke to his companion as the opponents changed courts. "I still think, though, the young hussy ought to wear some clothes—those white nylon shorts make her look nakeder even than usual. I told her so, too, the jade, but she keeps on wearing less and less."

"Of course," Commissioner Roderick K. Kinnison laughed quietly. "What did you expect? She got her hair and eyes from you, why not your hard-headedness, too? One thing, though, that's all to the good—she's got what it takes to strip ship that way, and most of 'em haven't. But what I can't understand is why they don't . . . ." He paused.

"I don't either. Lord knows we've thrown them at each other hard enough, and Jack Kinnison and Jill Samms would certainly make a pair to draw to. But if they won't . . . but maybe they will yet. They're still youngsters, and they're friendly enough."

If Samms père could have been out on the court, however, instead of in the box, he would have been surprised; for young Kinnison, although smiling enough as to face, was addressing his gorgeous partner in terms which carried little indeed of friendliness.

"Listen, you bird-brained, knot-headed, grand-standing half-wit!" he stormed, voice low but bitterly intense. "I ought to beat your alleged brains out! I've told you a thousand times to watch your own territory and *stay out of mine!* If you had been where you belonged, or even taken my signal, Frank couldn't have made that thirty-all point; and if Lois hadn't netted she'd've caught you flat-footed, a kilometer out of position, and made it deuce. What do you think you're doing, anyway—playing tennis or seeing how many innocent bystanders you can bring down out of control?"

"What do *you* think?" the girl sneered, sweetly. Her tawny eyes, only a couple of inches below his own, almost emitted sparks. "And just look at who's trying to tell who how to do what! For your information, Master Pilot John K. Kinnison, I'll tell you that just because you can't quit being 'Killer' Kinnison even long enough to let two good friends of ours get a point now and then, or maybe even a game, is no reason why I've got to turn into 'Killer' Samms. And I'll also tell you . . . ."

"You'll tell me nothing, Jill—I'm telling *you!* Start giving away points in anything and you'll find out some day that you've given away too many. I'm not having any of that kind of game—and as long as you're playing with me you aren't either—or else. If you louse up this match just once more, the next ball I serve will hit the tightest part of those fancy white shorts of yours—right where the hip pocket would be if they had any—and it'll raise a welt that will make you eat off of the mantel for three days. So watch your step!"

"You insufferable lug! I'd like to smash this racket over your head! I'll do it, too, and walk off the court, if you don't . . . ."

The whistle blew. Virgilia Samms, all smiles, toed the base-line and became the personification and embodiment of smoothly flowing motion. The ball whizzed over the net, barely clearing it—a sizzling service ace. The game went on.

And a few minutes later, in the shower room, where Jack Kinnison was caroling lustily while plying a towel, a huge young man strode up and slapped him ringingly between the shoulder blades.

"Congratulations, Jack, and so forth. But there's a thing I want to ask you. Confidential, sort of . . . ?"

"Shoot! Haven't we been eating out of the same dish for lo, these many moons? Why the diffidence all of a sudden, Mase? It isn't in character."

"Well . . . it's . . . I'm a lip-reader, you know."

"Sure. We all are. What of it?"

"It's only that . . . well, I saw what you and Miss Samms said to each other out there, and if that was lovers' small talk I'm a Venerian mud-puppy."

"*Lovers!* Who the hell ever said we were lovers? . . . Oh, you've been inhaling some of dad's balloon-juice. *Lovers!* Me and that red-headed stinker—that jelly-brained sapadilly? *Hardly!*"

"Hold it, Jack!" The big officer's voice was slightly edged. "You're off course—a hell of a long flit off. That girl has got everything. She's the class of the Reservation—why, she's a regular twelve-nineteen!"

"Huh?" Amazed, young Kinnison stopped drying himself and stared. "You mean to say you've been giving her a miss just because . . . ." He had started to say "because you're the best friend I've got in the System," but he did not.

"Well, it would have smelled slightly cheesy, I thought." The other man did not put into words, either, what both of them so deeply knew to be the truth. "But if you haven't got . . . if it's O.K. with you, of course . . . ."

"Stand by for five seconds—I'll take you around."

Jack threw on his uniform, and in a few minutes the two young officers, immaculate in the space-black-and-silver of the Patrol, made their way toward the women's dressing rooms.

" . . . but she's all right, at that . . . in most ways . . . I guess." Kinnison was half-apologizing for what he had said. "Outside of being chicken-hearted and pig-headed, she's a good egg. She really qualifies . . . most of the time. But I wouldn't have her, bonus attached, any more than she would have me. It's strictly mutual. You won't fall for her, either, Mase; you'll want to pull one of her legs off and beat the rest of her to death with it inside of a week—but there's nothing like finding things out for yourself."

In a short time Miss Samms appeared; dressed somewhat less revealingly than before in the blouse and kilts which were the mode of the moment.

"Hi, Jill! This is Mase—I've told you about him. My boat-mate. Master Electronicist Mason Northrop."

"Yes, I've heard about you, 'Troncist—a lot." She shook hands warmly.

"He hasn't been putting tracers on you, Jill, on accounta he figured he'd be poaching. Can you feature that? I straightened him out, though, in short order. Told him why, too, so he ought to be insulated against any voltage you can generate."

"Oh, you did? How sweet of you! But how . . . oh, those?" She gestured at the powerful prism binoculars, a part of the uniform of every officer of space.

"Uh-huh." Northrop wriggled, but held firm.

"If I'd only been as big and husky as you are," surveying admiringly some six feet two of altitude and two hundred-odd pounds of hard meat, gristle, and bone, "I'd have grabbed him by one ankle, whirled him around my head, and flung him into the fifteenth row of seats. What's the matter with him, Mase, is that he was born centuries and centuries too late. He should have been an overseer when they built the pyramids—flogging slaves because they wouldn't step just so. Or better yet, one of those people it told about in those funny old books they dug up last year—liege lords, or something like that, remember? With the power of life and death—'high, middle, and low justice', whatever that was—over their vassals and their families, serfs, and serving-wenches. *Especially* serving-wenches! He likes little, cuddly baby-talkers, who pretend to be utterly spineless and completely brainless—eh, Jack?"

"Ouch! Touché, Jill—but maybe I had it coming to me, at that. Let's call it off, shall we? I'll be seeing you two, hither or yon." Kinnison turned and hurried away.

"Want to know why he's doing such a quick flit?" Jill grinned up at her companion; a bright, quick grin. "Not that he was giving up. The blonde over there—the one in rocket red. Very few blondes can wear such a violent shade. Dimples Maynard."

"And is she . . . er . . . ?"

"Cuddly and baby-talkish? Uh-uh. She's a grand person. I was just popping off; so was he. You know that neither of us really meant half of what we said . . . or . . . at least . . . ." Her voice died away.

"I don't know whether I do or not," Northrop replied, awkwardly but honestly. "That was savage stuff if there ever was any. I can't see for the life of me why you two—two of the world's finest people—should have to tear into each other that way. Do you?"

"I don't know that I ever thought of it like that." Jill caught her lower lip between her teeth. "He's splendid, really, and I like him a lot—usually. We get along perfectly most of the time. We don't fight at all except when we're too close together . . . and then we fight about anything and everything . . . say, suppose that that could be it? Like charges, repelling each other inversely as the square of the distance? That's about the way it seems to be."

"Could be, and I'm glad." The man's face cleared. "And I'm a charge of the opposite sign. Let's go!"

*

And in Virgil Samms' deeply-buried office, Civilization's two strongest men were deep in conversation.

" . . . troubles enough to keep four men of our size awake nights." Samms' voice was light, but his eyes were moody and somber. "You can probably whip yours, though, in time. They're mostly in one solar system; a short flit covers the rest. Languages and customs are known. But how—how—can legal processes work efficiently—work at all, for that matter—when a man can commit a murder or a pirate can loot a space-ship and be a hundred parsecs away before the crime is even discovered? How can a Tellurian John Law find a criminal on a strange world that knows nothing whatever of our Patrol, with a completely alien language—maybe no language at all—where it takes months even to find out who and where—if any—the native police officers are? But there must be a way, Rod—there's *got* to be a way!" Samms slammed his open hand resoundingly against his desk's bare top. "And by God I'll find it—the Patrol *will* come out on top!"

"'Crusader' Samms, now and forever!" There was no trace of mockery in Kinnison's voice or expression, but only friendship and admiration. "And I'll bet you do. Your Interstellar Patrol, or whatever . . . ."

"Galactic Patrol. I know what the name of it is going to be, if nothing else."

" . . . is just as good as in the bag, right now. You've done a job so far, Virge. This whole system, Nevia, the colonies on Aldebaran II and other planets, even Valeria, as tight as a drum. Funny about Valeria, isn't it . . . ."

There was a moment of silence, then Kinnison went on:

"But wherever diamonds are, there go Dutchmen. And Dutch women go wherever their men do. And, in spite of medical advice, Dutch babies arrive. Although a lot of the adults died—three G's is no joke—practically all of the babies keep on living. Developing bones and muscles to fit—walking at a year and a half old—living normally—they say that the third generation will be perfectly at home there."

"Which shows that the human animal is more adaptable than some ranking medicos had believed, is all. Don't try to side-track me, Rod. You know as well as I do what we're up against; the new headaches that inter-stellar commerce is bringing with it. New vices—drugs—thionite, for instance; we haven't been able to get an inkling of an idea as to where that stuff is coming from. And I don't have to tell you what piracy has done to insurance rates."

"I'll say not—look at the price of Aldebaranian cigars, the only kind fit to smoke! You've given up, then, on the idea that Arisia is the pirates' GHQ?"

"Definitely. It isn't. The pirates are even more afraid of it than tramp spacemen are. It's out of bounds—absolutely forbidden territory, apparently—to everybody, my best operatives included. All we know about it is the name—Arisia—that our planetographers gave it. It is the first completely incomprehensible thing I have ever experienced. I am going out there myself as soon as I can take the time—not that I expect to crack a thing that my best men couldn't touch, but there have been so many different and conflicting reports—no two stories agree on anything except in that no one could get anywhere near the planet—that I feel the need of some first-hand information. Want to come along?"

"Try to keep me from it!"

"But at that, we shouldn't be too surprised," Samms went on, thoughtfully. "Just beginning to scratch the surface as we are, we should expect to encounter peculiar, baffling—even completely inexplicable things. Facts, situations, events, and beings for which our one-system experience could not possibly have prepared us. In fact, we already have. If, ten years ago, anyone had told you that such a race as the Rigellians existed, what would you have thought? One ship went there, you know—once. One hour in any Rigellian city—one minute in a Rigellian automobile—drives a Tellurian insane."

"I see your point." Kinnison nodded. "Probably I would have ordered a mental examination. And the Palainians are even worse. People—if you can call them that—who live on Pluto and *like* it! Entities so alien that nobody, as far as I know, understands them. But you don't have to go even that far from home to locate a job of unscrewing the inscrutable. Who, what, and why—and for how long—was Gray Roger? And, not far behind him, is this young Bergenholm of yours. And by the way, you never did give me the lowdown on how come it was the 'Bergenholm', and not the 'Rodebush-Cleveland', that made trans-galactic commerce possible and caused nine-tenths of our headaches. As I get the story, Bergenholm wasn't—isn't—even an engineer."

"Didn't I? Thought I did. He wasn't, and isn't. Well, the original Rodebush-Cleveland free drive was a killer, you know . . . ."

"*How* I know!" Kinnison exclaimed, feelingly.

"They beat their brains out and ate their hearts out for months, without getting it any better. Then, one day, this kid Bergenholm ambles into their shop—big, awkward, stumbling over his own feet. He gazes innocently at the thing for a couple of minutes, then says:

"'Why don't you use uranium instead of iron and rewind it so it will put out a wave-form like this, with humps here, and here; instead of there, and there?' and he draws a couple of free-hand, but really beautiful curves.

"'Why should we?' they squawk at him.

"'Because it will work that way,' he says, and ambles out as unconcernedly as he came in. Can't—or won't—say another word.

"Well in sheer desperation, they tried it—and it WORKED! And nobody has ever had a minute's trouble with a Bergenholm since. That's why Rodebush and Cleveland both insisted on the name."

"I see; and it points up what I just said. But if he's such a mental giant, why isn't he getting results with his own problem, the meteor? Or is he?"

"No . . . or at least he wasn't as of last night. But there's a note on my pad that he wants to see me sometime today—suppose we have him come in now?"

"Fine! I'd like to talk to him, if it's O.K. with you and with him."

The young scientist was called in, and was introduced to the Commissioner.

"Go ahead, Doctor Bergenholm," Samms suggested then. "You may talk to both of us, just as freely as though you and I were alone."

"I have, as you already know, been called psychic," Bergenholm began, abruptly. "It is said that I dream dreams, see visions, hear voices, and so on. That I operate on hunches. That I am a genius. Now I very definitely am *not* a genius—unless my understanding of the meaning of that word is different from that of the rest of mankind."

Bergenholm paused. Samms and Kinnison looked at each other. The latter broke the short silence.

"The Councillor and I have just been discussing the fact that there are a great many things we do not know; that with the extension of our activities into new fields, the occurrence of the impossible has become almost a commonplace. We are able, I believe, to listen with open minds to anything you have to say."

"Very well. But first, please know that I am a scientist. As such, I am trained to observe; to think calmly, clearly, and analytically; to test every hypothesis. I do not believe at all in the so-called supernatural. This universe did not come into being, it does not continue to be, except by the operation of natural and immutable laws. And I mean *immutable*, gentlemen. Everything that has ever happened, that is happening now, or that ever is to happen, was, is, and will be statistically connected with its predecessor event and with its successor event. If I did not believe that implicitly, I would lose all faith in the scientific method. For if one single 'supernatural' event or thing had ever occurred or existed it would have constituted an entirely unpredictable event and would have initiated a series—a succession—of such events; a state of things which no scientist will or can believe possible in an orderly universe.

"At the same time, I recognize the fact that I myself have done things—caused events to occur, if you prefer—that I cannot explain to you or to any other human being in any symbology known to our science; and it is about an even more inexplicable—call it 'hunch' if you like—that I asked to have a talk with you today."

"But you are arguing in circles," Samms protested. "Or are you trying to set up a paradox?"

"Neither. I am merely clearing the way for a somewhat startling thing I am to say later on. You know, of course, that any situation with which a mind is unable to cope; a really serious dilemma which it cannot resolve; will destroy that mind—frustration, escape from reality, and so on. You also will realize that I must have become cognizant of my own peculiarities long before anyone else did or could?"

"Ah. I see. Yes, of course." Samms, intensely interested, leaned forward. "Yet your present personality is adequately, splendidly integrated. How could you possibly have overcome—reconciled—a situation so full of conflict?"

"You are, I think, familiar with my parentage?" Samms, keen as he was, did not consider it noteworthy that the big Norwegian answered his question only by asking one of his own.

"Yes . . . oh, I'm beginning to see . . . but Commissioner Kinnison has not had access to your dossier. Go ahead."

"My father is Dr. Hjalmar Bergenholm. My mother, before her marriage, was Dr. Olga Bjornson. Both were, and are, nuclear physicists—very good ones. Pioneers, they have been called. They worked, and are still working, in the newest, outermost fringes of the field."

"Oh!" Kinnison exclaimed. "A mutant? Born with second sight—or whatever it is?"

"Not second sight, as history describes the phenomenon, no. The records do not show that any such faculty was ever demonstrated to the satisfaction of any competent scientific investigator. What I have is something else. Whether or not it will breed true is an interesting topic of speculation, but one having nothing to do with the problem now in hand. To return to the subject, I resolved my dilemma long since. There is, I am absolutely certain, a science of the mind which is as definite, as positive, as immutable of law, as is the science of the physical. While I will make no attempt to prove it to you, I *know* that such a science exists, and that I was born with the ability to perceive at least some elements of it.

"Now to the matter of the meteor of the Patrol. That emblem was and is purely physical. The pirates have just as able scientists as we have. What physical science can devise and synthesize, physical science can analyze and duplicate. There is a point, however, beyond which physical science cannot go. It can neither analyze nor imitate the tangible products of that which I have so loosely called the science of the mind.

"I know, Councillor Samms, what the Triplanetary Service needs; something vastly more than its meteor. I also know that the need will become greater and greater as the sphere of action of the Patrol expands. Without a really efficient symbol, the Solarian Patrol will be hampered even more than the Triplanetary Service; and its logical extension into the Space Patrol, or whatever that larger organization may be called, will be definitely impossible. We need something which will identify any representative of Civilization, positively and unmistakably, wherever he may be. It must be impossible of duplication, or even of imitation, to which end it must kill any unauthorized entity who attempts imposture. It must operate as a telepath between its owner and any other living intelligence, of however high or low degree, so that mental communication, so much clearer and faster than physical, will be possible without the laborious learning of language; or between us and such peoples as those of Rigel Four or of Palain Seven, both of whom we know to be of high intelligence and who must already be conversant with telepathy."

"Are you or have you been, reading my mind?" Samms asked quietly.

"No," Bergenholm replied flatly. "It is not and has not been necessary. Any man who can think, who has really considered the question, and who has the good of Civilization at heart, must have come to the same conclusions."

"Probably so, at that. But no more side issues. You have a solution of some kind worked out, or you would not be here. What is it?"

"It is that you, Solarian Councillor Samms, should go to Arisia as soon as possible."

"Arisia!" Samms exclaimed, and:

"Arisia! Of all the hells in space, why Arisia? And how can we make the approach? Don't you know that *nobody* can get anywhere near that damn planet?"

Bergenholm shrugged his shoulders and spread both arms wide in a pantomime of complete helplessness.

"How do you know—another of your hunches?" Kinnison went on. "Or did somebody tell you something? *Where* did you get it?"

"It is not a hunch," the Norwegian replied, positively. "No one told me anything. But I *know*—as definitely as I know that the combustion of hydrogen in oxygen will yield water—that the Arisians are very well versed in that which I have called the science of the

185

mind; that if Virgil Samms goes to Arisia he will obtain the symbol he needs; that he will never obtain it otherwise. As to *how* I know these things . . . I can't . . . I just . . . I *know* it, I tell you!"

Without another word, without asking permission to leave, Bergenholm whirled around and hurried out. Samms and Kinnison stared at each other.

"Well?" Kinnison asked, quizzically.

"I'm going. Now. Whether I can be spared or not, and whether you think I'm out of control or not. I believe him, every word—and besides, there's the Bergenholm. How about you? Coming?"

"Yes. Can't say that I'm sold one hundred percent; but, as you say, the Bergenholm is a hard fact to shrug off. And at minimum rating, it's got to be tried. What are you taking? Not a fleet, probably—the *Boise*? Or the *Chicago*?" It was the Commissioner of Public Safety speaking now, the Commander-in-Chief of the Armed Forces. "The *Chicago*, I'd say—the fastest and strongest thing in space."

"Recommendation approved. Blast-off; twelve hundred hours tomorrow!"

CHAPTER 3

The superdreadnought *Chicago*, as she approached the imaginary but nevertheless sharply defined boundary, which no other ship had been allowed to pass, went inert and crept forward, mile by mile. Every man, from Commissioner and Councillor down, was taut and tense. So widely variant, so utterly fantastic, were the stories going around about this Arisia that no one knew what to expect. They expected the unexpected—and got it.

"Ah, Tellurians, you are precisely on time." A strong, assured, deeply resonant pseudo-voice made itself heard in the depths of each mind aboard the tremendous ship of war. "Pilots and navigating officers, you will shift course to one seventy eight dash seven twelve fifty three. Hold that course, inert, at one Tellurian gravity of acceleration. Virgil Samms will now be interviewed. He will return to the consciousnesses of the rest of you in exactly six of your hours."

Practically dazed by the shock of their first experience with telepathy, not one of the *Chicago's* crew perceived anything unusual in the phraseology of that utterly precise, diamond-clear thought. Samms and Kinnison, however, precisionists themselves, did. But, warned although they were and keyed up although they were to detect any sign of hypnotism or of mental suggestion, neither of them had the faintest suspicion, then or ever, that Virgil Samms did not as a matter of fact leave the *Chicago* at all.

Samms *knew* that he boarded a lifeboat and drove it toward the shimmering haze beyond which Arisia was. Commissioner Kinnison *knew*, as surely as did every other man aboard, that Samms did those things, because he and the other officers and most of the crew watched Samms do them. They watched the lifeboat dwindle in size with distance; watched it disappear within the peculiarly iridescent veil of force which their most penetrant ultra-beam spy-rays could not pierce.

They waited.

And, since every man concerned *knew*, beyond any shadow of doubt and to the end of his life, that everything that seemed to happen actually did happen, it will be so described.

Virgil Samms, then, drove his small vessel through Arisia's innermost screen and saw a planet so much like Earth that it might have been her sister world. There were the white ice-caps, the immense blue oceans, the verdant continents partially obscured by fleecy banks of cloud.

Would there, or would there not, be cities? While he had not known at all exactly what to expect, he did not believe that there would be any large cities upon Arisia. To qualify for the role of *deus ex machina*, the Arisian with whom Samms was about to deal would have to be a super-man indeed—a being completely beyond man's knowledge or experience in power of mind. Would such a race of beings have need of such things as cities? They would not. There would be no cities.

Nor were there. The lifeboat flashed downward—slowed—landed smoothly in a regulation dock upon the outskirts of what appeared to be a small village surrounded by farms and woods.

"This way, please." An inaudible voice directed him toward a two-wheeled vehicle which was almost, but not quite, like a Dillingham roadster.

This car, however, took off by itself as soon as Samms closed the door. It sped smoothly along a paved highway devoid of all other traffic, past farms and past cottages, to stop of itself in front of the low, massive structure which was the center of the village and, apparently, its reason for being.

"This way, please," and Samms went through an automatically-opened door; along a short, bare hall; into a fairly large central room containing a vat and one deeply-holstered chair.

"Sit down, please." Samms did so, gratefully. He did not know whether he could have stood up much longer or not.

He had expected to encounter a tremendous mentality; but this was a thing far, far beyond his wildest imaginings. This was a brain—just that—nothing else. Almost globular; at least ten feet in diameter; immersed in and in perfect equilibrium with a pleasantly aromatic liquid—a BRAIN!

"Relax," the Arisian ordered, soothingly, and Samms found that he *could* relax. "Through the one you know as Bergenholm I heard of your need and have permitted you to come here this once for instruction."

"But this . . . none of this . . . it isn't . . . it *can't* be real!" Samms blurted. "I am—I must be—imagining it . . . and yet I know that I *can't* be hypnotized—I've been psyched against it!"

"What is reality?" the Arisian asked, quietly. "Your profoundest thinkers have never been able to answer that question. Nor, although I am much older and a much more capable thinker than any member of your race, would I attempt to give you its true answer. Nor, since your experience has been so limited, is it to be expected that you could believe without reservation any assurances I might give you in thoughts or in words. You must, then, convince yourself—definitely, by means of your own five senses—that I and everything about you are real, as you understand reality. You saw the village and this building; you see the flesh that houses the entity which is I. You feel your own flesh; as you tap the woodwork with your knuckles you feel the impact and hear the vibrations as sound. As you entered this room you must have perceived the odor of the nutrient solution in which and by virtue of which I live. There remains only the sense of taste. Are you by any chance either hungry or thirsty?"

"Both."

"Drink of the tankard in the niche yonder. In order to avoid any appearance of suggestion I will tell you nothing of its content except the one fact that it matches perfectly the chemistry of your tissues."

Gingerly enough, Samms brought the pitcher to his lips—then, seizing it in both hands, he gulped down a tremendous draught. It was GOOD! It smelled like all appetizing kitchen aromas blended into one; it tasted like all of the most delicious meals he had ever eaten; it quenched his thirst as no beverage had ever done. But he could not empty even that comparatively small container—whatever the stuff was, it had a satiety value immensely higher even than old, rare, roast beef! With a sigh of repletion Samms replaced the tankard and turned again to his peculiar host.

"I am convinced. That was real. No possible mental influence could so completely and unmistakably satisfy the purely physical demands of a body as hungry and as thirsty as mine was. Thanks, immensely, for allowing me to come here, Mr . . . .?"

"You may call me Mentor. I have no name, as you understand the term. Now, then, please think fully—you need not speak—of your problems and of your difficulties; of what you have done and of what you have it in mind to do."

Samms thought, flashingly and cogently. A few minutes sufficed to cover Triplanetary's history and the beginning of the Solarian Patrol; then, for almost three hours, he went into the ramifications of the Galactic Patrol of his imaginings. Finally he wrenched himself back to reality. He jumped up, paced the floor, and spoke.

"But there's a vital flaw, one inherent and absolutely ruinous fact that makes the whole thing impossible!" he burst out, rebelliously. "No one man, or group of men, no matter who they are, can be trusted with that much power. The Council and I have already been called everything imaginable; and what we have done so far is literally nothing at all in comparison with what the Galactic Patrol could and must do. Why, I myself would be the first to protest against the granting of such power to *anybody*. Every dictator in history, from Philip of Macedon to the Tyrant of Asia, claimed to be—and probably was, in his beginnings—motivated solely by benevolence. How am I to think that the proposed Galactic Council, or even I myself, will be strong enough to conquer a thing that has corrupted utterly every man who has ever won it? Who is to watch the watchmen?"

"The thought does you credit, youth," Mentor replied, unmoved. "That is one reason why you are here. You, of your own force, can not know that you are in fact incorruptible. I, however, know. Moreover, there is an agency by virtue of which that which you now believe to be impossible will become commonplace. Extend your arm."

Samms did so, and there snapped around his wrist a platinum-iridium bracelet carrying, wrist-watch-wise, a lenticular something at which the Tellurian stared in stupefied amazement. It seemed to be composed of thousands—millions—of tiny gems, each of which emitted pulsatingly all the colors of the spectrum; it was throwing out—broadcasting—a turbulent flood of writhing, polychromatic light!

"The successor to the golden meteor of the Triplanetary Service," Mentor said, calmly. "The Lens of Arisia. You may take my word for it, until your own experience shall have convinced you of the fact, that no one will ever wear Arisia's Lens who is in any sense unworthy. Here also is one for your friend, Commissioner Kinnison; it is not necessary for him to come physically to Arisia. It is, you will observe, in an insulated container, and does not glow. Touch its surface, but lightly and very fleetingly, for the contact will be painful."

Samms' finger-tip barely touched one dull, gray, lifeless jewel: his whole arm jerked away uncontrollably as there swept through his whole being the intimation of an agony more poignant by far than any he had ever known.

"Why—it's *alive!*" he gasped.

"No, it is not really alive, as you understand the term . . . " Mentor paused, as though seeking a way to describe to the Tellurian a thing which was to him starkly incomprehensible. "It is, however, endowed with what you might call a sort of pseudo-life; by virtue of which it gives off its characteristic radiation while, and only while, it is in physical circuit with the living entity—the ego, let us say—with whom it is in exact resonance. Glowing, the Lens is perfectly harmless; it is complete—saturated—satiated—fulfilled. In the dark condition it is, as you have learned, dangerous in the extreme. It is then incomplete—unfulfilled—frustrated—you might say seeking or yearning or demanding. In that condition its pseudo-life interferes so strongly with any life to which it is not attuned that that life, in a space of seconds, is forced out of this plane or cycle of existence."

"Then I—I alone—of all the entities in existence, can wear this particular Lens?" Samms licked his lips and stared at it, glowing so satisfyingly and contentedly upon his wrist. "But when I die, will it be a perpetual menace?"

"By no means. A Lens cannot be brought into being except to match some one living personality; a short time after you pass into the next cycle your Lens will disintegrate."

"Wonderful!" Samms breathed, in awe. "But there's one thing . . . these things are . . . priceless, and there will be millions of them to make . . . and you don't . . . ."

"What will we get out of it, you mean?" The Arisian seemed to smile.

"Exactly." Samms blushed, but held his ground. "Nobody does anything for nothing. Altruism is beautiful in theory, but it has never been known to work in practice. I will pay a tremendous price—any price within reason or possibility—for the Lens; but I will have to know what that price is to be."

"It will be heavier than you think, or can at present realize; although not in the sense you fear." Mentor's thought was solemnity itself. "Whoever wears the Lens of Arisia will carry a load that no weaker mind could bear. The load of authority; of responsibility; of knowledge that would wreck completely any mind of lesser strength. Altruism? No. Nor is it a case of good against evil, as you so firmly believe. Your mental picture of glaring white and of unrelieved black is not a true picture. Neither absolute evil nor absolute good do or can exist."

"But that would make it still worse!" Samms protested. "In that case, I can't see any reason at all for your exerting yourselves—putting yourselves out—for us."

"There is, however, reason enough; although I am not sure that I can make it as clear to you as I would wish. There are in fact three reasons; any one of which would justify us in exerting—would compel us to exert—the trivial effort involved in the furnishing of Lenses to your Galactic Patrol. First, there is nothing either intrinsically right or intrinsically wrong about liberty or slavery, democracy or autocracy, freedom of action or complete regimentation. It seems to us, however, that the greatest measure of happiness and of well-being for the greatest number of entities, and therefore the optimum advancement toward whatever sublime Goal it is toward which this cycle of existence is trending in the vast and unknowable Scheme of Things, is to be obtained by securing for each and every individual the greatest amount of mental and physical freedom compatible with the public welfare. We of Arisia are only a small part of this cycle; and, as goes the whole, so goes in greater or lesser degree each of the parts. Is it impossible for you, a fellow citizen of this cycle-universe, to believe that such fulfillment alone would be ample compensation for a much greater effort?"

"I never thought of it in that light . . . ." It was hard for Samms to grasp the concept; he never did understand it thoroughly. "I begin to see, I think . . . at least, I believe you."

"Second, we have a more specific obligation in that the life of many, many worlds has sprung from Arisian seed. Thus, *in loco parentis*, we would be derelict indeed if we refused to act. And third, you yourself spend highly valuable time and much effort in playing chess. Why do you do it? What do you get out of it?"

"Why, I . . . uh . . . mental exercise, I suppose . . . I like it!"

"Just so. And I am sure that one of your very early philosophers came to the conclusion that a fully competent mind, from a study of one fact or artifact belonging to any given universe, could construct or visualize that universe, from the instant of its creation to its ultimate end?"

"Yes. At least, I have heard the proposition stated, but I have never believed it possible."

"It is not possible simply because no fully competent mind ever has existed or ever will exist. A mind can become fully competent only by the acquisition of infinite knowledge, which would require infinite time as well as infinite capacity. Our equivalent of your chess, however, is what we call the 'Visualization of the Cosmic All'. In my visualization a descendant of yours named Clarrissa MacDougall will, in a store called Brenleer's upon the planet . . . but no, let us consider a thing nearer at hand and concerning you personally, so that its accuracy will be subject to check. Where you will be and exactly what you will be doing, at some definite time in the future. Five years, let us say?"

"Go ahead. If you can do that you're *good*."

"Five Tellurian calendar years then, from the instant of your passing through the screen of 'The Hill' on this present journey, you will be . . . allow me, please, a moment of thought . . . you will be in a barber shop not yet built; the address of which is to be fifteen hundred fifteen Twelfth Avenue, Spokane, Washington, North America, Tellus. The barber's name will be Antonio Carbonero and he will be left-handed. He will be engaged in cutting your hair. Or rather, the actual cutting will have been done and he will be shaving, with a razor trade-marked 'Jensen-King-Byrd', the short hairs in front of your left ear. A comparatively small, quadrupedal, grayish-striped entity, of the race called 'cat'—a young cat, this one will be, and called Thomas, although actually of the female sex—will jump into your lap, addressing you pleasantly in a language with which you yourself are only partially familiar. You call it mewing and purring, I believe?"

"Yes," the flabbergasted Samms managed to say. "Cats do purr—especially kittens."

"Ah—very good. Never having met a cat personally, I am gratified at your corroboration of my visualization. This female youth erroneously called Thomas, somewhat careless in computing the elements of her trajectory, will jostle slightly the barber's elbow with her tail; thus causing him to make a slight incision, approximately three millimeters long, parallel to and just above your left cheek-bone. At the precise moment in question, the barber will be applying a styptic pencil to this insignificant wound. This forecast is, I trust, sufficiently detailed so that you will have no difficulty in checking its accuracy or its lack thereof?"

"Detailed! *Accuracy!*" Samms could scarcely think. "But listen—not that I want to cross you up deliberately, but I'll tell you now that a man doesn't like to get sliced by a barber, even such a little nick as that. I'll remember that address—and the cat—and I'll never go into the place!"

"Every event does affect the succession of events," Mentor acknowledged, equably enough. "Except for this interview, you would have been in New Orleans at that time, instead of in Spokane. I have considered every pertinent factor. You will be a busy man. Hence, while you will think of this matter frequently and seriously during the near future, you will have forgotten it in less than five years. You will remember it only at the touch of the astringent, whereupon you will give voice to certain self-derogatory and profane remarks."

"I ought to," Samms grinned; a not-too-pleasant grin. He had been appalled by the quality of mind able to do what Mentor had just done; he was now more than appalled by the Arisian's calm certainty that what he had foretold in such detail would in every detail come to pass. "If, after all this Spokane—let a tiger-striped kitten jump into my lap—let a left-handed Tony Carbonero nick me—uh-uh, Mentor, UH-UH! *If* I do, I'll deserve to be called everything I can think of!"

"These that I have mentioned, the gross occurrences, are problems only for inexperienced thinkers." Mentor paid no attention to Samms' determination never to enter that shop. "The real difficulties lie in the fine detail, such as the length, mass, and exact place and position of landing, upon apron or floor, of each of your hairs as it is severed. Many factors are involved. Other clients passing by—opening and shutting doors—air currents—sunshine—wind—pressure, temperature, humidity. The exact fashion in which the barber will flick his shears, which in turn depends upon many other factors—what he will have been doing previously, what he will have eaten and drunk, whether or not his home life will have been happy . . . you little realize, youth, what a

191

priceless opportunity this will be for me to check the accuracy of my visualization. I shall spend many periods upon the problem. I cannot attain perfect accuracy, of course. Ninety nine point nine nines percent, let us say . . . or perhaps ten nines . . . is all that I can reasonably expect . . . ."

"But, Mentor!" Samms protested. "I can't help you on a thing like that! How can I know or report the exact mass, length, and orientation of single hairs?"

"You cannot; but, since you will be wearing your Lens, I myself can and will compare minutely my visualization with the actuality. For know, youth, that wherever any Lens is, there can any Arisian be if he so desires. And now, knowing that fact, and from your own knowledge of the satisfactions to be obtained from chess and other such mental activities, and from the glimpses you have had into my own mind, do you retain any doubts that we Arisians will be fully compensated for the trifling effort involved in furnishing whatever number of Lenses may be required?"

"I have no more doubts. But this Lens . . . I'm getting more afraid of it every minute. I see that it is a perfect identification; I can understand that it can be a perfect telepath. But is it something else, as well? If it has other powers . . . what are they?"

"I cannot tell you; or, rather, I will not. It is best for your own development that I do not, except in the most general terms. It has additional qualities, it is true; but, since no two entities ever have the same abilities, no two Lenses will ever be of identical qualities. Strictly speaking, a Lens has no real power of its own; it merely concentrates, intensifies, and renders available whatever powers are already possessed by its wearer. You must develop your own powers and your own abilities; we of Arisia, in furnishing the Lens, will have done everything that we should do."

"Of course, sir; and much more than we have any right to expect. You have given me a Lens for Roderick Kinnison; how about the others? Who is to select them?"

"You are, for a time." Silencing the man's protests, Mentor went on: "You will find that your judgment will be good. You will send to us only one entity who will not be given a Lens, and it is necessary that that one entity should be sent here. You will begin a system of selection and training which will become more and more rigorous as time goes on. This will be necessary; not for the selection itself, which the Lensmen themselves could do among babies in their cradles, but because of the benefits thus conferred upon the many who will not graduate, as well as upon the few who will. In the meantime you will select the candidates; and you will be shocked and dismayed when you discover how few you will be able to send.

"You will go down in history as First Lensman Samms; the Crusader, the man whose wide vision and tremendous grasp made it possible for the Galactic Patrol to become what it is to be. You will have highly capable help, of course. The Kinnisons, with their irresistible driving force, their indomitable will to do, their transcendent urge; Costigan, back of whose stout Irish heart lie Erin's best of brains and brawn; your cousins George and Ray Olmstead; your daughter Virgilia . . . ."

"Virgilia! Where does *she* fit into this picture? What do you know about her—and how?"

"A mind would be incompetent indeed who could not visualize, from even the most fleeting contact with you, a fact which has been in existence for some twenty three of your years. Her doctorate in psychology; her intensive studies under Martian and Venerian masters—even under one reformed Adept of North Polar Jupiter—of the involuntary, uncontrollable, almost unknown and hence highly revealing muscles of the face, the hands, and other parts of the human body. You will remember that poker game for a long time."

"I certainly will." Samms grinned, a bit shamefacedly. "She gave us clear warning of what she was going to do, and then cleaned us out to the last millo."

"Naturally. She has, all unconsciously, been training herself for the work she is destined to do. But to resume; you will feel yourself incompetent, unworthy—that, too, is a part of a Lensman's Load. When you first scan the mind of Roderick Kinnison you will feel that he, not you, should be the prime mover in the Galactic Patrol. But know now that no mind, not even the most capable in the universe, can either visualize truly or truly evaluate itself. Commissioner Kinnison, upon scanning your mind as he will scan it, will know the truth and will be well content. But time presses; in one minute you leave."

"Thanks a lot . . . thanks." Samms got to his feet and paused, hesitantly. "I suppose that it will be all right . . . that is, I can call on you again, if . . . ?"

"No," the Arisian declared, coldly. "My visualization does not indicate that it will ever again be either necessary or desirable for you to visit or to communicate with me or with any other Arisian."

Communication ceased as though a solid curtain had been drawn between the two. Samms strode out and stepped into the waiting vehicle, which whisked him back to his lifeboat. He blasted off; arriving in the control room of the *Chicago* precisely at the end of the sixth hour after leaving it.

"Well, Rod, I'm back . . . " he began, and stopped; utterly unable to speak. For at the mention of the name Samms' Lens had put him fully en rapport with his friend's whole mind; and what he perceived struck him—literally and precisely—dumb.

He had always liked and admired Rod Kinnison. He had always known that he was tremendously able and capable. He had known that he was big; clean; a square shooter; the world's best. Hard; a driver who had little more mercy on his underlings in selected undertakings than he had on himself. But now, as he saw spread out for his inspection Kinnison's ego in its entirety; as he compared in fleeting glances that terrific mind with those of the other officers—good men, too, all of them—assembled in the room; he knew that he had never even begun to realize what a giant Roderick Kinnison really was.

"What's the matter, Virge?" Kinnison exclaimed, and hurried up, both hands outstretched. "You look like you're seeing ghosts! What did they do to you?"

"Nothing—much. But 'ghosts' doesn't half describe what I'm seeing right now. Come into my office, will you, Rod?"

Ignoring the curious stares of the junior officers, the Commissioner and the Councillor went into the latter's quarters, and in those quarters the two Lensmen remained in close consultation during practically all of the return trip to Earth. In fact, they were still conferring deeply, via Lens, when the *Chicago* landed and they took a ground-car into The Hill.

"But who are you going to send first, Virge?" Kinnison demanded. "You must have decided on at least some of them, by this time."

"I know of only five, or possibly six, who are ready," Samms replied, glumly. "I would have sworn that I knew of a hundred, but they don't measure up. Jack, Mason Northrop, and Conway Costigan, for the first load. Lyman Cleveland, Fred Rodebush, and perhaps Bergenholm—I haven't been able to figure him out, but I'll know when I get him under my Lens—next. That's all."

"Not quite. How about your identical-twin cousins, Ray and George Olmstead, who have been doing such a terrific job of counter-spying?"

"Perhaps . . . Quite possibly."

"And if I'm good enough, Clayton and Schweikert certainly are, to name only two of the commodores. And Knobos and DalNalten. And above all, how about Jill?"

"Jill? Why, I don't . . . she measures up, of course, but . . . but at that, there was nothing said against it, either . . . I wonder . . . ."

"Why not have the boys in—Jill, too—and thrash it out?"

The young people were called in; the story was told; the problem stated. The boys' reaction was instantaneous and unanimous. Jack Kinnison took the lead.

"Of course Jill's going, if anybody does!" he burst out vehemently. "Count *her* out, with all the stuff she's got? *Hardly!*"

"Why, Jack! This, from *you?*" Jill seemed highly surprised. "I have it on excellent authority that I'm a stinker; a half-witted one, at that. A jelly-brain, with come-hither eyes."

"You are, and a lot of other things besides." Jack Kinnison did not back up a millimeter, even before their fathers. "But even at your sapadilliest your half wits are better than most other people's whole ones; and I never said or thought that your brain couldn't function, whenever it wanted to, back of those sad eyes. Whatever it takes to be a Lensman, sir," he turned to Samms, "she's got just as much of as the rest of us. Maybe more."

"I take it, then, that there is no objection to her going?" Samms asked.

There was no objection.

"What ship shall we take, and when?"

"The *Chicago*. Now." Kinnison directed. "She's hot and ready. We didn't strike any trouble going or coming, so she didn't need much servicing. Flit!"

They flitted, and the great battleship made the second cruise as uneventfully as she had made the first. The *Chicago's* officers and crew knew that the young people left the vessel separately; that they returned separately, each in his or her lifeboat. They met, however, not in the control room, but in Jack Kinnison's private quarters; the three young Lensmen and the girl. The three were embarrassed; ill at ease. The Lenses were—definitely—not working. No one of them would put his Lens on Jill, since she did not have one . . . . The girl broke the short silence.

"Wasn't she the most perfectly *beautiful* thing you ever saw?" she breathed. "In spite of being over seven feet tall? She looked to be about twenty—except her eyes—but she must have been a hundred, to know so much—but what are you boys staring so about?"

"*She!*" Three voices blurted as one.

"Yes. She. Why? I know we weren't together, but I got the impression, some way or other, that there was only the one. What did *you* see?"

All three men started to talk at once, a clamor of noise; then all stopped at once.

"You first, Spud. Whom did you talk to, and what did he, she, or it say?" Although Conway Costigan was a few years older than the other three, they all called him by nickname as a matter of course.

"National Police Headquarters—Chief of the Detective Bureau," Costigan reported, crisply. "Between forty three and forty five; six feet and half an inch; one seventy five. Hard, fine, keen, a Big Time Operator if there ever was one. Looked a lot like your father, Jill; the same dark auburn hair, just beginning to gray, and the same deep orange-yellow markings in his eyes. He gave me the works; then took this Lens out of his safe, snapped it onto my wrist, and gave me two orders—get out and stay out."

Jack and Mase stared at Costigan, at Jill, and at each other. Then they whistled in unison.

"I see this is not going to be a unanimous report, except possibly in one minor detail," Jill remarked. "Mase, you're next."

"I landed on the campus of the University of Arisia," Northrop stated, flatly. "Immense place—hundreds of thousands of students. They look me to the Physics Department—to the private laboratory of the Department Head himself. He had a panel with about a million meters and gauges on it; he scanned and measured every individual component element of my brain. Then he made a pattern, on a milling router just about as complicated as his panel. From there on, of course, it was simple—just like a dentist making a set of china choppers or a metallurgist embedding a test-section. He snapped a couple of sentences of directions at me, and then said 'Scram!' That's all."

"Sure that was all?" Costigan asked. "Didn't he add 'and *stay* scrammed'?"

"He didn't *say* it, exactly, but the implication was clear enough."

"The one point of similarity," Jill commented. "Now you, Jack. You have been looking as though we were all candidates for canvas jackets that lace tightly up the back."

"Uh-uh. As though maybe *I* am. I didn't see anything at all. Didn't even land on the planet. Just floated around in an orbit inside that screen. The thing I talked with was a pattern of pure force. This Lens simply appeared on my wrist, bracelet and all, out of thin air. He told me plenty, though, in a very short time—his last word being for me not to come back or call back."

"Hm . . . m . . . m." This of Jack's was a particularly indigestible bit, even for Jill Samms.

"In plain words," Costigan volunteered, "we all saw exactly what we expected to see."

"Uh-uh," Jill denied. "I certainly did not expect to see a woman . . . no; what each of us saw, I think, was what would do us the most good—give each of us the highest possible lift. I am wondering whether or not there was anything at all really there."

"That might be it, at that." Jack scowled in concentration. "But there must have been *something* there—these Lenses are real. But what makes me mad is that they wouldn't give you a Lens. You're just as good a man as any one of us—if I didn't know it wouldn't do a damn bit of good I'd go back there right now and . . . ."

"Don't pop off so, Jack!" Jill's eyes, however, were starry. "I know you mean it, and I could almost love you, at times—but I don't need a Lens. As a matter of fact, I'll be much better off without one."

"Jet back, Jill!" Jack Kinnison stared deeply into the girl's eyes—but still did not use his Lens. "Somebody must have done a terrific job of selling, to make you believe that . . . or *are* you sold, actually?"

"Actually. Honestly. That Arisian was a thousand times more of a woman than I ever will be, and she didn't wear a Lens—never had worn one. Women's minds and Lenses don't fit. There's a sex-based incompatibility. Lenses are as masculine as whiskers—and at that, only a very few men can ever wear them, either. Very special men, like you three and Dad and Pops Kinnison. Men with tremendous force, drive, and scope. Pure killers, all of you; each in his own way, of course. No more to be stopped than a glacier, and twice as hard and ten times as cold. A woman simply *can't* have that kind of a mind! There is going to be a woman Lensman some day—just one—but not for years and years; and I wouldn't be in her shoes for anything. In this job of mine, of . . . ."

"Well, go on. What is this job you're so sure you are going to do?"

"Why, I don't know!" Jill exclaimed, startled eyes wide. "I thought I knew all about it, but I don't! Do you, about yours?"

They did not, not one of them; and they were all as surprised at that fact as the girl had been.

"Well, to get back to this Lady Lensman who is going to appear some day, I gather that she is going to be some kind of a freak. She'll have to be, practically, because of the sex-based fundamental nature of the Lens. Mentor didn't say so, in so many words, but she made it perfectly clear that . . . ."

"Mentor!" the three men exclaimed.

Each of them had dealt with Mentor!

"I am beginning to see," Jill said, thoughtfully. "Mentor. Not a real name at all. To quote the Unabridged verbatim—I had occasion to look the word up the other day and I am appalled now at the certainty that there was a connection—quote; Mentor, a wise and faithful counselor; unquote. Have any of you boys anything to say? I haven't; and I am beginning to be scared blue."

Silence fell; and the more they thought, those three young Lensmen and the girl who was one of the two human women ever to encounter knowingly an Arisian mind, the deeper that silence became.

CHAPTER 4

"So you didn't find anything on Nevia." Roderick Kinnison got up, deposited the inch-long butt of his cigar in an ashtray, lit another, and prowled about the room; hands jammed deep into breeches pockets. "I'm surprised. Nerado struck me as being a B.T.O . . . . I thought sure he'd qualify."

"So did I." Samms' tone was glum. "He's Big Time, and an Operator; but not big enough, by far. I'm—we're both—finding out that Lensman material is *damned* scarce stuff. There's none on Nevia, and no indication whatever that there ever will be any."

"Tough . . . and you're right, of course, in your stand that we'll have to have Lensmen from as many different solar systems as possible on the Galactic Council or the thing won't work at all. So damned much jealousy—which is one reason why we're here in New York instead of out at The Hill, where we belong—we've found that out already, even in such a small and comparatively homogeneous group as our own system—the Solarian Council will not only have to be made up mostly of Lensmen, but each and every inhabited planet of Sol will have to be represented—even Pluto, I suppose, in time. And by the way, your Mr. Saunders wasn't any too pleased when you took Knobos of Mars and DalNalten of Venus away from him and made Lensmen out of them—and put them miles over his head."

"Oh, I wouldn't say that . . . exactly. I convinced him . . . but at that, since Saunders is not Lensman grade himself, it was a trifle difficult for him to understand the situation completely."

"You say it easy—'difficult' is not the word I would use. But back to the Lensman hunt." Kinnison scowled blackly. "I agree, as I said before, that we need non-human Lensmen, the more the better, but I don't think much of your chance of finding any. What makes you think . . . Oh, I see . . . but I don't know whether you're justified or not in assuming a high positive correlation between a certain kind of mental ability and technological advancement."

"No such assumption is necessary. Start anywhere you please, Rod, and take it from there; including Nevia."

"I'll start with known facts, then. Interstellar flight is new to us. We haven't spread far, or surveyed much territory. But in the eight solar systems with which we are most familiar there are seven planets—I'm not counting Valeria—which are very much like Earth in point of mass, size, climate, atmosphere, and gravity. Five of the seven did not have any intelligent life and were colonized easily and quickly. The Tellurian worlds of Procyon and Vega became friendly neighbors—thank God we learned something on Nevia—because they were already inhabited by highly advanced races: Procia by people as human as we are, Vegia by people who would be so if it weren't for their tails. Many other worlds of these systems are inhabited by more or less intelligent non-human races. Just how intelligent they are we don't know, but the Lensmen will soon find out.

"My point is that no race we have found so far has had either atomic energy or any form of space-drive. In any contact with races having space-drives we have not been the discoverers, but the discovered. *Our* colonies are all within twenty six light-years of Earth except Aldebaran II, which is fifty seven, but which drew a lot of people, in spite of the distance, because it was so nearly identical with Earth. On the other hand, the Nevians, from a distance of over a hundred light-years, found *us* . . . implying an older race and a higher development . . . but you just told me that they would *never* produce a Lensman!"

"That point stopped me, too, at first. Follow through; I want to see if you arrive at the same conclusion I did."

"Well . . . I . . . I . . . " Kinnison thought intensely, then went on: "Of course, the Nevians were not colonizing; nor, strictly speaking, exploring. They were merely hunting for iron—a highly organized, intensively specialized operation to find a raw material they needed desperately."

"Precisely," Samms agreed.

"The Rigellians, however, were *surveying*, and Rigel is about four hundred and forty light-years from here. We didn't have a thing they needed or wanted. They nodded at us in passing and kept on going. I'm still on your track?"

"Dead center. And just where does that put the Palainians?"

"I see . . . you may have something there, at that. Palain is so far away that nobody knows even where it is—probably thousands of light-years. Yet they have not only explored this system; they colonized Pluto long before our white race colonized America. But damn it, Virge, I don't like it—any part of it. Rigel Four you may be able to take, with your Lens . . . even one of their damned automobiles, if you stay solidly en rapport with the driver. But *Palain*, Virge! Pluto is bad enough, but the home planet! You can't. Nobody can. It simply can't be done!"

"I know it won't be easy," Samms admitted, bleakly, "but if it's got to be done, I'll do it. And I have a little information that I haven't had time to tell you yet. We discussed once before, you remember, what a job it was to get into any kind of communication with the Palainians on Pluto. You said then that nobody could understand them, and you were right—then. However, I re-ran those brain-wave tapes, wearing my Lens, and could understand them—the thoughts, that is—as well as though they had been recorded in precisionist-grade English."

"*What?*" Kinnison exclaimed, then fell silent. Samms remained silent. What they were thinking of Arisia's Lens cannot be expressed in words.

"Well, go on," Kinnison finally said. "Give me the rest of it—the stinger that you've been holding back."

"The messages—*as messages*—were clear and plain. The backgrounds, however, the connotations and implications, were not. Some of their codes and standards seem to be radically different from ours—so utterly and fantastically different that I simply cannot reconcile either their conduct or their ethics with their obviously high intelligence and their advanced state of development. However, they have at least some minds of tremendous power, and none of the peculiarities I deduced were of such a nature as to preclude Lensmanship. Therefore I am going to Pluto; and from there—I hope—to Palain Seven. If there's a Lensman there, I'll get him."

"You will, at that," Kinnison paid quiet tribute to what he, better than anyone else, knew that his friend had.

"But enough of me—how are you doing?"

"As well as can be expected at this stage of the game. The thing is developing along three main lines. First, the pirates. Since that kind of thing is more or less my own line

I'm handling it myself, unless and until you find someone better qualified. I've got Jack and Costigan working on it now.

"Second; drugs, vice, and so on. I hope you find somebody to take this line over, because, frankly, I'm in over my depth and want to get out. Knobos and DalNalten are trying to find out if there's anything to the idea that there may be a planetary, or even inter-planetary, ring involved. Since Sid Fletcher isn't a Lensman I couldn't disconnect him openly from his job, but he knows a lot about the dope-vice situation and is working practically full time with the other two.

"Third; pure—or rather, decidedly impure—politics. The more I studied *that* subject, the clearer it became that politics would be the worst and biggest battle of the three. There are too many angles I don't know a damned thing about, such as what to do about the succession of foaming, screaming fits your friend Senator Morgan will be throwing the minute he finds out what our Galactic Patrol is going to do. So I ducked the whole political line.

"Now you know as well as I do—better, probably—that Morgan is only the Pernicious Activities Committee of the North American Senate. Multiply him by the thousands of others, all over space, who will be on our necks before the Patrol can get its space-legs, and you will see that all that stuff will have to be handled by a Lensman who, as well as being a mighty smooth operator, will have to know *all* the answers and will have to have plenty of guts. I've got the guts, but none of the other prime requisites. Jill hasn't, although she's got everything else. Fairchild, your Relations ace, isn't a Lensman and can never become one. So you can see quite plainly who has got to handle politics himself."

"You may be right . . . but this Lensman business comes first . . . ." Samms pondered, then brightened. "Perhaps—probably—I can find somebody on this trip—a Palainian, say—who is better qualified than any of us."

Kinnison snorted. "If you can, I'll buy you a week in any Venerian relaxerie you want to name."

"Better start saving up your credits, then, because from what I already know of the Palainian mentality such a development is distinctly more than a possibility." Samms paused, his eyes narrowing. "I don't know whether it would make Morgan and his kind more rabid or less so to have a non-Solarian entity possess authority in our affairs political—but at least it would be something new and different. But in spite of what you said about 'ducking' politics, what have you got Northrop, Jill and Fairchild doing?"

"Well, we had a couple of discussions. I couldn't give either Jill or Dick orders, of course . . . ."

"Wouldn't, you mean," Samms corrected.

"Couldn't," Kinnison insisted. "Jill, besides being your daughter and Lensman grade, had no official connection with either the Triplanetary Service or the Solarian Patrol. And the Service, including Fairchild, is still Triplanetary; and it will have to stay Triplanetary until you have found enough Lensmen so that you can spring your twin surprises—Galactic Council and Galactic Patrol. However, Northrop and Fairchild are keeping their eyes and ears open and their mouths shut, and Jill is finding out whatever she can about drugs and so on, as well as the various political angles. They'll report to you—facts, deductions, guesses, and recommendations—whenever you say the word."

"Nice work, Rod. Thanks. I think I'll call Jill now, before I go—wonder where she is? . . . but I wonder . . . with the Lens perhaps telephones are superfluous? I'll try it."

"JILL!" he thought intensely into his Lens, forming as he did so a mental image of his gorgeous daughter as he knew her. But he found, greatly to his surprise, that neither elaboration nor emphasis was necessary.

"Ouch!" came the almost instantaneous answer, long before his thought was complete. "Don't think so hard, Dad, it hurts—I almost missed a step." Virgilia was actually there with him; inside his own mind; in closer touch with him than she had ever before been. "Back so soon? Shall we report now, or aren't you ready to go to work yet?"

"Skipping for the moment your aspersions on my present activities—not quite." Samms moderated the intensity of his thought to a conversational level. "Just wanted to check with you. Come in, Rod." In flashing thoughts he brought her up to date. "Jill, do you agree with what Rod here has just told me?"

"Yes. Fully. So do the boys."

"That settles it, then—unless, of course, I can find a more capable substitute."

"Of course—but we will believe that when we see it."

"Where are you and what are you doing?"

"Washington, D.C. European Embassy. Dancing with Herkimer Third, Senator Morgan's Number One secretary. I was going to make passes at him—in a perfectly lady-like way, of course—but it wasn't necessary. He thinks he can break down my resistance."

"Careful, Jill! That kind of stuff . . . ."

"Is very old stuff indeed, Daddy dear. Simple. And Herkimer Third isn't really a menace; he just thinks he is. Take a look—you can, can't you, with your Lens?"

"Perhaps . . . Oh, yes. I see him as well as you do." Fully en rapport with the girl as he was, so that his mind received simultaneously with hers any stimulus which she was willing to share, it seemed as though a keen, handsome, deeply tanned face bent down from a distance of inches toward his own. "But I don't like it a bit—and him even less."

"That's because you aren't a girl," Jill giggled mentally. "This is fun; and it won't hurt him a bit, except maybe for a slightly bruised vanity, when I don't fall down flat at his feet. And I'm learning a lot that he hasn't any suspicion he's giving away."

"Knowing you, I believe that. But don't . . . that is . . . well, be very careful not to get your fingers burned. The job isn't worth it—yet."

"Don't worry, Dad." She laughed unaffectedly. "When it comes to playboys like this one, I've got millions and skillions and whillions of ohms of resistance. But here comes Senator Morgan himself, with a fat and repulsive Venerian—he's calling my boy-friend away from me, with what he thinks is an imperceptible high-sign, into a huddle—and my olfactory nerves perceive a rich and fruity aroma, as of skunk—so . . . I hate to seem to be giving a Solarian Councillor the heave-ho, but if I want to read what goes on—and I certainly do—I'll have to concentrate. As soon as you get back give us a call and we'll report. Take it easy, Dad!"

"You're the one to be told that, not me. Good hunting, Jill!"

Samms, still seated calmly at his desk, reached out and pressed a button marked "GARAGE". His office was on the seventeenth floor; the garage occupied level after level of sub-basement. The screen brightened; a keen young face appeared.

"Good evening, Jim. Will you please send my car up to the Wright Skyway feeder?"

"At once, sir. It will be there in seventy five seconds."

Samms cut off; and, after a brief exchange of thought with Kinnison, went out into the hall and along it to the "DOWN" shaft. There, going free, he stepped through a doorless, unguarded archway into over a thousand feet of air. Although it was long after conventional office hours the shaft was still fairly busy, but that made no difference—inertialess collisions cannot even be felt. He bulleted downward to the sixth floor, where he brought himself to an instantaneous halt.

Leaving the shaft, he joined the now thinning crowd hurrying toward the exit. A girl with meticulously plucked eyebrows and an astounding hair-do, catching sight of his Lens, took her hands out of her breeches pockets—skirts went out, as office dress, when up-and-down open-shaft velocities of a hundred or so miles per hour replaced elevators—nudged her companion, and whispered excitedly:

"Look there! Quick! I never saw one close up before, did you? That's him—himself! First Lensman Samms!"

At the Portal, the Lensman as a matter of habit held out his car-check, but such formalities were no longer necessary, or even possible. Everybody knew, or wanted to be thought of as knowing, Virgil Samms.

"Stall four sixty five, First Lensman, sir," the uniformed gateman told him, without even glancing at the extended disk.

"Thank you, Tom."

"This way, please, sir, First Lensman," and a youth, teeth gleaming white in a startlingly black face, strode proudly to the indicated stall and opened the vehicle's door.

"Thank you, Danny," Samms said, as appreciatively as though he did not know exactly where his ground-car was.

He got in. The door jammed itself gently shut. The runabout—a Dillingham eleven-forty—shot smoothly forward upon its two fat, soft tires. Half-way to the exit archway he was doing forty; he hit the steeply-banked curve leading into the lofty "street" at ninety. Nor was there shock or strain. Motorcycle-wise, but automatically, the "Dilly" leaned against its gyroscopes at precisely the correct angle; the huge low-pressure tires clung to the resilient synthetic of the pavement as though integral with it. Nor was there any question of conflicting traffic, for this thoroughfare, six full levels above Varick Street proper, was not, strictly speaking, a street at all. It had only one point of access, the one which Samms had used; and only one exit—it was simply and only a feeder into Wright Skyway, a limited-access superhighway.

Samms saw, without noting particularly, the maze of traffic-ways of which this feeder was only one tiny part; a maze which extended from ground-level up to a point well above even the towering buildings of New York's metropolitan district.

The way rose sharply; Samms' right foot went down a little farther; the Dillingham began to pick up speed. Moving loud-speakers sang to him and yelled and blared at him, but he did not hear them. Brilliant signs, flashing and flaring all the colors of the spectrum—sheer triumphs of the electrician's art—blazed in or flamed into arresting words and eye-catching pictures, but he did not see them. Advertising—designed by experts to sell everything from aardvarks to Martian zyzmol ("bottled ecstacy")—but the First Lensman was a seasoned big-city dweller. His mind had long since become a perfect filter, admitting to his consciousness only things which he wanted to perceive: only so can big-city life be made endurable.

Approaching the Skyway, he cut in his touring roadlights, slowed down a trifle, and insinuated his low-flyer into the stream of traffic. Those lights threw fifteen hundred watts apiece, but there was no glare—polarized lenses and wind-shields saw to that.

He wormed his way over to the left-hand, high-speed lane and opened up. At the edge of the skyscraper district, where Wright Skyway angles sharply downward to ground level, Samms' attention was caught and held by something off to his right—a blue-white, whistling something that hurtled upward into the air. As it ascended it slowed down; its monotone shriek became lower and lower in pitch; its light went down through the spectrum toward the red. Finally it exploded, with an earth-shaking crash; but the lightning-like flash of the detonation, instead of vanishing almost instantaneously, settled itself upon a low-hanging artificial cloud and became a picture and four words—two bearded faces and "SMITH BROS. COUGH DROPS"!

"Well, I'll be damned!" Samms spoke aloud, chagrined at having been compelled to listen to and to look at an advertisement. "I thought I had seen everything, but *that* is really new!"

Twenty minutes—fifty miles—later, Samms left the Skyway at a point near what had once been South Norwalk, Connecticut; an area transformed now into the level square miles of New York Spaceport.

New York Spaceport; then, and until the establishment of Prime Base, the biggest and busiest field in existence upon any planet of Civilization. For New York City, long the financial and commercial capital of the Earth, had maintained the same dominant position in the affairs of the Solar System and was holding a substantial lead over her rivals, Chicago, London, and Stalingrad, in the race for inter-stellar supremacy.

And Virgil Samms himself, because of the ever-increasing menace of piracy, had been largely responsible for the policy of basing the war-vessels of the Triplanetary Patrol upon each space-field in direct ratio to the size and importance of that field. Hence he was no stranger in New York Spaceport; in fact, master psychologist that he was, he had made it a point to know by first name practically everyone connected with it.

No sooner had he turned his Dillingham over to a smiling attendant, however, than he was accosted by a man whom he had never seen before.

"Mr. Samms?" the stranger asked.

"Yes." Samms did not energize his Lens; he had not yet developed either the inclination or the technique to probe instantaneously every entity who approached him, upon any pretext whatever, in order to find out what that entity *really* wanted.

"I'm Isaacson . . . " the man paused, as though he had supplied a world of information.

"Yes?" Samms was receptive, but not impressed.

"Interstellar Spaceways, you know. We've been trying to see you for two weeks, but we couldn't get past your secretaries, so I decided to buttonhole you here, myself. But we're just as much alone here as we would be in either one of our offices—yes, more so. What I want to talk to you about is having our exclusive franchise extended to cover the outer planets and the colonies."

"Just a minute, Mr. Isaacson. Surely you know that I no longer have even a portfolio in the Council; that practically all of my attention is, and for some time to come will be, directed elsewhere?"

"Exactly—*officially*." Isaacson's tone spoke volumes. "But you're still the Boss; they'll do anything you tell them to. We couldn't try to do business with you before, of course, but in your present position there is nothing whatever to prevent you from getting into the biggest thing that will ever be. We are the biggest corporation in existence now, as you know, and we are still growing—fast. We don't do business in a small way, or with small men; so here's a check for a million credits, or I will deposit it to your account . . . ."

"I'm not interested."

"As a binder," the other went on, as smoothly as though his sentence had not been interrupted, "with twenty-five million more to follow on the day that our franchise goes through."

"I'm still not interested."

"No . . . o . . . o . . . ?" Isaacson studied the Lensman narrowly: and Samms, Lens now wide awake, studied the entrepreneur. "Well . . . I . . . while I admit that we want you pretty badly, you are smart enough to know that we'll get what we want anyway, with or without you. With you, though, it will be easier and quicker, so I am authorized to offer you, besides the twenty six million credits . . . " he savored the words as he uttered them: "twenty two and one-half percent of Spaceways. On today's market that is worth fifty million credits; ten years from now it will be worth fifty *billion*. That's my high bid; that's as high as we can possibly go."

"I'm glad to hear that—I'm *still* not interested," and Samms strode away, calling his friend Kinnison as he did so.

"Rod? Virgil." He told the story.

"Whew!" Kinnison whistled expressively. "They're not pikers, anyway, are they? What a *sweet* set-up—and you could wrap it up and hand it to them like a pound of coffee . . . ."

"Or you could, Rod."

"Could be . . . ." The big Lensman ruminated. "But *what* a hookup! Perfectly legitimate, and with plenty of precedents—and arguments, of a sort—in its favor. The outer planets. Then Alpha Centauri and Sirius and Procyon and so on. Monopoly—all the traffic will bear . . . ."

"Slavery, you mean!" Samms stormed. "It would hold Civilization back for a thousand years!"

"Sure, but what do *they* care?"

"That's it . . . and he said—and actually believed—that they would get it without my help . . . . I can't help wondering about that."

"Simple enough, Virge, when you think about it. He doesn't know yet what a Lensman is. Nobody does, you know, except Lensmen. It will take some time for that knowledge to get around . . . ."

"And still longer for it to be *believed*."

"Right. But as to the chance of Interstellar Spaceways ever getting the monopoly they're working for, I didn't think I would have to remind you that it was not entirely by accident that over half of the members of the Solarian Council are Lensmen, and that any Galactic Councillor will automatically *have* to be a Lensman. So go right ahead with what you started, my boy, and don't give Isaacson and Company another thought. We'll bend an optic or two in that direction while you are gone."

"I was overlooking a few things, at that, I guess." Samms sighed in relief as he entered the main office of the Patrol.

The line at the receptionist's desk was fairly short, but even so, Samms was not allowed to wait. That highly decorative, but far-from-dumb blonde, breaking off in mid-sentence her business of the moment, turned on her charm as though it had been a battery of floodlights, pressed a stud on her desk, and spoke to the man before her and to the Lensman:

"Excuse me a moment, please. First Lensman Samms, sir . . . ?"

"Yes, Miss Regan?" her communicator—"squawk-box", in every day parlance—broke in.

"First Lensman Samms is here, sir," the girl announced, and broke the circuit.

"Good evening, Sylvia. Lieutenant-Commander Wagner, please, or whoever else is handling clearances," Samms answered what he thought was to have been her question.

"Oh, no, sir; you are cleared. Commodore Clayton has been waiting for you . . . here he is, now."

"Hi, Virgil!" Commodore Clayton, a big, solid man with a scarred face and a shock of iron-gray hair, whose collar bore the two silver stars which proclaimed him to be the commander-in-chief of a continental contingent of the Patrol, shook hands vigorously. "I'll zip you out. Miss Regan, call a bug, please."

"Oh, that isn't necessary, Alex!" Samms protested. "I'll pick one up outside."

"Not in any Patrol base in North America, my friend; nor, unless I am very badly mistaken, anywhere else. From now on, Lensmen have absolute priority, and the quicker everybody realizes exactly what that means, the better."

The "bug"—a vehicle something like a jeep, except more so—was waiting at the door. The two men jumped aboard.

"The *Chicago*—and blast!" Clayton ordered, crisply.

The driver obeyed—literally. Gravel flew from beneath skidding tires as the highly maneuverable little ground-car took off. A screaming turn into the deservedly famous Avenue of Oaks. Along the Avenue. Through the Gate, the guards saluting smartly as the bug raced past them. Past the barracks. Past the airport hangars and strips. Out into the space-field, the scarred and blackened area devoted solely to the widely-spaced docks of the tremendous vessels which plied the vacuous reaches of inter-planetary and inter-stellar space. Spacedocks were, and are, huge and sprawling structures; built of concrete and steel and asbestos and ultra-stubborn refractory and insulation and vacuum-breaks; fully air-conditioned and having refrigeration equipment of thousands of tons per hour of ice; designed not only to expedite servicing, unloading, and loading, but also to protect materials and personnel from the raving, searing blasts of take-off and of landing.

A space-dock is a squat and monstrous cylinder, into whose hollow top the lowermost one-third of a space-ship's bulk fits as snugly as does a baseball into the "pocket" of a veteran fielder's long-seasoned glove. And the tremendous distances between those docks minimize the apparent size, both of the structures themselves and of the vessels surmounting them. Thus, from a distance, the *Chicago* looked little enough, and harmless enough; but as the bug flashed under the overhanging bulk and the driver braked savagely to a stop at one of the dock's entrances, Samms could scarcely keep from flinching. That featureless, gray, smoothly curving wall of alloy steel loomed so incredibly high above them—extended so terrifyingly far outward beyond its visible means of support! It *must* be on the very verge of crashing!

Samms stared deliberately at the mass of metal towering above him, then smiled—not without effort—at his companion.

"You'd think, Alex, that a man would get over being afraid that a ship was going to fall on him, but I haven't—yet."

"No, and you probably never will. I never have, and I'm one of the old hands. Some claim not to mind it—but not in front of a lie detector. That's why they had to make the passenger docks bigger than the liners—too many passengers fainted and had to be carried aboard on stretchers—or cancelled passage entirely. However, scaring hell out of them on the ground had one big advantage; they felt so safe inside that they didn't get the colly-wobbles so bad when they went free."

"Well, I've got over *that*, anyway. Good-bye, Alex; and thanks."

Samms entered the dock, shot smoothly upward, followed an escorting officer to the captain's own cabin, and settled himself into a cushioned chair facing an ultra-wave view-plate. A face appeared upon his communicator screen and spoke.

"Winfield to First Lensman Samms—you will be ready to blast off at twenty one hundred?"

"Samms to Captain Winfield," the Lensman replied. "I will be ready."

Sirens yelled briefly; a noise which Samms knew was purely a formality. Clearance had been issued; Station PiXNY was filling the air with warnings. Personnel and material close enough to the *Chicago's* dock to be affected by the blast were under cover and safe.

The blast went on; the plate showed, instead of a view of the space-field, a blaze of blue-white light. The war-ship was inertialess, it is true; but so terrific were the forces released that incandescent gases, furiously driven, washed the dock and everything for hundreds of yards around it.

The plate cleared. Through the lower, denser layers of atmosphere the *Chicago* bored in seconds; then, as the air grew thinner and thinner, she rushed upward faster and faster. The terrain below became concave . . . then convex. Being completely without inertia, the ship's velocity was at every instant that at which the friction of the medium through which she blasted her way equaled precisely the force of her driving thrust.

Wherefore, out in open space, the Earth a fast-shrinking tiny ball and Sol himself growing smaller, paler, and weaker at a startling rate, the *Chicago's* speed attained an almost constant value; a value starkly impossible for the human mind to grasp.

CHAPTER 5

For hours Virgil Samms sat motionless, staring almost unseeing into his plate. It was not that the view was not worth seeing—the wonder of space, the ever-changing, constantly-shifting panorama of incredibly brilliant although dimensionless points of light, against that wondrous background of mist-besprinkled black velvet, is a thing that never fails to awe even the most seasoned observer—but he had a tremendous load on his mind. He had to solve an apparently insoluble problem. How . . . *how* . . . HOW could he do what he had to do?

Finally, knowing that the time of landing was approaching, he got up, unfolded his fans, and swam lightly through the air of the cabin to a hand-line, along which he drew himself into the control room. He could have made the trip in that room, of course, if he had so chosen; but, knowing that officers of space do not really like to have strangers in that sanctum, he did not intrude until it was necessary.

Captain Winfield was already strapped down at his master conning plate. Pilots, navigators, and computers worked busily at their respective tasks.

"I was just going to call you, First Lensman." Winfield waved a hand in the general direction of a chair near his own. "Take the Lieutenant-Captain's station, please." Then, after a few minutes: "Go inert, Mr. White."

"Attention, all personnel," Lieutenant-Captain White spoke conversationally into a microphone. "Prepare for inert maneuvering, Class Three. Off."

A bank of tiny red lights upon a panel turned green practically as one. White cut the Bergenholm, whereupon Virgil Samms' mass changed instantly from a weight of zero to one of five hundred and twenty five pounds—ships of war then had no space to waste upon such non-essentials as artificial gravity. Although he was braced for the change and cushioned against it, the Lensman's breath *whooshed!* out sharply; but, being intensely interested in what was going on, he swallowed convulsively a couple of times, gasped a few deep breaths, and fought his way back up to normalcy.

The Chief Pilot was now at work, with all the virtuoso's skill of his rank and grade; one of the hall-marks of which is to make difficult tasks look easy. He played trills and runs and arpeggios—at times veritable glissades—upon keyboards and pedals, directing with micrometric precision the tremendous forces of the superdreadnaught to the task of matching the intrinsic velocity of New York Spaceport at the time of his departure to the I. V. of the surface of the planet so far below.

Samms stared into his plate; first at the incredibly tiny apparent size of that incredibly hot sun, and then at the barren-looking world toward which they were dropping at such terrific speed.

"It doesn't seem possible . . . " he remarked, half to Winfield, half to himself, "that a sun could be that big and that hot. Rigel Four is almost two hundred times as far away from it as Earth is from Sol—something like eighteen billion miles—it doesn't look much, if any, bigger than Venus does from Luna—yet this world is hotter than the Sahara Desert."

"Well, blue giants are both big and hot," the captain replied, matter-of-factly, "and their radiation, being mostly invisible, is deadly stuff. And Rigel is about the biggest in this region. There are others a lot worse, though. Doradus S, for instance, would make Rigel, here, look like a tallow candle. I'm going out there, some of these days, just to take a look at it. But that's enough of astronomical chit-chat—we're down to twenty miles of altitude and we've got your city just about stopped."

The *Chicago* slowed gently to a halt; perched motionless upon softly hissing jets. Samms directed his visibeam downward and sent along it an exploring, questing thought. Since he had never met a Rigellian in person, he could not form the mental image or pattern necessary to become en rapport with any one individual of the race. He did know, however, the type of mind which must be possessed by the entity with whom he wished to talk, and he combed the Rigellian city until he found one. The rapport was so incomplete and imperfect as to amount almost to no contact at all, but he could, perhaps, make himself understood.

"If you will excuse this possibly unpleasant and certainly unwarranted intrusion," he thought, carefully and slowly, "I would like very much to discuss with you a matter which should become of paramount importance to all the intelligent peoples of all the planets in space."

"I welcome you, Tellurian." Mind fused with mind at every one of uncountable millions of points and paths. This Rigellian professor of sociology, standing at his desk, was physically a monster . . . the oil-drum of a body, the four blocky legs, the multi-branchiate tentacular arms, that immobile dome of a head, the complete lack of eyes and of ears . . . nevertheless Samms' mind fused with the monstrosity's as smoothly, as effortlessly, and almost as completely as it had with his own daughter's!

And *what* a mind! The transcendent poise; the staggeringly tremendous range and scope—the untroubled and unshakeable calm; the sublime quietude; the vast and placid certainty; the ultimate stability, unknown and forever unknowable to any human or near-human race!

"Dismiss all thought of intrusion, First Lensman Samms . . . I have heard of you human beings, of course, but have never considered seriously the possibility of meeting one of you mind to mind. Indeed, it was reported that none of our minds could make any except the barest and most unsatisfactory contact with any of yours they chanced to encounter. It is, I now perceive, the Lens which makes this full accord possible, and it is basically about the Lens that you are here?"

"It is," and Samms went on to cover in flashing thoughts his conception of what the Galactic Patrol should be and should become. That was easy enough; but when he tried to describe in detail the qualifications necessary for Lensmanship, he began to bog down. "Force, drive, scope, of course . . . range . . . power . . . but above all, an absolute integrity . . . an ultimate incorruptibility . . . ." He could recognize such a mind after meeting it and studying it, but as to finding it . . . It might not be in any place of power or authority.

207

His own, and Rod Kinnison's, happened to be; but Costigan's was not . . . and both Knobos and DalNalten had made inconspicuousness a fine art . . . .

"I see," the native stated, when it became clear that Samms could say no more. "It is evident, of course, that I cannot qualify; nor do I know anyone personally who can. However . . . ."

"What?" Samms demanded. "I was sure, from the feel of your mind, that you . . . but with a mind of such depth and breadth, such tremendous scope and power, you must be incorruptible!"

"I am," came the dry rejoinder. "We all are. No Rigellian is, or ever will be or can be, what you think of as 'corrupt' or 'corruptible'. Indeed, it is only by the narrowest, most intense concentration upon every line of your thought that I can translate your meaning into a concept possible for any of us even to understand."

"Then what . . . Oh, I see. I was starting at the wrong end. Naturally enough, I suppose, I looked first for the qualities rarest in my own race."

"Of course. Our minds have ample scope and range; and, perhaps, sufficient power. But those qualities which you refer to as 'force' and 'drive' are fully as rare among us as absolute mental integrity is among you. What you know as 'crime' is unknown. We have no police, no government, no laws, no organized armed forces of any kind. We take, practically always, the line of least resistance. We live and let live, as your thought runs. We work together for the common good."

"Well . . . I don't know what I expected to find here, but certainly not this . . . ." If Samms had never before been completely thunderstruck, completely at a loss, he was then. "You don't think, then, that there is any chance?"

"I have been thinking, and there may be a chance . . . a slight one, but still a chance," the Rigellian said, slowly. "For instance, that youth, so full of curiosity, who first visited your planet. Thousands of us have wondered, to ourselves and to each other, about the peculiar qualities of mind which compelled him and others to waste so much time, effort, and wealth upon a project so completely useless as exploration. Why, he had even to develop energies and engines theretofore unknown, and which can never be of any real use!"

Samms was shaken by the calm finality with which the Rigellian dismissed all possibility of the usefulness of inter-stellar exploration, but stuck doggedly to his purpose.

"However slight the chance, I must find and talk to this man. I suppose he is now out in deep space somewhere. Have you any idea where?"

"He is now in his home city, accumulating funds and manufacturing fuel with which to continue his pointless activities. That city is named . . . that is, in your English you might call it . . . Suntown? Sunberg? No, it must be more specific . . . Rigelsville? Rigel City?"

"Rigelston, I would translate it?" Samms hazarded.

"Exactly—Rigelston." The professor marked its location upon a globular mental map far more accurate and far more detailed than the globe which Captain Winfield and his lieutenant were then studying.

"Thanks. Now, can you and will you get in touch with this explorer and ask him to call a meeting of his full crew and any others who might be interested in the project I have outlined?"

"I can. I will. He and his kind are not quite sane, of course, as you know; but I do not believe that even they are so insane as to be willing to subject themselves to the environment of your vessel."

"They will not be asked to come here. The meeting will be held in Rigelston. If necessary, I shall insist that it be held there."

"You would? I perceive that you would. It is strange . . . yes, fantastic . . . you are quarrelsome, pugnacious, anti-social, vicious, small-bodied and small-brained; timid, nervous, and highly and senselessly excitable; unbalanced and unsane; as sheerly monstrous mentally as you are physically . . . ." These outrageous thoughts were sent as casually and as impersonally as though the sender were discussing the weather. He paused, then went on: "And yet, to further such a completely visionary project, you are eager to subject yourself to conditions whose counterparts I could not force myself, under any circumstances whatever, to meet. It may be . . . it must be true that there is an extension of the principle of working together for the common good which my mind, for lack of pertinent data, has not been able to grasp. I am now en rapport with Dronvire the explorer."

"Ask him, please, not to identify himself to me. I do not want to go into that meeting with any preconceived ideas."

"A balanced thought," the Rigellian approved. "Someone will be at the airport to point out to you the already desolated area in which the space-ship of the explorers makes its so-frightful landings; Dronvire will ask someone to meet you at the airport and bring you to the place of meeting."

The telepathic line snapped and Samms turned a white and sweating face to the *Chicago's* captain.

"God, what a strain! Don't ever try telepathy unless you positively have to—especially not with such an outlandishly *different* race as these Rigellians are!"

"Don't worry; I won't." Winfield's words were not at all sympathetic, but his tone was. "You looked as though somebody was beating your brains out with a spiked club. Where next, First Lensman?"

Samms marked the location of Rigelston upon the vessel's chart, then donned ear-plugs and a special, radiation-proof suit of armor, equipped with refrigerators and with extra-thick blocks of lead glass to protect the eyes.

The airport, an extremely busy one well outside the city proper, was located easily enough, as was the spot upon which the Tellurian ship was to land. Lightly, slowly, she settled downward, her jets raving out against a gravity fully twice that of her native Earth. Those blasts, however, added little or nothing to the destruction already accomplished by the craft then lying there—a torpedo-shaped cruiser having perhaps one-twentieth of the *Chicago's* mass and bulk.

The superdreadnaught landed, sinking into the hard, dry ground to a depth of some ten or fifteen feet before she stopped. Samms, en rapport with the entity who was to be his escort, made a flashing survey of the mind so intimately in contact with his own. No use. This one was not and never could become Lensman material. He climbed heavily down the ladder. This double-normal gravity made the going a bit difficult, but he could stand that a lot better than some of the other things he was going to have to take. The Rigellian equivalent of an automobile was there, waiting for him, its door invitingly open.

Samms had known—in general—what to expect. The two-wheeled chassis was more or less similar to that of his own Dillingham. The body was a narrow torpedo of steel, bluntly pointed at both ends, and without windows. Two features, however, were both unexpected and unpleasant—the hard, tough steel of which that body was forged was an inch and a half thick, instead of one-sixteenth; and even that extraordinarily armored body was dented and scarred and marred, especially about the fore and rear quarters, as deeply and as badly and as casually as are the fenders of an Earthly jalopy!

The Lensman climbed, not easily or joyously, into that grimly forbidding black interior. Black? It was so black that the port-hole-like doorway seemed to admit no light at all. It was blacker than a witch's cat in a coal cellar at midnight! Samms flinched; then, stiffening, thought at the driver.

"My contact with you seems to have slipped. I'm afraid that I will have to cling to you rather more tightly than may be either polite or comfortable. Deprived of sight, and without your sense of perception, I am practically helpless."

"Come in, Lensman, by all means. I offered to maintain full engagement, but it seemed to me that you declined it; quite possibly the misunderstanding was due to our unfamiliarity with each others' customary mode of thought. Relax, please, and come in . . . there! Better?"

"Infinitely better. Thanks."

And it was. The darkness vanished; through the unexplainable perceptive sense of the Rigellian he could "see" everything—he had a practically perfect three-dimensional view of the entire circumambient sphere. He could see both the inside and the outside of the ground car he was in and of the immense space-ship in which he had come to Rigel IV. He could see the bearings and the wrist-pins of the internal-combustion engine of the car, the interior structure of the welds that held the steel plates together, the busy airport outside, and even deep into the ground. He could see and study in detail the deepest-buried, most heavily shielded parts of the atomic engines of the *Chicago*.

But he was wasting time. He could also plainly see a deeply-cushioned chair, designed to fit a human body, welded to a stanchion and equipped with half a dozen padded restraining straps. He sat down quickly; strapped himself in.

"Ready?"

"Ready."

The door banged shut with a clangor which burst through space-suit and ear-plugs with all the violence of a nearby thunderclap. And that was merely the beginning. The engine started—an internal-combustion engine of well over a thousand horsepower, designed for maximum efficiency by engineers in whose lexicon there were no counterparts of any English words relating to noise, or even to sound. The car took off; with an acceleration which drove the Tellurian backward, deep into the cushions. The scream of tortured tires and the crescendo bellowing of the engine combined to form an uproar which, amplified by and reverberating within the resonant shell of metal, threatened to addle the very brain inside the Lensman's skull.

"You suffer!" the driver exclaimed, in high concern. "They cautioned me to start and stop gently, to drive slowly and carefully, to bump softly. They told me you are frail and fragile, a fact which I perceived for myself and which has caused me to drive with the utmost possible care and restraint. Is the fault mine? Have I been too rough?"

"Not at all. It isn't that. It's the ungodly noise." Then, realizing that the Rigellian could have no conception of his meaning, he continued quickly:

"The vibrations in the atmosphere, from sixteen cycles per second up to about nine or ten thousand." He explained what a second was. "My nervous system is very sensitive to those vibrations. But I expected them and shielded myself against them as adequately as I could. Nothing can be done about them. Go ahead."

"Atmospheric vibrations? *Atmospheric* vibrations? Atmospheric *vibrations?*" The driver marveled, and concentrated upon this entirely new concept while he—

1. Swung around a steel-sheathed concrete pillar at a speed of at least sixty miles per hour, grazing it so closely that he removed one layer of protective coating from the metal.

2. Braked so savagely to miss a wildly careening truck that the restraining straps almost cut Samms' body, space-suit and all, into slices.

3. Darted into a hole in the traffic so narrow that only tiny fractions of inches separated his hurtling Juggernaut from an enormous steel column on one side and another speeding vehicle on the other.

4. Executed a double-right-angle reverse curve, thus missing by hair's breadths two vehicles traveling in the opposite direction and one in his own.

5. As a grand climax to this spectacular exhibition of insane driving, he plunged at full speed into a traffic artery which seemed so full already that it could not hold even one more car. But it could—just barely could. However, instead of near misses or grazing hits, this time there were bumps, dents—little ones, nothing at all, really, only an inch or so deep—and an utterly hellish concatenation and concentration of noise.

"I fail completely to understand what effect such vibrations could have," the Rigellian announced finally, sublimely unconscious that anything at all out of the ordinary had occurred. For him, nothing had. "But surely they cannot be of any use?"

"On this world, I am afraid not. No," Samms admitted, wearily. "Here, too, apparently, as everywhere, the big cities are choking themselves to death with their own traffic."

"Yes. We build and build, but never have roads enough."

"What are those mounds along the streets?" For some time Samms had been conscious of those long, low, apparently opaque structures; attracted to them because they were the only non-transparent objects within range of the Rigellian's mind. "Or is it something I should not mention?"

"What? Oh, those? By no means."

One of the nearby mounds lost its opacity. It was filled with swirling, gyrating bands and streamers of energy so vivid and so solid as to resemble fabric; with wildly hurtling objects of indescribable shapes and contours; with brilliantly flashing symbols which

Samms found, greatly to his surprise, made sense—not through the Rigellian's mind, but through his own Lens:

"EAT TEEGMEE'S FOOD!"

"Advertising!" Samms' thought was a snort.

"Advertising. You do not perceive yours, either, as you drive?" This was the first bond to be established between two of the most highly advanced races of the First Galaxy!

The frightful drive continued; the noise grew worse and worse. Imagine, if you can, a city of fifteen millions of people, throughout whose entire length, breadth, height, and depth no attempt whatever had ever been made to abate any noise, however violent or piercing! If your imagination has been sufficiently vivid and if you have worked understandingly enough, the product may approximate what First Lensman Samms was forced to listen to that day.

Through ever-thickening traffic, climbing to higher and ever higher roadways between towering windowless walls of steel, the massive Rigellian automobile barged and banged its way. Finally it stopped, a thousand feet or so above the ground, beside a building which was still under construction. The heavy door clanged open. They got out.

And then—it chanced to be daylight at the time—Samms saw a tangle of fighting, screaming *colors* whose like no entity possessing the sense of sight had ever before imagined. Reds, yellows, blues, greens, purples, and every variation and inter-mixture possible; laid on or splashed on or occurring naturally at perfect random, smote his eyes as violently as the all-pervading noise had been assailing his ears.

He realized then that through his guide's sense of perception he had been "seeing" only in shades of gray, that to these people "visible" light differed only in wave-length from any other band of the complete electromagnetic spectrum of vibration.

Strained and tense, the Lensman followed his escort along a narrow catwalk, through a wall upon which riveters and welders were busily at work, into a room practically without walls and ceiled only by story after story of huge I-beams. Yet *this* was the meeting-place; almost a hundred Rigellians were assembled there!

And as Samms walked toward the group a craneman dropped a couple of tons of steel plate, from a height of eight or ten feet, upon the floor directly behind him.

"I just about jumped right out of my armor," is the way Samms himself described his reactions; and that description is perhaps as good as any.

At any rate, he went briefly out of control, and the Rigellian sent him a steadying, inquiring, wondering thought. He could no more understand the Tellurian's sensitivity than Samms could understand the fact that to these people, even the concept of physical intrusion was absolutely incomprehensible. These builders were not workmen, in the Tellurian sense. They were Rigellians, each working his few hours per week for the common good. They would be no more in contact with the meeting than would their fellows on the other side of the planet.

Samms closed his eyes to the riot of clashing colors, deafened himself by main strength to the appalling clangor of sound, forced himself to concentrate every fiber of his mind upon his errand.

"Please synchronize with my mind, as many of you as possible," he thought at the group as a whole, and went en rapport with mind after mind after mind. And mind after mind after mind lacked something. Some were stronger than others, had more initiative and drive and urge, but none would quite do. Until—

"Thank God!" In the wave of exultant relief, of fulfillment, Samms no longer saw the colors or heard the din. "You, sir, are of Lensman grade. I perceive that you are Dronvire."

"Yes, Virgil Samms, I am Dronvire; and at long last I know what it is that I have been seeking all my life. But how of these, my other friends? Are not some of them . . . ?"

"I do not know, nor is it necessary that I find out. You will select . . . " Samms paused, amazed. The other Rigellians were still in the room, but mentally, he and Dronvire were completely alone.

"They anticipated your thought, and, knowing that it was to be more or less personal, they left us until one of us invites them to return."

"I like that, and appreciate it. You will go to Arisia. You will receive your Lens. You will return here. You will select and send to Arisia as many or as few of your fellows as you choose. These things I require you, by the Lens of Arisia, to do. Afterward—please note that this is in no sense obligatory—I would like very much to have you visit Earth and accept appointment to the Galactic Council. Will you?"

"I will." Dronvire needed no time to consider his decision.

The meeting was dismissed. The same entity who had been Samms' chauffeur on the in-bound trip drove him back to the *Chicago*, driving as "slowly" and as "carefully" as before. Nor, this time, did the punishment take such toll, even though Samms knew that each terrific lunge and lurch was adding one more bruise to the already much-too-large collection discoloring almost every square foot of his tough hide. He had succeeded, and the thrill of success had its usual analgesic effect.

The *Chicago's* captain met him in the air-lock and helped him remove his suit.

"Are you *sure* you're all right, Samms?" Winfield was no longer the formal captain, but a friend. "Even though you didn't call, we were beginning to wonder . . . you look as though you'd been to a Valerian clambake, and I sure as hell don't like the way you're favoring those ribs and that left leg. I'll tell the boys you got back in A-prime shape, but I'll have the doctors look you over, just to make sure."

Winfield made the announcement, and through his Lens Samms could plainly feel the wave of relief and pleasure that spread throughout the great ship with the news. It surprised him immensely. Who was *he*, that all these boys should care so much whether he lived or died?

"I'm perfectly all right," Samms protested. "There's nothing at all the matter with me that twenty hours of sleep won't fix as good as new."

"Maybe; but you'll go to the sick-bay first, just the same," Winfield insisted. "And I suppose you want me to blast back to Tellus?"

"Right. And fast. The Ambassadors' Ball is next Tuesday evening, you know, and that's one function I can't stay away from, even with a Class A Double Prime excuse."

*

THE LENSMAN

CHAPTER 6

The Ambassadors' Ball, one of the most ultra-ultra functions of the year, was well under way. It was not that everyone who was anyone was there; but everyone who was there was, in one way or another, very emphatically someone. Thus, there were affairs at which there were more young and beautiful women, and more young and handsome men; but none exhibiting newer or more expensive gowns, more ribbons and decorations, more or costlier or more refined jewelry, or a larger acreage of powdered and perfumed epidermis.

And even so, the younger set was well enough represented. Since pioneering appeals more to youth than to age, the men representing the colonies were young; and their wives, together with the daughters and the second (or third or fourth, or occasionally the fifth) wives of the human personages practically balanced the account.

Nor was the throng entirely human. The time had not yet come, of course, when warm-blooded, oxygen-breathing monstrosities from hundreds of other solar systems would vie in numbers with the humanity present. There were, however, a few Martians on the floor, wearing their light "robes du convention" and dancing with meticulously mathematical precision. A few Venerians, who did not dance, sat in state or waddled importantly about. Many worlds of the Solarian System, and not a few other systems, were represented.

One couple stood out, even against that opulent and magnificent background. Eyes followed them wherever they went.

The girl was tall, trim, supple; built like a symphony. Her Callistan vexto-silk gown, of the newest and most violent shade of "radio-active" green, was phosphorescently luminous; fluorescent; gleaming and glowing. Its hem swept the floor, but above the waist it vanished mysteriously except for wisps which clung to strategic areas here and there with no support, apparently, except the personal magnetism of the wearer. She, almost alone of all the women there, wore no flowers. Her only jewelry was a rosette of huge, perfectly-matched emeralds, perched precariously upon her bare left shoulder. Her hair, unlike the other women's flawless coiffures, was a flamboyant, artistically-disarranged, red-bronze-auburn mop. Her soft and dewy eyes—Virgilia Samms could control her eyes as perfectly as she could her highly educated hands—were at the moment gold-flecked, tawny wells of girlish innocence and trust.

"But I *can't* give you this next dance, too, Herkimer—*Honestly* I can't!" she pleaded, snuggling just a trifle closer into the embrace of the young man who was just as much man, physically, as she was woman. "I'd just *love* to, really, but I just simply *can't*, and you know why, too."

"You've got some duty-dances, of course . . . "

"*Some?* I've got a list as long as from here to there! Senator Morgan first, of course, then Mr. Isaacson, then I sat one out with Mr. Ossmen—I can't *stand* Venerians, they're so slimy and fat and repulsive!—and that leathery horned toad from Mars and that Jovian hippopotamus . . . "

She went down the list, and as she named or characterized each entity another finger of her left hand pressed down upon the back of her partner's right, to emphasize the count of her social obligations. But those talented fingers were doing more—far, far more—than that.

Herkimer Third, although no little of a Don Juan, was a highly polished, smoothly finished, thoroughly seasoned diplomat. As such, his eyes and his other features—particularly his eyes—had been schooled for years to reveal no trace of whatever might be going on inside his brain. If he had entertained any suspicion of the beautiful girl in his arms, if anyone had suggested that she was trying her best to pump him, he would have smiled the sort of smile which only the top-drawer diplomat can achieve. He was not suspicious of Virgilia Samms. However, simply because she was Virgil Samms' daughter, he took an extra bit of pain to betray no undue interest in any one of the names she recited. And besides, she was not looking at his eyes, nor even at his face. Her glance, demurely downcast, was all too rarely raised above the level of his chin.

There were some things, however, that Herkimer Herkimer Third did not know. That Virgilia Samms was the most accomplished muscle-reader of her times. That she was so close to him, not because of his manly charm, but because only in that position could she do her prodigious best. That she could work with her eyes alone, but in emergencies, when fullest possible results were imperative, she had to use her exquisitely sensitive fingers and her exquisitely tactile skin. That she had studied intensively, and had tabulated the reactions of, each of the entities on her list. That she was now, with his help, fitting those reactions into a pattern. And finally, that that pattern was beginning to assume the grim shape of MURDER!

And Virgilia Samms, working now for something far more urgent and vastly more important than a figmental Galactic Patrol, hoped desperately that this Herkimer was not a muscle-reader too; for she knew that she was revealing her secrets even more completely than was he. In fact, if things got much worse, he could not help but feel the pounding of her heart . . . but she could explain that easily enough, by a few appropriate wiggles . . . No, he wasn't a reader, definitely not. He wasn't watching the right places; he was looking where that gown had been designed to make him look, and nowhere else . . . and no tell-tale muscles lay beneath any part of either of his hands.

As her eyes and her fingers and her lovely torso sent more and more information to her keen brain, Jill grew more and more anxious. She was sure that murder was intended, but who was to be the victim? Her father? Probably. Pops Kinnison? Possibly. Somebody else? Barely possibly. And when? And where? And how? She *didn't know*! And she would have to be *sure* . . . Mentioning names hadn't been enough, but a personal appearance . . . Why *didn't* dad show up—or did she wish he wouldn't come at all . . . ?

Virgil Samms entered the ball-room.

"And dad told me, Herkimer," she cooed sweetly, gazing up into his eyes for the first time in over a minute, "that I must dance with every one of them. So you see . . . Oh, there he is now, over there! I've been wondering where he's been keeping himself." She nodded toward the entrance and prattled on artlessly. "He's almost *never* late, you know, and I've . . . "

He looked, and as his eyes met those of the First Lensman, Jill learned three of the facts she needed so badly to know. Her father. Here. Soon. She never knew how she managed to keep herself under control; but, some way and just barely, she did.

Although nothing showed, she was seething inwardly: wrought up as she had never before been. What could she do? She *knew*, but she did not have a scrap or an iota of visible or tangible evidence; and if she made one single slip, however slight, the consequences could be immediate and disastrous.

After this dance might be too late. She could make an excuse to leave the floor, but that would look very bad, later . . . and none of them would Lens her, she knew, while she was with Herkimer—*damn* such chivalry! . . . She *could* take the chance of waving at her father, since she hadn't seen him for so long . . . no, the smallest risk would be with Mase. He looked at her every chance he got, and she'd *make* him use his Lens . . .

Northrop looked at her; and over Herkimer's shoulder, for one fleeting instant, she allowed her face to reveal the terrified appeal she so keenly felt.

"Want me, Jill?" His Lensed thought touched only the outer fringes of her mind. Full rapport is more intimate than a kiss: no one except her father had ever really put a Lens on Virgilia Samms. Nevertheless:

"*Want* you! I never wanted anybody so much in my life! Come in, Mase—quick—*please!*"

Diffidently enough, he came; but at the first inkling of the girl's news all thought of diffidence or of privacy vanished.

"Jack! Spud! Mr. Kinnison! Mr. Samms!" he Lensed sharp, imperative, almost frantic thoughts. "Listen in!"

"Steady, Mase, I'll take over," came Roderick Kinnison's deeper, quieter mental voice. "First, the matter of guns. Anybody except me wearing a pistol? You are, Spud?"

"Yes, sir."

"You would be. But you and Mase, Jack?"

"We've got our Lewistons!"

"You would have. Blasters, my sometimes-not-quite-so-bright son, are fine weapons indeed for certain kinds of work. In emergencies, it is of course permissible to kill a few dozen innocent bystanders. In such a crowd as this, though, it is much better technique to kill only the one you are aiming at. So skip out to my car, you two, right now, and change—and make it *fast*." Everyone knew that Roderick Kinnison's car was at all times an arsenal on wheels. "Wish you were in uniform, too, Virge, but it can't be helped now. Work your way—*slowly*—around to the northwest corner. Spud, do the same."

"It's impossible—starkly unthinkable!" and "I'm not *sure* of anything, really . . . " Samms and his daughter began simultaneously to protest.

"Virgil, you talk like a man with a paper nose. Keep still until after you've used your brain. And I'm sure enough of what you know, Jill, to take plenty of steps. You can relax now—take it easy. We're covering Virgil and I called up support in force. You *can* relax a little, I see. Good! I'm not trying to hide from anybody that the next few minutes may be critical. Are you pretty sure, Jill, that Herkimer is a key man?"

"Pretty sure, Pops." *How* much better she felt, now that the Lensmen were on guard! "In this one case, at least."

"Good! Then let him talk you into giving him every dance, right straight through until something breaks. Watch him. He must know the signal and who is going to operate, and if you can give us a fraction of a second of warning it will help no end. Can do?"

"I'll say I can—and I would love to, the big, slimy, stinking skinker!" As transliterated into words, the girl's thought may seem a trifle confused, but Kinnison knew exactly what she meant.

"One more thing, Jill; a detail. The boys are coming back in and are working their partners over this way. See if Herkimer notices that they have changed their holsters."

"No, he didn't notice," Jill reported, after a moment. "But I don't notice any difference, either, and I'm looking for it."

"Nevertheless, it's there, and the difference between a Mark Seventeen and a Mark Five is something more than that between Tweedledum and Tweedledee," Kinnison returned, dryly. "However, it may not be as obvious to non-military personnel as it is to us. That's far enough, boys, don't get too close. Now, Virge, keep solidly en rapport with Jill on one side and with us on the other, so that she won't have to give herself and the show away by yelling and pointing, and . . . "

"But this is preposterous!" Samms stormed.

"Preposterous, hell," Roderick Kinnison's thought was still coldly level; only the fact that he was beginning to use non-ballroom language revealed any sign of the strain he was under. "Stop being so goddam heroic and start using your brain. You turned down fifty billion credits. Why do you suppose they offered that much, when they can get anybody killed for a hundred? And what would they do about it?"

"But they couldn't get away with it, Rod, at an Ambassadors' Ball. They *couldn't*, possibly."

"Formerly, no. That was my first thought, too. But it was you who pointed out to me, not so long ago, that the techniques of crime have changed of late. In the new light, the swankier the brawl the greater the confusion and the better the chance of getting away clean. Comb *that* out of your whiskers, you red-headed mule!"

"Well . . . there might be something in it, after all . . . " Samms' thought showed apprehension at last.

"You know damn well there is. But you boys—Jack and Mase especially—loosen up. You can't do good shooting while you're strung up like a couple of cocoons. Do something—talk to your partners or think at Jill . . . "

"That won't be hard, sir." Mason Northrop grinned feebly. "And that reminds me of something, Jill. Mentor certainly bracketed the target when he—or she, or it, maybe—said that you would never need a Lens."

"Huh?" Jill demanded, inelegantly. "I don't see the connection, if any."

"No? Everybody else does, I'll bet. How about it?" The other Lensmen, even Samms, agreed enthusiastically. "Well, do you think that any of those characters, particularly Herkimer Herkimer Third, would let a harness bull in harness—even such a beautiful one as you—get close enough to him to do such a Davey the Dip act on his mind?"

"Oh . . . I never thought of that, but it's right, and I'm glad . . . but Pops, you said something about 'support in force.' Have you any idea how long it will be? I *hope* I can hold out, with you all supporting me, but . . . "

"You can, Jill. Two or three minutes more, at most."

"Support? In force? What do you mean?" Samms snapped.

"Just that. The whole damned army," Kinnison replied. "I sent Two-Star Commodore Alexander Clayton a thought that lifted him right out of his chair. Everything he's got, at full emergency blast. Armor—mark eighty fours—six by six extra heavies—a ninety sixty for an ambulance—full escort, upstairs and down—way-friskers—'copters—cruisers and big stuff—in short, the works. I would have run with you before this, if I dared; but the minute the relief party shows up, we do a flit."

"If you *dared?*" Jill asked, shaken by the thought.

"Exactly, my dear. I don't dare. If they start anything we'll do our damnedest, but I'm praying they won't."

But Kinnison's prayers—if he made any—were ignored. Jill heard a sharp, but very usual and insignificant sound; someone had dropped a pencil. She felt an inconspicuous muscle twitch slightly. She saw the almost imperceptible tensing of a neck-muscle which would have turned Herkimer's head in a certain direction if it had been allowed to act. Her eyes flashed along that line, searched busily for milli-seconds. A man was reaching unobtrusively, as though for a handkerchief. But men at Ambassadors' Balls do not carry blue handkerchiefs; nor does any fabric, however dyed, resemble at all closely the blued steel of an automatic pistol.

Jill would have screamed, then, and pointed; but she had time to do neither. Through her rapport with her father the Lensmen saw everything that she saw, in the instant of her seeing it. Hence five shots blasted out, practically as one, before the girl could scream, or point, or even move. She did scream, then; but since dozens of other women were screaming, too, it made no difference—then.

Conway Costigan, trigger-nerved spacehound that he was and with years of gun-fighting and of hand-to-hand brawling in his log, shot first; even before the gunman did. It was Costigan's blinding speed that saved Virgil Samms' life that day; for the would-be assassin was dying, with a heavy slug crashing through his brain, before he finished pulling the trigger. The dying hand twitched upward. The bullet intended for Samms' heart went high; through the fleshy part of the shoulder.

Roderick Kinnison, because of his age, and his son and Northrop, because of their inexperience, were a few milli-seconds slow. They, however, were aiming for the body, not for the head; and any of those three resulting wounds would have been satisfactorily fatal. The man went down, and stayed down.

Samms staggered, but did not go down until the elder Kinnison, as gently as was consistent with the maximum of speed, threw him down.

"Stand back! Get back! Give him air!" Men began to shout, the while pressing closer themselves.

"You men, stand back. Some of you go get a stretcher. You women, come here." Kinnison's heavy, parade-ground voice smashed down all lesser noises. "Is there a doctor here?"

There was; and, after being "frisked" for weapons, he went busily to work.

"Joy—Betty—Jill—Clio," Kinnison called his own wife and their daughter, Virgilia Samms, and Mrs. Costigan. "You four first. Now you—and you—and you—and you . . . ." he went on, pointing out large, heavy women wearing extremely extreme gowns, "Stand here, right over him. Cover him up, so that nobody else can get a shot at him. You other women, stand behind and between these—closer yet—fill those spaces up solid—there! Jack, stand there. Mase, there. Costigan, the other end; I'll take this one. Now, everybody, listen. I know damn well that none of you women are wearing guns above the waist, and you've all got long skirts—thank God for ballgowns! Now, fellows, if any one of these women makes a move to lift her skirt, blow her brains out, right then, without waiting to ask questions."

"Sir, I protest! This is outrageous!" one of the dowagers exclaimed.

"Madam, I agree with you fully. It is." Kinnison smiled as genuinely as he could under the circumstances. "It is, however, *necessary*. I will apologize to all you ladies, and to you, doctor—in writing if you like—after we have Virgil Samms aboard the *Chicago*; but until then I would not trust my own grandmother."

The doctor looked up. "The *Chicago*? This wound does not appear to be a very serious one, but this man is going to a hospital at once. Ah, the stretcher. So . . . please . . . easy . . . there, that is excellent. Call an ambulance, please, immediately."

"I did. Long ago. But no hospital, doctor. All those windows—open to the public—or the whole place bombed—by no means. I'm taking no chances whatever."

"Except with your own life!" Jill put in sharply, looking up from her place at her father's side. Assured that the First Lensman was in no danger of dying, she had begun to take interest in other things. "You are important, too, you know, and you're standing right out there in the open. Get another stretcher, lie down on it, and we'll guard you, too . . . and don't be too stiff-necked to take your own advice!" she flared, as he hesitated.

"I'm not, if it were necessary, but it isn't. If they had killed him, yes. I'd probably be next in line. But since he got only a scratch, there'd be no point at all in killing even a *good* Number Two."

"A *scratch*!" Jill fairly seethed. "Do you call that horrible wound a *scratch*?"

"Huh? Why, certainly—that's all it is—thanks to you," he returned, in honest and complete surprise. "No bones shattered—no main arteries cut—missed the lung—he'll be as good as new in a couple of weeks."

"And now," he went on aloud, "if you ladies will please pick up this stretcher we will move en masse, and *slowly*, toward the door."

The women, no longer indignant but apparently enjoying the sensation of being the center of interest, complied with the request.

"Now, boys," Kinnison Lensed a thought. "Did any of you—Costigan?—see any signs of a concerted rush, such as there would have been to get the killer away if we hadn't interfered?"

"No, sir," came Costigan's brisk reply. "None within sight of me."

"Jack and Mase—I don't suppose you looked?"

They hadn't—had not thought of it in time.

"You'll learn. It takes a few things like this to make it automatic. But I couldn't see any, either, so I'm fairly certain there wasn't any. Smart operators—quick on the uptake."

"I'd better get at this, sir, don't you think, and let Operation Boskone go for a while?" Costigan asked.

"I don't think so." Kinnison frowned in thought. "This operation was *planned*, son, by people with brains. Any clues you could find now would undoubtedly be plants. No, we'll let the regulars look; we'll stick to our own . . . "

Sirens wailed and screamed outside. Kinnison sent out an exploring thought.

"Alex?"

"Yes. Where do you want this ninety-sixty with the doctors and nurses? It's too wide for the gates."

"Go through the wall. Across the lawn. Right up to the door, and never mind the frippery they've got all over the place—have your adjutant tell them to bill us for damage. Samms is shot in the shoulder. Not too serious, but I'm taking him to the Hill, where I know he'll be safe. What have you got on top of the umbrella, the *Boise* or the *Chicago*? I haven't had time to look up yet."

"Both."

"Good man."

Jack Kinnison started at the monstrous tank, which was smashing statues, fountains, and ornamental trees flat into the earth as it moved ponderously across the grounds, and licked his lips. He looked at the companies of soldiers "frisking" the route, the grounds, and the crowd—higher up, at the hovering helicopters—still higher, at the eight light cruisers so evidently and so viciously ready to blast—higher still, at the long streamers of fire which, he now knew, marked the locations of the two most powerful engines of destruction ever built by man—and his face turned slowly white.

"Good Lord, Dad!" he swallowed twice. "I had no idea . . . but they might, at that."

"Not 'might', son. They damn well would, if they could get here soon enough with heavy enough stuff." The elder Kinnison's jaw-muscles did not loosen, his darting eyes did not relax their vigilance for a fraction of a second as he Lensed the thought. "You boys can't be expected to know it all, but right now you're learning fast. Get this—paste it in your iron hats. *Virgil Samms' life is the most important thing in this whole damned universe!* If they had got him then it would not, strictly speaking, have been my fault, but if they get him now, it will be."

The land cruiser crunched to a stop against the very entrance, and a white-clad man leaped out.

"Let me look at him, please . . . "

"Not yet!" Kinnison denied, sharply. "Not until he's got four inches of solid steel between him and whoever wants to finish the job they started. Get your men around him, and get him aboard—fast!"

Samms, protected at every point at every instant, was lifted into the maw of the ninety-sixty; and as the massive door clanged shut Kinnison heaved a tremendous sigh of relief. The cavalcade moved away.

"Coming with us, Rod?" Commodore Clayton shouted.

"Yes, but got a couple minutes' work here yet. Have a staff car wait for me, and I'll join you." He turned to the three young Lensmen and the girl. "This fouls up our plans a little, but not too much—I hope. No change in Mateese or Boskone; you and Costigan, Jill, can go ahead as planned. Northrop, you'll have to brief Jill on Zwilnik and find out what she knows. Virgil was going to do it tonight, after the brawl here, but you know as much about it now as any of us. Check with Knobos, DalNalten, and Fletcher—while Virgil is laid up you and Jack may have to work on both Zabriska and Zwilnik—he'll Lens you. Get the dope, then do as you think best. Get going!" He strode away toward the waiting staff-car.

"Boskone? Zwilnik?" Jill demanded. "What gives? What are they, Jack?"

"We don't know yet—maybe we're going to name a couple of planets . . . "

"Piffle!" she scoffed. "Can *you* talk sense, Mase? What's Boskone?"

"A simple, distinctive, pronounceable coined word; suggested, I believe, by Dr. Bergenholm . . . " he began.

"You know what I mean, you . . . " she broke in, but was silenced by a sharply Lensed thought from Jack. His touch was very light, barely sufficient to make conversation possible; but even so, she flinched.

"Use your brain, Jill; you aren't thinking a lick—not that you can be blamed for it. Stop talking; there may be lip-readers or high-powered listeners around. This feels funny, doesn't it?" He twitched mentally and went on: "You already know what Operation Mateese is, since it's your own dish—politics. Operation Zwilnik is drugs, vice, and so on. Operation Boskone is pirates; Spud is running that. Operation Zabriska is Mase and me checking some peculiar disturbances in the sub-ether. Come in, Mase, and do your stuff—I'll see you later, aboard. Clear ether, Jill!"

Young Kinnison vanished from the fringes of her mind and Northrop appeared. And what a difference! His mind touched hers as gingerly as Jack's had done; as skittishly, as instantaneously ready to bolt away from anything in the least degree private. However, Jack's mind had rubbed hers the wrong way, right from the start—and Mase's didn't!

"Now, about this Operation Zwilnik," Jill began.

"Something else first. I couldn't help noticing, back there, that you and Jack . . . well, not out of phase, exactly, or really out of sync, but sort of . . . well, as though . . . "

"'Hunting'?" she suggested.

"Not exactly . . . 'forcing' might be better—like holding a tight beam together when it wants to fall apart. So you noticed it yourself?"

"Of course, but I thought Jack and I were the only ones who did. Like scratching a blackboard with your finger-nails—you *can* do it, but you're awfully glad to stop . . . and I *like* Jack, too, darn it—at a distance."

"And you and I fit like precisely tuned circuits. Jack really meant it, then, when he said that you . . . that is, he . . . I didn't quite believe it until now, but if . . . you know, of course, what you've already done to me."

Jill's block went on, full strength. She arched her eyebrows and spoke aloud—"why, I haven't the *faintest* idea!"

"Of course not. That's why you're using voice. I've found out, too, that I can't lie with my mind. I feel like a heel and a louse, with so much job ahead, but you've simply got to tell me something. Then—whatever you say—I'll hit the job with everything I've got. Do I get heaved out between planets without a space-suit, or not?"

"I don't think so." Jill blushed vividly, but her voice was steady. "You would rate a space-suit, and enough oxygen to reach another plan—another goal. And now we'd better get to work, don't you think?"

"Yes. Thanks, Jill, a million. I know as well as you do that I was talking out of turn, and how much—but I had to know." He breathed deep. "And that's all I ask—for now. Cut your screens."

She lowered her mental barriers, finding it surprisingly easy to do so in this case; let them down almost as far as she was in the habit of doing with her father. He explained in flashing thoughts everything he knew of the four Operations, concluding:

"I'm not assigned to Zabriska permanently; I'll probably work with you on Mateese after your father gets back into circulation. I'm to act more as a liaison man—neither Knobos nor DalNalten knows you well enough to Lens you. Right?"

"Yes, I've met Mr. Knobos only once, and have never even seen Dr. DalNalten."

"Ready to visit them, via Lens?"

"Yes. Go ahead."

The two Lensmen came in. They came into his mind, not hers. Nevertheless their thoughts, superimposed upon Northrop's, came to the girl as clearly as though all four were speaking to each other face to face.

"What a *weird* sensation!" Jill exclaimed. "Why, I never *imagined* anything like it!"

"We are sorry to trouble you, Miss Samms . . . ." Jill was surprised anew. The silent voice deep within her mind was of characteristically Martian timbre, but instead of the harshly guttural consonants and the hissing sibilants of any Martian's best efforts at English, pronunciation and enunciation were flawless.

"Oh, I didn't mean that. It's no trouble at all, really, I just haven't got used to this telepathy yet."

"None of us has, to any noticeable degree. But the reason for this call is to ask you if you have anything new, however slight, to add to our very small knowledge of Zwilnik?"

"Very little, I'm afraid; and that little is mostly guesses, deductions, and jumpings at conclusions. Father told you about the way I work, I suppose?"

"Yes. Exact data is not to be expected. Hints, suggestions, possible leads, will be of inestimable value."

"Well, I met a very short, very fat Venerian, named Ossmen, at a party at the European Embassy. Do either of you know him?"

"I know of him," DalNalten replied. "A highly reputable merchant, with such large interests on Tellus that he has to spend most of his time here. He is not in any one of our books . . . although there is nothing at all surprising in that fact. Go on, please, Miss Samms."

"He didn't come to the party with Senator Morgan; but he came to some kind of an agreement with him that night, and I am pretty sure that it was about thionite. That's the only new item I have."

"*Thionite!*" The three Lensmen were equally surprised.

"Yes. Thionite. Definitely."

"How *sure* are you of this, Miss Samms?" Knobos asked, in deadly earnest.

"I am not *sure* that this particular agreement was about thionite, no; but the probability is roughly nine-tenths. I *am* sure, however, that both Senator Morgan and Ossmen know a lot about thionite that they want to hide. Both gave very high positive reactions—well beyond the six-sigma point of virtual certainty."

There was a pause, broken by the Martian, but not by a thought directed at any one of the three.

"Sid!" he called, and even Jill could feel the Lensed thought speed.

"Yes, Knobos? Fletcher."

"That haul-in you made, out in the asteroids. Heroin, hadive, and ladolian, wasn't it? No thionite involved anywhere?"

"No thionite. However, you must remember that part of the gang got away, so all I can say positively is that we didn't see, or hear about, any thionite. There was some gossip, of course: but you know there always is."

"Of course. Thanks, Sid." Jill could feel the brilliant Martian's mental gears whirl and click. Then he went into such a flashing exchange of thought with the Venerian that the girl lost track in seconds.

"One more question, Miss Samms?" DalNalten asked. "Have you detected any indications that there may be some connection between either Ossmen or Morgan and any officer or executive of Interstellar Spaceways?"

"*Spaceways!* Isaacson?" Jill caught her breath. "Why . . . nobody even thought of such a thing—at least, nobody ever mentioned it to me—I never thought of making any such tests."

"The possibility occurred to me only a moment ago, at your mention of thionite. The connection, if any exists, will be exceedingly difficult to trace. But since most, if not all, of the parties involved will probably be included in your Operation Mateese, and since a finding, either positive or negative, would be tremendously significant, we feel emboldened to ask you to keep this point in mind."

"Why, of course I will. I'll be very glad to."

"We thank you for your courtesy and your help. One or both of us will get in touch with you from time to time, now that we know the pattern of your personality. May immortal Grolossen speed the healing of your father's wound."

CHAPTER 7

Late that night—or, rather, very early the following morning—Senator Morgan and his Number One secretary were closeted in the former's doubly spy-ray-proofed office. Morgan's round, heavy, florid face had perhaps lost a little of its usual color; the fingers of his left hand drummed soundlessly upon the glass top of his desk. His shrewd gray eyes, however, were as keen and as calculating as ever.

"This thing smells, Herkimer . . . it *reeks* . . . but I can't figure any of the angles. That operation was *planned*. Sure fire, it *couldn't* miss. Right up to the last split second it worked perfectly. Then—blooie! A flat bust. The Patrol landed and everything was under control. There *must* have been a leak somewhere—but where in hell could it have been?"

"There couldn't have been a leak, Chief; it doesn't make sense." The secretary uncrossed his long legs, recrossed them in the other direction, threw away a half-smoked cigarette, lit another. "If there'd been any kind of a leak they would have done a lot more than just kill the low man on the ladder. You know as well as I do that Rocky Kinnison is the hardest-boiled character this side of hell. If he had known anything, he would have killed everybody in sight, including you and me. Besides, if there had been a leak, he would not have let Samms get within ten thousand miles of the place—that's one sure thing. Another is he wouldn't have waited until after it was all over to get his army there. No, Chief, there couldn't have been a leak. Whatever Samms or Kinnison found out—probably Samms, he's a hell of a lot smarter than Kinnison is, you know—he learned right there and then. He must have seen Brainerd start to pull his gun."

"I thought of that. I'd buy it, except for one fact. Apparently you didn't time the interval between the shots and the arrival of the tanks."

"Sorry, Chief." Herkimer's face was a study in chagrin. "I made a bad slip there."

"I'll say you did. One minute and fifty eight seconds."

"*What!*"

Morgan remained silent.

"The patrol is fast, of course . . . and always ready . . . and they would yank the stuff in on tractor beams, not under their own power . . . but even so . . . five minutes, is my guess, Chief. Four and a half, absolute minimum."

"Check. And where do you go from there?"

"I see your point. I don't. That blows everything wide open. One set of facts says there was a leak, which occurred between two and a half and three minutes before the signal was given. I ask you, Chief, does that make sense?"

"No. That's what is bothering me. As you say, the facts seem to be contradictory. Somebody must have learned something before anything happened; but if they did, why didn't they do more? And Murgatroyd. If they didn't know about him, why the ships—especially the big battlewagons? If they did think he might be out there somewhere, why didn't they go and find out?"

"Now I'll ask one. Why didn't our Mr. Murgatroyd do something? Or wasn't the pirate fleet supposed to be in on this? Probably not, though."

"My guess would be the same as yours. Can't see any reason for having a fleet cover a one-man operation, especially as well-planned a one as this was. But that's none of our

224

business. These Lensmen are. I was watching them every second. Neither Samms nor Kinnison did anything whatever during that two minutes."

"Young Kinnison and Northrop each left the hall about that time."

"I know it. So they did. Either one of them *could* have called the Patrol—but what has that to do with the price of beef C. I. F. Valeria?"

Herkimer refrained tactfully from answering the savage question. Morgan drummed and thought for minutes, then went on slowly:

"There are two, and only two, possibilities; neither of which seem even remotely possible. It was—*must* have been—either the Lens or the girl."

"The girl? Act your age, Senator. I knew where *she* was, and what she was doing, every second."

"That was evident." Morgan stopped drumming and smiled cynically. "I'm getting a hell of a kick out of seeing you taking it, for a change, instead of dishing it out."

"Yes?" Herkimer's handsome face hardened. "That game isn't over, my friend."

"That's what *you* think," the Senator jibed. "Can't believe that any woman *can* be Herkimer-proof, eh? You've been working on her for six weeks now, instead of the usual six hours, and you haven't got anywhere yet."

"I will, Senator." Herkimer's nostrils flared viciously. "I'll get her, one way or another, if it's the last thing I ever do."

"I'll give you eight to five you don't; and a six-month time limit."

"I'll take five thousand of that. But what makes you think that she's anything to be afraid of? She's a trained psychologist, yes; but so am I; and I'm older and more experienced than she is. That leaves that yoga stuff—her learning how to sit cross-legged, how to contemplate her navel, and how to try to get in tune with the infinite. How do you figure *that* puts her in my class?"

"I told you, I don't. Nothing makes sense. But she is Virgil Samms' daughter."

"What of it? You didn't gag on George Olmstead—you picked him yourself for one of the toughest jobs we've got. By blood he's just about as close to Virgil Samms as Virgilia is. They might as well have been hatched out of the same egg."

"Physically, yes. Mentally and psychologically, no. Olmstead is a realist, a materialist. He wants his reward in this world, not the next, and is out to get it. Furthermore, the job will probably kill him, and even if it doesn't, he will never be in a position of trust or where he can learn much of anything. On the other hand, Virgil Samms is—but I don't need to tell you what *he* is like. But you don't seem to realize that she's just like him—she isn't playing around with you because of your overpowering charm . . . ."

"Listen, Chief. She didn't know anything and she didn't do anything. I was dancing with her all the time, as close as that," he clasped his hands tightly together, "so I know what I'm talking about. And if you think she could *ever* learn anything from me, skip it. You know that nobody on Earth, or anywhere else, can read my face; and besides, she was playing coy right then—wasn't even looking at me. So count her out."

"We'll have to, I guess." Morgan resumed his quiet drumming. "If there were any possibility that she pumped you I'd send you to the mines, but there's no sign . . . that leaves the Lens. It has seemed, right along, more logical than the girl—but a lot more fantastic. Been able to find out anything more about it?"

"No. Just what they've been advertising. Combination radio-phone, automatic language-converter, telepath, and so on. Badge of the top skimmings of the top-bracket cops. But I began to think, out there on the floor, that they aren't advertising everything they know."

"So did I. You tell me."

"Take the time zero minus three minutes. Besides the five Lensmen—and Jill Samms—the place was full of top brass; scrambled eggs all over the floor. Commodores and lieutenant-Commodores from all continental governments of the Earth, the other planets, and the colonies, all wearing full-dress side-arms. Nobody knew anything then; we agree on that. But within the next few seconds, somebody found out something and called for help. One of the Lensmen could possibly have done that without showing signs. BUT—at zero time all four Lensmen had their guns out—and *not* Lewistons, please note—and were shooting; whereas none of the other armed officers knew that anything was going on until after it was all over. That puts the finger on the Lens."

"That's the way I figured it. But the difficulties remain unchanged. *How?* Mind-reading?"

"Space-drift!" Herkimer snorted. "My mind can't be read."

"Nor mine."

"And besides, if they could read minds, they wouldn't have waited until the last possible split second to do it, unless . . . say, wait a minute! . . . Did Brainerd act or look nervous, toward the last? I wasn't to look at him, you know."

"Not nervous, exactly; but he did get a little tense."

"There you are, then. Hired murderers aren't smart. A Lensman saw him tighten up and got suspicious. Turned in the alarm on general principles. Warned the others to keep on their toes. But even so, it doesn't look like mind-reading—they'd have killed him sooner. They were watchful, and mighty quick on the draw."

"That could be it. That's about as thin and as specious an explanation as I ever saw cooked up, but it *does* cover the facts . . . and the two of us will be able to make it stick . . . but take notice, pretty boy, that certain parties are not going to like this at all. In fact, they are going to be very highly put out."

"That's a nice hunk of understatement, boss. But notice one beautiful thing about this story?" Herkimer grinned maliciously. "It lets us pass the buck to Big Jim Towne. We can be—and will be—sore as hell because he picks such weak-sister characters to do his killings!"

*

In the heavily armored improvised ambulance, Virgil Samms sat up and directed a thought at his friend Kinnison, finding his mind a turmoil of confusion.

"What's the matter, Rod?"

"Plenty!" the big Lensman snapped back. "They were—maybe still are—too damn far ahead of us. Something has been going on that we haven't even suspected. I stood by, as innocent as a three-year-old girl baby, and let you walk right into that one—and I emphatically do not enjoy getting caught with my pants down that way. It makes me jumpy. This may be all, but it may not be—not by eleven thousand light-years—and I'm trying to dope out what is going to happen next."

"And what have you deduced?"

"Nothing. I'm stuck. So I'm tossing it into your lap. Besides, that's what you are getting paid for, thinking. So go ahead and think. What would you be doing, if you were on the other side?"

"I see. You think, then, that it might not be good technique to take the time to go back to the spaceport?"

"You get the idea. But—can you stand transfer?"

"Certainly. They got my shoulder dressed and taped, and my arm in a sling. Shock practically all gone. Some pain, but not much. I can walk without falling down."

"Fair enough. Clayton!" He Lensed a vigorous thought. "Have any of the observers spotted anything, high up or far off?"

"No, sir."

"Good. Kinnison to Commodore Clayton, orders. Have a 'copter come down and pick up Samms and myself on tractors. Instruct the *Boise* and the cruisers to maintain utmost vigilance. Instruct the *Chicago* to pick us up. Detach the *Chicago* and the *Boise* from your task force. Assign them to me. Off."

"Clayton to Commissioner Kinnison. Orders received and are being carried out. Off."

The transfers were made without incident. The two super-dreadnaughts leaped into the high stratosphere and tore westward. Half-way to the Hill, Kinnison called Dr. Frederick Rodebush.

"Fred? Kinnison. Have Cleve and Bergenholm link up with us. Now—how are the Geigers on the outside of the Hill behaving?"

"Normal, all of them," the physicist-Lensman reported after a moment. "Why?"

Kinnison detailed the happenings of the recent past. "So tell the boys to unlimber all the stuff the Hill has got."

"My God!" Cleveland exclaimed. "Why, that's putting us back to the days of the Interplanetary Wars!"

"With one notable exception," Kinnison pointed out. "The attack, if any, will be strictly modern. I hope we'll be able to handle it. One good thing, the old mountain's got a lot of sheer mass. How much radioactivity will it stand?"

"Allotropic iron, U-235, or plutonium?" Rodebush seized his slide-rule.

"What difference does it make?"

"From a practical standpoint . . . perhaps none. But with a task force defending, not many bombs could get through, so I'd say . . . "

"I wasn't thinking so much of bombs."

"What, then?"

"Isotopes. A good, thick blanket of dust. Slow-speed, fine stuff that neither our ships nor the Hill's screens could handle. We've got to decide, first, whether Virgil will be safer there in the Hill or out in space in the *Chicago*; and second, for how long."

"I see . . . I'd say here, *under* the Hill. Months, perhaps years, before anything could work down this far. And we can *always* get out. No matter how hot the surface gets, we've got enough screen, heavy water, cadmium, lead, mercury, and everything else necessary to get him out through the locks."

"That's what I was hoping you'd say. And now, about the defense . . . I wonder . . . I don't want everybody to think I've gone completely hysterical, but I'll be damned if I want to get caught again with . . . ." His thought faded out.

"May I offer a suggestion, sir?" Bergenholm's thought broke the prolonged silence.

"I'd be very glad to have it—your suggestions so far haven't been idle vaporings. Another hunch?"

"No, sir, a logical procedure. It has been some months since the last emergency call-out drill was held. If you issue such another call now, and nothing happens, it can be simply another surprise drill; with credit, promotion, and monetary awards for the best performances; further practice and instruction for the less proficient units."

"Splendid, Dr. Bergenholm!" Samms' brilliant and agile mind snatched up the thought and carried it along. "And what a chance, Rod, for something vastly larger and more important than a Continental, or even a Tellurian, drill—make it the first maneuver of the Galactic Patrol!"

"I'd like to, Virge, but we can't. My boys are ready, but you aren't. No top appointments and no authority."

"That can be arranged in a very few minutes. We have been waiting for the psychological moment. This, especially if trouble should develop, is the time. You yourself expect an attack, do you not?"

"Yes. I would not start anything unless and until I was ready to finish it, and I see no reason for assuming that whoever it was that tried to kill you is not at least as good a planner as I am."

"And the rest of you . . . ? Dr. Bergenholm?"

"My reasoning, while it does not exactly parallel that of Commissioner Kinnison, leads to the same conclusion; that an attack in great force is to be expected."

"Not *exactly* parallel?" Kinnison demanded. "In what respects?"

"You do not seem to have considered the possibility, Commissioner, that the proposed assassination of First Lensman Samms could very well have been only the first step in a comprehensive operation."

"I didn't . . . and it *could* have been. So go ahead, Virge, with . . . ."

The thought was never finished, for Samms had already gone ahead. Simultaneously, it seemed, the minds of eight other Lensmen joined the group of Tellurians. Samms, intensely serious, spoke aloud to his friend:

"The Galactic Council is now assembled. Do you, Roderick K. Kinnison, promise to uphold, in as much as you conscientiously can and with all that in you lies, the authority of this Council throughout all space?"

"I promise."

"By virtue of the authority vested in me its president by the Galactic Council, I appoint you Port Admiral of the Galactic Patrol. My fellow councillors are now inducting the armed forces of their various solar systems into the Galactic Patrol . . . It will not take long . . . There, you may make your appointments and issue orders for the mobilization."

The two super-dreadnaughts were now approaching the Hill. The *Boise* stayed "up on top"; the *Chicago* went down. Kinnison, however, paid very little attention to the landing or to Samms' disembarkation, and none whatever to the *Chicago's* reascent into the high heavens. He knew that everything was under control; and, now alone in his cabin, he was busy.

"All personnel of all armed forces just inducted into the Galactic Patrol, attention!" He spoke into an ultra-wave microphone, the familiar parade-ground rasp very evident in his deep and resonant voice. "Kinnison of Tellus, Port Admiral, speaking. Each of you has taken oath to the Galactic Patrol?"

They had.

"At ease. The organization chart already in your hands is made effective as of now. Enter in your logs the date and time. Promotions: Commodore Clayton of North America, Tellus . . . ."

In his office at New York Spaceport Clayton came to attention and saluted crisply; his eyes shining, his deeply-scarred face alight.

" . . . to be Admiral of the First Galactic Region. Commodore Schweikert of Europe, Tellus . . . "

In Berlin a narrow-waisted, almost foppish-seeming man, with roached blond hair and blue eyes, bowed stiffly from the waist and saluted punctiliously.

" . . . to be Lieutenant-Admiral of the First Galactic Region."

And so on, down the list. A marshal and a lieutenant-marshal of the Solarian System; a general and a lieutenant-general of the planet Sol Three. Promotions, agreed upon long since, to fill the high offices thus vacated. Then the list of commodores upon other planets—Guindlos of Redland, Mars; Sesseffsen of Talleron, Venus; Raymond of the Jovian Sub-System; Newman of Alphacent; Walters of Sirius; van-Meeter of Valeria; Adams of Procyon; Roberts of Altair; Barrtell of Fomalhout; Armand of Vega; and Coigne of Aldebaran—each of whom was actually the commander-in-chief of the armed forces of a world. Each of these was made general of his planet.

"Except for lieutenant-commodores and up, who will tune their minds to me—dismissed!" Kinnison stopped talking and went onto his Lens.

"That was for the record. I don't need to tell you, fellows, how glad I am to be able to do this. You're tops, all of you—I don't know of anybody I'd rather have at my back when the ether gets rough . . . "

"Right back at you, chief!" "Same to you Rod!" "Rocky Rod, Port Admiral!" "Now we're blasting!" came a melange of thoughts. Those splendid men, with whom he had shared so much of danger and of stress, were all as jubilant as schoolboys.

"But the thing that makes this possible may also make it necessary for us to go to work; to earn your extra stars and my wheel." Kinnison smothered the welter of thoughts and outlined the situation, concluding: "So you see it may turn out to be only a drill—but on the other hand, since the outfit is big enough to have built a war-fleet alone, if it wanted one, and since it may have had a lot of first-class help that none of us knows anything about, we may be in for the damndest battle that any of us ever saw. So come prepared for *anything*. I am now going back onto voice, for the record.

"Kinnison to the commanding officers of all fleets, sub-fleets, and task-forces of the Galactic Patrol. Information. Subject, tactical problem; defense of the Hill against a postulated Black Fleet of unknown size, strength, and composition; of unknown nationality or origin; coming from an unknown direction in space at an unknown time.

"Kinnison to Admiral Clayton. Orders. Take over. I am relinquishing command of the *Boise* and the *Chicago*."

"Clayton to Port Admiral Kinnison. Orders received. Taking over. I am at the *Chicago's* main starboard lock. I have instructed Ensign Masterson, the commanding officer of this gig, to wait; that he is to take you down to the Hill."

"WHAT? Of all the damned . . . ." This was a thought, and unrecorded.

"Sorry, Rod—I'm sorry as hell, and I'd like no end to have you along." This, too, was a thought. "But that's the way it is. Ordinary Admirals ride the ether with their fleets. Port Admirals stay aground. I report to you, and you run things—in broad—by remote control."

"I see." Kinnison then Lensed a fuming thought at Samms. "Alex *couldn't* do this to me—and wouldn't—and knows damn well that I'd burn him to a crisp if he had the guts to try it. So it's *your* doing—what in hell's the big idea?"

"Who's being heroic now, Rod?" Samms asked, quietly. "Use *your* brain. And then come down here, where you belong."

And Kinnison, after a long moment of rebellious thought and with as much grace as he could muster, came down. Down not only to the Patrol's familiar offices, but down into the deepest crypts beneath them. He was glum enough, and bitter, at first: but he found much to do. Grand Fleet Headquarters—*his* headquarters—was being organized, and the best efforts of the best minds and of the best technologists of three worlds were being devoted to the task of strengthening the already extremely strong defenses of THE HILL. And in a very short time the plates of GFHQ showed that Admiral Clayton and Lieutenant-Admiral Schweikert were doing a very nice job.

All of the really heavy stuff was of Earth, the Mother Planet, and was already in place; as were the less numerous and much lighter contingents of Mars, of Venus, and of Jove. And the fleets of the outlying solar systems—cutters, scouts, and a few light cruisers—were neither maintaining fleet formation nor laying course for Sol. Instead, each individual vessel was blasting at maximum for the position in space in which it would form one unit of a formation englobing at a distance of light-years the entire Solarian System, and each of those hurtling hundreds of ships was literally combing all circumambient space with its furiously-driven detector beams.

"Nice." Kinnison turned to Samms, now beside him at the master plate. "Couldn't have done any better myself."

"After you get it made, what are you going to do with it in case nothing happens?" Samms was still somewhat skeptical. "How long can you make a drill last?"

"Until all the ensigns have long gray whiskers if I have to, but don't worry—if we have time to get the preliminary globe made I'll be the surprisedest man in the system."

And Kinnison was not surprised; before full englobement was accomplished, a loud-speaker gave tongue.

"Flagship *Chicago* to Grand Fleet Headquarters!" it blatted, sharply. "The Black Fleet has been detected. RA twelve hours, declination plus twenty degrees, distance about thirty light-years . . . ."

Kinnison started to say something; then, by main force, shut himself up. He wanted intensely to take over, to tell the boys out there exactly what to do, but he couldn't. He was now a Big Shot—damn the luck! He could be and must be responsible for broad policy and for general strategy, but, once those vitally important decisions had been made, the actual work would have to be done by others. He didn't like it—but there it was. Those flashing thoughts took only an instant of time.

" . . . which is such extreme range that no estimate of strength or composition can be made at present. We will keep you informed."

"Acknowledge," he ordered Randolph; who, wearing now the five silver bars of major, was his Chief Communications Officer. "No instructions."

He turned to his plate. Clayton hadn't had to be told to pull in his light stuff; it was all pelting hell-for-leather for Sol and Tellus. Three general plans of battle had been mapped out by Staff. Each had its advantages—and its disadvantages. Operation Acorn—long distance—would be fought at, say, twelve light-years. It would keep everything, particularly the big stuff, away from the Hill, and would make automatics useless . . . *unless* some got past, or *unless* the automatics were coming in on a sneak course, or *unless* several other things—in any one of which cases *what* a God-awful shellacking the Hill would take!

He grinned wryly at Samms, who had been following his thought, and quoted: "A vast hemisphere of lambent violet flame, through which neither material substance nor destructive ray can pass."

"Well, that dedicatory statement, while perhaps a bit florid, was strictly true at the time—before the days of allotropic iron and of polycyclic drills. Now I'll quote one: 'Nothing is permanent except change'."

"Uh-huh," and Kinnison returned to his thinking. Operation Adack. Middle distance. Uh-uh. He didn't like it any better now than he had before, even though some of the Big Brains of Staff thought it the ideal solution. A compromise. All of the disadvantages of both of the others, and none of the advantages of either. It *still* stunk, and unless the Black fleet had an utterly fantastic composition Operation Adack was out.

And Virgil Samms, quietly smoking a cigarette, smiled inwardly. Rod the Rock could scarcely be expected to be in favor of any sort of compromise.

That left Operation Affick. Close up. It had three tremendous advantages. First, the Hill's own offensive weapons—as long as they lasted. Second, the new Rodebush-Bergenholm fields. Third, no sneak attack could be made without detection and interception. It had one tremendous disadvantage; some stuff, and probably a lot of it, would get through. Automatics, robots, guided missiles equipped with super-speed drives, with polycyclic drills, and with atomic war-heads strong enough to shake the whole world.

But with those new fields, shaking the world wouldn't be enough; in order to get deep enough to reach Virgil Samms they would damn near have to destroy the world.

Could *anybody* build a bomb that powerful? He didn't think so. Earth technology was supreme throughout all known space; of Earth technologists the North Americans were, and always had been, tops. Grant that the Black Fleet was, basically, North American. Grant further that they had a man as good as Adlington—or that they could spy-ray Adlington's brain and laboratories and shops—a tall order. Adlington himself was several months away from a world-wrecker, unless he could put one a hundred miles down before detonation, which simply was not feasible. He turned to Samms.

"It'll be Affick, Virge, unless they've got a composition that is radically different from anything I ever saw put into space."

"So? I can't say that I am very much surprised."

The calm statement and the equally calm reply were beautifully characteristic of the two men. Kinnison had not asked, nor had Samms offered, advice. Kinnison, after weighing the facts, made his decision. Samms, calmly certain that the decision was the best that could be made upon the data available, accepted it without question or criticism.

"We've still got a minute or two," Kinnison remarked. "Don't quite know what to make of their line of approach. Coma Berenices. I don't know of anything at all out that way, do you? They could have detoured, though."

"No, I don't." Samms frowned in thought. "Probably a detour."

"Check." Kinnison turned to Randolph. "Tell them to report whatever they know; we can't wait any . . . "

As he was speaking the report came in.

The Black Fleet was of more or less normal make-up; considerably larger than the North American contingent, but decidedly inferior to the Patrol's present Grand Fleet. Either three or four capital ships . . .

"And we've got six!" Kinnison said, exultantly. "Our own two, Asia's *Himalaya*, Africa's *Johannesburg*, South America's *Bolivar*, and Europe's *Europa*."

. . . Battle cruisers and heavy cruisers, about in the usual proportions; but an unusually high ratio of scouts and light cruisers. There were either two or three large ships which could not be classified definitely at that distance; long-range observers were going out to study them.

"Tell Clayton," Kinnison instructed Randolph, "that it is to be Operation Affick, and for him to fly at it."

"Report continued," the speaker came to life again. "There are three capital ships, apparently of approximately the *Chicago* class, but tear-drop-shaped instead of spherical . . . "

"Ouch!" Kinnison flashed a thought at Samms. "I don't like that. They can both fight and run."

" . . . The battle cruisers are also tear-drops. The small vessels are torpedo-shaped. There are three of the large ships, which we are still not able to classify definitely. They are spherical in shape, and very large, but do not seem to be either armed or screened, and are apparently carriers—possibly of automatics. We are now making contact—off!"

Instead of looking at the plates before them, the two Lensmen went en rapport with Clayton, so that they could see everything he saw. The stupendous Cone of Battle had long since been formed; the word to fire was given in a measured two-second call. Every firing officer in every Patrol ship touched his stud in the same split second. And from the gargantuan mouth of the Cone there spewed a miles-thick column of energy so raw, so stark, so incomprehensibly violent that it must have been seen to be even dimly appreciated. It simply cannot be described.

Its prototype, Triplanetary's Cylinder of Annihilation, had been a highly effective weapon indeed. The offensive beams of the fish-shaped Nevian cruisers of the void were even more powerful. The Cleveland-Rodebush projectors, developed aboard the original *Boise* on the long Nevian way, were stronger still. The composite beam projected by this fleet of the Galactic Patrol, however, was the sublimation and quintessence of each of these, redesigned and redesigned by scientists and engineers of ever-increasing knowledge, rebuilt and rebuilt by technologists of ever-increasing skill.

Capital ships and a few of the heaviest cruisers could mount screen generators able to carry that frightful load; but every smaller ship caught in that semi-solid rod of indescribably incandescent fury simply flared into nothingness.

But in the instant before the firing order was given—as though precisely timed, which in all probability was the case—the ever-watchful observers picked up two items of fact which made the new Admiral of the First Galactic Region cut his almost irresistible weapon and break up his Cone of Battle after only a few seconds of action. One: those three enigmatic cargo scows had fallen apart *before* the beam reached them, and hundreds—yes, thousands—of small objects had hurtled radially outward, out well beyond the field of action of the Patrol's beam, at a speed many times that of light. Two: Kinnison's forebodings had been prophetic. A swarm of Blacks, all small—must have been hidden right on Earth somewhere!—were already darting at the Hill from the south.

"Cease firing!" Clayton rapped into his microphone. The dreadful beam expired. "Break cone formation! Independent action—light cruisers and scouts, *get those bombs!* Heavy cruisers and battle cruisers, engage similar units of the Blacks, two to one if possible. *Chicago* and *Boise*, attack Black Number One. *Bolivar* and *Himalaya*, Number Two. *Europa* and *Johannesburg*, Number Three!"

Space was full of darting, flashing, madly warring ships. The three Black super-dreadnaughts leaped forward as one. Their massed batteries of beams, precisely synchronized and aimed, lashed out as one at the nearest Patrol super heavy, the *Boise*. Under the vicious power of that beautifully-timed thrust that warship's first, second, and third screens, her very wall-shield, flared through the spectrum and into the black. Her Chief Pilot, however, was fast—*very* fast—and he had a fraction of a second in which to work. Thus, practically in the instant of her wall-shield's failure, she went free; and while she was holed badly and put out of action, she was not blown out of space. In fact, it was learned later that she lost only forty men.

The Blacks were not as fortunate. The *Chicago*, now without a partner, joined beams with the *Bolivar* and the *Himalaya* against Number Two; then, a short half-second later, with her other two sister-ships against Number Three. And in that very short space of time two Black super-dreadnaughts ceased utterly to be.

But also, in that scant second of time, Black Number One had all but disappeared! Her canny commander, with no stomach at all for odds of five to one against, had ordered flight at max; she was already one-sixtieth of a light-year—about one hundred thousand million miles—away from the Earth and was devoting her every energy to the accumulation of still more distance.

"*Bolivar! Himalaya!*" Clayton barked savagely. "Get him!" He wanted intensely to join the chase, but he couldn't. He had to stay here. And he didn't have time even to swear. Instead, without a break, the words tripping over each other against his teeth: "*Chicago! Johannesburg! Europa!* Act at will against heaviest craft left. Blast'em down!"

He gritted his teeth. The scouts and light cruisers were doing their damndest, but they were out-numbered three to one—Christ, what a lot of stuff was getting through! The Blacks wouldn't last long, between the Hill and the heavies . . . but maybe long enough, at that—the Patrol globe was leaking like a sieve! He voiced a couple of bursts of deep-space profanity and, although he was almost afraid to look, sneaked a quick peek to see how much was left of the Hill. He looked—and stopped swearing in the middle of a four-letter Anglo-Saxon word.

What he saw simply did not make sense. Those Black bombs should have peeled the armor off of that mountain like the skin off of a nectarine and scattered it from the Pacific to the Mississippi. By now there should be a hole a mile deep where the Hill had been. But there wasn't. The Hill was still there! It might have shrunk a little—Clayton couldn't see very well because of the worse-than-incandescent radiance of the practically continuous, sense-battering, world-shaking atomic detonations—*but the Hill was still there!*

And as he stared, chilled and shaken, at that indescribably terrific spectacle, a Black cruiser, holed and helpless, fell toward that armored mountain with an acceleration starkly impossible to credit. And when it struck it did not penetrate, and splash, and crater, as it should have done. Instead, it simply spread out, *in a thin layer*, over an acre or so of the fortress' steep and apparently still armored surface!

"You saw that, Alex? Good. Otherwise you could scarcely believe it," came Kinnison's silent voice. "Tell all our ships to stay away. There's a force of over a hundred thousand G's acting in a direction normal to every point of our surface. The boys are giving it all the decrement they can—somewhere between distance cube and fourth power—but even so it's pretty fierce stuff. How about the *Bolivar* and the *Himalaya*? Not having much luck catching Mr. Black, are they?"

"Why, I don't know. I'll check . . . No, sir, they aren't. They report that they are losing ground and will soon lose trace."

"I was afraid so, from that shape. Rodebush was about the only one who saw it coming . . . well, we'll have to redesign and rebuild . . . "

*

Port Admiral Kinnison, shortly after directing the foregoing thought, leaned back in his chair and smiled. The battle was practically over. The Hill had come through. The Rodebush-Bergenholm fields had held her together through the most God-awful session of saturation atomic bombing that any world had ever seen or that the mind of man had ever conceived. And the counter-forces had kept the interior rock from flowing like water. So far, so good.

Her original armor was gone. Converted into . . . what? For hundreds of feet inward from the surface she was hotter than the reacting slugs of the Hanfords. Delousing her would be a project, not an operation; millions of cubic yards of material would have to be hauled off into space with tractors and allowed to simmer for a few hundred years; but what of that?

Bergenholm had said that the fields would tend to prevent the radioactives from spreading, as they otherwise would—and *Virgil Samms was still safe!*

"Virge, my boy, come along." He took the First Lensman by his good arm and lifted him out of his chair. "Old Doctor Kinnison's peerless prescription for you and me is a big, thick, juicy, porterhouse steak."

CHAPTER 8

That murderous attack upon Virgil Samms, and its countering by those new super-lawmen, the Lensmen, and by an entire task force of the North American Armed Forces, was news of Civilization-wide importance. As such, it filled every channel of Universal Telenews for an hour. Then, in stunning and crescendo succession, came the staccato reports of the creation of the Galactic Patrol, the mobilization—allegedly for maneuvers—of Galactic Patrol's Grand Fleet, and the ultimately desperate and all-too-nearly successful attack upon The Hill.

"Just a second, folks; we'll have it very shortly. You'll see something that nobody ever saw before and that nobody will ever see again. We're getting in as close as the Law will let us." The eyes of Telenews' ace reporter and the telephoto lens of his cameraman stared down from a scooter at the furiously smoking, sputteringly incandescent surface of Triplanetary's ancient citadel; while upon dozens of worlds thousands of millions of people packed themselves tighter and tighter around tens of millions of visiplates and loud-speakers in order to see and to hear the tremendous news.

"There it is, folks, look at it—the only really impregnable fortress ever built by man! A good many of our experts had it written off as obsolete, long ago, but it seems these Lensmen had something up their sleeves besides their arms, heh-heh! And speaking of Lensmen, they haven't been throwing their weight around, so most of us haven't noticed them very much, but this reporter wants to go on record right now as saying there must be a lot more to the Lens than any of us has thought, because otherwise nobody would have gone to all that trouble and expense, to say nothing of the tremendous loss of life, just to kill the Chief Lensman, which seems to have been what they were after.

"We told you a few minutes ago, you know, that every Continent of Civilization sent official messages denying most emphatically any connection with this outrage. It's still a mystery, folks; in fact, it is getting more and more mysterious all the time. *Not one single man of the Black Fleet was taken alive!* Not even in the ships that were only holed—they blew themselves up! And there were no uniforms or books or anything of the kind to be found in any of the wrecks—no identification whatever!

"And now for the scoop of all time! Universal Telenews has obtained permission to interview the two top Lensmen, both of whom you all know—Virgil Samms and 'Rod the Rock' Kinnison—personally for this beam. We are now going down, by remote control, of course, right into the Galactic patrol office, right in The Hill itself. Here we are. Now if you will step just a little closer to the mike, please, Mr. Samms, or should I say . . . ?"

"You should say 'First Lensman Samms'," Kinnison said bruskly.

"Oh, yes, First Lensman Samms. Thank you, Mr. Kinnison. Now, First Lensman Samms, our clients all want to know all about the Lens. We all know what it *does*, but what, really, *is* it? Who invented it? How does it work?"

Kinnison started to say something, but Samms silenced him with a thought.

"I will answer those questions by asking you one." Samms smiled disarmingly. "Do you remember what happened because the pirates learned to duplicate the golden meteor of the Triplanetary Service?"

"Oh, I see." The Telenews ace, although brash and not at all thin-skinned, was quick on the uptake. "Hush-hush? T. S.?"

"Top Secret. Very much so," Samms confirmed, "and we are going to keep some things about the Lens secret as long as we possibly can."

"Fair enough. Sorry folks, but you will agree that they're right on that. Well, then, Mr. Samms, who do you think it was that tried to kill you, and where do you think the Black Fleet came from?"

"I have no idea," Samms said, slowly and thoughtfully. "No. No idea whatever."

"What? Are you *sure* of that? Aren't you holding back maybe just a little bit of a suspicion, for diplomatic reasons?"

"I am holding nothing back; and through my Lens I can make you certain of the fact. Lensed thoughts come from the mind itself, direct, not through such voluntary muscles as the tongue. The mind does not lie—even such lies as you call 'diplomacy'."

The Lensman demonstrated and the reporter went on:

"He is *sure*, folks, which fact knocked me speechless for a second or two—which is quite a feat in itself. Now, Mr. Samms, one last question. What is all this Lens stuff really about? What are all you Lensmen—the Galactic Council and so on—really up to? What do you expect to get out of it? And why would anybody want to make such an all-out effort to get rid of you? And give it to me on the Lens, please, if you can do it and talk at the same time—that was a wonderful sensation, folks, of getting the dope straight and *knowing* that it was straight."

"I can and will answer both by voice and by Lens. Our basic purpose is . . . " and he quoted verbatim the resounding sentences which Mentor had impressed so ineradicably upon his mind. "You know how little happiness, how little real well-being, there is upon any world today. We propose to increase both. What we expect to get out of it is happiness and well-being for ourselves, the satisfaction felt by any good workman doing the job for which he is best fitted and in which he takes pride. As to why anyone should want to kill me, the logical explanation would seem to be that some group or organization or race, opposed to that for which we Lensmen stand, decided to do away with us and started with me."

"Thank you, Mr. Samms. I am sure that we all enjoyed this interview very much. Now, folks, you all know 'Rocky Rod', 'Rod the Rock', Kinnison . . . just a little closer, please . . . thank you. I don't suppose you have any suspicions, either, any more than . . . ."

"I certainly have!" Kinnison barked, so savagely that five hundred million people jumped as one. "How do you want it; voice, or Lens, or both?" Then on the Lens: "Think it over, son, because *I suspect everybody!*"

"Bub-both, please, Mr. Kinnison." Even Universal's star reporter was shaken by the quiet but deadly fury of the big Lensman's thought, but he rallied so quickly that his hesitation was barely noticeable. "Your Lensed thought to me was that you suspect *everybody*, Mr. Kinnison?"

"Just that. Everybody. I suspect every continental government of every world we know, including that of North America of Tellus. I suspect political parties and organized minorities. I suspect pressure groups. I suspect capital and I suspect labor. I suspect an organization of criminals. I suspect nations and races and worlds that no one of us has as yet heard of—not even you, the top-drawer newshawk of the universe."

"But you have nothing concrete to go on, I take it?"

"If I did have, do you think I'd be standing here talking to you?"

*

First Lensman Samms sat in his private quarters and thought.

Lensman Dronvire of Rigel Four stood behind him and helped him think.

Port Admiral Kinnison, with all his force and drive, began a comprehensive program of investigation, consolidation, expansion, redesigning, and rebuilding.

Virgilia Samms went to a party practically every night. She danced, she flirted, she talked. *How* she talked! Meaningless small talk for the most part—but interspersed with artless questions and comments which, while they perhaps did not put her partner of the moment completely at ease, nevertheless did not quite excite suspicion.

Conway Costigan, Lens under sleeve, undisguised but inconspicuous, rode the ether-lanes; observing minutely and reporting fully.

Jack Kinnison piloted and navigated and computed for his friend and boat-mate:

Mason Northrop; who, completely surrounded by breadboard hookups of new and ever-more-fantastic complexity, listened and looked; listened and tuned; listened and rebuilt; listened and—finally—took bearings and bearings and bearings with his ultra-sensitive loops.

DalNalten and Knobos, with dozens of able helpers, combed the records of three worlds in a search which produced as a by-product a monumental "who's who" of crime.

Skilled technicians fed millions of cards, stack by stack, into the most versatile and most accomplished machines known to the statisticians of the age.

And Dr. Nels Bergenholm, abandoning temporarily his regular line of work, devoted his peculiar talents to a highly abstruse research in the closely allied field of organic chemistry.

The walls of Virgil Samms' quarters became covered with charts, diagrams, and figures. Tabulations and condensations piled up on his desk and overflowed into baskets upon the floor. Until:

"Lensman Olmstead, of Alphacent, sir," his secretary announced.

"Good! Send him in, please."

The stranger entered. The two men, after staring intently at each other for half a minute, smiled and shook hands vigorously. Except for the fact that the newcomer's hair was brown, they were practically identical!

"I'm certainly glad to see you, George. Bergenholm passed you, of course?"

"Yes. He says that he can match your hair to mine, even the individual white ones. And he has made me a wig-maker's dream of a wig."

"Married?" Samms' mind leaped ahead to possible complications.

"Widower, same as you. And . . . ."

"Just a minute—going over this once will be enough." He Lensed call after call. Lensmen in various parts of space became en rapport with him and thus with each other.

"Lensmen—especially you, Rod—George Olmstead is here, and his brother Ray is available. I am going to work."

"I still don't like it!" Kinnison protested. "It's too dangerous. I told the Universe I was going to keep you covered, and I meant it!"

"That's what makes it perfectly safe. That is, if Bergenholm is sure that the duplication is close enough . . . "

"I am sure." Bergenholm's deeply resonant pseudo-voice left no doubt at all in any one of the linked minds. "The substitution will not be detected."

" . . . and that nobody knows, George, or even suspects, that you got your Lens."

"I am sure of that." Olmstead laughed quietly. "Also, nobody except us and your secretary knows that I am here. For a good many years I have made a specialty of that sort of thing. Photos, fingerprints, and so on have all been taken care of."

"Good. I simply can not work efficiently here," Samms expressed what all knew to be the simple truth. "Dronvire is a much better analyst-synthesist than I am; as soon as any significant correlation is possible he will know it. We have learned that the Towne-Morgan crowd, Mackenzie Power, Ossmen Industries, and Interstellar Spaceways are all tied in together, and that thionite is involved, but we have not been able to get any further. There is a slight correlation—barely significant—between deaths from thionite and the arrival in the Solarian System of certain Spaceways liners. The fact that certain officials of the Earth-Screen Service have been and are spending considerably more than they earn sets up a slight but definite probability that they are allowing space-ships or boats from space-ships to land illegally. These smugglers carry contraband, which may or may not be thionite. In short, we lack fundamental data in every department, and it is high time for me to begin doing my share in getting it."

"I don't check you, Virge." None of the Kinnisons ever did give up without a struggle. "Olmstead is a mighty smooth worker, and you are our prime coordinator. Why not let him keep up the counter-espionage—do the job you were figuring on doing yourself—and you stay here and boss it?"

"I have thought of that, a great deal, and have . . . ."

"Because Olmstead can not do it," a hitherto silent mind cut in, decisively. "I, Rularion of North Polar Jupiter, say so. There are psychological factors involved. The ability to separate and to evaluate the constituent elements of a complex situation; the ability to make correct decisions without hesitation; as well as many others not as susceptible to concise statement, but which collectively could be called power of mind. How say you, Bergenholm of Tellus? For I have perceived in you a mind approximating in some respects the philosophical and psychological depth of my own." This outrageously egotistical declaration was, to the Jovian, a simple statement of an equally simple truth, and Bergenholm accepted it as such.

"I agree. Olmstead probably could not succeed."

"Well, then, can Samms?" Kinnison demanded.

"Who knows?" came Bergenholm's mental shrug, and simultaneously:

"Nobody knows whether I can or not, but I am going to try," and Samms ended—almost—the argument by asking Bergenholm and a couple of other Lensmen to come into his office and by taking off his Lens.

"And that's another thing I don't like." Kinnison offered one last objection. "Without your Lens, *anything* can happen to you."

"Oh, I won't have to be without it very long. And besides, Virgilia isn't the only one in the Samms family who can work better—sometimes—without a Lens."

The Lensmen came in and, in a surprisingly short time, went out. A few minutes later, two Lensmen strolled out of Samms' inner office into the outer one.

"Good-bye, George," the red-headed man said aloud, "and good luck."

"Same to you, Chief," and the brown-haired one strode out.

Norma the secretary was a smart girl, and observant. In her position, she had to be. Her eyes followed the man out, then scanned the Lensman from toe to crown.

"I've never seen anything like it, Mr. Samms," she remarked then. "Except for the difference in coloring, and a sort of . . . well, stoopiness . . . he could be your identical twin. You two must have had a common ancestor—or several—not too far back, didn't you?"

"We certainly did. Quadruple second cousins, you might call it. We have known of each other for years, but this is the first time we have met."

"Quadruple second cousins? What does that mean? How come?"

"Well, say that once upon a time there were two men named Albert and Chester . . . ."

"What? Not two Irishmen named Pat and Mike? You're slipping, boss." The girl smiled roguishly. During rush hours she was always the fast, cool, efficient secretary, but in moments of ease such persiflage as this was the usual thing in the First Lensman's private office. "Not at all up to your usual form."

"Merely because I am speaking now as a genealogist, not as a raconteur. But to continue, we will say that Chester and Albert had four children apiece, two boys and two girls, two pairs of identical twins, each. And when they grew up—half way up, that is . . . ."

"Don't tell me that we are going to suppose that all those identical twins married each other?"

"Exactly. Why not?"

"Well, it would be stretching the laws of probability all out of shape. But go ahead—I can see what's coming, I think."

"Each of those couples had one, and only one, child. We will call those children Jim Samms and Sally Olmstead; John Olmstead and Irene Samms."

The girl's levity disappeared. "James Alexander Samms and Sarah Olmstead Samms. Your parents. I didn't see what was coming, after all. This George Olmstead; then, is your . . . ."

"Whatever it is, yes. I can't name it, either—maybe you had better call Genealogy some day and find out. But it's no wonder we look alike. And there are three of us, not two—George has an identical twin brother."

The red-haired Lensman stepped back into the inner office, shut the door, and Lensed a thought at Virgil Samms.

"It worked, Virgil! I talked to her for five solid minutes, practically leaning on her desk, and she didn't tumble! And if this wig of Bergenholm's fooled *her* so completely, the job he did on you would fool *anybody!*"

"Fine! I've done a little testing myself, on the keenest men I know, without a trace of recognition so far."

His last lingering doubt resolved, Samms boarded the ponderous, radiation-proof, neutron-proof shuttle-scow which was the only possible means of entering or leaving the Hill. A fast cruiser whisked him to Nampa, where Olmstead's "accidentally" damaged transcontinental transport was being repaired, and from which city Olmstead had been gone so briefly that no one had missed him. He occupied Olmstead's space; he surrendered the remainder of Olmstead's ticket. He reached New York. He took a 'copter to Senator Morgan's office. He was escorted into the private office of Herkimer Herkimer Third.

"Olmstead. Of Alphacent."

"Yes?" Herkimer's hand moved, ever so little, upon his desk's top.

"Here." The Lensman dropped an envelope upon the desk in such fashion that it came to rest within an inch of the hand.

"Prints. Here." Samms made prints. "Wash your hands, over there." Herkimer pressed a button. "Check all these prints, against each other and the files. Check the two halves of the torn sheet, fiber to fiber." He turned to the Lensless Lensman, now standing quietly before his desk. "Routine; a formality, in your case, but necessary."

"Of course."

Then for long seconds the two hard men stared into the hard depths of each other's eyes.

"You may do, Olmstead. We have had very good reports of you. But you have never been in thionite?"

"No. I have never even seen any."

"What do you want to get into it for?"

"Your scouts sounded me out; what did they tell you? The usual thing—promotion from the ranks into the brass—to get to where I can do myself and the organization some good."

"Yourself first, the organization second?"

"What else? Why should I be different from the rest of you?"

This time the locked eyes held longer; one pair smoldering, the other gold-flecked, tawny ice.

"Why, indeed?" Herkimer smiled thinly. "We do not advertise it, however."

"Outside, I wouldn't, either; but here I'm laying my cards flat on the table."

"I see. You *will* do, Olmstead, if you live. There's a test, you know."

"They told me there would be."

"Well, aren't you curious to know what it is?"

"Not particularly. *You* passed it, didn't you?"

"What do you mean by *that* crack?" Herkimer leaped to his feet; his eyes, smoldering before, now ablaze.

"Exactly what I said, no more and no less. You may read into it anything you please." Samms' voice was as cold as were his eyes. "You picked me out because of what I am. Did you think that moving upstairs would make a boot-licker out of me?"

"Not at all." Herkimer sat down and took from a drawer two small, transparent, vaguely capsule-like tubes, each containing a few particles of purple dust. "You know what this is?"

"I can guess."

"Each of these is a good, heavy jolt; about all that a strong man with a strong heart can stand. Sit down. Here is one dose. Pull the cover, stick the capsule up one nostril, squeeze the ejector, and sniff. If you can leave this other dose sitting here on the desk you will live, and thus pass the test. If you can't, you die."

Samms sat, and pulled, and squeezed, and sniffed.

His forearms hit the desk with a thud. His hands clenched themselves into fists, the tight-stretched tendons standing boldly out. His face turned white. His eyes jammed themselves shut; his jaw-muscles sprang into bands and lumps as they clamped his teeth hard together. Every voluntary muscle in his body went into a rigor as extreme as that of death itself. His heart pounded; his breathing became stertorous.

This was the dreadful "muscle-lock" so uniquely characteristic of thionite; the frenzied immobility of the ultimately passionate satisfaction of every desire.

The Galactic Patrol became for him an actuality; a force for good pervading all the worlds of all the galaxies of all the universes of all existing space-time continual. He knew what the Lens was, and why. He understood time and space. He knew the absolute beginning and the ultimate end.

He also saw things and did things over which it is best to draw a kindly veil, for *every* desire—mental or physical, open or sternly suppressed, noble or base—that Virgil Samms had ever had was being *completely satisfied*. EVERY DESIRE.

As Samms sat there, straining motionlessly upon the verge of death through sheer ecstasy, a door opened and Senator Morgan entered the room. Herkimer started, almost imperceptibly, as he turned—had there been, or not, an instantaneously-suppressed flash of guilt in those now completely clear and frank brown eyes?

"Hi, Chief; come in and sit down. Glad to see you—this is not exactly my idea of fun."

"No? When did you stop being a sadist?" The senator sat down beside his minion's desk, the fingertips of his left hand began soundlessly to drum. "You wouldn't have, by any chance, been considering the idea of . . . ?" He paused significantly.

"What an idea." Herkimer's act—if it was an act—was flawless. "He's too good a man to waste."

"I know it, but you didn't act as though you did. I've never seen you come out such a poor second in an interview . . . and it wasn't because you didn't know to start with just what kind of a tiger he was—that's why he was selected for this job. And it would have been so easy to give him just a wee bit more."

"That's preposterous, Chief, and you know it."

"Do I? However, it couldn't have been jealousy, because he isn't being considered for your job. He won't be over you, and there's plenty of room for everybody. What was the matter? Your bloodthirstiness wouldn't have taken you *that* far, under these circumstances. Come clean, Herkimer."

"Okay—I hate the whole damned family!" Herkimer burst out, viciously.

"I see. That adds up." Morgan's face cleared, his fingers became motionless. "You can't make the Samms wench and aren't in position to skin her alive, so you get allergic to all her relatives. That adds up, but let me tell you something." His quiet, level voice carried more of menace than most men's loudest threats. "Keep your love life out of business and keep that sadistic streak under control. Don't let anything like this happen again."

"I won't, Chief. I got off the beam—but he made me so *damn* mad!"

"Certainly. That's exactly what he was trying to do. Elementary. If he could make you look small it would make him look big, and he just about did. But watch now, he's coming to."

Samms' muscles relaxed. He opened his eyes groggily; then, as a wave of humiliated realization swept over his consciousness, he closed them again and shuddered. He had always thought himself pretty much of a man; how could he *possibly* have descended to such nauseous depths of depravity, of turpitude, of sheer moral degradation? And yet every cell of his being was shrieking its demand for more; his mind and his substance alike were permeated by an over-mastering craving to experience again the ultimate thrills which they had so tremendously, so outrageously enjoyed.

There was another good jolt lying right there on the desk in front of him, even though thionite-sniffers always saw to it that no more of the drug could be obtained without considerable physical exertion; which exertion would bring them to their senses. If he took that jolt it would kill him. What of it? What was death? What good was life, except to enjoy such thrills as he had just had and was about to have again? And besides, thionite couldn't kill *him*. He was a super-man; he had just proved it!

He straightened up and reached for the capsule; and that effort, small as it was, was enough to bring First Lensman Virgil Samms back under control. The craving, however, did not decrease. Rather, it increased.

Months were to pass before he could think of thionite, or even of the color purple, without a spasmodic catching of the breath and a tightening of every muscle. Years were to pass before he could forget, even partially, the theretofore unsuspected dwellers in the

242

dark recesses of his own mind. Nevertheless, from the store of whatever it was that made him what he was, Virgil Samms drew strength. Thumb and forefinger touched the capsule, but instead of picking it up, he pushed it across the desk toward Herkimer.

"Put it away, bub. One whiff of that stuff will last me for life." He stared unfathomably at the secretary, then turned to Morgan and nodded. "After all, he did not *say* that he ever passed this or any other test. He just didn't contradict me when I said it."

With a visible effort Herkimer remained silent, but Morgan did not.

"You talk too much, Olmstead. Can you stand up yet?"

Gripping the desk with both hands, Samms heaved himself to his feet. The room was spinning and gyrating; every individual thing in it was moving in a different and impossible orbit; his already splintered skull threatened more and more violently to emulate a fragmentation bomb; black and white spots and vari-colored flashes filled his cone of vision. He wrenched one hand free, then the other—and collapsed back into the chair.

"Not yet—quite," he admitted, through stiff lips.

Although he was careful not to show it, Morgan was amazed—not that the man had collapsed, but that he had been able so soon to lift himself even an inch. "Tiger" was not the word; this Olmstead must be seven-eighths dinosaur.

"It takes a few minutes; longer for some, not so long for others," Morgan said, blandly. "But what makes you think Herkimer here never took one of the same?"

"Huh?" Again two pairs of eyes locked and held; and this time the duel was longer and more pregnant. "What do *you* think? How do you suppose I lived to get as old as I am now? By being dumb?"

Morgan unwrapped a Venerian cigar, settled it comfortably between his teeth, lit it, and drew three slow puffs before replying.

"Ah, a student. An analytical mind," he said, evenly, and—apparently—irrelevantly. "Let's skip Herkimer for the moment. Try your hand on me."

"Why not? From what we hear out in the field, you have always been in the upper brackets, so you probably never had to prove that you could take it or let it alone. My guess would be, though, that you could."

"The good old oil, eh?" Morgan allowed his face and voice to register a modicum, precisely metered, of contempt. "How to get along in the world; Lesson One: Butter up the Boss."

"Nice try, Senator, but I'll have to score you a clean miss." Samms, now back almost to normal, grinned companionably. "We both know that if I were still in the kindergarten I wouldn't be here now."

"I'll let that one pass—this time." Under that look and tone Morgan's underlings were wont to cringe, but this Olmstead was not the cringing type. "Don't do it again. It might not be safe."

"Oh, it would be safe enough—for today, at least. There are two factors which you are very carefully ignoring. First, I haven't accepted the job yet."

"Are you innocent enough to think you'll get out of this building alive if I don't accept you?"

"If you want to call it innocence, yes. Oh, I know you've got gunnies all over the place, but they don't mean a thing."

"No?" Morgan's voice was silkily venomous.

"No." Olmstead was completely unimpressed. "Put yourself in my place. You know I've been around a long time; and not just around my mother. I was weaned quite a number of years ago."

"I see. You don't scare worth a damn. A point. And you are testing me, just as I am testing you. Another point. I'm beginning to like you, George. I think I know what your second point is, but let's have it, just for the record."

"I'm sure you do. Any man, to be my boss, has got to be at least as good a man as I am. Otherwise I take his job away from him."

"Fair enough. By God, I *do* like you, Olmstead!" Morgan, his big face wreathed in smiles, got up, strode over, and shook hands vigorously; and Samms, scan as he would, could not even hazard a guess as to how much—if any—of this enthusiasm was real. "Do you want the job? And when can you go to work?"

"Yes, sir. Two hours ago, sir."

"That's fine!" Morgan boomed. Although he did not comment upon it, he noticed and understood the change in the form of address. "Without knowing what the job is or how much it pays?"

"Neither is important, sir, at the moment." Samms, who had got up easily enough to shake hands, now shook his head experimentally. Nothing rattled. Good—he was in pretty good shape already. "As to the job, I can either do it or find out why it can't be done. As to pay, I've heard you called a lot of things, but 'piker' was never one of them."

"Very well. I predict that you will go far." Morgan again shook the Lensman's hand; and again Samms could not evaluate the Senator's sincerity. "Tuesday afternoon. New York Spaceport. Space-ship *Virgin Queen*. Report to Captain Willoughby in the dock office at fourteen hundred hours. Stop at the cashier's office on your way out. Good-bye."

CHAPTER 9

Piracy was rife. There was no suspicion, however, nor would there be for many years, that there was anything of very large purpose about the business. Murgatroyd was simply a Captain Kidd of space; and even if he were actually connected with Galactic Spaceways, that fact would not be surprising. Such relationships had always existed; the most ferocious and dreaded pirates of the ancient world worked in full partnership with the First Families of that world.

Virgil Samms was thinking of pirates and of piracy when he left Senator Morgan's office. He was still thinking of them while he was reporting to Roderick Kinnison. Hence:

"But that's enough about this stuff and me, Rod. Bring me up to date on Operation Boskone."

"Branching out no end. Your guess was right that Spaceways' losses to pirates are probably phony. But it wasn't the *known* attacks—that is, those cases in which the ship was found, later, with some or most of the personnel alive—that gave us the real information.

They were all pretty much alike. But when we studied the total disappearances we really hit the jack-pot."

"That doesn't sound just right, but I'm listening."

"You'd better, since it goes farther than even you suspected. It was no trouble at all to get the passenger lists and the names of the crews of the independent ships that were lost without a trace. Their relatives and friends—we concentrated mostly on wives—could be located, except for the usual few who moved around so much that they got lost. Spacemen average young, you know, and their wives are still younger. Well, these young women got jobs, most of them remarried, and so on. In short, normal."

"And in the case of Spaceways, not normal?"

"Decidedly not. In the first place, you'd be amazed at how little publication was ever done of passenger lists, and apparently crew lists were not published at all. No use going into detail as to how we got the stuff, but we got it. However, nine tenths of the wives had disappeared, and none had remarried. The only ones we could find were those who did not care, even when their husbands were alive, whether they ever saw them again or not. But the big break was—you remember the disappearance of that girls'-school cruise ship?"

"Of course. It made a lot of noise."

"An interesting point in connection with that cruise is that two days before the ship blasted off the school was robbed. The vault was opened with thermite and the whole Administration Building burned to the ground. All the school's records were destroyed. Thus, the list of missing had to be made up from statements made by friends, relatives, and what not."

"I remember something of the kind. My impression was, though, that the space-ship company furnished . . . . Oh!" The tone of Samms' thought alerted sharply. "That was Spaceways, under cover?"

"Definitely. Our best guess is that there were quite a few shiploads of women disappeared about that time, instead of one. Austine's College had more students that year than ever before or since. It was the extras, not the regulars, who went on that cruise; the ones who figured it would be more convenient to disappear in space than to become ordinary missing persons."

"But Rod! That would mean . . . but where?"

"It means just that. And finding out 'where' will run into a project. There are over two thousand million suns in this galaxy, and the best estimate is that there are more than that many planets habitable by beings more or less human in type. You know how much of the galaxy has been explored and how fast the work of exploring the rest of it is going. Your guess is just as good as mine as to where those spacemen and engineers and their wives and girl-friends are now. I am sure, though, of four things; none of which we can ever begin to prove. One; they didn't die in space. Two; they landed on a comfortable and very well equipped Tellurian planet. Three; they built a fleet there. Four; that fleet attacked the Hill."

"Murgatroyd, do you suppose?" Although surprised by Kinnison's tremendous report, Samms was not dismayed.

"No idea. No data—yet."

"And they'll keep on building," Samms said. "They had a fleet much larger than the one they expected to meet. Now they'll build one larger than all our combined forces. And since the politicians will always know what we are doing . . . or it might be . . . I wonder . . . ?"

"You can stop wondering." Kinnison grinned savagely.

"What do you mean?"

"Just what you were going to think about. You know the edge of the galaxy closest to Tellus, where that big rift cuts in?"

"Yes."

"Across that rift, where it won't be surveyed for a thousand years, there's a planet that could be Earth's twin sister. No atomic energy, no space-drive, but heavily industrialized and anxious to welcome us. Project Bennett. Very, *very* hush-hush. Nobody except Lensmen know anything about it. Two friends of Dronvire's—smart, smooth operators—are in charge. It's going to be the Navy Yard of the Galactic Patrol."

"But Rod . . . " Samms began to protest, his mind leaping ahead to the numberless problems, the tremendous difficulties, inherent in the program which his friend had outlined so briefly.

"Forget it, Virge!" Kinnison cut in. "It won't be easy, of course, but we can do anything they can do, and do it better. You can go calmly ahead with your own chores, knowing that when—and notice that I say 'when', not 'if'—we need it we'll have a fleet up our sleeves that will make the official one look like a task force. But I see you're at the rendezvous, and there's Jill. Tell her 'hi' for me. And as the Vegians say—'Tail high, brother!'"

Samms was in the hotel's ornate lobby; a couple of uniformed "boys" and Jill Samms were approaching. The girl reached him first.

"You had no trouble in recognizing me, then, my dear?"

"None at all, Uncle George." She kissed him perfunctorily, the bell hops faded away. "So nice to see you—I've heard *so* much about you. The Marine Room, you said?"

"Yes. I reserved a table."

And in that famous restaurant, in the unequalled privacy of the city's noisiest and most crowded night spot, they drank sparingly; ate not-so-sparingly; and talked not sparingly at all.

"It's perfectly safe here, you think?" Jill asked first.

"Perfectly. A super-sensitive microphone couldn't hear anything, and it's so dark that a lip-reader, even if he could read us, would need a pair of twelve-inch night-glasses."

"Goody! They did a marvelous job, Dad. If it weren't for your . . . well, your personality, I wouldn't recognize you even now."

"You think I'm safe, then?"

"Absolutely."

"Then we'll get down to business. You, Knobos, and DalNalten all have keen and powerful minds. You can't all be wrong. Spaceways, then, is tied in with both the Towne-

Morgan gang and with thionite. The logical extension of that—Dal certainly thought of it, even though he didn't mention it—would be . . . " Samms paused.

"Check. That the notorious Murgatroyd, instead of being just another pirate chief, is really working for Spaceways and belongs to the Towne-Morgan-Isaacson gang. But dad—what an idea! Can things be *that* rotten, really?"

"They may be worse than that. Now the next thing. Who, in your opinion, is the real boss?"

"Well, it certainly is not Herkimer Herkimer Third." Jill ticked him off on a pink forefinger. She had been asked for an opinion; she set out to give it without apology or hesitation. "He could—just about—direct the affairs of a hot-dog stand. Nor is it Clander. He isn't even a little fish; he's scarcely a minnow. Equally certainly it is neither the Venerian nor the Martian. They may run planetary affairs, but nothing bigger. I haven't met Murgatroyd, of course, but I have had several evaluations, and he does not rate up with Towne. And Big Jim—and this surprised me as much as it will you—is almost certainly not the prime mover." She looked at him questioningly.

"That would have surprised me tremendously yesterday; but after today—I'll tell you about that presently—it doesn't."

"I'm glad of that. I expected an argument, and I have been inclined to question the validity of my own results, since they do not agree with common knowledge—or, rather, what is supposed to be knowledge. That leaves Isaacson and Senator Morgan." Jill frowned in perplexity; seemed, for the first time, unsure. "Isaacson is of course a big man. Able. Well-informed. Extremely capable. A top-notch executive. Not only *is*, would *have* to be, to run Spaceways. On the other hand, I have always thought that Morgan was nothing but a windbag . . . ." Jill stopped talking; left the thought hanging in air.

"So did I—until today," Samms agreed grimly. "I thought that he was simply an unusually corrupt, greedy, rabble-rousing politician. Our estimates of him may have to be changed very radically."

Samms' mind raced. From two entirely different angles of approach, Jill and he had arrived at the same conclusion. But, if Morgan were really the Big Shot, would he have deigned to interview personally such small fry as Olmstead? Or was Olmstead's job of more importance than he, Samms, had supposed?

"I've got a dozen more things to check with you," he went on, almost without a pause, "but since this leadership matter is the only one in which my experience would affect your judgment, I had better tell you about what happened today . . . ."

*

Tuesday came, and hour fourteen hundred; and Samms strode into an office. There was a big, clean desk; a wiry, intense, gray-haired man.

"Captain Willoughby?"

"Yes."

"George Olmstead reporting."

"Fourth Officer." The captain punched a button; the heavy, sound-proof door closed itself and locked.

"*Fourth* Officer? New rank, eh. What does the ticket cover?"

"New, and special. Here's the articles; read it and sign it." He did not add "or else", it was not necessary. It was clearly evident that Captain Willoughby, never garrulous, intended to be particularly reticent with his new subordinate.

Samms read. " . . . Fourth Officer . . . shall . . . no duties or responsibilities in the operation or maintenance of said space-ship . . . cargo . . . " Then came a clause which fairly leaped from the paper and smote his eyes: "when in command of a detail outside the hull of said space-ship he shall enforce, by the infliction of death or such other penalty as he deems fit . . . ."

The Lensman was rocked to the heels, but did not show it. Instead, he took the captain's pen—his own, as far as Willoughby was concerned, could have been filled with vanishing ink—and wrote George Olmstead's name in George Olmstead's bold, flowing script.

Willoughby then took him aboard the good ship *Virgin Queen* and led him to his cabin.

"Here you are, Mr. Olmstead. Beyond getting acquainted with the super-cargo and the rest of your men, you will have no duties for a few days. You have full run of the ship, with one exception. Stay out of the control room until I call you. Is that clear?"

"Yes, sir." Willoughby turned away and Samms, after tossing his space-bag into the rack, took inventory.

The room was of course very small; but, considering the importance of mass, it was almost extravagantly supplied. There were shelves, or rather, tight racks, of books; there were sun-lamps and card-shelves and exercisers and games; there was a receiver capable of bringing in programs from almost anywhere in space. The room had only one lack; it did not have an ultra-wave visiplate. Nor was this lack surprising. "They" would scarcely let George Olmstead know where "they" were taking him.

Samms was surprised, however, when he met the men who were to be directly under his command; for instead of one, or at most two, they numbered exactly forty. And they were all, he thought at first glance, the dregs and sweepings of the lowest dives in space. Before long, however, he learned that they were not all space-rats and denizens of Skid Rows. Six of them—the strongest physically and the hardest mentally of the lot—were fugitives from lethal chambers; murderers and worse. He looked at the biggest, toughest one of the six—a rock-drill-eyed, red-haired giant—and asked:

"What did they tell you, Tworn, that your job was going to be?"

"They didn't say. Just that it was dangerous, but if I done exactly what my boss would tell me to do, and nothing else, I might not even get hurt. An' I was due to take the deep breath the next week, see? That's just how it was, boss."

"I see," and one by one Virgil Samms, master psychologist, studied and analyzed his motley crew until he was called into the control room.

The navigating tank was covered; no charts were to be seen. The one "live" visiplate showed a planet and a fiercely blue-white sun.

"My orders are to tell you, at this point, all I know about what you've got to do and about that planet down there. Trenco, they call it." To Virgil Samms, the first adherent of Civilization ever to hear it, that name meant nothing whatever. "You are to take about five of your men, go down there, and gather all the green leaves you can. Not green in color; sort of purplish. What they call broadleaf is the best; leaves about two feet long and a foot wide. But don't be too choosy. If there isn't any broadleaf handy, grab anything you can get hold of."

"What is the opposition?" Samms asked, quietly. "And what have they got that makes them so tough?"

"Nothing. No inhabitants, even. Just the planet itself. Next to Arisia, it's the God damndest planet in space. I've never been any closer to it than this, and I never will, so I don't know anything about it except what I hear; but there's something about it that kills men or drives them crazy. We spend seven or eight boats every trip, and thirty-five or forty men, and the biggest load that anybody ever took away from here was just under two hundred pounds of leaf. A good many times we don't get any."

"They go crazy, eh?" In spite of his control, Samms paled. But it couldn't be like Arisia. "What are the symptoms? What do they say?"

"Various. Main thing seems to be that they lose their sight. Don't go blind, exactly, but can't see where anything is; or, if they do see it, it isn't there. And it rains over forty feet deep every night, and yet it all dries up by morning. The worst electrical storms in the universe, and wind-velocities—I can show you charts on that—of over eight hundred miles an hour."

"Whew! How about time? With your permission, I would like to do some surveying before I try to land."

"A smart idea. A couple of the other boys had the same, but it didn't help—they didn't come back. I'll give you two Tellurian days—no, three—before I give you up and start sending out the other boats. Pick out your five men and see what you can do."

As the boat dropped away, Willoughby's voice came briskly from a speaker. "I know that you five men have got ideas. Forget'em. Fourth Officer Olmstead has the authority and the orders to put a half-ounce slug through the guts of any or all of you that don't jump, and jump fast, to do what he tells you. And if that boat makes any funny moves I blast it out of the ether. Good harvesting!"

For forty-eight Tellurian hours, taking time out only to sleep, Samms scanned and surveyed the planet Trenco; and the more he studied it, the more outrageously abnormal it became.

Trenco was, and is, a peculiar planet indeed. Its atmosphere is not air as we know air; its hydrosphere does not resemble water. Half of that atmosphere and most of that hydrosphere are one chemical, a substance of very low heat of vaporization and having a boiling point of about seventy-five degrees Fahrenheit. Trenco's days are intensely hot; its nights are bitterly cold.

At night, therefore, it rains: and by comparison a Tellurian downpour of one inch per hour is scarcely a drizzle. Upon Trenco it really *rains*—forty seven feet and five inches of precipitation, every night of every Trenconian year. And this tremendous condensation of course causes wind. Willoughby's graphs were accurate. Except at Trenco's very poles there is not a spot in which or a time at which an Earthly gale would not constitute a dead calm; and along the equator, at every sunrise and every sunset, the wind blows from the day side into the night side at a velocity which no Tellurian hurricane or cyclone, however violent, has even distantly approached.

Also, therefore, there is lightning. Not in the mild and occasional flashes which we of gentle Terra know, but in a continuous, blinding glare which outshines a normal sun; in battering, shattering, multi-billion-volt discharges which not only make darkness unknown there, but also distort beyond recognition and beyond function the warp and the woof of space itself. Sight is almost completely useless in that fantastically altered medium. So is the ultra-beam.

Landing on the daylight side, except possibly at exact noon, would be impossible because of the wind, nor could the ship stay landed for more than a couple of minutes. Landing on the night side would be practically as bad, because of the terrific charge the boat would pick up—unless the boat carried something that could be rebuilt into a leaker. Did it? It did.

Time after time, from pole to pole and from midnight around the clock, Samms stabbed Visibeam and spy-ray down toward Trenco's falsely-visible surface, with consistently and meaninglessly impossible results. The planet tipped, lurched, spun, and danced. It broke up into chunks, each of which began insanely to follow mathematically impossible paths.

Finally, in desperation, he rammed a beam down and held it down. Again he saw the planet break up before his eyes, but this time he held on. He *knew* that he was well out of the stratosphere, a good two hundred miles up. Nevertheless, he *saw* a tremendous mass of jagged rock falling straight down, with terrific velocity, upon his tiny lifeboat!

Unfortunately the crew, to whom he had not been paying overmuch attention of late, saw it, too; and one of them, with a bestial yell, leaped toward Samms and the controls. Samms, reaching for pistol and blackjack, whirled around just in time to see the big red-head lay the would-be attacker out cold with a vicious hand's-edge chop at the base of the skull.

"Thanks, Tworn. Why?"

"Because I want to get out of this alive, and he'd've had us all in hell in fifteen minutes. You know a hell of a lot more than we do, so I'm playin' it your way. See?"

"I see. Can you use a sap?"

"An artist," the big man admitted, modestly. "Just tell me how long you want a guy to be out and I won't miss it a minute, either way. But you'd better blow that crumb's brains out, right now. He ain't no damn good."

"Not until after I see whether he can work or not. You're a Procian, aren't you?"

"Yeah. Midlands—North Central."

"What did you do?"

"Nothing much, at first. Just killed a guy that needed killing; but the goddam louse had a lot of money, so they give me twenty five years. I didn't like it very well, and acted rough, so they give me solitary—boot, bandage, and so on. So I tried a break—killed six or eight, maybe a dozen, guards—but didn't quite make it. So they slated me for the big whiff. That's all, boss."

"I'm promoting you, now, to squad leader. Here's the sap." He handed Tworn his blackjack. "Watch'em—I'll be too busy to. This landing is going to be tough."

"Gotcha, boss." Tworn was calibrating his weapon by slugging himself experimentally on the leg. "Go ahead. As far as these crumbs are concerned, you've got this air-tank all to yourself."

Samms had finally decided what he was going to do. He located the terminator on the morning side, poised his little ship somewhat nearer to dawn than to midnight, and "cut the rope". He took one quick reading on the sun, cut off his plates, and let her drop, watching only his pressure gages and gyros.

One hundred millimeters of mercury. Three hundred. Five hundred. He slowed her down. He was going to hit a thin liquid, but if he hit it too hard he would smash the boat, and he had no idea what the atmospheric pressure at Trenco's surface would be. Six hundred. Even this late at night, it might be greater than Earth's . . . and it might be a lot less. Seven hundred.

Slower and slower he crept downward, his tension mounting infinitely faster than did the needle of the gage. This was an instrument landing with a vengeance! Eight hundred. How was the crew taking it? How many of them had Tworn had to disable? He glanced quickly around. None! Now that they could not see the hallucinatory images upon the plates, they were not suffering at all—he himself was the only one aboard who was feeling the strain!

Nine hundred . . . nine hundred forty. The boat "hit the drink" with a crashing, splashing impact. Its pace was slow enough, however, and the liquid was deep enough, so that no damage was done. Samms applied a little driving power and swung his craft's sharp nose into the line toward the sun. The little ship plowed slowly forward, as nearly just awash as Samms could keep her; grounded as gently as a river steam-boat upon a mud-flat. The starkly incredible downpour slackened; the Lensman knew that the second critical moment was at hand.

"Strap down, men, until we see what this wind is going to do to us."

The atmosphere, moving at a velocity well above that of sound, was in effect not a gas, but a solid. Even a spaceboat's hard skin of alloy plate, with all its bracing, could not take what was coming next. Inert, she would be split open, smashed, flattened out, and twisted into pretzels. Samms' finger stabbed down; the Berg went into action; the lifeboat went free just as that raging blast of quasi-solid vapor wrenched her into the air.

The second descent was much faster and much easier than the first. Nor, this time, did Samms remain surfaced or drive toward shore. Knowing now that this ocean was not deep enough to harm his vessel, he let her sink to the bottom. More, he turned her on her side and drove her at a flat angle into the bottom; so deep that the rim of her starboard lock was flush with the ocean's floor. Again they waited; and this time the wind did not blow the lifeboat away.

Upon purely theoretical grounds Samms had reasoned that the weird distortion of vision must be a function of distance, and his observations so far had been in accord with that hypothesis. Now, slowly and cautiously, he sent out a visibeam. Ten feet . . . twenty . . . forty . . . all clear. At fifty the seeing was definitely bad; at sixty it became impossible.

He shortened back to forty and began to study the vegetation, growing with such fantastic speed that the leaves, pressed flat to the ground by the gale and anchored there by heavy rootlets, were already inches long. There was also what seemed to be animal life, of sorts, but Samms was not, at the moment, interested in Trenconian zoology.

"Are them the plants we're going to get, boss?" Tworn asked, staring into the plate over Samms' shoulder. "Shall we go out now an' start pickin''em?"

"Not yet. Even if we could open the port the blast would wreck us. Also, it would shear your head off, flush with the coaming, as fast as you stuck it out. This wind should ease off after a while; we'll go out a little before noon. In the meantime we'll get ready. Have the boys break out a couple of spare Number Twelve struts, some clamps and chain, four snatch blocks, and a hundred feet of heavy space-line . . . ."

"Good," he went on, when the order had been obeyed. "Rig the line from the winch through snatch blocks here, and here, and here, so I can haul you back against the wind. While you are doing that I'll rig a remote control on the winch."

Shortly before Trenco's fierce, blue-white sun reached meridian, the six men donned space-suits and Samms cautiously opened the air-lock ports. They worked. The wind was now scarcely more than an Earthly hurricane; the wildly whipping broadleaf plants, struggling upward, were almost half-way to the vertical. The leaves were apparently almost fully grown.

Four men clamped their suits to the line. The line was paid out. Each man selected two leaves; the largest, fattest, purplest ones he could reach. Samms hauled them back and received the loot; Tworn stowed the leaves away. Again—again—again.

With noon there came a few minutes of "calm". A strong man could stand against the now highly variable wind; could move around without being blown beyond the horizon; and during those few minutes all six men gathered leaves. That time, however, was very short. The wind steadied into the reverse direction with ever-increasing fury; winch and space-line again came into play. And in a scant half hour, when the line began to hum an almost musical note under its load, Samms decided to call it quits.

"That'll be all for today, boys," he announced. "About twice more and this line will part. You've done too good a job to lose you. Secure ship."

"Shall I blow the air, sir?" Tworn asked.

"I don't think so." Samms thought for a moment. "No. I'm afraid to take the chance. This stuff, whatever it is, is probably as poisonous as cyanide. We'll keep our suits on and exhaust into space."

Time passed. "Night" came; the rain and the flood. The bottom softened. Samms blasted the lifeboat out of the mud and away from the planet. He opened the bleeder valves, then both air-lock ports; the contaminated air was replaced by the ultra-hard vacuum of the inter-planetary void. He signaled the *Virgin Queen*; the lifeboat was taken aboard.

"Quick trip, Olmstead," Willoughby congratulated him. "I'm surprised that you got back at all, to say nothing of with so much stuff and not losing a man. Give me the weight, mister, fast!"

"Three hundred and forty eight pounds, sir," the super-cargo reported.

"My God! And all pure broadleaf! *Nobody* ever did *that* before! How did you do it, Olmstead?"

"I don't know whether that would be any of your business or not." Samms' mien was not insulting; merely thoughtful. "Not that I give a damn, but my way might not help anybody else much, and I think I had better report to the main office first, and let them do the telling. Fair enough?"

"Fair enough," the skipper conceded, ungrudgingly. "What a load! And no losses!"

"One boatload of air, is all; but air is expensive out here." Samms made a point, deliberately.

"Air!" Willoughby snorted. "I'll swap you a hundred flasks of air, any time, for any one of those leaves!" Which was what Samms wanted to know.

Captain Willoughby was smart. He knew that the way to succeed was to use and then to trample upon his inferiors; to toady to such superiors as were too strong to be pulled down and thus supplanted. He knew this Olmstead had what it took to be a big shot. Therefore:

"They told me to keep you in the dark until we got to Trenco," he more than half apologized to his Fourth Officer shortly after the *Virgin Queen* blasted away from the Trenconian system. "But they didn't say anything about afterwards—maybe they figured you wouldn't be aboard any more, as usual—but anyway, you can stay right here in the control room if you want to."

"Thanks, Skipper, but mightn't it be just as well," he jerked his head inconspicuously toward the other officers, "to play the string out, this trip? I don't care where we're going, and we don't want anybody to get any funny ideas."

"That'd be a lot better, of course—as long as you know that your cards are all aces, as far as I'm concerned."

"Thanks, Willoughby. I'll remember that."

Samms had not been entirely frank with the private captain. From the time required to make the trip, he knew to within a few parsecs Trenco's distance from Sol. He did not know the direction, since the distance was so great that he had not been able to recognize any star or constellation. He did know, however, the course upon which the vessel then was, and he would know courses and distances from then on. He was well content.

A couple of uneventful days passed. Samms was again called into the control room, to see that the ship was approaching a three-sun solar system.

"This where we're going to land?" he asked, indifferently.

"We ain't going to land," Willoughby told him. "You are going to take the broadleaf down in your boat, close enough so that you can parachute it down to where it has to go. Way 'nuff, pilot, go inert and match intrinsics. Now, Olmstead, watch. You've seen systems like this before?"

"No, but I know about them. Those two suns over there are a hell of a lot bigger and further away than they look, and this one here, much smaller, is in the Trojan position. Have those big suns got any planets?"

"Five or six apiece, they say; all hotter and dryer than the brazen hinges of hell. This sun here has seven, but Number Two—'Cavenda', they call it—is the only Tellurian planet in the system. The first thing we look for is a big, diamond-shaped continent . . . there's only one of that shape . . . there it is, over there. Notice that one end is bigger than the other—that end is north. Strike a line to split the continent in two and measure from the north end one-third of the length of the line. That's the point we're diving at now . . . see that crater?"

"Yes." The *Virgin Queen*, although still hundreds of miles up, was slowing rapidly. "It must be a big one."

"It's a good fifty miles across. Go down until you're dead sure that the box will land somewhere inside the rim of that crater. Then dump it. The parachute and the sender are automatic. Understand?"

"Yes, sir; I understand," and Samms took off.

He was vastly more interested in the stars, however, than in delivering the broadleaf. The constellation directly beyond Sol from wherever he was might be recognizable. Its shape would be smaller and more or less distorted; its smaller stars, brilliant to Earthly eyes only because of their nearness, would be dimmer, perhaps invisible; the picture would be further confused by intervening, nearby, brilliant strangers; but such giants as Canopus and Rigel and Betelgeuse and Deneb would certainly be highly visible if he could only recognize them. From Trenco his search had failed; but he was still trying.

There was something vaguely familiar! Sweating with the mental effort, he blocked out the too-near, too-bright stars and studied intensively those that were left. A blue-white and a red were most prominent. Rigel and Betelgeuse? Could that constellation be Orion? The Belt was very faint, but it was there. Then Sirius ought to be about there, and Pollux about there; and, at this distance, about equally bright. They were. Aldebaran would be orange, and about one magnitude brighter than Pollux; and Capella would be yellow, and half a magnitude brighter still. There they were! Not too close to where they should be, but close enough—it was Orion! And this thionite way-station, then, was somewhere near right ascension seventeen hours and declination plus ten degrees!

He returned to the *Virgin Queen*. She blasted off. Samms asked very few questions and Willoughby volunteered very little information; nevertheless the First Lensman learned more than anyone of his fellow pirates would have believed possible. Aloof, taciturn, disinterested to a degree, he seemed to spend practically all of his time in his cabin when he was not actually at work; but he kept his eyes and his ears wide open. And Virgil Samms, as has been intimated, had a brain.

The *Virgin Queen* made a quick flit from Cavenda to Vegia, arriving exactly on time; a proud, clean space-ship as high above suspicion as Calpurnia herself. Samms unloaded her cargo; replaced it with one for Earth. She was serviced. She made a fast, eventless run to Tellus. She docked at New York Spaceport. Virgil Samms walked unconcernedly into an ordinary-looking rest-room; George Olmstead, fully informed, walked unconcernedly out.

As soon as he could, Samms Lensed Northrop and Jack Kinnison.

"We lined up a thousand and one signals, sir," Northrop reported for the pair, "but only one of them carried a message, and it didn't make sense."

"Why not?" Samms asked, sharply. "With a Lens, *any* kind of a message, however garbled, coded, or interrupted, makes sense."

"Oh, we understood what it said," Jack came in, "but it didn't say enough. Just 'READY—READY—READY'; over and over."

"What!" Samms exclaimed, and the boys could feel his mind work. "Did that signal, by any chance, originate anywhere near seventeen hours and plus ten degrees?"

"Very near. Why? How did you know?"

"Then it does make sense!" Samms exclaimed, and called a general conference of Lensmen.

"Keep working along these same lines," Samms directed, finally. "Keep Ray Olmstead in the Hill in my place. I am going to Pluto, and—I hope—to Palain Seven."

Roderick Kinnison of course protested; but, equally of course, his protests were overruled.

CHAPTER 10

Pluto is, on the average, about forty times as far away from the sun as is Mother Earth. Each square yard of Earth's surface receives about sixteen hundred times as much heat as does each of Pluto's. The sun as seen from Pluto is a dim, wan speck. Even at perihelion, an event which occurs only once in two hundred forty eight Tellurian years, and at noon and on the equator, Pluto is so bitterly cold that climatic conditions upon its surface simply cannot be described by or to warm-blooded, oxygen-breathing man.

As good an indication as any can be given, perhaps, by mentioning the fact that it had taken the Patrol's best engineers over six months to perfect the armor which Virgil Samms then wore. For no ordinary space-suit would do. Space itself is not cold; the only loss of heat is by radiation into or through an almost perfect vacuum. In contact with Pluto's rocky, metallic soil, however, there would be conduction; and the magnitude of the inevitable heat-loss made the Tellurian scientists gasp.

"Watch your feet, Virge!" had been Roderick Kinnison's insistent last thought. "Remember those psychologists—if they stayed in contact with that ground for five minutes they froze their feet to the ankles. Not that the boys aren't good, but slipsticks sometimes slip in more ways than one. If your feet ever start to get cold, drop whatever you're doing and drive back here at max!"

Virgil Samms landed. His feet stayed warm. Finally, assured that the heaters of his suit could carry the load indefinitely, he made his way on foot into the settlement near which he had come to ground. And there he saw his first Palainian.

Or, strictly speaking, he saw part of his first Palainian; for no three-dimensional creature has ever seen or ever will see in entirety any member of any of the frigid-blooded, poison-breathing races. Since life as we know it—organic, three-dimensional life—is based upon liquid water and gaseous oxygen, such life did not and could not develop upon planets whose temperatures are only a few degrees above absolute zero. Many, perhaps most, of these ultra-frigid planets have an atmosphere of sorts; some have no atmosphere at all. Nevertheless, with or without atmosphere and completely without oxygen and water, life—highly intelligent life—did develop upon millions and millions of such worlds.

That life is not, however, strictly three-dimensional. Of necessity, even in the lowest forms, it possesses an extension into the hyper-dimension; and it is this metabolic extension alone which makes it possible for life to exist under such extreme conditions.

The extension makes it impossible for any human being to see anything of a Palainian except the fluid, amorphous, ever-changing thing which is his three-dimensional aspect of the moment; makes any attempt at description or portraiture completely futile.

Virgil Samms stared at the Palainian; tried to see what it looked like. He could not tell whether it had eyes or antennae; legs, arms, or tentacles, teeth or beaks, talons or claws or feet; skin, scales, or feathers. It did not even remotely resemble anything that the Lensman had ever seen, sensed, or imagined. He gave up; sent out an exploring thought.

"I am Virgil Samms, a Tellurian," he sent out slowly, carefully, after he made contact with the outer fringes of the creature's mind. "Is it possible for you, sir or madam, to give me a moment of your time?"

"Eminently possible, Lensman Samms, since my time is of completely negligible value." The monster's mind flashed into accord with Samms' with a speed and precision that made him gasp. That is, a part of it became en rapport with a part of his: years were to pass before even the First Lensman would know much more about the Palainian than he learned in that first contact; no human beings except the Children of the Lens ever were to understand even dimly the labyrinthine intricacies, the paradoxical complexities, of the Palainian mind.

"'Madam' might be approximately correct," the native's thought went smoothly on. "My name, in your symbology, is Twelfth Pilinipsi; by education, training, and occupation I am a Chief Dexitroboper. I perceive that you are indeed a native of that hellish Planet Three, upon which it was assumed for so long that no life could possibly exist. But communication with your race has been almost impossible heretofore . . . Ah, the Lens. A remarkable device, truly. I would slay you and take it, except for the obvious fact that only you can possess it."

"What!" Dismay and consternation flooded Samms' mind. "You already know the Lens?"

"No. Yours is the first that any of us has perceived. The mechanics, the mathematics, and the basic philosophy of the thing, however, are quite clear."

"What!" Samms exclaimed again. "You can, then, produce Lenses yourselves?"

"By no means, any more than you Tellurians can. There are magnitudes, variables, determinants, and forces involved which no Palainian will ever be able to develop, to generate, or to control."

"I see." The Lensman pulled himself together. For a First Lensman, he was making a wretched showing indeed . . . .

"Far from it, sir," the monstrosity assured him. "Considering the strangeness of the environment into which you have voluntarily flung yourself so senselessly, your mind is well integrated and strong. Otherwise it would have shattered. If our positions were reversed, the mere thought of the raging heat of your Earth would—come no closer, please!" The thing vanished; reappeared many yards away. Her thoughts were a shudder of loathing, of terror, of sheer detestation. "But to get on. I have been attempting to analyze and to understand your purpose, without success. That failure is not too surprising, of course, since my mind is weak and my total power is small. Explain your mission, please, as simply as you can."

Weak? Small? In view of the power the monstrosity had just shown, Samms probed for irony, for sarcasm or pretense. There was no trace of anything of the kind.

He tried, then, for fifteen solid minutes, to explain the Galactic Patrol, but at the end the Palainian's only reaction was one of blank non-comprehension.

"I fail completely to perceive the use of, or the need for, such an organization," she stated flatly. "This altruism—what good is it? It is unthinkable that any other race would take any risks or exert any effort for us, any more than we would for them. Ignore and be ignored, as you must already know, is the Prime Tenet."

"But there is a little commerce between our worlds; your people did not ignore our psychologists; and you are not ignoring me," Samms pointed out.

"Oh, none of us is perfect," Pilinipsi replied, with a mental shrug and what seemed to be an airy wave of a multi-tentacled member. "That ideal, like any other, can only be approached asymptotically, never reached; and I, being somewhat foolish and silly, as well as weak and vacillant, am much less perfect than most."

Flabbergasted, Samms tried a new tack. "I might be able to make my position clearer if I knew you better. I know your name, and that you are a woman of Palain Seven"—it is a measure of Virgil Samms' real size that he actually thought "woman", and not merely "female"—"but all I can understand of your occupation is the name you have given it. What does a Chief Dexitroboper do?"

"She—or he—or, perhaps, it . . . is a supervisor of the work of dexitroboping." The thought, while perfectly clear, was completely meaningless to Samms, and the Palainian knew it. She tried again. "Dexitroboping has to do with . . . nourishment? No—with nutrients."

"Ah. Farming—agriculture," Samms thought; but this time it was the Palainian who could not grasp the concept. "Hunting? Fishing?" No better. "Show me, then, please."

She tried; but demonstration, too, was useless; for to Samms the Palainian's movements were pointless indeed. The peculiarly flowing subtly changing thing darted back and forth, rose and fell, appeared and disappeared; undergoing the while cyclic changes in shape and form and size, in aspect and texture. It was now spiny, now tentacular, now scaly, now covered with peculiarly repellent feather-like fronds, each oozing a crimson slime. But it apparently did not *do* anything whatever. The net result of all its activity was, apparently, zero.

"There, it is done." Pilinipsi's thought again came clear. "You observed and understood? You did not. That is strange—baffling. Since the Lens did improve communication and understanding tremendously, I hoped that it might extend to the physical as well. But there must be some basic, fundamental difference, the nature of which is at present obscure. I wonder . . . if I had a Lens, too—but no . . . ."

"But yes!" Samms broke in, eagerly. "Why don't you go to Arisia and be tested for one? You have a magnificent, a really *tremendous* mind. It is of Lensman grade in every respect except one—you simply don't *want* to use it!"

"Me? Go to Arisia?" The thought would have been, in a Tellurian, a laugh of scorn. "How utterly silly—how abysmally stupid! There would be personal discomfort, quite possibly personal danger, and two Lenses would be little or no better than one in resolving differences between our two continua, which are probably in fact incommensurable."

"Well, then," Samms thought, almost viciously, "can you introduce me to someone who is stupider, sillier, and more foolish than you are?"

"Not here on Pluto, no." The Palainian took no offense. "That was why it was I who interviewed the earlier Tellurian visitors and why I am now conversing with you. The others avoided you."

"I see." Samms' thought was grim. "How about the home planet, then?"

"Ah. Undoubtedly. In fact, there is a group, a club, of such persons. None of them is, of course, as insane—as aberrant—as you are, but they are all much more so than I am."

"Who of this club would be most interested in becoming a Lensman?"

"Tallick was the least stable member of the New-Thought Club when I left Seven; Kragzex a close second. There may of course have been changes since then. But I cannot believe that even Tallick—even Tallick at his outrageous worst—would be crazy enough to join your Patrol."

"Nevertheless, I must see him myself. Can you and will you give me a chart of a routing from here to Palain Seven?"

"I can and I will. Nothing you have thought will be of any use to me; that will be the easiest and quickest way of getting rid of you." The Palainian spread a completely detailed chart in Samms' mind, snapped the telepathic line, and went unconcernedly about her incomprehensible business.

Samms, mind reeling, made his way back to his boat and took off. And as the light-years and the parsecs screamed past, he sank deeper and deeper into a welter of unproductive speculation. What were—really—those Palainians? How could they—really—exist as they seemed to exist? And why had some of that dexitroboper's—whatever *that* meant!—thoughts come in so beautifully sharp and clear and plain while others . . . ?

He knew that his Lens would receive and would convert into his own symbology any thought or message, however coded or garbled or however sent or transmitted. The Lens was not at fault; his symbology was. There were concepts—things—actualities—occurrences—so foreign to Tellurian experience that no referents existed. Hence the human mind lacked the channels, the mechanisms, to grasp them.

He and Roderick Kinnison had glibly discussed the possibility of encountering forms of intelligent life so alien that humanity would have no point whatever of contact with them. After what Samms had just gone through, that was more of a possibility than either he or his friend had believed; and he hoped grimly, as he considered how seriously this partial contact with the Palainian had upset him, that the possibility would never become a fact.

He found the Palainian system easily enough, and Palain Seven. That planet, of course, was almost as dark upon its sunward side as upon the other, and its inhabitants had no use for light. Pilinipsi's instructions, however, had been minute and exact; hence Samms had very little trouble in locating the principal city—or, rather, the principal village, since there were no real cities. He found the planet's one spaceport. What a thing to call a *port!* He checked back; recalled exactly this part of his interview with Pluto's Chief Dexitroboper.

"The place upon which space-ships land," had been her thought, when she showed him exactly where it was in relationship to the town. Just that, and nothing else. It had been his mind, not hers, that had supplied the docks and cradles, the service cars, the officers, and all the other things taken for granted in space-fields everywhere as Samms knew them. Either the Palainian had not perceived the trappings with which Samms had invested her visualization, or she had not cared enough about his misapprehension to go to the trouble of correcting it; he did not know which.

The whole area was as bare as his hand. Except for the pitted, scarred, slagged-down spots which showed so clearly what driving blasts would do to such inconceivably cold rock and metal, Palainport was in no way distinguishable from any other unimproved portion of the planet's utterly bleak surface.

There were no signals; he had been told of no landing conventions. Apparently it was everyone for himself. Wherefore Samms' tremendous landing lights blazed out, and with their aid he came safely to ground. He put on his armour and strode to the air-lock; then changed his mind and went to the cargo-port instead. He had intended to walk, but in view of the rugged and deserted field and the completely unknown terrain between the field and the town, he decided to ride the "creep" instead.

This vehicle, while slow, could go—literally—anywhere. It had a cigar-shaped body of magnalloy; it had big, soft, tough tires; it had cleated tracks; it had air- and water-propellers; it had folding wings; it had driving, braking, and steering jets. It could traverse the deserts of Mars, the oceans and swamps of Venus, the crevassed glaciers of Earth, the jagged, frigid surface of an iron asteroid, and the cratered, fluffy topography of the moon; if not with equal speed, at least with equal safety.

Samms released the thing and drove it into the cargo lock, noting mentally that he would have to exhaust the air of that lock into space before he again broke the inner seal. The ramp slid back into the ship; the cargo port closed. Here he was!

Should he use his headlights, or not? He did not know the Palainians' reaction to or attitude toward light. It had not occurred to him while at Pluto to ask, and it might be important. The landing lights of his vessel might already have done his cause irreparable harm. He could drive by starlight if he had to . . . but he needed light and he had not seen a single living or moving thing. There was no evidence that there was a Palainian within miles. While he had known, with his brain, that Palain would be dark, he had expected to find buildings and traffic—ground-cars, planes, and at least a few space-ships—and not this vast nothingness.

If nothing else, there *must* be a road from Palain's principal city to its only spaceport; but Samms had not seen it from his vessel and he could not see it now. At least, he could not recognize it. Wherefore he clutched in the tractor drive and took off in a straight line toward town. The going was more than rough—it was really rugged—but the creep was built to stand up under punishment and its pilot's chair was sprung and cushioned to exactly the same degree. Hence, while the course itself was infinitely worse than the smoothly paved approaches to Rigelston, Samms found this trip much less bruising than the other had been.

Approaching the village, he dimmed his roadlights and slowed down. At its edge he cut them entirely and inched his way forward by starlight alone.

What a town! Virgil Samms had seen the inhabited places of almost every planet of Civilization. He had seen cities laid out in circles, sectors, ellipses, triangles, squares, parallelopipeds—practically every plan known to geometry. He had seen structures of all shapes and sizes—narrow skyscrapers, vast-spreading one-stories, polyhedra, domes, spheres, semi-cylinders, and erect and inverted full and truncated cones and pyramids. Whatever the plan or the shapes of the component units, however, those inhabited places had, without exception, been understandable. But this!

Samms, his eyes now completely dark-accustomed, could see fairly well, but the more he saw the less he grasped. There was no plan, no coherence or unity whatever. It was as though a cosmic hand had flung a few hundreds of buildings, of incredibly and senselessly varied shapes and sizes and architectures, upon an otherwise empty plain, and as though each structure had been allowed ever since to remain in whatever location and attitude it had chanced to fall. Here and there were jumbled piles of three or more utterly incongruous structures. There were a few whose arrangement was almost orderly. Here and there were large, irregularly-shaped areas of bare, untouched ground. There were no streets—at least, nothing that the man could recognize as such.

Samms headed the creep for one of those open areas, then stopped—declutched the tracks, set the brakes, and killed the engines.

"Go slow, fellow," he advised himself then. "Until you find out what a dexitroboper actually does while working at his trade, don't take chances of interfering or of doing damage!"

No Lensman knew—then—that frigid-blooded poison-breathers were not strictly three-dimensional; but Samms did know that he had actually seen things which he could not understand. He and Kinnison had discussed such occurrences calmly enough; but the actuality was enough to shake even the mind of Civilization's First Lensman.

He did not need to be any closer, anyway. He had learned the Palainians' patterns well enough to Lens them from a vastly greater distance than his present one; this personal visit to Palainopolis had been a gesture of friendliness, not a necessity.

"Tallick? Kragzex?" He sent out the questing, querying thought. "Lensman Virgil Samms of Sol Three calling Tallick and Kragzex of Palain Seven."

"Kragzex acknowledging, Virgil Samms," a thought snapped back, as diamond-clear, as precise, as Pilinipsi's had been.

"Is Tallick here, or anywhere on the planet?"

"He is here, but he is emmfozing at the moment. He will join us presently."

Damnation! There it was again! First "dexitroboping", and now this!

"One moment, please," Samms requested. "I fail to grasp the meaning of your thought."

"So I perceive. The fault is of course mine, in not being able to attune my mind fully to yours. Do not take this, please, as any aspersion upon the character or strength of your own mind."

"Of course not. I am the first Tellurian you have met?"

"Yes."

"I have exchanged thoughts with one other Palainian, and the same difficulty existed. I can neither understand nor explain it; but it is as though there are differences between us so fundamental that in some matters mutual comprehension is in fact impossible."

"A masterly summation and undoubtedly a true one. This emmfozing, then—if I read correctly, your race has only two sexes?"

"You read correctly."

"I cannot understand. There is no close analogy. However, emmfozing has to do with reproduction."

"I see," and Samms saw, not only a frankness brand-new to his experience, but also a new view of both the powers and the limitations of his Lens.

It was, by its very nature, of precisionist grade. It received thoughts and translated them precisely into English. There was some leeway, but not much. If any thought was such that there was no extremely close counterpart or referent in English, the Lens would not translate it at all, but would simply give it a hitherto meaningless symbol—a symbol which would from that time on be associated, by all Lenses everywhere, with that one concept and no other. Samms realized then that he might, some day, learn what a dexitroboper actually did and what the act of emmfozing actually was; but that he very probably would not.

Tallick joined them then, and Samms again described glowingly, as he had done so many times before, the Galactic Patrol of his imaginings and plannings. Kragzex refused to have anything to do with such a thing, almost as abruptly as Pilinipsi had done, but Tallick lingered—and wavered.

"It is widely known that I am not entirely sane," he admitted, "which may explain the fact that I would very much like to have a Lens. But I gather, from what you have said, that I would probably not be given a Lens to use purely for my own selfish purposes?"

"That is my understanding," Samms agreed.

"I was afraid so." Tallick's mien was . . . "woebegone" is the only word for it. "I have work to do. Projects, you know, of difficulty, of extreme complexity and scope, sometimes even approaching danger. A Lens would be of tremendous use."

"How?" Samms asked. "If your work is of enough importance to enough people, Mentor would certainly give you a Lens."

"This would benefit me; only me. We of Palain, as you probably already know, are selfish, mean-spirited, small-souled, cowardly, furtive, and sly. Of what you call 'bravery' we have no trace. We attain our ends by stealth, by indirection, by trickery and deceit." Ruthlessly the Lens was giving Virgil Samms the uncompromisingly exact English equivalent of the Palainian's every thought. "We operate, when we must operate at all openly, with the absolutely irreducible minimum of personal risk. These attitudes and attributes will, I have no doubt, preclude all possibility of Lensmanship for me and for every member of my race."

"Not necessarily."

Not necessarily! Although Virgil Samms did not know it, this was one of the really critical moments in the coming into being of the Galactic Patrol. By a conscious, a tremendous effort, the First Lensman was lifting himself above the narrow, intolerant prejudices of human experience and was consciously attempting to see the whole through Mentor's Arisian mind instead of through his Tellurian own. That Virgil Samms was the first human being to be born with the ability to accomplish that feat even partially was one of the reasons why he was the first wearer of the Lens.

"Not necessarily," First Lensman Virgil Samms said and meant. He was inexpressibly shocked—revolted in every human fiber—by what this unhuman monster had so frankly and callously thought. There were, however, many things which no human being ever could understand, and there was not the shadow of a doubt that this Tallick had a really tremendous mind. "You have said that your mind is feeble. If so, there is no simple expression of the weakness of mine. I can perceive only one, the strictly human, facet of the truth. In a broader view it is distinctly possible that your motivation is at least as 'noble' as mine. And to complete my argument, you work with other Palainians, do you not, to reach a common goal?"

"At times, yes."

"Then you can conceive of the desirability of working with non-Palainian entities toward an end which would benefit both races?"

"Postulating such an end, yes; but I am unable to visualize any such. Have you any specific project in mind?"

"Not at the moment." Samms ducked. He had already fired every shot in his locker. "I am quite certain, however, that if you go to Arisia you will be informed of several such projects."

There was a period of silence. Then:

"I believe that I *will* go to Arisia, at that!" Tallick exclaimed, brightly. "I will make a deal with your friend Mentor. I will give him a share—say fifty percent, or forty—of the time and effort I save on my own projects!"

"Just so you *go*, Tallick." Samms concealed right manfully his real opinion of the Palainian's scheme. "When can you go? Right now?"

"By no means. I must first finish this project. A year, perhaps—or more; or possibly less. Who knows?"

Tallick cut communications and Samms frowned. He did not know the exact length of Seven's year, but he knew that it was long—*very* long.

CHAPTER 11

A small, black scout-ship, commanded jointly by Master Pilot John K. Kinnison and Master Electronicist Mason M. Northrop, was blasting along a course very close indeed to RA17: D+10. In equipment and personnel, however, she was not an ordinary scout. Her control room was so full of electronics racks and computing machines that there was scarcely footway in any direction; her graduated circles and vernier scales were of a size and a fineness usually seen only in the great vessels of the Galactic Survey. And her crew, instead of the usual twenty-odd men, numbered only seven—one cook, three engineers, and three watch officers. For some time the young Third Officer, then at the board, had been studying something on his plate; comparing it minutely with the chart clipped into the rack in front of him. Now he turned, with a highly exaggerated deference, to the two Lensmen.

"Sirs, which of your Magnificences is officially the commander of this here bucket of odds and ends at the present instant?"

"Him." Jack used his cigarette as a pointer. "The guy with the misplaced plucked eyebrow on his upper lip. I don't come on duty until sixteen hundred hours—one precious Tellurian minute yet in which to dream of the beauties of Earth so distant in space and in both past and future time."

"Huh? Beauties? Plural? Next time I see a party whose pictures are cluttering up this whole ship I'll tell her about your polygamous ideas. I'll ignore that crack about my mustache, though, since you can't raise one of your own. I'm ignoring you, too—like this, see?" Ostentatiously turning his back upon the lounging Kinnison, Northrop stepped carefully over three or four breadboard hookups and stared into the plate over the watch officer's shoulder. He then studied the chart. "*Was ist los*, Stu? I don't see a thing."

"More Jack's line than yours, Mase. This system we're headed for is a triple, and the chart says it's a double. Natural enough, of course. This whole region is unexplored, so the charts are astronomicals, not surveys. But that makes us Prime Discoverers, and our Commanding Officer—and the book says 'Officer', not 'Officers'—has got to . . . ."

"That's me, now," Jack announced, striding grandly toward the plate. "Amscray, oobsbay. *I* will name the baby. *I* will report. *I* will go down in history . . . ."

"Bounce back, small fry. You weren't at the time of discovery." Northrop placed a huge hand flat against Jack's face and pushed gently. "You'll go down, sure enough—not in history, but from a knock on the knob—if you try to steal any thunder away from *me*. And besides, you'd name it 'Dimples'—what a *revolting* thought!"

"And what would you name it? '*Virgilia*', I suppose?"

"Far from it, my boy." He had intended doing just that, but now he did not quite dare. "After our project, of course. The planet we're heading for will be Zabriska; the suns will be A-, B-, and C-Zabriskae, in order of size; and the watch officer then on duty, Lieutenant L. Stuart Rawlings, will engross these and all other pertinent data in the log. Can you classify 'em from here, Jack?"

"I can make some guesses—close enough, probably, for Discovery work." Then, after a few minutes: "Two giants, a blue-white and a bluish yellow; and a yellow dwarf."

"Dwarf in the Trojan?"

"That would be my guess, since that is the only place it could stay very long, but you can't tell much from one look. I can tell you one thing, though—unless your Zabriska is in a system straight beyond this one, it's got to be a planet of the big fellow himself; and brother, that sun is *hot*!"

"It's got to be here, Jack. I haven't made *that* big an error in reading a beam since I was a sophomore."

"I'll buy that . . . well, we're close enough, I guess." Jack killed the driving blasts, but not the Bergenholm; the inertialess vessel stopped instantaneously in open space. "Now we've got to find out which one of those twelve or fifteen planets was on our line when that last message was sent . . . . There, we're stable enough, I hope. Open your cameras, Mase. Pull the first plate in fifteen minutes. That ought to give me enough track so I can start the job, since we're at a wide angle to their ecliptic."

The work went on for an hour or so. Then:

"Something coming from the direction of Tellus," the watch officer reported. "Big and fast. Shall I hail her?"

"Might as well," but the stranger hailed first.

"Space-ship *Chicago*, NA2AA, calling. Are you in trouble? Identify yourself, please."

"Space-ship NA774J acknowledging. No trouble . . . ."

"Northrop! Jack!" came Virgil Samms' highly concerned thought. The superdreadnaught flashed alongside, a bare few hundred miles away, and stopped. "Why did you stop *here*?"

"This is where our signal came from, sir."

"Oh." A hundred thoughts raced through Samms' mind, too fast and too fragmentary to be intelligible. "I see you're computing. Would it throw you off too much to go inert and match intrinsics, so that I can join you?"

"No sir; I've got everything I need for a while."

Samms came aboard; three Lensmen studied the chart.

"Cavenda is there," Samms pointed out. "Trenco is there, off to one side. I felt sure that your signal originated on Cavenda; but Zabriska, here, while on almost the same line, is less than half as far from Tellus." He did not ask whether the two young Lensmen were sure of their findings. He knew. "This arouses my curiosity no end—does it merely complicate the thionite problem, or does it set up an entirely new problem? Go ahead, boys, with whatever you were going to do next."

Jack had already determined that the planet they wanted was the second out; A-Zabriskae Two. He drove the scout as close to the planet as he could without losing complete coverage; stationed it on the line toward Sol.

"Now we wait a bit," he answered. "According to recent periodicity, not less than four hours and not more than ten. With the next signal we'll nail that transmitter down to within a few feet. Got your spotting screens full out, Mase?"

"*Recent* periodicity?" Samms snapped. "It has improved, then, lately?"

"Very much, sir."

"That helps immensely. With George Olmstead harvesting broadleaf, it would. It is still one problem. While we wait, shall we study the planet a little?"

They explored; finding that A-Zabriskae Two was a disappointing planet indeed. It was small, waterless, airless, utterly featureless, utterly barren. There were no elevations, no depressions, no visible markings whatever—not even a meteor crater. Every square yard of its surface was apparently exactly like every other.

"No rotation," Jack reported, looking up from the bolometer. "That sand-pile is not inhabited and never will be. I'm beginning to wonder."

"So am I, now," Northrop admitted. "I still say that those signals came from this line and distance, but it looks as though they must have been sent from a ship. If so, now that we're here—particularly the *Chicago*—there will be no more signals."

"Not necessarily." Again Samms' mind transcended his Tellurian experience and knowledge. He did not suspect the truth, but he was not jumping at conclusions. "There may be highly intelligent life, even upon such a planet as this."

They waited, and in a few hours a communications beam snapped into life.

"READY—READY—READY . . . ." it said briskly, for not quite one minute, but that was time enough.

Northrop yelped a string of numbers; Jack blasted the little vessel forward and downward; the three watch officers, keen-eyed at their plates, stabbed their visibeams, ultra-beams, and spy-rays along the indicated line.

"And bore straight through the planet if you have to—they may be on the other side!" Jack cautioned, sharply.

"They aren't—it's here, on this side!" Rawlings saw it first. "Nothing much to it, though . . . it looks like a relay station."

"A *relay*! I'll be a . . . ." Jack started to express an unexpurgated opinion, but shut himself up. Young cubs did not swear in front of the First Lensman. "Let's land, sir, and look the place over, anyway."

"By all means."

They landed, and cautiously disembarked. The horizon, while actually quite a little closer than that of Earth, seemed much more distant because there was nothing whatever—no tree, no shrub, no rock or pebble, not even the slightest ripple—to break the geometrical perfection of that surface of smooth, hard, blindingly reflective, fiendishly hot white sand. Samms was highly dubious at first—a ground-temperature of four hundred seventy-five degrees was not to be taken lightly; he did not at all like the looks of that ultra-fervent blue-white sun; and in his wildest imaginings he had never pictured such a desert. Their space-suits, however, were very well insulated, particularly as to the feet, and highly polished; and in lieu of atmosphere there was an almost perfect vacuum. They could stand it for a while.

The box which housed the relay station was made of non-ferrous metal and was roughly cubical in shape, perhaps five feet on a side. It was so buried that its upper edge was flush with the surface; its top, which was practically indistinguishable from the surrounding sand, was not bolted or welded, but was simply laid on, loose.

Previous spy-ray inspection having proved that the thing was not booby-trapped, Jack lifted the cover by one edge and all three Lensmen studied the mechanisms at close range; learning nothing new. There was an extremely sensitive non-directional receiver, a highly directional sender, a beautifully precise uranium-clock director, and an "eternal" powerpack. There was nothing else.

"What next, sir?" Northrop asked. "There'll be an incoming signal, probably, in a couple of days. Shall we stick around and see whether it comes in from Cavenda or not?"

"You and Jack had better wait, yes." Samms thought for minutes. "I do not believe, now, that the signal will come from Cavenda, or that it will ever come twice from the same direction, but we will have to make sure. But I can't see any *reason* for it!"

"I think I can, sir." This was Northrop's specialty. "No space-ship could possibly hit Tellus from here except by accident with a single-ended beam, and they can't use a double-ender because it would have to be on all the time and would be as easy to trace as the Mississippi River. But this planet did all its settling ages ago—which is undoubtedly why they picked it out—and that director in there is a Marchanti—the second Marchanti I have ever seen."

"Whatever *that* is," Jack put in, and even Samms thought a question.

"The most precise thing ever built," the specialist explained. "Accuracy limited only by that of determination of relative motions. Give me an accurate enough equation to feed into it, like that tape is doing, and two sighting shots, and I'll guarantee to pour an eighteen-inch beam into any two foot cup on Earth. My guess is that it's aimed at some particular bucket-antenna on one of the Solar planets. I could spoil its aim easily enough, but I don't suppose that is what you're after."

"Decidedly not. We want to trace them, without exciting any more suspicion than is absolutely necessary. How often, would you say, do they have to come here to service this station—change tapes, and whatever else might be necessary?"

"Change tapes, is all. Not very often, by the size of those reels. If they know the relative motions exactly enough, they could compute as far ahead as they care to. I've been timing that reel—it's got pretty close to three months left on it."

"And more than that much has been used. It's no wonder we didn't see anything." Samms straightened up and stared out across the frightful waste. "Look there—I thought I saw something move—it *is* moving!"

"There's something moving closer than that, and it's really funny." Jack laughed deeply. "It's like the paddle-wheels, shaft and all, of an old-fashioned river steam-boat, rolling along as unconcernedly as you please. He won't miss me by over four feet, but he isn't swerving a hair. I think I'll block him off, just to see what he does."

"Be careful, Jack!" Samms cautioned, sharply. "Don't touch it—it may be charged, or worse."

Jack took the metal cover, which he was still holding, and by working it back and forth edgewise in the sand, made of it a vertical barrier squarely across the thing's path. The traveler paid no attention, did not alter its steady pace of a couple of miles per hour. It measured about twelve inches long over all; its paddle-wheel-like extremities were perhaps two inches wide and three inches in diameter.

"Do you think it's actually *alive*, sir? In a place like this?"

"I'm sure of it. Watch carefully."

It struck the barrier and stopped. That is, its forward motion stopped, but its rolling did not. Its rate of revolution did not change; it either did not know or did not care that its drivers were slipping on the smooth, hard sand; that it could not climb the vertical metal plate; that it was not getting anywhere.

266

"What a brain!" Northrop chortled, squatting down closer. "Why doesn't it back up or turn around? It may be alive, but it certainly isn't very bright."

The creature, now in the shadow of the 'Troncist's helmet, slowed down abruptly—went limp—collapsed.

"Get out of his light!" Jack snapped, and pushed his friend violently away; and as the vicious sunlight struck it, the native revived and began to revolve as vigorously as before. "I've got a hunch. Sounds screwy—never heard of such a thing—but it acts like an energy-converter. Eats energy, raw and straight. No storage capacity—on this world he wouldn't need it—a few more seconds in the shade would probably have killed him, but there's no shade here. Therefore, he can't be dangerous."

He reached out and touched the middle of the revolving shaft. Nothing happened. He turned it at right angles to the plate. The thing rolled away in a straight line, perfectly contented with the new direction. He recaptured it and stuck a test-prod lightly into the sand, just ahead of its shaft and just inside one paddle wheel. Around and around that slim wire the creature went: unable, it seemed, to escape from even such a simple trap; perfectly willing, it seemed, to spend all the rest of its life traversing that tiny circle.

"'What a brain!' is right, Mase," Jack exclaimed. "*What* a brain!"

"This is wonderful, boys, really wonderful; something completely new to our science." Samms' thought was deep with feeling. "I am going to see if I can reach its mind or consciousness. Would you like to come along?"

"*Would* we!"

Samms tuned low and probed; lower and lower; deeper and deeper; and Jack and Mase stayed with him. The thing was certainly alive; it throbbed and vibrated with vitality: equally certainly, it was not very intelligent. But it had a definite consciousness of its own existence; and therefore, however tiny and primitive, a mind. Although its rudimentary ego could neither receive nor transmit thought, it knew that it was a fontema, that it must roll and roll and roll, endlessly, that by virtue of determined rolling its species would continue and would increase.

"Well, that's one for the book!" Jack exclaimed, but Samms was entranced.

"I would like to find one or two more of them, to find out . . . I think I'll *take* the time. Can you see any more of them, either of you?"

"No, but we can find some—Stu!" Northrop called.

"Yes?"

"Look around, will you? Find us a couple more of these fontema things and flick them over here with a tractor."

"Coming up!" and in a few seconds they were there.

"Are you photographing this, Lance?" Samms called the Chief Communications Officer of the *Chicago*.

"We certainly are, sir—all of it. What are they, anyway? Animal, vegetable, or mineral?"

"I don't know. Probably no one of the three, strictly speaking. I'd like to take a couple back to Tellus, but I'm afraid that they'd die, even under an atomic lamp. We'll report to the Society."

Jack liberated his captive and aimed it to pass within a few feet of one of the newcomers, but the two fontemas did not ignore each other. Both swerved, so that they came together wheel to wheel. The shafts bent toward each other, each into a right angle. The angles touched and fused. The point of fusion swelled rapidly into a double fist-sized lump. The half-shafts doubled in length. The lump split into four; became four perfect paddle-wheels. Four full-grown fontemas rolled away from the spot upon which two had met; their courses forming two mutually perpendicular straight lines.

"Beautiful!" Samms exclaimed. "And notice, boys, the method of avoiding inbreeding. Upon a perfectly smooth planet such as this, no two of those four can ever meet, and the chance is almost vanishingly small that any of their first-generation offspring will ever meet. But I'm afraid I've been wasting time. Take me back out to the *Chicago*, please, and I'll be on my way."

"You don't seem at all optimistic, sir," Jack ventured, as the NA774J approached the *Chicago*.

"Unfortunately, I am not. The signal will almost certainly come in from an unpredictable direction, from a ship so far away that even a super-fast cruiser could not get close enough to her to detect—just a minute. Rod!" He Lensed the elder Kinnison so sharply that both young Lensmen jumped.

"What is it, Virge?"

Samms explained rapidly, concluding: "So I would like to have you throw a globe of scouts around this whole Zabriskan system. One detet out and one detet apart, so as to be able to slap a tracer onto any ship laying a beam to this planet, from any direction whatever. It would not take too many scouts, would it?"

"No; but it wouldn't be worth while."

"Why not?"

"Because it wouldn't prove a thing except what we already know—that Spaceways is involved in the thionite racket. The ship would be clean. Merely another relay."

"Oh. You're probably right." If Virgil Samms was in the least put out at this cavalier dismissal of his idea, he made no sign. He thought intensely for a couple of minutes. "You *are* right. I will have to work from the Cavenda end. How are you coming with Operation Bennett?"

"Nice!" Kinnison enthused. "When you get a couple of days, come over and see it grow. This is a fine world, Virge—it'll be ready!"

"I'll do that." Samms broke the connection and called Dronvire.

"The only change here is for the worse," the Rigellian reported, tersely. "The slight positive correlation between deaths from thionite and the arrival of Spaceways vessels has disappeared."

There was no need to elaborate on that bare statement. Both Lensmen knew what it meant. The enemy, either in anticipation of statistical analysis or for economic reasons, was rationing his small supply of the drug.

And DalNalten was very much unlike his usual equable self. He was glum and unhappy; so much so that it took much urging to make him report at all.

"We have, as you know, put our best operatives to work on the inter-planetary lines," he said finally, half sullenly. "We have secured quite a little data. The accumulating facts, however, point more and more definitely toward an utterly preposterous conclusion. Can you think of any valid reason why the exports and imports of thionite between Tellus and Mars, Mars and Venus, and Venus and Tellus, should all be exactly equal to each other?"

"*What!*"

"Precisely. That is why Knobos and I are not yet ready to present even a preliminary report."

Then Jill. "I can't prove it, any more than I could before, but I'm pretty sure that Morgan is the Boss. I have drawn every picture I can think of with Isaacson in the driver's seat, but none of them fit?" She paused, questioningly.

"I am already reconciled to adopting that view; at least as a working hypothesis. Go ahead."

"The fact seems to be that Morgan has always had all the left-wingers of the Nationalists under his thumb. Now he and his man Friday, Representative Flierce, are wooing all the radicals and so-called liberals on our side of both Senate and House—a new technique for him—and they're offering plenty of the right kind of bait. He has the commentators guessing, but there's no doubt whatever in my mind that he is aiming at next Election Day and our Galactic Council."

"And you and Dronvire are sitting idly by, doing nothing, of course?"

"Of course!" Jill giggled, but sobered quickly. "He's a smooth, *smooth* worker, Dad. We are organizing, of course, and putting out propaganda of our own, but there's so pitifully little that we can actually *do*—look and listen to this for a minute, and you'll see what I mean."

In her distant room Jill manipulated a reel and flipped a switch. A plate came to life, showing Morgan's big, sweating, passionately earnest face.

" . . . and who *are* these Lensmen, anyway?" Morgan's voice bellowed, passionate conviction in every syllable. "They are the hired minions of the classes, stabbers in the back, crooks and scoundrels, TOOLS OF RUTHLESS WEALTH! They are hirelings of the inter-planetary bankers, those unspeakable excrescences on the body politic who are still grinding down into the dirt, under an iron heel, the face of the common man! In the guise of democracy they are trying to set up the worst, the most outrageous tyranny that this universe has ever . . . ." Jill snapped the switch viciously.

"And a lot of people *swallow* that . . . that *bilge!*" she almost snarled. "If they had the brains of a . . . of even that Zabriskan fontema Mase told me about, they wouldn't, but they *do!*"

"I know they do. We have known all along that he is a masterly actor; we now know that he is more than that."

"Yes, and we're finding out that no appeal to reason, no psychological counter-measures, will work. Dronvire and I agree that you'll *have* to arrange matters so that you can do solid months of stumping yourself. Personally."

"It may come to that, but there's a lot of other things to do first."

Samms broke the connection and thought. He did not consciously try to exclude the two youths, but his mind was working so fast and in such a disjointed fashion that they could catch only a few fragments. The incomprehensible vastness of space—tracing—detection—Cavenda's one tiny, fast moving moon—back, and solidly, to DETECTION.

"Mase," Samms thought then, carefully. "As a specialist in such things, why is it that the detectors of the smallest scout—lifeboat, even—have practically the same range as those of the largest liners and battleships?"

"Noise level and hash, sir, from the atomics."

"But can't they be screened out?"

"Not entirely, sir, without blocking reception completely."

"I see. Suppose, then, that all atomics aboard were to be shut down; that for the necessary heat and light we use electricity, from storage or primary batteries or from a generator driven by an internal-combustion motor or a heat-engine. Could the range of detection then be increased?"

"Tremendously, sir. My guess is that the limiting factor would then be the cosmics."

"I hope you're right. While you are waiting for the next signal to come in, you might work out a preliminary design for such a detector. If, as I anticipate, this Zabriska proves to be a dead end, Operation Zabriska ends here—becomes a part of Zwilnik—and you two will follow me at max to Tellus. You, Jack, are very badly needed on Operation Boskone. You and I, Mase, will make appropriate alterations aboard a J-class vessel of the Patrol."

CHAPTER 12

Approaching Cavenda in his dead-black, converted scout-ship, Virgil Samms cut his drive, killed his atomics, and turned on his super-powered detectors. For five full detets in every direction—throughout a spherical volume over ten detets in diameter—space was void of ships. Some activity was apparent upon the planet dead ahead, but the First Lensman did not worry about that. The drug-runners would of course have atomics in their plants, even if there were no space-ships actually on the planet—which there probably were. What he did worry about was detection. There would be plenty of detectors, probably automatic; not only ordinary sub-ethereals, but electros and radars as well.

He flashed up to within one and a quarter detets, stopped, and checked again. Space was still empty. Then, after making a series of observations, he went inert and established an intrinsic velocity which, he hoped, would be close enough. He again shut off his atomics and started the sixteen-cylinder Diesel engine which would do its best to replace them.

That best was none too good, but it would do. Besides driving the Bergenholm it could furnish enough kilodynes of thrust to produce a velocity many times greater than any attainable by inert matter. It used a lot of oxygen per minute, but it would not run for very many minutes. With her atomics out of action his ship would not register upon the plates of the long-range detectors universally used. Since she was nevertheless traveling faster than light, neither electromagnetic detector-webs nor radar could "see" her. Good enough.

Samms was not the System's best computer, nor did he have the System's finest instruments. His positional error could be corrected easily enough; but as he drove nearer and nearer to Cavenda, keeping, toward the last, in line with its one small moon, he wondered more and more as to how much of an allowance he should make for error in his intrinsic, which he had set up practically by guess. And there was another variable, the cut-off. He slowed down to just over one light; but even at that comparatively slow speed an error of one millisecond at cut-off meant a displacement of two hundred miles! He switched the spotter into the Berg's cut-off circuit, set it for three hundred miles, and waited tensely at his controls.

The relays clicked, the driving force expired, the vessel went inert. Samms' eyes, flashing from instrument to instrument, told him that matters could have been worse. His intrinsic was neither straight up, as he had hoped, nor straight down, as he had feared, but almost exactly half-way between the two—straight out. He discovered that fact just in time; in another second or two he would have been out beyond the moon's protecting bulk and thus detectable from Cavenda. He went free, flashed back to the opposite boundary of his area of safety, went inert, and put the full power of the bellowing Diesel to the task of bucking down his erroneous intrinsic, losing altitude continuously. Again and again he repeated the maneuver; and thus, grimly and stubbornly, he fought his ship to ground.

He was very glad to see that the surface of the satellite was rougher, rockier, ruggeder, and more cratered even than that of Earth's Luna. Upon such a terrain as this, it would be next to impossible to spot even a moving vessel—if it moved carefully.

By a series of short and careful inertialess hops—correcting his intrinsic velocity after each one by an inert collision with the ground—he maneuvered his vessel into such a position that Cavenda's enormous globe hung directly overhead. Breathing a profoundly deep breath of relief he killed the big engine, cut in his fully-charged accumulators, and turned on detector and spy-ray. He would see what he could see.

His detectors showed that there was only one point of activity on the whole planet. He located it precisely; then, after cutting his spy-ray to minimum power, he approached it gingerly, yard by yard. Stopped! As he had more than half expected, there was a spy-ray block. A big one, almost two miles in diameter. It would be almost directly beneath him—or rather, almost straight overhead—in about three hours.

Samms had brought along a telescope, considerably more powerful than the telescopic visiplate of his scout. Since the surface gravity of this moon was low—scarcely one-fifth that of Earth—he had no difficulty in lugging the parts out of the ship or in setting the thing up.

But even the telescope did not do much good. The moon was close to Cavenda, as astronomical distances go—but really worth-while astronomical optical instruments simply are not portable. Thus the Lensman saw something that, by sufficient stretch of the imagination, could have been a factory; and, eyes straining at the tantalizing limit of visibility, he even made himself believe that he saw a toothpick-shaped object and a darkly circular blob, either of which could have been the space-ship of the outlaws. He was sure, however, of two facts. There were no real cities upon Cavenda. There were no modern spaceports, or even air-fields.

He dismounted the 'scope, stored it, set his detectors, and waited. He had to sleep at times, of course; but any ordinary detector rig can be set to sound off at any change in its status—and Samms' was no ordinary rig. Wherefore, when the drug-mongers' vessel took off, Samms left Cavenda as unobtrusively as he had approached it, and swung into that vessel's line.

Samms' strategy had been worked out long since. On his Diesel, at a distance of just over one detet, he would follow the outlaw as fast as he could; long enough to establish his line. He would then switch to atomic drive and close up to between one and two detets; then again go onto Diesel for a check. He would keep this up for as long as might prove necessary.

As far as any of the Lensmen knew, Spaceways always used regular liners or freighters in this business, and this scout was much faster than any such vessel. And even if—highly improbable thought!—the enemy ship was faster than his own, it would still be within range of *those* detectors when it got to wherever it was that it was going. But how wrong Samms was!

At his first check, instead of being not over two detets away the quarry was three and a half; at the second the distance was four and a quarter; at the third, almost exactly five. Scowling, Samms watched the erstwhile brilliant point of light fade into darkness. That circular blob that he had almost seen, then, had been the space-ship, but it had not been a sphere, as he had supposed. Instead, it had been a tear-drop; sticking, sharp tail down, in the ground. Ultra-fast. This was the result. But ideas had blown up under him before, they probably would again. He resumed atomic drive and made arrangements with the Port Admiral to rendezvous with him and the *Chicago* at the earliest possible time.

"What is there along that line?" he demanded of the superdreadnaught's Chief Pilot, even before junction had been made.

"Nothing, sir, that we know of," that worthy reported, after studying his charts.

He boarded the gigantic ship of war, and with Kinnison pored over those same charts.

"Your best bet is Eridan, I think," Kinnison concluded finally. "Not too near your line, but they could very easily figure that a one-day dogleg would be a good investment. And Spaceways owns it, you know, from core to planetary limits—the richest uranium mines in existence. Made to order. Nobody would suspect a uranium ship. How about throwing a globe around Eridan?"

Samms thought for minutes. "No . . . not yet, at least. We don't know enough yet."

"I know it—that's why it looks to me like a good time and place to learn something," Kinnison argued. "We know—almost know, at least—that a super-fast ship, carrying thionite, has just landed there. This is the hottest lead we've had. I say englobe the planet, declare martial law, and not let anything in or out until we find it. Somebody there must know something, a lot more than we do. I say hunt him out and make him talk."

"You're just popping off, Rod. You know as well as I do that nabbing a few of the small fry isn't enough. We can't move openly until we can strike high."

"I suppose not," Kinnison grumbled. "But we know so *damned* little, Virge!"

"Little enough," Samms agreed. "Of the three main divisions, only the political aspect is at all clear. In the drug division, we know where thionite comes from and where it is processed, and Eridan may be—probably is—another link. On the other end, we know a lot of peddlers and a few middlemen—nobody higher. We have no actual knowledge whatever as to who the higher-ups are or how they work; and it's the bosses we want. Concerning the pirates, we know even less. 'Murgatroyd' may be no more a man's name than 'zwilnik' is . . . ."

"Before you get too far away from the subject, what are you going to do about Eridan?"

"Nothing, for the moment, would be best, I believe. However, Knobos and DalNalten should switch their attention from Spaceways' passenger liners to the uranium ships from Eridan to all three of the inner planets. Check?"

"Check. Particularly since it explains so beautifully the merry-go-round they have been on so long—chasing the same packages of dope backwards and forwards so many times that the corners of the boxes got worn round. We've got to get the top men, and they're smart. Which reminds me—Morgan as Big Boss does not square up with the Morgan that you and Fairchild smacked down so easily when he tried to investigate the Hill. A loud-mouthed, chiseling politician might have a lock-box full of documentary evidence about party bosses and power deals and chorus girls and Martian tekkyl coats, but the man we're after very definitely would not."

"You're telling me?" This point was such a sore one that Samms relapsed into idiom. "The boys should have cracked that box a week ago, but they struck a knot. I'll see if they know anything yet. Tune in, Rod. Ray!" He Lensed a thought at his cousin.

"Yes, Virge?"

"Have you got a spy-ray into that lock-box yet?"

"Glad you called. Yes, last night. Empty. Empty as a sub-deb's skull—except for an atomic-powered gimmick that it took Bergenholm's whole laboratory almost a week to neutralize."

"I see. Thanks. Off." Samms turned to Kinnison. "Well?"

"Nice. A mighty smart operator." Kinnison gave credit ungrudgingly. "Now I'll buy your picture—what a man! But now—and I've got my ears pinned back—what was it you started to say about pirates?"

"Just that we have very little to go on, except for the kind of stuff they seem to like best, and the fact that even armed escorts have not been able to protect certain types of shipments of late. The escorts, too, have disappeared. But with these facts as bases, it seems to me that we could arrange something, perhaps like this . . . ."

*

A fast, sleek freighter and a heavy battle-cruiser bored steadily through the inter-stellar void. The merchantman carried a fabulously valuable cargo: not bullion or jewels or plate of price, but things literally above price—machine tools of highest precision, delicate optical and electrical instruments, fine watches and chronometers. She also carried First Lensman Virgil Samms.

And aboard the war-ship there was Roderick Kinnison; for the first time in history a mere battle-cruiser bore a Port Admiral's flag.

As far as the detectors of those two ships could reach, space was empty of man-made craft; but the two Lensmen knew that they were not alone. One and one-half detets away, loafing along at the freighter's speed and paralleling her course, in a hemispherical formation open to the front, there flew six tremendous tear-drops; super-dreadnaughts of whose existence no Tellurian or Colonial government had even an inkling. They were the fastest and deadliest craft yet built by man—the first fruits of Operation Bennett. And they, too, carried Lensmen—Costigan, Jack Kinnison, Northrop, Dronvire of Rigel Four, Rodebush, and Cleveland. Nor was there need of detectors: the eight Lensmen were in as close communication as though they had been standing in the same room.

"On your toes, men," came Samms' quiet thought. "We are about to pass within a few light-minutes of an uninhabited solar system. No Tellurian-type planets at all. This may be it. Tune to Kinnison on one side and to your captains on the other. Take over, Rod."

At one instant the ether, for one full detet in every direction, was empty. In the next, three intensely brilliant spots of detection flashed into being, in line with the dead planet so invitingly close at hand.

This development came as a surprise, since only two raiders had been expected: a battleship to take care of the escort, a cruiser to take the merchantman. The fact that the pirates had become cautious or suspicious and had sent three super-dreadnaughts on the mission, however, did not operate to change the Patrol's strategy; for Samms had concluded, and Dronvire and Bergenholm and Rularion of Jupiter had agreed, that the real commander of the expedition would be aboard the vessel that attacked the freighter.

In the next instant, then—each Lensman saw what Roderick Kinnison saw, in the very instant of his seeing it—six more points of hard, white light sprang into being upon the plates of guileful freighter and decoying cruiser.

"Jack and Mase, take the leader!" Kinnison snapped out the thought. "Dronvire and Costigan, right wing—he's the one that's going after the freighter. Fred and Lyman, left wing. Hipe!"

The pirate ships flashed up, filling ether and sub-ether alike with a solid mush of interference through which no call for help could be driven; two super-dreadnaughts against the cruiser, one against the freighter. The former, of course, had been expected to offer more than a token resistance. Battle cruisers of the Patrol were powerful vessels, both on offense and defense, and it was a known and recognized fact that the men of the Patrol were men. The pirate commander who attacked the freighter, however, was a surprised pirate indeed. His first beam, directed well forward, well ahead of the precious cargo, should have wrought the same havoc against screens and wall-shields and structure as a white-hot poker would against a pat of luke-warm butter. Practically the whole nose-section, including the control room, should have whiffed outward into space in gobbets and streamers of molten and gaseous metal. But nothing of the sort happened—this merchantman was *no* push-over!

SUPER PACK

No ordinary screens protected that particular freighter and the person of First Lensman Samms—Roderick Kinnison had very thoroughly seen to that. In sheer mass her screen generators out-weighed her entire cargo, heavy as that cargo was, by more than two to one. Thus the pirate's beams stormed and struck and clawed and clung—uselessly. They did not penetrate. And as the surprised attacker shoved his power up and up, to his absolute ceiling of effort, the only result was to increase the already tremendous pyrotechnic display of energies cascading in all directions from the fiercely radiant defenses of the Tellurian freighter.

And in a few seconds the commanding officers of the other two attacking battleships were also surprised. The battle-cruiser's screens did not go down, even under the combined top effort of two super-dreadnaughts! And she did not have a beam hot enough to light a match—she must be *all screen*! But before the startled outlaws could do anything about the realization that they, instead of being the trappers, were in cold fact the trapped, all three of them were surprised again—the last surprise that any of them was ever to receive. Six mighty tear-drops—vastly bigger, faster, more powerful than their own—were rushing upon them, blanketing all channels of communication as efficiently and as enthusiastically as they themselves had been doing an instant before.

Being out simply and ruthlessly to kill, and not to capture, four of the newcomers from Bennett polished off the cruiser's two attackers in very short order. They simply flashed in, went inert at the four corners of an imaginary tetrahedron, and threw everything they had—and they had plenty. Possibly—just barely possibly—there may have been, somewhere, a space-battle shorter than that one; but there certainly was never one more violent.

Then the four set out after their two sister-ships and the one remaining pirate, who was frantically devoting his every effort to the avoidance of engagement. But with six ships, each one of which was of vastly greater individual power than his own, at the six corners of an octahedron of which he was the geometrical center, his ability to cut tractor beams and to "squirt out" from between two opposed pressors did him no good whatever. He was englobed; or, rather, to apply the correct terminology to an operation involving so few units, he was "boxed".

To blow the one remaining raider out of the ether would have been easy enough, but that was exactly what the Patrolmen did not want to do. They wanted information. Wherefore each of the Patrol ships directed a dozen or so beams upon the scintillating protective screens of the enemy; enough so that every square yard of defensive web was under direct attack. As rapidly as it could be done without losing equilibrium or synchronization, the power of each beam was stepped up until the wildly violet incandescence of the pirate screen showed that it was hovering on the very edge of failure. Then, in the instant, needle-beamers went furiously to work. The screen was already loaded to its limit; no transfer of defensive energy was possible. Thus, tremendously overloaded locally, locally it flared through the ultra-violet into the black and went down; and the fiercely penetrant daggers of pure force stabbed and stabbed and stabbed.

The engine room went first, even though the needlers had to gnaw a hundred-foot hole straight through the pirate craft in order to find the vital installations. Then, enough damage done so that spy-rays could get in, the rest of the work was done with precision and dispatch. In a matter of seconds the pirate hulk lay helpless, and the Patrolmen peeled her like an orange—or, rather, more like an amateur cook very wastefully peeling a potato. Resistless knives of energy sheared off tail-section and nose-section, top and bottom, port and starboard sides; then slabbed off the corners of what was left, until the control room was almost bared to space.

Then, as soon as the intrinsic velocities could possibly be matched, board and storm! With Dronvire of Rigel Four in the lead, closely followed by Costigan, Northrop, Kinnison the Younger, and a platoon of armed and armored Space Marines!

Samms and the two scientists did not belong in such a melee as that which was to come, and knew it. Kinnison the Elder did not belong, either, but did not know it. In fact, he cursed fluently and bitterly at having to stay out—nevertheless, out he stayed.

Dronvire, on the other hand, did not like to fight. The very thought of actual, bodily, hand-to-hand combat revolted every fiber of his being. In view of what the spy-ray men were reporting, however, and of what all the Lensmen knew of pirate psychology, Dronvire had to get into that control room first, and he had to get there *fast*. And if he *had* to fight, he could; and, physically, he was wonderfully well equipped for just such activity. To his immense physical strength, the natural concomitant of a force of gravity more than twice Earth's, the armor which so encumbered the Tellurian battlers was a scarcely noticeable impediment. His sense of perception, which could not be barred by any material substance, kept him fully informed of every development in his neighborhood. His literally incredible speed enabled him not merely to parry a blow aimed at him, but to bash out the brains of the would-be attacker before that blow could be more than started. And whereas a human being can swing only one space-axe or fire only two ray-guns at a time, the Rigellian plunged through space toward what was left of the pirate vessel, swinging not one or two space-axes, but four; each held in a lithe and supple, but immensely strong, tentacular "hand".

Why axes? Why not Lewistons, or rifles, or pistols? Because the space armor of that day could withstand almost indefinitely the output of two or three hand-held projectors; because the resistance of its defensive fields varied directly as the cube of the velocity of any material projectile encountering them. Thus, and strangely enough, the advance of science had forced the re-adoption of that long-extinct weapon.

Most of the pirates had died, of course, during the dismemberment of their ship. Many more had been picked off by the needle-beam gunners. In the control room, however, there was a platoon of elite guards, clustered so closely about the commander and his officers that needles could not be used; a group that would have to be wiped out by hand.

If the attack had come by way of the only doorway, so that the pirates could have concentrated their weapons upon one or two Patrolmen, the commander might have had time enough to do what he was under compulsion to do. But while the Patrolmen were still in space a plane of force sheared off the entire side of the room, a tractor beam jerked the detached wall away, and the attackers floated in en masse.

Weightless combat is not at all like any form of gymnastics known to us ground-grippers. It is much more difficult to master, and in times of stress the muscles revert involuntarily and embarrassingly to their wonted gravity-field techniques. Thus the endeavors of most of the battlers upon both sides, while earnest enough and deadly enough of intent, were almost comically unproductive of result. In a matter of seconds frantically-struggling figures were floating from wall to ceiling to wall to floor; striking wildly, darting backward from the violence of their own fierce swings.

The Tellurian Lensmen, however, had had more practice and remembered their lessons better. Jack Kinnison, soaring into the room, grabbed the first solid thing he could reach; a post. Pulling himself down to the floor, he braced both feet, sighted past the nearest foeman, swung his axe, and gave a tremendous shove. Such was his timing that in the instant of maximum effort the beak of his atrociously effective weapon encountered the pirate's helmet—and that was that. He wrenched his axe free and shoved the corpse away in such a direction that the reaction would send him against a wall at the floor line, in position to repeat the maneuver.

Since Mason Northrop was heavier and stronger than his friend, his technique was markedly different. He dove for the chart-table, which of course was welded to the floor. He hooked one steel-shod foot around one of the table's legs and braced the other against its top. Weightless but inert, it made no difference whether his position was vertical or horizontal or anywhere between; from this point of vantage, with his length of body and arm and axe, he could cover a lot of room. He reached out, hooked bill of axe into belt or line-snap or angle of armor, and pulled; and as the helplessly raging pirate floated past him, he swung and struck. And that, too, was that.

Dronvire of Rigel Four did not rush to the attack. He had never been and was not now either excited or angry. Indeed, it was only empirically that he knew what anger and excitement were. He had never been in any kind of a fight. Therefore he paused for a couple of seconds to analyze the situation and to determine his own most efficient method of operation. He would not have to be in physical contact with the pirate captain to go to work on his mind, but he would have to be closer than this and he would have to be free from physical attack while he concentrated. He perceived what Kinnison and Costigan and Northrop were doing, and knew why each was working in a different fashion. He applied that knowledge to his own mass, to his own musculature, to the length and strength of his arms—each one of which was twice as long and ten times as strong as the trunk of an elephant. He computed forces and leverages, actions and reactions, points of application, stresses and strains.

He threw away two of his axes. The two empty arms reached out, each curling around the neck of a pirate. Two axes flashed, grazing each pinioning arm so nearly that it seemed incredible that the sharp edges did not shear away the Rigellian's own armor. Two heads floated away from two bodies and Dronvire reached for two more. And two—and two—and two. Calm and dispassionate, but not wasting a motion or a millisecond, Dronvire accomplished more, in less time, than all the Tellurians in the room.

"Costigan, Northrop, Kinnison—attend!" he launched a thought. "I have no time to kill more of them. The commander is dying of a self-inflicted wound and I have important work to do. See to it, please, that these remaining creatures do not attack me while I am doing it."

Dronvire tuned his mind to that of the pirate and probed. Although dying, the pirate captain offered fierce resistance, but the Rigellian was not alone. Attuned to his mind, working smoothly with it, giving it strengths and qualities which no Rigellian ever had had or ever would have, were the two strongest minds of Earth: that of Rod the Rock Kinnison, with the driving force, the indomitable will, the transcendent urge of all human heredity; and that of Virgil Samms, with all that had made him First Lensman.

"TELL!" that terrific triple mind demanded, with a force which simply could not be denied. "WHERE ARE YOU FROM? Resistance is useless; yours or that of those whom you serve. Your bases and powers are smaller and weaker than ours, since Spaceways is only a corporation and we are the Galactic Patrol. TELL! WHO ARE YOUR BOSSES? TELL—TELL!"

Under that irresistible urge there appeared, foggily and without any hint of knowledge of name or of spatial co-ordinates, an embattled planet, very similar in a smaller way to the Patrol's own Bennett, and—

Even more foggily, but still not so blurred but that their features were unmistakeably recognizable, the images of two men. That of Murgatroyd, the pirate chief, completely strange to both Kinnison and Samms; and—

Back of Murgatroyd and above him, that of—

BIG JIM TOWNE!

CHAPTER 13

"First, about Murgatroyd." In his office in The Hill Roderick Kinnison spoke aloud to the First Lensman. "What do you think should be done about him?"

"Murgatroyd. Hm . . . m . . . m." Samms inhaled a mouthful of smoke and exhaled it slowly; watched it dissipate in the air. "Ah, yes, Murgatroyd." He repeated the performance. "My thought, at the moment, is to let him alone."

"Check," Kinnison said. If Samms was surprised at his friend's concurrence he did not show it. "Why? Let's see if we check on that."

"Because he does not seem to be of fundamental importance. Even if we could find him . . . and by the way, what do you think the chance is of our spies finding him?"

"Just about the same chance that theirs have of finding out about the Samms-Olmstead switch or our planet Bennett. Vanishingly small. Zero."

"Right. And even if we could find him—even find their secret base, which is certainly as well hidden as ours is—it would do us no present good, because we could take no positive action. We have, I think, learned the prime fact; that Towne is actually Murgatroyd's superior."

"That's the way I see it. We can almost draw an organization chart now."

"I wouldn't say 'almost'." Samms smiled half-ruefully. "There are gaping holes, and Isaacson is as yet a highly unknown quantity. I've tried to draw one a dozen times, but we haven't got enough information. An incorrect chart, you know, would be worse than none at all. As soon as I can draw a correct one, I'll show it to you. But in the meantime, the position of our friend James F. Towne is now clear. He is actually a Big Shot in both piracy and politics. That fact surprised me, even though it did clarify the picture tremendously."

"Me, too. One good thing, we won't have to hunt for him. You've been working on him right along, though, haven't you?"

"Yes, but this new relationship throws light on a good many details which have been obscure. It also tends to strengthen our working hypothesis as to Isaacson—which we can't prove yet, of course—that he is the actual working head of the drug syndicate. Vice-President in charge of Drugs, so to speak."

"Huh? That's a new one on me. I don't see it."

"There is very little doubt that at the top there is Morgan. He is, and has been for some time, the real boss of North America. Under him, probably taking orders direct, is President Witherspoon."

"Undoubtedly. The Nationalist party is strictly *a la* machine, and Witherspoon is one of the world's slimiest skinkers. Morgan is Chief Engineer of the Machine. Take it from there."

"We know that Boss Jim is also in the top echelon—quite possibly the Commander-in-Chief—of the enemy's Armed Forces. By analogy, and since Isaacson is apparently on the same level as Towne, immediately below Morgan . . . ."

"Wouldn't there be three? Witherspoon?"

"I doubt it. My present idea is that Witherspoon is at least one level lower. Comparatively small fry."

"Could be—I'll buy it. A nice picture, Virge; and beautifully symmetrical. His Mightiness Morgan. Secretary of War Towne and Secretary of Drugs Isaacson; and each of them putting a heavy shoulder behind the political bandwagon. *Very* nice. That makes Operation Mateese tougher than ever—a triple-distilled toughie. Glad I told you it wasn't my dish—saves me the trouble of backing out now."

"Yes, I have noticed how prone you are to duck tough jobs." Samms smiled quietly. "However, unless I am even more mistaken than usual, you will be in it up to your not-so-small ears, my friend, before it is over."

"Huh? How?" Kinnison demanded.

"That will, I hope, become clear very shortly." Samms stubbed out the butt of his cigarette and lit another. "The basic problem can be stated very simply. How are we going to persuade the sovereign countries of Earth—particularly the North American Continent—to grant the Galactic Patrol the tremendous power and authority it will have to have?"

"Nice phrasing, Virge, and studied. Not off the cuff. But aren't you over-drawing a bit? Little if any conflict. The Patrol would be pretty largely inter-systemic in scope . . . with of course the necessary inter-planetary and inter-continental . . . and . . . um . . . m . . . ."

"Exactly."

"But it's logical enough, Virge, even at that, and has plenty of precedents, clear back to ancient history. 'Way back, before space-travel, when they first started to use atomic energy, and the only drugs they had to worry about were cocaine, morphine, heroin, and other purely Tellurian products. I was reading about it just the other day."

Kinnison swung around, fingered a book out of a matched set, and riffled its leaves. "Russia was the world's problem child then—put up what they called an iron curtain—wouldn't play with the neighbors' children, but picked up her marbles and went home. But yet—here it is. Original source unknown—some indications point to a report of somebody named Hoover, sometime in the nineteen forties or fifties, Gregorian calendar. Listen:

"'This protocol'—he's talking about the agreement on world-wide Narcotics Control—'was signed by fifty-two nations, including the U.S.S.R.'—that was Russia—'and its satellite states. It was the only international agreement to which the Communist countries'—you know more about what Communism was, I suppose, than I do."

"Just that it was another form of dictatorship that didn't work out."

"' . . . to which the Communist countries ever gave more than lip service. This adherence is all the more surprising, in view of the political situation then obtaining, in that all signatory nations obligated themselves to surrender national sovereignty in five highly significant respects, as follows:

"'First, to permit Narcotics agents of all other signatory nations free, secret, and unregistered entry into, unrestricted travel throughout, and exit from, all their lands and waters, wherever situate:

"'Second, upon request, to allow known criminals and known contraband to enter and to leave their territories without interference:

"'Third, to cooperate fully, and as a secondary and not as a prime mover, in any Narcotics Patrol program set up by any other signatory nation:

"'Fourth, upon request, to maintain complete secrecy concerning any Narcotics operation: and

"'Fifth, to keep the Central Narcotics Authority fully and continuously informed upon all matters hereinbefore specified.'

"And apparently, Virge, it worked. If they could do that, 'way back then, we certainly should be able to make the Patrol work now."

"You talk as though the situations were comparable. They aren't. Instead of giving up an insignificant fraction of their national sovereignty, all nations will have to give up practically all of it. They will have to change their thinking from a National to a Galactic viewpoint; will have to become units in a Galactic Civilization, just as counties used to be units of states, and states are units of the continents. The Galactic Patrol will not be able to stop at being the supreme and only authority in inter-systemic affairs. It is bound to become intra-systemic, intra-planetary, and intra-continental. Eventually, it must and it shall be the *sole* authority, except for such purely local organizations as city police."

"*What* a program!" Kinnison thought silently for minutes. "But I'm still betting that you can bring it off."

"We'll keep on driving until we do. What gives us our chance is that the all-Lensman Solarian Council is already in existence and is functioning smoothly; and that the government of North America has no jurisdiction beyond the boundaries of its continent. Thus, and even though Morgan has extra-legal powers both as Boss of North America and as the head of an organization which is in fact inter-systemic in scope, he can do nothing whatever about the fact that the Solarian Council has been enlarged into the Galactic Council. As a matter of fact, he was and is very much in favor of that particular move—just as much so as we are."

"You're going too fast for me. How do you figure that?"

"Unlike our idea of the Patrol as a coordinator of free and independent races, Morgan sees it as the perfect instrument of a Galactic dictatorship, thus: North America is the most powerful continent of Earth. The other continents will follow her lead—or else. Tellus can very easily dominate the other Solarian planets, and the Solar System can maintain dominance over all other systems as they are discovered and colonized. Therefore, whoever controls the North American Continent controls all space."

"I see. Could be, at that. Throw the Lensmen out, put his own stooges in. Wonder how he'll go about it? A *tour de force*? No. The next election, would be my guess. If so, that will be the most important election in history."

"If they decide to wait for the election, yes. I'm not as sure as you seem to be that they will not act sooner."

"They can't," Kinnison declared. "Name me one thing they think they can do, and I'll shoot it fuller of holes than a target."

"They can, and I am very much afraid that they will," Samms replied, soberly. "At any time he cares to do so, Morgan—through the North American Government, of course—can abrogate the treaty and name his own Council."

"Without my boys—the backbone and the guts of North America, as well as of the Patrol? Don't be stupid, Virge. They're *loyal*."

"Admitted—but at the same time they are being paid in North American currency. Of course, we will soon have our own Galactic credit system worked out, but . . . ."

"What the hell difference would *that* make?" Kinnison wanted savagely to know. "You think they'd last until the next pay-day if they start playing that kind of ball? What in hell do you think *I'd* be doing? And Clayton and Schweikert and the rest of the gang? Sitting on our fat rumps and crying into our beers?"

"You would do nothing. I could not permit any illegal . . . ."

"Permit!" Kinnison blazed, leaping to his feet. "Permit—hell! Are you loose-screwed enough to actually think I would ask or need your permission? Listen, Samms!" The Port Admiral's voice took on a quality like nothing his friend had ever before heard. "The first thing I would do would be to take off your Lens, wrap you up—especially your mouth—in seventeen yards of three-inch adhesive tape, and heave you into the brig. The second would be to call out everything we've got, including every half-built ship on Bennett able to fly, and declare martial law. The third would be a series of summary executions, starting with Morgan and working down. And if he's got any fraction of the brain I credit him with, Morgan knows damned well *exactly* what would happen."

"Oh." Samms, while very much taken aback, was thrilled to the center of his being. "I had not considered anything so drastic, but you probably would . . . ."

"Not 'probably'," Kinnison corrected him grimly. "'Certainly'."

" . . . and Morgan does know . . . except about Bennett, of course . . . and he would not, for obvious reasons, bring in his secret armed forces. You're right, Rod, it will be the election."

"Definitely; and it's plain enough what their basic strategy will be." Kinnison, completely mollified, sat down and lit another cigar. "His Nationalist party is now in power, but it was our Cosmocrats of the previous administration who so basely slipped one over on the dear pee-pul—who betrayed the entire North American Continent into the claws of rapacious wealth, no less—by ratifying that unlawful, unhallowed, unconstitutional, and so on, treaty. Scoundrels! Bribe-takers! Betrayers of a sacred trust! *How* Rabble-Rouser Morgan will thump the tub on that theme—he'll make the welkin ring as it never rang before."

Kinnison mimicked savagely the demagogue's round and purple tones as he went on: "'Since they had no mandate from the pee-pul to trade their birthright for a mess of pottage that nefarious and underhanded treaty is, *a prima vista* and *ipso facto* and *a priori*, completely and necessarily and positively null and void. People of Earth, arouse! Arise! Rise in your might and throw off this stultifying and degrading, this paralyzing yoke of the Monied Powers—throw out this dictatorial, autocratic, wealth-directed, illegal, monstrous Council of so-called Lensmen! Rise in your might at the polls! Elect a Council of your own choosing—not of Lensmen, but of ordinary folks like you and me. Throw *off* this hellish yoke, I say!'—and here he begins to positively froth at the mouth—'so that government of the people, by the people, and for the people shall not perish from the Earth!'

"He has used that exact peroration, ancient as it is, so many times that practically everybody thinks he originated it; and it's always good for so many decibels of applause that he'll keep on using it forever."

"Your analysis is vivid, cogent, and factual, Rod—but the situation is not at all funny."

"Did I act as though I thought it was? If so, I'm a damned poor actor. I'd like to kick the bloodsucking leech all the way from here to the Great Nebula in Andromeda, and if I ever get the chance I'm going to!"

"An interesting, but somewhat irrelevant idea." Samms smiled at his friend's passionate outburst. "But go on. I agree with you in principle so far, and your viewpoint is—to say the least—refreshing."

"Well, Morgan will have so hypnotized most of the dear pee-pul that they will think it their own idea when he re-nominates this spineless nincompoop Witherspoon for another term as President of North America, with a solid machine-made slate of hatchet-men behind him. They win the election. Then the government of the North American Continent—not the Morgan-Towne-Isaacson machine, but all nice and legal and by mandate and in strict accordance with the party platform—abrogates the treaty and names its own Council. And right then, my friend, the boys and I will do our stuff."

"Except that, in such a case, you wouldn't. Think it over, Rod."

"Why not?" Kinnison demanded, in a voice which, however, did not carry much conviction.

"Because we would be in the wrong; and we are even less able to go against united public opinion than is the Morgan crowd."

"We'd do *something*—I've got it!" Kinnison banged the desk with his fist. "That would be a strictly unilateral action. North America would be standing alone."

"Of course."

"So we'll pull all the Cosmocrats and all of our friends out of North America—move them to Bennett or somewhere—and make Morgan and Company a present of it. We won't declare martial law or kill anybody, unless they decide to call in their reserves. We'll merely isolate the whole damned continent—throw a screen around it and over it that a microbe won't be able to get through—one that would make that iron curtain I read about look like a bride's veil—and we'll *keep* them isolated until they beg to join up on our terms. Strictly legal, and the perfect solution. How about me giving the boys a briefing on it, right now?"

"Not yet." Samms' mien, however, lightened markedly. "I never thought of that way out . . . . It *could* be done, and it would probably work, but I would not recommend it except as an ultimately last resort. It has at least two tremendous drawbacks."

"I know it, but . . . ."

"It would wreck North America as no nation has ever been wrecked; quite possibly beyond recovery. Furthermore, how many people, including yourself and your children, would like to renounce their North American citizenship and remove themselves, permanently and irrevocably, from North American soil?"

"Um . . . m . . . m. Put that away, it doesn't sound so good, does it? But what the hell else can we do?"

"Just what we have been planning on doing. We must win the election."

"Huh?" Kinnison's mouth almost fell open. "You say it easy. How? With whom? By what stretch of the imagination do you figure that you can find anybody with a loose enough mouth to out-lie and out-promise Morgan? And can you duplicate his machine?"

"We can not only duplicate his machine; we can better it. The truth, presented to the people in language they can understand and appreciate, by a man whom they like, admire, and respect, will be more attractive than Morgan's promises. The same truth will dispose of Morgan's lies."

"Well, go on. You've answered my questions, after a fashion, except the stinger. Does the Council think it's got a man with enough dynage to lift the load?"

"Unanimously. They also agreed unanimously that we have only one. Haven't you any idea who he is?"

"Not a glimmering of one." Kinnison frowned in thought, then his face cleared into a broad grin and he yelled: "*What* a damn fool I am—*you*, of course!"

"Wrong. I was not even seriously considered. It was the concensus that I could not possibly win. My work has been such as to keep me out of the public eye. If the man in the street thinks of me at all, he thinks that I hold myself apart and above him—the ivory tower concept."

"Could be, at that; but you've got my curiosity aroused. How can a man of that caliber have been kicking around so long without me knowing anything about him?"

"You do. That's what I've been working around to all afternoon. You."

"Huh?" Kinnison gasped as though he had received a blow in the solar plexus. "Me? ME? Hell's—Brazen—Hinges!"

"Exactly. You." Silencing Kinnison's inarticulate protests, Samms went on: "First, you'll have no difficulty in talking to an audience as you've just talked to me."

"Of course not—but did I use any language that would burn out the transmitters? I don't remember whether I did or not."

"I don't, either. You probably did, but that would be nothing new. Telenews has never yet cut you off the ether because of it. The point is this: while you do not realize it, you are a better tub-thumper and welkin-ringer than Morgan is, when something—such as just now—really gets you going. And as for a machine, what finer one is possible than the Patrol? Everybody in it or connected with it will support you to the hilt—you know that."

"Why, I . . . I suppose so . . . probably they would, yes."

"Do you know why?"

"Can't say that I do, unless it's because I treat them fair, so they do the same to me."

"Exactly. I don't say that everybody likes you, but I don't know of anybody who doesn't respect you. And, most important, everybody—all over space—knows 'Rod the Rock' Kinnison, and why he is called that."

"But that very 'man on horseback' thing may backfire on you, Virge."

"Perhaps—slightly—but we're not afraid of that. And finally, you said you'd like to kick Morgan from here to Andromeda. How would you like to kick him from Panama City to the North Pole?"

"I said it, and I wasn't just warming up my jets, either. I'd like it." The big Lensman's nostrils flared, his lips thinned. "By God, Virge, I will!"

"Thanks, Rod." With no display whatever of the emotion he felt, Samms skipped deliberately to the matter next in hand. "Now, about Eridan. Let's see if they know anything yet."

The report of Knobos and DalNalten was terse and exact. They had found—and that finding, so baldly put, could have filled and should fill a book—that Spaceways' uranium vessels were, beyond any reasonable doubt, hauling thionite from Eridan to the planets of Sol. Spy-rays being useless, they had considered the advisability of investigating Eridan in person, but had decided against such action. Eridan was closely held by Uranium, Incorporated. Its population was one hundred percent Tellurian human. Neither DalNalten nor Knobos could disguise himself well enough to work there. Either would be caught promptly, and as promptly shot.

"Thanks, fellows," Samms said, when it became evident that the brief report was done. Then, to Kinnison, "That puts it up to Conway Costigan. And Jack? Or Mase? Or both?"

"Both," Kinnison decided, "and anybody else they can use."

"I'll get them at it." Samms sent out thoughts. "And now, I wonder what that daughter of mine is doing? I'm a little worried about her, Rod. She's too cocky for her own good—or strength. Some of these days she's going to bite off more than she can chew, if she hasn't already. The more we learn about Morgan, the less I like the idea of her working on Herkimer Herkimer Third. I've told her so, a dozen times, and why, but of course it didn't do any good."

"It wouldn't. The only way to develop teeth is to bite with 'em. You had to. So did I. Our kids have got to, too. We lived through it. So will they. As for Herky the Third . . . ." He thought for moments, then went on: "Check. But she's done a job so far that nobody else could do. In spite of that fact, if it wasn't for our Lenses I'd say to pull her, if you have to heave the insubordinate young jade into the brig. But with the Lenses, and the way you watch her . . . to say nothing of Mase Northrop, and he's a lot of man . . . I can't see her getting in either very bad or very deep. Can you?"

"No, I can't." Samms admitted, but the thoughtful frown did not leave his face. He Lensed her: finding, as he had supposed, that she was at a party; dancing, as he had feared, with Senator Morgan's Number One Secretary.

"Hi, Dad!" she greeted him gaily, with no slightest change in the expression of the face turned so engagingly to her partner's. "I have the honor of reporting that all instruments are still dead-centering the green."

"And have you, by any chance, been paying any attention to what I have been telling you?"

"Oh, lots," she assured him. "I've collected reams of data. He could be almost as much of a menace as he thinks he is, in some cases, but I haven't begun to slip yet. As I have told you all along, this is just a game, and we're both playing it strictly according to the rules."

"That's good. Keep it that way, my dear." Samms signed off and his daughter returned her full attention—never noticeably absent—to the handsome secretary.

The evening wore on. Miss Samms danced every dance; occasionally with one or another of the notables present, but usually with Herkimer Herkimer Third.

"A drink?" he asked. "A small, cold one?"

"Not so small, and *very* cold," she agreed, enthusiastically.

Glass in hand, Herkimer indicated a nearby doorway. "I just heard that our host has acquired a very old and very fine bronze—a Neptune. We should run an eye over it, don't you think?"

"By all means," she agreed again.

But as they passed through the shadowed portal the man's head jerked to the right. "*There's* something you really ought to see, Jill!" he exclaimed. "Look!"

She looked. A young woman of her own height and build and with her own flamboyant hair, identical as to hair-do and as to every fine detail of dress and of ornamentation, glass in hand, was strolling back into the ball-room!

Jill started to protest, but could not. In the brief moment of inaction the beam of a snub-nosed P-gun had played along her spine from hips to neck. She did not fall—he had given her a very mild jolt—but, rage as she would, she could neither struggle nor scream. And, after the fact, she knew.

But he *couldn't*—couldn't *possibly*! Nevian paralysis-guns were as outlawed as was Vee Two gas itself! Nevertheless, he had.

And on the instant a woman, dressed in crisp and spotless white and carrying a hooded cloak, appeared—and Herkimer now wore a beard and heavy, horn rimmed spectacles. Thus, very shortly, Virgilia Samms found herself, completely helpless and completely unrecognizable, walking awkwardly out of the house between a businesslike doctor and a solicitous nurse.

"Will you need me any more, Doctor Murray?" The woman carefully and expertly loaded the patient into the rear seat of a car.

"Thank you, no, Miss Childs." With a sick, cold certainty Jill knew that this conversation was for the benefit of the doorman and the hackers, and that it would stand up under any examination. "Mrs. Harman's condition is . . . er . . . well, nothing at all serious."

The car moved out into the street and Jill, really frightened for the first time in her triumphant life, fought down an almost overwhelming wave of panic. The hood had slipped down over her eyes, blinding her. She could not move a single voluntary muscle. Nevertheless, she knew that the car traveled a few blocks—six, she thought—west on Bolton Street before turning left.

Why didn't somebody Lens her? Her father wouldn't, she knew, until tomorrow. Neither of the Kinnisons would, nor Spud—they never did except on direct invitation. But Mase would, before he went to bed—or would he? It was past his bed-time now, and she had been pretty caustic, only last night, because she was doing a particularly delicate bit of reading. But he would . . . he *must*!

"Mase! *Mase!* MASE!"

And, eventually, Mase did.

Deep under The Hill, Roderick Kinnison swore fulminantly at the sheer physical impossibility of getting out of that furiously radiating mountain in a hurry. At New York Spaceport, however, Mason Northrop and Jack Kinnison not only could hurry, but did.

"Where are you, Jill?" Northrop demanded presently. "What kind of a car are you in?"

"Quite near Stanhope Circle." In communication with her friends at last, Jill regained a measure of her usual poise. "Within eight or ten blocks, I'm sure. I'm in a black Wilford sedan, last year's model. I didn't get a chance to see its license plates."

"That helps a lot!" Jack grunted, savagely. "A ten-block radius covers a hell of a lot of territory, and half the cars in town are black Wilford sedans."

"Shut up, Jack! Go ahead, Jill—tell us all you can, and keep on sending us anything that will help at all."

"I kept the right and left turns and distances straight for quite a while—about twenty blocks—that's how I know it was Stanhope Circle. I don't know how many times he went around the circle, though, or which way he went when he left it. After leaving the Circle, the traffic was very light, and here there doesn't seem to be any traffic at all. That brings us up to date. You'll know as well as I do what happens next."

With Jill, the Lensmen knew that Herkimer drove his car up to the curb and stopped—parked without backing up. He got out and hauled the girl's limp body out of the car, displacing the hood enough to free one eye. Good! Only one other car was visible; a bright yellow convertible parked across the street, about half a block ahead.

SUPER PACK

There was a sign—"NO PARKING ON THIS SIDE 7 TO 10." The building toward which he was carrying her was more than three stories high, and had a number—one, four—if he would *only* swing her a little bit more, so that she could see the rest of it—one four-seven-nine!

"Rushton Boulevard, you think, Mase?"

"Could be. Fourteen seventy nine would be on the downtown-traffic side. Blast!"

Into the building, where two masked men locked and barred the door behind them. "And keep it locked!" Herkimer ordered. "You know what to do until I come back down."

Into an elevator, and up. Through massive double doors into a room, whose most conspicuous item of furniture was a heavy steel chair, bolted to the floor. Two masked men got up and placed themselves behind that chair.

Jill's strength was coming back fast; but not fast enough. The cloak was removed. Her ankles were tied firmly, one to each front leg of the chair. Herkimer threw four turns of rope around her torso and the chair's back, took up every inch of slack, and tied a workmanlike knot. Then, still without a word, he stood back and lighted a cigarette. The last trace of paralysis disappeared, but the girl's mad struggles, futile as they were, were not allowed to continue.

"Put a double hammerlock on her," Herkimer directed, "but be damned sure not to break anything at this stage of the game. That comes later."

Jill, more furiously angry than frightened until now, locked her teeth to keep from screaming as the pressure went on. She could not bend forward to relieve the pain; she could not move; she could only grit her teeth and glare. She was beginning to realize, however, what was actually in store; that Herkimer Herkimer Third was in fact a monster whose like she had never known.

He stepped quietly forward, gathered up a handful of fabric, and heaved. The strapless and backless garment, in no way designed to withstand such stresses, parted; squarely across at the upper strand of rope. He puffed his cigarette to a vivid coal—took it in his fingers—there was an audible hiss and a tiny stink of burning flesh as the glowing ember was extinguished in the clear, clean skin below the girl's left armpit. Jill flinched then, and shrieked desperately, but her tormentor was viciously unmoved.

"That was just to settle any doubt as to whether or not I mean business. I'm all done fooling around with you. I want to know two things. First, everything you know about the Lens; where it comes from, what it really is, and what it does besides what your press-agents advertise. Second, what really happened at the Ambassadors' Ball. Start talking. The faster you talk, the less you'll get hurt."

"You can't get away with this, Herkimer." Jill tried desperately to pull her shattered nerves together. "I'll be missed—traced . . . ." She paused, gasping. If she told him that the Lensmen were in full and continuous communication with her—and if he believed it—he would kill her right then. She switched instantly to another track. "That double isn't good enough to fool anybody who really knows me."

"She doesn't have to be." The man grinned venomously. "Nobody who knows you will get close enough to her to tell the difference. This wasn't done on the spur of the

287

moment, Jill; it was planned—minutely. You haven't got the chance of the proverbial celluloid dog in hell."

"Jill!" Jack Kinnison's thought stabbed in. "It isn't Rushton—fourteen seventy-nine is a two-story. What other streets could it be?"

"I don't know . . . ." She was not in very good shape to think.

"Damnation! Got to get hold of somebody who knows the streets. Spud, grab a hacker at the Circle and I'll Lens Parker . . . ." Jack's thought snapped off as he tuned to a local Lensman.

Jill's heart sank. She was starkly certain now that the Lensmen could not find her in time.

"Tighten up a little, Eddie. You, too, Bob."

"Stop it! Oh, God, STOP IT!" The unbearable agony relaxed a little. She watched in horrified fascination a second glowing coal approach her bare right side. "Even if I do talk you'll kill me anyway. You couldn't let me go now."

"Kill you, my pet? Not if you behave yourself. We've got a lot of planets the Patrol never heard of, and you could keep a man interested for quite a while, if you really tried. And if you beg hard enough maybe I'll let you try. However, I'd get just as much fun out of killing you as out of the other, so it's up to you. Not sudden death, of course. Little things, at first, like we've been doing. A few more touches of warmth here and there—so . . . ."

"Scream as much as you please. I enjoy it, and this room is sound-proof. Once more, boys, about half an inch higher this time . . . up . . . steady . . . down. We'll have half an hour or so of this stuff"—Herkimer knew that to the quivering, sensitive, highly imaginative girl his words would be practically as punishing as the atrocious actualities themselves—"then I'll do things to your finger-nails and toe-nails, beginning with burning slivers of double-base flare powder and working up. Then your eyes—or no, I'll save them until last, so you can watch a couple of Venerian slasher-worms work on you, one on each leg, and a Martian digger on your bare belly."

Gripping her hair firmly in his left hand, he forced her head back and down; down almost to her hard-held hands. His right hand, concealing something which he had not mentioned and which was probably starkly unmentionable, approached her taut-stretched throat.

"Talk or not, just as you please." The voice was utterly callous, as chill as the death she now knew he was so willing to deal. "But listen. If you elect to talk, tell the truth. You won't lie twice. I'll count to ten. One."

Jill uttered a gurgling, strangling noise and he lifted her head a trifle.

"Can you talk now?"

"Yes."

"Two."

Helpless, immobile, scared now to a depth of terror she had never imagined it possible to feel, Jill fought her wrenched and shaken mind back from insanity's very edge; managed with a pale tongue to lick bloodless lips. Pops Kinnison always said a man could die only once, but he didn't know . . . in battle, yes, perhaps . . . but she had already died a dozen times—but she'd keep on dying forever before she'd say a word. But—

"Tell him, Jill!" Northrop's thought beat at her mind. He, her lover, was unashamedly frantic; as much with sheer rage as with sympathy for her physical and mental anguish. "For the nineteenth time I say tell him! We've just located you—Hancock Avenue—we'll be there in two minutes!"

"Yes, Jill, quit being a damned stubborn jackass and tell him!" Jack Kinnison's thought bit deep; but this time, strangely enough, the girl felt no repugnance at his touch. There was nothing whatever of the lover; nor of the brother, except of the fraternity of arms. She belonged. She would come out of this brawl right side up or none of them would. "Tell the goddam rat the truth!" Jack's thought drove on. "It won't make any difference—he won't live long enough to pass it on!"

"But I can't—I won't!" Jill stormed. "Why, Pops Kinnison would . . . ."

"Not this time I wouldn't, Jill!" Samms' thought tried to come in, too, but the Port Admiral's vehemence was overwhelming. "No harm—he's doing this strictly on his own—if Morgan had had any idea he'd've killed him first. Start talking or I'll spank you to a rosy blister!"

They were to laugh, later, at the incongruity of that threat, but it did produce results.

"Nine." Herkimer grinned wolfishly, in sadistic anticipation.

"Stop it—I'll tell!" she screamed. "Stop it—take that thing away—I can't stand it—I'll tell!" She burst into racking, tearing sobs.

"Steady." Herkimer put something in his pocket, then slapped her so viciously that fingers-long marks sprang into red relief upon the chalk-white background of her cheek. "Don't crack up; I haven't started to work on you yet. What about that Lens?"

She gulped twice before she could speak. "It comes from—ulp!—Arisia. I haven't got one myself, so I don't know very much—ulp!—about it at first hand, but from what the boys tell me it must be . . . ."

*

Outside the building three black forms arrowed downward. Northrop and young Kinnison stopped at the sixth level; Costigan went on down to take care of the guards.

"Bullets, not beams," the Irishman reminded his younger fellows. "We'll have to clean up the mess without leaving a trace, so don't do any more damage to the property than you absolutely have to."

Neither made any reply; they were both too busy. The two thugs standing behind the steel chair, being armed openly, went first; then Jack put a bullet through Herkimer's head. But Northrop was not content with that. He slid the pin to "full automatic" and ten more heavy slugs tore into the falling body before it struck the floor.

Three quick slashes and the girl was free.

"Jill!"

"Mase!"

Locked in each other's arms, straining together, no bystander would have believed that this was their first kiss. It was plainly—yes, quite spectacularly—evident, however, that it would not be their last.

Jack, blushing furiously, picked up the cloak and flung it at the oblivious couple.

"P-s-s-t! *P-s-s-t! Jill!* Wrap 'em up!" he whispered, urgently. "All the top brass in space is coming at full emergency blast—there'll be scrambled eggs all over the place any second now—*Mase! Damn* your thick, hard skull, snap out of it! He's always frothing at the mouth about her running around half naked and if he sees her like this—especially with *you*—he'll simply have a litter of lizards! You'll get a million black spots and seven hundred years in the clink! That's better—'bye now—I'll see you up at New York Spaceport."

Jack Kinnison dashed to the nearest window, threw it open, and dived headlong out of the building.

CHAPTER 14

The employment office of any concern with personnel running into the hundreds of thousands is a busy place indeed, even when its plants are all on Tellus and its working conditions are as nearly ideal as such things can be made. When that firm's business is Colonial, however, and its working conditions are only a couple of degrees removed from slavery, procurement of personnel is a first-magnitude problem; the Personnel Department, like Alice in Wonderland, must run as fast as it can go in order to stay where it is. Thus the "Help Wanted" advertisements of Uranium, Incorporated covered the planet Earth with blandishment and guile; and thus for twelve hours of every day and for seven days of every week the employment offices of Uranium, Inc. were filled with men—mostly the scum of Earth.

There were, of course, exceptions; one of which strode through the motley group of waiting men and thrust a card through the "Information" wicket. He was a chunky-looking individual, appearing shorter than his actual five feet nine because of a hundred and ninety pounds of weight—even though every pound was placed exactly where it would do the most good. He looked—well, slouchy—and his mien was sullen.

"Birkenfeld—by appointment," he growled through the wicket, in a voice which could have been pleasantly deep.

The coolly efficient blonde manipulated plugs. "Mr. George W. Jones, sir, by appointment . . . . Thank you, sir," and Mr. Jones was escorted into Mr. Birkenfeld's private office.

"Have a chair, please, Mr. . . . . er . . . Jones."

"So you know?"

"Yes. It is seldom that a man of your education, training, and demonstrated ability applies to us for employment of his own initiative, and a very thorough investigation is indicated."

"What am I here for, then?" the visitor demanded, truculently. "You could have turned me down by mail. Everybody else has, since I got out."

"You are here because we who operate on the frontiers cannot afford to pass judgment upon a man because of his past, unless that past precludes the probability of a useful future. Yours does not; and in some cases, such as yours, we are very deeply interested in the future." The official's eyes drilled deep.

Conway Costigan had never been in the limelight. On the contrary, he had made inconspicuousness a passion and an art. Even in such scenes of violence as that which had occurred at the Ambassadors' Ball he managed to remain unnoticed. His Lens had never been visible. No one except Lensmen—and Clio and Jill—knew that he had one; and Lensmen—and Clio and Jill—did not talk. Although he was calmly certain that this Birkenfeld was not an ordinary interviewer, he was equally certain that the investigators of Uranium, Inc. had found out exactly and only what the Patrol had wanted them to find.

"So?" Jones' bearing altered subtly, and not because of the penetrant eyes. "That's all I want—a chance. I'll start at the bottom, as far down as you say."

"We advertise, and truthfully, that opportunity on Eridan is unlimited." Birkenfeld chose his words with care. "In your case, opportunity will be either absolutely unlimited or zero, depending entirely upon yourself."

"I see." Dumbness had not been included in the fictitious Mr. Jones' background. "You don't need to draw a blue-print."

"You'll do, I think." The interviewer nodded in approval. "Nevertheless, I must make our position entirely clear. If the slip was—shall we say accidental?—you will go far with us. If you try to play false, you will not last long and you will not be missed."

"Fair enough."

"Your willingness to start at the bottom is commendable, and it is a fact that those who come up through the ranks make the best executives; in our line at least. Just how far down are you willing to start?"

"How low do you go?"

"A mucker, I think would be low enough; and, from your build, and obvious physical strength, the logical job."

"Mucker?"

"One who skoufers ore in the mine. Nor can we make any exception in your case as to the routines of induction and transportation."

"Of course not."

"Take this slip to Mr. Calkins, in Room 6217. He will run you through the mill."

And that night, in an obscure boarding-house, Mr. George Washington Jones, after a meticulous Service Special survey in every direction, reached a large and somewhat grimy hand into a screened receptacle in his battered suitcase and touched a Lens.

"Clio?" The lovely mother of their wonderful children appeared in his mind. "Made it, sweetheart, no suspicion at all. No more Lensing for a while—not too long, I hope—so . . . so-long, Clio."

"Take it easy, Spud darling, and *be careful*." Her tone was light, but she could not conceal a stark background of fear. "Oh, I *wish* I could go, too!"

"I wish you could, Tootie." The linked minds flashed back to what the two had done together in the red opacity of Nevian murk; on Nevia's mighty, watery globe—but that kind of thinking would not do. "But the boys will keep in touch with me and keep you posted. And besides, you know how hard it is to get a baby-sitter!"

*

THE LENSMAN

It is strange that the fundamental operations of working metalliferous veins have changed so little throughout the ages. Or is it? Ores came into being with the crusts of the planets; they change appreciably only with the passage of geologic time. Ancient mines, of course, could not go down very deep or follow a seam very far; there was too much water and too little air. The steam engine helped, in degree if not in kind, by removing water and supplying air. Tools improved—from the simple metal bar through pick and shovel and candle, through drill and hammer and low explosive and acetylene, through Sullivan slugger and high explosive and electrics, through skoufer and rotary and burley and sourceless glow, to the complex gadgetry of today—but what, fundamentally, is the difference? Men still crawl, snake-like, to where the metal is. Men still, by dint of sheer brawn, jackass the precious stuff out to where our vaunted automatics can get hold of it. And men still die, in horribly unknown fashions and in callously recorded numbers, in the mines which supply the stuff upon which our vaunted culture rests.

But to resume the thread of narrative, George Washington Jones went to Eridan as a common laborer; a mucker. He floated down beside the skip—a "skip" is a mine elevator—some four thousand eight hundred feet. He rode an ore-car a horizontal distance of approximately eight miles to the brilliantly-illuminated cavern which was the Station of the Twelfth and lowest level. He was assigned to the bunk in which he would sleep for the next fifteen nights: "Fifteen down and three up," ran the standard underground contract.

He walked four hundred yards, yelled "Nothing Down!" and inched his way up a rise—in many places scarcely wider than his shoulders—to the stope some three hundred feet above. He reported to the miner who was to be his immediate boss and bent his back to the skoufer—which, while not resembling a shovel at all closely, still meant hard physical labor. He already knew ore—the glossy, sub-metallic, pitchy black luster of uraninite or pitchblende; the yellows of autunite and carnotite; the variant and confusing greens of tobernite. No values went from Jones' skoufer into the heavily-timbered, steel-braced waste-pockets of the stope; very little base rock went down the rise.

He became accustomed to the work; got used to breathing the peculiarly lifeless, dry, oily compressed air. And when, after a few days, his stentorian "Nothing Down!" called forth a "Nothing but a little fine stuff!" and a handful of grit and pebbles, he knew that he had been accepted into the undefined, unwritten, and unofficial, yet nevertheless intensely actual, fellowship of hard-rock men. He belonged.

He knew that he must abandon his policy of invisibility; and, after several days of thought, he decided how he would do it. Hence, upon the first day of his "up" period, he joined his fellows in their descent upon one of the rawest, noisiest dives of Danapolis. The men were met, of course, by a bevy of giggling, shrieking, garishly painted and strongly perfumed girls—and at this point young Jones' behavior became exceedingly unorthodox.

"Buy me a drink, mister? And a dance, huh?"

"On your way, sister." He brushed the importunate wench aside. "I get enough exercise underground, an' you ain't got a thing I want."

SUPER PACK

Apparently unaware that the girl was exchanging meaningful glances with a couple of husky characters labelled "BOUNCER" in billposter type, the atypical mucker strode up to the long and ornate bar.

"Gimme a bottle of pineapple pop," he ordered bruskly, "an' a package of Tellurian cigarettes—Sunshines."

"P-p-pine . . . ?" The surprised bartender did not finish the word.

The bouncers were fast, but Costigan was faster. A hard knee took one in the solar plexus; a hard elbow took the other so savagely under the chin as to all but break his neck. A bartender started to swing a bung-starter, and found himself flying through the air toward a table. Men, table, and drinks crashed to the floor.

"I pick my own company an' I drink what I damn please," Jones announced, grittily. "Them lunkers ain't hurt none, to speak of . . . " His hard eyes swept the room malevolently, "but I ain't in no gentle mood an' the next jaspers that tackle me will wind up in the repair shop, or maybe in the morgue. See?"

This of course was much too much; a dozen embattled roughnecks leaped to mop up on the misguided wight who had so impugned the manhood of all Eridan. Then, while six or seven bartenders blew frantic blasts upon police whistles, there was a flurry of action too fast to be resolved into consecutive events by the eye. Conway Costigan, one of the fastest men with hands and feet the Patrol has ever known, was trying to keep himself alive; and he succeeded.

"What the hell goes on here?" a chorus of raucously authoritative voices yelled, and sixteen policemen—John Law did not travel singly in that district, but in platoons—swinging clubs and saps, finally hauled George Washington Jones out from the bottom of the pile. He had sundry abrasions and not a few contusions, but no bones were broken and his skin was practically whole.

And since his version of the affair was not only inadequate, but also differed in important particulars from those of several non-participating witnesses, he spent the rest of his holiday in jail; a development with which he was quite content.

The work—and time—went on. He became in rapid succession a head mucker, a miner's pimp (which short and rugged Anglo-Saxon word means simply "helper" in underground parlance) a miner, a top-miner, and then—a long step up the ladder!—a shift-boss.

And then disaster struck; suddenly, paralyzingly, as mine disasters do. Loud-speakers blared briefly—"Explosion! Cave-in! Flood! Fire! Gas! Radiation! Damp!"—and expired. Short-circuits; there was no way of telling which, if any, of those dire warnings were true.

The power failed, and the lights. The hiss of air from valves, a noise which by its constant and unvarying and universal presence soon becomes unheard, became noticeable because of its diminution in volume and tone. And then, seconds later, a jarring, shuddering rumble was felt and heard, accompanied by the snapping of shattered timbers and the sharper, utterly unforgettable shriek of rending and riven steel. And the men, as men do under such conditions, went wild; yelling, swearing, leaping toward where, in the rayless dark, each thought the rise to be.

It took a couple of seconds for the shift-boss to break out and hook up his emergency battery-lamp; and three or four more seconds, and by dint of fists, feet, and a two-foot length of air-hose, to restore any degree of order. Four men were dead; but that wasn't too bad—considering.

"Up there! Under the hanging wall!" he ordered, sharply. "*That* won't fall—unless the whole mountain slips. Now, how many of you jaspers have got your emergency kits on you? Twelve—out of twenty-six—what brains! Put on your masks. You without 'em can stay up here—you'll be safe for a while—I hope."

Then, presently: "There, that's all for now. I guess." He flashed his light downward. The massive steel members no longer writhed; the crushed and tortured timbers were still.

"That rise may be open, it goes through solid rock, not waste. I'll see. Wright, you're all in one piece, aren't you?"

"I guess so—yes."

"Take charge up here. I'll go down to the drift. If the rise is open I'll give you a flash. Send the ones with masks down, one at a time. Take a jolly-bar and bash the brains out of anybody who gets panicky again."

Jones was not as brave as he sounded: mine disasters carry a terror which is uniquely and peculiarly poignant. Nevertheless he went down the rise, found it open, and signalled. Then, after issuing brief orders, he led the way along the dark and silent drift toward the Station; wondering profanely why the people on duty there had not done something with the wealth of emergency equipment always ready there. The party found some cave-ins, but nothing they could not dig through.

The Station was also silent and dark. Jones, flashing his head-lamp upon the emergency panel, smashed the glass, wrenched the door open, and pushed buttons. Lights flashed on. Warning signals flared, bellowed and rang. The rotary air-pump began again its normal subdued, whickering whirr. But the water-pump! Shuddering, clanking, groaning, it was threatening to go out any second—but there wasn't a thing in the world Jones could do about it—yet.

The Station itself, so buttressed and pillared with alloy steel as to be little more compressible than an equal volume of solid rock, was unharmed; but in it nothing lived. Four men and a woman—the nurse—were stiffly motionless at their posts; apparently the leads to the Station had been blasted in such fashion that no warning whatever had been given. And smoke, billowing inward from the main tunnel, was growing thicker by the minute. Jones punched another button; a foot-thick barrier of asbestos, tungsten, and vitrified refractory slid smoothly across the tunnel's opening. He considered briefly, pityingly, those who might be outside, but felt no urge to explore. If any lived, there were buttons on the other side of the fire-door.

The eddying smoke disappeared, the flaring lights winked out, air-horns and bells relapsed into silence. The shift-boss, now apparently the Superintendent of the whole Twelfth Level, removed his mask, found the Station walkie-talkie, and snapped a switch. He spoke, listened, spoke again then called a list of names—none of which brought any response.

"Wright, and you five others," picking out miners who could be depended upon to keep their heads, "take these guns. Shoot if you have to, but not unless you have to. Have the muckers clear the drift, just enough to get through. You'll find a shift-boss, with a crew of nineteen, up in Stope Sixty. Their rise is blocked. They've got light and power again now, and good air, and they're working on it, but opening the rise from the top is a damned slow job. Wright, you throw a chippie into it from the bottom. You others, work back along the drift, clear to the last glory hole. Be sure that all the rises are open—check all the stopes and glory holes—tell everybody you find alive to report to me here . . . ."

"Aw, what good!" a man shrieked. "We're all goners anyway—I want *water* an' . . . ."

"Shut up, fool!" There was a sound as of fist meeting flesh, the shriek was stilled. "Plenty of water—tanks full of the stuff." A grizzled miner turned to the self-appointed boss and twitched his head—toward the laboring pump. "Too damn much water too soon, huh?"

"I wouldn't wonder—but get busy!"

As his now orderly and purposeful men disappeared, Jones picked up his microphone and changed the setting of a dial.

"On top, somebody," he said crisply. "On top . . . ."

"Oh, there's somebody alive down in Twelve, after all!" a girl's voice screamed in his ear. "Mr. Clancy! Mr. Edwards!"

"To hell with Clancy, and Edwards, too," Jones barked. "Gimme the Chief Engineer and the Head Surveyor, and gimme 'em *fast*."

"Clancy speaking, Station Twelve." If Works Manager Clancy had heard that pointed remark, and he must have, he ignored it. "Stanley and Emerson will be here in a moment. In the meantime, who's calling? I don't recognize your voice, and it's been so long . . . ."

"Jones. Shift-boss, Stope Fifty Nine. I had a little trouble getting here to the Station."

"What? Where's Pennoyer? And Riley? And . . . ?"

"Dead. Everybody. Gas or damp. No warning."

"Not enough to turn on *anything*—not even the purifiers?"

"Nothing."

"Where were you?"

"Up in the stope."

"Good God!" That news, to Clancy, was informative enough.

"But to hell with all that. What happened, and where?"

"A skip-load, and then a magazine, of high explosive, right at Station Seven—it's right at the main shaft, you know." Jones did not know, since he had never been in that part of the mine, but he could see the picture. "Main shaft filled up to above Seven, and both emergency shafts blocked. Number One at Six, Number Two at Seven—must have been a fault—But here's Chief Engineer Stanley." The works manager, not too unwillingly, relinquished the microphone.

A miner came running up and Jones covered his mouth-piece. "How about the glory holes?"

"Plugged solid, all four of 'em—by the vibro, clear up to Eleven."

"Thanks." Then, as soon as Stanley's voice came on:

"What I want to know is, why is this damned water-pump overloading? What's the circuit?"

"You must be . . . yes, you are pumping against too much head. Five levels above you are dead, you know, so . . . ."

"Dead? Can't you raise *anybody?*"

"Not yet. So you're pumping through dead boosters on Eleven and Ten and so on up, and when your overload-relief valve opens . . . ."

"*Relief* valve!" Jones almost screamed, "Can I dog the damn thing down?"

"No, it's internal."

"Christ, what a design—I could eat a handful of iron filings and *puke* a better emergency pump than that!"

"When it opens," Stanley went stolidly on, "the water will go through the by-pass back into the sump. So you'd better rod out one of the glory holes and . . . ."

"Get conscious, fat-head!" Jones blazed. "What would we use for time? Get off the air—gimme Emerson!"

"Emerson speaking."

"Got your maps?"

"Yes."

"We got to run a sag up to Eleven—fast—or drown. Can you give me the shortest possible distance?"

"Can do." The Head Surveyor snapped orders. "We'll have it for you in a minute. Thank God there was somebody down there with a brain."

"It doesn't take super-human intelligence to push buttons."

"You'd be surprised. Your point on glory holes was very well taken—you won't have much time after the pump quits. When the water reaches the Station . . . ."

"Curtains. And it's all done now—running free and easy—recirculating. Hurry that dope!"

"Here it is now. Start at the highest point of Stope Fifty Nine. Repeat."

"Stope Fifty-Nine." Jones waved a furious hand as he shouted the words; the tight-packed miners turned and ran. The shift-boss followed them, carrying the walkie-talkie, aiming an exasperated kick of pure frustration at the merrily-humming water pump as he passed it.

"Thirty two degrees from the vertical—anywhere between thirty and thirty five."

"Thirty to thirty five off vertical."

"Direction—got a compass?"

"Yes."

"Set the blue on zero. Course two hundred seventy five degrees."

"Blue on zero. Course two seven five."

"Dex sixty nine point two zero feet. That'll put you into Eleven's class yard—so big you can't miss it."

"Distance sixty nine point two—*that* all? Fine! Maybe we'll make it, after all. They're sinking a shaft, of course. From where?"

"About four miles in on Six. It'll take time."

"If we can get up into Eleven we'll have all the time on the clock—it'll take a week or more to flood Twelve's stopes. But this sag is sure as hell going to be touch and go. And say, from the throw of the pump and the volume of the sump, will you give me the best estimate you can of how much time we've got? I want at least an hour, but I'm afraid I won't have it."

"Yes. I'll call you back."

The shift-boss elbowed his way through the throng of men and, dragging the radio behind him, wriggled and floated up the rise.

"Wright!" he bellowed, the echoes resounding deafeningly all up and down the narrow tube. "You up there ahead of me?"

"Yeah!" that worthy bellowed back.

"More men left than I thought—how many—half of 'em?"

"Just about."

"Good. Sort out the ones you got up there by trades." Then, when he had emerged into the now brilliantly illuminated stope, "Where are the timber-pimps?"

"Over there."

"Rustle timbers. Whatever you can find and wherever you find it, grab it and bring it up here. Get some twelve-inch steel, too, six feet long. Timbermen, grab that stuff off of the face and start your staging right here. You muckers, rig a couple of skoufers to throw muck to bury the base and checkerwork up to the hanging wall. Doze a sluice-way down into that waste pocket there, so we won't clog ourselves up. Work fast, fellows, but make it *solid*—you know the load it'll have to carry and what will happen if it gives."

They knew. They knew what they had to do and did it; furiously, but with care and precision.

"How wide a sag you figurin' on, Supe?" the boss timberman asked. "Eight foot checkerwork to the hangin', anyway, huh?"

"Yes. I'll let you know in a minute."

The surveyor came in. "Forty one minutes is my best guess."

"From when?"

"From the time the pump failed."

"That was four minutes ago—nearer five. And five more before we can start cutting. Forty one less ten is thirty one. Thirty one into sixty nine point two goes . . . ."

"Two point two three feet per minute, my slip-stick says."

"Thanks. Wright, what would you say is the biggest sag we can cut in this kind of rock at two and a quarter feet a minute?"

"Um . . . m . . . m". The miner scratched his whiskery chin. "That's a tough one, boss. You'll hafta figure damn close to a hundred pounds of air to the foot on plain cuttin'—that's two hundred and a quarter. But without a burley to pimp for 'er, a rotary can't take that kind of air—she'll foul herself to a standstill before she cuts a foot. An' with a burley riggin' she's got to make damn near a double cut—seven foot inside figger—so any way you look at it you ain't goin' to cut no two foot to the minute."

"I was hoping you wouldn't check my figures, but you do. So we'll cut five feet. Saw your timbers accordingly. We'll hold that burley by hand."

Wright shook his head dubiously. "We don't want to die down here any more than you do, boss, so we'll do our damndest—but how in *hell* do you figure you can hold her to her work?"

"Rig a yoke. Cut a stretcher up for canvas and padding. It'll pound, but a man can stand almost anything, in short enough shifts, if he's got to or die."

And for a time—two minutes, to be exact, during which the rotary chewed up and spat out a plug of rock over five feet deep—things went very well indeed. Two men, instead of the usual three, could run the rotary; that is, they could tend the complicated pneumatic walking jacks which not only oscillated the cutting demon in a geometrical path, but also rammed it against the face with a steadily held and enormous pressure, even while climbing almost vertically upward under a burden of over twenty thousand pounds.

An armored hand waved a signal—voice was utterly useless—up! A valve was flipped; a huge, flat, steel foot arose; a timber slid into place, creaking and groaning as that big flat foot smashed down. Up—again! Up—a third time! Eighteen seconds—less than one-third of a minute—ten inches gained!

And, while it was not easy, two men could hold the burley—in one-minute shifts. As has been intimated, this machine "pimped" for the rotary. It waited on it, ministering to its every need with a singleness of purpose impossible to any except robotic devotion. It picked the rotary's teeth, it freed its linkages, it deloused its ports, it cleared its spillways of compacted debris, it even—and this is a feat starkly unbelievable to anyone who does not know the hardness of neocarballoy and the tensile strength of ultra-special steels—it even changed, while in full operation, the rotary's diamond-tipped cutters.

Both burley and rotary were extremely efficient, but neither was either quiet or gentle. In their quietest moments they shrieked and groaned and yelled, producing a volume of sound in which nothing softer than a cannon-shot could have been heard. But when, in changing the rotary's cutting teeth, the burley's "fingers" were driven into and through the solid rock—a matter of merest routine to both machines—the resultant blasts of sound cannot even be imagined, to say nothing of being described.

And always both machines spewed out torrents of rock, in sizes ranging from impalpable dust up to chunks as big as a fist.

As the sag lengthened and the checkerwork grew higher, the work began to slow down. They began to lose the time they had gained. There were plenty of men, but in that narrow bore there simply was not room for enough men to work. Even through that storm of dust and hurtling rock the timbermen could get their blocking up there, but they could not place it fast enough—there were too many other men in the way. One of them had to get out. Since one man could not *possibly* run the rotary, one man would have to hold the burley.

They tried it, one after another. No soap. It hammered them flat. The rotary, fouled in every tooth and channel and vent under the terrific thrust of two hundred thirty pounds of air, merely gnawed and slid. The timbermen now had room—but nothing to do. And

Jones, who had been biting at his mustache and ignoring the frantic walkie-talkie for minutes, stared grimly at watch and tape. Three minutes left, and over eight feet to go.

"Gimme that armor!" he rasped, and climbed the blocks. "Open the air wide open—give 'er the whole two-fifty! Get down, Mac—I'll take it the rest of the way!"

He put his shoulders to the improvised yoke, braced his feet, and heaved. The burley, screaming and yelling and clamoring, went joyously to work—both ways—God, what punishment! The rotary, free and clear, chewed rock more viciously than ever. An armored hand smote his leg. Lift! He lifted that foot, set it down two inches higher. The other one. Four inches. Six. One foot. Two. Three. Lord of the ancients! Was this lifetime of agony only one minute? Or wasn't he holding her—had the damn thing stopped cutting? No, it was still cutting—the rocks were banging against and bouncing off of his helmet as viciously and as numerously as ever; he could sense, rather than feel, the furious fashion in which the relays of timbermen were laboring to keep those high-stepping jacks in motion.

No, it had been only one minute. Twice that long yet to go. God! Nothing *could* be that brutal—a bull elephant couldn't take it—but by all the gods of space and all the devils in hell, he'd stay with it until that sag broke through. And grimly, doggedly, toward the end nine-tenths unconsciously, Lensman Conway Costigan stayed with it.

And in the stope so far below, a new and highly authoritative voice blared from the speaker.

"Jones! God damn it, Jones, answer me! If Jones isn't there, somebody else answer me—*anybody!*"

"Yes, sir?" Wright was afraid to answer that peremptory call, but more afraid not to.

"Jones? This is Clancy."

"No, sir. Not Jones. Wright, sir—top miner."

"Where's Jones?"

"Up in the sag, sir. He's holding the burley—alone."

"*Alone!* Hell's purple fires! Tell him to—how many men has he got on the rotary?"

"Two, sir. That's all they's room for."

"Tell him to quit it—put somebody else on it—I *won't* have him killed, damn it!"

"He's the only one strong enough to hold it, sir, but I'll send up word." Word went up via sign language, and came back down. "Beggin' your pardon, sir, but he says to tell you to go to hell, sir. He won't have no time for chit-chat, he says, until this goddam sag is through or the juice goes off, sir."

A blast of profanity erupted from the speaker, of such violence that the thoroughly scared Wright threw the walkie-talkie down the waste-chute, and in the same instant the rotary crashed through.

Dazed, groggy, barely conscious from his terrific effort, Jones stared owlishly through the heavy, steel-braced lenses of his helmet while the timbermen set a few more courses of wood and the rotary walked itself and the clinging burley up and out of the hole. He climbed stiffly out, and as he stared at the pillar of light flaring upward from the sag, his gorge began to rise.

"Wha's the idea of that damn surveyor lying to us like that?" he babbled. "We had oodles an' oodles of time—didn't have to kill ourselves—damn water ain't got there yet—wha's the big . . . ." He wobbled weakly, and took one short step, and the lights went out. The surveyor's estimate had been impossibly, accidentally close. They had had a little extra time; but it was measured very easily in seconds.

And Jones, logical to the end in a queerly addled way, stood in the almost palpable darkness, and wobbled, and thought. If a man couldn't see anything with his eyes wide open, he was either blind or unconscious. He wasn't blind, therefore he must be unconscious and not know it. He sighed, wearily and gratefully, and collapsed.

Battery lights were soon reconnected, and everybody knew that they had holed through. There was no more panic. And, even before the shift-boss had recovered full consciousness, he was walking down the drift toward Station Eleven.

There is no need to enlarge upon the rest of that grim and grisly affair. Level after level was activated; and, since working upward in mines is vastly faster than working downward, the two parties met on the Eighth Level. Half of the men who would otherwise have died were saved, and—much more important from the viewpoint of Uranium, Inc.—the deeper and richer half of the biggest and richest uranium mine in existence, instead of being out of production for a year or more, would be back in full operation in a couple of weeks.

And George Washington Jones, still a trifle shaky from his ordeal, was called into the front office. But before he arrived:

"I'm going to make him Assistant Works Manager," Clancy announced.

"I think not."

"But listen, Mr. Isaacson—please! How do you expect me to build up a staff if you snatch every good man I find away from me?"

"You didn't find him. Birkenfeld did. He was here only on a test. He is going into Department Q."

Clancy, who had opened his mouth to continue his protests, shut it wordlessly. He knew that department Q was—

DEPARTMENT Q.

CHAPTER 15

Costigan was not surprised to see the man he had known as Birkenfeld in Uranium's ornate conference room. He had not expected, however, to see Isaacson. He knew, of course, that Spaceways owned Uranium, Inc., and the planet Eridan, lock, stock, and barrel; but it never entered his modest mind that his case would be of sufficient importance to warrant the personal attention of the Big Noise himself. Hence the sight of that suave and unrevealing face gave the putative Jones a more than temporary qualm. Isaacson was top-bracket stuff, 'way out of his class. Virgil Samms ought to be taking this assignment, but since he wasn't—

But instead of being an inquisition, the meeting was friendly and informal from the start. They complimented him upon the soundness of his judgment and the accuracy of his decisions. They thanked him, both with words and with a considerable sum of expendable credits. They encouraged him to talk about himself, but there was nothing whatever of the star-chamber or of cross-examination. The last question was representative of the whole conference.

"One other thing, Jones, has me slightly baffled," Isaacson said, with a really winning smile. "Since you do not drink, and since you were not in search of feminine . . . er . . . companionship, just why did you go down to Roaring Jack's dive?"

"Two reasons," Jones said, with a somewhat shamefaced grin. "The minor one isn't easy to explain, but . . . well, I hadn't been having an exactly easy time of it on Earth . . . you all know about that, I suppose?"

They knew.

"Well, I was taking a very dim view of things in general, and a good fight would get it out of my system. It always does."

"I see. And the major reason?"

"I knew, of course, that I was on probation. I would have to get promoted, and fast, or stay sunk forever. To get promoted fast, a man can either be enough of a boot-licker to be pulled up from on high, or he can be shoved up by the men he is working with. The best way to get a crowd of hard-rock men to like you is to lick a few of 'em—off hours, of course, and according to Hoyle—and the more of 'em you can lick at once, the better. I'm pretty good at rough-and-tumble brawling, so I gambled that the cops would step in before I got banged up too much. I won."

"I see," Isaacson said again, in an entirely different tone. He did see, now. "The first technique is so universally used that the possibility of the second did not occur to me. Nice work—*very* nice." He turned to the other members of the Board. "This, I believe, concludes the business of the meeting?"

For some reason or other Isaacson nodded slightly as he asked the question; and one by one, as though in concurrence, the others nodded in reply. The meeting broke up. Outside the door, however, the magnate did not go about his own business nor send Jones about his. Instead:

"I would like to show you, if I may, the above-ground part of our Works?"

"My time is yours, sir. I am interested."

It is unnecessary here to go into the details of a Civilization's greatest uranium operation; the storage bins, the grinders, the Wilfley tables and slime tanks, the flotation sluices, the roasters and reducers, the processes of solution and crystallization and recrystallization, of final oxidation and reduction. Suffice it to say that Isaacson showed Jones the whole immensity of Uranium Works Number One. The trip ended on the top floor of the towering Administration Building, in a heavily-screened room containing a desk, a couple of chairs, and a tremendously massive safe.

"Smoke up." Isaacson indicated a package of Jones' favorite brand of cigarettes and lighted a cigar. "You knew that you were under test. I wonder, though, if you knew how much of it was testing?"

"All of it." Jones grinned. "Except for the big blow, of course."

"Of course."

"There were too many possibilities, of too many different kinds, too pat. I might warn you, though—I could have got away clear with that half-million."

"The possibility existed." Surprisingly, Isaacson did not tell him that the trap was more subtle than it had appeared to be. "It was, however, worth the risk. Why didn't you?"

"Because I figure on making more than that, a little later, and I might live longer to spend it."

"Sound thinking, my boy—really sound. Now—you noticed, of course, the vote at the end of the meeting?"

Jones had noticed it; and, although he did not say so, he had been wondering about it ever since. The older man strolled over to the safe and opened it, revealing a single, startlingly small package.

"You passed, unanimously; you are now learning what you have to know. Not that we trust you unreservedly. You will be watched for a long time, and before you can make one false step, you will die."

"That would seem to be good business, sir."

"Glad you look at it that way—we thought you would. You saw the Works. Quite an operation, don't you think?"

"Immense, sir. The biggest thing I ever saw."

"What would you say, then, to the idea of this office being our real headquarters, of that little package there being our real business?" He swung the safe door shut, spun the knob.

"It would have been highly surprising a couple of hours ago." Costigan could not afford to appear stupid, nor to possess too much knowledge. He had to steer an extremely difficult middle course. "After the climax of this build-up, though, it wouldn't seem at all impossible. Or that there were wheels—plenty of 'em!—within wheels."

"Smart!" Isaacson applauded. "And what would you think might be in that package? This room is ray-proof."

"Against anything the Galactic Patrol can swing?"

"Positively."

"Well, then, it *might* be something beginning with the letter" he flicked two fingers, almost invisibly fast, into a T and went on without a break "M, as in morphine."

"Your caution and restraint are commendable. If I had any remaining doubt as to your ability, it is gone." He paused, frowning. As belief in ability increased, that in sincerity lessened. This doubt, this questioning, existed every time a new executive was initiated into the mysteries of Department Q. The Board's judgment was good. They had slipped only twice, and those two errors had been corrected easily enough. The fellow had been warned once; that was enough. He took the plunge. "You will work with the Assistant Works Manager here until you understand the duties of the position. You will be transferred to Tellus as Assistant Works Manager there. Your principal duties will, however, be concerned with Department Q—which you will head up one day if you make good. And, just incidentally, when you go to Tellus, a package like that one in the safe will go with you."

"Oh . . . I see. I'll make good, sir." Jones let Isaacson see his jaw-muscles tighten in resolve. "It may take a little time for me to learn my way around, sir, but I'll learn it."

"I'm sure you will. And now, to go into greater detail . . . ."

*

Virgil Samms had to be sure of his facts. More than that, he had to be able to prove them; not merely to the satisfaction of a law-enforcement officer, but beyond any reasonable doubt of the hardest-headed member of a cynical and skeptical jury. Wherefore Jack Kinnison and Mase Northrop took up the thionite trail at the exact point where, each trip, George Olmstead had had to abandon it; in the atmosphere of Cavenda. And fortunately, not too much preparation was required.

Cavenda was, as has been intimated, a primitive world. Its native people, humanoid in type, had developed a culture approximating in some respects that of the North American Indian at about the time of Columbus, in others that of the ancient Nomads of Araby. Thus a couple of wandering natives, unrecognizable under their dirty stormproof blankets and their scarcely thinner layers of grease and grime, watched impassively, incuriously, while a box floated pendant from its parachute from sky to ground. Mounted upon their uncouth steeds, they followed that box when it was hauled to the white man's village. Unlike many of the other natives, these two did not shuffle into that village, to lean silently against a rock or a wall awaiting their turns to exchange a few hours of simple labor for a container of a new and highly potent beverage. They did, however, keep themselves constantly and minutely informed as to everything these strange, devil-ridden white men did. One of these pseudo-natives wandered off into the wilderness two or three days before the huge thing-which-flies-without-wings left ground; the other immediately afterward.

Thus the departure of the space-ship from Cavenda was recorded, as was its arrival at Eridan. It had been extremely difficult for the Patrol's engineers to devise ways and means of tracing that ship from departure to arrival without exciting suspicion, but it had not proved impossible.

And Jack Kinnison, lounging idly and elegantly in the concourse of Danopolis Spaceport, seethed imperceptibly. Having swallowed a tiny Service Special capsule that morning, he knew that he had been under continuous spy-ray inspection for over two hours. He had not given himself away—practically everybody screened their inside coat pockets and hip pockets, and the cat-whisker lead from Lens to leg simply could not be seen—but for all the good they were doing him his ultra-instruments might just as well have been back on Tellus.

"Mase!" he sent, with no change whatever in the vapid expression then on his face. "I'm still covered. Are you?"

"Covered!" the answering thought was a snort. "They're covering me like water covers a submarine!"

"Keep tuned. I'll call Spud. Spud!"

"Come in, Jack." Conway Costigan, alone now in the sanctum of Department Q, did not seem to be busy, but he was.

"That red herring they told us to drag across the trail was too damned red. They must be touchier than fulminate to spy-work on their armed forces—neither Mase nor I can do a lick of work. Anybody else covered?"

"No. All clear."

"Good. Tell them the zwilnik blockers took us out."

"I'll do that. Distance only, or is somebody on your tail?"

"Somebody; and I mean *some body*. A slick chick with a classy chassis; a blonde, with great, big come-hither eyes. Too good to be true; especially the falsies. Wiring, my friend—and I haven't been able to get a close look, but I wouldn't wonder if her nostrils had a skillionth of a whillimeter too much expansion. I want a spy-ray op—is it safe to use Fred?" Kinnison referred to the grizzled engineer now puttering about in a certain space-ship; not the one in which he and Northrop had come to Eridan.

"Definitely not. I can do it myself and still stay very much in character . . . . No, I don't know her. Not surprising, of course, since the policy here is never to let the right hand know what the left is doing. How about you, Mase? Have you got a little girl-friend, too?"

"Yea, verily, brother; but not little. More my size." Northrop pointed out a tall, trim brunette, strolling along with the effortless, consciously unconscious poise of the professional model.

"Hm . . . m . . . m. I don't know her, either," Costigan reported, "but both of them are wearing four-inch spy-ray blocks and are probably wired up like Christmas trees. By inference, P-gun proof. I can't penetrate, of course, but maybe I can get a viewpoint . . . . You're right, Jack. Nostrils plugged. Anti-thionite, anti-Vee-Two, anti-everything. In fact, anti-social. I'll spread their pictures around and see if anybody knows either of them."

He did so, and over a hundred of the Patrol's shrewdest operatives—upon this occasion North America had invaded Eridan in force—studied and thought. No one knew the tall brunette, but—

"I know the blonde." This was Parker of Washington, a Service ace for twenty five years. "'Hell-cat Hazel' DeForce, the hardest-boiled babe unhung. Watch your step around her; she's just as handy with a knife and knock-out drops as she is with a gun."

"Thanks, Parker. I've heard of her." Costigan was thinking fast. "Free-lance. No way of telling who she's working for at the moment." This was a statement, not a question.

"Only that it would have to be somebody with a lot of money. Her price is high. That all?"

"That's all, fellows." Then, to Jack and Northrop: "My thought is that you two guys are completely out-classed—out-weighed, out-numbered, out-manned, and out-gunned. Undressed, you're sitting ducks; and if you put out any screens it'll crystallize their suspicions and they'll grab you right then—or maybe even knock you off. You'd better get out of here at full blast; you can't do any more good here, the way things are."

"Sure we can!" Kinnison protested. "You wanted a diversion, didn't you?"

"Yes, but you already . . . ."

"What we've done already isn't a patch to what we can do next. We can set up such a diversion that the boys can walk right on the thionite-carrier's heels without anybody paying any attention. By the way, you don't know yet who is going to carry it, do you?"

"No. No penetration at all."

"You soon will, bucko. Watch our smoke!"

"What do you think you're going to do?" Costigan demanded, sharply.

"This." Jack explained. "And don't try to say no. We're on our own, you know."

"We . . . l . . . l . . . it sounds good, and if you can pull it off it will help no end. Go ahead."

The demurely luscious blonde stared disconsolately at the bulletin board, upon which another thirty minutes was being added to the time of arrival of a ship already three hours late. She picked up a book, glanced at its cover, put it down. Her hand moved toward a magazine, drew back, dropped idly into her lap. She sighed, stifled a yawn prettily, leaned backward in her seat—in such a position, Jack noticed, that he could not see into her nostrils—and closed her eyes. And Jack Kinnison, coming visibly to a decision, sat down beside her.

"Pardon me, miss, but I feel just like you look. Can you tell me why convention decrees that two people, stuck in this concourse by arrivals that nobody knows when will arrive, have got to suffer alone when they could have so much more fun suffering together?"

The girl's eyes opened slowly; she was neither startled, nor afraid, nor—it seemed—even interested. In fact, she gazed at him with so much disinterest and for so long a time that he began to wonder—was she going to play sweet and innocent to the end?

"Yes, conventions *are* stupid, sometimes," she admitted finally, her lovely lips curving into the beginnings of a smile. Her voice, low and sweet, matched perfectly the rest of her charming self. "After all, perfectly nice people do meet informally on shipboard; why not in concourses?"

"Why not, indeed? And I'm perfectly nice people, I assure you. Willi Borden is the name. My friends call me Bill. And you?"

"Beatrice Bailey; Bee for short. Tell me what you like, and we'll talk about it."

"Why talk, when we could be eating? I'm with a guy. He's out on the field somewhere—a big bruiser with a pencil-stripe black mustache. Maybe you saw him talking to me a while back?"

"I think so, now that you mention him. Too big—*much* too big." The girl spoke carelessly, but managed to make it very clear that Jack Kinnison was just exactly the right size. "Why?"

"I told him I'd have supper with him. Shall we hunt him up and eat together?"

"Why not? Is he alone?"

"He was, when I saw him last." Although Jack knew exactly where Northrop was, and who was with him, he had to play safe; he did not know how much this "Bee Bailey" really knew. "He knows a lot more people around here than I do, though, so maybe he isn't now. Let me carry some of that plunder?"

"You might carry those books—thanks. But the field is so *big*—how do you expect to find him? Or do you know where he is?"

"Uh-uh!" he denied, vigorously. This was the critical moment. She certainly wasn't suspicious—yet—but she was showing signs of not wanting to go out there, and if she refused to go . . . . "To be honest, I don't care whether I find him or not—the idea of ditching him appeals to me more and more. So how about this? We'll dash out to the third dock—just so I won't have to actually lie about looking for him—and dash right back here. Or wouldn't you rather have it a twosome?"

"I refuse to answer, by advice of counsel." The girl laughed gaily, but her answer was plain enough.

Their rate of progress was by no means a dash, and Kinnison did not look—with his eyes—for Northrop. Nevertheless, just south of the third dock, the two young couples met.

"My cousin, Grace James," Northrop said, without a tremor or a quiver. "Wild Willi Borden, Grace—usually called Baldy on account of his hair."

The girls were introduced; each vouchsafing the other a completely meaningless smile and a colorlessly conventional word of greeting. Were they, in fact as in seeming, total strangers? Or were they in fact working together as closely as were the two young Lensmen themselves? If that was acting, it was a beautiful job; neither man could detect the slightest flaw in the performance of either girl.

"Whither away, pilot?" Jack allowed no lapse of time. "You know all the places around here. Lead us to a good one."

"This way, my old and fragrant fruit." Northrop led off with a flourish, and again Jack tensed. The walk led straight past the third-class, apparently deserted dock of which a certain ultra-fast vessel was the only occupant. If nothing happened for fifteen more seconds . . . .

Nothing did. The laughing, chattering four came abreast of the portal. The door swung open and the Lensmen went into action.

They did not like to strong-arm women, but speed was their first consideration, with safety a close second; and it is impossible for a man to make speed while carrying a conscious, lithe, strong, heavily-armed woman in such a position that she cannot use fists, feet, teeth, gun or knife. An unconscious woman, on the other hand, can be carried easily and safely enough. Therefore Jack spun his partner around, forced both of her hands into one of his. The free hand flashed upward toward the neck; a hard finger pressed unerringly against a nerve; the girl went limp. The two victims were hustled aboard and the space-ship, surrounded now by full-coverage screen, took off.

Kinnison paid no attention to ship or course; orders had been given long since and would be carried out. Instead, he lowered his burden to the floor, spread her out flat, and sought out and removed item after item of wiring, apparatus, and offensive and defensive armament. He did not undress her—quite—but he made completely certain that the only weapons left to the young lady were those with which Nature had endowed her. And, Northrop having taken care of his alleged cousin with equal thoroughness, the small-arms were sent out and both doors of the room were securely locked.

"Now, Hell-cat Hazel DeForce," Kinnison said, conversationally, "You can snap out of it any time—you've been back to normal for at least two minutes. You've found out that your famous sex-appeal won't work. There's nothing loose you can grab, and you're too smart an operator to tackle me bare-handed. Who's the captain of your team—you or the clothes-horse?"

"Clothes-horse!" the statuesque brunette exclaimed, but her protests were drowned out. The blonde could—and did—talk louder, faster, and rougher.

"Do you think you can get away with *this?*" she demanded. "Why, you . . . " and the unexpurgated, trenchant, brilliantly detailed characterization could have seared its way through four-ply asbestos. "And just what do you think you're going to do with me?"

"As to the first, I think so," Kinnison replied, ignoring the deep-space verbiage. "As to the second—as of now I don't know. What would you do if our situations were reversed?"

"I'd blast you to a cinder—or else take a knife and . . . ."

"Hazel!" the brunette cautioned sharply. "Careful! You'll touch them off and they'll . . . ."

"Shut up, Jane! They won't hurt us any more than they have already; it's psychologically impossible. Isn't that true, copper?" Hazel lighted a cigarette, inhaled deeply, and blew a cloud of smoke at Kinnison's face.

"Pretty much so, I guess," the Lensman admitted, frankly enough, "but we can put you away for the rest of your lives."

"Space-happy? Or do you think I am?" she sneered. "What would you use for a case? We're as safe as if we were in God's pocket. And besides, our positions *will* be reversed pretty quick. You may not know it, but the fastest ships in space are chasing us, right now."

"For once you're wrong. We've got plenty of legs ourselves and we're blasting for rendezvous with a task-force. But enough of this chatter. I want to know what job you're on and why you picked on us. Give."

"Oh, does 'oo?" Hazel cooed, venomously. "Come and sit on mama's lap, itty bitty soldier boy, and she'll tell you everything you want to know."

Both Lensmen probed, then, with everything they had, but learned nothing of value. The women did not know what the Patrolmen were trying to do, but they were so intensely hostile that their mental blocks, unconscious although they were, were as effective as full-driven thought screens against the most insidious approaches the men could make.

"Anything in their hand-bags, Mase?" Jack asked, finally.

"I'll look . . . . Nothing much—just this," and the very tonelessness of Northrop's voice made Jack look up quickly.

"Just a letter from the boy-friend." Hazel shrugged her shoulders. "Nothing hot—not even warm—go ahead and read it."

"Not interested in what it says, but it might be smart to develop it, envelope and all, for invisible ink and whatnot." He did so, deeming it a worth-while expenditure of time. He already knew what the hidden message was; but no one not of the Patrol should know that no transmission of intelligence, however coded or garbled or disguised or by whatever means sent, could be concealed from any wearer of Arisia's Lens.

"Listen, Hazel," Kinnison said, holding up the now slightly stained paper. "'Three six two'—that's you, I suppose, and you're the squad leader—'Men mentioned previously being investigated stop assign three nine eight'—that must be you, Jane—'and make acquaintance stop if no further instructions received by eighteen hundred hours liquidate immediately stop party one'."

The blond operative lost for the first time her brazen control. "Why . . . that code is *unbreakable!*" she gasped.

"Wrong again, Gentle Alice. Some of us are specialists." He directed a thought at Northrop. "This changes things slightly, Mase. I was going to turn them loose, but now I don't know. Better we take it up with the boss, don't you think?"

"Pos-i-*tive*-ly!"

Samms was called, and considered the matter for approximately one minute. "Your first idea was right, Jack. Let them go. The message may be helpful and informative, but the women would not. They know nothing. Congratulations, boys, on the complete success of Operation Red Herring."

"Ouch!" Jack grimaced mentally to his partner after the First Lensman had cut off. "They know enough to be in on bumping you and me off, but that ain't important, says he!"

"And it ain't, bub," Northrop grinned back. "Moderately so, maybe, if they had got us, but not at all so now they can't. The Lensmen have landed and the situation is well in hand. It is written. Selah."

"Check. Let's wrap it up." Jack turned to the blonde. "Come on, Hazel. Out. Number Four lifeboat. Do you want to come peaceably or shall I work on your neck again?"

"You could think of other places that would be more fun." She got up and stared directly into his eyes, her lip curling. "That is, if you were a *man* instead of a sublimated Boy Scout."

Kinnison, without a word, wheeled and unlocked a door. Hazel swaggered forward, but the taller girl hung back. "Are you sure there's air—and they'll pick us up? Maybe they're going to make us breathe space . . . ."

"Huh? They haven't got the guts," Hazel sneered. "Come on, Jane. Number Four, you said, darling?"

She led the way. Kinnison opened the portal. Jane hurried aboard, but Hazel paused and held out her arms.

"Aren't you even going to kiss mama goodbye, baby boy?" she taunted.

"Better not waste much more time. We blow this boat, sealed or open, in fifteen seconds." By what effort Kinnison held his voice level and expressionless, he hoped the wench would never know.

She looked at him, started to say something, looked again. She had gone just about as far as it was safe to go. She stepped into the boat and reached for the lever. And as the valve was swinging smoothly shut the men heard a tinkling laugh, reminiscent of icicles breaking against steel bells.

"Hell's—Brazen—Hinges!" Kinnison wiped his forehead as the lifeboat shot away. Hazel was something brand new to him; a phenomenon with which none of his education, training, or experience had equipped him to cope. "I've heard about the guy who got hold of a tiger by the tail, but . . . ." His thought expired on a wondering, confused note.

"Yeah." Northrop was in no better case. "We won—technically—I guess—or did we? That was a God-awful drubbing we took, mister."

"Well, we got away alive, anyway . . . . We'll tell Parker his dope is correct to the proverbial twenty decimals. And now that we've escaped, let's call Spud and see how things came out."

And Costigan-Jones assured them that everything had come out very well indeed. The shipment of thionite had been followed without any difficulty at all, from the space-ship clear through to Jones' own office, and it reposed now in Department Q's own safe, under Jones' personal watch and ward. The pressure had lightened tremendously, just as Kinnison and Northrop had thought it would, when they set up their diversion. Costigan listened impassively to the whole story.

"Now *should* I have shot her, or not?" Jack demanded. "Not whether I *could* have or not—I couldn't—but *should* I have, Spud?"

"I don't know." Costigan thought for minutes. "I don't think so. No—not in cold blood. I couldn't have, either, and wouldn't if I could. It wouldn't be worth it. Somebody will shoot her some day, but not one of us—unless, of course, it's in a fight."

"Thanks, Spud; that makes me feel better. Off."

Costigan-Jones' desk was already clear, since there was little or no paper-work connected with his position in Department Q. Hence his preparations for departure were few and simple. He merely opened the safe, stuck the package into his pocket, closed and locked the safe, and took a company ground-car to the spaceport.

Nor was there any more formality about his leaving the planet. Eridan had, of course, a Customs frontier of sorts; but since Uranium Inc. owned Eridan in fee simple, its Customs paid no attention whatever to company ships or to low-number, gold-badge company men. Nor did Jones need ticket, passport, or visa. Company men rode company ships to and from company plants, wherever situated, without let or hindrance. Thus, wearing the aura of power of his new position—and Gold Badge Number Thirty Eight—George W. Jones was whisked out to the uranium ship and was shown to his cabin.

Nor was it surprising that the trip from Eridan to Earth was completely without incident. This was an ordinary freighter, hauling uranium on a routine flight. Her cargo was valuable, of course—the sine qua non of inter-stellar trade—but in no sense precious. Not pirate-bait, by any means. And only two men knew that this flight was in any whit different from the one which had preceded it or the one which would follow it. If this ship was escorted or guarded the fact was not apparent: and no Patrol vessel came nearer to it than four detets—Virgil Samms and Roderick Kinnison saw to that.

The voyage, however, was not tedious. Jones was busy every minute. In fact, there were scarcely minutes enough in which to assimilate the material which Isaacson had given him—the layouts, flow-sheets, and organization charts of Works Number Eighteen, on Tellus.

And upon arrival at the private spaceport which was an integral part of Works Number Eighteen, Jones was not surprised (he knew more now than he had known a few weeks before; and infinitely more than the man on the street) to learn that the Customs men of this particular North American Port of Entry were just as complaisant as were those of Eridan. They did not bother even to count the boxes, to say nothing of inspecting them. They stamped the ship's papers without either reading or checking them. They made a perfunctory search, it is true, of crewmen and quarters, but a low number gold badge was still a magic talisman. Unquestioned, sacrosanct, he and his baggage were escorted to the ground-car first in line.

"Administration Building," Jones-Costigan told the hacker, and that was that.

CHAPTER 16

It has been said that the basic drive of the Eddorians was a lust for power; a thought which should be elucidated and perhaps slightly modified. Their warrings, their strifes, their internecine intrigues and connivings were inevitable because of the tremendousness and capability—and the limitations—of their minds. Not enough *could* occur upon any one planet to keep such minds as theirs even partially occupied; and, unlike the Arisians, they could not satiate themselves in a static philosophical study of the infinite possibilities of the Cosmic All. They had to be *doing* something; or, better yet, making other and lesser beings do things to make the physical universe conform to their idea of what a universe should be.

Their first care was to set up the various echelons of control. The second echelon, immediately below the Masters, was of course the most important, and after a survey of both galaxies they decided to give this high honor to the Ploorans. Ploor, as is now well known, was a planet of a sun so variable that all Plooran life had to undergo radical cyclical changes in physical form in order to live through the tremendous climatic changes involved in its every year. Physical form, however, meant nothing to the Eddorians. Since no other planet even remotely like theirs existed in this, our normal plenum, physiques like theirs would be impossible; and the Plooran mentality left very little to be desired.

In the third echelon there were many different races, among which the frigid-blooded, poison-breathing Eich were perhaps the most efficient and most callous; and in the fourth there were millions upon millions of entities representing thousands upon thousands of widely-variant races.

Thus, at the pinpoint in history represented by the time of Virgil Samms and Roderick Kinnison, the Eddorians were busy; and if such a word can be used, happy. Gharlane of Eddore, second in authority only to the All-Highest, His Ultimate Supremacy himself, paid little attention to any one planet or to any one race. Even such a mind as his, when directing the affairs of twenty million and then sixty million and then a hundred million worlds, can do so only in broad, and not in fine.

And thus the reports which were now flooding in to Gharlane in a constantly increasing stream concerned classes and groups of worlds, and solar systems, and galactic regions. A planet might perhaps be mentioned as representative of a class, but no individual entity lower than a Plooran was named or discussed. Gharlane analyzed those tremendous reports; collated, digested, compared, and reconciled them; determined trends and tendencies and most probable resultants. Gharlane issued orders, the carrying out of which would make an entire galactic region fit more and ever more exactly into the Great Plan.

But, as has been pointed out, there was one flaw inherent in the Boskonian system. Underlings, then as now, were prone to gloss over their own mistakes, to cover up their own incompetences. Thus, since he had no reason to inquire specifically, Gharlane did not know that anything whatever had gone amiss on Sol Three, the pestiferous planet which had formerly caused him more trouble than all the rest of his worlds combined.

After the fact, it is easy to say that he should have continued his personal supervision of Earth, but can that view be defended? Egotistical, self-confident, arrogant, Gharlane *knew* that he had finally whipped Tellus into line. It was the same now as any other planet of its class. And even had he thought it worth while to make such a glaring exception, would not the fused Elders of Arisia have intervened?

Be those things as they may, Gharlane did not know that the new-born Galactic Patrol had been successful in defending Triplanetary's Hill against the Black Fleet. Nor did the Plooran Assistant Director in charge. Nor did any member of that dreadful group of Eich which was even then calling itself the Council of Boskone. The highest-ranking Boskonian who knew of the fiasco, calmly confident of his own ability, had not considered this minor reverse of sufficient importance to report to his immediate superior. He had already taken steps to correct the condition. In fact, as matters now stood, the thing was more fortunate than otherwise, in that it would lull the Patrol into believing themselves in a position of superiority—a belief which would, at election time, prove fatal.

This being, human to the limit of classification except for a faint but unmistakable blue coloration, had been closeted with Senator Morgan for a matter of two hours.

"In the matters covered, your reports have been complete and conclusive," the visitor said finally, "but you have not reported on the Lens."

"Purposely. We are investigating it, but any report based upon our present knowledge would be partial and inconclusive."

"I see. Commendable enough, usually. News of this phenomenon has, however, gone farther and higher than you think and I have been ordered to take cognizance of it; to decide whether or not to handle it myself."

"I am thoroughly capable of . . . ."

"I will decide that, not you." Morgan subsided. "A partial report is therefore in order. Go ahead."

"According to the procedure submitted and approved, a Lensman was taken alive. Since the Lens has telepathic properties, and hence is presumably operative at great distances, the operation was carried out in the shortest possible time. The Lens, immediately upon removal from the Patrolman's arm, ceased to radiate and the operative who held the thing died. It was then applied by force to four other men—workers, these, of no importance. All four died, thus obviating all possibility of coincidence. An attempt was made to analyze a fragment of the active material, without success. It seemed to be completely inert. Neither was it affected by electrical discharges or by sub-atomic bombardment, nor by any temperatures available. Meanwhile, the man was of course being questioned, under truth-drug and beams. His mind denied any knowledge of the nature of the Lens; a thing which I am rather inclined to believe. His mind adhered to the belief that he obtained the Lens upon the planet Arisia. I am offering for your consideration my opinion that the high-ranking officers of the Patrol are using hypnotism to conceal the real source of the Lens."

"Your opinion is accepted for consideration."

"The man died during examination. Two minutes after his death his Lens disappeared."

"Disappeared? What do you mean? Flew away? Vanished? Was stolen? Disintegrated? Or what?"

"No. More like evaporation or sublimation, except that there was no gradual diminution in volume, and there was no detectable residue, either solid, liquid, or gaseous. The platinum-alloy bracelet remained intact."

"And then?"

"The Patrol attacked in force and our expedition was destroyed."

"You are sure of these observational facts?"

"I have the detailed records. Would you like to see them?"

"Send them to my office. I hereby relieve you of all responsibility in the matter of the Lens. In fact, even I may decide to refer it to a higher echelon. Have you any other material, not necessarily facts, which may have bearing?"

"None," Morgan replied; and it was just as well for Virgilia Samms' continued well-being that the Senator did not think it worth while to mention the traceless disappearance of his Number One secretary and a few members of a certain unsavory gang. To his way of thinking, the Lens was not involved, except perhaps very incidentally. Herkimer, in spite of advice and orders, had probably got rough with the girl, and Samms' mob had rubbed him out. Served him right.

"I have no criticism of any phase of your work. You are doing a particularly nice job on thionite. You are of course observing all specified precautions as to key personnel?"

"Certainly. Thorough testing and unremitting watchfulness. Our Mr. Isaacson is about to promote a man who has proved very capable. Would you like to observe the proceedings?"

"No. I have no time for minor matters. Your results have been satisfactory. Keep them that way. Good-bye." The visitor strode out.

Morgan reached for a switch, then drew his hand back. No. He would like to sit in on the forthcoming interview, but he did not have the time. He had tested Olmstead repeatedly and personally; he knew what the man was. It was Isaacson's department; let Isaacson handle it. He himself must work full time at the job which only he could handle; the Nationalists must and would win this forthcoming election.

And in the office of the president of Interstellar Spaceways, Isaacson got up and shook hands with George Olmstead.

"I called you in for two reasons. First, in reply to your message that you were ready for a bigger job. What makes you think that any such are available?"

"Do I need to answer that?"

"Perhaps not . . . no." The magnate smiled quietly. Morgan was right; this man could not be accused of being dumb. "There is such a job, you are ready for it, and you have your successor trained in the work of harvesting. Second, why did you cut down, instead of increasing as ordered, the weight of broadleaf per trip? This, Olmstead, is really serious."

"I explained why. It would have been more serious the other way. Didn't you believe I knew what I was talking about?"

"Your reasoning may have been distorted in transmittal. I want it straight from you."

"Very well. It isn't smart to be greedy. There's a point at which something that has been merely a nuisance becomes a thing that *has* to be wiped out. Since I didn't want to be in that ferry when the Patrol blows it out of the ether, I cut down the take, and I advise you to keep it down. What you're getting now is a lot more than you ever got before, and a *hell* of a lot more than none at all. Think it over."

"I see. Upon what basis did you arrive at the figure you established?"

"Pure guesswork, nothing else. I guessed that about three hundred percent of the previous average per month ought to satisfy anybody who wasn't too greedy to have good sense, and that more than that would ring a loud, clear bell right where we don't want any noise made. So I cut it down to three, and advised Ferdy either to keep it at three or quit while he was still all in one piece."

"You exceeded your authority . . . and were insubordinate . . . but it wouldn't surprise me if you were right. You are certainly right in principle, and the poundage can be determined by statistical and psychological analysis. But in the meantime, there is tremendous pressure for increased production."

"I know it. Pressure be damned. My dear cousin Virgil is, as you already know, a crackpot. He is visionary, idealistic, full of sweet and beautiful concepts of what the universe would be like if there weren't so many people like you and me in it; but don't ever make the mistake of writing him off as anybody's fool. And you know, probably better than I do, what Rod Kinnison is like. If I were you I'd tell whoever is doing the screaming to shut their damn mouths before they get their teeth kicked down their throats."

"I'm very much inclined to take your advice. And now as to this proposed promotion. You are of course familiar in a general way with our operation at Northport?"

"I could scarcely help knowing *something* about the biggest uranium works on Earth. However, I am not well enough qualified in detail to make a good technical executive."

"Nor is it necessary. Our thought is to make you a key man in a new and increasingly important branch of the business, known as Department Q. It is concerned neither with production nor with uranium."

"Q as in 'quiet', eh? I'm listening with both ears. What duties would be connected with this . . . er . . . position? What would I really do?"

Two pairs of hard eyes locked and held, staring yieldlessly into each other's depths.

"You would not be unduly surprised to learn that substances other than uranium occasionally reach Northport?"

"Not *too* surprised, no," Olmstead replied dryly. "What would I do with it?"

"We need not go into that here or now. I offer you the position."

"I accept it."

"Very well. I will take you to Northport, and we will continue our talk en route."

And in a spy-ray-proof, sound-proof compartment of a Spaceways-owned stratoliner they did so.

"Just for my information, Mr. Isaacson, how many predecessors have I had on this particular job, and what happened to them? The Patrol get them?"

"Two. No; we have not been able to find any evidence that the Samms crowd has any suspicion of us. Both were too small for the job; neither could handle personnel. One got funny ideas, the other couldn't stand the strain. If you don't get funny ideas, and don't crack up, you will make out in a big—and I mean *really* big—way."

"If I do either I'll be more than somewhat surprised." Olmstead's features set themselves into a mirthless, uncompromising, somehow bitter grin.

"So will I." Isaacson agreed.

He knew what this man was, and just how case-hardened he was. He knew that he had fought Morgan himself to a scoreless tie after twisting Herkimer—and he was no soft touch—into a pretzel in nothing flat. At the thought of the secretary, so recently and so mysteriously vanished, the magnate's mind left for a moment the matter in hand. What was at the bottom of that affair—the Lens or the woman? Or both? If he were in Morgan's shoes . . . but he wasn't. He had enough grief of his own, without worrying about any of Morgan's stinkeroos. He studied Olmstead's inscrutable, subtly sneering smile and knew that he had made a wise decision.

"I gather that I am going to be one of the main links in the primary chain of deliveries. What's the technique, and how do I cover up?"

"Technique first. You go fishing. You are an expert at that, I believe?"

"You might say so. I won't have to do any faking there."

"Some week-end soon, and *every* week-end later on, we hope, you will indulge in your favorite sport at some lake or other. You will take the customary solid and liquid refreshments along in a lunch-box. When you have finished eating you will toss the lunch-box overboard."

"That all?"

"That's all."

"The lunch-box, then, will be slightly special?"

"More or less, although it will look ordinary enough. Now as to the cover-up. How would 'Director of Research' sound?"

"I don't know. Depends on what the researchers are doing. Before I became an engineer I was a pure scientist of sorts; but that was quite a while ago and I was never a specialist."

"That is one reason why I think you will do. We have plenty of specialists—too many, I often think. They dash off in all directions, without rhyme or reason. What we want is a man with enough scientific training to know in general what is going on, but what he will need mostly is hard common sense, and enough ability—mental force, you might call it—to hold the specialists down to earth and make them pull together. If you can do it—and if I didn't think you could I wouldn't be talking to you—the whole force will know that you are earning your pay; just as we could not hide the fact that your two predecessors weren't."

"Put that way it sounds good. I wouldn't wonder if I could handle it."

The conversation went on, but the rest of it is of little importance here. The plane landed. Isaacson introduced the new Director of Research to Works Manager Rand, who in turn introduced him to a few of his scientists and to the svelte and spectacular red-head who was to be his private secretary.

It was clear from the first that the Research Department was not going to be an easy one to manage. The top men were defiant, the middle ranks were sullen, the smaller fry were apprehensive as well as sullen. The secretary flaunted chips on both shapely shoulders. Men and women alike expected the application of the old wheeze "a new broom sweeps clean" for the third time in scarcely twice that many months, and they were defying him to do his worst. Wherefore they were very much surprised when the new boss did nothing whatever for two solid weeks except read reports and get acquainted with his department.

"How d'ya like your new boss, May?" another secretary asked, during a break.

"Oh, not too bad . . . I guess." May's tone was full of reservations. "He's quiet—sort of reserved—no passes or anything like that—it'd be funny if I finally got a boss that had something on the ball, wouldn't it? But you know what, Molly?" The red-head giggled suddenly. "I had a camera-fiend first, you know, with a million credits' worth of stereo-cams and such stuff, and then a golf-nut. I wonder what this Dr. Olmstead does with his spare cash?"

"You'll find out, dearie, no doubt." Molly's tone gave the words a meaning slightly different from the semantic one of their arrangement.

"I intend to, Molly—I *fully* intend to." May's meaning, too, was not expressed exactly by the sequence of words used. "It must be tough, a boss's life. Having to sit at a desk or be in conference six or seven hours a day—when he isn't playing around somewhere—for a measly thousand credits or so a month. How do they get that way?"

"You said it, May. You *really* said it. But we'll get ours, huh?"

Time went on. George Olmstead studied reports, and more reports. He read one, and re-read it, frowning. He compared it minutely with another; then sent red-headed May to hunt up one which had been turned in a couple of weeks before. He took them home that evening, and in the morning he punched three buttons. Three stiffly polite young men obeyed his summons.

"Good morning, Doctor Olmstead."

"Morning, boys. I'm not up on the fundamental theory of any one of these three reports, but if you combine this, and this, and this," indicating heavily-penciled sections of the three documents, "would you, or would you not, be able to work out a process that would do away with about three-quarters of the final purification and separation processes?"

They did not know. It had not been the business of any one of them, or of all them collectively, to find out.

THE LENSMAN

"I'm making it your business as of now. Drop whatever you're doing, put your heads together, and find out. Theory first, then a small-scale laboratory experiment. Then come back here on the double."

"Yes, sir," and in a few days they were back.

"Does it work?"

"In theory it should, sir, and on a laboratory scale it does." The three young men were, if possible, even stiffer than before. It was not the first time, nor would it be the last, that a Director of Research would seize credit for work which he was not capable of doing.

"Good. Miss Reed, get me Rand . . . Rand? Olmstead. Three of my boys have just hatched out something that may be worth quite a few million credits a year to us . . . . Me? Hell, no! Talk to them. I can't understand any one of the three parts of it, to say nothing of inventing it. I want you to give 'em a class AAA priority on the pilot plant, as of right now. If they can develop it, and I'm betting they can, I'm going to put their pictures in the Northport News and give 'em a couple of thousand credits apiece and a couple of weeks vacation to spend it in . . . . Yeah, I'll send 'em in." He turned to the flabbergasted three. "Take your dope in to Rand—now. Show him what you've got; then tear into that pilot plant."

And, a little later, Molly and May again met in the powder room.

"So your new boss is a *fisherman!*" Molly snickered. "And they say he paid over *two hundred credits* for a *reel!* You were right, May; a boss's life must be mighty hard to take. And he sits around more and does less, they say, than any other exec in the plant."

"*Who* says so, the dirty, sneaking liars?" the red-head blazed, completely unaware that she had reversed her former position. "And even if it *was* so, which it isn't, he can do more work sitting perfectly still than any other boss in the whole Works can do tearing around at forty parsecs a minute, so there!"

George Olmstead was earning his salary.

His position was fully consolidated when, a few days later, a tremor of excitement ran through the Research Department. "Heads up, everybody! Mr. Isaacson—himself—is coming—*here!* What for, I wonder? Y'don't s'pose he's going to take the Old Man away from us already, do you?"

He came. He went through, for the first time, the entire department. He observed minutely, and he understood what he saw.

Olmstead led the Big Boss into his private office and flipped the switch which supposedly rendered that sanctum proof against any and all forms of spying, eavesdropping, intrusion, and communication. It did not, however, close the deeper, subtler channels which the Lensmen used.

"Good work, George. So *damned* good that I'm going to have to take you out of Department Q entirely and make you Works Manager of our new plant on Vegia. Have you got a man you can break in to take your place here?"

"Including Department Q? No." Although Olmstead did not show it, he was disappointed at hearing the word "Vegia". He had been aiming much higher than that—at the secret planet of the Boskonian Armed Forces, no less—but there might still be enough time to win a transfer there.

"Excluding. I've got another good man here now for that. Jones. Not heavy enough, though, for Vegia."

"In that case, yes. Dr. Whitworth, one of the boys who worked out the new process. It'll take a little time, though. Three weeks minimum."

"Three weeks it is. Today's Friday. You've got things in shape, haven't you, so that you can take the week-end off?"

"I was figuring on it. I'm not going where I thought I was, though, I imagine."

"Probably not. Lake Chesuncook, on Route 273. Rough country, and the hotel is something less than fourth rate, but the fishing can't be beat."

"I'm glad of that. When I fish, I like to catch something."

"It would smell if you didn't. They stock lunch-boxes in the cafeteria, you know. Have your girl get you one, full of sandwiches and stuff. Start early this afternoon, as soon as you can after I leave. Be sure and see Jones, with your lunch-box, before you leave. Good-bye."

"Miss Reed, please send Whitworth in. Then skip down to the cafeteria and get me a lunch-box. Sandwiches and a thermos of coffee. Provender suitable for a wet and hungry fisherman."

"Yes, *sir*!" There were no chips now; the red-head's boss was the top ace of the whole plant.

"Hi, Ned. Take the throne." Olmstead waved his hand at the now vacant chair behind the big desk. "Hold it down 'til I get back. Monday, maybe."

"Going fishing, huh?" Gone was all trace of stiffness, of reserve, of unfriendliness. "You big, lucky stiff!"

"Well, my brilliant young squirt, maybe you'll get old and fat enough to go fishing yourself some day. Who knows? 'Bye."

Lunch-box in hand and encumbered with tackle, Olmstead walked blithely along the corridor to the office of Assistant Works Manager Jones. While he had not known just what to expect, he was not surprised to see a lunch-box exactly like his own upon the side-table. He placed his box beside it.

"Hi, Olmstead." By no slightest flicker of expression did either Lensman step out of character. "Shoving off early?"

"Yeah. Dropped by to let the Head Office know I won't be in 'til Monday."

"O.K. So'm I, but more speed for me. Chemquassabamticook Lake."

"Do you pronounce that or sneeze it? But have fun, my boy. I'm combining business with pleasure, though—breaking in Whitworth on my job. That Fairplay thing is going to break in about an hour, and it'll scare the pants off of him. But it'll keep until Monday, anyway, and if he handles it right he's just about in."

Jones grinned. "A bit brutal, perhaps, but a sure way to find out. 'Bye."

"So long." Olmstead strolled out, nonchalantly picking up the wrong lunch box on the way, and left the building.

He ordered his Dillingham, and tossed the lunch-box aboard as carelessly as though it did not contain an unknown number of millions of credits' worth of clear-quill, uncut thionite.

"I hope you have a nice week-end, sir," the yard-man said, as he helped stow baggage and tackle.

"Thanks, Otto. I'll bring you a couple of fish Monday, if I catch that many," and it should be said in passing that he brought them. Lensmen keep their promises, under whatever circumstances or however lightly given.

It being mid-afternoon of Friday, the traffic was already heavy. Northport was not a metropolis, of course; but on the other hand it did not have metropolitan multi-tiered, one-way, non-intersecting streets. But Olmstead was in no hurry. He inched his spectacular mount—it was a violently iridescent chrome green in color, with highly polished chromium gingerbread wherever there was any excuse for gingerbread to be—across the city and into the north-bound side of the superhighway. Even then, he did not hurry. He wanted to hit the inspection station at the edge of the Preserve at dusk. Ninety miles an hour would do it. He worked his way into the ninety-mile lane and became motionless relative to the other vehicles on the strip.

It was a peculiar sensation; it seemed as though the cars themselves were stationary, with the pavement flowing backward beneath them. There was no passing, no weaving, no cutting in and out. Only occasionally would the formation be broken as a car would shift almost imperceptibly to one side or the other; speeding up or slowing down to match the assigned speed of the neighboring way.

The afternoon was bright and clear, neither too hot nor too cold. Olmstead enjoyed his drive thoroughly, and arrived at the turn-off right on schedule. Leaving the wide, smooth way, he slowed down abruptly; even a Dillingham Super-Sporter could not make speed on the narrow, rough, and hilly road to Chesuncook Lake.

At dusk he reached the Post. Instead of stopping on the pavement he pulled off the road, got out, stretched hugely, and took a few drum-major's steps to take the kinks out of his legs.

"A lot of road, eh?" the smartly-uniformed trooper remarked. "No guns?"

"No guns." Olmstead opened up for inspection. "From Northport. Funny, isn't it, how hard it is to stop, even when you aren't in any particular hurry? Guess I'll eat now—join me in a sandwich and some hot coffee or a cold lemon sour or cherry soda?"

"I've got my own supper, thanks; I was just going to eat. But did you say a *cold* lemon sour?"

"Uh-huh. Ice-cold. Zero degrees Centigrade."

"I *will* join you, in that case. Thanks."

Olmstead opened a frost-lined compartment; took out two half-liter bottles; placed them and his open lunch-box invitingly on the low stone wall.

"Hm . . . m . . . m. Quite a zipper you got there, mister." The trooper gazed admiringly at the luxurious, two-wheeled monster; listened appreciatively to its almost inaudible hum. "I've heard about those new supers, but that is the first one I ever saw. Nice. All the comforts of home, eh?"

"Just about. Sure you won't help me clean up on those sandwiches, before they get stale?"

Seated on the wall, the two men ate and talked. If that trooper had known what was in the box beside his leg he probably would have fallen over backward; but how was he even to suspect? There was nothing crass or rough or coarse about any of the work of any of Boskone's high-level operators.

Olmstead drove on to the lake and took up his reservation at the ramshackle hotel. He slept, and bright and early the next morning he was up and fishing—and this part of the performance he really enjoyed. He knew his stuff and the fish were there; big, wary, and game. He loved it.

At noon he ate, and quite openly and brazenly consigned the "empty" box to the watery deep. Even if he had not had so many fish to carry, he was not the type to lug a cheap lunch-box back to town. He fished joyously all afternoon, without getting quite the limit, and as the sun grazed the horizon he started his putt-putt and skimmed back to the dock.

The thing hadn't sent out any radiation yet, Northrop informed him tensely, but it certainly would, and when it did they'd be ready. There were Lensmen and Patrolmen all over the place, thicker than hair on a dog.

And George Olmstead, sighing wearily and yet blissfully anticipatory of one more day of enthralling sport, gathered up his equipment and his fish and strolled toward the hotel.

CHAPTER 17

Forty thousand miles from Earth's center the *Chicago* loafed along a circular arc, inert, at a mere ten thousand miles an hour; a speed which, and not by accident, kept her practically stationary above a certain point on the planet's surface. Nor was it by chance that both Virgil Samms and Roderick Kinnison were aboard. And a dozen or so other craft, cruisers and such, whose officers were out to put space-time in their logs, were flitting aimlessly about; but never very far away from the flagship. And farther out—well out—a cordon of diesel-powered detector ships swept space to the full limit of their prodigious reach. The navigating officers of those vessels knew to a nicety the place and course of every ship lawfully in the ether, and the appearance of even one unscheduled trace would set in motion a long succession of carefully-planned events.

And far below, grazing atmosphere, never very far from the direct line between the *Chicago* and Earth's core, floated a palatial pleasure yacht. And this craft carried not one Lensman, or two, but eight; two of whom kept their eyes fixed upon their observation plates. They were watching a lunch-box resting upon the bottom of a lake.

"Hasn't it radiated yet?" Roderick Kinnison demanded. "Or been approached, or moved?"

"Not yet," Lyman Cleveland replied, crisply. "Neither Northrop's rig nor mine has shown any sign of activity."

He did not amplify the statement, nor was there need. Mason Northrop was a Master Electronicist; Cleveland was perhaps the world's greatest living expert. Neither of them had detected radiation. Ergo, none existed.

Equally certainly the box had not moved, or been moved, or approached. "No change, Rod," Doctor Frederick Rodebush Lensed the assured thought. "Six of us have been watching the plates in five-minute shifts."

A few minutes later, however: "Here is a thought which may be of interest," DalNalten the Venerian announced, spraying himself with a couple pints of water. "It is natural enough, of course, for any Venerian to be in or on any water he can reach—I would enjoy very much being on or in that lake myself—but it may not be entirely by coincidence that one particular Venerian, Ossmen, is visiting this particular lake at this particular time."

"What!" Nine Lensmen yelled the thought practically as one.

"Precisely. Ossmen." It was a measure of the Venerian Lensman's concern that he used only two words instead of twenty or thirty. "In the red boat with the yellow sail."

"Do you see any detector rigs?" Samms asked.

"He wouldn't need any," DalNalten put in. "He will be able to see it. Or, if a little colane had been rubbed on it which no Tellurian could have noticed, any Venerian could smell it from one end of that lake to the other."

"True. I didn't think of that. It may not have a transmitter after all."

"Maybe not, but keep on listening, anyway," the Port Admiral ordered. "Bend a plate on Ossmen, and a couple more on the rest of the boats. But Ossmen is clean, you say, Jack? Not even a spy-ray block?"

"He couldn't have a block, Dad. It'd give too much away, here on our home grounds. Like on Eridan, where their ops could wear anything they could lift, but we had to go naked." He flinched mentally as he recalled his encounter with Hazel the Hell-cat, and Northrop flinched with him.

"That's right, Rod," Olmstead in his boat below agreed, and Conway Costigan, in his room in Northport, concurred. The top-drawer operatives of the enemy depended for safety upon perfection of technique, not upon crude and dangerous mechanical devices.

"Well, since you're all so sure of it, I'll buy it," and the waiting went on.

Under the slight urge of the light and vagrant breeze, the red boat moved slowly across the water. A somnolent, lackadaisical youth, who very evidently cared nothing about where the boat went, sat in its stern, with his left arm draped loosely across the tiller. Nor was Ossmen any more concerned. His only care, apparently, was to avoid interference with the fishermen; his under-water jaunts were long, even for a Venerian, and he entered and left the water as smoothly as only a Venerian—or a seal—could.

"However, he could have, and probably has got, a capsule spy-ray detector," Jack offered, presently. "Or, since a Venerian can swallow anything one inch smaller than a kitchen stove, he could have a whole analyzing station stashed away in his stomach. Nobody's put a beam on him yet, have you?"

Nobody had.

"It might be smart not to. Watch him with 'scopes . . . and when he gets up close to the box, better pull your beams off of it. DalNalten, I don't suppose it would be quite bright for you to go swimming down there too, would it?"

"Very definitely not, which is why I am up here and dry. None of them would go near it."

They waited, and finally Ossmen's purposeless wanderings brought him over the spot on the lake's bottom which was the target of so many Tellurian eyes. He gazed at the discarded lunch-box as incuriously as he had looked at so many other sunken objects, and swam over it as casually—and only the ultra-cameras caught what he actually did. He swam serenely on.

"The box is still there," the spy-ray men reported, "but the package is gone."

"Good!" Kinnison exclaimed, "Can you 'scopists see it on him?"

"Ten to one they can't," Jack said. "He swallowed it. I expected him to swallow it box and all."

"We can't see it, sir. He must have swallowed it."

"Make sure."

"Yes, sir . . . . He's back on the boat now and we've shot him from all angles. He's clean—nothing outside."

"Perfect! That means he isn't figuring on slipping it to somebody else in a crowd. This will be an ordinary job of shadowing from here on in, so I'll put in the umbrella."

The detector ships were recalled. The *Chicago* and the various other ships of war returned to their various bases. The pleasure craft floated away. But on the other hand there were bursts of activity throughout the forest for a mile or so back from the shores of the lake. Camps were struck. Hiking parties decided that they had hiked enough and began to retrace their steps. Lithe young men, who had been doing this and that, stopped doing it and headed for the nearest trails.

For Kinnison *pere* had erred slightly in saying that the rest of the enterprise was to be an ordinary job of shadowing. No ordinary job would do. With the game this nearly in the bag it must be made absolutely certain that no suspicion was aroused, and yet Samms had to have *facts*. Sharp, hard, clear facts; facts so self-evidently facts that no intelligence above idiot grade could possibly mistake them for anything but facts.

Wherefore Ossmen the Venerian was not alone thenceforth. From lake to hotel, from hotel to car, along the road, into and in and out of train and plane, clear to an ordinary-enough-looking building in an ordinary business section of New York, he was *never* alone. Where the traveling population was light, the Patrol operatives were few and did not crowd the Venerian too nearly; where dense, as in a metropolitan station, they ringed him three deep.

He reached his destination, which was of course spy-ray proofed, late Sunday night. He went in, remained briefly, came out.

"Shall we spy-ray him, Virge? Follow him? Or what?"

"No spy-rays. Follow him. Cover him like a blanket. At the usual time give him the usual spy-ray going-over, but not until then. This time, make it *thorough*. Make certain that he hasn't got it on him, in him, or in or around his house."

"There'll be nothing doing here tonight, will there?"

"No, it would be too noticeable. So you, Fred, and Lyman, take the first trick; the rest of us will get some sleep."

THE LENSMAN

When the building opened Monday morning the Lensmen were back, with dozens of others, including Knobos of Mars. There were also present or nearby literally hundreds of the shrewdest, most capable detectives of Earth.

"So *this* is their headquarters—one of them at least," the Martian thought, studying the trickle of people entering and leaving the building. "It is as we thought, Dal, why we could never find it, why we could never trace any wholesaler backward. None of us has ever seen any of these persons before. Complete change of personnel per operation; probably inter-planetary. Long periods of quiescence. Check?"

"Check: but we have them now."

"Just like that, huh?" Jack Kinnison jibed; and from his viewpoint his idea was the more valid, for the wholesalers were very clever operators indeed.

From the more professional viewpoint of Knobos and DalNalten, however, who had fought a steadily losing battle so long, the task was not too difficult. Their forces were beautifully organized and synchronized; they were present in such overwhelming numbers that "tails" could be changed every fifteen seconds; long before anybody, however suspicious, could begin to suspect any one shadow. Nor was it necessary for the tails to signal each other, however inconspicuously, or to indicate any suspect at change-over time. Lensed thoughts directed every move, without confusion or error.

And there were tiny cameras with tremendous, protuberant lenses, the "long eyes" capable of taking wire-sharp close ups from five hundred feet; and other devices and apparatus and equipment too numerous to mention here.

Thus the wholesalers were traced and their transactions with the retail peddlers were recorded. And from that point on, even Jack Kinnison had to admit that the sailing was clear. These small fry were not smart, and their customers were even less so. None had screens or detectors or other apparatus; their every transaction could be and was recorded from a distance of many miles by the ultra-instruments of the Patrol. And not only the transactions. Clearly, unmistakeably, the purchaser was followed from buying to sniffing; nor was the time intervening ever long. Thionite, then as now, was bought at retail only to use, and the whole ghastly thing went down on tape and film. The gasping, hysterical appeal; the exchange of currency for drug; the headlong rush to a place of solitude; the rigid muscle-lock and the horribly ecstatic transports; the shaken, soul-searing recovery or the entranced death. It all went on record. It was sickening to have to record such things. More than one observer did sicken in fact, and had to be relieved. But Virgil Samms had to have concrete, positive, irrefutable evidence. He got it. Any possible jury, upon seeing that evidence, would know it to be the truth; no possible jury, after seeing that evidence, could bring in any verdict other than "guilty".

Oddly enough, Jack Kinnison was the only casualty of that long and hectic day. A man—later proved to be a middle-sized potentate of the underworld—who was not even under suspicion at the time, for some reason or other got the idea that Jack was after him. The Lensman had, perhaps, allowed some part of his long eye to show; a fast and efficient long-range telephoto lens is a devilishly awkward thing to conceal. At any rate the racketeer sent out a call for help, just in case his bodyguards would not be enough, and in the meantime his personal attendants rallied enthusiastically around.

SUPER PACK

They had two objects in view; One, to pass a knife expeditiously and quietly through young Kinnison's throat from ear to ear; and: Two, to tear the long eye apart and subject a few square inches of super-sensitive emulsion to the bright light of day. And if the Big Shot had known that the photographer was not alone, that the big, hulking bruiser a few feet away was also a bull, they might have succeeded.

Two of the four hoods reached Jack just fractionally ahead of the other two; one to seize the camera, the other to swing the knife. But Jack Kinnison was fast; fast of brain and nerve and muscle. He saw them coming. In three flashing motions he bent the barrel of the telephoto into a neat arc around the side of the first man's head, ducked frantically under the fiercely-driven knife, and drove the toe of his boot into the spot upon which prize-fighters like to have their rabbit-punches land. Both of those attackers lost interest promptly. One of them lost interest permanently; for a telephoto lens in barrel is heavy, very rigid, and very, *very* hard.

While Battling Jack was still off balance, the other two guards arrived—but so did Mason Northrop. Mase was not quite as fast as Jack was; but, as has been pointed out, he was bigger and much stronger. When he hit a man, with either hand, that man dropped. It was the same as being on the receiving end of the blow of a twenty-pound hammer falling through a distance of ninety seven and one-half feet.

The Lensmen had of course also yelled for help, and it took only a split second for a Patrol speedster to travel from any given point to any other in the same county. It took no time at all for that speedster to fill a couple of square blocks with patterns of force through which neither bullets nor beams could be driven. Therefore the battle ended as suddenly as it began; before more thugs, with their automatics and portables, could reach the scene.

Kinnison *fils* cursed and damned fulminantly the edict which had forbidden arms that day, and swore that he would never get out of bed again without strapping on at least two blasters; but he had to admit finally that he had nothing to squawk about. Kinnison *pere* explained quite patiently—for him—that all he had got out of the little fracas was a split lip, that young Northrop's hair wasn't even mussed, and that if everybody had been packing guns some scatter-brained young damn fool like him would have started blasting and blown everything higher than up—would have spoiled Samms' whole operation maybe beyond repair. Now would he please quit bellyaching and get to hell out?

He got.

*

"That buttons thionite up, don't you think?" Rod Kinnison asked. "And the lawyers will have plenty of time to get the case licked into shape and lined up for trial."

"Yes and no." Samms frowned in thought. "The *evidence* is complete, from original producer to ultimate consumer; but our best guess is that it will take years to get the really important offenders behind bars."

"Why? I thought you were giving them altogether too much time when you scheduled the blow-off for three weeks ahead of election."

"Because the drug racket is only a small part of it. We're going to break the whole thing at once, you know, and Mateese covers a lot more ground—murder, kidnapping, bribery, corruption, misfeasance—practically everything you can think of."

"I know. What of it?"

"Jurisdiction, among other things. With the President, over half of the Congress, much of the judiciary, and practically all of the political bosses and police chiefs of the Continent under indictment at once, the legal problem becomes incredibly difficult. The Patrol's Department of Law has been working on it twenty four hours a day, and the only thing they seem sure of is a long succession of bitterly-contested points of law. There are no precedents whatever."

"Precedents be damned! They're guilty and everybody knows it. We'll change the laws so that . . . ."

"We will *not!*" Samms interrupted, sharply. "We want and we will have government by law, not by men. We have had too much of that already. Speed is not of the essence; justice very definitely is."

"'Crusader' Samms, now and forever! But I'll buy it, Virge—now let's get back down to earth. Operation Zwilnik is all set. Mateese is going good. Zabriska tied into Zwilnik. That leaves Operation Boskone, which is, I suppose, still getting nowhere fast."

The First Lensman did not reply. It was, and both men knew it. The shrewdest, most capable and experienced operatives of the Patrol had hit that wall with everything they had, and had simply bounced. Low-level trials had found no point of contact, no angle of approach. Middle level, ditto. George Olmstead, working at the highest possible level, was morally certain that he had found a point of contact, but had not been able to do anything with it.

"How about calling a Council conference on it?" Kinnison asked finally. "Or Bergenholm at least? Maybe he can get one of his hunches on it."

"I have discussed it with them all, just as I have with you. No one had anything constructive to offer, except to go ahead with Bennett as you are doing. The concensus is that the Boskonians know just as much about our military affairs as we know about theirs—no more."

"It *would* be too much to expect them to be dumb enough to figure us as dumb enough to depend only on our visible Grand Fleet, after the warning they gave us at The Hill," Kinnison admitted.

"Yes. What worries me most is that they had a running start."

"Not enough to count," the Port Admiral declared. "We can out-produce 'em and out-fight 'em."

"Don't be over-optimistic. You can't deny them the possession of brains, ability, man-power and resources at least equal to ours."

"I don't have to." Kinnison remained obstinately cheerful. "Morale, my boy, is what counts. Man-power and tonnage and fire-power are important, of course, but morale has won every war in history. And our morale right now is higher than a cat's back—higher than any time since John Paul Jones—and getting higher by the day."

"Yes?" The question was monosyllabic but potent.

"Yes. I mean just that—*yes*. From what we know of their system they *can't* have the morale we've got. Anything they can do we can do more of and better. What you've got, Virge, is a bad case of ingrowing nerves. You've never been to Bennett, in spite of the number of times I've asked you to. I say take time right now and come along—it'll be good for what ails you. It will also be a very fine thing for Bennett and for the Patrol—you'll find yourself no stranger there."

"You may have something there . . . I'll do it."

Port Admiral and First Lensman went to Bennett, not in the *Chicago* or other superdreadnaught, but in a two-man speedster. This was necessary because space-travel, as far as that planet was concerned, was a strictly one-way affair except for Lensmen. Only Lensmen could leave Bennett, under any circumstances or for any reason whatever. There was no out-going mail, express, or freight. Even the war-vessels of the Fleet, while on practice maneuvers outside the bottle-tight envelopes surrounding the system, were so screened that no unauthorized communication could possibly be made.

"In other words," Kinnison finished explaining, "we slapped on everything anybody could think of, including Bergenholm and Rularion; and believe me, brother, that was a lot of stuff."

"But wouldn't the very fact of such rigid restrictions operate against morale? It is a truism of psychology that imprisonment, like everything else, is purely relative."

"Yeah, that's what I told Rularion, except I used simpler and rougher language. You know how sarcastic and superior he is, even when he's wrong?"

"*How* I know!"

"Well, when he's right he's too damned insufferable for words. You'd've thought he was talking to the prize boob of a class of half-wits. As long as nobody on the planet knew that there was any such thing as space-travel, or suspected that they were not the only form of intelligent life in the universe, it was all right. No such concept as being planet-bound could exist. They had all the room there was. But after they met us, and digested all the implications, they would develop the colly-wobbles no end. This, of course, is an extreme simplification of the way the old coot poured it into me; but he came through with the solution, so I took it like a little man."

"What was the solution?"

"It's a shame you were too busy to come in on it. You'll see when we land."

But Virgil Samms was quick on the uptake. Even before they landed, he understood. When the speedster slowed down for atmosphere he saw blazoned upon the clouds a welter of one many-times repeated signal; as they came to ground he saw that the same set of symbols was repeated, not only upon every available cloud, but also upon airships, captive balloons, streamers, roofs and sides of buildings—even, in multi-colored rocks and flower-beds, upon the ground itself.

"Twenty Haress," Samms translated, and frowned in thought. "A date of the Bennettan year. Would it by any chance happen to coincide with our Tellurian November fourteenth of this present year?"

"Bright boy!" Kinnison applauded. "I thought you'd get it, but not so fast. Yes—election day."

"I see. They know what is going on, then?"

"Everything that counts. They know what we stand to win—and lose. They've named it Liberation Day, and everything on the planet is building up to it in a grand crescendo. I was a little afraid of it at first, but if the screens are really tight it won't make any difference how many people know it, and if they aren't the beans would all be spilled anyway. And it really works—I get a bigger thrill every time I come here."

"I can see where it might work."

Bennett was a fully Tellurian world in mass, in atmosphere and in climate; her native peoples were human to the limit of classification, both physically and mentally. And First Lensman Samms, as he toured it with his friend, found a world aflame with a zeal and an ardor unknown to blasé Earth since the days of the Crusades. The Patrol's cleverest and shrewdest psychologists, by merely sticking to the truth, had done a marvelous job.

Bennett knew that it was the Arsenal and the Navy Yard of Civilization, and it was proud of it. Its factories were humming as they had never hummed before; every industry, every business, every farm was operating at one hundred percent of capacity. Bennett was dotted and spattered with spaceports already built, and hundreds more were being rushed to completion. The already staggering number of ships of war operating out of those ports was being augmented every hour by more and ever more ultra-modern, ultra-fast, ultra-powerful shapes.

It was an honor to help build those ships; it was a still greater one to help man them. Competitive examinations were being held constantly, nor were all or even most of the applicants native Bennettans.

Samms did not have to ask where these young people were coming from. He knew. From all the planets of Civilization, attracted by carefully-worded advertisements of good jobs at high pay on new and highly secret projects on newly discovered planets. There were hundreds of such ads. Most were probably the Patrol's, and led here; many were of Spaceways, Uranium Incorporated, and other mercantile firms. The possibility that some of them might lead to what was now being called Boskonia had been tested thoroughly, but with uniformly negative results. Lensmen had applied by scores for those non-Patrol jobs and had found them bona-fide. The conclusion was unavoidable—Boskone was doing its recruiting on planets unknown to any wearer of Arisia's Lens. On the other hand, more than a trickle of Boskonians were applying for Patrol jobs, but Samms was almost certain that none had been accepted. The final screening was done by Lensmen, and in such matters Lensmen did not make many or serious mistakes.

Bennett had been informed of the First Lensman's arrival, and Kinnison had been guilty of a gross understatement indeed in telling Samms that he would not be regarded as a stranger. Wherever Samms went he was met by wildly enthusiastic crowds. He had to make speeches, each of which was climaxed by a tremendous roar of "TO LIBERATION DAY!"

"No Lensman material here, you say, Rod?" Samms asked, after the first city-shaking demonstration was over. One of his prime concerns, throughout his life, was this. "With all this enthusiasm? Sure?"

"We haven't found any good enough to refer to you yet. However, in a few years, when the younger generation gets a little older, there certainly will be."

"Check." The tour of inspection and acquaintance was finished, the two Lensmen started back to Earth.

"Well, my skeptical and pessimistic friend, was I lying, or not?" Kinnison asked, as soon as the speedster's ports were sealed. "Can they match that or not?"

"You weren't—and I don't believe they can. I have never seen anything like it. Autocracies have parades and cheers and demonstrations, of course, but they have always been forced—artificial. Those were spontaneous."

"Not only that, but the enthusiasm will carry through. We'll be piping hot and ready to go. But about this stumping—you said I'd better start as soon as we get back?"

"Within a few days, I'd say."

"I wouldn't wonder, so let's use this time in working out a plan of campaign. My idea is to start out like this . . . ."

CHAPTER 18

Conway Costigan, leaving behind him scores of clues, all highly misleading, severed his connection with Uranium, Inc. as soon as he dared after Operation Zwilnik had been brought to a successful close. The technical operation, that is; the legal battles in which it figured so largely were to run on for enough years to make the word "zwilnik" a common noun and adjective in the language.

He came to Tellus as unobtrusively as was his wont, and took an inconspicuous but very active part in Operation Mateese, now in full swing.

"Now is the time for all good men and true to come to the aid of the party, eh?" Clio Costigan giggled.

"You can play that straight across the keyboard of your electric, pet, and not with just two fingers, either. Did you hear what the boss told 'em today?"

"Yes." The girl's levity disappeared. "They're so *dirty*, Spud—I'm really afraid."

"So am I. But we're not too lily-fingered ourselves if we have to be, and we're covering 'em like a blanket—Kinnison and Samms both."

"Good."

"And in that connection, I'll have to be out half the night again tonight. All right?"

"Of course. It's so nice having you home at all, darling, instead of a million light-years away, that I'm practically delirious with delight."

It was sometimes hard to tell what impish Mrs. Costigan meant by what she said. Costigan looked at her, decided she was taking him for a ride, and smacked her a couple of times where it would do the most good. He then kissed her thoroughly and left. He had very little time, these days, either to himself or for his lovely and adored wife.

For Roderick Kinnison's campaign, which had started out rough and not too clean, became rougher and rougher, and no cleaner, as it went along. Morgan and his crew were swinging from the heels, with everything and anything they could dig up or invent, however little of truth or even of plausibility it might contain, and Rod the Rock had never held even in principle with the gentle precept of turning the other cheek. He was rather an Old Testamentarian, and he was no neophyte at dirty fighting. As a young operative, skilled in the punishing, maiming techniques of hand-to-hand rough-and-tumble combat, he had brawled successfully in most of the dives of most of the solarian planets and of most of their moons. With this background, and being a quick study, and under the masterly coaching of Virgil Samms, Nels Bergenholm, and Rularion of North Polar Jupiter, it did not take him long to learn the various gambits and ripostes of this non-physical, but nevertheless no-holds-barred, political mayhem.

And the "boys and girls" of the Patrol worked like badgers, digging up an item here and a fact there and a bit of information somewhere else, all for the day of reckoning which was to come. They used ultra-wave scanners, spy-rays, long eyes, stool-pigeons—everything they could think of to use—and they could not *always* be blocked out or evaded.

"We've *got* it, boss—now let's *use* it!"

"No. Save it! Nail it down, solid! Get the facts—names, dates, places, and amounts. Prove it first—then save it!"

Prove it! Save it! The joint injunction was used so often that it came to be a slogan and was accepted as such. Unlike most slogans, however, it was carefully and diligently put to use. The operatives proved it and saved it, over and over, over and over again; by dint of what unsparing effort and selfless devotion only they themselves ever fully knew.

Kinnison stumped the Continent. He visited every state, all of the big cities, most of the towns, and many villages and hamlets; and always, wherever he went, a part of the show was to demonstrate to his audiences how the Lens worked.

"Look at me. You know that no two individuals are or ever can be alike. Robert Johnson is not like Fred Smith; Joe Jones is entirely different from John Brown. Look at me again. Concentrate upon whatever it is in your mind that makes me Roderick Kinnison, the individual. That will enable each of you to get into as close touch with me as though our two minds were one. I am not talking now; you are reading my mind. Since you are reading my very mind, you know exactly what I am *really* thinking, for better or for worse. It is impossible for my mind to lie to yours, since I can change neither the basic pattern of my personality nor my basic way of thought; nor would I if I could. Being in my mind, you know that already; you know what my basic quality is. My friends call it strength and courage; Pirate Chief Morgan and his cut-throat crew call it many other things. Be that as it may, you now know whether or not you want me for your President. I can do nothing whatever to sway your opinion, for what your minds have perceived you know to be the truth. That is the way the Lens works. It bares the depths of my mind to yours, and in return enables me to understand your thoughts.

"But it is in no sense hypnotism, as Morgan is so foolishly trying to make you believe. Morgan knows as well as the rest of us do that even the most accomplished hypnotist, with all his apparatus, CAN NOT AFFECT A STRONG AND DEFINITELY OPPOSED WILL. He is therefore saying that each and every one of you now receiving this thought is such a spineless weakling that—but you may draw your own conclusions.

"In closing, remember—nail this fact down so solidly that you will never forget it—a sound and healthy mind CAN NOT LIE. The mouth can, and does. So does the typewriter. But the mind—NEVER! I can hide my thoughts from you, while we are en rapport, like this . . . but I CAN NOT LIE TO YOU. That is why, some day, all of your highest executives will have to be Lensmen, and not politicians, diplomats, crooks and boodlers. I thank you."

As that long, bitter, incredibly vicious campaign neared its vitriolic end tension mounted higher and ever higher: and in a room in the Samms home three young Lensmen and a red-haired girl were not at ease. All four were lean and drawn. Jack Kinnison was talking.

" . . . not the party, so much, but Dad. He started out with bare fists, and now he's wading into 'em with spiked brass knuckles."

"You can play *that* across the board," Costigan agreed.

"He's really giving 'em hell," Northrop said, admiringly.

"Did you boys listen in on his Casper speech last night?"

They hadn't; they had been too busy.

"I could give it to you on your Lenses, but I couldn't reproduce the tone—the exquisite way he lifted large pieces of hide and rubbed salt into the raw places. When he gets excited you know he can't help but use voice, too, so I got some of it on a record. He starts out on voice, nice and easy, as usual; then goes onto his Lens without talking; then starts yelling as well as thinking. Listen:"

"You ought to have a Lensman president. You may not believe that any Lensman is, and as a matter of fact *must* be incorruptible. That is my belief, as you can feel for yourselves, but I cannot *prove* it to you. Only time can do that. It is a self-evident fact, however, which you can feel for yourselves, that a Lensman president could not lie to you except by word of mouth or in writing. You could demand from him at any time a Lensed statement upon any subject. Upon some matters of state he could and should refuse to answer; but not upon any question involving moral turpitude. If he answered, you would know the truth. If he refused to answer, you would know why and could initiate impeachment proceedings then and there.

"In the past there have been presidents who used that high office for low purposes; whose very memory reeks of malfeasance and corruption. One was impeached, others should have been. Witherspoon never should have been elected. Witherspoon should have been impeached the day after he was inaugurated. Witherspoon should be impeached now. We know, and at the Grand Rally at New York Spaceport three weeks from tonight we are going to PROVE, that Witherspoon is simply a minor cog-wheel in the Morgan-Towne-Isaacson machine, 'playing footsie' at command with whatever group happens to be the highest bidder at the moment, irrespective of North America's or the System's good. Witherspoon is a gangster, a cheat, and a God damn liar, but he is of very little actual importance; merely a boodling nincompoop. Morgan is the real boss and the real menace, the Operating Engineer of the lowest-down, lousiest, filthiest, rottenest, most corrupt machine of murderers, extortionists, bribe-takers, panderers, perjurers, and other pimples on the body politic that has ever disgraced any so-called civilized government. Good night."

"Wow!" Jack Kinnison yelped. "That's high, even for him!"

"Just a minute, Jack," Jill cautioned. "The other side, too. Listen to this choice bit from Senator Morgan."

"It is not exactly hypnotism, but something infinitely worse; something that steals away your very minds; that makes anyone listening believe that white is yellow, red, purple, or pea-green. Until our scientists have checked this menace, until we have every wearer of that cursed Lens behind steel bars, I advise you in all earnestness not to listen to them at all. If you do listen your minds will surely be insidiously decomposed and broken; you will surely end your days gibbering in a padded cell.

"And murders? *Murders!* The feeble remnants of the gangs which our government has all but wiped out may perhaps commit a murder or so per year; the perpetrators of which are caught, tried, and punished. But how many of your sons and daughters has Roderick Kinnison murdered, either personally or through his uniformed slaves? Think! Read the record! Then make him explain, if he can; but do not listen to his lying, mind-destroying Lens.

"Democracy? Bah! What does 'Rod the Rock' Kinnison—the hardest, most vicious tyrant, the most relentless and pitiless martinet ever known to any Armed Force in the long history of our world—know of democracy? Nothing! He understands only force. All who oppose him in anything, however small, or who seek to reason with him, die without record or trace; and if he is not arrested, tried, and executed, all such will continue, tracelessly and without any pretense of trial, to die.

"But at bottom, even though he is not intelligent enough to realize it, he is merely one more in the long parade of tools of ruthless and predatory wealth, the MONIED POWERS. *They,* my friends, never sleep; they have only one God, one tenet, one creed—the almighty CREDIT. *That* is what they are after, and note how craftily, how stealthily, they have done and are doing their grabbing. Where is your representation upon that so-called Galactic Council? How did this criminal, this vicious, this outrageously unconstitutional, this irresponsible, uncontrollable, and dictatorial monstrosity come into being? How and when did you give this bloated colossus the right to establish its own currency—to have the immeasurable effrontery to debar the solidest currency in the universe, the credit of North America, from inter-planetary and inter-stellar commerce? Their aim is clear; they intend to tax you into slavery and death. Do not forget for one instant, my friends, that the power to tax is the power to destroy. THE POWER TO TAX IS THE POWER TO DESTROY. Our forefathers fought and bled and died to establish the principle that taxation without rep . . . ."

"And so on, for one solid hour!" Jill snarled, as she snapped the switch viciously. "How do you like *them* potatoes?"

"Hell's—Blazing—Pinnacles!" This from Jack, silent for seconds, and:

"Rugged stuff . . . very, *very* rugged," from Northrop. "No wonder you look sort of pooped, Spud. Being Chief Bodyguard must have developed recently into quite a chore."

"You ain't just snapping your choppers, bub," was Costigan's grimly flippant reply. "I've yelled for help—in force."

"So have I, and I'm going to yell again, right now," Jack declared. "I don't know whether Dad is going to kill Morgan or not—and don't give a damn—but if Morgan isn't going all out to kill Dad it's because they've forgotten how to make bombs."

He Lensed a call to Bergenholm.

"Yes, Jack? . . . I will refer you to Rularion, who has had this matter under consideration."

"Yes, John Kinnison, I have considered the matter and have taken action," the Jovian's calmly assured thought rolled into the minds of all, even Lensless Jill's. "The point, youth, was well taken. It was your thought that some thousands—perhaps five—of spy-ray operators and other operatives will be required to insure that the Grand Rally will not be marred by episodes of violence."

"It was," Jack said, flatly. "It still is."

"Not having considered all possible contingencies nor the extent of the field of necessary action, you err. The number will approach nineteen thousand very nearly. Admiral Clayton has been so advised and his staff is now at work upon a plan of action in accordance with my recommendation. Your suggestions, Conway Costigan, in the matter of immediate protection of Roderick Kinnison's person, are now in effect, and you are hereby relieved of that responsibility. I assume that you four wish to continue at work?"

The Jovian's assumption was sound.

"I suggest, then, that you confer with Admiral Clayton and fit yourselves into his program of security. I intend to make the same suggestion to all Lensmen and other qualified persons not engaged in work of more pressing importance."

Rularion cut off and Jack scowled blackly. "The Grand Rally is going to be held three weeks before election day. I *still* don't like it. I'd save it until the night before election—knock their teeth out with it at the last possible minute."

"You're wrong, Jack; the Chief is right," Costigan argued. "Two ways. One, we can't play that kind of ball. Two, this gives them just enough rope to hang themselves."

"Well . . . maybe." Kinnison-like, Jack was far from being convinced. "But that's the way it's going to be, so let's call Clayton."

"First," Costigan broke in. "Jill, will you please explain why they have to waste as big a man as Kinnison on such a piffling job as president? I was out in the sticks, you know—it doesn't make sense."

"Because he's the only man alive who can lick Morgan's machine at the polls," Jill stated a simple fact. "The Patrol can get along without him for one term, after that it won't make any difference."

"But Morgan works from the side-lines. Why couldn't he?"

"The psychology is entirely different. Morgan *is* a boss. Pops Kinnison isn't. He's a leader. See?"

"Oh . . . I guess so . . . . Yes. Go ahead."

*

Outwardly, New York Spaceport did not change appreciably. At any given moment of day or night there were so many hundreds of persons strolling aimlessly or walking purposefully about that an extra hundred or so made no perceptible difference. And the spaceport was only the end-point. The Patrol's activities began hundreds or thousands or millions or billions of miles away from Earth's metropolis.

A web was set up through which not even a grain-of-sand meteorite could pass undetected. Every space-ship bound for Earth carried at least one passenger who would not otherwise have been aboard; passengers who, if not wearing Lenses, carried Service Special equipment amply sufficient for the work in hand. Geigers and other vastly more complicated mechanisms flew toward Earth from every direction in space; streamed toward New York in Earth's every channel of traffic. Every train and plane, every bus and boat and car, every conveyance of every kind and every pedestrian approaching New York City was searched; with a search as thorough as it was unobtrusive. And every thing and every entity approaching New York Spaceport was combed, literally by the cubic millimeter.

No arrests were made. No package was confiscated, or even disturbed, throughout the ranks of public check boxes, in private offices, or in elaborate or casual hiding-places. As far as the enemy knew, the Patrol had no suspicion whatever that anything out of the ordinary was going on. That is, until the last possible minute. Then a tall, lean, space-tanned veteran spoke softly aloud, as though to himself:

"Spy-ray blocks—interference—umbrella—on. Report."

That voice, low and soft as it was, was picked up by every Service Special receiver within a radius of a thousand miles, and by every Lensman listening, wherever he might be. So were, in a matter of seconds, the replies.

"Spy-ray blocks on, sir."

"Interference on, sir."

"Umbrella on, sir."

No spy-ray could be driven into any part of the tremendous port. No beam, communicator or detonating, could operate anywhere near it. The enemy would now know that something had gone wrong, but he would not be able to do anything about it.

"Reports received," the tanned man said, still quietly. "Operation Zunk will proceed as scheduled."

And four hundred seventy one highly skilled men, carrying duplicate keys and/or whatever other specialized apparatus and equipment would be necessary, quietly took possession of four hundred seventy one objects, of almost that many shapes and sizes. And, out in the gathering crowd, a few disturbances occurred and a few ambulances dashed busily here and there. Some women had fainted, no doubt, ran the report. They always did.

And Conway Costigan, who had been watching, without seeming even to look at him, a porter loading a truck with opulent-looking hand-luggage from a locker, followed man and truck out into the concourse. Closing up, he asked:

"Where are you taking that baggage, Charley?"

"Up Ramp One, boss," came the unflurried reply. "Flight Ninety will be late taking off, on accounta this jamboree, and they want it right up there handy."

"Take it down to the . . . ."

SUPER PACK

Over the years a good many men had tried to catch Conway Costigan off guard or napping, to beat him to the punch or to the draw—with a startlingly uniform lack of success. The Lensman's fist traveled a bare seven inches: the supposed porter gasped once and traveled—or rather, staggered backward—approximately seven feet before he collapsed and sprawled unconscious upon the pavement.

"Decontamination," Costigan remarked, apparently to empty air, as he picked the fellow up and draped him limply over the truckful of suitcases. "Deke. Front and center. Area forty-six. Class Eff-ex—hotter than the middle tailrace of hell."

"You called Deke?" A man came running up. "Eff-ex six—nineteen. This it?"

"Check. It's yours, porter and all. Take it away."

Costigan strolled on until he met Jack Kinnison, who had a rapidly-developing mouse under his left eye.

"How did *that* happen, Jack?" he demanded sharply. "Something slip?"

"Not exactly." Kinnison grinned ruefully. "I have the *damndest* luck! A woman—an old lady at that—thought I was staging a hold-up and swung on me with her hand-bag—southpaw and from the rear. And if you laugh, you untuneful harp, I'll hang one right on the end of your chin, so help me!"

"Far be it from such," Costigan assured him, and did not—quite—laugh. "Wonder how we came out? They should have reported before this—p-s-s-t! Here it comes!"

Decontamination was complete; Operation Zunk had been a one-hundred-percent success; there had been no casualties.

"Except for one black eye," Costigan could not help adding; but his Lens and his Service Specials were off. Jack would have brained him if any of them had been on.

Linking arms, the two young Lensmen strode away toward Ramp Four, which was to be their station.

This was the largest crowd Earth had ever known. Everybody, particularly the Nationalists, had wondered why this climactic political rally had been set for three full weeks ahead of the election, but their curiosity had not been satisfied. Furthermore, this meeting had been advertised as no previous one had ever been; neither pains nor cash had been spared in giving it the greatest build-up ever known. Not only had every channel of communication been loaded for weeks, but also Samms' workers had been very busily engaged in starting rumors; which grew, as rumors do, into things which their own fathers and mothers could not recognize. And the baffled Nationalists, trying to play the whole thing down, made matters worse. Interest spread from North America to the other continents, to the other planets, and to the other solar systems.

Thus, to say that everybody was interested in, and was listening to, the Cosmocrats' Grand Rally would not be too serious an exaggeration.

Roderick Kinnison stepped up to the battery of microphones; certain screens were cut.

"Fellow entities of Civilization and others: while it may seem strange to broadcast a political rally to other continents and to beam it to other worlds, it was necessary in this case. The message to be given, while it will go into the political affairs of the North American Continent of Tellus, will deal primarily with a far larger thing; a matter which will be of paramount importance to all intelligent beings of every inhabited world. You know how to attune your minds to mine. Do it now."

He staggered mentally under the shock of encountering practically simultaneously so many minds, but rallied strongly and went on, via Lens:

"My first message is not to you, my fellow Cosmocrats, nor to you, my fellow dwellers on Earth, nor even to you, my fellow adherents to Civilization; but to THE ENEMY. I do not mean my political opponents, the Nationalists, who are almost all loyal fellow North Americans. I mean the entities who are using the leaders of that Nationalist party as pawns in a vastly larger game.

"I know, ENEMY, that you are listening. I know that you had goon squads in this audience, to kill me and my superior officer. Know now that they are impotent. I know that you had atomic bombs, with which to obliterate this assemblage and this entire area. They have been disassembled and stored. I know that you had large supplies of radio-active dusts. They now lie in the Patrol vaults near Weehauken. All the devices which you intended to employ are known, and all save one have been either nullified or confiscated.

"That one exception is your war-fleet, a force sufficient in your opinion to wipe out all the Armed Forces of the Galactic Patrol. You intended to use it in case we Cosmocrats win this forthcoming election; you may decide to use it now. Do so if you like; you can do nothing to interrupt or to affect this meeting. This is all I have to say to you, Enemy of Civilization.

"Now to you, my legitimate audience. I am not here to deliver the address promised you, but merely to introduce the real speaker—First Lensman Virgil Samms . . . ."

A mental gasp, millions strong, made itself tellingly felt.

" . . . Yes—First Lensman Samms, of whom you all know. He has not been attending political meetings because we, his advisers, would not let him. Why? Here are the facts. Through Archibald Isaacson, of Interstellar Spaceways, he was offered a bribe which would in a few years have amounted to some fifty billion credits; more wealth than any individual entity has ever possessed. Then there was an attempt at murder, which we were able—just barely—to block. Knowing there was no other place on Earth where he would be safe, we took him to The Hill. You know what happened; you know what condition The Hill is in now. This warfare was ascribed to pirates.

"The whole stupendous operation, however, was made in a vain attempt to kill one man—Virgil Samms. The Enemy knew, and we learned, that Samms is the greatest man who has ever lived. His name will last as long as Civilization endures, for it is he, and *only* he, who can make it possible for Civilization *to* endure.

"Why was I not killed? Why was I allowed to keep on making campaign speeches? Because I do not count. I am of no more importance to the cause of Civilization than is my opponent Witherspoon to that of the Enemy.

"I am a wheel-horse, a plugger. You all know me—'Rocky Rod' Kinnison, the hard-boiled egg. I've got guts enough to stand up and fight for what I *know* is right. I've got the guts and the inclination to stand up and slug it out, toe to toe, with man, beast, or devil. I would make and WILL MAKE a good president; I've got the guts and inclination to keep on slugging after you elect me; before God I promise to smash down every machine-made crook who tries to hold any part of our government down in the reeking muck in which it now is.

"I am a plugger and a slugger, with no spark of the terrific flame of inspirational genius which makes Virgil Samms what he so uniquely is. My *kind* may be important, but I individually am not. There are *so* many of us! If they had killed me another slugger would have taken my place and the effect upon the job would have been nil.

"Virgil Samms, however, *can not be replaced* and the Enemy knows it. He is unique in all history. No one else can do his job. If he is killed before the principles for which he is working are firmly established Civilization will collapse back into barbarism. It will not recover until another such mind comes into existence, the probability of which occurrence I will let you compute for yourselves.

"For those reasons Virgil Samms is not here in person. Nor is he in The Hill, since the Enemy may now possess weapons powerful enough to destroy not only that hitherto impregnable fortress, but also the whole Earth. And they would destroy Earth, without a qualm, if in so doing they could kill the First Lensman.

"Therefore Samms is now out in deep space. Our fleet is waiting to be attacked. If we win, the Galactic Patrol will go on. If we lose, we hope you shall have learned enough so that we will not have died uselessly."

"Die? Why should *you* die? *You* are safe on Earth!"

"Ah, one of the goons sent that thought. If our fleet is defeated no Lensman, anywhere, will live a week. The Enemy will see to that.

"That is all from me. Stay tuned. Come in, First Lensman Virgil Samms . . . take over, sir."

It was psychologically impossible for Virgil Samms to use such language as Kinnison had just employed. Nor was it either necessary or desirable that he should; the ground had been prepared. Therefore—coldly, impersonally, logically, tellingly—he told the whole terrific story. He revealed the most important things dug up by the Patrols' indefatigable investigators, reciting names, places, dates, transactions, and amounts. Only in the last couple of minutes did he warm up at all.

"Nor is this in any sense a smear campaign or a bringing of baseless charges to becloud the issue or to vilify without cause and upon the very eve of election a political opponent. These are facts. Formal charges are now being preferred; every person mentioned, and many others, will be put under arrest as soon as possible. If any one of them were in any degree innocent our case against him could be made to fall in less than the three weeks intervening before election day. That is why this meeting is being held at this time.

"Not one of them is innocent. Being guilty, and knowing that we can and will prove guilt, they will adopt a policy of delay and recrimination. Since our courts are, for the most part, just, the accused will be able to delay the trials and the actual presentation of evidence until after election day. Forewarned, however, you will know exactly why the trials will have been delayed, and in spite of the fog of misrepresentation you will know where the truth lies. You will know how to cast your votes. You will vote for Roderick Kinnison and for those who support him.

THE LENSMAN

"There is no need for me to enlarge upon the character of Port Admiral Kinnison. You know him as well as I do. Honest, incorruptible, fearless, you know that he will make the best president we have ever had. If you do not already know it, ask any one of the hundreds of thousands of strong, able, clear-thinking young men and women who have served under him in our Armed Forces.

"I thank you, everyone who has listened, for your interest."

CHAPTER 19

As long as they were commodores, Clayton of North America and Schweikert of Europe had stayed fairly close to the home planet except for infrequent vacation trips. With the formation of the Galactic Patrol, however, and their becoming Admiral and Lieutenant-Admiral of the First Galactic Region, and their acquisition of Lenses, the radius of their sphere of action was tremendously increased. One or the other of them was always to be found in Grand Fleet Headquarters at New York Spaceport, but only very seldom were both of them there at once. And if the absentee were not to be found on Earth, what of it? The First Galactic Region included all of the solar systems and all of the planets adherent to Civilization, and the absentee could, as a matter of business and duty, be practically anywhere.

Usually, however, he was not upon any of the generally-known planets, but upon Bennett—getting acquainted with the officers, supervising the drilling of Grand Fleet in new maneuvers, teaching classes in advanced strategy, and holding skull-practice generally. It was hard work, and not too inspiring, but in the end it paid off big. They knew their men; their men knew them. They could work together with a snap, a smoothness, a precision otherwise impossible; for imported top brass, unknown to and unacquainted with the body of command, can not have and does not expect the deep regard and the earned respect so necessary to high morale.

Clayton and Schweikert had both. They started early enough, worked hard enough, and had enough stuff, to earn both. Thus it came about that when, upon a scheduled day, the two admirals came to Bennett together, they were greeted as enthusiastically as though they had been Bennettans born and bred; and their welcome became a planet-wide celebration when Clayton issued the orders which all Bennett had been waiting so long and so impatiently to hear. Bennettans were at last to leave Bennett!

Group after group, sub-fleet after sub-fleet, the component units of the Galactic Patrol's Grand Fleet took off. They assembled in space; they maneuvered enough to shake themselves down into some semblance of unity; they practiced the new maneuvers; they blasted off in formation for Sol. And as the tremendous armada neared the Solar System it met—or, rather, was joined by—the Patrol ships about which Morgan and his minions already knew; each of which fitted itself into its long-assigned place. Every planet of Civilization had sent its every vessel capable of putting out a screen or of throwing a beam, but so immense was the number of warships in Grand Fleet that this increment, great as it intrinsically was, made no perceptible difference in its size.

On Rally Day Grand Fleet lay poised near Earth. As soon as he had introduced Samms to the intensely interested listeners at the Rally, Roderick Kinnison disappeared. Actually,

336

he drove a bug to a distant corner of the spaceport and left the Earth in a light cruiser, but to all intents and purposes, so engrossed was everyone in what Samms was saying, Kinnison simply vanished. Samms was already in the *Boise*; the Port Admiral went out to his old flagship, the *Chicago*. Nor, in case any observer of the Enemy should be trying to keep track of him, could his course be traced. Cleveland and Northrop and Rularion and all they needed of the vast resources of the Patrol saw to that.

Neither Samms nor Kinnison had any business being with Grand Fleet in person, of course, and both knew it; but everyone knew why they were there and were glad that the two top Lensmen had decided to live or die with their Fleet. If Grand Fleet won, they would probably live; if Grand Fleet lost they would certainly die—if not in the pyrotechnic dissolution of their ships, then in a matter of days upon the ground. With the Fleet their presence would contribute markedly to morale. It was a chance very much worth taking.

Nor were Clayton and Schweikert together, or even near each other. Samms, Kinnison, and the two admirals were as far away from each other as they could get and still remain in Grand Fleet's fighting cylinder.

Cylinder? Yes. The Patrol's Board of Strategy, assuming that the enemy would attack in conventional cone formation and knowing that one cone could defeat another only after a long and costly engagement, had long since spent months and months at war-games in their tactical tanks, in search of a better formation. They had found it. Theoretically, a cylinder of proper composition could defeat, with negligible loss and in a very short time, the best cones they were able to devise. The drawback was that the ships composing a theoretically efficient cylinder would have to be highly specialized and vastly greater in number than any one power had ever been able to put into the ether. However, with all the resources of Bennett devoted to construction, this difficulty would not be insuperable.

This, of course, brought up the question of what would happen if cylinder met cylinder—if the Black strategists should also have arrived at the same solution—and this question remained unanswered. Or, rather, there were too many answers, no two of which agreed; like those to the classical one of what would happen if an irresistible force should strike an immovable object. There would be a lot of intensely interesting by-products!

Even Rularion of Jove did not come up with a definite solution. Nor did Bergenholm; who, although a comparatively obscure young Lensman-scientist and not a member of the Galactic Council, was frequently called into consultation because of his unique ability to arrive at correct conclusions via some obscurely short-circuiting process of thought.

"Well," Port Admiral Kinnison had concluded, finally, "*If* they've got one, too, we'll just have to shorten ours up, widen it out, and pray."

"Clayton to Port Admiral Kinnison," came a communication through channels. "Have you any additional orders or instructions?"

"Kinnison to Admiral Clayton. None," the Port Admiral replied, as formally, then went on via Lens: "No comment or criticism to make, Alex. You fellows have done a job so far and you'll keep on doing one. How much detection have you got out?"

"Twelve detets—three globes of diesels. If we sit here and do nothing the boys will get edgy and go stale, so if you and Virge agree we'll give 'em some practice. Lord knows they need it, and it'll keep 'em on their toes. But about the Blacks—they may be figuring on delaying any action until we've had time to crack from boredom. What's your idea on that?"

"I've been worried about the same thing. Practice will help, but whether enough or not I don't know. What do you think, Virge? Will they hold it up deliberately or strike fast?"

"Fast," the First Lensman replied, promptly and definitely. "As soon as they possibly can, for several reasons. They don't know our real strength, any more than we know theirs. They undoubtedly believe, however, the same as we do, that they are more efficient than we are and have the larger force. By their own need of practice they will know ours. They do not attach nearly as much importance to morale as we do; by the very nature of their regime they can't. Also, our open challenge will tend very definitely to force their hands, since face-saving is even more important to them than it is to us. They will strike as soon as they can and as hard as they can."

Grand Fleet maneuvers were begun, but in a day or so the alarms came blasting in. The enemy had been detected; coming in, as the previous Black Fleet had come, from the direction of Coma Berenices. Calculating machines clicked and whirred; orders were flashed, and a brief string of numbers; ships by the hundreds and the thousands flashed into their assigned positions.

Or, more precisely, *almost* into them. Most of the navigators and pilots had not had enough practice yet to hit their assigned positions exactly on the first try, since a radical change in axial direction was involved, but they did pretty well; a few minutes of juggling and jockeying were enough. Clayton and Schweikert used a little caustic language—via Lens and to their fellow Lensmen only, of course—but Samms and Kinnison were well enough pleased. The time of formation had been very satisfactorily short and the cone was smooth, symmetrical, and of beautifully uniform density.

The preliminary formation was a cone, not a cylinder. It was not a conventional Cone of Battle in that it was not of standard composition, was too big, and had altogether too many ships for its size. It was, however, of the conventional shape, and it was believed that by the time the enemy could perceive any significant differences it would be too late for him to do anything about it. The cylinder would be forming about that time, anyway, and it was almost believed—at least it was strongly hoped—that the enemy would not have the time or the knowledge or the equipment to do anything about that, either.

Kinnison grinned to himself as his mind, en rapport with Clayton's, watched the enemy's Cone of Battle enlarge upon the Admiral's conning plate. It was big, and powerful; the Galactic Patrol's publicly-known forces would have stood exactly the chance of the proverbial snowball in the nether regions. It was not, however, the Port Admiral thought, big enough to form an efficient cylinder, or to handle the Patrol's real force in any fashion—and unless they shifted within the next second or two it would be too late for the enemy to do anything at all.

As though by magic about ninety-five percent of the Patrol's tremendous cone changed into a tightly-packed double cylinder. This maneuver was much simpler than the previous one, and had been practiced to perfection. The mouth of the cone closed in and lengthened; the closed end opened out and shortened. Tractors and pressors leaped from ship to ship, binding the whole myriad of hitherto discrete units into a single structure as solid, even comparatively as to size, as a cantilever bridge. And instead of remaining quiescent, waiting to be attacked, the cylinder flashed forward, inertialess, at maximum blast.

Throughout the years the violence, intensity, and sheer brute power of offensive weapons had increased steadily. Defensive armament had kept step. One fundamental fact, however, had not changed throughout the ages and has not changed yet. Three or more units of given power have always been able to conquer one unit of the same power, if engagement could be forced and no assistance could be given; and two units could practically always do so. Fundamentally, therefore, strategy always has been and still is the development of new artifices and techniques by virtue of which two or more of our units may attack one of theirs; the while affording the minimum of opportunity for them to retaliate in kind.

The Patrol's Grand Fleet flashed forward, almost exactly along the axis of the Black cone; right where the enemy wanted it—or so he thought. Straight into the yawning mouth, erupting now a blast of flame beside which the wildest imaginings of Inferno must pale into insignificance; straight along that raging axis toward the apex, at the terrific speed of the two directly opposed velocities of flight. But, to the complete consternation of the Black High Command, nothing much happened. For, as has been pointed out, that cylinder was not of even approximately normal composition. In fact, there was not a normal war-vessel in it. The outer skin and both ends of the cylinder were purely defensive. Those vessels, packed so closely that their repellor fields actually touched, were all screen; none of them had a beam hot enough to light a match. Conversely, the inner layer, or "Liner", was composed of vessels that were practically all offense. They had to be protected at every point—but how they could ladle it out!

The leading and trailing edges of the formation—the ends of the gigantic pipe, so to speak—would of course bear the brunt of the Black attack, and it was this factor that had given the Patrol's strategists the most serious concern. Wherefore the first ten and the last six double rings of ships were special indeed. They were all screen—nothing else. They were drones, operated by remote control, carrying no living thing. If the Patrol losses could be held to eight double rings of ships at the first pass and four at the second—theoretical computations indicated losses of six and two—Samms and his fellows would be well content.

All of the Patrol ships had, of course, the standard equipment of so-called "violet", "green", and "red" fields, as well as duodecaplylatomate and ordinary atomic bombs, dirigible torpedoes and transporters, slicers, polycyclic drills, and so on; but in this battle the principal reliance was to be placed upon the sheer, brutal, overwhelming power of what had been called the "macro beam"—now simply the "beam". Furthermore, in the incredibly incandescent frenzy of the chosen field of action—the cylinder was to attack the cone at its very strongest part—no conceivable material projectile could have lasted a single microsecond after leaving the screens of force of its parent vessel. It could have flown fast enough; ultra-beam trackers could have steered it rapidly enough and accurately enough; but before it could have traveled a foot, even at ultra-light speed, it would have ceased utterly to be. It would have been resolved into its sub-atomic constituent particles and waves. Nothing material could exist, except instantaneously, in the field of force filling the axis of the Black's Cone of Battle; a field beside which the exact center of a multi-billion-volt flash of lightning would constitute a dead area.

That field, however, encountered no material object. The Patrol's "screeners", packed so closely as to have a four hundred percent overlap, had been designed to withstand precisely that inconceivable environment. Practically all of them withstood it. And in a fraction of a second the hollow forward end of the cylinder engulfed, pipe-wise, the entire apex of the enemy's war-cone, and the hitherto idle "sluggers" of the cylinder's liner went to work.

Each of those vessels had one heavy pressor beam, each having the same push as every other, directed inward, toward the cylinder's axis, and backward at an angle of fifteen degrees from the perpendicular line between ship and axis. Therefore, wherever any Black ship entered the Patrol's cylinder or however, it was driven to and held at the axis and forced backward along that axis. None of them, however, got very far. They were perforce in single file; one ship opposing at least one solid ring of giant sluggers who did not have to concern themselves with defense, but could pour every iota of their tremendous resources into offensive beams. Thus the odds were not merely two or three to one; but never less than eighty, and very frequently over two hundred to one.

Under the impact of those unimaginable torrents of force the screens of the engulfed vessels flashed once, practically instantaneously through the spectrum, and went down. Whether they had two or three or four courses made no difference—in fact, even the ultra-speed analyzers of the observers could not tell. Then, a couple of microseconds later, the wall-shields—the strongest fabrics of force developed by man up to that time—also failed. Then those ravenous fields of force struck bare, unprotected metal, and every molecule, inorganic and organic, of ships and contents alike, disappeared in a bursting flare of energy so raw and so violent as to stagger even those who had brought it into existence. It was certainly vastly more than a mere volatilization; it was deduced later that the detonating unstable isotopes of the Black's own bombs, in the frightful temperatures already existing in the Patrol's quasi-solid beams, had initiated a chain reaction which had resulted in the fissioning of a considerable proportion of the atomic nuclei of usually completely stable elements!

The cylinder stopped; the Lensmen took stock. The depth of erosion of the leading edge had averaged almost exactly six double rings of drones. In places the sixth ring was still intact; in others, which had encountered unusually concentrated beaming, the seventh was gone. Also, a fraction of one percent of the manned war-vessels had disappeared. Brief though the time of engagement had been, the enemy had been able to concentrate enough beams to burn a few holes through the walls of the attacking cylinder.

It had not been hoped that more than a few hundreds of Black vessels could be blown out of the ether at this first pass. General Staff had been sure, however, that the heaviest and most dangerous ships, including those carrying the enemy's High Command, would be among them. The mid-section of the apex of the conventional Cone of Battle had always been the safest place to be; therefore that was where the Black admirals had been and therefore they no longer lived.

In a few seconds it became clear that if any Black High Command existed, it was not in shape to function efficiently. Some of the enemy ships were still blasting, with little or no concerted effort, at the regulation cone which the cylinder had left behind; a few were attempting to get into some kind of a formation, possibly to attack the Patrol's cylinder. Indecision was visible and rampant.

To turn that tremendous cylindrical engine of destruction around would have been a task of hours, but it was not necessary. Instead, each vessel cut its tractors and pressors, spun end for end, reconnected, and retraced almost exactly its previous course; cutting out and blasting into nothingness another "plug" of Black warships. Another reversal, another dash; and this time, so disorganized were the foes and so feeble the beaming, not a single Patrol vessel was lost. The Black fleet, so proud and so conquering of mien a few minutes before, had fallen completely apart.

"That's enough, Rod, don't you think?" Samms thought then. "Please order Clayton to cease action, so that we can hold a parley with their senior officers."

"Parley, hell!" Kinnison's answering thought was a snarl. "We've got 'em going—mop 'em up before they can pull themselves together! Parley be damned!"

"Beyond a certain point military action becomes indefensible butchery, of which our Galactic Patrol will never be guilty. That point has now been reached. If you do not agree with me, I'll be glad to call a Council meeting to decide which of us is right."

"That isn't necessary. You're right—that's one reason I'm not First Lensman." The Port Admiral, fury and fire ebbing from his mind, issued orders; the Patrol forces hung motionless in space. "As President of the Galactic Council, Virge, take over."

Spy-rays probed and searched; a communicator beam was sent. Virgil Samms spoke aloud, in the lingua franca of deep space.

"Connect me, please, with the senior officer of your fleet."

There appeared upon Samms' plate a strong, not unhandsome face; deep-stamped with the bitter hopelessness of a strong man facing certain death.

"You've got us. Come on and finish us."

"Some such indoctrination was to be expected, but I anticipate no trouble in convincing you that you have been grossly misinformed in everything you have been told concerning us; our aims, our ethics, our morals, and our standards of conduct. There are, I assume, other surviving officers of your rank, although of lesser seniority?"

"There are ten other vice-admirals, but I am in command. They will obey my orders or die."

"Nevertheless, they shall be heard. Please go inert, match our intrinsic velocity, and come aboard, all eleven of you. We wish to explore with all of you the possibilities of a lasting peace between our worlds."

"Peace? Bah! Why lie?" The Black commander's expression did not change. "I know what you are and what you do to conquered races. We prefer a clean, quick death in your beams to the kind you deal out in your torture rooms and experimental laboratories. Come ahead—I intend to attack you as soon as I can make a formation."

"I repeat, you have been grossly, terribly, *shockingly* misinformed." Samms' voice was quiet and steady; his eyes held those of the other. "We are civilized men, not barbarians or savages. Does not the fact that we ceased hostilities so soon mean anything to you?"

For the first time the stranger's face changed subtly, and Samms pressed the slight advantage.

"I see it does. Now if you will converse with me mind to mind . . . ." The First Lensman felt for the man's ego and began to tune to it, but this was too much.

"I will not!" The Black put up a solid block. "I will have nothing to do with your cursed Lens. I know what it is and will have none of it!"

"Oh, what's the use, Virge!" Kinnison snapped. "Let's get on with it!"

"A great deal of use, Rod," Samms replied, quietly. "This is a turning-point. I *must* be right—I *can't* be that far wrong," and he again turned his attention to the enemy commander.

"Very well, sir, we will continue to use spoken language. I repeat, please come aboard with your ten fellow vice-admirals. You will not be asked to surrender. You will retain your side-arms—as long as you make no attempt to use them. Whether or not we come to any agreement, you will be allowed to return unharmed to your vessels before the battle is resumed."

"What? Side-arms? Returned? You swear it?"

"As President of the Galactic Council, in the presence of the highest officers of the Galactic Patrol as witnesses, I swear it."

"We will come aboard."

"Very well. I will have ten other Lensmen and officers here with me."

The *Boise*, of course, inerted first; followed by the *Chicago* and nine of the tremendous tear-drops from Bennett. Port Admiral Kinnison and nine other Lensmen joined Samms in the *Boise's* con room; the tight formation of eleven Patrol ships blasted in unison in the space-courtesy of meeting the equally tight formation of Black warships half-way in the matter of intrinsic velocity.

Soon the two little sub-fleets were motionless in respect to each other. Eleven Black gigs were launched. Eleven Black vice-admirals came aboard, to the accompaniment of the full military honors customarily granted to visiting admirals of friendly powers. Each was armed with what seemed to be an exact duplicate of the Patrol's own current blaster; Lewiston, Mark Seventeen. In the lead strode the tall, heavy, gray-haired man with whom Samms had been dealing; still defiant, still sullen, still concealing sternly his sheer desperation. His block was still on, full strength.

The man next in line was much younger than the leader, much less wrought up, much more intent. Samms felt for this man's ego, tuned to it, and got the shock of his life. This Black vice-admiral's mind was not at all what he had expected to encounter—it was, in every respect, of Lensman grade!

"Oh . . . how? You are not speaking, and . . . I see . . . the Lens . . . THE LENS!" The stranger's mind was for seconds an utterly indescribable turmoil in which relief, gladness, and high anticipation struggled for supremacy.

In the next few seconds, even before the visitors had reached their places at the conference table, Virgil Samms and Corander of Petrine exchanged thoughts which would require many thousands of words to express; only a few of which are necessary here.

"The LENS . . . I have dreamed of such a thing, without hope of realization or possibility. *How* we have been misled! They are, then, actually available upon your world, Samms of Tellus?"

"Not exactly, and not at all generally," and Samms explained as he had explained so many times before. "You will wear one sooner than you think. But as to ending this warfare. You survivors are practically all natives of your own world. Petrine?"

"Not 'practically', we are Petrinos all. The 'teachers' were all in the Center. Many remain upon Petrine and its neighboring worlds, but none remain alive here."

"Ohlanser, then, who assumed command, is also a Petrino? So hard-headed, I had assumed otherwise. He will be a stumbling-block. Is he actually in supreme command?"

"Only by and with our consent, under such astounding circumstances as these. He is a reactionary, of the old, die-hard, war-dog school. He would ordinarily be in supreme command and would be supported by the teachers if any were here; but I will challenge his authority and theirs; standing upon my right to command my own fleet as I see fit. So will, I think, several others. So go ahead with your meeting."

"Be seated, Gentlemen." All saluted punctiliously and sat down. "Now, Vice-Admiral Ohlanser . . . ."

"How do you, a stranger, know my name?"

"I know many things. We have a suggestion to offer which, if you Petrinos will follow it, will end this warfare. First, please believe that we have no designs upon your planet, nor any quarrel with any of its people who are not hopelessly contaminated by the ideas and the culture of the entities who are back of this whole movement; quite possibly those whom you refer to as the 'teachers'. You did not know whom you were to fight, or why." This was a statement, with no hint of question about it.

"I see now that we did not know all the truth," Ohlanser admitted, stiffly. "We were informed, and given proof sufficient to make us believe, that you were monsters from outer space—rapacious, insatiable, senselessly and callously destructive to all other forms of intelligent life."

"We suspected something of the kind. Do you others agree? Vice-Admiral Corander?"

"Yes. We were shown detailed and documented proofs; stereos of battles, in which no quarter was given. We saw system after system conquered, world after world laid waste. We were made to believe that our only hope of continued existence was to meet you and destroy you in space; for if you were allowed to reach Petrine every man, woman, and child on the planet would either be killed outright or tortured to death. I see now that those proofs were entirely false; completely vicious."

"They were. Those who spread that lying propaganda and all who support their organization must be and shall be weeded out. Petrine must be and shall be given her rightful place in the galactic fellowship of free, independent, and cooperative worlds. So must any and all planets whose peoples wish to adhere to Civilization instead of to tyranny and despotism. To further these ends, we Lensmen suggest that you re-form your fleet and proceed to Arisia . . . ."

"Arisia!" Ohlanser did not like the idea.

"Arisia," Samms insisted. "Upon leaving Arisia, knowing vastly more than you do now, you will return to your home planet, where you will take whatever steps you will then know to be necessary."

"We were told that your Lenses are hypnotic devices," Ohlanser sneered, "designed to steal away and destroy the minds of any who listen to you. I believe *that*, fully. I will not go to Arisia, nor will any part of Petrine's Grand Fleet. I will not attack my home planet. I will not do battle against my own people. This is final."

"I am not saying or implying that you should. But you continue to close your mind to reason. How about you, Vice-Admiral Corander? And you others?"

In the momentary silence Samms put himself en rapport with the other officers, and was overjoyed at what he learned.

"I do not agree with Vice-Admiral Ohlanser," Corander said, flatly. "He commands, not Grand Fleet, but his sub-fleet merely, as do we all. I will lead my sub-fleet to Arisia."

"Traitor!" Ohlanser shouted. He leaped to his feet and drew his blaster, but a tractor beam snatched it from his grasp before he could fire.

"You were allowed to wear side-arms, not to use them," Samms said, quietly. "How many of you others agree with Corander; how many with Ohlanser?"

All nine voted with the younger man.

"Very well. Ohlanser, you may either accept Corander's leadership or leave this meeting now and take your sub-fleet directly back to Petrine. Decide now which you prefer to do."

"You mean you aren't going to kill me, even now? Or even degrade me, or put me under arrest?"

"I mean exactly that. What is your decision?"

"In that case . . . I was—must have been—wrong. I will follow Corander."

"A wise choice. Corander, you already know what to expect; except that four or five other Petrinos now in this room will help you, not only in deciding what must be done upon Petrine, but also in the doing of it. This meeting will adjourn."

"But . . . no reprisals?" Corander, in spite of his newly acquired knowledge, was dubious, almost dumbfounded. "No invasion or occupation? No indemnities to your Patrol, or reparations? No punishment of us, our men, or our families?"

"None."

"That does not square up even with ordinary military usage."

"I know it. It does conform, however, to the policy of the Galactic Patrol which is to spread throughout our island universe."

"You are not even sending your fleet, or heavy units of it, with us, to see to it that we follow your instructions?"

"It is not necessary. If you need any form of help you will inform us of your requirements via Lens, as I am conversing with you now, and whatever you want will be supplied. However, I do not expect any such call. You and your fellows are capable of handling the situation. You will soon know the truth, and know that you know it; and when your house-cleaning is done we will consider your application for representation upon the Galactic Council. Good-bye."

Thus the Lensmen—particularly First Lensman Virgil Samms—brought another sector of the galaxy under the aegis of Civilization.

CHAPTER 20

After the Rally there were a few days during which neither Samms nor Kinnison was on Earth. That the Cosmocrats' presidential candidate and the First Lensman were both with the Fleet was not a secret; in fact, it was advertised. Everyone was told why they were out there, and almost everyone approved.

Nor was their absence felt. Developments, fast and terrific, were slammed home. Cosmocratic spellbinders in every state of North America waved the flag, pointed with pride, and viewed with alarm, in the very best tradition of North American politics. But above all, there appeared upon every news-stand and in every book-shop of the Continent, at opening time of the day following Rally Day, a book of over eighteen hundred pages of fine print; a book the publication of which had given Samms himself no little concern.

"But I'm afraid of it!" he had protested. "We know it's true; but there's material on almost every page for the biggest libel and slander suits in history!"

"I know it," the bald and paunchy Lensman-attorney had replied. "Fully. I hope they do take action against us, but I'm absolutely certain they won't."

"You hope they do?"

"Yes. If they take the initiative they can't prevent us from presenting our evidence in full; and there is no court in existence, however corrupt, before which we could not win. What they want and must have is delay; avoidance of any issue until after the election."

"I see." Samms was convinced.

The location of the Patrol's Grand Fleet had been concealed from all inhabitants of the Solarian system, friends and foes alike; but the climactic battle—liberating as it did energies sufficient to distort the very warp and woof of the fabric of space itself—could not be hidden or denied, or even belittled. It was not, however, advertised or blazoned abroad. Then as now the newshawks wanted to know, instantly and via long-range communicators, vastly more than those responsible for security cared to tell; then as now the latter said as little as it was humanly possible to say.

Everyone knew that the Patrol had won a magnificent victory; but nobody knew who or what the enemy had been. Since the rank and file knew it, everyone knew that only a fraction of the Black fleet had actually been destroyed; but nobody knew where the remaining vessels went or what they did. Everyone knew that about ninety five percent of the Patrol's astonishingly huge Grand Fleet had come from, and was on its way back to, the planet Bennett, and knew—since Bennettans would in a few weeks be scampering gaily all over space—in general *what* Bennett was; but nobody knew *why* it was.

Thus, when the North American Contingent landed at New York Spaceport, everyone whom the newsmen could reach was literally mobbed. However, in accordance with the aphorism ascribed to the wise old owl, those who knew the least said the most. But the Telenews ace who had once interviewed both Kinnison and Samms wasted no time upon small fry. He insisted on seeing the two top Lensmen, and kept on insisting until he did see them.

"Nothing to say," Kinnison said curtly, leaving no doubt whatever that he meant it. "All talking—if any—will be done by First Lensman Samms."

"Now, all you millions of Telenews listeners, I am interviewing First Lensman Samms himself. A little closer to the mike, please, First Lensman. Now, sir, what everybody wants to know is—who are the Blacks?"

"I don't know."

"You don't know? On the Lens, sir?"

"On the Lens. I still don't know."

"I see. But you have suspicions or ideas? You can guess?"

"I can guess; but that's all it would be—a guess."

"And my guess, folks, is that his guess would be a very highly informed guess. Will you tell the public, First Lensman Samms, what your guess is?"

"I will." If this reply astonished the newshawk, it staggered Kinnison and the others who knew Samms best. It was, however, a coldly calculated political move. "While it will probably be several weeks before we can furnish detailed and unassailable proof, it is my considered opinion that the Black fleet was built and controlled by the Morgan-Towne-Isaacson machine. That they, all unknown to any of us, enticed, corrupted, and seduced a world, or several worlds, to their program of domination and enslavement. That they intended by armed force to take over the Continent of North America and through it the whole earth and all the other planets adherent to Civilization. That they intended to hunt down and kill every Lensman, and to subvert the Galactic Council to their own ends. This is what you wanted?"

"That's fine, sir—*just* what we wanted. But just one more thing, sir." The newsman had obtained infinitely more than he had expected to get; yet, good newsmanlike, he wanted more. "Just a word, if you will, Mr. Samms, as to these trials and the White Book?"

"I can add very little, I'm afraid, to what I have already said and what is in the book; and that little can be classed as 'I told you so'. We are trying, and will continue to try, to force those criminals to trial; to break up, to prohibit, an unending series of hair-splitting delays. We want, and are determined to get, legal action; to make each of those we have accused defend himself in court and under oath. Morgan and his crew, however, are working desperately to avoid any action at all, because they know that we can and will prove every allegation we have made."

The Telenews ace signed off, Samms and Kinnison went to their respective offices, and Cosmocratic orators throughout the nation held a field-day. They glowed and scintillated with triumph. They yelled themselves hoarse, leather-lunged tub-thumpers though they were, in pointing out the unsullied purity, the spotless perfection of their own party and its every candidate for office; in shuddering revulsion at the never-to-be-sufficiently-condemned, proved and demonstrated villainy and blackguardy of the opposition.

And the Nationalists, although they had been dealt a terrific and entirely unexpected blow, worked near-miracles of politics with what they had. Morgan and his minions ranted and raved. They were being jobbed. They were being crucified by the Monied Powers. All those allegations and charges were sheerest fabrications—false, utterly vicious, containing nothing whatever of truth. They, not the Patrol, were trying to force a show-down; to vindicate themselves and to confute those unspeakably unscrupulous Lensmen before Election Day. And they were succeeding! Why, otherwise, had not a single one of the thousands of accused even been arrested? Ask that lying First Lensman, Virgil Samms! Ask that rock-hearted, iron-headed, conscienceless murderer, Roderick Kinnison! But do not, at peril of your sanity, submit your minds to their Lenses!

And why, the reader asks, were not at least some of those named persons arrested before Election Day? And your historian must answer frankly that he does not know. He is not a lawyer. It would be of interest—to some few of us—to follow in detail at least one of those days of legal battling in one of the high courts of the land; to quote verbatim at least a few of the many thousands of pages of transcript: but to most of us the technicalities involved would be boring in the extreme.

But couldn't the voters tell easily enough which side was on the offensive and which on the defensive? Which pressed for action and which insisted on postponement and delay? They could have, easily enough, if they had cared enough about the basic issues involved to make the necessary mental effort, but almost everyone was too busy doing something else. And it was so much easier to take somebody else's word for it. And finally, *thinking* is an exercise to which all too few brains are accustomed.

But Morgan neither ranted nor raved nor blustered when he sat in conference with his faintly-blue superior, who had come storming in as soon as he had learned of the crushing defeat of the Black fleet. The Kalonian was very highly concerned; so much so that the undertone of his peculiar complexion was turning slowly to a delicate shade of green.

"How did *that* happen? How *could* it happen? Why was I not informed of the Patrol's real power—how could you be guilty of such stupidity? Now I'll have to report to Scrwan of the Eich. He's pure, undiluted poison—and if word of this catastrophe ever gets up to Ploor . . . !!!"

"Come down out of the stratosphere, Fernald," Morgan countered, bitingly. "Don't try to make *me* the goat—I won't sit still for it. It happened because they could build a bigger fleet than we could. You were in on that—all of it. You knew what we were doing, and approved it—all of it. You were as badly fooled as I was. You were not informed because I could find out nothing—I could learn no more of their Bennett than they could of our Petrine. As to reporting, you will of course do as you please; but I would advise you not to cry too much before you're really hurt. This battle isn't over yet, my friend."

The Kalonian had been a badly shaken entity; it was a measure of his state of mind that he did not liquidate the temerarious Tellurian then and there. But since Morgan was as undisturbed as ever, and as sure of himself, he began to regain his wonted aplomb. His color became again its normal pale blue.

"I will forgive your insubordination this time, since there were no witnesses, but use no more such language to me," he said, stiffly. "I fail to perceive any basis for your optimism. The only chance now remaining is for you to win the election, and how can you do that? You are—must be—losing ground steadily and rapidly."

"Not as much as you might think." Morgan pulled down a large, carefully-drawn chart. "This line represents the hide-bound Nationalists, whom nothing we can do will alienate from the party; this one the equally hide-bound Cosmocrats. The balance of power lies, as always, with the independents—these here. And many of them are not as independent as is supposed. We can buy or bring pressure to bear on half of them—that cuts them down to this size here. So, no matter what the Patrol does, it can affect only this relatively small block here, and it is this block we are fighting for. We are losing a little ground, and steadily, yes; since we can't conceal from anybody with half a brain the fact that we're doing our best to keep the cases from ever coming to trial. But here's the actual observed line of sentiment, as determined from psychological indices up to yesterday; here is the extrapolation of that line to Election Day. It forecasts us to get just under forty nine percent of the total vote."

"And is there anything cheerful about that?" Fernald asked frostily.

"I'll say there is!" Morgan's big face assumed a sneering smile, an expression never seen by any voter. "This chart deals only with living, legally registered, bona-fide voters. Now if we can come that close to winning an absolutely honest election, how do you figure we can possibly lose the kind this one is going to be? We're in power, you know. We've got this machine and we know how to use it."

"Oh, yes, I remember—vaguely. You told me about North American politics once, a few years ago. Dead men, ringers, repeaters, ballot-box stuffing, and so on, you said?"

"'And so on' is right, Chief!" Morgan assured him, heartily. "Everything goes, this time. It'll be one of the biggest landslides in North American history."

"I will, then, defer any action until after the election."

"That will be the smart thing to do, Chief; then you won't have to take any, or make any report at all," and upon this highly satisfactory note the conference closed.

And Morgan was actually as confident as he had appeared. His charts were actual and factual. He knew the power of money and the effectiveness of pressure; he knew the capabilities of the various units of his machine. He did not, however, know two things: Jill Samms' insidious, deeply-hidden Voters' Protective League and the bright flame of loyalty pervading the Galactic Patrol. Thus, between times of bellowing and screaming his carefully-prepared, rabble-rousing speeches, he watched calmly and contentedly the devious workings of his smooth and efficient organization.

Until the day before election, that is. Then hordes of young men and young women went suddenly and briefly to work; at least four in every precinct of the entire nation. They visited, it seemed, every residence and every dwelling unit, everywhere. They asked questions, and took notes, and vanished; and the machine's operatives, after the alarm was given, could not find man or girl or notebook. And the Galactic Patrol, which had never before paid any attention to elections, had given leave and ample time to its every North American citizen. Vessels of the North American Contingent were grounded and practically emptied of personnel; bases and stations were depopulated; and even from every distant world every Patrolman registered in any North American precinct came to spend the day at home.

Morgan began then to worry, but there was nothing he could do about the situation—or was there? If the civilian boys and girls were checking the registration books—and they were—it was as legally-appointed checkers. If the uniformed boys and girls were all coming home to vote—and they were—that, too, was their inalienable right. But boys and girls were notoriously prone to accident and to debauchery . . . but again Morgan was surprised; and, this time, taken heavily aback. The web which had protected Grand Rally so efficiently, but greatly enlarged now, was functioning again; and Morgan and his minions spent a sleepless and thoroughly uncomfortable night.

Election Day dawned clear, bright, and cool; auguring a record turn-out. Voting was early and extraordinarily heavy; the polls were crowded. There was, however, very little disorder. Surprisingly little, in view of the fact that the Cosmocratic watchers, instead of being the venal wights of custom, were cold-eyed, unreachable men and women who seemed to know by sight every voter in the precinct. At least they spotted on sight and challenged without hesitation every ringer, every dead one, every repeater, and every imposter who claimed the right to vote. And those challenges, being borne out in every case by the carefully-checked registration lists, were in every case upheld.

Not all of the policemen on duty, especially in the big cities, were above suspicion, of course. But whenever any one of those officers began to show a willingness to play ball with the machine a calm, quiet-eyed Patrolman would remark, casually:

"Better see that this election stays straight, bud, and strictly according to the lists and signatures—or you're apt to find yourself listed in the big book along with the rest of the rats."

It was not that the machine liked the way things were going, or that it did not have goon squads on the job. It was that there were, everywhere and always, more Patrolmen than there were goons. And those Patrolmen, however young in years some of them might have appeared to be, were space-bronzed veterans, space-hardened fighting men, armed with the last word in blasters—Lewiston, Mark Seventeen.

To the boy's friends and neighbors, of course, his Lewiston was practically invisible. It was merely an article of clothing, the same as his pants. It carried no more of significance, of threat or of menace, than did the pistol and the club of the friendly Irish cop on the beat. But the goon did not see the Patrolman as a friend. He saw the keen, clear, sharply discerning eyes; the long, strong fingers; the smoothly flowing muscles, so eloquent of speed and of power. He saw the Lewiston for what it was; the deadliest, most destructive hand-weapon known to man. Above all he saw the difference in numbers: six or seven or eight Patrolmen to four or five or six of his own kind. If more hoods arrived, so did more spacemen; if some departed, so did a corresponding number of the wearers of the space-black and silver.

"Ain't you getting tired of sticking around here, George?" One mobster asked confidentially of one Patrolman. "I am. What say we and some of you fellows round up some girls and go have us a party?"

"Uh-uh," George denied. His voice was gay and careless, but his eyes were icy cold. "My uncle's cousin's stepson is running for second assistant dog-catcher, and I can't leave until I find out whether he wins or not."

Thus nothing happened; thus the invisible but nevertheless terrific tension did not erupt into open battle; and thus, for the first time in North America's long history, a presidential election was ninety nine and ninety nine one-hundredths percent pure!

Evening came. The polls closed. The Cosmocrats' headquarters for the day, the Grand Ballroom of the Hotel van der Voort, became the goal of every Patrolman who thought he stood any chance at all of getting in. Kinnison had been there all day, of course. So had Joy, his wife, who for lack of space has been sadly neglected in these annals. Betty, their daughter, had come in early, accompanied by a husky and personable young lieutenant, who has no other place in this story. Jack Kinnison arrived, with Dimples Maynard—dazzlingly blonde, wearing a screamingly red wisp of silk. She, too, has been shamefully slighted here, although she was never slighted anywhere else.

"The first time I ever saw her," Jack was wont to say, "I went right into a flat spin, running around in circles and biting myself in the small of the back, and couldn't pull out of it for four hours!"

That Miss Maynard should be a very special item is not at all surprising, in view of the fact that she was to become the wife of one of THE Kinnisons and the mother of another.

The First Lensman, who had been in and out, came in to stay. So did Jill and her inseparable, Mason Northrop. And so did others, singly or by twos or threes. Lensmen and their wives. Conway and Clio Costigan, Dr. and Mrs. Rodebush, and Cleveland, Admiral and Mrs. Clayton, ditto Schweikert, and Dr. Nels Bergenholm. And others. Nor were they all North Americans, or even human. Rularion was there; and so was blocky, stocky Dronvire of Rigel Four. No outsider could tell, ever, what any Lensman was thinking, to say nothing of such a monstrous Lensman as Dronvire—but that hotel was being covered as no political headquarters had ever been covered before.

The returns came in, see-sawing maddeningly back and forth. Faster and faster. The Maritime Provinces split fifty-fifty. Maine, New Hampshire, and Vermont, Cosmocrat. New York, upstate, Cosmocrat. New York City, on the basis of incomplete but highly significant returns, was piling up a huge Nationalist majority. Pennsylvania—labor—Nationalist. Ohio—farmers—Cosmocrat. Twelve southern states went six and six. Chicago, as usual, solidly for the machine; likewise Quebec and Ottawa and Montreal and Toronto and Detroit and Kansas City and St. Louis and New Orleans and Denver.

Then northern and western and far southern states came in and evened the score. Saskatchewan, Alberta, Britcol, and Alaska, all went Cosmocrat. So did Washington,

Idaho, Montana, Oregon, Nevada, Utah, Arizona, Newmex, and most of the states of Mexico.

At three o'clock in the morning the Cosmocrats had a slight but definite lead and were, finally, holding it. At four o'clock the lead was larger, but California was still an unknown quantity—California could wreck everything. *How* would California go? Especially, how would California's two metropolitan districts—the two most independent and free-thinking and least predictable big cities of the nation—how *would* they go?

At five o'clock California seemed safe. Except for Los Angeles and San Francisco, the Cosmocrats had swept the state, and in those two great cities they held a commanding lead. It was still mathematically possible, however, for the Nationalists to win.

"It's in the bag! Let's start the celebration!" someone shouted, and others took up the cry.

"Stop it! No!" Kinnison's parade-ground voice cut through the noise. "No celebration is in order or will be held until the result becomes certain or Witherspoon concedes!"

The two events came practically together: Witherspoon conceded a couple of minutes before it became mathematically impossible for him to win. Then came the celebration, which went on and on interminably. At the first opportunity, however, Kinnison took Samms by the arm, led him without a word into a small office, and shut the door. Samms, also saying nothing, sat down in the swivel chair, put both feet up on the desk, lit a cigarette, and inhaled deeply.

"Well, Virge—satisfied?" Kinnison broke the silence at last. His Lens was off. "We're on our way."

"Yes, Rod. Fully. At last." No more than his friend did he dare to use his Lens; to plumb the depths he knew so well were there. "Now it will roll—under its own power—no one man now is or ever will be indispensable to the Galactic Patrol—*nothing* can stop it now!"

EPILOGUE

The murder of Senator Morgan, in his own private office, was never solved. If it had occurred before the election, suspicion would certainly have fallen upon Roderick Kinnison, but as it was it did not. By no stretch of the imagination could anyone conceive of "Rod the Rock" kicking a man after he had knocked him down. Not that Morgan did not have powerful and vindictive enemies in the underworld: he had so many that it proved impossible to fasten the crime to any one of them.

Officially, Kinnison was on a five-year leave of absence from the Galactic Patrol, the office of Port Admiral had been detached entirely from the fleet and assigned to the Office of the President of North America. Actually, however, in every respect that counted, Roderick Kinnison was still Port Admiral, and would remain so until he died or until the Council retired him by force.

Officially, Kinnison was taking a short, well-earned vacation from the job in which he had been so outstandingly successful. Actually, he was doing a quick flit to Petrine, to get personally acquainted with the new Lensmen and to see what kind of a job they were doing. Besides, Virgil Samms was already there.

He arrived. He got acquainted. He saw. He approved.

"How about coming back to Tellus with me, Virge?" he asked, when the visiting was done. "I've got to make a speech, and it'd be nice to have you hold my head."

"I'd be glad to," and the *Chicago* took off.

Half of North America was dark when they neared Tellus; all of it, apparently, was obscured by clouds. Only the navigating officers of the vessel knew where they were, nor did either of the two Lensmen care. They were having too much fun arguing about the talents and abilities of their respective grandsons.

The *Chicago* landed. A bug was waiting. The two Lensmen, without an order being given, were whisked away. Samms had not asked where the speech was to be given, and Kinnison simply did not realize that he had not told him all about it. Thus Samms had no idea that he was just leaving Spokane Spaceport, Washington.

After a few miles of fast, open-country driving the bug reached the city. It slowed down, swung into brightly-lighted Maple Street, and passed a sign reading "Cannon Hill" something-or-other—neither of which names meant anything to either Lensman.

Kinnison looked at his friend's red-thatched head and glanced at his watch.

"Looking at you reminds me—I need a haircut," he remarked. "Should have got one aboard, but didn't think of it Joy told me if I come home without it she'll braid it in pigtails and tie it up with pink ribbons, and you're shaggier than I am. You've got to get one or else buy yourself a violin. What say we do it now?"

"Have we got time enough?"

"Plenty." Then, to the driver: "Stop at the first barber shop you see, please."

"Yes, sir. There's a good one a few blocks further along."

The bug sped down Maple Street, turned sharply into plainly-marked Twelfth Avenue. Neither Lensman saw the sign.

"Here you are, sir."

"Thanks."

There were two barbers and two chairs, both empty. The Lensmen, noticing that the place was neatly kept and meticulously clean, sat down and resumed their discussion of two extremely unusual infants. The barbers went busily to work.

"Just as well, though—better, really—that the kids didn't marry each other, at that," Kinnison concluded finally. "The way it is, we've each got a grandson—it'd be tough to have to share one with *you*."

Samms made no reply to this sally, for something was happening. The fact that this fair-skinned, yellow-haired blue-eyed barber was left-handed had not rung any bells—there were lots of left-handed barbers. He had neither seen nor heard the cat—a less-than-half-grown, gray, tiger-striped kitten—which, after standing up on its hind legs to sniff ecstatically at his nylon-clad ankles, had uttered a couple of almost inaudible "meows" and had begun to purr happily. Crouching, tensing its strong little legs, it leaped almost vertically upward. Its tail struck the barber's elbow.

Hastily brushing the kitten aside, and beginning profuse apologies both for his awkwardness and for the presence of the cat—he had never done such a thing before and he would drown him forthwith—the barber applied a styptic pencil and recollection hit Samms a pile-driver blow.

"Well, I'm a . . . !" He voiced three highly un-Samms-like, highly specific expletives which, as Mentor had foretold so long before, were both self-derogatory and profane. Then, as full realization dawned, he bit a word squarely in two.

"Excuse me, please, Mr. Carbonero, for this outrageous display. It was not the scratch, nor was any of it your fault. Nothing you could have done would have . . . ."

"You know my name?" the astonished barber interrupted.

"Yes. You were . . . ah . . . recommended to me by a . . . a friend . . . ." Whatever Samms could say would make things worse. The truth, wild as it was, would have to be told, at least in part. "You do not look like an Italian, but perhaps you have enough of that racial heritage to believe in prophecy?"

"Of course, sir. There have always been prophets—*true* prophets."

"Good. This event was foretold in detail; in such complete detail that I was deeply, terribly shocked. Even to the kitten. You call it Thomas."

"Yes, sir. Thomas Aquinas."

"It is actually a female. In here, Thomasina!" The kitten had been climbing enthusiastically up his leg; now, as he held a pocket invitingly open, she sprang into it, settled down, and began to purr blissfully. While the barbers and Kinnison stared pop-eyed Samms went on:

"She is determined to adopt me, and it would be a shame not to requite such affection. Would you part with her—for, say, ten credits?"

"*Ten credits!* I'll be glad to give her to you for nothing!"

"Ten it is, then. One more thing. Rod, you always carry a pocket rule. Measure this scratch, will you? You'll find it's mighty close to three millimeters long."

"Not 'close', Virge—it's *exactly* three millimeters, as near as this vernier can scale it."

"And just above and parallel to the cheek-bone."

"Check. Just above and as parallel as though it had been ruled there by a draftsman."

"Well, that's that. Let's get finished with the haircuts, before you're late for your speech," and the barbers, with thoughts which will be left to the imagination, resumed their interrupted tasks.

"Spill it, Virge!" Kinnison Lensed the pent-up thought. If Carbonero, who did not know Samms at all, had been amazed at what had been happening, Kinnison, who had known him so long and so well, had been literally and completely dumbfounded. "What in hell's behind this? What's the story? GIVE!"

Samms told him, and a mental silence fell; a silence too deep for intelligible thought. Each was beginning to realize that he never would and never could know what Mentor of Arisia really was.

GALACTIC PATROL

Dominating twice a hundred square miles of campus, parade ground, airport, and space port, a ninety-story edifice of chromium and glass sparkled dazzlingly in the bright sunlight of a June morning. This monumental pile was Wentworth Hall, in which the Tellurian candidates for the Lens of the Galactic Patrol live and move and have their being. One wing of its topmost floor seethed with tense activity, for that wing was the habitat of the lordly five-year men, this was graduation day, and in a few minutes Class 5 was due to report in Room A.

Room A, the private office of the commandant himself; the dreadful lair into which an undergraduate was summoned only to disappear from the Hall and from the cadet corps; the portentous chamber into which each year the handful of graduates marched and from which they emerged, each man in some subtle fashion changed.

In their cubicles of steel the graduates scanned each other narrowly, making sure that no wrinkle or speck of dust marred the black-and-silver perfection of the dress uniform of the patrol; that not even the tiniest spot of tarnish or dullness violated the glittering golden meteors upon their collars or the resplendently polished ray pistols and other equipment at their belts. The microscopic mutual inspection over, the kit boxes were snapped shut and racked, and the embryonic Lensmen made their way out into the assembly hall.

In the wardroom Kimball Kinnison, captain of the class by virtue of graduating at its head, and his three lieutenants, Clifford Maitland, Raoul LaForge, and Widel Holmberg, had inspected each other minutely and were now simply awaiting, in ever-increasing tension, the zero minute.

"Now, fellows, remember that drop!" the young captain jerked out. "We're dropping the shaft free, at higher velocity and in tighter formation than any class ever tried before. If anybody hashes the formation—our last show and with the whole corps looking on——"

"Don't worry about the drop, Kim," advised Maitland. "All three platoons will take that like clockwork. What's got me all of a dither is what is really going to happen in Room A."

"Uh-*huh*!" exclaimed LaForge and Holmberg as one.

"You can play that across the board for the whole class," Kinnison agreed. "Well, we'll soon know. It's time to get going."

The four officers stepped out into the assembly hall, the class springing to attention at their approach.

Kinnison, now all brisk captain, stared along the mathematically exact lines and snapped: "Report!"

"Class 5 present in full, sir!" The sergeant major touched a stud at his belt and all vast Wentworth Hall fairly trembled under the impact of an all-pervading, lilting, throbbing melody as the world's finest military band crashed into "Our Patrol."

"Squads left—march!" Although no possible human voice could have been heard in that gale of soul-stirring sound, and although Kinnison's lips did not move, his command was carried to the very bones of those for whom it was intended—and to no one else—by the tight-beam ultra-communicators strapped upon their chests. "Close formation—forward—march!"

*

In perfect alignment and cadence, the little column marched down the hall. In their path yawned the shaft—a vertical pit some twenty feet square extending from main floor to roof of the Hall; more than a thousand sheer feet of unobstructed air, cleared now of all traffic by flaring red lights. Five left heels clicked sharply, simultaneously upon the lip of the stupendous abyss. Five right legs swept out into emptiness. Five right hands snapped to belts and five bodies, rigidly erect, arrowed downward at such an appalling velocity that to unpracticed vision they simply vanished.

Six tenths of a second later, precisely upon a beat of the stirring march, those ten heels struck the main floor of Wentworth Hall, but not with a click. Dropping with a velocity of almost two thousand feet per second though they were at the instant of impact, yet those five husky bodies came from full speed to an instantaneous, shockless, effortless halt at contact. The drop had been made under complete neutralization of inertia—"free," in space parlance. Inertia restored, the march was resumed—or rather continued—in perfect time with the band. Five left feet swung out, and as the right toes left the floor the second rank, with only bare inches to spare, plunged down into the space its predecessor had occupied a moment before.

Rank after rank landed and marched away with machinelike precision. The dread door of Room A opened automatically at the approach of the cadets and closed behind them.

"Column right—march!" Kinnison commanded inaudibly, and the class obeyed in clockwork perfection. "Column left—march! Squads right—march! Company—halt! Salute!"

In company front, in a huge, square room devoid of furniture, the class faced the ogre—Inspector General Fritz von Hohendorff, commandant of cadets. Martinet, tyrant, dictator—he was known throughout the system as the embodiment of soullessness; and, insofar as he had ever been known to show emotion or feeling before any undergraduate, he seemed to glory in his repute of being the most pitilessly rigid disciplinarian that Earth had ever known. His thick, white hair was roached fiercely upward into a stiff pompadour. His left eye was of glass and his face bore dozens of tiny, thread-like scars; for not even the marvelous plastic surgery of that age could repair entirely the havoc wrought by the lethal rays of space combat. Also, his right leg and left arm, although practically normal to all outward seeming, were in reality largely products of science and art instead of nature.

Kinnison faced, then, this reconstructed potentate, saluted crisply, and snapped: "Sir, Class 5 reports to the commandant."

"Take your post, sir." The veteran saluted as punctiliously; and as he did so a semicircular desk rose around him from the floor—a desk whose most striking feature was an intricate mechanism surrounding a splintlike form so shaped as to receive a man's left arm.

"No. 1, Kimball Kinnison!" Von Hohendorff barked. "Front and center—march! The oath, sir."

THE LENSMAN

"Before the omnipotent witness I promise never to lower the standard of the Galactic Patrol," Kinnison said reverently; and, baring his left arm, thrust it into the hollow form.

*

From a small container labeled: "No. 1, Kimball Kinnison," the commandant shook out what was apparently an ornament—a lenticular jewel fabricated of hundreds of tiny, dead-white gems. Taking it up with a pair of insulated forceps, he touched it momentarily to the bronzed skin of the arm before him, and at that fleeting contact a flash as of many-colored fire swept over the stones. Satisfied, he dropped the jewel into a recess provided for it in the mechanism, which at once burst into activity.

The forearm was wrapped in thick insulation; molds and shields snapped into place, and there flared out an instantly suppressed flash of brilliance intolerable. Then the molds fell apart; the insulation was removed; there was revealed the Lens. Clamped to Kinnison's brawny wrist by a massive bracelet of imperishable, almost unbreakable, metal in which it was embedded it shone in all its lambent splendor—no longer a whitely inert piece of jewelry, but a lenticular polychrome of writhing, almost fluid radiance, which proclaimed to all observers in symbols of ever-changing flame that here was a Lensman of the Galactic Patrol.

In similar fashion each man of the class was invested with the symbol of his rank. Then the stern-faced inspector general touched a button and from the bare metal floor there arose deeply upholstered chairs, one for each graduate.

"Fall out!" he commanded, then smiled almost boyishly—the first intimation any of the class had ever had that the hard-boiled old tyrant *could* smile—and went on in a strangely altered voice: "Sit down, men, and smoke up. We have an hour in which to talk things over, and now I can tell you what it is all about. Each of you will find his favorite refreshment in the arm of his chair.

"No, there's no catch to it," he continued, in answer to amazedly doubtful stares, and lighted a huge black cigar of Venus-grown tobacco as he spoke. "You are Lensmen now, and henceforth each of you is accountable only to himself and to GHQ. Of course, you have yet to go through the formalities of commencement, but they don't count. Each of you really graduated when the Lens was welded around his arm.

"We know your individual preferences, and each of you has his favorite weed, from Tillotson's Pittsburgh stogies up to Snowden's Alsakanite cigarettes—even though Alsakan is just about as far away from here as a planet can be and still lie within the galaxy.

"We also know that you are all immune to the lure of noxious drugs. If you were not, you would not be here to-day. So smoke up and speak up. Ask any questions you care to, and I will try to answer them. Nothing is barred now. This room is shielded against any spy ray or communicator beam operable upon any known frequency."

There was a brief and rather uncomfortable silence. Then Kinnison suggested, diffidently: "Might it not be best, sir, to tell us all about it, from the ground up? I imagine that most of us are in too much of a daze to ask intelligent questions."

*

"Perhaps. While some of you undoubtedly have your suspicions, I will begin by telling you what is behind what you have been put through during the last five years. Feel

356

perfectly free to break in with questions at any time. You know that every year one million eighteen-year-old boys of Earth are chosen as cadets by competitive examinations. You know that during the first year, before any of them see Wentworth Hall, that number shrinks to less than fifty thousand. You know that by graduation day there are only, approximately, one hundred left in the class. Now I am allowed to tell you that you graduates are those who have come with flying colors through the most brutally rigid, the most fiendishly thorough process of elimination that it has been possible to develop.

"Every man who can be made to reveal any sign of weakness is dropped. Most of these are dismissed from the patrol. There are many splendid men, however, who, for some reason not involving moral turpitude, are not quite what a Lensman must be. These men make up our organization, from grease monkeys up to the highest commissioned officers below the rank of Lensman. This explains what you already know—that the Galactic Patrol is the finest body of intelligent beings yet to serve under one banner.

"Of the million who started, you few are left. As must every being who has ever worn or who ever will wear the Lens, each of you has proven repeatedly, to the cold verge of death itself, that he is in every possible respect worthy to wear it. For instance, Kinnison here once had a highly adventurous interview with a lady of Aldebaran II and her friends. He did not know that we knew all about it, but we did."

Kinnison's very ears burned scarlet, but the commandant went imperturbably on: "So it was with Voelker and the hypnotist of Karalon; with LaForge and the bentlam eaters; with Flewelling when the Ganymede-Venus thionite smugglers tried to bribe him with ten million in gold."

"Good Heavens, commandant!" broke in one outraged youth. "Didn't we do any real work at all?"

"Plenty of it; but at the same time each of you underwent enough testing to prove definitely that you could not be cracked. And none of you need be ashamed, for you have passed every test. Those who did not pass them were those who were dropped.

"Nor is it any disgrace to have been dismissed from the service before graduation into the patrol. The million who started with you were the pick of the planet, yet we knew in advance that of that selected million scarcely one in ten thousand would measure up in every essential. Therefore, it would be manifestly unfair to stigmatize the rest of them because they were not born with that extra something, that ultimate quality of fiber which does, and of stern necessity *must*, characterize the wearers of the Lens. For that reason not even the man himself knows why he was dismissed, and no one save those who wear the Lens knows why they were selected—and a member of the patrol does not talk.

"It is necessary to consider the history and background of the patrol in order to bring out clearly the necessity for such care in the selection of its personnel. You are all familiar with it, but probably very few of you have thought of it in that connection. The patrol is, of course, an outgrowth of the old planetary police systems; and, until its development, law enforcement always lagged behind law violation. Thus, in the old days following the invention of the automobile, State troopers could not cross State lines. Then, when the national police finally took charge, they could not follow the rocket-equipped criminals across national boundaries.

*

"Still later, when interplanetary flight became a commonplace, the planetary police were at the same old disadvantage. They had no authority off their own worlds, while the public enemies flitted unhampered from planet to planet. And finally, with the invention of the inertialess drive and the consequent traffic between the worlds of hundreds of thousands of solar systems, crime became so rampant, so utterly uncontrollable, that it threatened the very foundations of civilization. A man could perpetrate any crime imaginable without fear of consequences, for in an hour he could be thousands of light years away from the scene and safely beyond the reach of the law.

"And helping powerfully toward utter chaos were the new vices, which were spreading from world to world; among others the taking of new and horrible drugs. Thionite, for instance; occurring only upon Trenco; a drug as much deadlier than heroin as that compound is than coffee, and which even now commands such a fabulous price that a man can carry a fortune in one hollow boot heel.

"Thus our patrol came into being. At first it was a pitiful enough organization. It was handicapped from without by politics and politicians, and at the same time it was honeycombed from within by the usual small but utterly poisonous percentage of the unfit—grafters, corruptionists, bribe takers, and out-and-out criminals. It was also hampered by the fact that there was then no emblem or credential which could not be counterfeited. No one could tell with certainty that the man in uniform was a patrolman and not a criminal in disguise.

"Slowly the patrol perfected itself. One of its greatest advances came with the invention of the Lens; which, being proof against counterfeiting or imitation, renders identification of all Lensmen automatic. The patrol then set up its own military courts and executed the few of its members guilty of misconduct. Standards of entrance were raised ever higher, and when it had become evident that the patrol was, to a man, incorruptible, it was granted more and ever more authority.

"Now its power is practically absolute. Its armament and equipment are the ultimate; its members can follow the lawbreaker wherever he may go. Furthermore, a Lensman can commandeer any material or assistance, wherever and whenever required; and the Lens is so respected throughout the galaxy that any wearer of it may be called upon at any time to be judge, jury, and executioner. Wherever he goes, upon, in, or through any land, water, air, or space, anywhere within the confines of our Island Universe, his word is *law*.

"That, I think, explains what you have been forced to undergo. The only excuse for its severity is that it produces results. In the last hundred years no wearer of the Lens has disgraced it. Any questions? About the Lens, for instance?"

"We have all wondered about the Lens, sir, of course," Maitland ventured. "The outlaws apparently keep up with us in science. Boskone himself is supposed to be a genius, and to have surrounded himself with a scientific staff second to none in the known universe. I have always supposed that what science can build, science can duplicate. Surely more than one Lens has fallen into the hands of the outlaws?"

"If it had been a scientific invention it would have been duplicated long ago," the commandant made surprising answer. "It is, however, not essentially scientific in nature. It is almost entirely philosophical, and was developed for us by the Arisians.

"Yes, each of you was sent to Arisia quite recently," Von Hohendorff went on, as the newly commissioned officers glanced at each other in dawning understanding. "What did you think of them, Murphy?"

"At first, sir, I thought that they were some new kind of dragon; but dragons with brains that you could actually *feel*. I was glad to get away, sir. They fairly gave me the creeps, even though I never did see one of them so much as move."

*

"They are a peculiar race," the commandant went on. "Essentially antisocial—or rather, supremely indifferent to all material things. For hundreds of thousands of generations they have devoted themselves to thinking; mainly of the essence of life. They say that they know scarcely anything fundamental concerning it; but even so they know more about it than does any other known race. While ordinarily they will have no intercourse whatever with outsiders, they did consent to help the patrol, for the good of all intelligence.

"Thus, each being about to graduate into the patrol is sent to Arisia, where a Lens is built to match its individual life force. While no mind other than that of an Arisian can understand its operation, thinking of your Lens as being synchronized with, or in exact resonance with your own vital principle or ego will give you a rough idea of it. The Lens is not really alive, as we understand the term. It is, however, endowed with a sort of pseudolife, by virtue of which it gives off its strong, characteristically changing light as long as it is in metal-to-flesh circuit with the living mentality for which it was designed. Also, by virtue of that pseudolife, it acts as a telepath through which you may converse with other intelligences, even though they may possess no organs either of sight or of hearing as we know those senses. It also has other highly important uses.

"The Lens cannot be removed by any one except its wearer without dismemberment; it glows as long as its rightful owner wears it; and it ceases to glow in the instant of its owner's death. Also—and here is the thing that renders impossible the impersonation of a Lensman—not only does the Lens not glow if worn by an impostor; but if a patrolman be dismembered and his Lens removed, that Lens kills, in a space of minutes, any living being who attempts to wear it. Its pseudolife interferes so strongly with any life to which it is not attuned that that life force cannot exist in this plane."

*

A brief silence fell, during which the young men absorbed the stunning import of what their commandant had been saying. More, there was striking into each young consciousness a realization of the stark heroism of the grand old Lensman before them; a man of such fiber that although physically incapacitated and long past the retirement age, he had conquered his human emotions sufficiently to accept deliberately his ogre's rôle, because in that way he could best further the progress of his patrol!

"I have scarcely broken the ground," Von Hohendorff continued. "I have merely given you an introduction to your new status. During the next few weeks, before you are assigned to duty, other officers will make clear to you the many things about which you

359

are still in the dark. Our time is growing short, but perhaps we have time for one more question."

"Not a question, sir, but something more important," Kinnison spoke up. "I speak for the class when I say that we have misjudged you grievously, and we wish to apologize."

"I thank you sincerely for the thought, although it is unnecessary. You could not have thought otherwise of me than as you did. It is not a particularly pleasant task that we old men have—that of weeding out the unfit. But we are too old for active duty in space—we no longer have the instantaneous nervous responses that are for that duty imperative—so we do what we can. However, the work has its brighter side, since each year there are about a hundred found worthy of the Lens. This, my one hour with the graduates, more than makes up for the year that precedes it; and the other oldsters have somewhat similar compensations.

"In conclusion, you are now able to understand fully what kind of mentalities compose our patrol. You know that any creature wearing the Lens is in every sense a Lensman, whether he be human or, hailing from some strange and distant planet, a monstrosity of a shape you have as yet not even imagined. Whatever his form, you may rest assured that he has been tested even as you have been; that he is as worthy of trust as are you yourselves. My last word is this—men of the Galactic Patrol die, but they do not fold up; individuals come and go, but the patrol goes on!"

Then, again all martinet: "Class 5, attention!" he barked. "Report upon the stage of the main auditorium!"

The class, again a rigidly military unit, marched out of Room A and down the long corridor toward the great theater in which, before the massed cadet corps and a throng of civilians, they were to be formally graduated.

As they marched along the graduates realized in what way the wearers of the Lens who emerged from Room A were different from the candidates who had entered it such a short time before. They had gone in as boys—nervous, apprehensive, and still somewhat unsure of themselves, in spite of their survival through the five long years of grueling tests which now lay behind them. They emerged from Room A as men; men knowing for the first time the real meaning of the physical and mental tortures they had undergone; men able to wield justly the vast powers whose scope and scale they could even now but dimly comprehend.

II.

Barely a month after his graduation, even before he had entirely completed the postgraduate tours of duty mentioned by Von Hohendorff, Kinnison was summoned to Prime Base by no less a personage than Port Admiral Haynes himself. There, in the admiral's private aëro, whose flaring lights cleared a path as though by magic through the swarming traffic, the novice and the veteran flew slowly over the vast establishment of the base.

Shops and factories, citylike barracks, landing fields stretching beyond the far horizon; flying craft ranging from tiny, one-man helicopters through small and large scouts, patrol ships and cruisers up to the immense, globular superdreadnaughts of space—all these were observed and commented upon. Finally, the aëro landed beside a long, comparatively low building—a structure heavily guarded, inside the base although it was—within which Kinnison saw a thing that fairly snatched away his breath.

A space ship it was—but what a ship! In bulk it was vastly larger even than the superdreadnaughts of the patrol; but, unlike them, it was, in shape, a perfect teardrop, streamlined to the ultimate possible degree.

"What do you think of her?" the port admiral asked.

"Think of her!" The young officer gulped twice before he attained coherence. "I can't put it in words, sir; but some day, if I live long enough and develop enough force, I hope to command a ship like that."

"Sooner than you think, Kinnison," Haynes told him, flatly. "You are in command of her beginning to-morrow morning."

"Huh? Me?" Kinnison exclaimed, but sobered quickly. "Oh, I see, sir. It takes ten years of proved accomplishment to rate command of a first-class enforcement vessel, and I have no rating at all. You have already intimated that this ship is experimental. There is, then, something about her that is new and untried, and so dangerous that you do not want to risk an experienced commander in her. I am to give her a work-out, and if I can bring her back in one piece I turn her over to her real captain. But that's all right with me, admiral—thanks a lot for picking me out. What a chance! *What* a chance!" Kinnison's eye gleamed at the prospect of even a brief command of such a creation.

"Right—and wrong," the old admiral made surprising answer. "It is true that she is new, untried, and dangerous, so much so that we are unwilling to give her to any of our present captains. No, she is not really new, either. Rather, her basic idea is so old that it has been abandoned for centuries. She uses explosives, of a type that cannot be tried out fully except in actual combat. Her primary weapon is what we have called the 'Q-gun.' The propellent is heptadetonite; the shell carries a charge of twenty metric tons of duodecaplylatomate."

"But, sir——" Kinnison began.

*

"Just a minute, I'll go into that later. While your premises were correct, your conclusion is not. You graduated No. 1, and in every respect, save experience, you are as well qualified to command as is any captain of the fleet; and since the *Brittania* is such a radical departure from any conventional type, battle experience is not a prerequisite. Therefore, if she holds together through one engagement she is yours for good. In other words, to make up for the possibility of having yourself scattered all over space, you have a chance to win that ten years' rating you mentioned a minute ago, all in one trip. Fair enough?"

"Fair? It's fine—wonderful! And thanks a——"

"Never mind the thanks until you get back. You were about to comment, I believe, upon the impossibility of using explosives against a free opponent?"

"It can't be impossible, of course, since the *Brittania* has been built. I just don't quite see how it could have been made effective."

"You lock to the pirate with tractors, screen to screen—dex about ten kilometers. You blast a hole through his screens to his wall shield. The muzzle of the Q-gun mounts an annular multiplex projector which puts out a Q-type tube of force—Q47SM9, to be exact. As you can see from the type formula, this helix extends the gun barrel from ship to ship and confines the propellent gases behind the projectile, where they belong. When the shell strikes the wall shield of the pirate and detonates, *something* will have to give way.

"The tube and tractors, being pure force and computed for this particular combination of explosions, will hold; and our physicists have calculated that the ten-kilometer column of inert propellent gases will offer so much inertia and resistance that any possible wall shield will have to go down. That is the point that cannot be tried out experimentally. It is quite within the bounds of possibility that the pirates may have been able to develop wall screens as powerful as our Q-type helices.

"It should not be necessary to point out to you that if they *have* been able to develop a wall shield that will stand up under detonating duodecaplylatomate, the back blast through the breech of the Q-gun will blow the *Brittania* apart as though she were made of matchwood. That is only one of the chances—and perhaps not the greatest one—that you and your crew will have to take. They are all volunteers, by the way, and will get plenty of extra rating if they come through alive. Do you want the job?"

"You don't have to ask me that, chief—you *know* I want it!"

"Of course, but I had to go through the formality of asking, sometime. But to get on with the discussion. This pirate situation is entirely out of control, as you already know. We don't even know whether Boskone is a reality, a figurehead, a symbol, or simply a figment of somebody's imagination. But whoever or whatever Boskone really is, some being or some group of beings has perfected a mighty efficient organization of outlaws; so efficient that we haven't been able to locate their main base.

*

"You may as well know now a fact that is not yet public property; that even convoyed vessels are no longer safe. The pirates have developed ships of a new and extraordinary type; ships that are much faster than our heavy battleships, and yet vastly more heavily armed than our fast cruisers. Thus, they can outfight any enforcement vessel that can catch them, and can outrun anything of ours armed heavily enough to stand up against their beams."

"That accounts for the recent heavy losses," Kinnison mused.

"Yes," Haynes went on, grimly. "Ship after ship of our best has been blasted out of the ether, doomed before it pointed a beam, and more will be. We cannot force an engagement on our terms; we must fight on theirs.

"That is the present intolerable situation. We *must* learn what the pirates' new power system is. Our scientists say that it may be anything, from cosmic-energy receptors and converters down to a controlled space warp—whatever that may be. Anyway, they haven't been able to duplicate it, so it is up to us to find out what it is. The *Brittania* is the tool our engineers have designed to get that information. She is the fastest thing in space, developing at full blast an inert acceleration of *ten gravities*. Figure out for yourself what velocity that means free in open space!"

"You have just said that we can't have everything in one ship," Kinnison said, thoughtfully. "What did they sacrifice to get that speed?"

"All the conventional offensive armament," Haynes replied frankly. "She has no long-range beams at all, and only enough short-range stuff to help drive the Q-helix through the enemy's screens. Practically her only offense is the Q-gun. But she has plenty of defensive screens; she has speed enough to catch anything afloat; and she has the Q-gun—which we hope will be enough.

"Now we'll go over the general plan of action. The engineers will go into all the technical details with you, during a test flight that will last as long as you like. When you and your crew are thoroughly familiar with every phase of her operation, bring the engineers back here to base and go out on patrol.

"Somewhere in the galaxy you will find a pirate vessel of the new type. You lock to him, as I said before. You attach the Q-gun well forward, being sure that the point of attachment is far enough away from the power rooms so that the essential mechanisms will not be destroyed. You board and storm—another revival of the technique of older times. Specialists in your crew, who will have done nothing much up to that time, will then find out what our scientists want to know. If at all possible, they will send it in instantly via tight-beam communicator. If, because of distance or for any other reason, it should be impossible for them to communicate, the whole thing is again up to you."

The port admiral paused, his eyes boring into those of the younger man, then went on impressively: "That information *must* get back to base. If it does not, the *Brittania* is a failure; we will be right back where we started from; the slaughter of our men and the destruction of our ships will continue unchecked. As to how you are to do it, we cannot give you even general instructions. All I can say is that you have the most important assignment in the universe to-day, and repeat—*that information must get back to base*. Now come aboard and meet your crew and the engineers."

*

Under the expert tutelage of the designers and builders of the *Brittania* Vice Commander Kinnison drove her hither and thither through the trackless wastes of the galaxy. Inert and "free," under every possible degree of power he maneuvered her; attacking imaginary foes and actual meteorites with equal zeal. Maneuvered and attacked until he and his ship were one; until he reacted automatically to her slightest demand; until he and every man of his eager and highly trained crew knew to the final volt and to the ultimate ampere her Gargantuan capacity both to give it and to take it.

Then and only then did he return to base, unload the engineers, and set out upon the quest. Trail after trail he followed, but all were cold. Alarm after alarm he answered, but always he arrived too late; arrived to find gutted merchantmen and riddled enforcement vessel, with no life in either and with nothing to indicate in which direction the marauders might have gone.

Finally, however: "QBT! Calling QBT!" The *Brittania's* code call blared from the sealed-band speaker, and a string of numbers followed—the spatial coördinates of the luckless vessel's position.

THE LENSMAN

Chief Pilot Henry Henderson punched the figures upon his locator, and in the "tank"—the enormous, minutely cubed model of the galaxy—there appeared a redly brilliant point of light. Kinnison rocketed out of his narrow bunk, digging the sleep out of his eyes, and shot himself into his place beside the pilot.

"Right in our laps!" he exulted. "Scarcely ten light years away! Start scrambling the ether!" And as the vengeful cruiser darted toward the scene of depredation all space became filled with blast after blast of static interference through which, it was hoped, the pirate could not summon the help he was so soon to need.

But that howling static gave the pirate commander pause. Surely this was something new? Before him lay a richly laden freighter, its two convoying enforcement ships already practically *hors de combat*. A few more minutes and the prize would be his. Nevertheless, he darted away, swept the ether with his detectors, saw the *Brittania*, and turned in headlong flight. For if this streamlined freighter was sufficiently convinced of its prowess to try to blanket the ether against *him*, that information was something that Boskone would value far above one shipload of material wealth.

*

But the pirate craft was now upon the visiplates of the *Brittania*, and, entirely ignoring the crippled space ships, Henderson flung his vessel after the other. Manipulating his incredibly complex controls purely by touch, the while staring into his plate not only with his eyes, but with every fiber of his being as well, he hurled his huge mount hither and thither in frantic leaps. After what seemed an age he snapped down a toggle switch and relaxed long enough to grin at Kinnison.

"Holding 'em?" the young commander demanded.

"Got 'em, skipper," the pilot replied, positively. "It was touch and go for ninety seconds, but I've got a CRX tracer on him now at full pull. He can't put out enough jets to get away from *that*. I can hold him forever!"

"Fine work, Hen!" Kinnison strapped himself into his seat and donned his headset. "General call! Attention! Battle stations! By stations, report!"

"Station 1, tractor beams—hot!"

"Station 2, repellers—hot!"

"Station 3, projector 1—hot!"

Thus station after station of the warship of the void reported, until: "Station 58, the Q-gun—hot!" Kinnison himself reported; then gave to the pilot the words which throughout the space-ways of the galaxy had come to mean complete readiness to face any emergency.

"Hot and tight, Hen—let's take 'em!"

The pilot shoved his blast lever, already almost at maximum, clear out against its stop and hunched himself even more intently over his instruments. As moved his pointers, so varied the direction of the thrust that was driving the *Brittania* toward the enemy at the unimaginable velocity of ninety parsecs an hour—a velocity possible only to inertialess matter being urged through an almost perfect vacuum by a driving blast capable of lifting the stupendous normal tonnage of the immense sky rover against a gravity ten times that of her native Earth.

SUPER PACK

Unimaginable? Completely so—the ship of the Galactic Patrol was hurling herself through space at a pace in comparison with which any speed that the mind can grasp would be the merest crawl: a pace to make light itself seem stationary.

Ordinary vision would have been useless, but the observers of that day used no antiquated optical system. Their detector beams, converted into light only at their plates, were heterodyned upon and were carried by subethereal ultra-waves; vibrations residing far below the level of the ether and thus possessing a velocity and a range infinitely greater than those of any possible ether-borne wave.

Although stars moved across the visiplates in flaming, zigzag lines of light, as pursued and pursuer passed system after solar system in fantastic, light-years long hops, yet Henderson kept his cruiser upon the pirate's tail and steadily cut down the distance between them. Soon a tractor beam licked out from the patrol ship, touched the fleeing marauder lightly, and the two space ships flashed toward each other.

*

Nor was the enemy unprepared for combat. One of the crack raiders of Boskone, master pirate of the known universe, she had never before found difficulty in conquering any vessel fleet enough to catch her. Therefore, her commander made no attempt to cut the beam. Or rather, since the two inertialess vessels flashed together to repeller-zone contact in such a minute fraction of a second that any human action within that time was impossible, it would be more correct to say that the pirate captain changed his tactics instantly from those of flight to those of combat.

He thrust out tractor beams of his own, and from the already white-hot refractory throats of his projectors there raved out horribly potent beams of annihilation, beams of dreadful power which tore madly at the straining defensive screens of the patrol ship. Screens flared vividly, radiating all the colors of the spectrum. Space itself seemed a rainbow gone mad, for there were being exerted there forces of a magnitude to stagger the imagination—forces to be yielded only by the atomic might from which they sprang—forces whose neutralization set up visible strains in the very fabric of the ether itself.

The young commander, seated at his conning plate, clenched his fists and swore a startled, deep-space oath as his eyes swept over the delicately accurate meters and gauges before him; for under the frightful impact of that instantaneously launched attack his outer screen was already down and his second was beginning to crack!

"We'll have to scrap the regulation battle plan!" he barked into his microphone. "Open all motors to absolute top; cut all resistance out of No. 3 Circuit. Dalhousie, cut all repellers, bring us right up to their zone. All you beamers, concentrate on area K. *Break down those screens!*" Kinnison was hunched rigidly over his panel; his voice came grittily through locked teeth. "Cut *all* your resistors if you have to, the motors and accumulators will hold long enough. There, that's better. Our third is up again and theirs is going down. Come on, boys, burn 'em down! Give 'em everything you can put through the bare bus bars! No matter what it takes, get through to that wall shield, so that I can use this Q-gun!"

365

THE LENSMAN

Little by little, under the stupendous force of the *Brittania's* attack the defenses of the enemy began to fail, and Kinnison's hands flew over his controls. A port opened in the patrol ship's armored side and an ugly snout protruded—the projector-ringed muzzle of a squat and monstrous cannon. From its projector bands there leaped out, with the velocity of light, a tube of quasi-solid force which was, in effect, a continuation of the rifle's grim barrel; a tube which crashed through the weakened third screen of the enemy with a space-racking shock and struck savagely, with writhing, twisting thrusts, at the second.

Aided by the massed concentration of the *Brittania's* every battery of short-range beams, it went through—and through the first. Now it struck the very wall shield of the outlaw—that impregnable screen which, designed to bear the brunt of any possible inert collision, had never been pierced or ruptured by any material substance, however applied.

To this inner defense the immaterial gun barrel clung. Simultaneously, the tractor beams, hitherto exerting only a few dynes of force, stiffened into unbreakable, inflexible rods of energy, binding the two ships of space into one rigid system; each, relative to the other, immovable.

*

Then Kinnison's flying finger tip touched a button and the Q-gun spoke. From its sullen throat there erupted a huge torpedo. Slowly the giant projectile crept along, watched in awe and amazement by the officers of both vessels. For to those space-hardened veterans the velocity of light was a veritable crawl; and here was a thing that would require four or five whole seconds to cover a mere ten kilometers of distance!

But, although slow, this bomb *might* prove dangerous, therefore the pirate commander threw his every resource into attempts to cut the tube of force, to blast away from the tractor beams, to explode the sluggish missile before it could reach his wall shields. In vain; for the *Brittania's* every beam was set to protect the torpedo and the mighty rods of energy without whose grip the inertialess mass of the enemy vessel would offer no resistance whatever to the force of the proposed explosion.

Slowly, *so* slowly, as the age-long seconds crawled into eternity, there extended from enforcement vessel almost to pirate wall a raging, white-hot-pillar—the gases of combustion of the propellent heptadetonite—ahead of which there rushed the Q-gun's tremendous shell with its horribly destructive freight. What would happen? Could even the almost immeasurable force of that frightful charge of duodecaplylatomate break down a wall shield designed to withstand the cosmic assaults of meteoric missiles? And what would happen if that wall screen held?

In spite of himself Kinnison's mind insisted upon painting the ghastly picture: the awful explosion; the pirate's screen still intact; the raving gases driven backward along the tube of force. The bare metal of the Q-gun's breech, he knew, was not and could not be reënforced by the infinitely stronger, although immaterial shields of pure energy which protected the hull; and no conceivable substance, however resistant, could impede, save momentarily, the unimaginable forces about to be unleashed.

Nor would there be time to release the Q-tube after the explosion but before the *Brittania's* own destruction; for if the enemy's shield stayed up for even a fraction of a second, the unthinkable pressure of the blast would propagate backward through the already densely compressed gases in the tube, would sweep away as though it were nothing the immensely thick metallic barrier of the gun breech, and would wreak within the bowels of the patrol ship a destruction even more complete than that intended for the foe.

Nor were his men in better case. Each knew that this was the climactic instant of his whole existence; that life itself hung poised upon the issue of the next split second. Hurry it up! Snap into it! Will that crawling, creeping thing *never* strike? Some prayed briefly; some swore bitterly; but prayers and curses were alike unconscious and had precisely the same meaning—each man, white of face and grim of jaw, clenched his hands and waited, tense and straining, for the impact.

III.

The missile struck, and in the instant of its striking the coldly brilliant stars were blotted from sight in a vast globe of intolerable flame. The pirate's shield had failed, and under the cataclysmic force of that horrible detonation the entire nose section of the enemy vessel had flashed into incandescent vapor and had added itself to the rapidly expanding cloud of fire. As it expanded, the cloud cooled. Its fierce glare subsided to a rosy glow, through which the stars again began to shine. It faded, cooled, darkened, revealing the crippled hulk of the pirate ship. She was still fighting; but ineffectually, now that all her heavy forward batteries were gone.

"Needlers, fire at will!" barked Kinnison, and even that feeble resistance was ended. Keen-eyed needle-ray men, working at spy-ray visiplates, bored hole after hole into the captive, seeking out and destroying the control-panels of the remaining beams and screens.

"Pull 'er up!" came the next order. The two ships of space flashed together—the yawning, blasted-open fore end of the once cigar-shaped raider solidly against the *Brittania's* armored side. A great port opened.

"Now, Bus, it's all yours. Classification to three places—A point A A. They're human or approximately so. Board and storm!"

Back of that port there had been massed a hundred fighting men—dressed in full panoply of space armor, armed with the deadliest weapons known to the science of the age, and powered by the gigantic accumulators of their ship. At their head was Sergeant VanBuskirk, six and a half feet of Dutch-Valerian dynamite, who had fallen out of Valeria's cadet corps only because of an innate inability to master the intricacies of higher mathematics. Now the attackers swept forward in a black-and-silver wave.

Four squatly massive semiportable projectors crashed down upon their magnetic clamps and in the fierce ardor of their beams the thick bulkhead before them ran the gamut of the spectrum and puffed outward. Some score of defenders were revealed, likewise clad in armor, and battle again was joined. Explosive and solid bullets detonated against and ricocheted from that highly efficient armor, the beams of DeLameter hand projectors splashed in torrents of man-made lightning off its protective fields of force.

But that skirmish was soon over. The semiportables, whose vast energies no ordinary personal armor could withstand, were brought up and clamped down; and in their holocaust of vibratory destruction all life vanished from the pirates' compartment.

"One more bulkhead and we're in their control room!" VanBuskirk cried. "Beam it down!"

But when the beams pressed their switches nothing happened. The pirates had managed to jury rig a screen generator, and with it had cut the power beams behind the invading forces. Also they had cut loopholes in this bulkhead, through which, in frantic haste, they were trying to bring heavy projectors of their own into alignment.

"Bring up the ferral paste," the sergeant commanded. "Get up as close to that wall as you can, so they can't blast us!"

The paste—an ultra-modern development of thermite—was brought up and the giant Dutchman himself troweled it on in furious swings, from floor up and around in a huge arc and back down to floor. He fired it, and simultaneously some of the enemy gunners managed to angle a projector sharply enough to reach the farther ranks of the enforcement men. Then mingled the flashing, scintillating, gassy glare of the thermite and the raving energy of the pirates' beam to make of that confined space a veritable inferno.

*

But the paste had done its work, and as the semicircle of wall fell out the soldiers of the Lens leaped through the hole in the still-glowing wall to struggle hand to hand against the pirates, now making a desperate last stand. The semiportables and other heavy ordnance powered from the *Brittania's* accumulators were, of course, useless. Pistols were ineffective against the pirates' armor of hard alloy; hand rays were equally impotent against its defensive shields.

Now heavy hand grenades began to rain down among the combatants, blowing enforcement men and no few pirates to bits. For the outlaw chiefs cared nothing that they killed some of their own men, if in so doing they could take a proportionately greater toll of the law. And worse, a crew of gunners was swiveling a mighty projector around upon its hastily improvised mount, to cover that sector of the great compartment in which the policemen were most densely massed.

But the minions of the law had one remaining weapon, carried expressly for this eventuality, and no mean weapon it proved to be. The space ax—a combination and sublimation of battle ax, mace, and bludgeon—a massively needle-pointed implement of potentialities limited only by the physical strength and bodily agility of its wielder.

Now, all the men of the *Brittania's* storming party were Valerians, and therefore were big, hard, fast, and agile; and of them all, their sergeant leader was the biggest, hardest, fastest, and most agile. When the space-tempered apex of that thirty-pound monstrosity, driven by the four-hundred-odd pounds of rawhide and whalebone that was his body, struck pirate armor, that armor gave way. Nor did it matter whether or not that hellish beak of steel struck a vital part after crashing through the armor. Head or body, leg or arm, the net result was the same; a man does not fight effectively when he is breathing space in lieu of atmosphere.

VanBuskirk perceived the danger to his men in the slowly turning ray projector, and for the first time called his chief.

"Kim," he spoke in level tones into his microphone. "Blast that delta ray, will you? . . . Or have they cut this beam, so you can't hear me? . . . Guess they have."

"They've cut our communication," he informed his troopers then. "Keep them off me as much as you can and I'll attend to that delta-ray outfit myself."

Aided by the massed interference of his men, he plunged toward the threatening mechanism, hewing to right and to left as he strode. Beside the temporary projector mount at last, he aimed a tremendous blow at the man at the delta-ray controls; only to feel the ax flash instantaneously to its mark and strike it with a gentle push, and to see his intended victim float effortlessly away from the blow. The pirate commander had played his last card: VanBuskirk floundered, not only weightless, but inertialess as well!

But the huge Dutchman's mind, while not mathematical, was even faster than his lightninglike muscles, and not for nothing had he spent arduous weeks in inertialess tests of strength and skill. Hooking feet and legs around a convenient wheel, he seized the enemy operator and jammed his helmeted head down between the base of the mount and the long, heavy steel lever by means of which it was turned. Then, throwing every ounce of his wonderful body into the effort, he braced both feet against the projector's grim barrel and heaved. The helmet flew apart like an eggshell; blood and brains gushed out in nauseous blobs. But the delta-ray projector was so jammed that it would not soon again become a threat.

Then VanBuskirk drew himself across the room toward the main control panel of the warship. Officer after officer he pushed aside, then reversed two double-throw switches, restoring gravity and inertia to the riddled cruiser.

*

In the meantime the tide of battle had continued in favor of enforcement. Few survivors though there were of the black-and-silver force, of the pirates there were still fewer, fighting now a desperate and hopeless defensive. But in this combat quarter was not, *could* not be thought of, and Sergeant VanBuskirk again waded into the fray. Four times more his horribly effective hybrid weapon descended like the irresistible hammer of Thor, cleaving and crushing its way through steel and flesh and bone. Then, striding to the control board, he manipulated switches and dials, then again spoke evenly to Kinnison.

"You can hear me now, can't you? . . . All mopped up. Come and get the dope!"

The specialists, headed by Chief Technician LaVerne Thorndyke, had been waiting strainingly for that word for minutes. Now they literally flew at their tasks, in furious haste, but following rigidly and in perfect coördination a prearranged schedule. Every control and lead, every bus bar and immaterial beam of force was traced and checked. Instruments and machines were dismantled; sealed mechanisms were ruthlessly torn apart by jacks or sliced open with cutting beams. And everywhere, everything and every movement was being photographed, charted, and diagramed.

"Getting the idea now, Kim," the chief technician said finally, during a brief lull in his work. "A sweet system—"

"Look at this!" a mechanic interrupted. "Here's a machine that's all shot to pieces!"

The shielding cover had been torn from a monstrous fabrication of metal, apparently a motor or generator of an exceedingly complex type. The insulation of its coils and windings had fallen away in charred fragments; its copper had melted down in sluggish, viscous streams.

"That's what we've been looking for," Thorndyke declared. "Check those leads! Alpha!"

"Seven-three-nine-four!" And the minutely careful study went on until: "That's enough; we've got everything we need now. Have you draftsmen and photographers got everything down solid?"

"On the boards!" and "In the cans!" rapped out the two reports as one.

"Then let's go!"

"And go *fast!*" Kinnison ordered, brusquely. "I'm afraid that we're going to run out of time as it is!"

All hands hurried back into the *Brittania*, paying no attention to the bodies littering the decks. So desperate was the emergency, each man knew, that nothing could be done about the dead, whether friend or foe. Every resource of mechanism, of brain and of brawn, must needs be strained to the utmost if they themselves were not soon to be in similar case.

"Can you talk, Nels?" demanded Kinnison of his communications officer, even before the air lock had closed.

"No, sir. They're blanketing us plenty," that worthy replied instantly. "Space's so full of static that you couldn't drive a power beam through it, let alone a communicator. Couldn't talk direct, anyway. Look where we are." He pointed out in the tank their present location.

"Hm-m-m. We couldn't have got much farther away from Earth without jumping the galaxy entirely. Boskone got a warning, either from that ship back there or from the disturbance. They are undoubtedly concentrating on us now. One of them will spear us with a tractor, just as sure as hell's a man-trap——"

*

The fledgling commander rammed both hands into his pockets and thought in black intensity. He *must* get this data back to base. But how? HOW? Henderson was already driving the vessel back toward the solar system with every iota of her inconceivable top speed, but it was out of the question even to hope that she would ever get there. The life of the *Brittania* was now, he was coldly certain, to be measured in hours—and all too scant measure, even of them. For there were hundreds of pirate vessels tearing through the void, forming a gigantic net to cut off her return to base. Fast though she was, one of that barricading horde would certainly manage to clamp a tracer ray upon her—and when that happened her flight was done.

Nor could she fight. She had conquered one first-class war vessel of the public enemy, it was true; but at what awful cost her captain knew only too well. The prodigious drain of power had almost emptied her accumulators. Also, and worse, the refractories of her main projectors were burned away practically to the shells. Without vastly heavier bracing fields than the *Brittania* carried, no substance, however stable, could stand up long under such hellish loads as they had had to handle.

The Q-gun was as useless as a fountain pen without full-driven offensive beams. One fresh vessel, similar to the one they had just left, could very easily blast his crippled mount out of space. Nor would there be only one. Within a space of minutes after the attachment of a tracer ray, the enforcement vessel would be surrounded by the cream of Boskone's fighters. There was apparently only one way out offering any chance at all of success; and slowly, thoughtfully, and finally grimly, young Vice Commander Kinnison—now and briefly Captain Kinnison—decided to take it.

"Everybody open your communicators and listen!" he ordered. "We must get this information back to base, and we can't do it in the *Brittania*. The pirates are bound to catch us, and our chance in another fight is exactly zero. We'll have to abandon ship and take to the lifeboats, in the hope that at least one of us will be able to get through their lines.

"The technicians and specialists will take all the data they got—information, descriptions, diagrams, pictures, everything—boil it down, and put it on a spool of tape. They will make thirty-nine copies of it, since there are just forty of us left, and one spool will be given to each man.

"There will be twenty boats, two men to a boat. We will start launching them after we have gone as far toward base as it is safe to go in this ship. Once away, use very little detectable power, or, better yet, no power at all, until you are sure that the pirates have chased the *Brittania* a good many parsecs away from where you are. From then on you'll be strictly on your own. Do it any way you can; but some way, *any* way, get your spool back to base. There's no use in me trying to impress you with the importance of this stuff; you know what it means as well as I do.

"Boat mates will be drawn by lot. The quartermaster will write all our names on slips of paper and draw them out of a helmet two at a time. The only exception to this is that if two navigators, such as Henderson and I, are drawn together, both names go back into the helmet. Get to work!"

*

Twice the name of Kinnison came out together with that of another skilled in astronautics and was replaced. The third time, however, it came out paired with VanBuskirk, to the manifest joy of the giant policeman and to the approval of the crowd as well.

"That was a break for me, chief!" the sergeant called over the cheers of his fellows. "I'm dead sure of getting back now!"

"Pretty strong talk, I'm afraid, but I don't know of any one I'd rather have at my back than you," Kinnison replied, with a boyish grin.

The pairings were made; DeLameters, spare batteries, and other equipment were checked and tested; the spools of tape were sealed in their corrosionproof containers and distributed; and Kinnison sat talking with the chief technician.

"So they've solved the problem of the really efficient reception and conversion of cosmic radiation!" Kinnison whistled softly through his teeth. "And a sun—even a small

371

one—radiates the energy given off by the annihilation of one-to-several million tons of matter per second! *Some* power!"

"That's the story, skip, and it explains completely why their ships have been so much superior to ours. They could have installed faster drives even than the *Brittania's*. They probably will, now that it has become necessary. Also, if the bus bars in that receptor-converter had been a few square centimeters larger in cross section, they could have held their wall shield, even against our duodec bomb. Then what? They had plenty of intake, but not quite enough distribution."

"They have atomic motors, the same as ours, just as big and just as efficient," Kinnison cogitated. "But those motors are all we *have* got, while they use them, and at full power, too, simply as first-stage exciters for the cosmic-energy screens. Blinding blue blazes, what power! Some of us *have* to get back, Verne. If we don't, Boskone's got the whole galaxy by the tail, and civilization is sunk without a trace."

"I'll say so; but also I'll say this for those of us who don't get back—it won't be for lack of trying. Well, I'd better go check up on my boat. If I don't see you again, Kim old man, clear ether!"

They shook hands briefly and Thorndyke strode away. En route, however, he paused beside the quartermaster and signaled to him to disconnect his communicator.

"Clever lad, Allerdyce!" Thorndyke whispered, with a grin. "Kinda loaded the dice a trifle once or twice, didn't you? I don't think anybody but me smelled a rat, though. Certainly neither the skipper nor Henderson did, or you'd 've had it to do over again."

"At least one team has got to get through," the quartermaster replied, quietly and obliquely, "and the strongest teams we can muster will find the going none too easy. Any team made up of strength and weakness is a weak team. Captain Kinnison, our only Lensman, is, of course, the best man aboard this buzz buggy. Who would you pick for No. 2?"

"VanBuskirk, of course, the same as you did. I wasn't criticizing you, man, I was complimenting you; and thanking you, in a roundabout way, for giving me Henderson. He's got plenty of what it takes, too."

"It wasn't 'VanBuskirk, of course,' by any means," the quartermaster rejoined. "It's mighty hard to figure either you or Henderson third, to say nothing of fourth, in any kind of company, however fast—mentally or physically. However, it seemed to me that you fitted in better with the pilot. I could hand pick only two teams without getting caught at it—you spotted me as it was—but I think that I picked the two strongest teams possible. At least one of you will get through, for all the tea there is in China. If none of you four can make it, nobody could."

"Well, here's hoping, anyway. Thanks again. See you again sometime, maybe. Clear ether!"

Chief Pilot Henderson had, a few minutes since, changed the course of the cruiser from right-line flight to fantastic, zigzag leaps through space, and now he turned frowningly to Kinnison.

"We'd better begin dumping them out pretty soon now, I think," he suggested. "We haven't detected anything yet, but according to the figures it won't be long now; and after they get their traps set we'll run out of time mighty quick."

"Right."

And then, one after another, but even so several light years apart in space, eighteen of the small boats were launched into the void. In the control room there were left only Henderson and Thorndyke with VanBuskirk and Kinnison, who were to be the last to leave.

"All right, Hen, now we'll try out your roulette-wheel director by chance," Kinnison said, then went on, in answer to Thorndyke's questioning glance. "A bouncing ball on an oscillating table. Every time the ball caroms off a pin it shifts the course through a fairly large, but entirely unpredictable angle. Pure chance—we thought it might cross them up a little."

Hair-line beams were connected from panels to pins, and soon four interested spectators looked on while, with no human guidance, the *Brittania* lurched and leaped even more erratically than she had done under Henderson's direction. Now, however, the ever-changing vectors of her course were as unexpected and surprising to her passengers as to any possible external observer.

*

One more lifeboat left the enforcement vessel, and only the Lensman and his giant aide remained. While they were waiting the required few minutes before their own departure, Kinnison spoke.

"Bus, there's one more thing we ought to do, and I've just figured out how to do it. We don't want this ship to fall into the pirates' hands intact, as there's a lot of stuff in her that would probably be as new to them as it was to us. They know that we got the best of that ship of theirs, but they don't know what we did or how we did it. On the other hand, we want her to drive on as long as possible after we leave her. The farther away from us she gets, the better our chance of making our get-away.

"We should have something that will touch off those duodec torpedoes we have left—all seven of them at once—at the first touch of a spy beam; both to keep them from studying her and to do a little damage if possible. They'll go inert and pull her up close as soon as they get a tracer on her. Of course, we can't do it by stopping the spy ray altogether, with a spy screen, but I think I can establish an R7TX7M field outside our regular screens that will interfere with a TX7 just enough—say one tenth of one per cent—to actuate a relay in the field-supporting beam."

"One tenth of one per cent of one milliwatt is one microwatt, isn't it? Not much power, I'd say, but that's a little out of my line. You can do it, and do it before we run out of time, or you wouldn't have suggested it. Go ahead. I'll observe while you're busy."

Thus it came about that, a few minutes later, the immense sky rover of the Galactic Patrol darted along entirely untenanted. And it was her nonhuman helmsman, operating solely by chance, that prolonged the chase far more than even the most optimistic member of her crew could have hoped. For the pilots of the pirate pursuers were intelligent, and assumed that their quarry also was directed by intelligence. Therefore, they aimed their vessels for points toward which the *Brittania* should logically go; only and maddeningly to watch her go somewhere else.

Senselessly, she hurled herself directly toward enormous suns, once grazing one so nearly that the harrying pirates gasped at the foolhardiness of such exposure to lethal radiation. For no reason at all she shot straight backward, almost into a cluster of pirate craft, only to dash off on another unexpected tangent before the startled outlaws could lay a beam against her.

But finally she did it once too often. Flying between two vessels, she held her line the merest fraction of a second too long. Two tractors lashed out and the three vessels flashed together, zone to zone to zone. Then, instantly, the two pirate ships became inert, to anchor in space their wildly fleeing prey. Then spy beams licked out, to explore the *Brittania's* interior.

*

At the touch of those beams, light and delicate as they were, the relay clicked and the torpedoes let go. Those frightful shells were so designed and so charged that one of them could demolish any inert structure known to man. What of seven? There was an explosion to stagger the imagination and which must be left to the imagination, since no words in any language of the galaxy can describe it adequately.

The *Brittania*, literally blown to bits, partially fused and even partially volatilized by the inconceivable fury of the outburst, was hurled in all directions in streamers, droplets, chunks, and masses, each component part urged away from the center of pressure by the ragingly compressed gases of detonation. Furthermore, each component was now, of course, inert and therefore capable of giving up its full measure of kinetic energy to any inert object with which it should come in contact.

One mass of wreckage, so fiercely sped that its victim had time neither to dodge nor become inertialess, crashed full against the side of the nearer attacker. Meteorite screens flared brilliantly violet and went down. The full-driven wall shield held; but so terrific was the concussion that what few of the crew were not killed outright would take no interest in current events for many hours to come.

The other, slightly more distant attacker was more fortunate. Her commander had had time to render her inertialess, and as she rode lightly away, ahead of the outermost, most tenuous fringe of vapor, he reported succinctly to his headquarters all that had transpired. There was a brief interlude of silence.

Then a speaker gave tongue. "Helmuth, speaking for Boskone," snapped from it. "Your report is neither complete nor conclusive. Find, study, photograph, and bring in to headquarters every fragment and particle pertaining to the wreckage, paying particular attention to all bodies or portions thereof.

"Helmuth, speaking for Boskone!" roared from the general-wave unscrambler. "Commanders of all vessels, of every class and tonnage, upon whatever mission bound, attention! The vessel referred to in our previous message has been destroyed, but it is feared that some or all of her personnel were allowed to escape. Every unit of that personnel must be killed before he has opportunity to communicate with any patrol base. Therefore cancel your present orders, whatever they may be, and proceed at maximum blast to the region previously designated. Scour that entire volume of space. Beam out of existence every vessel whose papers do not account unquestionably for every intelligent being aboard. Investigate every possible avenue of escape. More detailed orders will be given each of you upon your nearer approach to the neighborhood under search."

*

IV.

Space-suited complete, except for helmets, and with those ready at hand, Kinnison and VanBuskirk sat in the tiny control room of their lifeboat as it drifted inert through interstellar space. Kinnison was poring over charts taken from the *Brittania's* pilot room; the sergeant gazed idly into a detector plate.

"No clear ether yet, I don't suppose," the captain remarked, as he rolled up a chart and tossed it aside.

"No let-up for a second; they're not taking any chances at all. Found out where we are? Alsakan ought to be hereabouts somewhere, hadn't it?"

"I've got our coördinate roughly. Alsakan would be fairly close for a ship, but it's out of the question for us. Nothing much inhabited around here, either, apparently; to say nothing of being civilized. Scarcely one to the block. Don't think I've been out here before. Have you?"

"Off my beat entirely. How long do you figure it'll be before it's safe for us to blast off?"

"Can't start blasting until your plates are clear. Anything we can detect can detect us as soon as we start putting out power."

"We may be in for a spell of waiting then—" VanBuskirk broke off suddenly and his tone changed to one of tense excitement. "Great blasts of fire! Look at that!"

"Blinding blue blazes!" Kinnison exclaimed, staring into the plate. "With all macro-universal space and all the time in eternity to play around in, the blind god of chance had to bring her back here and now!"

For there, right in their laps, not a hundred miles away, lay the *Brittania* and her two pirate captors!

"Better go free, hadn't we?" whispered VanBuskirk.

"Daren't!" grunted Kinnison. "At this range they'd spot us in a split second. Acting like a hunk of loose metal's our only chance. We'll be able to dodge any flying chunks, I think. There she goes!"

From their coign of vantage the two patrolmen saw their gallant ship's terrific end, saw the one pirate vessel suffer collision with the flying fragment, saw the other escape inertialess, saw her disappear.

The inert pirate vessel had now almost exactly the same velocity as the lifeboat, both in speed and in direction; only very slowly were the large craft and the small approaching each other. Kinnison stood rigid, staring into his plate, his nervous hands grasping the switches whose closing, at the first sign of detection, would render them inertialess and would pour full blast into their driving projectors. But minute after minute passed and nothing happened.

375

"Why don't they do something?" he burst out, finally. "They know we're here. There isn't a detector made that could be badly enough out of order to miss us at this distance. Why, they can *see* us from there, with no detectors at all!"

"Asleep, unconscious, or dead," VanBuskirk diagnosed. "And they certainly are not asleep. And believe me, Kim, that ship was nudged. It's quite possible that she was hit hard enough to lay out most of her crew cold—anyway enough of them to put her out of control. And say, it's a practical certainty that she has a standard emergency inlet port. How about it, huh?"

*

Kinnison's mind leaped eagerly at the daring suggestion of his subordinate, but he did not reply at once. Their first, their *only* duty, concerned the safety of two spools of tape. But if the lifeboat lay there inert until the pirates regained control of their craft, detection and capture were certain. The same fate was as certain should they attempt flight with all near-by space so full of enemy fliers. Therefore, hare-brained though it appeared at first glance, VanBuskirk's wild idea was actually the safest course!

"All right, Bus, we'll try it. We'll take a chance on going free and using a tenth of a dyne of drive for a hundredth of a second. Get into the lock with your magnets."

The lifeboat flashed against the pirate's armored side and the sergeant, by deftly manipulating his two small hand magnets, worked it rapidly along the steel plating toward the driving jets. There, in the conventional location just forward of the main driving projectors, was indeed the emergency inlet port, with its galactic-standard controls.

In a few minutes the two warriors were inside, dashing toward the control room. There Kinnison glanced at the board and heaved a sigh of relief.

"Fine! Same type as the one we studied. Same race, too," he went on, eyeing the motionless forms scattered about the floor. Seizing one of the bodies, he propped it against a panel, thus obscuring a multiple lens.

"That's the eye overlooking the control room," he explained unnecessarily. "We can't cut their headquarters visibeams without creating suspicion, but we don't want them looking around in here until after we have done a little stage setting for them."

"But they'll get suspicious anyway when we go free," VanBuskirk protested.

"Sure, but we'll arrange for that later. First thing we've got to do is to make sure that all the crew, except possibly one or two in here, are really dead. Don't beam unless you have to; we want to make it look as though everybody got killed or fatally injured in the crash."

A complete tour of the vessel, with a grim and distasteful accompaniment, was made. Not all of the pirates were dead, or even disabled; but, unarmored as they were and taken completely by surprise, the survivors could offer but little resistance. A cargo port was opened and the *Brittania's* lifeboat was drawn inside. Then back to the control room, where Kinnison picked up another body and strode to the main panels.

"This fellow," he announced, "was hurt badly, but managed to get to the board. He threw in the free switch, like this, and then full-blast drive, so. Then he pulled himself over to the steering globe and tried to lay the pointers back toward headquarters, but couldn't quite make it. He died with the course set right there. Not exactly toward the solar system, you notice—that would be too much of a coincidence—but close enough to help a lot. His bracelet got caught in the guard, like this. There is clear evidence as to exactly what happened. Now we'll get out of range of that eye, and let the body that's covering it float away naturally."

"Now what?" asked VanBuskirk, after the two had hidden themselves.

"Nothing whatever until we have to," was the reply. "Wish we could go on like this for a couple of weeks, but there's not a chance. Headquarters will get curious pretty quick as to why we're shoving off."

*

Even as he spoke a furious burst of noise erupted from the communicator; a noise which meant:

"Vessel F47U596! Where are you going, and why? Report!"

At that brusque command one of the still forms struggled weakly to its knees and tried to frame words, but fell back dead.

"Perfect!" Kinnison breathed into VanBuskirk's ear. "Couldn't have been better. Now they'll probably take their time about rounding us up. Listen, here comes some more."

The communicator was again sending. "See if you can get a direction on their transmitter!"

"If there are any survivors able to report, do so at once!" Kinnison understood the dynamic cone to say. Then the voice moderating, as though the speaker had turned from his microphone to someone near-by, it went on, "No one answers, sir. This, you know, is the ship that was lying closest to the new patrol ship when she exploded; so close that her navigator did not have time to go free before collision with the débris. The crew were apparently all killed or incapacitated by the shock."

"If any of the officers survive have them brought in for trial," a more distant voice commanded, savagely. "Boskone has no use for bunglers except to serve as examples. Have the ship seized and returned here as soon as possible."

"Could you trace it, Bus?" Kinnison demanded. "Even one line on their headquarters would be mighty useful."

"No, it came in scrambled—couldn't separate it from the rest of the static out there. Now what?"

"Now we eat and sleep. Particularly and most emphatically, we sleep."

"Watches?"

"No need; I'll be awakened in plenty of time if anything happens. My Lens, you know."

They ate ravenously and slept prodigiously; then ate and slept again. Rested and refreshed, they studied charts, but VanBuskirk's mind was very evidently not upon the maps before them.

"You understand that jargon, and it doesn't even sound like a language to me," he pondered. "It's the Lens, of course. Maybe it's something that shouldn't be talked about?"

"No secret—not among us, at least," Kinnison assured him. "The Lens receives as pure thought any pattern of force which represents, or is in any way connected with, thought. My brain receives this thought in English, since that is my native language. At the same time my ears are practically out of circuit, so that I actually hear the English language

377

instead of whatever noise is being made. I do not hear the foreign sounds at all. Therefore, I haven't the slightest idea what the pirates' language sounds like, since I have never heard any of it.

"Conversely, when I want to talk to some one who doesn't know any language I do, I simply think into the Lens and direct its force at him. He thinks I'm talking to him in his own mother tongue. Thus, you are hearing me now in perfect Valerian Dutch, even though you know that I can speak only a dozen or so words of it, and those with a vile American accent. Also, you are hearing it in my voice, even though you know I am actually not saying a word, since you can see that my mouth is wide open and that neither my lips, tongue, nor vocal cords are moving. If you were a Frenchman you would be hearing this in French; or, if you were a Manarkan and couldn't talk at all, you would be getting it as regular Manarkan telepathy."

"Oh—I see—I think," the astounded Dutchman gulped. "Then why couldn't you talk back to them through their phones?"

"Because the Lens, although a mighty fine and versatile thing, is not omnipotent," Kinnison replied, dryly. "It sends out only thought; and thought waves, lying below the level of the ether, cannot affect a microphone. The microphone, not being itself intelligent, cannot receive thought. Of course, I can broadcast a thought—everybody does; more or less—but even with the full amplification of the Lens the range is very limited. In Lens-to-Lens communication we can cover real distances, but without a Lens at the other end I can cover only a few thousand kilometers. Of course, power increases with practice, and I'm not very good at it yet."

"You can receive a thought——Everybody broadcasts——Then you can read minds?" VanBuskirk stated, rather than asked.

"When I so will it, yes. That was what I was doing while we were mopping up. I demanded the galactic coördinates of their base from every one of them alive, but none of them knew them. I got a lot of pictures and descriptions of the buildings, layout, arrangements and personnel of the base, but not a hint as to its location in space. The navigators were all dead, and not even the Arisians understand death. But that's getting pretty deeply into philosophy and it's time to eat again. Let's go!"

*

Days passed uneventfully, but finally the communicator again began to talk. Two pirate ships were closing in upon the supposedly derelict cruiser, discussing with each other the exact point of convergence of the three courses.

"I was hoping that we'd be able to communicate with base before they caught up with us," Kinnison remarked. "But I guess it's no dice—the ether's as full of interference as ever. They're a suspicious bunch, and they aren't going to let us get away with a single thing if they can help it. You've got that duplicate of their communications unscrambler built?"

"Yes. That was it you just listened to. I built it out of our own stuff, and I've gone over the whole ship with a cleaner. As far as I can see there isn't a trace, not even a fingerprint, to show that anybody except her own crew has ever been aboard."

"Good work! This course takes us right through a planetary system in a few minutes and we'll have to unload there. Let's see. This chart marks planets two and three as inhabited, but with a red reference number, twenty-seven. That means practically unexplored and unknown. No patrol representation or connection—no commerce—state of civilization unknown—visited only once, in the Third Galactic Survey. That was in the days of the semi-inert drive, when it took years to cross the galaxy. Not so good, apparently—but maybe all the better for us, at that. Anyway, it's a forced landing, so get ready to shove off."

They boarded their lifeboat, placed it in the cargo lock, opened the outer port upon its automatic block, and waited. At their awful galactic speed the diameter of a solar system would be traversed in such a small fraction of a second that observation would be impossible, to say nothing of computation. They would have to act first and compute later.

They flashed into the strange system. A planet loomed terrifyingly close—at their frightful velocity almost invisible even upon their ultra-vision plates. The lifeboat shot out, becoming inert as it passed the screen. The cargo port swung shut. Luck had been with them; the planet was scarcely a million miles away. While VanBuskirk drove toward it, Kinnison made hasty observations.

"Could have been better—but could have been a lot worse," he reported. "This is Planet 4. Uninhabited, which is very good. Three, though, is clear over across the Sun, and Two isn't any too close for a space-sun flight—better than eighty million miles. Easy enough as far as distance goes—we've all made longer hops in our suits—but we'll be open to detection for at least twenty minutes. Can't be helped, though. Here we are!"

"Going to land her free, huh?" VanBuskirk whistled. "What a chance!"

"It'd be a bigger one to take the time to land her inert. Her power will hold—I hope. We'll inert her and match velocities with her when we come back. We'll have more time then."

*

The lifeboat stopped instantaneously, in a free landing, upon the uninhabited, desolate, rocky soil of the strange world. Without a word the two men leaped out, carrying fully packed knapsacks. A portable projector was then dragged out and its fierce beam directed into the base of the hill beside which they had landed. A cavern was quickly made, and while its glassy walls were still smoking-hot the lifeboat was driven within it. With their DeLameters the two wayfarers then undercut the hill, so that a great slide of soil and rock obliterated every sign of the visit. Kinnison and VanBuskirk could find their vessel again, from their accurately taken bearings; but, they hoped, no one else could.

Then, still without a word, the two adventurers flashed upward. The atmosphere of the planet, tenuous and cold though it was, nevertheless, so sorely impeded their progress, that minutes of precious time were required for the driving projectors of their suits to force them through its thin layer. Eventually, however, they were in interplanetary space and were flying at quadruple the speed of light. Then VanBuskirk spoke.

"Landing the boat, hiding it, and this trip are the danger spots. Heard anything yet?"

"No, and I don't believe we will. I think probably we've lost them completely. Won't know definitely, though, until after they catch the ship, and that won't be for ten minutes yet. We'll be landed by then."

A world now loomed beneath them, a pleasant, Earthly-appearing world of scattered clouds, green forests, rolling plains, wooded and snow-capped mountain ranges, and rolling oceans. Here and there were to be seen what looked like cities, but Kinnison gave them a wide berth, electing to land upon an open meadow in the shelter of a towering black and glassy cliff.

"Ah, just in time; they're beginning to talk," Kinnison announced. "Unimportant stuff yet, opening the ship and so on. I'll relay the talk as nearly verbatim as possible when it gets interesting." He fell silent, then went on in a singsong tone, as though he were reciting from memory, which, in effect, he was:

"'Captains of ships P4J263 and EQ769B47 calling Helmuth! We have stopped and have boarded the F47U569. Everything is in order and as deduced and reported by your observers. Every one aboard is dead. They did not all die at the same time, but they all died from the effects of the collision. There is no trace of outside interference and all the personnel are accounted for.'

"'Helmuth, speaking for Boskone. Your report is inconclusive. Search the ship minutely for tracks, prints, scratches. Note any missing supplies or misplaced items of equipment. Study carefully all mechanisms, particularly converters and communicators, for signs of tampering or dismantling.'

"Whew!" whistled Kinnison. "They'll find where you took that communicator apart, Bus, just as sure as hell's a man-trap!"

"No, they won't," declared VanBuskirk as positively. "I did it with rubber-nosed pliers, and if I left a scratch or a scar or a print on it I'll eat it, tubes and all!"

A pause.

"'We have studied everything most carefully, O Helmuth, and find no trace of tampering or visit.'

"Helmuth again: 'Your report is still inconclusive. Whoever did what has been done is probably a Lensman, and certainly has *brains*. Give me the present recorded serial number of all port openings, and the exact number of times you have opened each port.'

"Ouch!" groaned Kinnison. "If that means what I think it does, all hell's out for noon. Did you see any numbering recorders on those ports? I didn't. Of course, neither of us thought of such a thing. Shut up, here comes some more stuff.

"'Port-opening recorder serial numbers are as follows.' They don't mean a thing to us. 'We have opened the emergency inlet port once and the starboard lock twice. No other port at all.'

"And here's Helmuth again: 'Ah, as I thought. The emergency port was opened once by outsiders, and the starboard cargo port twice. The Lensman came aboard, headed the ship toward Sol, took his lifeboat aboard, listened to us, and departed at his leisure. And this in the very midst of our fleet, the entire personnel of which was supposed to be looking for him! How supposedly intelligent spacemen could be guilty of such utter and indefensive stupidity?'

"He's tellin' 'em plenty, Bus, but there's no use repeating it. The tone can't be reproduced, and it's simply taking the hide right off their backs. Here's some more: 'General broadcast! Ship F47U596 in its supposedly derelict condition flew from the point of destruction of the patrol ship, on course longitude three five one point two seven degrees, latitude five point two three degrees, distance twenty-four thousand seven hundred parsecs. Cancel all previous orders and investigate.' No use repeating it, Bus, he's simply giving directions for scouring our whole line of flight. Fading out—they're going on, or back. This outfit, of course, is good for only the closest kind of close-up work."

"And we're out of the frying pan into the fire, huh?"

"Oh, no; we're a lot better off than we were. We're on a planet and not using any power that they can trace. Also, they've got to cover so much territory that they can't comb it very fine, and that gives the rest of the fellows a break. Furthermore——"

*

A crushing weight descended upon his back, and the two found themselves fighting for their lives. From the bare, supposedly safe rock face of the cliff there had emerged rope-tentacled monstrosities in a ravenously attacking swarm. In the raving blasts of DeLameters hundreds of the gargoyle horde vanished in vivid flashes of radiance, but on they came, by thousands and, it seemed, by millions, dashing madly toward them.

Eventually, the batteries energizing the projectors became exhausted. Then flailing coil met shearing steel, fierce-driven parrot beaks clanged against space-tempered armor, bulbous heads pulped under hard-swung axes; but not for the fractional second necessary for inertialess flight could the two patrolmen win clear. Then Kinnison sent out his S O S.

"A Lensman calling help! A Lensman calling help!" he broadcast with the full power of mind and Lens.

Immediately a high, girlish voice poured into his brain: "Coming, wearer of the Lens! Coming at speed to the cliff of the Catlats. Hold until I come! I arrive in thirty——"

Thirty what? What possible intelligible relative measure of that unknown and unknowable concept, time, can be conveyed by thought alone?

"Keep slugging, Bus!" Kinnison panted. "Help is on the way. A local cop—voice sounds like a woman—will be here in thirty somethings. Don't know whether it's thirty minutes or thirty days; but we'll still be here."

"Maybe so and maybe not," grunted the Dutchman. "Something's coming besides help. Look up and see if you see what I think I do."

Kinnison did. Through the air from the top of the cliff there was hurtling downward toward them a veritable dragon: a nightmare's horror of hideously reptilian head, of leathern wings, of viciously fanged jaws, of frightfully taloned feet, of multiple knotty arms, of long, sinuous, heavily scaled serpent's body. In fleeting glimpses through the writhing tentacles of his opponents Kinnison perceived, little by little, the full picture of that unbelievable monstrosity; and, accustomed as he was to the outlandish denizens of worlds even yet scarcely known to man, his very senses reeled at the sight.

As the quasi-reptilian organism descended, the cliff dwellers went mad. Their attack upon the two patrolmen, already vicious, became insanely frantic. Abandoning the gigantic Dutchman entirely, every Catlat within reach threw himself upon Kinnison and so enwrapped the Lensman's head, arms, and torso that he could scarcely move a muscle. Then entwining captors and helpless man moved slowly toward the largest of the openings in the cliff's obsidian face.

Upon that slowly moving mélange VanBuskirk hurled himself, deadly space ax swinging. But, hew and smite as he would, he could neither free his chief from the grisly horde enveloping him nor impede, measurably, that horde's progress toward its goal. However, he could and did cleave away the comparatively few cables confining Kinnison's legs.

"Clamp a leg lock around my waist, Kim," he directed, the flashing thought in no whit interfering with his prodigious ax play, "and as soon as I get a chance, before the real tussle comes, I'll couple us together with all the belt snaps I can reach. Wherever we're going we're going together! Wonder why they haven't ganged up on me, too, and what that lizard is doing? Been too busy to look, but thought he'd have been on my back before this."

"He won't be on your back. That's Worsel, the lad who answered my call. I told you his voice was funny? They can't talk or hear—use telepathy, like the Manarkans. He's cleaning them out in great shape. If you can hold me for three minutes, he'll have the lot of them whipped."

"I can hold you for three minutes against all the vermin between here and Andromeda," VanBuskirk declared. "There, I've got four snaps on you."

"Not too tough, Bus," Kinnison cautioned. "Leave enough slack so that you can cut me loose if you have to. Remember that the spools are more important than any one of us. Once inside that cliff we'll all be washed up—even Worsel can't help us there—so drop me rather than go in yourself."

"Um," grunted the Dutchman, non-committally. "There, I've tossed my spool out onto the ground. Tell Worsel that if they get us he is to pick it up and carry on. We'll go ahead with yours, inside the cliff if necessary."

"I said cut me loose if you can't hold me!" Kinnison snapped, "and I meant it. That's an official order. Remember it!"

"Official order be damned!" snorted VanBuskirk, still plying his ponderous mace. "They won't get you into that hole without breaking me in two, and that will be a job of breaking in anybody's language. Now shut your pan," he concluded grimly. "We're here, and I'm going to be too busy, even to think, very shortly."

He spoke truly. He had already selected his point of resistance, and as he reached it he thrust the head of his mace into the crack behind the open trap-door, jammed its shaft into the shoulder socket of his armor, set blocky legs and Herculean arms against the side of the cliff, arched his mighty back, and held. And the surprised Catlats, now inside the gloomy fastness of their tunnel, thrust anchoring tentacles in the wall and pulled harder, ever harder.

SUPER PACK

Under the terrific stress Kinnison's heavy armor creaked as its air-tight joints accommodated themselves to their new and unusual positions. That armor, of space-tempered alloy, would, of course, not give way—but what of its human anchor?

*

Well it was for Kimball Kinnison that day, and well for our present civilization, that the *Brittania's* quartermaster selected Peter VanBuskirk for the Lensman's mate; for death, inevitable and horrible, resided within that cliff, and no human frame of Earthly upbringing, however armored, could have borne, for even a fraction of a second, the violence of the Catlats' pull.

But Peter VanBuskirk, although of Earthly Dutch ancestry, had been born and reared upon the planet Valeria, and that massive planet's gravity—over two and one half times Earth's—had given him a physique and a strength almost inconceivable to us life-long dwellers upon small, green Terra. His head, as has been said, towered seventy-eight inches above the ground; but at that he appeared squatty because of his enormous spread of shoulder and his startling girth. His bones were elephantine—they had to be, to furnish adequate support and leverage for the incredible masses of muscle overlaying and surrounding them. But even VanBuskirk's Valerian strength was now being taxed to the uttermost.

The anchoring chains hummed and snarled as the clamps bit into the rings. Muscles writhed and knotted; tendons stretched and threatened to snap; sweat rolled down his mighty back. His jaws locked in agony and his eyes started from their sockets with the effort; but still VanBuskirk held.

"Cut me loose!" commanded Kinnison at last. "Even you can't take much more of that. No use letting them break your back. *Cut*, I tell you. I said *cut*, you big, dumb, Valerian ape!"

But if VanBuskirk heard or felt the savagely voiced commands of his chief, he gave no heed. Straining to the very ultimate fiber of his being, exerting every iota of loyal mind and every atom of Brobdingnagian frame, grimly, tenaciously, stubbornly the gigantic Dutchman held.

Held while Worsel of Velantia, that grotesquely hideous, that fantastically reptilian ally, plowed toward the two patrolmen through the horde of Catlats; a veritable tornado of rending fang and shearing talon, of beating wing and crushing snout, of mailed hand and trenchant tail.

Held while that demon incarnate drove closer and closer, hurling entire Catlats and numberless dismembered fragments of Catlats to the four winds as he came.

Held while the raging tumult, whose center was Worsel, swept over his rigid body like an ocean wave breaking over an immovable rock.

Held until Worsel's snakelike body, a supple and sentient cable of living steel, tipped with its double-edged, razor-keen, scimitarlike sting, slipped into the tunnel beside Kinnison and wrought grisly havoc among the Catlats close-packed there!

As the terrific tension upon him was suddenly released VanBuskirk's own efforts hurled him away from the cliff. He fell to the ground, his overstrained muscles twitching uncontrollably, and on top of him fell the fettered Lensman. Kinnison, his hands now

383

free, unfastened the clamps linking his armor to that of VanBuskirk and whirled to confront the foe. But the fighting was over. The Catlats had had enough of Worsel of Velantia; and, shrieking in baffled rage, the last of them were disappearing into their caves. He turned back to VanBuskirk, who was getting shakily to his feet.

"Thanks a lot, Worsel; we were just about to run out of time——" VanBuskirk began, only to be silenced by an insistent thought from the grotesque stranger.

"Stop that radiating! Do not think at all if you cannot screen your minds!" came the urgent mental commands. "These Catlats are a very minor pest of this planet Delgon. There are others worse by far. Fortunately, your thoughts are upon a frequency never used here—if I had not been so very close to you I would not have heard you at all—but should the Overlords have a listener upon that band, your unshielded thinking may already have done irreparable harm. Follow me. I will slow my speed to yours, but hurry all possible!"

"You tell 'im, chief," VanBuskirk said, and fell silent; his mind as nearly a perfect blank as his iron will could make it.

"This is a screened thought, through my Lens," Kinnison took up the conversation. "You don't need to slow down on our account. We can develop any speed you wish. Lead on!"

*

The Velantian leaped into the air and flashed away in headlong flight. Much to his surprise, the two human beings kept up with him effortlessly upon their inertialess drives, and after a moment Kinnison directed another thought.

"If time is an object, Worsel, know that my companion and I can carry you anywhere you wish to go at a speed hundreds of times greater than this that we are using," he vouchsafed.

It developed that time was of the utmost possible importance and the three closed in. Mighty wings folded back, hands and talons gripped armor chains, and the group, inertialess all, shot away at a pace that Worsel of Velantia had never even imagined in his wildest dreams of speed. Their goal, a small, featureless tent of thin sheet metal, occupying a barren spot in a writhing, crawling expanse of lushly green jungle, was reached in a space of minutes. Once inside, Worsel sealed the opening and turned to his armored guests.

"We can now think freely in open converse. This wall is the carrier of a screen through which no thought can make its way."

"This world you call by a name I have interpreted as Delgon," Kinnison began, slowly. "You are a native of Velantia, a planet now beyond the Sun. Therefore, I assumed that you were taking us to your space ship. Where is that ship?"

"I have no ship," the Velantian replied, composedly, "nor have I need of one. For the remainder of my life—which is now to be measured in a few of your hours—this tent is my only——"

"No ship!" VanBuskirk broke in. "I hope we won't have to stay on this God-forsaken planet forever—and I'm not very keen on going much farther in that lifeboat, either."

"We may not have to do either of those things," Kinnison reassured his sergeant. "Worsel comes of a long-lived tribe, and the fact that he thinks his enemies are going to get him in a few hours doesn't make it true, by any means. There are three of us to reckon with now. Also, when we need a space ship we'll get one, if we have to build it. Now, let's find out what this is all about. Worsel, start at the beginning and don't skip a thing. Between us we can surely find a way out, for all of us."

*

Then the Velantian told his story. There was much repetition, much roundabout thinking, as some of the concepts were so bizarre as to defy transmission, but finally the Earthman had a fairly complete picture of the situation within that strange solar system.

The inhabitants of Delgon were bad, being characterized by a type and a depth of depravity impossible for a mind of Earth to visualize. Not only were the Delgonians enemies of the Velantians in the ordinary sense of the word; not only were they pirates and robbers; not only were they their masters, taking them both as slaves and as food cattle; but there was something more, something deeper and worse, something only partially transmissible from mind to mind—a horribly and repulsively Saturnalian type of mental and intellectual, as well as biological, parasitism. This relationship had gone on for ages.

Finally, however, a thought-screen had been devised, behind which Velantia developed a high science of her own. The students of this science lived with but one purpose in life: to free Velantia from the tyranny of the Overlords of Delgon. Each student, as he reached the zenith of his mental power, went to Delgon, to study and if possible destroy the tyrants. And after disembarking upon the soil of that dread planet no Velantian, whether student or scientist or private adventurer, had ever returned to Velantia.

"But why don't you lay a complaint against them before the council?" demanded VanBuskirk. "They'd straighten things out in a hurry."

"We have not heretofore known, save by the most unreliable and roundabout reports, that such an organization as your Galactic Patrol really exists," the Velantian replied, obliquely. "Nevertheless, many years since, we launched a space ship toward its nearest reputed base. However, since that trip requires three normal lifetimes, with deadly peril in every moment, it will be a miracle if the ship ever completes it.

"Furthermore, even if the ship should reach its destination, our complaint will probably not even be considered, because we have not a single shred of real evidence with which to support it. No living Velantian has ever seen a Delgonian, nor can any one testify to the truth of anything I have told you. While we believe that that is the true condition of affairs, our belief is based, not upon evidence admissible in a court of law, but upon deductions from occasional thoughts radiated from this planet. Nor were these thoughts alike in tenor——"

"Skip that for a minute—we'll take the picture as correct," Kinnison broke in. "Nothing you have said so far shows any necessity for you to die in the next few hours."

"The only object in life for a trained Velantian is to liberate his planet from the horrors of subjection to Delgon. Many such have come here, but not one has found a workable idea; not one has either returned to or even communicated with Velantia after starting work here. I am a Velantian. I am here. Soon I shall open that door and get in touch with the enemy. Since better men than I am have failed, I do not expect to succeed. Nor shall I return to my native planet. As soon as I start to work the Delgonians will command me to come to them. In spite of myself I will obey that command, and very shortly thereafter I shall die, in what fashion I do not know."

*

"Snap out of it, Worsel!" barked Kinnison, roughly. "That's the rankest kind of defeatism, and you know it. Nobody ever got to the first check station on that kind of fuel."

"You are talking about something now about which you know nothing whatever." For the first time Worsel's thoughts showed passion. "Your thoughts are idle—ignorant—vain. You know nothing whatever of the mental power of the Delgonians."

"Maybe not—I make no claim of being a mental giant—but I do know that mental power alone cannot overcome a definitely and positively opposed *will*. An Arisian could probably break my will, but I'll stake my life that no other mentality in the known universe can do it!"

"You think so, Earthling?" And a seething sphere of mental force encompassed the Tellurian's brain. Kinnison's senses reeled at the terrific impact; but he shook off the attack and smiled.

"Come again, Worsel. That one jarred me to the heels, but it didn't quite ring the bell."

"You flatter me," the Velantian declared in surprise. "I could scarcely touch your mind—could not penetrate even its outermost defenses, and I exerted all my force. But that fact gives me hope. My mind is, of course, inferior to theirs, but since I could not influence you at all, even in direct contact and at full power, you may be able to resist the minds of the Delgonians. Are you willing to hazard the stake you mentioned a moment ago? Or rather, I ask you, by the Lens you wear, so to hazard it—with the liberty of an entire people dependent upon the outcome."

"Why not? The spools come first, of course—but without you our spools would both be buried now inside the cliff of the Catlats. Fix it so that your people will find these spools and carry on with them in case we fail, and I'm your man. There—now tell me what we're apt to be up against, and then let loose your dogs."

"That I cannot do. I know only that they will direct against you mental forces such as you never even imagined. I cannot forewarn you in any respect whatever as to what forms those forces may appear to assume. I know, however, that I shall succumb to the first bolt of force. Therefore, bind me with these chains before I open the shield. Physically, I am extremely strong, as you know; therefore, be sure to put on enough chains so that I cannot possibly break free, for if I can break away I shall undoubtedly kill both of you."

"How come all these things here, ready to hand?" asked VanBuskirk, as the two patrolmen so loaded the passive Velantian with chains, manacles, handcuffs, leg irons and straps that he could not move even his tail.

"It has been tried before, many times," Worsel replied bleakly, "but the rescuers, being Velantians, also succumbed to the force and took off the irons. Now I caution you, with all the power of my mind—no matter what you see, no matter what I may command you or beg of you, no matter how urgently you yourself may wish to do so—*do not liberate me under any circumstances* unless and until things appear exactly as they do now and that door is shut. Know fully and ponder well the fact that if you release me while that door is open it will be because you have yielded to Delgonian force, and that not only will all three of us die, lingeringly and horribly, but also, and worse, that our deaths will not have been of any benefit to civilization. Do you understand? Are you ready?"

"I understand. I am ready," thought Kinnison and VanBuskirk as one.

"Open that door."

*

Kinnison did so. For a few minutes nothing happened. Then three-dimensional pictures began to form before their eyes—pictures which they knew existed only in their own minds, yet which were composed of such solid substance that they obscured from vision everything else in the material world. At first hazy and indistinct, the scene—for it was in no sense now a picture—became clear and sharp. And, piling horror upon horror, sound was added to sight. And directly before their eyes, blotting out completely even the solid metal of the wall only a few feet distant from them, the two outlanders saw and heard something which can be represented only vaguely by imagining Dante's Inferno an actuality and raised to the nth power!

In a dull and gloomy cavern there lay, sat, and stood hordes of *things*. These beings—the "nobility" of Delgon—had reptilian bodies, somewhat similar to Worsel's, but they had no wings and their heads were distinctly apish rather than crocodilian. Every greedy eye in the vast throng was fixed upon an enormous screen which, like that in a motion-picture theater, walled off one end of the stupendous cavern.

Slowly, shudderingly, Kinnison's mind began to take in what was happening upon that screen. And it was really happening, Kinnison was sure of that. This was not a picture any more than this whole scene was an illusion. It was all an actuality—somewhere.

Upon that screen there were stretched out victims. Hundreds of these were Velantians, more hundreds were winged Delgonians, and scores were creatures whose like Kinnison had never seen. And all these were being tortured; tortured to death both in fashions known to the Inquisitors of old and ways of which even those experts had never an inkling.

Some were being twisted outrageously in three-dimensional frames. Others were being stretched upon racks. Many were being pulled horribly apart, chains intermittently but relentlessly extending each helpless member. Still others were being lowered into pits of constantly increasing temperatures or were being attacked by gradually increasing concentrations of some foully corrosive vapor which ate away their tissues, little by little. And, apparently the pièce de résistance of the hellish exhibition, one luckless Velantian, in a spot of hard, cold light, was being pressed out flat against the screen, as an insect might be pressed between two panes of glass. Thinner and thinner he became, under the influence of some awful, invisible force, in spite of every exertion of inhumanely powerful muscles driving body, tail, wings, arms, legs, and head in every frantic maneuver which grim and imminent death could call forth.

387

Physically nauseated, brainsick at the atrocious visions blasting his mind and at the screaming of the damned assailing his ears, Kinnison strove to wrench his mind away, but was curbed savagely by Worsel.

"You *must* stay! You *must* pay attention!" commanded the Velantian. "This is the first time any living being has seen so much! You *must* help me now! They have been attacking me from the first; but, braced by the powerful negatives in your mind, I have been able to resist and have transmitted a truthful picture so far. But they are surprised at my resistance and are concentrating more force. I am slipping fast. You *must* brace my mind! And when the picture changes—as change it must, and soon—do not believe it. Hold fast, brothers of the Lens, for your own lives and for the people of Velantia. There is more—and worse!"

Kinnison stayed. So did VanBuskirk, fighting with all his stubborn Dutch mind. Revolted, outraged, nauseated as they were at the sights and sounds, they stayed. Flinching with the victims as they were fed into the hoppers of slowly turning mills; wincing at the unbelievable acts of the boilers, the beaters, the scourgers, the flayers; suffering themselves every possible and many apparently impossible nightmares.

The light in the cavern now changed to a strong, greenish-yellow glare; and in that hard illumination it was to be seen that each dying being was surrounded by a palely glowing aura. And now, crowning horror of that unutterably horrible orgy of sadism resublimed, from the eyes of each one of the monstrous audience there leaped out visible beams of force. These beams touched the aura of the dying prisoners—touched and clung. And as they clung the aura shrank and disappeared.

The Overlords of Delgon were actually *feeding* upon the ebbing life forces of their tortured, dying victims!

VI.

Gradually and so insidiously that the Velantian's dire warnings might as well never have been uttered, the scene changed. Or rather, the scene itself did not change, but the observers' perception of it slowly underwent such a radical transformation that it was in no sense the same scene it had been a few minutes before; and they felt almost abjectly apologetic as they realized how unjust their previous ideas had been.

For the cavern was not a torture chamber, as they had supposed. It was, in reality, a hospital, and the beings they had thought victims of brutalities unspeakable were, in reality, patients undergoing treatments and operations for various ills. In proof whereof the patients—who should have been dead by this time were the early ideas well-founded—were now being released from the screenlike operating theater. And not only was each one completely whole and sound in body, but he was also possessed of a mental clarity, power, and grasp undreamed of before his hospitalization and treatment by Delgon's super surgeons!

Also, the intruders had misunderstood completely the audience and its behavior. They were really medical students, and the beams which had seemed to be devouring rays were simply visibeams, by means of which each student could follow, in close-up detail, each step of the operation in which he was most interested. The patients themselves were living, vocal witnesses of the visitors' mistakenness, for each, as he made his way through the assemblage of students, was voicing his thanks for the marvelous results of his particular treatment or operation.

Kinnison now became acutely aware that he himself was in need of immediate surgical attention. His body, which he had always regarded so highly, he now perceived to be sadly inefficient; his mind was in even worse shape than his physique; and both body and mind would be improved immeasurably if he could get to the Delgonian hospital before the surgeons departed. In fact, he felt an almost irresistible urge to rush away toward that hospital instantly, without the loss of a single precious second. And, since he had had no reason to doubt the evidence of his own senses, his conscious mind was not aroused to active opposition. However, in his subconscious, or his essence, or whatever you choose to call that ultimate something of his that made him a Lensman, a "dead, slow bell" began to sound.

"Release me and we'll all go, before the surgeons leave the hospital," came an insistent thought from Worsel. "But hurry—we haven't much time!"

VanBuskirk, completely under the influence of the frantic compulsion, leaped toward the Velantian, only to be checked bodily by Kinnison, who was foggily trying to isolate and identify one thing about the situation that did not ring quite true.

"Just a minute, Bus. Shut that door first!" he commanded.

"Never mind the door!" Worsel's thought came in a roaring crescendo. "Release me instantly! Hurry, or it will be too late, for all of us!"

"All this terrific rush doesn't make any kind of sense at all," Kinnison declared, closing his mind resolutely to the clamor of the Velantian's thoughts. "I want to go just as badly as you do, Bus, or maybe more so—but I can't help feeling that there's something screwy somewhere. Anyway, remember the last thing Worsel said, and let's shut the door before we unsnap a single chain."

Then something clicked in the Lensman's mind.

"Hypnotism, through Worsel!" he barked, opposition now aflame. "So gradual that it never occurred to me to build up a resistance. Holy rackets, what a fool I've been! Fight 'em, Bus—*fight* 'em! Don't let 'em kid you any more, and pay no attention to anything Worsel sends at you!" Whirling around, he leaped toward the open door of the tent.

But as he leaped his brain was invaded by such a concentration of force that he fell flat upon the floor, physically out of control. He must *not* shut the door. He *must* release the Velantian. They *must* go to the Delgonian cavern. Fully aware now, however, of the source of the waves of compulsion, he threw the sum total of his mental power into an intense negation and struggled, inch-wise, toward the opening.

*

Upon him now, in addition to the Delgonians' compulsion, beat at point-blank range the full power of Worsel's mighty mind, demanding release and compliance. Also, and worse, he perceived that some powerful mentality was being exerted to make VanBuskirk kill him. One blow of the Valerian's ponderous mace would shatter helmet and skull, and all would be over. Once more the Delgonians would have triumphed. But the stubborn Dutchman, although at the very verge of surrender, was still fighting. He would take one step forward, bludgeon poised aloft, only to throw it convulsively backward.

Again and again VanBuskirk repeated his futile performance, while the Lensman struggled nearer and nearer the door. Finally, he reached it and kicked it shut. Instantly, the mental turmoil ceased and the two white and shaking patrolmen released the limp, unconscious Velantian from his bonds.

"Wonder what we can do to help him revive," gasped Kinnison. But his solicitude was unnecessary; the Velantian recovered consciousness as he spoke.

"Thanks to your wonderful power of resistance, I am alive, unharmed, and know more of our foes and their methods than any other of my race has ever learned," Worsel thought, feelingly. "But it is of no value whatever unless I can send it back to Velantia. The thought-screen is carried only by the metal of these walls; and if I make an opening in the wall to think through, however small, it will now mean death. Of course, the science of your patrol has not perfected an apparatus to drive through such a screen."

"No. Anyway, it seems to me that we'd better be worrying about something besides thought-screens," Kinnison suggested. "Surely, now that they know where we are, they'll be coming out here after us, and we haven't got much of any defense."

"They don't know where we are, or care——" began the Velantian.

"Why not?" broke in VanBuskirk. "Any spy ray capable of such scanning as you showed us—I never saw anything like it before—would certainly be as easy to trace as an out-and-out gas blast!"

"I sent out no spy ray or anything of the kind," Worsel thought, carefully. "Since our science is so foreign to yours, I am not sure that I can explain satisfactorily, but I shall try to do so. First, as to what you saw. When that door is open, no barrier to thought exists. I merely broadcast a thought, placing myself en rapport with the Delgonian Overlords in their retreat. This condition established, of course I heard and saw exactly what they heard and saw—and so, equally of course, did you, since you were also en rapport with me. That is all."

"That's all!" echoed VanBuskirk. "What a system! You can do a thing like that, without apparatus of any kind, and yet say 'that's all'!"

"It is results that count," Worsel reminded him gently. "While it is true that we have done much—this is the first time in history that any Velantian has encountered the mind of a Delgonian Overlord and lived. It is equally true that it was the will power of you patrolmen that made it possible, not my mentality. Also, it remains true that we cannot leave this room and live."

"Why won't we need weapons?" asked Kinnison, returning to his previous line of thought.

"Thought screens are the only defense we will require," Worsel stated, positively, "for they use no weapons except their minds. By mental power alone they make us come to them; and, once there, their slaves do the rest. Of course, if my race is ever to rid the planet of them, we must employ offensive weapons of power. We have such, but we have never been able to use them. For, in order to locate the enemy, either by telepathy or by spy ray, we must open our metallic shields—and the instant we release those screens we are lost. From those conditions there is no escape," Worsel concluded, hopelessly.

"Don't be such a pessimist," Kinnison commanded. "There are a lot of things not tried yet. For instance, from what I have seen of your generator equipment and that screen, you don't need a metallic conductor any more than a snake needs hips. Maybe I'm wrong, but I think we're a bit ahead of you there. If a DeVilbiss projector can handle that screen—and I think it can, with special tuning—VanBuskirk and I can fix things in an hour so that all three of us can walk out of here in perfect safety—from mental interference, at least. While we're trying it out, tell us all the new stuff you got on them just now, and anything else that, by any possibility, may prove useful. And remember you said this is the first time any of you had been able to cut them off. That fact ought to make them sit up and take notice. Probably they'll stir around more than they ever did before. Come on, Bus—let's tear into it!"

*

The DeVilbiss projectors were rigged and tuned. Kinnison had been right; they worked. Then plan after plan was made, only to be discarded as its weaknesses were pointed out.

"Whichever way we look there are too many 'ifs' and 'buts' to suit me," Kinnison summed up the situation finally. "*If* we can find them, and *if* we can get up close to them without losing our minds to them, we could clean them out *if* we had some power in our accumulators. So I'd say the first thing for us to do is to get our batteries charged. We saw some cities from the air, and cities always have power. Lead us to power, Worsel—almost *any* kind of power—and we'll soon have it in our guns."

"There are cities, yes"—Worsel was not at all enthusiastic—"dwelling places of the ordinary Delgonians, the people you saw being eaten in the cavern of the Overlords. As you saw, they resemble us Velantians to a certain extent. Since they are of a lower culture and are much weaker in life force than we are, however, the Overlords prefer us to their own slave races.

"To visit any city of Delgon is out of the question. Every inhabitant of every city is an abject slave and his brain is an open book. Whatever he sees, whatever he thinks, is communicated instantly to his master. And I now perceive that I may have misinformed you as to the Overlords' ability to use weapons. While the situation has never arisen, it is only logical to suppose that as soon as we are seen by any Delgonian the controllers will order all the inhabitants of the city to capture us and bring us to them."

"What a guy!" interjected VanBuskirk. "Did you ever see his top for looking at the bright side of life?"

"Only in conversation," the Lensman replied. "When the ether gets crowded, you notice, he's right in here, blasting away and not saying a word. But there's one thing we haven't thought of: power. I've got only eight minutes of free flight left in my battery; and with your mass, you must be about out. Come to think of it, didn't you land a trifle hard when we sat down here?"

"Practically inert."

"That means we've *got* to get some power. Well, it's not so bad, at that; there's a city right close."

"Yes, but as far as I'm concerned it might as well be on Mars. You know as well as I do what's between here and there. You can take my batteries and I'll wait here."

"On your emergency food, water, and air? That's out!"

"What else, then?"

"I can spread my field to cover all three of us," proposed Kinnison. "That will give us at least one minute of free flight—almost, if not quite, enough to clear the jungle. They have night here; and, like us, the Delgonians are night sleepers. We start at dusk, and to-night we recharge our batteries."

*

The following hour, during which the huge, hot Sun dropped to the horizon, was spent in intense discussion, but no significant improvement upon the Lensman's plan could be devised.

"It is time to go," Worsel announced, curling out one extensile eye toward the vanishing orb. "I have recorded all my findings. Already I have lived longer and, through you, have accomplished more, than any one believed possible. I am ready to die. I should have been dead long since."

"Living on borrowed time's a lot better than not living at all," Kinnison replied, with a grin. "Link up. Ready? Go!"

He snapped his switches and the close-linked group of three shot into the air and away. As far as the eye could reach in any direction extended the sentient, ravenous growth of the jungle; but Kinnison's eyes were not upon that fantastically inimical green carpet. His whole attention was occupied by two all-important meters and by the task of so directing their flight as to gain the greatest possible horizontal distance with the power at his command.

Fifty seconds of flashing flight, then: "All right, Worsel, get out in front and get ready to pull!" Kinnison snapped. "Ten seconds of drive left, but I can hold us free for five seconds after my driver quits. Pull!"

Kinnison's driver expired, its small accumulator completely exhausted; and Worsel, with his mighty wings, took up the task of propulsion. Inertialess still, with Kinnison and VanBuskirk grasping his tail, each beat a mile-long leap, he struggled on. But all too soon the battery powering the neutralizers also went dead and the three began to plummet downward at a sharper and sharper angle, in spite of the Velantian's Herculean efforts to keep them aloft.

Some distance ahead of them the green of the jungle ended in a sharply cut line, beyond which there was a heavy growth of fairly open forest. A couple of miles of this and there was the city, their objective—so near and yet so far!

"We'll either just make the timber or we just won't," Kinnison, mentally plotting the course, announced dispassionately. "Just as well if we land in the jungle, I think. It'll break our fall, anyway; and hitting solid ground inert at this speed might be pretty serious."

"If we land in the jungle we will never leave it"—Worsel's thought did not slow the incredible tempo of his prodigious pinions—"but it makes little difference whether I die now or later."

"It does to us, you pessimistic croaker!" flared Kinnison. "Forget that dying complex of yours for a minute! Remember the plan and follow it! We're going to strike the jungle, about ninety or a hundred meters in. If you come in with us you die at once, and the rest of our scheme is all shot to pieces. So when we let go, you go ahead and land in the woods. We'll join you there, never fear; our armor will hold long enough for us to cut our way through a hundred meters of any jungle that ever grew—even this one. Get ready, Bus. Leggo!"

*

They dropped. Through the lush succulence of close-packed upper leaves and tentacles they crashed—through the heavier, wooded main branches below, through to the ground. And there they fought for their lives; for those voracious plants nourished themselves not only upon the soil in which their roots were embedded, but also upon anything organic unlucky enough to come within reach. Flabby but tough tentacles encircled them; ghastly sucking disks, exuding a potent corrosive, slobbered wetly at their armor; knobbed and spiky bludgeons whanged against tempered steel as the monstrous organisms began dimly to realize that these particular titbits were encased in something more resistant far than skin, scales, or bark.

But the Lensman and his giant companion were not quiescent. They came down oriented and fighting. VanBuskirk, in the van, swung his frightful space ax as a reaper swings his scythe—one solid, short step forward with each swing. And close behind the Valerian strode Kinnison, his own flying ax guarding the giant's head and back.

Masses of that obscene vegetation crashed down upon their heads from above, revolting cupped orifices sucking and smacking; and they were showered continually with floods of the opaque, corrosive sap to the action of which even their armor was not entirely immune. But, hampered as they were and almost blinded, they struggled indomitably on; while behind them an ever-lengthening corridor of demolition marked their progress.

"Ain't we got fun?" grunted the Dutchman, in time with his swing. "But we're quite a team at that, chief—brains and brawn, huh?"

"Uh-huh," dissented Kinnison, his flying weapon a solid disk of steel to the eye. "Grace and poise; or, if you want to be really romantic, ham and eggs."

"Rack and ruin will be more like it if we don't break out before this confounded goo eats through our armor. But we're making it—the stuff's thinning out and I think I can see trees up ahead."

"It is well if you can," came a cold, clear thought from Worsel, "for I am sorely beset. Hasten or I perish!"

At that thought the two patrolmen forged ahead in a burst of furious activity. Crashing through the thinning barriers of the jungle's edge, they wiped their lenses partially clear, glanced quickly about, and saw the Velantian. That worthy was "sorely beset" indeed. Six animals—huge, reptilian, but lithe and active—had him down. So helplessly immobile was

Worsel that he could scarcely move his tail, and the monsters were already beginning to gnaw at his scaly, armored hide.

"I'll put a stop to that, Worsel!" called Kinnison, referring to the fact, well known to all us moderns, that any real animal, no matter how savage, can be controlled by any wearer of the Lens. For, no matter how low in the scale of intelligence the animal is, the Lensman can get in touch with whatever mind the creature has and reason with it.

But these monstrosities, as Kinnison learned immediately, were not really animals. Even though of animal form and mobility, they were purely vegetable in motivation and behavior, reacting only to the stimuli of food and of reproduction. Weirdly and completely inimical to all other forms of created life, they were so utterly noisome, so completely alien that the full power of mind and Lens failed entirely to gain rapport.

*

Upon that confusedly writhing heap the patrolmen flung themselves, terrible axes destructively a-swing. In turn, they were attacked viciously; but this battle was not long to endure. VanBuskirk's first terrific blow knocked one adversary away, almost spinning end over end. Kinnison took out one, the Dutchman another, and the remaining three were no match at all for the humiliated and furiously raging Velantian. But it was not until the monstrosities had been gruesomely carved and torn apart, literally limb from hideous limb, that they ceased their insensately voracious attacks.

"They took me by surprise," explained Worsel, unnecessarily, as the three made their way through the night toward their goal, "and six of them at once were too much for me. I tried to hold their minds, but apparently they have none."

"How about the Overlords?" asked Kinnison. "Suppose they have received any of our thoughts? We patrolmen at least have been doing a lot of unguarded radiating lately."

"No," Worsel made positive reply. "The thought-screen batteries, while small and of very little actual power, have, nevertheless, a very long service life. Now let us again go over the next steps of our plan of action."

Since no more untoward events marred their progress toward the Delgonian city, they soon reached it. It was for the most part dark and quiet, its somber buildings merely blacker blobs against a background of black. Here and there, however, were to be seen automotive vehicles moving about, and the three invaders crouched against a convenient wall, waiting for one to come along the "street" in which they were. Eventually one did.

As it passed them Worsel sprang into headlong, gliding flight, Kinnison's heavy knife in one gnarled fist. And as he sailed he struck—lethally. Before that luckless Delgonian's brain could radiate a single thought it was in no condition to function at all; for the head containing it was bouncing in the gutter. Worsel backed the peculiar conveyance along the curb and his two companions leaped into it, lying flat upon its floor and covering themselves from sight as best they could.

Worsel, familiar with things Delgonian and looking enough like a native of the planet to pass a casual inspection in the dark, drove the car. Streets and thoroughfares he traversed at reckless speed, finally drawing up before a long, low building, entirely dark. He scanned his surroundings with care, in every direction. Not a creature was in sight.

"All is clear, friends," he thought, and the three adventurers sprang to the building's entrance. The door—it had a door, of sorts—was locked, but VanBuskirk's ax made short work of that difficulty. Inside, they braced the wrecked door against intrusion. Then Worsel led the way into the unlighted interior. Soon he flashed his lamp about him and stepped upon a black, peculiarly marked tile set into the floor; whereupon a harsh, white light illuminated the room.

"Cut it, before somebody takes alarm!" snapped Kinnison.

"No danger of that," replied the Velantian. "There are no windows in any of these rooms; no light can be seen from outside. This is the control room of the city's power plant. If you can convert any of this power to your uses, help yourselves to it. In this building is also Delgon's closest approximation to a munitions plant. Whether or not anything in it can be of service to you is, of course, for you to say. I am now at your disposal."

While the Velantian was thinking these things Kinnison had been studying the panels and instruments. Now he and VanBuskirk tore open their armor—they had already learned that the atmosphere of Delgon, while not as wholesome for them as that in their suits, would, for a time at least, support human life—and wrought diligently with pliers, screw drivers, and other tools of the electrician. Soon their exhausted batteries were upon the floor beneath the instrument panel, greedily absorbing the electrical fluid from the busbars of the Delgonians.

"Now, while they're getting filled up, let's see what they mean by 'munitions' in these parts," Kinnison ordered. "Lead on, Worsel!"

VII.

With Worsel in the lead, the three interlopers hastened along a corridor, past branching and intersecting hallways, to a distant wing of the structure. There, it was evident, manufacturing of weapons was carried on; but a quick study of the queer-looking devices and mechanisms upon the benches and inside the storage racks lining its walls convinced Kinnison that the room could yield them nothing of permanent benefit. There were high-powered beam projectors, it was true; but they were so heavy that they were not even semiportable. There were also hand weapons of various peculiar patterns, but without exception they were ridiculously inferior to the DeLameters of the patrol in every respect of power, range, controllability, and storage capacity. Nevertheless, after testing them out sufficiently to make certain of the above findings, Kinnison selected an armful of the most powerful models and turned to his companions.

"Let's go back to the power room," he urged. "I'm nervous as a cat. I feel stark naked without my batteries; and if any one should happen to drop in there and do away with them, we'd be sunk without a trace."

Loaded down with Delgonian weapons, they hurried back the way they had come. Much to Kinnison's relief he found that his forebodings had been groundless; the batteries were still there, still absorbing myriawatt hour after myriawatt hour from the Delgonian generators. Staring fixedly at the innocuous-looking containers, he frowned in thought.

"Better we insulate those leads a little heavier and put the cans back in our armor," he suggested finally. "They'll charge just as well in place, and it doesn't stand to reason that this drain of power can go on for the rest of the night without *somebody* noticing it. And when that happens those Overlords are bound to take plenty of steps—the nature of none of which we can even guess at."

"We must have power enough now so that we can all fly away from any possible trouble," Worsel suggested.

"But that's just exactly what we are *not* going to do!" Kinnison declared, with finality. "Now that we've found a good charger, we aren't going to leave it until our accumulators are chocka-block. It's coming in faster than full draft will take it out, and we're going to get a full charge if we have to stand off all the vermin of Delgon to do it."

Far longer than Kinnison had thought possible they were unmolested, but finally a couple of Delgonian engineers came to investigate the unprecedented shortage in the output of their completely automatic generators. At the entrance they were stopped, for no ordinary tools could force the barricade VanBuskirk had erected behind that portal. With leveled weapons the patrolmen stood, awaiting the expected attack. But none developed. Hour by hour the long night wore away, uneventfully. At daybreak, however, a storming party appeared and massive battering-rams were brought into play.

As the dull, heavy concussions reverberated throughout the building the patrolmen each picked up two of the weapons piled before them and Kinnison addressed the Velantian.

"Drag a couple of those metal benches across that corner and coil up behind them," he directed. "They'll be enough to ground any stray charges. If they can't see you they won't know you're here, so probably nothing much will come your way direct."

The Velantian demurred, declaring that he would not hide while his two companions were fighting his battle.

But Kinnison silenced him fiercely. "Don't be a fool!" the Lensman snapped. "One of these beams would fry you to a crisp in ten seconds, whereas the defensive fields of our armor could neutralize a thousand of them, from now on. Do as I say, and do it quick, or I'll beam you unconscious and toss you in there myself!"

*

Realizing that Kinnison meant exactly what he said, and knowing that, unarmored as he was, he was utterly unable to resist either the Tellurian or their common foe, Worsel unwillingly erected his metallic barrier and coiled his sinuous length behind it. He hid himself just in time.

The outer barricade had fallen, and now a wave of reptilian forms flooded into the control room. Nor was this any ordinary investigation. The Overlords had studied the situation from afar, and this wave was one of heavily armed—for Delgon—soldiery. On they came, projectors fiercely aflame, confident in their belief that nothing could stand before their blasts.

But how wrong they were! The two repulsively erect bipeds before them neither burned nor fell. Beams, no matter how powerful, did not reach them.

Nor were these outlandish beings inoffensive. Utterly careless of the service life of the pitifully weak Delgonian projectors, they were using them at maximum drain and at extreme aperture—and in the resultant beams the Delgonian soldier slaves fell in scorched and smoking heaps. On came reserves, platoon after platoon, only and continuously to meet the same fate; for as soon as one projector weakened the invincibly armored man would toss it aside and pick up another. But finally the last commandeered weapon was exhausted and the beleaguered pair brought their own DeLameters—the most powerful portable weapons known to the military scientists of the Galactic Patrol—into play.

And what a difference! In *those* beams the attacking reptiles did not smoke or burn. They simply vanished in a blaze of flaming light, so did also the near-by walls and a good share of the building beyond! The Delgonian hordes having disappeared, VanBuskirk shut off his DeLameter.

Kinnison, however, left his on, angling its beam sharply upward, blasting into fiery vapor the ceiling and roof over their heads, remarking: "While we're at it we might as well fix things so that we can make a quick get-away if we want to."

Then they waited. Waited, watching the needles of their meters creep ever closer to the "full-charge" marks; waited while, as they shrewdly suspected, the distant, cowardly hiding Overlords planned some other, more promising line of physical attack.

Nor was it long in developing. Another small army appeared, armored this time; or, more accurately, advancing behind metallic shields. Knowing what to expect, Kinnison was not surprised when the beam of his DeLameter not only failed to pierce one of those shields, but did not in any way impede the progress of the Delgonian column.

"Well, we're all done here, anyway, as far as I'm concerned." Kinnison grinned at the Dutchman as he spoke. "My cans've been showing full back pressure for the last five minutes. How about yours?"

"Same here," VanBuskirk reported, and the two leaped lightly into the Velantian's refuge. Then, inertialess all, the three shot into the air at such a pace that to the slow senses of the Delgonian slaves they simply disappeared. Indeed, it was not until the barrier had been blasted away and every room, nook, and cranny of the immense structure had been literally and minutely combed that the Delgonians—and through their enslaved minds the Overlords—became convinced that their prey had in some uncanny and unknown fashion eluded them.

*

Now high in the air, the three troopers traversed, in a matter of minutes, the same distance that had cost them so much time and strife the day before. Over the monster-infected forest they sped, over the deceptively peaceful green lushness of the jungle, to slant down toward Worsel's thoughtproof tent. Inside that refuge they snapped off their thought-screens and Kinnison yawned prodigiously.

"Working days and nights both is all right for a while, but it gets monotonous in time. Since this seems to be the only really safe spot on the planet, I suggest that we take a day or so off and catch up on our eats and sleeps."

They slept and ate; slept and ate again.

"The next thing on the program," Kinnison announced then, "is to clean out that den of Overlords. Then Worsel will be free to help us get going about our own business."

"You speak lightly indeed of the impossible," Worsel, again all glum despondency, reproved him. "I have already explained why the task is, and must remain, beyond our power."

"Yes, but you don't quite grasp the possibilities of the stuff we've got to work with now," the Tellurian replied. "Listen: you could never do anything because you couldn't see through or work through your thought-screens. Neither we nor you could, even now, enslave a Delgonian and make him lead us to the cavern, because the Overlords would know all about it 'way ahead of time and the slave would lead us anywhere else except to the cavern. However, one of us can cut his screen and surrender; possibly keeping just enough screen up to keep the enemy from possessing his mind fully enough to learn that the other two are coming along. The big question is—which of us is to surrender?"

"That is already decided," Worsel made instant reply. "I am the logical—in fact, the *only* one—to do it. Not only would they think it perfectly natural that they should overpower me, but also I am the only one of us three sufficiently able to control his thoughts so as to keep from them the knowledge that I am being accompanied. Furthermore, you both know that it would not be good for your minds, unaccustomed as they are to the practice, to surrender their control voluntarily to an enemy."

"I'll say it wouldn't!" Kinnison agreed, feelingly. "I might do it if I had to, but I wouldn't like it and don't think I'd ever quite get over it. I hate to put such a horrible job off onto you, Worsel, but you're undoubtedly the best equipped to handle it—and even you may have your hands full."

"Yes," the Velantian said, thoughtfully. "While the undertaking is no longer an absolute impossibility, it is difficult—very. In any event you will probably have to beam me yourselves, if we succeed in reaching the cavern. The Overlords will see to that. If so, do it without regret. Know that I expect it and am well content to die in that fashion. Thousands of better men than I am would be only too glad to be in my place, meaning what it does to all Velantia. Know also that I have already reported what is to occur, and that your welcome to Velantia is assured, whether or not I accompany you there."

"I don't think I'll have to kill you, Worsel," Kinnison replied, slowly, picturing in detail exactly what that steel-hard reptilian body would be capable of doing when, unshackled, its directing mind was completely taken over by an utterly soulless and conscienceless Overlord. "If we can't keep from going off the deep end, of course you'll get pretty tough and I know that you're hard to handle. However, as I told you back there, I think I can beam you unconscious without killing you. I may have to burn off a few scales, but I'll try not to do any damage that can't be repaired."

"If you can so stop me it will be wonderful indeed. Are we ready?"

They were ready. Worsel opened the door and in a moment was hurtling through the air, his giant wings arrowing him along at a pace no winged creature of Earth would even approach. And, following him easily at a little distance, floated the two patrolmen upon their inertialess drives.

*

398

During that long flight scarcely a thought was exchanged, even between Kinnison and VanBuskirk. To direct a thought at the Velantian was, of course, out of the question. All lines of communication with him had been cut; and, furthermore, his mind, able as it was, was being taxed to the ultimate cell in doing what he had set out to do. And the two patrolmen were reluctant to converse with each other, even upon their tight beams, radios, or sounders, for fear that some slight leakage of thought energy might reveal their presence to the ever-watchful Overlords. If this opportunity were lost, they knew, another chance to wipe out that hellish horde might never present itself.

Land was traversed, and sea; but finally a stupendous range of mountains reared before them and Worsel, folding back his tireless wings, shot downward in a screaming, full-weight dive. In his line of flight Kinnison saw the mouth of a cave, a darker spot of blackness in the black rock of the mountain's side. Upon the ledged approach there lay a Delgonian—a guard or lookout, of course.

The Lensman's DeLameter was already in his hand, and at sight of the guardian reptile he sighted and fired in one incredibly fast motion. But, rapid as it was, it was still too slow. The Overlords had seen that the Velantian had companions of whom he had been able to keep them in ignorance theretofore.

Instantly, Worsel's wings again began to beat, bearing him off at a wide angle; and, although the patrolmen were insulated against his thought, the meaning of his antics was very plain. He was telling them in every possible way that the hole below was *not* the cavern of the Overlords, that it was over this way, that they were to keep on following him to it. Then, as they refused to follow him, he rushed upon Kinnison in mad attack.

"Beam him down, Kim!" VanBuskirk yelled. "Don't take any chances with that bird!" He leveled his own DeLameter.

"Lay off, Bus!" the Lensman snapped. "I can handle him—a lot easier out here than on the ground."

And so it proved. Inertialess as he was, the buffetings of the Velantian affected him not at all; and when Worsel coiled his supple body around him and began to apply pressure, Kinnison simply expanded his thought-screen to cover them both, thus releasing the mind of his temporarily inimical friend from the Overlord's grip. Instantly the Velantian became himself, snapped on his own shield, and the three continued, as one, their interrupted downward course.

Worsel came to a halt upon the ledge, beside the practically incinerated corpse of the lookout, knowing, unarmored as he was, that to go farther meant sudden death. The armored pair, however, shot on into the gloomy passage. At first they were offered no opposition. The Overlords had had no time to muster an adequate defense. Scattering handfuls of slaves rushed them, only to be blasted out of existence as their hand weapons proved useless against the armor of the Galactic Patrol. Defenders became more numerous as the cavern itself was approached; but neither were they allowed to stay the patrolmen's progress. Finally, a palely shimmering barrier of metal appeared to bar their way. Its fields of force neutralized or absorbed the blasts of the DeLameters, but its material substance offered but little resistance to a thirty-pound sledge swung by one of the strongest men ever produced by any planet colonized by the humanity of Earth.

THE LENSMAN

*

Now they were in the cavern itself—the sanctum sanctorum of the Overlords of Delgon. There was the hellish torture screen, with its burden of mental and physical pain. There was the horribly avid audience, now milling about in a mob frenzy of panic. There, upon a raised balcony, were the "big shots" of this nauseous clan; now doing their utmost to marshal some force able to cope effectively with this unheard-of violation of their age-old immunity.

A last wave of Delgonian slaves hurled themselves forward, futile projectors furiously aflame, only to disappear in the DeLameters' fans of force. The patrolmen hated to kill those mindless slaves, but it was a nasty job that had to be done. The slaves out of the way, those ravening beams bored on into the massed Overlords.

And now Kinnison and VanBuskirk killed, if not joyously, at least relentlessly, mercilessly, and with neither sign nor sensation of compunction. For this unbelievably monstrous tribe needed killing, root and branch. Not a scion or shoot of it should be allowed to survive, to continue to contaminate the civilization of the galaxy. Back and forth, to and fro, up and down swept the raging beams of the DeLameters, playing on until in all the vast volume of that gruesome chamber nothing lived save the two grim figures in its portal.

Assured of this fact, but with DeLameters still in hand, the two destroyers retraced their way to the tunnel's mouth, where Worsel anxiously awaited them. Lines of communication again established, Kinnison informed the Velantian of all that had taken place, and the latter gradually cut down the power of his thought-screen. Soon it was at zero strength and he reported jubilantly that for the first time in untold ages, the Overlords of Delgon were off the air!

"But surely the danger isn't over yet!" protested Kinnison. "We couldn't have got them all in this one raid. Some of them must have escaped, and there must be other dens of them on this planet somewhere?"

"Possibly; possibly." The Velantian waved his tail airily—the first sign of joyousness he had shown. "But their power is broken, definitely and forever. With these new screens, and with the arms and armament which, thanks to you, we can now fabricate, the task of wiping them out completely will be comparatively simple. Now you will accompany me to Velantia where, I assure, the resources of the planet will be put solidly behind you in your own endeavors. I have already summoned a space ship. In less than twelve days we will be back in Velantia and at work upon your projects. In the meantime——"

"Twelve *days*! Holy jumping rockets!" VanBuskirk exploded.

Kinnison said, "Sure—you forget that they knew nothing of our free drive. We'd better hop over and get our lifeboat, I think. It's not so good, either way, but in our own boat we'll be open to detection less than two hours, as against twelve days in the Velantians'. And the pirates may be here any minute. It's as good as certain that their ship will be stopped and searched long before it gets back to Velantia, and if we were aboard it would be just too bad."

"And, since the crew knows about us, the pirates soon will, and it'll be just too bad, anyway," VanBuskirk reasoned.

"Not at all," interposed Worsel. "The few of my people who know of you have been instructed to seal that knowledge. I must admit, however, that I am greatly disturbed by your conceptions of these pirates of space. You see, until I met you I knew nothing more of the pirates than I did of your patrol."

"What a world!" VanBuskirk exclaimed. "No patrol and no pirates! But at that, life might be simpler without both of them and without the free space drive—more like it used to be in the good old airplane days that the novelists rave about."

"Of course, I could not judge as to that." The Velantian was very serious. "This in which we live seems to be an out-of-the-way section of the galaxy; or it may be that we have nothing that the pirates want."

"More likely it's simply that, like the patrol, they haven't got organized into this district yet," suggested Kinnison. "There are so many millions of solar systems in the galaxy that it will probably be thousands of years yet before the patrol gets into them all."

"But about these pirates," Worsel went back to his point. "If they have such minds as those of the Overlords, they will be able to break the seals of our minds. However, I gather from your thoughts that their minds are not of that strength?"

"Not so far as I know," Kinnison replied. "You folks have the most powerful brains I ever heard of, short of the Arisians. And speaking of mental power, you can hear thoughts a lot farther than I can, even with my Lens or with this pirate receiver I've got. See if you can find out whether there are any pirates in space around here, will you?"

*

While the Velantian was concentrating, VanBuskirk asked: "Why, if his mind is so strong, could the Overlords put him under so much easier than they could us 'weak-minded' humans?"

"You are confusing 'mind' with 'will,' I think. Ages of submission to the Overlords made the Velantians' will power zero, as far as the bosses were concerned. On the other hand, you and I could raise stubbornness to sell to most people. In fact, if the Overlords had succeeded in really breaking us down, back there, I believe that we would have been insane for the rest of our lives."

"Probably you're right. We break, but don't bend, huh?"

Then the Velantian was ready to report. "I have scanned space to the nearer stars—some eleven of your light years—and have encountered no intruding entities," he announced.

"Eleven light years—what a range!" Kinnison exclaimed. "However, that's only a shade over two minutes for a pirate ship at full blast. But we've got to take a chance sometime, and the quicker we get started the sooner we'll get back. We'll pick you up here, Worsel. No use in you going back to your tent—we'll be back here long before you could reach it. You'll be safe enough, I think, especially with our spare DeLameters. Let's get going, Bus!"

Again they shot into the air; again they traversed the airless depths of interplanetary space. To locate the temporary tomb of their lifeboat required only a few minutes, to disinter her only a few more. Then again they braved detection in the void; Kinnison tense at his controls, VanBuskirk in strained attention listening to and staring at his

401

unscramblers and detectors. But the ether was still blank as they materialized in an inertialess landing beside the waiting Velantian.

"All right, Worsel, snap it up!" Kinnison called, and went on to VanBuskirk, "Now, you big, flat-footed Valerian space hound, I hope that that spaceman's god of yours will see to it that our luck holds good for just seven minutes more. We've had more luck already than we had any right to expect, but we can put a little more to most gosh-awful good use!"

"Noshabkeming *does* bring spacemen luck," insisted the giant, grimacing a peculiar salute toward a small, golden image set inside his helmet, "and the fact that you warty, runty little space fleas of Tellus haven't got sense enough to know it, doesn't change matters at all."

"That's tellin' 'em, Bus!" Kinnison applauded. "But if it helps charge your batteries, go to it. Ready to blast! Lift!"

The Velantian had come aboard; the tiny air lock was again tight, and the little vessel shot away from Delgon toward far Velantia. And still the ether remained empty as far as the detectors could reach. Nor was this fact surprising, in spite of the Lensman's fears to the contrary; for the patrolmen had given the pirates such an extremely long line to cover that many days must yet elapse before the minions of Boskone would get around to visit that unimportant, unexplored, and almost unknown solar system.

*

En route to his home planet Worsel got in touch with the crew of the Velantian vessel already in space, ordering them to return to port posthaste and instructing them in detail what to think and how to act should they be stopped and searched by one of Boskone's raiders. By the time these instructions had been given, Velantia loomed large beneath the flying midget. Then, with Worsel as guide, Kinnison drove over a mighty ocean upon whose opposite shore lay the great city in which Worsel lived.

"But I would like to have them welcome you as befits what you have done, and have you go to the dome!" mourned the Velantian. "Think of it! You have done a thing which for ages the massed power of the planet has been trying vainly to accomplish, and yet you insist that I alone take full and complete credit for it!"

"I don't insist on any such thing," argued Kinnison, "even though it's practically all yours, anyway. I insist only on your keeping us and the patrol out of it, and you know as well as I do why you've got to do that. Tell them anything else you want to. Say that a couple of pink-haired Chickladorians helped you and then beat it back home. *That* planet's far enough away so that if the pirates chase them they'll get a real run for their money. After this blows over you can tell the truth—but *not until then.*

"And as for us going to the dome for a grand hocus-pocus, that is completely and definitely *out.* We're not going anywhere except to the biggest space yard you've got. You're not going to give us anything except a lot of material and a lot of highly trained help that can keep their thoughts sealed.

"We've got to build a lot of heavy stuff fast; and we've got to get started on it just as quickly as the gods of space will let us!"

*

VIII.

Worsel knew his council of scientists, as well he might, since it developed that he himself ranked high in that select circle. True to his promises, the largest space port of the planet was immediately emptied of its customary personnel, which was replaced the following morning by an entirely new group of workmen.

Nor were these replacements ordinary laborers. They were young, keen, and highly trained, taken, to a man, from behind the thought-screens of the scientists. It is true that they had no inkling of what they were to do, since none of them had ever dreamed of the possibility of such engines as they were to be called upon to construct.

But, upon the other hand, they were well versed in the fundamental theories and operations of mathematics, and from pure mathematics to applied mechanics is but a step. Furthermore, they had *brains*—knew how to think logically, coherently, and effectively, and needed neither driving nor supervision—only instruction. And best of all, practically every one of the required mechanisms already existed, in miniature, within the *Brittania's* lifeboat, ready at hand for their dissection, analysis, and enlargement. It was not lack of understanding which was to slow up the work; it was simply that the planet did not boast machine tools and equipment large enough or strong enough to handle the necessarily huge and heavy parts and members required.

While the construction of this heavy machinery was being rushed through, Kinnison and VanBuskirk devoted their efforts to the fabrication of an ultra-sensitive receiver, tunable to the pirates' scrambled wave bands. With their exactly detailed knowledge, and with the cleverest technicians and the choicest equipment of Velantia at their disposal, the set was soon completed.

Kinnison was giving its exceedingly delicate coils their final alignment when Worsel wriggled blithely into the radio laboratory.

"Hi, Kimball Kinnison of the Lens!" he called gayly. Throwing some twenty feet of his serpent's body in lightning loops about a convenient pillar, he made a horizontal bar of the rest of himself and dropped one wing tip to the floor. Then, nonchalantly upside down, he thrust out three or four eyes and curled their stalks over the Lensman's shoulder, the better to inspect the results of the mechanics' efforts. Gone was the morose, pessimistic, death-haunted Worsel who had wrought and fought beside the armored pair upon fantastically inimical Delgon. This was a new Worsel entirely; gay, happy, carefree, and actually frolicsome—if you can imagine a thirty-foot-long, crocodile-headed, leather-winged python as being frolicsome!

"Hi, your royal snakeship!" Kinnison retorted in kind. "Still here, huh? Thought you'd be back on Delgon by this time, cleaning up the rest of that mess."

"The equipment is not ready, but there's no hurry about that." The playful reptile unwrapped ten or twelve feet of tail from the pillar and waved it airily about. "Their power is broken; their race is done. You are about to try out the new receiver?"

"Yes—going out after them right now." Kinnison began deftly to manipulate the micrometric verniers of his dials.

*

THE LENSMAN

Eyes fixed upon meters and gauges, he listened—listened—increased his power and listened again. More and more power he applied to his apparatus, listening continually. Suddenly he stiffened, his hands becoming rock-still. He listened, if possible even more intently than before; and as he listened his face grew grim and granite-hard. Then the micrometers began again, crawlingly, to move, as though he were tracing a beam.

"Bus! Hook on the focusing beam antenna!" he snapped. "It's going to take every milliwatt of power we've got in this hook-up to tap his beam, but I think that I've got Helmuth direct, instead of through a pirate-ship relay!"

Again and again he checked the readings of his dials and of the directors of his antenna; each time noting the exact time of the Velantian day.

"There! As soon as we get some time, Worsel, I'd like to work out these figures with some of your astronomers. They'll give me a right line through to Helmuth's headquarters—I hope. Some day, if I'm spared, I'll get another!"

"What kind of news did you get?" asked VanBuskirk.

"Good and bad both," replied the Lensman. "Good in that Helmuth doesn't believe that we stayed with his ship as long as we did. He's a suspicious devil, you know, and is pretty well convinced that we tried to run the same kind of a blazer on him that we did the other time. Since he hasn't got enough ships on the job to work the whole line, he's concentrating on the other end. That means that we've got plenty of days left. The bad part of it is that they've got four of our boats already and are bound to get more. Lord, how I wish I could call the rest of them! Some of them could certainly make it here before they got caught."

"Might I then offer a suggestion?" asked Worsel, suddenly diffident.

"Surely!" the Lensman replied in surprise. "Your ideas have never been any kind of poppycock. Why so bashful all at once?"

"Because this one is so—ah—so peculiarly personal, since you men regard so highly the privacy of your minds. Our two sciences, as you have already observed, are vastly different. You are far beyond us in mechanics, physics, chemistry, and the other applied sciences. We, on the other hand, have delved much deeper than have you into psychology and the other introspective studies. For that reason I know positively that the Lens you wear is capable of enormously greater things than you are at present able to perform. Of course, I cannot use your Lens directly, since it is attuned to your own ego. However, if the idea appeals to you, I could, with your consent, occupy your mind and use your Lens to put you en rapport with your fellows. I have not volunteered the suggestion before because I know how averse your mind is to any foreign control."

"Not necessarily to foreign control," Kinnison corrected him. "Only to enemy control. The idea of friendly control never occurred to me. That would be an entirely different breed of cats. Go to it!"

*

Kinnison relaxed his mind completely, and that of the Velantian came welling in, wave upon friendly, surging wave of benevolent power. And not only—or not precisely—power. It was more than power; it was a calm, cool, placid certainty, a depth and clarity of perception that Kinnison in his most cogent moments had never dreamed a possibility.

The possessor of that mind knew things, cameo-clear in microscopic detail, which the keenest minds of Earth could perceive only as chaotically indistinct masses of mental light and shade, of no recognizable pattern whatever!

"Give me the thought pattern of him with whom you wish first to converse," came Worsel's thought, this time from deep within the Lensman's own brain.

Kinnison felt a subtle thrill of uneasiness at that new and ultra-strange dual personality, but thought back steadily, "Sorry—I can't."

"Excuse me, I should have known that you cannot think in our patterns. Think, then, of him as a person—an individual. That will give me, I believe, sufficient data."

Into the Earthman's mind there leaped a picture of Henderson, sharp and clear. He felt his Lens actually tingle and throb as a concentration of vital force such as he had never known poured through his whole being and into that almost-living creation of the Arisians, and immediately thereafter he was in full mental communication with the chief pilot of the ill-fated *Brittania*! And there, seated across the tiny mess table of their lifeboat, was Thorndyke, the master technician.

Henderson came to his feet with a yell as the telepathic message bombarded into his brain, and it required several seconds to convince him that he was not the victim of space insanity or suffering from any other form of hallucination. Once convinced, however, he acted. His lifeboat shot toward far Velantia at maximum blast.

Then: "Nelson! Allerdyce! Thompson! Jenkins! Uhlenhuth! Smith! Chatway—" Kinnison called the roll of the survivors.

Nelson, the *Brittania's* communications officer, answered his captain's call. So did Allerdyce, the juggling quartermaster. So did Uhlenhuth, a technician. So did those in three other boats. Two of these three were apparently well within the danger zone, and might get nipped in their dash, but their crews elected without hesitation to take the chance. Four boats, it was already known, had been captured by the pirates. The remaining eight were either so distant as to be out of range of even the Worsel-driven Lens, or they had been taken by pirates who had not yet reported to Helmuth.

"Eight out of twenty," Kinnison mused. "Not so good, but it could have been a lot worse. They might very well have taken us all by this time."

Then he turned to the Velantian, who had withdrawn his mind as soon as its task was done. "Thanks, Worsel," he said simply. "Some of those lads coming in have got plenty of just what it takes, and *how* we can use them!"

*

One by one the lifeboats of the *Brittania* came into port, where their crews were welcomed briefly, but feelingly, before they were put to work. Nelson, the communications officer, among the last to arrive, was to the Lensman particularly welcome.

"Nels, we need you badly," Kinnison informed him as soon as greetings had been exchanged. "The pirates have a beam, carrying a peculiarly scrambled wave that they can receive and decode through any kind of ordinary blanketing interference, and you're the best man of us all to study their system. Some of these Velantian scientists can probably help you a lot on that—any race that can develop a screen against thought figures to know more than somewhat about vibration in general. We've got working models of the pirates' instruments, so that you can figure out their patterns and formulas. That ought to be simple.

"When you've done that, I want you and your Velantians to design something that will scramble all the pirates' communicator beams in space, from here to the near rim of the galaxy. If you can fix things so that they can't talk, any more than we can, it'll help a lot, believe me!"

"QX, chief, we'll give it the works." And the radio man called for tools, apparatus and electricians.

Then throughout the great space port the many Velantians and the handful of patrolmen labored mightily, side by side, and to very good effect indeed. Slowly, the port became ringed about by, and studded everywhere with, monstrous mechanisms. Everywhere there were projectors: refractory-throated demons ready to vomit forth every force known to the expert technicians of the patrol. There were absorbers, too, backed by their bleeder resistors, air gaps, ground rods, and racks for discharged accumulators. There, too, were receptors and converters for the cosmic energy which was to empower many of the devices. There were, of course, atomic motor generators by the score, and battery upon battery of gigantic accumulators. And Nelson's high-powered scrambler was ready to go to work.

These machines appeared crude, rough, unfinished; for neither time nor labor had been wasted upon nonessentials. But inside each one the moving parts fitted with micrometric accuracy and with hair-spring balance. All, without exception, functioned perfectly.

At Worsel's call, Kinnison climbed up out of a great beamproof pit, the top of whose wall was practically composed of tractor-beam projectors. Pausing only to make sure that a sticking switch on one of the screen-dome generators had been replaced, he hurried to the heavily armored control room, where his little force of fellow patrolmen awaited him.

"They're coming, boys," he announced. "You all know what to do. There are a lot more things that we could have done if we'd had more time, but as it is we'll just go to work on them with what we've got." And Kinnison, again all brisk captain, bent over his instruments.

In the ordinary course of events the pirate would have flashed up to the planet with spy rays out and issuing a peremptory demand for the planet to show a clean bill of health or to surrender instantly such fugitives as might lately have landed upon it. But Kinnison did not—could not—wait for that. The spy rays, he knew, would reveal the presence of his armament; and such armament most certainly did not belong to this planet. Therefore, the instant that the pirate ship came within range of his detectors he acted; and forthwith everything happened at once, with furious swiftness.

A tracer lashed out, the pilot ray of the rim battery of extraordinarily powerful tractors. Under the urge of those beams the inertialess ship flashed toward their center of action, which was the geometrical center of the space port's deep rayproof pit. At the same moment Nelson's scrambler burst into activity, a dome-screen against cosmic-energy intake, and a full circle of super-powered attacking rays.

SUPER PACK

*

All these things occurred in the twinkling of an eye, and the vessel was being slowed down by the atmosphere of Velantia before her startled commander could even realize that he was being attacked. Only the presence of automatically reacting defensive screens saved that ship from instant destruction; but they did so save it and in seconds the pirates' every weapon was furiously ablaze.

In vain. The defenses of that pit could take it. They were driven by mechanisms easily able to absorb the output of any equipment mountable upon a mobile base, and to his consternation the pirate found that his cosmic-energy intake was at, and remained at, zero. He sent out call after call for help, but could not make contact with any other pirate station. Ether and subether alike were closed to him; his signals were blanketed completely. Nor could his drivers, even though operating at ruinous overload, move him from the geometrical center of that incandescently flaming pit, so inconceivably rigid were the tractors' clamps upon him.

And soon his power began to fail. His vessel, designed to operate upon cosmic-energy intake, carried only enough accumulators for stabilization of power flow, an amount ridiculously inadequate for a combat as profligate of energy as this. But, strangely enough, as his defense weakened, so lessened the power of the attack. It was no part of the Lensman's plan to destroy this superdreadnaught of the void.

"That was one good thing about the old *Brittania*," he gritted as he cut down, step by step, the power of his beams, "nobody could block her off from what power she had!"

Soon the stored-up energy of the battleship was exhausted and she lay there, quiescent. Then giant pressers went into action and she was lifted over the wall of the pit, to settle down in an open space beside it—open, but still under the domes of force.

Kinnison had no needle rays as yet, the time at his disposal having been sufficient only for the construction of the absolutely essential items of equipment. Now, while he was debating with his fellows as to what part of the vessel to destroy in order to wipe out its crew, the pirates themselves ended the debate. Ports yawned in the vessel's armored side and they came out fighting.

For they were not a breed to die like rats in a trap, and they knew that to remain inside their vessel was to die whenever and however their captors willed. They knew also that die they must if they could not conquer. Their surrender, even if it should be accepted, would mean only a somewhat later death in the lethal chambers of the law. In the open, they could at least take some of their foes with them.

Furthermore, not being men as we know men, they had nothing in common with either human beings or Velantians. Both of them were vermin, as they themselves were to the beings manning this surprisingly impregnable fortress here in this waste corner of the galaxy. Therefore, space-hardened veterans all, they fought, with the insane ferocity and desperation of the ultimately last stand; but they did not conquer. Instead, and to the last man, they died.

*

As soon as the battle was over, before the interference blanketing the pirates' communicators was cut off, Kinnison went through the captured vessel, destroying the headquarters visiplates and every automatic sender which could transmit any kind of a message to any pirate base.

Then the interference was stopped; the domes were released; the ship was removed from the field of operations. Then, while Thorndyke and his reptilian aides—themselves now radio experts of no mean attainments—busied themselves at installing a high-powered scrambler aboard her, Kinnison and Worsel scanned space in search of more prey. Soon they found it, more distant than the first one had been—two solar systems away—and in an entirely different direction. Tracers and tractors and interference and domes of force again became the order of the day. Projectors again raved out in their incandescent might, and soon another immense cruiser of the void lay beside her sister ship. Another and another; then, for a long time, space was blank.

The Lensman then energized his ultra-receiver, pointing his antenna carefully into the galactic line to Helmuth's base, as laid down for him by the Velantian astronomers. Again, so tight and hard was Helmuth's beam, he had to drive his apparatus so unmercifully that the tube noise almost drowned out the signals, but again he was rewarded by hearing faintly the voice of the pirate director of operations.

"—four vessels, all within or near one of those five solar systems, have ceased communicating; each cessation being accompanied by a period of blanketing interference of a pattern never before registered. You two vessels who are receiving these orders are instructed to investigate that region with the utmost care. Go with screens out and everything on the trips, and with automatic recorders set on me here.

"It is not believed that the patrol has anything to do with this, as ability has been shown transcending anything it has been known to possess. As a working hypothesis it is assumed that one of those solar systems, hitherto practically unexplored and unknown, is, in reality, the seat of a highly advanced race, which perhaps has taken offense at the attitude or conduct of our first ship to visit them. Therefore, proceed with extreme caution, with a thorough spy-ray search at extreme range before approaching at all. If you land, use tact and diplomacy instead of the customary tactics. Find out whether our ships and crews have been destroyed, or are only being held. And remember, automatic reporters on at all times. Helmuth, speaking for Boskone—off!"

For minutes Kinnison manipulated his micrometer in vain. He could not get another sound.

"What are you trying to get, Kim?" asked Thorndyke. "Wasn't that enough?" The message had been re-broadcast to the minds of the others by Worsel, as fast as it had entered the Lensman's ears.

"No, that's only half of it," Kinnison returned. "Helmuth's nobody's fool. He's certainly trying to plot the boundaries of our interference, and I want to see how he's coming out with it. But no dice. He's so far away and his beam's so hard that I can't work him unless he happens to be talking almost directly toward us. Well, it won't be long now until we'll give him some real interference to plot. Now we'll see what we can do about those two other ships that are heading this way. On your toes, everybody."

*

Carefully as those two ships investigated, and sedulously, as they sought to obey Helmuth's instructions, all their precautions amounted to exactly nothing. As ordered, they began a spy-ray survey at extreme range; but even at that range Kinnison's tracers were effective and those two ships also ceased communicating in a blaze of interference. Then recent history repeated itself. The details were changed somewhat, since there were two vessels instead of one; but the pit was of ample size to accommodate two ships, and the tractors could hold two as well and as rigidly as one. The conflict was a little longer, the beaming a little hotter and more coruscant, but the ending was the same. Scramblers were quickly installed and Kinnison addressed his men, already in the ships.

"Well, we're about ready to shove off again. Running away has worked twice so far, with very good results—once in the old *Brittania*, and once in the pirate's own ships. It should work again, if we can ring in enough variations on the theme to keep Helmuth guessing a while longer. Maybe, if the supply of pirate ships keeps up, we'll be able to make Helmuth furnish us transportation all the way back to base!

"Here's the idea. We've got six ships, and there's enough of us to drive them. Some of the younger Velantians have joined us, in spite of the fact that I've told them the chances are against them ever getting back. Enough of them, in fact, to make up almost full crews of us all. But six ships isn't enough of a squadron to fight through the fleets that Helmuth will have organized if we go in a body. So we'll spread out radially, covering thousands of parsecs before we get halfway to base, and broadcasting every watt of interference we can put out all along the way, in as many different shapes and powers as our apparatus will permit. We can't talk to each other, of course, but nothing else can talk anywhere in the same sector of the galaxy, either, and that will give us the edge. Each ship will be on its own, as we were before in the boats; the big difference being that we'll be in superdreadnaughts instead of lifeboats.

"Now, Worsel, if the pirates check up and follow the disturbance we are going to make sure they won't bother you folks at all. In fact, if they ever succeed in finding the center of that interference there will be nothing there except empty space. But if they don't follow us—and Helmuth is apt to insist upon a thorough study of this region before he does anything else—you folks are due for an inspection; and the next inspection will mean a real battle instead of a slaughter. The first spy ray will reveal this stuff here. But I don't suppose you want to hide it or destroy it?"

"We do not," the Velantian replied, positively. "Let them come, in whatever force they care to bring. The more that attack here, the less there will be to halt your progress. This armament represents the best of that possessed by both your patrol and the pirates, with improvements developed by your scientists and ours in full coöperation. We understand thoroughly its construction, operation, and maintenance. You may rest assured that the pirates will never levy tribute upon us, and that any pirate visiting this system will remain in it, permanently!"

"'At-a-snake, Worsel—long may you wiggle!" Kinnison exclaimed. Then, more seriously, "Maybe, after this is all over, I'll see you again sometime. If not, good-by. Good-by, all Velantia! All set, boys? Clear ether and light landings to you all! Blast off!"

Six ships, once pirate craft, now vessels of the Galactic Patrol, hurled themselves into and through Velantian air, into and through interplanetary space, out into the larger, wider, more unobstructed emptiness of the interstellar void. Six, each broadcasting with prodigious power and volume an all-inclusive interference through which no pirate communicator or visiray beam could possibly be driven!

IX.

Kimball Kinnison sat at his controls, smoking a rare, festive cigarette and smiling, at peace with the entire universe. For this new picture was in every element a different one from the old. Instead of being in a pitifully weak and defenseless lifeboat, skulking and hiding, he was in one of the most powerful battleships afloat, driving boldly at full blast almost directly toward home. Instead of only two, the patrolmen were now three in number, and LaVerne Thorndyke, master technician, was a telling addition to their force. Also, they had under them almost a normal crew of alert and highly trained Velantians.

Best of all, the enemy, instead of being a close-knit group, keeping Helmuth informed moment by moment of the situation and instantly responsive to his orders, were now entirely out of communication with each other and with their headquarters, groping helplessly. Literally, as well as figuratively, the pirates were in the dark—the absolute blackness of interstellar space. Then Thorndyke entered the room, frowning slightly.

"You look like the fabled Cheshire Cat, Kim," he remarked. "I hate to spoil such perfect bliss, but I'm here to tell you that we ain't out of the woods yet, by seven thousand rows of trees."

"Maybe not," the Lensman returned, blithely, "but compared to the jam we were in a while ago we're not only sitting on top of the world; we're perched right on the exact apex of the universe. They can't send or receive reports or orders, and they can't communicate. Even their detectors are mighty lame. You know how far they can get on electromagnetic detectors and visual apparatus. Furthermore, there isn't an identification number, symbol, or name on the outside of this buzz buggy. If it ever had one the friction and attrition have worn it off, clear down to the armor. What can happen that we can't cope with?"

"These engines can happen," the technician responded, bluntly. "The Bergenholm is developing a meter jump that I don't like a little bit."

"Does she knock? Or even tick?" demanded Kinnison.

"Not yet," Thorndyke confessed, reluctantly.

"How big a jump?"

"Pretty near two thousandths maximum. Average a thousandth and a half."

"That's hardly a wiggle on the recorder line. Drivers run for months with bigger jumps than that."

"Yeah—drivers. But of all the troubles anybody ever had with Bergenholms, a meter kick was never one of them, and that's what's got me guessing as to the whichness of the why. I'm not trying to scare you—yet. I'm just telling you."

The machine referred to was the neutralizer of inertia, the *sine qua non* of interstellar speed, and it was not to be wondered at that the slightest irregularity in its performance was to the technician a matter of grave concern. Day after day passed, however, and the huge converter continued to function, taking in and sending out its wonted torrents of power. It developed not even a tick, and the meter jump did not grow worse. And during those days they put an inconceivable distance behind them.

During all this time their visual instruments remained blank; to all optical apparatus space was empty save for the normal tenancy of celestial bodies. From time to time something invisible or beyond the range of vision registered upon one of the electromagnetic detectors, but so slow were these instruments that nothing came of their signals. In fact, by the time the warnings were recorded, the objects causing the disturbances were probably far astern.

*

One day, however, the Bergenholm quit—cold. There was no laboring, no knocking, no heating up, no warning at all. One instant the ship was speeding along in free flight; the next she was lying inert in space. She was practically motionless, for any possible velocity built up by inert acceleration is scarcely a crawl, as free space speeds go!

Then the whole crew labored like mad. As soon as they had the massive covers off, Thorndyke scanned the interior of the machine and turned to Kinnison.

"I think we can patch her up, but it'll take quite a while. Maybe you'd be of more use in the control room—this ain't quite as safe as a church, is it, lying here inert?"

"Most of the stuff is on automatic trip, but maybe I'd better keep an eye on things, at that. Let me know occasionally how you're getting along." And the Lensman went back to his controls—none too soon.

For one pirate ship was already beaming him viciously. Only the fact that his defensive armament was upon its automatic trips had saved the stolen battleship from practically instantaneous destruction.

As Kinnison had already remarked more than once, Helmuth was far from being a fool, and that new and amazingly effective blanketing of his every means of communication was a problem whose solution was of paramount importance. Almost every available ship had been, for days, upon the fringe of that interference, observing and reporting continuously. So rapidly was it moving, however, so peculiar was its apparent shape, and so contradictory were the directional readings obtained, that Helmuth's computers had been baffled.

Then Kinnison's Bergenholm failed and his ship went inert. In a space of minutes the location of one center of interference was known. Its coördinates were determined and half a dozen warships were ordered to rush that spot. The raider first to arrive had signaled, visually and audibly; then, obtaining no response, had anchored with a tractor and had loosed his bolts. Nor would the result have been different had every one aboard, instead of no one, been in the control room at the time of the signaling. Kinnison could have read the messages, but neither he nor any one else then aboard the erstwhile pirate craft could have answered them in kind.

Soon the two space ships attacking the turncoat became three, then four, and still the Lensman sat unworried at his board. His meters showed no overload; his noble craft was easily taking everything her sister ships could send.

Then Thorndyke stepped into the room, no longer a natty officer of space. Instead, he was stripped to sweat-soaked undershirt and overalls. He was covered with grease and grime, and what of his thickly smeared face was visible was almost haggard with fatigue. He opened his mouth to say something, then snapped it shut, as his eye was caught by a flaring visiplate.

"Holy jumping rockets!" he exclaimed. "At us already? Why didn't you yell?"

"How much good would that have done?" Kinnison wanted to know. "Of course, if I had known that you were loafing on the job and could have snapped it up a little, I would have. But there's no particular hurry about this. It'll take more than four of them to break us down, and I was hoping that before they can overload us you'd have us traveling. What was on your mind?"

"I came up here—one, to tell you that we're ready to blast; two, to suggest that you hit her easy at first; and three, to ask if you know where there's any grease soap. But you can cancel two and three. We don't want to play around with these boys much longer—they play too rough—and I ain't going to wash up until I see whether she holds together or not. Blast away—and won't those guys be surprised!"

"I'll say so. We were, too, when the Velantians showed us how to compute a screen that would cut a tractor like so much cheese. Here she goes!"

*

The Lensman twirled a couple of knobs, then punched down hard upon three buttons. As he did so the flaring plates became dark; they were again alone in space. To the dumfounded pirates, inert as they were and with their supposedly unbreakable tractors locked in full grip, it was as though their prey had slipped off into the fourth dimension. Their tractors gripped nothing whatever, their ravening beams bored unimpeded through the space occupied an instant before by resisting screens. They did not know what had happened, or how; and, being deep in the field of interference, they could neither report to nor be guided by the master mind of Boskone.

For minutes Thorndyke, VanBuskirk, and Kinnison waited tensely for they knew not what would happen; but nothing happened and the tension gradually relaxed.

"What was the matter with it?" Kinnison asked, finally.

"Overloaded," was Thorndyke's terse reply.

"Overloaded—hooey!" snapped the Lensman. "How *could* they overload a Bergenholm? And, even if they could, why in all the nine hells of Valeria would they want to?"

"They *could* do it easily enough, in just the way they *did* do it—by banking accumulators onto it in series parallel. As to why, I'll let you do the guessing. With no load on the Bergenholm you've got full inertia, with full load you've got zero inertia—you can't go any farther. It looks just plain dumb to me. But then, I think all pirates are short a few jets somewhere. If they weren't they wouldn't be pirates."

"I don't know whether you're right or not. Hope so, but afraid not. Personally, I don't believe these folks are pirates at all, in the ordinary sense of the word."

"Huh? What are they, then?"

"Piracy implies similarity of culture, I would think," the Lensman said, thoughtfully. "Ordinary pirates are usually renegades, deficient somehow, as you suggested, rebelling against a constituted authority which they themselves have at one time acknowledged and of which they are still afraid. That pattern doesn't fit into this matrix at all, anywhere."

"So what? Now I say 'hooey' right back at you. Anyway, why worry about it?"

"Not worrying about it exactly, but somebody has got to do some thinking about it, or else——"

"I don't like to think; it makes my head ache," interrupted VanBuskirk. "Besides, we're getting away from the Bergenholm."

"You'll get a real headache there"—Kinnison laughed—"because I'll bet a good Tellurian beefsteak that the pirates were trying to set up a negative inertia when they overloaded the Bergenholm; and thinking about that state of matter is enough to make *anybody's* head ache!"

"I knew that some of the dippier Ph.D.'s in higher mechanics have been speculating about it," Thorndyke offered, "but it can't be done that way, can it?"

"Nor any other way that anybody has tried yet, and if such a thing is possible the results may prove really startling. But you two had better shove off; you're dead from the neck up. The Berg's spinning like a top—as smooth as that much green velvet. You'll find a can of soap in my locker, I think."

*

"Maybe she'll hold together long enough for us to get some sleep." The technician eyed a meter dubiously, although its needle was not wavering a hair's breadth from the green line. "But I'll tell the cockeyed universe that that was a jury rigging we gave it, if there ever was one. You can't depend on it for an hour until after it's been pulled and gone over; and that, you know as well as I do, takes a real shop, with plenty of equipment. If you take my advice you'll sit down somewhere while you can and as soon as you can. That Bergenholm is in bad shape, believe me. We can hold her together for a while by main strength and awkwardness, but before very long she's going out for keeps—and when she goes out you don't want to find yourself fifty years from a machine shop instead of fifty minutes."

"I'll say not," the Lensman agreed. "But on the other hand, we don't want those birds jumping us the minute we land, either. Let's see, where are we? And where are the bases? Um—um—sector bases are white rings, you know, sub-sector bases red stars——" Three heads bent over charts.

"The nearest red-star marker seems to be in System 240-16-37," Kinnison finally announced. "Don't know the name of the planet—never been there and——"

"Too far," interrupted Thorndyke. "We'll never make it. Might as well try direct for Prime Base on Tellus. If you can't find a red closer than that, look for an orange or a yellow."

"Bases of any kind seem to be scarce out here," the Lensman commented. "Wish they had scattered them around a little thicker. Here's a violet star, but that wouldn't help us—just an outpost."

"Guess that purple one there's our best bet," concluded Thorndyke. "It's probably several breakdowns away, but maybe we can make it if we have to. Purples are pretty low-grade space ports, but they've got tools, anyway. What's the name of it, Kim—or is it only a number?"

"It's that very famous planet, Trenco," the Lensman announced, after looking up the reference numbers in the atlas.

"*Trenco!*" exclaimed Thorndyke in disgust. "The nuttiest, dopiest, wooziest planet in the galaxy! We *would* draw something like that to sit down on for repairs, wouldn't we? Well, I'm on minus time for sleep. Call me if we go inert before I wake up, will you?"

"I sure will; and I'll try to figure out a way of getting down to ground without bringing all the pirates in space along with us."

Then Thorndyke and VanBuskirk slept; Kinnison planned, and the mighty Bergenholm continued to hold the vessel inertialess. In fact, all three men were thoroughly rested and refreshed before the expected breakdown came. And when it did come they were more or less prepared for it. The delay was not sufficiently long to enable the pirates to find them again.

*

The sweating, grunting, swearing engineers made one seemingly impossible repair after another, by dint of what dodge, improvisation, and makeshift only the fertile brain of LaVerne Thorndyke ever did know. The master technician, one of the keenest and most highly trained engineers of the whole solarian system, was not used to working with his hands. Although young in years, he was wont to use only his head, in directing the labors and the energies of others.

Nevertheless, he was now working like a stevedore. He was permanently grimy and greasy—their one can of mechanics' soap had been used up long since. His finger nails were black and broken; his hands and face were burned, blistered and cracked. His muscles ached and shrieked at the unaccustomed effort, until now they were on the build. But through it all he had stuck uncomplainingly, even buoyantly, to his task. One day, during an interlude of free flight, he strode into the control room and glanced at the course-plotting goniometer, then stared into the "tank."

"Still on the original course, I see. Have you got anything doped out yet?"

"Nothing very good. That's why I'm staying on this course until we reach the point closest to Trenco. I've figured until my alleged brain back-fired on me, and here's all I can get:

"I've been shrinking and expanding our interference zone, changing its shape as much as I could with reflectors, and cutting it off entirely now and then, to cross up their surveyors as much as I could. When we come to the jumping-off place we'll simply cut off everything that is sending out traceable vibrations. The Berg will have to run, of course, but it doesn't radiate much and we can ground out practically all of that. The drive is the bad feature. It looks as though we'll have to cut down to where we can ground out the radiation."

"How about the flare?" Thorndyke took the inevitable slide rule from a pocket of his overalls and began to work it.

"I've already had the Velantians build us some baffles—we've got lots of spare tantalum, tungsten, carballoy, and refractory, you know—just in case we should want to use them."

"Radiation—detection—decrement—cosine squared theta—um—call it Point 0038," the engineer mumbled, operating his calculator. "We'll have to cut down to about ten or twelve lights. Mighty slow, but we would get there sometime—maybe. Now about the baffles." And he went into another bout with his slide rule, during which could be distinguished a few such words as "temperature—inert corpuscles—velocity—fusion point—Weinberger's Constant——"

Then he said, "It figures that at about fourteen lights your baffles go out. Pretty close check with the radiation limit. QX, I guess—but I shudder to think of what we may have to do to that Bergenholm to hold it together that long."

"It's not so hot. I don't think much of the scheme myself," admitted Kinnison frankly. "Probably you can think up something better before——"

"Who, me? What with?" Thorndyke interrupted, with a laugh. "Looks to me like our best bet. Anyway, ain't you the master mind of this outfit? Blast off!"

*

Thus it came about that, long later, the Lensman cut off his interference, cut off his driving power, cut off every mechanism whose operation generated vibrations which would reveal to enemy detectors the location of his cruiser. Space-suited mechanics emerged from the stern lock and fitted over the still white-hot vents of the driving projectors the baffles they had previously built.

It is, of course, well known that all ships of space are propelled by the inert projection, by means of high-potential static fields, of nascent fourth-order particles or "corpuscles," which are formed inert, inside the inertialess projector, by the conversion of some form of energy into matter. This conversion liberates some heat, and a vast amount of light. This light, or "flare," shining as it does directly upon and through the highly tenuous gas formed by the projected corpuscles, makes of a speeding space ship one of the most gorgeous spectacles known to man; and it was this very spectacular effect that Kinnison and his crew must do away with if their bold scheme was to have any chance at all of success.

The baffles were in place. Now, instead of shooting out in telltale luminescence, the light was shut in—but so, alas, was approximately three per cent of the heat. And the generation of heat *must* be cut down to a point at which the radiation-equilibrium temperature of the baffles would be below the point of fusion of the refractories of which they were composed. This would cut down their speed tremendously; but, on the other hand, they were practically safe from detection and would reach Trenco eventually—if the Bergenholm held out.

Of course, there was still the chance of visual or electromagnetic detection, but that chance was vanishingly small. The proverbial task of finding a needle in a haystack would be an easy one indeed, compared to that of seeing in a telescope or upon visiplate or magne-plate a dead-black, lightless ship in the infinity of space. No, the Bergenholm was their great, their only concern; and the engineers lavished upon that monstrous fabrication of metal a devotion to which could be likened only that of a corps of nurses attending the ailing baby of a multimillionaire.

This concentration of attention did get results. The engineers still found it necessary to sweat and to grunt and to swear, but they did somehow keep the thing running—most of the time. Nor were they detected—then.

For the attention of the pirate high command was very much taken up with that fast-moving, that ever-expanding, that peculiarly-fluctuating volume of interference—utterly enigmatic as it was, and impenetrable to their very instrument of communication. Its center was moving toward the solarian system. In that system was the Prime Base of the Galactic Patrol. Therefore, it *was* the Lensman's work—undoubtedly the same Lensman who had conquered one of their superships and, after having learned its every secret, had escaped in a *lifeboat* through the fine-meshed net set to catch him! And, piling Ossa upon Pelion, this same Lensman had—*must* have—captured ship after unconquerable ship of their best and was even now sailing calmly home with them!

Therefore, using as tools every pirate ship in that sector of space, Helmuth and his computers and navigators were slowly but grimly solving the equations of motion of that volume of interference. Smaller and smaller became the uncertainties. Then ship after ship bored into the subethereal murk, to match course and velocity with, and ultimately to come to grips with, each focus of disturbance as it was determined.

Thus in a sense, and although Kinnison and his friends did not then know it, it was only the failure of the Bergenholm that was to save their lives, and with those lives our present civilization.

*

Slowly, haltingly, and, for reasons already given, undetected, Kinnison made pitiful progress toward Trenco—impatiently cursing his ship, the crippled generator, its designer and its previous operators as he went. But at long last Trenco loomed large beneath them and the Lensman used his Lens.

"Lensman of Trenco space port, or any other Lensman within call!" he sent out clearly. "Kinnison of Tellus—Sol III—calling. My Bergenholm is almost out and I must sit down at Trenco space port for repairs. I have avoided the pirates so far, but they may be either behind me or ahead of me, or both. What is the situation there?"

"I fear that I can be of no help," came back a weak thought, without the customary identification. "I am out of control. However, Tregonsee is in the——"

Kinnison felt a poignant, unbearably agonizing mental impact that jarred him to the very core: a shock that, while of sledge-hammer force, was still of such a keenly, penetrant timbre that it almost exploded every cell of his brain.

Communication ceased, and the Lensman knew, with a sick, shuddering certainty, that while in the very act of talking to him a Lensman had died.

X.

Judged by any Earthly standards, the planet Trenco was—and is—a peculiar one indeed. Its atmosphere, which is not air, and its liquid, which is not water, are its two outstanding peculiarities and the sources of most of its others. Almost half of that atmosphere and by far the greater part of the liquid phase of the planet is a substance of extremely low latent heat of vaporization, with a boiling point such that during the

416

daytime it is a vapor and at night a liquid. To make matters worse, the other constituents of Trenco's gaseous envelope are of very feeble blanketing power, low specific heat, and of high permeability, so that its days are intensely hot and its nights are bitterly cold.

At night, therefore, it rains. Words are entirely inadequate to describe to any one who has never been there just how it does rain during Trenco's nights. Upon Earth one inch of rainfall in an hour is a terrific downpour. Upon Trenco that amount of precipitation would scarcely be considered a mist; for along the equatorial belt, in less than thirteen Tellurian hours, it rains exactly forty-seven feet and five inches every night—no more and no less, each and every night of every year.

Also there is lightning. Not in Terra's occasional flashes, but in one continuous, blinding glare which makes night as we know it unknown there—in nerve-wracking, battering, sense-destroying discharges which make ether and subether alike impenetrable to any ray or signal short of a full-driven power beam. The days are practically as bad. The lightning is not so violent then, but the bombardment of Trenco's monstrous sun, through that outlandishly peculiar atmosphere, produces almost the same effect.

Because of the difference in pressure set up by the enormous precipitation, always and everywhere upon Trenco there is wind—and what a wind! Except at the very poles, where it is too cold for even Trenconian life to exist, there is hardly a spot in which or a time at which an Earthy gale would not be considered a dead calm; and along the equator, at every sunrise and at every sunset, the wind blows from the day side to the night side at the rate of a trifle over eight hundred miles an hour!

Through countless thousands of years wind and wave have planed and scoured the planet Trenco to a geometrically perfect oblate spheroid. It has no elevations and no depressions. Nothing fixed in an Earthly sense grows or exists upon its surface; no structure has ever been built there able to stay in one place through one whole day of the cataclysmic meteorological phenomena which constitute the natural Trenconian environment.

*

There live upon Trenco two types of vegetation, each type having innumerable subdivisions. One type sprouts in the mud of the morning; flourishes flatly, by dint of deeply sent and powerful roots, during the wind and the heat of the day; comes to full fruit in late afternoon; and at sunset dies and is swept away by the flood. The other type is free-floating. Some of its genera are remotely like footballs; others resemble tumbleweeds; still others thistledown; hundreds of others have not their remotest counterparts upon Earth. Essentially, however, they are alike in habits of life. They can sink in the "water" of Trenco; they can burrow in its mud, from which they derive part of their sustenance; they can emerge therefrom into the sunlight; they can, undamaged, float in or roll along before the ever-present Trenconian wind; and they can enwrap, entangle, or otherwise seize and hold anything with which they come in contact which by any chance may prove edible.

Animal life, too, while abundant and diverse, is characterized by three qualities. From lower to very highest it is amphibious; it is streamlined; and it is omnivorous. Life upon Trenco is hard, and any form of life to evolve there must of stern necessity be willing, yes, even anxious, to eat literally *anything* available. And for that reason all surviving forms of life, vegetable and animal, have a voracity and a fecundity almost unknown anywhere else in the galaxy.

Thionite, the noxious drug referred to earlier in this narrative, is the sole reason for Trenco's galactic importance. As chlorophyll is to Earthly vegetation, so is thionite to that of Trenco. Trenco is the only planet thus far known upon which this substance occurs, nor have our scientists even yet been able either to analyze or to synthesize it. Thionite is capable of affecting only those races who breathe oxygen and possess warm blood, red with haemoglobin.

However, the planets peopled by such races are legion, and very shortly after the drug's discovery hordes of addicts, smugglers, peddlers, and out-and-out pirates were rushing toward the new bonanza. Thousands of these adventurers died, either from each other's ray guns or under an avalanche of hungry Trenconian life; but, thionite being what it is, thousands more kept coming. Also came the patrol, to curb the evil traffic at its source by beaming down ruthlessly any being attempting to gather any Trenconian vegetation.

Thus between the patrol and the drug syndicate there rages a bitterly continuous battle to the death. Arrayed against both factions is the massed life of the noisome planet, omnivorous as it is, eternally ravenous, and of an individual power and ferocity and a collective aggregate of numbers none of which is to be despised. And eternally raging against all these contending parties are the wind, the lightning, the rain, the flood, and the hellish vibratory output of Trenco's enormous, malignant, blue-white sun.

*

This, then, was the planet upon which Kinnison had to land in order to repair his crippled Bergenholm—and in the end how well it was to be that such was the case!

"Kinnison of Tellus, greetings. Tregonsee of Rigel IV calling from Trenco space port. Have you ever landed on this planet before?"

"No, but what—"

"Skip that for a time; it is most important that you land here quickly and safely. Where are you in relation to this planet?"

"Your apparent diameter is a shade under six degrees. We are near the plane of your ecliptic and almost in the plane of your terminator, on the morning side."

"That is well; you have ample time. Place your ship between Trenco and the sun. Enter the atmosphere exactly fifteen G-P minutes from . . . check . . . at twenty degrees after meridian, as nearly as possible on the ecliptic, which is also our equator. Go inert as you enter atmosphere; for a free landing upon this planet is impossible. Synchronize with our rotation, which is twenty-six point two G-P hours. Descend vertically until the atmospheric pressure is seven hundred millimeters of mercury, which will be at an altitude of approximately one thousand meters. Since you rely largely upon that sense called sight, allow me to caution you now not to trust it. When your external pressure is seven hundred millimeters of mercury your altitude will be one thousand meters, whether you believe it or not. Stop at that pressure and inform me of the fact, meanwhile holding yourself as nearly stationary as you can. Check so far?"

"QX. But do you mean to tell me that we can't locate each other at a *thousand meters?*" Kinnison's amazed thought escaped him. "What kind of—"

"I can locate you, but you cannot locate me," came the dry reply. "Every one knows that Trenco is peculiar, but no one who has never been here can realize even dimly how peculiar it really is. Detectors and spy rays are useless, electromagnetics are practically paralyzed, and optical apparatus is distinctly unreliable. You cannot trust your vision here. Do not believe all that you see. It used to require days to land a ship at this port. But with our Lenses and my "sense of perception," as you call it, it will be a matter of minutes."

Kinnison had flashed his ship to the designated position.

"Cut the Berg, Thorndyke, we're all done with it. I've got to build up an inert velocity to match the rotation, and land inert."

"Thanks be to all the gods of space for that." The engineer heaved a sigh of relief. "I've been expecting it to blow its top for the last hour, and I don't know whether we'd ever have got it meshed in again or not."

"QX on location and orbit," Kinnison reported to the as yet invisible space port a few minutes later. "Now, what about that Lensman? What happened?"

"The usual thing," came the emotionless response. "It happens to altogether too many Lensmen who can see, in spite of everything we can tell them. He insisted upon going out after his zwilniks in a ground car, and, of course, we had to let him go. He became confused, lost control, let something—possibly a zwilnik's bomb—get under his leading edge, and the wind and the Trencos did the rest. He was Lageston of Mercator V—a good man, too. What is the pressure now?"

"Five hundred millimeters."

"Slow down. Now, if you cannot conquer the tendency to believe your eyes, you had better shut off your visiplates and watch only the pressure gauge."

"Being warned, I can disbelieve my eyes, I think." For a minute or so communication ceased.

*

At a startled oath from VanBuskirk, Kinnison glanced into the plate. It needed all his self-control to keep from wrenching savagely at the controls. For the whole planet was tipping, lurching, spinning, gyrating madly in a frenzy of impossible motions.

"Sheer off, Kim!" yelled the Valerian.

"Hold it, Bus," cautioned the Lensman, "That's what we've got to expect, you know. I passed all the stuff along as I got it. Everything, that is, except that a zwilnik is anything or anybody that comes after thionite, and that a Trenco is anything, animal or vegetable, that lives on the planet. QX, Tregonsee—seven hundred, and I'm holding steady—I hope!"

"Steady enough, but you are too far away for our landing bars. Direct a thought, rotating the prime axis of your Lens while inclining it somewhat downward . . . . Stop! Mark that line on your circles. Now think of the alignment of your ship in relation to that line. Swing your prow away from that line, clear around, to approach it from the other side . . . slow . . . hold it! Apply normal acceleration . . . ."

In a few minutes the crew felt a gentle, snubbing shock, and Kinnison again translated to his companions the stranger's thoughts: "We have grasped you with our landing bars. Cut off all your power and set all controls in neutral. Do nothing more until I instruct you to come out."

Kinnison obeyed; and, released from all duty, the three visitors stared in fascinated incredulity into the visiplate. For that at which they stared was and must forever remain impossible of duplication upon Earth, and only in imagination can it be even faintly pictured. Imagine all the fantastic and monstrous creatures of a delirium-tremens vision incarnate and actual. Imagine them being hurled through the air, borne by a dust-laden gale more severe than any the great American "dust bowl" or Africa's Sahara Desert ever endured. Imagine this scene as being viewed, not in an ordinary, solid, distorting mirror, but in one whose falsely reflecting contours were changing constantly, with no logical or intelligible rhythm, into new and ever more grotesque warps. If imagination has been equal to the task, the resultant is what the three patrolmen tried to see.

At first they could make nothing whatever of it. Upon nearer approach, however, the ghastly distortion grew less and the flatly level expanse of sun-baked mud took on a semblance of rigidity. Directly beneath them they made out something that looked like an immense, flat blister upon the otherwise featureless terrain. Their ship was drawn toward this blister.

*

A port opened, dwarfed in apparent size to a mere window by the immensity of the structure. Through this port the vast bulk of the space ship was wafted upon the landing bars, and behind it the mighty bronze-and-steel gates clanged shut. The lock was pumped to a vacuum; there was a hiss of entering air; a spray of vaporous liquid bathed every inch of the vessel's surface, and Kinnison felt again the calm voice of Tregonsee, the Rigellian Lensman.

"You may now open your air lock and emerge. If I have read aright, our atmosphere is sufficiently like your own in oxygen content so that you will suffer no ill effects from it. It may be well, however, to wear your armor until you have become accustomed to its considerably greater density."

"That'll be a relief!" growled VanBuskirk's deep base, when his chief had transmitted the thought. "I've been breathing this thin stuff so long I'm getting light-headed."

"That's gratitude!" Thorndyke retorted. "We've been running our air so heavy that all the rest of us are thick-headed now. If the air in this space port is any heavier than what we've been having, I'm going to wear armor as long as we stay here!"

Kinnison had opened the air lock, found the atmosphere of the space port satisfactory, and now stepped out, to be greeted cordially by Tregonsee, the Lensman.

This—this apparition was at least erect, which was something. His body was the size and shape of an oil drum. Beneath this massive cylinder of a body were four short, blocky legs upon which he waddled about with surprising speed. Midway up the body, above each leg, there sprouted out a ten-foot-long, writhing, boneless, tentacular arm, which toward the extremity branched out into dozens of lesser tentacles, ranging in size from hairlike tendrils up to mighty fingers two inches or more in diameter. Tregonsee's head was merely a neckless, immobile, bulging dome in the center of the flat, upper surface of his body—a dome bearing neither eyes nor ears, but only four equally spaced toothless mouths and four single, flaring nostrils.

But Kinnison felt no qualm of repugnance at Tregonsee's monstrous appearance, for embedded in the leathery flesh of one arm was the Lens. Here, the Lensman knew, was in every essential a *man*—and probably a superman.

"Welcome to Trenco, Kinnison of Tellus," Tregonsee was saying. "While we are near neighbors in space, I have never happened to visit your planet. I have encountered Tellurians here, of course, but they were not of a type to be received as guests."

"No, a zwilnik is not a high type of Tellurian," Kinnison agreed. "I have often wished that I could have your sense of perception, if only for a day. It must be wonderful indeed to be able to perceive a thing as a whole, inside and out, instead of having vision stopped at its surface, as is ours. And to be independent of light or darkness, never to be lost or in need of instruments, to know definitely where you are in relation to every other object or thing around you—that, I think, is the most marvelous sense in the universe."

"Just as I have wished for sight and hearing, those two remarkable and to us entirely unexplainable senses. I have dreamed; I have studied volumes, on color and sound: color in art and in nature; sound in music and in the voices of loved ones. But they remain meaningless symbols upon a printed page. However, such thoughts are vain. In all probability neither of us would enjoy the other's equipment if he had it, and this interchange is of no material assistance to you."

*

In flashing thoughts Kinnison then communicated to the other Lensman everything that had transpired since he left Prime Base.

"I perceive that your Bergenholm is of Standard 14 Rating," Tregonsee said, as the Tellurian finished his story. "We have several spares here; and, while they all have regulation patrol mountings, it would take much less time to change mounts than to overhaul your machine."

"That's so, too. I never thought of the possibility of your having spare machines—and we've lost a lot of time already. How long will it take?"

"One night of labor to change mounts—at least eight to rebuild yours enough to be sure that it will get you home."

"We'll change mounts, then, by all means. I'll call the boys——"

"There is no need of that. We are amply equipped, and neither of you humans nor the Velantians could handle our tools." Tregonsee made no visible motion nor could Kinnison perceive a break in his thought, but while he was conversing with the Tellurian half a dozen of his blocky Rigellians had dropped whatever they had been doing and were scuttling toward the visiting ship. "Now I must leave you for a time, as I have one more trip to make this afternoon."

"Is there anything I can do to help you?" asked Kinnison.

"No," came the definite negative. "I will return in three hours, as well before sunset the wind makes it impossible to get even a ground car into the port. I will then show you why you can be of little assistance to us."

Kinnison spent those three hours watching the Rigellians work upon the Bergenholm; there was no need for direction or advice. They knew what to do and they did it. Those tiny, hairlike fingers, literally hundreds of them at once, performed delicate tasks with surpassing nicety and dispatch; when it came to heavy tasks the larger digits or even whole arms wrapped themselves around the work and, with the solid bracing of the four blocklike legs, exerted forces that even VanBuskirk's giant frame could not have approached.

As the end of the third hour neared, Kinnison watched with a spy ray—there were no windows in the Trenco space port—the leeward groundway of the structure. In spite of the weird antics of Trenco's sun—gyrating, jumping, appearing and disappearing—he knew that it was going down. Soon he saw the ground car coming in, scuttling crab-wise, nose into the wind but actually moving backward and sidewise. Although the "seeing" was very poor, at this close range the distortion was minimized and he could see that, like its parent craft, the ground car was in the shape of a blister. Its edges actually touched the ground all around, sloping upward and over the top in such a smooth reverse curve that the harder the wind blew the more firmly was the vehicle pressed downward.

The ground flap came up just enough to clear the car's top and the tiny craft crept up. But before the landing bars could seize her the ground car struck an eddy from the flap—an eddy in a medium which, although gaseous, was at that velocity practically solid. Earth blasted away in torrents from the leading edge; the car leaped bodily into the air and was flung away, end over end. But Tregonsee, with consummate craftsmanship, forced her flat again, and again she crawled up toward the flap. This time the landing bars took hold and, although the little vessel fluttered like a leaf in a gale, she was drawn inside the port and the flap went down behind her. She was then sprayed, and Tregonsee came out.

"Why the spray?" thought Kinnison, as the Rigellian entered his control room.

"Trencos. Much of the life of this planet starts from almost imperceptible spores. It develops rapidly, attains considerable size, and consumes anything organic it touches. This port was depopulated time after time before the lethal spray was developed. Now turn your spy ray again to the lee of the port."

*

During the few minutes that had elapsed the wind had increased in fury to such an extent that the very ground was boiling away from the trailing edge in the tumultuous eddy formed there, ultra-streamlined though the space port was. And that eddy, far surpassing in violence any storm known to Earth, was to the denizens of Trenco a miraculously appearing quiet spot in which they could stop and rest, eat and be eaten.

A globular monstrosity had thrust pseudopodia deep into the boiling dirt. Other limbs now shot out, grasping a tumbleweedlike growth. The latter fought back viciously, but could make no impression upon the rubbery integument of the former. Then a smaller creature, slipping down the polished curve of the shield, was enmeshed by the tumbleweed. There ensued the amazing spectacle of one half of the tumbleweed devouring the newcomer, even while its other half was being devoured by the globe!

"Now look out farther—still farther," directed Tregonsee.

422

"I can't. Things take on impossible motions and become so distorted as to be unrecognizable."

"Exactly. If you saw a zwilnik out there, where would you shoot?"

"At him, I suppose. Why?"

"Because if you shot at where you think you see him, not only would you miss him, but the ray might very well swing around and enter your own back. Many men have been killed by their own weapons in precisely that fashion. Since we know, not only what the object is, but exactly where it is, we can correct our beams for the then existing values of distortion. This is, of course, the reason why we Rigellians and other races possessing the sense of perception are the only ones who can efficiently police this planet."

"Reason enough, I'd say, from what I've seen."

Silence fell. For minutes the two Lensmen watched, while creatures of a hundred kinds streamed into the lee of the space port and killed and ate each other. Finally, something came crawling upwind, against that unimaginable gale—a flatly streamlined creature somewhat resembling a turtle, but shaped as was the ground car.

Thrusting down long, hooked flippers into the dirt it inched along, paying no attention to the scores of lesser creatures who hurled themselves upon its armored back, until it was close beside the largest football-shaped creature in the eddy. Then, lightninglike, it drove a needle-sharp organ at least eight inches into the leathery mass of its victim. Struggling convulsively, the stricken thing lifted the turtle a fraction of an inch—and both were hurled instantly out of sight; the living ball still eating a luscious bit of soil.

"Good Lord, what was that?" exclaimed Kinnison.

"The flat? That was a representative of Trenco's highest life form. It may develop a civilization in time. It is quite intelligent now."

"But the difficulties!" protested the Tellurian. "Building cities, even homes and——"

"Neither cities nor homes are necessary, nor even desirable, here. Why build? Nothing is or can be fixed on this planet, and since one place is exactly like every other place, why wish to remain in any one particular spot? They do very well, in their own mobile way. Here, you will notice, comes the rain."

The rain came—forty-four inches per hour of rain—and the lightning. Such rain and such lightning must be seen to be even dimly appreciated; there is no use in attempting to describe the indescribable. The dirt first became mud, then muddy water being driven in fiercely flying gouts and masses.

The water grew deeper and deeper, its upper surface now whipped into frantic sheets of spray. The structure was now afloat, and Kinnison saw with astonishment that, small as was the exposed surface and flatly curved, yet it was pulling through the water at frightful speed the wide-spreading steel sea anchors which were holding its head to the gale.

"With no reference points how do you know where you're going?" he demanded.

"We know not, nor care," responded Tregonsee, with a mental shrug. "We are like the natives in that. Since one spot is like every other spot, why choose between them?"

"What a world—*what* a world! However, I am beginning to understand why thionite is so expensive." And, overwhelmed by the ever-increasing fury raging outside, Kinnison sought his bunk.

THE LENSMAN

*

Morning came, a reversal of the previous evening. The liquid evaporated; the mud dried; the flat-growing vegetation sprang up with shocking speed; the animals emerged and again ate and were eaten.

And eventually came Tregonsee's announcement that it was noon; and that now, for an hour or so, it would be calm enough for the space ship to leave the port.

"You are sure that I would be of no help to you?" asked the Rigellian, half pleadingly.

"Sorry, Tregonsee, but you would fit into my matrix just as I would into yours here. But here's the spool I told you about. If you will take it to your base on your next relief you will do civilization and the patrol more good than you could by coming with us. Thanks for the Bergenholm, which is covered by credits, and thanks a lot for your help and courtesy, which can't be covered. Good-by." The now entirely spaceworthy craft shot out through the port, through Trenco's noxiously peculiar atmosphere, into the vacuum of space.

XI.

"Shapley holds that these (star) clusters, under the gravitative control of the larger system, vibrate back and forth through the galaxy." Fath, "Elements of Astronomy," p. 297.

At some distance from the galaxy, yet shackled to it by the flexible yet powerful bonds of gravitation, the small but comfortable planet upon which was Helmuth's base circled about its parent sun. This planet had been chosen with the utmost care, and its location was a secret guarded jealously indeed. Scarcely one in a million of Boskone's teeming millions knew even that such a planet existed; and of the chosen few who had ever been asked to visit it, fewer still by far had been allowed to leave it.

Grand Base covered hundreds of square miles of that planet's surface. It was equipped with all the arms and armament known to the military genius of the age; and in the exact center of that immense citadel there arose a glittering metallic dome.

The inside surface of that dome was lined with visiplates and communicators, hundreds of thousands of them. Miles of catwalks clung precariously to the inward-curving wall. Control panels and instrument boards covered the floor in banks and tiers, with only narrow runways between them. And what a personnel! There were Solarians, Crevenians, Sirians. There were Antareans, Vandemarians, Arcturians. There were representatives of scores, yes, hundreds of other solar systems of the galaxy.

But whatever their external form they were all breathers of oxygen and they were all nourished by warm, red blood. Also, they were all alike mentally. Each had won his present high place by trampling down those beneath him and by pulling down those above him in the branch to which he had first belonged of the "pirate" organization.

Kinnison had been eminently correct in his belief that Boskone's was not a "pirate outfit" in any ordinary sense of the word, but even his ideas of its true nature fell far short indeed of the truth.

It was a tyranny, an absolute monarchy, a despotism not even remotely approximated by the dictatorships of earlier ages. It had only one creed: "The end justifies the means."

Anything—literally *anything at all*—that produced the desired result was commendable; to fail was the only crime.

Therefore, no weaklings dwelt within that fortress; and of all its cold, hard, ruthless crew far and away the coldest, hardest, and most ruthless was Helmuth, the "speaker for Boskone," who sat at the great desk in the dome's geometrical center. This individual was almost human in form and build, springing as he did from a planet closely approximating Earth in mass, atmosphere, and climate. Indeed, only his general, all-pervasive aura of blueness bore witness to the fact that he was not a native of Tellus.

His eyes were blue; his hair was blue; and even his skin was faintly blue beneath its coat of ultra-violet tan. His intensely dynamic personality fairly radiated blueness—not the gentle blue of an Earthly sky, not the sweetly innocuous blue of an Earthly flower; but the keenly merciless blue of a delta ray, the cold and bitter blue of a Polar iceberg, the unyielding, inflexible blue of chilled and tempered steel.

*

Now a frown sat heavily upon his arrogantly patrician face, as his eyes bored into the plate before him, from the base of which were issuing the words being spoken by the assistant pictured in its deep surface:

"—the fifth dived into the deepest ocean of Corvina II, in the depths of which all rays are useless. The ships which followed have not as yet reconnected. No trace of the sixth has been found, and it is therefore assumed that she was destroyed upon Velantia——"

"Who assumes so?" demanded Helmuth, coldly. "There is no justification whatever for such an assumption. Go on!"

"The Lensman, if there is one, must therefore be in the fifth ship, since he was not in any of the four which we have retaken."

"Your report is neither complete nor conclusive. I do not at all approve of your intimation that the Lensman is simply a figment of my imagination. That there is a Lensman is the only possible logical conclusion. None other of the patrol forces could have done what has been done. Postulating his reality, it seems to me that instead of being a rare possibility, it is highly probable that he has again escaped us, and again in one of our own vessels—this time in the one you have so conveniently 'assumed' to have been destroyed. Have you searched the line of flight?"

"Yes, sir. Everything in space and every planet within reach of that line has been examined with care; except, of course, Velantia and Trenco."

"Velantia is, for the time being, unimportant. It will be reduced later. Why Trenco?" and Helmuth pressed a series of buttons. "Ah, I see. To recapitulate, one ship, the one which in all probability is now carrying the Lensman, is still unaccounted for. *Where is it?* We assume that it left Velantia. We know that it has not landed upon or near any solarian planet. Incidentally, we must see to it that it does not so land. Now, I think, it has become necessary to have that planet Trenco combed, inch by inch."

"But sir, how——" began the anxious-eyed underling.

"When did it become necessary to draw diagrams and make blue prints for you?" demanded Helmuth, harshly. "We have ships manned by Rigellians and other races having the sense of perception. Find out where they are and get them there at full blast!"

He flipped over two double-throw switches, thus replacing the image upon his plate by another.

"It has now become of paramount importance that we complete our knowledge of the Lens of the patrol," he began, without salutation or preamble. "Have you traced its origin yet?"

"I believe so, but I do not certainly know. It has proved to be a task of such difficulty——"

"If it had been an easy one I would not have made a special assignment of it to you. Go on!"

"Everything seems to point to a planet named Arisia, but of that planet I can learn nothing definite whatever except that——"

"Just a moment!" Helmuth punched more buttons and listened. "Unexplored—unknown—shunned by all spacemen——"

"Superstition, eh?" he snapped. "Another of those haunted planets?"

"Something more than ordinary spacemen's superstition, sir, but just what I have not been able to discover. By combing my department I managed to make up a crew of those who either were not afraid of it or have never heard of it. That crew is now *en route* there."

"Whom have we in that sector of space? I find it desirable to check your findings."

The department head reeled off a list of names and numbers, which Helmuth considered at length.

"Gildersleeve, the Valerian," he announced finally. "He is a good man, coming along fast. Aside from a firm belief in his own peculiar gods, he has shown no signs of weakness. You considered him?"

"Certainly." The henchman, as cold as his icy chief, knew that explanations would not satisfy Helmuth, therefore he offered none. "He is raiding at the moment, but I will put you on him if you like."

"Do so." And upon Helmuth's plate there appeared a deep-space scene of rapine and pillage.

*

The convoying patrol ships, two of them, had already been blasted out of existence; only a few idly drifting masses of débris remaining to show that they had ever been. Needle rays were at work, and soon the merchantman hung inert and helpless. The pirates, scorning to use the emergency inlet port, simply blasted away the entire entrance panel. Then they boarded, an armored swarm, flaming DeLameters spreading death and destruction before them.

The sailors, outnumbered as they were and overarmed, fought heroically—but uselessly. In groups and singly they fell; those who were not already dead being callously tossed out into space in slitted space suits and with smashed motors. Only the younger women—the stewardesses, the nurses, the one or two such among the few passengers—were taken as booty; all others shared the fate of the crew.

Then the ship plundered from nose to after jets and every article or thing of value trans-shipped, the raider drew off, bathed in the blue-white glare of the atomic bombs that were destroying every trace of the merchant ship's existence. Then and only then did Helmuth reveal himself to Gildersleeve.

"A good, clean job of work, captain," he commended. "Now, how would you like to visit Arisia for me—for *me*, direct?"

A pallor overspread the normally ruddy face of the Valerian and an uncontrollable tremor shook his giant frame. But as he considered the implications resident in Helmuth's concluding phrase he licked his lips and spoke.

"I hate to say no, sir, if you order me to and if there was any way of making my crew do it. But we were near there once, sir, and we—I—they—it——Well, sir, I *saw* things, sir, and I was—was *warned*, sir!"

"Saw what? And was warned of what?"

"I can't describe what I saw, sir. I can't even think of it in thoughts that mean anything. As for the warning, though, it was very definite, sir. I was told very plainly that if I ever go near that planet again I will die a worse death than any I have dealt out to any other living being."

"But you will go there again?"

"I tell you, sir, that the crew will not do it," Gildersleeve replied, doggedly. "Even if I were anxious to go, every man aboard will mutiny if I tried it."

"Call them in right now and tell them that you have been ordered to Arisia!"

*

The captain did so. But he had scarcely started to talk when he was stopped in no uncertain fashion by his first officer—also, of course, a Valerian—who pulled his DeLameter and spoke savagely: "Cut it, chief! We are not going to Arisia, nor anywhere near there. I was with you before, you know. Point course within a quadrant of that accursed planet and I flash you where you sit!"

"Helmuth, speaking for Boskone!" ripped from the headquarters' speaker. "This is rankest mutiny. You know the penalty, do you not?"

"Certainly I do. What of it?" the first officer snapped back.

"Suppose that I *tell* you to go to Arisia?" Helmuth's voice was now soft and silky, but instinct with deadly menace.

"In that case *I* tell *you* to go to hell—or to Arisia, a million times worse!" snapped the officer.

"What? You dare speak thus to *me*?" demanded the archpirate, sheer amazement at the fellow's audacity blanketing his rising anger.

"I so dare," declared the rebel, brazen defiance and unalterable resolve in every line of his hard body and in every lineament of his hard face. "All you can do is kill us. You can order out enough ships to blast us out of the ether, but that's all you *can* do. That would be a clean, quick death and we would have the fun of taking a lot of the boys along with us. If we go to Arisia, though, it would be different—very, very different, believe me. No, Helmuth, and I say this to your face: If I ever go near Arisia again it will be in a ship in which you, Helmuth, in person, are sitting at the controls. If you think this is an empty dare and don't like it, you don't have to take it. Send on your dogs!"

THE LENSMAN

"That will do! Report yourselves to Base D under—" Then Helmuth's flare of anger passed and his cold reason took charge. Here was something utterly unprecedented: an entire crew of the hardest-bitten marauders in space offering open and barefaced mutiny—no, not mutiny, but actual rebellion—to him, Helmuth, in his very teeth. And not a typical, skulking, carefully planned uprising, but the immovably brazen desperation of men making an ultimately last-ditch stand.

Truly, it must be a powerful superstition, indeed, to make that crew of hard-boiled hellions choose certain death rather than face again the imaginary—they *must* be imaginary—perils of a planet unknown to and unexplored by Boskone's planetographers. But they were, after all, ordinary spacemen, of little mental force and of small real ability. Even so, it was clearly indicated that in this case precipitate action was to be avoided. Therefore, he went on calmly and almost without a break. "Cancel all this that has been spoken and that has taken place. Continue with your original orders pending further investigation." Helmuth switched his plate back to the department head.

"I have checked your conclusions and have found them correct," he announced, as though nothing at all out of the way had transpired. "You did well in sending a ship to investigate. No matter where I am or what I am doing, notify me instantly at the first sign of irregularity in the behavior of any member of that ship's personnel."

*

Nor was that call long in coming. The carefully selected crew—selected for complete lack of knowledge of the dread planet which was their objective—sailed along in blissful ignorance, both of the real meaning of their mission and of what was to be its ghastly end. Soon after Helmuth's unsatisfactory interview with Gildersleeve and his mate, the luckless exploring vessel reached the barrier which the Arisians had set around their system and through which no uninvited stranger was allowed to pass.

The free-flying ship struck that frail barrier and stopped. In the instant of contact a wave of mental force flooded the mind of the captain, who, gibbering with sheer, stark, panic terror, flashed his vessel away from that horror-impregnated barrier and hurled call after frantic call along his beam, back to headquarters. His first call, in the instant of reception, was relayed to Helmuth at his central desk.

"Steady, man; report intelligently!" that worthy snapped, and his eyes, large now upon the cowering captain's plate, bored steadily, hypnotically, into those of the expedition's leader. "Pull yourself together and tell me exactly what happened. Everything!"

"Well, sir, when we struck something—a screen of some sort—and stopped, something came aboard. It was——Oh—ay-ay-e-e!" his voice rose to a shriek. But under Helmuth's dominating glare he subsided quickly and went on. "A monster, sir, if there ever was one. A fire-breathing demon, sir, with teeth and claws and cruelly barbed tail. He spoke to me in my own Crevenian language. He said——"

"Never mind what he said. I did not hear it, but I can guess what it was. He threatened you with death in some horrible fashion, did he not?"

The coldly ironical tones did more to restore the shaking man's equilibrium than reams of remonstrance could have done. "Well, yes, that was about the size of it, sir," he admitted.

428

"And does that sound reasonable to you, the commander of a first-class battleship of Boskone's fleet?" sneered Helmuth.

"Well, sir, put in that way, it does seem a bit far-fetched," the captain replied, sheepishly.

"It *is* far-fetched." The director, in the safety of his dome, could afford to be positive. "We do not know exactly what caused that hallucination, apparition, or whatever it was. You were the only one who could see it, apparently; it certainly was not visible on our master plates here at base. It was probably some form of suggestion or hypnotism; and you know as well as we do that any suggestion can be thrown off by a definitely opposed will. But you did not oppose it, did you?"

"No, sir, I didn't have time."

"Nor did you have your screens out, nor automatic recorders on the trip. Not much of anything, in fact. I think that you had better report back here, at full blast."

"Oh, no, sir—please!" He knew what rewards were granted to failures, and Helmuth's carefully chosen words had already produced the effect desired by their speaker. "They took me by surprise then, but I'll go through this next time."

"Very well. We will give you one more chance. When you get close to the barrier, or whatever it is, go inert and put out all your screens. Man your plates and weapons, for whatever can hypnotize can be killed. Go ahead at full blast, with all the acceleration you can get. Crash through anything that opposes you, and beam anything that you can detect or see. Can you think of anything else?"

"That should be sufficient, sir." The captain's equanimity was completely restored, now that the warlike preparations were making more and more nebulous the sudden, but single, thought wave of the Arisian.

"Proceed!"

*

The plan was carried out to the letter. This time the pirate craft struck the frail barrier inert, and its slight force offered no tangible bar to the prodigious mass of metal. But this time, since the barrier was actually passed, there was no mental warning and no possibility of retreat.

Many men have skeletons in their closets. Many have phobias, things of which they are consciously afraid. Many others have them, not consciously, but buried deep in the subconscious, specters which seldom or never rise above the threshold of perception. Every sentient being has, if not such specters as these, at least a few active or latent dislikes, dreads, or outright fears. This is true, no matter how quiet and peaceful a life the being has led.

These particular pirates, however, were the scum of space. They were beings of hard and criminal lives and of violent and lawless passions. Their hates and conscience-searing deeds had been legion, their count of crimes long, black, and hideous. Therefore, slight indeed was the effort required to locate in their conscious minds—to say nothing of the noxious depths of their subconscious ones—visions of horror fit to blast stronger intellects than theirs.

429

And that is exactly what the Arisian guardsman did. From each pirate's total mind, a veritable charnel pit, he extracted the foulest, most unspeakable dregs, the deeply hidden things of which the subject was in the greatest fear. Of these things he formed a whole of horror incomprehensible and incredible, and this ghastly whole he made incarnate and visible to the pirate who was its unwilling parent; as visible as though it were composed of flesh and blood, of copper and steel. Is it any wonder that each member of that outlaw crew, seeing such an abhorrent materialization, went instantly mad?

It is of no use to go into the horribly monstrous shapes of the things, even were it possible; for each of them was visible to only one man, and none of them was visible to those who looked on from the safety of the distant base. To them the entire crew simply abandoned their posts and attacked each other, senselessly and in insane frenzy, with whatever weapons came first to hand. Indeed, many of them fought barehanded, weapons hanging unused in their belts, gouging, beating, clawing, biting until life had been rived horribly away. In other parts of the ship DeLameters flamed briefly; bars crashed crunchingly; knives and axes sheared and trenchantly bit. And soon it was over—almost. The pilot was still alive, unmoving and rigid at his controls.

Then he, too, moved, slowly, haltingly, as though in a trance. Without touching the controls of the Bergenholm, he nursed his driving projectors up to maximum, spun his ship and steadied her on course; and when Helmuth read that course even his iron nerves failed him momentarily. For the ship, still inert, was pointed, not for its own home port, but directly toward Grand Base, the jealously secret planet whose spatial coördinates neither that pilot nor any other creature of the pirates' rank and file had ever known!

*

Helmuth snapped out orders, to which the pilot gave no heed. His voice—for the first time in his career—rose almost to a howl. But the pilot still paid no attention. Instead, eyes bulging with horror and fingers curved tensely into veritable talons, he reared upright upon his bench and leaped as though to clutch and to rend some unutterably appalling foe. He leaped over his board into thin and empty air. He came down a-sprawl in a maze of naked, high-potential busbars. His body vanished in a flash of searing flame and a cloud of thick and greasy smoke.

The busbars cleared themselves of their gruesome "short" and the great ship, manned now entirely by corpses, bored on.

"—stinking klebots, the lily-livered cowards!" the department head, who had also been yelling orders, was still pounding his desk and cursing. "If they're *that* afraid—go mad and kill each other without being touched—I'll have to go myself——"

"No, Sansteed," Helmuth interrupted, curtly. "You will not have to go. There is, after all, I think, something there—something that you may not be able to handle. You see, you missed the one essential key fact." He referred to the course, the setting of which had shaken him to the very core.

"Let be," he silenced the other's flood of question and protest. "It would serve no purpose to detail it to you now. Have the ship taken back to port."

Helmuth knew now that it was not superstition that made spacemen shun Arisia. He knew that, from his standpoint at least, there was something very seriously amiss.

XII.

Helmuth sat at his desk, thinking—thinking with all the coldly analytical precision of which he was capable.

This Lensman was, in truth, a foeman worthy of his steel. The cosmic-energy drive, developed by the science of a world which the patrol did not know existed, was Boskone's one great item of superiority. If the patrol could be kept in ignorance of that drive the struggle would be over in a year; the culture of the iron hand would be unchallenged throughout the galaxy. If, however, the patrol did manage to learn the secret of power, to all intents and purposes unlimited, the war between the two cultures might well be prolonged indefinitely. This Lensman knew that secret and was still at large, of that he was all too certain. Therefore, the Lensman must be destroyed. And that brought up the Lens.

What was it? A peculiar bauble indeed, simple of ultimate quantitative analysis, but actually impossible of duplication because of some subtlety of intra-atomic arrangement. Also, it was of peculiar and dire potentiality. Not a man of his force could even wear one; he had watched several of them die horribly in attempting to do so. It must account in some way for the outstanding ability of the Lensmen, and it must tie in, somehow, both with Arisia and with the thought-screens. This Lens was the one thing possessed by the patrol which his own forces did not have. He must and would have it, for it was undoubtedly a powerful arm. Not to be compared, of course, with their own monopoly of cosmic energy—but that monopoly was now threatened, and seriously. That Lensman *must be destroyed.*

But how? It was easy to say "Comb Trenco, inch by inch," but doing it would prove a Herculean task. Suppose that the Lensman should again escape, in that volume of so fantastically distorted media? He had already escaped twice, in much clearer ether than Trenco's. However, if this information should never get back to Prime Base, little harm would be done. Ships could and would be thrown around the solarian system in such numbers that not even a grain-of-dust meteorite could pass that screen without detection. Nothing—nothing whatever—would be allowed to enter that system until this whole affair had been settled. There were other patrol bases, of course, but with the Prime Base isolated, nothing really serious could happen. So much for the Lensman. Now about getting the secret of the Lens.

Again, how? There was something upon Arisia, and that something was connected in some way with the Lens and with thought—possibly also with the new thought-screens. Whatever it was, it had mental power, of that there was no doubt. Out of the full sphere of space, what was the mathematical probability that the pilot of that death ship would have set, by accident, his course so exactly upon this planet? Vanishingly small. Treachery would not explain the facts. The pilot had been insane when he had laid the course. As an explanation, mental force alone seemed fantastic, but none other as yet presented itself as a possibility. Also, it was supported by the unbelievable, the absolutely definite refusal of Gildersleeve's normally fearless crew even to approach the planet. It would take an unheard-of mental force so to affect such crime-hardened veterans.

Helmuth was not one to underestimate an enemy. Was there a man beneath that dome, save himself, of sufficient mental caliber to undertake the now necessary mission to Arisia? There was not. He himself had the finest mind on the planet; else that other had deposed him long since and had sat at the control desk himself. He was sublimely confident that no outside thought could break down *his* definitely opposed will—and besides, there were the thought-screens, his own personal property as yet. Of no other will could he say the same; no other would he trust with those screens. Of all his force, he was the only one whom he could be *sure* of. Therefore, he would go himself.

It has already been made clear that Helmuth was not a fool. No more was he a coward. If he himself could best of all his force do a thing, that thing he did, with the coldly ruthless efficiency that marked alike his every action and his every thought.

*

How should he go? Should he accept that challenge, and take Gildersleeve's rebellious crew of cutthroats to Arisia? No. In the event of an outcome short of complete success, it would not do to lose face before that band of ruffians. Moreover, the idea of such a crew going insane behind him was not one to be relished. He would go alone.

"Wolmark, come to the center," he ordered. When that worthy appeared, he went on, "Be seated, as this is a serious conference. I have watched with admiration and appreciation, as well as some mild amusement, the development of your lines of information, particularly those covering affairs which are most distinctly not in your department. They are, however, efficient. You already know exactly what has happened." A definite statement this, is no wise a question.

"Yes, sir," Wolmark said quietly. He was somewhat taken aback, but not at all abashed.

"That is the reason you are here now. I thoroughly approve of you. I am leaving the planet for approximately twenty days, and you are the best man in the organization to take charge in my absence."

"I suspected that you would be leaving, sir."

"I know you did. But I am now informing you, merely to make sure that you develop no peculiar ideas in my absence, that there are at least a few things which you do not suspect at all. That safe, for instance," Helmuth said, nodding toward a peculiarly shimmering globe of force anchoring itself in air. "Even your highly efficient spy system has not been able to learn a thing about that."

"No, sir, we have not—yet," he could not forbear adding.

"Nor will you, with any skill or force known to man. But keep on trying; it amuses me. I know, you see, of all your attempts. But to get on. I now say, and for your own good I advise you to believe, that failure upon my part to return to this desk will prove highly unfortunate for you."

"I believe that, sir. Any man of intelligence would make some such arrangement, if he could. But sir, suppose that the Arisians——"

"If your 'if he could' implies a doubt, act upon it and learn wisdom," Helmuth advised him coldly. "You should know by this time that I neither gamble nor bluff. I have made

432

arrangements to protect myself, both from enemies, such as the Arisians and the patrol, and from friends, such as ambitious youngsters who are making arrangements to supplant me. If I were not entirely confident of getting back here safely, my dear Wolmark, I would not go."

"You misunderstood me, sir. Really, I have no idea of supplanting you."

"Not until you get a good opportunity, you mean. I understand you thoroughly; and, as I have said before, I approve of you. Go ahead with all your plans. I have kept at least one lap ahead of you so far, and if the time should ever come when I can no longer do so, I shall no longer be fit to speak for Boskone. You understand, of course, that the most important matter now in work is the search for the Lensman, of which the combing of Trenco and the screening of the solarian system are only two phases."

"Yes, sir."

"Very well. I can, I think, leave matters in your hands. If anything really serious comes up, such as a development in the Lensman case, let me know at once. Otherwise do not call me. Take the desk." Helmuth strode away.

He was whisked to the space port, where his special speedster awaited him.

*

For him the trip to Arisia was neither long nor tedious. The little racer was fully automatic, and as it tore through space he worked as coolly and efficiently as he was wont to do at his desk. Indeed, more so, for here he could concentrate without interruption. Many were the matters he planned and the decisions he made, the while his portfolio of notes grew thicker and thicker.

As he neared his destination he put away his work, actuated his special mechanisms, and waited. When the speedster struck the barrier and stopped, Helmuth wore a faint, hard smile; but that smile disappeared with a snap as a thought crashed into his supposedly shielded brain.

"You are surprised that your thought-screens are not effective?" The thought was coldly contemptuous. "Wherever, think you, originated those screens? We did not foresee your theft of them from Velantia, but think you that we would allow to remain at large a thing which we could not neutralize?

"Know, fool, once and for all, that Arisia does not want and will not tolerate uninvited visitors. Your presence is particularly distasteful, representing as you do a despotic, degrading, and antisocial culture. Evil and good are, of course, purely relative, so it cannot be said in absolute terms that your culture is evil. It is, however, based upon greed, hatred, corruption, violence, and fear. Justice it does not recognize, nor mercy, nor truth except as a scientific utility. It is basically opposed to liberty. Now liberty—of person, of thought, of action—is the basis and the goal of civilization to which you are opposed, and with which any really philosophical mind must find itself in accord.

"Inflated overweeningly by your warped and perverted ideas, by your momentary success in dominating your handful of minions, tied to you by bonds of greed, of passion, and of crime, you come here to wrest from us the secret of the Lens—from us, who were already an ancient race when the remotest ancestors of your own were still wriggling in their planet's primordial slime.

"You consider yourself cold, hard, ruthless. Comparatively you are weak, soft, tender as a child unborn. That you may learn and appreciate that fact is one reason why you are living at this present moment. Your lesson will now begin."

Then Helmuth, starkly rigid, unable to move a muscle, felt delicate probes enter his brain. One at a time they pierced his innermost being, each to a definitely selected center. It seemed that each thrust carried with it the ultimate measure of exquisitely poignant anguish possible of endurance, but each successive needle carried with it an even more keenly unbearable thrill of agony.

Helmuth was not calm and cold now. He would have screamed in wild abandon; but even that relief was denied him. He could not even scream; all he could do was sit there and suffer.

Then he began to see things. There, actually materializing in the empty air of the speedster, he saw, in endless procession, things he had done, either in person or by proxy, both during his ascent in his present high place in the pirates' organization and since the attainment of that place. Long was the list, and black. As it unfolded his torment grew more and ever more intense; until finally, after an interval that might have been a fraction of a second or might have been untold hours, he could stand no more. He fainted, sinking beyond the reach of pain into a sea of black consciousness.

*

He awakened white and shaking, wringing wet with perspiration and so weak that he could scarcely sit erect, but with a supremely blissful realization that, for the time being at least, his punishment was over.

"This, you will observe, has been a very mild treatment," the cold Arisian accents went on inside his brain. "Not only do you still live, you are even still sane. We now come to the second reason why you have not been destroyed. Your destruction by us would not be good for that struggling young civilization which you oppose.

"We have given that civilization an instrument by virtue of which it should become able to destroy you and everything for which you stand. If it cannot do so, it is not yet ready to become a civilization and your obnoxious culture shall be allowed to conquer and to flourish for a time.

"Now go back to your dome. Do not return. We well know that you will not have the temerity to do so in person. Do not attempt to do so by any form whatever of proxy."

There were no threats, no warnings, no mention of consequences; but the level and incisive tone of the Arisian put a fear into Helmuth's cold heart the like of which he had never before known.

He whirled his speedster about and hurled her at full blast toward his home planet. It was only after many hours that he was able to regain even a semblance of his customary poise, and days elapsed before he could think coherently enough to consider, as a whole, the shocking, the unbelievable thing that had happened to him.

He wanted to believe that the creature, whatever it was, had been bluffing—that it could not kill him, that it had done its worst. In a similar case he would have killed without mercy, and that course seemed to him the only logical one to pursue. His cold reason, however, would not allow him to entertain that comforting belief. Deep down he *knew* that the Arisian could have killed him as easily as it had slain the lowest member of his band, and the thought chilled him to the marrow.

What could he do? What *could* he do? Endlessly, as the miles and light years reeled off behind his hurtling racer, this question reiterated itself; and when his home planet loomed close it was still unanswered.

*

Since Wolmark believed implicitly Helmuth's statement that it would be poor technique to oppose his return, the planet's screens went down at Helmuth's signal. His first act was to call all the department heads to the center, for an extremely important council of war.

There he told them everything that had happened, calmly and concisely, concluding: "They are aloof, disinterested, unpartisan to a degree I find it impossible to understand. They disapprove of us on purely philosophical grounds, but they will take no active part against us as long as we stay away from their solar system. Therefore, we cannot obtain knowledge of the Lens by direct action, but there are other methods which shall be worked out in due course.

"The Arisians do approve of the patrol, and have helped them to the extent of giving them the Lens. There, however, they stop. If the Lensmen do not know how to use their Lenses efficiently—and I gather that they do not—we 'shall be allowed to conquer and to flourish for a time.' We *will* conquer, and we will see to it that the time of our flourishing will be a long one indeed.

"The whole situation, then, boils down to this: our cosmic energy against the Lens of the patrol. Ours is the much more powerful arm, but our only hope of immediate success lies in keeping the patrol in ignorance of our cosmic-energy receptors and converters. One Lensman already has that knowledge. Therefore, gentlemen, it is very clear that the death of that Lensman has now become absolutely imperative. We *must* find him, if it means the abandonment of our every other enterprise throughout the galaxy. Give me a full report upon the screening of the solarian system."

"It is done, sir," came the quick reply. "That system is completely blockaded. Ships are spaced so closely that even the electromagnetic detectors have a five-hundred-per-cent overlap. Visual detectors have at least two-hundred-fifty-per-cent overlap. Nothing as large as one centimeter in any dimension can get through without detection and observation."

"And how about the search of Trenco?"

"Results are still negative. One of our ships, a Rigellian, with papers all in order, visited Trenco space port openly. No one was there except the regular force of Rigellians. Our captain was in no position to be too inquisitive, but the missing ship was certainly not in the port and he gathered that he was the first visitor they had had in a month. We learned on Rigel IV that Tregonsee, the Lensman actually there, has been there for a month and will not be relieved for another month. He was the only Lensman there. We are, of course, carrying on the search for the rest of the planet. About half the personnel of each vessel to land has been lost. But they started with double crews and replacements are being sent."

"The Lensman Tregonsee's story may or may not be true," Helmuth mused. "It makes little difference. It would be impossible to hide that ship in the Trenco space port from even a casual inspection, and if the ship is not there the Lensman is not. He may be hiding somewhere else on the planet, but I doubt it. Continue to search, nevertheless. There are many things he may have done. I will have to consider them, one by one."

But Helmuth had very little time to consider what Kinnison might have done, for the Lensman had left Trenco long since. Because of the flare baffles upon his driving projectors his pace was slow; but to compensate for this condition the distance to be covered was short. Therefore, even as Helmuth was cogitating upon what next to do, the Lensman and his able crew were approaching the far-flung screen of Boskonian war vessels investing the entire solar system.

To approach that screen undetected was a physical impossibility, and before Kinnison realized that he was in a danger zone six tractors had flicked out, had seized his ship, and had jerked it up to combat range. But the Lensman was ready for anything, and again everything happened at once.

*

Warnings screamed into the distant pirate base and Helmuth, tense at his desk, took personal charge of his mighty fleet. On the field of action Kinnison's screens flamed out in stubborn defense; tracers and tractors snapped under his slashing shears; the baffles disappeared in an incandescent flare as he shot maximum blast into his drive; and space again became suffused with the output of his now ultra-powered multiplex scrambler.

And through that murk the Lensman directed a thought toward Earth, with the full power of mind and Lens.

"Port Admiral Haynes—Prime Base! Port Admiral Haynes—Prime Base! Urgent! Kinnison calling from the direction of Sirius—urgent!" he sent out the fiercely-driven message.

It so happened that at Prime Base it was deep night, and Port Admiral Haynes was sound asleep. But his ever-vigilant Lens received the message, and like the trigger-nerved old space cat that he was, the admiral came instantly awake. Scarcely had an eye flicked open than his answer had been hurled back: "Haynes acknowledging. Send it, Kinnison!"

"Coming in, in a pirate ship—VanBuskirk, Thorndyke, and I, and a crew of Velantians. All the pirates in space are on our necks. But we're coming in, in spite of hell and high water! Don't send up any ships to help us down. They could blast you out of space in a second, but they can't stop us. Get ready. It won't be long now!"

Then, after the port admiral had sounded the emergency alarm, Kinnison went on: "Our ship carries no markings, but there's only one of us and you'll know which one it is. We'll be doing the dodging. They'd be crazy to follow us down to base, with all the stuff you've got, but they act crazy enough to do almost anything. If they do follow us down, get ready to give 'em everything you've got. Here we are!"

Pursued and pursuers had touched the outermost fringe of the stratosphere; and, slowed down to optical visibility by even that highly rarefied atmosphere, the battle raged in incandescent splendor. One ship was spinning, twisting, looping, gyrating, jumping and darting hither and thither—performing every weird maneuver that the fertile and agile mind of the Lensman could improvise—to shake off the horde of attackers.

The pirates, on the other hand, were desperately determined that, whatever the cost, that Lensman should not land. Tractors would not hold and the inertialess ship could not be rammed. Therefore, their strategy was that which had worked so successfully four times before in similar case—to englobe the ship completely and thus beam her down. And while attempting this englobement they so massed their forces as to drive the Lensman's vessel as far as possible away from the grim and tremendously powerful fortifications of the patrol's Prime Base, almost directly below them.

*

But those four other patrol-manned pirate ships which the pirates had recaptured had not been driven by Lensmen; and in this ship Kinnison, the Lensman, was now calling upon his every resource of instantaneous nervous reaction, of brilliant brain and of lightning hand, to avoid that fatal trap. And avoid it he did, by series after series of fantastic maneuvers never set down in any manual of space combat.

Powerful as were the weapons of Prime Base, in that thick atmosphere their effective range was less than fifty miles. Therefore the gunners, idle at their controls, and the officers of the superdreadnaughts, chained by definite orders to the ground, fumed and swore as, powerless to help their battling fellows, they stood by and watched in their plates the furious engagement so high overhead.

But slowly, so slowly, Kinnison won his way downward, keeping as close over base as he could without being englobed. Finally he managed to get within range of the gigantic projectors of the patrol. Only the heaviest of the fixed-mount guns could reach that mad whirlpool of ships, but each one of them raved out against the same spot at precisely the same instant. In the inferno which that spot instantly became, not even a full-driven wall shield could endure, and a vast hole yawned where pirate ships had been. The beams flicked off, and, timed by his Lens, Kinnison shot his ship through that hole before it could be closed, and arrowed downward toward base at maximum blast.

Ship after ship of the pirate horde followed him down in madly suicidal last attempts to blast him out, down toward the terrific armament of the base. Prime Base itself, the most dreaded, the most heavily armed, the most impregnable fortress of the Galactic Patrol! Nothing afloat could even threaten that citadel. The overbold attackers simply disappeared in brief flashes of coruscant vapor.

Kinnison flashed to ground in a free landing and called his commander.

"Did any of the other boys beat us in, sir?" he asked.

"No, sir," came the curt response. Congratulations, felicitations, and celebration would come later; he was now the port admiral receiving an official report.

"Then, sir, I have the honor to report that the expedition has succeeded." And he could not help adding informally, youthfully exultant at the success of his first real mission, "We've brought home the bacon!"

THE LENSMAN

XIII.

A powerful fleet had been sent to rescue those of the *Brittania's* crew who might have managed to stay out of the clutches of the pirates. The wildly enthusiastic celebration inside Prime Base was over. Outside the force walls of the reservation, however, it was just beginning. Thorndyke, VanBuskirk, and the Velantians were in the thick of it. No one on Earth, except a few planetographers, had ever heard of Velantia, and those highly intelligent reptilian beings knew even less of Tellus. Nevertheless, simply because they had aided the patrolmen, the visitors were practically given the keys to the planet, and they were enjoying the experience tremendously.

"We want Kinnison! We want Kinnison!" the festive crowd, led by Universal Telenews men, had been yelling; and finally the Lensman came out. But after one pose before a lens and a few words into a microphone, he pleaded, "There's my call, now—urgent!" and fled back inside Reservation. Then the milling tide of celebrants rolled back toward the city, taking with it every patrolman who could get leave.

Engineers and designers were swarming through and over the pirate ship Kinnison had driven home, each armed with a sheaf of blue prints already prepared from the long-cherished data spool, each directing a corps of mechanics in dismantling some mechanism of the great space rover. It was to this hive of bustling activity that Kinnison had been called. He stood there, answering as best he could the multitude of questions being fired at him from all sides, until he was rescued by no less a personage than Port Admiral Haynes.

"You gentlemen can get your information from the data sheets better than you can from Kinnison," he remarked with a smile, "and I want to take his report without any more delay."

Hand under arm, the old Lensman led the young one away. But once inside his private office he summoned neither secretary nor recorder. Instead, he pushed the buttons which set up a complete-coverage shield and spoke.

"Now, son, open up. Out with it—everything that you have been holding back ever since you landed. I got your signal."

"Well, yes, I have been holding back," Kinnison admitted. "I haven't got enough jets to be sticking my neck out in fast company, even if it were something to be discussed in public, which it is not. I'm glad you could give me this time so soon. I want to go over an idea with you, and with *no one else*. It may be as cockeyed as Trenco's ether—you are to be the sole judge as to that—but you will know, no matter how goofy it is, that I mean well."

"That certainly is not an overstatement," Haynes replied, dryly. "Go ahead."

"The great peculiarity of space combat is that we fly free, but fight inert," Kinnison began, apparently irrelevantly, but choosing his phraseology with care. "To force an engagement one ship locks to the other first with tracers, then with tractors, and goes inert. Thus, relative speed determines the ability to force or to avoid engagement; but it is relative power that determines the outcome. Heretofore, the pirates——

*

"And by the way, we are belittling our opponents and building up a disastrous overconfidence in ourselves by calling them pirates. It has been thought before that they

438

were not pirates, and now we know definitely that they are not. It is more than a race or a system. It is actually a galaxy-wide culture. It is an absolute despotism, holding its authority by means of a rigid system of rewards and punishments. In our eyes it is fundamentally wrong, but it works. *How* it works! It is organized just as we are, and is apparently as strong in bases, vessels and personnel. In my own mind I have been calling the whole culture 'Boskonia,' since no one seems to know who or what Boskone really is. Perhaps Boskone really *is* the name of the entire organization?

"But to get on with the thought. Boskonia has had all the best of it, both in speed—except for the *Brittania's* momentary advantage—and in power. That advantage is now lost to them. We will have, then, two immense powers, each galactic in scope, each tremendously powerful in arms, equipment, and personnel; each having exactly the same weapons and defenses, and each determined to wipe out the other. A stalemate is inevitable; an absolute deadlock; a sheerly destructive war of attrition which will go on for centuries and which must end in the annihilation of both Boskonia and civilization."

"But our new shears and screens!" protested the older man. "They give us an overwhelming advantage. We can force or avoid engagement, as we please. You know the plan to crush them. You helped to develop it."

"Yes, I know the plan. I also know that we will not crush them. So do you. We both know that our advantage will be only temporary." The young Lensman, unimpressed, was in deadly earnest.

*

The admiral did not reply for a time. Deep down, he himself had felt the doubt; but neither he nor any other of his school had ever mentioned the thing that Kinnison had now so boldly put into words. He knew that whatever one side had, of weapon or armor or of equipment, would sooner or later become the property of the other—as was witnessed by the desperate venture which Kinnison himself had so recently and so successfully concluded. He knew that the devices installed in the vessels captured upon Velantia had been destroyed before falling into the hands of the enemy, but he also knew that with entire fleets so equipped the new arms could not be kept secret indefinitely.

Therefore, he finally replied: "That may be true." He paused, then went on like the indomitable veteran that he was, "But we have the advantage now and we'll drive it while we've got it. After all, we *may* be able to hold it long enough."

"I've just thought of one more thing that would help: communication." Kinnison did not argue the previous point, but went ahead. "It seems to be impossible to drive any kind of a communicator beam through the double interference—"

"*Seems* to be!" barked Haynes. "It *is* impossible! Nothing but a thought—"

"That's it exactly—*thought!*" interrupted Kinnison in turn. "The Velantians can do things with a Lens that nobody would believe possible. Why not examine some of them for Lensmen? I'm sure that Worsel could pass, and probably many others. They can drive thoughts through anything except their own thought-screens—and what communicators they would make!"

"That idea has distinct possibilities and will be followed up. However, it is not what you wanted to discuss. G.A.!"

"QX," Kinnison went into Lens-to-Lens communication. "I want some kind of a shield or screen that will neutralize or nullify a detector. I asked Hotchkiss, the communications expert, about it—under seal. He said that it had never been investigated, even as an academic problem in research, but that it was theoretically possible."

"This room is shielded, you know." Haynes was surprised at the use of the Lenses. "Is it *that* important?"

"I don't know. As I said before, I may be cockeyed; but if my idea is any good at all that nullifier is the most important thing in the universe, and if word of it gets out it will be absolutely useless. You see, sir, over the long route, the only really permanent advantage that we have over Boskonia, the one thing that they cannot get, is the Lens. There must be some way to use it. If that nullifier is possible, and if we can keep it a secret, I believe that I have found it. At least, I want to try something. It may not work—probably it won't; it's a mighty slim chance—but if it does, we may be able to wipe out Boskonia in a few months, instead of carrying on forever a war of attrition. First, I want to go to——"

"Hold on!" Haynes snapped. "I've been thinking, too. I can't see any possible relation between such a device and any real military weapon, or the Lens, either. If I can't, not many others can, and that's a point in your favor. If there is anything at all in your idea, it is too big to share with any one, even me. Keep it yourself."

"But it's a peculiar hook-up, and may not be any good at all," protested Kinnison. "You might want to cancel it."

"No danger of that," came the positive statement. "You know more about the pirates—pardon me, about Boskonia—than any other patrolman. You believe that your idea has some slight chance of success. Very well—that fact is enough to put every resource of the patrol back of you. Put your idea on a tape and seal the spool in your private box in the vault, so that it will not be lost in case of your death. Then go ahead. If it is possible to develop that nullifier, you shall have it. Hotchkiss will take charge of it, and have any other Lensmen he wants. No one except Lensmen will work on it or know anything about it. Only one will be made and no records will be kept. It will not even exist until you yourself release it to us."

"Thanks, sir." And Kinnison left the room.

*

Then for weeks Prime Base was the scene of an activity furious indeed. New apparatus was designed and tested; shears for tracers and tractors, generators of screens against cosmic-energy intake, scramblers for the communicators of the enemy, and many other things. Each item was designed and tested, redesigned and retested, until even the most skeptical of the patrol's engineers could no longer find in it anything to criticize. Then, throughout the galaxy, the ships of the patrol were called into their sector bases to be rebuilt.

There were to be two great classes of vessels. Those of the first were to have speed and defense—nothing else. They were to be the fastest things in space, and able to defend themselves against attack. That was all. Vessels of the second class had to be built from the keel upward, since nothing even remotely like them had theretofore been conceived. They were to be huge, ungainly, slow—simply storehouses of incomprehensibly vast powers of offense. They carried projectors of a size and power never before set upon movable foundations, nor were they dependent upon cosmic energy. They carried their own, in bank upon stupendous bank of Gargantuan accumulators. In fact, each of these monstrous floating fortresses was to be able to generate screens of such design and power that no vessel anywhere near them could receive cosmic energy!

This, then, was the bolt which civilization was preparing to hurl against Boskonia. In theory the thing was simplicity itself. The ultra-fast cruisers would catch the enemy, lock on with tractors, and go inert, thus anchoring in space. Then, while absorbing and dissipating everything that the opposition could send, they would put out a peculiarly patterned interference, the center of which could easily be located. The mobile fortresses would then come up, cut off the Boskonians' power intake, and finish up the job.

Not soon was that bolt forged; but in time civilization was ready to launch its stupendous and, it was generally hoped and believed, conclusive attack upon Boskonia. Every sector base and sub-base was ready; the zero hour had been set.

At Prime Base Kimball Kinnison, the youngest Tellurian ever to wear the four silver stripes of captain, sat at the conning plate of the cruiser *Brittania II*, so named at his own request. He thrilled inwardly as he thought of her speed. Such was her force of drive that, streamlined to the ultimate degree although she was, she had special wall shields, and special dissipators to radiate into space the heat of friction of the medium through which she tore so madly. Otherwise she would have destroyed herself in an hour of full blast, even in the hard vacuum of interstellar space!

And in his office Port Admiral Haynes watched a chronometer. Minutes to go—then seconds.

"Clear ether and light landings." His deep voice was gruff with unexpressed emotion. "Five seconds . . . . QX . . . . Lift!" And the fleet shot into the air.

*

The first objective of this solarian fleet was twofold, and this first hop was to be a short one indeed. For the Boskonians had established bases upon both Pluto and Neptune, right here in the solarian system. So close to Prime Base were these bases that only intensive screening and constant vigilance had kept their spy rays out; so powerful were they that the ordinary battleships of the patrol had been impotent against them. Now they were to be removed. Therefore the fleet, cruisers and "maulers" alike, divided into two parts; one part flashing toward Neptune, the other toward slightly more distant Pluto.

Short as was the time necessary to traverse any interplanetary distance, the solarians were detected and were met in force by the ships of Boskone. But scarcely had battle been joined when the enemy began to realize that this was to be a battle the like of which they had never before seen; and when they began to understand it, it was too late. They could not run, and all space was so full of interference that they could not even report to Helmuth what was going on. These first, peculiarly teardrop-shaped vessels of the patrol did not fight at all. They simply held on like bulldogs, taking without response everything that the white-hot projectors could hurl into them.

Their defensive screens radiated fiercely, high into the violet, under the appalling punishment being dealt out to them by the batteries of ship and shore, but they did not go down. Nor did the grip of a single tractor loosen from its anchorage. And in minutes the squat and monstrous maulers came up. Out went their cosmic-energy blocking screens, out shot their tractor beams, and out from the refractory throats of their stupendous projectors there raved the most terrifically destructive forces generable by man.

Boskonian outer screens scarcely even flickered as they went down before the immeasurable, the incredible violence of that thrust. The second course offered a briefly brilliant burst of violet radiance as it gave way. The inner screen resisted stubbornly as it ran the spectrum in a wildly coruscant display of pyrotechnic splendor; but it, too, went through the ultra-violet and into the black.

Now the wall shield itself—that inconceivably rigid fabrication of pure force, which only the instantaneous detonation of twenty metric tons of "duodec" had ever been known to rupture—was all that barred from the base metal of Boskonian walls the utterly indescribable fury of the maulers' beams. Now force was streaming from that shield in veritable torrents.

So terrible were the conflicting energies there at grips that their neutralization was actually visible and tangible. In sheets and masses, in terrific, ether-racking vortices, and in miles-long, pillaring streamers and flashes, those energies were being hurled away—hurled to all the points of the sphere's full compass, filling and suffusing all near-by space.

The Boskonian commanders stared at their instruments, first in bewildered amazement and then in sheer, stark, unbelieving horror as their power intake dropped to zero and their wall shields began to fail—and still the attack continued in never-lessening power. Surely that beaming *must* slacken down soon. No conceivable mobile plant could throw such a load for long!

But those mobile plants could—and did. The attack kept up, at the extremely high level upon which it had begun. No ordinary storage cells fed those mighty projectors; along no ordinary busbars were their Titanic amperages borne. Those maulers were designed to do just one thing—to *maul*—and that one thing they did well, relentlessly and thoroughly.

*

Higher and higher into the spectrum the defending wall shields began to radiate. At the first blast they had leaped almost through the visible spectrum, in one unbearably fierce succession of red, orange, yellow, green, blue, and indigo, up to a sultry, coruscating, blindingly hard violet. Now the doomed shields began leaping erratically into the ultra-violet. To the eye they were already invisible; upon the recorders they were showing momentary flashes of black.

Soon they went down; and in the instant of each failure one vessel of Boskonia was no more. For, that last defense gone, nothing save unresisting metal was left to withstand the ardor of those ultra-powerful, ravening beams. As has already been said, no substance, however refractory or resistant or inert, can endure even momentarily in such a field of force. Therefore, every atom, alike of vessel and of contents, went to make up the searing, seething burst of brilliant, incandescently luminous vapor which suffused all circumambient space.

Thus passed out of the scheme of things the vessels of the solarian detachment of Boskonia. Not a single vessel escaped; the cruisers saw to that. And then the attack thundered on to the bases themselves. Here the cruisers were useless; they merely formed an observant fringe, the while continuing to so blanket all channels of communication that the doomed bases could send out no word of what was happening to them. The maulers moved up and grimly, doggedly, methodically went to work.

Since a base is always much more powerfully armored than is a battleship, the reduction of these fortresses took longer than had the destruction of the fleet. But the bases could no longer draw power from the Sun or from any other heavenly body, and their other sources of power were comparatively weak. Therefore, their defenses also failed under that never-ceasing assault. Course after course their screens went down, and with the last one went the base. The maulers' beams went through metal and masonry as effortlessly as steel-jacketed bullets go through butter, and bored on, deep into the planet's bedrock, before their frightful force was spent.

Then around and around they spiraled, until nothing whatever was left of the Boskonian works; until only a seething, white-hot lake of molten lava in the midst of the planet's frigid waste was all that remained to show that anything had ever been built there.

Surrender had not been thought of. Quarter or clemency had not been asked, nor offered. Victory, of itself, was not enough. This was, and of stern necessity had to be, a war of utter, complete, and merciless extinction.

*

XIV.

The enemy strongholds so insultingly close to Prime Base having been obliterated, the solarian fleet sailed on into space. For a few weeks game was plentiful enough. Hundreds of raiding vessels were overtaken and held by the patrol cruisers, then blasted to vapor by the maulers.

Many Boskonian bases were also reduced. The locations of most of these had long been known to the intelligence service; others were detected or discovered by the fast-flying cruisers themselves. Marauding vessels revealed the sites of others by succeeding in reaching them before being overtaken by the cruisers. Others were found by the tracers and loops of the signal corps.

Very few of these bases were hidden or in any way difficult of access, and most of them fell before the blasts of a single mauler. But if one mauler was not enough, others were summoned until it did fall. One fortress, a hitherto unknown and surprisingly strong Sector Base, required the concentration of every mauler of the solarian fleet; but they were brought up and the fortress fell. As has been said, this was a war of extinction and every pirate base that was found was reduced.

But one day a cruiser found a base which had not even a spy-ray shield up, and a cursory inspection showed it to be completely empty. Machinery, equipment, stores, and personnel had all been evacuated. Suspicious, the patrol vessels stood off and beamed it from afar, but there were no untoward occurrences. The structures simply slumped down into lava, and that was all.

Every base discovered thereafter was in the same condition, and at the same time the ships of Boskone, formerly so plentiful, disappeared utterly from space. Day after day the cruisers sped hither and thither throughout the vast reaches of the void, at the peak of their unimaginably high pace, without finding a trace of any Boskonian vessel. More remarkable still, and for the first time in years, the ether was absolutely free from Boskonian interference.

Following an impulse, Kinnison asked and received permission to take his ship on scouting duty. At maximum blast, he drove toward the Velantian system, to the point at which he had picked up Helmuth's communication line. Along that line he drove for twenty-two solid days, halting only when a considerable distance outside the galaxy. Ahead of him there was nothing whatever except one or two distant and nebulous star clusters. Behind him there extended the immensity of the galactic lens in all its splendor. But Captain Kinnison had no eye for astronomical beauty that day.

*

He held the *Brittania II* there for an hour, while he mulled over in his mind what the apparent facts could mean. He knew that he had covered the line, from the point of determination out beyond the galaxy's edge. He knew that his detectors, operating as they had been in clear and undistorted ether, could not possibly have missed a thing as large as Helmuth's base must be, if it had been anywhere near that line; that their effective range was immensely greater than the largest possible error in the determination or the following of the line. There were, he concluded, three possible explanations, and only three.

First, Helmuth's base might also have been evacuated. This was almost unthinkable. From what he himself knew of Helmuth that base would be as nearly impregnable as anything could be made, and it was no more apt to be vacated than was the Prime Base of the patrol. Second, Helmuth might already have the device he himself wanted so badly, and upon which Hotchkiss and the other experts had been at work so long—a detector nullifier. This was possible, distinctly so. Possible enough, at least, to warrant filing the idea for future consideration. Third, that base might not be in the galaxy at all, but in that star cluster out there straight ahead of the *Brittania II*, or possibly in one even farther away. That idea seemed the best of the three. It would necessitate ultra-powerful communicators, of course, but Helmuth could very well have them. It squared up in other ways. Its pattern fitted into the matrix very nicely.

But if that base were out there—it could stay there—for a while. The *Brittania II* just wasn't enough ship for that job. Too much opposition out there, and not—enough—ship. Or too much ship? But he wasn't ready, yet, anyway. He needed, and would get, another line on Helmuth's base. Therefore, shrugging his shoulders, he whirled his vessel about and set out to rejoin the fleet.

While a full day short of junction, Kinnison was called to his plate, to see upon its lambent surface the visage of Port Admiral Haynes.

"Did you find out anything on your trip?" he asked.

"Nothing definite, sir. Just a couple of things to think about, is all. But I can say that I don't like this at all. I don't like anything about it or any part of it."

"No more do I," agreed the admiral. "It looks very much as though your forecast of a stalemate might be about to eventuate. Where are you headed for now?"

"Back to the fleet."

"Don't do it. Stay on scouting duty for a while longer. And, unless something more interesting turns up, report back here to base. We have something that may interest you. The boys have been——"

The admiral's picture was broken up into flashes of blinding light and his words became a meaningless, jumbled roar of noise. A distress call had begun to come in, only to be blotted out by a flood of the Boskonian static interference, of which the ether had for so long been clear.

"Got its center located?" Kinnison barked at his communications officer. "They're close—right in our laps!"

"Yes, sir!" And the radio man snapped out numbers.

"Blast!" the captain commanded, unnecessarily; for the alert pilot had already set the course and his levers were even then flashing across their arcs. "I don't know what we can do, since we haven't got a thing to do anything with, if that baby is what I think it is. But believe me, we'll try!"

*

Toward the center of disturbance shot *Brittania II*, herself emitting now a scream of peculiarly patterned interference which was not only a scrambler of all possible communication throughout that whole sector of the galaxy, but also an imperative call for any mauler within that sector. So close had the *Brittania II* been to the scene of depredation that for her to reach it required only minutes.

There lay the merchantman and her Boskonian assailant. Emboldened by the cessation of piratical activities, some shipping concern had sent out a freighter, loaded probably with highly "urgent" cargo; and this was the result. The marauder, inert, had gripped her with his tractors and was beaming her into submission. She was resisting, but feebly now; it was apparent that her screens were failing. Her crew must soon open ports in token of surrender, or roast to a man; and they would probably prefer to roast.

Thus the situation in one instant. The next instant it was changed; the Boskonian discovering suddenly that his beams, instead of boring through the weak defenses of the freighter, were not even exciting to a glow the mighty protective envelopes of a cruiser of the patrol.

He switched from the diffused heat beam he had been using upon the merchantman to the hardest, hottest, most penetrating beam of annihilation he mounted—with but little more to show for it and with no better results. For the *Brittania II's* screens had been designed to stand up almost indefinitely against the most potent beams of any space ship, and they stood up. Increase power as he would, to whatever ruinous overload, the pirate could not break down Kinnison's screens; nor, dodge as he would, could he again get in position to attack his former prey. And eventually the mauler arrived; fortunately it, too, had been fairly close by. Out reached its mighty tractors. Out raved one of its tremendous beams, striking the Boskonian's defenses squarely amidships.

That beam struck and the pirate ship disappeared—but not in a hazily incandescent flare of volatilized metal. The raider disappeared bodily, and still all in one piece. He had put out shears of his own, snapping even the mauler's tractors like threads; and the velocity of his departure was due almost as much to the pressor effect of the patrol beam as it was to the thrust of his own powerful drivers.

It was the beginning of the stalemate Kinnison had foreseen.

"I was afraid of that," the young captain muttered; and, paying no attention whatever to the merchantman, he called the commander of the mauler. At this close range, of course, no possible ether scrambler could interfere with visual apparatus, and there on his plate he saw the face of Clifford Maitland, the man who graduated No. 2 in his own class.

"Hi, Kim, you old space flea!" Maitland exclaimed in delight. "Oh, pardon me, sir," he went on in mock deference, with an exaggerated salute. "To a guy with four jets, I should say——"

"Seal that, Cliff, or I'll climb up you like a squirrel, first chance I get!" Kinnison retorted. "So they've got you skippering one of the big battle wagons, huh? Lucky stiff! Think of a mere infant like you being let play with so much high power. But what'll we do about this heap here?"

"Damn if I know. It isn't covered, so you'll have to tell me, captain."

"Who am I to be passing out orders? As you say, it isn't covered in the book. It's against G I regs for them to be cutting our tractors. But he's all yours, not mine. I've got to flit. You might find out what he's carrying, from where, to where, and why. Then, if you want to, you can escort him either back where he came from or on to where he's going, whichever you think best. If this interference dies out, you'd better report to Prime Base and get some real orders. If it doesn't, use your own judgment, if any. Clear ether, Cliff, I've got to buzz along."

"Free landings, space hound!"

"Now, Vic"—Kinnison turned to his pilot—"we've got urgent business at base. And when I say 'urgent' I don't mean perchance. Let's see you burn a hole in the ether." And that worthy snapped his levers over to maximum blast.

*

The *Brittania II* made the run to Prime Base in a few days, and scarcely had she touched ground when Kinnison was summoned to the office of the port admiral. As soon as he was announced, Haynes brusquely cleared his office and sealed it against any possible form of intrusion or eavesdropping before he spoke. He had aged noticeably since these two had had that memorable conference in this same room. His face was lined and careworn; his eyes and his entire mien bore witness to days and nights of sleeplessly continuous work.

"You were right, Kinnison," he began, abruptly. "A stalemate it is, a hopeless deadlock. I called you in to tell you that Hotchkiss has your nullifier done, and that it works perfectly against all long-range stuff. It works fairly well on vision, except at close range.

Against electromagnetics, however, it is not very effective. About all that can be done, it seems, is to shorten the range; it has not been possible, as yet, to develop a screen against magnetism. Perhaps we expected too much."

"I can get by with that, I think. I will be out of electromagnetic range most of the time, and nobody watches their electros very close, anyway. Thanks a lot. It's ready to install?"

"Doesn't need installation. It's such a little thing you can put it in your pocket. It's self-contained and will work anywhere."

"Better and better. In that case I'll need two of them—and a ship. I would like to have one of those new automatic speedsters. Lots of legs, cruising range, and screens. Only one beam, but I probably won't use even that one so——"

"Going *alone?*" interrupted Haynes. "Better take a battle cruiser, at least. I don't like the idea of your going out there alone."

"I don't particularly relish the prospect, either. But it's got to be that way. The whole fleet, maulers and all, isn't enough to do by force what's got to be done, and even two men are too many to do it in the only way it can be done. You see, sir——"

"No explanations, please. It's on the spool, where we can get it if we need it. Are you informed as to the latest developments?"

"No, sir. I heard a little coming in, but not much."

"We are almost back where we were before you took off in the *Brittania II.* Commerce is almost at a standstill, all over the galaxy. All shipping firms are practically idle. But that is neither all of it nor the worst of it. You may not realize how important interstellar trade is; but as a result of its stoppage general business has slowed down tremendously. As is only to be expected, perhaps, complaints are coming in by the thousand because we have not already blasted the pirates out of space, and demands that we do so at once. They do not understand the true situation, nor realize that we are doing all that we can do. We cannot send a mauler with every freighter and liner, and mauler-escorted vessels are the only ones to arrive at their destinations."

"But why? With tractor shears on all ships, how can they hold them?" asked Kinnison.

"Magnets!" snorted Haynes. "Plain, old-fashioned electromagnets. No pull to speak of, at a distance, of course, but with the raider running free, a millionth of a dyne is enough. Close up—lock on—board and storm—all done!"

"Hm-m-m. That changes things. I've got to find a pirate ship. I was planning on following a freighter or liner out toward Alsakan. But if there aren't any to follow—I'll have to hunt around some——"

"That is easily arranged. Lots of them want to go. We will let one go, with a mauler accompanying her, but well outside detector range."

"That covers everything, then, except the assignment. I can't very well ask for leave, but maybe I could be put on special assignment, reporting direct to you?"

*

"Something better than that." And Haynes smiled broadly, in genuine pleasure. "Everything is fixed. Your release has been entered in the books. Your commission as captain has been canceled, so leave your uniform in your former quarters. Here is your credit book and here is the rest of your kit. You are now an unattached Lensman."

THE LENSMAN

The release! The goal toward which all Lensmen strive, but which so comparatively few attain, even after years of work! He was now a free agent, responsible to no one and to nothing save his own conscience. He was no longer of Earth, nor of the solarian system, but of the galaxy as a whole. He was no longer a tiny cog in the immense machine of the Galactic Patrol; wherever he might go, throughout the immensity of the entire island universe, he *would be* the Galactic Patrol!

"Yes, it's real." The older man was enjoying the youngster's stupefaction at his release, reminding him as it did of the time, long years ago, when he had won his own. "You go anywhere you please and do anything you please, for as long as you please. You take anything you want, whenever you want it, with or without giving reasons—although you will usually give a thumb-printed credit slip in return. You report if, as, when, where, how, and to whom you please—or not, as you please. You don't even get a salary any more. You help yourself to that, too, wherever you may be—as much as you want, whenever you want it."

"But, sir—I—you——I mean—that is——" Kinnison gulped three times before he could speak coherently. "I'm not ready, sir. Why, I'm nothing but a kid. I haven't got enough jets to swing it. Just the bare thought of it scares me into hysterics!"

"It would. It always does." The admiral was very much in earnest now, but it was a glad, proud earnestness. "You are to be as nearly absolutely free an agent as it is possible for a living, flesh-and-blood creature to be. To the man on the street that would seem to spell a condition of perfect bliss. Only a gray Lensman knows what a frightful load it really is; but it is a load that such a Lensman is glad and proud to carry."

"Yes, sir, he would be, of course, if he——"

"That thought will bother you for a time—if it did not, you would not be here—but do not worry about it any more than you can help. All I can say is that in the opinion of those who should know, not only have you proved yourself ready for release, but also you have earned it."

"How do they figure that out?" Kinnison demanded, hotly. "All that saved my bacon on that trip was luck—a burned-out Bergenholm—and at the time I thought that it was bad luck, at that. And VanBuskirk and Worsel and the other boys and Heaven knows who else pulled me out of jam after jam. I'd like awfully well to believe that I'm ready, sir, but I'm not. I can't take credit for pure dumb luck and for other men's abilities."

"Well, coöperation is to be expected, and we like to make gray Lensmen out of the lucky ones." Haynes laughed deeply. "It may make you feel better, though, if I tell you two more things: first, that so far you have made the best showing of any man yet graduated from Wentworth Hall; second, that we of the court believe you would have succeeded in that almost impossible mission without VanBuskirk, without Worsel, and without the lucky failure of the Bergenholm. In a different, and now, of course, unguessable fashion, but succeeded, nevertheless. Nor is this to be taken as in any sense a belittlement of the very real abilities of those others, nor a denial that luck, or chance, does exist. It is merely our recognition of the fact that you have what it takes to be an unattached Lensman.

"Seal it now, and buzz off!" he commanded, as Kinnison tried to say something; and, clapping him on the shoulder, he turned him around and gave him a gentle shove toward the door. "Clear ether, lad!"

"Same to you, sir—all of it there is. I still think that you and all the rest of the court are cockeyed; but I'll try not to let you down." And the newly unattached Lensman blundered out. He stumbled over the threshold, bumped against a stenographer who was hurrying along the corridor, and almost barged into the jamb of the entrance door instead of going through the opening. Outside he regained his physical poise and walked on air toward his quarters; but he never could remember afterward what he did or whom he met on that long, fast hike. Over and over the one thought pounded in his brain: unattached! *Unattached!!* UNATTACHED!!

*

And behind him, in the port admiral's office, that high official sat and mused, smiling faintly with lips and eyes, staring unseeingly at the still-open doorway through which Kinnison had staggered. The boy had measured up in every particular. He would be a good man. He would marry. He did not think so now, of course—in his own mind his life was consecrate—but he would. If necessary, the patrol itself would see to it that he did. There were ways, and such stock was altogether too good not to be propagated. And, fifteen years or so from now—if he lived—when he was no longer fit for the grinding, grueling life to which he now looked forward so eagerly, he would select the Earthbound job for which he was best fitted and would become a good executive. For such were the executives of the patrol. But this daydreaming was getting him nowhere, fast; he shook himself and plunged again into his work.

Kinnison reached his quarters at last, realizing with a thrill that they were no longer his. He now had no quarters, no residence, no address. Wherever he might be, throughout the whole of illimitable space, there was his home. But, instead of being dismayed by the thought of the life he faced, he was filled by a fierce eagerness to be actually living it.

There was a tap at his door and an orderly entered, carrying a bulky package.

"Your grays, sir," he announced, with a crisp salute.

"Thanks." Kinnison returned the salute as smartly; and, almost before the door had closed, he was stripping off the space black-and-silver gorgeousness of the captain's uniform he wore, and was donning gray.

The gray—the unadorned, neutral-colored leather that was the proud garb of that branch of the patrol to which he was thenceforth to belong. It had been tailored to his measurements, and he could not help studying with approval his reflection in the mirror: the round, almost visorless cap, heavily and softly quilted in protection against the helmet of his armor; the heavy goggles, opaque to all radiation harmful to the eyes; the short jacket, emphasizing broad shoulders and narrow waist; the trim breeches and high-laced boots, incasing powerful, tapering legs.

"What an outfit—*what* an outfit!" he breathed. "And maybe I ain't such a bad-looking ape, at that, in these grays!" He did not then, and never did realize that he was wearing the plainest, drabbest, most strictly utilitarian uniform in the known universe; for to him,

THE LENSMAN

as to all others who knew it, the sheer, stark simplicity of the unattached Lensman's plain gray leather transcended by far the gaudy trappings of the other branches of the service. He admired himself boyishly, as men do, feeling a trifle ashamed in so doing; but he did not then and never did appreciate what a striking figure of a man he really was as he strode out of quarters and down the wide avenue toward the *Brittania II's* dock.

*

He was glad indeed that there had been no ceremony or public show connected with this, his real and only important graduation. For as his fellows—not only his own crew, but also his friends from all over the Reservation—thronged about him, mauling and pummeling him in congratulation and acclaim, he knew that he couldn't stand much more. If there were to be much more of it, he discovered suddenly, he would either pass out cold or cry like a baby. He didn't quite know which.

That whole howling, chanting mob clustered about him; and, considering it an honor to carry the least of his personal belongings, formed a yelling, cap-tossing escort. Traffic meant nothing whatever to that pleasantly mad crew, nor, temporarily, did regulations. Let traffic detour; let pedestrians, no matter how august, cool their heels; let cars, trucks, yes, even trains, wait until they got past; let everything wait, or turn around and go back, or go some other way. Here comes Kinnison! Kinnison, gray Lensman! Make way! And way was made—from the *Brittania II's* dock clear across base to the slip in which the Lensman's new speedster lay.

And what a ship this little speedster was! Trim, trig, streamlined to the ultimate she lay there, quiescent but surcharged with power. Almost sentient she was, this power-packed, ultra-racy little fabrication of space-toughened alloy, instantly ready at his touch to liberate those tremendous energies which were to hurl him through the infinite reaches of the cosmic void.

None of the mob came aboard, of course. They backed off, still frantically waving and throwing whatever came closest to hand; and as Kinnison touched a button and shot into the air he swallowed several times in a vain attempt to dispose of an amazing lump which had somehow appeared in his throat.

XV.

It so happened that for many long weeks there had been lying in New York space port an urgent shipment for Alsakan. And not only was that urgency a one-way affair. For, with the possible exception of a few packets, whose owners had locked them in vaults and would not part with them at any price, there was not a single Alsakanite cigarette left on Earth!

Luxuries, then as now, soared feverishly in price with scarcity. Only the rich smoked Alsakanite cigarettes, and to those rich the price of anything they really wanted was a matter of almost complete indifference. And plenty of them wanted, and wanted badly, their Alsakanite cigarettes. There was no doubt of that.

The current market report upon them was: "Bid, one thousand credits per packet of ten. Offered, none at any price."

SUPER PACK

With that ever-climbing figure in mind, a merchant prince named Matthews had been trying to get an Alsakanbound ship into the ether. He knew that one cargo of Alsakanite cigarettes safely landed in any Tellurian space port would yield more profit than could be made by his entire fleet in ten years of normal trading. Therefore, he had for weeks been pulling every wire, and even every string, that he could reach—political, financial, even at times verging altogether too close for comfort upon the criminal—but without results.

For, even if he could find a crew willing to take the risk, to launch the ship without an escort would be out of the question. There would be no profit in a ship that did not return to Earth. The ship was his, to do with as he pleased, but the escorting maulers were assigned solely by the Galactic Patrol, and that patrol would not give his ship an escort.

In answer to his first request, he had been informed that only cargoes classed as necessary were being escorted at all regularly; that seminecessary loads were escorted occasionally, when of a particularly useful or desirable commodity and if opportunity offered; that luxury loads, such as his, were not being escorted at all; that he would be notified if, as, and when the *Prometheus* could be given escort. Then the merchant prince began his siege.

*

Politicians of high rank, local and national, sent in "requests" of varying degrees of diplomacy. Financiers first offered inducements, then threatened to "bear down," then put on all the various kinds of pressure known to their pressure-loving ilk. Pleas, demands, threats, and pressures were alike, however, futile. The patrol could not be coaxed or bullied, cajoled, bribed, or cowed; and all further communications upon the subject, from whatever source originating, were ignored.

Having exhausted his every resource of diplomacy, politics, guile, and finance, the merchant prince resigned himself to the inevitable and stopped trying to get his ship off the ground.

Then, like the proverbial bolt from the blue, New York sub-base received from Prime Base an open message, not even coded, which read:

Authorize space ship *Prometheus* to clear for Alsakan at will, escorted by patrol ship B 42 TC 838, whose present orders are hereby canceled. Signed, Haynes.

A demolition bomb dropped into that sub-base would not have caused greater excitement than did that message. Neither the base commander, the captain of the mauler, the captain of the *Prometheus*, nor the highly pleased but equally surprised Matthews could explain it; but all of them did whatever they could to expedite the departure of the freighter. She was, and had been for a long time, practically ready to sail.

As the base commander and Matthews sat in the office, shortly before the scheduled time of departure, Kinnison arrived—or, more correctly, let them know that he was there. He invited them both into the control room of his speedster; and invitations from gray Lensmen were accepted without question or demur.

"I suppose that you are wondering what this is all about," he began. "I'll make it as short as I can. I asked you in here because this is the only convenient place in which I *know* that what we say will not be overheard. There are lots of spy rays around here, whether you know it or not. The *Prometheus* is to be allowed to go to Alsakan, because that is where pirates seem to be most numerous, and we do not want to waste time hunting all over space to find one.

"Your vessel was selected, Mr. Matthews, for three reasons, and in spite of the attempts you have been making to obtain special privileges, not because of them: first, because there is no necessary or seminecessary freight waiting for clearance into that region; second, because we do not want your firm to fail. We do not know of any other large shipping line in such a shaky position as yours, nor of any firm anywhere to which one single cargo would make such an immense financial difference."

"You are certainly right there, Lensman!" Matthews agreed, whole-heartedly. "It means bankruptcy on the one hand and a fortune on the other."

*

"Here's what is to happen. The ship and the mauler blast off on schedule, fourteen minutes from now. They get about to Valeria, when they are both recalled—urgent orders for the mauler to go on rescue work. The mauler comes back, but your captain will, in all probability, keep on going, saying that he started out for Alsakan and that's where he's going—"

"But he wouldn't. He wouldn't *dare!*" gasped the ship owner.

"Sure he would," Kinnison insisted, cheerfully enough. "That is the third good reason your vessel is being allowed to set out: because it certainly will be attacked. You didn't know it until now, but your captain and over half of your crew are pirates themselves, and—"

"What? Pirates!" Matthews bellowed. "I'll go down there and—"

"You'll do nothing whatever, Mr. Matthews, except watch things, and you will do that from here. The situation is entirely under control."

"But my ship! My cargo!" the shipper wailed. "We'll be ruined if—"

"Let me finish, please," the Lensman interrupted. "As soon as the mauler turns back it is practically certain that your captain will send out a message, letting the pirates know that he is easy prey. Within a minute after sending that message, he dies. So does every other pirate aboard. Your ship lands on Valeria and takes on a crew of space-fighting wildcats, headed by Peter VanBuskirk. Then it goes on toward Alsakan. When the pirates board that ship, after its prearranged, half-hearted resistance and easy surrender, they are going to think that all hell's out for noon. Especially since the mauler, back from her 'rescue work,' will be tagging along, not too far away."

"Then my ship will really go to Alsakan, and back, safely?" Matthews was almost dazed. Matters were entirely out of his hands, and things had moved so rapidly that he hardly knew what to think. "But if my own crews are pirates, some of them may—But I can, of course, get police protection if necessary."

"Unless something entirely unforseen happens, the *Prometheus* will make the round trip in safety, cargoes and all—under mauler escort all the way. You will, of course, have to take the other matter up with your local police."

"When is the attack to take place, sir?" asked the base commander.

"That's what the mauler skipper wanted to know when I told him what was ahead of him." Kinnison grinned. "He wanted to sneak up a little closer about that time. I'd like to know, myself, but unfortunately that will have to be decided by the pirates after they get the signal. It will be on the way out, though, because the cargo she has aboard now is a lot more valuable to Boskone than a load of Alsakanite cigarettes would be."

"But do you think you can take the pirate ship that way?" asked the commander, dubiously.

"No. But he will cut down his personnel to such an extent that he will have to head back for base."

"And that's what you want—the base. I see."

He did not see—quite—but the Lensman did not enlighten him further.

*

There was a brilliant double flare as freighter and mauler lifted into the air. Kinnison showed the ship owner out.

"Hadn't I better be going, too?" asked the commander. "Those orders, you know."

"A couple of minutes yet. I have another message for you—official. Matthews won't need a police escort long—if any. When that ship is attacked it is to be the signal for cleaning out every pirate in Greater New York—the worst pirate hotbed on Tellus. Neither you nor your force will be in on it directly, but you might pass the word around, so that our own men will be informed ahead of the Telenews outfits."

"Good! That has needed doing for a long time."

"Yes. But you know it takes a long time to line up every man in such a big organization. They want to get them all, without getting any innocent by-standers."

"Who's doing it? Prime Base?"

"Yes. Enough men will be thrown in here to do the whole job in an hour."

"That is good news. Clear ether, Lensman!" And the base commander went back to his post.

As the air-lock toggles rammed home, sealing the exit behind the departing visitor, Kinnison eased his speedster into the air and headed for Valeria. Since the two vessels ahead of him had left atmosphere inertialess, as would he, and since several hundred seconds had elapsed since their take-off, he was, of course, some ten thousand miles off their line as well as being uncounted millions of miles behind them. But the larger distance meant no more than the smaller, and neither of them meant anything at all to the patrol's finest speedster. Kinnison, on easy touring blast, caught up with them in minutes. Closing up to less than one light year, he slowed his pace to match theirs and held his distance.

Any ordinary ship would have been detected instantly—long since, in fact—but Kinnison rode no ordinary ship. His speedster was immune to all detection save electromagnetic or visual, and, therefore, even at that close range—the travel of half a minute for even a slow space ship in open space—he was safe. For electromagnetics are useless at that distance; and visual apparatus, even with subether converters, is reliable only up to a few mere thousands of miles, unless the observer knows exactly what to look for and where to look for it.

THE LENSMAN

Kinnison, then, closed up and followed the *Prometheus* and her mauler escort; and as they approached the Valerian solar system, sure enough, the recall messages came booming in. Also, as had been expected, the renegade captain of the freighter sent back, first his defiant answer, and then his message to the pirate high command. The mauler turned back; the merchantman kept on. Suddenly, however, she stopped, inert, and from her ports were ejected discrete bits of matter—probably the bodies of the Boskonian members of her crew. Then the *Prometheus*, again inertialess, flashed directly toward the planet Valeria.

An inertialess landing is, of course, highly irregular, and is made only when the ship is to take off again immediately. It saves all the time ordinarily lost in spiraling and deceleration, and saves the computation of a landing orbit, which is no task for an amateur computer. It is, however, dangerous.

It takes power, plenty of it, to maintain the force which neutralizes the inertia of mass, and if that force fails, even for an instant, while a ship is upon a planet's surface, the consequences are usually highly disastrous. For in the neutralization of inertia there is no magic, no getting of something for nothing, no violation of Nature's law of the conservation of matter and energy. The instant that force becomes inoperative the ship possesses exactly the same velocity, momentum, and inertia that it possessed at the instant the force took effect.

Thus, if a space ship takes off from Earth, with its orbital velocity of about eighteen and one half miles per second relative to the Sun, goes free, dashes to Mars, lands free, and then goes inert, its original velocity, both in speed and in direction, is instantly restored, with consequences better imagined than described. Such a velocity, of course, *might* take the ship harmlessly into the air; but it probably would not.

But the *Prometheus* landed free, and so did Kinnison. He stepped out, fully armored against Valeria's extremely heavy atmosphere and laboring a trifle under its terrific gravitation, to be greeted cordially by *Lieutenant* VanBuskirk, whose fighting men were already streaming aboard the freighter.

"Hi, chief!" the Dutchman called, gayly. "Everything went off like clockwork. Won't hold you up long—be blasting off in ten minutes."

"Ho, Lefty!" the Lensman acknowledged, as cordially, but saluting the newly commissioned officer with an exaggerated formality. "Say, Bus, I've been doing some thinking. Why wouldn't it be a good idea to——"

"Uh-uh, it would *not*," denied the fighter, positively. "I know what you're going to say—that you want in on this party—but don't say it."

"But I——" Kinnison began to argue.

"Nix," the Valerian declared flatly. "You've got to stay with your speedster. No room for her inside, as she's full to the last meter with cargo and with my men. You can't clamp on outside, as that would give the whole thing away. And besides, for the first and last time in my life I've got a chance to give a gray Lensman orders. Those orders are to stay out of and away from this ship—and I'll see to it that you do, too, you little Tellurian wart! Boy, what a kick I get out of that!"

454

"You would, you big, dumb Valerian ape. You always were a small-souled type!" Kinnison retorted. "Piggy-piggy—Haynes, huh?"

"Uh-huh." VanBuskirk nodded. "How else could I talk so rough to *you* and get away with it? However, don't feel too bad. You aren't missing a thing, really. This thing is in the cans already, and your fun is up ahead somewhere. And by the way, Kim, congratulations. You had it coming. We're all behind you, from here to the next universe and back."

"Thanks. And the same to you, Bus, and many of 'em. Well, if you won't let me stow away, I'll tag along behind, I guess. Clear ether—or rather, I hope it's full of pirates by to-morrow morning. Won't be, though, probably; don't imagine they'll move until we're almost there."

*

And tag along Kinnison did, through thousands and thousands of parsecs of uneventful voyage.

Part of the time he spent in the speedster, dashing hither and yon. Most of it, however, he spent in the vastly more comfortable mauler; to the armored side of which his tiny vessel clung with its magnetic clamps while he slept and ate, gossiped and read, exercised and played with the mauler's officers and crew, in deep-space comradery. It so happened, however, that when the long-waited attack developed he was out in his speedster, and thus saw and heard everything from the beginning.

Space was filled with the old, familiar interference. The raider flashed up, locked on with magnets, and began to beam. Not heavily—scarcely enough to warm up the defensive screens—and Kinnison probed into the pirate with his spy ray.

"Terrestrials—and Americans!" he exclaimed, half aloud, startled for an instant. "But naturally they would be, since this is a put-up job and over half the crew were New York gangsters."

"The blighter's got his spy-ray screens up," the pilot was grumbling to his captain. The fact that he spoke in English was immaterial to the Lensman; he would have understood equally well any other possible form of communication or of thought exchange. "That wasn't part of the plan, was it?"

If Helmuth, or one of the able minds at his base, had been directing that attack it would have stopped right there. The pilot had shown a flash of feeling that, with a little encouragement, might have grown into a suspicion.

But the captain was not an imaginative man. Therefore: "Nothing was said about it, either way," he replied. "Probably the mate's on duty. He is not one of us, you know. All the better if he is. The captain will open up. If he doesn't do it pretty quick, I'll open her up myself. There, the port's opening. Slide a little forward . . . . Hold it! Go get 'em, men!"

Then men, hundreds of them, armed and armored, swarmed through the freighter's locks. But as the last man of the boarding party passed the portal something happened that was most decidedly not on the program: the outer port slammed shut and its toggles drove home!

"Blast those screens! Knock them down! Get in there with a spy ray!" barked the pirate captain. He was not one of those hardy and valiant souls who, like Gildersleeve, led, in person, the attacks of his cutthroats. He emulated, instead, the higher Boskonian officials and directed his raids from the safety of his control room; but, as has been intimated, he was unlike those officials in that he lacked directorial ability. Thus it was only after it was too late that he became suspicious. "I wonder if somebody could have double-crossed us? Hi-jackers?"

"We'll soon know," the pilot growled, and even as he spoke the spy ray got through, revealing a very shambles.

For VanBuskirk and his Valerians had not been caught napping, nor were they a crew—unarmored, partially armed, and rendered even more impotent by internal mutiny, strife, and slaughter—such as the pirates had expected to find.

*

Instead of such a crew the boarders met a force that was overwhelmingly superior to their own—not only in point of numbers, but even more markedly in the strength and agility of its units. Also, the defenders were more capably armed than were the attackers, since, in addition to the efficient armor of the patrol and its ultra-deadly portable weapons, at least one of those terrific semiportable projectors commanded every corridor of the freighter. In the blasts of those projectors most of the pirates died instantly, not knowing what struck them, not even knowing that they died.

They were the fortunate ones. The others knew what was coming and saw it as it came, for the Valerians did not even draw their DeLameters. They knew that the pirates' armor could withstand for many minutes any hand weapon's beams, and they disdained to remount the heavy semiportables. They came in with their space axes, and at the sight the pirates broke and ran screaming in panic fear. But they could not escape. The toggles of the exit port were not only in their sockets, but they were also locked in them.

Therefore, the storming party died to the last man; and, as VanBuskirk had foretold, it was scarcely even a struggle. For any ordinary space armor is just so much tin against a Valerian swinging a space ax.

The spy ray of the pirate captain got through just in time to see the ghastly finale of the massacre, and his face turned first purple, then white.

"The patrol!" he gasped. "Valerians—a whole company of them! I'll say we've been double-crossed!"

"Right-o—we've jolly well been," the pilot agreed. "You don't know the half of it yet, either. Somebody's coming, and it isn't a boy scout. If a mauler should suck us in, we'd be very much a spent force, what?"

"Cut out the conversation!" snapped the captain. "Is it a mauler, or not?"

"A bit too far away yet to say, but it probably is. They wouldn't have sent those jaspers out without cover, old bean. They knew that we can burn that freighter's screens down in an hour. Better cut the beams and get ready to run, what?"

The commander did so, wild thoughts racing through his mind. If a mauler got close enough to him to use magnets, he was done. Cutting arcs would burn through his armor like cheese, and he had no fighting men left. And even if he had—even a full crew of the most savage fighters known would have to be inescapably cornered before they would mix it with what that mauler had aboard. He would have to go back to base, anyway—

"Tally ho, old fruit!" The pilot slammed his levers over to maximum blast. "It's a mauler and we've been bloody well jobbed. Back to base?"

"Yes." And the discomfited captain energized his communicator, to report to his immediate superior the humiliating outcome of the supposedly carefully planned coup.

XVI.

As the pirate fled into space Kinnison followed, matching his quarry in course and speed. He then cut in the automatic controller on his drive, the automatic recorder on his plate, and began to tune in his beam tracer; only to be brought up short by the realization that the spy ray's point would not stay in the pirate's control room without constant attention and manual adjustment. He had known that, too. Even the most precise of automatic controllers, driven by the most carefully stabilized electronic currents, are prone to slip twenty feet or so at even such close range as ten million miles, especially in the bumpy ether near solar systems, and there was nothing to correct the slip. He had not thought of that before; the pilot always made those minor corrections as a matter of course.

But now he was torn between two desires. He wanted to listen to the conversation that would ensue as soon as the pirate captain got into communication with his superior officers; and, especially should Helmuth put in his beam, he very much wanted to trace it and thus secure another line on the headquarters he was so anxious to locate. He now feared that he could not do both—a fear that soon was to prove well-grounded—and wished fervently that for a few minutes he could be two men—or at least a Velantian; they had eyes and hands and separate brain compartments enough so that they could do half a dozen things at once and do each one well. He could not; but he could try. Maybe he should have brought one of the boys along, at that. No, that would wreck everything, later on; he would have to do the best he could.

Communication was established and the pirate captain began to make his report. By using one hand on the ray and the other on the tracer, Kinnison managed to get a partial line and to record scraps of the conversation. He missed, however, the essential part of the entire episode, that part in which the base commander turned the unsuccessful captain over to Helmuth himself. Therefore, Kinnison was surprised indeed at the disappearance of the beam he was so laboriously tracing, and to hear Helmuth conclude his castigation of the unlucky captain with:

"—not entirely your fault. We will not punish you at all severely this time. Report to our base on Aldebaran I. Turn your vessel over to base commander there and do anything he tells you to do for thirty of the days of that planet."

Frantically, Kinnison drew back his tracer and searched for Helmuth's beam; but before he could synchronize with it the message of the pirates' high chief was finished and his beam was gone. The Lensman sat back in thought.

Aldebaran! Practically next door to his own solarian system, from which he had come so far. How had they possibly managed to keep concealed, or to re-establish, a base so close to Sol, through all the intensive searching that had been done? But they *had*. That was the important thing. Anyway, he knew where he was going, and that helped.

One other thing he hadn't thought of—and one that might have spoiled everything—was the fact that he couldn't stay awake indefinitely to follow that ship! He had to sleep sometime, and while he was asleep his quarry was bound to escape. He, of course, had a CRX tracer, which would hold a ship without attention as long as it was anywhere within even extreme range; and it would have been a simple enough matter to have had a photo-cell relay put in between the plate of the CRX and the automatic controls of the spacer and driver—but he had not asked for it. Well, luckily, he now knew where he was going, and the trip to Aldebaran would be long enough for him to build a dozen such controls. He had all the necessary parts and plenty of tools. It would give him something to do to break the monotony of the voyage.

*

Therefore, following the pirate ship easily as it tore through space, Kinnison built his automatic "chaser," as he called it. During each of the first four or five "nights" he lost the vessel he was pursuing, but found it without any great difficulty upon awakening. Thereafter he held it continuously, improving day by day the performance of his apparatus until it could do almost anything except talk.

After that he devoted his time to an intensive study of the general problem before him. His results were highly unsatisfactory; for in order to solve any problem one must have enough data to set it up, either in actual equations or in logical sequences, and Kinnison found that he did not have enough data. He had altogether too many unknowns and not enough knowns.

The first specific problem was that of getting into the pirate base. Since the searchers of the patrol had not found it, that base must be very well hidden indeed. And hiding anything as large as a base on Aldebaran I, as he remembered it, would be quite a feat in itself. He had been in that system only once, but—

Alone in his ship, and in deep space although he was, he blushed painfully as he remembered what had happened to him during that visit. He had chased a couple of dope runners to Aldebaran II, and there he had encountered the most vividly, the most flawlessly, the most remarkably and intriguingly beautiful girl he had ever seen. He had seen beautiful girls and women, of course, before and in plenty. He had seen beauties amateur and professional—social butterflies, dancers, actresses, models, and posturers, both in the flesh and in Telenews plates—but he had never supposed that such an utterly ravishing creature as she was could exist outside of a thionite dream. As a timidly innocent damsel in distress she had been perfect, and if she had held that pose a little longer Kinnison shuddered to think of what might have happened.

But, having known too many dope runners and too few patrolmen, she misjudged entirely, not only the cadet's sentiments, but also his reactions. For, even as she came amorously into his arms, he had known that there was something screwy. Women like that did not play that kind of game for nothing. She must be mixed up with the two he had been chasing. He got away from her, with only a couple of scratches, just in time to capture her confederates as they were making their escape. He had been afraid of beautiful women ever since. He'd like to see that Aldebaranian hell-cat again—just once. He'd been just a kid then, but now——

*

But that line of thought was getting him nowhere, fast. It was Aldebaran I that he had better be thinking of: barren, lifeless, desolate, airless, waterless; bare as his hand, covered with extinct volcanoes, cratered, jagged, and torn. To hide a base on that planet would take plenty of doing, and, conversely, it would be correspondingly difficult of approach. If on the surface at all, which he doubted very strongly, it would be covered.

In any event, all its approaches would be thoroughly screened and equipped with lookouts on the ultra-violet and on the infra-red, as well as on the visible. His detector nullifier wouldn't help him much there. Those screens and lookouts were bad—very, very bad. Question: could *anything* get into that base without setting off an alarm?

His speedster could not even get close; that was certain. Could he, alone? He would have to wear armor, of course, to hold his air, and it would radiate. Not necessarily—he could land out of range and walk, without power; but there were still the screens and the lookouts. If the pirates were on their toes it simply wasn't in the cards; and he had to assume that they would be alert.

What, then, could pass those barriers? Prolonged consideration of every facet of the situation gave definite answer and marked out clearly the course he must take. Something admitted by the pirates themselves was the only thing that could get in. The vessel ahead of his was going in. Therefore, he must and would enter that base within the pirate vessel itself. With that point decided there remained only the working out of a method, which proved to be almost ridiculously simple.

Once inside the base, what should he—or rather, what *could* he—do? For days he made and discarded plans, but finally he tossed them all out of his mind. So much depended upon the location of the base, its personnel, its arrangement, and its routine, that he could develop not even the rough draft of a working plan. He knew what he wanted to do, but he had not even the remotest idea as to how he could go about doing it. Of the opening that appeared, he would have to choose the most feasible and fit his actions to whatever situation then and there obtained.

So deciding, he shot his spy ray toward the planet and studied it with care. It was, indeed, as he had remembered it—or worse. Bleakly, hotly arid, it had no soil whatever, its entire surface being composed of igneous rock, lava, and pumice. Stupendous ranges of mountains crisscrossed and intersected each other at random, each range a succession of dead volcanic peaks and blown-off craters. Mountainside and rocky plain, crater wall and valley floor, alike and innumerably were pock-marked with subcraters and with immensely yawning shell holes, as though the whole planet had been, throughout geologic ages, the target of an incessant cosmic bombardment.

*

Over its surface and through and through its volume he drove his spy ray, finding nothing. He bored into its substance with his detectors and his tracers, with results completely negative. Of course, closer up, his electromagnetics would report iron—plenty

459

of it—but that information would also be meaningless. Practically all planets had iron cores.

As far as his instruments could tell—and he had given Aldebaran I a more thorough going over, by far, than any ordinary surveying ship would have given it—there was no base of any kind upon or within the planet. Yet he *knew* that a base was there. So what? So—maybe—Helmuth's base might be inside the galaxy after all, protected from detection in the same way, probably by solid miles of iron or of iron ore. A second line upon that base had now become imperative. But they were approaching the system fast; he had better get ready.

He belted on his personal equipment, including a nullifier, then inspected his armor, checking its supplies and apparatus carefully before he hooked it ready to his hand. Glancing into the plate, he noted with approval that his chaser was functioning perfectly. Pursued and pursuer were now both well inside the solar system of Aldebaran; and, as slowed the pirate, so slowed the speedster.

Finally, the leader went inert in preparation for his spiral. But Kinnison was no longer following. Before he went inert he flashed down to within fifty thousand miles of the planet's forbidding surface. He then cut his Bergenholm, threw the speedster into an almost circular orbit, well away from the landing orbit selected by the pirate, cut off all his power, and drifted. He stayed in the speedster, observing and computing, until he had so exactly defined its path that he could find it unerringly at any future instant. Then he went into the air lock, stepped out into space, and, waiting only to be sure that the portal had snapped shut behind him, set his course toward the pirate's spiral.

Inert now, his progress was so slow as to seem imperceptible, but he had plenty of time. And it was only relatively that his speed was low. He was actually hurtling through space at the rate of well over two thousand miles an hour, and his powerful little driver was increasing that speed constantly by an acceleration of two Earth gravities.

Soon the vessel crept up, beneath him now, and Kinnison, increasing his drive to five gravities, shot toward it in a long, slanting dive. This was the most ticklish minute of the trip, but the Lensman had assumed correctly that the officers of the badly undermanned ship would be looking ahead of them and down, not backward and up. They were, and he made his approach unseen. The approach itself, the boarding of an inert space ship at its frightful landing-spiral velocity, was elementary to any competent space man—simplicity itself. There was not even a flare to bother him or to reveal him to sight, as the braking jets were now doing all the work. Matching course and velocity ever more closely, he crept up—flung his magnet—pulled up, hand over hand—opened the emergency inlet lock—and there he was.

Unconcernedly, he made his way along the sternway and into the now deserted quarters of the fighters. There he lay down in a hammock, snapped the acceleration straps, and shot his spy ray into the control room. And there, in the pirate captain's own visiplate, he observed the rugged and torn topography of the terrain below, as the pilot fought his ship down, mile by mile.

Tough going, this, Kinnison reflected, and the bird was doing a nice job, even if he was taking it the hard way, bringing her down straight on her nose instead of taking one more spiral around the planet and then sliding in on her under jets, which were designed and placed specifically for such work. But taking it the hard way he was, and his vessel was bucking, kicking, bouncing, and spinning on the terrific blast from her braking jets. Down she came, fast; and it was only after she was actually inside one of those stupendous craters, well below the level of its rim, that the pilot flattened her out and assumed normal landing position.

They were still going too fast, Kinnison thought. But the pirate pilot knew what he was doing. Five miles the vessel dropped, straight down that Titanic shaft, before the bottom was reached. The shaft's wall was studded with windows; in front of the craft loomed the outer gate of a gigantic air lock. It opened; the ship was trundled inside, landing cradle and all, and the massive gate closed behind it. This was the pirates' base, and Kinnison was inside it!

"Men, attention!" The pirate commander snapped then. "This air is deadly poison, so put on your armor and be sure your tanks are full. They have rooms for us, having good air, but don't open your suits a crack until I tell you to. Assemble! All of you that are not here in this control room in five minutes will stay on board and take your own chances!"

Kinnison decided instantly to assemble with the crew. He could do nothing in the ship, and it would be inspected, of course. He had plenty of air, but space armor all looked alike, and his Lens would warn him in time of any unfriendly or suspicious thought. He had better go. If they called a roll——But he would cross that bridge when he came to it.

No roll was called; in fact, the captain paid no attention at all to his men. They could come along or not, just as they pleased. But since to stay in the ship meant death, every man was prompt. At the expiration of the five minutes the captain strode away, followed by the crowd. Through a doorway, left turn, and the captain was met by a creature whose shape Kinnison could not make out. A pause, a straggling forward, then a right turn.

Kinnison decided that he would not take that turn. He would stay here, close to the shaft—where he could blast his way out if necessary—until he had studied the whole base thoroughly enough to map out a plan of campaign. He soon found an empty and apparently unused room, and assured himself that through its heavy, crystal-clear window he could indeed look out into the vastly cylindrical emptiness of the volcanic shaft.

*

Then, with his spy ray, he watched the pirates as they were escorted to the quarters prepared for them. Those might have been rooms of state, but it looked to Kinnison very much as though his former shipmates were being jailed ignominiously, and he was glad that he had taken leave of them. Shooting his ray here and there throughout the structure, he finally found what he was looking for: the communicator room. That room was fairly well lighted, and at what he saw there his jaw dropped in sheerest amazement.

He had expected to see men, since Aldebaran II, the only inhabited planet in the system, had been colonized from Tellus and its people were as truly human and Caucasian as those of Chicago or of Paris. But these—these *things*—He had been around quite a bit, but he had never seen nor heard of their like. They were wheels, really. When they went anywhere they rolled. Heads where hubs ought to be—eyes—arms, dozens of them, and very capable-looking hands——

"Vogenar!" a crisp thought flashed from one of the peculiar entities to another, impinging also upon Kinnison's Lens. "Some one—some outsider—is looking at me. Relieve me while I abate this intolerable nuisance."

"One of those creatures from Tellus? We will teach them very shortly that such intrusion is not to be borne for an instant."

"No, it is not one of them. The touch is similar, but the tone is entirely different. Nor could it be one of them, for not one of them is equipped with the instrument which is such a clumsy substitute for the sense of perception with which all really intelligent races are endowed in their minds. There, I will now begin to——"

Kinnison snapped on his thought-screen, but the damage had already been done.

In the violated communications room the angry observer went on: "—attune myself and trace the origin of that prying look. It has disappeared now, but its sender cannot be distant, since our walls are shielded and screened. Ah, there is a blank space which I cannot penetrate, in the seventh room of the fourth corridor. In all probability it is one of our guests, hiding now behind a thought screen." Then his orders boomed out to a corps of guards. "Take him and put him with the others!"

Kinnison had not heard the order, but he was ready for anything, and those who came to take him found that it was easier far to issue such orders than to carry them out.

"Halt!" snapped the Lensman, his Lens carrying the crackling command deep into the wheelmen's minds. "I do not wish to harm you, but come no closer!"

"You? Harm us?" came a cold, clear thought, and the creatures vanished. But not for long. They, or others like them, were back in moments, this time armed and armored for strife.

Again Kinnison found that rays were useless. The armor of the foe-mounted generators as capable as his own; and, although the air in the room soon became one intolerably glaring field of force, in which the very walls themselves began to crumble and to vaporize, neither he nor his attackers were harmed. Again, then, the Lensman had recourse to his medieval weapon, sheathing his DeLameter and wading in with his ax. Although not a VanBuskirk, he was, for an Earthman, of unusual strength, skill, and speed; and to those opposing him he was a very Hercules.

*

Therefore, as he struck and struck and struck again, the cell became a gorily reeking slaughter pen, its every corner high-piled with the shattered corpses of the wheelmen and its floor running with blood and slime. The last few of the attackers, unwilling to face longer that irresistible steel, wheeled away, and Kinnison thought flashingly of what he should do next.

This trip was a bust so far. He couldn't do himself a bit of good here now, and he'd better buzz off while he was still in one piece. How? The door? No. Couldn't make it. He'd run out of time quick that way. Better take out the wall. That would give those Wheelmen something else to think about, too, while he was doing his flit.

Only a fraction of a second was taken up by these thoughts; then Kinnison was at the wall. He set his DeLameter to minimum aperture and at maximum blast, to throw a cutting pencil against which no material substance could stand. Through the wall that pencil pierced—up, over, and around.

But, fast as the Lensman had acted, he was still too late. There came trundling into the room behind him, upon four low wheels, a truck, bearing a squat and monstrous mechanism. Kinnison whirled to face it. As he turned the section of the wall upon which he had been at work blew outward with a deafening crash. The ensuing rush of escaping atmosphere picked the Lensman up as though he had been a straw and hurled him out through the opening and into the shaft. In the meantime the mechanism upon the truck had begun a staccato, grinding roar, and as it roared Kinnison felt slugs ripping through his armor and tearing through his flesh, each as crushing, crunching, paralyzing a blow as though it had been inflicted by VanBuskirk's space ax.

This was the first time that Kinnison had ever been really badly wounded, and it made him sick. But, sick and numb, senses reeling at the shock to his slug-torn body, his right hand flashed to the external controller of his neutralizer. For he was falling inert. It was only ten or fifteen meters to the bottom, as he remembered it. He had mighty little time to waste if he were not to land inert. He snapped the controller. Nothing happened. Something had been shot away. His driver, too, was dead. Snapping the sleeve of his armor into its clamps he began to withdraw his arm in order to operate the internal controls, but he ran out of time. He crashed, on the top of a subsiding pile of masonry which had preceded him, but which had not yet attained a state of equilibrium, underneath a shower of similar material which rebounded from his armor in a boiler-shop clangor of noise.

Well it was that that heap of masonry had not yet had time to settle into form, for in some slight measure it acted as a cushion to break the Lensman's fall. But an inert fall of forty feet, even cushioned by rocks, is in no sense a light one. Kinnison crashed. It seemed as though a thousand pile drivers struck him at once. Surges of almost unbearable agony swept over him, as bones snapped and bruised flesh gave way. He knew dimly that a merciful tide of oblivion was reaching up to engulf his shrieking, suffering mind.

But, foggily at first in the stunned confusion of his entire being, something stirred, that unknown and unknowable something, that indefinable ultimate quality that had made him worthy of the Lens he wore. He lived, and while a Lensman lived he did not quit. To quit was to die then and there, since he was losing air fast. He had plastic in his kit, of course, and the holes were small. He *must* plug those leaks, and plug them quick.

His left arm, he found, he could not move at all. It must be smashed pretty badly. Every shallow breath was a searing pain. That meant a rib or two gone out. Luckily, however, he was not breathing blood; therefore, his lungs must still be intact. He could move his right arm, although it seemed like a lump of clay or a limb belonging to some one else.

But, mustering all his power of will, he made it move. He dragged it out of the armor's clamped sleeve, forced the leaden hand to slide through the welter of blood that seemed almost to fill the bulge of his armor. He found his kit box, and, after an eternity of pain-racked time, he compelled his sluggish hand to open it and to take out the plastic.

*

Then, in a continuously crescendo throbbing of agony, he forced his maimed, crushed, and broken body to writhe and to wriggle about, so that his one sound hand could find and stop the holes through which his precious air was whistling out and away. Find them he did, and quickly, and sealed them tight; but when he had plugged the last one he slumped down, spent and exhausted. He did not hurt so much, now; his suffering had mounted to such terrific heights of intolerable keenness that the nerves themselves, in outraged protest at carrying such a load, had blocked it off.

There was much more to do, but he simply could not do it without a rest. Even his iron will could not drive his tortured muscles to any further effort until after they had been allowed to recuperate a little from what they had gone through.

How much air did he have left, if any, he wondered, foggily and with an entirely detached and disinterested impersonalness. Maybe his tanks were empty. Of course, it couldn't have taken him as long to plug those leaks as it had seemed to, or he wouldn't have had any air left at all, in tanks or suit. He couldn't, however, have much left. He would look at his gauges and see.

But now he found that he could not move even his eyeballs, so deep was the coma that was enveloping him. Away off somewhere there was a billowing expanse of blackness, utterly heavenly in its deep, softly-cushioned comfort; and from that sea of peace and surcease there came reaching to embrace him huge, soft, tender arms. Why suffer, something crooned at him. It was *so* much easier to let go!

XVII.

Kinnison did not lose consciousness—quite. There was too much to do, too much that *had* to be done. He had to get out of here. He had to get back to his speedster. He had, by hook or by crook, to get back to Prime Base! Therefore, grimly, doggedly, teeth tight-locked in the enhancing agony of every movement, he drew again upon those hidden, those deeply buried resources which even he had no idea he possessed. His code was simple: the code of the Lens. While a Lensman lived he did not quit. Kinnison was a Lensman. Kinnison lived. Kinnison did not quit.

He fought back that engulfing tide of blackness, wave by wave as it came. He beat down by sheer force of will those tenderly beckoning, those sweetly seducing arms of oblivion. He forced the mass of protesting putty that was his body to do what *had* to be done. He thrust styptic gauze into the most copiously bleeding of his wounds. He was burned, too, he discovered then—they must have had a high-powered needle ray on that truck, as well as the rifle—but he could do nothing about burns. There simply wasn't time.

He found the power lead that had been severed by a bullet. Stripping the insulation was an almost impossible job, but it was finally accomplished, after a fashion. Bridging the gap proved to be even a worse one. Since there was no slack, the ends could not be twisted together, but had to be joined by a short piece of spare wire, which, in turn, had to be stripped and then twisted with each end of the severed lead. That task, too, he finally finished, although he was working purely by feel and half conscious withal in a wracking haze of pain.

Soldering those joints was, of course, out of the question. He was afraid even to try to insulate them with tape, lest the loosely twined strands should fall apart in the attempt. He did have some dry handkerchiefs, however, if he could reach them. He could, and did, and wrapped one carefully about the wires' bare joints. Then, apprehensively, he tried his neutralizer. Wonder of wonders, it worked! So did his driver!

In moments then he was rocketing up the shaft, and as he passed the opening out of which he had been blown, he realized with amazement that what had seemed to him like hours must have been minutes only, and few even of them. For the frantic Wheelmen were just then lifting into place the temporary shield which was to stem the mighty outrush of their atmosphere. Wonderingly, Kinnison looked at his air gauges. He had enough—if he hurried.

And hurry he did. He *could* hurry, since there was practically no atmosphere to impede his flight. Up the five-mile-deep shaft he shot and out into space. His chronometer, built to withstand even severer shocks than that of his fall, told him where his speedster was to be found, and in a matter of minutes he found her. Against her side he flashed in inertialess collision. He forced his rebellious right arm into the sleeve of his armor and fumbled at the lock. It yielded. The port swung open. He was inside his own ship.

Again the encroaching universe of blackness threatened, but again he fought it off. He *could not* pass out—yet! Dragging himself to the board, he laid his course upon distant Tellus, too distant by far to permit of the selection of such a tiny objective as Prime Base. He connected the automatic controls.

He was weakening fast, and knew it. But from somewhere and in some fashion he *must* get strength to do what *must* be done—and somehow he did it. He shoved his levers out to maximum blast. Hang on, Kim! Hang on for just a second more! He disconnected the spacer. He killed the detector nullifiers. Then, with the utterly last remnant of his strength he thought into his Lens.

"Haynes." The thought went out blurred, distorted, weak. "Kinnison. I'm coming—com——"

He was done—out cold, utterly spent. He had already done too much—far, far too much. He had driven that pitifully mangled body of his to its ultimately last possible movement; his wracked and tortured mind to its ultimately last possible thought. The last iota of even his tremendous reserve of vitality was consumed and he plunged, parsecs deep, into the black depths of oblivion which had so long and so unsuccessfully been trying to engulf him.

*

But Kimball Kinnison, gray Lensman, had done everything that had *had* to be done before he blacked out. His final thought, feeble though it was, and incomplete, did its work.

Port Admiral Haynes was seated at his desk, discussing matters of import with an officeful of executives, when that thought arrived. Hardened old space hound that he was, and survivor of many encounters and hospitalizations, he knew instantly what that thought connoted and from the depths of what dire need it had been sent.

Therefore, to the amazement of the officers in the room, he suddenly leaped to his feet, seized his microphone and snapped out orders. Orders, and still more orders. Every vessel in seven sectors, of whatever class or tonnage, was to shove its detectors out to the limit. Kinnison's speedster is out there somewhere. Find her—get her—kill her drive and drag her in here, to No. 10 landing field. Get a pilot here, fast—no, two pilots, in armor. Get them off the top of the board, too—Watson and Schermerhorn if they're anywhere within range. He then called Base Hospital.

"Lacy!" he barked at the dignified chief surgeon. "I've got a boy out that's badly hurt. He's coming in free. You know what that means. Send over a good doctor. And have you got a nurse who knows how to use a personal neutralizer and who isn't afraid to go into the net?"

"Coming myself. Yes." The doctor's voice was as crisp as the admiral's. "When do you want us?"

"As soon as they get their tractors on that speedster. You'll know when that happens."

Then, neglecting all other business, the port admiral directed in person the far-flung screen of ships searching for Kinnison's flying midget.

Eventually she was found; and Haynes, cutting off his plates, leaped to a closet in which was hanging his own armor. Unused for years, nevertheless it was kept in readiness for instant service; and now, at long last, the old space flea had a good excuse to use it again.

Armored, he strode out into the landing field across the paved way. There awaiting him were two armored figures, the two top-ranking pilots. There were the doctor and the nurse. He barely saw—or, rather, he saw without noticing—a saucy white cap atop a riot of red-bronze-auburn curls, a symmetrical young body in its spotless white. He did not notice the face at all. What he saw was that there was a neutralizer strapped snugly into the curve of her back, that it was fitted properly, and that it was not yet functioning.

*

For this that faced them was no ordinary job. The speedster would land free. Worse, the admiral feared—and rightly—that Kinnison would also be free, but independently, with a latent velocity different from that of his ship. They must enter the speedster, take her out into space and inert her. Kinnison must be taken out of the speedster, inerted, his velocity matched to that of the flier, and brought back aboard. Then and only then could doctor and nurse begin to work on him. Then they would have to land as fast as a landing could be made. The boy should have been in the hospital long ago.

And during all these evolutions and until their return to ground the rescuers themselves would remain inertialess. Ordinarily such visitors left the ship, inerted themselves, and came back to it inert, under their own power. But now there was no time for that. They had to get Kinnison to the hospital; and besides, the doctor and the nurse—particularly the nurse—could not be expected to be space-suit navigators. They would all take it in the net, and that was another reason for haste. For while they were gone their latent velocity would remain unchanged, while the actual velocity of their present surroundings would be changing constantly. The longer they were gone the greater would become the discrepancy. Hence the net.

The net—a leather-and-canvas sack, lined with softly padded inner-spring mattresses, anchored to ceiling and to walls and to floor through every shock-absorbing artifice of steel spring and of rubber cable that the mind of man had been able to devise. It takes something to absorb and to dissipate the kinetic energy which may reside within a human body when its latent velocity does not match exactly the actual velocity of its surroundings—that is, if that body is not to be mashed to a pulp. It takes something, also, to enable any human being to face without flinching the prospect of going into that net, especially in ignorance of exactly how much kinetic energy will have to be dissipated.

Haynes cogitated, studying the erect, supple young back, then spoke, "Maybe we'd better cancel the nurse, Lacy, or get her a suit——"

"Time is too important," the girl herself put in, crisply. "Don't worry about me, admiral; I've been in the net before."

She turned toward Haynes as she spoke, and for the first time he really saw her face. Why, she was a raving beauty—a knock-out—a seven-sector call-out——

"Here she is!" In the grip of a tractor the speedster had flashed to ground in front of the waiting five, and they hurried aboard.

They hurried, but there was no flurry, no confusion. Each knew exactly what to do, and each did it.

Out into space shot the little vessel, jerking savagely downward and sidewise as one of the pilots cut the Bergenholm. Out of the air lock flew the port admiral and the helpless, unconscious Kinnison, inertialess both and now chained together. Off they darted, in a new direction and with tremendous speed, as Haynes cut Kinnison's neutralizer. There was a mighty double flare as the drivers of both space suits struggled against that which had been the young Lensman's latent velocity.

As soon as it was safe to do so, out darted an armored figure with a space line, whose grappling end clinked into a socket of the old man's armor as the pilot rammed it home. Then, as an angler plays a fish, two husky pilots, feet wide-braced against the steel portal of the air lock and bodies sweating with effort, heaving when they could and giving line only when they must, helped the laboring drivers to overcome the difference in velocity.

Soon the Lensmen, young and old, were inside. Doctor and nurse went instantly to work, with the calmness and precision so characteristic of their highly skilled crafts. In a trice they had him out of his armor, out of his leather, and into a hammock, perceiving at once that except for a few pads of gauze they could do nothing for their patient until they had him upon an operating table. Meanwhile the pilots, having swung the hammocks, had been observing, computing, and conferring.

"She's got a lot of speed, admiral—most of it straight down," Watson reported. "On her landing jets it'll take two G's on a full revolution to bring her in. With both of us at the controls we can balance her down, but it'll have to be on her tail and it'll mean over five G's all the way. Which do you want?"

"Which is more important, Lacy, time or pressure?" Haynes transferred decision to the surgeon.

"Time." Lacy decided instantly. "Fight her down!" His patient had been through so much already of force and pressure that a little more would not do additional hurt, and time was most decidedly of the essence.

Starkly incandescent flares ripped and raved from driving jets and side jets. The speedster spun around viciously, only to be curbed, skillfully if savagely, at the precisely right instant. Without an orbit, without even a corkscrew or other spiral, she was going down—straight down. And not upon her under jets was this descent to be, nor upon her more powerful braking jets. Those two master pilots, Prime Base's best, were going to kill the awful inertia of the speedster by "balancing her down on her tail." Or, to translate from the jargon of space, they were going to hold the tricky, cranky little vessel upright upon the terrific blasts of her driving projectors, against the Earth's gravitation and against all other perturbing forces, while her driving force counteracted, overcame, and dissipated the full frightful measure of the kinetic energy of her mass and speed!

And balance her down they did. Haynes was afraid for a while that that intrepid pair were actually going to *land* the speedster on her tail. They didn't—quite—but they had only a scant hundred feet to spare when they nosed her over and eased her to ground on her under jets.

The crash-wagon and its crew were waiting, and as Kinnison was rushed to the hospital the others hurried to the net room. Doctor Lacy first, of course, then the nurse; and, to Haynes' approving surprise, she took it like a veteran. Hardly had the surgeon let himself out of the "cocoon" than she was in it; and hardly had the terrific surges and recoils of her own not inconsiderable one hundred and forty-five pounds of mass abated than she herself was out and sprinting across the sward toward the hospital.

*

Haynes went back to his office and tried to work, but he could not concentrate. He made his way back to the hospital. There he waited, and as Lacy came out of the operating room he buttonholed him.

"How about it, Lacy, will he live?" he demanded.

"Live? Of course he'll live," the surgeon replied, gruffly. "Can't tell you details yet—won't know, ourselves, for a couple of hours yet. Buzz off, Haynes. Come back at six o'clock—not a second before—and I'll tell you all about it."

Since there was no help for it the port admiral did "buzz off," but he was back promptly on the tick of the designated hour.

"How is he?" he began, without preamble. "Will he really live, or were you just giving me a shot in the arm?"

"Better than that, much better," the surgeon assured him. "Definitely so; yes. He is in much better shape than we dared hope. Must have been a very light crash indeed—nothing seriously the matter with him at all. We won't even have to amputate, from what we can see now. He should make a one-hundred-per-cent recovery, not only without artificial members, but with scarcely a scar. He couldn't have been in a space crack-up at all, or he would not have come out with so little injury."

"Fine, doc—wonderful! Now the details."

"Here's the picture." And the doctor unrolled a full-length X-ray print, showing every anatomical detail of the Lensman's interior structure. "First, just notice that skeleton. It is really remarkable. Slightly out of true here and there right now, of course, but I believe that it is going to turn out to be the second absolutely perfect male skeleton I have ever seen. That young man will go far, Haynes."

"Sure he will. Why else do you suppose we put him in gray? But I didn't come over here to be told that. Show me the damage."

"Look at the picture—see for yourself. Multiple and compound fractures, you notice, of legs and arm, and a few ribs. Scapula, of course—there. Oh, yes, there's a skull fracture, too, but it doesn't amount to much. That's all. The spine, you see, isn't injured at all."

"What d'you mean, 'that's all'? How about his wounds? I saw some of them myself, and they were not pin pricks."

"Nothing of the least importance. A few punctured wounds and a couple of incised ones, but nothing even close to a vital part. He won't need even a transfusion, since he stopped the major hemorrhages himself, shortly after he was wounded. There are a few burns, of course, but they are mostly superficial—none that will not yield quite readily to treatment."

"Mighty glad of that. He'll be here six weeks then?"

"Better call it twelve, I think—ten at least. You see, some of the fractures, especially those in the left leg, and a couple of the burns, are rather severe, as such things go. Then, too, the length of time elapsing between injury and treatment didn't do anything a bit of good."

"In two weeks he'll be wanting to get up and go places and do things; and in six he'll be tearing down your hospital, stone by stone."

"Yes." The surgeon smiled. "He is not the type to make an ideal patient; but, as I have told you before, I like to have patients that we do not like."

*

"And another thing. I want the files on his nurses, particularly the red-headed one."

"I suspected that you would, so I had them sent down. Here you are. Glad you noticed MacDougall—she's by way of being my favorite. Clarrissa MacDougall—Scotch, of course, with that name—twenty years old. Height, one hundred sixty-eight centimeters; weight, sixty-six kilos. Here are her pictures. Never mind the conventional photo; this X-ray is the one that counts. Man, look at that skeleton! Beautiful! The only really perfect skeleton I ever saw in a woman——"

"It isn't the skeleton I'm interested in," grunted Haynes. "It's what is outside the skeleton that my Lensman will be looking at."

"You needn't worry about MacDougall," declared the surgeon. "One good look at that picture will tell you that. She classifies. With that skeleton she *has* to. She couldn't leave the beam a millimeter, even if she wanted to. Good, bad, or indifferent; male or female; physical, mental, moral, and psychological; the skeleton tells the whole story."

"Maybe it does to you, but not to me." And Haynes took up the "conventional" photograph—a stereoscope in full and absolutely true color, an almost living duplicate of the girl in question. Her thick, heavy hair was not red, but was a vividly intense and indescribable auburn, a gorgeous mass of coppery bronze, flashed with red and gold. Her eyes—bronze was all that he could think of, with flecks of topaz and of tawny gold. Her skin, too, was faintly bronze, glowing with even more than healthy youth's normal measure of sparkling vitality. Not only was she beautiful, the port admiral decided; in the words of the surgeon, she "classified."

"Hm-m-m. Worse even than I thought," he muttered. "She's a menace to civilization." And he went on to read the documents. "Family—hm-m-m. History . . . . Experiences . . . . Reactions and characteristics . . . behavior . . . psychology . . . mentality—"

"She'll do, Lacy," he advised the surgeon finally. "Keep her on with him."

"But see here, Haynes, you suspicious old granny!" snorted the doctor. "He won't be falling for anybody yet. Why, he's just been unattached. He'll be bulletproof for quite a while. You ought to know that young Lensmen—especially young gray Lensmen—can't see anything but their jobs, for a couple of years, anyway."

"His skeleton tells you that, too, huh?" Haynes grunted, skeptically. "Ordinarily, yes! but you never can tell, especially in hospitals."

"More of your layman's misinformation!" Lacy snapped. "Contrary to popular belief, romance does not thrive in hospitals; except, of course, among the staff. Patients oftentimes think that they fall in love with nurses, but it takes two people to make one romance. Nurses do not fall in love with patients, because a man is never at his best under hospitalization. In fact, the better a man is, the poorer a showing he is apt to make."

"And, as I forget who said, a long time ago, 'no generalization is ever true, not even this one,'" retorted the port admiral. "When it does hit him it will hit hard, and we'll take no chances. How about the black-haired one?"

"Well, I just told you that MacDougall has the only perfect skeleton I ever saw in a woman. Brownlee is very good, too, of course, but—"

"But not good enough to rate Lensman's mate, eh?" Haynes completed the thought. "Then take her out. Pick the best skeletons you've got for this job, and see that no others come anywhere near him. Transfer them to some other hospital—to some other floor of this one, at least. Any woman that he ever falls for will fall for him, in spite of your ideas as to the one-wayness of hospital romance; and I don't want him to have such a good chance of making a dive at something that doesn't rate up. Am I right or wrong, you old sawbones, and for how much?"

"Well, I haven't had time yet to really study his skeleton, but—"

"Better take a week off and study it. I've studied a lot of people in the last sixty-five years, and I'll match my experience against your knowledge of bones, any time. Not saying that he *will* fall this trip, you understand—just playing safe. Good-by, Lacy!"

XVIII.

Kinnison was dragged out of unconsciousness by the knowledge that he had landed his speedster inertialess. He came to—or, rather, to say that he came half to would be a more accurate statement—with a yell directed at the blurrily seen figure in white which he knew must be a nurse.

"Nurse!" Then, as a searing stab of pain shot through him at the effort, he went on, thinking at the figure in white through his Lens: "My speedster! I landed her free! Get the space port—"

"There, there, Lensman," a low, rich voice crooned, and a red head bent over him. "The speedster has been taken care of. Everything is on the needles; go to sleep and rest."

"But my ship—"

"Never mind your ship," the unctuous voice went on. "It was landed and put away—"

"Listen, dumb-bell!" snapped the patient, speaking aloud now, in spite of the pain, the better to drive home his meaning. "Don't try to soothe me! What do you think I am, delirious? Get this and get it straight. I said that I landed that speedster *free*. If you don't know what that means, tell somebody that does. Get the space port—get Haynes—get—"

"We got them, Lensman, long ago." Although her voice was still creamily, sweetly soft, an angry color burned into the nurse's face. "I said everything is on zero. Your speedster was inerted; how else could you be here, inert? I helped do it myself, so I *know* that she is inert."

"QX." The patient relapsed instantly into unconsciousness and the nurse turned to an interne standing by. (Wherever *that* nurse was, at least one doctor could almost always be found.)

"Dumb-bell!" she flared. "What a sweet mess *he's* going to be to take care of! He's not even conscious yet, and he's calling names and picking fights already!"

In a few days Kinnison was fully and alertly conscious. In a week most of the pain had left him, and he was beginning to chafe under restraint. In ten days he was "fit to be tied," and his acquaintance with his head nurse, so inauspiciously begun, developed even more inauspiciously as time went on. For, as Haynes and Lacy had each more than anticipated, the Lensman was by no means an ideal patient. In fact, he was most decidedly the opposite.

Nothing that could be done would satisfy him. All doctors were fatheads, even Lacy, the man who had put him together. All nurses were dumb-bells, even—or specially?—Mac, who with almost superhuman skill, tact and patience had been holding him together. Why, even fatheads and dumb-bells, even high-grade morons, ought to know that a man needed food!

Accustomed to eating everything that he could reach, three or four or five times a day, he did not realize—nor did his stomach—that his now quiescent body could no longer use the five thousand or more calories that it had been wont to burn up, each twenty-four hours, in intense effort. He was always hungry, and he was forever demanding food.

And food, to him, did not mean orange juice or grape juice or tomato juice or milk. Nor did it mean weak tea and hard, dry toast and an occasional soft-boiled egg. If he ate eggs at all he wanted them fried—three or four of them, accompanied by two or three thick slices of ham.

He wanted—and demanded in no uncertain terms, argumentatively and persistently—a big, thick, rare beefsteak. He wanted baked beans, with plenty of fat pork. He wanted bread in thick slices, piled high with butter, and not this quadruply-and-unmentionably-qualified toast. He wanted roast beef, rare, in great chunks. He wanted potatoes and thick

471

brown gravy. He wanted corned beef and cabbage. He wanted pie—any kind of pie—in large, thick quarters. He wanted peas and corn and asparagus and cucumbers, and also various other worldly staples of diet which he often and insistently mentioned by name.

But above all, he wanted beefsteak. He thought about it days and dreamed about it nights. One night in particular he dreamed about it—an especially luscious porterhouse, fried in butter and smothered in mushrooms—only to wake up, mouth watering, literally starved, to face again the weak tea, dry toast, and, horror of horrors, this time a flabby, pallid, flaccid *poached* egg! It was the last straw.

"Take it away," he said, weakly; then, when the nurse did not obey, he reached out and pushed the breakfast, tray and all, off the table. As it crashed to the floor, he turned away, and, in spite of all his efforts, two hot tears forced themselves between his eyelids.

*

It was a particularly trying ordeal, and one requiring all of even Mac's skill, diplomacy, and forbearance, to make the recalcitrant patient eat the breakfast prescribed for him. She was finally successful, however, and as she stepped out into the corridor she met the ubiquitous interne.

"How's your Lensman?" he asked, in the privacy of the diet kitchen.

"Don't call him *my* Lensman!" she stormed. She was about to explode with the pent-up feelings which she, of course, could not vent upon such a pitiful, helpless thing as her star patient. "Beefsteak! I almost wish they *would* give him a beefsteak, and that he'd choke on it—which, of course, he would. He's worse than a baby. I never saw such a—such a *brat* in my life. I'd like to spank him! He needs it. I'd like to know how *he* ever got to be a Lensman, the big, cantankerous clunker! I'm *going* to spank him, too, one of these days; see if I don't!"

"Don't take it so hard, Mac," the interne urged. He was, however, very much relieved that relations between the handsome young Lensman and the gorgeous redhead were not upon a more cordial basis. "He won't be here very long. But I never saw a patient clog *your* jets before."

"You probably never saw a patient like *him* before, either. I certainly hope he never gets cracked up again."

"Huh?"

"Do I have to draw you a chart?" she asked, sweetly. "Or, if he does get cracked up again, I hope they send him to some other hospital." And she flounced out.

Nurse MacDougall thought that when the Lensman could eat the meat he craved, her troubles would be over; but she was mistaken, Kinnison was nervous, moody, brooding, by turns irritable, sullen, and pugnacious. Nor is it to be wondered at. He was chained to that bed, and in his mind was the gnawing consciousness that he had failed. And not only failed—he had made a complete fool of himself. He had underestimated an enemy, and as a result of his own stupidity the whole patrol had taken a setback. He was anguished and tormented.

Therefore: "Listen, Mac," he pleaded one day. "Bring me some clothes and let me take a walk. I need the exercise."

"Not yet, Kim," she denied him gently, but with her entrancing smile in full evidence. "But pretty quick, when that leg looks a little less like a Chinese puzzle, you and nursie go bye-bye."

"Beautiful, but dumb!" the Lensman growled. "Can't you and those cockeyed croakers realize that I'll *never* get any strength back if you keep me in bed all the rest of my life? And don't talk baby talk at me, either. I'm well enough at least so that you can wipe that professional smile off your pan and cut that soothing bedside manner of yours."

"Very well—I think so, too!" she snapped, patience at long last gone. "Somebody should tell you the truth. I always supposed that Lensmen had to have *brains*, but you've acted like a spoiled brat ever since you've been here. First you wanted to eat yourself sick, and now you want to get up, with bones half knit and burns half healed, and undo everything that has been done for you. Why don't you snap out of it and act your age for a change?"

"I never did think nurses had much sense, and now I know they haven't." Kinnison eyed her with intense disfavor, not at all convinced. "I'm not talking about going back to work. I mean a little gentle exercise, and I know what I need."

"You'd be surprised at what you don't know." And the nurse walked out, chin in air. In five minutes, however, she was back, her radiant smile again flashing.

"Sorry, Kim, I shouldn't have blasted off that way, I know that you're bound to back-fire and to have brain storms. I would, too, if I were—"

"Cancel it, Mac," he began, awkwardly. "I don't know why I have to be such a mutt as to be crabbing at you all the time."

"QX, Lensman," she replied, entirely serene now. "I do. You are not the type to stay in bed without it griping you; but when a man has been ground up into such hamburger as you are, he has to stay in bed whether he likes it or not, and no matter how much he pops off about it. Roll over here, now, and I'll give you an alcohol rub. But it won't be long now, really—pretty soon we'll have you out in a wheel chair—"

Thus it went for weeks. Kinnison knew his behavior was atrocious, abominable; but he simply could not help it. Every so often the accumulated pressure of his bitterness and anxiety *would* blow off; and, like a jungle tiger with a toothache, he would bite and claw anything or anybody within reach.

*

Finally, however, the last picture was studied, the last bandage was removed, and he was discharged as fit. And he was not discharged, bitterly although he resented his "captivity," as he called it, until he really *was* fit. Haynes saw to that. And Haynes had allowed only the most sketchy interviews during that long convalescence. Discharged, however, Kinnison sought him out.

"Let me talk first," Haynes instructed him at sight. "No self-reproaches, no destructive criticism. Everything constructive. Now, Kimball, I'm mighty glad to hear that you made a perfect recovery. You were in bad shape. Go ahead."

"You have just about shut my mouth by your first order." Kinnison smiled sourly as he spoke. "Two words—flat failure. No, let me add two more—as yet."

"That's the spirit!" Haynes exclaimed. "Nor do we agree with you that it was a failure. It was merely not a success—so far—which is an altogether different thing. Also, I may add that we had very fine reports indeed on you from the hospital."

"Huh?" Kinnison was amazed to the point of being inarticulate.

"You just about tore it down, of course, but that was only to be expected."

"But, sir, I made such a——"

"Exactly. As Lacy tells me quite frequently, he likes to have patients over there that they don't like. Mull that one over for a bit. You may understand it better as you get older. The thought, however, may take some of the load off your mind."

"Well, sir, I am feeling a trifle low, but if you and the rest of them still think——"

"We do so think. Cheer up and get on with the story."

"I've been doing a lot of thinking, and before I go around sticking out my neck again I'm going to——"

"You don't need to tell me, you know."

"No, sir, but I think I'd better. I'm going to Arisia to see if I can get me a few treatments for swelled head and lame brain. I still think that I know how to use the Lens to good advantage, but I simply haven't got enough jets to do it. You see, I——" He stopped. He would not offer anything that might sound like an alibi; but his thoughts were plain as print to the old Lensman.

"Go ahead, son. We know you wouldn't."

"If I thought at all, I assumed that I was tackling men, since those on the ship were men, and men were the only known inhabitants of the Aldebaranian system. But when those Wheelmen took me so easily and so completely, it became very evident that I didn't have enough stuff. I ran like a scared pup, and I was lucky to get home at all. It wouldn't have happened if——" He paused.

"If what? Reason it out, son," Haynes advised, pointedly. "You are wrong, dead wrong. You made no mistake, either in judgment or in execution. You have been blaming yourself for assuming that they were men. Let us suppose that you had assumed that they were the Arisians themselves. Then what? After close scrutiny, even in the light of after-knowledge, we do not see how you could have changed the outcome." It did not occur, even to the sagacious old admiral, that Kinnison need not have gone in. Lensmen always went in.

"Well, anyway, they licked me, and that hurts," Kinnison admitted, frankly. "So I'm going back to Arisia for more training, if they'll give it to me. I may be gone quite a while, as it may take even them a long time to increase the permeability of my skull enough so that an idea can filter through it in something under a century."

"Um-m-m." Haynes pondered. "It has never been done. They are a peculiar race, incomprehensible—but not vindictive. They may refuse you, but nothing worse—that is, if you do not cross the barrier without invitation. It's a splendid idea, I think; but be very careful to strike that barrier free and at almost zero power—or else don't strike it at all."

*

They shook hands, and in a space of minutes the speedster was again tearing through space. Kinnison now knew exactly what he wanted to get, and he utilized every waking hour of that long trip in physical and mental exercise to prepare himself to take it. Thus the time did not seem long. He crept up to the barrier at a snail's pace, stopping instantly as he touched it, and through that barrier he sent a thought.

"Is it permitted that I approach your planet?" he asked, neither brazenly nor obsequiously. He was matter-of-factly asking a simple question and expecting a simple reply. He knew that to these beings, whatever they really were, salutations and identifications were alike superfluous. Nor was he met as Helmuth had been met.

"Ah, 'tis Kimball Kinnison, of Earth," a slow, deep, measured voice resounded in his brain. "Neutralize your controls. You will be landed."

He did so, and the inert speedster shot forward, to come to ground in a perfect landing at a regulation space port. He strode into the office, to confront the same grotesque, dragonlike entity who had measured him for his Lens not so long ago. Now, however, he stared straight into that entity's unblinking eyes, in silence.

"Ah, you have progressed. You realize now that vision is not always reliable. At our previous interview you took it for granted that what you saw must really exist, and did not wonder as to what our true shapes might be."

"I am wondering now, seriously," Kinnison replied. "And if it is permitted, I intend to stay here until I can see your true shapes."

"This?" And the figure changed instantly into that of an old, white-bearded, scholarly gentleman.

"No. There is a vast difference between seeing something myself and having you show it to me. I realize only too well that you can make me see you as anything you choose. You could appear to me as a perfect copy of myself, or as any other thing, person or object conceivable to my mind."

"Ah, you have indeed progressed. While you were expected to return, you are ahead of time by several of your years. When you approached the barrier it was supposed that you came to ask for some particular information, but now that I search your mind I perceive that what you seek is not mere information, but is indeed knowledge."

"You say that you expected me. How could you know that I was coming? I didn't decide definitely myself until only a couple of weeks ago."

"It was inevitable. When we fitted your Lens we knew that you would return if you lived. As we recently informed that one known as Helmuth——"

"*Helmuth!* You know, then, where——" Kinnison choked himself off. He would not ask for help in that. He would fight his own battles and bury his own dead. If they volunteered the information, well and good; but he would not ask it. Nor did the Arisian furnish it.

"You are right," the sage remarked, imperturbably. "For strong development it is essential that you secure that information for yourself."

Then he continued his previous thought: "As we told Helmuth recently, we have given your civilization an instrumentality—the Lens—by virtue of which it should be able to make itself secure throughout the galaxy. Having given it, we could do nothing more of real or permanent benefit until you Lensmen yourselves began to realize what it was that we had given you. That realization has been inevitable; from the first it has been certain that in time your minds would become strong enough to discover the theretofore unknown depths of power of your Lenses. As soon as any mind made that discovery it would, of course, return to Arisia, the source of the Lens, for additional instruction; which, equally of course, that mind could not have borne previously.

"Decade by decade your minds have become stronger. Finally you came to be fitted with a Lens. Your mind, while pitifully undeveloped, had a latent capacity and a power that made your return here certain. Since your enlensment there has been one other who will return. Indeed, it has become a topic of discussion among us as to whether you or that other would be the first advanced student."

"Who is that other, if I may ask?"

"Your friend, Worsel, the Velantian."

"He's got a real mind—'way, 'way ahead of mine," the Lensman stated, as a matter of self-evident fact.

"In some ways, yes. In other and highly important characteristics, no."

"Huh?" Kinnison exclaimed. "In what possible way have I got it over him?"

"I am not certain that I can explain it exactly in thoughts which you can understand. Broadly speaking, his mind is the better trained, the more fully developed. It is of more grasp and reach, and of vastly greater present power. It is more controllable, more responsive, more adaptable than is yours—now. But your mind, while undeveloped, is of considerably greater capacity than his, and of greater and more varied latent capabilities. Above all, you have a driving force, a will to do, an undefeatable mental urge that no one of his race will be able to develop for many cycles of time to come. Since I selected you as the first to return, I am naturally gratified that you have developed so rapidly."

"Well, I have been more or less under pressure, and I got quite a few lucky breaks. But at that, it seemed to me that I was progressing backward instead of forward."

"It is ever thus with the really competent. Prepare yourself!"

He launched a mental bolt, at the impact of which Kinnison's mind literally turned inside out in a wildly gyrating spiral vortex of dizzyingly confused images.

"Resist!" came the harsh command.

"Resist! How?" demanded the writhing, sweating Lensman. "You might as well tell a fly to resist an inert space ship!"

"Use your will—your force—your adaptability. Shift your mind to meet mine at every point. Apart from these fundamentals neither I nor any one else can tell you how; each mind must find its own medium and develop its own technique. But this is a very mild treatment indeed, one conditioned to your present strength. I will increase it gradually in severity, but rest assured that I will at no time raise it to the point of permanent damage. Constructive exercises will come later; the first step must be to build up your resistance. Therefore, resist!"

The force, which had not slackened for an instant, waxed slowly to the very verge of intolerability; and grimly, doggedly, the Lensman fought it. Teeth locked, muscles straining, fingers digging savagely into the hard leather upholstery of his chair he fought it; mustering his every ultimate resource to the task——

Suddenly, the torture ceased and the Lensman slumped down, a mental and physical wreck. He was white, trembling, sweating, shaken to the very core of his being. He was ashamed of his weakness. He was humiliated and bitterly disappointed at the showing he had made; but from the Arisian there came a calm, encouraging thought.

"You need not feel ashamed; you should instead feel proud, for you have made a start which is really surprising, even to me, your sponsor. This may seem to you like needless punishment, but it is not. This is the only possible way in which that which you seek may be found."

"In that case, go to it," the Lensman declared. "I can take it."

*

Day after day and week after week the "advanced instruction" went on, with the pupil becoming ever stronger, until he was taking without damage thrusts that would have slain him instantly a few weeks since. The bouts became shorter and shorter, requiring as they did such terrific outpourings of mental force that not even the master could stand the awful strain for more than half an hour at a time.

And now these savage conflicts of wills and minds were interspersed with real instruction, with lessons neither painful nor unpleasant. In these the aged scientist probed gently into the youngster's mind, opening it and exposing to its owner's gaze vast caverns whose very presence he had never even suspected. Some of these storehouses were already partially or completely filled, needing only arrangement and connection. Others were nearly empty. These were catalogued and made accessible. And in all, permeating everything, was the Lens.

"Just like clearing out a clogged-up water system; with the Lens the pump that wouldn't work!" exclaimed Kinnison one day.

"More like that than you at present realize," assented the Arisian. "You have observed, of course, that I have not given you any detailed instructions nor pointed out any specific abilities of the Lens which you have not known how to use. You will have to operate the pump yourself; and you have many surprises awaiting you as to what your Lens will pump, and how. Our sole task is to prepare your mind to work with the Lens, and that task is not yet done. Let us on with it."

Eventually the time came when Kinnison could block out entirely the suggestions of his mentor, but he did not reveal that fact; nor, now blocked out, could the Arisian discern it. The Lensman gathered all his force together, concentrated it, and hurled it back at his teacher; and there ensued a struggle none the less Titanic because of its essential friendliness. The very ether seethed and boiled with the fury of the mental forces there at grips, but finally the Lensman beat down the other's screens. Then, boring deep into his eyes, he willed with all his force to see that Arisian as he really was. And instantly the scholarly old man subsided into a—a *brain*! There were a few appendages, of course, and other appurtenances and incidentals to nourishment, locomotion, and the like, but to all intents and purposes the Arisian was simply and solely a brain.

Tension ended; conflict ceased; and Kinnison apologized.

"Think nothing of it." And the brain actually smiled into Kinnison's mind. "Any mind of power sufficient to block mine is, of course, able to hurl no feeble bolts of its own. See to it, however, that you thrust no such force at any lesser mind, or it dies instantly."

Kinnison started to stammer a reply, but the Arisian went on: "No, son, I knew and know that the warning is superfluous. If you were not worthy of this power and were you not able to control it properly you would not have it. You have obtained that which you sought. Go, then, with power."

"But this is only one phase, barely a beginning!" protested Kinnison.

"Ah, you realize even that? Truly, youth, you have come far and fast. But you are not yet ready for more, and it is a truism that the reception of forces for which a mind is not prepared will destroy that mind. Thus, when you came to me you knew exactly what you wanted. Do you know with equal certainty what more you want from us?"

"No."

"Nor will you for years, if ever. Indeed, it may well be that only your descendants will be ready for that for which you now so dimly grope. Again I say, young man, go with power."

Kinnison went.

XIX.

It had taken the Lensman a long time to work out in his mind exactly what it was that he had wanted from the Arisians, and from no single source had the basic idea come. Part of it had come from his own knowledge of ordinary hypnosis; part from the ability of the Overlords of Delgon to control from a distance the minds of others; part from Worsel, who, working through Kinnison's own mind, had done such surprising things with a Lens; and a great part indeed from the Arisians themselves, who had the astounding ability literally and completely to superimpose their own mentalities upon those of others, wherever situate. Part by part and bit by bit the Tellurian Lensman had built up his plan, but he had not had the sheer power of intellect to make it work. Now he had that, and was ready to go.

Where? His first impulse was to return to Aldebaran I and to invade again the stronghold of the Wheelmen, who had routed him so ignominiously in his one encounter with them. Ordinary prudence, however, counseled against that course.

"You'd better lay off them a while, Kim old boy," he told himself quite frankly. "They've got a lot of jets and you don't know how to use this new stuff of yours yet. Better pick out something easier to take!"

Ever since leaving Arisia he had been subconsciously aware of a difference in his eyesight. He was seeing things much more clearly than he had ever seen them before, more sharply and in greater detail. Now this awareness crept into his consciousness and he glanced toward his tube lights. They were out—except for the tiny lamps and bull's-eyes of his instrument board the vessel must be in complete darkness. He remembered then, with a shock, that when he entered the speedster he had not turned on his lights. He could see, and had not thought of them at all!

This, then, was the first of the surprises the Arisian had promised him. He now had the sense of perception of the Rigellians. Or was it that of the Wheelmen? Or both? Or were they the same sense? Intently aware now, he focused his attention upon a meter before him. First upon its dial, noting that the needle was exactly upon the green hair line of normal operation. Then deeper. Instantly, the face of the instrument disappeared—moved behind his point of sight, or so it seemed—so that he could see its coils, pivots, and other interior parts. He could look into and study the grain and particle size of the dense, hard condensite of the board itself. His vision was limited, apparently, only by his will to see!

"Well—ain't—that—something!" he demanded of the universe at large; then, as a thought struck him: "I wonder if they blinded me in the process?"

He switched on his lamps, discovering that his vision was unimpaired and normal in every respect; and a rigid investigation proved to him conclusively that in addition to ordinary vision he now had an extra sense—or perhaps two of them—and that he could change from one to the other, or use them simultaneously, at will! But the very fact of this discovery made Kinnison pause.

He hadn't better go anywhere, or do anything, until he had found out something about his new equipment. The fact was that he didn't even know what he had, to say nothing of knowing how to use it. If he had the sense of a hoot owl he would go somewhere where he could do a little experimenting without getting his jets burned off in case something slipped at a critical moment. Where was the nearest patrol base—a big one, fully defended? Let's see—Radelix would be about the closest Sector Base, he guessed. He'd find out if he could raid that outfit without getting caught at it.

Off he shot, and in due course a fair, green, Earthlike planet lay beneath his vessel's keel. Since it was Earthlike in climate, age, atmosphere, and mass, its people were, of course, more or less similar to humanity in general characteristics, both of body and of mind. If anything, they were even more intelligent than Earthlings, and their patrol base was a very strong one indeed. His spy ray would be useless, since all patrol bases were screened thoroughly and continuously. He would see what a sense of perception would do. From Tregonsee's explanation, it ought to work at this range.

*

It did. When Kinnison concentrated his attention upon the base he saw it. He advanced toward it at the speed of thought and entered it; passing through screens and metal walls without hindrance and without giving alarm. He saw men at their accustomed tasks and heard, or rather sensed, their conversation: the everyday chat of their professions. A thrill shot through him at a dazzling possibility thus revealed.

If he could make one of those fellows down there do something without his knowing that he was doing it, the problem was solved. That computer, say; make him uncover that calculator and set up a certain integral on it. It would be easy enough to get into touch with him and have him do it, but this was something altogether different.

Kinnison got into the computer's mind easily enough, and willed intensely what he was to do; but the officer did not do it. He got up; then, staring about him in bewilderment, sat down again.

"What's the matter?" asked one of his fellows. "Forget something?"

"Not exactly." The computer still stared. "I was going to set up an integral. I didn't want it, either. I could swear that somebody *told* me to set it up."

"Nobody did," grunted the other, "and you'd better start staying home nights. Then maybe you wouldn't get funny ideas."

This wasn't so good, Kinnison reflected. The guy should have done it and shouldn't have remembered a thing about it. Well, he hadn't really thought he could put it across at that distance, anyway. He didn't have the brain of an Arisian. He'd have to follow his original plan, of close-up work.

Waiting until the base was well into the night side of the planet and making sure that his flare baffles were in place, he allowed the speedster to drop downward, landing at some little distance from the fortress. There he left the ship and made his way toward his objective in a rapid series of long, inertialess hops. Lower and shorter became the hops. Then he cut off his power entirely and walked until he saw before him, rising from the ground and stretching interminably upward, an almost invisibly shimmering web of force. This, the prowler knew, was the curtain which marked the border of the reservation, the trigger upon which a touch, either of solid object or of beam, would liberate a veritable inferno of the most destructive agencies generable.

To the eye that base was not impressive, being merely a few square miles of level ground, outlined with low, broad pill boxes and studded here and there with harmless-looking, bulging domes. There were a few clusters of buildings. That was all—to the eye—but Kinnison was not deceived. He knew that the base itself was a thousand feet underground; that the pill boxes housed lookouts and detectors; and that those domes were simply weather shields which, rolled back, would expose projectors second in power not even to those of Prime Base itself.

Far to the right, between two tall pylons of metal, was the gate, the only opening in the web. Kinnison had avoided it purposely; it was no part of his plan to subject himself yet to the scrutiny of the all-inclusive photo cells of that entrance. Instead, with his new sense of perception, he sought out the conduits leading to those cells and traced them down, through concrete and steel and masonry, to the control room far below.

He then superimposed his mind upon that of the man at the board and flew boldly toward the entrance. He now actually had a dual personality; since one part of his mind was in his body, darting through the air toward the portal, while the other part was deep in the base below, watching him come and acknowledging his signals!

*

A trap lifted, revealing a sloping, tunneled ramp, down which the Lensman shot. He soon found a convenient storeroom. Slipping within it, he withdrew his control carefully from the mind of the observer, wiping out all traces of that control as he did so. He then watched apprehensively for a possible reaction. He was almost sure that he had performed the operation correctly, but he had to be absolutely certain; more than his life depended upon the outcome of this test. The observer, however, remained calm and placid at his post; and a close reading of his thoughts showed that he had not the faintest suspicion that anything untoward had occurred.

SUPER PACK

One more test and he was through. He must find out how many minds he could control simultaneously, but he'd better do that openly. No use making a man feel like a fool needlessly. He'd done that once already, and once was too many times.

Therefore, reversing the procedure by which he had come, he went back to his speedster, took her out into the ether, and slept. Then, when the light of morning flooded the base, he cut his detector nullifier and approached it boldly.

"Radelix base! Lensman Kinnison of Tellus asking permission to land. I wish to confer with your Lensman. My screens are down."

A spy ray swept through the speedster, the web disappeared, and Kinnison landed, to be greeted by four fellow Lensmen with a quiet and cordial respect—cordiality for his Lens and respect for his gray. The base commander knew that his visitor was not there purely for pleasure. Gray Lensmen did not take pleasure jaunts. Therefore, he led the way into his private office and shielded it.

"My announcement was not at all informative," Kinnison admitted then, "but my errand is nothing to be advertised. I've got to try out something, and I want to ask you four Lensmen to coöperate with me for a few minutes."

"You need not ask——" began the commander.

"No, this is not an order at all, simply a request. You see, I've been working a long time on a mind controller, and I want to see if it works. I'll put four books on this table, one in front of each of you. Now I would like to try to make two or three of you—all four of you if I can—each bend over, pick up his book, and hold it. Your part of the game will be for each of you to try not to pick it up, and to put it back as soon as you possibly can if I do make you obey. Will you?"

"Sure!" the three of them chorused.

"There will be no mental damage, of course?" asked the commander.

"None whatever, and no after effects. I've had it worked on myself, a lot."

"Do you want any apparatus?"

"No, I have everything necessary. Remember, I want top resistance."

"Let her come! You'll get plenty of resistance. If you can make any one of us pick up a book, after all this warning, I'll say you've got something."

*

Lensman after Lensman, in spite of strainingly resisting mind and body, lifted his book from the table, only to drop it again as Kinnison's control relaxed for an instant. He could control two of them—*any* two of them—but he could not quite handle three. Satisfied, he ceased his efforts.

As the base commander poured long, cold drinks for the sweating five, one of his fellows asked: "What did you do, anyway, Kinnison? Oh, pardon me, I shouldn't have asked."

"Sorry," the Tellurian replied uncomfortably, "but it isn't ready yet. You'll all know about it as soon as possible, but not just now."

"Sure," the Radeligian replied. "I knew I shouldn't have blasted off as soon as I spoke."

"Well, thanks a lot, fellows." Kinnison set his empty glass down with a click. "I can make a nice progress report on this dojig now. And one more thing. I did a little long-range experimenting on one of your computers last night."

"Desk 12? The one who thought he wanted to integrate something?"

"That's the one. Tell him I was using him for a mind-ray subject, will you, and give him this fifty-credit bill? Don't want the boys needling him *too* much."

"Yes, and thanks. And—I wonder——" The base commander evidently had something on his mind. "Say, can you make a man tell the truth with that? And if you can, will you?"

"I think so. Certainly I will, if I can. Why?" Kinnison knew that he could do so, but he did not wish to seem cock-sure.

"There's been a murder." The other three glanced at each other in understanding and sighed with profound relief. "A particularly fiendish murder of a woman—girl, rather. Two men have been accused. Each has a perfect alibi, supported by honest witnesses; but you know how much an alibi means now. Both men tell perfectly straight stories under the Lens and all other lie detectors. Either one of those men is lying with a polish I would never have believed possible, or both are innocent. And one of them *must* be guilty; these are the only suspects. If we try them now we make fools of ourselves; and we can't put off the trial very much longer without losing face. If you can help us out you'll be doing a lot for the patrol throughout this whole sector."

"I can help you," Kinnison declared. "For this, though, better have some props. Make me a box—double Burbank controls, with five baby spots on it—orange, blue, green, purple and red. I want the biggest set of head phones you've got, and a thick, black blindfold. How soon can you try 'em?"

"The sooner the better. It can be arranged for this afternoon."

*

The trial was announced, and long before the appointed hour the great courtroom of that world's largest city was thronged. The hour struck. Quiet reigned. Kinnison, the Lensman, in somber gray, strode to the judge's desk and sat down behind the peculiar box upon it. In dead silence two other Lensmen approached. The first invested him reverently with the head phones; the second so enwrapped his head in black cloth that it was apparent to all observers that his vision was completely obscured.

"Although from a world far distant in space, I have been asked to try two suspects for the crime of murder," Kinnison intoned. "I do not know the details of the crime nor the identity of the suspects. I do know that they and their witnesses are within these railings. I shall now select those who are about to be examined."

Piercing beams of intense, varicolored light played over the two groups, and the deep, impressive voice went on: "I know now who the suspects are. They are about to rise, to walk, and to seat themselves as I shall direct."

They did so, it being plainly evident to all observers that they were under some awful compulsion.

"The witnesses may be excused. Truth is the only thing of importance here; and witnesses, being human and therefore frail, obstruct truth more frequently than they further its progress. I shall now examine these two accused."

Again the vivid, weirdly distorting glares of light lashed out, bathing in intense monochrome and in various ghastly combinations first one prisoner, then the other; the while Kinnison drove his mind into theirs, plumbing their deepest depths. The silence, already profound, became the utter stillness of outer space as the throng, holding its very breath now, sat enthralled by that portentous examination.

"I have examined them fully. You are all aware that any Lensman of the Galactic Patrol may, in case of need, serve as judge, jury, and executioner. I am, however, none of these; nor is this proceeding to be a trial as you may have understood the term. I have said that witnesses are superfluous. I will now add that neither judge nor jury is necessary. All that is required is to discover the truth, since truth is all-powerful. For that reason, also, not even an executioner is needed here—the discovered truth will in and of itself serve us in that capacity.

"One of these men is guilty; the other is innocent. From the mind of the guilty one I am about to construct a composite, not of this one fiendish crime alone, but of all the crimes he has ever committed. I shall project that composite into the air before him. No innocent mind will be able to see any iota of it. The guilty man, however, will perceive its every revolting detail; and, so perceiving, he will forthwith cease to exist in this plane of life."

One of the men had nothing to fear—Kinnison had told him so, long since. The other had been trembling for minutes in uncontrollable paroxysms of terror. Now this one leaped from his seat, clawing savagely at his eyes and screaming in mad abandon.

"I did it! Help! Mercy! Take her away! Oh-h-h——" he shrieked, and died, horribly, even as he shrieked.

Nor was there noise in the courtroom after the thing was over. The stunned spectators slunk away, scarcely daring even to breathe until they were safely outside.

*

Nor were the Radeligian Lensmen much more at ease. Not a word was said until the five were back in the commander's office at base. Then Kinnison, still white of face and set of jaw, spoke. The others knew that he had found the guilty man, and that he had in some peculiarly terrible fashion executed him. He knew that they knew that the man was hideously guilty.

Nevertheless, the Tellurian said, "He was guilty—guilty as all the devils in all the hells of the entire universe. I never had to do that before, and it gripes me—but I couldn't shove the job off onto you fellows. I wouldn't want anybody to see that picture who didn't have to, and without it you could never begin to understand just how atrociously and damnably guilty that hell hound really was."

"Thanks, Kinnison," the commander said, simply. "Kinnison. Kinnison of Tellus. I'll remember that name, in case we ever need you as badly again. But, after what you just did, it will be a long time—if ever. You didn't know, did you, that all the inhabitants of four planets were watching you?"

"Holy rockets, no! Were they?"

"They were. And if the way you scared *me* is any criterion, it will be a long, cold day before anything like that comes up again in this system. And thanks again, gray Lensman. You have done something for our whole patrol this day."

"Be sure to dismantle that box so thoroughly that nobody will recognize any of its component parts." Kinnison managed a rather feeble grin. "One more thing and I'll buzz along. Do you fellows happen to know where there's a good, strong pirate base around here anywhere? And, while I don't want to seem fussy, I would like it all the better if they were warm-blooded oxygen breathers, so that I won't have to wear armor all the time."

"What are you trying to do, give us the needle, or something?" This is not precisely what the Radeligian said, but it conveys the thought Kinnison received as the base commander stared at him in amazement.

"Don't tell me that there *is* such a base around here!" exclaimed the Tellurian in delight. "Is there, really?"

"There is. It is so strong that we have not been able to touch it, and it is manned and staffed by natives of your own planet, Tellus of Sol. We reported it to Prime Base some eighty-three days ago, just after we discovered it. You're direct from there——" He fell silent. This was no way to be talking to a gray Lensman.

"I was in the hospital then, fighting with my nurse because she wouldn't give me anything to eat," Kinnison explained with a laugh. "When I left Tellus I didn't check up on the late data—didn't think I would need it quite so soon. If you've got it, though——"

"Hospital! You?" queried one of the younger Lensmen.

"Yeah—bit off more than I could chew." And the Tellurian briefly described his misadventure with the Wheelmen of Aldebaran I. "This other thing has come up since then, though, and I won't be sticking my neck out that way again. If you've got such a made-to-order base as that in this region, it'll save me a long trip. Where is it?"

They gave him its coördinates and what little information they had been able to secure concerning it. They did not ask him why he wanted that data. They may have wondered at his temerity in daring to scout alone a fortress whose strength had kept at bay the massed patrol forces of the sector; but if they did so they kept their thoughts well screened. For this was a gray Lensman, and very evidently a super-powered individual, even of that select group whose weakest members were powerful indeed. If he felt like talking they would listen; but Kinnison did not talk. He did the listening.

Then, when he had learned everything they knew of the Boskonian base, he said, "Well, I'd better be buzzing. Clear ether, fellows!" And he was gone.

XX.

Out from Radelix and into deep space shot the speedster, bearing the gray Lensman toward Boyssia II, where the Boskonian base was situated. The patrol forces had not even yet been able to locate it definitely; therefore, it must be cleverly hidden indeed. It was manned and staffed by Tellurians—and this was fairly close to the line first taken by the pilot of the pirate vessel whose crew had been so decimated by VanBuskirk and his Valerians. There couldn't be so many Boskonian bases with Tellurian personnel,

Kinnison reflected. It was well within the bounds of possibility, even of probability, that he might again encounter here his former, but unsuspecting, shipmates.

Since the Boyssian system was less than a hundred parsecs from Radelix, a couple of hours found the Lensman staring down upon another green and Earthly world. Very Earthly indeed was this one. There were polar ice caps, areas of intensely dazzling white. There was an atmosphere, deep and sweetly blue, filled for the most part with sunlight, but flecked here and there with clouds, some of which were slow-moving storms. There were continents, bearing mountains and plains, lakes and rivers. There were oceans, studded with islands great and small.

But Kinnison was no planetographer, nor had he been gone from Tellus sufficiently long so that the sight of this beautiful and homelike world aroused in him any qualm of nostalgia. He was looking for a pirate base; and, dropping his speedster as low into the night side as he dared, he began his search.

Of man or of the works of man he at first found little enough trace. All human or pseudohuman life was apparently still in a savage state of development; and, except for a few scattered races, or rather tribes, of burrowers and of cliff or cave dwellers, it was still nomadic, wandering here and there without permanent habitation or structure. Animals of scores of genera and species were there in myriads, but neither was Kinnison a biologist. He wanted pirates; and, it seemed, that was the one form of life which he was *not* going to find!

But finally, through sheer, grim, bulldog pertinacity, he was successful. That base was there, somewhere. He would find it, no matter how long it took. He would find it if he had to examine the entire crust of the planet, land and water alike, kilometer by plotted cubic kilometer! He set out to do just that; and it was thus that he found the Boskonian stronghold.

It had been built directly beneath a towering range of mountains, protected from detection by mile upon mile of native copper and of iron ore.

Its entrances, invisible before, were even now not readily perceptible, camouflaged as they were by outer layers of rock which matched exactly in form, color, and texture the rocks of the cliffs in which they were placed. Once those entrances were located, the rest was easy. Again he set his speedster into a carefully observed orbit and came to ground in his armor. Again he crept forward, furtively and skulkingly, until he could perceive a shimmering web of force.

With minor variations, his method of entry into the Boskonian base was similar to that he had used in making his way into the patrol base upon Radelix. He was, however, working now with a surety and a precision which had then been entirely lacking. His practice upon the patrolmen and his terrific bout with the four Lensmen had given him knowledge and technique. His sitting in judgment, during which he had touched almost every mind in the vast assemblage, had taught him much. And, above all, the grisly finale of that sitting, horribly distasteful and soul-wracking as it had been, had given him training of inestimable value; necessitating as it had the infliction of the ultimate penalty.

*

THE LENSMAN

He knew that he might have to stay inside that base for some time; therefore he selected his hiding place with care. He could, of course, blank out the knowledge of his presence in the mind of any one chancing to discover him; but since such an interruption might come at a critical instant, he preferred to take up his residence in a secluded place. There were, of course, many vacant suites in the officers' quarters—all bases must have accommodations for visitors—and the Lensman decided to occupy one of them. It was a simple matter to obtain a key, and, inside the bare but comfortable little room, he stripped off his armor with a sigh of relief.

Leaning back in a deeply upholstered leather arm chair, he closed his eyes and let his sense of perception roam throughout the great establishment. With all his newly developed power he studied it, hour after hour and day after day. When he was hungry the pirate cooks fed him, not knowing that they did so. He had lived on iron rations long enough. When he was tired he slept, with his eternally vigilant Lens on guard.

Finally, he knew everything there was to be known about that stronghold, and was ready to act. He did not take over the mind of the base commander, but chose instead the chief communications officer as the one most likely and most intimately to have dealings with Helmuth. For Helmuth, he who spoke for Boskone, had for many long months been the Lensman's definite objective.

But this game could not be hurried. Bases, no matter how important, did not call Grand Base except upon matters of the most dire urgency, and no such matter eventuated. Nor did Helmuth call that base, since nothing out of the ordinary was happening—to any pirates' knowledge, that is—and his attention was more necessary elsewhere.

One day, however, there came crackling in a triumphant report: a ship working out of that base had taken noble booty indeed; no less a prize than a fully supplied hospital ship of the patrol itself! As the report progressed, Kinnison's heart went down into his boots and he swore bitterly to himself. How in all the nine hells of Valeria had they managed to take such a ship as that? Hadn't she been escorted?

Nevertheless, as chief communications officer, he took the report and congratulated heartily, through the ship's radio man, its captain, its officers, and its crew.

"Mighty fine work; Helmuth himself shall hear of this," he concluded his words of praise. "How did you do it? With one of the new maulers?"

"Yes, sir," came the reply. "Our mauler, accompanying us just out of range, came up and engaged theirs. That left us free to take this ship. We locked on with magnets, cut our way in, and here we are."

There they were indeed. The hospital ship was red with blood; patients, doctors, internes, officers and operating crew alike had been butchered with the horribly ruthless savagery which was the customary technique of all the agencies of Boskone. Of all that ship's personnel only the nurses lived. They were not to be put to death—yet. In fact, and under certain conditions, they need not die at all.

*

They huddled together, a little knot of white-clad misery in that corpse-littered room, and even now one of them was being dragged away. She was fighting viciously, with fists

486

and feet, with nails and teeth. No one pirate could handle her; it took two of the huskies to subdue that struggling fury. They hauled her upright and she threw back her head, in panting defiance. There was a cascade of red-bronze hair and Kinnison saw—Clarrissa MacDougall! He remembered that there *had* been some talk that they were going to put her back into space service! The Lensman decided instantly what to do.

"Stop, you swine!" he roared through his pirate mouthpiece. "Where do you think you're going with that nurse?"

"To the captain's cabin, sir." The huskies stopped short in amazement as that roar filled the room, but answered the question concisely.

"Let her go!" Then, as the girl fled back to the huddled group in the corner, he said, "Tell the captain to come out here and assemble every officer and man of the crew. I want to talk to everybody at once."

He had a minute or two in which to think, and he thought furiously, but accurately. He had to do something, but whatever he did must be done strictly according to the pirates' own standards of ethics; if he made one slip it might be Aldebaran I all over again. He knew how to keep from making that slip, he thought. But also, and this was the hard part, he must work in something that would let those nurses know that there was still hope, that there were a few more acts of this drama yet to come. Otherwise he knew with a stark, cold certainty what would happen. He knew of what stuff the space nurses of the patrol were made, knew that they could be driven just so far, and no further—alive.

There was a way out of that, too. In the childishness of his hospitalization he had called Nurse MacDougall a dumb-bell. He had thought of her, and had spoken to her quite frankly, in uncomplimentary terms. But he knew that there was a real brain back of that beautiful countenance, that a quick and keen intelligence resided under that red-bronze thatch. Therefore, when the assembly was complete he was ready, and in no uncertain or ambiguous language he opened up.

"Listen, you—all of you!" he barked, savagely. "This is the first time in months that we have made such a haul as this, and you fellows have the brazen gall to start helping yourselves to the choicest stuff before anybody else gets a look at it. I tell you now to lay off, and that goes exactly as it lays. I, personally, will kill any man that touches one of those women before they arrive here at base. Now you, captain, are the first and worst offender of the lot." And he stared directly into the eyes of the officer whom he had last seen entering the dungeon of the Wheelmen.

"I admit that you're a good picker." Kinnison's voice was now venomously soft, his intonation distinct with thinly veiled sarcasm. "Unfortunately, however, your taste agrees too well with mine. You see, captain, I'm going to need a nurse myself. I think I'm coming down with something. And, since I've got to have a nurse, I'll take that red-headed one. I had a nurse once with hair just that color, who insisted on feeding me tea and toast and a soft-boiled egg when I wanted beefsteak; and I am going to take my grudge out on this one here for all the red-headed nurses that ever lived. I trust that you will pardon the length of this speech, but I want to give you my reasons in full for cautioning you that that particular nurse is my own particular personal property. Mark her for me, and see to it that she gets here—exactly as she is now."

The captain had been afraid to interrupt his superior, but now he erupted.

"But see here, Blakeslee!" he stormed. "She ought to be mine, by every right. I captured her; I saw her first; I've got her here——"

"Enough of that back talk, captain!" Kinnison sneered elaborately. "You know, of course, that you are violating every rule by taking booty for yourself before division at base, and that you can be shot for doing it."

"But everybody does it!" protested the captain.

"Except when a superior officer catches him at it. Superiors get first pick, you know," the Lensman reminded him, suavely.

"But I protest, sir! I'll take it up with——"

"Shut up!" Kinnison snarled, with cold finality. "Take it up with whom you please, but remember this, my last warning: Bring her in to me as she is and you live. Touch her and you die! Now, you nurses, come over here to the board!"

*

Nurse Macdougall had been whispering furtively to the others, and now she led the way, head high and eyes blazing defiance. She was an actress, as well as a nurse.

"Take a good, long look at this button, right here, marked 'Relay 46,'" came curt instructions. "If anybody aboard this ship touches any one of you, or even looks at you as though he wants to, press this button and I'll do the rest. Now, you big, red-headed dumb-bell, look at me. Don't start begging—yet. I just want to be sure that you'll know me when you see me."

"I'll know you, never fear, you—you *brat*!" she flared, thus informing the Lensman that she had received his message. "I'll not only know you—I'll scratch your eyes out on sight!"

"That'll be a good trick if you can do it," Kinnison sneered, and cut off.

"What's it all about, Mac? What has got into you?" demanded one of the nurses, as soon as the women were alone.

"I don't know," she whispered. "Watch out; they may have spy rays on us. I don't know anything, really, and the whole thing is too wildly impossible, too utterly fantastic to be even partially true. But pass the word along to all the girls to ride this out, because my gray Lensman is in on it, somewhere and somehow. I don't see how he can be, possibly, but I just know that he is."

For, at the first mention of tea and toast, before she perceived even an inkling of the true situation, her mind had flashed back instantly to Kinnison, the most stubborn and rebellious patient she had ever had—more, the only man she had ever known who had treated her precisely as though she were a part of the hospital's very furniture. As is the way of women—particularly of beautiful women—she had orated of women's rights and of women's status in the scheme of things. She had decried all special privileges, and had stated, often and with heat, that she asked no odds of any man living or yet to be born. Nevertheless, and also beautiful-woman-like, the thought had bitten deep that here was a man who had never even realized that she *was* a woman, to say nothing of realizing that she was an extraordinarily beautiful one! And deep within her and sternly suppressed the thought had still rankled.

At the mention of beefsteak she all but screamed, gripping her knees with frantic hands to keep her emotion down. For she had had no real hope; she was simply fighting with everything she had until the hopeless end, which she had known could not long be delayed. Now she gathered herself together and began to act.

When the word "dumb-bell" boomed from the speaker she knew, beyond doubt or peradventure, that it was Kinnison, the gray Lensman, who was really doing that talking. It was crazy; it didn't make any kind of sense at all; but it was, it must be, true. And, again, woman-like, she knew with a calm certainty that as long as that gray Lensman were alive and conscious, he would be completely the master of any situation in which he might find himself. Therefore, she passed along her illogical but cheering thought, and the nurses, also being women, accepted it without question as the actual and accomplished fact.

They carried on, and when the captured hospital ship had docked at base, Kinnison was completely ready to force matters to a conclusion. In addition to the chief communications officer, he now had under his control a highly capable observer. To handle two such minds was child's play to the intellect which had directed, against their full fighting wills, the minds of two and three quarters alert, powerful, and fully warned Lensmen!

"Good girl, Mac!" he put his mind *en rapport* with hers and sent his message. "Glad you got the idea. You did a good job of acting, and if you can do some more as good we'll be all set. Can do?"

"I'll say I can!" she assented fervently. "I don't know what you are doing, how you can possibly do it, or where you are, but that can wait. Tell me what to do and I'll do it!"

"Make a pass at the base commander," he instructed her. "Hate me—the ape I'm working through, you know—all over the place. Go into it big. You maybe could love him, but if I get you you'll blow out your brains—if any. You know the line—play up to him with everything you can bring to bear, and hate me all to pieces. Help all you can to start a fight between us. If he falls for you hard enough the blow-off comes then and there. If not, he'll be able to do us all plenty of dirt. I can kill a lot of them, but not enough of them quick enough."

"He'll fall," she promised him gleefully, "like ten thousand bricks falling down a well. Just watch my jets!"

*

And fall he did. He had not even seen a woman for months, and he expected nothing except bitter resistance and suicide from any of these women of the patrol. Therefore, he was rocked to the heels—set back upon his very haunches—when the most beautiful woman he had ever seen came of her own volition into his arms, seeking in them sanctuary from his own chief communications officer.

"I hate him!" she sobbed, nestling against the huge bulk of the base commander's body and turning upon him the full blast of the high-powered projectors which were her eyes. "*You* wouldn't be so mean to me, I just know you wouldn't!" And her subtly perfumed head sank upon his shoulder. The base commander was just so much soft wax.

"I'll say I wouldn't be mean to you!" his voice dropped to a gentle bellow. "Why, you little sweetheart, I'll *marry* you. I will, by all the gods of space!"

It thus came about that nurse and base commander entered the control room together, arms about each other.

"There he is!" she shrieked, pointing at the chief communications officer. "He's the one! Now let's see you start something, you rat-faced clunker! There's one real man around here, and he won't let you touch me—ya-a-a!" She gave him a resounding Bronx cheer, and her escort swelled visibly.

"Is—that—so——?" Kinnison sneered. "Get this, baby-face, and get it straight. You were marked as mine as soon as I looked the ship over, and mine you're going to be, whether you like it or not, and no matter what anybody else says or does about it. And as for you, chief, you're too late. I saw her first. And now, you red-headed hussy, come over here where you belong!"

She snuggled closer into the commander's embrace and the big man turned purple.

"What do you mean, too late?" he roared. "You took her away from the ship's captain, didn't you? You said that superior officers get first choice, and they do. I am the boss here and I am taking her away from you. Get me? You'll stand for it, too—yes, and you'll like it. One word out of you and I'll have you spread-eagled across the mouth of No. 6 Projector!"

"Superior officers do not *always* get first choice," Kinnison replied, with bitter, cold ferocity, but choosing his words with care. "It depends entirely upon who the two men are."

Now was the time to strike. Kinnison knew that if the base commander kept his head, the lives of those valiant women were forfeit, and the Lensman's whole plan seriously endangered. He himself could get away, of course—but he could not see himself doing it under these conditions. No, he must goad the commander to a frenzy. Mac would help. In fact, and without his suggestion, she was even then hard at work fomenting trouble between the two men.

"You don't have to take that from anybody, big boy," she was whispering, urgently. "Don't call in a crew to spread-eagle him, either; beam him out yourself. You're a better man than he is, any time. Blast him down. That'll show him who's who around this base!"

"When the inferior is such a man as I am, and the superior such a one as you are," the biting, contemptuously sneering voice went on without a break, "such a bloated swine, such a mangy, low-down cur, such a pussy-gutted tub of lard, such a worthless, brainless spawn of the lowest dregs of the sourest scum of space, such an utterly incompetent and self-opinionated ass as you are——"

The outraged pirate chief, bellowing incoherently in wildly mounting rage, was leaping toward a cabinet in which were kept the DeLameters.

"—then, in that case, the inferior keeps the red-headed wench himself. Put that on a tape, chief, and eat it. Then, if you are too much of a lily-livered coward to do anything about it yourself, have me spread-eagled," the Lensman concluded, cuttingly.

"Blast him! Blast him down!" the nurse had been shrieking; and, as the raging commander neared the cabinet, no one noticed that her latest and loudest scream was "Kim! Blast him down! Don't wait any longer—beam him down before he gets a gun!"

But the Lensman did not act—yet. Although almost every man of the pirate crew stared spellbound, Kinnison's enslaved observer had for many seconds been jamming the subether with Helmuth's personal and urgent call. It was of almost vital importance to his plan that Helmuth himself should see the climax of this scene. Therefore, the communications officer stood immobile, while the profanely raving base commander reached the cabinet, tore it open, seized a DeLameter, and swung it savagely toward him!

XXI.

But Blakeslee, the chief communications officer whose mind and body Kinnison was using, was already armed. Kinnison had seen to that. And as the base commander wrenched open the arms cabinet that happened for which the Lensman had been waiting. Helmuth's private lookout set began to draw current; that potentate himself was now looking on, and the enslaved observer had already begun to trace his beam. Therefore, as the raging commander of Boyssia's pirate base swung about with raised DeLameter he faced one already ablaze; and in a matter of seconds there was only a charred and smoking heap where the commander had stood.

Kinnison wondered that Helmuth's cold voice was not already snapping from the speaker, but he was soon to discover the reason for that silence. Unobserved by the Lensman, one of the observers had recovered sufficiently from his shocked amazement to turn in a riot alarm to the guard room. Five armed men answered that call on the double, stopped and glanced around.

"Guards! Blast Blakeslee down!" Helmuth's unmistakable voice blared from his speaker.

Obediently and manfully enough the five guards tried; and, had it actually been Blakeslee confronting them so defiantly, they probably would have succeeded. It was the body of the communications officer, it is true. The mind operating the muscles of that body, however, was the mind of Kimball Kinnison, gray Lensman, the fastest man with a ray pistol old Tellus had ever produced; keyed up, expecting the move, and with two DeLameters out and poised at hip! This was the being whom Helmuth was so nonchalantly ordering his minions to slay! Faster than any watching eye could follow, five bolts of lightning flicked from Blakeslee's DeLameters. The last guard went down, his head a shriveled cinder, before a single pirate bolt could be loosed.

"You see, Helmuth," Kinnison spoke conversationally to the board, his voice dripping vitriol, "playing it safe from a distance, and making other men pull your chestnuts out of the fire, is a very fine trick as long as it works. But when it fails to work, as now, it puts your tail right into the wringer. I, for one, have been for a long time completely fed up on taking orders from a mere voice; especially from the voice of one whose entire method of operation proves him to be the most pitifully arrant coward in the galaxy."

"Observer! You other at the board!" snarled Helmuth, paying no attention to Kinnison's barbed shafts. "Sound the assembly—armed!"

"No use, Helmuth, he is stone deaf," Kinnison explained, voice sweetly venomous. "I am the only man in this base that you can talk to, and you won't be able to do even that very much longer."

"And you really think that you can get away with this mutiny—this barefaced insubordination—this defiance of *my* authority?"

"Sure I can. That's what I have been explaining to you. If you were here in person, or ever had been; if any of the boys had ever seen you, or had ever known you as anything except a disembodied voice, maybe I couldn't. But, since nobody has ever seen even your face, that gives me a chance——"

*

In his distant base Helmuth's mind had flashed over every aspect of this unheard-of situation. He decided to play for time; therefore, even as his hands darted to buttons here and there, he spoke. "Do *you* want to see my face?" he demanded. "If you do see it, no power in the galaxy——"

"Skip it, chief," sneered Kinnison. "Don't try to kid me into believing that you wouldn't kill me now, under any conditions, if you possibly could. As for your face, it makes no difference whatever to me, now, whether I ever see your ugly pan or not."

"Well, you shall!" And Helmuth's visage appeared, concentrating upon the rebellious officer a glare of such fury and such power that any ordinary man must have quailed. But not Blakeslee-Kinnison!

"Well! Not so bad, at that—the guy looks almost human!" Kinnison exclaimed, in the tone most carefully designed to drive even more frantic the helpless and inwardly raging pirate chieftain. "But I've got things to do. You can guess at what goes on around here from now on." And in the blaze of a DeLameter Helmuth's plate, set, and "eye" disappeared. Kinnison had also been playing for time, and his enslaved observer had checked and rechecked this second and highly important line to Helmuth's ultra-secret base.

Then, throughout the fortress, there blared out the urgent assembly call, to which the Lensman added, verbally: "This is a one-hundred-per-cent call-out, including crews of ships in dock as well as regular base personnel. Bring also the patrol nurses. Come as you are and come fast. The doors of the auditorium will be locked in five minutes and any man outside those doors will be given ample reason to wish that he had been on time."

*

The auditorium was right off the control room, and was so arranged that when a partition was rolled back the control room became its stage. All Boskonian bases were arranged thus, in order that the supervising officers at Grand Base could oversee, through their instruments upon the main panel, just such assemblies as this one was supposed to be. Every man hearing that call assumed that it came from Grand Base, and every man hurried to obey it.

Kinnison rolled back the partition between the two rooms and watched for ray pistols, as the men came streaming into the auditorium. Ordinarily only the guards went armed—three of them were left—but possibly a few of the ship's officers would be wearing their DeLameters .... Four—five—six—the captain and the pilot of the battleship that had

492

captured the nurses, and a vice commander of another, besides the three guards. Knives, billies, and such did not count.

"Time's up. Lock the doors. Bring the keys and the nurses up here," he ordered the six armed men, calling each by name. "You women take these chairs over here; you men sit there."

Then, when all were seated, Kinnison touched a button and the steel partition slid smoothly into place.

"What's coming off here?" demanded a guard. "Where's the commander? How about Grand Base? Look at that board!"

"Sit tight," Kinnison directed. "Hands on knees. I'll burn any or all of you that make a move. I have already burned the old man and five guards, and have put Grand Base out of the picture. Now I want to find out just how we seven stand." The Lensman already knew, but he was not tipping his hand.

"Why we seven?"

"Because we are the only ones who happened to be wearing guns. Every one else of the entire personnel is unarmed and is now locked in the auditorium. You know how apt they are to get out until one of us lets them out."

"But Helmuth—he'll have you blasted for this!"

"Hardly. My plans were not made yesterday. How many of you fellows are with me?"

"What's your scheme?" demanded the vice commander.

"To take these nurses to some patrol base and surrender. I'm sick of this whole game; and, since none of them have been hurt, I figure they'll bring us a pardon and a fresh start—a light sentence at least."

"Oh, so that's the reason——" growled the captain.

"Exactly. But I don't want any one with me whose only thought would be to burn me down at the first opportunity."

"Count me in," declared the pilot. "I've got a strong stomach, but enough of these jobbies is altogether too much. If you can wangle anything short of a life sentence for me I'll go back, but I bloody well won't help you against the——"

"Sure not. Not until after we're out in space. I don't need any help here."

"Do you want my DeLameter?"

"No, keep it. You won't use it on me. Anybody else?"

One guard joined the pilot, standing aside; the other four wavered.

"Time's up!" Kinnison snapped. "Now, you four fellows, either go for your guns or else turn your backs, and do it right now!"

They elected to turn their backs and Kinnison collected their weapons, one by one. Having disarmed them, he again rolled back the partition and ordered them to join the wondering throng in the auditorium. He then addressed the assemblage, telling them what he had done and what he had it in mind to do.

"A good many of you must be fed up on this lawless game of piracy and anxious to resume association with decent men, if you can do so without incurring too great a punishment," he concluded. "I feel quite certain that those of us who man the hospital ship in order to return these nurses to the patrol will get light sentences, at most. Miss MacDougall is head nurse. We will ask her what she thinks."

"Better than that," Mac replied clearly. "I am not merely 'quite certain,' either—I am absolutely sure that whatever men Mr. Blakeslee selects for his crew will not be given any sentences at all. They will be pardoned, and will be given chances at jobs in the merchant service."

"How do you know, miss?" asked one. "We're a black lot."

"I know you are," she replied serenely. "I won't say how I know, but you can take my word for it that I *do* know."

*

"Those of you who want to take a chance with us line up over here," Kinnison directed, and walked rapidly down the line, reading the mind of each man in turn. Many of them he waved back into the main group, as he found thoughts of treachery or signs of inherent criminality. Those he selected were those who were really sincere in their desire to quit forever the ranks of Boskone, those who were in those ranks because of some press of circumstance rather than because of a mental taint. As each man passed inspection he armed himself from the cabinet and stood at ease before the group of women.

Having selected his crew, the Lensman operated the controls that opened the exit nearest the hospital ship, blasted away the panel, so that that exit could not be closed, unlocked a door, and turned to the pirates.

"Vice Commander Krimsky, as senior officer you are now in command of this base," he remarked. "While I am in no sense giving you orders, there are a few matters about which you should be informed. First, I set no definite time as to when you may leave this room. I merely state that you will find it decidedly unhealthy to follow us at all closely as we go from here to the hospital ship. Second, you haven't a ship fit to take the ether, as your blast levers have all been broken off at the pivots. If your mechanics work at top speed, new ones can be put on in exactly two hours. Third, there is going to be a very severe earthquake in precisely two hours and thirty minutes, one which should make this base merely a memory."

"An earthquake! Don't bluff, Blakeslee. You couldn't do *that!*"

"Well, perhaps not a regular earthquake, but something that will do just as well. If you think I am bluffing, wait and find out. But common sense should give you the answer to that. I know exactly what Helmuth is doing now, whether you do or not. At first I intended to wipe you all out without warning, but I changed my mind. I decided that I would rather leave you alive, so that you could report to Helmuth exactly what happened. I wish that I could be watching him when he finds out how badly one man rooked him, and how far from foolproof his system is. But we can't have everything. Let's go, folks!"

As the group hurried away, Mac loitered until she was near the form of Blakeslee, who was bringing up the rear.

"Where are you, Kim?" she whispered urgently.

"I'll join up at the next corridor. Keep further ahead, and get ready to run when we do!"

As they passed that corridor a figure in gray leather, carrying an extremely heavy object, stepped out of it. Kinnison himself set his burden down, yanked a lever, and ran. And as he ran fountains of intolerable heat erupted and cascaded from the mechanism he had left upon the floor. Just ahead of him, but at some distance behind the others, ran Blakeslee and Mac.

"Gosh, I'm glad to see you, Kim!" she panted, as the Lensman caught up with them and all three slowed down. "What is that thing back there?"

"Nothing much—just a KJ4Z hot-shot. Won't do any real damage—just melt this tunnel down so that they can't interfere with our get-away."

"Then you *were* bluffing about the earthquake?" she asked, a shade of disappointment in her tone.

"Hardly," he reproved her. "That isn't due for two hours and a half yet, but it'll happen on schedule time."

"How?"

"You remember about the curious cat, don't you? However, no particular secret about it, I guess—ten duodec bombs placed where they'll do the most good, and timed for exactly simultaneous detonation. Here we are. Don't tell anybody I'm here."

Aboard the vessel, Kinnison disappeared into a stateroom while Blakeslee continued in charge. Men were divided into watches; duties were assigned; inspections were made, and the ship shot into the air. There was a brief halt to pick up Kinnison's speedster; then, again on the way, Blakeslee turned the board over to Crandall, the pilot, and went into Kinnison's room.

There the Lensman withdrew his control, leaving intact the memory of everything that had happened. For minutes Blakeslee was almost in a daze, but struggled through it and held out his hand.

"Mighty glad to meet you, Lensman. Thanks. All I can say is that after I got sucked in I couldn't—"

"Sure, I know all about it. That was one of the reasons I picked you out. Your subconsciousness didn't fight back a bit, at any time. You are to be in charge, from here to Tellus. Please go and chase everybody out of the control room except Crandall."

"Say, I just thought of something!" exclaimed Blakeslee, when Kinnison joined the two officers at the board. "You must be that particular Lensman who has been getting in Helmuth's hair so much lately!"

"Probably. That's my chief aim in life."

"I'd like to see Helmuth's face when he gets the report of this. I've said that before, haven't I? But I mean it now, even more than I did before."

"I'm thinking of Helmuth, too, but not that way." The pilot had been scowling at his plate, and now turned to Blakeslee and the Lensman, glancing curiously from one to the other. "Oh, I say—A Lensman, what? A bit of good old light begins to dawn; but that can wait. Helmuth is after us, foot, horse, and marines. Look at that plate!"

"Four of them already!" exclaimed Blakeslee. "And there's another! And we haven't got a beam hot enough to light a cigarette, nor a screen strong enough to stop a firecracker.

We've got legs, but not as many as Helmuth's fliers. You knew all about that, though, of course, before we started; and from what you have pulled off so far you've got something left on the hooks. What is it? What's the answer?"

"Indetectability," replied Kinnison. "We can detect them, but they can't detect us. All you have to do is to stay out of range of their electros and drill for Tellus."

"That's hard to believe, but it must be true. There are nine ships on the plates now: all Boskonians and all certainly looking for us, but not a one of them has paid any attention to us."

"Nor will they. And, by the way, who or what is Boskone?"

"Nobody knows. Helmuth speaks for Boskone, and nobody else ever does, not even Boskone himself—if there is such a person. Nobody can prove it, but everybody knows that Helmuth and Boskone are simply two names for the same man. Helmuth, you know, is only a voice. Nobody ever saw his face until to-day."

"I'm beginning to think so, myself." And Kinnison strode away, to call at the office of Head Nurse MacDougall.

"Mac, here's a small, but highly important box," he told her, taking the neutralizer from his pocket and handing it to her. "Put it in your locker until you get to Tellus. Then take it, yourself, and give it to Haynes, himself, in person, and to nobody else. Just tell him I sent it. He'll know all about it."

"But why not keep it and give it to him yourself? You're coming with us, aren't you?"

"Probably not all the way. I imagine I'll have to shove off before we get back to Tellus."

"But I want to talk to you!" she exclaimed. "Why, I've got a million questions to ask you!"

"That would take a long time"—he grinned at her—"and time is just what we don't have right now, either of us." And he strode back to the board.

*

He labored for hours at a calculating machine and in the tank; finally to squat down upon his heels, staring at two needlelike rays of light in the tank and whistling softly between his teeth. For those two lines, while exactly in the same plane, did not intersect in the tank at all! Estimating as carefully as he could the point of intersection of the lines, he punched the "cancel" key to wipe out all traces of his work and went to the chart room. Chart after chart he hauled down, and for many minutes he worked with calipers, compass, goniometer, and a carefully set adjustable triangle. Finally he marked a point—exactly upon a small, plain dot already upon the chart—and again whistled.

"Huh!" he grunted. He rechecked all his figures and retraversed the chart, only to have his needle pierce again the same tiny, unmarked dot. He stared at it for a full minute, studying the map all around his marker.

"Star Cluster AC 257-4736," he ruminated. "The smallest, most insignificant, least-known star cluster he could find, and my largest possible error can't put it anywhere else. Kind of thought it might be in a cluster, but I never would have looked *there*. No wonder it took a lot of stuff to trace his beam. It would have to be four numbers Brinnell harder than a diamond drill to work from there."

Again whistling tunelessly to himself, he rolled up the chart upon which he had been at work, stuck it under his arm, replaced the others in their compartments, and went back to the control room.

"How's tricks, fellows?" he asked.

"QX," replied Blakeslee. "We're through them and into clear ether. Not a ship on the plate, and nobody gave us even a tumble."

"Fine! You won't have any trouble, then, from here in to Prime Base. Glad of it, too. I've got to flit. That'll mean long watches for you two, but it can't very well be helped."

"But I say, old bird, I don't mind the watches, but——"

"Don't worry about that, either. This crew can be trusted, to a man. Not one of you joined the pirates of your own free will, and not one of you has ever taken an active part——"

"What are you, a mind reader or something?" Crandall burst out.

"Something like that," Kinnison assented with a grin.

Blakeslee put in, "More than that, you mean. Something like hypnosis, only more so. You think that I had something to do with this, but I didn't. The Lensman did it all himself."

"Um-m-m." Crandall stared at Kinnison, new respect in his eyes. "I knew that unattached Lensmen were good, but I had no idea they were *that* good. No wonder Helmuth has been getting his wind up about you. I'll string along with any one who can take a whole base, single-handed, and make such a bally ass to boot out of such a keen old bird as Helmuth is. But I'm in a bit of a dither, not to say a funk, about what is going to happen when we pop into Prime Base without you. Every man jack of us, you know, is slated for the lethal chamber without trial. Miss MacDougall will do her bit, of course, but what I mean is, has she enough jets to swing it?"

"I think that she has; but to avoid all argument I've fixed that up, too. Here's a tape, telling all about what happened. It ends up with my recommendation for a full pardon for each of you, and for a job at whatever he is found best fitted for. It is signed with my thumb print. Give it or send it to Port Admiral Haynes as soon as you land. I've got enough jets, I think, so that it will go as it lays."

"Jets? You? Right-o! You've got jets enough to lift fourteen freighters off the North Pole of Valeria. What next?"

"Stores and supplies for my speedster. I'm doing a long flit and this ship has supplies to burn, so I'd like to have my little can loaded, Plimsoll down."

*

The speedster was stocked forthwith. Then, with nothing more than a casually waved salute in the way of farewell, Kinnison boarded his tiny space ship and shot away toward his distant goal. Crandall, the pilot, sought his bunk; while Blakeslee started his long trick at the board. In an hour or so the head nurse strolled in.

"Kim?" she queried, doubtfully.

"No, Miss MacDougall. It's Blakeslee. Sorry——"

"Oh, I'm glad of that. That means that everything is settled. Where's the Lensman—in bed?"

"He has gone, miss."

"Gone! Without a word? Where?"

"He didn't say."

"He wouldn't, of course." The nurse turned away, exclaiming inaudibly, "Gone! I'd like to cuff him for that, the lug! *Gone!* Why, the great, big, lobsterly clunker!"

XXII.

But Kinnison was not heading for Helmuth's base—yet. He was splitting the ether toward Aldebaran instead, as fast as his speedster could go; and she was one of the fastest things in the galaxy. He had two good reasons for going there before he attempted Boskone's Grand Base: first, to try out his skill upon nonhuman intellects—if he could handle the Wheelmen he was ready to take the far greater hazard; second, he owed those Wheelmen something, and he did not like to call in the whole patrol to help him pay his debts. He could, he thought, handle that base himself.

Knowing exactly where it was, he had no difficulty in finding the volcanic shaft which formed the entrance to that Aldebaranian base. Down that shaft his sense of perception sped. He found the lookout plates and followed their power leads. Gently, carefully, he insinuated his mind into that of the Wheelman at the board, discovering, to his great relief, that that monstrosity was no more difficult to handle than had been the Radeligian observer. Mind or intellect, he found, were not affected at all by the shape of the brains concerned; quality, reach, and power were the essential factors.

Therefore, he let himself in and took position in the same room from which he had been driven so violently. Kinnison examined with interest the wall through which he had been blown, noting that it had been repaired so perfectly that he could scarcely find the joints which had been made.

These Wheelmen, the Lensman knew, had explosives; since the bullets which had torn their way through his armor and through his flesh had been propelled by that agency. Therefore, to the mind within his grasp he suggested "the place where explosives are kept?" and the thought of that mind flashed to the storeroom in question. Similarly, the thought of the one who had access to that room pointed out to the Lensman the particular Wheelman he wanted. It was as easy as that. And since he took care not to look at any of the weird beings, he gave no alarm.

Kinnison withdrew his mind delicately, leaving no trace of its occupancy, and went to investigate the arsenal. There he found a few cases of machine-rifle cartridges, and that was all. Then he went into the mind of the munitions officer, where he discovered that the heavy bombs were kept in a distant crater, so that no damage would be done by any possible explosion.

"Not quite as simple as I thought," Kinnison ruminated. "But there's a way out of that, too."

There was. It took an hour or so of time; and he had to control two Wheelmen instead of one, but he found that he could do that. When the munitions master took out a bomb-scow after a load of H.E., the crew had no idea that it was anything except a routine job. The only Wheelman who would have known differently, the one at the lookout board, was the other whom Kinnison had to keep under control. The scow went out, got its load, and came back. Then, while the Lensman was flying out into space, the scow dropped down the shaft. So quietly was the whole thing done that not a creature in that whole establishment knew that anything was wrong until it was too late to act—and then none of them knew anything at all. Not even the crew of the scow realized that they were dropping too fast.

Kinnison didn't know what would happen if a mind—to say nothing of two of them—died while in his mental grasp, and he did not care to find out. Therefore, a fraction of a second before the crash, he jerked free and watched.

The explosion and its consequences did not look at all impressive from the Lensman's coign of vantage. The mountain trembled a little, then subsided noticeably. From its summit there erupted an unimportant little flare of flame, some smoke, and an insignificant shower of rock and débris.

However, when the scene had cleared there was no longer any shaft leading downward from that crater; a floor of solid rock began almost at its lip. Nevertheless, the Lensman explored thoroughly all the region where the stronghold had been, making sure that the clean-up had been one-hundred-per-cent effective.

Then, and only then, did he point the speedster's streamlined nose toward Star Cluster AC 257-4736.

*

In his hidden retreat so far from the galaxy's crowded suns and worlds, Helmuth was in no enviable or easy frame of mind. Four times he had declared that that accursed Lensman, whoever he might be, must be destroyed, and had mustered his every available force to that end, only to have his intended prey slip from his grasp as effortlessly as a droplet of mercury eludes the clutching fingers of a child.

That Lensman, with nothing except a speedster and a bomb, had taken and had studied one of Boskone's new battleships, thus obtaining for his patrol the secret of cosmic energy. Abandoning his own vessel, then crippled and doomed to capture or destruction, he had stolen one of the ships searching for him and in it he had calmly sailed to Velantia, right through Helmuth's screen of blockading vessels. He had in some way so fortified Velantia as to capture six more Boskonian battleships. In one of those ships he had won his way back to the Prime Base of the patrol, with information of such immense importance that it had robbed the Boskonian organization of its then overwhelming superiority.

More, he had found or had developed new items of equipment which, save for Helmuth's own success in obtaining them, would have given the patrol a definite and decisive superiority over Boskonia. Now both sides were again equal, except for that Lensman and—the Lens.

Helmuth still quailed inwardly whenever he thought of what he had undergone at the Arisian barrier, and he had given up all thought of securing the secret of the Lens by force or from Arisia. But there must be other ways of getting it——

And just then there came in the urgent call from Boyssia II, followed by the stunningly successful revolt of the hitherto innocuous Blakeslee, culminating as it did in the destruction of Helmuth's every Boyssian device of vision or of communication. Blue-white with fury, the Boskonian high chief flung his net abroad to take the renegade; but as he settled back to await results a thought struck him like a blow from a fist: Blakeslee *was* innocuous. He never had had, did not now and never would have, the cold nerve and the sheer, dominating power he had just shown. Toward what conclusion did that fact point?

The furious anger disappeared from Helmuth's face as though it had been wiped therefrom with a sponge, and he became again the coldly calculating mechanism of flesh and blood that he ordinarily was. This conception changed matters entirely. This was not an ordinary revolt of an ordinary subordinate. The man had done something which he could not possibly do. So what? The Lens again. Again that accursed Lensman, the one who had somehow learned really to *use* his Lens!

"Wolmark, call every vessel at Boyssia base," he directed, crisply. "Keep on calling them until some one answers. Get whoever is in charge there now and put him on me here."

A few minutes of silence followed, then Vice Commander Krimsky reported in full everything that had happened and told of the threatened destruction of the base.

"You have an automatic speedster there, have you not?"

"Yes, sir."

"Turn over command to the next in line, with orders to move to the nearest base, taking with him as much equipment as is possible. Caution him to leave on time, however, for I very strongly suspect that it is now too late to do anything to prevent the destruction of the base. You, alone, take the speedster and bring away the personal files of the men who went with Blakeslee. A speedster will meet you at a point to be designated later and relieve you of the records."

*

An hour passed—two, then three.

"Wolmark! Blakeslee and the hospital ship have vanished, I presume?"

"They have." The underling, expecting a verbal flaying, was greatly surprised at the mildness of his chief's tone and at the studious serenity of his face.

"Come to the center." Then, when the lieutenant was seated, "I do not suppose that you as yet realize what—or rather, who—it is that is doing this?"

"Why, Blakeslee is doing it, of course."

"I thought so, too, at first. That was what the one who really did it wanted us to think."

"It must have been Blakeslee. We saw him do it, sir. How could it have been any one else?"

"I do not know. I do know, however, and so should you, that he could not have done it. Blakeslee, of himself, is of no importance whatever."

"We'll catch him, sir, and make him talk. He can't get away."

"You will find that you will not catch him and that he can get away. Blakeslee alone, of course, could not do so, any more than he could have done the things he apparently did do. No, Wolmark, we are not dealing with Blakeslee."

"Who then, sir?"

"Haven't you deduced that yet? The Lensman, fool—the same Lensman who has been thumbing his nose at us ever since he took one of our first-class battleships with a speed boat and a firecracker."

"But—great blinding rockets, how?"

"Again I admit that I do not know—yet. The connection, however, is quite evident—thought. Blakeslee was thinking thoughts utterly beyond him. The Lens comes from Arisia. The Arisians are masters of thought—of mental forces and processes incomprehensible to any of us. These are the elements which, when fitted together, will give us the complete picture."

"Still I don't see how they fit."

"Neither do I—yet. However, it should be clear to you that we do not want that Lensman thinking such thoughts as that into this base."

"We certainly do not. However, surely he can't trace——"

"Just a moment! The time has come when it is no longer safe to say what that Lensman cannot do. Our communicator beams are hard and tight, yes. But any beam can be tapped if enough power be applied to it, and any beam that can be tapped can be traced. I expect him to visit us here, and we shall be prepared for his visit. That is the reason for this conference with you. Here is a device which generates a field through which no thought can penetrate. I have had this device for some time, but for obvious reasons have not released it. Here are the diagrams and complete constructional data. Have a few hundred of them made with all possible speed, and see to it that every being upon this planet wears one continuously. Impress upon every one, and I will also, that it is of the utmost importance that absolutely continuous protection be maintained, even while changing batteries.

"Experts have been working for some time upon the problem of protecting the entire planet with such a screen, and there is some little hope of success in the near future; but individual protection will still be of the utmost importance. We cannot impress it too forcibly upon every one that every man's life is dependent upon each one maintaining his thought-screen in full operation at all times. That is all."

*

When the messenger brought in the personal files of Blakeslee and the other deserters, Helmuth and his psychologists went over them with minutely painstaking care. The more they studied them the clearer it became that the chief's conclusion was the correct one. Some one had, in some way, brought an extraordinary mental pressure to bear.

Reason and logic told Helmuth that the Lensman's only purpose in attacking the Boyssian base was to get a line on Grand Base; that Blakeslee's flight and the destruction of the base were merely diversions to obscure the real purpose of the visit; that the Lensman had staged that theatrical performance especially to hold him, Helmuth, while his beam was being traced, and that was the only reason why the visiset was not sooner put out of action; and, finally, that the Lensman had scored another clean hit.

He, Helmuth himself, had been caught flat-footed. His face hardened and his jaw set at the thought. But he had not been taken in. He was forewarned and he would be ready, for he was coldly certain that Grand Base and he himself were the real objectives of the

Lensman. That Lensman knew full well that any number of ordinary bases, ships, and men could be destroyed without damaging, materially, the Boskonian cause.

Steps must be taken to make Grand Base as impregnable to mental forces as it already was to physical ones. Otherwise, it might well be that even Helmuth's own life would presently be at stake, and that life was a thing precious indeed. Therefore, council after council was held; every contingency that could be thought of was brought up and discussed; every possible precaution was taken. In short, every resource of Grand Base was devoted to the warding off of any possible mental threat which might be forthcoming.

*

Kinnison approached that star cluster with care. Small though it was, as cosmic groups go, it yet was composed of some hundreds of stars and an unknown number of planets. Any one of those planets might be the one he sought, and to approach it unknowingly might prove disastrous. Therefore, he slowed down to a crawl and crept up, light year by light year, with his ultra-powered detectors fanning out before him to the limit of their unimaginable reach.

He had more than half expected that he would have to search that cluster, world by world; but in that, at least, he was pleasantly disappointed. One corner of one of his plates began to show a dim glow of detection. A bell tinkled and Kinnison directed his most powerful master plate into the region indicated. This plate, while of very narrow field, had tremendous resolving power and magnification; and in it he saw that there were eighteen small centers of radiation surrounding one vastly larger one.

There was no doubt then as to the location of Helmuth's base, but there arose the question of approach. The Lensman had not considered the possibility of a screen of lookout ships. If they were close enough together so that their electromagnetics had even a fifty-per-cent overlap, he might as well go back home. What were those outposts, and exactly how closely were they spaced? He observed, advanced, and observed again; computing finally that, whatever they were, they were so far apart that there could be no possibility of any electro overlap at all. He could get between them easily enough. He wouldn't even have to baffle his flares.

They could not be guards at all, Kinnison concluded, but must be simply outposts, set far outside the solar system of the planet they guarded; not to ward off one-man speedsters, but to warn Helmuth of the possible approach of a force large enough to threaten the Grand Base of Boskonia.

Closer and closer Kinnison flashed, discovering that the central object was indeed a base, startling in its immensity and completely and intensively fortified; and that the outposts were huge, floating fortresses, practically stationary in space relative to the sun of the solar system they surrounded. The Lensman aimed at the center of the imaginary square formed by four of the outposts and drove in as close to the planet as he dared. Then, going inert, he set his speedster into an orbit—he did not care particularly about its shape, provided that it was not too narrow an ellipse—and cut off all his power. He was now safe from detection. Leaning back in his seat and closing his eyes, he hurled his sense of perception into and through the massed fortifications of Grand Base.

For a long time he did not find a single living creature. He traversed hundreds of miles, perceiving only automatic machinery, bank after towering, mile-square bank of accumulators, and remote-controlled projectors and other weapons and apparatus. Finally, however, he came to Helmuth's dome; and in that dome he received another severe shock. The personnel in that dome were to be numbered by the hundreds, but he could not make mental contact with any one of them. He could not touch their minds at all; he was stopped cold. Every member of Helmuth's band was protected by a thought-screen as effective as the Lensman's own!

Around and around the planet the speedster circled, while Kinnison struggled with this new and entirely unexpected setback. This looked as though Helmuth knew what was coming. Helmuth was nobody's fool, Kinnison knew; but how could he possibly have suspected that a mental attack was in the book? Perhaps he was just playing safe. If so, the Lensman's chance would come. Men would be careless; batteries weakened and would have to be changed.

But this hope was also vain, as continued watching revealed that each battery was listed, checked, and timed. Nor was any screen released, even for an instant, when its battery was changed; the fresh power source being slipped into service before the weakening one was disconnected.

"Well, that proves that Helmuth *knows*," Kinnison cogitated, after watching vainly several such changes. "He's a wise old bird. The guy really has jets. I still don't see what I did that could have put him wise to what was going on."

*

Day after day the Lensman studied every detail of construction, operation, and routine of that base, and finally an idea began to dawn. He shot his attention toward a barracks he had inspected frequently of late, but stopped, irresolute.

"Uh-uh, Kim, maybe better not," he advised himself. "Helmuth's mighty quick on the trigger, to figure out that Boyssian thing so fast——"

His projected thought was sheared off without warning, thus settling the question definitely. Helmuth's big apparatus was at work; the whole planet was screened against thought.

"Oh, well, probably better, at that," Kinnison went on arguing with himself. "If I'd tried it out maybe he'd have got onto it and laid me a stymie next time, when I really need it."

Since he had accomplished everything that he could do for the time being, he went free and hurled his speedster toward Earth, now distant indeed. Several times during that long trip he was sorely tempted to call Haynes through his Lens and get things started; but he always thought better of it. This was altogether too important a thing to be sent through so much subether, or even to be thought about except inside an absolutely thought-tight room. And besides, every waking hour of even that long trip could be spent very profitably in digesting and correlating the information he had obtained and in mapping out the salient features of the campaign that was to come. Therefore, before time began to drag, Kinnison landed at Prime Base and was granted instant audience with Port Admiral Haynes.

"Mighty glad to see you, son," Haynes greeted the young Lensman cordially, as he sealed the room thought-tight. "Since you came in under your own power, I assume that you are here to make a constructive report?"

"Better than that, sir. I'm here to start something in a big way. I know at last where their Grand Base is, and have detailed plans of it. I think that I know who and where Boskone is. I know where Helmuth is, and I have worked out a plan whereby, if it works, we can wipe out that base, Boskone, Helmuth, and all the lesser master minds, at one wipe."

"Holy jumping rockets!" For the first time since Kinnison had known him the old man lost his poise. He leaped to his feet and seized Kinnison by the arm. "I knew you were good, but not *that* good! The Arisians gave you the treatments you wanted, then?"

"They sure did," and the younger man reported as briefly as possible everything that had happened, then outlined the plan upon which he had been working so long.

"I am just as sure that Helmuth is Boskone as I can be of anything that can't be proved," Kinnison declared, bending over a huge chart and sketching rapidly. "Helmuth speaks for Boskone, and nobody else ever does, not even Boskone himself. None of the other big shots know anything about Boskone or ever heard him speak; but they all jump through their hoops when Helmuth, 'speaking for Boskone,' cracks the whip. And I couldn't get a trace of Helmuth ever taking anything up with any higher-ups. Therefore, I am dead certain that when we get Helmuth we get Boskone.

*

"But that's going to be a real job of work. I scouted his headquarters from stem to gudgeon, as I told you; and Grand Base is absolutely impregnable as it stands. I never imagined anything like it. It makes Prime Base here look like a deserted cross roads after a hard winter. They've got screens, pits, projectors, accumulators, all on a gigantic scale. In fact, they've got everything. But you can get all that from the tape. I have learned definitely that we cannot take them by any possible direct frontal attack. Even if we attacked with every ship and mauler we've got throughout the galaxy they could stand us off. And they can match us, ship for ship. We'd never get near that base at all if they knew that we were coming."

"Well, if it's such an impossible job, what——"

"I'm coming to that. It is impossible as it stands; but there's a good chance that I'll be able to soften Grand Base up. You know, like a worm—bore from within. Anyway, that's the only possible way to do it, so I've got to try it. You'll have to put detector nullifiers on every ship assigned to the job, but that'll be easy. I would suggest sending all the maulers and first-class battleships we've got, but you will, of course, work that out later."

"The important thing, as I gather it, is timing."

"Absolutely to the minute, since I won't be able to communicate, once I get inside their thought-screens. How long will it take to concentrate everything we've got and put it in that cluster?"

"Seven weeks—eight at the outside."

"Plus two for allowances. QX. At exactly Hour 20, ten weeks from to-day, let every projector of every vessel that you can possibly get there cut loose on that base with everything they can pour in. Where's that other print? Here—twenty-six main objectives, you see. Blast them all, simultaneously to the second. If they all go down, the rest will be possible. If not, it will be just too bad. Then work along these lines here, straight from those twenty-six stations to the dome, blasting everything as you go. Make it last exactly fifteen minutes, not a minute more or less. If, by fifteen minutes after twenty, the main dome hasn't surrendered by cutting its screens, blast that, too, if you can. It'll take a lot of blasting, I'm afraid. From then on you and the fleet commander will have to do whatever is appropriate to the occasion."

"Your plan doesn't cover that, apparently. Where will you be? How will *you* be fixed—if the main dome does not cut its screens?"

"I'll be dead, and you'll be just starting the damnedest war that this galaxy ever saw."

XXIII.

While servicing and checking over the speedster required only a couple of hours, Kinnison did not leave Earth for almost two days. He had requisitioned much special equipment, the construction of one item of which—a suit of armor such as had never been seen upon Earth before—caused almost all of the delay. When it was ready the greatly interested port admiral accompanied the young Lensman out to the steel-lined, sand-filled concrete dugout, in which the suit had already been mounted upon a remote-controlled dummy. Fifty feet from that dummy there was a heavy, water-cooled machine rifle, with its armored crew standing by. As the two approached the crew leaped to attention.

"As you were," Haynes instructed.

"You checked those cartridges against those I brought in from Aldebaran I?" asked Kinnison of the officer in charge, as, accompanied by the port admiral, he crouched down behind the shields of the control panel.

"Yes, sir. These are twenty-five per cent over, as you specified."

"QX—commence firing!" Then, as the weapon clamored out its stuttering, barking roar, Kinnison made the dummy stoop, turn, bend, twist, and dodge, so as to bring its every plate, joint, and member into the hail of steel. The uproar stopped.

"One thousand rounds, sir," the officer reported.

"No holes—no dents—not a scratch or a scar," Kinnison reported, after a minute examination, and got into the thing. "Now give me two thousand rounds, unless I tell you to stop. Shoot!"

Again the machine rifle burst into its ear-shattering song of hate; and, strong as Kinnison was and powerfully braced by the blast of his drivers, he could not stand against the awful force of those bullets. Over he went, backward, and the firing ceased.

"Keep it up!" he snapped. "Think they're going to quit shooting at me because I fall down?"

"But you had had nineteen hundred!" protested the officer.

"Keep on pecking until you run out of ammunition or until I tell you to stop," ordered Kinnison. "I've got to learn how to handle this thing under fire." The storm of metal again began to crash against the reverberating shell of steel.

It hurled the Lensman down, rolled him over and over, slammed him against the backstop. Again and again he struggled upright, only to be hurled again to ground as the riflemen, really playing the game now, swung their leaden hail from part to part of the armor, and varied their attack from steady fire to short, but savage, bursts. But finally, in spite of everything the gun crew could do, Kinnison learned his controls.

*

Then, drivers flaring, he faced that howling, chattering muzzle and strode straight into the stream of smoke- and flame-enshrouded steel. Now the air was literally full of metal. Bullets and fragments of bullets whined and shrieked in mad abandon as they ricocheted off that armor in all directions. Sand and bits of concrete flew hither and yon, filling the atmosphere of the dugout. The rifle yammered at maximum, with its sweating crew laboring mightily to keep its voracious maw full-fed. But, in spite of everything, Kinnison held his line and advanced. He was a bare ten feet from that raving, steel-vomiting muzzle when the firing again ceased.

"Twenty thousand, sir," the officer reported, crisply. "We'll have to change barrels before we can give you any more."

"That's enough!" snapped Haynes. "Come out of there!"

Out Kinnison came. He removed heavy ear plugs, swallowed four times, blinked and grimaced. Finally he spoke. "It works perfectly, sir, except for the noise. It's a good thing I've got a Lens. Even though I was wearing plugs, I won't be able to hear a sound for three days!"

"How about the springs and shock absorbers? Are you bruised anywhere? You took some real bumps."

"Perfect—not a bruise. Let's look her over."

Every inch of that armor's surface was now marked by blurs, where the metal of the bullets had rubbed on the shining alloy, but that surface was neither scratched, scored, nor dented.

"QX, boys—thanks," Kinnison dismissed the riflemen. They probably wondered how any man could see through a helmet built up of inches-thick laminated alloys, with neither window nor port through which to look; but if so, they made no mention of their curiosity. They, too, were patrolmen.

"Is that thing an armor or a personal tank?" asked Haynes. "I aged ten years while that was going on; but, at that, I'm glad you insisted on testing it as you did. You can get away with anything now."

"I've found that it is much better technique to learn things among friends here, than among enemies." Kinnison laughed. "It's heavy, of course—over three hundred kilos, net. I won't be walking around in it much, though; and even that little I'll be flying it instead of walking it. Well, sir, since everything's all set, I think I'd better fly it over to the speedster and start flitting, don't you? I don't know exactly how much time I am going to need on Trenco."

"Might as well," the port admiral agreed, as casually, and Kinnison was gone.

"What a man!" Haynes stared after the monstrous figure until it vanished in the distance, then strolled slowly toward his office, thinking as he went.

SUPER PACK

*

Nurse MacDougall had been highly irked and incensed at Kinnison's casual departure, without idle conversation or formal leave takings. Not so Haynes. That seasoned campaigner knew that gray Lensmen—particularly young gray Lensmen—were prone to get that way. He knew, in a way she never would and never could know, that Kinnison was no longer of Earth.

He was now only of the galaxy, not of any one tiny dust grain of it. He was of the patrol. He *was* the patrol, and he was taking his new responsibilities very seriously indeed. In his fierce zeal to drive his campaign through to a successful end he would use man or woman, singly or in groups, ships, even Prime Base itself, exactly as he had used them: as pawns, as mere tools, as means to an end. And, having used them, he would leave them as unconcernedly and as unceremoniously as he would drop pliers and spanner, and with no realization that he had violated any of the nicer amenities of life as it is lived!

And as he strolled along and thought, the port admiral smiled quietly to himself. He knew, as Kinnison would learn in time, that the universe was vast, that time was long, and that the Scheme of Things, comprising the whole of eternity and the cosmic all, was a something incomprehensibly immense indeed. With which cryptic thought the space-hardened veteran sat down at his desk and resumed his interrupted labors.

But Kinnison had not yet attained Haynes' philosophic viewpoint, any more than he had his age, and to him the trip to Trenco seemed positively interminable. Eager as he was to put his plan of campaign to the test, he found that mental urgings, or even audible invectives, would not make the speedster go any faster than the already incomprehensible top speed of her drivers' maximum blast. Nor did pacing up and down the little control room seem to help very much. Physical exercise he had to perform, but it did not satisfy him. Mental exercise was impossible; he could think of nothing except Helmuth's base.

*

Eventually, however, he approached Trenco and located, without difficulty, the patrol's space port. Fortunately, it was then at about eleven o'clock, so that he did not have to wait long to land. He drove downward inert, sending a thought ahead of him: "Lensman of Trenco Space Port—Tregonsee or his relief? Lensman Kinnison of Sol III asking permission to land."

"It is Tregonsee," came back the thought. "Welcome, Kinnison. You are on the correct line. You have, then, perfected an apparatus to see truly in this distorting medium?"

"I didn't perfect it—it was given to me."

The landing bars lashed out, seized the speedster, and eased her down into the lock; and, as soon as she had been disinfected, Kinnison went into consultation with Tregonsee. The Rigellian was a highly important factor in the Tellurian's scheme; and, since he was also a Lensman, he was to be trusted implicitly.

Therefore, Kinnison told him briefly what occurred and what he had it in mind to do, concluding: "So you see, I need about fifty kilograms of thionite. Not fifty milligrams, or even grams, but fifty *kilograms*; and, since there probably isn't that much of the stuff loose in the whole galaxy, I came over here to ask you to make it for me."

507

THE LENSMAN

Just like that. Calmly asking a Lensman, whose sworn duty it was to kill any being even attempting to gather a single Trenconian plant, to make for him more of the prohibited drug than was ordinarily processed throughout the galaxy during a solarian month! It would be just such an errand were one to walk into the treasury department in Washington and inform the chief of the narcotics bureau, quite nonchalantly, that he had dropped in to pick up ten tons of heroin! But Tregonsee did not flinch or question—he was not even surprised. This was a gray Lensman, and his plan would work.

"That should not be too difficult," Tregonsee replied, after a moment's study. "We have several thionite processing units, confiscated from zwilnik ships and not yet picked up by headquarters; and all of us are, of course, quite familiar with the technique of extracting and purifying the drug."

He issued orders and shortly Trenco Space Port presented the astounding spectacle of a full crew of the Galactic Patrol devoting its every energy to the whole-hearted breaking of the one law it was supposed most rigidly, and without fear or favor, to enforce!

*

It was a little after noon, the calmest hour of Trenco's day. The wind had died to "nothing"; which, on that planet, meant that a strong man could stand against it; could even, if he were agile as well as strong, walk about in it. Therefore, Kinnison donned his light armor and was soon busily harvesting the purple-leaved plants, which, he had been informed, were the richest sources of thionite.

He had been working for only a few minutes when one of the "natives" came crawling up to him; and, after ascertaining that his hard steel armor was not good to eat, drew off and observed him intently. Here was another opportunity for practice, and in a flash the Lensman availed himself of it. Having practiced for hours upon the minds of various Earthly animals, he entered this mind easily enough, finding that the Trenconian "flat" was considerably more intelligent than a dog. So much so, in fact, that the race had already developed a fairly comprehensive language.

Therefore, it did not take long for the Lensman to learn to use his subject's peculiar limbs and other members, and soon the flat was working like a Trojan. And, since he was ideally adapted for his wildly raging Trenconian environment, he actually accomplished more than all the rest of the force combined.

"It's a dirty trick I'm playing on you, fellow," Kinnison told his helper after a while. "Come on into the receiving room and I'll see if I can square it with you."

Since food was the only logical tender, Kinnison brought out from his speedster a small can of salmon, a package of cheese, a bar of chocolate, a few lumps of sugar, and a potato, offering them to the Trenconian in order. The salmon and the cheese were both highly acceptable fare. The morsel of chocolate was a delightfully surprising delicacy. The lump of sugar, however, was what really rang the bell. Kinnison's own mind felt the shock of pure ecstasy as that wonderful substance dissolved in the trenco's mouth. He also ate the potato, of course—any Trenconian animal will, at any time, eat anything containing carbon, even limerock, gasoline, or truck grease—but it was merely food, nothing to rave about.

Knowing now what to do, Kinnison led his assistant out into the howling, shrieking gale and released him from control, throwing a lump of sugar upwind as he did so. The trenco seized it in the air, ate it, and went into a very hysteria of joy.

"More! More!" he insisted, attempting to climb up the Lensman's armored leg.

"You must work for more of it, if you want it," Kinnison explained. "Break off these plants here and carry them over into that empty thing over there, and you get more."

This was an entirely new idea to the native, but after Kinnison had taken hold of his mind and had shown him how to do consciously that which he had been doing unconsciously for an hour, he worked willingly enough. In fact, before it started to rain, thereby putting an end to the labor of the day, there were a dozen of them toiling at the harvest and the crop was coming in as fast as the entire crew of Rigellians could process it. And even after the space port was sealed they crowded up, paying no attention to the rain, bringing in their small loads of leaves and plaintively asking admittance.

*

It took some little time for Kinnison to make them understand that the day's work was done, but that they were to come back to-morrow morning. Finally, however, he succeeded in getting the idea across, and the last disconsolate turtle-man went reluctantly away. But sure enough, next morning, even before the mud had dried, the same twelve were back on the job. The two Lensmen wondered simultaneously how those trencos could have found the space port. Or had they stayed near it through the storm and flood of the night?

"I don't know," Kinnison answered the unasked question, "but I can find out." Again and more carefully he examined the minds of two or three of them. "No, they didn't follow us," he reported then. "They're not as dumb as I thought they were. They have a sense of perception, Tregonsee, about the same thing, I judge, as yours—perhaps even more so. I wonder—why couldn't they be trained into mighty efficient police assistants on this planet?"

"The way you handle them, yes. I can converse with them a little, of course, but they have never before shown any willingness to coöperate with us."

"You never fed them sugar." Kinnison laughed. "You have sugar, of course—or do you? I was forgetting that many races do not use it at all."

"We Rigellians are one of those races. Starch is so much tastier and so much better adapted to our body chemistry that sugar is used only as a chemical. We can, however, obtain it easily enough. But there is something else. You can tell these trencos what to do and make them really understand you. I cannot."

"I can fix that up with a simple mental treatment that I can give you in five minutes. Also, I can let you have enough sugar to carry on with until you can get in a supply of your own."

In the few minutes during which the Lensmen had been discussing their potential allies, the mud had dried and the amazing coverage of dense, succulent "grass" was springing visibly into being. So incredibly rapid was its growth that in ten minutes more the plants were large enough to be gathered. The leaves were lush and rank, in color a vivid, crimsonish purple.

"These early-morning plants are the richest of any in thionite, but the zwilniks can never get more than a handful of them because of the wind," remarked the Rigellian. "Now, if you will give me that treatment, I will see what I can do with the Flats."

Kinnison did so, and the trencos worked for Tregonsee as industriously as they had for Kinnison—and ate his sugar as rapturously.

"That is enough," decided the Rigellian presently. "This will finish your fifty kilograms and to spare."

He then "paid off" his now enthusiastic helpers, with instructions to return when the sun was directly overhead, for more work and more sugar. And this time they did not complain, nor did they loiter around or bring in unwanted vegetation. They were learning fast.

Well before noon the last kilogram of impalpable, purplish-blue powder was put into its impermeable sack. The machinery was cleaned; the untouched leaves, the waste, and the contaminated air were blown out of the space port; and the room and its occupants were sprayed with anti-thionite. Then and only then did the crew remove their masks and air filters. Trenco Space Port was again a patrol post, no longer a zwilnik's paradise.

"Thanks, Tregonsee, and all you fellows——" Kinnison paused, then went on, dubiously, "I don't suppose that you will——"

"We will not," declared Tregonsee. "Our time is yours, as you know, without payment; and time is all that we gave you, really."

"Sure—that and about a thousand million credits' worth of thionite."

"That, of course, does not count, as you also know. You have helped us, I think, even more than we have helped you."

"I hope that I have done you some good, anyway. Well, I've got to flit. Thanks again. I'll see you sometime, maybe." And again the Tellurian Lensman was on his way.

XXIV.

Kinnison approached Star Cluster AC 257-4736 warily, as before; and as before he insinuated his speedster through the loose outer cordon of guardian fortresses. This time, however, he did not steer even remotely near Helmuth's world. He would be there too long; there was altogether too much risk of electromagnetic detection to set his ship into any kind of an orbit around *that* planet. Instead, he had computed a long, narrow, elliptical orbit around its sun, well inside the zone guarded by the maulers. He could compute it only approximately, of course, since he did not know exactly either the masses involved or the perturbing forces; but he thought that he could find his ship again with an electro. If not, she would not be an irreplaceable loss. He set the speedster, then, into the outward leg of that orbit and took off in his new armor.

He knew that there was a thought-screen around Helmuth's planet, and suspected that there might be other screens as well. Therefore, shutting off every watt of power, he dropped straight down into the night side, well clear of the citadel's edge. His flares were, of course, heavily baffled; but even so he did not put on his brakes until it was absolutely necessary. He landed heavily, then sprang away in long, free hops, until he reached his previously selected destination: a great cavern thickly shielded with iron ore and fully five thousand miles from his point of descent. Deep within that cavern he hid himself, then searched intently for any sign that his approach had been observed. There was no such sign. So far, so good.

But during his search he had perceived with a slight shock that Helmuth had tightened his defenses even more. Not only was every man in the dome screened against thought, but also each was now wearing full armor. Had he protected the dogs, too? Or killed them? No real matter if he had—any kind of a pet animal would do; or, in a pinch, even a wild rock-lizard! Nevertheless, he shot his perception into the particular barracks he had noted so long before, and found with some relief that the dogs were still there, and that they were still unprotected. It had not occurred, even to Helmuth's cautious mind, that a dog could be a source of mental danger.

With all due precaution against getting even a single grain of the stuff into his own system, Kinnison transferred his thionite into the special container in which it was to be used. Another day sufficed to observe and to memorize the personnel of the gateway observers, their positions, and the sequence in which they took the boards. Then the Lensman, still almost a week ahead of schedule, settled down to await the time when he should make his next move. Nor was this waiting unduly irksome; now that everything was ready he could be as patient as a cat on duty at a mouse hole.

*

The time came to act. Kinnison took over the mind of the dog, which at once moved over to the bunk in which one particular observer lay asleep. There would be no chance whatever of gaining control of any observer while he was actually on the board, but here in barracks it was almost ridiculously easy. The dog crept along on soundless paws; a long, slim nose reached out and up; sharp teeth closed delicately upon a battery lead; out came the plug. The thought-screen went down, and instantly Kinnison was in charge of the fellow's mind.

And when that observer went on duty his first act was to admit Kimball Kinnison, gray Lensman, to the Grand Base of Boskone! Low and fast Kinnison flew, while the observer so placed his body as to shield from any chance passer-by the all-too-revealing surface of his visiplate. In a few minutes the Lensman reached a portal of the dome itself. Those doors also opened—and closed behind him. He released the mind of the observer and watched briefly. Nothing happened. All was still well!

Then, in every barracks save one, using whatever came to hand in the way of dog or other unshielded animal, Kinnison wrought briefly but effectively. He did not slay by mental force—he did not have enough of that to spare—but the mere turn of an inconspicuous valve would do just as well. Some of those now idle men would probably live to answer Helmuth's call to extra duty, but not too many—nor would those who obeyed that summons live long thereafter.

Down stairway after stairway he dived, down to the compartment in which was housed the great air purifier. Now let them come! Even if they had a spy ray on him, now it would be too late to do them a bit of good. And now, by all the gods of space, that fleet had better be out there, getting ready to blast!

THE LENSMAN

It was. From all over the galaxy that grand fleet had been assembled; every patrol base had been stripped of almost everything mobile that could throw a beam. Every vessel carried either a Lensman or some other highly trusted officer; and each such officer had two detector nullifiers—one upon his person, the other in his locker—either one of which would protect his whole ship from detection.

In long lines, singly and at intervals, those untold thousands of ships had crept between the vessels guarding Grand Base. Nor were the outpost crews to blame. They had been on duty for months, and not even an asteroid had relieved the monotony. Nothing had happened or would. They watched their plates steadily enough—and, if they did nothing more, why should they? And what could they have done? How could they suspect that such a thing as a detector nullifier had been invented?

*

The patrol's grand fleet, then, was already massing over its primary objectives, each vessel in a rigidly assigned position. The pilots, captains, and navigators were chatting among themselves jerkily and in low tones, as though even to raise their voices might reveal prematurely to the enemy the concentration of the patrol forces. The firing officers were already at their boards, eyeing hungrily the small switches which they could not throw for so many long minutes yet.

And far below, beside the pirates' air purifier, Kinnison released the locking toggles of his armor and leaped out. To burn a hole in the primary duct took only a second. To drop into that duct his container of thionite, to drench that container with the reagent which would in sixty seconds dissolve completely that container's substance without affecting either its contents or the metal of the duct, to slap a flexible adhesive patch over the hole in the duct, and to leap back into his armor—all these things required only a trifle over one minute. Eleven minutes to go—QX.

Then in the last barracks, even while the Lensman was arrowing up the stairways, a dog again deprived a sleeping man of his thought screen. That man, however, instead of going to work, took up a pair of pliers and proceeded to cut the battery leads of every sleeper in the barracks, severing them so close that no connection could be made without removing the armor.

As those leads were severed, men woke up and dashed into the dome. Along catwalk after catwalk they raced, and apparently that was all that they were doing. But each runner, as he passed a man on duty, flicked a battery plug out of its socket; and that observer, at Kinnison's command, opened the face plate of his armor and breathed deeply of the now drug-laden atmosphere.

Thionite, as has been intimated, is perhaps the worst of all known habit-forming drugs. In almost infinitesimal doses it gives rise to a state in which the victim seems actually to experience the gratification of his every desire, whatever that desire may be. The larger the dose, the more intense the sensation, until—and very quickly—the dosage is reached at which he passes into such an ecstatic stupor that not a single nerve can force a stimulus into his frenzied brain. In this stage he dies.

Thus there was no alarm, no outcry, no warning. Each observer sat or stood entranced, holding exactly the pose he had been in at the instant of opening his face plate. But now, instead of paying attention to his duty, he was plunging deeper and deeper into the paroxysmally ecstatic profundity of a thionite debauch from which there was to be no awakening. Therefore, half of that mighty dome was unmanned before Helmuth even realized that anything at all out of order was going on.

As soon as he realized that something was amiss, however, he sounded the "all-hands-on-duty" alarm and rapped out instructions to the officers in the barracks. But the cloud of death had arrived there first, and to his consternation not one quarter of those officers responded. Quite a number of men did get into the dome, but every one of them collapsed before reaching the catwalks. And three fourths of his working force were *hors de combat* before he located Kinnison's speeding messengers.

"Blast them down!" Helmuth shrieked, pointing, gesticulating madly.

Blast whom down? The minions of the Lensman were themselves blasting away now, right and left, shouting contradictory but supposedly authoritative orders.

"Blast those men not on duty!" Helmuth's raging voice now filled the dome. "You, at Board 479! Blast that man on Catwalk 28, at Board 495!"

With such detailed instructions, Kinnison's agents, one by one, ceased to be. But as one was beamed down another took his place, and soon every one of the few remaining living pirates in the dome was blasting indiscriminately at every other one. And then, to cap the Saturnalian climax, came the zero second.

*

The grand fleet of the Galactic Patrol had assembled. Every cruiser, every battleship, every mauler hung poised above its assigned target. Every vessel was stripped for action. Every accumulator cell was full to its ultimate watt; every generator and every arm was tuned and peaked to its highest attainable efficiency. Every firing officer upon every ship sat tensely at his board, his hand hovering near, but not touching, his firing keys, his eyes fixed glaringly upon the second hand of his synchronized electric timer, his ears scarcely hearing the droning, soothing voice of Port Admiral Haynes.

For the old man had insisted upon giving the firing order himself, and he now sat at the master timer, speaking into the master microphone. Beside him sat von Hohendorff, the grand old commandant of cadets. Both of these veterans had thought long since that they were done with space war forever; but only an order of the full Galactic Council could have kept either of them at home. They were grimly determined that they were going to be in at the death, even though they were not at all certain whose death it was to be. If it should turn out that it was to be Helmuth's, all well and good—everything would be on the green. If, on the other hand, young Kinnison had to go, they would, in all probability, have to go, too—and so be it.

"Now remember, boys, keep your hands off those keys until I give you the word." Haynes' soothing voice droned on, giving no hint of the terrific strain he himself was under. "I'll give you lots of warning. I am going to count the last five seconds for you. I know that you all want to shoot the first bolt, but remember that I, personally, will strangle any and every one of you who beats my signal by a thousandth of a second. It won't be long now; the second hand is starting around on its last lap. Keep your hands off those keys. Keep away from them, I tell you, or I'll smack you down. Fifteen seconds yet. Stay away, boys; let 'em alone. Going to start counting now." His voice dropped lower and lower. "Five—four—three—two—one—*fire!*" he yelled.

Perhaps some of the boys did beat the gun a trifle; but not many, or much. To all intents and purposes it was one simultaneous blast of destruction that flashed down from a hundred thousand projectors, each delivering the maximum blast of which it was capable. There was no thought now of service life, of equipment or of holding anything back for a later effort. They had to hold that blast for only fifteen minutes; and if the task ahead of them could not be done in those fifteen minutes it probably could not be done at all.

Therefore, it is entirely useless even to attempt to describe what happened then, or to portray the spectacle that ensued when beam met screen. Why try to describe high C to a man born deaf? Suffice it to say that those patrol beams bored down, and that Helmuth's automatic screens resisted to the limit of their ability. Nor was that resistance small. It was of such power that, years later, astronomers observed and recorded a peculiarly behaving Nova in Star Cluster AC 257-4736.

Had Helmuth's customary staff of keen-eyed, quick-witted lieutenants been at their posts, to reënforce those primary screens with the practically unlimited power which could have been put behind them, his defenses would not have failed, even under the unimaginable force of that Titanic thrust; but those lieutenants were not at their posts. The screens of the twenty-six primary objectives failed, and the twenty-six stupendous flotillas moved slowly, grandly, voraciously, each along its designated line.

*

Every alarm in Helmuth's dome had burst into frantic warning as the massed might of the Galactic Patrol was first hurled against the twenty-six vital points of Grand Base; but those alarms clamored in vain. No hands were raised to the switches whose closing would unleash the hellish energies of Boskone's irresistible projectors; no eyes were upon the sighting devices which would align them against the attacking ships of war.

Only Helmuth, in his inner-shielded control compartment, was left; and Helmuth was the directing intelligence, the master mind, and not a mere operator. And, now that he had no operators to direct, he was utterly helpless. He could see the stupendous fleet of the patrol; he could understand fully its dire menace; but he could neither stiffen his screens nor energize a single beam. He could only sit, grinding his teeth in helpless fury, and watch the destruction of the armament which, if it could only have been in operation, would have blasted those battleships and maulers from the skies as though they had been so many fluffy bits of thistledown.

Time after time he leaped to his feet, as if about to dash across to one of the control stations; but each time he sank back into his seat at the desk. One firing station would be little, if any, better than none at all. Besides, that accursed Lensman was back of this. He was—must be—right here in the dome, somewhere. He *wanted* him to leave this desk; that was what he was waiting for! As long as he stayed at the desk he himself was safe. For that matter, this whole dome was safe. The projector had never been mounted that could break down *those* screens. No—no matter what happened, he would stay at the desk!

Kinnison, watching, marveled at his fortitude. He himself could not have stayed there, he knew; and he also knew now that Helmuth was going to stay. Time was flying; five of the fifteen minutes were gone. He had hoped that Helmuth would leave that well-protected inner sanctum, with its unknown potentialities; but if the pirate would not come out, the Lensman would go in. The storming of that inner stronghold was what his new armor had been designed for.

*

In he went, but he did not catch Helmuth napping. Even before he crashed the screens his own defensive zones burst into furiously coruscant activity, and through that flame there came tearing the metallic slugs of a high-caliber machine rifle.

Ha! There *was* a rifle, even though he had not been able to find it! Clever guy, that Helmuth! And what a break that he had taken time to learn how to hold this suit up against the trickiest kind of machine-rifle fire!

Kinnison's screens were almost those of a battleship; his armor almost, relatively, as strong. And he could hold that armor upright. Therefore, through the raging beam of the semiportable projector he plowed, and straight up that torrent of raging steel he drove his way. And now from his own mighty projector, against Helmuth's armor, there raved out a beam scarcely less potent than that of a semiportable. The Lensman's armor did not mount a water-cooled machine rifle—there was a limit to what even that powerful structure could carry—but grimly, with every faculty of his newly enlarged mind concentrated upon that thought-screened, armored head behind the belching gun, Kinnison held his line and forged ahead.

Well it was that the Lensman *was* concentrating upon that screened head; for when the screen weakened slightly and a thought began to seep through it toward an enigmatically sparkling ball of force, Kinnison was ready. He blanketed the thought savagely, before it could take form, and attacked the screen so viciously that Helmuth had either to restore full coverage instantly or die then and there. For the Lensman had studied that ball long and earnestly. It was the one thing about the whole base that he could not understand, the one thing, therefore, of which he had been uneasily afraid.

But he was afraid of it no longer. It was operated, he now knew, by thought; and, no matter how terrific its potentialities might be, it now was and would remain perfectly harmless; for if the pirate chief softened his screen enough to emit a thought, he would never think again.

Therefore, Kinnison rushed. At full blast he hurdled the rifle and crashed full against the armored figure behind it. Magnetic clamps locked and held; and, driving projectors furiously ablaze, he whirled around and forced the madly struggling Helmuth back, toward the line along which the bellowing rifle was still spewing forth a continuous storm of metal.

Helmuth's utmost efforts sufficed only to throw the Lensman out of balance, and both figures crashed to the floor. Now the madly fighting armored pair rolled over and over—straight into the line of fire.

First Kinnison—the bullets whining, shrieking off the armor of his personal battleship and crashing through or smashing ringingly against whatever happened to be in the ever-changing line of ricochet. Then Helmuth—and the fierce-driven metal slugs tore, in their multitudes, through his armor and through his body, riddling his every vital organ.

GRAY LENSMAN

PROLOGUE

This is not, strictly speaking, a biography. It is not, it cannot be, comprehensive enough to be called that. Nor, since of necessity it must be limited, both in length and in scope, can it be called a history. It is, perhaps, best described as a record—the record of the activities of Galactic Co-ordinator Kimball Kinnison, Gray Lensman, of Tellus, during the Boskonian War.

Nevertheless this record, what there is of it, is in essence biographical; and the biographer of such a man as Kinnison has a peculiar task. In one way it is easy, in two others it is difficult in the extreme.

"Nuts!" he is wont to exclaim in answer to a direct question as to some particular event or situation. "Why in all the nine hells of Valeria are you still wasting time writing about *me?*" But eventually I get the data I need, and thus it is comparatively easy to make this work completely authentic, as far as the Gray Lensman himself is concerned.

It may be objected that I have recorded as facts certain minutiae which, considering what happened to the planet of the Eich and in the light of other happenings elsewhere, cannot be known so exactly by any living entity. This objection is untenable; as profound research upon every debatable point has shown conclusively that something very similar to, if not in fact identical with, each such detail must have occurred.

Of the two great difficulties, one lies in the selection of material. The story of Kimball Kinnison easily could—and really should—fill a dozen encyclopedic spools; it is a Galactic shame and an almost impossible undertaking to compress it into one two-hour tape. The other sticking point is the diversity of my audience. For in the First Galaxy alone there are millions of planets, peopled by races as divergent in mentality and in physique as they are far apart in space. Some races will read this chronicle from printed pages; some will see it; some will hear it; some will both see it and hear it; some, unable either to see or to hear, will receive it telepathically. Still others, in other Galaxies, will undoubtedly acquire it in fashions starkly incomprehensible to me, its compiler.

Numberless races of intelligent beings already know Kinnison well, since his fame has spread north, south, east, west, zenith and nadir, to the six points of the three-dimensional galactic-inductor compasses of two galaxies. On the other hand, many know him not at all. Many have never even heard of Tellus, nor of Sol, our parent sun; even though it was upon that proud planet of this, our Solarian System, that the Galactic Patrol came into being. Indeed, it is inevitable that this biography will in days to come be of interest to races which, inhabiting planets not yet reached by the Cosmic Survey, have not even heard of the Galactic Patrol, to say nothing of knowing its origin and its history.

In view of the above inescapable facts, and after a great deal of thought and care, I have decided to write this Prologue, which will summarize very simply that which is already most widely known; namely, the happenings up to and including the first phase of the Boskonian War. Even that condensation, however, leaves me all too little space in which to do justice to the part that Kimball Kinnison played in enabling the civilization of the Galactic Council to triumph over the monstrous culture of Boskone.

SUPER PACK

With the understanding, then, that the more informed mentality may skip from here to Chapter I, I proceed.

*

Should I begin with Arisia? That forbidding, forbidden planet whose inhabitants, having achieved sheerly unimaginable heights of philosophical and mental power, withdrew almost completely into themselves, leaving traces only in Galaxy-wide folk tales and legends of supermen and gods? Probably not. I should, it seems to me, begin with Earth's almost prehistoric bandits and gangsters, gentry who flourished in the days when space flight was mentioned only in fantastic fiction.

Know, then, that for ages law enforcement lagged behind law violation because the minions of the law were limited in their spheres of action, while criminals were not. Thus, in the days following the invention of the automobile, State troopers could not cross State lines. Later, when what were then known as the "G-men" combined with the various State constabularies to form the National Police, they could not follow the stratosphere planes of the lawbreakers across national boundaries.

Still later, when interplanetary flight became commonplace, the Planetary Guards were at the same old disadvantage. They had no authority off their own worlds, while the public enemies flitted unhampered from planet to planet. And finally, with the development of the inertialess drive and the consequent traffic between hundreds of thousands of solar systems, crime became so rampant as to threaten the very foundations of civilization.

Then the Galactic Patrol came into being. At first it was a pitiful-enough organization. It was handicapped from within by the usual small, but utterly disastrous percentage of grafters and criminals; from without by the fact that there was then no emblem or credential which could not be counterfeited. No one could tell with certainty that the man in uniform was a Patrolman and not an outlaw in disguise.

The second difficulty was overcome first. One old-time Patrolman had heard of the Arisians. He visited their planet and—this should be a saga by itself—persuaded those Masters of Mentality that they should help right against wrong, at least to the extent of furnishing a positive means of identification. They did, and still do—The Lens.

Each being about to graduate as a Lensman is sent to Arisia; where, although the candidate does not then know it, a Lens—a lenticular jewel composed of thousands of tiny crystalloids—is built to match his individual life force. While no mind other than that of an Arisian can understand its functioning, thinking of the Lens as being synchronized with, or in exact resonance with the life principle—personality, ego, call it what you will—of its owner will give a rough idea of it. It is not really alive, as we understand the term. It is, however, endowed with a sort of pseudolife, by virtue of which it gives off its strong, characteristically changing, polychromatic light as long as it is in circuit with the living mentality for which it was designed. It is inimitable, unforgettable. Anyone who has ever seen a Lens, or even a picture of one, will never forget it; nor will he ever be deceived by any possible counterfeit or imitation of it.

The Lens cannot be removed by anyone except its wearer without actual dismemberment of that wearer; it shines as long as its rightful owner wears it, and in the

517

instant of its owner's death, it ceases forever to shine. And not only does a Lens refuse to shine if any impostor attempts to wear it—any Lens not in circuit with its owner kills in a space of minutes any other who touches it, so strongly does its pseudolife interfere with any life to which it is not attuned.

Also by virtue of that pseudolife the Lens acts as a telepath through which its owner may communicate with any other intelligence, high or low; even though the other entity may possess no organs either of sight or of hearing, as we know these senses. The Lens has also many other highly important uses, which lack of space forbids even mentioning here.

*

Having the Lens, it was an easy matter for the Patrol to purify itself of its few unworthy members. Standards of entrance were raised higher and higher; and, as it became evident that it was to a man incorruptible, it was granted more and ever more authority.

Now its power is practically unlimited; the Lensman can follow the lawbreaker, wherever he may go. He can commandeer any material or assistance, whenever and wherever required. The Lens is so respected throughout the Galactic Union that any wearer of it may at any time be called upon to act as judge, jury, and executioner. Wherever he goes, throughout the Universe of Civilization, he not only carries the law with him—he *is* the law.

How are these Lensmen chosen? An Earthman myself, and proud of the fact that Tellus was the cradle of Galactic Civilization, I will describe only how Tellurian Lensmen are selected. Upon other planets the methods and means vary widely; but the results are the same: Wherever he may be found or however monstrous he may appear, a Lensman is always a *Lensman*.

Each year one million boys are picked, by competitive examination, from all the eighteen-year-olds of Earth. During the first year of training, before any of them set foot inside Wentworth Hall, that number shrinks to less than fifty thousand. Then, for four years more, they are put through the most poignantly searching, the most pitilessly rigid process of elimination possible to develop, during the course of which every man who can be made to reveal any sign of unworthiness or of weakness is dropped. Of each class, only about a hundred win through to the Lens; but each of those few has proven repeatedly, to the cold verge of death itself, that he is in every sense fit to wear it.

Of those who drop out alive, most are dismissed from the Patrol. There are many splendid men, however, who for some reason not involving moral turpitude are not quite what a Lensman must be. These men make up the organization, from grease monkeys up to the highest commissioned officers below the rank of Lensman. This fact explains what is already so widely known: that the Galactic Patrol is the finest body of intelligent beings yet to serve under one banner.

But even Lensmen are not all alike; some are more richly endowed than others. Most Lensmen work more or less under direction; that is, they have headquarters and, at the completion of one investigation or project, are assigned to another by the port admiral. Occasionally, however, a Lensman shows himself to be of such outstanding ability, even for a Lensman, that he is given his Release. Technically, he is now an "Unattached

Lensman"; in popular parlance he is a "Gray Lensman," from the color of the leather he wears.

*

The Release! The goal toward which all Lensmen strive, but which so relatively few attain, even after years of work! The Gray Lensman is as nearly absolutely free an agent as it is possible for any flesh-and-blood being to be. He is responsible to no one and to nothing save his own conscience. He is no longer of Earth, nor of the Solarian System, but of the Universe as a whole. He is no longer a cog in the immense machine of the Galactic Patrol; wherever he may go throughout the reaches of unbounded space, he is the Galactic Patrol:

He goes anywhere he pleases and does anything he pleases, for as long as he pleases. He takes what he wants, when he wants it, with or without giving reasons or anything except a thumb-printed credit slip in return—if he chooses to do so. He reports when, where, and to whom he pleases—or not, as he pleases. He has no headquarters, no address; he can be reached only through his Lens. He no longer gets even a formal salary; he takes that, too, as he goes, whatever he finds needful.

To the man on the street that would seem to be a condition of perfect bliss. It is not. All Lensmen strive mightily for the Release, even though they realize dimly what it will mean—but only an Unattached Lensman really understands what a frightful, what a man-killing load the Release brings with it. However, Gray Lensmen being what they must be, it is a load which they are glad and proud to bear.

Hence, to say that Kimball Kinnison ranked Number One in his graduating class is to say a great deal—but even more revealing of his quality is to add that he was the first to perceive that what was known as Boskonia was not merely an organization of outlaws and pirates, but was in fact a Galaxy-wide culture diametrically opposed in fundamental philosophy to that of Galactic Civilization. The most illuminating thing I can say of him in a few words, however, is this:

Of all the millions of entities who through the years had worn the symbol of the Lens, Kinnison was the first to perceive that the Arisians had endowed the Lens with powers theretofore undreamed of, powers which no brain without special training could either evoke or control. Thus, he was the first Lensman to return to Arisia for that advanced training; and during that instruction he learned why no other Lensman had been so trained before. It was such an ordeal that only a mind of power sufficient to perceive of itself the real need of such treatment could endure it without becoming starkly insane.

Shortly after Kinnison won his Lens, he was called to Prime Base by Port Admiral Haynes, the Patrol's chief of staff. There, in a room sealed against spy rays, an appalling situation was bared. Space piracy, always rife enough, had become an organized force; and, under the leadership of a half-mythical entity about whom nothing was known save the name "Boskone," had risen to such heights of power as to threaten seriously the Galactic Patrol itself. Indeed, in one respect, Boskonia was ahead of the Patrol, its scientists having developed a source of power vastly greater than any known to Galactic Civilization. It had fighting ships of a new and extraordinary type, from which even convoyed shipping was no longer safe. Being faster than the Patrol's fast cruisers, and

519

more heavily armed than its heaviest battleships, they had been doing practically as they pleased in space.

For one particular purpose, the engineers of the Patrol had designed and built one ship—the *Brittania*. She was the fastest thing in space, but for offensive armament she had only one weapon, the "Q-gun." This depended upon chemical explosives, which, in warfare at least, had been obsolete for centuries. Nevertheless, Kinnison was put in command of the *Brittania* and was told to take her out, capture a pirate war vessel of late model, learn her secrets of power, and transmit the information to Prime Base with the least possible delay.

He was successful in finding and in defeating such a vessel. Peter van Buskirk led the storming party of Valerians—men of remote Earth-human ancestry, but of extraordinary size, strength and agility because of the enormous gravitation of generations of life on the planet Valeria—in wiping out those of the pirate crew not killed in the combat between the two vessels.

The *Brittania's* scientists secured the required data, but were unable to report immediately to Prime Base, as the pirates were blanketing all available channels of communication. Boskonian ships were gathering for the kill, and the crippled Patrol ship could neither run nor fight. Therefore each man was given a spool of tape bearing a complete record of everything that had occurred; and, after setting up a director-by-chance to make the empty ship pursue an unpredictable course in space, and after rigging bombs to explode her at the first touch of a ray, the Patrolmen paired off by lot and took to the lifeboats.

The erratic course of the cruiser brought her near the lifeboat in which Kinnison and Van Buskirk were, and there the pirates attempted to stop her. The ensuing explosion was so violent that flying wreckage disabled practically the entire personnel of one of the attacking ships, which did not have time to go free—inertialess—before the crash. The two Patrolmen captured the pirate vessel and drove her toward Earth. They reached the solar system of Velantia before the Boskonians blocked them off, thus compelling them again to take to their lifeboat. They landed upon the planet Delgon, where they were rescued from a horde of Catlats by Worsel, a highly intelligent winged reptile, a native of the neighboring planet of Velantia.

By means of improvements upon Velantian thought-screens the three destroyed most of the Overlords of Delgon, a sadistic race of monsters who had been preying upon the other people of the system by sheer power of mind. Worsel then accompanied the two Patrolmen to Velantia, where all the resources of the planet were devoted to the preparation of defense against the expected attack of the Boskonians. Several other of the *Brittania's* lifeboats reached Velantia, guided by Worsel's mind working through Kinnison's mind and Lens.

Kinnison intercepted a message from Helmuth, who "spoke for Boskone," and traced his communicator beam, thus getting his first line upon Boskonia's Grand Base. The pirates attacked Velantia, and six of their vessels were captured. In these six ships, manned by Velantian crews and blanketing ether and subether against the pirates' own communicators, the Patrolmen again set out toward Earth and the Prime Base of the Galactic Patrol.

Then Kinnison's Bergenholm broke down. The Bergenholm, the generator of the force that neutralizes inertia—the *sine qua non* of interstellar speed. For, while any mass in the free condition can assume an almost unlimited velocity, inert matter cannot equal even that of light—the veriest crawl, as space speeds go. Also, there is no magic, no getting of something for nothing, in the operation of a Bergenholm. It takes power, plenty of power, to run one, and whenever one goes out, the ship dependent upon it is, to all intents and purposes, anchored in space.

Therefore the Patrolmen were forced to land upon Trenco—which, as almost everyone knows, is the planet upon which is produced thionite, perhaps the deadliest of all habit-forming drugs—for repairs.

Meanwhile Helmuth, the Boskonian, had deduced that it was a Lensman who had been giving him so much trouble. He had already connected the Lens with Arisia; therefore he set out for Arisia to find out for himself just what it was that made the Lens such a powerful thing. He discovered that he was no match at all for an Arisian. He was given terrific mental punishment, but was allowed to return to his Grand Base alive and sane; being informed that he was spared because his destruction would not be good for the budding Civilization to which Boskonian culture was opposed. He was told further that the Arisians had given Civilization the Lens; that by its intelligent use, Civilization should be able to conquer Boskone's alien, abhorrent culture; that if it could not learn to use the Lens, it was not yet ready to become a Civilization, and Boskonia would be allowed to flourish for a time.

After various adventures upon Trenco—a peculiar planet indeed—Kinnison secured a new Bergenholm and went on. This time he managed to reach Tellus, and, after a spectacular battle in the stratosphere with a blockading fleet of the enemy, got down to Prime Base with his precious data. There he first revealed his conviction that the Boskonians were not ordinary pirates, but in fact composed a culture almost, if not quite, as strong as Civilization itself; and asked that certain scientists of the Patrol should try to develop a detector nullifier. He predicted a stalemate, and intimated that such a nullifier might well prove to be the deciding factor in the entire war.

By building ultrapowerful battleships, called "maulers," the Patrol gained a temporary advantage, but the stalemate soon ensued. Kinnison thought out a plan of action, in the pursuit of which he scouted a pirate base upon Aldebaran I. The personnel of this base, however, instead of being human or near-human beings, were Wheelmen, beings possessed of a sense of perception unknown to man. The Lensman was discovered before he could accomplish anything, and in the fight which followed he was very seriously wounded.

However, he managed to get back to his speedster and sent a thought to Port Admiral Haynes, who forthwith sent ships to his aid. In the hospital, Chief Surgeon Lacy put him together without the use of artificial members; and, during a long and quarrelsome convalescence, Nurse Clarrissa MacDougall held him together.

THE LENSMAN

As soon as he could leave the hospital he went to Arisia in the hope that he might be permitted to take advanced training—an unheard-of idea. Much to his surprise, he learned that he had been expected to return for exactly such training. Getting it almost killed him, but he emerged from the ordeal infinitely stronger of mind than any man had ever been before; and possessed of a new sense of perception as well—a sense somewhat analogous to sight, but of vastly greater power, depth, and scope, and not dependent upon light, a sense only vaguely forecast by ancient experiments with clairvoyance.

After trying out his new mental equipment by solving a murder mystery upon Radelix, he succeeded in entering an enemy base upon Boyssia II. There he took over the mind of the communications officer and waited for the opportunity of getting the second, all-important line upon Boskonia's Grand Base. An enemy ship of this base captured a hospital ship of the Patrol and brought it in. Nurse MacDougall, head nurse of the captured ship, working under Kinnison's instructions, stirred up trouble which soon became mutiny. Helmuth, from Grand Base, took a hand, thus enabling Kinnison to get his second line.

The hospital ship, undetectable by virtue of the Lensman's nullifier, escaped from Boyssia II and headed for Earth at full blast. Kinnison, convinced that Helmuth was really Boskone himself, found that the intersection of his two lines—and therefore the pirates' Grand Base—lay in a star cluster AG 257-4736, well outside the Galaxy. Pausing only long enough to destroy the Wheelmen of Aldebaran I, the project in which his first attempt had failed so dismally, he set out to investigate Helmuth's headquarters. He found a stronghold impregnable to any massed attack the Patrol could throw against it, manned by beings each wearing a thought-screen. His sense of perception was suddenly cut off—the pirates had thrown a thought-screen around the entire planet. He then returned to Prime Base, deciding en route that boring from within was the only possible way in which that stupendous fortress could be taken.

In consultation with Port Admiral Haynes, the zero hour was set, at which time the massed Grand Fleet of Patrol was to begin raying Helmuth's base with every projector that could be brought to bear.

Pursuant to his plan, Kinnison again visited Trenco, where the Patrol forces extracted for him fifty kilograms of thionite, the noxious drug which, in microgram inhalations, makes the addict experience all the sensations of doing whatever it is that he wishes most ardently to do. The larger the dose, the more intense the sensations; the slightest overdose resulting in an ecstatic death. Thence to Helmuth's planet; where, finding a dog whose brain was unshielded, he let himself into the central dome. Here, just before the zero minute, he released his thionite into the air stream, thus wiping out all the pirate personnel except Helmuth, who, in his inner sanctum, could not be affected.

The Grand Fleet of the Patrol attacked, but Helmuth would not leave his retreat, even to try to save his Base. Therefore Kinnison would have to go in after him. Poised in the air of Helmuth's inner sphere there was an enigmatic, sparkling ball of force which the Lensman could not understand, and of which he was in consequence extremely suspicious.

But the storming of that quadruply-defended inner stronghold was precisely the task for which Kinnison's new and ultracumbersome armor had been designed; and in the Gray Lensman went.

I.

Among the world-girdling fortifications of a planet distant indeed from star cluster AG 257-4736 there squatted sullenly a fortress quite similar to Helmuth's own. Indeed, in some respects it was even superior to the base of him who spoke for Boskone. It was larger and stronger. Instead of one dome, it had many. It was dark and cold withal, for its occupants had practically nothing in common with humanity save the possession of high intelligence.

In the central sphere of one of the domes there sparkled several of the peculiarly radiant globes whose counterpart had given Kinnison so seriously to think, and near them there crouched or huddled or lay at ease a many-tentacled creature indescribable to man. It was not exactly like an octopus. Though spiny, it did not resemble at all closely a sea-cucumber. Nor, although it was scaly and toothy and wingy, was it, save in the vaguest possible way, similar to a lizard, a sea serpent, or a vulture. Such a description by negatives is, of course, pitifully inadequate; but, unfortunately, it is the best that can be done.

The entire attention of this being was focused within one of the globes, the obscure mechanism of which was relaying to his sense of perception from Helmuth's globe and mind a clear picture of everything which was happening within Grand Base. The corpse-littered dome was clear to his sight; he knew that the Patrol was attacking from without; knew that that ubiquitous Lensman, who had already unmanned the citadel, was about to attack from within.

"You have erred seriously," the entity was thinking coldly, emotionlessly, into the globe, "in not deducing until after it was too late to save your base that the Lensman had perfected a nullifier of subethereal detection. Your contention that I am equally culpable is, I think, untenable. It was your problem, not mine; I had, and still have, other things to concern me. Your base is of course lost; whether or not you yourself survive will depend entirely upon the adequacy of your protective devices."

"But, Eichlan, you yourself pronounced them adequate!"

There followed an interval of silence, as though those conferring were separated by such a gulf of space that even thought, with its immeasurable velocity of propagation, required finite time to traverse it.

"Pardon me—I said that they *seemed* adequate."

"If I survive—or, rather, after I have destroyed this Lensman—what are your orders?" Another interval.

"Go to the nearest communicator and concentrate our forces; half of them to engage this Patrol fleet, the remainder to wipe out all the life of Sol III. I have not tried to give those orders direct, since all the beams are keyed to your board and, even if I could reach them, no commander in that Galaxy knows that I speak for Boskone. After you have done that, report to me here."

THE LENSMAN

"Instructions received and understood. Helmuth, ending message."

"Set your controls as instructed. I will observe and record. Prepare yourself, the Lensman comes. Eichlan, speaking for Boskone, ending message."

The Lensman rushed. Even before he crashed the pirate's screens his own defensive zone flamed white in the beam of semiportable projectors, and through that blaze came tearing the metallic slugs of a high-caliber machine rifle. But the Lensman's screens were almost those of a battleship, his armor relatively as strong; he had at his command projectors scarcely inferior to those opposing his advance. Therefore, with every faculty of his newly enlarged mind concentrated upon that thought-screened, armored head behind the bellowing gun and the flaring projectors, Kinnison held his line and forged ahead.

*

Attentive as he was to Helmuth's thought-screens, the Patrolman was ready when it weakened slightly and a thought began to seep through, directed at that peculiar ball of force. He blanketed it savagely, before it could even begin to take form, and attacked the screen so viciously that the Boskonian had either to restore full coverage instantly or else die there and then.

Kinnison feared that force-ball no longer. He still did not know what it was; but he had learned that, whatever its nature might be, it was operated or controlled by thought. Therefore it was and would remain harmless. If the pirate chief softened his screen enough to emit a thought he would never think again.

Doggedly the Lensman drove in, closer and closer. Magnetic clamps locked and held. Two steel-clad, warring figures rolled into the line of fire of the ravening automatic rifle. Kinnison's armor, designed and tested to withstand even heavier stuff, held; wherefore he came through that storm of metal unscathed. Helmuth's, however, even though stronger far than the ordinary personal armor of space, failed; and thus the Boskonian died.

Blasting himself upright, the Patrolman shot across the inner dome to the control panel and paused, momentarily baffled. He could not throw the switches controlling the defensive screens of the gigantic outer dome! His armor, designed for the ultimate of defensive strength, could not and did not bear any of the small and delicate external mechanisms so characteristic of the ordinary spacesuit. To leave his personal tank at that time and in that environment was unthinkable; yet he was fast running out of time. A scant fifteen seconds was all that remained before zero, the moment at which the hellish output of every watt generable by the massed fleet of the Galactic Patrol would be hurled against those screens in their furiously raging destructive might. To release the screens after that zero moment would mean his own death, instantaneous and inevitable.

Nevertheless, he could open those circuits—the conservation of Boskonian property meant nothing to him. He flipped on his own projector and flashed its beam briefly across the banked panels in front of him. Insulation burst into flame, fairly exploding in its haste to disintegrate; copper and silver ran in brilliant streams or puffed away in clouds of sparkling vapor: high-tension arcs ripped, crashed, and cracked among the writhing, dripping, flaring bus-bar. The shorts burned themselves clear or blew their fuses, every circuit opened, every Boskonian defense came down; and then, and only then, could Kinnison get into communication with his friends.

524

"Haynes!" he thought crisply into his Lens. "Kinnison calling!"

"Haynes acknowledging!" a thought instantly snapped back. "Congrat—"

"Hold it! We're not done yet! Have every ship in the Fleet go free at once. Have them all, except yours, put out full-coverage screens, so that they can't look at or think into this Base."

A moment passed. "Done!"

"Don't come in any closer—I'm on my way out there to you. Have your ship block every band except your personal frequency, which you and I are now on, and caution all Lensmen aboard with you to stay off that channel until further notice. Now as to you, personally, I don't like to seem to be giving orders to the Admiral of the Fleet, but it may be quite essential that you concentrate upon me, and think of nothing else, for the next few minutes."

"Right! I don't mind taking orders from *you.*"

"QX. Now we can take things a bit easier." Kinnison had so arranged matters that no one except himself could think into that stronghold, and he himself would not. He would not think into that tantalizing enigma, nor toward it, nor even of it, until he was completely ready to do so. And how many persons, I wonder, really realize just how much of a feat that was? Realize the sort of mental training that required?

"How many gamma-zeta tracers can you put out, chief?" Kinnison asked then, more conversationally.

A brief consultation; then, "Ten in regular use. By tuning in all our spares we can put out sixty."

"At two diameters' distance forty-eight fields will surround this planet at one-hundred-percent overlap. Please have that many set that way. Of the other twelve, set three to go well outside the first sphere—say at four diameters out—covering the line from this planet to Lundmark's Nebula. Set the last nine to be thrown out as far as you can read them accurately to only the first decimal on your screens, centering on the same line. Not much overlap is necessary on these backing fields—bare contact is enough. Release nothing, of course, until I get there. And while the boys are setting things up, you might go inert—it's safe enough now—so that I can match your intrinsic velocity and come aboard."

*

There followed the maneuvering necessary for one inert body to approach another in space, then Kinnison's incredible housing of steel was hauled into the airlock by means of space lines attached to magnetic clamps. The outer door of the lock closed behind him, the inner one opened, and the Lensman entered the flagship.

First to the armory, where he clambered stiffly out of his small battleship and gave orders concerning its storage. Then to the control room, stretching and bending hugely as he went, in vast relief at his freedom from the narrow and irksome confinement which he had endured so long.

Of all the men in that control room, only two knew Kinnison personally. All knew of him, however, and as the tall gray-clad figure entered there was a loud, quick cheer.

"Hi, fellows—thanks." Kinnison waved a salute to the room as a whole. "Hi, Port Admiral! Hi, Commandant!" He saluted Haynes and von Hohendorff as perfunctorily, and greeted them as casually, as though he had last seen them an hour, instead of ten weeks, before; as though the intervening time had been spent in the veriest idleness, instead of in the fashion in which it actually had been spent.

Old von Hohendorff greeted his erstwhile pupil cordially enough, but: "Out with it!" Haynes demanded. "What did you do? How did you do it? What does all this confounded rigmarole mean? Tell us all about it—all you can, I mean," he added, hastily.

"There's no need of secrecy now, I think," and in flashing thoughts the Gray Lensman went on to describe everything that had happened.

"So you see," he concluded, "I don't really *know* anything. It's all surmise, suspicion, and deduction. It may be that nothing at all will happen: in which case these precautions, while they will have been wasted effort, will have done us no harm. In case something *does* happen, however—and I'll bet all the tea in China that something will—we'll be ready for it."

"But if what you are beginning to suspect is really true, it means that Boskonia is inter-Galactic in scope—wider spread even than the Patrol!"

"Probably, but not necessarily—it may mean only that they have bases further outside. And remember that I'm arguing on a mighty slim thread of evidence. That screen was hard and tight, and I couldn't touch the external beam—if there was one—at all. I got just part of a thought, here and there. However, the thought was 'that' galaxy; not just 'galaxy,' or 'this' or 'the' galaxy—and why think that way if the guy was already in this galaxy?"

"But nobody has ever—But skip it for now—the boys are ready for you. Take over!"

"QX. First we'll go free again. Don't think much, if any, of the stuff can come out here, but no use taking chances. Cut your screens. Now, all you gamma-zeta men, throw out your fields, and if any of you get a puncture, or even a flash, measure its position. You recording observers, step your scanners up to fifty thousand. QX?"

"QX!" the observers and recorders reported, almost as one, and the Gray Lensman sat down at a plate.

*

His mind, free at last to make the investigation from which it had been so long and so sternly barred, flew down into and through the dome, to and into that cryptic globe so tantalizingly poised in the air of the Center.

The reaction was practically instantaneous; so rapid that any ordinary mind could have perceived nothing at all; so rapid that even Kinnison's consciousness recorded only a confusedly blurred impression. But he did see something: in that fleeting millionth of a second he sensed a powerful, malignant mental force; a force backing multiplex scanners and subethereal stress-fields interlocked in peculiarly unidentifiable patterns.

For that ball was, as Kinnison had more than suspected, a potent agency indeed. It was, as he had thought that it must be, a communicator; but it was far more than that. Ordinarily harmless enough, it could be so set as to become an infernal machine at the vibrations of any thought not in a certain coded sequence; and Helmuth had so set it.

Therefore at the touch of the Patrolman's thought it exploded: liberating instantaneously the unimaginable forces with which it was charged. More, it sent out waves which, attuned to detonating receivers, touched off strategically placed stores of duodecaplylatomate. "Duodec," that concentrated essence of atomic violence than which science has even yet failed to develop a more devastating!

"Hell's—jingling—bells!" Port Admiral Haynes grunted in stunned amazement, then subsided into silence, eyes riveted upon his plate; for to the human eye dome, fortress, and planet had disappeared in one cataclysmically incandescent sphere of flame.

But the observers of the Galactic Patrol did not depend upon eyesight alone. Their scanners had been working at ultrafast speed; and, as soon as it became clear that none of the ships of the Fleet had been endangered, Kinnison asked that certain of the spools be run into a visitank at normal tempo.

There, slowed to a speed at which the eye could clearly discern sequences of events, the two old Lensmen and the young one studied with care the three-dimensional pictures of what had happened; pictures taken from points of projection close to and even within the doomed structure itself.

Deliberately, the ball of force opened up, followed an inappreciable instant later by the secondary centers of detonation; all expanding magically into spherical volumes of blindingly brilliant annihilation. There were as yet no flying fragments: no inert fragment *can* fly from duodec in the first few instants of its detonation. For the detonation of duodec is propagated at the velocity of light, so that the entire mass disintegrates in a period of time to be measured only in fractional trillionths of a second. Its detonation pressure and temperature have never been measured save indirectly, since nothing will hold it except a Q-type helix of pure force. And even those helices, which perforce must be practically open at both ends, have to be designed and powered to withstand pressures and temperatures obtaining only in the cores of suns.

Imagine, if you can, what would happen if some fifty thousand metric tons of material from the innermost core of Sirius B were to be taken to Grand Base, separated into twenty-five packages, each package placed at a strategic point, and all restraint instantaneously removed. What would have happened then, was what actually *was* happening!

As has been said, for moments nothing moved except the ever-expanding spheres of destruction. Nothing *could* move—the inertia of matter itself held it in place until it was too late—everything close to those centers of action simply flared into turgid incandescence and added its contribution to the already hellish whole.

As the spheres expanded, their temperatures and pressures decreased and the action became somewhat less violent. Matter no longer simply disappeared. Instead, plates and girders, even gigantic structural members, bent, buckled, and crumbled. Walls blew outward and upward. Huge chunks of metal and of masonry, many with fused and dripping edges, began to fly in all directions.

And not only, or principally, upward was directed the force of those inconceivable explosions. Downward the effect was, if possible, even more catastrophic, since conditions there approximated closely the oft-argued meeting between the irresistible force and the immovable object. The planet was to all intents and purposes immovable, the duodec to the same degree irresistible. The result was that the entire planet was momentarily blown apart. A vast chasm was blasted deep into its interior, and, gravity temporarily overcome, stupendous cracks and fissures began to yawn. Then, as the pressure decreased, the core-stuff of the planet became molten and began to wreak its volcanic havoc.

Gravity, once more master of the situation, took hold. The cracks and chasms closed, extruding uncounted cubic miles of fiery lava and metal. The entire world shivered and shuddered in a Gargantuan cosmic ague.

*

The explosion blew itself out. The hot gases and vapors cooled. The steam condensed. The volcanic dust disappeared. There lay the planet; but changed—hideously and awfully changed. Where Grand Base had been there remained nothing whatever to indicate that anything wrought by man had ever been there. Mountains were leveled, valleys were filled. Continents and oceans had shifted, and were still shifting; visibly. Earthquakes, volcanoes, and other seismic disturbances, instead of decreasing, were increasing in violence, minute by minute.

Helmuth's planet was, and would for years remain, a barren and uninhabitable world.

"Well!" Haynes, who had been holding his breath unconsciously, released it in an almost explosive sigh. "That is inescapably and incontrovertibly *that*. I was going to use that base, but it looks as though we'll have to get along without it."

Without comment Kinnison turned to the gamma-zeta observers. "Any traces?" he asked.

It developed that three of the fields had shown activity. Not merely traces or flashes, but solid punctures showing the presence of a hard, tight beam. And those three punctures were in the same line; a line running straight out into inter-Galactic space.

Kinnison took careful readings on the line, then stood motionless. Feet wide apart, hands jammed into pockets, head slightly bent, eyes distant, he stood there unmoving; thinking with all the power of his brain.

"I want to ask three questions," the old Commandant of Cadets interrupted his cogitations finally. "Was Helmuth Boskone, or not? Have we got them licked, or not? What do we do next, besides the mopping up of those eighteen super-maulers?"

"To all three the answer is 'I don't know'." Kinnison's face was stern and hard. "You know as much about the whole thing as I do—I haven't held back a thing that I even suspect. I did not tell you that Helmuth was Boskone; I said that everyone in any position to judge, including myself, was as sure that he was as one could be about anything that could not be proved. I firmly believed that he was. The presence of this communicator line, and the other stuff I have told you about, has destroyed that belief in my mind. However, we do not actually *know* any more than we did before. It is no more certain now that Helmuth was *not* Boskone than it was before that he *was* Boskone. The second question ties in with the first, and so does the third—but I see that the mopping up has started."

SUPER PACK

While von Hohendorff and Kinnison had been talking, Haynes had issued orders and the Grand Fleet, divided roughly and with difficulty into eighteen parts, went raggedly outward to surround the eighteen outlying fortresses. But, and surprisingly enough to the Patrol forces, the reduction of those hulking monsters was to prove no easy task.

The Boskonians had witnessed the destruction of Helmuth's Grand Base. Their master plates were dead. Try as they would, they could get in touch with no one with authority to give them orders, with no one to whom they could report their present plight. Nor could they escape: the slowest mauler in the Patrol Fleet could have caught any one of them in space of minutes.

To surrender was not even thought of—better far to die a clean death in the blazing holocaust of space battle than to be thrown ignominiously into the lethal chambers of the Patrol. There was not, there could not be, any question of pardon or of sentence to any mere imprisonment, for the strife between Civilization and Boskonia in no respect resembled the wars between two fundamentally similar and friendly nations which small, green Terra knew so frequently of old. It was a Galaxy-wide struggle for survival between two diametrically opposed, mutually exclusive, and absolutely incompatible cultures; a duel to the death in which quarter was neither asked nor given; a conflict which, except for the single instance which Kinnison himself had engineered, was, and of stern necessity had to be, one of ruthless, complete, and utter extinction.

*

Die, then, the pirates knew they must; and, although adherents to a scheme of existence monstrous indeed to our way of thinking, they were in no sense cowards. Not like cornered rats did they conduct themselves, but fought like what they were; courageous beings hopelessly outnumbered and outpowered, unable either to escape or to choose the field of operations, grimly resolved that in their passing they would take full toll of the minions of that detested and despised Galactic Civilization. Therefore, in suicidal glee, Boskonian engineers rigged up a fantastically potent weapon of offense, tuned in their defensive screens and hung poised in space, awaiting calmly the massed attack so sure to come.

Up flashed the heavy cruisers of the Patrol, serenely confident. Although of little offensive strength, these vessels mounted tractors and pressors of prodigious power, as well as defensive screens which—theoretically—no projector-driven beam of force could puncture. They had engaged mauler after mauler of Boskonia's mightiest, and never yet had one of those screens gone down. Theirs the task of immobilizing the opponent; since, as is of course well known, it is under any ordinary conditions impossible to wreak any hurt upon an object which is both inertialess and at liberty to move in space. It simply darts away from the touch of the harmful agent, whether it be immaterial beam or material substance.

Formerly the attachment of two or three tractors was all that was necessary to insure immobility, and thus vulnerability; but with the Velantian development of a shear-plane to cut tractor beams, a new technique became necessary. This was englobement, in which a dozen or more vessels surrounded the proposed victim in space and held it motionless at the center of a sphere by means of pressors, which could not be cut or evaded. Serene, then, and confident, the heavy cruisers rushed out to englobe the Boskonian fortress.

Flash! Flash! Flash! Three points of light, as unbearably brilliant as atomic vortices, sprang into being upon the fortress' side. Three needle rays of inconceivable energy lashed out, hurtling through the cruisers' outer screens as though they had been so much inactive webbing. Through the second and through the first. Through the wall shield, even that ultrapowerful field scarcely flashing as it went down. Through the armor, violating the prime tenet then held and which has just been referred to, that no object free in space can be damaged—in this case, so unthinkably vehement was the thrust, the few atoms of substances in the space surrounding the doomed cruisers afforded resistance enough. Through the ship itself, a ravening cylinder of annihilation.

For perhaps a second—certainly no longer—those incredible, those undreamed-of beams persisted before winking out into blackness; but that second had been long enough. Three riddled hulks lay dead in space, and as the three original projectors went black three more flared out. Then three more. Nine of the mightiest of Civilization's ships of war were riddled before the others could hurl themselves backward out of range!

*

Most of the officers of the flagship were stunned into temporary inactivity by that shocking development, but two reacted almost instantly.

"Thorndyke!" the Admiral snapped. "What did they do, and how?"

And Kinnison, not speaking at all, leaped to a certain panel, to read for himself the analysis of those incredible beams of force.

"They made superneedle rays out of their main projectors," Master Technician Laverne Thorndyke reported, crisply. "They must have shorted everything they've got onto them to burn them out that fast."

"Those beams were hot—plenty hot," Kinnison corroborated the findings. "These recorders go to five billion and have a factor of safety of ten. Even that wasn't anywhere nearly enough—everything in the recorder circuits blew."

"But how could they handle them—" von Hohendorff began to ask.

"They didn't. They pointed them and died," Thorndyke explained, grimly. "They traded one projector and its crew for one cruiser and *its* crew—a good trade from their viewpoint."

"There will be no more such trades," Haynes declared.

Nor were there. The Patrol had maulers enough to englobe the enemy craft at a distance greater even than the effective range of those suicidal beams, and it did so.

Shielding screens cut off the Boskonians' intake of cosmic power and the relentless beaming of the bulldog maulers began. For hour after hour it continued, the cordon ever tightening as the victims' power lessened. And finally even the Gargantuan accumulators of the immense fortresses were drained. Their screens went down under the hellish fury of the maulers' incessant attack, and in a space of minutes thereafter the structures and their contents ceased to exist save as atomic detritus.

The Grand Fleet of the Galactic Patrol remade its formation after a fashion and set off toward the Galaxy at touring blast.

530

And in the control room of the flagship three Lensmen brought a very serious conference to a close.

"You saw what happened to Helmuth's planet," Kinnison's voice was oddly hard, "and I gave you all I could get of the thought about the destruction of all life upon Sol III. A big-enough duodec bomb in the bottom of an ocean would do it. I don't really *know* anything except that we hadn't better let them catch us asleep at the switch again—we've got to be up on our toes every second."

And the Gray Lensman, face set and stern, strode off to his quarters.

II.

During practically all of the long trip back to Earth, Kinnison kept pretty much to his cabin, thinking deeply, blackly, and, he admitted ruefully to himself, to very little purpose. And at Prime Base, through week after week of its feverish activity, he continued to think. Finally, however, he was snatched out of his dark abstraction by no less a personage than Surgeon General Lacy.

"Snap out of it, lad," that worthy advised, smilingly. "When you concentrate on one thing too long, you know, the vortices of thought occupy narrower and narrow loci, until finally the effective volume becomes infinitesimal. Or, mathematically, the then range of cogitation, integrated between the limits of plus and minus infinity, approaches zero as a limit—"

"Huh? What are you talking about?" the Lensman demanded.

"Poor mathematics, perhaps, but sound psychology," Lacy grinned. "It got your undivided attention, didn't it? That was what I was after. In plain English, if you keep on thinking around in circles you'll soon be biting yourself in the small of the back. Come on, you and I are going places."

"Where?"

"To the Grand Ball in honor of the Grand Fleet, my boy—old Dr. Lacy prescribes it for you as a complete and radical change of atmosphere. Let's go!"

The city's largest ballroom was a blaze of light and color. A thousand polychromic lamps flooded their radiance downward through draped bunting upon an even more colorful throng. Two thousand items of feminine loveliness were there, in raiment whose fabrics were the boast of hundreds of planets, whose hues and shades put the spectrum itself to shame. There were over two thousand men, clad in plain or beribboned or bemedaled full civilian dress, or in the variously panoplied dress uniforms of the many Services.

"You're dancing with Miss Forrester first, Kinnison," the surgeon introduced them informally, and the Lensman found himself gliding away with a stunning blonde, ravishingly and revealingly dressed in a dazzlingly blue wisp of Manarkan glamorette—fashion's *dernier cri*.

To the uninformed, Kinnison's garb of plain gray leather might have seemed incongruous indeed in that brilliantly and fastidiously dressed assemblage. But to those people, as to us of today, the drab, starkly utilitarian uniform of the Unattached Lensman transcended far any other, however resplendent, worn by men: and literally hundreds of eyes followed the strikingly handsome couple as they slid rhythmically out upon the polished floor. But a measure of the tall beauty's customary poise had deserted her. She was slimly taut in the circle of the Lensman's arm, her eyes were downcast, and suddenly she missed a step.

"'Scuse me for stepping on your feet," he apologized. "A fellow gets out of practice, flitting around in a speedster so much."

"Thanks for taking the blame, but it's my fault entirely—I know it as well as you do," she replied, flushing uncomfortably. "I *do* know how to dance, too, but—Well, you're a Gray Lensman, you know."

"Huh?" he ejaculated, in honest surprise, and she looked up at him for the first time. "What has that fact got to do with the price of Venerian orchids in Chicago—or with my clumsy walking all over your slippers?"

*

"Everything in the world," she assured him. Nevertheless, her stiff young body relaxed and she fell into the graceful, accurate dancing which she really knew so well how to do. "You see, I don't suppose that any of us has ever seen a Gray Lensman before, except in pictures, and actually to be dancing with one is so thrilling that it is really a shock—I have to get used to it gradually, so to speak. Why, I don't even know how to talk to you! One couldn't possibly call you plain mister, as one would any ord—"

"It'll be QX if you just call me 'say'!" he informed her. "Maybe you'd rather not dance with a dub? What say we go get us a sandwich and a bottle of fayalin or something?"

"No—never!" she exclaimed. "I didn't mean it that way at all. I'm going to have this full dance with you, and enjoy every second of it. And later I am going to pack this dance card—which I hope you will sign for me—away in lavender, so it will go down in history that in my youth I really did dance with Gray Lensman Kinnison. I see that I have recovered enough so that I can talk and dance at the same time. Do you mind if I ask you some silly questions about space?"

"Go ahead. They won't be silly, if I'm any judge. Elementary, perhaps, but not silly."

"I hope so, but I think you're being charitable again. Like most of the girls here, I suppose, I have never been out in deep space at all. Besides a few hops to the Moon, I have taken only two flits, and they were both only interplanetary. One to Mars and one to Venus. I never could see how you deep-space men can really understand what you're doing—either the frightful speeds at which you travel, the distance you cover, or the way your communicators work. In fact, a professor told us that no human mind can understand figures of those magnitudes at all. But you must understand them, I should think . . . oh, perhaps—"

"Or maybe the guy isn't human?" Kinnison laughed deeply, infectiously. "No, your professor was right. We can't understand the figures, but we don't have to—all we have to do is to work with them. And, now that it has just percolated through my skull who you really are, that you are *Gladys* Forrester, it is quite clear that you are in that same boat."

"Me? How?" she exclaimed.

"The human mind cannot really understand a million of anything. Yet your father, an immensely wealthy man, gave you clear title to a million credits in cash, to train you in finance in the only way that really produces results—the hard way of actual experience. You lost a lot of it at first, of course; but at last accounts you had got it all back, and some besides, in spite of all the smart guys trying to take it away from you. The fact that your brain cannot envisage a million credits has not interfered with your manipulation of that amount, has it?"

"No, but that's entirely different!" she protested.

"Not in any essential feature," he countered. "I can explain it best, perhaps, by analogy. You can't visualize, mentally, the size of North America, either, yet that fact does not bother you in the least while you are driving around on it in an automobile. What do you drive? On the ground, I mean, not in the air?"

"A De Khotinsky sporter."

"Um. Top speed a hundred and forty miles per hour, and I suppose you cruise between ninety and a hundred. We'll have to pretend that you drive a Crownover sedan, or some other big, slow jalopy, so that you will tour at about sixty and have an absolute top of ninety. Also, you have a radio. On the broadcast bands you can hear a program from three or four thousand miles away; or, on short wave, from anywhere on Tellus—"

"I can get tight-beam short-wave programs from the Moon," the girl broke in. "I've heard them lots of times."

"Yes," Kinnison assented dryly, "at such times as there didn't happen to be any interference."

"Static *is* pretty bad, lots of times," the heiress agreed.

*

"Well, change 'miles' to 'parsecs' and you've got the picture of deep-space speeds and operations," Kinnison informed her. "Our speed varies, of course, with the density of matter in space; but on the average—say one atom of substance per ten cubic centimeters in space—we tour at about sixty parsecs an hour, and full blast is about ninety. And our ultra-wave communicators, working below the level of the ether, in the subether—"

"Whatever that is," she interrupted.

"That's as good a description or definition of it as any," he grinned at her. "We don't know what even the ether is, or whether or not it exists as an objective reality; to say nothing of what we so nonchalantly call the subether. We do not understand gravity, although we can make it to order. No scientist yet has been able to say how it is propagated, or even whether or not it is propagated. No one has been able to devise any kind of an apparatus or meter or method by which its nature, period, or velocity can be determined. Neither do we know anything about time or space. In fact, fundamentally, we don't really *know* much of anything at all," he concluded.

"Says you. But that makes me feel better, anyway," she confided, snuggling a little closer. "Go on about the communicators."

"Ultra-waves are faster than ordinary radio waves, which of course travel through the ether with the velocity of light, in just about the same ratio as that of the speed of our ships to the speed of slow automobiles—that is, the ratio of a parsec to a mile. Roughly nineteen billion to one. Range, of course, is proportional to the square of the speed."

"Nineteen billion!" she exclaimed. "And you just said that nobody could understand even a million!"

"That's the point exactly," he went on, undisturbed. "You don't have to understand or to visualize it. All you have to do is to remember that deep-space vessels and communicators can cover distance in parsecs at practically the same rate that Tellurian automobiles can cover miles. So, when some space-flea talks to you about parsecs, just think of miles in terms of an automobile and a radio and you won't be far off."

"I never heard it explained that way before—it does make it ever so much simpler. Will you sign this, please?"

"Just one more point." The music had ceased and he was signing her card, preparatory to escorting her back to her place. "Like your supposedly tight-beam Luna-Tellus hookups, our long range, equally tight-beam communicators are very sensitive to interference, either natural or artificial. So, while under perfect conditions we can communicate clear across the Galaxy, there are times—particularly when the pirates are scrambling the channels—that we can't drive a beam from here to Alpha Centauri. Thanks a lot for the dance."

*

The other girls did not quite come to blows as to which of them was to get him next; and shortly—he never did know exactly how it came about—he found himself dancing with a luscious, cuddly little brunette, clad—partially clad, at least—in a high-slitted, flame-colored sheath of some new fabric which the Lensman had never seen before. It looked like solidified, tightly woven electricity!

"Oh, Mr. Kinnison!" his new partner cooed, ecstatically. "I think that all spacemen, and you Lensmen particularly, are just too perfectly darn *heroic* for anything! Why, I think that space is just *terrible*! I simply can't *cope* with it at *all*!"

"Ever been out, miss?" he grinned. He had never known many social butterflies, and temporarily he had forgotten that such girls as this one really existed.

"Why, of *course*!" The young woman kept on being exclamatory.

"Clear out to the Moon, perhaps?" he hazarded.

"Don't be ridic! *Ever* so much farther than *that*! Why, I went clear to *Mars*! And it gave me the screaming *meamies*, no less. I thought I would *collapse*!"

That dance ended ultimately, and other dances with other girls followed; but Kinnison could not throw himself into the gaiety surrounding him. During his cadet days he had enjoyed such revels to the full, but now the whole thing left him cold. His mind insisted upon reverting to its problem. Finally, in the throng of young people on the floor, he saw a girl with a mass of red-bronze hair and a supple, superbly molded figure. He did not need to await her turning to recognize his erstwhile nurse and later assistant, whom he had last seen just this side of far-distant Boyssia II.

"Mac!" To her mind alone he sent out a thought through his Lens. "For the love of Klono, lend a hand—rescue me! How many dances have you got ahead?"

"None at all—I'm not dating ahead." She jumped as though someone had jabbed her with a needle, then paused in panic; eyes wide, breath coming fast, breast pounding. She had felt Lensed thoughts before, but this was something else, something entirely different. Every cell of her brain was open to that Lensman's mind—and what *was* she seeing! She blanketed her thoughts desperately, tried with all her might not to think at all!

"QX, Mac," the thought went quietly on within her mind, quite as though nothing unusual were occurring. "No intrusion meant. You didn't think it; I already knew that if you started dating ahead you'd be tied up until day after tomorrow. Can I have the next one?"

"Sure, Kim."

"Thanks—the Lens is off for the rest of the evening."

She sighed in relief as he snapped the telepathic line as though he were hanging up the receiver of a telephone.

"I'd like to dance with you all, kids," he addressed a large group of buds surrounding him and eying him hungrily, "but I've got this next one. See you later, perhaps," and he was gone.

"Sorry, fellows," he remarked casually, as he made his way through the circle of men around the gorgeous redhead. "Sorry, but this dance is mine, isn't it, Miss MacDougall?"

She nodded, flashing the radiant smile which had so aroused his ire during his hospitalization. "I heard you invoke your spaceman's god, but I was beginning to be afraid that you had forgotten this dance."

"And she said she wasn't dating ahead—the diplomat!" murmured an ambassador, aside.

"Don't be a dope," a captain of Marines muttered in reply. "She meant with *us*. That's a Gray Lensman!"

*

Although the nurse, as has been said, was anything but small, she appeared almost petite against the Lensman's mighty frame as they took off. Silently the two circled the great hall once; lustrous, goldenly green gown—of Earthly nylon, this one, and less revealing than most—swishing in perfect cadence against deftly and softly stepping high-laced boots.

"This is better, Mac," Kinnison sighed, finally, "but I lack just seven thousand kilocycles of being in tune with this. Don't know what's the matter, but it's clogging my jets. I must be getting to be a space-louse."

"A space-louse—you? Uh-uh!" She shook her head. "You know very well what the matter is. You're just too much of a man to mention it."

"Huh?" he demanded.

"Uh-huh," she asserted, positively if obliquely. "Of course you're not in tune with this crowd. How could you be? I don't fit into it any more myself, and what I'm doing isn't even a muffled flare compared to your job. Not one in ten of these fluffs here tonight has ever been beyond the stratosphere; not one in a hundred has ever been out as far as Jupiter, or has ever had a serious thought in her head except about clothes or men; not one of them all has any more idea of what a Lensman really is than I have of hyperspace or of non-Euclidean geometry!"

"Kitty, kitty!" he laughed. "Sheathe the little claws, before you scratch somebody!"

"That isn't cattishness; it's the barefaced truth. Or perhaps," she amended, honestly, "it's both true and cattish, but it's certainly true. And that isn't half of it. No one in the Universe except yourself really *knows* what you are doing, and I'm pretty sure that only two others even suspect. And Dr. Lacy is not one of them," she concluded, surprisingly.

Though shocked, Kinnison did not miss a step. "You *don't* fit into this matrix, any more than I do," he agreed, quietly. "S'pose you and I could do a little flit somewhere?"

"Surely, Kim," and, breaking out of the crowd, they strolled out into the grounds. Not a word was said until they were seated upon a broad, low bench beneath the spreading foliage of a tree.

Then: "What did you come here for tonight, Mac—the real reason?" he demanded, abruptly.

"I . . . me . . . you . . . I mean—Oh, skip it!" the girl stammered, a wave of scarlet flooding her face and down even to her superb, bare shoulders. Then she steadied herself and went on: "You see, I agree with you—as you say, I check you to nineteen decimals. Even Dr. Lacy, with all his knowledge, can be slightly screwy at times, I think."

"Oh, so that's it!" It was not, it was only a very minor part of her reason; but the nurse would have bitten her tongue off rather than admit that she had come to that dance solely and only because Kimball Kinnison was to be there. "You knew, then, that this was old Lacy's idea?"

"Of course. You would never have come, else. He thinks that you may begin wobbling on the beam pretty soon unless you put out a few braking jets."

"And you?"

"Not in a million, Kim. Lacy is as cockeyed as Trenco's ether, and I as good as told him so. He may wobble a bit, but *you* won't. You've got a job to do, and you're doing it. You'll finish it, too, in spite of all the vermin infesting all the galaxies of the macro-cosmic Universe!" she finished, passionately.

"Klono's brazen whiskers, Mac!" He turned suddenly and stared intently down into her wide, gold-flecked, tawny eyes. She stared back for a moment, then looked away.

"Don't look at me like that!" she almost screamed. "I can't stand it—you make me feel stark naked! I know that your Lens is off—I'd simply die if it wasn't—but I think that you're a mind-reader, even without it!"

*

She did know that that powerful telepath was off and would remain off, and she was glad indeed of that fact; for her mind was seething with thoughts which that Lensman must not know, then or ever. And for his part, the Lensman knew what she did not even suspect; that had he chosen to exert the powers at his command she would have been naked, mentally and physically, to his perception; but he did not exert those powers—then. The amenities of human relationship demanded that some fastnesses of reserve remain inviolate, but he had to know what this woman knew. If necessary, he would take the knowledge away from her by force, so completely that she would never know that she had ever known it. Therefore:

"Just what do you know, Mac, and how did you find it out?" he demanded; quietly, but with a stern finality of inflection that made a quick chill run up and down the nurse's back.

"I know a lot, Kim." The girl shivered slightly, even though the evening was warm and balmy. "I learned it from your own mind. When you called me, back there on the floor, you didn't send just a single, sharp thought, just as though you were speaking to me, as you always did before. Instead, it seemed as though I was actually inside your own mind—the whole of it. I have heard Lensman speak of a wide-open two-way, but I never had even the faintest inkling of what it would be like—no one could who has never experienced it. Of course I didn't—I couldn't—understand a millionth of what I saw, or seemed to see. It was too vast, too incredibly immense. I never dreamed any mortal *could* have a mind like that, Kim! But it was ghastly, too. It gave me the creepy jitters. It sent me down completely out of control for a second. And you didn't even know it—I know you didn't! I didn't want to look, really, but I couldn't help seeing, and I'm glad I did—I wouldn't have missed it for the world!" she finished, almost incoherently.

"Hm-m-m. That changes the picture entirely." Much to her surprise, the man's voice was calm and thoughtful; not at all incensed. Not even disturbed. "So I spilled the beans myself, on a wide-open two-way, and didn't even realize it. I knew that you were back-firing about something, but thought it was because I might think you guilty of petty vanity. And I called *you* a dumbbell once!" he marveled.

"Twice," she corrected him, "and the second time I was never so glad to be called names in my whole life."

"Now I *know* that I was getting to be a space-louse."

"Uh-uh, Kim," she denied again, gently. "And you aren't a brat or a lug or a clunker, either, even though I have thought at times that you were all of those things. But, now that I've actually got all this stuff, what can you—what can we—do about it?"

"Perhaps . . . probably . . . I think, since I gave it to you myself, I'll let you keep it," Kinnison decided, slowly.

"Keep it!" she exclaimed. "Of course, I'll keep it! Why, it's in my mind—I'll *have* to keep it—nobody can take *knowledge* away from anyone!"

"Oh, sure—of course," he murmured, absently. There were a lot of things that Mac didn't know, and probably no good end would be served my enlightening her further. "You see, there's a lot of stuff in my mind that I don't know much about myself, yet. Since I gave you an open channel, there must have been a good reason for it, even though, consciously, I don't know myself what it was." He thought intensely for moments, then went on: "Undoubtedly the subconscious. Probably it recognized the necessity of discussing the whole situation with someone having a fresh viewpoint, someone whose ideas can help me develop a fresh angle of attack. Haynes and I think too much alike for him to be of much help."

"You trust *me* that much?" the girl asked, dumfounded.

"Certainly," he replied without hesitation. "I know enough about you to know that you can keep your mouth shut."

THE LENSMAN

*

Thus unromantically did Kimball Kinnison, Gray Lensman, acknowledge the first glimmerings of the dawning perception of a vast fact—that this nurse and he were two between whom there never would nor could exist any iota of doubt or of question.

Then they sat and talked. Not idly, as is the fashion of lovers, of the minutiae of their own romantic affairs, did these two converse, but cosmically, of the entire Universe and of the already existent conflict between the culture of Civilization and Boskonia.

They sat there, romantically enough to all outward seeming; their privacy assured by Kinnison's Lens and by his ever-watchful sense of perception. Time after time, completely unconsciously, that sense reached out to other couples who approached, to touch and to affect their minds so insidiously that they did not know that they were being steered away from the tree in whose black moon-shadow sat the Lensman and the nurse.

Finally the long conversation came to an end and Kinnison assisted his companion to her feet. His frame was straighter, his eyes held a new and brighter light.

"By the way, Kim," she asked idly as they strolled back toward the ballroom, "who is this Klono, by whom you were swearing a while ago? Another spaceman's god, like Noshabkeming, of the Valerians?"

"Something like him, only more so," he laughed. "A combination of Noshabkeming, some of the gods of the ancient Greeks and Romans, all three of the Fates, and quite a few other things as well. I think, originally, from Corvina, but fairly widespread through certain sections of the Galaxy now. He's got so much stuff—teeth and horns, claws and whiskers, tail and everything—that he's much more satisfactory to swear by than any other space-god I know of."

"But why do men have to swear at all, Kim?" she queried, curiously. "It's so silly."

"For the same reason that women cry," he countered. "A man swears to keep from crying, a woman cries to keep from swearing. Both are sound psychology. Safety valves—means of blowing off excess pressure that would otherwise blow fuses or burn out tubes."

III.

In the library of the Port Admiral's richly comfortable home, a room as heavily guarded against all forms of intrusion as was his private office, two old but active Lensmen sat and grinned at each other like the two conspirators which in fact they were. One took a squat, red bottle of fayalin from a cabinet and filled two small glasses. The glasses clinked, rim to rim.

"Here's to love!" Haynes gave the toast.

"Ain't it grand!" Surgeon General Lacy responded.

"Down the hatch!" they chanted in unison, and action followed word.

"You aren't asking if everything stayed on the beam." This from Lacy.

"No need. I had a spy ray on the whole performance."

"You would—you're the type. However, I would have, too, if I had a panel full of them in my office. Well, say it, you old space-hellion!" Lacy grinned again, albeit a trifle wryly.

538

"Nothing to say, sawbones. You did a grand job, and you've got nothing to blow a jet about."

"No? How would you like to have a red-headed spitfire who's scarcely dry behind the ears yet tell you to your teeth that you've got softening of the brain? That you had the mental capacity of a gnat, the intellect of a Zabriskan fontema? And to have to take it, without even heaving the insubordinate young jade into the can for about twenty-five well-earned black spots?"

"Oh, come, now, you're just blasting. It wasn't that bad."

"Perhaps not quite—but it was bad enough."

"She'll grow up, some day, and realize that you were foxing her six ways from the origin."

"Probably. In the meantime, it's all part of the bigger job. Thank God I'm not young any more. They suffer so."

"Check. *How* they suffer!"

"But you saw the ending and I didn't. How did it turn out?" Lacy asked.

"Partly good, partly bad." Haynes slowly poured two more drinks and thoughtfully swirled the crimson, pungently aromatic liquid around and around in his glass before he spoke again. "Hooked—but she knows it, and I'm afraid she'll do something about it."

"She's a smart girl—I told you she was. She doesn't fox herself about anything. Hm-m-m. And separation is indicated, it would seem."

"Check. Can you send out a hospital ship somewhere, so as to get rid of her for two or three weeks?"

"Can do. Three weeks be enough? We can't send him anywhere, you know."

"Plenty. He'll be gone in two." Then, as Lacy glanced at him questioningly, Haynes continued: "Ready for a shock? He's going to Lundmark's Nebula."

"But he *can't*! That would take years! Nobody has ever got back from there yet, and there's this new job of his. Besides, this separation is only supposed to last until you can spare him for a while!"

"If it takes very long he's coming back. The idea has always been, you know, that intergalactic matter may be so thin—one atom per liter or so—that such a flit won't take one tenth the time supposed. We recognize the danger. He's going well heeled."

"How well?"

"The best that we can give him."

"I hate to clog their jets this way, but it's got to be done. We'll give her a raise when I send her out—make her sector chief. Huh?"

"Did I hear any such words lately as 'spitfire,' 'hussy,' and 'jade,' or did I dream them?" Haynes asked, quizzically.

"She's all of them, and more—but she's one of the best nurses and one of the finest women this side of Hades, too!"

"QX, Lacy, give her her raise. Of course she's good, or she wouldn't be in on this deal at all. In fact, they're about as fine a couple of youngsters as old Tellus has produced."

"They are that. Man, *what* a pair of skeletons!"

*

And in the Nurses' Quarters a young woman with a wealth of red-bronze-auburn hair and tawny eyes was staring at her own reflection in a mirror.

"You half-wit, you ninny, you lug!" she stormed, bitterly if almost inaudibly, at that reflection. "You lame-brained moron, you red-headed, idiotic imbecile, you microcephalic dumbbell, you clunker! Of all the men in this whole cockeyed galaxy, you would have to make a dive at Kimball Kinnison, the one man who never has realized that you are even alive. At a Gray Lensman—" Her expression changed and she whispered softly: "A . . . Gray . . . Lensman. He can't love any woman as long as he's carrying that load. They can't let themselves be human—quite; perhaps loving him will be enough—"

She straightened up, shrugged, and smiled; but even that pitiful travesty of a smile could not long endure. Shortly it was buried in waves of pain and the girl threw herself down upon her bed.

"Oh Kim, Kim!" she sobbed. "I wish . . . why can't you—Oh, why did I ever have to be born!"

*

Three weeks later, far out in space, Kimball Kinnison was thinking thoughts entirely foreign to his usual pattern. He was in his bunk, smoking dreamily, staring unseeing at the metallic ceiling. He was not thinking of Boskone.

When he had thought of Mac, back there at that dance, he had, for the first time in his life, failed to narrow down his beam to the exact thought being sent. Why? The explanation he had given the girl was totally inadequate. For that matter, why had he been so glad to see her there? And why, at every odd moment, did visions of her keep coming into his mind—her form and features, her eyes, her lips, her startling hair?

She was beautiful, of course, but not nearly such a seven-sector callout as that thionite dream he had met on Aldebaran II—and his only thought of her was an occasional faint regret that he had not half wrung her lovely neck. Why, she wasn't really as good-looking as, and didn't have half the je ne sais quoi of, that blond heiress—what was her name?—oh, yes, Forrester—

There was only one answer, and it jarred him to the core—he would not admit it, even to himself. He couldn't love anybody—it just simply was not in the cards. He had a job to do. The Patrol had spent a million credits making a Lensman out of him, and it was up to him to give them some kind of a run for their money. No Lensman had any business with a wife, especially a Gray Lensman. He couldn't sit down anywhere, and she couldn't flit with him. Besides, nine out of every ten Gray Lensmen got killed before they finished their jobs, and the one that did happen to live long enough to retire to a desk was almost always half machinery and artificial parts—

No, not in seven thousand years. No woman deserved to have her life made into such a hell on earth as that would be—years of agony, of heartbreaking suspense, climaxed by untimely widowhood; or, at best, the wasting of the richest part of her life upon a husband who was half steel, rubber, and phenoline plastic. Red in particular was much too splendid a person to be let in for anything like that—

But hold on—jet back! What made him think that he rated any such girl? That there was even a possibility—especially in view of the way he had behaved while under her care in Base Hospital—that she would ever feel like being anything more to him than a strictly impersonal nurse? Probably not. He had Klono's own brazen gall to think that she would marry him, under any conditions, even if he made a full-power dive at her.

Just the same, she might. Look at what women did fall in love with, sometimes. So he would never make any kind of a dive at her; no, not even a pass. She was too sweet, too fine, too vital a woman to be tied to any space-louse; she deserved happiness, not heartbreak. She deserved the best there was in life, not the worst; the whole love of a whole man for a whole lifetime, not the fractions which were all that he could offer any woman. As long as he could think a straight thought he wouldn't make any motions toward spoiling her life. In fact, he hadn't better see Reddy again. He wouldn't go near any planet she was on, and if he saw her out in space he'd go somewhere else at ten gravities.

With a bitter imprecation Kinnison sprang out of his bunk, hurled his half-smoked cigarette at an ash tray, and strode toward the control room.

*

The ship he rode was of the Patrol's best. Superbly powered for flight, defense, and offense, she was withal a complete space-laboratory and observatory; and her personnel, over and above her regular crew, was as varied as her equipment. She carried ten Lensmen—a circumstance unique in the annals of space, even for such a trouble-shooting battle wagon as the *Dauntless* was; a scientific staff which was practically a cross section of the Tree of Knowledge. She carried Lieutenant Peter van Buskirk and his company of Valerian wild cats; Worsel of Velantia and threescore of his reptilian kinsmen; Tregonsee, the blocky Rigellian Lensman, and a dozen or so of his fellows; Master Technician LaVerne Thorndyke and his crew. She carried three Master Pilots, Prime Base's best—Henderson, Schermerhorn, and Watson.

The *Dauntless* was an immense vessel. She had to be, in order to carry, in addition to the men and the things requisitioned by Kinnison, the personnel and the equipment which Port Admiral Haynes had insisted upon sending with him.

"But great Klono, chief, think of what a hole you're making in Prime Base if we don't get back!" Kinnison had protested.

"You're coming back, Kinnison," the Port Admiral had replied gravely. "That is why I am sending these men and this stuff along—to be as sure as I possibly can that you *do* get back."

Now they were out in intergalactic space, and the Gray Lensman, lying flat upon his back with his eyes closed, sent his sense of perception out beyond the confining iron walls and let it roam the void. This was better than a visiplate; with no material barriers or limitations he was feasting upon a spectacle scarcely to be pictured in the most untrammeled imaginings of man. There were no planets, no suns, no stars, no meteorites, no particles of cosmic débris. All nearby space was empty, with an indescribable perfection of emptiness at the very thought of which the mind quailed in uncomprehending horror. And, accentuating that emptiness, at such mind-searing distances as to be dwarfed into buttons, and yet, because of their intrinsic massiveness, starkly apparent in their three-dimensional relationships, there hung poised and motionlessly stately the component galaxies of a universe.

Behind the flying vessel the First Galaxy was a tiny, brightly shining lens, so far away that such minutiae as individual solar systems were invisible, so distant that even the gigantic masses of its accompanying globular star clusters were merged indistinguishably into its sharply lenticular shape. In front of her, to right and to left of her, above and beneath her were other galaxies, never explored by man or by any other beings subscribing to the code of Galactic Civilization. Some, edge on, were thin, waferlike. Others appeared as full disks, showing faintly or boldly the prodigious, mathematically inexplicable spiral arms by virtue of whose obscure functioning they had come into being. Between these two extremes there was every possible variant in angular displacement.

Utterly incomprehensible although the speed of the space-flyer was, yet those galaxies remained relatively motionless, hour after hour. What distances! What magnificence! What grandeur! What awful, what poignantly solemn calm!

Despite the fact that Kinnison had gone out there expecting to behold that very scene, he felt awed to insignificance by the overwhelming, the cosmic immensity of the spectacle. What business had he, a sub-electronic midge from an ultra-microscopic planet, venturing out into macro-cosmic space, a demesne comprehensible only to the omniscient and omnipotent Creator?

*

He got up, shaking off the futile mood. This wouldn't get him to the first check station, and he had a job to do. And, after all, wasn't man as big as space? Could he have come out here, otherwise? He was. Yes, man was bigger even than space. Man, by his very envisionment of macro-cosmic space, had already mastered it.

Besides, the Boskonians, whoever they might be, had certainly mastered it; he was now certain that they were operating upon an intergalactic scale. Even after leaving Tellus he had hoped and had really expected that his line would lead to a stronghold in some star cluster belonging to his own Galaxy, so distant from it, or perhaps so small, as to have escaped the notice of the chartmakers; but such was not the case. No possible error in either the determination or the following of that line placed it anywhere near any such cluster. It led straight to and only to Lundmark's Nebula; and that Galaxy was, therefore, his present destination.

Man was certainly as good as the pirates; probably better, on the basis of past performance. Of all the races of the Galaxy, man had always taken the initiative, had always been the leader and commander. And, with the exception of the Arisians, man had the best brain in the Galaxy.

The thought of that eminently philosophical race gave Kinnison pause. His Arisian sponsor had told him that by virtue of the Lens the Patrol should be able to make Civilization secure throughout the Galaxy. Just what did that mean—that it could not go outside? Or did even the Arisians suspect that Boskonia was in fact intergalactic? Probably. The mentor had said that, given any one definite fact, a really competent mind could envisage the entire Universe; even though he had added carefully that his own mind was not a really competent one.

But this, too, was idle speculation, and it was time to receive and to correlate some more reports. Therefore, one by one, he got in touch with scientists and observers.

The density of matter in space, which had been lessening steadily, was now approximately constant at one atom per four hundred cubic centimeters. Their speed was therefore about a hundred thousand parsecs per hour; and, even allowing for the slowing up at both ends due to the density of the medium, the trip should not take over ten days.

The power situation, which had been his gravest care, since it was almost the only factor not amenable to theoretical solution, was even better than anyone had dared hope; the cosmic energy available in space had actually been increasing as the matter content decreased—a fact which seemed to bear out the contention than energy was continually being converted into matter in such regions. It was taking much less excitation of the intake screens to produce a given flow of power than any figure ever observed in the denser media within the Galaxy.

Thus, the atomic motors which served as exciters had a maximum power of four hundred pounds an hour; that is, each exciter could transform that amount of matter into pure energy and employ the output usefully in energizing the intake screen to which it was connected. Each screen, operating normally on a hundred-thousand-to-one ratio, would then furnish its receptor on the ship with energy equivalent to the annihilation of four million pounds per hour of material substance. Out there, however, it was being observed that the intake-exciter ratio, instead of being less than a hundred thousand to one, was actually almost a million to one.

*

It would serve no useful purpose here to go further into the details of any more of the reports, or to dwell at any great length upon the remainder of the journey to the Second Galaxy. Suffice it to say that Kinnison and his highly trained crew observed, classified, recorded, and conferred; and that they approached their destination with every possible precaution. Detectors full out, observers were at every plate, the ship was as immune to detection as Hotchkiss' nullifiers could make it.

Up to the Second Galaxy the *Dauntless* flashed, and into it. Was this island universe essentially like the First Galaxy as to planets and peoples? If so, had they been won over or wiped out by the horrid culture of Boskonia or was the struggle still going on?

"If we assume, as we must, that the line we followed was the trace of Boskone's beam," argued the sagacious Worsel, "the probability is very great that the enemy is in virtual control of this entire Galaxy. Otherwise—if they were in a minority or were struggling seriously for dominion—they could neither have spared the forces which invaded our Galaxy, nor would they have been in condition to rebuild their vessels as they did to match the new armaments developed by the Patrol."

"Very probably true," agreed Kinnison, and that was the consensus of opinion. "Therefore we want to do our scouting very quietly. But in some ways that makes it all the better. If they are in control, they won't be unduly suspicious."

And thus it proved. A planet-bearing sun was soon located, and while the *Dauntless* was still light-years distant from it, several ships were detected. At least, the Boskonians were not using nullifiers!

THE LENSMAN

Spy rays were sent out. Tregonsee, the Rigellian Lensman, exerted to the full his powers of perception, and Kinnison hurled downward to the planet's surface a mental viewpoint and communications center. That the planet was Boskonian was soon learned, but that was all. It was scarcely fortified: no trace could be found of a beam communicating with Boskone.

Solar system after solar system was found and studied, with like result. But finally, out in space, one of the screens showed activity; a beam was in operation between a vessel then upon the plates and some other station. Kinnison tapped it quickly; and, while observers were determining its direction, hardness, and power, a thought flowed smoothly into the Lensman's brain.

"—proceed at once to relieve vessel P4K730. Eichlan, speaking for Boskone, ending message."

"Follow that ship, Hen!" Kinnison directed, crisply. "Not too close, but don't lose him!" He then relayed to the others the orders which had been intercepted.

"The same formula, huh?" Van Buskirk roared, and "Just another lieutenant, that sounds like, not Boskone himself." Thorndyke added.

"Perhaps so, perhaps no." The Gray Lensman was merely thoughtful. "It doesn't prove a thing except that Helmuth was not Boskone, which was already fairly certain. If we can prove that there is such a being as Boskone, and that he is not in this Galaxy—well, in that case, we'll go somewhere else," he concluded, with grim finality.

*

The chase was comparatively short, leading toward a yellowish star around which swung eight average-sized planets. Toward one of these flew the unsuspecting pirate, followed by the Patrol vessel, and it soon became apparent that there was a battle going on. One spot upon the planet's surface, either a city or a tremendous military base, was domed over by a screen which was one blinding glare of radiance. And for miles in every direction ships of space were waging spectacularly devastating warfare.

Kinnison shot a thought down into the fortress, and with the least possible introduction or preamble, got into touch with one of its high officers. He was not surprised to learn that those people were more or less human in appearance, since the planet was quite similar to Tellus in age, climate, atmosphere, and mass.

"Yes, we are fighting Boskonia," the answering thought came coldly clear. "We need help, and badly. Can you—"

"We're detected!" Kinnison's attention was seized by a yell from the board. "They're all coming at us at once!"

Whether the scientists of Boskone developed the detector-nullifier before or after Helmuth's failure to deduce the Lensman's use of such an instrument is a nice question, and one upon which a great deal has been said. While interesting, the point is really immaterial here; the facts remaining the same—that the pirates not only had it at the time of the Patrol's first visit to the Second Galaxy, but had used it to such good advantage that the denizens of that recalcitrant planet had been forced, in the sheer desperation of self-preservation, to work out a scrambler for that nullification and to surround their world with its radiations. They could not restore perfect detection, but the conditions for

544

complete nullification were so critical that it was a comparatively simple matter to upset it sufficiently so that an image of a sort was revealed. And, at that close range, any sort of an image was enough.

The *Dauntless*, approaching the planet, entered the zone of scrambling and stood revealed plainly enough upon the plates of enemy vessels. They attacked instantly and viciously; within a second after the lookout had shouted his warning the outer screens of the Patrol ship were blazing incandescent under the furious assaults of a dozen Boskonian beams.

IV.

For a moment all eyes were fixed apprehensively upon meters and recorders, but there was no immediate cause for alarm. The builders of the *Dauntless* had built well; her outer screen, the lightest of her series of four, was carrying the attackers' load with no sign of distress.

"Strap down, everybody," the expedition's commander ordered then. "Inert her, Hen. Match velocity with that base," and as Master Pilot Henry Henderson cut his Bergenholm, the vessel lurched wildly aside as its intrinsic velocity was restored.

Henderson's fingers swept over his board as rapidly and as surely as those of an organist over the banked keys of his console; producing, not chords and arpeggios of harmony, but roaring blasts of precisely controlled power. Each keylike switch controlled one jet. Lightly and fleetingly touched, it produced a gentle urge; at sharp, full contact it yielded a mighty, solid shove; depressed still farther, so as to lock into any one of a dozen notches, it brought into being a torrent of propulsive force of any desired magnitude, which ceased only when its key-release was touched.

And Henderson was a virtuoso. Smoothly, effortlessly, but in a space of seconds the great vessel rolled over, spiraled, and swung until her landing jets were in line and exerting five gravities of thrust. Then, equally smoothly, almost imperceptibly, the line of force was varied until the flame-enshrouded dome was stationary below them. Nobody, not even the two other Master Pilots, and least of all Henderson himself, paid any attention to the polished perfection, the consummate artistry, of the performance. That was his job. He was a Master Pilot, and one of the hallmarks of his rating was the habit of making difficult maneuvers look easy.

"Take 'em now, chief? Can't we, huh?" Chatway, the chief firing officer, did not say those words. He did not need to. The attitude and posture of the C.F.O. and his subordinates made the thought tensely plain.

"Not yet, Chatty," the Lensman answered the unsent thought. "We'll have to wait until they englobe us, so that we can get them all. It's got to be all or none. If even one of them gets away, or even has time to analyze and report on the stuff we're going to use, it'll be just too bad."

He then got in touch with the officer within the beleaguered base and renewed the conversation at the point at which it had been broken off.

"We can help you, I think; but to do so effectively we must have clear ether. Will you please order your ships away, out of even extreme range?"

"For how long? They can do us irreparable damage in one rotation of the planet."

"One-twentieth of that time, at most—if we cannot do it in that time we cannot do it at all. Nor will they direct many beams at you, if any. They will be working on us."

Then, as the defending ships darted away, Kinnison turned to his C. F. O. "QX, Chatty. Open up with your secondaries. Fire at will!"

Then from projectors of a power theretofore carried only by maulers, there raved out against the nearest Boskonian vessels beams of a vehemence compared to which the enemies' own seemed weak, futile. And those were the secondaries!

As has been intimated, the *Dauntless* was an unusual ship. She was enormous. She was bigger even than a mauler in actual bulk and mass; and from needle-beaked prow to jet-studded stern she was literally packed with power—power for any emergency conceivable to the fertile minds of Port Admiral Haynes and his staff of designers and engineers. Instead of two, or at most three intake-screen exciters, she had two hundred. Her bus bars, instead of being the conventional rectangular coppers, of a few square inches cross-sectional area, were laminated members built up of co-axial tubing of pure silver to a diameter of over a yard—multiple and parallel conductors, each of whose current-carrying capacity was to be measured only in millions of amperes. And everything else aboard that mighty engine of destruction was upon the same Gargantuan scale.

*

Titanic though those thrusts were, not a pirate ship was seriously hurt. Outer screens went down, and more than a few of the second lines of defense also failed. But that was the Patrolmen's strategy; to let the enemy know that they had weapons of offense somewhat superior to their own, but not quite powerful enough to be a real menace.

In minutes, therefore, the Boskonians rushed up and englobed the newcomer; supposing, of course, that she was a product of the world below, that she was manned by the race who had so long and so successfully fought off Boskonian encroachment.

They attacked, and under the concentrated fury of their beams, the outer screen of the Patrol ship began to fail. Higher and higher into the spectrum it radiated, blinding white—blue—an intolerable violet glare; then, patchily, through the invisible ultraviolet and into the black of extinction. The second screen resisted longer and more stubbornly, but finally it also went down; the third automatically taking up the burden of defense. Simultaneously, the power of Civilization's projectors weakened, as though the *Dauntless* were shifting her power from offense to defense in order to stiffen her third, and supposedly her last, shielding screen.

"Pretty soon, now, Chatway," Kinnison observed. "Just as soon as they can report that they have us in a bad way; that it is just a matter of time until they blow us out of the ether. Better report now—I'll put you on the spool."

"We are equipped to energize simultaneously eight of the new, replaceable-unit primary projectors," the C.F.O. stated, crisply. "There are twenty-one vessels englobing us, and no others within detection. With a discharge period of point six oh second and a switching interval of point oh nine, the entire action should occupy one point nine eight seconds."

"Chief Communications Officer Nelson on the spool. Can the last surviving ship of the enemy report enough in two seconds to do us material harm?"

"In my opinion it cannot, sir," Nelson reported, formally. "The communications officer is neither an observer nor a technician; he merely transmits whatever material is given him by other officers for transmission. If he is already working a beam to his base at the moment of our first blast, he might be able to report the destruction of vessels, but he could not be specific as to the nature of the agent used. Such a report could do no harm, as the fact of the destruction of the vessels will in any event become apparent shortly. Since we are apparently being overcome easily, however, and this is a routine action, the probability is that this detachment is not in direct communication with Base at any given moment. If not, he could not establish working control in two seconds."

"Kinnison now reporting. Having determined to the best of my ability that engaging the enemy at this time will not enable them to send Boskone any information regarding our primary armament, I now give the word to—*fire*."

*

The underlying principle of the destructive beam produced by overloading a regulation projector had, it is true, been discovered by a Boskonian technician. In so far as Boskonia was concerned, however, the secret had died with its inventor, since the pirates had at that time no headquarters in the First Galaxy. And the Patrol had had months of time in which to perfect it, for that work was begun before the last of Helmuth's guardian fortress had been destroyed.

The projector was not now fatal to its crew, since they were protected from the lethal back-radiation, not only by shields of force, but also by foot after impenetrable foot of lead, osmium, carbon, and paraffin. The refractories were of neo-cargalloy, backed and permeated by M K R fields; the radiators were constructed of the most ultimately resistant materials known to the science of the age. But even so, the unit had a useful life of but little over half a second, so frightful was the overload at which it was used. Like a rifle cartridge, it was good for only one shot. Then it was thrown away, to be replaced by a new unit.

Those problems were relatively simple of solution. Switching those enormous energies was the great stumbling block. The old Kimmerling block-dispersion circuit breaker was prone to arc over under loads much in excess of a hundred billion KW, hence could not even be considered in this new application. However, the Patrol force finally succeeded in working out a combination of the immersed-antenna and the semi-permeable-condenser types, which they called the Thorndyke heavy-duty switch. It was cumbersome, of course—any device to interrupt voltages and amperages of the really astronomical magnitude in question could not at that time be small—but it was positive, fast-acting, and reliable.

At Kinnison's word of command, eight of those indescribable primary beams lashed out; stilettos of irresistibly penetrant energy which not even a Q-type helix could withstand. Through screens, through wall shields, and through metal they hurtled in a space of time almost too brief to be measured. Then, before each beam expired, it was swung a little, so that the victim was literally split apart or carved into sections. Performance exceeded by far that of the hastily improvised weapon which had so easily destroyed the heavy cruisers of the Patrol; in fact, it checked almost exactly with the theoretical figures of the designers.

As the first eight beams winked out, eight more came into being, then five more; and meanwhile the mighty secondaries were sweeping the heavens with full-aperture cones of destruction. Metal meant no more to those rays than did organic material; everything solid or liquid whiffed into vapor and disappeared. The *Dauntless* lay alone in the sky of that new world.

"Marvelous—wonderful!" the thought beat into Kinnison's brain as soon as he re-established rapport with the being so far below. "We have recalled our ships. Will you please come down to our spaceport at once, so that we can put into execution a plan which has been long in preparation?"

"As soon as your ships are down," the Tellurian acquiesced. "Not sooner, as your landing conventions are doubtless very unlike our own and we do not wish to cause disaster. Give me the word when your field is entirely clear."

*

That word came soon, and Kinnison nodded to the pilots. Once more inertialess, the *Dauntless* shot downward, deep into atmosphere, before her inertia was restored. Rematching velocity this time was a simple matter, and upon the towering, powerfully resilient pillars of her landing-jets the inconceivable mass of the Tellurian ship of war settled toward the ground, as lightly seeming as a wafted thistle-down.

"Their cradles wouldn't fit us, of course, even if they were big enough—which they aren't, by half," Schermerhorn commented. "Where do they want us to put her?"

"'Anywhere,' they say," the Lensman answered, "but we don't want to take that too literally—without a solid dock she'll make an awful hole, wherever we set her down. Won't hurt her any. She's designed for it. We couldn't expect to find cradles to fit her anywhere except on Tellus. I'd say to lay her down on her belly over there in that corner, out of the way, as close to that big hangar as you can work without blasting it out with your jets."

As Kinnison had intimated, the lightness of the vessel was indeed only seeming. Superbly and effortlessly the big boat seeped downward into the designated corner; but when she touched the pavement she did not stop. Still easily and without jar or jolt she settled—a full twenty feet into the concrete, reinforcing steel and hard-packed earth of the field before she came to a halt.

"What a monster! Who are they? Where could they have come from?" Kinnison caught a confusion of startled thoughts as the real size and mass of the visitor became apparent to the natives. Then again came the clear thought of the officer.

"We would like very much to have you and as many as possible of your companions come to confer with us as soon as you have tested our atmosphere. Come in spacesuits if you must."

The air was tested and found suitable. True, it did not match exactly that of Tellus, or Rigel IV, or Velantia; but then, neither did that of the *Dauntless*, since that gaseous mixture was a compromise one, and mostly artificial to boot.

"Worsel, Tregonsee, and I will go to this conference," Kinnison decided. "The rest of you sit tight. I don't need to tell you to keep on your toes, that anything is apt to happen, anywhere, without warning. Keep your detectors full out and keep your noses clean—be ready like the good little endeavorers you are, 'to do with all your might what your hands find to do.' Come on, fellows," and the three Lensmen strode, wriggled, and waddled across the field, to and into a spacious room of the Administration Building.

"Strangers, or, I should say friends, I introduce you to Wise, our president," Kinnison's acquaintance said, clearly enough, although it was plain to all three Lensmen that he was shocked at the sight of the Earthman's companions.

"I am informed that you understand our language—" the president began doubtfully.

He, too, was staring at Tregonsee and Worsel. He had been told that Kinnison, and therefore, supposed, the rest of the visitors, were beings fashioned more or less after his own pattern. But these two creatures!

*

For they were not even remotely human in form. Tregonsee, the Rigellian, with his leathery, multiappendaged, oil-drumlike body, his immobile dome of a head and his four blocky pillars of legs must at first sight have appeared fantastic indeed. And Worsel, the Velantian, was infinitely worse. He was repulsive, a thing materialized from sheerest nightmare—a leather-winged, crocodile-headed, crooked-armed, thirty-foot long, pythonish, reptilian monstrosity!

But the President of Medon saw at once that which the three outlanders had in common. The Lenses, each glowingly aflame with its own innate pseudo-vitality—Kinnison's clamped to his brawny wrist by a band of iridium-osmium-tungsten alloy; Tregonsee's embedded in the glossy black flesh of one mighty, sinuous arm; Worsel's apparently driven deep and with cruel force into the horny, scaly hide squarely in the middle of his forehead, between two of his weirdly stalked, repulsively extensible eyes.

"It is not your language we understand, but your thoughts, by virtue of these our Lenses which you have already noticed." The president gasped as Kinnison bulleted the information into his mind. "Go ahead . . . . Just a minute!" as an unmistakable sensation swept through his being. "We've gone *free*! The whole planet, I perceive. In that respect, at least, you are in advance of us. As far as I know, no scientist of any of our races has even thought of a Bergenholm big enough to free a world."

"It was long in the designing; many years in the building of its units," Wise replied. "We are leaving this sun in an attempt to escape from our enemy and yours; Boskone. It is our only chance of survival. The means have long been ready, but the opportunity which you have just made for us is the first that we have had. This is the first time in many, many years that not a single Boskonian vessel is in position to observe our flight."

"Where are you going? Surely the Boskonians will be able to find you if they wish."

"That is possible, but we must run that risk. We must have a respite or perish; after a long lifetime of continuous warfare, our resources are at the point of exhaustion. There is a part of this Galaxy in which there are very few planets, and of those few, none are inhabited or habitable. Since nothing is to be gained, ships seldom or never go there. If we can reach that region undetected, the probability is that we shall be unmolested long enough to recuperate."

Kinnison exchanged flashing thoughts with his two fellow Lensmen, then turned again to Wise.

"We come from a neighboring Galaxy," he informed him, and pointed out to his mind just which Galaxy he meant. "You are fairly close to the edge of this one. Why not move over to ours? You have no friends here, since you think that yours may be the only remaining independent planet. We can assure you of friendship. We can also give you some hope of peace—or at least semipeace—in the near future, for we are driving Boskonia out of our Galaxy."

"What you think of as 'semipeace' would be tranquillity incarnate to us," the old man replied with feeling. "We have, in fact, considered long that very move. We decided against it for two reasons: first, because we knew nothing about conditions there, and hence might be going from bad to worse; and second and more important, because of lack of reliable data upon the density of matter in intergalactic space. Lacking that, we could not estimate the time necessary for the journey, and we could have no assurance that our sources of power, great as they are, would be sufficient to make up the heat lost by radiation."

"We have already given you an idea of conditions and we can give you the data you lack."

*

They did so, and for a matter of minutes the Medonians conferred. Meanwhile Kinnison went on a mental expedition to one of the power plants. He expected to see supercolossal engines; bus bars ten feet thick, perhaps cooled in liquid helium; and other things in proportion. But what he actually saw made him gasp for breath and call Tregonsee's attention. The Rigellian sent out his sense of perception with Kinnison's, and he also was almost stunned.

"What's the answer, Trig?" the Earthman asked, finally. "This is more down your alley than mine. That motor's about the size of my foot, and if it isn't eating a thousand pounds an hour I'm Klono's maiden aunt. And the whole output is going out on two wires no bigger than number four, jacketed together like ordinary parallel pair. Perfect insulator? If so, how about switching?"

"That must be it, a substance of practically infinite resistance," the Rigellian replied absently, studying intently the peculiar mechanism. "Must have a better conductor than silver, too, unless they can handle voltages of ten to the fifteenth or so, and don't see how they could break such potentials . . . . Guess they don't use switches . . . don't see any . . . must shut down the prime sources . . . . No, there it is—so small that I overlooked it completely. In that little box there! Sort of a jam-plate type; a thin sheet of insulation with a knife on the leading edge, working in a slot to cut the two conductors apart—kills the arc by jamming into the tight slot at the end of the box. The conductors must fuse together at each make and burn away a little at each break, that's why they have renewable tips. Kim, they've really got something! I certainly am going to stay here and do some studying."

"Yes, and we'll have to rebuild the *Dauntless*—"

The two Lensmen were called away from their study by Worsel—the Medonians had decided to accept the invitation to attempt to move to the First Galaxy. Orders were given, the course was changed and the planet, now a veritable spaceship, shot away in the new direction.

"Not as many legs as a speedster, of course, but at that, she's no slouch—we're making plenty of lights," Kinnison commented, then turned to the president. "It seems rather presumptuous for us to call you simply 'Wise,' especially as I gather that that is not really your formal name—"

"That is what I am called, and that is what you are to call me," the oldster replied: "We of Medon do not have names. Each has a number; or, rather, a symbol composed of numbers and letters of our alphabet—a symbol which gives his full classification. Since these things are too clumsy for regular use, however, each of us is given a nickname, usually an adjective, which is supposed to be more or less descriptive. You of Earth we could not give a complete symbol, your two companions we could not give any at all. However, you may be interested in knowing that you three have already been named?"

"Very much so."

"You are to be called 'Keen.' He of Rigel IV is 'Strong,' and he of Velantia is 'Agile.'"

"Quite complimentary to me, but—"

"Not bad at all, I'd say," Tregonsee broke in. "But hadn't we better be getting on with more serious business?"

"We should indeed," Wise agreed. "We have much to discuss with you; particularly the weapon you used."

"Could you get an analysis of it?" Kinnison asked, sharply.

"No. No one beam was in operation long enough. However, a study of the recorded data, particularly the figure for intensity—figures so high as to be almost unbelievable—lead us to believe that the beam is the result of an enormous overload upon a projector otherwise of more or less conventional type. Some of us have wondered why we did not think of the idea ourselves—"

"So did we, when it was used on us," Kinnison grinned and went off to explain the origin of the primary. "But before we go into details, I noticed that your fixed-mount stuff could not work effectively through atmosphere. We have what we call Q-type helices, with which we incase such beams so that they work in a tube of vacuum. We will give you the Q-formulæ and also the working hookup—including the protective devices, because they're mighty dangerous without plenty of force-backing—of the primaries, in exchange for some lessons in power-plant design."

"Such an exchange of knowledge would be helpful indeed," Wise agreed.

"The Boskonians know nothing whatever of this beam, and we do not want them to learn of it," Kinnison cautioned. "Therefore I have two suggestions to make. First, that you try everything else before you use this primary beam. Second, that you don't use it even then unless you can wipe out, as nearly simultaneously as we did out there, every Boskonian who may be able to report back to his base as to what really happened. Fair enough?"

"Eminently so. We agree without reservation—it is to our interest as much as yours that such a secret be kept from Boskone."

"QX. Fellow, let's go back to the ship for a couple of minutes." Then, aboard the *Dauntless*: "Tregonsee, you and your crew want to stay with the planet, to show the Medonians what to do and to help them along generally, as well as to learn about their power system. Thorndyke, you and your gang, and probably Lensman Hotchkiss, had better study these things, too—you'll know what you want as soon as they show you the hookup. Worsel, I'd like to have you stay with the ship. You're in command of her until further orders. Keep her here for, say, a week or ten days, until the planet is well out of the Galaxy. Then, if Hotchkiss and Thorndyke haven't got all the dope they want, leave them here to ride back with Tregonsee on the planet and drill the *Dauntless* for Tellus. Keep yourself more or less disengaged for a while, and sort of keep tuned to me. I may not need an ultra-long-range communicator, but you never can tell."

"Why such comprehensive orders, Kim?" asked Hotchkiss. "Who ever heard of a commander abandoning his expeditions? Aren't you sticking around?"

"Nope—got to do a flit. Think maybe I'm getting an idea. Break out my speedster, will you, Allerdyce?"—and the Gray Lensman was gone.

V.

Kinnison's speedster shot away and made an undetectable, uneventful voyage back to the Earth. In due time, therefore, the Gray Lensman was again closeted with Port Admiral Haynes.

"Why the foliage?" the chief of staff asked, almost at sight, for the Gray Lensman was wearing a more-than-half-grown beard.

"I may need to be Chester Q. Fordyce for a while. If I don't, I can shave it off quick. If I do, a real beard is a lot better than an imitation," and he plunged into his subject.

"Very fine work, son, very fine indeed," Haynes congratulated the younger man at the conclusion of his report. "We shall begin at once, and be ready to rush things through when the technicians bring back the necessary data from Medon. But there's one more thing I want to ask you. How did you come to place those spotting-screens so exactly? The beam practically dead-centered them. You said that it was surmise and suspicion before it happened, but I thought then and still think that you had a much firmer foundation than any kind of a mere hunch. What was it?"

"Deduction, based upon an unproved, but logical, cosmogonic theory—but you probably know more about that stuff than I do."

"Highly improbable. I read just a smattering now and then of the doings of the astronomers and astrophysicists. I didn't know that that was one of your specialties, either."

"It isn't, but I had to do a little cramming. We'll have to go back quite a while to make it clear. You know, of course, that a long time ago, before even interplanetary ships were developed, the belief was general that not more than about four planetary solar systems could be in existence at any one time in the whole Galaxy?"

"Yes, I am familiar with that belief—a consequence of the binary-dynamic-encounter theory in a too-limited application. The theory itself is still good, isn't it?"

"Eminently so—every other theory is wrecked by its failure to account for the quantity and above all, the distribution, of angular momentum of planetary systems. But you know what I'm going to say—that 'limited application' proves it!"

"No, just let's say that a bit of light is beginning to dawn. Go ahead."

"QX. Well, when it was discovered that there were millions of times as many planets in the Galaxy as could be accounted for by a dynamic encounter occurring once in two times ten to the tenth years or so, some way had to be figured out to increase, millionfold, the number of such encounters. Manifestly, the random motion of the stars within the Galaxy could not account for it. Neither could the vibration or oscillation of the globular clusters through the Galaxy. The meeting of two Galaxies—the passage of them completely through each other, edgewise—would account for it very nicely. It would also account for the fact that the solar systems on one side of the Galaxy tend to be somewhat older than the ones on the apposite side. Question; find the Galaxy. It was van der Schleiss, I believe, who found it. Lundmark's Nebula. It is edge on to us, with a receding velocity of twelve hundred and forty-six miles per second—the exact velocity which, corrected for gravitational decrement, will put Lundmark's Nebula right here at the time when, according to our best geophysicists and geochemists, old Earth was being born. If that theory was correct, Lundmark's Nebula should also be full of planets. Four expeditions went out to check the theory, and none of them came back. We know why, now—Boskone got them. We got back, because of you, and only you."

"Holy Klono!" the old man breathed, paying no attention to the tribute. "It checks—*how* it checks!"

"To nineteen decimals."

*

"But still it doesn't explain why you set your traps on that line."

"Sure it does. How many Galaxies are there in the Universe, do you suppose, that are full of planets?"

"Why, all of them I suppose—or no, not so many perhaps—I don't know—I don't remember of having read anything on that question."

"No, and you probably won't. Only loose-screwed space detectives, like me, and crackpot science-fiction writers, like Wacky Willison, have noodles vacuous enough to harbor such thin ideas. But, according to our admittedly highly tenuous reasoning, there are only two such Galaxies—Lundmark's Nebula and ours."

"Huh? Why?" demanded Haynes.

"Because Galaxies don't collide much, if any, oftener than binaries within a Galaxy do," Kinnison asserted. "True, they are closer together in space, relative to their actual linear dimensions, than are stars; but on the other hand, their relative motions are slower—that is, a star will traverse the average interstellar distance much quicker than a Galaxy will the intergalactic one—so that the whole thing evens up. As nearly as Wacky and I could figure it, two Galaxies will collide deeply enough to produce a significant number of planetary solar systems on an average of once in just about one point eight times ten to the tenth years. Pick up your slide rule and check me on it, if you like."

"I'll take your word for it," the old Lensman murmured absently. "But any Galaxy probably has at least a couple of solar systems all the time—but I see your point. The probability is overwhelmingly great that Boskone would be in a Galaxy having hundreds of millions of planets rather than in one having only a dozen or less inhabitable worlds. But at that, they *could* all have lots of planets. Suppose that our wilder thinkers are right, that Galaxies are grouped into Universes, which are spaced, roughly, about the same as the Galaxies are. Two of *them* could collide, couldn't they?"

"They could, but you're getting 'way out of my range now. At this point the detective withdraws, leaving a clear field for you and the science-fiction imaginationeer."

"Well, finish the thought—that I'm wackier even than he is!" Both men laughed, and the Port Admiral went on: "It's a fascinating speculation—it does no harm to let the fancy roam at times—but at that, there are things of much greater importance. You think, then, that the thionite ring enters into this matrix?"

"Bound to. Everything ties in. The most intelligent races of this Galaxy are oxygen-breathers, with warm, red blood: the only kind of physique which thionite affects. The more of us who get the thionite habit, the better for Boskone. It explains why we have never got to the first check station in getting any of the real higher-ups in the thionite game; instead of being an ordinary criminal ring they've got all the brains and all the resources of Boskonia back of them. But if they are that big—and as good as we know they are—I wonder why—" Kinnison's voice trailed off into silence; his brain raced.

*

"I want to ask you a question that is none of my business," the young Lensman went on almost immediately, in a voice strangely altered. "Just how long ago was it that you started losing fifth-year men just before graduation? I mean, that boys sent to Arisia to be measured for their Lenses supposedly never got there? Or at least, they never came back and no Lenses were ever received for them?"

"About ten years. Twelve, I think, to be ex—" Haynes broke off in the middle of the word and his eyes bored into those of the younger man. "What makes you think that there were any such?"

"Deduction again, but this time I know that I'm right. At least one every year. Usually two or three."

"Right, but there have always been space accidents . . . or they were caught by the pirates . . . you think, then, that—"

"I don't think. I *know!*" Kinnison declared. "They got to Arisia, *and they died there.* All I can say is, thank God for the Arisians! We can still trust our Lenses; they are seeing to that."

"But why didn't they tell us?" Haynes asked, perplexed.

"They wouldn't; that isn't their way," Kinnison stated, flatly and with conviction. "They have given us an instrumentality, the Lens, by virtue of which we should be able to do the job, and they are seeing to it that that instrumentality remains untarnished. If we cannot handle it properly, that is our lookout. We've got to fight our own battles and bury our own dead. Now that we have smeared up the enemy's military organization in this Galaxy by wiping out Helmuth and his headquarters, the drug syndicate seems to be my best chance of getting a line on the real Boskone. While you are mopping up and keeping them from establishing another war base here, I think I'd better be getting at it, don't you?"

"Probably so—you know your own oysters best. Mind if I ask where you're going to start in?" Haynes looked at Kinnison quizzically as he spoke. "Have you deduced that, too?"

The Gray Lensman returned the look in kind. "No. Deduction couldn't take me quite that far," he replied in the same tone. "You are going to tell me that, when you get around to it."

"Me? Where do I come in?" the Port Admiral feigned surprise.

"As follows. Helmuth probably had nothing to do with the dope running, so its organization must still be intact. If so, they would take over as much of the other branch as they could get hold of, and hit us harder than ever. I haven't heard of any unusual activity around here, so it must be somewhere else. Wherever it is, you would know about it, since you are a member of Galactic Council; and Councillor Ellington, in charge of Narcotics, would hardly take any very important step without conferring with you, as port admiral and chief of staff. How near right am I?"

*

"On the center of the beam, all the way—your deducer is blasting at maximum," Haynes said, in admiration. "Radelix is the worst—they're hitting it mighty hard. We sent a full unit over there last week. Shall we recall them, or do you want to work independently?"

"Let them go on; I'll be of more use working on my own, I think. I did the boys over there a favor a while back—they would co-operate anyway, of course, but it's a little nicer to have them sort of owe it to me. We'll all be able to play together very nicely if the opportunity arises."

"I'm mighty glad you're taking this on. The Radeligians are stuck, and we had no real reason for thinking that our men could do any better. With this new angle of approach, however, and with you working behind the scenes, the picture looks entirely different."

"I'm afraid that's unjustifiably high—"

"Not a bit of it, lad. Just a minute—I'll break out a couple of beakers of fayalin—Luck!"

"Thanks, chief!"

"Down the hatch!" and again the Gray Lensman was gone. To the spaceport, into his speedster, and away—hurtling through the void at the maximum blast of the fastest space-flier then boasted by the Galactic Patrol.

During the long trip, Kinnison exercised, thought, and studied spool after spool of tape—the Radeligian language. Thoughts of the red-headed nurse obtruded themselves strongly at times, but he put them aside resolutely. He was, he assured himself, off women forever—all women. He cultivated his new beard; trimming it, with the aid of a triplex mirror and four stereoscopic photographs, into something which, although neat and spruce enough, was too full and bushy by half to be a Vandyke. Also, he moved his

555

Lens bracelet up his arm and rayed the white skin thus exposed until his whole wrist was the same even shade of tan.

He did not drive his speedster to Radelix, for that racy little fabrication would have been recognized anywhere for what she was; and private citizens simply did not drive ships of that type. Therefore, with every possible precaution of secrecy, he landed her in a Patrol base four solar systems away. In that base Kimball Kinnison disappeared; but the tall, shock-haired, bushy-bearded Chester Q. Fordyce—cosmopolite, man of leisure, and dilettante in science—who took the next space liner for Radelix was not precisely the same individual who had come to that planet a few days before with that name and those unmistakable characteristics.

Mr. Chester Q. Fordyce, then, and not Gray Lensman Kimball Kinnison, disembarked at Ardith, the world-capital of Radelix. He took up his abode at the Hotel Ardith-Splendide and proceeded, with neither too much nor too little fanfare, to be his cosmopolitan self in those circles of society in which, wherever he might find himself, he was wont to move.

As a matter of course, he entertained, and was entertained by, the Tellurian Ambassador. Equally as a matter of course, he attended divers and sundry functions, at which he made the acquaintance of hundreds of persons, many of them personages. That one of these should have been Vice-Admiral Gerrond, Lensman in charge of the Patrol's Radeligian base, was inevitable.

*

It was, then, a purely routine and logical development that at a reception one evening Vice-Admiral Gerrond stopped to chat for a moment with Mr. Fordyce; and it was purely accidental that the nearest bystander was a few yards distant. Hence, Mr. Fordyce's conduct was strange enough.

"Gerrond!" he said without moving his lips and in a tone almost inaudible, the while he was offering the Admiral an Alsakanite cigarette. "Don't look at me particularly right now, and don't show surprise. Study me for the next ten minutes, then put your Lens on me and tell me whether you have ever seen me before or not." Then, glancing at the watch upon his left wrist—a time-piece just about as large and as ornate as a wrist watch could be and still remain in impeccable taste—he murmured something conventional and strolled away.

The ten minutes passed and he felt Gerrond's thought. A peculiar sensation, this, being on the receiving end of a single beam, instead of using his own Lens.

"As far as I can tell, I have never seen you before. You are certainly not one of our agents, and if you are one of Haynes' whom I have ever worked with you have done a wonderful job of disguising. I must have met you somewhere, sometime, else there would be no point to your question; but beyond the evident—and admitted—fact that you are a white Tellurian, I can't seem to place you."

"Does this help?" This question was shot through Kinnison's own Lens.

"Since I have known so few Tellurian Lensmen it tells me that you must be Kinnison, but I do not recognize you at all readily. You seem changed—older—besides, who ever heard of an Unattached Lensman doing the work of an ordinary agent?"

"I am both older and changed—partly natural and partly artificial. As for the work, it's a job that no ordinary agent can handle—it takes a lot of special equipment—"

"You've got *that*, indubitably! I get goose-flesh yet every time I think of that trial."

"You think that I'm proof against recognition, then, as long as I don't use my Lens?" Kinnison stuck to the issue.

"Absolutely so. You're here, then, on thionite?" No other issue, Gerrond knew, could be grave enough to account for this man's presence. "But your wrist? I studied it. You can't have worn your Lens there for months—those Tellurian bracelets leave white streaks an inch wide."

"I tanned it with a pencil beam. Nice job, eh? But what I want to ask you about is a little co-operation. As you supposed, I'm here to work on this drug ring."

"Surely—anything we can do. But Narcotics is handling that, not us—but you know that, as well as I do—" the officer broke off, puzzled.

"I know. That's why I want you—that and because you handle the secret service. Frankly, I'm scared to death of leaks. For that reason I'm not saying anything to anyone except Lensmen, and I'm having no dealings with anyone connected with Narcotics. I have as unimpeachable an identity as Haynes could furnish—"

"There's no question as to its adequacy, then," the Radeligian interposed.

"I would like to have you pass the word around among your boys and girls that you know who I am and that I'm safe to play with. That way, if Boskone's agents spot me, it will be for an agent of Haynes, and not for what I really am. That's the first thing. Can do?"

"Easily and gladly. Consider it done. Second?"

"To have a boatload of good, tough marines on hand if I should call you. There are some Valerians coming over later, but I may need help in the meantime. I may want to start a fight—quite possibly even a riot."

"They'll be ready, and they'll be big, tough, and hard. Anything else?"

*

"Not just now, except for one question. You know Countess Avondrin, the woman I was dancing with a while ago. Got any dope on her?"

"Certainly not—what do you mean?"

"Huh? Don't you know even that she's a Boskonian agent of some kind?"

"Man, you're crazy! She isn't an agent, she can't be. Why, she's the daughter of a Planetary Councillor, the wife of one of our most loyal officers."

"She would be. That's the type they like to get hold of."

"Prove it!" the Admiral snapped. "Prove it or retract it!" He almost lost his poise, almost looked toward the distant corner in which the bewhiskered gentleman was sitting so idly.

"QX. If she isn't an agent, why is she wearing a thought-screen? You haven't tested her, of course."

Of course not. The amenities, as has been said, demanded that certain reserves of privacy remain inviolate. The Tellurian went on: "You didn't, but I did. On this job I can recognize nothing of good taste, of courtesy, of chivalry, or even of ordinary common decency. I suspect *everyone* who does not wear a Lens."

"A thought-screen!" exclaimed Gerrond. "How could she, without armor?"

"It's a late model—brand new. Just as good and just as powerful as the one I myself am wearing," Kinnison explained. "The mere fact that she's wearing it gives me a lot of highly useful information."

"What do you want me to do about her?" the Admiral asked. He was mentally asquirm, but he was a Lensman.

"Nothing whatever—except possibly, for our own information, to find out how many of her friends have become thionite-sniffers lately. If you do anything, you may warn them, although I know nothing definite about which to caution you. I'll handle her. Don't worry too much, though; I don't think she's anybody we really want. Afraid she's small fry—no such luck as that I'd get hold of a big one so soon."

"I hope she's small fry." Gerrond's thought was a grimace of distaste. "I hate Boskonia as much as anybody does, but I don't relish the idea of having to put that girl into the Chamber."

"If my picture is half right she can't amount to much," Kinnison replied. "A good lead is the best I can expect. I'll see what I can do."

For days, then, the searching Lensman pried into minds: so insidiously that he left no trace of his invasions. He examined men and women, of high and of low estate. Waitresses and ambassadors, flunkies and bankers, ermined prelates and truck drivers. He went from city to city. Always, but with only a fraction of his brain, he played the part of Chester Q. Fordyce; ninety-nine percent of his stupendous mind was probing, searching and analyzing. Into what charnel pits of filth and corruption he delved, into what fastnesses of truth and loyalty and high courage and ideals, must be left entirely to the imagination; for the Lensman never has spoken and never will speak of these things.

He went back to Ardith and, late at night, approached the dwelling of Count Avondrin. A servant arose and admitted the visitor, not knowing then or ever that he did so. The bedroom door was locked from the inside, but what of that? What resistance can any mechanism offer to a master craftsman, plentifully supplied with tools, who can perceive every component part, however deeply buried?

The door opened. The countess was a light sleeper, but before she could utter a single scream one powerful hand clamped her mouth, another snapped the switch of her supposedly carefully concealed thought-screen generator. What followed was done very quickly.

Mr. Fordyce strolled back to his hotel and Lensman Kinnison directed a thought at Vice-Admiral Gerrond.

"Better fake up some kind of an excuse for having a couple of guards or policemen in front of Count Avondrin's town house at eight twenty-five this morning. The countess is going to have a brainstorm."

"What *have* . . . what will she do?" Gerrond mastered his emotions sufficiently to keep from swearing.

"Nothing much. Scream a bit, rush out of doors half dressed, and fight anything and everybody that touches her. Warn the officers that she'll kick, scratch, and bite. There are plenty of signs of a prowler having been in her room, but if they can find him they're good—*very* good. She'll have all the signs and symptoms, even to the puncture, of having been given a shot in the arm of some brand-new drug, which the doctors won't be able to find or to identify. But there will be no question raised of insanity or of any other permanent damage—she'll be right as rain in a couple of months."

"Oh, that mind-ray machine of yours again, eh? And that's all you're going to do to her?"

"That's all. I can let her off easy and still be just, I think. She's helped me a lot. She'll be a good girl from now on, too; I've thrown a scare into her that will last her the rest of her life."

"Thanks, Gray Lensman! What else?"

"I'd like to have you at the Tellurian Ambassador's Ball day after tomorrow, if it's convenient."

"I've been planning on it, since it's on the 'must' list. Shall I bring anything or anyone special?"

"No. I just want you on hand to give me any information you can on a person who will probably be there to investigate what happened to the countess."

"I'll be there," and he was.

*

It was a gay and colorful throng, but neither of the two Lensmen was in any mood for gaiety. They acted, of course. They neither sought nor avoided each other but, somehow, they were never alone together.

"Man or woman?" asked Gerrond.

"I don't know. All I've got is the recognition."

The Radeligian did not ask what that recognition was to be. He knew that that information might prove dangerous indeed to any unauthorized possessor. He did not want to know it; he was glad that the Tellurian had not thrust it upon him.

Suddenly the Vice-Admiral's attention was wrenched toward the doorway, to see the most marvelously, the most flawlessly beautiful woman he had ever seen. But not long did he contemplate that beauty, for the Tellurian Lensman's thoughts were fairly seething, despite his iron control.

"Do you mean . . . you can't mean—" Gerrond faltered.

"Yes—definitely!" Kinnison rasped. "She looks like an angel, but take it from me, *she isn't*. She's one of the slimiest snakes that ever lived—she's so low that she could put on a tall silk hat and walk under a duck. I know she's beautiful. She's a riot, a seven-sector callout, a thionite dream. So what? She is also Dessa Desplaines, formerly of Aldebaran II. Does that mean anything to you?"

"Not a thing, Kinnison."

"She's in it, clear to her neck. I had a chance to wring her neck once, too, damn it all, and didn't. She's got a brazen crust, coming here now, with all our Narcotics on the

559

job—Wonder if they think they've got Enforcement so badly whipped that they can get away with stuff as rough as this—Sure you don't know her, or know of her?"

"I never saw her before, or heard of her."

"Perhaps she isn't known, out this way. Or maybe they think they're ready for a show-down . . . or don't care. Her being here ties me up hand and foot, anyway. *She'll* recognize me, for all the tea in China. Gerrond! You know the Narcotics' Lensmen, don't you?"

"Certainly."

"Call one of them right now. Tell him that Dessa Desplaines, the zwilnik houri, is right here on the floor—What! He doesn't know her, either! And none of our boys are Lensmen! Make it a three-way. Lensman Winstead? Kinnison of Sol III—unattached. Sure that none of you recognize this picture?" and he transmitted a perfect image of the ravishing creature then moving regally across the floor. "Nobody does? Good! Maybe that's why she's here, after all—thinks she can get away with it. Anyway, she's your meat. Here's the chance for a real capture. Come and get her."

"You will appear against her, of course?"

"If necessary—but it won't be necessary. As soon as she sees that the game's up, all hell will be out for noon."

*

As soon as the connection had been broken, Kinnison realized that the thing could not be done that way; that he could not stay out of it. No man alive save himself could prevent her from flashing a warning—badly as he hated it, he had to do it. Gerrond glanced at him curiously: he had received a few of those racing thoughts.

"Tune in on this," Kinnison grinned wryly. "If the last meeting I had with her is any criterion, it ought to be good. S'pose anybody around here understands the language of Aldebaran II?"

"Never heard it mentioned if they do."

The Tellurian walked blithely up to the radiant visitor, held out his hand in Earthly—and Aldebaranian—greeting, and spoke: "Madam Desplaines would not remember Chester Q. Fordyce, of course. It is of the piteousness that I should be so accursedly of the ordinariness; for to see madam but the one time, as I did at the New Year's ball in High Altamont, is to remember her forever."

"Such a flatterer!" The woman laughed. "I trust that you will forgive me, Mr. Fordyce, but one meets so many interesting—" Her eyes widened in surprise, an expression which changed rapidly to one of flaming hatred, not unmixed with fear.

"So you do recognize me, you bedroom-eyed, Aldebaranian hell-cat," he remarked, evenly. "I rather expected that you would."

"Yes, you sweet, uncontaminated sissy, you overgrown super-Boy Scout, I do," she hissed, malevolently, and made a quick motion toward her corsage. These two, as has been intimated, were friends of old.

Quick though she was, the man was quicker. His left hand darted out to seize her left wrist; his right, flashing around her body, grasped her right and held it rigidly in the small of her back. Thus they walked away.

"Stop!" she flared. "You're making a spectacle of me!"

"Now isn't that something to worry about?" His lips smiled, for the benefit of the observers, but his eyes held no glint of mirth. "These folks will think that this is the way all Aldebaranian friends walk together. If you think for a second that I'm going to give you a chance to touch that sounder you're wearing you haven't got the sense of a Zabriskan fontema. Stop wriggling!" he counseled, sharply. "Even if you can do enough hula-hula shimmying to work it, before it contacts once I'll crush your brain to a pulp, right here and right now!"

Outside, in the grounds, "Oh, Lensman, let's sit down and talk this over!" and the girl brought into play everything she had. It was a distressing scene, but it left the Lensman cold.

"Save your breath," he advised her finally, wearily. "To me you're just another zwilnik, no more and no less. A female louse is still a louse; and calling a zwilnik a louse is sheerest flattery."

He said that; and, saying it, knew it to be the exact and crystal truth: but not even that knowledge could mitigate in any iota the recoiling of his every fiber from the deed which he was about to do. He could not even pray, with immortal Merritt's *Dwayanu*:

"Luka—turn your wheel so I need not slay this woman!"

It had to be. Why in all the nine hells of Valeria did he have to be a Lensman? Why did he have to be the one to do it? But it had to be done, and soon; they'd be here shortly.

"There's just one thing you can do to make me believe that you're even partially innocent," he ground out, "that you have even one decent thought or one decent instinct anywhere in you."

"What is that, Lensman? I'll do it, whatever it is!"

"Release your thought-screen and send out a call to the Big Shot."

The girl stiffened. This big cop wasn't so dumb—he really *knew* something. He must die, and at once. How could she get word to—

Simultaneously Kinnison perceived that for which he had been waiting; the Narcotics men were coming.

He tore open the woman's gown, flipped the switch of her thought-screen, and invaded her mind. But, fast as he was, he was late—almost too late altogether. He could get neither direction line nor location; but only, and faintly, a picture of a space-dock saloon, of a repulsively obese man in a luxuriously furnished back room. Then her mind went completely blank and her body slumped down, bonelessly.

Thus Narcotics found them; the woman inert and flaccid upon the bench, the man staring down at her in black abstraction.

VI.

"Suicide? Or did you—" Gerrond paused, delicately. Winstead, the Lensman of Narcotics, said nothing, but looked on intently.

"Neither," Kinnison replied, still studying. "I would have had to, but she beat me to it."

"What d'you mean, 'neither'? She's dead, isn't she? How did it happen?"

"Not yet, and unless I'm more cockeyed even than usual, she won't be. She isn't the type to rub herself out—ever, under any conditions. As to 'how,' that was easy. A hollow false tooth. Simple, but new—and clever. But why? WHY?" Kinnison was thinking to himself more than addressing his companions. "If they had killed her, yes. As it is, it doesn't make any kind of sense—any of it."

"But the girl's dying!" protested Gerrond. "What're you going to do?"

"I wish to Klono I knew." The Tellurian was puzzled, groping. "No hurry doing anything about her—what was done to her has been done, and no one this side of Hades can undo it—unless I can fit these pieces together into some kind of a pattern I'll never know what it's all about—none of it makes sense—" He shook himself and went on: "One thing is plain. She won't die. If they had intended to kill her, she would have died almost instantly. They figure she's worth saving; in which I agree with them. At the same time, they certainly are not planning on letting me tap her knowledge. They may be planning on taking her away from us. Therefore, as long as she stays alive—or even not dead, the way she is now—guard her so heavily that an army can't get her. If she should happen to die, don't leave her body unguarded for a second until she's been autopsied, and you know she'll *stay* dead. The minute she recovers, day or night, call me. Might as well take her to the hospital now, I guess."

The call came soon that the patient had indeed recovered.

"She's talking, but I haven't answered her," Gerrond reported. "There's something strange here, Kinnison."

"There would be—bound to be. Hold everything until I get there," and he hurried to the hospital.

"Good morning, Dessa," he greeted her in Aldebaranian. "You are feeling better, I hope?"

Her reaction was surprising. "You really know me?" she almost shrieked, and flung herself into the Lensman's arms. Not deliberately; not with her wonted, highly effective technique of bringing into play the s.a. equipment with which she was so overpoweringly armed. No; this was the utterly innocent, the wholly unselfconscious abandon of a very badly frightened young girl. "What happened?" she sobbed, frantically, "Where am I? Why are all these strangers here?"

Her wide, childlike, tear-filled eyes sought his; and as he probed them, deeper and deeper into the brain behind them; his face grew set and hard. Mentally, she now *was* a young and innocent girl! Nowhere in her mind, not even in the deepest recesses of her subconscious, was there the slightest inkling that she had even existed since her fifteenth year. It was staggering; it was unheard of; but it was indubitably a fact. For her, now, the intervening time had lapsed instantaneously—five or six years of her life had disappeared so utterly as never to have been!

"You have been very ill, Dessa," he told her gravely, "and you are no longer a child." He led her into another room and up to a triple mirror. "See for yourself."

"But that isn't I?" she protested. "It can't be! Why, she's beautiful!"

"You're all of that," the Lensman agreed, casually. "You've had a bad shock. Your memory will return shortly, I think. Now you must go back to bed."

She did so, but not to sleep. Instead, she went into a trance; and so, almost, did Kinnison. For over an hour he lay intensely asprawl in an easy-chair, the while he engraved, day by day, a memory of missing years into that bare storehouse of knowledge. And finally the task was done.

"Sleep, Dessa," he told her then. "Sleep. Waken in eight hours; whole."

"Lensman, you're a *man*!" Gerrond realized vaguely what had been done. "You didn't give her the truth, of course?"

"Far from it. Only that she was married and is a widow. The rest of it is highly fictitious—just enough like the real thing so that she can square herself with herself, if she meets old acquaintances. Plenty of lapses, of course, but they're covered by shock."

"But the husband?" queried the curious Radeligian.

"That's her business," Kinnison countered, callously. "She'll tell you, if she ever feels like it. One thing I did do, though—they'll never use her again. The next man that tries to hypnotize her will be lucky if he gets away alive."

*

The advent of Dessa Desplaines, however, and his curious adventure with her, had altered markedly the Lensman's situation. No one else in the throng had worn a screen, but there might have been agents—anyway, the observed facts would enable the higher-ups to link Fordyce up with what had happened—they would know, of course, that the real Fordyce hadn't done it—he could be Fordyce no longer.

Wherefore the real Chester Q. Fordyce took over and a strange Unattached Lensman appeared. A Posenian, supposedly, since against the air of Radelix he wore that planet's unmistakable armor. No other race of even approximately human shape could "see" through a helmet of solid, opaque metal.

And in this guise Kinnison continued his investigations. That place and that man must be on this planet somewhere; the sending outfit worn by the Desplaines woman could not possibly reach any other. He had a good picture of the room and a fair picture—several pictures, in fact—of the man. The room was an actuality; all he had had to do was to fill in the details which definitely, by unmistakable internal evidence, belonged there. The man was different. How much of the original picture was real, and how much of it was the girl's impression?

She was, he knew, physically fastidious almost to an extreme. He knew that no possible hypnotism could nullify completely the basic, the fundamental characteristics of the subconscious. The intrinsic ego could not be changed. Was the man really such a monster, or was the picture in the girl's mind partially or largely the product of her physical revulsion?

For hours he had sat at a recording machine, covering yard after yard of tape with every possible picture of the man he wanted. Pictures ranging from a man almost of normal build up to a thing duplicating in every detail the woman's mental image.

Now he ran the tape again, time after time. The two extremes, he concluded, were highly improbable. Somewhere in between—the man *was* fat, he guessed. Fat, and had a mean pair of eyes. And, no matter how Kinnison changed the man's physical shape he had found it impossible to eradicate a personality that was definitely bad.

"The guy's a louse," Kinnison decided, finally. "Needs killing. Glad of that—if I have to keep on fighting women much longer I'll go completely nuts. Got enough dope to identify him now, I think."

And again the Tellurian Lensman set out to comb the planet, city by city. Since he was not now dealing with Lensmen, every move he made had to be carefully planned and as carefully concealed. It was heartbreaking; but at long last he found a bartender who had once seen his quarry. He *was* fat, Kinnison discovered, and he was a bad egg. From that point on, progress was rapid. He went to the indicated city, which was, ironically enough, the very Ardith from which he had set out; and, from a bit of information here and a bit there, he tracked down his man. He found the room first, and then the man. The girl wasn't so far wrong, at that. Her aversion was somewhat worse than the actuality, but not too much.

Now what to do? The technique he had used so successfully upon Boyssia II and in other bases could not succeed here; there were thousands of people instead of dozens, and someone would certainly catch him at it. Nor could he work at a distance. He was no Arisian, he had to be right beside his job. He would have to turn dock-walloper.

Therefore a dock-walloper he became. Not like one, but actually one. He labored prodigiously, his fine hands and his entire being becoming coarse and hardened. He ate prodigiously, and drank likewise. But, wherever he drank, his liquor was poured from the bartender's own bottle or from one of similarly innocuous contents; for then, as now, bartenders did not themselves imbibe the corrosively potent distillates in which they dealt. Nevertheless, Kinnison became intoxicated—boisterously, flagrantly, and pugnaciously so, as did his fellows.

He lived scrupulously within his dock-walloper's wages. Eight credits per week went to the company, in advance, for room and board; the rest he spent over the fat man's bar or gambled away at the fat man's crooked games—for Bominger, although engaged in vaster commerce far, nevertheless, allowed no scruple to interfere with his esurient rapacity. Money was money, whatever its amount or source or however despicable its means of acquirement.

The Lensman knew that the games were crooked, certainly. He could see, however they were concealed, the crooked mechanisms of the wheels. He could see the crooked workings of the dealers' minds as they manipulated their crooked decks. He could read as plainly as his own the cards his crooked opponents held. But to win or to protest would have set him apart, hence he was always destitute before pay day. Then, like his fellows, he spent his spare time loafing in the same saloon, vaguely hoping for a free drink or for a stake at cards, until one of the bouncers threw him out.

*

But in his every waking hour, working, gambling, or loafing, he studied Bominger and Bominger's various enterprises. The Lensman could not pierce the fat man's thought-screen, and he could never catch him without it. However, he could and did learn much. He read volume after volume of locked account books, page by page. He read secret documents, hidden in the deepest recesses of massive vault. He listened in on conference after conference; for a thought-screen of course, does not interfere with either sight or sound. The Big Shot did not own—legally—the saloon, nor the ornate, almost palatial back room which was his office. Nor did he own the dance hall and boudoirs upstairs, nor the narrow, cell-like rooms in which addicts of twice a score of different noxious drugs gave themselves over libidinously to their addictions. Nevertheless, they were his; and they were only a part of that which was his.

Kinnison detected, traced, and identified agent after agent. With his sense of perception he followed passages, leading to other scenes, utterly indescribable here. One comparatively short gallery, however, terminated in a different setting altogether; for there, as here and perhaps everywhere, ostentation and squalor lie almost back to back. Nalizok's Café, the high-life hot-spot of Radelix! Downstairs was innocuous enough; nothing rough—that is, too rough—was ever pulled there. Most of the robbery there was open and above-board, plainly written upon the checks. But there were upstairs rooms, and cellar rooms, and back rooms. And there were addicts, differing only from those others in wearing finer raiment and being of a self-styled higher stratum. Basically they were the same.

Men, women, girls ever were there, in the rigid muscle-lock of thionite. Teeth hard-set, every muscle tense and staring, eyes jammed closed, fists clenched, faces white as though carved from marble, immobile in the frenzied emotion which characterized the ultimately passionate fulfillment of every suppressed desire; in the release of their every inhibition crowding perilously close to the dividing line beyond which lay death from sheer ecstasy. That was the technique of the thionite-sniffer—to take every microgram that he could stand, to come to, shaken and too weak even to walk; to swear that he would never so degrade himself again; to come back after more as soon as he had recovered strength to do so; and finally, with an irresistible craving for stronger and ever stronger thrills, to take a larger dose than his rapidly-weakening body could endure, and so to cross the fatal line.

There also were the idiotically smiling faces of the hadive smokers, the twitching members of those who preferred the Centralian nitrolabe-needle, the helplessly stupefied eaters of bentlam—but why go on? Suffice it to say that in that one city block could be found every vice and every drug enjoyed by Radeligians and the usual run of visitors; and if perchance you were an unusual visitor, desiring something unusual, Bominger could get it for you—at a price.

Kinnison studied, perceived, and analyzed. Also, he reported, via Lens, daily and copiously, to Narcotics, under Lensman's Seal.

"But Kinnison!" Winstead protested one day. "How much longer are you going to make us wait?"

"Until I get what I came after or until they get onto me," Kinnison replied, flatly. For weeks his Lens had been hidden in the side of his shoe, in a flat sheath of highly charged metal, proof against any except the most minutely searching spy-ray inspection; but this new location did not in any way interfere with its functioning.

"Any danger of that?" the Narcotics head asked, anxiously.

"Plenty—and getting worse every day. More actors in the drama. Some day I'll make a slip—I can't keep this up forever."

"Let us go, then," Winstead urged. "We've got enough now to blow this ring out of existence, all over the planet."

"Not yet. You're making good progress, aren't you?"

"Yes, but considering—"

"Don't consider it yet. Your present progress is normal for your increased force. Any more would touch off an alarm. You could take this planet's drug personnel, yes, but that isn't what I'm after. I want big game, not small fry. So sit tight until I give you the g.a. QX?"

"Got to be QX if you say so, Kinnison. Be careful!"

"I am. Won't be long now, I'm sure. Bound to break very shortly, one way or the other. If possible, I'll give you and Gerrond warning."

*

Kinnison had everything lined up except the one thing he had come after. This was, in fact, the headquarters of the drug syndicate for the entire planet of Radelix. He knew where the stuff came in, and when, and how. He knew who received it, and the principal distributors of it. He knew almost all of the secret agents of the ring, and not a few even of the small-fry peddlers. He knew where the remittances went, and how much, and what for. But every lead had stopped at Bominger. Apparently the fat man was the absolute head of the drug syndicate; and that appearance didn't make sense—it *had* to be false. Bominger and the other planetary lieutenants—themselves only small fry if the Lensman's ideas were only half right—*must* get orders from, and send reports and, in probability, payments to some Boskonian authority; of that Kinnison felt certain, but he had not been able to get even the slightest trace of that higher-up.

That the communication would be established upon a thought-beam the Tellurian was equally certain. The Boskonian would not trust any ordinary, tappable communicator beam, and he certainly would not be such a fool as to send any written or taped or otherwise permanently recorded message, however coded. No, that message, when it came, would come as thought, and to receive it the fat man would have to release his screen. Then, and not until then, could Kinnison act. Action at that time might not prove simple—judging from the precautions Bominger was taking already, he would not release his screen without taking plenty more—but until then the Lensman could do nothing.

That screen had not yet been released, Kinnison could swear to that. True, he had had to sleep at times, but he had slept in a very hair-trigger, with his subconscious and his Lens set to guard that screen and to give the alarm at its first sign of weakening.

As the Lensman had foretold, the break came soon. Not in the middle of the night, as he had half-thought that it would come; nor yet in the quiet of the daylight hours. Instead, it came well before midnight, while revelry was at its height. It did not come suddenly, but was heralded by a long period of gradually increasing tension, of a mental stress very apparent to the mind of the watcher.

Agents of the drug baron came in, singly and in groups, to an altogether unprecedented number. Some of them were their usual viciously self-contained selves, others were slightly but definitely ill at ease. Kinnison, seated alone at a small table,

566

playing a game of Radeligian solitaire, divided his attention between the big room as a whole and the office of Bominger; in neither of which was anything definite happening.

Then a wave of excitement swept over the agents as five men wearing thought-screens entered the room and, sitting down at a reserved table, called for cards and drinks; and Kinnison thought it time to send his warning.

"Gerrond! Winstead! Three-way! It's going to break soon, now, I think—tonight. Agents all over the place—five men with thought-screens here on the floor. Nervous tension high. Lots more agents outside, for blocks. General precaution, I think, not specific. Not suspicious of me, at least not exactly. Afraid of spies with a sense of perception—Rigellians or Posenians or such. Just killed an Ordovik on general principles, over on the next block. Get your gangs ready, but don't come too close—just close enough so that you can be here in thirty seconds after I call you."

"What do you mean 'not exactly suspicious'? What have you done?"

"Nothing that I know of—any one of a million possible small slips I may have made. Nothing serious, though, or they wouldn't have let me hang around this long."

"You're in danger. No armor, no DeLameter, no anything. Better come out while you can."

"And miss what I've spent all this time building up? Not a chance; I'll be able to take care of myself, I think—Here comes one of the boys in a screen, to talk to me. I'll leave my Lens open, so that you can sort of look on."

*

Just then Bominger's screen went down and Kinnison invaded his mind; taking complete possession of it. Under his domination the fat man reported to the Boskonian, reported truly and fully. In turn, he received orders and instructions. Had any inquisitive stranger been around, or anyone on the planet using any kind of a mind-ray machine since that quadruply-accursed Lensman had held that trial? (Oh, that was what had touched them off! Kinnison was glad to know it.) No, nothing unusual at all—

And just at that critical moment, when the Lensman's mind was so busy with its task, the stranger came up to his table and stared down at him dubiously, questioningly.

"Well, what's on *your* mind?" Kinnison growled. He could not spare much of his mind just then, but it did not take much of it to play his part as a dock-walloper. "You another of these smoking house-numbers, snooping around to see if I'm trying to run a blazer on myself? By the devil and his imps, if I hadn't lost so much money here already I'd tear up this deck and go over to Croleo's and *never* come near this crummy joint again—his rotgut can't be any worse than yours is."

"Don't burn out a jet, pal." The agent, apparently reassured, adopted a conciliatory tone.

"Who in hell ever said you was a pal of mine, you Radelig-gig-gigian pimp?" The supposedly three quarters drunken, certainly three quarters naked, Lensman got up, wobbled a little, and sat down again, heavily. "Don't 'pal' me, ape—I'm partic-hic-hicular about who I pal with."

"That's all right, big fellow; no offense intended," soothed the other. "Come on, I'll buy you a drink."

"Don't want no drink until after I've finished this game," Kinnison grumbled, and took an instant to flash a thought via Lens. "All set, boys? Thing's moving fast. If I have to take this drink—it's doped, of course—I'll bust this bird wide open. When I yell, shake the lead out of your pants!"

"Of course you want a drink!" the pirate urged. "Come and get it—it's on me, you know."

"And who are you to be buying me, a Tellurian gentleman, a drink?" the Lensman roared, flaring into one of the sudden, senseless rages of the character he had cultivated so assiduously. "Did I ask you for a drink? I'm educated, I am, and I've got money, I have. I'll buy myself a drink when I want one." His rage mounted higher and higher, visibly. "Did I *ever* ask you for a drink, you—" (unprintable here for the space of two long breaths).

This was the blow-off. If the fellow was even half honest, there would be a fight, which Kinnison could make as long as necessary. If he did not start slugging after what Kinnison had just called him, he was not what he seemed and the Lensman was surely suspected; for the Earthman had dredged out the noisomest depths of the foulest vocabularies in space for the terms he had just employed.

"If you weren't drunk I'd break every bone in your laxlo-soaked carcass." The other man's anger was sternly suppressed, but he looked at the dock-walloper with no friendship in his eyes. "I don't ask lousy spaceport bums to drink with me every day, and when I do, they do—or else. Do you want to take that drink now or do you want a couple of the boys to work you over first? Barkeep! Bring two glasses of laxlo over here!"

Now the time was short, indeed, but Kinnison would not—could not—act yet. Bominger's conference was still on; the Lensman didn't know enough yet. The fellow wasn't very suspicious, certainly, or he would have made a pass at him before this. Bloodshed meant less than nothing to these gentry; the stranger did not want to incur Bominger's wrath by killing a steady customer. The fellow probably thought the whole mind ray story was hocus-pocus, anyway—not a chance in a million of it being true. Besides, he needed a machine, and Kinnison couldn't hide a thing, let alone anything as big as that mind-ray machine had been, because he didn't have clothes enough on to flag a handcar with. But that free drink was certainly doped—Oh, they wanted to question him. It would be a truth-dope in the laxlo, then—he certainly couldn't take *that* drink!

Then came the all-important second; just as the bartender set the glasses down Bominger's interview ended. At the signing off, Kinnison got additional data, just as he had thought that he would; and in that instant, before the drugmaster could restore his screen, the fat man died—his brain literally blasted. And in that same instant Kinnison's Lens fairly throbbed with the power of the call he sent out to his allies.

But not even Kinnison could hurl such a mental bolt without some outward sign. His face stiffened, perhaps, or his eyes may have lost their drunken, vacant stare, to take on momentarily the keen, cold ruthlessness that was for the moment his. At any rate, the enemy agent was now definitely suspicious.

"Drink that, bum, and drink it quick—or burn!" he snapped, DeLameter out and poised.

SUPER PACK

The Tellurian's hand reached out for the glass, but his mind also reached out, and faster by a second, to the brains of two nearby agents. Those worthies drew their own weapons and, with wild yells, began firing. Seemingly indiscriminately, yet in those blasts two of the thought-screened minions died. For a fraction of a second even the hard-schooled mind of Kinnison's opponent was distracted, and that was long enough for the Gray Lensman's instantaneous nervous reactions and his mighty muscles.

*

A quick flick of the wrist sent the potent liquor into the Boskonian's eyes; a lightning thrust of the knee sent the little table hurtling against his gun-hand, flinging the weapon afar. Simultaneously, the Lensman's hamlike fist, urged by all the strength and all the speed of his two hundred and sixteen pounds of rawhide and whalebone, drove forward. Not for the jaw. Not for the head or the face. Lensmen know better than to mash bare hands, break fingers and knuckles, against bone. For the solar plexus. The big Patrolman's fist sank forearm-deep. The stricken zwilnik uttered one shrieking grunt, doubled up, and collapsed; never to rise again. Kinnison leaped for the fellow's DeLameter—too late, he was already hemmed in.

One—two—three—four of the nearest men died without having received a physical blow; again and again Kinnison's heavy fists and far heavier feet crashed deep into vital spots. One thought-screened enemy dived at him bodily in a Tomingan donganeur, to fall with a broken neck as the Lensman opposed instantly the only possible parry—a savage chop, edge-handed, just below the base of the skull; the while he disarmed the surviving thought-screened stranger with an accurately-hurled chair. The latter, feinting a swing, launched a vicious French kick. The Lensman, expecting anything, perceived the foot coming. His big hands shot out like striking snakes, closing and twisting savagely in the one fleeting instant, then jerking upward and backward. A hard and heavy dock-walloper's boot crashed thuddingly to a mark. A shriek rent the air and that foeman, too, was done.

Not fair fighting, no; nor cluvvy. Lensmen did not and do not fight according to the tenets of the late Marquis of Queensberry. They use the weapons provided by Mother Nature only when they must; but they can, and do use them with telling effect indeed, when body-to-body brawling becomes necessary. For they are skilled in the art—every Lensman has a completely detailed knowledge of all the lethal tricks of foul combat known to all the dirty fighters of ten thousand planets for twice ten thousand years.

And then the doors and windows crashed in, admitting those whom no other bifurcate race has ever faced willingly in hand-to-hand combat—full-armed Valerians, swinging their space-axes!

The gangsters broke then, and fled in panic disorder; but escape from Narcotics' fine-meshed net was impossible. They were cut down to a man.

"QX, Kinnison?" came two hard, sharp thoughts. The Lensmen did not see the Tellurian, but Lieutenant Peter van Buskirk did. That is, he saw him, but did not look at him.

"Hi, Kim, you little Tellurian wart!" That worthy's thought was a yell. "Ain't we got fun?"

"QX fellows—thanks," to Gerrond and to Winstead, and—

"Ho, Bus! Thanks, you big, Valerian ape!" to the gigantic Dutch-Valerian with whom he had shared so many experiences in the past. "A good clean-up, fellows?"

"One hundred per cent, thanks to you. We'll put you—"

"Don't, please. You will probably clog my jets if you do. I don't appear in this anywhere—it's just one of your good, routine jobs of mopping up. Clear ether, fellows, I've got to do a flit."

"Where?" all three wanted to ask, but they didn't—the Gray Lensman was gone.

VII.

Kinnison did start his flit, but he did not get far. In fact, he did not even reach his squalid room before cold reason told him that the job was only half done—yes, less than half. He had to give Boskone credit for having brains, and it was not at all likely that even such a comparatively small unit as a planetary headquarters would have only one string to its bow. They certainly would have been forced to install duplicate controls of some sort or other by the trouble they had had after Helmuth's supposedly impregnable Grand Base had been destroyed.

There were other straws pointing the same way. Where had those five strange thought-screened men come from? Bominger hadn't known of them apparently. If that idea was sound, the other headquarters would have a spy ray on the whole thing. Both sides used spy rays freely, of course, and to block them was, ordinarily, worse than to let them come. The enemies' use of the thought-screen was different. They realized that it made it easy for the unknown Lensman to discover their agents, but they were forced to use it because of the deadliness of the supposed mind-ray. Why hadn't he thought of this sooner, and had the whole area blocked off? Too late to cry about it now, though.

Assume the idea correct. They certainly knew now that he was a Lensman; probably were morally certain that he was *the* Lensman. His instantaneous change from a drunken dock-walloper to a cold-sober, deadly-skilled rough-and-tumble brawler—and the unexplained deaths of half-a-dozen agents, as well as that of Bominger himself—this was bad. Very, *very* bad—a flare lit tip-off, if there ever was one. Their spy rays would have combed him, millimeter by plotted cubic millimeter: they knew exactly where his Lens was, as well as he did himself. He had put his tail right into the wringer—wrecked the whole job right at the start—unless he could get that other headquarters outfit, too, and get them before they reported in detail to Boskone.

In his room, then, he sat and thought, harder and more intensely than he had ever thought before. No ordinary method of tracing would do. It might be anywhere on the planet, and it certainly would have no connection whatever with the thionite gang. It would be a small outfit; just a few men, but under smart direction. Their purpose would be to watch the business end of the organization, but not to touch it save in an emergency. All that the two groups would have in common would be recognition signals, so that the reserves could take over in case anything happened to Bominger—as it already had. They had him, Kinnison, cold—What to do? *What to do?*

The Lens. That must be the answer—it *had* to be. The Lens—what was it, really, anyway? Simply an aggregation of crystalloids. Not really alive; just a pseudolife, a sort of a reflection of his own life—he wondered—great Klono's brazen teeth and tail, could *that* be it? An idea had struck him, an idea so stupendous in its connotations and ramifications that he gasped, shuddered, and almost went faint at the shock. He started to reach for his Lens, then forced himself to relax and shot a thought to Base.

"Gerrond! Send me a portable spy-ray block, quick!"

"But that would give everything away!" protested the vice-admiral. "That's why we haven't been using them."

"Are you telling me?" the Lensman demanded. "Shoot it along—I'll explain while it's on the way." He went on to tell the Base commander everything that he thought it well for him to know, concluding: "So you see, it's a virtual certainty that I am already as wide open as intergalactic space, and that nothing but fast and sure moves will do us a bit of good."

The block arrived, and as soon as the messenger had departed Kinnison set it going. He was now the center of a sphere into which no spy-ray beam could penetrate. He was also an object of suspicion to anyone using a spy ray, but that fact made no difference, then. He snatched off his shoe, took out his Lens, and tossed that ultra-precious fabrication across the room. Then, just as though he still wore it, he directed a thought at Winstead.

"All serene, Lensman?" he asked, quietly.

"Everything's on the beam," came instant reply. "Why?"

"Just checking, is all." Kinnison did not specify exactly what it was that he was checking!

*

He then did something which, so far as he knew, no Lensman had ever before even thought of doing. Although he felt stark naked without his Lens, he hurled a thought three quarters of the way across the Galaxy to that dread planet Arisia; a thought narrowed down to the exact pattern of that gigantic, fearsome Brain who had been his mentor and his sponsor.

"Ah, 'tis Kimball Kinnison, of Earth," that entity responded, in precisely the same modulation it had employed once before. "You have perceived, then, youth, that the Lens is not the supremely important thing you have supposed it to be?"

"I . . . you . . . I mean—" The flustered Lensman, taken completely aback, was cut off by a sharp rebuke.

"Stop! You are thinking muddily—conduct ordinarily inexcusable! Now, youth, to redeem yourself, you will explain the phenomenon to me, instead of asking me to explain it to you. I realize that you have just discovered another facet of the Cosmic Truth, I know what a shock it has been to your immature mind; hence for this once it may be permissible for me to overlook your crime. But strive not to repeat the offense; for I tell you again in all possible seriousness—I cannot urge upon you too strongly the fact—that in clear and precise thinking lies your only safeguard through that which you are attempting. Confused, wandering thought will assuredly bring disaster inevitable and irreparable."

"Yes, sir," Kinnison replied meekly; a small boy reprimanded by his teacher. "It must be this way. In the first stage of training the Lens is a necessity; just as is the crystal ball or some other hypnotic object in a séance. In the more advanced stage the mind is able to work without aid. The Lens, however, may be—in fact, it must be—endowed with uses other than that of a symbol of identification; uses about which I as yet know nothing. Therefore, while I can work without it, I should not do so except when it is absolutely necessary, as its help will be imperative if I am to advance to any higher stage. It is also clear that you were expecting my call. May I ask if I am on time?"

"You are—your progress has been highly satisfactory. Also, I note with approval that you are not asking for help in your admittedly difficult present problem."

"I know that it wouldn't do me any good—and why." Kinnison grinned wryly. "But I'll bet that Worsel, when he comes up for his second treatment, will know on the spot what it has taken me all this time to find out."

"You deduce truly. He did."

"What? He has been back there already? And you told me—"

"What I told you was true and is. His mind is more fully developed and more responsive than yours; yours is of vastly greater latent capacity, capability, and force—" and the line of communication snapped.

Calling a conveyance, Kinnison was whisked to Base, the spy-ray block full on all the way. There, in a private room, he put his heavily-insulated Lens and a full spool of tape into a ray-proof container, sealed it, and called in the Base commander.

"Gerrond, here is a package of vital importance," he informed him. "Among other things, it contains a record of everything I have done to date. If I don't come back to claim it myself, please send it to Prime Base for personal delivery to Port Admiral Haynes. Speed will be no object, but safety very decidedly of the essence."

"QX—we'll send it in by special messenger."

"Thanks a lot. Now I wonder if I could use your visiphone a minute? I want to talk to the zoo."

"Certainly."

"Zoological Gardens?" and the image of an elderly, white-bearded man appeared upon the plate. "Lensman Kinnison of Tellus—Unattached. Have you as many as three oglons, caged together?"

"Yes. In fact, we have four of them in one cage."

"Better yet. Will you please send them over here to Base at once? Vice-admiral Gerrond, here, will confirm."

"It is most unusual, sir—" the gray-beard began, but broke off at a curt word from Gerrond. "Very well, sir," he agreed, and disconnected.

"Oglons?" the surprised commander demanded. "*Oglons!*"

*

For the oglon, or Radeligian cateagle, is one of the fiercest, most intractable beasts of prey in existence; it assays more concentrated villainy and more sheerly vicious ferocity to the gram than any other creature known to science. It is not a bird, but a winged mammal; and is armed not only with the gripping, tearing talons of the eagle, but also with the heavy, cruel, needle-sharp fangs of the wildcat. And its mental attitude toward all other forms of life is anti-social to the nth degree.

"Oglons." Kinnison confirmed, shortly. "I can handle them."

"You can, of course. But—" Gerrond stopped. This Gray Lensman was forever doing amazing, unprecedented, incomprehensible things. But, so far, he had produced eminently satisfactory results, and he could not be expected to spend all his time in explanations.

"But you think I'm screwy, huh?"

"Oh, no, Kinnison, I wouldn't say that. I only . . . well . . . after all, there isn't much real evidence that we didn't mop up one hundred percent."

"Much? Real evidence? There isn't any," the Tellurian assented, cheerfully enough. "But you've got the wrong slant entirely on these people. You are still thinking of them as gangsters, desperadoes, renegade scum of our own civilization. They are not. They are just as smart as we are; some of them are smarter. Perhaps I am taking too many precautions; but, if so, there is no harm done. On the other hand, there are two things at stake which, to me at least, are extremely important; this whole job of mine and my life: and remember this—the minute I leave this Base both of those things are in your hands."

To that, of course, there could be no answer.

While the two men had been talking and while the oglons were being brought out, two trickling streams of men had been passing, one into and one out of the spy ray shielded confines of Base. Some of these men were heavily bearded, some were shaven clean, but all had two things in common. Each one was human in type and each one in some respect or other resembled Kimball Kinnison.

"Now remember, Gerrond," the Gray Lensman said impressively as he was about to leave. "They're probably right here in Ardith, but they may be anywhere on the planet. Keep a spy ray on me wherever I go, and trace theirs if you can. That will take some doing, as the head one is bound to be an expert. Keep those oglons at least a mile—thirty seconds flying time—away from me; get all the Lensmen you can on the job; keep a cruiser and a speedster hot, but not too close. I may need one of them, or all, or none of them, I can't tell; but I do know this—if I need anything at all, I'll need it fast. Above all, Gerrond, by the Lens you wear, do nothing whatever, no matter what happens around me or to me, until I give you the word. QX?"

"QX, Gray Lensman. Clear ether!"

Kinnison took a ground-cab to the mouth of the narrow street upon which was situated his dock-walloper's mean lodging. This was a desperate, a fool-hardy trick—but in its very boldness, in its insolubly paradoxical aspects, lay its strength. Probably Boskone could solve its puzzles, but—he hoped—this ape, not being Boskone, couldn't. And, paying off the cabman, he thrust his hands into his tattered pockets and, whistling blithely if a bit raucously through his stained teeth, he strode off down the narrow way as though he did not have a care in the world. But he was doing the finest job of acting of his short career; even though, for all he really knew, he might not have any audience at all. For, inwardly, he was strung to highest tension. His sense of perception, sharply alert, was covering the full hemisphere around and above him; his mind was triggered to jerk any muscle of his body into instantaneous action.

*

Meanwhile, in a heavily guarded room, there sat a manlike being, faintly but definitely blue; not only as to eyes, but also as to hair, teeth, and complexion. For two hours he had been sitting at his spy ray plate, studying with ever-growing uneasiness the human beings so suddenly and so surprisingly numerously having business at the Patrol's Base. For minutes he had been studying minutely a man in a ground-cab, and his uneasiness reached panic heights.

"It *is* the Lensman!" he burst out. "It's *got* to be, Lens or no Lens. Who else would have the cold nerve to go back there when he knows that he has exposed himself?"

"Well, get him, then," advised his companion. "All set, aren't you?"

"But it *can't* be!" the chief went on, reversing himself in mid-flight. "A Lensman without a Lens is unthinkable, and invisible Lens is preposterous. And this fellow has not now, and never has had, a mind-ray machine. He hasn't got *anything!* And besides, the Lensman we're after wouldn't think of doing a thing like this—he always disappears the instant a job is finished, whether or not there is any chance of his having been discovered."

"Well, drop him and chase somebody else, then," the lieutenant advised, unfeelingly.

"But there's nobody nearly enough like him!" snarled the chief, in desperation. He was torn by doubt and indecision. This whole situation was a mess—it didn't add up right, from any possible angle. "It's got to be him—it *can't* be anybody else. I've checked and rechecked him. It *is* him, and not a double. He thinks that he's safe enough; he doesn't suspect that we're here at all. Besides, his only good double, Fordyce—and *he's* not good enough to stand the inspection I just gave him—hasn't appeared anywhere."

"Probably inside Base yet. Maybe this is a better double. Perhaps this *is* the real Lensman pretending he isn't, or maybe the real Lensman is slipping out while you're watching the man in the cab," the junior suggested, helpfully.

"Shut up!" the superior yelled. He started to reach for a switch, but paused, hand in air.

"Go ahead. That's it, call District and toss it into their laps, if it's too hot for you to handle. I think myself that whoever did this job is a warm number—plenty warm."

"And get my ears bunted off with that 'your report is neither complete nor conclusive' of his?" the chief sneered. "And get reduced for incompetence besides? No, we've got to do it ourselves, and do it right—but that man there isn't the Lensman—he can't be!"

"Well, you'd better make up your mind—you haven't got all day. And nix on that 'we' stuff. It's *you* that's got to do it—you're the boss, not me," the underling countered, callously. For once, he was really glad that he was not the one in command. "And you'd better get busy and do it, too."

"I'll do it," the chief declared, grimly. "There's a way."

There was a way. One only. He must be brought in alive and compelled to divulge the truth. There was no other way.

574

The blue man touched a stud and spoke. "Don't kill him—bring him in alive. If you kill him even accidentally, I'll kill both of you, myself."

*

The Gray Lensman made his carefree way down the alleylike thoroughfare, whistling inharmoniously and very evidently at peace with the Universe.

It takes something, friends, to walk knowingly into a trap; without betraying emotion or stress even while a blackjack, wielded by a strong arm, is descending toward the back of your head. Something of quality, something of fiber. But whatever it took, Kinnison in ample measure had.

He did not wink, flinch, or turn an eye as the billy came down. Only as it touched his hair did he act, exerting all his marvelous muscular control to jerk forward and downward, with the weapon and ahead of it, to spare himself as much as possible of the terrific blow.

The blackjack crunched against the base of the Lensman's skull in a shower of coruscating constellations. He fell. He lay there, twitching feebly.

VIII.

As has been said, Kinnison rode the blow of the blackjack forward and downward, thus robbing it of some of its power. It struck him hard enough so that the thug did not suspect the truth; he thought that he had all but taken the Lensman's life. And, for all the speed with which the Tellurian had yielded before the blow, he was hurt; but he was not stunned. Therefore, although he made no resistance when the two bullies rolled him over, lashed his feet together, tied his hands behind him, and lifted him into a car, he was fully conscious throughout the proceedings.

When the cab was perhaps half an hour upon its way the Lensman struggled back, quite realistically, to consciousness.

"Take it easy, pal," the larger of his thought-screened captors advised, dandling the blackjack suggestively before his eyes. "One yelp out of you, or a signal, if you've got one of them Lenses, and I bop you another one."

"What the blinding blue hell's coming off here?" demanded the dock-walloper, furiously. "Wha'd'ya think you're doing, you lop-eared—" and he cursed the two, viciously and comprehensively.

"Shut up or he'll knock you kicking," the smaller thug advised from the driver's seat, and Kinnison subsided. "Not that it bothers me any, but you're making too much noise."

"But what's the matter?" Kinnison asked, more quietly. "What'd you slug me for and drag me off? I ain't done nothing and I ain't got nothing."

"I don't know nothing," the big agent replied. "The boss will tell you all you need to know when we get to where we're going. All I know is the boss says to bop you easylike and bring you in alive if you don't act up. He says to tell you not to yell and not to use no Lens. If you yell we burn you out. If you use any Lens, the boss he's got his eyes on all the bases and space-ports and everything, and if any help starts to come this way he'll tell us and we burn you out. Then we buzz off. We can kill you and flit before any help can get near you, he says."

"Your boss ain't got the brains of a fontema," Kinnison growled. He knew that boss, wherever he was, could hear every word. "Hell's hinges, if I was a Lensman you think I'd be walloping junk on a dock? Use your head, cully, if you got one."

"I wouldn't know nothing about that," the other returned, stolidly.

"But I ain't got no Lens!" the dock-walloper stormed, in exasperation. "Look at me—frisk me! You'll see I ain't!"

"All that ain't none of my dish." The thug was entirely unmoved. "I don't know nothing and I don't do nothing except what the boss tells me, see? Now take it easy, all nice and quietlike. If you don't," and he flicked the blackjack lightly against the Lensman's knee, "I'll put out your landing-lights. I'll lay you like a mat, and I don't mean maybe. See?"

Kinnison saw, and relapsed into silence. The automobile rolled along. And, flitting industriously about upon its delivery duties, but never much more or less than one measured mile distant, a panel job pursued its devious way. Oddly enough, its chauffeur was a Lensman. Here and there, high in the heavens, were a few airplanes, gyros, and copters; but they were going peacefully and steadily about their business—even though most of them happened to have Lensmen as pilots.

And, not at Base at all, but high in the stratosphere and so thoroughly screened that a spy-ray observer could not even tell that his gaze was being blocked, Base's swiftest cruiser, Lensman-commanded, rode poised upon flare-baffled, softly hissing under jets. And, equally high and as adequately protected against observation, a keen-eyed Lensman sat at the controls of a speedster, jazzing her muffled jets and peering eagerly through a telescopic sight. As far as the Patrol was concerned, everything was on the trips.

The car approached the gates of a suburban estate and stopped. It waited. Kinnison knew that the Boskonian within was working his every beam, alert for any sign of Patrol activity; knew that if there were any such sign the car would be off in an instant. But there was no activity. Kinnison sent a thought to Gerrond, who relayed micro-metric readings of the objective to various Lensmen. Still everyone waited. Then the gate opened of itself, the two thugs jerked their captive out of the car to the ground, and Kinnison sent out his signal.

*

Base remained quiet, but everything else erupted at once. The airplanes wheeled, cruiser and speedster plummeted downward at maximum blast. The panel job literally fell open, as did the cage within it, and four ravening cateagles, with the silent ferocity of their kind, rocketed toward their goal.

Although the oglons were not as fast as the flying ships they did not have nearly as far to go, wherefore they got there first. The thugs had no warning whatever. One instant everything was under control; in the next the noiselessly arrowing destroyers struck their prey with the mad fury that only a striking cateagle can exhibit. Barbed talons dug viciously into eyes, faces, mouths; tearing, rending, wrenching; fierce-driven fangs tore deeply, savagely into defenseless throats.

Once each the thugs screamed in mad, lethal terror, but no warning was given; for by that time every building upon that pretentious estate had disappeared in the pyrotechnic flare of detonating duodec. The pellets were small, of course—the gunners did not wish either to destroy the nearby residences or to injure Kinnison—but they were powerful enough for the purpose intended. Mansion and outbuildings disappeared, and not even the most thoroughgoing spy-ray search revealed the presence of anything animate or structural where those buildings had been.

The panel job drove up and Kinnison, perceiving that the cateagles had done their work, sent them back into their cage. The Radeligian Lensman, after securely locking cage and truck, cut the Earthman's bonds.

"QX, Kinnison?" he asked.

"QX, Barknett—thanks," and the two Lensmen, one in the panel truck and the other in the gangsters' car, drove back to Base. There Kinnison recovered his package.

"This has got me all of a soapy lather, but you have called the turn on every play yet," Winstead told the Tellurian, later. "Is this all of the big shots, do you think, or are there some more of them around here?"

"Not around here, I'm pretty sure," Kinnison replied. "No, two main lines is all they would have had, I think—this time. Next time—"

"There won't be any next time," Winstead declared.

"Not on this planet, no. Knowing what to expect, you fellows can handle anything that comes up. I was thinking then of my next step."

"Oh. But you'll get 'em, Gray Lensman!"

"I hope so"—soberly.

"Luck, Kinnison!"

"Clear ether, Winstead!" and this time the Tellurian really did flit.

As his speedster ripped through the void Kinnison did more thinking, but he was afraid that his Arisian mentor would have considered the product muddy, indeed. He couldn't seem to get to the first check station. One thing was limpidly clear; this line of attack or any very close variation of it would never work again. He'd have to think up something new. So far, he had got away with his stuff because he had kept one lap ahead of them, but how much longer could he manage to keep up the pace?

Bominger had been no mental giant, of course; but this other lad was nobody's fool and this next higher-up, with whom he had had an interview via Bominger, would certainly prove to be a really shrewd number.

"'The higher the fewer,'" he repeated to himself the old saying, adding, "and in this case, the smarter." He had to put out some jets, but where he was going to get the fuel he had no idea.

*

Again the trip to Tellus was uneventful, and the Gray Lensman, the symbol of his rank again flashing upon his wrist, sought interview with Haynes.

"Send him in, certainly—send him in!" Kinnison heard the communicator crackle, and the receptionist passed him along. He paused in surprise, however, at the doorway of the office, for Chief Surgeon Lacy and a Posenian were in conference with the Port Admiral.

"Come in, Kinnison," Haynes invited. "Lacy wants to see you a minute, too. Dr. Phillips–Lensman Kinnison, Unattached. His name is not Phillips, of course; that is merely one we gave him in self-defense. His real name is utterly unpronounceable."

Phillips, the Posenian, was as tall as Kinnison, and heavier. His figure was somewhat human in shape, but not in detail. He had four arms instead of two, each arm had two opposed hands, and each hand had two thumbs, one situated about where a little finger would be expected. He had no eyes, not even vestigial ones. He had two broad, flat noses and two toothful mouths; one of each in what would ordinarily be called the front of his round, shining, hairless head; the other in the back. Upon the sides of his head were large, volute, highly dirigible ears. And, like most races having the faculty of perception instead of that of sight, his head was relatively immobile, his neck being short, massive, and tremendously strong.

"You look well, very well," Lacy reported, after feeling and prodding vigorously the members which had been in splints and casts so long. "Have to take a picture, of course, before saying anything definite. No, we won't, either, now. Phillips, look at his"–an interlude of technical jargon–"and see what kind of a recovery he has made." Then, while the Posenian was examining Kinnison's interior mechanisms, the Chief Surgeon went on:

"Wonderful diagnosticians and surgeons, these Posenians–can see into the patient without taking him apart. In another few centuries every doctor will have to have the sense of perception. Phillips is doing a research in neurology–more particularly a study of the neural synapse and the proliferation of neural dendrites–"

"La–cy-y-y!" Haynes drawled the word in reproof. "I've told you a thousand times to talk English when you're talking to me. How about it, Kinnison?"

"It might be more comprehensible, although we must admit that any scientist likes to speak with precision, which he cannot do in the ordinary language of the layman."

"Right, boy–surprisingly and pleasingly right!" Lacy exclaimed. "Why can't you adopt that attitude, Haynes, and learn enough words so that you can understand what a man is talking about? But to reduce it to monosyllabic simplicity, Phillips is studying a thing that has baffled us for centuries–yes, for millennia. The lower forms of cells are able to regenerate themselves; wounds heal, bones knit. Higher types, such as nerve cells, regenerate imperfectly, if at all; and the highest type, the brain cells, do not do so under any conditions." He turned a reproachful gaze upon Haynes. "This is terrible. Those statements are pitiful–inadequate–false. Worse than that–practically meaningless. What I wanted to say, and what I'm going to say, is that–"

"Oh, no you aren't, not in this office," his old friend interrupted. "We got the idea perfectly. The question is, why can't human beings repair nerves or spinal cords, or grow new ones? If such a worthless beastie as a starfish can grow a whole new body to one leg, including a brain, if any, why can't a really intelligent victim of simple infantile paralysis–or a ray–recover the use of a leg that is otherwise in perfect shape?"

"Well, that's something like it, but I hope you can aim closer than that at a battleship," Lacy grunted. "We'll buzz off now, Phillips, and leave these two war horses alone."

*

"Here is my report in detail." Kinnison placed the package upon the Port Admiral's desk as soon as the room was sealed behind the visitors. "I talked to you direct about most of it—this is for the record."

"Of course. Mighty glad you found Medon, for our sake as well as theirs. They have things that we need, badly."

"Where did they put them? I suggested a sun near Sol, so as to have them handy to Prime Base."

"Right next door—Alpha Centauri. Didn't get to do much scouting, did you?"

"I'll say we didn't. Boskonia owns that Galaxy; lock, stock, and barrel. Maybe some other independent planets—bound to be, of course; probably a lot of them—but it's too dangerous, hunting them at this stage of the game. But at that, we did enough, for the time being. We proved our point. Boskone, if there is any such being, is certainly in the Second Galaxy. However, it will be a long time before we're ready to carry the war there to him, and in the meantime we've got a lot to do. Check?"

"To nineteen decimals."

"It seems to me, then, that while you are rebuilding our first-line ships, super-powering them with Medonian insulation and conductors, I had better keep on tracing Boskone along the line of drugs. I have proved to my own satisfaction that they are back of almost all of that drug business."

"And in some ways their drugs are more dangerous to Civilization than their battleships. More insidious and, ultimately, more fatal."

"I'm convinced of it. And since I am perhaps as well equipped as any of the other Lensmen to cope with that particular problem—" Kinnison paused, questioningly.

"That certainly is no overstatement," the Port Admiral replied, dryly. "You're the *only* one equipped to cope with it."

"None of the other boys except Worsel, then? I heard that a couple—"

"They thought that they had a call, but they didn't. All they had was a wish. They came back."

"Too bad—but I can see how that would be. A man has to know exactly what he needs, and his brain must be ready to take it, or it burns it out. It almost does, anyway—mind is a funny thing. But that isn't getting us anywhere. Can you take time to let me talk at you a few minutes?"

"I certainly can. You have what is perhaps the most important assignment in the Galaxy, and I would like to know more about it, if it's anything you can pass on."

"Nothing that need be sealed from any Lensman. The main object of all of us, as you know, is to push Boskonia out of this Galaxy. From a military standpoint they practically *are* out. Their drug syndicate, however, is very decidedly in, and getting in deeper all the time. Therefore, we next push the zwilniks out. They have peddlers and such small fry, who deal with distributors and so on. These, as it were, form the bottom layer. Above them are the secret agents, the observers, and the wholesale handlers; runners and importers. All these folks are directed and controlled by one man, the boss of each planetary organization. Thus, Bominger was the boss of all zwilnik activities on the whole planet of Radelix.

"In turn the planetary bosses report to, and are synchronized and controlled by, a Regional Director, who supervises the activities of a couple of hundred or so planetary outfits. I got a line on the one over Bominger, you know—Prellin, the Kalonian. By the way, you knew, didn't you, that Helmuth was a Kalonian, too?"

"I got it from the tape. Smart people, they must be, but not my idea of good neighbors."

"I'll say not. Well, that's all I really *know* of their organization. It seems logical to suppose, though, that the structure is coherent all the way up. If so, the Regional Directors would be under some higher-up, possibly a Galactic Director, who in turn might be under Boskone himself—or one of his cabinet officers, at least. Perhaps the Galactic Director might even be a cabinet officer in their government, whatever it is?"

"An ambitious program you've got mapped out for yourself. How are you figuring on swinging it?"

*

"That's the rub—I don't know," Kinnison confessed, ruefully. "But if it's done at all, that's the way I've got to go about it. Any other way would take a thousand years and more men than we'll ever have. This way works fine, when it works at all."

"I can see that—lop off the head and the body dies," Haynes agreed.

"That's the way it works—especially when the head keeps detailed records and books covering the activities of all the members of his body. With Bominger and the others gone, and with full transcripts of his accounts, the boys mopped up Radelix in a hurry. From now on it will be simple to keep it clean, except of course, for the usual bootleg trickle, and that can be reduced to a minimum. Similarly, if we can put this Prellin away and take a good look at his ledgers, it will be easy to clear up his two hundred planets. And so on."

"Very clear, and quite simple—in theory." The older man was thoughtful and frankly dubious. "In practice, difficult in the extreme."

"But necessary," the younger insisted.

"I suppose so," Haynes assented finally. "Useless to tell you not to take chances—you'll have to—but for all of our sakes, if not for your own, be as careful as you can."

"I'll do that, chief. I think a lot of me, really. You know that story about the guy who was all right in his place, but the place hadn't been dug yet? Well, I don't want anybody digging my proper place for a long time to come."

Haynes laughed, but the concern did not leave his features. "Anything special you want done?" he asked.

"Yes, very special," Kinnison surprised him by answering in the affirmative. "You know that the Medonians developed a scrambler for a detector-nullifier. Hotchkiss and the boys developed a new line of attack on that—against long-range stuff we're probably safe—but they haven't been able to do a thing on electromagnetics. Well, the Boskonians, beginning with Prellin, are going to start wondering what has been happening. Then, if I succeed in getting Prellin, they are bound to start doing things. One thing they will do will be to fix up their headquarters so that they will have about five hundred percent overlap on their electros. Perhaps they will have outposts, too, close enough together to have the same thing there—possibly two or three hundred even on visuals."

"In that case, I would say that you'd stay out."

"Not necessarily. What do electros work on?"

"Iron, I suppose—they did when I went to school last."

"The answer, then, is to build me a speedster that is inherently indetectable—absolutely non-ferrous. Berylumin and other alloys for all the structural parts—"

"But you've got to have silicon-steel cores for your electrical equipment!"

"I was coming to that. Have you? I was reading in the 'Transactions' the other day that force fields had been used in big units, and were more efficient. Some of the smaller units, instruments and so on, might have to have some iron, but wouldn't it be possible to so saturate those small pieces with a dense field of detector frequencies that they wouldn't react?"

"I don't know. Never thought of it. Would it?"

"I don't know, either—I'm not telling you, I'm just making suggestions. I do know one thing, however. We've got to keep ahead of them—think of things first and oftenest, and be ready to abandon them for something else as soon as we have used them once."

"Except for those primary projectors." Haynes grinned wryly. "They can't be abandoned—even with Medonian power we haven't been able to develop a screen that will stop them cold. We've got to keep them secret from Boskone—and in that connection I want to compliment you on the suggestion of having Velantian Lensmen as mind readers wherever those projectors are even being thought of."

"You caught spies, then? How many?"

"Not many—three or four in each Base—but enough to have done the damage. Now, I believe, for the first time in history, we can be *sure* of our entire personnel."

"I think so. The Arisian said that the Lens was enough, if we used it properly. That's up to us."

"But how about visuals?" Haynes was still worrying, and to good purpose.

*

"Well, we have a black coating now that is ninety-nine percent absorptive, and I don't need ports or windows. At that, though, one percent reflection would be enough to give me away at a critical time. How'd it be to put a couple of the boys on that job? Have them put a decimal point after the ninety-nine and see how many nines they can tack on behind it?"

"That's a thought, Kinnison, and they have lots of time to work on it while the engineers are trying to fill your specifications as to a speedster. But you're right, dead right, in everything you have said. We—or rather, you—have got to out-think them; and it certainly is up to us to do everything that can be done to build the apparatus to put your thoughts into practice. And it is not at some vague time in the future that Boskone is going to start thinking seriously about you and what you have done. It is now; or even more probably, a week or so ago. In fact, if there were any way of learning the truth, I think we should find that they have begun acting already, instead of waiting until you abate the nuisance which is Prellin, the Kalonian. But you haven't said a word yet about the really big job you have in mind."

"I've been putting that off until the last." The Gray Lensman's voice held obscure puzzlement. "The fact is that I simply can't get a tooth into it—can't get a grip in it anywhere. I don't know enough about math or physics. Everything comes out negative for me; not only inertia, but also force, velocity, and even mass itself. Final results always contain an 'i', too, the square root of minus one. I can't get rid of it, and I don't see how it can be built into any kind of apparatus. It may not be workable at all, but before I give up the idea I would like to call a conference, if it's QX with you and the Council."

"Certainly it is QX with us. You're forgetting again, aren't you, that you're a Gray Lensman?" Haynes' voice held no reproof, he was positively beaming with a super-fatherly pride.

"Not exactly." Kinnison blushed, almost squirmed. "I'm just too much of a cub to be sticking my neck out so far, that's all. The idea may be—probably is—wilder than a Radeligian cateagle. The only kind of a conference that could even begin to handle it would cost a young fortune, and I don't want to spend that much money on my own responsibility."

"To date your ideas have worked out well enough so that the Council is backing you one hundred percent," the older man said, dryly. "Expense is no object." Then, his voice changing markedly, "Kim, have you any idea at all of the financial resources of the Patrol?"

"Very little, sir, if any, I'm afraid," Kinnison confessed.

"Here on Tellus alone we have an expendible reserve of over ten thousand million credits. With the restriction of government to its proper sphere and its concentration into our organization, resulting in the liberation of man-power into wealth-producing enterprise, and especially with the enormous growth of inter-world commerce, world-income increased to such a point that taxation could be reduced to a minimum; and the lower the taxes the more flourishing business became and the greater the income.

"Now the tax rate is the lowest in recorded history. The total income tax, for instance, in the highest bracket, is only three point five nine two percent. At that, however, if it had not been for the recent slump, due to Boskonian interference with inter-systemic commerce, we would have had to reduce the tax rate again to avoid serious financial difficulty due to the fact that too much of the galactic total of circulating credit would have been concentrated in the expendable funds of the Galactic Patrol. So don't even think of money. Whether you want to spend a thousand credits, a million, or a thousand million; go ahead."

"Thanks, chief; glad you explained. I'll feel better now about spending money that doesn't belong to me. Now if you'll give me, for about a week, the use of the librarian in charge of science files and a galactic beam, I'll quit bothering you."

"I'll do that." The Port Admiral touched a button and in a few minutes a trimly attractive blonde entered the room. "Miss Hostetter, this is Lensman Kinnison, Unattached. Please turn over your regular duties to an assistant and work with him until he releases you. Whatever he says, goes; the sky's the limit."

*

In the Library of Science Kinnison outlined his problem briefly to his new aide, concluding:

"I want only about fifty, as a larger group could not co-operate efficiently. Are your lists arranged so that you can skim off the top fifty?"

"Such a group can be selected, I think." The girl stood for a moment, lower lip held lightly between white teeth. "That is not a standard index, but each scientist has a rating upon his card. I can set the acceptor . . . no, the rejector would be better . . . to throw out all the cards above any given rating. If we take out all ratings over seven hundred we will have only the highest of the geniuses."

"How many, do you suppose?"

"I have only a vague idea—a couple of hundred, perhaps. If too many, we can run them again at a higher level, say seven ten. But there won't be very many, since there are only two galactic ratings higher than seven fifty. There will be duplications, too—such people as Sir Austin Cardynge will have two or three cards in the final rejects."

"QX—we'll want to hand-pick the fifth, anyway. Let's go!"

Then for hours, bale after bale of cards went through the machine; thousands of records per minute. Occasionally one card would flip out into a rack, rejected. Finally:

"That's all, I think. Mathematicians, physicists," the librarian ticked off upon pink fingers. "Astronomers, philosophers, and this new classification, which has not been named yet."

"The H.T.T.'s." Kinnison glanced at the label, lightly lettered in pencil, fronting the slim packet of cards. "Aren't you going to run them through, too?"

"No. These are the two I mentioned a minute ago—the only ones rating over seven hundred fifty."

"A choice pair, eh? Sort of a *crème de la crème*? Let's look 'em over," and he extended his hand. "What do the initials stand for?"

"I'm awfully sorry, sir, really," the girl flushed in embarrassment as she relinquished the cards in high reluctance. "If I'd had any idea, we wouldn't have dared—we call you, among ourselves, the 'High-Tension Thinkers.'"

"Us!" It was the Lensman's turn to flush. Nevertheless, he took the packet and read sketchily the facer: "Class XIX—Unclassifiable at present—lack of adequate methods—minds of range and scope far beyond any available indices—Ratings above high genius (750)—yet no instability—power beyond any heretofore known—assigned rating tentative and definitely minimum."

He then read the cards.

"Worsel, Velantia, eight hundred five."

And:

"Kimball Kinnison, Tellus, nine hundred twenty-five!"

IX.

The Port Admiral was eminently correct in supposing that Boskone, whoever or whatever he or it might be, was already taking action upon what the Tellurian Lensman had done. For, even as Kinnison was at work in the Library of Science, a meeting which was indirectly to affect him no little was being called to order.

In the immensely distant Second Galaxy was that meeting being held; upon the then planet Jarnevon of the Eich; within that sullen fortress already mentioned briefly. Presiding over it was the indescribable entity known to history as Eichlan; or, more properly, Lan of the Eich.

"Boskone is now in session," that entity announced to the eight other like monstrosities who in some fashion indescribable to man were stationed at the long, low, wide bench of stonelike material which served as a table of State. "Nine days ago each of us began to search for whatever new facts might bear upon the activities of the as-yet-entirely-hypothetical Lensman who, Helmuth believed, was the real force back of our recent intolerable reverses in the Tellurian Galaxy.

"As First of Boskone I will report as to the military situation. As you know, our positions there became untenable with the fall of our Grand Base and all our mobile forces were withdrawn. In order to facilitate reorganization, co-ordinating ships were sent out. Some of these ships went to planets held in toto by us. Not one of these vessels has been able to report any pertinent facts whatever. Ships approaching bases of the Patrol, or encountering Patrol ships of war in space, simply ceased communicating. Even their automatic recorders, tuned to my desk as commander-in-chief, ceased to function without transmitting any intelligible data, indicating complete destruction of those ships. A cascade system, in which one ship followed another at long range and with analytical instruments set to determine the nature of any beam or weapon employed, was attempted. The enemy, however, threw out blanketing zones of tremendous power; and we lost six more vessels without obtaining the desired data. These are the facts, all negative. Theorizing, deduction, summation, and integration will as usual, come later. Eichmil, Second of Boskone, will now report."

"My facts are also entirely negative," the Second began. "As soon as our operations upon the planet Radelix began to be really productive of results, a contingent of Tellurian narcotic agents arrived; which may or may not have included the Lensman—"

"Stick to facts for the time being," Eichlan ordered, curtly.

"Shortly thereafter a minor agent, a female instructed to wear a thought-screen at all times, lost her usefulness by suffering a mental disorder which incapacitated her quite seriously. Then another agent, also a female, this time one of the third order and who had been very useful up to that time, ceased reporting. A few days later Bominger, the Planetary Director, failed to report, as did the Planetary Observer; who, as you know, was entirely unknown to, and had no connection with, the operating staff. Reports from other sources, such as importers and shippers—these, I believe, are here admissible as facts—indicate that our entire personnel upon Radelix has been put to death. No unusual developments have occurred upon any other planet, nor has any significant fact, however small, been discovered."

"Eichnor, Third of Boskone."

"Also negative. Our every source of information from within the bases of the Patrol has been shut off. Every one of our representatives—some of whom have been reporting regularly for many years—has been silent, and every effort to reach any of them has failed."

"Eichsnap, Fourth of Boskone."

"Utterly negative. We have been able to find no trace whatever of the planet Medon, or of any one of the twenty-one warships investing it at the time of its disappearance."

And so on, through nine reports, while the tentacles of the mighty First of Boskone played intermittently over the keys of a complex instrument or machine before him.

"We will now reason, theorize, and draw conclusions," the First announced, and each of the organisms fed his ideas and deductions into the machine. It whirred briefly, then ejected a tape, which Eichlan took up and scanned narrowly.

*

"Rejecting all conclusions having a probability of less than ninety-five percent," he announced, "we have: First, a set of three probabilities of a value of ninety-nine and ninety-nine one-hundredths—virtual certainties—that some one Tellurian Lensman is the prime mover behind what has happened; that he has acquired a mental power heretofore unknown to his race; and that he has been in large part responsible for the development of the Patrol's new and formidable weapons. Second, a probability of ninety-nine percent that he and his organization are no longer on the defensive, but have assumed the offensive. Third, one of ninety-seven percent that it is not primarily Tellus which is an obstacle, even though the Galactic Patrol and Civilization did originate upon that planet, but Arisia; that Helmuth's report was at least partially true. Fourth, one of ninety-five and one half percent that the Lens is also concerned in the disappearance of the planet Medon. There is a lesser probability, but still of some ninety-four percent, that that same Lensman is involved here.

"I will interpolate here that the vanishment of that planet is a much more serious matter than it might appear, on the surface, to be. In situ, it was a thing of no concern—gone, it becomes an affair of almost vital import. To issue orders impossible of fulfillment, as Helmuth did when he said 'Comb Trenco, inch by inch,' is easy. To comb this Galaxy star by star for Medon would be an even more difficult and longer task; but what can be done is being done.

"To return to the conclusions, they point out a state of things which I do not have to tell you is really grave. This is the first major setback which the culture of the Boskone has encountered since it began its rise, thousands of years ago. You are familiar with that rise; how we of the Eich took over in turn a city, a race, a planet, a solar system, a region, a galaxy. How we extended our sway into the Tellurian Galaxy, as a preliminary to the extension of our authority throughout all the populated galaxies of the macro-cosmic Universe.

"You know our creed; to the victor the power. He who is strongest and fittest shall survive and shall rule. This so-called Civilization which is opposing us, which began upon Tellus but whose driving force is that which dwells upon Arisia, is a soft, weak, puny-spirited thing indeed to resist the mental and material power of our culture. Myriads of beings upon each planet, each one striving for power and, so striving, giving of that power to him above. Myriads of planets, each, in return for our benevolently despotic

585

control, delegating and contributing power to the Eich. All this power, delegated to the thousands of millions of the Eich of this planet, culminates in and is wielded by the nine of us who comprise Boskone.

"Power! Our forefathers thought that control of one planet was enough. Later it was declared that mastery of a galaxy, if realized, would sate ambition. We of Boskone, however, now know that our power shall be limited only by the bounds of the Material Cosmic All—every world that exists throughout space shall and must pay homage and tribute to Boskone! What, gentlemen, is the sense of this meeting?"

"Arisia must be visited!" There was no need of integrating this thought; it was dominant and unanimous.

"I would advise caution, however," the Eighth of Boskone amended his ballot. "We are an old race, it is true, and able; we have demonstrated our superiority over every other race of our Galaxy, much more conclusively than the Tellurians have shown their supremacy on theirs, I cannot help but believe, however, that in Arisia there exists an unknown quality, an 'x' which we as yet are unable to evaluate. It must be borne in mind that Helmuth, while not of the Eich, was, nevertheless, an able being; yet he was handled so mercilessly there that he could not render a complete or conclusive report of his expedition, then or ever. With these thoughts in mind I suggest that no actual landing be made, but that the torpedo be launched from a distance."

"The suggestion is eminently sound," the First approved. "As to Helmuth, he was, for an oxygen-breather, fairly able. He was however, mentally soft, as are all such. Do you, our foremost psychologist, believe that any existent or conceivable mind could break yours, with no application whatever of physical force or device, as Helmuth's reports seemed to indicate that his was broken? I use the word 'seemed' advisedly, for I do not believe that Helmuth reported the actual truth. In fact, I was about to replace him with an Eich, however unpleasant such an assignment would be to any of our race, because of that weakness."

"No," agreed the Eighth. "I do not believe that there exists in the Universe a mind of sufficient power to break mine. It is a truism that no mental influence, however powerful, can affect a strong, definitely and positively opposed will. For that reason I voted against the use of thought-screens by our agents. Such screens expose them to detection and can be of no real benefit. Physical means were—must have been—used first, and, after physical subjugation, the screens were, of course, useless."

*

"I am not sure that I agree with you entirely," the Ninth put in. "We have here cogent evidence that there have been employed mental forces of a type or pattern with which we are entirely unfamiliar. While it is the consensus of opinion that the importance of Helmuth's report should be minimized, it seems to me that we have enough corroborative evidence to indicate that this mentality may be able to operate without material aid. If so, rigid screening should be retained, as offering the only possible safeguard from such force."

"Sound in theory, but in practice dubious," the psychologist countered. "If there were any evidence whatever that the screens had done any good I would agree with you. But have they? Screening failed to save Helmuth or his base; and there is nothing to indicate that the screens impeded, even momentarily, the progress of the suppositious Lensman upon Radelix. You speak of 'rigid' screening. The term is meaningless. Perfectly effective screening is impossible. If, as we seem to be doing, we postulate the ability of one mind to control another without physical, bodily contact—or is the idea at all far fetched, considering what I myself have done to the minds of many of our agents?—the Lensman can work through any unshielded mentality whatever to attain his ends. As you know, Helmuth deduced, too late, that it must have been through the mind of a dog that the Lensman invaded Grand Base."

"Poppycock!" snorted the Seventh. "Or, if not, we can kill the dogs—or screen their minds, too," he sneered.

"Admitted," the psychologist returned, unmoved. "You might conceivably kill all the animals that run and all the birds that fly. You cannot, however, destroy all life in any locality at all extended, clear down to the worms in their burrows and the termites in their hidden retreats; and the mind has not yet existed which is keen enough to draw a line of demarcation and say 'here begins intelligent life.'"

"This discussion is interesting, but futile," put in Eichlan, forestalling a scornful reply. "It is more to the point, I think, to discuss that which must be done; or, rather, who is to do it, since the thing itself admits of only one solution—an atomic bomb of sufficient power to destroy every trace of life upon that accursed planet. Shall we send someone, or shall some of us ourselves go? To overestimate a foe is at worst only an unnecessary precaution; to underestimate this one may well be fatal. Therefore, it seems to me, that the decision in this matter should lie with our psychologist. I will, however, if you prefer, integrate our various conclusions."

Recourse to the machine was unnecessary; it was agreed by all that Eichamp, the Eighth of Boskone, should decide.

"My decision will be evident," that worthy said, measuredly, "when I say that I myself, for one, am going. The situation is admittedly a serious one. Moreover, I believe, to a greater extent than do the rest of you, that there is a certain amount of truth in Helmuth's version of his experiences. My mind is the only one in existence of whose power I am absolutely certain; the only one which I definitely *know* will not give way before any conceivable mental force, whatever its amount or whatever its method of application. I want none with me save of the Eich, and even those I will examine carefully before permitting them aboard ship with me."

"You decide as I thought," said the First. "I also shall go. My mind will hold, I think."

"It will hold—in your case examination is unnecessary," agreed the psychologist.

"And I! And I!" arose what amounted to a chorus.

"No," came curt denial from the First. "Two are enough to operate all machinery and weapons. To take any more of the Boskone would weaken us here injudiciously; well you know how many are working, and in what fashions, for seats at this table. To take any weaker mind, even of the Eich, might conceivably be to court disaster. We two should be safe; I because I have proven repeatedly my right to hold the title of First of this Council, the rulers and masters of the dominant race of the Universe; Eichamp because of his unparalleled knowledge, of all intelligence. Our vessel is ready. We go."

*

As has been indicated, none of the Eich were, or ever had been, cowards. Tyrants they were, it is true, and dictators of the harshest, sternest, and most soulless kind; callous and merciless they were; cold as the rocks of their frigid world and as utterly ruthless and remorseless as the fabled Juggernaut; but they were as logical as they were hard. He, who of them all was best fitted to do anything, did it unquestioningly and, as a matter of course; did it with the calmly emotionless efficiency of the machine which in actual fact he was. Therefore, it was the First and the Eighth of Boskone who went.

Through the star-studded purlieus of the Second Galaxy the black, airless, lightless vessel sped; through the reaches, vaster and more tenuous far, of intergalactic space; into the Tellurian Galaxy; up to a solar system shunned then as now, by all uninvited intelligences—dread and dreaded Arisia.

Not close to the planet did even the two of Boskone venture; but stopped at the greatest distance at which a torpedo could be directed surely against the target. But even so the vessel of the Eich had punctured a screen of mental force; and as Eichlan extended a tentacle toward the firing mechanism of the missiles, watched in as much suspense as they were capable of feeling by the planet-bound seven of Boskone, a thought as penetrant as a needle and yet as binding as a cable tempered steel drove into his brain.

"Hold!" That thought commanded, and Eichlan held, as did also his fellow Boskonian.

Both remained rigid, unable to move any single voluntary muscle; while the other seven of the Council looked on in uncomprehending amazement. Their instruments remained dead—since those mechanisms were not sensitive to thought, to them nothing at all was occurring. Those seven leaders of the Eich knew that something was happening; something dreadful, something untoward, something very decidedly not upon the program they had helped to plan. They, however, could do nothing about it; they could only watch and wait.

"Ah, 'tis Lan and Amp of the Eich," the thought resounded within the minds of the helpless twain. "Truly, the Elders are correct. My mind is not yet competent, for, although I have had many facts instead of but a single one upon which to cogitate, and no dearth of time in which to do so, I now perceive that I have erred grievously in my visualization of the Cosmic All. You do, however, fit nicely into the now enlarged Scheme, and I am really grateful to you for furnishing new material with which for many cycles of time to come, I shall continue to build.

"Indeed, I believe that I shall permit you to return unharmed to your own planet. You know the warning we gave Helmuth, your minion, hence your lives are forfeit for violating knowingly the privacy of Arisia; but wanton or unnecessary destruction is not conducive to mental growth. You are, therefore, at liberty to depart. I repeat to you the instructions given your underling: do not return, either in person or by any form whatever of proxy."

SUPER PACK

The Arisian had as yet exerted scarcely a fraction of his power; although the bodies of the two invaders were practically paralyzed, their minds had not been punished. Therefore the psychologist said, coldly:

"You are not now dealing with Helmuth, nor with any other weak, mindless oxygen-breather, but with the *Eich*," and, by sheer effort of will, he moved toward the controls.

"What boots it?" the Arisian compressed upon the Eighth's brain a searing force which sent shrieking waves of pain throughout all nearby space. Then, taking over the psychologist's mind, he forced him to move to the communicator panel, upon whose plate could be seen the other seven of Boskone, gazing in wonder.

"Set up planetary coverage," he directed, through Eichamp's organs of speech, "so that each individual member of the entire race of the Eich can understand what I am about to transmit." There was a brief pause, then the deep, measured voice rolled on:

"I am Eukonidor of Arisia, speaking to you through this mass of undead flesh which was once your chief psychologist, Eichamp, the Eighth of that high council which you call Boskone. I had intended to spare the lives of these two simple creatures, but I perceive that such action would be useless. Their minds and the minds of all you who listen to me are warped, perverted, incapable of reason. They and you would have misinterpreted the gesture completely; would have believed that I did not slay them only because I could not do so. Some of you would have offended again and again, until you were so slain; you can be convinced of such a fact only by an unmistakable demonstration of superior force. Force is the only thing you are able to understand. Your one aim in life is to gain material power; greed, corruption, and crime are your chosen implements.

"You consider yourselves hard and merciless. In a sense, and according to your abilities you are, although your minds are too callow to realize that there are depths of cruelty and of depravity which you cannot even faintly envision.

"You love and worship power. Why? To any thinking mind it should be clear that such a lust intrinsically is, and forever must by its very nature be, futile. For, even if any one of you could command the entire material Universe, what good would it do him? None. What would he have? Nothing. Not even the satisfaction of accomplishment, for that lust is in fact insatiable—it would then turn upon itself and feed upon itself. I tell you as a fact that there is only one power which is at one and the same time illimitable and yet finite; insatiable yet satisfying; one which, while eternal, yet invariably returns to its possessor the true satisfaction of real accomplishment in exact ratio to the effort expended upon it. That power is the power of the mind. You, being so backward and so wrong of development, cannot understand how this can be, but if any one of you will concentrate upon one single fact, or a small object, such as a pebble or the seed of a plant or other creature, for as short a period of time as one hundred of your years, you will begin to perceive its truth.

"You boast that your planet is old. What of that? We of Arisia dwelt in turn upon a thousand planets, from planetary youth to cosmic old age, before we became independent of the chance formation of such celestial bodies.

"You prate that you are an ancient race. Compared to us you are sheerly infantile. We of Arisia did not originate upon a planet formed during the recent interpassage of these

589

two galaxies, but upon one which came into being in an antiquity so distant that the figure in years would be entirely meaningless to your minds. We were of an age to your mentalities starkly incomprehensible when your most remote ancestors began to wriggle about in the slime of your parent world.

"'Do the men of the Patrol know—?' I perceive the question in your minds. They do not. None save a few of the most powerful of their minds has the slightest inkling of the truth. To reveal any portion of it to Civilization as a whole would blight that Civilization irreparably. Though Seekers after Truth in the best sense, they are essentially juvenile and their life spans are ephemeral indeed. The mere realization that there is in existence such a race as ours would place upon them such an inferiority complex as would make further advancement impossible. In your case such a course of events is not to be expected. You will close your minds to all that has happened, declaring to yourselves that it was impossible and that therefore, it could not have taken place and did not. Nevertheless, you will stay away from Arisia henceforth.

"But to resume. You consider yourselves long-lived. Know then, insects, that your life span of a thousand of your years is but a moment. I, myself, have already lived eleven thousand such lifetimes, and I am but a youth—a mere Guardian, not yet to be entrusted with really serious thinking.

"I have spoken overlong; the reason for my prolixity being that I do not like to see the energy of a race so misused, so corrupted to material conquest for its own sake. I would like to set your minds upon the Way of Truth, if perchance such a thing should be possible. I have pointed out that Way; whether or not you follow it is for you to decide. Indeed, I fear that most of you, in your short-sighted pride, have already cast my message aside; refusing point-blank to change your habits of thought. It is, however, in the hope that some few of you will perceive the Way and will follow it by abandoning your planet and its Eich before it is too late, that I have discoursed at such length.

"Whether or not you change your habits of thought, I advise you to heed this, my warning. Arisia does not want and will not tolerate intrusion. As a lesson, watch these two violators of our privacy destroy themselves."

The giant voice ceased. Eichlan's tentacles moved toward the controls. The vast torpedo launched itself.

But instead of hurtling toward distant Arisia it swept around in a mighty circle and struck in direct central impact the great cruiser of the Eich. There was an appalling crash, a space-wracking detonation, a flare of incandescence incredible and indescribable as the energy calculated to disrupt—almost to volatilize—a world expended itself upon the insignificant mass of one Boskonian battleship and upon the unresisting texture of the void.

X.

Considerably more than the stipulated week passed before Kinnison was done with the librarian and with the long-range communicator beam, but eventually he succeeded in enlisting the aid of the fifty-three most eminent scientists and thinkers of all the planets of Galactic Civilization. From all over the Galaxy were they selected; from Vandemar and

Centralia and Alsakan; from Chickladoria and Radelix; from the solar systems of Rigel and Sirius and Antares. Millions of planets were not represented at all; and of the few which were, Tellus alone had more than one delegate.

This was necessary, Kinnison explained carefully to each of the chosen. Sir Austin Cardynge, the man whose phenomenal brain had developed a new mathematics to handle the positron and the negative energy levels, was the one who would do the work; he himself was present merely as a co-ordinator and observer. The meeting place, even, was not upon Tellus, but upon Medon, the newly acquired and hence entirely neutral planet. For the Gray Lensman knew well the minds with which he would have to deal.

They were all the geniuses of the highest rank, but in all too many cases their stupendous mentalities merged altogether too closely upon insanity for any degree of comfort. Even before the conclave assembled it became evident that jealousy was to be rife and rampant; and after the initial meeting, at which the problem itself was propounded, it required all of Kinnison's ability, authority, and drive, and all of Worsel's vast diplomacy and tact, to keep those mighty brains at work.

Time after time, some essential entity, his dignity outraged and his touchy ego infuriated by some real or fancied insult, stalked off in high dudgeon to return to his own planet; only to be coaxed or bullied, or even mentally man-handled by Kinnison or Worsel, or both, into returning to his task.

Nor were those insults all, or even mostly, imaginary. Quarreling and bickering were incessant, violent flare-ups and passionate scenes of denunciation and vituperation were of almost hourly occurrence. Each of those minds had been accustomed to world-wide adulation, to the unquestioned acceptance as gospel of his every idea or pronouncement, and to have to submit his work to the scrutiny and to the unworshipful criticisms of lesser minds—actually to have to give way, at times, to those inferior mentalities—was a situation quite definitely intolerable.

But at length most of them began to work together, as they appreciated the fact that the problem before them was one which none of them singly had been able even partially to solve; and Kinnison let the others, the most fanatically non-co-operative, go home. The progress began—and none too soon. The Gray Lensman had lost twenty-five pounds of weight, and even the iron-thewed Worsel was a wreck. He could not fly, he declared, because his wings buckled in the middle; he could not crawl, because his belly-plate clashed against his backbone!

And finally the thing was done; reduced to a set of equations which could be written upon a single sheet of paper. It is true that those equations would have been meaningless to almost anyone then alive, since they were based upon a system of mathematics which had been brought into existence at that very meeting, but Kinnison had taken care of that.

No Medonian had been allowed in the Conference—the admittance of one to membership would have caused a massed exodus of the high-strung, temperamental maniacs working so furiously there—but the Tellurian Lensman had had recorded every act, almost every thought, of every one of those geniuses. Those records had been studied for weeks, not only by Wise of Medon and his staff, but also by a corps of the less brilliant, but infinitely better balanced scientists of the Patrol proper.

"Now you fellows can really get to work." Kinnison heaved a sigh of profound relief as the last member of the Conference figuratively shook the dust of Medon off his robe as he departed homeward. "I'm going to sleep for a week. Call me, will you, when you get the model done?"

*

This was sheerest exaggeration, of course, for nothing could have kept the Lensman from watching the construction of that first apparatus. He watched the erection of a spherical shell of loosely latticed truss-work some twenty feet in diameter. He watched the installation, at its six cardinal points, of atomic exciters, each capable of transforming ten thousand pounds per hour of substance into pure energy. He knew that those exciters were driving their intake screens at a ratio of at least twenty thousand to one; that energy equivalent to the annihilation of at least six hundred thousand tons per hour of material was being hurled into the center of that web from the six small mechanisms which were in fact, super-Bergenholms. Nor is that word adequate to describe them. They were engines at whose power the late Dr. Bergenholm himself would have quailed; demons whose fabrication would have been utterly impossible without Medonian conductors and insulation.

He watched the construction of a conveyor and a chute and looked on intently while a hundred thousand tons of refuse—rocks, sand, concrete, scrap iron, loose metal, débris of all kinds—were dropped into that innocuous-appearing sphere, only to vanish as though they had never existed.

"But we ought to be able to see it by this time, I should think!" Kinnison protested once.

"Not yet, Kim," Master Technician LaVerne Thorndyke informed him. "Just forming the vortex—microscopic yet. I haven't the faintest idea of what is going on in there; but man, dear man, *am* I glad that I'm here to help make it go on!"

"But *when?*" demanded the Lensman. "How soon will you know whether it's going to work or not? I want to do a flit."

"You can flit any time—now, if you like," the technician told him, brutally. "We don't need *you* any more—you've done your bit. It's working now. If it wasn't, do you think we could pack all that stuff into that little space? But we'll have it done long before you'll need it."

"But I want to see it work, you big lug!" Kinnison retorted, only half playfully.

"Come back in three-four days—maybe a week; but don't expect to see anything but a hole."

"That's exactly what I want to see, a hole in space," and that was precisely what, a few days later, the Lensman did see.

The spherical framework was unchanged, the machines were still carrying easily their incredible working load. Material—any and all kinds of stuff—was still disappearing; instantaneously, invisibly, quietly, with no flash or fury to mark its passing.

592

But at the center of that massive sphere there now hung poised a—a *something*. Or was it a nothing? Mathematically, it was a sphere, or rather a negasphere, about the size of a baseball; but the eye, while it could see something, could not perceive it analytically. Nor could the mind envision it in three dimensions, for it was not essentially three-dimensional in nature. Light sank into the thing, whatever it was, and vanished. The peering eye could see nothing whatever of shape or of texture; the mind behind the eye reeled away before infinite vistas of nothingness.

Kinnison hurled his extrasensory perception into it and jerked back, almost stunned. It was neither darkness nor blackness, he decided, after he recovered enough poise to think coherently. It was worse than that—worse than anything imaginable—an infinitely vast and yet non-existent realm of the total absence of everything whatever—*absolute negation!*

"That's it, I guess," the Lensman said then. "Might as well stop feeding it now."

"We would have to stop soon, in any case," Wise replied, "for your available waste material is becoming scarce. It will take the substance of a fairly large planet to produce that which you require. You have, perhaps, a planet in mind which is to be used for the purpose?"

"Better than that. I have in mind the material of just such a planet, but already broken up into sizes convenient for handling."

"Oh, the asteroid belt!" Thorndyke exclaimed. "Fine! Kill two birds with one stone, huh? Build this thing and at the same time clear out the menaces to inert interplanetary navigation? But how about the miners?"

"All covered. The ones actually in development will be let alone. They're not menaces, anyway, as they all have broadcasters. The tramp miners we send—at Patrol expense and grubstake—to some other system to do their mining. But there's one more point before we flit. Are you sure that you can shift to the second stage without an accident?"

"Positive. Build another one around it, mount new Bergs, exciters, and screens on it, and let this one, machines and all, go in to feed the kitty—whatever it is," the technician finished.

"QX. Let's go, fellows!"

*

Two huge Tellurian freighters were at hand; and, holding the small framework between them in a net of tractors and pressors, they set off blithely toward Sol. They took a couple of hours for the journey—and there was no hurry, and in the handling of this particular freight caution was decidedly of the essence.

Arrived at destination, the crews tackled with zest and zeal this new game. Tractors lashed out, seizing chunks of iron—

"Pick out the little ones, men," cautioned Kinnison. "Nothing over about ten feet in section-dimension will go into this frame. Better wait for the second frame before you try to handle the big ones."

"We can cut 'em up," Thorndyke suggested. "What've we got these shear-planes for?"

"QX if you like. Just so you keep the kitty fed."

"We'll feed her!" and the game went on.

Chunks of débris—some rock, but mostly solid meteoric nickel-iron—shot toward the vessels and the ravening sphere, becoming inertialess as they entered a wide-flung zone. Pressors seized them avidly, pushing them through the interstices of the framework, holding them against the voracious screen. As they touched the screen they disappeared; no matter how fast they were driven the screen ate them away, silently and unspectacularly, as fast as they could be thrown against it. A weird spectacle indeed, to see a jagged fragment of solid iron, having a mass of thousands of tons, drive against that screen and disappear! For it vanished, utterly, along a geometrically perfect spherical surface. From the opposite side the eye could see the mirror sheen of the metal at the surface of disintegration! It was as though the material were being shoved out of our familiar three-dimensional space into another universe—which, as a matter of cold fact, may have been the case.

For not even the men who were doing the work made any pretense of understanding what was happening to that iron. Indeed, the only entities who did have any comprehension of the phenomenon—the forty-odd geniuses whose mathematical wizardry had made it possible—thought of it and discussed it, not in the limited, three-dimensional symbols of everyday existence, but only in the language of high mathematics; a language in which few indeed, are able to really and readily to think.

And while the crews became more and more expert at the new technique, so that metal came in faster and faster—huge, hot-sliced bars of iron ten feet square and a quarter of a mile long were being driven into that enigmatic sphere of extinction—an outer framework a hundred and fifty miles in diameter was being built. Nor, contrary to what might be supposed, was a prohibitive amount of metal or of labor necessary to fabricate that mammoth structure. Instead of six there were six cubed—two hundred and sixteen—working stations, complete with generators and super-Bergenholms and screen generators, each mounted upon a massive platform; but, instead of being connected together and supported by stupendous beams and trusses of metal, those platforms were linked by infinitely stronger bonds of pure force. It took a lot of ships to do the job, but the technicians of the Patrol had at call enough floating machine shops and to spare.

When the sphere of negation grew to be about a foot in apparent diameter it had been found necessary to surround it with a screen opaque to all visible light, for to look into it long or steadily then meant insanity. Now the opaque screen was sixteen feet in diameter, nearing dangerously the sustaining framework, and the outer frame was ready. It was time to change.

The Lensman held his breath, but the Medonians and the Tellurian technicians did not turn a hair as they mounted their new stations and tested their apparatus.

"Ready." "Ready." "Ready." Station after station reported: then, as Thorndyke threw in the master switch, the primary sphere—invisible now, through distance, to the eye, but plain upon the visiplates—disappeared; a mere morsel to those new, gigantic forces.

"Swing into it, boys!" Thorndyke yelled into his transmitter. "We don't have to feed her with a teaspoon any more. Let her have it!"

*

And "let her have it" they did. No more cutting up of the larger meteorites; asteroids ten, fifteen, twenty miles in diameter, along with hosts of smaller stuff, were literally hurled through the black screen into the even lusher blackness of that which was inside it, without complaint from the quietly humming motors.

"Satisfied, Kim?" Master Technician Thorndyke asked.

"Uh-*huh*!" the Lensman assented, vigorously. "Nice! Slick, in fact," he commended. "I'll buzz off now, I guess."

"Might as well—everything's on the green. Clear ether, spacehound!"

"Same to you, big fella. I'll be seeing you, or sending you a thought. There's Tellus, right over there. Funny, isn't it, doing a flit to a place you can actually see before you start?"

The trip to Earth was scarcely a hop, even in a supply-boat. To Prime Base the Gray Lensman went, where he found that his new non-ferrous speedster was done; and during the next few days he tested it out thoroughly. It did not register at all, neither upon the regular, long-range ultra-instruments nor upon the short-range emergency electros. Nor could it be seen in space, even in a telescope at point-blank range. True, it occulted an occasional star; but since even the direct rays of a searchlight failed to reveal its shape to the keenest eye—the Lensman chemists who had worked out that ninety-nine point nine nine percent absolute black coating had done a wonderful job—the chance of discovery through that occurrence was very slight.

"QX, Kim?" the Port Admiral asked. He was accompanying the Gray Lensman on a last tour of inspection.

"Fine, chief. Couldn't be better—thanks a lot."

"Sure you're non-ferrous yourself?"

"Absolutely. Not even an iron nail in my shoes."

"What is it, then? You look worried. Want something expensive?"

"You hit the thumb, admiral, right on the nail. The trouble is not only that it's expensive; I'm afraid that probably we'll never have any use for it."

"Better build it, anyway. Then if you want it you'll have it, and if you don't want it we can always use it for something. What is it?"

"A nutcracker. There are a lot of cold planets around, aren't there, that aren't good for anything?"

"Thousands of them—perhaps millions."

"The Medonians put Bergenholms on their planet and flew it from Lundmark's Nebula to here in a few weeks. Why wouldn't it be a sound idea to have the planetographers pick out a couple of useless worlds which, at some points in their orbits, have diametrically opposite velocities, to within a degree or two?"

"You've got something there, my boy. It shall be done, and at once. A thing like that is very much worth having, just for its own sake, if we never have any use for it. Anything else?"

"Not a thing in the universe. Clear ether, chief!"

"Light landings, Kinnison!" and gracefully, effortlessly, the dead-black sliver of semi-precious metal lifted herself away from Earth.

THE LENSMAN

*

Through Bominger, the Radeligian Big Shot, Kinnison had had a long and eminently satisfactory interview with Prellin, the Regional Director of all surviving Boskonian activities. Thus he knew where the latter was, even to the address, and knew the name of the firm which was his alias—Ethan D. Wembleson & Sons, Inc., 4627 Boulevard Dezalies, Cominoche, Quadrant Eight, Bronseca. That name was Kim's first shock, for that firm was one of the largest and most conservative houses in galactic trade; one having an unquestioned AAA1 rating in every mercantile index.

However, that was the way they worked, Kinnison reflected, as his speedster reeled off the parsecs. It wasn't far to Bronseca—easy Lens distance—he'd better call somebody there and start making arrangements. He had heard about the planet, although he'd never been there. Somewhat warmer than Tellus, but otherwise very Earthlike. Millions of Tellurians lived there and liked it.

His approach to the planet Bronseca was characterized by all possible caution, as was his visit to Cominoche, the capital city. He found that 4627 Boulevard Dezalies was a structure covering an entire city block and some eighty stories high, owned and occupied exclusively by Wembleson's. No visitors were allowed except by appointment. His first stroll past it showed him that an immense cylinder, comprising almost the whole interior of the building, was shielded by thought-screens. He rode up and down in the elevators of nearby buildings—no penetration. He visited a dozen offices in the neighborhood upon various errands, choosing his time with care so that he would have to wait in each an hour or so in order to see his man.

These leisurely scrutinies of his objective failed to reveal a single fact of value. Ethan D. Wembleson & Sons, Inc., did a tremendous business, but every ounce of it was legitimate! That is, the files in the outer offices covered only legitimate transactions, and the men and women busily at work there were all legitimately employed. And the inner offices—vastly more extensive than the outer, to judge by the number of employees entering in the morning and leaving at the close of business—were sealed against his prying, every second of every day.

He tapped in turn the minds of dozens of those clerks, but drew only blanks. As far as they were concerned, there was nothing "queer" going on anywhere in the organization. The "Old Man"—Howard Wembleson, a grandnephew or something of Ethan—had developed a complex lately that his life was in danger. Scarcely left the building—not that he had any need to, as he had always had palatial quarters there—and then only under heavy guard.

A good many thought-screened persons came and went, but a careful study of them and their movements convinced the Gray Lensman that he was wasting his time.

"No soap," he reported to a Lensman at Bronseca's Base. "Might as well try to stick a pin quietly into a cateagle. He's been told that he's the next link in the chain, and he's got the jitters right. I'll bet he's got a dozen loose observers, instead of only one. I'll save time, I think, by tracing another line. I have thought before that my best bet is in the asteroid dens instead of on the planets. I let them talk me out of it—it's a dirty job and

I've got to establish an identity of my own, which will be even dirtier—but it looks as though I'll have to go back to it."

"But the others are warned, too," suggested the Bronsecan. "They'll probably be just as bad. Let's blast it open and take a chance on finding the data you want."

"No," Kinnison said, emphatically. "Not a chance in the universe that there's anything there that would do me a bit of good on the big hunt. The others are probably warned, yes, but since they aren't on my direct line to the throne, they probably aren't taking it as seriously as this Prellin—or Wembleson—is. Or if they are, they won't keep it up as long. They can't, and get any joy out of life at all.

"And you can't say a word to Prellin about his screens, either," the Tellurian went on in reply to a thought. "They're legal enough; just as much so as spy-ray blocks. Every man has a right to privacy. Just one question here, or just one suspicious move, is apt to blow everything into a cocked hat. You fellows keep on working along the lines we laid out and I'll try another line. If it works, I'll come back and we'll open this can the way you want to. That way, we may be able to get the low-down on about four hundred planetary organizations at one haul."

*

Thus it came about that Kinnison took his scarcely-used indetectable speedster back to Prime Base; and that, in a solar system prodigiously far removed from both Tellus and Bronseca, there appeared another tramp meteor-miner.

Peculiar people, these toilers in the interplanetary voids; flotsam and jetsam; for the most part the very scum of space. Some solar systems contain vastly greater amounts of asteroidal and meteoric débris than did ours of Sol; others somewhat less; but all have at least some. In the main this material is either nickel-iron or rock, but some of these fragments carry prodigious values in platinum, osmium, and other noble metals, and occasionally there are discovered diamonds and other gems of tremendous size and value. Hence, in the asteroid belts of every solar system there are to be found those universally despised, but nevertheless bold and hardy souls who, risking life and limb from moment to moment though they are, yet live in hope that the next lump of cosmic detritus will prove to be a bonanza.

Some of these men are the sheer misfits of life. Some are petty criminals, fugitives from the justice of their own planets, but not of sufficient importance to be upon the "wanted" lists of the Patrol. Some are of those who for some reason or other—addiction to drugs, perhaps, or the overwhelming urge occasionally to go on a spree—are unable or unwilling to hold down the steady jobs of their more orthodox brethren. Still others, and these are many, live that horridly adventurous life because it is in their blood; like the lumberjacks who in ancient times dwelt upon Tellus, they labor tremendously and unremittingly for weeks, only and deliberately to "blow in" the fruits of their toil in a few wild days and still wilder nights of hectic, sanguine, and lustful debauchery in one or another of the spacemen's hells of which every inhabited solar system has its quota.

But, whatever their class, they have much in common. They all live for the moment only, from hand to mouth. They all are intrepid spacemen. They have to be—all others die during their first venture. They all live dangerously, violently. They are men of red and gusty passions, and they have, if not an actual contempt, at least a loud-voiced scorn of the law in its every phase and manifestation. "Law ends with atmosphere" is the galaxy-wide creed of the clan, and it is a fact that no law save that of the ray-gun is even yet really enforced in the badlands of the asteroid belts.

Indeed, the meteor miners as a matter of course, take their innate lawlessness with them into their revels in the crimson-lit resorts already referred to. In general the nearby Planetary Police adopt a laissez faire attitude, particularly since the asteroids are not within their jurisdictions, but independent worlds, each with its own world-government. If they kill a dozen or so of each other and of the bloodsuckers who batten upon them, what of it? If everybody in those hells could be killed at once, the Universe would be that much better off!—and if the Galactic Patrol is compelled, by some unusually outrageous performance, to intervene in the revelry, it comes in, not as single policemen, but in platoons or in companies of armed, full-armored infantry going to war!

Such, then, were those among whom Kinnison chose to cast his lot, in a new effort to get in touch with the Galactic Director of the drug ring.

XI.

Although Kinnison left Bronseca, abandoning that line of attack completely—thereby, it might be thought, forfeiting all the work he had theretofore done upon it—the Patrol was not idle, nor was Prellin-Wembleson of Cominoche, the Boskonian Regional Director, neglected. Lensman after Lensman came and went, unobtrusively, but grimly determined. There came Tellurians, Manarkans, Borovans; Lensmen of every human breed, any of whom might have been, as far as the minions of Boskone knew, the one foe whom they had such good cause to fear.

Rigellian Lensmen came also, and Poenians, and Ordoviks; representatives, in fact, of almost every available race possessing any type or kind of extrasensory perception, came to test out their skill and cunning. Even Worsel of Velantia came, hurled for days his mighty mind against those screens, and departed.

Whether or not business went on as usual no one could say, but the Patrol was certain of three things. First, that while the Boskonians might be destroying some of their records, they were moving none away, by air, land, or tunnel; second, that there was no doubt in any zwilnik mind that the Lensmen were there to stay until they won, in one way or another; and third, that Prellin's life was not a happy one!

And while his brothers of the Lens were so efficiently pinch-hitting for him—even though they were at the same time trying to show him up and thereby win kudos for themselves—in mentally investing the Regional stronghold of Boskone, Kinnison was establishing an identity as a wandering hellion of the asteroid belts.

There would be no slips this time. He would *be* a meteor miner in every particular, down to the last, least detail. To this end he selected his equipment with the most exacting care. It must be thoroughly adequate and dependable, but neither new nor of such outstanding quality or amount as to cause comment.

His ship, a stubby, powerful space-tug with an oversized air lock, was a used job—hard-used, too—some ten years old. She was battered, pitted, and scarred; but it should be noted here, perhaps parenthetically, that when the technicians finished their rebuilding she was actually as stanch as a battleship. His space-armor, Spalding drills, DeLameters, tractors and pressors, and "spee-gee"—torsion specific-gravity apparatus—were of the same grade. All bore unmistakable evidence of years of hard use, but all were in perfect working condition. In short, his outfit was exactly that which a successful meteor miner—even such a one as he was going to become—would be expected to own.

He cut his own hair, and his whiskers, too, with ordinary shears, as was good technique. He learned the polyglot of the trade; the language which, made up of words from each of hundreds of planetary tongues, was and is the everyday speech of human or near-human meteor miners, wherever found. By "near-human" is meant a six-place classification of A A point A A A A—meaning erect, bifurcate, warm-blooded, oxygen-breathing, bilaterally duo-symmetrical, and possessing eyes. For, even in meteor-mining, like has a tendency to run with, and especially to play with, like. Thus, warm-blooded oxygen-breathers find neither welcome nor enjoyment in a pleasure-resort operated by and for such a race, say, as the Trocanthers, who are cold-blooded, quasi-reptilian beings who abhor light of all kinds and who breath a gaseous mixture not only paralyzingly cold in temperature but also chemically fatal to man.

Above all, he had to learn how to drink strong liquors and how to take drugs, for he knew that no drink that had ever been distilled, and no drug, with the possible exception of thionite, could enslave the mind he then had. Thionite was out, anyway. It was too scarce and too expensive for meteor miners; they simply didn't go for it. Hadive, heroin, opium, nitrolabe, bentlam—that was it, bentlam. He could get it anywhere, all over the Galaxy, and it was very much in character. Easy to take, potent in results, and not as damaging—if you didn't become a real addict—to the system as most of the others. He would become a bentlam-eater.

*

Bentlam, known also to the trade by such nicknames as "benny," "benweed," "happy-sleep," and others, is a shredded, moistly fibrous material of about the same consistency and texture as fine-cut chewing tobacco. Through his friends in Narcotics the Gray Lensman obtained a supply of "the clear quill, first chop, in the original tins" from a prominent bootlegger, and had it assayed for potency.

The drinking problem required no thought; he would learn to drink, and apparently to like, anything and everything that would pour. Meteor miners did.

Therefore, coldly, deliberately, dispassionately, and with as complete a detachment as though he were calibrating a burette or analyzing an unknown solution, he set about the task. He determined his capacity as impersonally as though his physical body were a volumetric flask; he noted the effect of each measured increment of high-proof beverage and of habit-forming drug as precisely as though he were studying a chemical reaction in which he himself was not concerned save as a purely scientific observer.

He detested the stuff. Every fiber of his being rebelled at the sensations evoked—the loss of co-ordination and control, the inflation, the aggrandizement, the falsity of values, the sheer hallucinations—nevertheless he went through with the whole program, even to the extent of complete physical helplessness for periods of widely varying duration. And when he had completed his researches he was thoroughly well informed.

He knew to a nicety, by feel, how much active principle he had taken, no matter how strong, how weak, or how adulterated the liquor or the drug had been. He knew to a fraction how much more he could take; or, having taken too much, almost exactly how long he would be incapacitated. He learned for himself what was already widely known, that it was better to get at least moderately illuminated before taking the drug; that bentlam rides better on top of liquor than vice versa. He even determined roughly the rate of increase with practice of his tolerances. Then, and only then, did he begin working as a meteorite miner.

Working in an asteroid belt of one solar system might have been enough, but the Gray Lensman took no chances at all of having his new identity traced back to its source. Therefore he worked, and caroused, in five; approaching step-wise to the solar system of Borova which was his goal.

Arrived at last, he gave his chunky space-boat the average velocity of an asteroid belt just outside the orbit of the fourth planet, shoved her down into it, turned on his Bergenholm, and went to work. His first job was to "set up"; to install in the extra-large air lock, already equipped with duplicate controls, his tools and equipment. He donned space-armor, made sure that his DeLameters were sitting pretty—all meteor miners go armed as routine, and the Lensman had altogether too much at stake in any case to forgo his accustomed weapons—pumped the air of the lock back into the body of the ship, and opened the outer port. For meteor miners do not work inside their ships. It takes too much time to bring the metal in through the air locks. It also wastes air, and air is precious; not only in money, although that is no minor item, but also because no small ship, stocked for a six-weeks' run, can carry any more air than is really needed.

Set up, he studied his electros and flicked his tractor beams out to a passing fragment of metal, which flashed up to him, almost instantaneously. Or, rather, the inertialess tugboat flashed across space to the comparatively tiny, but inert, bit of metal which he was about to investigate. With expert ease Kinnison clamped the meteorite down and rammed into it his Spalding drill, the tool which in one operation cuts out and polishes a cylindrical sample exactly one inch in diameter and exactly one inch long. Kinnison took the sample, placed it in the jaw of his spee-gee, and cut his Berg. Going inert in an asteroid belt is dangerous business, but it is only one of a meteor miner's hazards and it is necessary; for the torsiometer is the quickest and simplest means of determining the specific gravity of metal out in space, and no torsion instrument will work upon inertialess matter.

He read the scale even as he turned on the Berg. Seven point nine. Iron. Worthless. Big operators could use it—the asteroid belts had long since supplanted the mines of the worlds as sources of iron—but it wouldn't do him a bit of good. Therefore, tossing it aside, he speared another. Another, and another. Hour after hour, day after day; the back-breaking, lonely labor of the meteor miner. But very few of the bona-fide miners had the Gray Lensman's physique or his stamina, and not one of them all had even a noteworthy fraction of his brain. And brain counts, even in meteor-mining. Hence

Kinnison found pay-metal; quite a few really good, although not phenomenally dense, pieces.

*

Then one day there happened a thing which, if it was not in actual fact premeditated, was as mathematically improbable, almost, as the formation of a planetary solar system; an occurrence that was to exemplify in startling and hideous fashion the doctrine of tooth and fang which is the only law of the asteroid belts. Two tractor beams seized, at almost the same instant, the same meteor! Two ships, flashing up to zone contact in the twinkling of an eye, the inoffensive meteor squarely between them! And in the air lock of the other tug there were two men, not one; two men already going for their guns with the practiced ease of space-hardened veterans to whom the killing of a man was the veriest bagatelle!

They must have been hijackers, killing and robbing as a business, Kinnison concluded, afterward. Bona-fide miners almost never work two to a boat, and the fact that they actually beat him to the draw, and yet were so slow in shooting, argued that they had not been taken by surprise, as had he. Indeed, the meteor itself, the bone of contention, might very well have been a bait.

He could not follow his natural inclination to let go, to let them have it. The tale would have spread far and wide, branding him as a coward and a weakling. He would have had to kill, or been killed by, any number of lesser bullies who would have attacked him on sight. Nor could he have taken over their minds quickly enough to have averted death. One, perhaps, but not two; he was no Arisian. These thoughts, as has been intimated, occurred to him long afterward. During the actual event there was no time to think at all. Instead, he acted; automatically and instantaneously.

Kinnison's hands flashed to the worn grips of his DeLameters, sliding them from the leather and bringing them to bear at the hip with one smoothly flowing motion that was a marvel of grace and speed. But, fast as he was, he was almost too late. Four bolts of lightning blasted, almost as one. The two desperadoes dropped, cold; the Lensman felt a stab of agony sear through his shoulder and the breath whistled out of his mouth and nose as his spacesuit collapsed. Gasping terribly for air that was no longer there, holding onto his senses doggedly and grimly, he made shift to close the outer door of the lock and to turn a valve. He did not lose consciousness—quite—and as soon as he recovered the use of his muscles he stripped off his suit and examined himself narrowly in a mirror.

Eyes, plenty bloodshot. Nose, bleeding copiously. Ears bleeding, but not too badly; drums not ruptured, fortunately—he had been able to keep the pressure fairly well equalized. Felt like some internal bleeding, but he could see nothing really serious. He hadn't breathed space long enough to do any permanent damage, he guessed.

Then, baring his shoulder, he treated the wound with Zinmaster burn-dressing. This was no trifle, but at that, it wasn't so bad. No bone gone—it'd heal in two or three weeks. Lastly, he looked over his suit. If he'd only had his G-P armor on—but that, of course, was out of the question. He had a spare suit, but he'd rather—Fine, he could replace the burned section easily enough. QX.

601

He donned his other suit, re-entered the air lock, neutralized the screens, and crossed over; where he did exactly what any other meteor miner would have done. He divested the bloated corpses of their spacesuits and shoved them off into space. He then ransacked the ship, transferring from it to his own, as well as four heavy meteors, every other item of value which he could move and which his vessel could hold. Then inerting her, he gave her a couple of notches of drive and cut her loose, for so a real miner would have done. It was not compunction or scruple that would have prevented any miner from taking the ship, as well as the supplies. Ships were registered, and otherwise were too hot to be handled except by organized criminal rings.

As a matter of routine he tested the meteor which had been the innocent cause of all this strife—or had it been a bait?—and found it worthless iron. Also as routine he kept on working. He had almost enough metal now, even at Miners' Rest prices, for a royal binge, but he couldn't go in until his shoulder was well. And a couple of weeks later he got the shock of his life.

*

He had brought in a meteor; a mighty big one, over four feet in its smallest diameter. He sampled it, and as soon as he cut the Berg and flicked the sample experimentally from hand to hand, his skilled muscles told him that that metal was astoundingly dense. Heart racing, he locked the test-piece into the spee-gee; and that vital organ almost stopped beating entirely as the indicator needle went up and up and up—stopping at a full twenty-two, and the scale went only to twenty-four!

"Klono's brazen hoofs and diamond-tipped horns!" he ejaculated. He whistled stridently through his teeth, then measured his find as accurately as he could. Then, speaking aloud, "Just about thirty thousand kilograms of something noticeably denser than pure platinum—thirty million credits or I'm a Zabriskan fontema's maiden aunt. What to do?"

This find, as well it might, gave the Gray Lensman pause. It upset his calculations. It was unthinkable to take that meteor to such a fence's hide-out as Miners' Rest. Men had been murdered, and would be again, for a thousandth of its value. No matter where he took it, there would be publicity galore, and that wouldn't do. If he called a Patrol ship to take the white elephant off his hands he might be seen; and he had put in too much work on this identity to jeopardize it. He would have to bury it, he guessed—he had maps of the System, and the fourth planet was close by.

He cut off a chunk of a few pounds' weight and made a nugget—a tiny meteor—of it, then headed for the planet, a plainly visible disk some fifteen degrees from the Sun. He had a fairly large-scale chart of the System, with notes. Borova IV was uninhabited, except by low forms of life, and by outposts. Cold. Atmosphere thin—good, that meant no clouds. No oceans. No volcanic activity. Very good! He'd look it over, and the first striking landmark he saw, from one diameter out, would be his cache.

He circled the planet once at the equator, observing a formation of five mighty peaks arranged in a semicircle, cupped toward the world's north pole. He circled it again, seeing nothing as prominent, and nothing else resembling it at all closely. Scanning his plate narrowly, to be sure nothing was following him, he drove downward in a screaming dive toward the middle mountain.

It was an extinct volcano, he discovered, with a level-floored crater more than a hundred miles in diameter. Practically level, that is, except for a smaller cone which reared up in the center of that vast, desolate plain of craggy, tortured lava. Straight down into the cold vent of the inner cone the Lensman steered his ship; and in its exact center he dug a hole and buried his treasure. He then lifted his tugboat fifty feet and held her there, poised on her raving underjets, until the lava in the little crater again began sluggishly to flow, and thus to destroy all evidence of his visit. This detail attended to, he shot out into space and called Haynes, to whom he reported in full.

"I'll bring the meteor in when I come—or do you want to send somebody out here after it? It belongs to the Patrol, of course."

"No, it doesn't, Kim—it belongs to you."

"Huh? Isn't there a law that any discoveries made by any employees of the Patrol belong to the Patrol?"

"Nothing as broad as that, that I know of. Certain scientific discoveries, by scientists assigned to an exact research, yes. But you're forgetting again that you're an Unattached Lensman, and as such are accountable to no one in the Universe. Even the ten percent treasure-trove law couldn't touch you. Besides, your meteor is not in that category, as you are its first owner, as far as we know. If you insist I will mention it to the Council, but I know in advance that the Patrol can claim none of it, even if we wanted to—which we definitely do not."

"QX, chief—thanks," and the connection was broken.

There, that was that. He had got rid of the white elephant, yet it wouldn't be wasted. If the zwilniks got him, the Patrol would dig it up; if he lived long enough to retire to a desk job he wouldn't have to take any more of the Patrol's money as long as he lived. Financially, he was all set.

And physically, he was all set for his first real binge as a meteor miner. His shoulder and arm were as good as new. He had a lot of metal; enough so that its proceeds would finance, not only his next venture into space, but also a really royal celebration in any spaceman's resort, even the one he had already picked out.

For the Lensman had devoted a great deal of thought to that item. For his purpose, the bigger the resort the better. The man he was after would not be a small operator, nor would he deal directly with such. Also, the big kingpins did not murder drugged miners for their ships and outfits, as the smaller ones sometimes did. The big ones realized that there was more long-pull profit in repeat business.

Therefore, Kinnison set his course toward the great asteroid Euphrosyne and its festering hell-hole, Miners' Rest. Miners' Rest, to all highly moral citizens the disgrace not only of a solar system but of a sector; the very name of which was—and is—a byword and a hissing to the blue-noses of twice a hundred inhabited and civilized worlds.

XII.

As has been implied, Miners' Rest was the biggest, widest-open, least restrained joint in that entire sector of the Galaxy. And through the underground activities of his fellows of the Patrol, Kinnison knew that of all the king-snipes of that lawless asteroid, the man called Strongheart was the big shot.

Therefore, the Lensman landed his battered craft at Strongheart's dock, loaded the equipment of the hijacker's boat into a hand truck, and went in to talk to Strongheart himself. "Supplies—Equipment—Metal—Bought and Sold" the sign read; but to any experienced eye it was evident that the sign was conservative indeed; that it did not cover Strongheart's business, by half. There were dance halls, there were long and ornate bars, there were rooms in plenty devoted to various games of so-called chance, and most significant, there were scores of the unmistakable cubicles in which the basest passions and lusts of man were satisfied.

"Welcome, stranger! Glad to see you. Have a good trip?" The divekeeper always greeted new customers effusively. "Have a drink on the house!"

"Business before pleasure," Kinnison replied, tersely. "Pretty good, yes. Here's some stuff I don't need any more that I aim to sell. What'll you gimme for it?"

The dealer inspected the suits and instruments, then bored a keen stare into the miner's eyes; a scrutiny under which Kinnison neither flushed nor wavered.

"Two hundred and fifty credits for the lot," Strongheart decided.

"Best you can do?"

"Tops. Take it or leave it."

"QX, they're yours. Gimme it."

"Why, this just starts our business, don't it? Ain't you got cores? Sure you have."

"Yeah, but not for no"—doubly and unprintably qualified—"damn robber. I like a louse, but you suit me altogether too damn well. Them suits alone, just as they lay, are worth a thousand."

"So what? For why go to insult me, a business man? Sure I can't give what that stuff is worth—who could? You ought to know how I got to get rid of hot goods. You killed, ain't it, the guys what owned it, so how could I treat it except like it's hot? Now be your age—don't burn out no jets," as the Lensman turned with a blistering, sizzling deep-space oath. "I know they shot first, they always do, but how does that change things? But keep your shirt on yet. I don't tell nobody nothing. For why should I? How could I make any money on hot goods if I talk too much with my mouth, huh? But on cores, that's something else again. Meteors is legitimate merchandise, and I pay you as much as anybody, maybe more."

"QX," and Kinnison tossed over his cores. He had sold the bandits' spacesuits and equipment deliberately, in order to minimize further killing.

This was his first visit to Miners' Rest, but he intended to become an habitue of the place; and before he would be accepted as a "regular" he knew that he would have to prove his quality. Buckoes and bullies would be sure to try him out. This way was much better. The tale would spread; and any gunman who had drilled two hijackers, dead-center through the face-plates, was not one to be challenged lightly. He might have to kill one or two, but not many, nor frequently.

And the fellow was honest enough in his buying of the metal. His Spaldings cut honest cores—Kinnison put micrometers on them to be sure of that fact. He did not under-read his torsiometer, and he weighed the meteors upon certified balances. He used Galactic Standard average-value-density tables, and offered exactly half of the calculated average value; which, Kinnison knew, was fair enough. By taking his metal to a mint or rare-metals station of the Patrol, any miner could get the precise value of any meteor, as shown by detailed analysis. However, instead of making the long trip and waiting—and paying—for the exact analyses, the miners usually preferred to take the "fifty-percent-of-average-density-value" which was the customary offer of the outside dealers.

*

Then, the meteors unloaded and hauled away. Kinnison dickered with Strongheart concerning the supplies he would need during his next trip; the hundred-and-one items which are necessary to make a tiny spaceship a self-contained, self-sufficient, warm and inhabitable worldlet in the immense and unfriendly vacuity of space. Here, too, the Lensman was overcharged shamelessly; but that, too, was routine. No one would, or could be expected to, do business in any such place as Miners' Rest in any sane or ordinary percentage of profit.

When Strongheart counted out to him the net proceeds of the voyage, Kinnison scratched reflectively at his whiskery chin.

"That ain't hardly enough, I don't think, for the real, old-fashioned, stem-winding bender I was figuring on," he ruminated. "I been out a long time and I was figuring on doing the thing up brown. Have to let go of my nugget, too, I guess. Kinda hate to—been packing it around quite a while—but here she is." He reached into his kit-bag and tossed over the lump of really precious metal. "Let you have it for fifteen hundred credits."

"Fifteen hundred! An idiot you must be, or you should think I'm one, I don't know?" Strongheart yelped, as he juggled the mass lightly from hand to hand. "Two hundred, you mean . . . well two fifty, then, but that's an awful high bid, mister, believe me. I tell you, I couldn't give my own mother over three hundred—I'd lose money on the goods. You ain't tested it, what makes you think it's such a much?"

"No, and I notice you ain't testing it, neither," Kinnison countered. "Me and you both know metal well enough so we don't need to test no such nugget as that. Fifteen hundred or I flit to a mint and get full value for it. I don't have to stay here, you know, by all the nine hells of Valeria. There's millions of other places where I can get just as drunk and have just as good a time as I can here."

There ensued howls of protest, but Strongheart finally yielded, as the Lensman had known that he would. He could have forced him higher, but fifteen hundred was enough.

"Now, sir, just the guarantee and you're all set for a lot of fun." Strongheart's anguish had departed miraculously upon the instant of the deal's closing. "We take your keys, and when your money's gone and you come back to get 'em, to sell your supplies or your ship or whatever, we takes you, without hurting you a bit more than we have to, and sober you up, quick as scat. A room here, whenever you want it, included. Padded, sir, very nice and comfortable—you can't hurt yourself, possibly. We been in business here for years, with perfect satisfaction. Not one of our customers—and we got hundreds who never go nowhere else—have we ever let sell any of the stuff he had laid in for his next trip, and we never steal none of his supplies, neither. Only two hundred credits for the whole service, sir. Cheap, sir—very, *very* cheap at the price."

"Um-m-m"—Kinnison again scratched meditatively, this time at the nape of his neck—"I'll take your guarantee, I guess, because sometimes, when I get to going real good, I don't know just exactly when to stop. But I won't need no padded cell. Me, I don't never get violent. I always taper off on twenty-four units of bentlam. That gives me twenty-four hours on the shelf, and then I'm all set for another stretch out in the ether. You couldn't get me no benny, I don't suppose, and if you could it wouldn't be no damn good."

This was the critical instant, the moment the Lensman had been approaching so long and so circuitously. Mind was already reading mind, Kinnison did not need the speech which followed.

"Twenty-four units!" Strongheart exclaimed. That was a heroic dose—but the man before him was of heroic mold. "Sure of that?"

"Sure I'm sure; and if I get cut weight or cut quality I cut the guy's throat that peddles it to me. But I ain't out. I got a few good jolts left. Guess I'll use my own, and when it gets gone go buy some from a fella I know that's about half honest."

"Don't handle it myself," this, the Lensman knew, was at least partially true, "but I know a man who has a friend who can get it. Good stuff, too, in the original tins; special import from Corvina II. That'll be four hundred altogether. Gimme it and you can start your helling around."

"Whatja mean, four hundred?" Kinnison snorted. "Think I'm just blasting off about having some left, huh? Here's two hundred for your guarantee, and that's all I want out of you."

"Wait a minute. Jet back, miner!" Strongheart had thought that the newcomer was entirely out of his drug, and could therefore be charged eight prices for it. "How much do you get it for, mostly, the clear quill?"

"One credit per unit—twenty-four for the jolt," Kinnison replied tersely and truly. That was the prevailing price charged by retail peddlers. "I'll pay you that, and I don't mean twenty-five, neither."

"QX, gimme it. You don't need to be afraid of being bumped off or rolled here, neither. We got a reputation, we have."

"Yeah, I been told you run a high-class joint," Kinnison agreed, amiably. "That's why I'm here. But you wanna be mighty sure that the ape don't gyp me on the dose—looky here!"

*

As the Lensman spoke he shrugged his shoulders and the divekeeper leaped backward with a shriek; for faster than sight two ugly DeLameters had sprung into being in the miner's huge, dirty paws and were pointing squarely at his midriff!

"Put 'em away!" Strongheart yelled.

"Look 'em over first," and Kinnison handed them over, butts first. "These ain't like them buzzards' cap-pistols what I sold you. These are my own, and they're hot and tight. You know guns, don't you? Look 'em over, pal—real close."

The renegade did know weapons, and he studied these two with care, from the worn, rough-checkered grips and full-charged magazines to the burned, scarred, deeply-pitted orifices. Definitely and unmistakably they were weapons of terrific power; weapons, withal, which had seen hard and frequent service; and Strongheart personally could bear witness to the blinding speed of this miner's draw.

"And remember this," the Lensman went on. "I never yet got so drunk that anybody could take my guns away from me, and if I don't get a full jolt of benny I get mighty peevish."

The publican knew that—it was a characteristic of the drug—and he certainly did not want that miner running amuck with those two weapons in his highly capable hands. He would, he assured him, get his full dose.

And, for his part, Kinnison knew that he was reasonably safe, even in this hell of hells. As long as he was active he could take care of himself, in any kind of company, and he was fairly certain that he would not be slain, during his drug-induced physical helplessness, for the value of his ship and supplies. This one visit had yielded Strongheart a profit of four or five times what he had left, and each subsequent visit should yield a similar amount.

"The first drink's on the house, always," Strongheart derailed his guest's train of thought. "What'll it be? Tellurian ain't you—whiskey?"

"Uh-huh. Close, though—Aldebaran II. Got any good old Aldebaranian bolega?"

"No, but we got some good old Tellurian whiskey, about the same thing."

"QX—gimme a shot." He poured a stiff three fingers, downed it at a gulp, shuddered ecstatically, and emitted a wild yell. "Yip-yip-yipee! I'm Wild Bill Williams, the ripping, roaring, ritoo-dolorum from Aldebaran II, and this is my night to howl. Whee . . . yow . . . owrie-e-e!" Then, quieting down, "This rotgut wasn't never within a million parsecs of Tellus, but it ain't bad—not bad at all. Got the teeth and claws of holy old Klono himself—goes down your throat just like swallowing a mad Radeligian cateagle. Clear ether, pal, I'll be back shortly."

For his first care was to tour the entire Rest, buying scrupulously one good stiff drink, of whatever first came to hand, at each hot spot as he came to it.

"A good-will tour," he explained joyously to Strongheart upon his return. "Got to do it, pal, to keep 'em from calling down the curse of Klono on me, but I'm going to do all my serious drinking right here."

And he did. He drank various and sundry beverages, mixing them with a sublime disregard for consequences which surprised even the hard-boiled booze fighters assembled there. "Anything that'll pour," he declared, loud and often, and acted accordingly. Potent or mild; brewed, fermented, or distilled; loaded, cut, or straight, all one. "Down the hatch!" and down it went. Here was a two-fisted drinker whose like had not been seen for many a day, and his fame spread throughout the Rest.

Being a "happy jag," the more he drank the merrier he became. He bestowed largess hither and yon, in joyous abandon. He danced blithely with the hostesses and tipped them extravagantly. He did not gamble, explaining frequently and painstakingly that that wasn't none of his dish; he wanted to have fun with his money.

He fought, even, without anger or rancor; but gayly, laughing with Homeric gusto the while. He missed with terrific swings that would have felled a horse had they landed; only occasionally getting in, as though by chance, a paralyzing punch. Thus he accumulated an entirely unnecessary mouse under each eye and a sadly bruised nose.

However, his good humor was, as is generally the case in such instances, quite close to the surface, and was prone to turn into passionate anger with less real cause even than the trivialities which started the friendly fist-fights. During various of these outbursts of wrath he smashed four chairs, two tables, and assorted glassware.

But only once did he have to draw a deadly weapon—the news, as he had known it would, had spread abroad that with a DeLameter he was nobody to monkey with—and even then he didn't have to kill the guy. Just winging him—a little bit of a burn through his gun-arm—had been enough.

*

So it went for days. And finally, it was an immense relief that the hilariously drunken Lensman, his money gone to the last millo, went roistering up the street with a two-quart bottle in each hand; swigging now from one, then from the other; inviting bibulously the while any and all chance comers to join him in one last, fond drink. The sidewalk was not wide enough for him, by half; indeed, he took up most of the street. He staggered and reeled, retaining any semblance of balance only by a miracle and by his rigorous spaceman's training.

He threw away one empty bottle, then the other. Then, as he strode along, so purposefully and yet so futilely, he sang. His voice was not particularly musical, but what it lacked in quality of tone it more than made up in volume. Kinnison had a really remarkable voice, a bass of tremendous power, timbre, and resonance; and, pulling out all the stops, in tones audible for two thousand yards against the wind, he poured out his zestfully lusty reveler's soul. His song was a deep-space chanty that would have blistered the ears of any of the gentler spirits who had known him as Kimball Kinnison, of Earth; but which, in Miners' Rest, was merely a humorous and sprightly ballad.

Up the full length of the street he went. Then back, as he put it, to "Base." Even if this final bust did make him sicker at the stomach than a ground-gripper going free for the first time, the Lensman reflected, he had done a mighty good job. He had put Wild Bill Williams, meteor miner, of Aldebaran II, on the map in a big way. It wasn't a faked and therefore fragile identity, either; it was solidly, definitely his own.

Staggering up to his friend Strongheart he steadied himself with two big hands upon the latter's shoulders and breathed a forty-thousand-horsepower breath into his face.

"I'm boiled like a Tellurian hoot-owl," he announced, still happily. "When I'm this stewed I can't say 'partic-hic-hicu-lar-ly' without hick-hicking, but I would partic-hic-hicularly just like one more quart. How about me borrowing a hundred on what I'm going to bring in next time, or selling you—"

"You've had plenty, Bill. You've had lots of fun. How about a good chew of sleep-happy, huh?"

"That's a thought!" the miner exclaimed eagerly. "Lead me to it!"

*

A stranger came up unobtrusively and took him by one elbow. Strongheart took the other, and between them they walked him down a narrow hall and into a cubicle. And while he walked flabbily along Kinnison studied intently the brain of the newcomer. *This* was what he was after!

The ape had had a screen; but it was such a nuisance he took it off for a rest whenever he came here. No Lensman on Euphrosyne! They had combed everybody, even this drunken bum here. This was one place that no Lensman would ever come to; or, if he did, he wouldn't last long. Kinnison had been pretty sure that Strongheart would be in cahoots with somebody bigger than a peddler, and so it had proved. This guy knew plenty, and the Lensman was taking the information—all of it. Six weeks from now, eh? Just right—time to find enough metal for another royal binge here. And during that binge he would really do things.

Six weeks. Quite a while . . . but . . . QX. It would take some time yet, anyway, probably, before the Regional Directors would, like this fellow, get over their scares enough to relax a few of their most irksome precautions. And, as has been intimated, Kinnison, while impatient enough at times, could hold himself in check like a cat watching a mouse hole whenever it was really necessary.

Therefore, in the cell, he seated himself upon the bunk and seized the packet from the hand of the stranger. Tearing it open, he stuffed the contents into his mouth; and, eyes rolling and muscles twitching, he chewed vigorously; expertly allowing the potent juice to trickle down his gullet just fast enough to keep his head humming like a swarm of angry bees. Then, the cud sucked dry, he slumped down upon the mattress, physically dead to the world for the ensuing twenty-four G-P hours.

He awakened; weak, flimsy, and supremely wretched. He made heavy going to the office, where Strongheart returned to him the keys of his boat.

"Feeling low, sir." It was a statement, not a question.

"I'll say so," the Lensman groaned. He was holding his spinning head, trying to steady the gyrating universe. "I'd have to look up—'way, 'way up, with a number nine visiplate—to see a snake's belly in a swamp. Make that damn cat quit stomping his feet, can't you?"

"Too bad, but it won't last long." The voice was unctuous enough, but totally devoid of feeling. "Here's a pickup—you need it."

The Lensman tossed off the potion, without thanks, as was good technique in those parts. His head cleared miraculously, although the stabbing ache remained.

"Come in again next time. Everything's been on the green, ain't it, sir?"

"Uh-huh, very nice," the Lensman admitted. "Couldn't ask for better. I'll be back in five or six weeks, if I have any luck at all."

As the battered but stanch and powerful meteorboat floated slowly upward a desultory conversation was taking place in the dive he had left. At that early hour business was

609

slack to the point of nonexistence, and Strongheart was chatting idly with a bartender and one of the hostesses.

"If more of the boys was like him, we wouldn't have no trouble at all," Strongheart stated with conviction. "Nice, quiet, easygoing—why, he didn't hardly damage a thing, for all his fun."

"Yeah, but at that maybe it's a good gag nobody riled him up too much," the barkeep opined. "He could be rough if he wanted to, I bet a quart. Drunk or sober, he's chain lightning with them DeLameters."

"He's so refined, such a perfect gentleman," sighed the woman. "He's nice." To her, he had been. She had had plenty of credits from the big miner, without having given anything save smiles and dances in return. "Them two guys he drilled must have needed killing, or he wouldn't have burned 'em."

And that was that. As the Lensman had intended, Wild Bill Williams was an old, known, and highly respected resident of Miners' Rest!

*

Out among the asteroids again; more muscle-tearing, back-breaking, lonesome labor. Kinnison did not find any more fabulously rich meteors—such things happen only once in a hundred lifetimes—but he was getting his share of heavy stuff. Then one day when he had about half a load there came, screaming in upon the emergency wave, a call for help; a call so loud that the ship broadcasting it must be very close indeed. Yes, there she was, right in his lap; startlingly large even upon the low-power plates of his spacetramp.

"Help! Spaceship *Hyperion*, position—" a rattling string of numbers. "Bergenholm dead, meteorite screens practically disabled, intrinsic velocity throwing us into the asteroids. Any spacetugs, any vessels with tractors—hurry!"

At the first word Kinnison had shoved his blast-lever full over. A few seconds of free flight, a minute of inert maneuvering that taxed to the utmost his Lensman's skill and powerful frame, and he was within the liner's air lock.

"I know something about Bergs!" he snapped. "Take this boat of mine and pull! Are you evacuating passengers?" he shot at the mate as they ran toward the engine room.

"Yes, but afraid we haven't boats enough—overloaded," was the gasped reply.

"Use mine—fill 'er up!" If the mate was surprised at such an offer from the despised spacerat he did not show it. There were many more surprises in store.

In the engine room Kinnison brushed aside a crew of helplessly futile gropers and threw in switch after switch. He looked. He listened. Above all, he pried into that sealed monster of power with all his sense of perception. How glad he was now that he and Thorndyke had struggled so long and so furiously with a balky Bergenholm on that trip to tempestuous Trenco! For as a result of that trip he *did* know Bergs, with a sure knowledge.

"Number four lead is shot somewhere," he reported. "Must be burned off where it clears the pilaster. Careless overhaul last time—got to take off the lower port third cover. No time for wrenches—get me a cutting beam, and get the lead out of your pants!"

The beam was brought on the double and the Lensman himself blasted away the designated cover. Then, throwing an insulated plate over the red-hot casing he lay on his back—"Hand me a light!"—and peered briefly upward into the bowels of the Gargantuan mechanism.

"I thought so," he grunted. "Piece of four-oh stranded, eighteen inches long. Ditmars number six clip ends, spaced to twenty inches between hole-centers. Myerbeer insulation on center section, doubled. Snap it up! One of you other fellows, bring me a short, heavy screwdriver and a Ditmars six wrench!"

The technicians worked fast and in a matter of seconds the stuff was there. The Lensman labored briefly but hugely; and much more surely than if he were dependent upon the rays of the hand-lamp to penetrate the smoky, steamy, greasy murk in which he toiled. Then:

"QX—give her the juice!" he snapped.

They gave it, and to the stunned surprise of all, she took it. The liner again was free!

"Kind of a jury-rigging I gave it, but it'll hold long enough to get you into port, sir," he reported to the captain in his sanctum, saluting crisply. He was in for it now, he knew, as the officer stared at him. But he *couldn't* have let that shipload of passengers get ground up into hamburger. Anyway, there was no way out.

*

In apparent reaction he turned pale and trembled, and the officer hastily took from his medicinal stores a bottle of choice brandy.

"Here, drink this," he directed, proffering the glass:

Kinnison did so. More, he seized the bottle from the captain's hand and drank that, too—all of it—a draft which would have literally turned him inside out a few months since. Then, to the captain's horrified disgust, he took from his filthy dungarees a packet of bentlam and began to chew it, idiotically blissful. Thence, and shortly, into oblivion.

"Poor devil—you poor, poor devil," the commander murmured, and had him put into a bunk.

When he had come to and had had his pickup, the captain came and regarded him soberly.

"You were a man once. An engineer, and a crackerjack; or I'm an oiler's pimp," he said levelly.

"Maybe," Kinnison replied, white and weak. "I'm all right yet, except once in a while—"

"I know," the captain frowned. "No cure?"

"Not a chance. Tried dozens. So—" and the Lensman spread out his hands in a hopeless gesture.

"Better tell me your name, anyway—your real name. That'll let your planet know that you aren't—"

"Better not," the sufferer shook his aching head. "Folks think I'm dead. Better let them keep on thinking so. Williams is the name, sir; William Williams, of Aldebaran II."

"As you say."

"How far are we from where I boarded you?"

"Close. Less than half a billion miles. This, the second, is our home planet: your asteroid belt is just outside the orbit of the fourth."

"I can hop it in an hour, easy. Guess I'll buzz off."

611

"As you say," the officer agreed, again. "But we'd like to—" and he extended a sheaf of currency.

"Rather not, sir, thanks. You see, the longer it takes me to earn another stake, the longer it'll be before—"

"I see. Thanks, anyway, for us all," and captain and mate helped the derelict embark. They scarcely looked at him, scarcely dared look at each other, but—

Kinnison, for his part, was almost content. This story, too, would get around. It would be in Miners' Rest before he got back there, and it would help—help a lot.

He did not see how he could possibly, or ever, let those officers know the truth, even though he realized full well that at that very moment they were thinking, pityingly:

"The poor devil—the poor, brave devil!"

XIII.

The Gray Lensman went back to his mining with a will and with unimpaired vigor, for his distress aboard the ship he had rescued had been sheerest acting. One small bottle of good brandy was scarcely a cocktail to the physique that had stood up under quart after quart of the crudest, wickedest, fieriest beverage known to space; that tiny morsel of bentlam—scarcely half a unit—affected him no more than a lozenge of licorice.

Three weeks. Twenty-one days, each of twenty-four G-P hours. At the end of that time, he had learned from the mind of the zwilnik that the Boskonian director of this, the Borovan solar system, would visit Miners' Rest, to attend some kind of a meeting. His informant did not know what the meeting was to be about, and he was not unduly curious about it. Kinnison, however, did and was.

The Lensman knew, or at least very shrewdly suspected, that that meeting was to be a regional conference of big-shot zwilniks; he was intensely curious to know all about everything that was to take place; and he was determined to be present.

Three weeks was lots of time. In fact, he should be able to complete his quota of heavy metal in two, or less. It was there, there was no question of that. Right out there were the meteors, unaccountable thousands of millions of them, and a certain proportion of them carried values. The more and the harder he worked, the more of these worthwhile wanderers of the void he would find. Therefore he labored long, hard, and rapidly, and his store of high-test meteors grew apace.

To such good purpose did he use beam and Spalding drill that he was ready more than a week ahead of time. That was QX—he'd much rather be early than late. Something might have happened to hold him up—things did happen, too often—and he had to be at that meeting!

Thus it came about that, a few days before the all-important date, Kinnison's battered treasure-hunter blasted herself down to her second landing at Strongheart's dock. This time the miner was welcomed, not as a stranger, but as a friend of long standing.

"Hi, Wild Bill!" Strongheart yelled at sight of the big spacehound. "Right on time, I see—glad to see you! Luck, too, I hope—lots of luck, and all good, I bet me—ain't it?"

"Ho, Strongheart!" the Lensman roared in return, pommeling the divekeeper affectionately. "Had a good trip, yeah—a fine trip. Struck a rich sector—twice as much as I got last time. Told you I'd be back in five or six weeks, and made it in five weeks and four days."

"Keeping tab on the days, huh?"

"I'll say I do. With a thirst like mine a guy can't do nothing else—I tell you all my guts're dryer than any desert on the whole of Mars. Well, what're we waiting for? Check this plunder of mine in and let me get to going places and doing things!"

The business end of the visit was settled with neatness and dispatch. Dealer and miner understood each other thoroughly, each knew what could and what could not be done to the other. The meteors were tested and weighed. Supplies for the ensuing trip were bought. The guarantee and twenty-four units of benny—QX. No argument. No hysterics. No bickering or quarreling or swearing. Everything on the green, all the way. Gentlemen and friends. Kinnison turned over his keys, accepted a thick sheaf of currency, and, after the first formal drink with his host, set out upon the self-imposed, superstitious tour of the other hot spots which would bring him favor—or at least would avert the active disfavor—of Klono, his spaceman's deity.

*

This time, however, that tour took longer. Upon his first ceremonial round he had entered each saloon in turn, had bought one drink of whatever was nearest, had tossed it down, and had gone on to the next place; unobserved and inconspicuous. Now, how different it all was! Wherever he went he was the center of attention.

Men who had met him before flung themselves upon him with whoops of welcome; men who had never seen him clamored to drink with him; women, whether or not they knew him, fawned upon him and brought into play their every lure and wile. For not only was this man a hero and a celebrity of sorts; he was a lucky—or a skillful—miner whose every trip resulted in wads of money big enough to clog the under jets of a Valerian freighter! Moreover, when he was lit up he threw it around regardless, and he was getting stewed as fast as he could swallow. Let's keep him here—or, if we can't do that, let's go along, wherever he goes!

This, too, was strictly according to the Lensman's expectations. Everybody knew that he did not do any serious drinking glass by glass at the bar, but bottle by bottle; that he did not buy individual drinks for his friends, but let them drink as deeply as they would from whatever container chanced then to be in hand; and his vast popularity gave him a sound excuse to begin his bottle-buying at the start instead of waiting until he got back to Strongheart's. He bought, then, several or many bottles and tins in each place, instead of a single drink. And, since everybody knew for a fact that he was a practically bottomless drinker, who was even to suspect that he barely moistened his gullet while the hangers-on were really emptying the bottles, flasks, and flagons?

And during his real celebration at Strongheart's, while he drank enough, he did not drink too much. He waxed exceedingly happy and frolicsome, as before. He was as profligate, as extravagant in tips. He had the same sudden flashes of hot anger. He fought enthusiastically and awkwardly, as Wild Bill Williams did, although only once or twice, that time; and he did not have to draw his DeLameters at all—he was so well known and so beloved! He sang as loudly and as raucously, and with the same good taste in madrigals.

Therefore, when the infiltration of thought-screened men warned him that the meeting was about to be called Kinnison was ready. He was in fact cold sober when he began his tuneful, last-two-bottles trip up the street, and he was almost as sober when he returned to "Base," empty of bottles and pockets, to make the usual attempt to obtain more money from Strongheart and to compromise by taking his farewell chew of bentlam instead.

Nor was he unduly put out by the fact that both Strongheart and the zwilnik were now wearing screens. He had taken it for granted that they might be, and had planned accordingly. He seized the packet as avidly as before, chewed its contents as ecstatically, and slumped down as helplessly and as idiotically. That much of the show, at least, was real. Twenty-four units of that drug will paralyze *any* human body, make it assume the unmistakable pose and stupefied mien of the bentlam-eater. But Kinnison's mind was not an ordinary one; the dose which would have rendered any bona-fide miner's brain as helpless as his body did not affect the Lensman's new equipment at all. Alcohol and bentlam together were bad, but the Lensman was sober. Therefore, if anything, the drugging of his body only made it easier to dissociate his new mind from it. Furthermore, he need not waste any thought in making it act. There was only one way it could act, now, and Kinnison let his new senses roam abroad without even thinking of the body he was leaving behind him.

*

In view of the rigorous orders from higher-up the conference room was heavily guarded by screened men; no one except old and trusted employees were allowed to enter it, and they were also protected. Nevertheless, Kinnison got in, by proxy.

A clever pickpocket brushed against a screened waiter who was about to enter the sacred precincts, lightning fingers flicking a switch. The waiter began to protest—then forgot what he was going to say, even as the pickpocket forgot completely the deed he had just done. The waiter in turn was a trifle clumsy in serving a certain big shot, but earned no rebuke thereby; for the latter forgot the offense almost instantly. Under Kinnison's control the director fumbled at his screen-generator for a moment, loosening slightly a small but important resister. That done, the Lensman withdrew delicately and the meeting was an open book.

"Before we do anything," the director began, "show me that all your screens are on." He bared his own—it would have taken an expert service man an hour to find that it was not functioning perfectly.

"Poppycock!" snorted the zwilnik. "Who in all the hells of space thinks that a Lensman would—or *could*—come to Euphrosyne?"

"No one can tell what this particular Lensman can or can't do, and nobody knows what he is doing until just before he dies. Hence the strictness. You've searched everybody here, of course?"

"Everybody," Strongheart averred, "even the drunks and dopes. The whole building is screened, besides the screens we're wearing."

"The dopes don't count, of course, provided they're really doped." No one, except the Gray Lensman himself, could possibly conceive of a Lensman being—not seeming to be, but actually *being*—a drunken sot, to say nothing of being a confirmed addict of any drug. "By the way, who is this Wild Bill Williams that I've been hearing about?"

Strongheart and his friend looked at each other and laughed.

"I checked up on him early," the zwilnik chuckled. "He isn't the Lensman, of course, but I thought at first he might be an agent. We frisked him and his ship thoroughly—no dice—and checked back on him as a miner, four solar systems back. He's clean, anyway; this is his second bender here. He's been guzzling everything in stock for a week, getting more pie-eyed every day, and Strongheart and I just put him to bed with twenty-four units of benny. You know what *that* means, don't you?"

"Your own benny or his?" the director asked.

"My own. That's why I know he's clean. All the other dopes are, too. The drunks we gave the bum's rush, like you told us to."

"QX. I don't think there's any danger, myself—I think that the hot-shot Lensman they're afraid of is still working Bronseca—but these orders not to take any chances at all come from 'way, 'way up."

"How about this new system they're working on, that nobody knows his boss any more?" asked the zwilnik. "Hooey, I call it."

"Not ready yet," the director answered. "They haven't been able to invent one that is safe enough for them and yet will handle the volume of work that has to be done. In the meantime, we're using these books. Cumbersome, but absolutely safe, they say, unless and until the enemy gets onto the idea. Then one group will go into the lethal chambers of the Patrol and the rest of us will use something else. Some say that this code can't be cracked without the key; others say any code can be read in time. Anyway here's your orders. Pass them along. Give me your stuff and we'll have supper and a few drinks."

They ate. They drank. They enjoyed an evening and a night of high revelry and low dissipation, each to his taste; each secure in the knowledge that his thought-screen was one-hundred-percent effective against the one enemy he really feared. Indeed, the screens were that effective—then. The Lensman, having learned from the director all that he knew, had restored the generator to full efficiency in the instant of his relinquishment of control.

Although the heads of the zwilniks, and therefore their minds, were secure against Kinnison's prying, the books of record were not. And, though his body was lying helpless, inert upon a drug-fiend's cot, his sense of perception read those books; if not as readily as though they were in his hands and open, yet readily enough. And, far off in space, a power-brained Lensman yclept Worsel, recorded upon imperishable metal a detailed account, including names, dates, facts, and figures, of all the doings of all the zwilniks of a solar system!

The information was coded, it is true; but, since Kinnison knew the key, it might just as well have been printed in English. To the later consternation of Narcotics, however, that tape was sent in under Lensman's seal—the spool could not be opened until the Gray Lensman gave the word.

THE LENSMAN

In twenty-four hours Kinnison recovered from the effects of his debauch. He got his keys from Strongheart. He left the asteroid. He knew the mighty intellect with whom he had next to deal, he knew where that entity was to be found; but, sad to say, he had positively no idea at all as to what he was going to do or how he was going to do it.

Wherefore it was that a sense of relief tempered, with no small degree, the natural apprehension he felt upon receiving an insistent call from Port Admiral Haynes. Truly this must be something really extraordinary, for while during the long months of his service Kinnison had called the chief of staff scores of times, Haynes had never before lensed him.

"Kinnison! Haynes calling!" the message beat into his consciousness.

"Kinnison acknowledging Haynes, sir!" the Gray Lensman thought back.

"Am I interrupting anything important?"

"No, sir, not at all. I'm just doing a little flit."

"A situation has come up which we feel you should study, not only in person, but also without advance information or preconceived ideas. Is it at all possible for you to come into Prime Base immediately?"

"Yes, sir, eminently so. In fact, a little time right now might do me good in two ways—let me mull a job over, and let a nut mellow down to a point where maybe I can crack it. At your orders, sir!"

"Not orders, Kinnison!" the old man reprimanded him sharply. "No one gives unattached Lensmen orders. We request or suggest, but you are the sole judge as to where your greatest usefulness lies."

"Please believe, sir, that your requests are orders, to me," Kinnison replied in all seriousness. Then, more lightly, "Your calling me in suggests an emergency, and traveling in this miner's scow of mine is just a trifle faster than going afoot. How about sending out something with some legs to pick me up?"

"The *Dauntless*, for instance?"

"Oh—you've got her rebuilt already?"

"Yes."

"I'll bet she's a sweet clipper! She was a mighty slick stepper before; now she must have more legs than a centipede!"

And so it came about that in a region of space entirely empty of all other vessels as far as ultrapowerful detectors could reach, the *Dauntless* met Kinnison's tugboat. The two went inert and maneuvered briefly, then the immense warship engulfed her tiny companion and flashed away.

"Hi, Kim, you old son-of-a-space-flea!" A general yell arose at sight of him, and irrepressible youth rioted, regardless of Regs, in this reunion of old comrades-in-arms who were yet scarcely more than boys in years.

"His Nibs says for you to call 'im, Kim, when we're about an hour out from Prime Base," Commander Maitland informed his classmate irreverently, as the *Dauntless* neared the Solarian System.

"Plate or Lens?"

"Didn't say—as you like, I suppose."

"Plate then, I guess—don't want to butt in."

In a few moments chief of staff and Gray Lensman were in image face-to-face.

"How are you making out, Kinnison?" The Port Admiral studied the young man's face intently, gravely, line by line. Then, upon his Lens, "We heard about the shows you put on, clear over here on Tellus. A man can't drink and dope the way you did without suffering consequences. I've been wondering if even you can fight it off. How about it? How do you feel now?"

"Some craving, of course," Kinnison replied, shrugging his shoulders. "That can't be helped—you can't make an omelette without breaking eggs. However, I can assure you as a fact that it's nothing I can't lick. I've got it pretty well boiled out of my system already."

"Mighty glad to hear that, son. Only Ellison and I know who Wild Bill Williams really is. You had us scared stiff for a while." Then, speaking aloud:

"I would like to have you come to my office as soon as is convenient after you land."

"I'll be there, chief, two minutes after we hit the bumpers," and he was.

"Right of way, Norma?" he asked, waving an airy salute at the attractive young woman in Haynes' outer office.

"Go right in, Lensman Kinnison, he's waiting for you," and opening the door for him, she stood aside as he strode into the sanctum.

*

The Port Admiral returned the younger man's punctilious salute, then the two shook hands warmly before Haynes referred to the third man in the room.

"Navigator Xylpic, this is Lensman Kinnison, unattached. Sit down, please; this may take some time. Now, Kinnison, I want to tell you that ships have been disappearing, right and left, disappearing without sending out an alarm or leaving a trace. Convoying makes no difference, as the escorts also disappear—"

"Any with the new projectors?" Kinnison flashed the question via Lens—this was nothing to talk about aloud.

"No," came the reassuring thought in reply. "Every one bottled up tight until we find out what it's all about. Sending out the *Dauntless* after you was the only exception."

"Fine. You shouldn't have taken even that much chance." This interplay of thought took but an instant; Haynes went on with scarcely a break in his voice:

"—with no more warning or report than the freighters and liners they are supposed to be protecting. Automatic reporting also fails—the instruments simply stop sending. The first and only sign of light—if it *is* such a sign; which, frankly, I doubt—came shortly before I called you in, when Xylpic here came to me with a tall story."

Kinnison looked then at the stranger. Pink. Unmistakably a Chickladorian—pink all over. Bushy hair, triangular eyes, teeth, skin; all that same peculiar color. Not the flush of red blood showing through translucent skin, but opaque pigment; the brick-reddish pink so characteristic of the near-humanity of that planet.

"We have investigated this Xylpic thoroughly." Haynes went on, discussing the Chickladorian as impersonally as though he were upon his home planet instead of there in the room, listening. "The worse of it is that the man is absolutely honest—or at least, he himself believes that he is—in telling this yarn. Also, except for this one thing—this obsession, fixed idea, hallucination, call it what you like; it seems incredible that it *can* be a fact—he not only seems to be, but actually *is*, absolutely sane.

"Now, Xylpic, tell Kinnison what you have told the rest of us. And Kinnison, I hope that you can make sense of it—none of the rest of us can."

"QX. Go ahead, I'm listening." But Kinnison did far more than listen. As the fellow began to talk the Gray Lensman insinuated his mind into that of the Chickladorian. He groped for moments, seeking the wave-length; then he, Kimball Kinnison, was actually reliving with the pink man an experience which harrowed his very soul.

"The Second Navigator of a Radeligian vessel died in space, and when it landed on Chickladoria I took the berth. About a week out, the whole crew went mad, all at once. The first I knew of it was when the pilot on duty beside me left his board, picked up a stool, and smashed the automatic recorder. Then he went inert and neutralized all the controls.

"I yelled at him, but he didn't answer me, and all the men in the control room acted funny. They just milled around like men in a trance. I buzzed the captain, but he didn't acknowledge either. Then the men around me left the control room and went down the companionway toward the main lock. I was scared—my skin prickled and the hair on the back of my neck stood straight up—but I followed along, quite a ways behind, to see what they were going to do. The captain, all the rest of the officers, and the whole crew joined them in the lock. Everybody was acting kind of crazy, and as if they were in an awful hurry to get somewhere.

"I didn't go any nearer—I wasn't going to go out into space without a suit on. I went back into the control room to get at a spy ray, then changed my mind. That was the first place they would come to if they boarded us, as they probably would—other ships had disappeared in space, plenty of them. Instead, I went over to a lifeboat and used its spy. And I tell you, sirs, there was nothing there—nothing at all!" The stranger's voice rose almost to a shriek, his mind quivered in an ecstasy of horror.

"Steady, Xylpic, steady," the Gray Lensman said, quietingly. "Everything you've said so far makes sense. It all fits right into the matrix. Nothing to go off the beam about, at all."

"What! You believe me!" the Chickladorian stared at Kinnison in amazement, an emotion very evidently shared by the Port Admiral.

"Yes," the man in gray leather asserted. "Not only that, but I have a very fair idea of what's coming next. G. A."

*

"The men walked out into space." The pink man offered this information diffidently, although positively—an oft-repeated but starkly incredible statement. "They did not float outward, sirs, they *walked*; and they acted as if they were breathing air, not space. And as they walked they sort of faded out; became thin, mistylike. This sounds crazy, sir"—to Kinnison alone—"I thought then maybe I was cuckoo, and everybody around here thinks I am now, too. Maybe I *am* nuts, sir—I don't know."

"I do. You aren't," Kinnison said, calmly.

"Well, and here comes the worst of it, they walked around just as though they were in a ship, growing fainter all the time. Then some of them lay down and something began to *skin* one of them—skin him alive, sir—but there was nothing there at all. I ran, then. I got into the fastest lifeboat on the far side and gave her all the oof she'd take. That's all, sir."

"Not quite all, Xylpic, unless I'm badly mistaken. Why didn't you tell the rest of it while you were at it?"

"I didn't dare to, sir. If I'd told any more they would have *known* I was crazy instead of just thinking so—" He broke sharply, his voice altering strangely as he went on: "What makes you think there was anything more, sir? Do you—" The question trailed off into silence.

"I do. If what I think happened really did happen, there was more—quite a lot more—and worse. Wasn't there?"

"I'll say there was!" The navigator almost exploded in relief. "Or rather, I think now that there was. But I can't describe any of it very well—everything was getting fainter all the time, and I thought that I must be imagining most of it."

"You weren't imagining a thing—" the Lensman began, only to be interrupted by Haynes.

"Hell's jingling bells!" that worthy almost shouted. "If you know what it was, tell me!"

"Think I know, but not quite sure yet—got to check it. Can't get it from him—he's told everything he really knows. He didn't really see anything, it was practically invisible. Even if he had tried to describe the whole performance you wouldn't have recognized it. Nobody could have, except Worsel and I, and possibly Van Buskirk. I'll tell you the rest of what actually happened and Xylpic can tell us if it checks." His features grew taut, his voice became hard and chill. "I saw it done, once. Worse, I heard it. Saw it and heard it, clear and plain. Also, I knew what it was all about, so I can describe it a lot better than Xylpic possibly can.

"Every man of that crew was killed by torture. Some were flayed alive, as Xylpic said; then they were carved up, slowly and piecemeal. Some were stretched, pulled apart by chains and hooks, on racks. Others twisted on frames. Boiled, little by little. Picked apart, bit by bit. Gassed. Eaten away by corrosives, one molecule at a time. Pressed out flat, as though between two plates of glass. Whipped. Scourged. Beaten gradually to a pulp. Other methods, lots of them—indescribable. All slow, though, and extremely painful. Greenish-yellow light, showing the aura of each man as he died. Beams from somewhere—possibly invisible—consuming the auras. Check, Xylpic?"

"Yes, sir, it checks!" The Chickladorian exclaimed in profound relief; then added, carefully: "That is, that's the way the torture was, exactly, sir, but there was something funny, a difference, about their fading away. I can't describe what was funny about it, but it didn't seem so much that they became invisible as that they went away, sir, even though they didn't go any place."

"That's due to the way that system of invisibility works. Got to be—nothing else will fit into—"

"The Overlords of Delgon!" Haynes rasped, sharply. "But if that's a true picture, how in all the hells of space did this Xylpic, alone of all the ship's personnel, get away clean? Tell me that!"

"Simple!" the Gray Lensman snapped back as sharply. "The rest were all Radeligians—he was the only Chickladorian aboard. The Overlords simply didn't know that he was there. They didn't feel him at all. Chickladorians think on a wave nobody else in the Galaxy uses—you must have noticed that when you felt of him with your Lens. It took me half a minute to synchronize with him.

"As for his escape, that makes sense, too. The Overlords are slow workers and when they're playing that game they really concentrate on it—they don't pay any attention to anything else. By the time they got done and were ready to take over the ship, he could be almost anywhere."

"But he says that there was no ship there—nothing at all!" Haynes protested.

"Invisibility isn't hard to understand," Kinnison countered. "We've almost got it ourselves—we undoubtedly could have it as good as that, with a little more work on it. There was a ship there, beyond question. Close. Hooked on with magnets, and with a spacetube, lock to lock.

"The only peculiar part of it, and the bad part, is something you haven't mentioned yet. What would the Overlords—if, as we must assume, some of them got away from Worsel and his crew—be doing with a ship? They never had any spaceships that I ever knew anything about, nor any other mechanical devices requiring any advanced engineering skill. Also, and most important, they never did and never could invent or develop such an invisibility apparatus as that."

*

Kinnison fell silent, and while he frowned in thought Haynes dismissed the Chickladorian, with orders that his every want be supplied.

"What do you deduce from those facts?" the Port Admiral presently asked.

"Plenty," the Gray Lensman said, darkly. "I smell a rat. In fact, it stinks to high Heaven. Boskone."

"You may be right," the chief of staff conceded. It was hopeless, he knew, for him to try to keep up with this man's mental processes. "But why, and above all, how?"

"'Why' is easy. They both owe us a lot, and want to pay us in full. Both hate us all to pieces. 'How' is immaterial. One found the other, some way. They're together, just as sure as hell's a mantrap, and that's what matters. It's bad. Very, *very* bad, believe me."

"Orders?" asked Haynes. He was a big man; big enough to ask instructions from anyone who knew more than he did—big enough to make no bones of such asking.

"One does not give orders to the Port Admiral," Kinnison mimicked him lightly, but meaningly. "One may request, perhaps, or suggest, but—"

"Skip it! I'll take a club to you yet, you young hellion! You said you'd take orders from me. QX—I'll take 'em from you. What are they?"

"No orders yet, I don't think—" Kinnison ruminated. "No . . . not until after we investigate. I'll have to have Worsel and Van Buskirk; we're the only three who have had experience. We'll take the *Dauntless*, I think—it'll be safe enough. Thought-screens will stop the Overlords cold, and a scrambler will take care of the invisibility business if they use the same principle we do, and they very probably do."

"Safe enough, then, you think, to let traffic resume, if they're protected with screens?"

"I wouldn't say so. They've got Boskonian superdreadnoughts now to use if they want to, and that's something else to think about. Another week or so won't hurt much—better wait until we see what we can see. I've been wrong once or twice before, too, and I may be again."

He was. Although his words were conservative enough, he was practically certain in his own mind that he knew all the answers. But how wrong he was—how terribly, how tragically wrong! For even his mentality had not as yet envisaged the incredible actuality; his deductions and perceptions fell far, far short of the appalling truth!

XIV.

The fashion in which the Overlords of Delgon had come under the ægis of Boskone, while obscure for a time, was in reality quite simple and logical; for upon distant Jarnevon the Eich had profited signally from Eichlan's disastrous raid upon Arisia. Not exactly in the sense suggested by Eukonidor, the Arisian guardian, it is true, but profited nevertheless. They had learned that thought, hitherto considered only a valuable adjunct to achievement, was actually an achievement in itself; that it could be used as a weapon of surpassing power.

Eukonidor's homily, as he more than suspected at the time, might as well never have been uttered, for all the effect it had upon the life or upon the purpose in life of any single member of the race of the Eich. Eichmil, who had been Second of Boskone, was now First; the others were advanced correspondingly; and a new Eighth and Ninth had been chosen to complete the roster of the council which was Boskone.

"The late Eichlan," Eichmil stated harshly after calling the new Boskone to order—which event took place within a day after it became apparent that the two bold spirits had departed to a bourne from which there was to be no returning—"erred seriously, in fact fatally, in underestimating an opponent, even though he himself was prone to harp upon the danger of that very thing.

"We are agreed that our objectives remain unchanged; and also that greater circumspection must be used until we have succeeded in discovering the hitherto unsuspected potentialities of pure thought. We will now hear from one of our new members, the Ninth, also a psychologist, who most fortunately had been studying this situation even before the inception of the expedition which yesterday came to such a catastrophic end."

"It is clear," the Ninth of Boskone began, "that Arisia is at present out of the question. Perceiving the possibility of some such dénouement—an idea to which I repeatedly called the attention of my predecessor psychologist, the late Eighth—I have been long at work upon certain alternative measures.

"Consider, please, that we learned first of the thought-screens from Helmuth; who was then of the opinion that they were first used in the Tellurian Galaxy by the natives of Velantia. This belief was amended later, in discredited reports, to one that said devices did in fact originate upon Arisia. This later conclusion we may now accept as a fact, since the Arisians could and did break such screens by the application of mental forces either of greater magnitude than they could withstand or of some new and as yet unknown composition or pattern.

"Such screens were, however, and probably still are, used largely and commonly upon the planet Velantia. Therefore they must have been both necessary and adequate. The deduction is, I believe, defensible that they were used as a protection against entities who were, and who still may be, employing against the Velantians the weapons of pure thought which we wish to investigate and to acquire.

"I propose, then, that I and a few others of my selection continue this research, not upon Arisia, but upon Velantia and perhaps elsewhere."

To this suggestion there was no demur and a vessel set out forthwith. The visit to Velantia was simple and created no untoward disturbance whatever. In this connection it must be remembered that the natives of Velantia, then in the early ecstasies of discovery by the Galactic Patrol and the consequent acquisition of inertialess flight, were fairly reveling in visits to and from the widely-variant peoples of the planets of hundreds of other suns. It must be borne in mind that, since the Eich were, if anything, physically more like the Velantians than were the men of Tellus, the presence of a group of such entities upon the planet would create no more interest or comment than that of a group of human beings. Therefore that fateful visit went unnoticed at the time, and as it was only by long and arduous research, after Kinnison had deduced that some such visit must have been made, that it was shown to have been an actuality.

Space forbids any detailed account of what the Ninth of Boskone and his fellows did, although that story of itself would be no mean epic. Suffice it to say, then, that they became well acquainted with the friendly Velantians; they studied and they learned. Particularly did they seek information concerning the noisome Overlords of Delgon, although the natives did not care to dwell at any length upon the subject.

"Their power is broken," they were wont to inform the questioners, with airy flirtings of tail and wing. "Every known cavern of them, and not a few hitherto unknown caverns, have been blasted out of existence. Whenever one of them dares to obtrude his mentality upon any one of us he is at once hunted down and slain. Even if they are not all dead, as we think, they certainly are no longer a menace to our peace and security."

*

Having secured all the information available upon Velantia, the Eich went to Delgon, where they devoted all the power of their admittedly first-grade minds and all the not inconsiderable resources of their ship to the task of finding and uniting the remnants of what had once been a flourishing race, the Overlords of Delgon.

The Overlords! That monstrous, repulsive, amoral race which, not excepting even the Eich themselves, achieved the most universal condemnation ever to have been given in the long history of the Galactic Union. The Eich, admittedly deserving of the fate which was theirs, had and have their apologists. The Eich were wrong-minded, all admit. They were anti-social, blood-mad, obsessed with an insatiable lust for power and conquest which nothing except complete extinction could extirpate. Their evil attributes were legion. They were, however, brave. They were organizers par excellence. They were, in their own fashion, creators and doers. They had the courage of their convictions and followed them to the bitter end.

Of the Overlords, however, nothing good has ever been said. They were debased, cruel, perverted to a degree starkly unthinkable to any normal intelligence, however housed. In their native habitat they had no weapons, nor need of any. Through sheer power of mind they reached out to their victims, even upon other planets, and forced them to come to the gloomy caverns in which they had their being. There the victims were tortured to death in numberless unspeakable fashions, and while they died the captors *fed*, ghoulishly, upon the departing life principle of the sufferer.

The mechanism of that absorption is entirely unknown; nor is there any adequate evidence as to what end was served by it in the economy of that horrid race. That these orgies were not essential to their physical well-being is certain, since many of the creatures survived for a long time after the frightful rites were rendered impossible.

Be that as it may, the Eich sought out and found many surviving Overlords. The latter tried to enslave the visitors and to bend them into their hideously sadistic purposes, but to no avail. Not only were the Eich protected by thought-screens; they had minds of a fierce power almost, if not quite, equal to the Overlord's own. And, after these first overtures had been made and channels of communication established, the alliance was a natural.

Much has been said and written of the binding power of love. That, and other noble emotions, have indeed performed wonders. It seems to this historian, however, that all too little has been said of the effectiveness of pure hate as a cementing material. Probably for good and sufficient moral reasons; perhaps because—and for the best—its application has been of comparatively infrequent occurrence. Here, in the case in hand, we have history's best example of two entirely dissimilar peoples working efficiently together under the urge, not of love or of any other lofty sentiment, but of sheer, stark, unalloyed and corrosive, but common, hate.

Both hated civilization and everything pertaining to it. Both wanted revenge; wanted it with a searing, furious need almost tangible; a gnawing, burning lust which neither countenanced palliation nor brooked denial. And above all, both hated vengefully, furiously, esuriently—every way except blindly—an as yet unknown and unidentified wearer of the million-times accursed Lens of the Galactic Patrol!

The Eich were hard, ruthless, cold; not even having such words in their language as "conscience," "mercy," or "scruple." Their hatred of the Lensman was then a thing of an intensity unknowable to any human mind. Even that emotion, however, grim as it was and fearsome, paled beside the passionately vitriolic hatred of the Overlords of Delgon for the being who had been the Nemesis of their race.

And when the sheer mental power of the Overlords, unthinkably great as it was and operative withal in a fashion sheerly incomprehensible to us of civilization, was combined with the ingenuity, resourcefulness, and drive, as well as with the scientific ability of the Eich, the results would in any case have been portentous indeed.

In this case they were more than portentous, and worse. Those prodigious intellects, fanned into fierce activity by fiery blasts of hatred, produced a thing incredible.

XV.

Before the *Dauntless* was serviced for the flight into the unknown Kinnison changed his mind. He was vaguely troubled about the trip. It was nothing as definite as a "hunch"; hunches are, the Gray Lensman knew, the results of the operation of an extrasensory perception possessed by all of us in greater or lesser degree. It was probably not an obscure warning to his super-sense from another, more pervasive dimension. It was, he thought, a repercussion of the doubt in Xylpic's mind that the fading out of the men's bodies had been due to simple invisibility.

"I think I'd better go alone, chief," he informed the Port Admiral one day. "I'm not quite as sure as I was as to just what they've got."

"What difference does that make?" Haynes demanded.

"Lives," was the terse reply.

"*Your* life is what I'm thinking about. You'll be safer with the big ship, you can't deny that."

"We-ll, perhaps. But I don't want—"

"What you want is immaterial."

"How about a compromise? I'll take Worsel and Van Buskirk. When the Overlords hypnotized him that time it made Bus so mad that he's been taking treatments from Worsel. Nobody can hypnotize him now, Worsel says, not even an Overlord."

"No compromise. I can't order you to take the *Dauntless*, since your authority is transcendent. You can take anything you like. I can, however, and shall, order the *Dauntless* to ride your tail wherever you go."

"QX, I'll have to take her then." Kinnison's voice grew somber. "But suppose half the crew don't get back—and that I do?"

"Isn't that what happened on the *Brittania?*"

"No," came flat answer. "We were all taking the same chance then—it was the luck of the draw. This is different."

"How different?"

"I've got better equipment than they have. I'd be a murderer, cold."

"Not at all, no more than then. You had better equipment then, too, you know, although not as much of it. Every commander of men has that same feeling when he sends men to death. But put yourself in my place. Would you send one of your best men, or let him go alone on a highly dangerous mission when more men or ships would improve his chances? Answer that, honestly."

"Probably I wouldn't," Kinnison admitted, reluctantly.

"QX. Take all the precautions you can—but I don't have to tell you that. I know you will."

*

Therefore it was the *Dauntless* in which Kinnison set out a day or two later. With him were Worsel and Van Buskirk, as well as the vessel's full operating crew of Tellurians. As they approached the region of space in which Xylpic's vessel had been attacked every man in the crew got his armor in readiness for instant use, checked his side arms, and took his emergency battle station. Kinnison turned then to Worsel.

"How d'you feel, fellow old snake?" he asked.

"Scared," the Velantian replied, sending a rippling surge of power the full length of the thirty-foot-long cable of supple, although almost steel-hard flesh that was his body. "Scared to the tip of my tail. Not that they can treat me as they did before—we three, at least, are safe from their minds—but at what they will *do*. Whatever it is to be, it will not be what we expect. They certainly will not do the obvious."

"That's what's clogging my jets." The Lensman agreed. "As a flapper told me once, I'm getting the screaming meamies."

"That's what you mugs get for being so brainy," Van Buskirk put in. With a flick of his massive wrist he brought his thirty-pound spaceax to the "ready" as lightly as though it were a Tellurian dress saber. "Bring on your Overlords—squish! Just like that!" and a whistling sweep of his atrocious weapon was illustration enough.

"May be something in that, too, Bus," he laughed. Then, to the Velantian, "About time to tune in one of 'em, I guess."

He was in no doubt whatever as to Worsel's ability to reach them. He knew that that incredibly powerful mind, without Lens or advanced Arisian instruction, had been able to cover eleven solar systems: he knew that, with his present ability, Worsel could cover half of space!

Although every fiber of his being shrieked protest against contact with the hereditary foe of his race, the Velantian put his mind en rapport with the Overlords and sent out his thought. He listened for seconds, motionless, then glided across the room to the thought-screened pilot and hissed directions. The pilot altered his course sharply and gave her the gun.

"I'll take her over now," Worsel said, presently. "It'll look better that way—more as though they had us all under control."

He cut the Bergenholm, then set everything on zero—the ship hung, inert and practically motionless, in space. Simultaneously twenty unscreened men—volunteers—dashed toward the main air lock, overcome by some intense emotion.

"Now! Screens on! Scramblers!" Kinnison yelled; and at his words a thought-screen enclosed the ship; high-powered scramblers—within whose fields no invisibility apparatus could hold—burst into action. Then the vessel was, right beside the *Dauntless*, a Boskonian in every line and member!

"Fire!"

But even as she appeared, before a firing-stud could be pressed, the enemy craft almost disappeared again; or rather, she did not really appear at all, except as the veriest wraith of what a good, solid ship of space-alloy ought to be. She was a ghost ship, as unsubstantial as fog. Mist, tenuous, immaterial; the shadow of a shadow. A dream ship, built of the gossamer of dreams, manned by figments of horror recruited from sheerest nightmare. Not invisibility this time, Kinnison knew with a profound shock. Something else—something entirely different—something utterly incomprehensible. Xylpic had said it as nearly as it could be put into understandable words—the Boskonian ship was *leaving*, although it was standing still! It was monstrous—it *couldn't be done!*

Then, at a range of only feet instead of the usual "point-blank" range of hundreds of miles, the tremendous secondaries of the *Dauntless* cut loose. At such a ridiculous range as that—why, the screens themselves kept anything farther away from them than that ship was—they *couldn't* miss. Nor did they; but neither did they hit. Those ravening beams went through and through the tenuous fabrication which should have been a vessel, but they struck nothing whatever. They went *past*—entirely harmlessly past—both the ship itself and the wraithlike but unforgettable figures which Kinnison recognized at a glance as Overlords of Delgon. His heart sank with a thud. He knew when he had had enough; and this was altogether too much.

"Go free!" he rasped. "Give 'er the oof!"

Energy poured into and through the great Bergenholm, but nothing happened; ship and contents remained inert. Not exactly inert, either, for the men were beginning to feel a new and unique sensation.

Energy raved from the driving jets, but still nothing happened. There was none of the thrust, none of the reaction of an inert start; there was none of the lashing, quivering awareness of speed which affects every mind, however hardened to free flight, in the instant of change from rest to a motion many times faster than that of light.

"Armor! Thought-screens! Emergency stations all!" Since they could not run away from whatever it was that was coming, they would face it.

*

And something was happening now, there was no doubt of that. Kinnison had been seasick and airsick and spacesick. Also, since cadets must learn to be able to do without artificial gravity, pseudo-inertia, and those other refinements which make space liners so comfortable, he had known the nausea and the queasily terrifying endless-fall sensations of weightlessness, as well as the even worse outrages of the sensibilities incident to inertialessness in its crudest, most basic applications. He thought that he was familiar with all the untoward sensations of every mode of travel known to science. This, however, was something entirely new.

He felt as though he were being compressed; not as a whole, but atom by atom. He was being twisted—cork-screwed in a monstrously obscure fashion which permitted him neither to move from his place nor to remain where he was. He hung there, poised, for hours—or was it for a thousandth of a second? At the same time he felt a painless, but revolting transformation progress in a series of waves throughout his entire body; a rearrangement, a writhing, crawling distortion, an incomprehensibly impossible extrusion of each ultimate corpuscle of his substance in an unknowable and non-existent direction!

As slowly—or as rapidly—as the transformation had waxed, it waned. He was again free to move. As far as he could tell, everything was almost as before. The *Dauntless* was about the same; so was the almost-invisible ship attached to her so closely. There was, however, a difference. The air seemed thick—familiar objects were seen blurrily, dimly—distorted—outside the ship there was nothing except a vague blur of grayness—no stars, no constellations.

A wave of thought came beating into his brain. He had to leave the *Dauntless*. It was most vitally important to go into that dimly-seen companion vessel without an instant's delay! And even as his mind instinctively reared a barrier, blocking out the intruding thought, he recognized it for what it was—the summons of the Overlords!

But how about the thought-screens, he thought in a semidaze, then reason resumed accustomed sway. He was no longer in space—at least, not in the space he knew. That new, indescribable sensation had been one of *acceleration*—when they attained constant velocity it stopped. Acceleration—velocity—in what? To what? He did not know. Out of space as he knew it, certainly. Time was distorted, unrecognizable. Matter did not necessarily obey the familiar laws. Thought? QX—thought, lying in the subether, probably was unaffected. Thought-screen generators, however, being material might not—in fact, did not—work. Worsel, Van Buskirk, and he did not need them, but those other poor devils—

He looked at them. The men—all of them, officers and all—had thrown off their armor, thrown away their weapons, and were again rushing toward the lock. With a smothered curse Kinnison followed them, as did the Velantian and the giant Dutch-Valerian. Into the lock. Through it, into the almost invisible spacetube, which, he noticed, was floored with a much denser-appearing substance. The air felt heavy; dense, like water, or even more like metallic mercury. It breathed, however, QX. Into the Boskonian ship, along corridors, into a room which was precisely such a torture chamber as Kinnison had described. There they were, ten of them; ten of the dragonlike, reptilian Overlords of Delgon!

*

They moved slowly, sluggishly, as did the Tellurians, in that thick, dense medium which was not, could not be, air. Ten chains were thrown, like pictures in slow motion, about ten human necks; ten entranced men were led unresistingly to anguished doom. This time the Gray Lensman's curse was not smothered—with a blistering deep-space oath he pulled his DeLameter and fired—once, twice, thrice. No soap—he knew it, but he had to try. Furious, he launched himself. His taloned fingers, ravening to tear, went past, not around, the Overlord's throat; and the scimitared tail of the reptile, fierce-driven, apparently went through the Lensman, screens, armor, and brisket, but touched none of them in passing. He hurled a thought a more disastrous bolt by far than he had sent against any mind since he had learned the art. In vain—the Overlords, themselves masters of mentality, could not be slain or even swerved by any forces at his command.

Kinnison reared back then in thought. There must be some ground, some substance common to the planes or dimensions involved, else they could not be here. The deck, for instance, was as solid to his feet as it was to the enemy. He thrust out a hand at the wall beside him—it was not there. The chains, however, held his suffering men, and the Overlords held the chains. The knives, also and the clubs, and the other implements of torture being wielded with such peculiarly horrible slowness.

To think was to act. He leaped forward, seized a maul, and made as though to swing it in terrific blow; only to stop, shocked. The maul did not move! Or rather, it moved, but *so* slowly, as though he were hauling it through putty! He dropped the handle, shoving it back, and received another shock, for it kept on coming under the urge of his first mighty heave—kept coming, knocking him aside as it came!

Mass! Inertia! The stuff must be a hundred times as dense as platinum!

"Bus!" he flashed a thought to the staring Valerian. "Grab one of these clubs here—a little one, even *you* can't swing a big one—and get to work!"

As he thought, he leaped again; this time for a small, slender knife, almost a scalpel, but with a long, keenly thin blade. Even though it was massive as a dozen broadswords he could swing it and he did so; plunging lethally as he swung. A full-arm sweep—razor-edge shearing, crunching through plated, corded throat—grisly head floating one way, horrid body the other!

Then an attack in waves of his own men! The Overlords knew what was toward. They commanded their slaves to abate the nuisance, and the Gray Lensman was buried under an avalanche of furious, although unarmed, humanity.

"Chase 'em off me, will you, Worsel?" Kinnison pleaded. "You're husky enough to handle 'em all—I'm not. Hold 'em off while Bus and I polish off this crowd, huh?" And Worsel did so.

Van Buskirk, scorning Kinnison's advice, had seized the biggest thing in sight, only to relinquish it sheepishly—he might as well have attempted to wield a bridge-girder! He finally selected a tiny bar, only half an inch in diameter and scarcely six feet long; but he found that even this sliver was more of a bludgeon than any spaceaxe he had ever swung.

Then the armed pair went joyously to war, the Tellurian with his knife, the Valerian with his magic wand. When the Overlords saw that a fight to the finish was inevitable they also seized weapons and fought with the desperation of the cornered rats they were. This, however, freed Worsel from guard duty, since the monsters were fully occupied in defending themselves. He seized a length of chain, wrapped six feet of tail in an unbreakable anchorage around a torture rack, and set viciously to work.

Thus again the intrepid three, the only minions of civilization theretofore to have escaped alive from the clutches of the Overlords of Delgon, fought side by side. Van Buskirk particularly was in his element. He was used to a gravity almost three times Earth's; he was accustomed to enormously heavy, almost viscous air. This stuff, thick as it was, tasted infinitely better than the vacuum that Tellurians liked to breathe. It let a man *use* his strength; and the gigantic Dutchman waded in happily, swinging his frightfully massive weapon with devastating effect. Crunch! Splash! THWUCK! When that bar struck it did not stop. It went through; blood, brains, smashed heads and dismembered limbs flying in all directions. And Worsel's lethal chain, driven irresistibly at the end of the twenty-five-foot lever of his free length of body, clanked, hummed, and snarled its way through reptilian flesh. And, while Kinnison was puny indeed in comparison with his two brothers-in-arms, he had selected a weapon which would make his skill count; and his wicked knife stabbed, sheared, and trenchantly bit.

And thus, instead of dealing out death, the Overlords died.

XVI.

The carnage over, Kinnison made his way to the control board, which was more or less standard in type. There were, however some instruments new to him; and these he examined with care, tracing their leads throughout their lengths with his sense of perception before he touched a switch. Then he pulled out three plungers, one after the other.

There was a jarring *thunk!* and a reversal of the inexplicable, sickening sensations he had experienced previously. They ceased; the ships, solid now and still locked side by side, lay again in open, familiar space.

"Back to the *Dauntless*," Kinnison directed, tersely, and they went; taking with them the bodies of the slain patrolmen. The ten who had been tortured were dead; twelve more had perished under the mental forces or the physical blows of the Overlords. Nothing could be done for any of them save to take their remains back to Tellus.

"What do we do with this ship? Let's burn her out, huh?" asked Van Buskirk.

"Not on Tuesdays—the College of Science would fry me to a crisp in my own lard if I did," Kinnison retorted. "We take her in, as is. Where are we, Worsel? Have you and the navigator found out yet?"

"'Way, 'way out—almost out of the Galaxy," Worsel replied, and one of the computers recited a string of numbers, then added, "I don't see how we could have come so far in that short a time."

"How much time was it—got any idea?" Kinnison asked, pointedly.

"Why, by the chronometers—Oh—" the man's voice trailed off.

"You're getting the idea. Wouldn't have surprised me much if we'd been clear out of the known universe. Hyperspace is funny that way, they say. Don't know a thing about it myself, except that we were in it for a while, but that's enough for me."

Back to Tellus they drove at the highest practicable speed, and at Prime Base scientists swarmed over and throughout the Boskonian vessel. They tore down, rebuilt, measured, analyzed, tested, and conferred.

"They got some of it. All of it, they say, except the stuff that is of real importance," Thorndyke reported to his friend Kinnison one day. "Old Cardynge is mad as a cateagle about your report of that vortex, or tunnel, or whatever it was. He says your lack of appreciation of the simplest fundamentals is something pitiful, or words to that effect. He's going to blast you to a cinder as soon as he gets hold of you."

"Vell, ve can't all be first violiners in der orchestra, some of us got to push vind through der trombone," Kinnison quoted, philosophically. "I done my darnedest. How's a guy going to report accurately on something he can't hear, see, feel, smell, taste, or sense? But I heard that they've solved that thing of the interpenetrability of the two kinds of matter. What's the low-down on that?"

"Cardynge says it's simple. Maybe it is, but I'm a technician myself, not a mathematician. As near as I can get it, the Overlords and their stuff were treated or conditioned with an oscillatory wave of some kind, so that under the combined action of the fields generated by the ship and the shore station all their substance was rotated almost out of space. Not out of space, exactly, either, more like, say, very nearly one hundred eighty degrees out of phase; so that two bodies—one untreated, our stuff—could occupy the same place at the same time without perceptible interference. The failure of either force, such as your cutting the ship's generators, would relieve the strain."

"It did more than that—it destroyed the vortex . . . but it might, at that," the Lensman went on, thoughtfully. "It could very well be that only that one special force, exerted in the right place relative to the home-station generator, could bring the vortex into being. But how about that heavy stuff, common to both planes, or phases, of matter?"

"Synthetic, they say. Not as dense as it appears—that's due largely to field-action, too. They're working on it now."

"Thanks for the dope. I've got to flit—got a date with Haynes. I'll see Cardynge later and let him get it off his chest," and the Lensman strode away toward the Port Admiral's office.

*

Haynes greeted him cordially; then, at sight of the storm signals flying in the Gray Lensman's eyes, he sobered.

"QX," he said, wearily. "If we have to go over this again, unload it, Kim."

"Twenty-two good men," Kinnison said, harshly. "I murdered them. Just as surely, if not quite as directly, as though I brained them with a spaceaxe."

"In one way, if you look at it fanatically enough, yes," the older man admitted, much to Kinnison's surprise. "I am not asking you to look at it in a broader sense, because you probably can't—yet. Some things you can do alone; some things you can do even better alone than with help. I have never objected; nor shall I ever object to your going alone on such missions, however dangerous they may be. That is, and will be, your job. What you are forgetting in the luxury of giving way to your emotions is that the Patrol comes first. The Patrol is of vastly greater importance than the lives of any man or group of men in it."

"But I know that, sir," protested Kinnison. "I—"

"You have a peculiar way of showing it, then," the Admiral broke in. "You say that you killed twenty-two men. Admitting it for the moment, which would you say was better for the Patrol—to lose those twenty-two good men in a successful and productive operation, or to lose the life of one Unattached Lensman without gaining any information or any other benefit whatever thereby?"

"Why . . . I—If you look at it that way, sir—" Kinnison still knew that he was right, but in that form the question answered itself.

"That is the only way it can be looked at," the old man returned, flatly. "No heroics on your part, no maudlin sentimentality. Now, as a Lensman, is it your considered judgment that it is best for the Patrol that you traverse that hyperspatial vortex alone, or with all the resources of the *Dauntless* at your command?"

Kinnison's face was white and strained. He could not lie to the Port Admiral. Nor could he tell the truth, for the dying agonies of those fiendishly tortured boys still wracked him to the core.

"But I can't order men into any such death as that," he broke out, finally.

"You must," Haynes replied, inexorably. "Either you take the ship as she is or else you call for volunteers—and you know what that would mean."

Kinnison did, too well. The surviving personnel of the two *Brittanias*, the full present complement of the *Dauntless*, the crews of every other ship in Base, practically everybody on the Reservation—Haynes himself certainly, even Lacy and old von Hohendorff, everybody, even or especially if they had no business on such a trip as that—would volunteer; and every man jack of them would yell his head off at being left out. Each would have a thousand reasons for going.

"QX, I suppose. You win." Kinnison submitted, although with ill grace, rebelliously. "But I don't like it, nor any part of it. It clogs my jets."

"I know it, Kim," Haynes put a hand upon the boy's shoulder, tightening his fingers. "We all have to do it, it's part of the job. But remember always, Lensman, that the Patrol is not an army of mercenaries or conscripts. Any one of them—just as would you yourself—would go out there, *knowing* that it meant death in the torture chamber of the Overlords, if in so doing he knew that he could help to end the torture and the slaughter of non-combatant men, women, and children that is now going on."

*

Kinnison walked slowly back to the Field; silenced, but not convinced. There was something screwy somewhere, but he couldn't—

"Just a moment, young man!" came a sharp, irritated voice. "I have been looking for you. At what time do you propose to set out for that which is being so loosely called the 'hyperspatial vortex'?"

He pulled himself out of his abstraction to see Sir Austin Cardynge. Testy, irascible, impatient, and vitriolic of tongue, he had always reminded Kinnison of a frantic hen attempting to mother a brood of ducklings.

"Hi, Sir Austin! Tomorrow—hour fifteen. Why?" The Lensman had too much on his mind to be ceremonious with this mathematical nuisance.

"Because I find that I must accompany you, and it is most damnably inconvenient, sir. The Society meets Tuesday week, and that ass Weingarde will—"

"Huh?" Kinnison ejaculated. "Who told you that you had to go along, or that you even *could*, for that matter?"

"Don't be a fool, young man!" the peppery scientist advised. "It should be apparent even to your feeble intelligence that after your fiasco, your inexcusable negligence in not reporting even the most elementary vectorial-tensorial analysis of that extremely important vortex, someone with at least a rudimentary brain should—"

"Hold on, Sir Austin!" Kinnison interrupted the harangue, "Do you mean to say that you want to come along just to study the mathematics of that damn—"

"*Just* to study it!" shrieked the old man, almost tearing his hair. "You dolt—you blockhead! My God, why should anything with such a brain be permitted to live? Don't you even know, Kinnison, that in that vortex lies the solution of one of the greatest problems in all science?"

"Never occurred to me," the Lensman replied, unruffled by the old man's acid fury. He had had weeks of it, at the Conference.

"It is imperative that I go." Sir Austin was still acerbic, but the intensity of his passion was abating. "I must analyze those fields, their patterns, interactions and reactions, myself. Unskilled observations are useless, as you learned to your sorrow, and this opportunity is priceless—possibly it is unique. Since the data must be not only complete but also entirely authoritative, I myself must go. That is clear, is it not, even to you?"

"No. Hasn't anybody told you that everybody aboard is simply flirting with the undertaker?"

"Nonsense! I have subjected the affair, every phase of it, to a rigid statistical analysis. The probability is significantly greater than zero—oh, ever so much greater, almost point one nine, in fact—that the ship will return, with my notes."

"But listen, Sir Austin," Kinnison explained patiently. "You won't have time to study the generators at the other end, even if the folks there felt inclined to give us the chance. Our object is to blow the whole thing clear out of space."

"Of course, of course—certainly! The mere generating mechanisms are immaterial. Analyses of the forces themselves are the sole desiderata. Vectors—tensors—performance of mechanisms in reception—ethereal and subethereal phenomena—propagation—xtinction—phase angles—complete and accurate data upon hundreds of such items—slighting even one would be calamitous. Having this material, however, the mechanism of energization becomes a mere detail—complete solution and design inevitable, absolute—childishly simple."

"Oh," the Lensman was slightly groggy under the barrage. "The ship may get back, but how about you, personally?"

"What difference does that make?" Cardynge snapped fretfully. "Even if, as is theoretically probable, we find that communication is impossible, my notes have a very good chance—very good indeed—of getting back. You do not seem to realize, young man, that to science that data is *necessary*. It is *so* evident that the persons or beings who are operating it do not know, or are at least not utilizing, one percent of its potentialities. They stumbled upon it—blundered into it—someone with at least a rudimentary knowledge of science must analyze it, so that the Conference may exhaust its real possibilities."

Kinnison looked down at the wispy little man in surprise. Here was something he had never suspected. Cardynge was a scientific wizard, he knew. That he had a phenomenal mind there was no shadow of doubt, but the Lensman had never thought of him as being physically brave. It was not merely courage, he decided. It was something bigger—better. Transcendent. An utter selflessness, a devotion to science so complete that neither physical welfare nor even life itself could be given any consideration whatever.

"You think, then, that this data is worth sacrificing the lives of four hundred men, including yours and mine, to get?" Kinnison asked, earnestly.

"Certainly, or a hundred times that many," Cardynge snapped, testily. "You heard me say, did you not, that this opportunity is priceless, and may very well be unique?"

"QX, you can come," and Kinnison went on into the *Dauntless*.

*

632

Kinnison went to bed wondering. Maybe the chief was right. He woke up, still wondering. Perhaps he was taking himself too seriously. Perhaps he was, as Haynes had more than intimated, indulging in mock heroics.

He prowled about. The two ships of space were still locked together. They would fly together to and along that dread tunnel, and he had to see that everything was on the green.

He went into the wardroom. One young officer was thumping the piano right tunefully and a dozen others were rending the atmosphere with joyous song. In that room any formality or "as you were" signal was unnecessary; the whole bunch fell upon their commander gleefully and with a complete lack of restraint, in a vociferous hilarity very evidently neither forced nor assumed.

Kinnison went on with his tour. "What was it?" he demanded of himself. Haynes didn't feel guilty. Cardynge was worse—he would kill forty thousand men, including the Lensman and himself, without batting an eye. These kids didn't give a damn. Their fellows had been slain by the Overlords, the Overlords had in turn been slain. All square—QX. Their turn next? So what? Kinnison himself did not want to die—he wanted to live—but if his number came up that was part of the game.

What was it, this willingness to give up life itself for an abstraction? Science, the Patrol, Civilization—notoriously ungrateful mistresses. Why? Some inner force—some compensation defying sense, reason, or analysis?

Whatever it was, he had it, too. Why deny it to others? What in all the nine hells of Valeria was he griping about?

"Maybe *I'm* nuts!" he concluded, and gave the word to blast off.

To blast off—to find and to traverse wholly that awful hypertube, at whose far terminus there would be lurking no man knew what.

XVII.

Out in space Kinnison called the entire crew to a mass meeting, in which he outlined to them as well as he could that which they were about to face.

"The Boskonian ship will undoubtedly return automatically to her dock," he concluded. "That there is probably docking space for only one ship is immaterial, since the *Dauntless* will remain free. That ship is not manned, as you know, because no one knows what is going to happen when the fields are released in the home dock. Consequences may be disastrous to any foreign, untreated matter within her. Some signal will undoubtedly be given upon landing, although we have no means of knowing what that signal will be and Sir Austin has pointed out that there can be no communication between that ship and her base until her generators have been cut.

"Since we also will be in hyperspace until that time, it is clear that the generator must be cut from within the vessel. Electrical and mechanical relays are out of the question. Therefore two of our personnel will keep alternate watches in her control room, to pull the necessary switches. I am not going to order any man to such a duty, nor am I going to ask for volunteers. If the man on duty is not killed outright—this is a distinct possibility, although not a probability—speed in getting back here will be decidedly of the essence. It seems to me that the best interests of the Patrol will be served by having the two fastest members of our force on watch. Time trials from the Boskonian panel to our air lock are, therefore, now in order."

This was Kinnison's device for taking the job himself. He was, he knew, the fastest man aboard, and he proved it. He negotiated the distance in seven seconds flat, over half a second faster than any other member of the crew. Then:

"Well, if you small, slow runts are done playing creepie-mousie, get out of the way and let folks run that really can," Van Buskirk boomed. "Come on, Worsel, I see where you and I are going to get ourselves a job."

"But see here, you can't!" Kinnison protested, aghast. "I said members of the crew."

"No, you didn't," the Valerian contradicted. "You said 'two of our personnel,' and if Worsel and I ain't personnel, what are we? We'll leave it to Sir Austin."

"Indubitably 'personnel,'" the arbiter decided, taking a moment from the apparatus he was setting up. "Your statement that speed is a prime requisite is also binding."

Whereupon the winged Velantian flew and wriggled the distance in two seconds, and the steel-thewed Dutch-Valerian ran it in three!

"You big, knot-headed Valerian ape!" Kinnison hissed a malevolent thought; not as the expedition's commander to a subordinate, but as an outraged friend speaking plainly to friend. "You knew I wanted that job myself, you clunker—damn your thick, hard crust!"

"Well, so did I, you poor, spindly little Tellurian wart, and so did Worsel," the giant warrior shot back in kind. "Besides it's for the good of the Patrol—you said so yourself! Comb *that* out of your whiskers, half-portion!" he added, with a wide and toothy grin, as he swaggered away, lightly brandishing his ponderous mace.

The run to the point in space where the vortex had been was made on schedule. Switches drove home, most of the fabric of the enemy vessel went out of phase, the voyagers experienced the weirdly uncomfortable acceleration along an impossible vector, and the familiar firmament disappeared into an impalpable but impenetrable murk of featureless, textureless gray.

Sir Austin was in his element. Indeed, he was in the seventh heaven of rapture as he observed, recorded, and calculated. He chuckled over his interferometers, he clucked over his meters, now and again he emitted shrill whoops of triumph as a particularly abstruse bit of knowledge was torn from its lair. He strutted, he gloated, he practically purred as he recorded upon the tape still another momentous conclusion or a gravid equation, each couched in terms of such incomprehensibly formidable mathematics that no one not a member of the Conference of Scientists could even dimly perceive its meaning.

Cardynge finished his work; and, after doing everything that could be done to insure the safe return to Science of his priceless records, he simply preened himself. He wasn't like an old hen, after all, Kinnison decided. More like a lean, gray tomcat. One that has just eaten the canary and, contemplatively smoothing his whiskers, is full of pleasant, if somewhat sanguine visions of what he is going to do to those other felines at that next meeting.

Time wore on. A long time? Or a short? Who could tell? What possible measure of that unknown and intrinsically unknowable concept exists or can exist in that fantastic region of—hyperspace? Interspace? Pseudospace? Call it what you like.

*

Time, as has been said, wore on. The ships arrived at the enemy base, the landing signal was given. Worsel, on duty at the time, recognized it for what it was—with his brain that was a foregone conclusion. He threw the switches, then flew and wriggled as even he had never done before, hurling a thought as he came.

And as the Velantian, himself in the throes of weird deceleration, tore through the thinning atmosphere, the queasy Gray Lensman watched the development about them of a forbiddingly inimical scene.

They were materializing upon a landing field of sorts, a smooth and level expanse of black igneous rock. Two suns, one hot and close, one pale and distant, cast the impenetrable shadows so characteristic of an airless world. Dwarfed by distance, but still massively, craggily tremendous, there loomed the encircling rampart of the volcanic crater upon whose floor the fortress lay.

And what a fortress! New—raw—crude—but fanged with armament of might. There was the typically Boskonian dome of control, there were powerful ships of war in their cradles, there beside the *Dauntless* was very evidently the power plant in which was generated the cryptic force which made interdimensional transit an actuality. But, and here was the saving factor which the Lensman had dared only half hope to find, those ultrapowerful defensive mechanisms were mounted to resist attack from without, not from within. It had not occurred to the foe, even as a possibility, that the Patrol might come upon them in panoply of war through their own hyperspatial tube!

Kinnison knew that it was useless to assault that dome. He could, perhaps, crack its screens with his primaries, but he did not have enough stuff to reduce the whole establishment and therefore could not use the primaries at all. Since the enemy had been taken completely by surprise, however, he had a lot of time—at least a minute, perhaps a trifle more—and in that time the old *Dauntless* could do a lot of damage. The power plant came first; that was what they had come out here to get.

"All secondaries fire at will!" Kinnison barked into his microphone. He was already at his conning board, every man of the crew was at his station. "All of you who can reach twenty-seven, three-oh-eight, hit it—hard. The rest of you do as you please."

Every beam which could be brought to bear upon the powerhouse, and there were plenty of them, flamed out practically as one. The building stood for an instant, starkly outlined in a raging inferno of incandescence, then slumped down flabbily; its upper, nearer parts flaring away in clouds of sparklingly luminous vapor even as its lower members flowed sluggishly together in streams of molted metal. Deeper and deeper bored the frightful beams; foundations, subcellars, structural members and Gargantuan mechanisms uniting with the obsidian of the crater's floor to form a lake of bubbling, frothing lava.

"QX—that's good!" Kinnison snapped. "Scatter your stuff, fellows—hit 'em!"

Kinnison then spoke to Henderson, his chief pilot. "Lift us up a bit, Hen, to give the boys a better sight. Be ready to flit, fast; all hell's going to be out for noon any second now!"

Ships—warships of Boskone's mightiest—caught cold. Some crewless; some half-manned; none ready for the stunning surprise attack of the Patrolmen. Through and through them the ruthless beams tore; leaving, not ships, but nondescript masses of half-fused metal. Hangars, machine shops, supply depots suffered the same fate; a good third of the establishment became a smoking, smoldering heap of junk.

Then, one by one, the fixed-mount weapons of the enemy, by dint of what Herculean efforts can only be surmised, were brought to bear upon the bold invader. Brighter and brighter flamed her prodigiously powerful defensive screens. Number One faded out; crushed flat by the hellish energies of Boskone's projectors. Number Two flared into ever more spectacular pyrotechnics, until soon even its tremendous resources of power became inadequate—blotchily, in discrete areas, clinging to existence when all the might of its Medonian generators and transmitters, it, too, began to fall.

"Better we flit, Hen, while we're all in one piece—right now," Kinnison advised the pilot then. "And I don't mean loaf, either. Let's see you burn a hole in the ether."

Henderson's fingers swept over his board, depressing to maximum and locking down key after key. Blast after blast flared from her jets of energies of an intensity almost to pale the brilliance of the madly warring screens, and to Boskone's observers the immense Patrol raider vanished from all ken.

*

At that drive, the *Dauntless* incomprehensible maximum, there was little danger of pursuit: for, as well as being the biggest and the most powerfully armed, she was also the fastest thing in space.

Out in open intergalactic space—safe—discipline went by the board as though on signal and all hands joined in a release of pent-up emotion. Kinnison threw off his armor and, seizing the scandalized and highly outraged Cardynge, spun him around in dizzying, though effortless circles.

"Didn't lose a man—NOT A MAN!" he yelled, exuberantly.

He plucked the now idle Henderson from his board and wrestled with him, only to drift lightly away, ahead of a tremendous slap aimed at his back by Van Buskirk. Inertialessness takes most of the edge off rough housing, but the performance did relieve the tension and soon the ebullient youths quieted down.

The enemy base was located well outside the Galaxy. Not, as Kinnison had feared, in the Second Galaxy, but in a star cluster not too far removed from the first. Hence the flight to Prime Base did not take long.

Sir Austin Cardynge was more like a self-satisfied tomcat than ever as he gathered up his records, gave a corps of aides minute instructions regarding the packing of his equipment, and set out, figuratively but very evidently licking his chops, rehearsing the scene in which he would confound his allegedly learned fellows, especially that insufferable puppy, that upstart Weingarde.

"And that's that," Kinnison concluded his informal report to Haynes. "They're all washed up, there, at least. Before they can rebuild, you can wipe out the whole nest. If there should happen to be one or two more such bases, the boys know now how to handle them. I think I'd better be getting back onto my own job, don't you?"

"Probably so," Haynes thought for moments, then continued: "Can you use help, or can you work better alone?"

"I've been thinking about that. The higher the tougher, and it might not be a bad idea at all to have Worsel standing by in my speedster; close by and ready all the time. He's pretty much of an army himself, mental and physical. QX?"

"Can do," and thus it came about that the good ship *Dauntless* flew again, this time out Borova way; her sole freight a sleek black speedster and a rusty, battered meteor-tug, her passengers a sinuous Velantian and a husky Tellurian.

"Sort of a thin time for you, old man, I'm afraid." Kinnison leaned unconcernedly against the towering pillar of his friend's tail, whereupon four or five grotesquely stalked eyes curled out at him speculatively. To these two, each other's appearance and shape were neither repulsive nor strange. They were friends, in the deepest, truest sense. "He's so hideous that he's positively distinguished-looking," each had boasted more than once of the other to friends of his own race.

"Nothing like that." The Velantian flashed out a leather wing and flipped his tail aside in a playfully unsuccessful attempt to catch the Earthman off balance. "Some day, if you ever learn really to think, you will discover that a few weeks' solitary, undisturbed and concentrated thought is a rare treat. To have such an opportunity in the line of duty makes it a pleasure unalloyed."

"I always did think that you were slightly screwy at times, and now I know it," Kinnison retorted, unconvinced. "Thought is—or should be—a means to an end, not an end in itself; but if that's your idea of a wonderful time I'm glad to be able to give it to you."

*

They disembarked carefully in far space, the complete absence of spectators assured by the warship's fullest reach of detectors, and Kinnison again went down to Miners' Rest. Not, this time, to carouse. Miners were not carousing there. Instead, the whole asteroid was buzzing with news of the fabulously rich finds which were being made in the distant solar system of Tressilia.

Kinnison had known that the news would be there, for it was at his instructions that those rich meteors had been placed there to be found. Tressilia III was the home of the Regional Director with whom the Gray Lensman had important business to transact; he had to have a solid reason, not a mere excuse, for Bill Williams to leave Borova for Tressilia.

The lure of wealth, then as ever, was stronger even than that of drink or of drug. Miners came to revel, but instead they outfitted in haste and hied themselves to the new Klondike. Nor was this anything out of the ordinary. Such stampedes occurred every once in a while, and Strongheart and his minions were not unduly concerned. They'd be back, and in the meantime there was the profit on a lot of metal and an excess profit due to the skyrocketing prices of supplies.

"You too, Bill?" Strongheart asked without surprise.

"I'll tell the Universe!" came ready answer. "If there's metal there, I'll find it, pal." In making this declaration he was not boasting, he was merely voicing a simple truth. By this time the meteor belts of a hundred solar systems knew for a fact that Wild Bill Williams, of Aldebaran II could find metal if metal was there to be found.

"If it's a bloomer, Bill, come back," the divekeeper urged. "Come back anyway when you've worked it a couple of drunks."

"I'll do that, Strongheart old pal, I sure will," the Lensman agreed, amiably enough. "You run a nice joint here and I like it."

Thus Kinnison went to the asteroid belts of Tressilia and there Bill Williams found rich metal. Or, more precisely, he dumped out into space and then recovered a very special meteor indeed—one in whose fabrication Kinnison's own treasure-trove had played a leading part. He did not find it the first day, of course, nor during the first week—it would be a trifle smelly to have even Wild Bill strike it rich too soon—but after a decent interval of time.

His Tressilian find had to be very much worth while, far too much so to be left to chance; for Edmund Crowninshield, the Regional Director, inhabited no such rawly obvious dive as Miners' Rest. He catered only to the upper crust; meteor miners and other similar scum were never permitted to enter his door.

When Kinnison repaired the Bergenholm of the Borovan spaceliner he had, by sheerest accident, laid the groundwork of a perfect approach, and now he was taking advantage of the circumstance. That incident had been reported widely: it was well known that Wild Bill Williams had been a gentleman once. If he should strike it rich—really rich—what would be more natural than that he should forsake the noisesome space hells he had been wont to frequent in favor of such gilded palaces of sin as the Crown-On-Shield?

In due time, then, Kinnison "found" his special meteor, which was big enough and rich enough so that any miner would have taken it to a Patrol station instead of to a space robber. He disposed of his whole load by analysis; then, with more money in the bank than William Williams had ever dreamed of having, he hesitated visibly before embarking upon one of the gorgeous, spectacular sprees from which he had derived his nickname. He hesitated; then, with an effort apparent to all observers, he changed his mind.

He had been a gentleman once, he would be again. He had his hair cut, he had himself shaved every day. Manicurists dug away and scrubbed away the ingrained grime from his hardened, meteor-miner's paws. His nails, even, became pink and glossy. He bought clothes, including the full-dress shorts, barrel-top jacket, and voluminous cloak of the Aldebaranian gentleman, and wore them with easy grace.

And in the meantime he was drinking steadily. He drank, however, only the choicest beverages; decorously and—for him—sparingly. Thus, while he was seldom what could be called strictly sober, he was never really drunk. He shunned low resorts, living in the best hotels and frequenting only the finest taverns. The finest, that is, with one exception, the

Crown-On-Shield. Not only did he not go there, he never spoke of or would discuss the place. It was as though for him it did not exist.

Occasionally he escorted—oh, so correctly!—a charming companion to supper or to the theater, but ordinarily he was alone. Alone by choice. Aloof, austere, possibly not quite sure of himself. He rebuffed all attempts to inveigle him into any one of the numerous cliques with which the "upper crust" abounded. He waited for what he knew would come.

*

Underlings of gradually increasing numbers and importance came to him with invitations to the Crown-On-Shield, but he refused them all; curtly, definitely, and without giving reason or excuse. In the light of what he was going to do there he could not be seen in the place unless and until it was clear to all that the visit was not of his design. Finally Crowninshield himself met the ex-miner as though by accident.

"Why haven't you been out to our place, Mr. Williams?" he asked, heartily.

"Because I didn't want to, and don't want to," Kinnison replied, flatly and definitely.

"But why?" demanded the Boskonian Director, this time in genuine surprise. "It's getting talked about—*everybody* comes to the Crown!—people are wondering why you never even look in on us."

"You know who I am, don't you?" The Lensman's voice was coldly level, uninflected.

"Certainly. William Williams, formerly of Aldebaran II."

"No. Wild Bill Williams, meteor miner. The Crown-On-Shield boasts that it does not solicit the patronage of men of my profession. If I go there, some dim-wit will start blasting off about miners. Then you'll have the job of mopping him up off the floor with a sponge and the Patrol will be after me with a speedster. Thanks just the same, but none of that for me."

"Oh, is *that* all?" Crowninshield smiled in relief. "Perhaps a natural misapprehension, Mr. Williams, but you are entirely mistaken. It is true that practicing miners do not find our society congenial, but you are no longer a miner and we never refer to any man's past. As an Aldebaranian gentleman we would welcome you. And, in the extremely remote contingency to which you refer, I assure you that you would not have to act. Any guest so boorish would be expelled."

"In that case I would really enjoy spending a little time with you. It has been a long time since I associated with persons of breeding," he explained, with engaging candor.

"I'll have a boy see to the transfer of your things," and thus the Gray Lensman allowed the zwilnik to persuade him to visit the one place in the Universe where he most ardently wished to be.

For days in the new environment everything went on with the utmost decorum and circumspection, but Kinnison was not deceived. They would feel him out some way, just as effectively if not as crassly as did the zwilniks of Miners' Rest. They would have to—this was Regional Headquarters. At first he had been suspicious of thionite, but since the high-ups were not wearing anti-thionite plugs in their nostrils, he wouldn't have to either.

Then one evening a girl—young, pretty, vivacious—approached him, a pinch of purple powder between her fingers. As the Gray Lensman he knew that the stuff was not thionite, but as William Williams he did not.

"*Do* have a tiny smell of thionite, Mr. Williams!" she urged, coquettishly, and made as though to blow it into his face.

Williams reacted strangely, but instantaneously. He ducked with startling speed and the flat of his palm smacked ringingly against the girl's cheek. He did not slap her hard—it looked and sounded much worse than it really was—the only actual force was in the follow-up push that sent her flying across the room.

"Whatja mean, you? You can't slap girls around like that here!" and the chief bouncer came at him with a rush.

This time the Lensman did not pull his punch. He struck with everything he had, from heels to fingertips. Such was the sheer brute power of the blow that the bouncer literally somersaulted the length of the room, bringing up with a crash against the distant wall; so accurate was its placement that the victim, while not killed outright, would be unconscious for many hours to come.

Others turned then, and paused; for Williams was not running away; he was not even giving ground. Instead, he stood lightly poised upon the balls of his feet, knees bent the veriest trifle, arms hanging at ready, eyes as hard and as cold as the iron meteorites of the space he knew so well.

"Any others of you damn zwilniks want to make a pass at me?" he demanded, and a concerted gasp arose: the word "zwilnik" was in those circles far worse than a mere fighting word. It was absolutely taboo: it was *never*, under any circumstance, uttered.

Nevertheless, no action was taken. At first the cold arrogance, the sheer effrontery of the man's pose held them in check; then they noticed one thing and remembered another, the combination of which gave them most emphatically to pause.

No garment, even by the most deliberate intent, could possibly have been designed as a better hiding place for DeLameters than the barrel-topped full-dress jacket of Aldebaran II; and—

Mr. William Williams, poised there in steel-spring readiness for action; so coldly self-confident; so inexplicably, so scornfully derisive of that whole roomful of men not a few of whom he knew must be armed; was also the Wild Bill Williams, meteor miner, who was widely known as the fastest and deadliest performer with twin DeLameters who had ever infested space!

XVIII.

Edmund Crowninshield sat in his office and seethed quietly, the all-pervasive blueness of the Kalonian brought out even more prominently than usual by his mood. His plan to find out whether or not the ex-miner was a spy had backfired, badly. He had had reports from Euphrosyne that the fellow was not—*could* not be—a spy, and now his test had confirmed that conclusion, too thoroughly by far. He would have to do some mighty quick thinking and perhaps some salve-spreading or lose him. He certainly didn't want to lose a client who had over a quarter of a million credits to throw away, and who could not possibly resist his cravings for alcohol and bentlam much longer! But curse him, what had the fellow meant by having a kit-bag built of indurite, with a lock on it that not even his cleverest artists could pick!

"Come in," he called, unctuously, in answer to a tap. "Oh, it's you! What did you find out?"

"Janice isn't hurt. He didn't make a mark on her—just gave her a shove and scared hell out of her. But Clovis was nudged, believe me. He's still out—will be for hours, the doctor says. What a sock that guy's got! Clovis looks like he'd been hit with a Valerian maul."

"You're sure he was armed?"

"Must have been. Typical gun fighter's crouch. He was ready, not bluffing, believe me. The man don't live that could bluff a roomful of us like that. He was betting that he could whiff us all before we could get a gun out, and I wouldn't wonder if he was right."

"QX. Beat it, and don't let anyone come near here except Williams."

Therefore the ex-miner was the next visitor.

"You wanted to see me, Crowninshield, before I flit." Kinnison was fully dressed, even to his flowing cloak, and he was carrying his own kit. This, in an Aldebaranian, implied the extremest height of dudgeon.

"Yes, Mr. Williams, I wish to apologize for the house. However," somewhat exasperated, "it does seem that you were abrupt, to say the least, in your reaction to a childish prank."

"Prank!" The Aldebaranian's voice was decidedly unfriendly. "Sir, to me thionite is no prank. I don't mind nitrolabe or heroin, and a little bentlam now and then is good for a man, but when anyone comes around me with thionite I object, sir, vigorously, and I don't care who knows it."

"Evidently. But that wasn't really thionite—we would never permit it—and Miss Carter is an exemplary young lady—"

"How was I to know it wasn't thionite?" Williams demanded. "And as for your Miss Carter, as long as a woman acts like a lady I treat her like a lady, but if she acts like a zwilnik—"

"Please, Mr. Williams—"

"—I treat her like a zwilnik, and that's that."

"Mr. Williams, please! Not that word, ever!"

"No? A planetary idiosyncrasy, perhaps?" The ex-miner's towering wrath abated into curiosity. "Now that you mention it, I do not recall having heard it lately, nor hereabouts. For its use please accept my apology."

Oh, this was better. Crowninshield was making headway. The big Aldebaranian didn't even know thionite when he saw it, and he had a rabid fear of it.

"There remains, then, only the very peculiar circumstance of your wearing arms here in a quiet hotel—"

"Who says I was armed?" Kinnison demanded.

"Why . . . I . . . it was assumed—" The proprietor was flabbergasted.

The visitor threw off his coat and removed his jacket, revealing a shirt of sheer glamorette through which could be plainly seen his hirsute chest and the smooth, bronzed skin of his brawny shoulders. He strode over to his kit-bag, unlocked it, and took out a double DeLameter harness, complete with instruments. He donned the contraption, put on jacket and cloak—open, now, this latter—shrugged his shoulders a few times to settle the new burden into its wonted position, and turned again to the hotelkeeper.

"This is the first time that I have worn this hardware since I came here," he said, quietly. "Having the name, however, you may take it upon the very best of authority that I will be armed during the remaining minutes of my visit here. With your permission, I shall leave now."

"Oh, no, that won't do, sir, really." Crowninshield was almost abject at the prospect. "We should be desolated. Mistakes will happen, sir—planetary prejudices—misunderstandings. Give us a little more time to get really acquainted, sir—" and thus it went.

Finally Kinnison let himself be mollified into staying on. With true Aldebaranian mulishness, however, he wore his armament, proclaiming to all and sundry his sole reason therefor: "An Aldebaranian gentleman, sir, keeps his word; however lightly or under whatever circumstances given. I said that I would wear these things as long as I stay here; therefore wear them I must and I shall. I will leave here any time, sir, gladly; but while here I remain armed, every minute of every day."

And he did. He never drew them, was always and in every way a gentleman. Nevertheless, the zwilniks were always uncomfortably conscious of the fact that those grim, formidable portables were there—always there and always ready. The fact that they themselves went armed with weapons deadly enough was all too little reassurance.

*

Always the quintessence of good behavior, Kinnison began to relax his barriers of reserve. He began to drink—to buy, at least—more and more. He had taken regularly a little bentlam; now, as though his will to moderation had begun to go down, he took larger and larger doses. It was not a significant fact to any one, except himself, that the nearer drew the time for a certain momentous meeting the more he apparently drank and the larger the doses of bentlam became.

Thus it was a purely unnoticed coincidence that it was upon the afternoon of the day during whose evening the conference was to be held that Williams' quiet and gentlemanly drunkenness degenerated into a noisy and obstreperous carousal. As a climax he demanded—and obtained—the twenty-four units of bentlam which, his host knew, comprised the highest-ceiling dose of the old, unregenerate mining days. They gave him the Titanic jolt, undressed him, put him carefully to bed upon a soft mattress covered with silken sheets and forgot him.

Before the meeting every possible source of interruption or spying was checked, rechecked, and guarded against; but no one even thought of suspecting the free-spending, hard-drinking, drug-soaked Williams. How could they?

And so it came about that the Gray Lensman attended that meeting also; as insidiously and as successfully as he had the one upon Euphrosyne. It took longer, this time, to read the reports, notes, orders, addresses, and so on, for this was a Regional meeting, not merely a local one. However, the Lensman had ample time and was a fast reader withal; and in Worsel he had an aide who could tape the stuff as fast as he could send it in. Wherefore, when the meeting broke up Kinnison was well content. He had forged another link in his chain—was one link nearer to Boskone, his goal.

As soon as Kinnison could walk without staggering he sought out his host. He was ashamed, embarrassed, bitterly and painfully humiliated; but he was still—or again—an Aldebaranian gentleman. He had made a resolution, and gentlemen of that planet did not take their gentlemanliness lightly.

"First, Mr. Crowninshield, I wish to apologize, most humbly, most profoundly, sir, for the fashion in which I have outraged your hospitality." He could slap down a girl and half-kill a guard without loss of self-esteem, but no gentleman, however inebriated, should descend to such depths of commonness and vulgarity as he had plumbed here. Such conduct was inexcusable. "I have nothing whatever to say in defense or palliation of my conduct. I can only say that in order to spare you the task of ordering me out, I am leaving."

"Oh, come, Mr. Williams, that is not at all necessary. Anyone is apt to take a drop too much occasionally. Really, my friend, you were not at all offensive, we have not even entertained the thought of your leaving us." Nor had he. The ten thousand credits which the Lensman had thrown away during his spree would have condoned behavior a thousand times worse; but Crowninshield did not refer to that.

"Thank you for your courtesy, sir, but I remember some of my actions, and I blush with shame," the Aldebaranian rejoined, stiffly. He was not to be mollified. "I could never look your other guests in the face again. I think, sir, that I can still be a gentleman; but until I am certain of the fact—until I know I can get drunk as a gentleman should—I am going to change my name and disappear. Until a happier day, sir, good-by."

Nothing could make the stiff-necked Williams change his mind, and leave he did, scattering five-credit notes abroad as he departed. However, he did not go far. As he had explained so carefully to Crowninshield, William Williams did disappear—forever, Kinnison hoped; he was all done with him—but the Gray Lensman made connections with Worsel.

"Thanks, old man," Kinnison shook one of the Velantian's gnarled, hard hands, even though Worsel never had had much use for that peculiarly human gesture. "Nice work. I won't need you for a while now, but I probably will later. If I succeed in getting the data I'll Lens it to you as usual for record—I'll be even less able than usual, I imagine, to take recording apparatus with me. If I can't get it I'll call you anyway, to help me make other arrangements. Clear ether, big fella!"

"Luck, Kinnison," and the two Lensmen went their separate ways; Worsel to Prime Base, the Tellurian on a long flit indeed. He had not been surprised to learn that the Galactic Director was not in the Galaxy proper, but in a star cluster; nor at the information that he whom he sought was one Jalte, a Kalonian. Boskone, Kinnison thought, was a highly methodical sort of a chap—he marked out the best way to do anything, and then stuck by it through thick and thin.

*

Kinnison was almost wrong there, for not long afterward Boskone was called in session and that very question was discussed seriously and at length.

"Granted that the Kalonians are good executives," the new Ninth of Boskone argued. "They are strong of mind and do produce results. It cannot be claimed, however, that they are in any sense comparable to us of the Eich. Eichlan was thinking of replacing Helmuth, but he put off acting until it was too late.

"There are many factors to consider," the First replied, gravely. "The planet is uninhabitable save for warm-blooded oxygen-breathers. The base is built for such, and such is the entire personnel. Years of time went into the construction there. One of us could not work efficiently alone, insulated against its heat and its atmosphere. If the whole dome were conditioned for us, we must needs train an entire new organization to man it. Then, too, the Kalonians have to work well in hand and, with all due respect to you and the others of your mind, it is by no means certain that even Eichlan could have saved Helmuth's base had he been there. Eichlan's own doubt upon this point had much to do with his delay in acting. In the end it comes down to efficiency, and some Kalonians are efficient. Jalte is one. And, while it may seem as though I am boasting of my own selection of directors, please note that Prellin, the Kalonian director upon Bronseca, seems to have been able to stop the advance of the Patrol."

"'Seems to' may be too exactly descriptive for comfort," said another, darkly.

"That is always a possibility," was conceded, "but whenever that Lensman has been able to act, he has acted. Our keenest observers can find no trace of his activities elsewhere, with the possible exception of the misfunctioning of the experimental hyperspatial tube of our allies of Delgon. Some of us have from the first considered that venture ill-advised, premature; and its seizure by the Patrol smacks more of their able mathematical physicists than of a purely hypothetical, superhuman Lensman. Therefore, it seems logical to assume that Prellin has stopped him. Our observers report that the Patrol is loath to act illegally without evidence, and no evidence can be obtained. Business was hurt, but Jalte is reorganizing as rapidly as may be."

"I still say that the Galactic Base should be rebuilt and manned by the Eich," Nine insisted. "It is our sole remaining Grand Headquarters there, and since it is both the brain of the peaceful conquest and the nucleus of our new military organization, it should not be subjected to any unnecessary risk."

"And you will, of course, be glad to take that highly important command, man the dome with your own people, and face the Lensman—if and when he comes—backed by the forces of the Patrol?"

"Why . . . ah . . . no," the Ninth managed. "I am of so much more use here—"

"That's what we all think," the first said, cynically. "While I would like very much to welcome that hypothetical Lensman here, I do not care to meet him upon any other planet. I really believe, however, that any change in our organization would weaken it seriously. Jalte is capable, energetic, and is as well informed as is any of us as to the possibilities of invasion by the Lensman or his Patrol. Beyond asking him whether he needs anything, and sending him everything he may wish of supplies and of reinforcements, I do not see how he can improve matters."

But even before the question was asked, Kinnison's blackly invisible, indetectable speedster was well within the star cluster. The guardian fortresses were closer spaced by far than Helmuth's had been. Electromagnetics had a three hundred percent overlap; ether and subether alike were suffused with vibratory fields in which nullification of detection was impossible, and the observers were alert and keen. To what avail? The speedster was non-ferrous, intrinsically indetectable; the Lensman slipped through the net with ease.

Sliding down the edge of the world's black shadow he felt for the expected thought-screen, found it, dropped cautiously through it, and poised there; observing during one whole rotation. This had been a fair, green world—once. It had had forests. It had once been peopled by intelligent, urban dwellers, who had had roads, works, and other evidences of advancement. But the cities had been melted down into vast lakes of lava and slag. Cold now for years, cracked, fissured, weathered; yet to Kinnison's probing sense they told tales of horror, revealed all too clearly the incredible ferocity and ruthlessness with which the conquerors had wiped out all the population of a world. What had been roads and works were jagged ravines and craters of destruction. The forests of the planet had been burned, again and again; only a few charred stumps remaining to mark where a few of the mightiest monarchs had stood. Except for the Boskonian base the planet was a scene of desolation and ravishment indescribable.

"They'll pay for that, too, the fiends," Kinnison gritted, and directed his attention toward the base. Forbidding indeed it loomed; thrice a hundred square miles of massively banked offensive and defensive armament, with a central dome of such colossal mass as to dwarf even the stupendous fabrications surrounding it. Typical Boskonian layout, Kinnison thought, very much like Helmuth's Grand Base. Fully as large and as strong, or stronger—but he had cracked that one and he was pretty sure that he could crack this. Exploringly he sent out his sense of perception; nor was he surprised to find that the whole aggregation of structures was screened. He had not thought that it would be as easy as that!

He did not need to get inside the dome this time, as he was not going to work directly upon the personnel. Inside the screen anywhere would do. But how to get there? The ground all around the thing was flat, as level as molten lava would cool, and every inch of it was bathed in the white glare of floodlights. They had observers, of course, and photocells, which were worse.

Approach then, either through the air or upon the ground, did not look so promising. That left only underground. They got water from somewhere—wells, perhaps—and their sewage went somewhere unless they incinerated it, which was highly improbable. There was a river over there, he'd see if there wasn't a trunk sewer running into it somewhere. There was. There was also a place within easy flying distance to hide his speedster, an overhanging bank of smooth black rock. The risk of his being seen was nil, anyway, for the only intelligent life left upon the planet inhabited the Boskonian fortress and did not leave it.

Donning his space-black, indetectable armor, Kinnison flew down the river to the sewer's mouth. He lowered himself into the placid stream and against the sluggish current of the sewer he made his way. The drivers of his suit were not as efficient in water as they were in air or in space, and in the dense medium his pace was necessarily slow. But he was in no hurry. It was fast enough—in a few hours he was beneath the stronghold.

*

He then began his study of the dome. It was like Helmuth's in some ways, entirely different from it in others. There were fully as many firing-stations, each with its operators ready at signal to energize and to direct the most terrifically destructive agencies known to the science of the time. There were fewer visiplates and communicators, fewer catwalks; but there were vastly more individual offices and there were ranks and tiers of filing cabinets. There would have to be; this was headquarters for the organized illicit commerce of an entire galaxy. There, in the familiar center, sat at his great desk Jalte the Kalonian, and beside him there sparkled the peculiar globe of force which the Lensman now knew was an intergalactic communicator.

"Ha!" Kinnison exclaimed triumphantly, if inaudibly, to himself, "the real boss of the outfit—Boskone—is in the Second Galaxy!"

He would have to wait until that communicator went into action, if it took a month. But in the meantime there was plenty to do. Those cabinets at least were not thought-screened, they held all the really vital secrets of the drug ring, and it would take many days to transmit the information which the Patrol must have if it were to make a one-hundred-percent clean-up of the whole zwilnik organization.

He called Worsel, and, upon being informed that the recorders were ready, he started in. Characteristically, he began with Prellin of Bronseca, and memorized the data covering that wight as he transmitted it. The next one to go down upon the steel tape was Crowninshield of Tressilia. Having exhausted all the filed information upon the organization controlled by those two Regional Directors, he took the rest of them in order.

He had finished his real task and had practically finished a detailed survey of the entire Base when the force-ball communicator burst into activity. Knowing approximately the analysis of the beam and exactly its location in space, it took only seconds for Kinnison to tap it; but the longer the interview went on the more disappointed the Lensman grew. Orders, reports, discussions of broad matters of policy—it was simply a conference between two high executives of a vast business firm.

"I assume from lack of mention that *the* Lensman has made no further progress," Eichmil concluded.

"Not so far as our best men can discover," Jalte replied, carefully, and Kinnison grinned like the Cheshire cat in his secure, if uncomfortable, retreat. It tickled his vanity immensely to be referred to so matter-of-factly as *the* Lensman, and he felt very smart and cagy indeed to be within a few hundred feet of Jalte as the Boskonian uttered the words. "Lensmen by the score are still working Prellin's base in Cominoche. Some twelve of these—human or approximately so—have been returning again and again. We are checking those with care, because of the possibility that one of them may be the one we want, but as yet I can make no conclusive report."

The connection was broken, and the Lensman's brief thrill of elated self-satisfaction died away.

"No soap," he growled to himself in disgust. "I've *got* to get into that guy's mind, some way or other!"

How could he make the approach? Every man in the Base wore a head-screen, and they were mighty careful. No dogs or other pet animals. There were few birds, but it would smell very cheesy indeed to have a bird flying around, pecking at screen generators. To anyone with half a brain that would tell the whole story, and these folks were really smart. What, then?

*

There was a nice spider up there in a corner. Big enough to do light work, but not big enough to attract much, if any, attention. Did spiders have minds? The power pack and the generator set were both open, being on Jalte's belt, while the screen itself was radiated from a collar-antenna round his neck. He would see what he could do.

The spider had more of a mind than he had supposed, and he got into it easily enough. She could not really think at all, and at the starkly terrible savagery of her tiny ego the Lensman actually winced, but at that she had redeeming features. She was willing to work hard and long for a comparatively small return of food. He could not fuse his mentality with hers smoothly, as he could do in the case of creatures of greater brain power, but he could handle her after a fashion. At least she knew that certain actions would result in nourishment.

Through the insect's compound eyes the room and all its contents were weirdly distorted, but the Lensman could make them out well enough to direct her efforts. She crawled along the ceiling and dropped upon a silken rope to Jalte's belt. She could not pull the plug of the power pack—it loomed before her eyes, a gigantic metal pillar as immovable as the Rock of Gibraltar—therefore she scampered on and began to explore the mazes of the set itself. She could not see the thing as a whole, it was far too immense a structure for that; so Kinnison, to whom the device was no larger than a hand, directed her to the first grid lead.

A tiny thing, thread-thin in gross; yet to the insect it was an ordinary cable of stranded soft-metal wire. Her powerful mandibles pried loose one of the component strands and with very little effort pulled it away from its fellows beneath the head of a binding screw. The strand bent easily, and as it touched the metal of the chassis the thought-screen vanished.

Instantly Kinnison insinuated his mind into Jalte's and began to dig for knowledge. Eichmil was his chief—Kinnison knew that already. His office was in the Second Galaxy, on the planet Jarnevon. Jalte had been there—co-ordinates so and so, courses such and such—Eichmil reported to Boskone—

The Lensman stiffened. Here was the first positive evidence he had found that his deductions were correct—or even that there really *was* such an entity as Boskone! He bored anew.

Boskone was not a single entity, but a council—probably of the Eich, the natives of Jarnevon—weird impressions of coldly intellectual reptilian monstrosities, horrific, indescribable—Eichmil must know exactly who and where Boskone was. Jalte did not.

Kinnison finished his research and abandoned the Kalonian's mind as insidiously as he had entered it. The spider opened the short, restoring the screen to usefulness. Then, before he did anything else, the Lensman directed his small ally to a whole family of young grubs just under the cover of his manhole. Lensmen paid their debts, even to spiders.

Then, with a profound sigh of relief, he dropped down into the sewer. The submarine journey to the river was made without incident, as was the flight to his speedster. Night fell, and through its blackness there darted the even blacker shape which was the Lensman's little ship. Out into intergalactic space she flashed, and homeward. And as she flew the Tellurian scowled.

He had gained much, but not enough by far. He had hoped to get all the data on Boskone, so that he could storm Headquarters in the van of Civilization's armada, invincible in its newly-devised might.

No soap. Before he could do that he would have to scout Jarnevon—in the Second Galaxy—alone. Alone? Better not. Better take the flying snake along. Good old dragon. That was a mighty long flit to be doing alone, and one with some mightily high-powered opposition at the other end of it.

XIX.

"Before you go anywhere; or, rather, whether you go anywhere or not, we want to knock down that Bronsecan base of Prellin's," Haynes declared to Kinnison in no uncertain voice. "It's a Galactic scandal, the way we've been letting them thumb their noses at us. Everybody in space thinks that the Patrol has gone soft all of a sudden. When are you going to let us smack them down? Do you know what they've done now?"

"No. What?"

"Gone out of business. We've been watching then so closely that they couldn't do any queer business—goods, letters, messages, or anything—so they closed up the Bronseca branch entirely. 'Unfavorable conditions,' they said. Locked up tight—telephones disconnected, communicators cut, everything."

"Hm-m-m. In that case we'd better take 'em, I guess. No harm done, anyway, now—maybe all the better. Let Boskone think that our strategy failed and we had to fall back on brute force."

"You say it easy. You think that it'll be a push-over, don't you?"

"Sure—why not?"

"You noticed the shape of their screens?"

"Roughly cylindrical"—in surprise. "They're hiding a lot of stuff, of course, but they can't possibly—"

"I'm afraid that they can, and will. I've been checking up on the building. Ten years old. Plans and permits QX except for the fact that nobody knows whether or not the inside of the building resembles the plans in any particular."

"Klono's whiskers!" Kinnison was aghast, his mind racing. "How could that be, chief? Inspectors—builders—contractors—workmen?"

"The city inspector who had the job came into money later, retired, and nobody has seen him since. Nobody can locate a single builder or workman who saw it constructed. No competent inspector has been in it since. Cominoche is lax—all cities are, for that matter—with an outfit as big as Wembleson's, that carries its own insurance, does its own inspecting, and won't allow outside interference. Wembleson's isn't alone in that attitude—they're not all zwilniks, either."

"You think that it's really fortified, then?"

"Sure of it. That's why we ordered a gradual, but complete, evacuation of the city, beginning a couple of months ago."

"How could you?" Kinnison was growing more surprised by the minute. "The businesses—the houses—the expense!"

"Martial law—the Patrol takes over in emergencies, you know. Businesses moved, and mostly carrying on very well. People ditto—very nice temporary camps, lake and river cottages, and so on. As for expense, the Patrol pays damages. We'll pay for rebuilding the whole city if we have to—much rather that than leave that Boskonian base standing there untouched."

"What a mess! Never thought of it that way, but you're right, as usual. They wouldn't be there at all unless they thought—but they must know, chief, that they can't hold off the stuff that you can bring to bear."

"Probably betting that we won't destroy our own city to get them—if so, they're wrong. Or possibly they hung on a few days too long."

"How about the observers?" Kinnison asked. "They have four auxiliaries there, you know."

"That's strictly up to you." Haynes was unconcerned. "Smearing that base is the only thing I insist on. We'll wipe out the observers or let them observe and report, whichever you say; but that base goes—it has been there far too long already."

"Be nicer to let them alone," Kinnison decided. "We're not supposed to know anything about them. You won't have to use the primaries, will you?"

"No. It's a fairly large building, as business blocks go, but it lacks a lot of being big enough to be a first-class base. We can burn the ground out from under all its foundations with our secondaries."

He called an adjutant. "Get me Sector 19." Then, as the seamed, scarred face of an old Lensman appeared upon a plate:

"You can go to work on Cominoche now, Parker. Twelve maulers. Twenty heavy caterpillars and about fifty units of Q-type screen, remote control. Supplies and service. Have them muster all available fire-fighting apparatus. If desirable, import some—we want to save as much of the place as we can. I'll come over in the *Dauntless*."

He glanced at Kinnison, one eye-brow raised quizzically.

"I feel as though I rate a little vacation; I think I'll go and watch this," he commented. "Got time to come along?"

"I think so. It's more or less on my way to Lundmark's Nebula."

649

THE LENSMAN

Upon Bronseca, then, as the *Dauntless* ripped her way through protesting space, there converged structures of the void from a dozen nearby systems; each ship emblazoned with the device of ray-emitting intertwined spirals which is the emblem of the Galactic Patrol. There came maulers; huge, ungainly flying fortresses of stupendous might. There came transports, bearing the commissariat and the service units. Vast freighters, under whose unimaginable mass the Gargantuanly braced and latticed and trussed docks yielded visibly and groaningly, crushed to a standstill and disgorged their varied cargoes.

What Haynes had so matter-of-factly referred to as "heavy" caterpillars were all of that; and the mobile screens were even heavier. Clanking and rumbling, but with their weight so evenly distributed over huge, flat treads that they sank only a foot or so into even ordinary ground, they made their ponderous way along Cominoche's deserted streets.

What thoughts seethed within the minds of the Boskonians can only be imagined. They knew that the Patrol had landed in force, but what could they do about it? At first, when the Lensmen began to infest the place, they could have fled in safety; but at that time they were too certain of their immunity to abandon their richly established position. Even now, they would not abandon it until that course became absolutely necessary.

They could have destroyed the city, true; but it was not until after the non-combatant inhabitants had unobtrusively moved out that that course suggested itself as a desirability. Now the destruction of property would be a gesture worse than meaningless; it would be a waste of energy which would all too certainly be needed—badly and soon.

Hence, as the Patrol's land forces ground clangorously into position the enemy made no demonstration. The mobile screens were in place, surrounding the doomed section with a wall of force to protect the rest of the city from the hellish energies so soon to be unleashed. The heavy caterpillars, mounting projectors quite comparable in size and power with the warships' own—weapons similar in purpose and function to the railway-carriage coast-defense guns of an earlier day—were likewise ready. Far back of the line, but still too close, as they were to discover later, heavily armored men crouched at their remote controls behind their shields; barriers both of hard-driven, immaterial fields of force and of solid, grounded, ultrarefrigerated walls of the most refractory materials possible of fabrication. In the sky hung the maulers, poised stolidly upon the towering pillars of flame erupting from their under jets.

Cominoche, Bronseca's capital city, witnessed then what no one there present had ever expected to see; the warfare designed for the illimitable reaches of empty space being waged in the very heart of its business district!

For Port Admiral Haynes had directed the investment of this minor stronghold almost as though it were a regulation base, and with good reason. He knew that from their coigns of vantage afar four separate Boskonian observers were looking on, charged with the responsibility of recording and reporting everything that transpired, and he wanted that report to be complete and conclusive. He wanted Boskone, whoever and wherever he might be, to know that when the Galactic Patrol started a thing, that thing it finished; that the mailed fist of civilization would not spare an enemy base simply because it was so located within one of humanity's cities that its destruction must inevitably result in severe property damage. Indeed, the chief of staff had massed there thrice the force necessary; specifically and purposely to drive that message home.

At the word of command there flamed out, almost as one, a thousand lances of energy intolerable. Masonry, brickwork, steel, glass, and chromium trim disappeared; flaring away in sparkling, hissing vapor or cascading away in brilliantly mobile streams of fiery, corrosive liquid. Disappeared, revealing the unbearably incandescent surface of the Boskonian defensive screen.

Full-driven, that barrier held, even against the titanic thrusts of the maulers above and of the heavy defense guns below. Energy rebounded in scintillating torrents, shot off in blinding streamers, released itself in bolts of lightning hurling themselves frantically to ground.

Nor was that superbly disguised citadel designed for defense alone. Knowing now that the last faint hope of continuing in business upon Bronseca was gone, and grimly determined to take full toll of the hated Patrol, the defenders in turn loosed their beams. Five of them shot out simultaneously, and five of the panels of mobile screen flamed instantly into eye-tearing violet. Then black. These were not the comparatively feeble, antiquated rays which Haynes had expected, but were the output of up-to-the-minute, first-line space artillery!

Defenses down, it took but a blink of time to lick up the caterpillars. On, then, the destroying beams tore, each in a direct line for a remote-control station. Through tremendous edifices of masonry and steel they drove, the upper floors collapsing into the cylinders of annihilation only to be consumed almost as fast as they could fall.

"All screen-control stations, back, fast!" Haynes directed crisply. "Back, dodging! Put your screens on automatic block until you get back beyond effective range. Spy-ray men! See if you can locate the enemy observers directing fire!"

But no matter how far back they went, Boskonian beams still sought them out in grimly persistent attempts to slay. Their shielding fields blazed white, their refractories wavered in the high blue as the overdriven refrigerators strove mightily to cope with the terrific load. The operators, stifling, almost roasting in their armor of proof, shook sweat from the eyes they could not reach as they drove themselves and their mechanisms on to even greater efforts; cursing luridly, fulminantly the while at carrying on a space war in the hotly reeking, the hellishly reflecting and heat-retaining environment of a metropolis!

And all around the embattled structure, within the Patrol's now partially open wall of screen, spread holocaust supreme; holocaust spreading wider and wider during each fractional split second. In an instant, it seemed, nearby buildings burst into flame. The fact that they were fireproof meant nothing whatever. The air inside them, heated in moments to a point far above the ignition temperature of organic material, fed furiously upon furniture, rugs, drapes, and whatever else had been left in place. Even without such adventitious aids the air itself, expanding tremendously, irresistibly, drove outward before it the glass of windows and the solid brickwork of walls. And as they fell, glass and brick ceased to exist as such. Falling, they fused; coalescing and again splashing apart as they descended through the inferno of annihilatory vibrations in an appalling rain which might very well have been sprinkled from the hottest middle of the central core of hell itself. And in this fantastically potent, this incredibly corrosive flood the ground itself, the metaled pavement, the sturdily immovable foundations of skyscrapers, dissolved as do lumps of sugar in boiling coffee. Dissolved, slumped down, flowed away in blindingly turbulent streams. Super-structures toppled into disintegration, each discrete particle contributing as it fell to the utterly indescribable fervency of the whole.

More and more panels of mobile screen went down. They were not designed to stand up under such heavy projectors as "Wemblesons" mounted, and the Boskonians blasted them down in order to get at the remote-control operators back of them. Swath after swath of flaming ruin was cut through the Bronsecan capital as the enemy gunners tried to follow the dodging caterpillar tractors.

"Drop down, maulers!" the commander-in-chief ordered. "Low enough so that your screens touch ground. Never mind damage—they'll blast the whole city if we don't stop those beams. Surround him!"

Down the maulers came, ringwise; mighty protective envelopes overlapping; down until the screens bit ground. Now the caterpillar and mobile-screen crews were safe; powerful as Prellin's weapons were, they could not break through those maulers' screens.

Now holocaust waxed doubly infernal. The wall was tight, the only avenue of escape of all that fiercely radiant energy straight upward; and adding to the furor were the flaring under jets—themselves destructive agents by no means to be despised!

Inside the screens, then, raged pure frenzy. At the line raved the maulers' prodigious lifting blasts. Out and away, down every avenue of escape, swept torrents of superheated air at whose touch anything and everything combustible burst into flame. But there could be no fire-fighting—yet. Outlying fires, along the lines of destruction previously cut, yes; but personal armor has never been designed to enable life to exist in such an environment as that near those screens then was.

"Burn out the ground under them!" came the order. "Tip them over—slag them down!"

Sharply downward angled twoscore of the beams which had been expending their energies upon Boskone's radiant defenses. Downward into the lake of lava which had once been pavement. That lake had already been seething and bubbling; emitting momently bursts of lambent flame. Now it leaped into a frenzy of its own; a transcendent fury of volatilization. High-explosive shells by the hundred dropped also into the incandescent mess, hurling the fiery stuff afar; deepening and broadening the sulphurous moat.

"Deep enough," Haynes spoke into his microphone. "Tractors and pressors as assigned—tip him over."

The intensity of the bombardment did not slacken, but from the maulers to the north there reached out pressors, from those upon the south came tractors; each a beam of terrific power, each backed by all the mass and all the driving force of a veritable flying fortress.

Slowly that which had been a building leaned from the perpendicular, its inner defensive screen still intact.

"Chief?" From his post as observer, Kinnison flashed a thought to Haynes. "Are you beginning to think any funny thoughts about that ape down there?"

"No. Are you? What?" asked the port admiral, surprised.

"Maybe I'm nuts, but it wouldn't surprise me if he'd start doing a flit pretty quick. I've got a CRX tracer on him, just in case, and it might be smart to caution Henderson to keep up on his toes."

"Your diagnosis—'nuts'—is correct, I think," came the answering thought; but the port admiral followed the suggestion, nevertheless.

*

And none too soon. Deliberately, grandly, the Colossus was leaning over, bowing in stately fashion toward the awful lake in which it stood. But only so far. Then there was a flash, visible even in the inferno of energies already there at war, and the already coruscant lava was hurled to all points of the compass as the full-blast drive of a superdreadnought was cut loose beneath its surface!

To the eye the thing simply and instantly disappeared; but not to the ultra-vision of the observers' plates, and especially not to the CRX tracers attached by Kinnison and by Henderson. They held, and the chief pilot, already warned, was on the trail as fast as he could punch his keys.

Through atmosphere, through stratosphere, into interplanetary space flew pursued and pursuer at ever-increasing speed. The *Dauntless* overtook her proposed victim fairly easily. The Boskonian was fast, but the Patrol's new flier was the fastest thing in space. But tractors would not hold against the now universal standard equipment of shears, and the heavy secondaries served only to push the fleeing vessel along all the faster. And the dreadful primary beams could not be used—yet.

"Not yet," cautioned the admiral. "Don't get too close—wait until there's nothing detectable in space."

Finally an absolutely empty region was entered, the word to close up was given, and Prellin drank of the bitter cup which so many commanders of vessels of the Patrol had had to drain—the gallingly fatal necessity of engaging a ship which was both faster and more powerful than his own. The Boskonian tried, of course. His beams raged out at full power against the screens of the larger ship, but without effect. Three primaries lashed out as one. The fleeing vessel, structure and contents, ceased to be. The *Dauntless* returned to the torn and ravaged city.

The maulers had gone. The lumbering caterpillars—what were left of them—were clanking away; reeking, smoking hot in every plate and member. Only the firemen were left, working like Trojans with explosives, rays, water, carbon-dioxide snow, clinging and smothering chemicals; anything and everything which would isolate, absorb, or dissipate any portion of the almost incalculable heat energy so recently and so profligately released.

Fire apparatus from four planets was at work. There were pumpers, ladder trucks, hose and chemical trucks. There were men in heavily insulated armor. Vehicles and men alike were screened against the specific wave lengths of heat; and under the direction of a fire marshal in his red speedster high in air they fought methodically and efficiently the conflagration which was the aftermath of battle. They fought, and they were winning.

And then it rained. As though the heavens themselves had been outraged by what had been done, they opened and rain sluiced down in level sheets. It struck hissingly the

653

nearby structures, but it did not touch the central area at all. Instead, it turned to steam in mid-air, and, rising or being blown aside by the tempestuous wind, it concealed the redly glaring, raw wound beneath a blanket of crimson fog.

"Well, that is that," the port admiral said slowly. His face was grim and stern. "A good job of clean-up—expensive, but worth the price. So be it to every pirate base and every zwilnik hide-out in the Galaxy! Henderson, land us at Cominoche Spaceport."

*

And from four other cities of the planet four Boskonian observers, each unknown to all the others, took off in four spaceships for four different destinations. Each had reported fully and accurately to Jalte everything that had transpired until the two fliers had faded into the distance. Then, highly elated—and probably, if the truth could be known, no little surprised as well—at the fact that he was still alive, each had left Bronseca at maximum blast.

The Galactic director had done all that he could, which was little enough. At the Patrol's first warlike move he had ordered a squadron of Boskone's ablest fighting craft to Prellin's aid. It was almost certainly a useless gesture, he knew as he did it. Gone were the days when pirate bases dotted the Tellurian Galaxy; only by a miracle could those ships reach the Bronsecan's line of flight in time to be of service.

Nor could they. The howl of interfering vibrations which was smothering Prellin's communicator beam snapped off into silence while the would-be rescuers were many hours away. For minutes, then, Jalte sat immersed in thought at his great desk in the Center, his normally bluish face turning a sickly green, before he called the planet Jarnevon to report to Eichmil, his chief.

"There is, however, a bright side to the affair," he concluded. "Prellin's records were destroyed with him. Also, there are two facts—that the Patrol had to use such force as practically to destroy the city of Cominoche, and that our four observers escaped unmolested—which furnish conclusive proof that the vaunted Lensman failed completely to penetrate with his mental powers the defenses we have been using against him."

"Not conclusive proof," Eichmil rebuked him harshly. "Not proof at all, in any sense—scarcely a probability. Indeed, the display of force may very well mean that he has already attained his objective. He may have allowed the observers to escape, to lull our suspicions. You yourself are probably the next in line. How certain are you that your own base has not already been invaded?"

"Absolutely certain, sir." Jalte's face, however, turned a shade greener at the thought.

"You use the term 'absolutely' very loosely—but I hope that you are right. Use all the men and all the equipment we have sent you to make sure that it remains impenetrable."

<h2 style="text-align:center">XX.</h2>

In their nonmagnetic, practically invisible speedster, Kinnison and Worsel entered the terra incognita of the Second Galaxy and approached the solar system of the Eich, slowing down to a crawl as they did so. They knew as much concerning dread Jarnevon, the planet which was their goal, as did Jalte, from whom the knowledge had been acquired; but that was all too little.

654

They knew that it was the fifth planet out from the Sun and that it was bitterly cold. It had an atmosphere, but one containing no oxygen; one poisonous to oxygen-breathers. It had no rotation—or rather, its day coincided with its year—and its people dwelt upon its eternally dark hemisphere. If they had eyes, a point upon which there was doubt, they did not operate upon the frequencies ordinarily referred to as "visible" light. In fact, about the Eich as persons or identities they knew next to nothing. Jalte had seen them, but either he did not perceive them clearly or else his mind could not retain their true likeness; his only picture of the Eichlan physique being a confusedly horrible blur.

"I'm scared, Worsel," Kinnison declared. "Scared purple, and the closer we come the more scared I get."

And he was scared. He was afraid as he had never before been, in all his short life. He had been in dangerous situations before, certainly; not only that, he had been wounded almost unto death. In those instances, however, peril had come upon him suddenly. He had reacted to it automatically, having had little if any time to think about it beforehand.

Never before had he gone into a place in which he knew in advance that the advantage was all upon the other side; from which his chance of getting out alive was so terrifyingly small. It was worse, much worse, than going into that vortex. There, while the road was strange, the enemy was known to be one whom he had conquered before; and furthermore, he had had the *Dauntless*, its eager young crew, and the scientific self-abnegation of old Cardynge to back him. Here he had the speedster and Worsel—and Worsel was just as scared as he was.

The pit of his stomach felt cold, his bones seemed bits of rubber tubing. Nevertheless, the two Lensmen were going in. That was their job. They had to go in, even though they knew that the foe was at least their equal mentally, was overwhelmingly their superior physically, and was upon his own ground.

"So am I," Worsel admitted. "I'm scared to the tip of my tail. I have one advantage over you, however—I've been that way before." He was referring to the time when he had gone to Delgon, abysmally certain that he would not return. Nor would he have returned save for Kinnison and Van Buskirk. "What is fated, happens. Shall we prepare?"

They had spent many hours in discussion of what could be done, and in the end had decided that the only possible preparation was to make sure that if Kinnison failed, his failure would not bring disaster to the Patrol.

"Might as well. Come in; my mind's wide open."

The Velantian insinuated his mind into Kinnison's and the Earthman slumped down, unconscious. Then for many minutes Worsel wrought within the plastic brain. Finally:

"Thirty seconds after you leave me these inhibitions will become operative. When I release them your memory and your knowledge will be exactly as they were before I began to operate," he thought, slowly, intensely, clearly. "Until that time you know nothing whatever of any of these matters. No mental search, however profound; no truth drug, however potent; no probing, even of the subconscious, will or can discover them. They do not exist. They never have existed. They shall not exist until I so allow. These other matters have been, are, and shall be the facts until that instant. Kimball Kinnison, awaken!"

The Tellurian came to, not knowing that he had been out. Nothing had occurred; for him no time whatever had elapsed. He could not perceive even that his mind had been touched.

"Sure it's done, Worsel? I can't find a thing!" Kinnison, who had himself operated upon so many minds as tracelessly, could scarcely believe that his own had been tampered with.

"It is done. If you could detect any trace of the work it would have been poor work, and wasted."

*

The speedster dropped as nearly as the Lensmen dared toward Jarnevon's tremendous primary base. They did not know whether they were being observed or not. For all they knew, these incomprehensible beings might be able to see or to sense them as plainly as though their ship were painted with radium and were landing openly, with searchlights ablaze and with bells a-clang. Muscles tense, ready to hurl their tiny flier away at the slightest alarm, they wafted downward.

Through the screens they dropped. Power off, even to the gravity pads; thought, even, blanketed to zero. Nothing happened. They landed. They disembarked. Foot by foot they made their cautious way forward.

In essence the plan was simplicity itself. Worsel would accompany Kinnison until both were within the thought-screens of the dome. Then the Tellurian would get, some way or other, the information the Patrol had to have, and the Velantian would get it back to Prime Base. If the Gray Lensman could go, too, well and good. After all, there was no real reason to think that he couldn't—he was merely playing safe, on general principles. If, however, worst came to worst, well—

They arrived.

"Now remember, Worsel, no matter what happens to me, or around me, you stay out. Don't come in after me. Help me all you can with your mind, but not otherwise. Take everything I get, and at the first sign of danger you flit back to the speedster and give her the oof, whether I'm around or not. Check?"

"Check," Worsel agreed, quietly. Kinnison's was the harder part. Not because he was the leader, but because he was the better qualified. They both knew it. The Patrol came first. It was bigger, vastly more important than any being or any group of beings in it.

The man strode away and in thirty seconds underwent a weird and striking mental transformation. Three quarters of his knowledge disappeared so completely that he had no inkling that he had ever had it. A new name, a new personality were his, so completely and indisputably his that he had no faint glimmering of a recollection that he had ever been otherwise.

He was wearing his Lens. It could do no possible harm, since it was almost inconceivable that the Eich could be made to believe that any ordinary agent could have penetrated so far, and the fact should not be revealed to the foe that any Lensman could work without his Lens. That would explain far too much of what had already happened. Furthermore, it was a necessity in the only really convincing rôle which Kinnison could play in the event of his capture.

He would not think into that base until he was far enough away from Worsel so that the Velantian's hiding place, if it were not already known, would not be revealed. He did not then know that such a being as Worsel existed; he did not think into the stronghold simply because he was not yet close enough to work efficiently.

Closer he crept. Closer. There were pits beneath the pavement, he observed, big enough to hold a speedster. Traps. He avoided them. There were various mechanisms within the blank walls he skirted. More traps. He avoided them. Photo-cells, trigger beams, invisible rays, networks. He avoided them all. Close enough.

*

Delicately he sent out a mental probe, and almost in the instant of its sending, cables of steel came whipping from afar. He perceived them as they came, but he was unable to dodge them all. His projectors flamed briefly, only to be sheared away. The cables wrapped about his limbs, binding him fast. Helpless, he was carried through the atmosphere, into the dome, through an air lock into a chamber housing much grimly unmistakable apparatus. And in the council room, where the nine of Boskone and one armored Delgonian Overlord held meeting, a communicator buzzed and snarled.

"Ah!" exclaimed Eichmil. "Our visitor has arrived and is awaiting us in the Delgonian hall of question. Shall we meet again, there?"

They did so; they of the Eich armored against the poisonous oxygen, the Overlord naked. All wore screens.

"Earthling, we are glad indeed to see you here," the First of Boskone welcomed the prisoner. "For a long time we have been anxious indeed—"

"I don't see how that can be," the Lensman blurted. "I just graduated. My first big assignment, and I have failed," he ended bitterly.

A start of surprise swept around the circle. Could this be?

"He is lying," Eichmil decided. "You of Delgon, take him out of his armor." The Overlord did so, the Tellurian's struggles meaningless to the reptile's superhuman strength. "Release your screen and see whether or not you can make him tell the truth."

After all, the man might not be lying. The fact that he could understand a strange language meant nothing at all. All Lensmen could.

"But in case he *should* be the one we seek—" The Overlord hesitated.

"We will see to it that no harm comes to you—"

"We cannot," the Ninth—the psychologist—broke in. "Before any screen is released I suggest that we question him verbally, under the influence of the drug which renders it impossible for any warm-blooded oxygen breather to tell anything except the complete truth."

The suggestion, so eminently sensible, was adopted forthwith.

"Are you the Lensman who has made it possible for the Patrol to drive us out of the Tellurian Galaxy?" came the sharp demand.

"No," was the flat and surprising reply.

"Who are you, then?"

"Philip Morgan, class of—"

657

"Oh, this will take forever!" snapped the Ninth. "Let me question him. Can you control minds at a distance and without previous treatment?"

"If they are not too strong, yes. All of us specialists in psychology can do that."

"Go to work upon him, Overlord!"

The now fully reassured Delgonian snapped off his screen and a battle of wills ensued which made the subether boil. For Kinnison, although he no longer knew what the truth was, still possessed a large part of his mental power, and the Delgonian's mind, as has already been made clear, was a capable one indeed.

"Desist!" came the command. "Earthman, what happened?"

"Nothing," Kinnison replied truthfully. "Each of us could resist the other; neither could penetrate or control."

"Ah!" and nine Boskonian screens snapped off. Since the Lensman could not master one Delgonian, he would not be a menace to the massed minds of the nine of Boskone, and the questioning need not wait upon the slowness of speech. Thoughts beat into Kinnison's brain from all sides.

*

This power of mind was relatively new, yes. He did not know what it was. He went to Arisia, fell asleep, and woke up with it. A refinement, he thought, of hypnotism. Only advanced students in psychology could do it. He knew nothing except by hearsay of the old *Brittania*—he was a cadet then. He had never heard of Blakeslee, or of anything unusual concerning any one hospital ship. He did not know who had scouted Helmuth's base, or put the thionite into it. He had no idea who it was who had killed Helmuth. As far as he knew, nothing had ever been done about any Boskonian spies in Patrol bases. He had never happened to hear of the planet Medon, or of anyone named Bominger, or Madame Desplaines, or Prellin. He was entirely ignorant of any unusual weapons of offense—he was a psychologist, not an engineer or a physicist. No, he was not unusually adept with DeLameters—

"Hold on!" Eichmil commanded. "Stop questioning him, everybody! Now, Lensman, instead of telling us what you do not know, give us positive information, in your own way. How do you work? I am beginning to suspect that the man we really want is a director, not an operator."

This was a more productive line. Lensmen, hundreds of them, each worked upon a definite assignment. None of them had ever seen or ever would see the man who issued orders. He had not even a name, but was a symbol—Star A Star. They received orders through their Lenses, wherever they might be in space. They reported back to him in the same way. Yes, Star A Star knew what was going on in that room. He was reporting constantly—

A knife descended viciously. Blood spurted. The stump was dressed, roughly but effectively. They did not wish their victim to bleed to death when he died, and he was not to die in any fashion—yet.

And in the instant that Kinnison's Lens went dead, Worsel, from his safely distant nook, reached out direct to the mind of his friend, thereby putting his own life in jeopardy. He knew that there was an Overlord in that room, and the grue of a thousand helplessly sacrificed generations of forebears swept his sinuous length at the thought, despite his inward certainty of the new powers of his mind. He knew that of all the entities in the Universe, the Delgonians were most sensitive to the thought vibrations of Velantians. Nevertheless, he did it.

He narrowed the beam down to the smallest possible coverage, employed a frequency as far as possible from that ordinarily used by the Overlords, and continued to observe. It was risky, but it was necessary. It was beginning to appear as though the Earthman might not be able to escape, and he must not die in vain.

"Can you communicate now?" In the ghastly chamber the relentless questioning went on.

"I cannot communicate."

"It is well. In one way I would not be averse to letting your Star A Star know what happens when one of his minions dares to spy upon the Council of Boskone itself, but the information is as yet a trifle premature. Later, he shall learn—"

Kinnison did not consciously thrill at that thought. He did not know that the news was going beyond his brain; that he had achieved his goal. Worsel, however, did; and Worsel thrilled for him. The Gray Lensman had finished his job; all that was left to do was to destroy this world and the power of Boskone would be broken. Kinnison could die, now, content.

But no thought of leaving entered Worsel's mind. He would, of course, stand by as long as there remained the slightest shred of hope, or until some development threatened his ability to leave the planet with his priceless information. And the pitiless inquisition went on.

*

Star A Star had sent him to investigate their planet, to discover whether or not there was any connection between it and the zwilnik organization. He had come alone, in a speedster. No, he could not tell them even approximately where the speedster was. It was so dark, and he had come such a long distance on foot. In an hour or so, though, it would start sending out a thought signal which he could detect—

"But you must have some ideas about this Star A Star!" This director was the man they wanted so desperately to get. They believed implicitly in this figment of a Lensman director. Fitting in so perfectly with their own ideas of efficient organization, it was more convincing by far than the actual truth would have been. They knew now that he would be hard to find. They did not now insist upon facts; they wanted every possible crumb of surmise. "You must have wondered who and where Star A Star is? You must have tried to trace him?"

Yes, he had tried, but the problem could not be solved. The Lens was non-directional, and the signals came in at practically the same strength, anywhere in the Galaxy. They were, however, very much fainter out here. That might be taken to indicate that Star A Star's office was in a star cluster, well out in either the zenith or the nadir direction—

The victim sucked dry, eight of the Council departed, leaving Eichmil and the Overlord with the Lensman.

"What you have in mind to do, Eichmil, is childish. Your basic idea is excellent, but your technique is pitifully inadequate."

"What could be worse?" Eichmil demanded. "I am going to dig out his eyes, smash his bones, flay him alive, roast him, cut him up into a dozen pieces, and send him back to his Star A Star with a warning that every creature he sends into this Galaxy will be treated the same way. What would *you* do?"

"You of the Eich lack finesse," the Delgonian sighed. "You have no subtlety, no conception of the nicer possibilities of torture, either of an individual or of a race. For instance, to punish Star A Star adequately this man must be returned to him alive, not dead."

"Impossible! He dies—*here!*"

"You misunderstand me. Not alive as he is now—but not entirely dead. Bones broken, yes, and eyes removed; but those minor matters are but a beginning. If I were doing it, I should then apply several of these devices here, successively; but none of them to the point of complete incompatibility with life. I should inoculate the extremities of his four limbs with an organism which grows—shall we say—unpleasantly? Finally, I should extract his life force and consume it—as you know, that essence is a rarely satisfying delicacy with us—taking care to leave just enough to maintain a bare existence. I would then put what is left of him aboard his ship, start it toward the Tellurian Galaxy, and send notice to the Patrol as to its exact course and velocity."

"But they would find him *alive!*" Eichmil stormed.

"Exactly. For the fullest vengeance they must, as I have said. Which is worse, think you? To find a corpse, however dismembered, and to dispose of it with full military honors, or to find and to have to take care of for a full lifetime a something that has not enough intelligence even to swallow food placed in its mouth? Remember also that the organism will be such that they themselves will be obliged to amputate all four of the creature's limbs to save its life."

While thinking thus the Delgonian shot out a slender tentacle which, slithering across the floor, flipped over the tiny switch of a small mechanism in the center of the room. This entirely unexpected action surprised Worsel. He had been debating for minutes whether or not to release the Gray Lensman's inhibitions. He would have done so instantly if he had had any warning of what the Delgonian was about to do. Now it was too late.

"I have set up a thought-screen about the room. I do not wish to share this titbit with any of my fellows, as there is not enough to divide," the monster explained, parenthetically. "Have you any suggestions as to how my plan may be improved?"

"No. You have shown that you understand torture better than we do."

"I should, since we Overlords have practiced it as a fine art since our beginnings as a race. Do you wish the pleasure of co-operating with me in the work?"

"I do not torture for pleasure. Since you do, you may carry out the procedure as outlined. All I require is the assurance that he will be a warning and an object lesson to Star A Star of the Galactic Patrol."

"I can assure you definitely that he will be both. More, I will show you the results when I have finished with him. Or, if you like, I would be glad to have you stay and look on—you will find the spectacle interesting, entertaining and highly instructive."

"No, thanks—that is, not if you are sure that you can handle him alone."

"Handle him! This pitiful weakling?" The Overlord snorted contemptuously. "I could handle seven like him. He is on the verge of fainting already. Observe, please, his reaction to the fungus-culture injections."

Four times the Delgonian rammed the needle home; and, true to prediction, Kinnison's body went limp in its shackles.

"Ah, yes; a weak race, physically—very weak," Eichmil observed, as he left the room; and the Overlord, alone with his victim, cast off the chains in order to stretch the Lensman out upon one of the sinister machines so close at hand.

*

But Kinnison had not fainted. He had not allowed himself to feel the hurt of the knife, of the needle, nor of the injected fluid. Never before had he been more coldly, intently alert than in this, the climactic minute of his life. The full of his powers he did not have, perhaps, yet even now he was better equipped, mentally and physically, than the Kinnison of even a short year ago, able to establish a nerve block that would permit full and unshaken concentration on every move of offense and defense he might make, whatever frightful toll of pain and injury the inhumanly powerful, semireptilian Delgonian might inflict in the struggle that the Lensman now proposed. Thus, upon the first instant of opportunity, he exploded into action with a violence which took even the trigger-nerved Overlord entirely by surprise.

In practically one motion he rolled, ducked, gathered himself together and launched a kick behind which there was the driving force of every ounce of his powerful body and the concentrated urge of every cell of his brain. It struck its mark squarely—the hard toe of the Lensman's heavy boot crashed squarely against the Overlord's plated neck at the exact base of the skull. That kick would have pulped any human or near-human head—it would have slain a horse—it staggered momentarily even the reptilianly armored monstrosity which was the Delgonian.

Kinnison went leaping across the room toward a rack of implements and weapons, only to be buried in mid-course beneath a hurtling avalanche of fury. For a moment man and monster stood poised, almost en tableau, then they crashed to the floor together—talons and fingers clawing, gouging at eyes; wings, feet, hard-gnarled hands, scimitared tail, balled fist, boots and teeth wreaking every ultimate possibility of damage. Against the frightfully armed and naturally armored body of the Delgonian, human physical weapons and human strength were near useless; but, insulated against the agony of snapping bones and bludgeon blows of the mighty tail by that hard-held nerve block, the Lensman's furiously active mind had a goal—a vaguely understood goal—toward which he directed the deadly struggle he could not control or hope to win—

Upon and over the thought-screen generator rolled the madly warring pair, and as the delicate mechanism disintegrated it ceased to function.

Worsel's prodigious mentality had been beating ceaselessly against that screen ever since its erection, and in the very instant of its fall Kinnison became again the Gray Lensman of old. And in the next instant both of those mighty minds—the two most powerful then known to civilization—had hurled themselves against that of the Delgonian. Bitter though the ensuing struggle was, it was brief. Nothing short of an Arisian mentality could have withstood the venomous intensity, the berserk power, of that concerted and synchronized attack.

Brain half burned out, the Overlord wilted; and, docility itself, he energized the communicator.

"Eichmil? The work is done. Thoroughly done, and well."

"So soon?"

"Yes. I was hungry—and, as I intimated, Tellurians are much too weak to furnish any real sport. Do you wish to inspect what is left of the Lensman?" This question was safe enough; Worsel knew exactly how Kinnison had fared during his whirlwind bodily encounter with the frightfully armed, heavily armored engine of destruction which was the Delgonian.

"No." Eichmil, as a high executive, was accustomed to delegating far more important matters to competent underlings. "If you say that it is well done, that is sufficient."

"Clear the way for me, then, please," the Overlord requested. Then, picking up the hideously mangled thing that was Kinnison's body, he incased it in its armor and, donning his own, wriggled boldly away with his burden. "I go to place this residuum within its ship and to return it to Star A Star."

"You will be able to find the speedster?"

"Certainly. He was to find it. Whatever he could have done, I, working through the cells of his brain, can likewise do."

"Can you handle him alone, Kinnison?" Worsel asked presently. "Can you hold out until you reach the boat?"

"Yes, to both. I can handle him—we softened him down plenty. I will last—I'll make myself last, long enough."

"I go, then, lest they be observing with spy rays."

To the black flier the completely subservient Delgonian then bore his physically disabled master, and carefully he put him aboard. Worsel helped openly there, for he had put out screens against all forms of intrusion. The vessel took off and the Overlord wriggled blithely back toward the dome. He was full of the consciousness of a good job, well done. He even felt the sensation of repletion concomitant with having consumed much vital force!

"I hate to let him go!" Worsel's thought was a growl of baffled fury. "It gripes me to the tail to let him think that he has done everything he set out to do; that he will never even know how he got those bruises and contusions. I wanted—I still want—to tear him apart for what he has done to you, my friend."

"Thanks, old snake." Kinnison's thought came faintly. "Just temporary. He's living on borrowed time. He'll get his. You've got everything under control, haven't you?"

"On the green. Why?"

"Because I can't hold this nerve block any longer . . . . It hurts . . . . I'm sick . . . . I think I'm going to—"

He fainted. More, he plunged parsecs deep into the blackest depths of oblivion as outraged nature took the toll she had been so long denied.

Worsel hurled a call to Earth, then turned to his maimed and horribly broken companion. He applied splints to the shattered limbs, he dressed and bandaged the hideous wounds and the raw sockets which had once held eyes, he ministered to the raging, burning thirst. Whenever Kinnison's mind wearied he held for him the nerve block, the priceless anodyne without which the Gray Lensman must have died from sheerest agony.

"Why not allow me, friend, to relieve you of all consciousness until help arrives?" the Velantian asked pityingly.

"Can you do it without killing me?"

"If you so allow, yes. If you offer any resistance, I do not believe that any mind in the Universe could."

"I won't resist you. Come in," and Kinnison's suffering ended.

But kindly Worsel could do nothing about the fantastically atrocious growths which were transforming the Earthman's legs and arms into monstrosities out of nightmare.

He could only wait—wait for the skilled assistance which he knew must be so long in coming.

XXI.

When Worsel's hard-driven call impinged upon the port admiral's lens, Haynes dropped everything to take the report himself. Characteristically Worsel sent first and Haynes first recorded a complete statement of the successful mission to Jarnevon. Last came personalities, the tale of Kinnison's ordeal and of his present plight.

"Are they following you in force, or can't you tell?"

"Nothing has been detectable, and at the time of our departure there had been no suggestion of any such action," Worsel replied carefully.

"We'll come in force, anyway, and fast. Keep him alive until we meet you," Haynes urged, and disconnected.

It was an unheard-of occurrence for the port admiral to turn over his very busy and extremely important desk to a subordinate without notice and without giving him detailed instructions, but Haynes did it now.

"Take charge of everything, Southworth!" he snapped. "I'm called away—emergency. Kinnison found Boskone—got away—hurt—I'm going after him in the *Dauntless*. Taking the new flotilla with me. Time indefinite—probably a few weeks."

He strode toward the communicator desk. The *Dauntless* was, as always, completely serviced and ready for any emergency. Where was that fleet of her sister ships, on its shakedown cruise? He'd shake them down! They had with them the new hospital ship, too—the only Red Cross ship in space that could leg it, parsec for parsec, with the *Dauntless*.

"Get me Navigations . . . . Figure best point of rendezvous for the *Dauntless* and Flotilla ZKD, both at full blast, en route to Lundmark's Nebula. Fifteen minutes departure. Figure approximate time of meeting with speedster, also at full blast, leaving that nebula hour nine fourteen today. Correction! Cancel speedster meeting; we can compute that more accurately later. Advise adjutant. Vice-Admiral Southworth will send order, through channels. Get me Base Hospital . . . . Lacy, please . . . . Kinnison's hurt, sawbones, bad. I'm going out after him. Coming along?"

"Yes. How about—"

"On the green. Flotilla ZKD, including your new two-hundred-million-credit hospital, is going along. Slip twelve, *Dauntless*, eleven and one half minutes from now. Hipe!" And the surgeon general "hiped."

Two minutes before the scheduled take-off Base Navigations called the chief navigating officer of the *Dauntless*.

"Course to rendezvous with Flotilla ZKD latitude three fifty-four dash thirty longitude nineteen dash forty-two time approximately twelve dash seven dash twenty-six place one dash three dash oh outside arbitrary galactic rim check and repeat," rattled from the speaker without pause or punctuation. Nevertheless, the chief navigator got it, recorded it, checked and repeated it.

"Figures only approximations because of lack of exact data on variations in density of medium and on distance necessarily lost in detouring stars," the speaker chattered on. "Suggest instructing your second navigator to communicate with navigating officers Flotilla ZKD at time twelve dash oh dash oh to correct courses to compensate unavoidably erroneous assumptions in computation Base Navigations off."

"I'll say he's off—'way off!" growled the second. "What does he think I am—a complete nitwit? Pretty soon he'll be telling me that two plus two equals four point oh."

*

The fifteen-second warning bell sounded. Every man came to the ready at his post, and precisely upon the designated second the superdreadnought blasted off. For six miles she rose inert upon her under jets, sirens and flaring lights clearing her way. Then she went free, her needle prow slanted sharply upward, her full battery of main driving projectors burst into action, and to all intents and purposes she vanished.

The Earth fell away from her at an incredible rate, dwindling away into invisibility in less than a minute. In two minutes the Sun itself was merely a bright star, in five it had merged indistinguishably into the sharply defined, brilliantly white belt of the Milky Way.

Hour after hour, day after day, the *Dauntless* hurtled through space, swinging almost imperceptibly this way and that to avoid the dense ether in the neighborhood of suns through which the designated course would have led; but never leaving far or for long the direct line, almost exactly in the equatorial plane of the Galaxy, between Tellus and the place of meeting. Behind her the Milky Way clotted, condensed, gathered itself together; before her and around her the stars began rapidly to thin out. Finally there were no more stars in front of her. She had reached the "arbitrary rim" of the Galaxy, and the second navigator plugged into Communications.

"Please get me Flotilla ZDK, Flagship Navigations," he requested; and, as a clean-cut young face appeared upon his plate: "Hi, Harvey, old spacehound! Fancy meeting you out here! It's a small Universe, ain't it? Say, did that crumb back there at Base tell you, too, to be sure and start checking course before you overran the rendezvous? If he was singling me out to make that pass at, I'm going to take steps, and not through channels, either."

"Yeah, he told me the same. I thought it was funny, too—an oiler's boy would know enough to do that without being told. We figured maybe he was jittery on account of us meeting the admiral or something. What's burned out all the jets, Paul, to get the big brass hats 'way out here and all dithered up, and to pull us offa the cruise this way? Must be a hell of an important flit! You're computing the Old Man himself; you oughta know something. What's all this about a speedster that we're going to escort? Spill it—give us the dope!"

"I don't know a thing, Harvey, honest, any more than you do. They didn't put out a word. Well, we'd better be getting onto the course—'to compensate unavoidably erroneous assumptions in computation,'" he mimicked caustically. "What do you read on my lambda? Fourteen—three—oh point six—decrement—"

The conversation became a technical jargon; because of which, however, the courses of the flying spaceships changed subtly. The flotilla swung around, through a small arc of a circle of prodigious radius, decreasing by a tenth its driving force. Up to it the *Dauntless* crept; through it and into the van. Then again in cone formation, but with fifty-five units instead of fifty-four, the flotilla screamed forward at maximum blast.

Well before the calculated time of meeting the speedster a Velantian Lensman who knew Worsel well put himself en rapport with him and sent a thought out far ahead of the flying squadron. It found its goal—Lensmen of that race, as has been brought out, have always been extraordinarily capable communicators—and once more the course was altered slightly. In due time Worsel reported that he could detect the fleet, and shortly thereafter:

"Worsel says to cut your drive to zero," the Velantian transmitted. "He's coming up. He's close. He's going to go inert and start driving. We're to stay free until we see what his intrinsic velocity is. Watch for his flare."

It was a weird sensation, this of knowing that a speedster—quite a sizable chunk of boat, really—was almost in their midst, and yet having all their instruments, even the electros, register empty space.

There it was! The flare of the driving blast, a brilliant streamer of fierce white light, sprang into being and drifted rapidly away to one side of their course. When it had attained a safe distance:

"All ships of the flotilla except the *Dauntless* go inert," Haynes directed. Then, to his own pilot, "Back us off a bit, Henderson, and do the same," and the new flagship also went inert.

"How can I get onto the *Pasteur* the quickest, Haynes?" Lacy demanded.

"Take a gig," the admiral grunted. "Strapped down, you can use as much acceleration as you like. Three G's is all we can use without warning and preparation."

*

There followed a curious and fascinating spectacle, for the hospital ship had an intrinsic velocity entirely different from that of either Kinnison's speedster or Lacy's powerful gig. The *Pasteur*, gravity pads cut to zero, was braking down by means of her under jets at a conservative one point four gravities, since hospital ships were not allowed to use the brutal inert accelerations employed as a matter of course by ships of war.

The gig was on her brakes at five gravities, all that Lacy wanted to take—but the speedster! Worsel had put his patient into a pressure pack and had hung him on suspension, and was "balancing her down on her tail" at everything he could stand—a full eleven gravities!

But even at that, the gig first matched the velocity of the hospital ship. The intrinsics of those two were at least of the same order of magnitude, since both had come from the same galaxy. Therefore, Lacy boarded the Red Cross vessel and was escorted to the office of the chief nurse while Worsel was still blasting at eleven G's—fifty thousand miles distant then and getting farther away by the second—to kill the speedster's Lundmarkian intrinsic velocity. Nor could the tractors of the warships be of any assistance—the speedster's own vicious jets were fully capable of supplying more acceleration than even unhuman Worsel could endure!

"How do you do, Dr. Lacy? Everything is ready." Clarrissa MacDougall met him, hand outstretched. Her saucy white cap was worn as jerkily cocked as ever; perhaps even more so, now that it was emblazoned with the cross-surmounted wedge which is the insignia of sector chief nurse. Her flaming hair was as gorgeous, her smile was as radiant, her bearing as confidently—Kinnison has said of her more than once that she is the only person he has ever known who can strut sitting down!—as calmly poised, "I'm very glad to see you, doctor. It's been quite a while—" Her voice died away, for the man was looking at her with an expression defying analysis.

For Lacy was thunderstruck. If he had ever known it—and he must have—he had forgotten completely that MacDougall had this ship. This was awful—terrible!

"Oh, yes . . . yes, of course. How do you do? Mighty glad to see you again. How's everything going?" He pumped her hand vigorously, thinking frantically the while what he would—what he *could*—say next. "Oh, by the way, who is to be in charge of the operating room?"

"Why, I am, of course," she replied in surprise. "Who else would be?"

"*Anyone* else," he wanted to say, but did not—then. "Why, that isn't at all necessary. I would suggest—"

"You'll suggest nothing of the kind!" She stared at him intently; then, as she realized what his expression really meant—she had never before seen such a look of pitying anguish upon his usually sternly professional face—her own turned white and both hands flew to her throat.

"Not Kim, Lacy!" she gasped. Gone now was everything of poise, of insouciance, which had so characterized her a moment before. She who had worked unflinchingly upon all sorts of dismembered, fragmentary, maimed and mangled men was now a pleading, stricken, desperately frightened girl. "Not Kim—please! Oh, merciful God, don't let it be my Kim!"

"You *can't* be there, Mac." He did not need to tell her. She knew; he knew that she knew. "Somebody else—*anybody* else."

"No!" came the hot negative, although the blood drained completely from the chief nurse's face, leaving it as white as the immaculate uniform she wore. Her eyes were black, burning holes. "It's my job, Lacy, in more ways than one. Do you think that I would *ever* let anyone else work on *him?*" she finished passionately.

"You'll have to," he declared. "I didn't want to tell you this, but he's a ghastly mess. Altogether too much so for any woman, to say nothing of one who loves him." This, from a surgeon of Lacy's long and wide experience, was an unthinkable statement. Nevertheless:

"All the more reason why I've got to do it. No matter what shape he's in, I'll let no one else work on my Kim."

"I say no. That's an order—official!"

"Damn such orders!" she flamed. "There's nothing back of it—you know that as well as I do!"

"See here, young woman—"

"Do you think that you can get away with ordering me not to perform the very duties I have taken an oath to do?" she stormed. "And even if it were not my job, I'd come in and work on him if I had to get a torch and cut the ship apart, plate by plate, to do it! The only way you can keep me out of that operating room, Lacy, is to have about ten of your men put me into a strait jacket—and if you do that I'll have you kicked out of the service bodily. You know that I could and that I would!"

"QX, MacDougall, you win." She had him there. This girl could and would do exactly that. "But if you faint, I swear that I'll make you wish—"

"You know me better than that, doctor." She was cold now as a woman of marble. "If he dies, I'll die, too, right then. But if he lives, I'll stand by as long as I can do a single thing, however small, to help."

"You would, at that," the surgeon admitted. "Probably you would be able to hold together better than anyone else could. But there'll be after-effects in your case, you know."

"I know." Her voice was bleak. "I'll live through them—if Kim lives." She became all nurse in the course of a breath. White, cold, inhuman; strung to highest tension and yet placidly calm, as only a truly loving woman in life's great crises can be. "You have had reports on him, doctor. What is your provisional diagnosis?"

"Something like elephantiasis, only worse, affecting both arms and both legs. Drastic amputations indicated. Eye sockets require attention. Various multiple and compound fractures. Punctured and incised wounds. Traumatism, ecchymosis, extensive extravasations, œdema. Profound systemic shock, of course. The prognosis, however, seems to be distinctly favorable, as far as we can tell."

"Oh, I'm glad of that!" she breathed, the woman for a moment showing through the armor of the nurse. She had not dared even to think of prognosis. Then she had a thought. "Is that really true, or are you just giving me a shot in the arm?" she demanded.

"The truth—strictly," he assured her. "Worsel has an excellent sense of perception, and he has reported fully and clearly. Kinnison's mind, brain, and spine are not affected in any way, and we should be able to save his life. That is the one good feature of the whole thing."

*

The speedster finally matched the velocity of the hospital ship. She went free, flashed up to the *Pasteur*, inerted, and maneuvered briefly. The larger vessel engulfed the smaller. The Gray Lensman was carried into the operating room. The anæsthetist approached the table and Lacy was stunned at a thought from Kinnison.

"Never mind the anæsthetic, Dr. Lacy. You can't make me unconscious without killing me. Go ahead with your work. I'll hold a nerve block while you're doing what has to be done. I can do it perfectly—I've had lots of practice."

"But we can't, man!" Lacy exclaimed. "You've got to be under a general for this job—we can't have you conscious. You're raving, I think. It will work, surely; it always has. Let us try it, anyway, won't you?"

"Sure. It'll save me the trouble of holding the block, even though it won't do anything else. Go ahead."

The attendant physician did so, with the same cool skill and to the same end point as in thousands of similar and successful undertakings. At its conclusion: "Gone now, aren't you, Kinnison?" Lacy asked, through his Lens.

"No," came the surprising reply. "Physically, it worked. I can't feel a thing and I can't move a muscle, but mentally I am as wide awake as I ever was."

"But you shouldn't be!" Lacy protested. "Perhaps you were right, at that—we can't give you much more without danger of collapse. But you've *got* to be unconscious! Isn't there some way in which you can be made so?"

"Yes, there is. But why do I have to be unconscious?" Kinnison asked curiously.

"To avoid mental shock—seriously damaging," the surgeon explained. "In your case particularly the mental aspect is much graver than the purely physical one."

"Maybe you're right but you can't do it with drugs. Call Worsel; he has done it before. He had me unconscious most of the way over here, except when he had to give me a drink or something to eat. He's the only man this side of Arisia who can operate on my mind."

Worsel came. "Sleep, my friend," he commanded, gently but firmly. "Sleep profoundly, body and mind, with no physical or mental sensations, no consciousness, no perception even of the passage of time. Sleep until someone having authority to do so bids you awaken."

And Kinnison slept; so deeply that even Lacy's probing Lens could elicit no response.

"He will *stay* that way?" the surgeon asked in awe.

"Yes."

"For how long?"

"Indefinitely. Until one of you doctors or nurses tells him to wake up, or until he dies for lack of food or water."

668

"We will see to it that he gets nourishment. He would make a much better recovery if we could keep him in that state until his injuries are almost healed. Would that do him harm, think you?"

"None whatever."

Then the surgeons and the nurses went to work. Lacy was not guilty of exaggeration when he described Kinnison as being a "ghastly mess." He was all of that. The job was long and hard. It was heartbreaking, even for those to whom Kinnison was merely another case, not a beloved personality. What they had to do they did, and the white marble chief nurse carried on through every soul-wrenching second, through every shocking, searing motion of it. She did her part, stoically, unflinchingly, as efficiently as though the patient upon the table were a total stranger undergoing a simple appendectomy and not the one man in her entire universe suffering radical dismemberment. Nor did she faint—then.

*

Back in Base Hospital, then, time wore on until Lacy decided that the Lensman could be aroused from his trance. Clarrissa it was who woke him up. She had fought for the privilege; first claiming it as a right and then threatening to commit mayhem upon the person of anyone else who dared even to think of doing it.

"Wake up, Kim, dear," she whispered. "The worst of it is over now. You are getting well."

The Gray Lensman came to instantly, in full command of every faculty, knowing everything that had happened up to the instant of his hypnosis by Worsel. He stiffened, ready to establish again the nerve block against the intolerable agony to which he had been subjected so long, but there was no need. His body was, for the first time in untold æons, free from pain; and he relaxed blissfully, reveling in the sheer comfort of it.

"I'm *so* glad that you're awake, Kim," the nurse went on. "I know that you can't talk to me—we can't unbandage your jaw until next week—and you can't think at me, either, because your new Lens hasn't come yet. But I can talk to you and you can listen. Don't be discouraged, Kim. Don't let it get you down. I love you just as much as I ever did, and as soon as you can talk we're going to get married. I am going to take care of you—"

"Don't 'poor dear' me, Mac," he interrupted her with a vigorous thought. "You didn't say it, I know, but you were thinking it. I'm not half as helpless as you think I am. I can still communicate, and I can see as well as I ever could, or better. And if you think that I'm going to let you marry me to take care of me, you're crazy."

"You're raving! Delirious! Stark, staring mad!" She started back, then controlled herself with an effort. "Maybe you can think at people without a Lens—of course you can, since you just did, at me—but you *can't* see, Kim, possibly. Believe me, boy, I *know* that you can't. I was there—"

"I can, though," he insisted. "I got a lot of stuff on my second trip to Arisia that I couldn't let anybody know about then, but I can now. I've got as good a sense of perception as Tregonsee has—maybe better. To prove it, you look thin, worn—whittled down to a nub. You've been working too hard—on me."

"Deduction," she scoffed. "You would know that I would."

"QX. How about those roses over there on the table? White ones, yellow ones, and red ones? With ferns?"

"You can smell them, perhaps"—dubiously. Then, with more assurance: "You would know that practically all the flowers known to botany would be here."

"Well, I'll count 'em and point 'em out to you, then—or, better, how about that little gold locket, with 'CM' engraved on it, that you're wearing under your uniform? I can't smell that, nor the picture in it—" The man's thought faltered in embarrassment. "My picture! Klono's whiskers, Mac, where did you get that—and why?"

"It's a reduction that Admiral Haynes let me have made. I am wearing it because I love you—I've said that before."

The girl's entrancing smile was now in full evidence. She knew now that he *could* see, that he would never be the helpless hulk which she had so gallingly thought him doomed to become, and her spirits rose in ecstatic relief. But he would *never* take the initiative now. Well, then, she would; and this was as good an opening as she ever would have with the stubborn brute. Therefore:

"More than that, as I said before, I am going to marry you, whether you like it or not." She blushed a heavenly—and discordant—magenta, but went on unfalteringly: "And not out of pity, either, Kim, or just to take care of you. It's older than that—much older."

"It can't be done, Mac." His thought was a protest to high Heaven at the injustice of Fate. "I've thought it over out in space a thousand times—thought until I was black in the face—but I get the same result every time. It's just simply no soap. You are much too fine a woman—too splendid, too vital, too much of everything a woman should be—to be tied down for life to a thing that's half steel, rubber, and phenoline. It just simply is not on the wheel, that's all."

"You're full of pickles, Kim." Gone was all her uncertainty and nervousness. She was calm, poised; glowing with a transcendent inward beauty. "I didn't really *know* until this minute that you love me, too, but I do now. Don't you realize, you big, dumb, wonderful clunker, that as long as there's one single, little bit of a piece of you left alive I'll love that piece more than I ever could any other man's entire being?"

"But I *can't*, I tell you!" He groaned the thought. "I can't and I won't! My job isn't done yet, either, and the next time they'll probably get me. I *can't* let you waste yourself, Mac, on a fraction of a man for a fraction of a lifetime!"

"QX, Gray Lensman." Clarissa was serene, radiantly untroubled. She could make things come out right now; everything was on the green. "We'll put this back up on the shelf for a while. I'm afraid that I have been terribly remiss in my duties as a nurse. Patients mustn't be excited or quarreled with, you know."

"That's another thing. How come you, a sector chief, to be on ordinary room duty, and night duty at that?"

"Sector chiefs assign duties, don't they?" she retorted sunnily. "Now I'll give you a rub and change some of these dressings."

XXII.

"Hi, Skeleton-gazer!"

"Ho, Big Chief Feet-on-the-desk!"

"I see that your red-headed sector chief is still occupying all strategic salients in force." Haynes had paused in the surgeon general's office on his way to another of his conferences with the Gray Lensman. "Can't you get rid of her or don't you want to?"

"Don't want to. Couldn't, anyway, probably. The young vixen would tear down the hospital—she might even resign, marry him out of hand, and lug him off somewhere. You want him to recover, don't you?"

"Don't be any more of an idiot than you have to. What a question!"

"Don't work up a temperature about MacDougall, then. As long as she's around him—and that's twenty-four hours a day—he'll get everything in the Universe that he can get any good out of."

"That's so, too. This other thing's out of our hands now, anyway. Kinnison can't hold his position long against her and himself both—overwhelmingly superior force. Just as well, too—civilization needs more like those two."

"Check, but the affair isn't out of our hands yet, by any means. We've got quite a little more fine work to do there, as you'll see, before it's a really good job. But about Kinnison—"

"Yes. When are you going to fit arms and legs on him? He should be practicing with them at this stage of the game, I should think—I was."

"You *should* think—but, unfortunately, you don't, about anything except war," was the surgeon's dry rejoinder. "If you did, you would have paid more attention to what Phillips has been doing. He is making the final test today. Come along—your conference with Kinnison can wait half an hour."

In the research laboratory which had been assigned to Phillips they found von Hohendorff with the Posenian. Haynes was surprised to see the old commandant of cadets, but Lacy quite evidently had known that he was to be there.

"Phillips," the surgeon general began, "explain to Admiral Haynes, in nontechnical language, what you are doing."

"The original problem was to discover what hormone or other agent caused proliferation of neural tissue—"

"Wait a minute; I'd better do it," Lacy broke in. "Anyway, you wouldn't do yourself justice. The first thing that Phillips found out was that the problem of repairing damaged nervous tissue was inextricably involved with several other unknown things, such as the original growth of such tissue, its relationship to growth in general, the regeneration of lost members in lower forms, and so on. You see, Haynes, it is a known fact that nerves do grow, or else they could not exist; and in some lower forms of life they regenerate. Those facts were all he had, at first. In higher forms, even during the growth stage, regeneration does not occur spontaneously. Phillips set out to find out why.

"The thyroid controls growth, but does not initiate it, he learned. This fact seemed to indicate that there was an unknown hormone involved—that certain lower types possess an endocrine gland which is either atrophied or non-existent in higher types. If the latter,

671

he was sunk. He reasoned, however, that, since higher types evolved from lower, the gland in question might very well exist in a vestigial stage. He studied animals, thousands of them, from the germ upward. He exhausted the patience of the Posenian authorities; and when they cut off his appropriation, on the ground that the thing was impossible, he came here. We gave him carte blanche.

"The man is a miracle of perseverence, a keen observer, a shrewd reasoner, and a mechanic par excellence—a born researcher. Therefore, in time he learned what it must be: to cut it short, the pineal body. Then he had to find the stimulant. Drugs, chemicals, and spectrum of radiation; singly and in combination. Years of plugging, with just enough progress to keep him at it. Visits to other planets peopled by races human to two places or more; learning everything that had been done along the line of his problem. When you fellows moved Medon over here he visited it as a matter of routine, and there he hit the jackpot. Wise himself is a surgeon, and the Medonians have for centuries been having warfare and grief enough, steadily and in heroic doses, to develop the medical and surgical arts no end.

"They knew how to stimulate the pineal—a combination of drugs and specific radiations—but their method was dangerous. With Phillips' fresh viewpoint, his wide, new knowledge, and his mechanical genius, they worked out a new and highly satisfactory technique. He was going to try it out on a pirate going into the lethal chamber, but von Hohendorff heard about it and insisted that it should be tried on him. Got up on his Unattached Lensman's high horse and won't come down. So here we are."

"Hm-m-m—interesting!" The admiral had listened attentively. "You're pretty sure that it will work, aren't you?"

"As sure as we can be of anything that hasn't been tried. Ninety-percent probability, say—certainly not over ninety-five."

*

"Good enough odds." Haynes turned to the commandant. "What do you mean, you old reprobate, by sneaking around behind my back and horning in on my reservation? I rate Unattached, too, you know, and it's mine. You're out, von."

"I saw it first and I refuse to relinquish." Von Hohendorff was adamant.

"You've got to," Haynes insisted. "He isn't your cub any more; he's my Lensman. Besides, I'm a better test than you are—I've got more parts to replace than you have."

"Four or five make just as good a test as a dozen," the commandant declared.

"Gentlemen, think!" the Posenian pleaded. "Please consider that the pineal is actually inside the brain. It is true that I have not been able to discover any brain injury so far, but the process has not yet been applied to a reasoning brain and I can offer no assurance whatever that some obscure injury will not result."

"What of it?" and the two old Unattached Lensmen resumed their battle, hammer and tongs. Neither would yield a millimeter.

"Operate on them both, then, since they are both above law or reason," Lacy finally ordered in exasperation. "There ought to be a law to reduce Gray Lensmen to the ranks when they begin to suffer from ossification of the intellect."

"Starting with yourself, perhaps?" the admiral shot back, not at all abashed.

Haynes relented enough to let von Hohendorff go first, and both were given the necessary injections. The commandant was then strapped solidly into a chair; his head was clamped so firmly that he could not move it in any direction.

The Posenian swung his needle rays into place; two of them, diametrically opposed, each held rigidly upon micrometered racks and each operated by two huge, double, rock-steady hands. The operator *looked* entirely aloof—being eyeless and practically headless, it is impossible to tell from a Posenian's attitude or posture anything about the focal point of his attention—but the watchers knew that he was observing in microscopic detail the tiny gland within the old Lensman's skull.

Then Haynes. "Is this all there is to it, or do we come back for more?" he asked, when he was released from his shackles.

"That's all," Lacy answered. "One stimulation lasts for life, as far as we know. But if the treatment is successful you'll come back—about day after tomorrow, I think—to go to bed here. Your spare equipment won't fit and your stumps may require surgical attention."

Sure enough, Haynes did come back to the hospital, but not to go to bed. He was too busy. Instead, he got a wheel chair, and in it he was taken back to his now-boiling office. And in a few more days he called Lacy in high exasperation.

"Know what you've done?" he demanded. "Not satisfied with taking my perfectly good parts away from me, you've taken my teeth, too. They don't fit—I can't eat a thing! And I'm hungry as a wolf—I was never so hungry before in all my life! I *can't* live on soup, man; I've got work to do. What are you going to do about it?"

"*Ho-ho-haw!*" Lacy roared. "Serves you right—von Hohendorff is taking it easy here; sitting right on top of the world. Easy, now, sailor, don't rupture your aorta. I'll send a nurse over with a soft-boiled egg and a spoon. *Teething—at your age—Haw-ho-haw!*"

But it was no ordinary nurse who came, a few minutes later, to see the port admiral; it was the sector chief herself. She looked at him pityingly as she trundled him into his private office and shut the door, thereby establishing complete coverage.

"I had no idea, Admiral Haynes, that you . . . that there—" She paused.

"That I was so much of a machine-shop rebuild?"—complacently. "Except in the matter of eyes—which he doesn't need, anyway—our mutual friend Kinnison has very little on me, my dear. I got so handy with the replacements that very few people knew how much of me was artificial. But it's these teeth that are taking all the joy out of life. I'm hungry, confound it! Have you got anything really satisfying that I can eat?"

"I'll say I have!" She fed him; then, bending over, she squeezed him tight and kissed him emphatically. "You and the commandant are just perfectly wonderful old darlings, and I love you all to pieces," she declared. "I think Lacy was simply poisonous to laugh at you the way he did. Why, you two are the world's greatest heroes! He knew perfectly well all the time, the lug, that of course you'd be hungry; that you'd have to eat twice as much as usual while your legs and things were growing. Don't worry, admiral, I'll feed you until you bulge. I want you to hurry up with this, so that they'll do it to Kim."

"Thanks, Mac," and as she wheeled him back into the main office he considered her anew. A ravishing creature, but sound. Rash, and a bit stubborn, perhaps; impetuous and head-strong; but clean, solid metal all the way through. She had what it takes—she qualified. She and Kinnison would make a mighty fine couple when the lad got some of that heroic damn nonsense knocked out of his head—but there was work to do.

*

There was. The Galactic Council had considered thoroughly Kinnison's reports; its every member had conferred with him and with Worsel at length. Throughout the First Galaxy the Patrol was at work in all its prodigious might, preparing to wipe out the menace to civilization which was Boskone. First-line superdreadnoughts—no others would go upon that mission—were being built and armed, rebuilt and rearmed.

Well it was that the Galactic Patrol had previously amassed an almost inexhaustible supply of wealth, for its "reserves of expendible credit" were running like water.

Weapons, supposedly of irresistible power, were made even more powerful. Screens already "impenetrable" were stiffened into even greater stubbornness.

Primary projectors were made to take even higher loads, for longer times. New and heavier Q-type helices were designed and built. Larger and more destructive duodec bombs were hurled against already ruined, torn, and quivering test planets. Uninhabited worlds were being equipped with super-Bergenholms and with driving projectors. The negasphere, the most incredible menace to navigation which had ever existed in space, was being patrolled by a cordon of guard ships.

And all this activity centered in one vast building and culminated in one man—Port Admiral Haynes, Galactic councilor and chief of staff. And Haynes could not get enough to eat because he was cutting a new set of teeth!

He cut them, all thirty-two of them. His new limbs grew perfectly, even to the nails. Hair grew upon what had for years been a shining expanse of pate. But, much to Lacy's relief, it was old skin, not young, which covered the new limbs. It was white hair, not brown, that was dulling the glossiness of Haynes' bald old head. His bifocals, unchanged, were still necessary if he were to see anything clearly, near or far.

"Our experimental animals aged and died normally," Lacy explained graciously, "but I was beginning to wonder if we had rejuvenated you two, or perhaps endowed you with eternal life. Glad to see that the new parts have the same physical age as the rest of you—it would be mildly embarrassing to have to kill two Gray Lensmen to get rid of them."

"You aren't even as funny as a rubber crutch," Haynes grunted. "When are you going to give young Kinnison the works? Don't you realize that we need him?"

"Pretty soon now—just as soon as we give you and von your psychological examinations."

"Bah! That isn't necessary—my brain's QX!"

"That's what you think, but what do you know about brains? Worsel will tell us what shape your mind—if any—is in."

The Velantian put both Haynes and von Hohendorff through a grueling examination, finding that their minds had not been affected in any way by the stimulants applied to their pineal glands.

Then and only then did Phillips operate upon Kinnison; and in his case, too, the operation was a complete success. Arms and legs and eyes replaced themselves flawlessly. The scars of his terrible wounds disappeared, leaving no sign of ever having been.

He was a little slower, however; somewhat clumsy, and woefully weak. Therefore, instead of discharging him from the hospital as cured, which procedure would have restored to him automatically all the rights and privileges of an Unattached Lensman, the Council decided to transfer him to a physical-culture camp. A few weeks there would restore to him entirely the strength, speed, and agility which had formerly been his, and he would then be allowed to resume active duty.

*

Just before he left the hospital, Kinnison strolled with Clarrissa out to a bench in the grounds.

"—and you're making a perfect recovery," the girl was saying. "You'll be exactly as you were before. But things between us aren't just as they were, and they never can be again. You know that, Kim. We've got unfinished business to transact—let's take it down off the shelf before you go."

"Better let it lay, Mac," and all the newfound joy of existence went out of the man's eyes. "I'm whole, yes, but that angle was really the least important of all. You never yet have faced squarely the fact that my job isn't done and that my chance of living through it is just about one in ten. Even Phillips can't do anything about a corpse."

"No, and I won't face it, either, unless and until I must." Her reply was tranquillity itself. "Most of the troubles people worry about in advance never do materialize. And even if I did, you ought to know that I . . . that any woman would rather . . . well, that half a loaf is better than no bread."

"QX. I haven't ever mentioned the worst thing. I didn't want to—but if you've got to have it, here it is," the man wrenched out. "Look at what I am. A barroom brawler. A rum-dum. A hard-boiled egg. A cold-blooded, ruthless murderer, even of my own men—"

"Not that, Kim, ever, and you know it," she rebuked him.

"What else can you call it?" he grated. "A killer besides; a red-handed butcher if there ever was one—then, now, and forever. I've got to be. I can't get away from it. Do you think that you, or any other decent woman, could stand it to live with me? That you could feel my arms around you, feel my gory paws touching you, without going sick at the stomach?"

"Oh, so *that's* what's really been griping you all this time!" Clarrissa was surprised and entirely unshaken. "I don't have to think about that, Kim—I know. If you were a murderer or had the killer instinct, that would be different, but you aren't and you haven't. You are hard, of course. You have to be—but do you think that I would ever run a temperature over a softy? You brawl, yes—like the world's champion you are. Anybody you ever killed needed killing, there's no question of that. You don't do those things for fun; and the fact that you can drive yourself to do the things that have to be done shows your true caliber.

"Nor have you ever thought of the obverse; that you lean over backward in wielding that terrific power of yours. The Desplaines woman, the countess—lots of other instances. I respect and honor you more than any other man I have ever known. Any woman who really knew you would—*she must! And I know!* Remember that wide-open two-way put me *in* your mind for an instant—long enough—that let me understand something of the

675

horrible weight you have to carry, something of the terrible power you must—for civilization—leash or release, direct and control. *I know*—no words you may say now can add to or change that single, full-view understanding I got then.

"Listen, Kim. Read my mind, all of it. You will know me then, and understand me better than I can ever explain myself."

"Have you got a picture of me doing that?" he asked flatly.

"No, you big, unreasonable clunker, I haven't!" she flared, "and that's just what's driving me mad!" Then, voice dropping to a whisper, almost sobbing: "Cancel that, Kim—I didn't mean it. You wouldn't—you couldn't, I suppose, and still be you, the man I love. But isn't there something—*anything*—that will make you understand what I really am?"

"I know what you are." Kinnison's voice was uninflected, weary. "As I told you before—the Universe's best. It's what I am that's clogging the jets. What I have been and what I have to keep on being. I simply don't rate up, and you'd better lay off me, Mac, while you can. There's a poem by one of the ancients—Kipling—the 'Ballad of Boh Da Thone'—that describes it exactly. You wouldn't know it—"

"You just think that I wouldn't"—nodding brightly. "The only trouble is that you always think of the wrong verses. Part of it really is descriptive of you. You know, where all the soldiers of the Black Tyrone thought so much of their captain?"

She recited:

"And worshiped with fluency, fervor, and zeal
The mud on the boot heels of Crook O'Neil.

"That describes you exactly."

"You're crazy for the lack of sense," he demurred. "I don't rate like that."

"Sure, you do," she assured him. "All the men think of you that way. And not only men. Women, too, darn 'em—and the very next time that I catch one of them at it I'm going to kick her cursed teeth out, one by one!"

*

Kinnison laughed, albeit a trifle sourly. "You're raving, Mac. Imagining things. But to get back to that poem, what I was referring to went like this—"

"I know how it goes. Listen:

"But the captain had quitted the long-drawn strife
And in far Simoorie had taken a wife;

"And she was a damsel of delicate mold,
With hair like the sunshine and heart of gold.

"And little she knew the arms that embraced
Had cloven a man from the brow to the waist;

"And little she knew that the loving lips
Had ordered a quivering life's eclipse,

"And the eyes that lit at her lightest breath
Had glared unawed in the Gates of Death.

"(For these be matters a man would hide,
As a general thing, from an innocent bride.)

676

"That's what you, mean, isn't it?" she asked quietly.

"Mac, you know a lot of things that you've got no business knowing." Instead of answering her question, he stared at her speculatively. "My sprees and brawls, Dessa Desplaines and the Countess Avondrin, and now this. Would you mind telling me how you get the stuff?"

"I'm closer to you than you suspect, Kim, and have been for a long time. Worsel calls it being 'en rapport,' I believe. You don't need to think at me—in fact, you have to put up a conscious block to keep me out. So I know a lot that I shouldn't, but Lensmen aren't the only ones who don't talk. You have been thinking about that poem a lot—it worried you—so I went to the library and looked it up. I memorized most of it."

"Well, to get the true picture of me you'll have to multiply that by a thousand. Also, don't forget that loose heads might be rolling onto your breakfast table almost any morning instead of only once."

"So what?" she countered evenly. "Do you think that I could sit for Kipling's portrait of Mrs. O'Neil? Nobody ever called my mold delicate, and he would have said of me:

"With hair like a conflagration

And a heart of solid brass!

"Captain O'Neil's bride, as well as being innocent and ignorant, strikes me as having been a good deal of a sissy, something of a weeping willow, and no little of a shrinking violet. Tell me, Kim, do you think that she would have made good as a sector chief nurse?"

"No, but that's neither here—"

"It is, too," she interrupted. "You've got to consider what I did, and that it's no job for a girl with a weak stomach. Besides, the Boh's head took the fabled Mrs. O'Neil by surprise. She didn't know that her husband used to be in the wholesale mayhem-and-killing business. I do.

"And lastly, you big lug, do you think that I'd be making such barefaced passes at you—playing the brazen hussy this way—unless I was very, *very* certain of the truth?"

"Huh?" he demanded, blushing furiously. "I thought that you were running a blazer on me before—you really do *know*, then, that—" He would not say it, even then.

"Of course I know!" She nodded; then, as the man spread his hands helplessly, she abandoned her attempts to keep the conversation upon a light level.

"I know, my dear; there is nothing we can do about it yet." Her voice was unsteady, her heart in every word. "You have to do your job, and I honor you for that, too; even if it does take you from me. It will be easier for you, though, I think, and I *know* that it will be easier for me, to have us both know the truth. Whenever you are ready, Kim, I'll be here—or somewhere—waiting. Clear ether, Gray Lensman!" and, rising to her feet, she turned back toward the hospital.

"Clear ether, Chris!" Unconsciously he used the pet name by which he had thought of her so much. He stared after her for a minute, hungrily. Then, squaring his shoulders, he strode away.

*

And upon far Jarnevon Eichmil, the First of Boskone, was conferring with Jalte via communicator. Long since, the Kalonian had delivered through devious channels the message of Boskone to an imaginary director of Lensmen; long since he had transmitted this cryptically direful reply:

"Lensman Morgan lives, and so does Star A Star."

Jalte had not been able to report to his chief any news concerning the fate of that which the speedster bore, since spies no longer existed within the reservations of the Patrol. He had learned of no discovery that any Lensman had made. He could not venture any hypothesis as to how this Star A Star had heard of Jarnevon or had learned of its location in space. He was sure of only one thing, and that was a grimly disturbing fact indeed. The Patrol was re-arming throughout the Galaxy, upon a scale theretofore unknown. Eichmil's thought was cold:

"That means but one thing. A Lensman invaded you and learned of us here—in no other way could knowledge of Jarnevon have come to them."

"Why me?" Jalte demanded. "If there exists a mind of power sufficient to break my screens and tracelessly to invade my mind, what of yours?"

"It is a thing proven by the outcome." The Boskonian's statement was a calm summation of fact. "The messenger sent against you succeeded; the one sent against us failed. The Patrol intends and is preparing: certainly to wipe out our remaining forces within the Tellurian Galaxy; probably to attack your stronghold; eventually to invade our own galaxy. It is well—for that reason, in part, was the Lensman Morgan sent back as he was sent."

"Let them come!" snarled the Kalonian. "We can and we will hold this planet forever against anything they can bring through space!"

"I would not be too sure of that," cautioned the superior. "In fact, if—as I am beginning to regard as a probability—the Patrol does make a concerted drive against any significant number of our planetary organizations, you should abandon your base there and return to Kalonia, after disbanding and so preserving for future use as many as possible of the planetary units."

"Future use? In that case there will be no future."

"There will be," Eichmil replied, coldly vicious. "We are strengthening the defenses of Jarnevon to withstand any conceivable assault. If they do not attack us here of their own free will, we shall compel them to do so. Then, after destroying their every mobile force, we shall again take over their galaxy. Arms for that purpose are even now in the building. Is the matter entirely clear?"

"It is clear. We shall warn all our groups that such orders may issue; and we shall prepare to abandon this base if such a step should become desirable."

So it was planned: neither Eichmil nor Jalte even suspecting two startling truths:

First, that when the Patrol was ready it would strike hard and without warning, and,

Second, that it would strike—not low, but high!

XXIII.

Kinnison played, worked, rested, ate, and slept. He boxed, strenuously and viciously, with masters of the craft. He practiced with his DeLameters until he had regained his old-time speed and dead-center accuracy. He swam for hours at a time, he ran in cross-country races. He lolled, practically naked, in hot sunshine. And finally, when his muscles were writhing and rippling as of yore beneath the bronzed satin of his skin, Lacy answered his insistent demands by coming to see him.

The Gray Lensman met the flier eagerly, but his face fell when he saw that the surgeon general was alone.

"No, MacDougall didn't come—she isn't around any more," he explained guilefully.

"Huh?" came the startled query. "How come?"

"Out in space—out Borova way somewhere. What do you care? After the way you acted you've got the crust of a rhinoceros to think that—"

"You're crazy, Lacy! Why, we . . . she—It's all fixed up."

"Funny kind of fixing. Moping around Base, crying her red head off. Finally, though, she decided that she had some Scotch pride left, and I let her go aboard again. If she isn't all done with you, she ought to be." This, Lacy figured, would be good for what ailed the big saphead. "Come on, and I'll see whether you're fit to go back to work or not."

He was fit. "QX, lad, flit!" Lacy discharged him informally with a slap upon the back. "Get dressed and I'll take you back to Haynes—he's been snapping at me like a turtle ever since you've been out here."

At Prime Base, Kinnison was welcomed enthusiastically by the admiral.

"Feel those fingers, Kim!" he exclaimed. "Perfect! Just like the originals!"

"Mine, too. They do feel good."

"It's a pity that you got your new ones so quick. You'd appreciate 'em much more after a few years without 'em. But to get down to business. The fleets have been taking off for a couple of weeks—we're to join up as the line passes. If you haven't anything better to do, I'd like to have you aboard the Z9M9Z."

"I don't know of any place I'd rather be, sir—thanks."

"QX. Thanks should be the other way. You can make yourself mighty useful between now and zero time." He eyed the young man speculatively.

Haynes had a special job for him, Kinnison knew. As a Gray Lensman, he could not be given any military rank or post, and he could not conceive of the admiral of Grand Fleet wanting him around as an aid-de-camp.

"Spill it, chief," he invited. "Not orders, of course—I understand that perfectly. Requests or . . . ah-hum . . . suggestions."

"I *will* crown you with something yet, you whelp!" Haynes snorted, and Kinnison grinned. These two were very close, in spite of their disparity in years; and very much of a piece. "As you get older you will realize that it is good tactics to stick pretty close to Gen Regs. Yes, I *have* got a job for you, and it's a nasty one. Nobody else has been able to handle it, not even two companies of Rigellians. Grand Fleet Operations."

"*Grand Fleet Operations!*" Kinnison was aghast. "Holy . . . Klono's . . . brazen . . . bowels! What makes you think I've got jets enough to swing *that* load, chief?"

"I haven't any idea whether you can or not. I know, however, that if you can't, nobody can; and in spite of all the work we've done on the thing we'll have to operate as a mob, as we did before, and not as a fleet. If so, I shudder to think of the results."

"QX. If you'll send for Worsel, we'll try it a fling or two. It'd be a shame to build a whole ship around an Operations tank and then not be able to use it; I'll see what I can do. By the way, I haven't seen my head nurse—Miss MacDougall, you know—any place lately. Have you? I ought to tell her 'thanks' or something—maybe send her a flower."

"Nurse? MacDougall? Oh, yes, the redhead. Let me see—did hear something about her the other day. Married? No, that wasn't it . . . . She took a hospital ship somewhere. Alsakan—Vandemar—somewhere; didn't pay any attention. She doesn't need thanks—or flowers, either—she's getting paid for her work. Much more important, don't you think, to get Operations straightened out?"

"Undoubtedly, sir," Kinnison replied stiffly, and as he went out Lacy came in.

The two old conspirators greeted each other with knowing grins. *Was* Kinnison taking it big! He was falling, like ten thousand bricks down a well.

"Do him good to undermine his position a bit. Too cocky altogether. But *how* they suffer!"

"Check!"

*

Kinnison rode toward the flagship in a mood which even he could not have described. He had expected to see her, as a matter of course—he wanted to see her—confound it, he *had* to see her! Why did she have to do a flit now, of all the times on the calendar? She knew that the fleet was shoving off, and that he'd have to go along—and nobody knew where she was. When he got back he'd find her if he had to chase her all over the Galaxy. He'd put an end to this. Duty was duty, of course—but Chris was CHRIS—and half a loaf *was* better than no bread!

He jerked back to reality as he entered the gigantic teardrop which was technically the Z9M9Z, socially the *Directrix*, and ordinarily GFHQ. She had been designed and built specifically to be Grand Fleet Headquarters, and nothing else. She bore no offensive armament; but since she had to protect the presiding geniuses of combat, she had every possible defense.

Port Admiral Haynes had learned a bitter lesson during the expedition to Helmuth's base. Long before that relatively small Grand Fleet got there he was sick to the core, realizing that fifty thousand vessels simply could not be controlled or maneuvered as a group. If that base had been capable of an offensive, or even of a real defensive, or if Boskone could have put their fleets into that star cluster in time, the Patrol would have been defeated ignominiously; and Haynes, wise old tactician that he was, knew it only too well.

Therefore, immediately after the return from that "triumphant" venture, he gave orders to design and to build, at whatever cost, a flagship capable of directing efficiently a million combat units.

The "tank"—the three-dimensional galactic chart which is a necessary part of every pilot room—had grown and grown as it became evident that it must be the prime agency in

Grand Fleet Operations. Finally, in this last rebuilding, the tank was seven hundred feet in diameter and eighty feet thick in the middle—over seventeen million cubic feet of space in which more than two million tiny lights crawled hither and thither in hopeless confusion. For, after the technicians and designers had put that tank into actual service, they had discovered that it was useless. No available mind had been able either to perceive any situation as a whole, or to identify with certainty any light or group of lights needing correction. And as for linking up any particular light with its individual, blanket-proof communicator in time to issue orders in space combat—

Kinnison looked at the tank, then around the full circle of the million-plug board encircling it. He observed the horde of operators, each one trying frantically to do something. Next he shut his eyes, the better to perceive everything at once, and studied the problem for an hour.

"Attention, everybody!" he thought then. "Open all circuits—do nothing at all for a while." He then called Haynes.

"I think that we can clean up this mess if you'll send over some Simplex analyzers and the crew of technicians. Helmuth had a sweet set-up on multiplex controls, and Jalte had some ideas that we can adapt to fit this tank. If we add them all together, we may have something."

*

And by the time Worsel arrived, they did.

"Red lights are fleets already in motion," Kinnison explained rapidly to the Velantian. "Greens are fleets still at their bases. Ambers are the planets the greens took off from—connected, you see, by Ryerson string-lights. The white star is us, the *Directrix*. That violet cross 'way over there is Jalte's planet, our first objective. The pink comets are our free planets, their tails showing their intrinsic velocities. Being so slow, they had to start long ago. The purple circle is the negasphere. It's on its way, too. You take that side, I'll take this. They were supposed to start from the edge of the twelfth sector. The idea was to make it a smooth, bowl-shaped sweep across the Galaxy, converging upon the objective, but each of the fleet commanders apparently wants to run this war to suit himself. Look at that guy there—he's beating the gun by nine thousand parsecs. Watch me pin his ears back!"

He pointed his Simplex at the red light which had so offendingly sprung into being. There was a whirring click and the number 449276 flashed above a board. An operator flicked a switch.

"Grand Fleet Operations!" Kinnison snapped. "Why are you taking off without orders?"

"Why, I . . . I'll give you the vice-admiral, sir—"

"No time! Tell your vice-admiral that one more such break will put him in irons. Land at once! GFO—off!"

"With around a million fleets to handle, we can't spend much time on anyone," he thought at Worsel, "but after we get them lined up and get our Rigellians broken in, it won't be so bad."

The breaking in did not take long; definite and meaningful orders flew faster and faster along the tiny, but steel-hard beams of the communicators.

"Take off . . . . Increase drive four point five . . . . Decrease drive two point seven . . . . Change course to—" and so it went, hour after hour and day after day.

And with the passage of time came order out of chaos. The red lights formed a gigantically sweeping, curving wall, its almost imperceptible crawl representing an actual velocity of almost one hundred parsecs an hour. Behind that wall blazed a sea of amber, threaded throughout with the brilliant filaments which were the Ryerson lights. Ahead of it lay a sparkling, almost solid blaze of green. Closer and closer the wall crept toward the bright white star.

And in the "reducer"—the standard, ten-foot tank in the lower well—the entire spectacle was reproduced in miniature. It was plainer there, clearer and much more readily seen; but it was so crowded that details were indistinguishable.

Haynes stood beside Kinnison's padded chair one day, staring up into the immense lens and shaking his head. He went down the flight of stairs to the reducer, studied that, and again shook his head.

"This is very pretty, but it doesn't mean a thing," he thought at Kinnison. "It begins to look as though I'm going along just for the ride. You—or you and Worsel—will have to do the fighting, too, I'm afraid."

"Uh-huh," Kinnison demurred. "What do we—or anyone else—know about tactics, compared to you? You've got to be the brains. That's why we had the boys rig up the original working model there, for a reducer. On that you can watch and figure out the gross developments and tell us in general terms what to do. Knowing that, we will know who ought to do what, from the big tank here, and we will pass your orders along."

"Say, that *will* work, at that!" and Haynes brightened visibly. "Looks as though a couple of those reds are going to knock our star out of the tank, doesn't it?"

"It'll be close in that reducer. They'll probably touch. Close enough in real space—less than three parsecs."

The zero hour came and the Tellurian armada of eighty-one sleek destroyers—eighty superdreadnoughts and the *Directrix*—spurned Earth and took its place in that hurtling wall of crimson. Solar system after solar system was passed; fleet after fleet leaped into the ether and fitted itself into the smoothly geometrical pattern which GFO was nursing along so carefully.

Through the Galaxy the formation swept, and out of it, toward a star cluster. It slowed its mad pace; the center hanging back, the edges advancing and folding in.

"Surround the cluster and close in," the admiral directed; and, under the guidance now of two hundred Rigellians, civilization's vast Grand Fleet closed smoothly in and went inert. Drivers flared white as they fought to match the intrinsic velocity of the cluster.

"Vice admirals of all fleets, attention! Using secondaries only, fire at will upon any enemy object coming within range. Engage outlying structures and such battle craft as may appear. Keep assigned distance from planet and stiffen cosmic screens to maximum. Haynes—off!"

From untold millions of projectors there raved out gigantic rods, knives, and needles of force, under the impact of which the defensive screens of Jalte's guardian citadels flamed into terrible refulgence. Duodec bombs were hurled—tight-beam-directed monsters of destruction which, swinging around in huge circles to attain the highest possible measure of momentum, flung themselves against Boskone's defenses in Herculean attempts to smash them down. They exploded; each as it burst filling all nearby space with blindingly intense violet light and with flying scraps of metal. Q-type helices, driven with all the frightful kilowattage possible to Medonian conductors and insulation, screwed in, biting, gouging, tearing in wild abandon. Shear-planes, hellish knives of force beside which Tellurian lightning is pale and wan, struck and struck and struck again—fiendishly, crunchingly.

But those grimly stolid fortresses could take it. They had been repowered; their defenses stiffened to such might as to defy, in the opinion of Boskone's experts, any projectors capable of being mounted upon mobile bases. And not only could they take it—those formidably armed and armored planetoids could dish it out as well. The screens of the Patrol ships flared high into the spectrum under the crushing force of sheer enemy power. Not a few of those defenses were battered down, clear to the wall shields, before the unimaginable ferocity of the Boskonian projectors could be neutralized.

*

And at this spectacularly frightful deep-space engagement Jalte, Boskone's galactic director, and through him Eichmil, First of Boskone itself, stared in stunned surprise.

"It is insane!" Jalte gloated. "The fools judged our strength by that of Helmuth; not considering that we, as well as they, would be both learning and doing during the intervening time. They have a myriad of ships, but mere numbers will never conquer my outposts, to say nothing of my works here."

"They are not fools. I am not sure—" Eichmil cogitated.

He would have been even less sure could he have listened to a conversation which was even then being held.

"QX, Thorndyke?" Kinnison asked.

"On the green," came instant reply. "Intrinsic, placement, releases—everything on the green!"

"Cut!" and the lone purple circle disappeared from tank and from reducer. The master technician had cut his controls and every pound of metal and other substance surrounding the negasphere had been absorbed by that enigmatic volume of nothingness. No connection or contact with it was now possible; and with its carefully established intrinsic velocity it rushed engulfingly toward the doomed planet. One of the mastodonic fortresses which lay in its path vanished utterly, with nothing save a burst of invisible cosmics to mark its passing. It approached its goal. It was almost upon the planet before any of the defenders perceived it; and even then they could neither understand nor grasp it. All detectors and other warning devices remained static, but:

"Look! There! Something's *coming*!" an observer jittered, and Jalte swung his plate.

Jalte saw—nothing. Eichmil saw the same thing. There was nothing to see. A vast, intangible nothing—yet a nothing tangible enough to occult everything material in a full

683

third of the cone of vision! Jalte's operators hurled into it their mightiest beams. Nothing happened. They struck nothing and disappeared. They loosed their heaviest duodec torpedoes; gigantic missiles whose warheads contained enough of that frightfully violent detonate to disrupt a world. Nothing happened—not even an explosion. Not even the faintest flash of light. Shell and contents alike merely and, oh, so incredibly peaceful, ceased to exist. There were important bursts of cosmics, but they were invisible and inaudible; and neither Jalte nor any member of his crew were to live long enough to realize how terribly they had already been burned.

Gigantic pressors shoved against it; beams of power sufficient to deflect a satellite; beams whose projectors were braced, in steel-laced concrete down to bedrock, against any conceivable thrust. But this was *negative*, not positive, matter—matter negative in every respect of mass, inertia, and force. To it a push was a pull. Pressors to it were tractors—at contact they pulled themselves up off their massive foundations and hurtled into the appalling blackness.

*

Then the negasphere struck. Or did it? Can nothing strike anything? It would be better, perhaps, to say that the spherical hyperplane which was the three-dimensional cross-section of the negasphere began to occupy the same volume of space as that in which Jalte's unfortunate world already was. And at the surface of contact of the two the materials of both disappeared. The substance of the planet vanished; the incomprehensible nothingness of the negasphere faded away into the ordinary vacuity of empty space.

Jalte's base, all the three hundred square miles of it, was taken at the first gulp. A vast pit opened where it had been, a hole which deepened and widened with horrifying rapidity. And as the yawning abyss enlarged itself the stuff of the planet fell into it, in turn to vanish. Mountains tumbled into it, oceans dumped themselves into it. The hot, frightfully compressed and nascent material of the planet's core sought to erupt—but instead of moving, it, too, vanished. Vast areas of the world's surface crust, tens of thousands of square miles in extent, collapsed into it, splitting off along crevasses of appalling depth, and became nothing. The stricken globe shuddered, trembled, ground itself to bits in paroxysm after ghastly paroxysm of disintegration.

What was happening? Eichmil did not know, since his "eye" was destroyed before any really significant developments could eventuate. He and his scientists could only speculate and deduce—which, with surprising accuracy, they did. The officers of the Patrol ships, however, *knew* what was going on, and they were scanning with intently narrowed eyes the instruments which were recording instant by instant the performance of the new cosmic super-screens which were being assaulted so brutally.

For, as has been said, the negasphere was composed of negative matter. Instead of electrons, its building blocks were positrons—the "Dirac holes" in an infinity of negative energy. Whenever the field of a positron encountered that of an electron, the two neutralized each other, giving rise to two quanta of hard radiation. And, since those encounters were occurring at the rate of countless trillions per second, there was tearing at the Patrol's defenses a flood of cosmic rays of an intensity which no spaceship had ever before been called upon to withstand. But the new screens had been figured with a factor of safety of five, and they stood up.

The planet dwindled with soul-shaking rapidity to a moon, to a moonlet, and finally to a discreetly conglomerate aggregation of meteorites before the mutual neutralization ceased.

"Primaries now," Haynes ordered briskly, as the needles of the cosmic-ray-screen meters dropped back to the points of normal functioning. The probability was that the defenses of the Boskonian citadels would now be automatic only, that no life had endured through that awful flood of lethal radiation; but he was taking no chances. Out flashed the penetrant super rays and the fortresses, too, ceased to exist save as the impalpable infradust of space.

And the massed Grand Fleet of the Galactic Patrol, making its formation, hurtled outward through the intergalactic void.

XXIV.

"They are not fools. I am not so sure—" Eichmil had said; and when the last force-ball, his last means of intergalactic communication, went dead, the First of Boskone became very unsure indeed. The Patrol undoubtedly had something new—he himself had had glimpses of it—but what was it?

That Jalte's base was gone was obvious. That Boskone's hold upon the Tellurian Galaxy was gone, followed as a corollary. That the Patrol was or would soon be wiping out Boskone's regional and planetary units was a logical inference. Star A Star, that accursed director of Lensmen, had—must have—succeeded in stealing Jalte's records, to be willing to destroy out of hand the base which had housed them.

Nor could Boskone do anything to help the underlings, now that the long-awaited attack upon Jarnevon itself was almost certainly coming. Let them come—Boskone was ready. Or was it—quite? Jalte's defenses had been strong, but they had not withstood that unknown weapon even for seconds.

Eichmil called a joint meeting of Boskone and the Academy of Science. Coldly and precisely he told them everything that he had seen. Discussion followed.

"Negative matter beyond a doubt," a scientist summed up the consensus of opinion. "It has long been surmised that in some other, perhaps hyperspatial universe there must exist negative matter of mass sufficient to balance the positive material of the universe we know. It is conceivable that by hyperspatial explorations and manipulations the Tellurians have discovered that other universe and have transported some of its substance into ours."

"Can they manufacture it?" Eichmil demanded.

"The probability that such material can be manufactured is exceedingly small," was the studied reply. "An entirely new mathematics would be necessary. In all probability they found it already existent."

"We must find it also, then, and at once."

"We will try. Bear in mind, however, that the field is large, and do not be optimistic of an early success. Note, also, that the substance is not necessary—perhaps not even desirable—in a defensive action."

"Why not?"

"Because, by directing pressors against such a bomb, Jalte actually pulled it into his base, precisely where the enemy wished it to go. As a surprise attack, against those ignorant of its true nature, such a weapon would be effective indeed; but against us it will prove a boomerang. All that is needful is to mount tractor heads upon pressor bases, and thus drive the bombs back upon those who send them." It did not occur, even to the coldest scientist of them all, that that bomb had been of planetary mass. Not one of the Eich suspected that all that remained of the entire world upon which Jalte's base had stood was a handful of meteorites.

"Let them come, then," the First of Boskone announced grimly. "Their dependence upon a new and supposedly unknown weapon explains what would otherwise be insane tactics. With that weapon impotent, they cannot possibly win a long war waged so far from their bases. We can match them ship for ship, and more; and our supplies and munitions are close at hand. We will wear them down—blast them out—the Tellurian Galaxy shall yet be ours!"

*

Admiral Haynes spent almost every waking hour setting up and knocking down tactical problems in the practice tank, and gradually his expression changed from one of strained anxiety to one of pleased satisfaction. He went over to his sealed-band transmitter, called all communications officers, and ordered:

"Each vessel will direct its longest-range detector, at highest possible power, centrally upon the objective galaxy. The first observer to find enemy activity will report it instantly to us here. We will send out a general C. B., at which every vessel will cease blasting at once, remaining motionless until further orders." He then called Kinnison.

"Look here," he directed the attention of the younger man into the reducer, which now represented intergalactic space, with a portion of the Second Galaxy filling one edge. "I have a solution, but its practicability depends upon whether or not it calls for the impossible from you, Worsel, and your Rigellians. You remarked at the start that I knew my tactics. I wish that I knew more—or at least could be certain that Boskone and I agree upon what constitutes good tactics. I feel quite safe in assuming, however, that we shall meet their Grand Fleet well outside the Galaxy—"

"Why?" asked the startled Kinnison. "If I were Eichmil, I'd pull every ship I had in around Jarnevon and keep it there; they can't force engagement with us!"

"Poor tactics. The very presence of their fleet out in space will force us to engage, and decisively at that. From his viewpoint, if he defeats us there, that ends it. If he loses, that is only his first line of defense. His observers will have reported fully. He will have invaluable data upon which to work, and much time before even his outlying fortresses can be threatened.

"From our viewpoint, we cannot refuse battle if his fleet is there. It would be suicidal for us to enter that Galaxy, leaving intact outside it a fleet as powerful as that one is bound to be."

"Why? Harrying us from the rear might be bothersome, but I don't see how it could be disastrous."

"Not that. They could, and would, attack Tellus."

"Oh—I never thought of that. But couldn't they, anyway—two fleets?"

"No. He knows that Tellus is very strongly held, and that this is no ordinary fleet. He will have to concentrate everything he has upon either one or the other—it is almost inconceivable that he would divide his forces."

"QX. I said that you're the brains of the outfit, and you are!"

"Thanks, lad. At the first sign of detection, we stop. They may be able to detect us, but I doubt it, since we are looking for them with special instruments. But that's immaterial. What I want to know is, can you and your crew split the fleet, making two big, hollow hemispheres of it? Let this group of ambers represent the enemy. Since they know that we will have to carry the battle to them, they will probably be in fairly close formation. Set your two hemispheres—the reds—there and there. Close in, making a sphere, like this—englobing their whole fleet. Can you do it?"

Kinnison whistled through his teeth; a long, low, unmelodious whistle. "Yes—but Klono's brazen claws, chief, suppose they catch you at it?"

"How can they? If you were using detectors, instead of double-ended, tight-beam binders, how many of our own vessels could you locate?"

"That's right, too—less than one percent of them. They couldn't tell that they were being englobed until long after it was done. They could, however, globe up inside us—"

"Yes—and that would give them the tactical advantage of position," the admiral admitted. "We probably have, however, enough superiority in firing power, if not in actual tonnage, to make up the difference. Also, we have speed enough, I think, so that we could retire in good order. But you are assuming that they can maneuver as rapidly and as surely as we can, a condition which I do not consider at all probable. If, as I believe much more likely, they have no better Grand Fleet Operations than we had in Helmuth's star cluster—if they haven't the equivalent of you and Worsel and this supertank here—then what?"

"In that case it'd be just too bad. Just like pushing baby chicks into a pond." Kinnison saw the possibilities clearly enough after they had been explained to him.

"How long will it take you?"

"With Worsel and both full crews of Rigellians I would guess it at about ten hours—eight to compute and assign positions and two to get there."

"Fast enough—faster than I would have thought possible. Oil up your calculating machines and Simplexes and get ready."

*

In due time the enemy fleet was detected and detection was confirmed. The "Cease Blasting" signal was sent out. Civilization's prodigious fleet stopped dead, hanging motionless in space with its nearest units at the tantalizing limit of detectability from the warships awaiting them. For eight hours two hundred Rigellians stood at whirring calculators, each solving course-and-distance problems at the rate of ten per minute. Two hours or less of free flight, and Haynes rejoiced audibly in the perfection of the two red hemispheres shown in his reducer. The two immense bowls flashed together, rim to rim. The sphere began inexorably to contract. Each ship put out a red K6T screen as a combined battle flag and identification, and the greatest naval engagement of the age was on.

It soon became evident that the Boskonians could not maneuver their forces efficiently. Their fleet was too huge, too unwieldy for their operations officers to handle. Against an equally uncontrollable mob of battle craft it would have made a showing, but against the carefully planned, chronometer-timed attack of the Patrol individual action, however courageous or however desperate, was useless.

Each red-sheathed destroyer hurtled along a definite course at a definite force of drive for a definite length of time. Orders were strict; no ship was to be lured from course, pace, or time. They could, however, fight en passant with their every weapon if occasion arose; and occasion did arise, some thousands of times. The units of Grand Fleet flashed inward, lashing out with their terrible primaries at everything in space not wearing the crimson robe of civilization. And whatever those beams struck did not need striking again.

The warships of Boskone fought back. Many of the Patrol's defensive screens blazed hot enough almost to mask the scarlet beacons; some of them went down. A few Patrol ships were englobed by the concerted action of two or three subfleet commanders more co-operative or more farsighted than the rest, and were blasted out of existence by an overwhelming concentration of power. But even those vessels took toll with their primaries as they went out; few, indeed, were the Boskonians who escaped through holes thus made.

At a predetermined instant each dreadnought stopped, to find herself one nut of an immense, red-flaming hollow sphere of ships packed almost screen to screen. And upon signal every primary projector that could be brought to bear hurled bolt after bolt, as fast as the burned-out shells could be replaced, into the ragingly incandescent inferno which that sphere's interior instantly became. For two hundred million discharges such as those will convert even a very large volume of space into something utterly impossible to describe.

The raving torrents of energy subsided and keen-eyed observers swept the scene of action. Nothing was there except jumbled and tumbling white-hot wreckage. A few vessels had escaped during the closing in of the sphere, but none inside it had survived this climactic action—not one in five thousand of Boskone's massed fleet made its way back to dark Jarnevon.

"Maneuver fifty-eight—hipe!" and Grand Fleet shot away. There was no waiting, no hesitation. Every course and time had been calculated and assigned.

Into the Second Galaxy the scarcely diminished armada of the Patrol hurtled—to Jarnevon's solar system—around it. Once again the crimson sheathing of civilization's messengers almost disappeared in blinding coruscance as the outlying fortresses unleashed their mighty weapons; once again a few ships, subjected to such concentrations of force as to overload their equipment, were lost; but this conflict, although savage in its intensity, was brief. Nothing mobile *could* endure for long the utterly hellish energies of the primaries, and soon the armored planetoids, too, ceased to be.

"Maneuver fifty-nine—hipe!" and Grand Fleet closed in upon somber Jarnevon itself.

"Sixty!" It rolled in space, forming an immense cylinder; the doomed planet the midpoint of its axis.

"Sixty-one!" Tractors and pressors leaped out, from ship to ship and from ship to shore. The Patrol did not know whether or not the scientists of the Eich could render their planet inertialess, but now it made no difference. Planet and fleet were for the time being one rigid system.

"Sixty-two—blast!" And against the world-girdling battlements of Jarnevon there flamed out in all their appalling might the dreadful beams against which the defensive webs of battleships and of mobile citadels alike had been so pitifully inadequate.

But these which they were attacking now were not the limited installations of a mobile structure. The Eich had at their command all the resources of a galaxy. Their generators and conductors could be of any desired number and size. Hence Eichmil, in view of prior happenings, had strengthened the defenses of his planet to a point which certain of his fellows derided as being beyond the bounds of sanity or reason.

*

Now those unthinkably powerful screens were being tested to the utmost. Bolt after bolt of quasi-solid lightning struck against them, spitting mile-long sparks in baffled fury as they raged to ground. Plain and incased in Q-type helices they came; biting, tearing, gouging. Often and often, under the thrust of half a dozen at once, local failures appeared; but these were only momentary, and not even the newly devised shells of the projectors could stand the load long enough to penetrate effectively Boskone's indescribably capable defenses. Nor were the enemies' offensive weapons less capable.

Rods, cones, planes, and shears of pure force bored, cut, stabbed, and slashed. Bombs and dirigible torpedoes charged to the skin with duodec sought out the red-cloaked ships. Beams, sheathed against atmosphere in Q-type helices, crashed against and through their armor—beams of an intensity almost to rival that of the Patrol's primary weapons and of a hundred times their effective aperture. And not singly did those beams come. Eight, ten, twelve at once they clung to and demolished dreadnought after dreadnought of the Expeditionary Force.

Eichmil was well content. "We can hold them and we are burning them down!" he gloated. "Let them loose their negative-matter bombs! Get the analysis of those beams—build them! They are burning out projectors, which means that they cannot keep this up indefinitely. They will have to retire, what there are left of them, for more munitions; and when they come back we will blast them out of space!"

He was wrong. Grand Fleet did not stay there long enough so that even the projectors of the Eich could destroy more than a few thousands of ships. For even while the cylinder was forming, Kinnison was in rapid but careful consultation with Thorndyke, checking intrinsic velocities, directions, and speeds.

"QX, Verne—*cut!*" he yelled.

Two planets, one well within each end of the combat cylinder, went inert at the word; resuming instantaneously their diametrically opposed intrinsic velocities, each of some thirty miles per second. And it was these two very ordinary, but utterly irresistible planets, instead of the negative-matter bombs with which the Eich were prepared to cope, which hurtled then along the axis of the immense tube of warships toward Jarnevon. Whether or not the Eich could make their planet inertialess has never been found out. Free or inert, the end would have been the same.

"Every Y14M officer of every ship of the Patrol, attention!" Haynes ordered. "Don't get all tensed up. Take it easy; there's lots of time. Any time within a second after I give the word will be p-l-e-n-t-y o-f t-i-m-e—*cut!*"

The two worlds rushed together, doomed Jarnevon squarely between them. Haynes snapped out his order as the three were within two seconds of contact, and as he spoke all the tractors and all the pressors were released. The ships of the Patrol were already free—none had been inert since leaving Jalte's ex-planet—and thus could not be harmed by flying débris.

The planets touched. They coalesced, squishingly at first, the encircling warships drifting lightly away before a cosmically violent blast of superheated atmosphere; Jarnevon burst open, all the way around, and spattered; billions upon billions of tons of hot core-magma being hurled afar in gouts and streamers. The two planets, crashing through what had been a world, met, crunched, crushed together in all the unimaginable momentum of their masses and velocities. They subsided, crashingly. Not merely mountains, but entire halves of worlds disrupted and fell, in such Gargantuan paroxysms as the eye of man had never elsewhere beheld. And every motion generated heat. The kinetic energy of translation of two worlds became heat. Heat added to heat, piling up ragingly, frantically, unable to escape!

The masses, still falling upon and through and past themselves and each other, melted—boiled—vaporized incandescently. The entire mass, the mass of three fused worlds, began to equilibrate; growing hotter and hotter as more and more of its terrific motion was converted into pure heat. Hotter! *Hotter!* HOTTER!

And as the Grand Fleet of the Galactic Patrol blasted through intergalactic space toward the First Galaxy and home, there glowed behind it a new, small, comparatively cool, and probably short-lived companion to an old and long-established star.

XXV.

The uproar of the landing of the Tellurian contingent was over; the celebration of victory had not yet begun. Haynes had, peculiarly enough, set a definite time for a conference with Kinnison and the two of them were in the admiral's private office, splitting a bottle of fayalin and discussing—apparently—nothing at all.

"Narcotics has been yelling for you." Haynes finally got around to business. "But they don't need you to help them clean up the zwilnik mess; they just want to have the honor of having you work with them—so I told Ellington, as diplomatically as possible, to take a swan dive off of an asteroid. Hicks wants you, too; and Spencer and Frelinghuysen and thousands of others. See that basketful of stuff? All requests for you, to be submitted to you for your consideration. I submit 'em, thus—into the wastebasket. You see, there's something really important—"

"Nix, chief, nix—jet back a minute, please!" Kinnison implored. "Unless it's something that's got to be done right away, gimme a break, can't you? I've got a couple of things to do first—stuff to attend to. Maybe a little flit somewhere, too, I don't know yet."

"More important than Patrol business?"—dryly.

"Until it's cleaned up, yes." Kinnison's face burned scarlet and his eyes revealed the mental effort necessary for him to make that statement. "The most important thing in the Universe," he finished, quietly but doggedly.

"Well, of course I can't give you orders—" Haynes' frown was distinct with disappointment.

"Don't, chief—that hurts. I'll be back, honest, as soon as I possibly can, and I'll do anything you want me to—"

"That's enough, son." Haynes stood up and grasped Kinnison's hands—hard—in both his own. "I know. Forgive me for taking you for this little ride, but you and Mac suffer so! You're so young, so intense, so insistent upon carrying the entire Cosmos upon your shoulders—I couldn't help it. You won't have to do much of a flit." He glanced at his chronometer. "You'll find all your unfinished business in Room 7295, Base Hospital."

"Huh? You know, then?" shouted the overjoyed young giant.

"Who doesn't?" was the admiral's quizzical rejoinder. "There may be a few members of some backward race somewhere who do not know all about you and your red-headed sector riot, but I don't happen to know—" He was addressing empty air.

Kinnison shot out of the building and, exerting his Gray Lensman's authority, he did a thing which he had always longed boyishly to do but which he had never before really considered doing. He whistled, shrill and piercingly, and waved a Lensed arm, even while he was directing a Lensed thought at the driver of the fast ground car always in readiness in front of GHQ.

"Base Hospital—full emergency blast!" he ordered, and the Jehu obeyed. That chauffeur loved emergency stuff, and the long, low, wide racer took off with a deafening roar of unmuffled exhaust and a scream of tortured, burning rubber.

"Thanks, Jack—you needn't wait." At the hospital's door Kinnison rendered tribute to fast service and strode along a corridor. An express elevator whisked him up to the seventy-second floor, and there his haste departed completely. This was Nurses' Quarters, he realized suddenly. He had no more business there than—yes, he did, too. He found Room 7295 and rapped upon its door. Boldly, he intended, but the resultant sound was surprisingly small.

"Come in!" called a clear contralto. Then, after a moment, "*Come in!*" more sharply; but the Lensman did not, could not obey the summons. She might be—dammitall, he *didn't* have any business on this floor! Why hadn't he called her up or sent her a thought or something? Why didn't he think at her now?

*

The door opened, revealing the mildly annoyed sector chief. At what she saw, her hands flew to her throat and her eyes widened in starkly unbelieving rapture.

"*Kim!*" she shrieked in ecstasy.

"Chris—my Chris!" Kinnison whispered unsteadily, and for minutes those two uniformed minions of the Galactic Patrol stood motionless upon the room's threshold, strong young arms straining, nurse's crisp and spotless white crushed unregarded against Lensman's pliant gray.

"Oh . . . I've missed you so terribly, my darling!" Clarrissa crooned. Her voice, always sweetly rich, was pure music.

"You don't know the half of it, Chris. This isn't real, I don't think. It can't be—nothing *can* feel this good!"

"You did come back to me—you really did!" she lilted. "I didn't dare to hope that you could come so soon."

"I had to." Kinnison drew a deep breath. "I simply couldn't stand it any longer. It'll be tough sometimes, but you were right—half a loaf *is* better than no bread."

"Of course it is!" She released herself—partially—after the first transports of their first embrace and eyed him shrewdly. "Tell me, Kim, did Lacy have a hand in this surprise?"

"Uh-huh," he denied. "I haven't seen him for ages—but jet back! Haynes told me—say, what'll you bet that those two old hardheads haven't been giving us the works?"

"Who are old hardheads?" Haynes—in person—demanded. So deeply immersed had Kinnison been in his rapturous delirium that even his sense of perception was in abeyance; and there, not two yards from the entranced couple, stood the two old Lensmen!

The culprits sprang apart, flushing guiltily, but Haynes went on imperturbably, quite as though nothing out of the ordinary had been either said or done:

"We gave you fifteen minutes, then came up to be sure to catch you before you flited off to the celebration or somewhere. We have matters to discuss—important matters, but pleasant."

"QX. Come in, all of you." As she spoke, the nurse stood aside in invitation. "You know, don't you, that it's exceedingly much contraregs for nurses to entertain visitors of the opposite sex in their rooms? Fifty demerits. Most girls never get a chance at even one Gray Lensmen, and here I've got three!" She giggled infectiously. "Wouldn't it be one for the book for me to get a hundred and fifty black spots for this? And to have Surgeon General Lacy, Port Admiral Haynes, and Unattached Lensman Kimball Kinnison all heaved into the clink to boot? Boy, oh, boy, ain't we got fun?"

"Lacy's too old and I'm too moral to be affected by the wiles even of the likes of you, my dear," Haynes explained equably, as he seated himself upon the davenport—the most comfortable thing in the room.

"Old? Moral? Tommyrot!" Lacy glared an "I'll-see-you-later" look at the admiral, then turned to the nurse. "Don't worry about that, MacDougall. No penalties accrue—regulations apply only to nurses actually in the service—"

"And what—" she started to blaze, but checked herself and her tone changed instantly. "Go on—you interest me strangely, sir. I'm just going to love this!" Her eyes sparkled, her voice was vibrant with unconcealed eagerness.

"Told you she was quick on the uptake!" Lacy gloated. "Didn't fox her for a second!"

"But say—listen—what's this all about, anyway?" Kinnison demanded.

"Never mind; you'll learn soon enough," from Lacy, and:

"Kinnison, you are very urgently invited to attend a meeting of the Galactic Council tomorrow afternoon," from Haynes.

"Huh? What's up now?" Kinnison protested. His arm tightened about the girl's supple waist and she snuggled closer, a trace of foreboding beginning to dim the eagerness in her eyes.

"Promotion. We want to make you something—galactic co-ordinator, director, something like that—the job hasn't been named yet. In plain language, the big shot of the Second Galaxy, formerly known as Lundmark's Nebula."

"But, Klono's brazen claws! Chief, I can't swing it—I haven't got jets enough!"

"You always yelp about a deficiency of jets whenever a new job is mentioned, but we notice that you usually deliver the goods. Think it over for a minute. Who else could we wish such a job as that onto?"

"Worsel," Kinnison declared without hesitation. "He's—"

"Balloon juice!" snorted the older man.

"Well, then . . . ah . . . er—" He stopped. Clarrissa opened her mouth; then shut it, ridiculously, without having uttered a word.

"Go ahead, MacDougall—you are an interested party, you know."

"No." She shook her spectacular head. "I'm not saying a word or thinking a thought to sway his decision one way or the other. Besides, he'd have to flit around as much then as now."

"Some travel involved, of course," Haynes admitted. "All over that Galaxy, some in this one, and back and forth between the two. However, the *Dauntless*—or something newer, bigger, and faster—will be his private yacht, and I do not see why it is either necessary or desirable that his flits be solo."

"Say, I never thought of that!" Kinnison blurted, and, as thoughts began to race through his mind of what he could do, with Chris beside him all the time, to straighten out the mess in the Second Galaxy:

"Oh, Kim!" Clarrissa squealed in ecstasy, squeezing his arm even tighter against her side.

"Hooked!" the surgeon general chortled in triumph.

"But I'd have to retire!" That thought was the only thorn in Kinnison's whole wreath of roses. "I wouldn't like that."

*

"Certainly you wouldn't," Haynes agreed. "But remember that all such assignments are conditional, subject to approval, and with a very definite cancellation agreement in case of what the Lensman regards as an emergency. If a Gray Lensman had to give up his right to serve the Patrol in any way he considered himself most able, they'd have to shoot us all before they could make executives out of us. And finally, I don't see how the job we're talking about can be figured as any sort of a retirement. You will be as active as you are now—yes, more so, I think."

"QX. I'll be there—I'll try it," Kinnison promised.

"Now for some more news," Lacy announced. "Haynes didn't tell you, but he has been made president of the Galactic Council. You are his first appointment. I hate to say anything good about the old scoundrel, but he has one outstanding ability. He doesn't know much or do much himself, but he certainly can pick the men who have to do the work for him!"

"There's something vastly more important than that," Haynes steered the acclaim away from himself.

"Just a minute," Kinnison interposed. "I haven't got this all straight yet. What was that crack about active nurses a while ago?"

"Why, Dr. Lacy was just intimating that I had resigned, goose," Clarrissa chuckled. "I didn't know a thing about it myself, but I imagine that it must have been just before this conference started. Am I right, doctor?" she asked innocently.

"Or tomorrow, or even yesterday—any convenient time will do," Lacy blandly assented. "You see, young man, MacDougall has been a mighty busy girl, and wedding preparations take time, too. Therefore, we have very reluctantly accepted her resignation."

"Especially, preparations take time when it's going to be such a wedding as the Patrol is going to stage," Haynes volunteered. "That was what I was starting to talk about when I was so rudely interrupted."

"Nix—not in seven thousand years!" Kinnison exploded. "Cancel that, right now. I won't stand for it. I'll not—"

"Close the pan, young fellow," the admiral advised him, firmly. "Bridegrooms are to be seen—just barely visible—but not heard, ever. A wedding is where the girls really strut their stuff. How about it, you gorgeous young menace to civilization?"

"I'll say so!" she exclaimed in high animation. "I'd just *love* it, admiral—" She broke off, aghast. Her face fell. "No, I didn't mean that, really. Kim's right. Thanks a million, just the same, but—"

"But nothing!" Haynes broke in. "I know what's the matter. Don't try to fib to an old campaigner, and don't be silly. I said the Patrol was throwing this wedding—*all* of it. All you have to do is to participate in the action. Got any money, Kinnison? On you, I mean."

"No," in surprise. "What would I be doing with money?"

"Here's ten thousand credits—Patrol funds. Take it and—"

"He will not!" the nurse stormed. "No! You can't, Admiral Haynes, really. Why, a bride has *got* to buy her own clothes!"

"She's right, Haynes," Lacy announced. The admiral stared at him in wrathful astonishment, and even the girl seemed disappointed at her easy victory. "But listen to this: As surgeon general, et cetera, in recognition of the unselfish services, et cetera, unflinching bravery under fire, performance beyond and above requirements or reasonable expectations, et cetera, et cetera, Sector Chief Nurse Clarrissa MacDougall, upon the occasion of her separation from the service, is hereby granted a bonus of ten thousand credits. That goes on the record as of hour twelve today. Now, you red-headed young spitfire, if you refuse to accept that bonus, I'll cancel your resignation and put you back to work! What do you say to that?"

"I say QX, Dr. Lacy. Thanks a million, both of you—you're perfect darlings and I love all two of you!" The gaspingly happy girl kissed them both, then turned to her betrothed.

"Let's go and walk about ten miles, shall we, Kim? I've got to do *something* or I'll explode all over the place!"

And the tall Lensman—no longer unattached—and the radiant nurse swung down the hall.

Side by side, in step, heads up, laughing; a beginning symbolical indeed of the life which they were to live together.

SECOND STAGE LENSMEN

HISTORICAL

Law enforcement lagged behind crime because the police were limited in their spheres of action, while criminals were not. Therefore, when Bergenholm invented the inertialess drive and commerce throughout the Galaxy became commonplace, crime became so rampant as to threaten the very existence of Civilization.

Thus came into being the Galactic Patrol, an organization whose highest members are called "Lensmen." Each is identified by wearing the Lens, a pseudoliving telepathic jewel matched to the ego of its wearer by those master philosophers, the Arisians. The Lens cannot be either imitated or counterfeited, since it glows with color when worn by its owner, and since it kills any other who attempts to wear it.

Of each million selected candidates for the Lens all except about a hundred fail to pass the grueling tests employed to weed out the unfit. Kimball Kinnison graduated No. 1 in his class and was put in command of the spaceship *Brittania*—a war vessel of a new type, using explosives, even though such weapons had been obsolete for centuries. The "pirates"—the Boskonian Conflict was just beginning, so that no one yet suspected that the Patrol faced anything worse than highly organized piracy—were gaining the upper hand because of a new and apparently almost unlimited source of power. Kinnison was instructed to capture one of the new-type pirate ships, in order to learn the secret of that power.

He found and defeated a Boskonian warship. Peter VanBuskirk led the storming party of Valerians—men of human type, but of extraordinary size, strength and agility because of the enormous gravitational force of their home planet—in wiping out those of the pirate crew not killed in the battle between the two ships.

The scientists of the expedition secured the information desired. It could not be transmitted to Prime Base, however, because the pirates blanketed all channels of communication. Boskonian warships were gathering, and the crippled *Brittania* could neither run nor fight. Therefore each man was given a spool of tape bearing the data and all the Patrolmen took to the lifeboats.

Kinnison and VanBuskirk, in one of the boats, were forced to land upon the planet Delgon, where they joined forces with Worsel—later to become Lensman Worsel—a winged, reptilian native of a neighboring planet, Velantia. The three destroyed a number of the Overlords of Delgon, a sadistic race of monsters who preyed upon the other races of their solar system by sheer power of mind. Worsel accompanied the Patrolmen to Velantia, where all the resources of the planet were devoted to preparing defenses against the expected Boskonian attack. Several others of the *Brittania's* lifeboats reached Velantia, called by Worsel's prodigious mind working through Kinnison's ego and Lens.

Kinnison finally succeeded in tapping a communicator beam, thus getting one line upon Helmuth, who "spoke for Boskone"—it was supposed then that Helmuth actually was Boskone instead of a comparatively unimportant Director of Operations—and upon his Grand Base.

SUPER PACK

The Boskonians attacked Velantia and six of their vessels were captured. In these ships, manned by Velantian crews, the Tellurians set out for Earth and the Prime Base of the Galactic Patrol. Kinnison's Bergenholm, the generator of the force which makes inertialess—"free," in space parlance—flight possible, broke down, wherefore he had to land upon the planet Trenco for repairs.

Trenco, the tempestuous, billiard ball-smooth planet where it rains forty-seven feet and five inches every night and where the wind blows eight hundred miles an hour. Trenco, the world upon which is produced thionite, the deadliest and most potent of all habit-forming drugs. Trenco, the Mecca of all the "zwilniks"—members of the Boskonian drug ring; sometimes loosely applied to any Boskonian—of the Galaxy. Trenco, whose weirdly charged ether and atmosphere so distort beams and vision that it can be policed only by such beings as the Rigellians, who possess the sense of perception instead of sight and hearing!

Lensman Tregonsee, of Rigel IV, then in command of the Patrol's wandering base upon Trenco, furnished Kinnison a new Bergenholm and he again set out for Tellus.

Meanwhile Helmuth, the Boskonian commander, had deduced that some one particular Lensman was back of all his setbacks; and that the Lens, a complete enigma to the Boskonians, was in some way connected with Arisia. That planet had always been dreaded and shunned by all spacemen. No one would ever say why, but no being who had ever approached that planet uninvited could be compelled, even by threat of death, to go near it again.

Helmuth, thinking himself secure by virtue of his thought-screens, the secret of which he had stolen from Velantia, went alone to Arisia, to learn how the Lens gave its wearer such power. He was stopped at the barrier. His thought-screens were useless—the Arisians had given them to Velantia, hence knew how to break them down. He was punished to the verge of insanity, but was finally permitted to return to his Grand Base, alive and sane: "Not for your own good, but for the good of that struggling young civilization which you oppose."

*

Kinnison finally reached Prime Base with the all-important data. By building superpowerful battleships, called "maulers," the Patrol gained a temporary advantage over Boskonia, but a stalemate soon ensued. Kinnison developed a plan of action whereby he hoped to locate Helmuth's Grand Base; and asked Port Admiral Haynes, Chief of Staff of the entire Patrol, for permission to follow it. In lieu of that, however, Haynes informed him that he had been given his Release; that he was an Unattached Lensman—a "Gray" Lensman, popularly so called, from the color of the plain leather uniforms they wear. Thus he earned the highest honor which the Galactic Patrol can bestow, for the Gray Lensman works under no direction whatever. He is as absolutely a free agent as it is possible to be. He is responsible to no one; to nothing save his own conscience. He is no longer of Tellus, nor of the Solarian System, but of the Universe as a whole. He is no longer a cog in the immense machine of the Patrol: wherever he may go, throughout the unbounded reaches of space, he *is* the Patrol!

THE LENSMAN

In quest of a second line upon Grand Base, Kinnison scouted a pirate stronghold upon Aldebaran I. Its personnel, however, were not even near-human, but were Wheelmen, possessed of the sense of perception; hence Kinnison was discovered before he could accomplish anything and was very seriously wounded. He managed to get back to his speedster and to send a thought to Port Admiral Haynes, who immediately rushed ships to his aid. In Base Hospital, Surgeon General Lacy put him together, and, during a long and quarrelsome convalescence, Nurse Clarrissa MacDougall held him together. Lacy and Haynes connived to promote a romance between nurse and Lensman.

As soon as he could leave the hospital he went to Arisia in the hope that he might be permitted to take advanced training; an unheard-of idea. Much to his surprise, he learned that he had been expected to return, for exactly such training. Getting it almost killed him, but he emerged infinitely stronger of mind than any man had ever been before. He also now had the sense of perception; a sense somewhat analogous to that of sight, but of vastly greater penetration, power and scope and not dependent upon light; a sense only vaguely forecast by ancient work upon clairvoyance.

By the use of his new mental equipment he succeeded in entering a Boskonian base upon Boyssia II. There he took over the mind of the communications officer and waited. A pirate ship working out of that base captured a hospital ship of the Patrol and brought it in. Clarrissa, now chief nurse of the captured vessel, working under Kinnison's instructions, stirred up trouble. Helmuth, from Grand Base, interfered, thus enabling the Lensman to get his second, all-important line.

The intersection of the two lines, Boskonia's Grand Base, lay in a star cluster well outside the Galaxy. Pausing only long enough to destroy the Wheelmen of Aldebaran I, the project in which his first attempt had failed so dismally, he investigated Helmuth's headquarters. He found fortifications impregnable to any massed attack of the Patrol, manned by beings wearing thought-screens. His sense of perception was suddenly cut off—the enemy had thrown a thought-screen around the whole planet.

He returned to Prime Base, deciding en route that boring from within was the only possible way in which that base could be reduced. In consultation with Haynes the zero hour was set, at which the Grand Fleet of the Patrol would start raying Helmuth's base with every available projector.

Pursuant to his plan, Kinnison again visited Trenco, where Tregonsee and his Rigellians extracted for him fifty kilograms of thionite, the noxious drug which, in microgram inhalations, makes the addict experience all the physical and mental sensations of doing whatever it is that he wishes most ardently to do. The larger the dose the more intense the sensations—but the slightest overdose means a sudden and super-ecstatic death.

Thence to Helmuth's planet; where, by controlling the muscles of a dog whose brain was unscreened, he let himself into the central dome. Here, just before zero time, he released his thionite into the primary air stream, thus wiping out all the pirate personnel except Helmuth; who, in his inner dome, could not be affected. The Patrol attacked on schedule. Kinnison killed Helmuth in hand-to-hand combat. Grand Base was blasted out of existence, largely by the explosion of bombs of duodecaplyl atomate placed by the

698

pirates themselves. These bombs were detonated by an enigmatic, sparkling force-ball which Kinnison had studied with care. He knew that it was operated by thought, and he suspected—correctly—that it was in reality an intergalactic communicator.

*

Kinnison's search for the real Boskone lead to Lundmark's Nebula, thenceforth called the Second Galaxy. His ship, the superpowerful *Dauntless*, met and defeated a squadron of Boskonian warships. The Tellurians landed upon the planet Medon, whose people were fighting a losing war against the forces of Boskone. The Medonians, electrical wizards who had been able to install inertia-neutralizers and a space drive upon their planet, moved their world over to our First Galaxy.

With the cessation of military activity, however, the illicit traffic in habit-forming drugs amongst all races of warm-blooded oxygen breathers had increased tremendously; and Kinnison, deducing that Boskone was back of the Drug Syndicate, decided that the best way to find the real leader of the enemy was to work upward through the drug ring.

Disguised as a dock walloper, he frequented the saloon of a drug baron, and helped to raid it; but, although he secured much information, his disguise was penetrated.

He called a Conference of Scientists, to devise means of building a gigantic bomb of negative matter. Then, impersonating a Tellurian secret-service agent who lent himself to the deception, he tried to investigate the stronghold of Prellin of Bronseca, one of Boskone's Regional Directors. This disguise also failed and he barely escaped.

Ordinary disguises having proved useless against Boskone's clever agents, Kinnison himself became Wild Bill Williams; once a gentleman of Aldebaran II, now a space rat meteor miner. Instead of pretending to drink he really drank; making of himself a practically bottomless drinker of the most vicious beverages known to space. He became a drug fiend—a bentlam eater—discovering that his Arisian-developed mind could function at full efficiency even while his physical body was stupefied. He became widely known as the fastest, deadliest performer with twin ray guns that had ever struck the asteroid belts. Thus, through solar system after solar system, he built up an unimpeachable identity as a hard-drinking, wildly carousing, bentlam-eating, fast-shooting space hellion; a lucky or a very skillful meteor miner; a derelict who had been an Aldebaranian gentleman once and who would be again if he should ever strike it rich and if he could conquer his weaknesses.

Physically helpless in a bentlam stupor, he listened in on a zwilnik conference and learned that Edmund Crowninshield, of Tressilia III, was also a Regional Director of the enemy.

Boskone formed an alliance with the Overlords of Delgon, and through a hyperspatial tube or vortex the combined forces again attacked humanity. Not simple slaughter this time, for the Overlords tortured their captives and consumed their life forces in sadistic orgies. The Conference of Scientists solved the mystery of the tube and the *Dauntless* attacked through it; returning victorious.

Wild Bill Williams struck it rich at last. Forthwith he abandoned the low dives in which he had been wont to carouse, and made an obvious effort to become again an Aldebaranian gentleman. He secured an invitation to visit Crowninshield's resort. The

699

Boskonian, believing that Williams was basically a drink and drug-soaked bum, took him in, to get his quarter-million credits. Relapsing into a characteristically wild debauch, Kinnison-Williams did squander a large part of his new fortune; but he learned from Crowninshield's mind that one Jalte, a Kalonian by birth, was Boskone's Galactic Director and that Jalte had his headquarters in a star cluster just outside the First Galaxy. Pretending bitter humiliation and declaring that he would change his name and disappear, the Gray Lensman left the planet—to investigate Jalte's base.

He learned that Boskone was not a single entity, but was a council. He also learned that, while the Kalonian did not know who or where Boskone was, Eichmil, Jalte's superior, who lived upon the planet Jarnevon in the Second Galaxy, would probably know all about it.

*

Kinnison and Worsel, therefore, set out to investigate Jarnevon. Kinnison was captured and tortured—there was at least one Delgonian upon Jarnevon—but Worsel rescued him before his mind was damaged and brought him back to the Patrol's Grand Fleet with his knowledge intact. Jarnevon was populated by the Eich, a race of monsters as bad as the Overlords of Delgon; the Council of Nine which ruled the noisome planet was, in fact, the long-sought, the utterly detested Boskone!

The greatest surgeons of the age—Phillips of Posenia and Wise of the newly acquired planet Medon—demonstrated that they could grow new nervous tissue; even new limbs and organs if necessary.

Again Clarrissa MacDougall nursed Kinnison back to health, and this time the love between them would not be denied.

The Grand Fleet of the Patrol was assembled, and with Kinnison in charge of Operations, swept outward from the First Galaxy. Jalte's planet was destroyed by means of the negasphere—the negative-matter bomb. Then on to the Second Galaxy.

There the Patrol forces destroyed Jarnevon, the planet of the Eich, by smashing it between two barren planets which had been driven there in the "free"—inertialess—condition. These planets, having opposite intrinsic velocities, were placed one upon each side of Jarnevon. Then their Bergenholms were cut, restoring inertia and intrinsic velocity; and when that frightful collision was over a minor star had come into being.

Grand Fleet returned to our Galaxy. Galactic Civilization rejoiced. Earth in particular made merry, and Prime Base was the center of celebration. And in Prime Base Kinnison, supposing that the war was over and that his problem was solved, threw off his Gray Lensman's burden and forgot all about the Boskonian menace. Marrying his Chris, he declared, was the most important thing in the Universe.

But how wrong he was! For, even as Lensman and Sector Chief Nurse were walking down a hallway of Base Hospital after a conference with Lacy and Haynes regarding that marriage—

*

I.

"Stop, youth!" The voice of that nameless, incredibly ancient Arisian who was Kinnison's instructor and whom he had thought of and spoken of simply as "Mentor" thundered silently, deep within the Lensman's brain.

He stopped convulsively, almost in midstride, and at the rigid, absent awareness in his eyes Nurse MacDougall's face went white.

"This is not merely the loose and muddy thinking of which you have all too frequently been guilty in the past," the deeply resonant, soundless voice went on, "it is simply not thinking at all. At times, Kinnison of Tellus, we almost despair of you. Think, youth, *think*! For know, Lensman, that upon the clarity of your thought and upon the trueness of your perception depends the whole future of your Patrol and of your Civilization; more so now by far than at any time in the past."

"Wha'dy'mean, 'think'?" Kinnison snapped back, thoughtlessly. His mind was a seething turmoil, his emotions an indescribable blend of surprise, puzzlement and incredulity.

For moments, as Mentor did not reply, the Gray Lensman's mind raced. Incredulity—becoming tinged with apprehension—turning rapidly into rebellion.

"Oh, Kim!" Clarrissa choked. A queer-enough tableau they made, these two, had any been there to see; the two uniformed figures standing there so strainedly, the nurse's two hands gripping those of the Lensman. She, completely en rapport with him, had understood his every fleeting thought. "Oh, Kim! They *can't* do that to us—"

"I'll say they can't!" Kinnison flared. "By Klono's tungsten teeth, I won't do it! We have a right to happiness, you and I, and we'll—"

"We'll what?" she asked, quietly. She knew what they had to face; and, strong-souled woman that she was, she was quicker to face it squarely than was he. "You were just blasting off, Kim, and so was I."

"I suppose so," glumly. "Why in all the nine hells of Valeria did I have to be a Lensman? Why couldn't I have stayed a—"

"Because you are you," the girl interrupted, gently. "Kimball Kinnison, the man I love. You couldn't do anything else." Chin up, she was fighting gamely. "And if I rate Lensman's Mate I can't be a sissy, either. It won't last forever, dear. Just a little longer to wait, that's all."

Eyes, steel-gray now, stared down into eyes of tawny, gold-flecked bronze. "QX, Chris? *Really* QX?" What a world of meaning there was in that cryptic question!

"Really, Kim." She met his stare unfalteringly. If not entirely unafraid, at least with whole-hearted determination. "On the beam and on the green, Gray Lensman, all the way. Every long, last millimeter. There, wherever it is—to the very end of whatever road it has to be—and back again. Until it's over. I'll be here. Or somewhere, Kim. Waiting."

The man shook himself and breathed deep. Hands dropped apart—both knew consciously as well as subconsciously that the less of physical demonstration the better for two such natures as theirs—and Kimball Kinnison, Unattached Lensman, came to grips with his problem.

He began really to think; to think with the full power of his prodigious mind; and as he did so he began to see what the Arisian could have—what he must have—meant. He,

Kinnison, had gummed up the works. He had made a colossal blunder in the Boskonian campaign. He knew that the Brain, although silent, was still en rapport with him; and as he coldly, grimly, thought the thing through to its logical conclusion he knew, with a dull, sick certainty, what was coming next. It came:

"Ah, you perceive at last some portion of the truth. You see that your confused, superficial thinking has brought about almost irreparable harm. I grant that, in specimens so young of such a youthful race, emotion has its place and its function; but I tell you now in all solemnity that for you the time of emotional relaxation has not yet come. *Think*, youth—THINK!" and the ancient sage of Arisia snapped the telepathic line.

As one, without a word, nurse and Lensman retraced their way to the room they had left so shortly before. Port Admiral Haynes and Surgeon General Lacy still sat upon the nurse's davenport, scheming roseate schemes having to do with the wedding they had so subtly engineered.

"Back so soon? Forget something, MacDougall?" Lacy asked, amiably. Then, as both men noticed the couple's utterly untranslatable expression:

"What happened? Break it out, Kim!" Haynes commanded.

"Plenty, chief," Kinnison answered, quietly. "Mentor—my Arisian, you know—stopped us before we got to the elevator. Told me that I'd put my foot in it clear up to the hip joint on that Boskonian thing. That instead of being all buttoned up, my fool blundering has put us further back than we were when we started."

"Mentor!"

"Your Arisian!"

"*Told* you!"

"Put us back!"

It was an entirely unpremeditated, unconscious duet. The two old officers were completely dumfounded. Arisians never had come out of their shells, they never would. Infinitely less disturbing would have been the authentic tidings that a brick house had fallen upstairs. They had nursed this romance along *so* carefully, had timed it so exactly, and now it had gone *p-f-f-t*—it had been taken out of their hands entirely. That thought flashed through their minds first. Then, as catastrophe follows lightning's flash, the real knowledge exploded within their consciousnesses that, in some unguessable fashion or other, the whole Boskonian campaign had gone *p-f-f-t*, too.

Port Admiral Hayes, master tactician, reviewed in his keen strategist's mind every phase of the recent struggle, without being able to find a flaw in it.

"There wasn't a loophole anywhere," he said aloud. "Where did they figure we slipped up?"

"We didn't slip—I slipped," Kinnison stated, flatly. "When we took Bominger—the fat Chief Zwilnik of Radelix, you know—I took a bop on the head to learn that Boskone had more than one string per bow. Observers, independent, for every station at all important. I learned that fact thoroughly then, I thought. At least, we figured on Boskone's having lines of communication past, not through, his Regional Directors, such as Prellin of Bronseca. Since I changed my line of attack at that point, I did not need to consider whether or not Crowninshield of Tressilia III was by-passed in the same way; and when I had worked my way up through Jalte in his star cluster to Boskone itself, on Jarnevon, I had forgotten the concept completely. Its possibility did not even occur to me. That is where I fell down."

"I still don't see it!" Haynes protested. "Boskone was the top!"

"Yeah?" Kinnison asked, pointedly. "That's what I thought—but prove it."

"Oh." The Port Admiral hesitated. "We had no reason to think otherwise—looked at it in that light, this intervention would seem to be conclusive—but before that there were no—"

"There were so," Kinnison contradicted, "but I didn't see them then. That's where my brain went sour; I should have seen them. Little things, mostly, but significant. Not so much positive as negative indices. Above all, there was nothing whatever to indicate that Boskone actually was the top. That idea was the product of my own wishful and very low-grade thinking, with no basis or foundation in fact or in theory. And now," he concluded bitterly, "because my skull is so thick that it takes an idea a hundred years to filter through it—because a sheer, bare fact has to be driven into my brain with a Valerian maul before I can grasp it—we're sunk without a trace."

"Wait a minute, Kim, we aren't sunk yet," the girl advised, shrewdly. "The fact that, for the first time in history, an Arisian has taken the initiative in communicating with a human being, means something big—*really* big. Mentor does not indulge in what he calls 'loose and muddy' thinking. Every part of every thought he sent carries meaning—plenty of meaning."

"What do you mean?" As one, the three men asked substantially the same question; the Lensman, by virtue of his faster reactions, being perhaps half a syllable in the lead.

*

"I don't know, exactly," Clarrissa admitted. "I've got only an ordinary mind, and it's firing on half its jets or less right now. But I do know that his thought was 'almost' irreparable, and that he meant precisely that—nothing else. If it had been wholly irreparable he not only would have expressed his thought that way, but he would have stopped you before you destroyed Jarnevon. I know that. Apparently it would have become wholly irreparable if we had got—" she faltered, blushing, then went on, "—if we had kept on about our own personal affairs. That's why he stopped us. We can win out, he meant, if you keep on working. It's your oyster, Kim—it's up to you to open it. You can do it, too—I just know that you can."

"But why didn't he stop you before you fellows smashed Boskone?" Lacy demanded, exasperated.

"I hope you're right, Chris—it sounds reasonable," Kinnison said, thoughtfully. Then, to Lacy:

"That's an easy one to answer, doctor. Because knowledge that comes the hard way is knowledge that really sticks with you. If he had drawn me a diagram before, it wouldn't have helped, the next time I get into a jam. This way it will. I've got to learn how to think, if it cracks my skull.

"*Really* think," he went on, more to himself than to the other three. "To think so that it counts."

"Well, what are we going to do about it?" Haynes was—he had to be, to get where he was and to stay where he was—quick on the uptake. "Or, more specifically, what are you going to do and what am I going to do?"

"What I am going to do will take a bit of mulling over," Kinnison replied, slowly. "Find some more leads and trace them up, is the best that occurs to me right now. Your job and procedure are rather clearer. You remarked out in space that Boskone knew that Tellus was very strongly held. That statement, of course, is no longer true."

"Huh?" Haynes half pulled himself up from the davenport, then sank back. "Why?" he demanded.

"Because we used the negasphere—a negative-matter bomb of planetary antimass—to wipe out Jalte's planet, and because we smashed Jarnevon between two colliding planets," the Lensman explained, concisely. "Can the present defenses of Tellus cope with either one of those offensives?"

"I'm afraid not—no," the port admiral admitted. "But—"

"We can admit no 'buts,' admiral," Kinnison declared, with grim finality. "Having used those weapons, we must assume that the Boskonian scientists—we'll have to keep on calling them 'Boskonians,' I suppose, until we find a truer name—had recorders on them and have now duplicated them. Tellus must be made safe against anything that we have ever used; against, as well, everything that, by the wildest stretch of the imagination, we can conceive of the enemy using."

"You're right—I can see that," Haynes nodded.

"We have been underestimating them right along," Kinnison went on. "At first we thought that they were merely organized outlaws and pirates. Then, when it was forced upon us that they could match us—overmatch us in some things—we still would not admit that they must be as large and as widespread as we are—galactic in scope. We know now that they were wider-spread than we are. Intergalactic. They penetrated into our Galaxy, riddled it, before we knew even that theirs was inhabited or inhabitable. Right?"

"To a hair, although I never thought of it in exactly that way before."

"None of us have—mental cowardice. And they have the advantage," Kinnison continued, inexorably, "in knowing that our Prime Base is upon Tellus; whereas, if Jarnevon was not in fact theirs, we have no idea whatever where it is. And another point. Does that fleet of theirs, as you look back on it, strike you as having been a planetary outfit?"

"Well, Jarnevon was a big planet, and the Eich were a mighty warlike race."

"Quibbling a bit, aren't you, chief?"

"Uh-huh," Haynes admitted, somewhat sheepishly. "The probability is very great that no one planet either built or maintained that fleet."

"And that leads us to expect what?"

"Counterattack. In force. Everything they can shove this way. However, they've got to rebuild their fleet, besides designing and building the new stuff. We'll have time enough, probably, if we get started right now."

"But, after all, Jarnevon *may* have been their vital spot," Lacy submitted.

"Even if that were true, which it probably isn't," the now thoroughly convinced port admiral sided in with Kinnison, "it doesn't mean a thing, Sawbones. If they should blow Tellus out of space, it wouldn't kill the Galactic Patrol. It would hurt it, of course, but it wouldn't cripple would, go ahead with it."

"My thought exactly," from Kinnison. "I check you to the proverbial nineteen decimals."

"Well, there's a lot to do and I'd better be getting at it," and Haynes and Lacy got up to go. Gone now was all thought of demerits or of infractions of rules—each knew what a wrenching the young couple had undergone. "See you in my office when convenient?"

"I'll be there directly, chief—as soon as I tell Chris, here, good-by."

At about the same time that Haynes and Lacy went to Nurse MacDougall's room, Worsel the Velantian arrowed downward through the atmosphere toward a certain flat roof. Leather wings shot out with a snap and in a blast of wind—Velantians can stand eleven Tellurian gravities—he came in to his customary appalling landing and dived unconcernedly down a nearby shaft. Into a corridor, along which he wriggled blithely to the office of his old friend, Master Technician LaVerne Thorndyke.

"Verne, I have been thinking," he announced, as he coiled all but about six feet of his sinuous length into a tight spiral upon the rug and thrust out half a dozen weirdly stalked eyes.

"That's nothing new," Thorndyke countered. No human mind can sympathize with or even remotely understand the Velantian passion for solid weeks of intense, uninterrupted concentration upon a single thought. "What about this time? The which-ness of the why?"

"That is the trouble with you Tellurians," Worsel grumbled. "Not only do you not know how to think, but you—"

"Hold on!" Thorndyke interrupted, unimpressed. "If you've got anything to say, old snake, why not say it? Why circumnavigate all the stars in space before you get to the point?"

"I have been thinking about thought—"

"So what?" The technician derided. "That's even worse. That's a dizzy spiral if there ever was one."

"Thought—and Kinnison," Worsel declared, with finality.

"Kinnison? Oh—that's different. I'm interested—very much so. Go ahead."

"And his weapons. His DeLameters, you know."

"No, I don't know, and you know that I don't know. What about them?"

"They are so . . . so . . . so *obvious*." The Velantian finally found the exact thought he wanted. "So big, and so clumsy, and so obtrusive. So inefficient, so wasteful of power. No subtlety—no finesse."

"But that's far and away the best hand weapon that has ever been developed!" Thorndyke protested.

"True. Nevertheless, a millionth of that power, properly applied, could be at least a million times as deadly."

"How?" The Tellurian, although shocked, was dubious.

"I have reasoned it out that thought, in any organic being, is and must be connected with one definite organic compound—this one," the Velantian explained didactically, the while there appeared within the technician's mind the space formula of an incredibly complex molecule; a formula which seemed to fill not only his mind, but the entire room as well. "You will note that it is a large molecule, and one of high molecular weight. Thus it is comparatively unstable. A vibration at the resonant frequency of any one of its component groups would break it down, and thought would therefore cease."

It took perhaps a minute for the full import of the ghastly thing to sink into Thorndyke's mind. Then, every fiber of him flinching from the idea, he began to protest.

"But he doesn't need it, Worsel. He's got a mind already that can—"

"It takes much mental force to kill," Worsel broke in, equably. "By that method one can slay only a few at a time, and it is exhausting work. My proposed method would require only a minute fraction of a watt of power and scarcely any mental force at all."

"And it would *kill*—it would have to. That reaction could not be made reversible."

"Certainly," Worsel concurred. "I never could understand why you soft-headed, soft-hearted, soft-bodied human beings are so reluctant to kill your enemies. What good does it do merely to stun them?"

"QX—skip it." Thorndyke knew that it was hopeless to attempt to convince the utterly unhuman Worsel of the fundamental rightness of human ethics. "But nothing has ever been designed small enough to project such a wave."

"I realize that. Its design and construction will challenge your inventive ability. Its smallness is its great advantage. He could wear it in a ring, in the bracelet of his Lens; or, since it will be actuated, controlled, and directed by thought, even imbedded surgically beneath his skin."

"How about backfires?" Thorndyke actually shuddered. "Projection—shielding—"

"Details—mere details," Worsel assured him, with an airy flip of his scimitared tail.

"That's nothing to be running around loose," the man argued. "Nobody could tell what killed them, could they?"

"Probably not." Worsel pondered briefly. "No. Certainly not. The substance must decompose in the instant of death, from any cause. And it would not be 'loose,' as you think; it should not become known, even. You would make only the one, of course."

"Oh. You don't want one, then?"

"Certainly not. What do I need of such a thing? Kinnison only—and only for his protection."

"Kim can handle it—but he's the only being this side of Arisia that I'd trust with one. QX, give me the dope on the frequency, wave form, and so on, and I'll see what I can do."

II.

Port Admiral Haynes, newly chosen President of the Galactic Council and by virtue of his double office probably the most powerful being in the First Galaxy, set instantly into motion the vast machinery which would make Tellus safe against any possible attack. He first called together his Board of Strategy; the same keen-minded tacticians who had helped him plan the invasion of the Second Galaxy and the eminently successful attack upon Jarnevon. Should Grand Fleet, many of whose component fleets had not yet reached their home planets, be recalled? Not yet—lots of time for that. Let them go home for a while first. The enemy would have to rebuild before they could attack, and there were many more pressing matters.

Scouting was most important. The planets near the galactic rim could take care of that. In fact, they should concentrate upon it, to the exclusion of everything else of warfare's activities. Every approach to the Galaxy—yes, the space between the two galaxies and as far into the Second Galaxy as it was safe to penetrate—should be covered as with a blanket. That way, they could not be surprised.

Kinnison, when he heard that, became vaguely uneasy. He did not really have a thought; it was as though he should have had one, but didn't. Deep down, far off, just barely above the threshold of perception an indefinite, formless something obtruded itself upon his consciousness. Tug and haul at it as he would, he could not get the drift. There was *something* he ought to be thinking of, but what in all the iridescent hells from Vandemar to Alsakan was it? So, instead of flitting about upon his declared business, he stuck around; helping the General Staff—and thinking.

And Defense Plan GBT went from the idea men to the draftsmen, then to the engineers. This was to be, primarily, a war of planets. Ships could battle ships, fleets fleets; but, postulating good tactics upon the other side, no fleet, however armed and powered, could stop a planet. That had been proved. A planet had a mass of the order of magnitude of one times ten to the twenty-fifth kilogram, and an intrinsic velocity of somewhere around forty kilometers per second. A hundred probably, relative to Tellus, if the planet came from the Second Galaxy. Kinetic energy, roughly, about five times ten to the forty-first ergs. No, that was nothing for any possible fleet to cope with.

Also, the attacking planets would of course be inertialess until the last strategic instant. Very well, they must be made inert prematurely, when the Patrol wanted them that way, not the enemy. How? The Bergenholms upon those planets would be guarded with everything the Boskonians had.

The answer to that question, as worked out by the engineers, was something they called a "super-mauler." It was gigantic, cumbersome and slow; but little faster, indeed, than a free planet. It was like Helmuth's fortresses of space, only larger. It was like the special defense cruisers of the Patrol, except that its screens were vastly heavier. It was like a regular mauler, except that it had only one weapon. All of its incomprehensible mass was devoted to one thing—*power*! It could defend itself; and, if it could get close enough to its objective, it could do plenty of damage—its dreadful primary was the first weapon ever developed capable of cutting a Q-type helix squarely in two.

And in various solar systems, uninhabitable and worthless planets were converted into projectiles. Dozens of them, possessing widely varying masses and intrinsic velocities. One by one they flitted away from their parent suns and took up positions—not too far away from our Solar System, but not too near.

And finally Kinnison, worrying at his tantalizing thought as a dog worries a bone, crystallized it. Prosaically enough, it was an extremely short and flamboyantly waggling pink shirt which catalyzed the reaction; which acted as the seed of the crystallization. Pink—a Chickladorian—Xylpic the Navigator—Overlords of Delgon. Thus flashed the train of thought, culminating in:

"Oh, so *that's it!*" he exclaimed, aloud. "That's IT, as sure as hell's a man trap!" He whistled raucously at a taxi, took the wheel himself, and broke—or at least bent—most of the city's traffic ordinances in getting to Haynes' office.

*

The port admiral was always busy, but he was never too busy to see Gray Lensman Kinnison; especially when the latter demanded the right of way in such terms as he used then.

"The whole defense set-up is screwy," Kinnison stated, baldly and at once. "I thought from the first that I was overlooking a bet, but I couldn't locate it. Why should they fight their way through intergalactic space and through sixty thousand parsecs of planet-infested galaxy when they don't have to?" he demanded. "Think of the length of the supply line, with our bases placed to cut it in a hundred places, no matter how they route it. It doesn't make sense. They'd have to outweigh us in an almost impossibly high ratio, unless they have an improbably superior armament."

"Check." The old warrior was entirely unperturbed. "Surprised that you didn't see that long ago. We did. We do not believe that they are going to attack at all."

"But you're going ahead with all this just as though—"

"Certainly. Something *may* happen, and we can't be caught off guard. Besides, it's good training for the boys. Helps morale, no end." Haynes' nonchalant air disappeared and he studied the younger man keenly for moments. "But Mentor's warning certainly meant something, and you said 'when they don't have to.' But even if they go clear around the Galaxy to the other side—an impossibly long haul—we're covered. Tellus is near enough to the center of this galaxy so that they can't possibly take us by surprise. So—spill it!"

"How about a hyperspatial tube? They know exactly where we are, you know."

"Hm-m-m!" Haynes was taken aback. "Never thought of it—possible, distinctly a possibility. A duodec bomb, say, just far enough underground—"

"Nobody else thought of it, either, until just now," Kinnison broke in. "However, I'm not afraid of duodec—don't see how they could control it accurately enough at this three-dimensional distance. Too deep, it wouldn't explode at all. What I don't like to think of, though, is a negasphere. Or a planet, perhaps."

"Ideas? Suggestions?" the admiral snapped.

"No—I don't know anything about the stuff. How about putting our Lenses on Cardynge?"

"That's a thought!" and in seconds they were in communication with Sir Austin Cardynge, Earth's mightiest mathematical brain.

"Kinnison, how many times must I tell you that I am not to be interrupted?" the aged scientist's thought was a crackle of fury. "How can I concentrate upon vital problems if every young whippersnapper in the System is to perpetrate such abominable, such outrageous intrusions—"

"Hold it, Sir Austin—hold everything!" Kinnison soothed. "I'm sorry. I wouldn't have intruded if it hadn't been a matter of life or death. But it would be a worse intrusion, wouldn't it, if the Boskonians sent a planet about the size of Jupiter—or a negasphere—through one of their extradimensional vortices into your study? That's exactly what they're figuring on doing."

"What . . . what . . . what?" Cardynge snapped, like a string of firecrackers. He quieted down, then, and thought. And Sir Austin Cardynge *could* think, upon occasion and when he felt so inclined; could think in the abstruse symbology of pure mathematics with a cogency equaled by few minds in the Universe. Both Lensmen perceived those thoughts, but neither could understand or follow them. No mind not a member of the Conference of Scientists could have done so.

"They can't!" of a sudden the mathematician cackled, gleefully disdainful. "Impossible—quite definitely impossible. There are laws governing such things, Kinnison, my impetuous and ignorant young friend. The terminus of the necessary hypertube could not be established within such proximity to the mass of the Sun. This is shown by—"

"Never mind the proof—the fact is enough," Kinnison interposed, hastily. "How close to the Sun could it be established?"

"I couldn't say, offhand," came the cautiously scientific reply. "More than two astronomical units, certainly, but the computation of the exact distance would require some little time. It would, however, be an interesting, if minor, problem. I will solve it for you, if you like, and advise you of the exact minimum distance."

"Please do so—thanks a million," and the Lensmen disconnected.

*

"The conceited old goat!" Haynes snorted. "I'd like to smack him down!"

"I've felt like it more than once, but it wouldn't do any good. You've got to handle him with gloves—besides, you can afford to make concessions to a man with a brain like that."

"I suppose so. But how about that infernal tube? Knowing that it cannot be set up within or very near Tellus helps some, but not enough. We've got to know where it is—*if* it is. Can you detect it?"

"Yes. That is, I can't, but the specialists can, I think. Wise of Medon would know more about that than anyone else. Why wouldn't it be a thought to call him over here?"

"It would that;" and it was done.

Wise of Medon and his staff came, conferred and departed.

Sir Austin Cardynge solved his minor problem, reporting that the minimum distance from the Sun's center to the postulated center of the terminus of the vortex—actually, the geometrical origin of the three-dimensional figure which was the hyperplane of intersection—was three point two six four seven, approximately, astronomical units; the last figure being tentative and somewhat uncertain because of the rapidly moving masses of Jupiter—

"Cover everything beyond three units out in every direction," Haynes directed, when he got that far along the tape. He had no time to listen to an hour of mathematical dissertation. What he wanted was *facts*.

Shortly thereafter, five-man speedsters, plentifully equipped with new instruments, flashed at full drive along courses carefully calculated to give the greatest possible coverage in the shortest possible time.

Unobtrusively the loose planets closed in upon the Solar System. Not close enough to affect appreciably the orbits of Sol's own children, but close enough so that at least three or four of them could reach any designated point in one minute or less. And the outlying units of Grand Fleet, too, were pulled in. That fleet was not actually mobilized—yet—but every vessel in it was kept in readiness for instant action.

"No trace," came the report from the Medonian surveyors, and Haynes looked at Kinnison, quizzically.

"QX, chief—glad of it," the Gray Lensman answered the unspoken query. "If it was up, that would mean that they were on the way. Hope they don't get a trace for two months yet. But I'm next to positive that that's the way they're coming and the longer they put it off the better—there's a possible new projector that will take a bit of doping out. I've got to do a flit—can I have the *Dauntless*?"

"Sure—anything you want. She's yours, anyway."

*

Kinnison went. And, wonder of wonders, he took Sir Austin Cardynge with him. From solar system to solar system, from planet to planet, the mighty *Dauntless* hurtled at the incomprehensible velocity of her full maximum blast; and every planet so visited was the home world of one of the most co-operative—or, more accurately, one of the least non-co-operative—members of the Conference of Scientists. For days brilliant but more or less unstable minds struggled with new and obdurate problems; struggled heatedly and with friction, as was their wont. Few, if any, of those mighty intellects would have really enjoyed a quietly studious session, even had such a thing been possible.

Then Kinnison returned his guests to their respective homes and shot his flying warship-laboratory back to Prime Base. And, even before the *Dauntless* landed, the first few hundreds of a fleet which was soon to be numbered in the millions of meteor miners' boats began working like beavers to build a new and exactly designed system of asteroid belts of iron meteors.

And soon, as such things go, new structures began to appear here and there in the void. Comparatively small, these things were; tiny, in fact, compared to the Patrol's maulers. Unarmed, too; carrying nothing except defensive screen. Each was, apparently, simply a powerhouse; stuffed skin full of atomic motors, exciters, intakes and generators of highly peculiar design and pattern. Unnoticed except by gauntly haggard Thorndyke and his experts, who kept dashing from one of the strange craft to another, each took its place in a succession of precisely determined relationships to the Sun.

Between the orbits of Mars and of Jupiter, the new, sharply defined rings of asteroids moved smoothly. Grand Fleet formed an enormous hollow globe, six astronomical units in diameter. Outside that globe the surveying speedsters and flitters rushed madly hither and yon. Uselessly, apparently, for not one needle of the vortex detectors stirred from its zero pin.

And as nearly as possible at the center of that globe, circling the Sun well inside the orbit of Venus, there floated the flagship. Technically the Z9M9Z, socially the *Directrix*, ordinarily simply *GFHQ*, that ship had been built specifically to control the operations of a million separate flotillas. At her million-plug board stood—they had no need, ever, to sit—two hundred blocky, tentacle-armed Rigellians. They were waiting, stolidly motionless.

Intergalactic space remained empty. Interstellar ditto, ditto. The flitters flitted, fruitlessly.

But if everything out there in the threatened volume of space seemed quiet and serene, things in the Z9M9Z were distinctly otherwise. Haynes and Kinnison, upon whom the heaviest responsibilities rested, were tensely ill at ease.

The admiral had his formation made, but he did not like it at all. It was too big, too loose, too cumbersome. The Boskonian fleet might appear anywhere outside that thin globe of Patrol ships, and it would take him far, far too long to get any kind of a fighting formation made, anywhere. So he worried. Minutes dragged—he wished that the pirates would hurry up and start something!

Kinnison was even less easy in his mind. He was not afraid of negaspheres, even if Boskonia should have them; but he was afraid of fortified, mobile planets. The supermaulers were big and powerful, of course, but they very definitely were not planets; and the big, new idea was mighty hard to jell. He did not like to bother Thorndyke by calling him—the master technician had troubles of his own—but the reports that were coming in were none too cheery. The excitation was wrong or the grid action was too unstable or the screen potentials were too high or too low or something. Sometimes they got a concentration, but it was just as apt as not to be a spread flood instead of a tight beam. To Kinnison, therefore, the minutes fled like seconds—but every minute that space remained clear was one more precious minute gained.

*

Then, suddenly, it happened. A needle leaped into significant figures. Relays clicked, a bright red light flared into being, a gong clanged out its raucous warning. A fractional instant later ten thousand other gongs in ten thousand other ships came brazenly to life as the discovering speedster automatically sent out its number and position; and those other ships—surveyors all—flashed toward that position and dashed frantically about. Theirs the task to determine, in the least number of seconds possible, the approximate location of the center of emergence.

For Port Admiral Haynes, canny old tactician that he was, had planned his campaign long since. It was standing plain in his tactical tank—to inglobe the entire space of emergence of the foe and to blast them out of existence before they could maneuver. If he could get into formation before the Boskonians appeared, it would be a simple slaughter—if not, it might be otherwise. Hence seconds counted; and hence he had had high-speed computers working steadily for weeks at the computation of courses for every possible center of emergence.

"Get me that center—fast!" Haynes barked at the surveyors, already blasting at maximum.

711

THE LENSMAN

It came in. The chief computer yelped a string of numbers. Selected loose-leaf binders were pulled down, yanked apart, and distributed on the double, leaf by leaf. And:

"Get it over there! Especially the shock globe!" the port admiral yelled.

For he himself could direct the engagement only in broad; details must be left to others. To be big enough to hold in any significant relationship the millions of lights representing vessels, fleets, planets, structures and objectives, the Operations tank of the *Directrix* had to be seven hundred feet in diameter; and it was a sheer physical impossibility for any ordinary mind either to perceive that seventeen million cubic feet of space as a whole or to make any sense at all out of the stupendously bewildering maze of multicolored lights crawling and flashing therein.

Kinnison and Worsel had handled Grand Fleet Operations during the Battle of Jarnevon, but they had discovered that they could have used some help. Four Rigellian Lensmen had been training for months for that all-important job, but they were not yet ready. Therefore the two old masters and one new one now labored at GFO: three tremendous minds, each supplying something that the others lacked. Kinnison of Tellus, with his hard, flat driving urge, his unconquerable, unstoppable will to do. Worsel of Velantia, with the prodigious reach and grasp which had enabled him, even without the Lens, to scan mentally a solar system eleven light-years distant. Tregonsee of Rigel IV, with the vast, calm certainty, the imperturbable poise peculiar to his long-lived, solemn race. Unattached Lensmen all; minds linked, basically, together into one mind by a wide-open three-way, superficially free, each to do his assigned third of the gigantic task.

Smoothly, effortlessly, those three linked minds went to work at the admiral's signal. Orders shot out along tight beams of thought to the stolid hundreds of Rigellian switchboard operators, and thence along communicator beams to the pilot rooms, wherever stationed. Flotillas, squadrons, subfleets flashed smoothly toward their newly assigned positions. Supermaulers moved ponderously toward theirs. The survey ships, their work done, vanished. They had no business anywhere near what was coming next. Small they were, and defenseless; a speedster's screens were as efficacious as so much vacuum against the forces about to be unleashed. The powerhouses also moved. Maintaining rigidly their cryptic mathematical relationships to each other and the Sun, they went as a whole into a new one with respect to the circling rings of tightly packed meteors and the invisible, nonexistent mouth of the Boskonian vortex.

Then, before Haynes' formation was nearly complete, the Boskonian fleet materialized. Just that—one instant space was empty; the next it was full of warships. A vast globe of battle wagons, in perfect fighting formation. They were not free, but inert and deadly.

Haynes swore viciously under his breath, the Lensmen pulled themselves together more tensely; but no additional orders were given. Everything that could possibly be done was already being done.

*

Whether the Boskonians expected to meet a perfectly placed fleet or whether they expected to emerge into empty space, to descend upon a defenseless Tellus, is not known or knowable. It is certain, however, that they emerged in the best possible formation to meet anything that could be brought to bear. It is also certain that, had the enemy had

712

a Z9M9Z and a Kinnison-Worsel-Tregonsee combination scanning its Operations tank, the outcome might well have been otherwise than it was.

For that ordinarily insignificant delay, that few minutes of time necessary for the Boskonians' orientation, was exactly that required for these two hundred smoothly working Rigellians to get Civilization's shock globe into position.

A million beams, primaries raised to the hellish heights possible only to Medonian conductors and insulation, lashed out almost as one. Screens stiffened to the urge of every generable watt of defensive power. Bolt after bolt of quasi-solid lightning struck and struck and struck again. Q-type helices bored, gouged and searingly hit. Rods and cones, planes and shears of incredibly condensed pure force clawed, tore and ground in mad abandon. Torpedo after torpedo, charged to the very skin with duodec, loosed its horribly detonant cargo against flinching wall shields, in such numbers and with such violence as to fill all circumambient space with an atmosphere of almost planetary density.

Screen after screen, wall shield after wall shield, in their hundreds and their thousands, went down. A full eighth of the Patrol's entire count of battleships were wrecked, riddled, blown apart or blasted completely out of space in the paralyzingly cataclysmic violence of that first, seconds-long, mind-shaking, space-racking encounter. Nor could it have been otherwise; for this encounter had not been at battle range. Not even at point-blank range; the warring monsters of the void were packed practically screen to screen.

But not a man died—upon Civilization's side at least—even though practically all of the myriad of ships composing the inner sphere, the shock globe, was lost. For they were automatic; manned by robots; what little superintendence was necessary had been furnished by remote control. Indeed it is possible, although perhaps not entirely probable, that the shock globe of the foe was similarly manned.

That first frightful meeting gave time for the reserves of the Patrol to get there, and it was then that the superior Operations control of the Z9M9Z made itself tellingly felt. Ship for ship, beam for beam, screen for screen, the Boskonians were, perhaps, equal to the Patrol; but they did not have the perfection of control necessary for unified action. The field was too immense, the number of contending units too enormously vast. But the mind of each of the three Unattached Lensmen read aright the flashing lights of his particular volume of the gigantic tank and spread their meaning truly in the infinitely smaller space model beside which Admiral Haynes, master tactician, stood. Scanning the entire space of battle as a whole, he rapped out general orders—orders applying, perhaps, to a hundred or to five hundred planetary fleets. Kinnison and his fellows broke these orders down for the operators, who in turn told the vice admirals and rear admirals of the fleets what to do. They gave detailed orders to the units of their commands, and the line officers, knowing exactly what to do and precisely how to do it, did it with neatness and dispatch.

There was no doubt, no uncertainty, no indecision or wavering. The line officers, even the rear and vice admirals, knew nothing, could know nothing whatever of the progress of the engagement as a whole. But they had worked under the Z9M9Z before. They knew that the maestro Haynes did know the battle as a whole. They knew that he was handling them as carefully and as skillfully as a master at chess plays his pieces upon the square-filled board. They knew that Kinnison or Worsel or Tregonsee was assigning no task too difficult of accomplishment. They knew that they could not be taken by surprise, attacked from some unexpected and unprotected direction; knew that, although in those hundreds of thousands of cubic miles of space there were hundreds of thousands of highly inimical and exceedingly powerful ships of war, none of them were, or shortly could be, in position to do them serious harm. If there had been, they would have been pulled out of there, *beaucoup* fast. They were as safe as anyone in a warship in such a war could expect, or even hope, to be. Therefore they acted instantly; directly, whole-heartedly and efficiently; and it was the Boskonians who were taken, repeatedly and by the thousands, by surprise.

For the enemy, as has been said, did not have the Patrol's smooth perfection of control. Thus several of Civilization's fleets, acting in full synchronizing, could and repeatedly did rush upon one unit of the foe; inglobing it, blasting it out of existence, and dashing back to stations; all before the nearest-by fleets of Boskone knew even that a threat was being made. Thus ended the second phase of the battle, the engagement of the two Grand Fleets, with the few remaining thousands of Boskone's battleships taking refuge upon or near the phalanx of planets which had made up their center.

*

Planets. Seven of them. Armed and powered as only a planet can be armed and powered; with fixed-mount weapons impossible of mounting upon any lesser mobile base, with fixed-mount intakes and generators which only planetary resources could excite or feed. Galactic Civilization's war vessels fell back. Attacking a full-armed planet was no part of their job. And as they fell back, the supermaulers moved ponderously up and went to work. This was their dish; for this they had been designed. Tubes, lances, stilettos of unthinkable energies raved against their mighty screens; bouncing off, glancing away, dissipating themselves in space-torturing discharges as they hurled themselves upon the nearest ground. In and in the monsters bored, inexorably taking up their positions directly over the ultra-protected domes which, their commanders knew, sheltered the vitally important Bergenholms and controls. Then they loosed forces of their own. Forces of such appalling magnitude as to burn out in the twinkling of an eye projector shells of a refractoriness to withstand for ten full seconds the maximum output of a first-class battleship's primary batteries!

The resultant beam was of very short duration, but of utterly intolerable poignancy. No material substance could endure it even momentarily. It pierced instantly the hardest, tightest wall shield known to the scientists of the Patrol. It was the only known thing which could cut or rupture the ultimately stubborn fabric of a Q-type helix. Hence it is not to be wondered at that as those incredible needles of ravening energy stabbed and stabbed and stabbed again at Boskonian domes every man of the Patrol, even Kimball Kinnison, fully expected those domes to go down.

But those domes held. And those fixed-mount projectors hurled back against the supermaulers forces at the impact of which course after course of fierce-driven defensive screen flamed through the spectrum and went down.

"Back! Get them back!" Kinnison whispered, white-lipped, and the attacking structures sullenly, stubbornly gave way.

"Why?" gritted Haynes. "They're all we've got."

"You forget the new one, chief—give us a chance."

"What makes you think it'll work?" the old admiral flashed the searing thought. "It probably won't—and if it doesn't—"

"If it doesn't," the younger man shot back, "we're no worse off than now to use the maulers. But we've got to use the sunbeam *now* while those planets are together and before they start toward Tellus."

"QX," the admiral assented; and, as soon as the Patrol's maulers were out of the way:

"Verne?" Kinnison flashed a thought. "We can't crack 'em. Looks like it's up to you—what do you say?"

"Jury-rigged—don't know whether she'll light a cigarette or not—but here she comes!"

*

The sun, shining so brightly, darkened almost to the point of invisibility. The war vessels of the enemy disappeared, each puffing out into a tiny, but brilliant, sparkle of light.

Then, before the beam could affect the enormous masses of the planets, the engineers lost it. The sun flashed up—dulled—brightened—darkened—wavered. The beam waxed and waned irregularly; the planets began to move away under the urgings of their now thoroughly scared commanders.

Again, while millions upon millions of tensely straining Patrol officers stared into their plates, haggard Thorndyke and his sweating crews got the sunbeam under control again—and, in a heart-stoppingly wavering fashion, held it together. It flared—sputtered—ballooned out—but very shortly, before they could get out of its way, the planets began to glow. Ice caps melted, then boiled. Oceans boiled, their surfaces almost exploding into steam. Mountain ranges melted and flowed sluggishly down into valleys. The Boskonian domes of force went down and stayed down.

"QX, Kim—let be," Haynes ordered. "No use overdoing it. Not bad-looking planets; maybe we can use them for something."

The sun brightened to its wonted splendor, the planets began visibly to cool—even the Titanic forces then at work had heated those planetary masses only superficially.

The battle was over.

"What in all the purple hells of Palain did you do, Haynes, and how?" demanded the Z9M9Z's captain.

"He used the whole damned solar system as a vacuum tube!" Haynes explained, gleefully. "Those power stations out there, with all their motors and intake screens, are simply the power leads. The asteroid belts, and maybe some of the planets, are the grids and plates. The sun is—"

"Hold on, chief!" Kinnison broke in. "That isn't quite it. You see, the directive field set up by the—"

"Hold on yourself!" Haynes ordered, brusquely. "You're too damned scientific, just like Sawbones Lacy. What do Rex and I care about technical details that we can't understand, anyway? The net result is what counts—and that was to concentrate upon those planets practically the whole energy output of the Sun. Wasn't it?"

"Well, that's the main idea," Kinnison conceded. "The energy equivalent, roughly, of four million one hundred and fifty thousand tons per second of disintegrating matter."

"*Whew!*" the captain whistled. "No wonder it frizzled 'em up."

"I can say now, I think, with no fear of successful contradiction, that Tellus *is* strongly held," Haynes stated, with conviction. "What now, Kim, old son?"

"I think they're done, for a while," the Gray Lensman pondered. "Cardynge can't communicate through the tube, so probably they can't; but if they managed to slip an observer through, they may know how almighty close they came to licking us. On the other hand, Verne says that he can get the bugs out of the sunbeam in a couple of weeks—and when he does, the next zwilnik he cuts loose at is going to get a surprise."

"I'll say so," Haynes agreed. "We'll keep the surveyors on the prowl, and some of the Fleet will always be close by. Not all of it, of course—we'll adopt a schedule of reliefs—but enough of it to be useful. That ought to be enough, don't you think?"

"I think so—yes," Kinnison answered, thoughtfully. "I'm just about positive that they won't be in shape to start anything here again for a long time. And I had better get busy, sir, on my own job—I've got to put out a few jets."

"I suppose so," Haynes admitted.

For Tellus *was* strongly held, now—so strongly held that Kinnison felt free to begin again the search upon whose successful conclusion depended, perhaps, the outcome of the struggle between Boskonia and Galactic Civilization.

III.

When the forces of the Galactic Patrol blasted Helmuth's Grand Base out of existence and hunted down and destroyed his secondary bases throughout this galaxy, Boskone's military grasp upon Civilization was definitely broken. Some minor bases may have escaped destruction, of course. Indeed, it is practically certain that some of them did so, for there are comparatively large volumes of our Island Universe which have not been mapped, even yet, by the planetographers of the Patrol. It is equally certain, however, that they were relatively few and of no real importance. For warships, being large, cannot be carried around or concealed in a vest pocket—a war fleet must of necessity be based upon a celestial object not smaller than a very large asteroid. Such a base, lying close enough to any one of Civilization's planets to be of any use, could not be hidden successfully from the detectors of the Patrol.

Reasoning from analogy, Kinnison quite justifiably concluded that the back of the drug syndicate had been broken in similar fashion when he had worked upward through Bominger and Strongheart and Crowninshield and Jalte to the dread council of Boskone itself. He was, however, wrong.

For, unlike the battleship, thionite is a vest-pocket commodity. Unlike the space-fleet base, a drug baron's headquarters can be, and frequently is, small, compact and highly mobile. Also, the Galaxy is huge, the number of planets in it immense, the total count of drug addicts utterly incomprehensible. Therefore it had been found more efficient to arrange the drug hookup in multiple series-parallel, instead of in the straight cascade sequence which Kinnison thought that he had followed up.

He thought so at first, that is, but he did not think so long. He had thought, and he had told Haynes, as well as Gerrond of Radelix, that the situation was entirely under control; that with the zwilnik headquarters blasted out of existence and with all of the regional heads and many of the planetary chiefs dead or under arrest, all that the Enforcement men would have to cope with would be the normal bootleg trickle. In that, too, he was wrong. Gerrond and the other lawmen of Narcotics had had a brief respite, it is true; but in a few days or weeks, upon almost as many planets as before, the illicit traffic was again in full swing.

After the Battle of Tellus, then, it did not take the Gray Lensman long to discover the above facts. Indeed, they were pressed upon him. He was, however, more relieved than disappointed at the tidings, for he knew that he would have material upon which to work. If his original opinion had been right, if all lines of communication with the now completely unknown ultimate authorities of the zwilniks had been destroyed, his task would have been an almost hopeless one.

It would serve no good purpose here to go into details covering his early efforts, since they embodied, in principle, the same tactics as those which he had previously employed. He studied, he analyzed, he investigated. He snooped and he spied. He fought; upon occasion he killed. And in due course—and not too long a course—he cut into the sign of what he thought must be a key zwilnik. Not upon Bronseca or Radelix or Chickladoria, or any other distant planet, but right upon Tellus!

But he could not locate him. He never saw him upon Tellus. As a matter of cold fact, he could not find a single person who had ever seen him or who knew anything definite about him except a number. These facts, of course, only whetted Kinnison's keenness to come to grips with the fellow. He might not be a very big shot, but the fact that he was covering himself up so thoroughly and so successfully made it abundantly evident that he was a fish well worth landing.

This wight, however, proved to be as elusive as the proverbial flea. He was never there when Kinnison pounced. In London he was a few minutes late. In Berlin he was a minute or so too early—and the ape didn't show up at all. He missed him in Paris and in San Francisco and in Shanghai. The guy settled down finally in New York, but still the Gray Lensman could not connect—it was always the wrong street, or the wrong house, or the wrong time, or something.

*

Then Kinnison set a snare which should have caught a microbe—and *almost* caught his zwilnik. He missed him by one mere second when he blasted off from New York Spaceport. He was so close that he saw his flare, so close that he could slap onto the fleeing vessel the beam of the CRX tracer which he always carried with him.

Unfortunately, however, the Lensman was in mufti at the time, and was driving a rented flitter. His speedster—altogether too spectacular and obvious a conveyance to be using in a hush-hush investigation—was at Prime Base. He didn't want the speedster, anyway, except inside the *Dauntless*. He'd go organized this time to chase the lug clear out of space, if he had to. He shot in a call for the big cruiser, and while it was coming he made luridly sulphurous inquiry.

Fruitless. His orders had been carried out to the letter, except in the one detail of not allowing any vessel to take off. This take-off absolutely could not be helped—it was just one of those things. The ship was a Patrol speedster from Deneb V, registry number so-and-so. Said he was coming in for servicing. Came in on the north beam, identified himself properly—Lieutenant Quirkenfal, of Deneb V, he said he was, and it checked—

It would check, of course. The zwilnik that Kinnison had been chasing so long certainly would not be guilty of any such raw, crude work as a faulty identification. In fact, right then he probably looked just as much like Quirkenfal as the lieutenant himself did.

"He wasn't in any hurry at all," the informant went on. "He waited around for his landing clearance, then slanted in on his assigned slide to the service pits. In the last hundred yards, though, he shot off to one side and sat down, *plop*, broadside on, clear over there in the far corner of the field. But he wasn't down but a second, sir. Long before anybody could get to him—before the cruisers could put a beam on him, even—he blasted off as though the devil were on his tail. Then you came along, sir, but we did put a CRX tracer on him—"

"I did that much, myself," Kinnison stated, morosely. "He stopped just long enough to pick up a passenger—my zwilnik, of course—then flitted—and you fellows let him get away with it."

"But we couldn't help it, sir," the official protested. "And, anyway, he couldn't possibly have—"

"He sure could. You'd be surprised no end at what that ape can do."

Then the *Dauntless* flashed in; not asking but demanding instant right of way.

"Look around, fellows, if you like, but you won't find a damned thing," Kinnison's uncheering conclusion came back as he sprinted toward the dock into which his battleship had settled. "The lug hasn't left a loose end dangling yet."

By the time the great Patrol ship had cleared the stratosphere, Kinnison's CRX, powerful and tenacious as it was, was just barely registering a line. But that was enough. Henry Henderson, master pilot, stuck the *Dauntless'* needle nose into that line and shoved into the driving projectors every watt of "oof" that those Brobdingnagian creations would take.

*

They had been following the zwilnik for three days now, Kinnison reflected, and his CRX's were none too strong yet. They were overhauling him mighty slowly; and the *Dauntless* was supposed to be the fastest thing in space. That can up ahead had plenty of legs—must have been souped up to the limit. This was apt to be a long chase, but he'd get that bozo if he had to chase him on a geodesic line along the hyper-dimensional curvature of space clear back to Tellus where he started from!

They did not have to circumnavigate total space, of course, but they did almost leave the Galaxy before they could get the fugitive upon their plates. The stars were thinning out fast; but still, hazily before them in a vastness of distance, there stretched a milky band of opalescence.

"What's coming up, Hen—a rift?" Kinnison asked.

"Uh-huh, Rift 94," the pilot replied. "And if I remember right, that arm up ahead is Dunstan's Region and it has never been explored. I'll have the chart room check up on it."

"Never mind! I'll go check it myself—I'm curious about this whole thing."

Unlike any smaller vessel, the *Dauntless* was large enough so that she could—and hence as a matter of course did—carry every space chart issued by all the various Boards and Offices and Bureaus concerned with space, astronomy, astrogation and planetography. She had to, for there were usually minds aboard which were apt at any time to become intensely and unpredictably interested in anything, anywhere. Hence it did not take Kinnison long to obtain what little information there was.

The vacancy they were approaching was Rift 94, a vast space, practically empty of stars, lying between the main body of the Galaxy and a minor branch of one of its prodigious spiral arms. The opalescence ahead was the branch—Dunstan's Region. Henderson was right; it had never been explored.

The Galactic Survey, which has not even yet mapped the whole of the Galaxy proper, had of course done no systematic work upon such outlying sections as the spiral arms. Some such regions were well known and well mapped, it is true; either because its own population, independently developing means of space flight, had come into contact with our Civilization upon its own initiative or because private exploration and investigation had opened up profitable lines of commerce. But Dunstan's Region was bare. No people resident in it had ever made themselves known; no private prospecting, if there had ever been any such, had revealed anything worthy of exploitation or development. And, with so many perfectly good uninhabited planets so much nearer to Galactic Center, it was, of course, much too far out for colonization.

Through the rift, then, and into Dunstan's Region the *Dauntless* bored at the unimaginable pace of her terrific full-blast drive. The tracers' beams grew harder and more taut with every passing hour; the fleeing speedster itself grew large and clear upon the plates. The opalescence of the spiral arm became a firmament of stars. A sun detached itself from that firmament; a dwarf of Type G—and planets.

One of these in particular, the second out, looked so much like Earth that it made some of the observers homesick. There were the familiar polar ice caps, the atmosphere and stratosphere, the high-piled, billowy masses of clouds. There were vast blue oceans, there were huge, unfamiliar continents glowing with chlorophyllic green.

*

At the spectroscopes, at the bolometers, at the many other instruments men went rapidly and skillfully to work.

"Hope the ape's heading for Two, and I think he is," Kinnison remarked, as he studied the results. "People living on that planet would be human to ten places, for all the tea in China. No wonder he was so much at home on Tellus—Yup, it's Two—there, he's gone inert."

719

"Whoever is piloting that can went to school just one day in his life and that day it rained and the teacher didn't come," Henderson snorted. "And he's trying to balance her down on her tail—look at her bounce and flop around! He's just begging for a crack-up."

"If he makes it, it'll be bad—plenty bad," Kinnison mused. "He'll gain a lot of time on us while we're rounding the globe on our landing spiral."

"Why spiral, Kim? Why not follow him down, huh? Our intrinsic is no worse than his—it's the same one, in fact."

"Get conscious, Hen. You haven't got a speedster under you now."

"So what? I can certainly handle this scrap heap a damn sight better than that ground-gripper is handling that speedster." Henry Henderson, Master Pilot No. 1 of the Service, was not bragging. He was merely voicing what to him was the simple and obvious truth.

"Mass is what. Mass and volume and velocity and inertia and power. You never stunted this much weight before, did you?"

"No; but what of it? I took a course in piloting once, in my youth." He was then a grand old man of twenty-eight or thereabouts. "I can line up the main rear center pipe onto any grain of sand you want to pick out on that field, and hold her there until she slags it down."

"If you think you can spell 'able,' hop to it!"

"QX, this is going to be fun." Henderson gleefully accepted the challenge, then clicked on his general alarm microphone. "Strap down, everybody, for inert maneuvering. Class 9. Four G's on the tail. Tail over to belly landing. Hipe!"

The Bergenholms were cut and as the tremendously massive superdreadnought, inert, shot off at an angle under its Tellurian intrinsic velocity, Master Pilot No. 1 proved his rating. As much a virtuoso of the banks and tiers of blast keys and levers before him as a concert organist is of his instrument, his hands and feet flashed hither and yon. Not music?—the bellowing, crescendo thunders of those jets *were* music to the hard-boiled spacehounds who heard them. And in response to the exact placement and the precisely measured power of those blasts the great sky rover spun, twisted and bucked as her prodigious mass was forced into motionlessness relative to the terrain beneath her.

Four G's, Kinnison reflected, while this was going on. Not bad—he had thought that it would take five; possibly six. He could sit up and take notice at four, and he did so.

*

This world wasn't very densely populated, apparently. Quite a few cities, but all just about on the equator. Nothing in the temperate zones at all; even the highest power revealed no handiwork of man. Virgin forest, untouched prairie. Lots of roads and things in the torrid zone, but nothing anywhere else. The speedster was making a rough and unskillful, but not catastrophic landing.

The field which was their destination lay just outside a large city. Funny—it wasn't a space-field at all. No docks, no pits, no ships. Low, flat buildings—hangars. An air-field, then, although not like any air-field upon Tellus. Too small. Gyros? 'Copters? Didn't see any—all little ships. Crates—biplanes and tripes. Made of wire and fabric. Wotta woil, wotta woil!

The *Dauntless* landed, fairly close to the now deserted speedster.

"Hold everything, men," Kinnison cautioned. "Something funny here. I'll do a bit of looking around before we open up."

He was not surprised that the people in and around the airport were human to at least ten places of classification; he had expected that from the planetary data. Nor was he surprised at the fact that they wore no clothing. He had learned long since that, while human or near-human races—particularly the women—wore at least a few ornaments, the wearing of clothing as such, except when it was actually needed for protection, was far more the exception than the rule. And, just as a Martian, out of deference to conventions, wears a light robe upon Tellus, Kinnison as a matter of course stripped to his evenly tanned hide when visiting planets upon which nakedness was *de rigueur*. He had attended more than one State function, without a quibble or a qualm, tastefully attired in a pair of sandals and his DeLameters.

No, the startling fact was that there was not a man in sight anywhere around the place; there was nothing male perceptible as far as his sense of perception could reach. Women were laboring, women were supervising, women were running the machines. Women were operating the airplanes and servicing them. Women were in the offices. Women and girls and little girls and girl babies filled the waiting rooms and the automobilelike conveyances parked near the airport and running along the streets.

And, even before Kinnison had finished uttering his warning, while his hand was in the air reaching for a spy-ray switch, he felt an alien force attempting to insinuate itself into his mind.

Fat chance! With any ordinary mind it would have succeeded, but in the case of the Gray Lensman it was just like trying to stick a pin unobtrusively into a panther. He put up a solid block automatically, instantaneously; then, a fraction of a second later, a thought-tight screen enveloped the whole vessel.

"Did any of you fellows—" he began, then broke off. They wouldn't have felt it, of course; their brains could have been read completely with them none the wiser. He was the only Lensman aboard, and even most Lensmen couldn't—this was *his* oyster. But that kind of stuff, on such an apparently backward planet as this? It didn't make sense, unless that zwilnik—Ah, this *was* his oyster, absolutely!

"Something funnier even than I thought—thought-waves," he calmly continued his original remark. "Thought I'd better undress to go out there, but I'm not going to. I'd wear full armor, except that I may need my hands or have to move fast. If they get insulted at my clothes, I'll apologize later."

"But, listen, Kim, you can't go out there alone—especially without armor!"

"Sure I can. I'm not taking any chances. You fellows couldn't do me much good out there, but you can here. Break out the 'copter and keep a spy-ray on me. If I give you the signal, go to work with a couple of narrow needle beams. Pretty sure that I won't need any help, but you can't always tell."

*

The air lock opened and Kinnison stepped out. He had a high-powered thought-screen, but he did not need it—yet. He had his DeLameters. He had also a weapon deadlier by far even than those mighty portables; a weapon so utterly deadly that he had not used it. He did not need to test it—since Worsel had said that it would work, it would. The trouble with it was that it could not merely disable; if used at all it killed, with complete and grim finality. And behind him he had the full awful power of the *Dauntless*. He had nothing to worry about.

Only when the spaceship had settled down upon and into the hard-packed soil of the airport could those at work there realize just how big and how heavy the visitor was. Practically everyone stopped work and stared, and they continued to stare as Kinnison strode toward the office. The Lensman had landed upon many strange planets, he had been met in divers fashions and with various emotions; but never before had his presence stirred up anything even remotely resembling the sentiments written so plainly upon these women's faces and expressed even more plainly in their seething thoughts.

Loathing, hatred, detestation—not precisely any one of the three, yet containing something of each. As though he were a monstrosity, a revolting abnormality that should be destroyed on sight. Beings such as the fantastically ugly, spiderlike denizens of Dekanore VI had shuddered at the sight of him, but their thoughts were mild compared to these. Besides, that was natural enough. Any human being would appear a monstrosity to such as those. But these women were human; as human as he was. He didn't get it, at all.

Kinnison opened the door and faced the manager, who was standing at that other-worldly equivalent of a desk. His first glance at her brought to the surface of his mind one of the peculiarities which he had already unconsciously observed. Here, for the first time in his life, he saw a woman without any touch whatever of personal adornment. She was tall and beautifully proportioned, strong and fine; her smooth skin was tanned to a rich and even brown. She was clean, almost blatantly so.

But she wore no jewelry, no bracelets, no ribbons; no decorations of any sort or kind. No paint, no powder, no touch of perfume. Her heavy, bushy eyebrows had never been either plucked or clipped. Some of her teeth had been expertly filled, and she had a two-tooth bridge that would have done credit to any Tellurian dentist—but her hair! It, too, was painfully clean, as was the white scalp beneath it, but aesthetically it was a mess. Some of it reached almost to her shoulders, but it was very evident that whenever a lock grew long enough to be a bother she was wont to grab it and hew it off, as close to the skull as possible, with whatever knife, shears or other implement came readiest to hand.

These thoughts and the general inspection did not take any appreciable length of time, of course. Before Kinnison had taken two steps toward the manager's desk, he directed a thought:

"Kinnison of Sol III—Lensman, Unattached. It is possible, however, that neither Tellus nor the Lens are known upon this planet?"

"Neither is known, nor do we care to know them," she replied, coldly. Her brain was keen and clear; her personality vigorous, striking, forceful. But, compared with Kinnison's doubly Arisian-trained mind, hers was woefully slow. He watched her assemble the mental bolt which was intended to slay him then and there. He let her send it, then struck back. Not lethally, not even paralyzingly, but solidly enough so that she slumped down, almost unconscious, into a nearby chair.

"It's good technique to size a man up before you tackle him, sister," he advised her when she had recovered. "Couldn't you tell from the feel of my mind-block that *you* couldn't crack it?"

"I was afraid so," she admitted, hopelessly, "but I had to kill you if I possibly could. Since you are the stronger you will, of course, kill me." Whatever else these peculiar women were, they were stark realists. "Go ahead—get it over with. But it *can't* be!" Her thought was a wail of protest. "I do not grasp your thought of 'a man,' but you are certainly a male; and no mere *male* can be—can *possibly* be, ever—as strong as a person."

*

Kinnison got that thought perfectly, and it rocked him. She did not think of herself as a woman, a female, at all. She was simply a *person*. She could not understand even dimly Kinnison's reference to himself as a man. To her, "man" and "male" were synonymous terms. Both meant sex, and nothing whatever except sex.

"I have no intention of killing you, or anyone else upon this planet," he informed her levelly, "unless I absolutely have to. But I have chased that speedster over there all the way from Tellus, and I intend to get the man that drove it here, if I have to wipe out half of your population to do it. Is that perfectly clear?"

"That is perfectly clear, male." Her mind was fuzzy with a melange of immiscible emotions. Surprise and relief that she was not to be slain out of hand; disgust and repugnance at the very idea of such a horrible, monstrous male creature having the audacity to exist; stunned, disbelieving wonder at his unprecedented power of mind; a dawning comprehension that there were perhaps some things which she did not know: these and numerous other conflicting thoughts surged through her mind. "But there was no male within the space-traversing vessel which you think of as a 'speedster,'" she concluded, surprisingly.

And he knew that she was not lying. No mentality in existence, not even that of Mentor the Arisian, could lie to Gray Lensman Kinnison against his will.

"Damnation!" he snorted to himself. "Fighting against *women* again!"

"Who was she, then—it, I mean?" he hastily corrected the thought.

"It was our elder sister—"

The thought so translated by the man was not really "sister." That term, having distinctly sexual connotations and implications, would never have entered the mind of any "person" of Lyrane II. "Elder child of the same heritage" was more like it.

"—and another person from what it claimed was another world," the thought flowed smoothly on. "An entity, rather, not really a person, but you would not be interested in that, of course."

"Of course I would," Kinnison assured her. "In fact, it is this other person, and not your elderly relative, in whom I am interested. But you say that it is an entity, not a person. How come? Tell me all about it."

"Well, it looked like a person, but it wasn't. Its intelligence was low, its brain power was small. And its mind was upon things . . . its thoughts were so—"

Kinnison grinned at the Lyranian's efforts to express clearly thoughts so utterly foreign to her mind as to be totally incomprehensible.

"You don't know what that entity was, but I do," he broke in upon her floundering. "It was a person who was also, and quite definitely, a female. Right?"

"But a person couldn't—couldn't *possibly*—be a female!" she protested. "Why, even biologically, it doesn't make sense. There are no such things as females—there *can't* be!" And Kinnison saw her viewpoint clearly enough. According to her sociology and conditioning there could not be.

"We'll go into that later," he told her. "What I want now is this female zwilnik. Is she—or it—with your elder relative now?"

"Yes. They will be having dinner in the hall very shortly."

"Sorry to be a bother, but you'll have to take me to them—right now."

"Oh, may I? Since I could not kill you myself, I must take you to them so that they can do it. I have been wondering how I could force you to go there," she explained, naïvely.

"Henderson?" The Lensman spoke into his microphone—thought-screens, of course, being no barrier to radio waves. "I'm going after the zwilnik. This woman here is taking me. Have the 'copter stay over me, ready to needle anything I tell them to. While I'm gone go over that speedster with a fine-tooth comb, and when you get everything we want, blast it. It and the *Dauntless* are the only space cans on the planet, and I haven't got a picture of them taking the cruiser away from you. But keep your thought-screens up. Don't let them down for a fraction of a second, because these janes here carry plenty of jets and they're just as sweet and reasonable as a cageful of cateagles. Got it?"

"On the tape, chief," came instant answer. "But don't take any chances, Kim. Sure you can swing it alone?"

"Jets enough and to spare," Kinnison assured him, curtly. Then, as the Tellurians' helicopter shot into the air, he again turned his thought to the manager.

"Let's go," he directed, and she led him across the way to a row of parked ground cars. She manipulated a couple of levers and smoothly, if slowly, the little vehicle rolled away.

*

The distance was long and the pace was slow. The woman was driving automatically, the while her every sense was concentrated upon finding some weak point, some chink in his barrier, through which to thrust at him. Kinnison was amazed—stumped—at her fixity of purpose; at her grimly single-minded determination to make an end of him. She was out to get him, and she was not fooling.

"Listen, sister," he thought at her, after a few minutes of it; almost plaintively, for him. "Let's be reasonable about this thing. I told you that I didn't want to kill you; why in all the iridescent hells of space are you so dead set on killing me? If you don't behave yourself, I'll give you a treatment that will make your head ache for the next six months. Why don't you snap out of it, you dumb little lug, and be friends?"

This thought jarred her so that she stopped the car, the better to stare directly and viciously into his eyes.

"Be *friends*? With a *male*?" The thought literally seared its way into the man's brain.

"Listen, half-wit!" Kinnison stormed, exasperated. "Forget your narrow-minded, one-planet prejudices and think for a minute, if you can think—use that pint of bean soup inside your skull for something besides hating me all over the place. Get this—I am no more a male than you are the kind of a female that you think, by analogy, such a creature would have to be if she could exist in a sane and logical world."

"Oh." The Lyranian was taken aback at such cavalier instruction. "But the others, those in your so-immense vessel, they are of a certainty males," she stated with conviction. "I understood what you told them via your telephone-without-conductors. You have mechanical shields against the thought which kills. Yet you do not have to use it, while the others—males indubitably—do. You yourself are not entirely a male; your brain is almost as good as a person's."

"Better, you mean," he corrected her. "You're wrong. All of us of the ship are men—all alike. But a man on a job can't concentrate all the time on defending his brain against attack, hence the use of thought-screens. I can't use a screen out here, because I've got to talk to you people. See?"

"You fear us, then, so little?" she flared, all of her old animosity blazing out anew. "You consider our power, then, so small a thing?"

"Right. Right to a hair," he declared, with tightening jaw. But he did not believe it—quite. This girl was just about as safe to play around with as five-feet-eleven of coiled bushmaster, and twice as deadly.

She could not kill him mentally. Nor could the elder sister—whoever she might be—and her crew; he was pretty sure of that. But if they couldn't do him in by dint of brain it was a foregone conclusion that they would try brawn. And brawn they certainly had. This jade beside him weighed a hundred sixty-five or seventy, and she was trained down fine. Hard, limber and fast. He might be able to lick three or four of them—maybe half a dozen—in a rough-and-tumble brawl; but more than that would mean either killing or being killed. Damn it all! He'd never killed a woman yet, but it looked as though he might have to start in pretty quick now.

*

"Well, let's get going again," he suggested, "and while we're en route let's see if we can't work out some basis of co-operation—a sort of live-and-let-live arrangement. Since you understood the orders I gave the crew, you realize that our ship carries weapons capable of razing this entire city in a space of minutes." It was a statement, not a question.

"I realize that." The thought was muffled in helpless fury. "Weapons, weapons—always *weapons*! The eternal *male*! If it were not for your huge vessel and the peculiar airplane hovering over us, I would claw your eyes out and strangle you with my bare hands!"

"That would be a good trick if you could do it," he countered, equably enough. "But listen, you frustrated young murderess. You have already shown yourself to be, basically, a realist in facing physical facts. Why not face mental, intellectual facts in the same spirit?"

"Why, I do, of course. I *always* do!"

"You do not," he contradicted, sharply. "Males, according to your lights, have two—and only two—attributes. One, they breed. Two, they fight. They fight each other, and everything else, to the death and at the drop of a hat. Right?"

"Right, but—"

725

"But nothing—let me talk. Why didn't you breed the combativeness out of your males, hundreds of generations ago?"

"They tried it once, but the race began to deteriorate," she admitted.

"Exactly. Your whole set-up is cockeyed—unbalanced. You can think of me only as a male—one to be destroyed on sight, since I am not like one of yours. Yet, when I could kill you and had every reason to do so, I didn't. We can destroy you all, but we won't unless we must. What's the answer?"

"I don't know," she confessed, frankly. Her frenzied desire for killing abated, although her ingrained antipathy and revulsion did not. "In some ways, you do seem to have some of the instincts and qualities of a . . . almost of a person."

"I am a person—"

"You are *not*! Do you think that I am to be misled by the silly coverings you wear?"

"Just a minute. I am a person of a race having two *equal* sexes. Equal in every way. Numbers, too—one man and one woman—" and he went on to explain to her, as well as he could, the sociology of Civilization.

"Incredible!" she gasped the thought.

"But true," he assured her. "And now are you going to lay off me and behave yourself, like a good little girl, or am I going to have to do a bit of massaging on your brain? Or wind that beautiful body of yours a couple of times around a tree? I'm asking this for your own good, kid, believe me."

"Yes, I do believe you," she marveled. "I am becoming convinced that . . . that perhaps you *are* a person—at least of a sort—after all."

"Sure I am—that's what I've been trying to tell you for an hour. And cancel that 'of a sort,' too—"

"But tell me," she interrupted, "a thought you used—'beautiful.' I do not understand it. What does it mean, 'beautiful body'?"

"Holy Klono's whiskers!" If Kinnison had never been stumped before, he was now. How could he explain beauty, or music, or art, to this . . . this matriarchal savage? How explain cerise to a man born blind? And, above all, who had ever heard of having to explain to a woman—to any woman, anywhere in the whole macrocosmic universe—that she in particular was beautiful?

But he tried. In her mind he spread a portrait of her as he had seen her first. He pointed out to her the graceful curves and lovely contours, the lithely flowing lines, the perfection of proportion and modeling and symmetry, the flawlessly smooth, firm-textured skin, the supple, hard-trained fineness of her whole physique. No soap. She tried, in brow-furrowing concentration, to get it, but in vain. It simply did not register.

"But that is merely efficiency, everything you have shown," she declared. "Nothing else. I must be so, for my own good and for the good of those to come. But I think that I have seen some of your beauty," and in turn she sent into his mind a weirdly distorted picture of a human woman. The zwilnik he was following, Kinnison decided instantly.

She would be jeweled, of course, but not that heavily—a horse couldn't carry that load. And no woman ever born put paint on that thick, or reeked so of violent perfume, or plucked her eyebrows to such a thread, or indulged in such a hairdo.

"If *that* is beauty, I want none of it," the Lyranian declared.

Kinnison tried again. He showed her a waterfall, this time, in a stupendous gorge, with appropriate cloud formations and scenery. That, the girl declared, was simply erosion. Geological formations and meteorological phenomena. Beauty still did not appear. Painting, it appeared to her, was a waste of pigment and oil. Useless and inefficient—for any purpose of record the camera was much more precise and truthful. Music—vibrations in the atmosphere—would of necessity be simply a noise; and noise—any kind of noise—was not efficient.

"You poor little devil." The Lensman gave up. "You poor, ignorant, soul-starved little devil. And the worst of it is that you don't even realize—and never can realize—what you are missing."

"Don't be silly." For the first time, the woman actually laughed. "You are utterly foolish to make such a fuss about such trivial things."

*

Kinnison quit, appalled. He knew, now, that he and this apparently human creature beside him were as far apart as the Galactic Poles in every essential phase of life. He had heard of matriarchies, but he had never considered what a real matriarchy, carried to its logical conclusion, would be like.

This was it. For ages there had been, to all intents and purposes, only one sex; the masculine element never having been allowed to rise above the fundamental necessity of reproducing the completely dominant female. And that dominant female had become, in every respect save the purely and necessitously physical one, absolutely and utterly sexless. Men, upon Lyrane II, were dwarfs about thirty inches tall. They had the temper and the disposition of a mad Radeligian cateagle, the intellectual capacity of a Zabriskan fontema. They were not regarded as people, either at birth or at any subsequent time. To maintain a static population, each person gave birth to one person, on the grand average. The occasional male baby—about one in a hundred—did not count. He was not even kept at home, but was taken immediately to the "maletorium," in which he lived until attaining maturity.

One man to a hundred or so women for a year, then death. The hundred persons had their babies at twenty-one or twenty-two years of age—they lived to an average age of a hundred years—then calmly blasted their male's mind and disposed of his carcass. The male was not exactly an outcast; not precisely a pariah. He was tolerated as a necessary adjunct to the society of persons, but in no sense whatever was he a member of it.

The more Kinnison pondered this hookup the more appalled he became. Physically, these people were practically indistinguishable from human, Tellurian, Caucasian women. But mentally, intellectually, in every other way, how utterly different! Shockingly, astoundingly so to any really human being, whose entire outlook and existence is fundamentally, however unconsciously or subconsciously, based upon and conditioned by the prime division of life into two fully co-operant sexes. It didn't seem, at first glance, that such a cause could have such terrific effects; but here they were. In cold reality, these women were no more human than were the . . . the Eich. Take the Posenians, or the Rigellians, or even the Velantians. Any normal, stay-at-home Tellurian woman would pass

727

out cold if she happened to stumble onto Worsel in a dark alley at night. Yet the members of his repulsively reptilian-appearing race, merely because of having a heredity of equality and co-operation between the sexes, were in essence more nearly human than were these tall, splendidly built, actually and intrinsically beautiful creatures of Lyrane II!

"This is the hall," the person informed him, as the car came to a halt in front of a large structure of plain gray stone. "Come with me."

"Gladly," and they walked across the peculiarly bare grounds. They were side by side, but a couple of feet apart. She had been altogether too close to him in the little car. She did not want this male—or *any* male—to touch her or to be near her. And, considerably to her surprise, if the truth were to be known, the feeling was entirely mutual. Kinnison would have preferred to touch a Borovan slime-lizard.

They mounted the granite steps. They passed through the dull, weather-beaten portal. They were still side by side—but they were now a full yard apart.

IV.

"Listen, my beautiful but dumb guide," Kinnison counseled the Lyranian girl as they neared their objective. "I see that you're forgetting all your good girl scout resolutions and are getting all hot and bothered again. I'm telling you now for the last time to watch your step. If that zwilnik person has even a split second's warning that I am on her tail, all hell will be out for noon—and I don't mean perchance."

"But I must notify the Elder One that I am bringing you in," she told him. "One simply does not intrude unannounced. It is not permitted."

"QX. Stick to the announcement, though, and don't put out any funny ideas. I'll send a thought along, just to make sure."

But he did more than that, for even as he spoke, his sense of perception was already in the room to which they were going. It was a large room, and bare; filled with tables except for a clear central space upon which at the moment a lithe and supple person was doing what seemed to be a routine of acrobatic dancing, interspersed with suddenly motionless posings and posturings of extreme technical difficulty. At the tables were seated a hundred or so Lyranians, eating.

Kinnison was not interested in the floor show, whatever it was, nor in the massed Lyranians. The zwilnik was what he was after. Ah, there she was, at a ringside table—a small, square table seating four—near the door. Her back was to it—good. At her left, commanding the central view of the floor, was a redhead, sitting in a revolving, reclining chair, the only such seat in the room. Probably the Big Noise herself—the Elder One. No matter, he wasn't interested in her, either—yet. His attention flashed back to his proposed quarry and he almost gasped.

For she, like Dessa Desplaines, was an Aldebaranian, and she was everything that the Desplaines woman had been—more so, if possible. She was a seven-sector call-out, a thionite dream if there ever was one. And jewelry! This Lyranian tiger hadn't exaggerated that angle very much, at that. Her breast shields were of gold and platinum filigree, thickly studded with diamonds, emeralds and rubies, in intricate designs. Her shorts, or rather trunks, were of Manarkan glamorette, blazing with gems. A cleverly concealed dagger, with a jeweled haft and a vicious little fang of a blade. Rings, even a thumb ring. A necklace which was practically a collar flashed all the colors of the rainbow. Bracelets, armlets, anklets and knee bands. High-laced dress boots, jeweled from stem to gudgeon. Earrings, and a meticulous, micrometrically precise coiffure held in place by at least a dozen glittering buckles, combs and barrettes.

"Holy Klono's brazen tendons!" the Lensman whistled to himself, for every last, least one of those stones was the clear quill. "Half a million credits if it's a millo's worth!"

But he was not particularly interested in this jeweler's vision of what the well-dressed lady zwilnik will wear. There were other, far more important things. Yes, she had a thought-screen. Its battery was mighty low now, but it would still work; good thing he had blocked the warning. And she had a hollow tooth, too, but he'd see to it that she didn't get a chance to swallow its contents. She knew plenty, and he hadn't chased her this far to let her knowledge be obliterated by that hellish Boskonian drug.

*

They were at the door now. Disregarding the fiercely driven mental protests of his companion, Kinnison flung it open, stiffening up his mental guard as he did so. Simultaneously he invaded the zwilnik's mind with a flood of force, clamping down so hard that she could not move a single voluntary muscle. Then, paying no attention whatever to the shocked surprise of the assembled Lyranians, he strode directly up to the Aldebaranian and bent her head back into the crook of his elbow. Forcibly but gently he opened her mouth. With thumb and forefinger he deftly removed the false tooth. Releasing her then, mentally and physically, he dropped his spoil to the cement floor and ground it savagely to bits under his hard and heavy heel.

The zwilnik screamed wildly, piercingly at first. However, finding that she was getting no results, from Lensman or Lyranian, she subsided quickly into alertly watchful waiting.

Still unsatisfied, Kinnison flipped out one of his DeLameters and flamed the remains of the capsule of worse than paralyzing fluid, caring not a whit that his vicious portable, even in that brief instant, seared a hole a foot deep into the floor. Then and only then did he turn his attention to the redhead in the boss' chair.

He had to hand it to Elder Sister—through all this sudden and to her entirely unprecedented violence of action she hadn't turned a hair. She had swung her chair around so that she was facing him. Her back was to the athletic dancer who, now holding a flawlessly perfect pose, was going on with the act as though nothing out of the ordinary were transpiring. She was leaning backward, far backward, in the armless swivel chair, her right foot resting upon its pedestal. Her left ankle was crossed over her right knee, her left knee rested lightly against the table's top. Her hands were clasped together at the nape of her neck, supporting her red-thatched head; her elbows spread abroad in easy, indolent grace. Her eyes, so deeply, darkly green as to be almost black, stared up unwinkingly into the Lensman's—"insolently" was the descriptive word that came first to his mind.

If the Elder Sister was supposed to be old, Kinnison reflected as he studied appreciatively the startlingly beautiful picture which the artless chief person of this tribe so unconsciously made, she certainly belied her looks. As far as looks went, she really qualified—whatever it took, she in abundant measure had. Her hair was not really red,

729

either. It was a flamboyant, gorgeous auburn, about the same color as Chris' own, and just as thick. And it wasn't all haggled up. Accidentally, of course, and no doubt because on her particular job her hair didn't get in the way very often, it happened to be a fairly even, shoulder-length bob. What a mop! And damned if it wasn't wavy! Just as she was, with no dolling up at all, she would be a primary beam on any man's planet. She had this zwilnik here, knockout that she was and with all her war paint and feathers, blasted clear out of the ether. But this queen bee had a sting; she was still boring away at his shield. He'd better let her know that she didn't even begin to have enough jets to swing *that* load.

*

"QX, ace, cut the gun!" he directed crisply. "Ace," from him, was a complimentary term indeed. "Pipe down—that is all of that kind of stuff from you. I stood for this much of it, just to show you that you can't get to the first check station with that kind of fuel, but enough is a great plenty." At the sheer cutting power of the thought, rebroadcast no doubt by the airport manager, Lyranian activity throughout the room came to a halt. This was decidedly out of the ordinary. For a male mind—*any* male mind—to be able even momentarily to resist that of the meanest person of Lyrane was starkly unthinkable. The Elder's graceful body tensed; into her eyes there crept a dawning doubt, a peculiar, wondering uncertainty. Of fear there was none; all these sexless Lyranian women were brave to the point of foolhardiness.

"You tell her, draggle-pate," he ordered his erstwhile guide. "It took me hell's own time to make you understand that I mean business, but you talk her language—see how fast you can get the thing through Her Royal Nibs' skull."

It did not take long. The lovely dark-green eyes held conviction now; but also a greater uncertainty.

"It will be best, I think, to kill you now, instead of allowing you to leave—" she began.

"*Allow* me to leave!" Kinnison exploded. "Where do you get such funny ideas as that killing stuff? Just who, Toots, is going to keep me from leaving?"

"This." At the thought a weirdly conglomerate monstrosity which certainly had not been in the dining hall an instant before leaped at Kinnison's throat. It was a frightful thing indeed, combining the worst features of the reptile and the feline, a serpent's head upon a panther's body. Through the air it hurtled, terrible claws unsheathed to rend and venomous fangs outthrust to stab.

Kinnison had never before met that particular form of attack, but he knew instantly what it was—knew that neither leather nor armor of proof nor screen of force could stop it. He knew that the thing was real only to the woman and himself, that it was not only invisible, but nonexistent to everyone else. He also knew how ultimately deadly the creature was, knew that if claw or fang should strike him, he would die then and there.

Ordinarily very efficient, to the Lensman this method of slaughter was crude and amateurish. No such figment of any other mind could harm him unless he knew that it was coming; unless his mind was given ample time in which to appreciate—in reality, to manufacture—the danger he was in. And in *that* time *his* mind could negate it. He had two defenses. He could deny the monster's existence, in which case it would simply disappear. Or, a much more difficult, but technically a much nicer course, would be to take over control and toss it back at her.

Unhesitatingly he did the latter. In midleap the apparition swerved, in a full right-angle turn, directly toward the quietly poised body of the Lyranian. She acted just barely in time; the madly reaching claws were within scant inches of her skin when they vanished. Her eyes widened in frightened startlement; she was quite evidently shaken to the core by the Lensman's viciously skillful riposte. With an obvious effort she pulled herself together.

"Or these, then, if I must," and with a sweeping gesture of thought she indicated the roomful of her Lyranian sisters.

"How?" Kinnison asked, pointedly.

"By force of numbers; by sheer weight and strength. You can kill many of them with your weapons, of course, but not enough or quickly enough."

"You yourself would be the first to die," he cautioned her; and, since she was en rapport with his very mind, she knew that it was not a threat, but the stern finality of fact.

"What of that?" He in turn knew that she, too, meant precisely that and nothing else.

He had another weapon, but she would not believe it without a demonstration, and he simply could not prove that weapon upon an unarmed, defenseless woman, even though she was a Lyranian.

Stalemate.

No, the 'copter. "Listen, Queen of Sheba, to what I tell my boys," he ordered, and spoke into his microphone.

"Ralph? Stick a three-second needle down through the floor here; close enough to make her jump, but far enough away so that you won't blister her. Say about fifteen feet or so back—Fire!"

*

At Kinnison's word a narrow, but ragingly incandescent pencil of destruction raved downward through ceiling and floor. So inconceivably hot was it that if it had been a fraction larger, it would have ignited the Elder Sister's very chair. Effortlessly, insatiably it consumed everything in its immediate path, radiating the while the entire spectrum of vibrations. It was unbearable, and the auburn-haired creature did indeed jump, in spite of herself—halfway to the door. The rest of the hitherto imperturbable persons clustered together in panic-stricken knots.

"You see, Cleopatra," Kinnison explained, as the dreadful needle beam expired, "I've got plenty of stuff if I want to—or have to—use it. The boys up there will stick a needle like that through the brain of anyone or everyone in this room if I give the word. I don't want to kill any of you unless it's necessary, as I explained to your misbarbered friend here, but I am leaving here alive and all in one piece, and I'm taking this Aldebaranian along with me, in the same condition. If I must, I'll lay down a barrage like that sample you just saw, and only the zwilnik and I will get out alive. How about it?"

"What are you going to do with the stranger?" the Lyranian asked, avoiding the issue.

"I'm going to take some information away from her, that's all. Why? What were you going to do with her yourselves?"

"We were—and are—going to kill it," came flashing reply. The lethal bolt came even before the reply; but, fast as the Elder One was, the Gray Lensman was faster. He blanked out the thought, reached over and flipped on the Aldebaranian's thought-screen.

"Keep it on until we get to the ship, sister," he spoke aloud in the girl's native tongue. "Your battery's low, I know, but it'll last long enough. These hens seem to be strictly on the peck."

"I'll say they are—you don't know the half of it." Her voice was low, rich, vibrant. "Thanks, Kinnison."

"Listen, Scarlet-top, what's the percentage in playing so dirty?" the Lensman complained then. "I'm doing my damnedest to let you off easy, but I'm all done dickering. Do we go out of here peaceably, or do we fry you and your crew to cinders in your own lard, and walk out over the grease spots? It's strictly up to you, but you'll decide right here and right now."

The Elder One's face was hard, her eyes flinty. Her fingers were curled into ball-tight fists. "I suppose, since we cannot stop you, we must let you go free," she hissed, in helpless but controlled fury. "If by giving my life and the lives of all these others we could kill you, here and now would you two die—but as it is, you may go."

"But why all the rage?" the puzzled Lensman asked. "You strike me as being, on the whole, reasoning creatures. You in particular went to Tellus with this zwilnik here, so you should know—"

"I *do* know," the Lyranian broke in. "That is why I would go to any length, pay any price whatever, to keep you from returning to your own world, to prevent the inrush of your barbarous hordes here—"

"Oh! So *that's* it!" Kinnison exclaimed. "You think that some of our people might want to settle down here, or to have traffic with you?"

"Yes." She went into a eulogy concerning Lyrane II, concluding, "I have seen the planets and the races of your so-called Civilization, and I detest them and it. Never again shall any of us leave Lyrane; nor, if I can help it, shall any stranger ever again come here."

"Listen, angel face!" the man commanded. "You're as mad as a Radeligian cateagle—you're as cockeyed as Trenco's ether. Get this, and get it straight. To any really intelligent being of any one of forty million planets, your whole Lyranian race would be a total loss with no insurance. You're a God-forsaken, spiritually and emotionally starved, barren, mentally ossified, and completely monstrous mess. If I, personally, never see either you or your planet again, that will be exactly twenty-seven minutes too soon. This girl here thinks the same of you as I do. If anybody else ever hears of Lyrane and thinks he wants to visit it, I'll take him out of . . . I'll knock a hip down on him if I have to, to keep him away from here. Do I make myself clear?"

"Oh, yes—perfectly!" she fairly squealed in schoolgirlish delight. The Lensman's tirade, instead of infuriating her further, had been sweet music to her peculiarly insular mind. "Go, then, at once—hurry! Oh, please, hurry! Can you drive the car back to your vessel, or will one of us have to go with you?"

"Thanks. I could drive your car, but it won't be necessary. The 'copter will pick us up."

He spoke to the watchful Ralph, then he and the Aldebaranian left the hall, followed at a careful distance by the throng. The helicopter was on the ground, waiting. The man and the woman climbed aboard.

*

"Clear ether, persons!" The Lensman waved a salute to the crowd and the Tellurian craft shot into the air.

Thence to the *Dauntless*, which immediately did likewise, leaving behind her, upon the little airport, a fused blob of metal that had once been the zwilnik's speedster. Kinnison studied the white face of his captive, then handed her a tiny canister.

"Fresh battery for your thought-screen generator; yours is about shot." Since she made no motion to accept it, he made the exchange himself and tested the result. It worked. "What's the matter with you, kid, anyway? I'd say that you were starved, if I hadn't caught you at a full table."

"I am starved," the girl said, simply. "I couldn't eat there. I knew that they were going to kill me, and it . . . it sort of took away my appetite."

"Well, what are we waiting for? I'm hungry, too—let's go eat."

"Not with you, either, any more than with them. I thanked you, Lensman, for saving my life there, and I meant it. I thought then and still think that I would rather have you kill me than those horrible, monstrous women, but I simply can't eat."

"But I'm not even thinking of killing you—can't you get that through your skull? I don't make war on women; you ought to know that by this time."

"You will have to." The girl's voice was low and level. "You didn't kill any of those Lyranians, no, but you didn't chase them a million parsecs, either. We have been taught ever since we were born that you Patrolmen always torture people to death. I don't quite believe that of you personally, since I have had a couple of glimpses into your mind, but you'll kill me before I'll talk. At least, I hope and I believe that I can hold out."

"Listen, girl." Kinnison was in deadly earnest. "You are in no danger whatever. You are just as safe as though you were in Klono's hip pocket. You have some information that I want, yes, and I will get it, but in the process I will neither hurt you nor do you mental or physical harm. The only torture you will undergo will be that which, as now, you give yourself."

"But you called me a . . . a zwilnik, and they *always* kill them," she protested.

"Not always. In battles and in raids, yes. Captured ones are tried in court. If found guilty, they used to go into the lethal chambers. Sometimes they do yet, but not usually. We have mental therapists now who can operate on a mind if there's anything there worth saving."

"And you think that I will wait to stand trial upon Tellus, in the entirely negligible hope that your bewhiskered, fossilized therapists will find something in me worth saving?"

"You won't have to," Kinnison laughed. "Your case has already been decided—in your favor. I am neither a policeman nor a narcotics man; but I happen to be qualified as judge, jury and executioner. I am a therapist to boot. I once saved a worse zwilnik than you are, even though she wasn't quite such a knockout. Now do we eat?"

"Really? You aren't just . . . just giving me the needle?"

*

The Lensman flipped off her screen and gave her unmistakable evidence. The girl, hitherto so unmovedly self-reliant, broke down. She recovered quickly, however, and in Kinnison's cabin she ate ravenously.

"Have you a cigarette?" she sighed with repletion when she could hold no more food.

"Sure. Alsakanite, Venerian, Tellurian, most anything—we carry a couple of hundred different brands. What would you like?"

"Tellurian, by all means. I had a package of Camerfields once—they were gorgeous. Would you have those, by any chance?"

"Uh-huh," he assured her. "Quartermaster! Carton Camerfields, please." It popped out of the pneumatic tube in seconds. "Here you are, sister."

The glittery girl drew the fragrant smoke deep down into her lungs.

"Ah, that tastes good! Thanks, Kinnison—for everything. I'm glad that you kidded me into eating; that was the finest meal I ever ate. But it won't take, really. I have never broken yet, and I don't believe that I will break now. And if I do, I'm dead certain that I won't be worth a damn, to myself or to anybody else, from then on." She crushed out the butt. "So let's get on with the third degree. Bring on your rubber hose and your lights and the drip can."

"You're still on the wrong foot, Toots," Kinnison said, pityingly. What a frightful contrast there was between her slimly rounded body, in its fantastically gorgeous costume, and the stark somberness of her eyes! "There'll be no third degree, no hose, no lights, nothing like that. In fact, I'm not even going to talk to you until you've had a good long sleep. You don't look hungry any more, but you're still not in tune, by seven thousand kilocycles. How long has it been since you really slept?"

"A couple of weeks, at a guess. Maybe a month."

"Thought so. Come on; you're going to sleep now."

The girl did not move. "With whom?" she asked, quietly. Her voice did not quiver, but stark terror lay in her mind and her hand crept unconsciously toward the hilt of her dagger.

"Holy Klono's claws!" Kinnison snorted, staring at her in wide-eyed wonder. "Just what kind of a bunch of hyenas do you think you've got into, anyway?"

"Bad," the girl replied, gravely. "Not the worst possible, but from my standpoint plenty bad enough. What can I expect from the Patrol except what I do expect? You don't need to kid me along, Kinnison. I can take it, and I'd a lot rather take it standing up, facing it, than have you sneak up on me with it after giving me your shots in the arm."

"What somebody has done to you is a sin and a shrieking shame," Kinnison declared, feelingly. "Come on, you poor little devil." He picked up sundry pieces of apparatus, then, taking her arm, he escorted her to another cabin.

"That door," he explained carefully, "is solid tool steel. The lock is on the inside, and it cannot be picked. There are only two keys to it in the Universe, and here they are. There is a bolt, too, that cannot be forced by anything short of a hydraulic jack. Here is a full-coverage screen, and here's a twenty-foot spy-ray block. There is your stuff out of the speedster. If you want help, or anything to eat or drink, or anything else that can be expected aboard a star wagon, there's the communicator. QX?"

"Then you really mean it? That I . . . that you . . . I mean—"

"Absolutely," he assured her. "Just that. You are completely the master of your destiny, the captain of your soul. Good night."

"Good night, Kinnison. Good night, and th . . . thanks." The girl threw herself face downward upon the bed in a storm of sobs.

Nevertheless, as Kinnison started back toward his own cabin, he heard the massive bolt click into its socket and felt the blocking screens go on.

V.

Some twelve or fourteen hours later, after the Aldebaranian girl had had her breakfast, Kinnison went to her cabin.

"Hi, Cutie, you look better. By the way, what's your name, so we'll know what to call you?"

"Illona."

"Illona what?"

"No what—just Illona, that's all."

"How do they tell you from other Illonas, then?"

"Oh, you mean my registry number. In the Aldebaranian language there are not the symbols—it would have to be 'The Illona who is the daughter of Porlakent the potter who lives in the house of—'"

"Hold everything—we'll call you Illona Potter." He eyed her keenly. "I thought your Aldebaranian wasn't so hot—didn't seem possible that I could have got *that* rusty. You haven't been on Aldebaran II for a long time, have you?"

"No, we moved to Lonabar when I was about six."

"Lonabar? Never heard of it—I'll check up on it later. Your stuff was all here, wasn't it? Did any of the red-headed person's things get mixed in?"

"Things?" She giggled sunnily, then sobered in quick embarrassment. "She didn't carry any. They're horrid, I think—positively *indecent*—to run around that way."

"Hm-m-m. Glad you brought the point up. You've got to put on some clothes aboard this ship, you know."

"Me?" she demanded, "Why, I'm fully dressed—" she paused, then shrank together visibly. "Oh, Tellurians—I remember, all those coverings! You mean, then . . . you think I'm shameless and indecent, too?"

"No. Not at all—yet." At his obvious sincerity Illona unfolded again. "Most of us—especially the officers—have been on so many different planets, had dealings with so many different types and kinds of entities, that we're used to anything. When we visit a planet that goes naked, we do also, as a matter of course; when we hit one that muffles up to complete invisibility we do that, too. 'When in Rome, be a Roman candle,' you know. The point is that we're at home here, you're the visitor. It's all a matter of convention, of course; but a rather important one. Don't you think so?"

"Covering up, certainly. Uncovering is different. They told me to be sure to, but I simply can't. I tried it back there, but I felt *naked!*"

"QX—we'll have the tailor make you a dress or two. Some of the boys haven't been around very much, and you'd look pretty bare to them. Everything you've got on, jewelry and all, wouldn't make a Tellurian sunsuit, you know."

"Then have them hurry up the dress, please. But this isn't jewelry, it is—"

"Jet back, beautiful. I know gold, and platinum, and—"

"The metal is expensive, yes," Illona conceded. "These alone," she tapped one of the delicate shields, "cost five days of work. But base metal stains the skin blue and green and black, so what can one do? As for the beads, they are synthetics—junk. Poor girls, if they buy it themselves, do not wear jewelry, but beads, like these. Half a day's work buys the lot."

"What!" Kinnison demanded.

"Certainly. Rich girls only, or poor girls who do not work, wear real jewelry, such as . . . the Aldebaranian has not the words. Let me think at you, please?"

"Sorry, nothing there that I recognize at all," Kinnison answered, after studying a succession of thought-images of multicolored, spectacular gems. "That's one to file away in the book, too, believe me. But as to that 'junk' you've got draped all over yourself—half a day's pay—what do you work at for a living, when you work?"

"I'm a dancer—like this." She leaped lightly to her feet and her left boot whizzed past her ear in a flashingly fast high kick. Then followed a series of gyrations and contortions, for which the Lensman knew no names, during which the girl seemed a practically boneless embodiment of suppleness and grace. She sat down; meticulous hairdress scarcely rumpled, not a buckle or bracelet awry, breathing hardly one count faster.

*

"Nice." Kinnison applauded briefly. "Hard for me to evaluate such talent as that. However, upon Tellus or any one of a thousand other planets I could point out to you, you can sell that 'junk' you're wearing for—at a rough guess—about fifty thousand days' work."

"Impossible!"

"True, nevertheless. So, before we land, you'd better give them to me, so that I can send them to a bank for you, under guard."

"If I land." As Kinnison spoke Illona's manner changed; darkened as though an inner light had been extinguished. "You have been so friendly and nice, I was forgetting where I am and the business ahead. Putting it off won't make it any easier. Better be getting on with it, don't you think?"

"Oh, that? That's all done, long ago."

"What?" she almost screamed. "It isn't! It *couldn't* be!"

"Sure. I got most of the stuff I wanted last night, while I was changing your thought-screen battery. Menjo Bleeko, your big-shot boss, and so on."

"You didn't! But . . . you must have, at that, to know it. You didn't hurt me, or anything. You couldn't have operated—changed me—because I have all my memories—or seem to. I'm not an idiot, I mean any more than usual—"

"You've been taught a good many sheer lies, and quite a few half-truths," he informed her, evenly. "For instance, what did they tell you that hollow tooth would do to you when you broke the seal?"

"Make my mind a blank. But one of their doctors would get hold of me very soon and give me the antidote that would restore me exactly as I was before."

"That is one of the half-truths. It would certainly have made your mind a blank, but only by blasting nine-tenths of your memory files out of existence. Their therapists would 'restore' you by substituting other memories for your own—whatever other ones they pleased."

"How horrible! How perfectly ghastly! That was why you treated it so, then; as though it were a snake. I wondered at your savagery toward it. But how, really, do I know that you are telling the truth?"

"You don't," he admitted. "You will have to make your own decisions after acquiring full information."

"You are a therapist," she remarked, shrewdly. "But if you operated upon my mind you didn't 'save' me, because I still think exactly the same as I always did about the Patrol and everything pertaining to it—or do I? Or is this—" Her eyes widened with a startling possibility.

"No, I didn't operate," he assured her. "No such operation can possibly be done without leaving scars—breaks in the memory chains—that you can find in a minute if you look for them. There are no breaks or blanks in any chain in your mind."

"No—at least, I can't find any," she reported after a few minutes' thought. "But why didn't you? You can't turn me loose this way, you know—a z . . . an enemy of your society."

"You don't need saving," he grinned. "You believe in absolute good and absolute evil, don't you?"

"Why, of course—certainly! *Everybody* must!"

"Not necessarily. Some of the greatest thinkers in the Universe do not." His voice grew somber, then lightened again. "Such being the case, however, all that you need to 'save' yourself is experience, observation and knowledge of both sides of the question. You're a colossal little fraud, you know."

"How do you mean?" She blushed vividly, her eyes wavered.

"Pretending to be such a hard-boiled egg. 'Never broke yet.' Why should you have broken, when you have never been under pressure?"

"I have so!" she flared. "What do you suppose I'm carrying this knife for?"

"Oh, that." He mentally shrugged the wicked little dagger aside as he pondered. "You little lamb in wolf's clothing—but at that, your memories may, I think, be altogether too valuable to monkey with. There's something funny about this whole matrix—*damned* funny. Come clean, angel face—why?"

*

"They told me," Illona admitted, wriggling slightly, "to act tough—really tough. As though I were an adventuress who had been everywhere and had done . . . done everything. That the worse I acted the better I would get along in your Civilization."

"I suspected something of the sort. And what did you zwil . . . excuse me, you folks . . . go to Lyrane for, in the first place?"

"I don't know. From chance remarks I gathered that we were to land upon one of the planets—any one, I supposed—and wait for somebody."

"What were you, personally, going to do?"

"I don't know that, either—not exactly, that is. Whoever it was that we were going to meet was going to give us instructions."

"How come those women killed your men? Didn't they have thought-screens, too?"

"No. They were not agents, just soldiers. They killed about a dozen of the Lyranians when we first landed—to demonstrate their power—then they dropped dead."

"Um. Poor technique, but typically Boskonian. Your trip to Tellus was more or less accidental, then?"

"Yes. I wanted her to take me back to Lonabar, but she wouldn't. She learned about Tellus and the Patrol from our minds—none of them could believe at first that there were any inhabited worlds except their own—and wanted to study them at first hand. So she took our ship and used me as . . . as a sort of blind, I think."

"I see. I'm not surprised. I thought that there was something remarkably screwy about those activities—they seemed so aimless and so barren of results—but I couldn't put my finger on it. And we crowded her so close that she decided to flit for home. You drove the ship and picked her up. You could see her, but nobody else could—that she didn't want to."

"That was it. She said that she was being hampered by a mind of power. That was you, of course?"

"And others. Well, that's that, for a while."

He called the tailor in. No, he didn't have a thing to make a girl's dress out of, especially not a girl like that. She should wear glamorette, and sheer—very sheer. He didn't know a thing about ladies' tailoring, either; he hadn't made a gown since he was knee-high to a duck. All he had in the shop was coat linings. Perhaps nylon would do, after a fashion. He remembered now, he did have a bolt of gray nylon that wasn't any good for linings—not stiff enough. Far too heavy, of course, but it would drape well.

It did. She came swaggering back, an hour or so later, the hem of her skirt swishing against the tops of her high-laced boots.

"Do you like it?" she asked, pirouetting gayly.

"Fine!" he applauded, and it was. The tailor had understated tremendously both his ability and the resources of his shop.

"Now what? I don't have to stay in my room all the time now, please?"

"I'll say not. The ship is yours. I want you to get acquainted with every man on board. Go anywhere you like—except the private quarters, of course—even to the control room. The boys all know that you're at large."

"The language—but I'm talking English now!"

"Sure. I've been giving it to you right along. You know it as well now as I do."

She stared at him in awe. Then, her natural buoyancy asserting itself, she flitted out of the room with a wave of her hand.

*

And Kinnison sat down to think. A girl—a kid who wasn't dry behind the ears yet—wearing beads worth a full-grown fortune, sent somewhere—to do what? Lyrane II, a perfect matriarchy. Lonabar, a planet of zwilniks that knew all about Tellus, but that Tellus had never even heard of, sending expeditions to Lyrane. To the System, perhaps not specifically to Lyrane II. Why? For what? To do what? Strange, new jewels of fabulous value. What was the hookup? It didn't make any kind of sense yet—not enough data.

And faintly, waveringly, barely impinging upon the outermost, most tenuous fringes of his mind he felt something: the groping, questing summons of an incredibly distant thought.

"Male of Civilization . . . Person of Tellus . . . Kinnison of Tellus . . . Lensman Kinnison of Sol III . . . . Any Lens-bearing officer of the Galactic Patrol—" Endlessly the desperately urgent, almost imperceptible thought implored.

Kinnison stiffened. He reached out with the full power of his mind, seized the thought, tuned to it, and hurled a reply—and when *that* mind really pushed a thought, it traveled.

"Kinnison of Tellus acknowledging!" His answer fairly crackled on its way.

"You do not know my name," the stranger's thought came clearly now. "I am the 'Toots,' the 'Queen of Sheba,' the 'Cleopatra,' the 'Elder Person' of Lyrane II. Do you know me, O Kinnison of Sol III?"

"I know you," he shot back. What a brain—what a *terrific* brain—that sexless woman had!

"We are invaded by manlike beings in ships of space, who wear screens against our thoughts and who slay without cause. Will you help us with your ship of might and your mind of power?"

"Just a sec, Toots—*Henderson!*" Orders snapped. The *Dauntless* spun end-for-end.

"QX, Helen of Troy," he reported then. "We're on our way back there at maximum blast. Say, that name 'Helen of Troy' fits you better than anything else I have called you. You don't know it, of course, but that other Helen launched a thousand ships. You're launching only one; but, believe me, Babe, the old *Dauntless* is SOME ship!"

"I hope so." The Person of Lyrane II, ignoring the byplay, went directly to the heart of the matter in her usual pragmatic fashion. "We have no right to ask; you have every reason to refuse—"

"Don't worry about that, Helen. We're all good little boy scouts at heart. We're supposed to do a good deed every day, and we have missed a lot of days lately."

"You are what you call 'kidding,' I think." A matriarch could not be expected to possess a sense of humor. "But I do not lie to you or pretend. We did not, do not now, and never will like you or yours. With us now, however, it is that you are much the lesser of two terrible evils. If you will aid us now, we will tolerate your Patrol."

"And that's big of you, Helen, no fooling." The Lensman was really impressed. The plight of the Lyranians must be desperate indeed. "Just keep a stiff upper lip, all of you. We're coming loaded for bear, and we are not exactly creeping."

Nor were they. The big cruiser had plenty of legs and she was using them all; the engineers were giving her all the oof that her drivers would take. She was literally blasting a hole through space; she was traveling so fast that the atoms of substance in the interstellar vacuum, merely wave forms though they were, simply could not get out of the flier's way. They were being blasted into nothingness against the *Dauntless'* wall shields.

And throughout her interior the Patrol ship, always in complete readiness for strife, was being gone over again with microscopic thoroughness, to be put into more readiness, if possible, even than that.

*

After a few hours Illona danced back to Kinnison's "con" room, fairly bubbling over.

"They're marvelous, Lensman!" she cried, "simply *marvelous!*"

"What are marvelous?"

"The boys," she enthused. "All of them. They're here because they *want* to be—why, the officers don't even have whips! They *like* them, actually! The officers who push the little buttons and things and those who walk around and look through the little glass things and even the gray-haired old man with the four stripes, why they like them all! And the boys were all putting on guns when I left—why, I never *heard* of such a thing!—and they're just simply *crazy* about you. I thought it was awfully funny that you took off your guns as soon as the ship left Lyrane and that you don't have guards around you all the time because I thought sure somebody would stab you in the back or something, but they don't even want to and that's what's so marvelous and Hank Henderson told me—"

"Save it!" he ordered. "Jet back, angel face, before you blow a fuse." He had been right in not operating—this girl was going to be a mine of information concerning Boskonian methods and operations, and all without knowing it. "That's what I have been trying to tell you about our Civilization; that it is founded upon the freedom of the individual to do pretty much as he pleases, as long as it is not to the public harm. And, as far as possible, equality of all the entities of Civilization."

"Uh-huh, I know you did," she nodded brightly, then sobered quickly, "but I couldn't understand it. I can't understand it yet; I can scarcely believe that you all are so—You know, don't you, what would happen if this were a Lonabarian ship and I would go running around talking to officers as though I were their equal?"

"No—what?"

"It's inconceivable, of course; it simply couldn't happen. But if it did, I would be punished terribly—perhaps, though, at a first offense, I might be given only a twenty-scar whipping." At his lifted eyebrow she explained, "One that leaves twenty scars that show for life.

"That's why I'm acting so intoxicated, I think. You see," she hesitated shyly, "I am not used to being treated as anybody's equal, except of course other girls like me. Nobody is, on Lonabar. Everybody is higher or lower than you are. I'm going to simply love this when I get accustomed to it." She spread both arms in a sweeping gesture. "I'd like to *squeeze* this whole ship and everybody in it—I just can't wait to get to Tellus and really *live* there!"

"That's a thing that has been bothering me," Kinnison confessed, and the girl stared wonderingly at his serious face. "We are going into battle, and we can't take time to land you anywhere before the battle starts."

"Of course not. Why should you?" she paused, thinking deeply. "You're not worrying about *me*, surely? Why, you're a high officer! Officers don't care whether a girl is shot or not, do they?" The thought was obviously, utterly new.

"We do. It's extremely poor hospitality to invite a guest aboard and then have her killed. All I can say, though, is that if our number goes up, I hope that you can forgive me for getting you into it!"

"Oh—thanks, Gray Lensman. Nobody ever spoke to me like that before. But I wouldn't land if I could. I like Civilization. If you . . . if you don't win, I couldn't go to Tellus, anyway, so I'd much rather take my chances here than not, sir, really. I'll *never* go back to Lonabar, in any case."

"'At a girl, Toots!" He extended his hand. She looked at it dubiously, then hesitantly stretched out her own. But she learned fast; she put as much pressure into the brief hand-clasp as Kinnison did. "You'd better blast off now, I've got work to do.

"Go anywhere you like until I call you. Before the trouble starts I'm going to put you down in the center, where you'll be as safe as possible."

*

The girl hurried away and the Lensman got into communication with Helen of Lyrane, who gave him then a resumé of everything that had happened. Two ships—big ships, immense space cruisers—appeared near the airport. Nobody saw them coming, they came so fast. They stopped, and without warning or parley destroyed all the buildings and all the people nearby with beams like Kinnison's needle beam, except much larger. Then the ships landed and men disembarked. The Lyranians killed ten of them by direct mental impact or by monsters of the mind, but after that everyone who came out of the vessel wore a thought-screen and the persons were quite helpless. The enemy had burned down and melted a part of the city, and as a further warning were then making formal plans to execute publicly a hundred leading Lyranians—ten for each man they had killed.

Because of the screens no communication was possible, but the invaders had made it clear that if there were one more sign of resistance, or even of non-co-operation, the entire city would be rayed and every living thing in it blasted out of existence. She herself had escaped so far. She was hidden in a crypt in the deepest subcellar of the city. She was, of course, one of the ones they wanted to execute, but finding any of Lyrane's leaders would be extremely difficult, if not impossible. They were still searching, with many persons as highly unwilling guides. They had indicated that they would stay there until the leaders were found; that they would make the Lyranians tear down their city, stone by stone, until they *were* found.

"But how could they know who your leaders are?" Kinnison wanted to know.

"Perhaps one of our persons weakened under their torture," Helen replied equably. "Perhaps they have among them a mind of power. Perhaps in some other fashion. What matters it? The thing of importance is that they do know."

"Another thing of importance is that it'll hold them there until we get there," Kinnison thought. "Typical Boskonian technique, I gather. It won't be many hours now. Hold them off if you can."

"I think that I can," came tranquil reply. "Through mental contact each person acting as guide knows where each of us hidden ones is, and is avoiding all our hiding places."

"Good. Tell me all you can about those ships, their size, shape and armament."

She could not, it developed, give him any reliable information as to size. She thought that the present invaders were smaller than the *Dauntless*, but she could not be sure. Compared to the little airships which were the only flying structures with which she was familiar, both Kinnison's ships and those now upon Lyrane were so immensely huge that trying to tell which was larger was very much like attempting to visualize the difference between infinity squared and infinity cubed. On shape, however, she was much better; she spread in the Lensman's mind an accurately detailed picture of the two space ships which the Patrolmen intended to engage.

In shape they were ultrafast, very much like the *Dauntless* herself. Hence they certainly were not maulers. Nor, probably, were they first-line battleships, such as had composed the fleet which had met Civilization's Grand Fleet off the edge of the Second Galaxy. Of course, the Patrol had had in that battle ultrafast ships which were ultrapowerful as well—such as this same *Dauntless*—and it was a fact that while Civilization was designing and building, Boskonia could very well have been doing the same thing. On the other hand, since the enemy could not logically be expecting real trouble in Dunstan's Region, these cans might very well be second-line or out-of-date stuff—

"Are those ships lying on the same field we landed on?" he asked at that point in his cogitations.

"Yes."

"You can give me pretty close to an actual measurement of the difference, then," he told her. "We left a hole in that field practically our whole length. How does it compare with theirs?"

"I can find that out, I think," and in due time she did so; reporting that the *Dauntless* was the longer, by some twelve times a person's height.

"Thanks, Helen." Then, and only then, did Kinnison leave his private conning room and call his officers into consultation in the control room.

He told them everything he had learned and deduced about the two Boskonian vessels which they were about to attack. Then, heads bent over a visitank, the Patrolmen began to discuss strategy and tactics.

VI.

As the *Dauntless* approached Lyrane II so nearly that the planet showed a perceptible disk upon the plates, the observers began to study their detectors carefully. Nothing registered, and a brief interchange of thoughts with the Chief Person of Lyrane informed the Lensman that the two Boskonian warships were still upon the ground. Indeed, they were going to stay upon the ground until after the hundred Lyranian leaders, most of whom were still safely hidden, had been found and executed, exactly as per announcement. The strangers had killed many persons by torture and were killing more in attempts to make them reveal the hiding places of the leaders, but little if any real information was being obtained.

"Good technique, perhaps, from a bullheaded, dictatorial standpoint, but it strikes me as being damned poor tactics," grunted Malcolm Craig, the *Dauntless'* grizzled captain, when Kinnison had relayed the information.

"I'll say it's poor tactics," the Lensman agreed. "If Helmuth or one of the living military hot shots of his caliber were down there, one of those cans would be out on guard, flitting all over space."

"But how could they be expecting trouble 'way out here, nine thousand parsecs from anywhere?" argued Chatway, the chief firing officer.

"They ought to be—that's the point." This from Henderson. "Where do we land, Kim? Did you find out?"

"Not exactly; they're on the other side of the planet from here, now. Good thing we don't have to get rid of a Tellurian intrinsic this time—it'll be a near thing as it is." And it was. Scarcely was the intrinsic velocity matched to that of the planet when the observers reported that the airport upon which the enemy lay was upon the horizon. Inertialess, the *Dauntless* flashed away, going inert and into action simultaneously when within range of the zwilnik ships. Within range of one of them, that is; for, short as the time had been, the crew of one of the Boskonian vessels had been sufficiently alert to get her away. The other one did not move; then or ever.

The Patrolmen acted with the flawless smoothness of long practice and perfect teamwork. At the first sign of zwilnik activity as revealed by his spy-rays, Nelson, the chief communications officer, loosed a barrage of ethereal and sub-ethereal static interference through which no communications beam or signal could be driven. Captain Craig barked a word into his microphone and every dreadful primary that could be brought to bear erupted as one weapon. Chief Pilot Henderson, after a casual glance below, cut in the Bergenholms, tramped in his blasts, and set the cruiser's narrow nose into his tracer's line. One glance was enough. He needed no orders as to what to do next. It would have been apparent to almost anyone, even to one of the persons of Lyrane, that that riddled, slashed, three-quarters fused mass of junk never again would be or could contain aught of menace. The Patrol ship had not stopped: had scarcely even paused. Now, having destroyed half of the opposition *en passant*, she legged it after the remaining half.

"Now what, Kim?" asked Captain Craig. "We can't inglobe him and he no doubt mounts tractor shears. We'll have to use the new tractor zone, won't we?"

Ordinarily the gray-haired four-striper would have made his own decisions, since he and he alone fought his ship; but these circumstances were far from ordinary. First, any Unattached Lensman, wherever he was, was the boss. Second, the tractor zone was new; so brand-new that even the *Dauntless* had not as yet used it. Third, the ship was on detached duty, assigned directly to Kinnison to do with as he willed. Fourth, said Kinnison was high in the confidence of the Galactic Council and would know whether or not the present situation justified the use of the new mechanism.

"If he can cut a tractor, yes," the Lensman agreed. "Only one ship. He can't get away and he can't communicate—safe enough. Go to it."

*

THE LENSMAN

The Tellurian ship was faster than the Boskonian; and, since she had been only seconds behind at the start, she came within striking distance of her quarry in short order. Tractor beams reached out and seized; but only momentarily did they hold. At the first pull they were cut cleanly away. No one was surprised; it had been taken for granted that all Boskonian ships would by this time have been equipped with tractor shears.

These shears had been developed originally by the scientists of the Patrol. Immediately following that invention, looking forward to the time when Boskone would have acquired it, those same scientists set themselves to the task of working out something which would be just as good as a tractor beam for combat purposes, but which could not be cut. They got it finally—a globular shell of force, very much like a meteorite screen except double in phase. That is, it was completely impervious to matter moving in either direction, instead of only to that moving inwardly. Even if exact data as to generation, gauging, distance, and control of this weapon were available—which they very definitely are not—it would serve no good end to detail them here. Suffice it to say that the *Dauntless* mounted tractor zones, and had ample power to hold them.

Closer up the Patrol ship blasted. The zone snapped on, well beyond the Boskonian, and tightened. Henderson cut the Bergenholms. Captain Craig snapped out orders and Chief Firing Officer Chatway and his boys did their stuff.

Defensive screens full out, the pirate stayed free and tried to run. No soap. She merely slid around upon the frictionless inner surface of the zone. She rolled and she spun. Then she went inert and rammed. Still no soap. She struck the zone and bounced; bounced with all of her mass and against all the power of her driving thrust. The impact jarred the *Dauntless* to her very skin; but the zone's anchorage had been computed and installed by top-flight engineers and they held. And the zone itself held. It yielded a bit, but it did not fail and the shear planes of the pirates could not cut it.

Then, no other course being possible, the Boskonians fought. Of course, theoretically, surrender was possible, but it simply was not done. No pirate ship ever had surrendered to a Patrol force, however large; none ever would. No Patrol ship had ever surrendered to Boskone—or would. That was the unwritten but grimly understood code of this internecine conflict between two galaxy-wide and diametrically opposed cultures; it was and had to be a war of utter and complete extermination. Individuals or small groups might be captured bodily; but no ship, no individual, even, ever, under any conditions, surrendered. The fight was—always and everywhere—to the death.

So this one was. The enemy was well armed of her type, but her type simply did not carry projectors of sufficient power to break down the *Dauntless'* hard-held defensive screens. Nor did she mount screens heavy enough to withstand for long the furious assault of the Patrol ship's terrific primaries.

As soon as the pirate's screens went down the firing stopped; that order had been given long since. Kinnison wanted information, he wanted charts, he wanted a few living Boskonians. He got nothing. Not a man remained alive aboard the riddled hulk; the chart room contained only heaps of fused ash. Everything which might have been of use to the Patrol had been destroyed, either by the Patrol's own beams or by the pirates themselves after they saw they must lose.

744

"Beam it out," Craig ordered, and the remains of the Boskonian warship disappeared.

*

Back toward Lyrane II, then, the *Dauntless* went, and Kinnison again made contact with Helen, the Elder Sister. She had emerged from her crypt and was directing affairs from her—"office" is perhaps the word—upon the top floor of the city's largest building. The search for the Lyranian leaders, the torture and murder of the citizens, and the destruction of the city had stopped, all at once, when the grounded Boskonian cruiser had been blasted out of commission. The directing intelligences of the raiders had remained, it developed, within the "safe" confines of their vessel's walls; and when they ceased directing, their minions in the actual theater of operations ceased operating. They had been grouped uncertainly in an open square, but at the first glimpse of the returning *Dauntless* they had dashed into the nearest large building, each man seizing one or sometimes two persons as he went. They were now inside, erecting defenses and very evidently intending to use the Lyranians both as hostages and as shields.

Motionless now, directly over the city, Kinnison and his officers studied through their spy-rays the number, armament, and disposition of the enemy force. There were one hundred and thirty of them, human to about six places. They were armed with the usual portable weapons carried by such parties.

Originally they had had several semiportable projectors, but since all heavy stuff must be powered from the mother ship, it had been abandoned long since. Surprisingly, though, they wore full armor. Kinnison had expected only thought-screens, since the Lyranians had no offensive weapons save those of the mind; but apparently either the pirates did not know that or else were guarding against surprise.

Armor was—and is—heavy, cumbersome, a handicap to fast action, and a nuisance generally; hence for the Boskonians to have dispensed with it would not have been poor tactics. True, the Patrol *did* attack, but that could not have been what was expected. In fact, had such an attack been in the cards, that Boskonian punitive party would not have been on the ground at all. It was equally true that canny old Helmuth, who took nothing whatever for granted, would have had his men in armor. However, he would have guarded much more completely against surprise—but few commanders indeed went to such lengths of precaution as Helmuth did. Thus Kinnison pondered.

"This ought to be as easy as shooting fish down a well—but you'd better put out space scouts just the same," he decided, as he punched a call for Lieutenant Peter Van Buskirk. "Bus? Do you see what we see?"

"Uh-huh, we've been peeking a bit," the huge Dutch-Valerian responded, happily.

"QX. Get your gang wrapped up in their tinware. I'll see you at the main lower stabbard lock in ten minutes." He switched off and turned to an orderly. "Break out my G-P cage for me, will you, Spike? And I'll want the 'copters—tell them to get hot."

"But listen, Kim!" and:

"You can't do that, Kinnison!" came simultaneously from chief pilot and captain, neither of whom could leave the ship in such circumstances as these. They, the vessel's two top officers, were bound to her; while the Lensman, although ranking both of them, even aboard ship, was not and could not be bound by anything.

"Sure, I can—you fellows are just jealous, that's all," Kinnison retorted, cheerfully. "I not only can, I've *got* to go with the Valerians. I need a lot of information, and I can't read a dead man's brain—yet."

*

While the storming party was assembling, the *Dauntless* settled downward, coming to rest in the already devastated section of the town, as close as possible to the building in which the Boskonians had taken refuge.

One hundred and two men disembarked: Kinnison, Van Buskirk, and the full company of one hundred Valerians. Each of those space-fighting wild cats measured seventy-eight inches or more from sole to crown; each was composed of four hundred or more pounds of the fantastically powerful, rigid, and reactive brawn, bone, and sinew necessary for survival upon a planet having a surface gravity almost three times that of small, feeble Terra.

Because of the women held captive by the pirates, the Valerians carried no machine rifles, no semiportables, no heavy stuff at all; only their DeLameters and, of course, their space axes. A Valerian trooper without his space ax? Unthinkable! A dire weapon indeed, the space ax. A combination and sublimation of battle-ax, mace, bludgeon, and lumberman's picaroon; thirty pounds of hard, tough, space-tempered alloy; a weapon of potentialities limited only by the physical strength and bodily agility of its wielder. And Van Buskirk's Valerians had both—plenty of both. One-handed, with simple flicks of his incredible wrist, the smallest Valerian of the *Dauntless* boarding party could manipulate his atrocious weapon as effortlessly as, and almost unbelievably faster than, a fencing master handles his rapier or an orchestra conductor waves his baton.

With machinelike precision the Valerians fell in and strode away; Van Buskirk in the lead, the helicopters hovering overhead, the Gray Lensman bringing up the rear. Tall and heavy, strong and agile as he was—for a Tellurian—he had no business in that front line, and no one knew that fact better than he did. The puniest Valerian of the company could do in full armor a standing high jump of over fourteen feet; and could dodge, feint, parry, and swing with a blinding speed starkly impossible to any member of any of the physically lesser breeds of man.

Approaching the building they spread out, surrounded it; and at a signal from a helicopter that the ring was complete, the assault began. Doors and windows were locked, barred, and barricaded, of course; but what of that? A few taps of the axes and a few blasts of the DeLameters took care of things very nicely; and through the openings thus made there leaped, dove, rolled, or strode the space black-and-silver warriors of the Galactic Patrol. Valerians, than whom no fiercer race of hand-to-hand fighters has ever been known—no bifurcate race, and but very few others, however built or shaped, have ever willingly come to grips with the armored axmen of Valeria!

Not by choice, then, but of necessity and in sheer desperation the pirates fought. In the vicious beams of their portables the stone walls of the room glared a baleful red; in spots even were pierced through. Old-fashioned pistols barked, spitting steel-jacketed lead. But the G-P suits were screened against lethal beams by generators capable of withstanding anything of lesser power than a semiportable projector; G-P armor was proof against any projectile possessing less energy than that hurled by the high caliber machine rifle. Thus the Boskonian beams splashed off the Valerian's screens in torrents of man-made lightning and in pyrotechnic displays of multicolored splendor, their bullets ricocheted harmlessly as spent, misshapen blobs of metal.

*

The Patrolmen did not even draw their DeLameters during their inexorable advance. They knew that the pirates' armor was as capable as theirs, and the women were not to die if death for them could possibly be avoided. As they advanced the enemy fell back toward the center of the great room; holding there with the Lyranians forming the outer ring of their roughly circular formation; firing over the women's heads and between their naked bodies.

Kinnison did not want those women to die. It seemed, however, that die they must, from the sheer, tremendous reflection from the Valerians' fiercely radiant screens, if the Patrolmen persisted in their advance. He studied the enemy formation briefly, then flashed an order.

There ensued a startling and entirely unorthodox maneuver, one possible only to the troopers there at work, as at Kinnison's command every Valerian left the floor in a prodigious leap. Over the women's heads, over the heads of the enemy; but in midleap, as he passed over, each Patrolman swung his ax at a Boskonian helmet with all the speed and all the power he could muster. Most of the enemy died then and there, for the helmet has never been forged which is able to fend the diamond beak of a space ax driven as each of those was driven. The fact that the Valerians were nine or ten feet off the floor at the time made no difference whatever. They were space fighters, trained to handle themselves and their weapons in any position or situation; with or without gravity, with or without even inertia.

"You persons—run! Get out of here! SCRAM!" Kinnison fairly shouted the thought as the Valerians left the floor, and the matriarchs obeyed—frantically. Through doors and windows they fled, in all directions and at the highest possible speed.

But in their enthusiasm to strike down the foe, not one of the Valerians had paid any attention to the exact spot upon which he was to land; or, if he did, someone else got there either first or just barely second. Besides, there was not room for them all in the center of the ring. For seconds, therefore, confusion reigned and a boiler-works clangor resounded for a mile around as a hundred and one extra-big and extra-heavy men, a writhing, kicking, pulling tangle of armor, axes, and equipment, jammed into a space which half their number would have filled overfull. Sulphurous Valerian profanity and sizzling deep-space oaths blistered the very air as each warrior struggled madly to right himself, to get one more crack at a pirate before somebody else beat him to it.

During this terrible melee some of the pirates released their screens and committed suicide. A few got out of the room, but not many. Nor far; the men in the helicopters saw to that. They had needle beams, powered from the *Dauntless*, which went through the screens of personal armor as a knife goes through ripe cheese.

"Save it, guys—hold everything!" Kinnison yelled as the tangled mass of Valerians resolved itself into erect and warlike units. "No more ax work—don't let them kill themselves—catch them ALIVE!"

They did so, quickly and easily. With the women out of the way, there was nothing to prevent the Valerians from darting right up to the muzzles of the foes' DeLameters. Nor could the enemy dodge, or run, half fast enough to get away. Armored, shielded hands batted the weapons away—if an arm or leg broke in the process, what the hell?—and the victim was held motionless until his turn came to face the mind-reading Kinnison.

Nothing. Nothing, flat. A string of zeros. And, bitterly silent, Kinnison led the way back to the *Dauntless*. The men he wanted, the ones who knew anything, were the ones who killed themselves, of course. Well, why not? In like case, officers of the Patrol had undoubtedly done the same. The live ones didn't know where their planet was, could give no picture even of where it lay in the Galaxy, did not know where they were going, nor why. Well, so what? Wasn't ignorance the prime characteristic of the bottom layers of dictatorships everywhere? If they had known anything, they would have been under orders to kill themselves, too, and would have done it.

In his con room in the *Dauntless* his black mood lightened somewhat and he called the Elder Person.

"Helen of Troy? I suppose that the best thing we can do now, for your peace of mind, prosperity, well-being, et cetera, is to drill out of here as fast as Klono and Noshabkeming will let us. Right?"

"Why, I . . . you . . . um . . . that is." The matriarch was badly flustered at the Lensman's bald summation of her attitude. She did not want to agree, but she certainly did not want these males around a second longer than was necessary.

"Just as well say it, because it goes double for me—you can play it clear across the board, toots, that if I ever see you again it will be because I can't get out of it." Then, to his chief pilot:

"QX, Hen, give her the oof—back to Tellus."

VII.

Through the ether the mighty *Dauntless* bored her serene way homeward, at the easy touring blast—for her—of some eighty parsecs an hour. The engineers inspected and checked their equipment, from instrument needles to blast nozzles; re-lining, repairing, replacing anything and everything which showed any sign of wear or strain because of what the big vessel had just gone through. Then they relaxed into their customary routine of killing time—the games of a dozen planets and the vying with each other in the telling of outrageously untruthful stories.

The officers on watch lolled at ease in their cushioned seats, making much ado of each tiny thing as it happened, even the changes of watch. The Valerians, as usual, remained invisible in their own special quarters. There the gravity was set at twenty-seven hundred instead of at the Tellurian normal of nine hundred eighty, there the atmospheric pressure was forty pounds to the square inch, there the temperature was ninety-six degrees Fahrenheit, and there Van Buskirk and his fighters lived and moved and had their daily drills of fantastic violence and stress. They were irked less than any of the others by monotony; being, as has been intimated previously, neither mental nor intellectual giants.

And Kinnison, mirror-polished gray boots stacked in all their majestic size upon a corner of his desk, leaned his chair precariously backward and thought in black concentration. It *still* didn't make any kind of sense. He had just enough clues—fragments of clues—to drive a man nuts. Menjo Bleeko was the man he wanted. On Lonabar. To find one was to find the other, but how in the steaming hells of Venus was he going to find either of them? It might seem funny not to be able to find a thing as big as a planet—but since nobody knew where it was, by fifty thousand parsecs, and since there were millions and skillions and whillions of planets in the Galaxy, a random search was quite definitely out. Bleeko was a zwilnik, or tied in with zwilniks, of course; but he could read a million zwilnik minds without finding, except by merest chance, one having any contact with or knowledge of the Lonabarian.

The Patrol had already scoured—fruitlessly—Aldebaran II for any sign, however slight, pointing toward Lonabar. The planetographers had searched the files, the charts, the libraries thoroughly. No Lonabar. Of course, they had suggested—what a help!—they might know it under some other name. Personally, he didn't think so, since no jeweler throughout the far-flung bounds of civilization had as yet been found who could recognize or identify any of the items he had described.

Whatever avenue or alley of thought Kinnison started along, he always ended up at the jewels and the girl. Illona, the squirrel-brained, romping, joyous little imp who by now owned in fee simple half of the ship and nine-tenths of the crew. Why in Palain's purple hells couldn't she have had a brain back of that beautiful pan? But at that, he had to admit, she was smarter than most—you couldn't expect any other woman in the Galaxy to have a mind like Mac's.

For minutes, then, he abandoned his problem and reveled in visions of the mental and physical perfections of his fiancée. But this was getting him nowhere, fast. The girl or the jewels—which? They were the only real angles he had.

He sent out a call for her, and in a few minutes she came swirling in. How different she was from what she had been! Gone were the somberness, the dread, the terror which had oppressed her; gone were the class-conscious inhibitions against which she had been rebelling, however subconsciously, since childhood. Here she was *free*! The boys were free, *everybody* was free! She had expanded tremendously—unfolded. She was living as she had never dreamed it possible to live. Each new minute was an adventure in itself. Her black eyes, once so dull, sparkled with animation; radiated her sheer joy in living. Even her jet-black hair seemed to have taken on a new luster and gloss, in its every precisely arranged wavelet.

*

"Hi, Lensman!" Illona burst out, before Kinnison could say a word or think a thought in greeting. "I'm *so* glad you sent for me, because there's something I've been wanting to ask you for days. The boys are going to throw a blowout, with all kinds of stunts, and they want me to do a dance. QX, do you think?"

"Sure. Why not?"

"Clothes," she explained. "I told them I couldn't dance in a dress, and they said that I wasn't supposed to, that acrobats didn't wear dresses when they performed on Tellus. I said they lied like thieves and they swore they didn't—said to ask the Old Man—" She broke off, two knuckles jammed into her mouth, expressive eyes wide in sudden fright. "Oh, excuse me, sir," she gasped. "I didn't—"

"'Smatter? What bit you?" Kinnison asked, then got it. "Oh . . . the 'Old Man,' huh? QX, angel face, that is standard nomenclature in the Patrol. Not with you folks, though, I take it?"

"I'll say not," she breathed. She acted as though a catastrophe had been averted by the narrowest possible margin. "Why, if anybody got caught even *thinking* such a thing, the whole crew would go into the steamer that very minute. And if I would dare to say 'Hi' to Menjo Bleeko—" She shuddered.

"Nice people," Kinnison commented.

"But are you sure that the . . . that I'm not getting any of the boys into trouble?" she pleaded. "For, after all, none of them ever dare call you that to your face, you know."

"You haven't been around enough yet," he assured her. "On duty, no; that's discipline—necessary for efficiency. And I haven't hung around the wardrooms much of late—been too busy. But at the party you'll be surprised at some of the things they call me—if you happen to hear them. You've been practicing—keeping in shape?"

"Uh-huh," she confessed. "In my room, with the spy-ray block on."

"Good. No need to hide, though, and no need to wear dresses any time you're practicing the boys were right on that. What do you think of this pseudoinertia as compared to the real thing?" He did not, actually, care what she thought of it; he was merely making conversation to cover up the fact that he was probing the deepest recesses of her mind.

"I like it, even better in some ways. Your legs and arms feel as though they were following through perfectly, but if you kick something, or come down too hard in a forward flip—back flips are easy—it doesn't hurt. It's nice."

"Must be," he agreed, absently. "Got to watch out for yourself, though, when you get back onto a planet. Now I want you to help me. Will you?"

"Yes, sir. In anything I can—*anything*, sir," she answered, instantly.

"I want you to give me every scrap of information you possibly can about Lonabar; its customs and habits, its work and its play—everything, even its money and its jewelry." This last apparently an afterthought. "To do so, you'll have to let me into your mind of your own free will—you'll have to co-operate to the limit of your capability. QX?"

"That will be quite all right, Lensman," she agreed, shyly. "I know now that you are not going to hurt me."

Illona did not like it at first, there was no question of that. And small wonder. It is an intensely disturbing thing to have your mind invaded, knowingly, by another; particularly when that other is the appallingly powerful mind of Gray Lensman Kimball Kinnison. There were lots of things she did not want exposed, and the very effort not to think of them brought them ever and ever more vividly to the fore. She squirmed, mentally and physically: her mind was for minutes a practically illegible turmoil. But she soon steadied down and, as she got used to the new sensations, she went to work with a will. She could not increase materially the knowledge of the planet which Kinnison had already obtained from her, but she was a mine of information concerning the peculiar gems. She knew all about every one of them, with the completely detailed knowledge one is all too apt to have of a thing long and intensely desired, but supposedly forever out of reach.

"Thanks, Illona." It was over; the Lensman knew as much as she did about everything which had any bearing upon his quest. "You have helped a lot—now you can flit."

"I'm glad to help, sir, really—any time. I'll see you at the party, then, if not before." Illona left the room in a far more subdued fashion than she had entered it. She had always been more than half afraid of Kinnison; just being near him did things to her which she did not quite like. And this last thing, this mind-searching interview, did not operate to quiet her fears. It gave her the screaming meamies, no less!

*

And Kinnison, alone in his room, called for a tight beam to Prime Base. He wanted something, he explained, when the visage of Port Admiral Haynes appeared upon his plate. Something big, something that had never been tried before. Namely, a wide-open, Lens-to-Lens conference with all the Lensmen—particularly all the Unattached Lensmen—of the whole Galaxy, at the same time. Could it be arranged?

"*Whew!*" the admiral whistled. "I was in on a wide-open ten-way, once, but that's as high as I ever tried it. What's your thought as to technique?"

"Set a definite time, far enough ahead to give everybody notice. At that time, have everybody tune to your frequency. Since everybody will be en *rapport* with you, we will all be en *rapport* with each other, automatically."

"Seems reasonable—can do, I think. It will take at least a day to arrange the hookup. Day and a half, maybe. Say hour twenty tomorrow."

"QX. Hour twenty, on the line."

The next day dragged, even for the always-busy Kinnison. He prowled about, aimlessly. He saw the beautiful Aldebaranian several times, noticing as he did so something which he had not hitherto really observed, but which tied in nicely with a fact he had half seen in the girl's own mind, before he could dodge it—that whenever she made a twosome with any man, the man was Chief Pilot Henderson.

"Blasted, Hen?" he asked, casually, as he came upon the pilot in a corner of a wardroom, staring fixedly at nothing.

"Out of the ether," Henderson admitted. "I want to talk to you."

"G. A., we're alone—or, better yet, on the Lens. About Illona, the Aldebaranian zwilnik, I suppose."

"Don't Kim," Henderson flinched. "She isn't a zwilnik, really—I'd bet my last millo on that?"

"Are you telling me, or asking me?" the Lensman asked.

"I don't know," Henderson hesitated. "I wanted to ask you . . . you know, you've got a lot of stuff that the rest of us haven't. I'm punctured plenty, and it's getting worse. Is there any reason, chief, why I shouldn't, well . . . er . . . get married?"

"Every reason in the book why you should, Hen. Why, when I get to be as old as you are, I hope to be retired, married, and the father of two or three kids."

"Damnation, Kim! That isn't what I meant, and you know it!"

"Think clearly, then; for your own sake and Illona's; not mine," Kinnison ordered. "Yes, I know what you mean, but you've got to bring it out into the open, yourself, to do any good."

"QX. Have I the permission of Kimball Kinnison, Unattached Lensman of the Galactic Patrol, to marry Illona Potter, if I've got jets enough to swing it?"

Mighty clever, the Lensman thought. Since all the men of the Patrol were notoriously averse to going sloppy or maudlin about it, he wondered just how the pilot was going to phrase his question. Hen had done it very neatly, by tossing the buck right back at him. But he wouldn't get sloppy, either. The "untarnished-meteors-upon-the-collars-of-the-Patrol" stuff was QX for Earthly spellbinders, but it didn't fit in anywhere else. So:

"That's better," Kinnison approved. "As far as I know—and in this case I bashfully admit that I know it all—everything is on the green. All you've got to worry about is the opposition of twelve hundred or so other guys in this can, and the fact that Illona will probably blast you to a cinder."

"Huh? Those apes? That? Watch my jets!" Henderson strode away, doubts all resolved; and Kinnison, seeing that hour twenty was very near, went to his own room.

*

Precisely upon the hour the Lensman tuned his—not his Lens, really, since he no longer needed that, but in all probability his very ego to that of Port Admiral Haynes. He had wondered frequently what it was going to feel like; but, having experienced it, he could never afterward describe it even in part.

It is difficult for any ordinary mind to conceive of its being in complete accord with any other, however closely akin. Consider, then, how utterly impossible it is to envision that merging of a hundred thousand, or five hundred thousand, or a million—nobody ever did know how many Lensmen tuned in that day—minds so utterly different that no one human being can live long enough even to see each of the races there represented! Probably less than half of them were even approximately human. Many were not mammals, many were not warm-blooded. Not all, by far, were even oxygen breathers—oxygen, to many of those races, was sheerest poison. Nevertheless, they had much in common. All were intelligent; most of them very highly so; and all were imbued with the principles of freedom and equality for which Galactic Civilization stood and upon which it was fundamentally based.

That meeting was staggering, even to Kinnison's mind. It was appalling—yet it was ultimately thrilling, too. It was one of the greatest, one of the most terrific thrills of the Lensman's long life.

"Thanks, fellows, for coming in," he began, simply. "I will make my message very short. As Haynes may have told you, I am Kinnison of Tellus. It will help greatly in locating the head of the Boskonian culture if I can find a certain planet, known to me only by the name of Lonabar. Its people are human beings to the last decimal; its rarest jewels are these," and he spread in the collective mind a perfect, exactly detailed and pictured

752

description of the gems. "Does any one of you know of such a planet? Has any one of you ever seen a stone like any of these?"

A pause—a heartbreakingly long pause. Then a faint, soft, diffident thought appeared; appeared as though seeping slowly from a single cell of that incredibly linked, million-fold-composite Lensmen's BRAIN.

"I waited to be sure that no one else would speak, as my information is very meager, and unsatisfactory, and old," the thought apologized.

"Whatever its nature, any information at all is very welcome," Kinnison replied. "Who is speaking, please?"

"Nadreck of Palain VII, Unattached. Many cycles ago I secured, and still have in my possession, a crystal—or rather, fragment of a supercooled liquid—like one of the red gems you showed us; the one having practically all its transmittance in a very narrow band centering at point seven, oh, oh."

"But you do not know what planet it came from—is that it?"

"Not exactly," the soft thought went on. "I saw it upon its native planet, but unfortunately I do not now know just what or where that planet was. We were exploring at the time, and had visited many planets. Not being interested in any world having an atmosphere of oxygen, we paused but briefly, nor did we map it. I was interested in the fusion because of its peculiar filtering effect, hence bought it from its owner. A scientific curiosity merely."

"Do you believe that you could find the planet again?"

"By checking back upon the planets we did map, and by retracing our route, I should be able to . . . yes, I am certain that I can do so."

"And when Nadreck of Palain VII says that he is certain of anything," another thought appeared, "nothing in the macrocosmic universe is more certain."

"I thank you, Twenty-four of Six, for the expression of confidence."

"And I thank both of you particularly, as well as all of you collectively," Kinnison broadcast. Then, as intelligences by the tens of thousands began to break away from the linkage, he continued to Nadreck:

"You will map this planet for me, then, and send the data in to Prime Base?"

"I will map the planet and will myself bring the data to you at Prime Base. Do you want some of the gems, also?"

"I don't think so," Kinnison thought swiftly. "No, better not. They'll be harder to get now, and it might tip our hand too much. I'll get them myself, later. Will you inform me, through Haynes, when to expect you upon Tellus?"

"I will so inform you. I will proceed at once, with speed."

"Thanks a million, Nadreck—clear ether!" and everyone cut loose.

*

The ship sped on, and as it sped, Kinnison continued to think. He attended the "blowout." Ordinarily he would have been right in the thick of it; but this time, young though he was and enthusiastic, he simply could not tune in. Nothing fitted, and until he could see a picture that made some kind of sense he could not let go. He listened to the music with half an ear, he watched the stunts with only half an eye.

He forgot his problem for a while when, at the end, Illona Potter danced. For Lonabarian acrobatic dancing is not like the Tellurian art of the same name. Or rather, it is like it, except more so—much more so. An earthly expert would be scarcely a novice on Lonabar, and Illona was a Lonabarian expert. She had been training, intensively, all her life, and even in Lonabar's chill social and psychological environment she had loved her work. Now, reveling as she was in the first realization of liberty of thought and of person, and inspired by the heartfelt applause of the spacehounds so closely packed into the hall, she put on something more than an exhibition of coldly impersonal skill and limberness. And the feelings, both of performer and of spectators, were intensified by the fact that, of all the repertoire of the *Dauntless'* superb orchestra, Illona liked best to dance to the stirring strains of "Our Patrol." "Our Patrol," which any man who has ever worn the space black-and-silver will say is the greatest, grandest, most glorious, most terrific piece of music that ever was or ever will be written, played, or sung! Small wonder, then, that the dancer really "gave," or that the mighty cruiser's walls almost bulged under the applause of Illona's "boys" at the end of her first number.

They kept her at it until Captain Craig stopped it, to keep the girl from killing herself. "She's worn down to a nub," he declared, and she was. She was trembling. She was panting; her almost lacquered-down hair stood out in wild disorder. Her eyes were starry with tears—happy tears. Then the ranking officers made short speeches of appreciation and the spectators carried the actors—actual carrying, in Illona's case, upon an improvised throne—off for refreshments.

Back in his quarters, Kinnison tackled his problem again. He could work out something on Lonabar now, but what about Lyrane? It tied in, too—there was an angle there, somewhere. To get it, though, somebody would have to get close to—really friendly with—the Lyranians. Just looking on from the outside wouldn't do. Somebody they could trust and would confide in—and they were so damnably, so fanatically non-co-operative! A man couldn't get a millo's worth of real information—he could read any one mind by force, but he'd never get the right one. Neither could Worsel or Tregonsee or any other nonhuman Lensman; the Lyranians just simply didn't have the galactic viewpoint. No, what he wanted was a human woman Lensman, and there weren't any—

At the thought he gasped; the pit of his stomach felt cold. Chris! She was more than half Lensman already—she was the only un-Lensed human being who had ever been able to read his thoughts. But he didn't have the gall, the sheer, brazen crust, to shove a load like that onto *her*—or did he? Didn't the job come first? Wouldn't Chris be big enough to see it that way? Sure, she would! As to what Haynes and the rest of the Lensmen would think—let them think! In this, he had to make his own decisions.

He couldn't. He sat there for an hour; teeth locked until his jaws ached, fists clenched. "I can't make that decision alone," he breathed, finally. "Not jets enough by half," and he shot a thought to distant Arisia and Mentor the Sage.

"This intrusion is necessary," he thought coldly, precisely. "It seems to me to be wise to do this thing which has never before been done. I have no data, however, upon which to base a decision and the matter is grave. I ask, therefore—is it wise?"

"You do not ask as to repercussions—consequences—either to yourself or to the woman?"

"I ask what I asked."

"Ah, Kinnison of Tellus, you truly grow. You at last learn to think. It is wise," and the telepathic link snapped.

Kinnison slumped down in relief. He had not known what to expect. He would not have been surprised if the Arisian had pinned his ears back; he certainly did not expect either the compliment or the clear-cut answer. He knew that Mentor would give him no help whatever in any problem which he could possibly solve alone; he was just beginning to realize that the Arisian *would* aid him in matters which were absolutely, intrinsically, beyond his reach.

Recovering, he flashed a call to Surgeon General Lacy.

"Lacy? Kinnison. I would like to have Sector Chief Nurse Clarrissa MacDougall detached at once. Please have her report to me here aboard the *Dauntless*, en route, at the earliest possible moment of rendezvous."

"Huh? What? You can't . . . you wouldn't—" the old Lensman gurgled.

"No, I wouldn't. The whole corps will know it soon enough, so I might as well tell you now that I'm going to make a Lensman out of her."

Lacy exploded then, but Kinnison had expected that.

"Seal it!" he counseled, sharply. "I am not doing it entirely on my own—Mentor of Arisia made the final decision. Prefer charges against me if you like, but in the meantime please do as I request."

And that was that.

VIII.

A few hours before the time of rendezvous with the cruiser which was bringing Chris out to him, the detectors picked up a vessel whose course, it proved, was set to intersect their own. A minute or so later a sharp, clear thought came through Kinnison's Lens.

"Kim? Raoul. Been flitting around out Arisia way, and they called me in and asked me to bring you a package. Said you'd be expecting it. QX?"

"Hi, Spacehound! QX." Kinnison had very decidedly not been expecting it—he had thought that he would have to do the best he could without it—but he realized instantly, with a thrill of gladness, what it was. "Inert? Or can't you stay?"

"Free. Got to make a rendezvous. Can't take time to inert—that is, if you'll inert the thing in your cocoon. Don't want it to hole out on you, though."

"Can do. Free it is. Pilot room! Prepare for inertialess contact with vessel approaching. Magnets. Messenger coming aboard—free."

The two speeding vessels flashed together, at all their unimaginable velocities, without a thump or jar. Magnetic clamps locked and held. Air-lock doors opened, shut, opened; and at the inner port Kinnison met Raoul la Forge, his classmate through the four years at Wentworth Hall. Brief but hearty greetings were exchanged, but the visitor could not stop. Lensmen are busy men.

"Fine seeing you, Kim—be sure and inert the thing—clear ether!"

"Same to you, ace. Sure, I will—think I want to tear a guy's arm off?"

Indeed, inerting the package was the Lensman's first care, for in the free condition it was a frightfully dangerous thing. Its intrinsic velocity was that of Arisia, while the ship's was that of Lyrane II. They might be forty or fifty miles per second apart; and if the *Dauntless* should go inert that harmless-looking package would instantly become a meteorite inside the ship. At the thought of that velocity he paused. The cocoon would stand it—but would the Lens? Oh, sure, the Arisian knew that this was coming; the Lens would be packed to stand it.

Kinnison wrapped the package in heavy gauze, then in roll after roll of spring steel mesh. He jammed heavy steel springs into the ends, then clamped the whole thing into a form with tool-steel bolts an inch in diameter. He poured in two hundred pounds of metallic mercury, filling the form to the top. Then a cover, also bolted on. This whole assembly went into the "cocoon," a cushioned, heavily padded affair suspended from all four walls, ceiling, and floor by every shock-absorbing device known to the engineers of the Patrol.

The *Dauntless* inerted briefly at Kinnison's word and it seemed as though a troop of elephants were running silently amuck in the cocoon room. The package to be inerted weighed no more than eight ounces—but eight ounces of mass, at a relative velocity of fifty miles per second, possesses a kinetic energy by no means to be despised.

The frantic lurchings and bouncings subsided, the cruiser resumed her free flight, and the man undid all that he had done. The Arisian package looked exactly as before, but it was harmless now; it had the same intrinsic velocity as did everything else aboard the vessel.

Then the Lensman pulled on a pair of thick rubber gloves and opened the package; finding, as he had expected, that the packing material was a dense, viscous liquid. He poured it out and there was the Lens—Chris' Lens! He cleaned it carefully, then wrapped it in heavy insulation. For of all the billions of unnumbered billions of living entities in existence, Clarrissa MacDougall was the only one whose flesh could touch that apparently innocuous jewel with impunity. Others could safely touch it while she wore it, while it glowed with its marvelously polychromatic cold flame; but until she wore it, and unless she wore it, its touch meant death to any life to which it was not attuned.

*

Shortly thereafter another Patrol cruiser hove in sight. This meeting, however, was to be no casual one, for the nurse could not be inerted from the free state in the *Dauntless'* cocoon. No such device ever built could stand it—and those structures are stronger far than is the human frame. Any adjustment which even the hardest, toughest spacehound can take in a cocoon is measured in feet per second, not in miles.

Hundreds of miles apart, the ships inerted and their pilots fought with supreme skill to make the two intrinsics match. And even so the vessels did not touch, even nearly. A space line was thrown; the nurse and her space roll were quite unceremoniously hauled aboard.

Kinnison did not meet her at the air lock, but waited for her in his con room; and the details of that meeting will remain unchronicled. They were young, they had not seen each other for a long time, and they were very much in love. It is evident, therefore, that Patrol affairs were not the first matters to be touched upon. Nor, if the historian has succeeded even partially in portraying truly the characters of the two persons involved, is it either necessary or desirable to go at any length into the argument they had as to whether or not she should be inducted so cavalierly into a service from which her sex had always, automatically, been barred. He did not want to make her carry that load, but he had to; she did not—although for entirely different reasons—want to take it.

He shook out the Lens and, holding it in a thick-folded corner of the insulating blanket, flicked one of the girl's fingertips across the bracelet. Satisfied by the fleeting flash of color which swept across the jewel, he snapped the platinum-iridium band around her left wrist, which it fitted exactly.

Chris stared for a minute at the smoothly, rhythmically flowing colors of the thing so magically sprung to life upon her wrist; awe and humility in her glorious eyes. Then:

"I can't, Kim. I simply can't. I'm not worthy of it," she choked.

"None of us is, Chris. We can't be—but we've got to do it, just the same."

"I suppose that's true—it would be so, of course. I'll do my best—but you know perfectly well, Kim, that I'm not—can't ever be—a real Lensman."

"Sure, you can. Do we have to go over all that again? You won't have some of the technical stuff that we got, of course, but you carry jets that no other Lensman ever has had. You're a real Lensman; don't worry about that—if you weren't, do you think that they would have made that Lens for you?"

"In a way I see that that must be true, even though I can't understand it. But I'm simply scared to death of the rest of it, Kim."

"You needn't be. It'll hurt, but not more than you can stand. Don't think we'd better start that stuff for a few days yet, though; not until you get used to using your Lens. Coming at you, Lensman!" and he went into Lens-to-Lens communication, broadening it gradually into a wide-open two-way.

She was appalled at first, but entranced some thirty minutes later, when he called the lesson to a halt.

"Enough for now," he decided. "It doesn't take much of that stuff to be a great plenty, at first."

"I'll say it doesn't," she agreed. "Put this away for me until next time, will you, Kim? I don't want to wear it all the time until I know more about it."

"Fair enough. In the meantime I want you to get acquainted with a new girl friend of mine," and he sent out a call for Illona Potter.

"Girl friend!"

"Uh-huh. Study her. Educational no end, and she may be important. Want to compare notes with you on her later, is why I'm not giving you any advance dope on her—here she comes."

"Mac, this is Illona," he introduced them informally. "I told them to give you the cabin next to hers," he added, to the nurse. "I'll go with you to be sure that everything's on the green."

It was, and the Lensman left the two together.

THE LENSMAN

"I'm awfully glad you're here," Illona said, shyly. "I've heard *so* much about you, Miss—"

"Mac to you, my dear—all of my friends call me that," the nurse broke in. "And you don't want to believe everything you hear, especially aboard this space can." Her lips smiled, but her eyes were faintly troubled.

"Oh, it was nice," Illona assured her. "About what a grand person you are, and what a wonderful couple you and Lensman Kinnison make . . . why, you really *are* in love with him, aren't you?" This in surprise, as she studied the nurse's face.

"Yes," unequivocally. "And you love him, too, and that makes it—"

"Good heavens, no!" the Aldebaranian exclaimed, so positively that Clarissa jumped.

"What? You don't? *Really?*" Gold-flecked, tawny eyes stared intensely into engagingly candid eyes of black. Mac wished then that she had left her Lens on, so that she could tell whether this bejeweled brunet hussy was telling the truth or not.

"Certainly not. That's what I meant—I'm simply scared to death of him. He's so—well—so over-powering. He's so much more—tremendous—than I am. I didn't see how any girl could possibly love him—but I understand now how you could, perhaps. You're sort of—terrific—yourself, you know. I feel as though I ought to call you 'Your Magnificence' instead of just plain Mac."

"Why, I'm no such thing!" Clarissa exclaimed; but she softened noticeably, none the less. "And I think that I'm going to like you a lot."

"Oh-h-h—honestly?" Illona squealed. "It sounds too good to be true, you're so marvelous. But if you do, I think that Civilization will be everything that I've been afraid—*so* afraid—that it couldn't possibly be!"

No longer was it a feminine Lensman investigating a female zwilnik; it was two girls—two young, intensely alive, human girls—who chattered on and on.

Days passed. Mac learned the use of her Lens as well as any first stage Lensman had ever known it. Then Kinnison, one of the few then existent second stage Lensmen, began really to bear down. Since the acquirement of the second stage of Lensmanship has been described in detail elsewhere, it need be said here only that Clarissa MacDougall had mental capacity enough to take it without becoming insane. He suffered as much as she did; after every mental bout he was as spent as she was; but both of them stuck relentlessly to it.

As is now well known, the prime requisite of all such advanced treatment is to know with the utmost precision exactly what knowledge or ability is required. Mac had no idea as to what she wanted or needed; but Kinnison did.

He could not give her everything that the Arisian had given him, of course. Much of it was too hazy yet; more of it did not apply. He gave her everything, however, which she could handle and which would be of any use to her in the work she was to do; including the sense of perception. He did it, that is, with a modicum of help; for, once or twice, when he faltered or weakened, not knowing exactly what to do or not being quite able to do it, a stronger mind than his was always there.

At length, approaching Tellus fast, Mac and Kim had a final conference; the consultation of two Lensmen settling the last details of procedure in a long-planned and highly important campaign.

"I agree with you that Lyrane II is a key planet," the nurse was saying, thoughtfully. "It must be, to have those expeditions from Lonabar and the as yet unknown planet 'X' centering there."

"'X' certainly, and don't forget the possibility of 'Y' and 'Z' and maybe others," he reminded her. "The Lyrane-Lonabar linkage is the only one we are sure of. With you on one end of that and me on the other, it'll be funny if we can't trace out some more. While I'm building up an authentic identity to tackle Bleeko, you'll be getting chummy with Helen of Lyrane. That's about as far ahead as we can plan definitely right now, since this ground-work can't be hurried too much."

"And I report to you often—frequently, in fact." Mac widened her expressive eyes at her man.

"At least," he agreed. "And I'll report to you between times."

"Oh, Kim, it's nice, being a Lensman!" She snuggled closer. Some way or other, the conference had become somewhat personal. "Being en rapport will be almost as good as being together—we can stand it, that way, at least."

"It'll help a lot, ace, no fooling. That was why I was afraid to go ahead with it on my own hook. I couldn't be sure that my feelings were not in control, instead of my judgment—if any."

"I'd have been certain that it was your soft heart instead of your hard head if it hadn't been for Mentor," she sighed, happily. "As it is, though, I know that everything is on the green."

"All done with Illona?"

"Yes, the darling. She's the *sweetest* thing, Kim—and a storehouse of information if there ever was one. You and I know more of Boskonian life than anyone of Civilization ever knew before, I am sure. And it's so ghastly! We *must* win, Kim—we simply *must*, for the good of all creation!"

"We will." Kinnison spoke with grim finality.

"But back to Illona. She can't go with me, and she can't stay here with Hank aboard the *Dauntless* taking me back to Lyrane, and you can't watch her. I'd hate to think of anything happening to her, Kim."

"It won't," he replied, comfortably. "Ilyowicz won't sleep nights until he has her as the top-flight solo dancer in his show—even though she doesn't have to work for a living any more."

"She will, though, I think. Don't you?"

"Probably. Anyway, a couple of Haynes' smart girls are going to be her best friends, wherever she goes. Sort of keep an eye on her until she learns the ropes—it won't take long. We owe her that much, I figure."

"That much, at least. You're seeing to the selling of her jewelry yourself, aren't you?"

"No, I had a new thought on that. I'm going to buy it myself—or rather, Cartiff is. They're making up a set of paste imitations. Cartiff has to buy a stock somewhere; why not hers?"

"That's a thought—there's certainly enough of them to stock a wholesaler. 'Cartiff'—I can see that sign," she snickered. "Almost microscopic letters, severely plain, in the lower right-hand corner of an immense plate-glass window. One gem in the middle of an acre of black velvet. Cartiff, the most peculiar, if not quite the most exclusive, jeweler in the Galaxy. And nobody except you and me knows anything about him. Isn't that something?"

"Everybody will know about Cartiff pretty soon," he told her. "Found any flaws in the scheme yet?"

"Nary a flaw." She shook her head. "That is, if none of the boys overdo it, and I'm sure they won't. I've got a picture of it," and she giggled merrily. "Think of a whole gang of sleuths from the homicide division chasing poor Cartiff, and never quite catching him!"

"Uh-huh—a touching picture indeed. But there goes the signal, and there's Tellus. We're about to land."

"Oh, I want to see!" and she started to get up.

"Look, then," pulling her down into her original place at his side. "You've got the sense of perception now, remember; you don't need visiplates."

And side by side, arms around each other, the two Lensmen watched the docking of their great vessel.

*

It landed. Jewelers came aboard with their carefully made wares. Assured that the metal would not discolor her skin, Illona made the exchange willingly enough. Beads were beads, to her. She could scarcely believe that she was now independently wealthy—in fact, she forgot all about her money after Ilyowicz had seen her dance.

"You see," she explained to Mac and Kinnison, "there were two things I wanted to do until Hank gets back—travel around a lot and learn all I can about your Civilization. I wanted to dance, too, but I didn't see how I could. Now I can do all three, and get paid for doing them besides—isn't that *marvelous*? And Mr. Ilyowicz said that you said that it was QX. Is it, really?"

"Right," and Illona was off.

The *Dauntless* was serviced and Mac was off, to far Lyrane.

Lensman Kinnison was supposedly off somewhere, also, when Cartiff appeared. Cartiff, the ultra-ultra; the, oh, so exclusive! Cartiff did not advertise. He catered, word spread fast, to only the very upper flakes of the upper crust. Simple dignity was Cartiff's keynote, his insidiously spread claim; the dignified simplicity of immense wealth and impeccable social position.

What he actually achieved, however, was something subtly different. His simplicity was just a hair off beam; his dignity was an affected, not a natural, quality. Nobody with less than a million credits ever got past his door, it is true. However, instead of being the real *crème de la crème* of Earth, Cartiff's clients were those who pretended to belong to, or who were trying to force an entrance into, that select stratum. Cartiff was a snob of

760

snobs; he built up a clientele of snobs; and, even more than in his admittedly fine and flawless gems, he dealt in equally high-proof snobbery.

Betimes came Nadreck, the Unattached Lensman of Palain VII, and Kinnison met him secretly at Prime Base. Soft-voiced as ever, apologetic, diffident; even though Kim had learned that the Palainian had a record of accomplishment as long as any one of his arms. But it was not an act, not affectation. It was simply a racial trait, for the intelligent and civilized race of that planet is in no sense human. Nadreck was utterly, startlingly unhuman. In his atmosphere there was no oxygen, in his body there flowed no aqueous blood. At his normal body temperature neither liquid water nor gaseous oxygen could exist.

The seventh planet out from any sun would, of course, be cold, but Kinnison had not thought particularly about the point until he felt the bitter radiation from the heavily insulated suit of his guest; perceived how fiercely its refrigerators were laboring to keep its internal temperature down.

"If you will permit it, please, I will depart at once," Nadreck pleaded, as soon as he had delivered his spool and his message. "My heat dissipators, powerful though they are, cannot cope much longer with this frightfully high temperature."

"QX, Nadreck—thanks a million," and the weird little monstrosity scuttled out. "Remember, Lensman's Seal on all this stuff until Prime Base releases it."

"Of course, Kinnison. You will understand, however, I am sure, that none of our races of Civilization are even remotely interested in Lonabar—it is as hot, as poisonous, as hellish generally as is Tellus itself!"

*

Kinnison went back to Cartiff's; and very soon thereafter it became noised abroad that Cartiff was a crook. He was a cheat, a liar, a robber. His stones were synthetic; he made them himself. The stories grew. He was a smuggler; he didn't have an honest gem in his shop. He was a zwilnik, an out-and-out pirate; a red-handed murderer who, if he wasn't there already, certainly ought to be in the big black book of the Galactic Patrol. This wasn't just gossip, either; everybody saw and spoke to men who had seen unspeakable things with their own eyes.

Thus Cartiff was arrested. He blasted his way out, however, before he could be brought to trial, and the newscasters blazed with that highly spectacular, murderous jail break. Nobody actually saw Cartiff escape, nobody actually saw any lifeless bodies. Everybody, however, saw the telenews broadcasts of the shattered walls and the sheeted forms; and, since such pictures are and always have been just as convincing as the real thing, everybody knew that there had been plenty of mangled corpses in those ruins and that Cartiff was a fugitive murderer. Also, everybody knew that the Patrol never gives up on a murderer.

Hence it was natural enough that the search for Cartiff, the jeweler-murderer, should spread from planet to planet and from region to region. Not exactly obtrusively, but inexorably, it did so spread; until finally anyone interested in the subject could find upon any one of a hundred million planets unmistakable evidence that the Patrol wanted one Cartiff, description so-and-so, for murder in the first degree.

761

And the Patrol was thorough. Wherever Cartiff went or how, they managed to follow him. At first he disguised himself, changed his name, and stayed in the legitimate jewelry business; apparently the only business he knew. But he never could get even a start. Scarcely would his shop open than he would be discovered and forced again to flee.

Deeper and deeper he went, then, into the noisome society of crime. A fence now—still and always he clung to jewelry. But always and ever the bloodhounds of the law were baying at his heels. Whatever name he used was nosed aside and "Cartiff" they howled; so loudly that a thousand million worlds came to know that despised and hated name.

Perforce he became a traveling fence, always on the go. He flew a dead-black ship, ultrafast, armed and armored like a superdreadnought, crewed—according to the newscasts—by the hardest-boiled gang of cutthroats in the known universe. He traded in, and boasted of trading in, the most bloodstained, the most ghost-ridden gems of a thousand worlds. And, so trading, hurling defiance the while into the teeth of the Patrol, establishing himself ever more firmly as one of Civilization's cleverest and most implacable foes, he worked zigzagwise and not at all obviously toward the unexplored spiral arm in which the planet Lonabar lay. And as he moved farther and farther away from the Solarian System his stock of jewels began to change. He had always favored pearls—the lovely, glorious things so characteristically Tellurian—and those he kept. The diamonds, however, he traded away; likewise the emeralds, the rubies, the sapphires, and some others. He kept and accumulated Borovan firestones, Manarkan star drops, and a hundred other gorgeous gems, none of which would be "beads" upon the planet which was his goal.

He visited planets only fleetingly now; the Patrol was hopelessly out-distanced. Nevertheless, he took no chances. His villainous crew guarded his ship; his bullies guarded him wherever he went—surrounding him when he walked, standing behind him while he ate, sitting at either side of the bed in which he slept. He was a king snipe now.

As such he was accosted one evening as he was about to dine in a garish restaurant. A tall, somewhat fish-faced man in faultless evening dress approached. His arms were at his sides, fingertips bent into the "I'm not shooting" sign.

*

"Captain Cartiff, I believe. May I seat myself at your table, please?" the stranger asked, politely, in the *lingua franca* of deep space.

Kinnison's sense of perception frisked him rapidly for concealed weapons. He was clean. "I would be very happy, sir, to have you as my guest," he replied, courteously.

The stranger sat down, unfolded his napkin, and delicately allowed it to fall into his lap, all without letting either of his hands disappear from sight, even for an instant, beneath the table's top. He was an old and skillful hand. And during the excellent meal the two men conversed brilliantly upon many topics, none of which were of the least importance. After it Kinnison paid the check, despite the polite protestations of his vis-à-vis. Then:

"I am simply a messenger, you will understand, nothing else," the guest observed. "No. 1 has been checking up on you, and has decided to let you come in. He will receive you tonight. The usual safeguards on both sides, of course—I am to be your guide and guarantee."

"Very kind of him, I'm sure." Kinnison's mind raced. Who could this No. 1 be? The ape had a thought-screen on, so he was flying blind. Couldn't be a real big shot, though, so soon—no use monkeying with him at all. "Please convey my thanks, but also my regrets."

"What?" the other demanded. His veneer of politeness had sloughed off; his eyes were narrow, keen, and cold. "You know what happens to independent operators around here, don't you? Do you think that you can fight *us?*"

"Not fight you, no." The Lensman elaborately stifled a yawn. He now had a clue. "Simply ignore you—if you act up, smash you like bugs, that's all. Please tell your No. 1 that I do not split my takes with anybody. Tell him also that I am looking for a choicer location to settle down upon than any I have found as yet. If I do not find such a place near here, I shall move on. If I do find it I shall take it, in spite of man or the devil."

The stranger stood up, glaring in quiet fury, but with both hands still above the table. "You want to make it a war, then, Captain Cartiff!" he gritted.

"Not 'Captain' Cartiff, please," Kinnison begged, dipping one paw delicately into his finger bowl. "'Cartiff' merely, my dear fellow, if you don't mind. Simplicity, sir, and dignity; those two are my key words."

"Not for long," prophesied the other. "No. 1 will blast you out of the ether before you can swap another necklace."

"The Patrol has been trying to do that for some time now, and I'm still here," Kinnison reminded him, gently. "Caution him, please, in order to avoid bloodshed, not to come after me in only one ship, but a fleet; and suggest that he have something hotter than Patrol primaries before he tackles me at all."

Surrounded by his bodyguards, Kinnison left the restaurant, and as he walked along he reflected. Nice going, this. It would get around fast. This No. 1 couldn't be Bleeko; but the king snipe of Lonabar and its environs would hear the news in short order. He was now ready to go. He would flit around a few more days—give this bunch of zwilniks a chance to make a pass at him if they felt like calling his bluff—then on to Lonabar.

IX.

Kinnison did not walk far, nor reflect much, before he changed his mind and retraced his steps; finding the messenger still in the restaurant.

"So you got wise to yourself and decided to crawl while the crawling's good, eh?" he sneered, before the Lensman could say a word. "I don't know whether the offer is still good or not."

"No—and I advise you to muffle your exhaust before somebody rams a ray gun down your throat." Kinnison's voice was coldly level. "I came back to tell you to tell your No. 1 that I'm calling his bluff. You know Checuster?"

"Of course." The zwilnik was plainly discomfited.

"Come along, then, and listen, so you'll know that I'm not running a blazer."

They sought a booth, wherein the native himself got Checuster on the visiplate.

"Checuster, this is Cartiff." The start of surprise and the expression of pleased interest revealed how well that name was known. "I'll be down at your old warehouse day after tomorrow night about this time. Pass the word around that if any of the boys have any stuff too hot for them to handle conveniently, I'll buy it; paying for it in either Patrol credits or bar platinum, whichever they like."

He then turned to the messenger. "Did you get that straight, Lizard Puss?"

The man nodded.

"Relay it to No. 1," Kinnison ordered and strode off. This time he got to his ship, which took off at once.

Cartiff had never made a habit of wearing visible arms, and his guards, while undoubtedly fast gunmen, were apparently only that. Therefore there was no reason for No. 1 to suppose that his mob would have any noteworthy difficulty in cutting this upstart, Cartiff, down. He was, however, surprised; for Cartiff did not come afoot or unarmed.

Instead, it was an armored car that brought the intruding fence through the truck entrance into the old warehouse. Not a car, either; it was more like a twenty-ton tank except for the fact that it ran upon wheels, not treads. It was screened like a cruiser; it mounted a battery of projectors whose energies, it was clear to any discerning eye, nothing short of battle screen could handle. The thing rolled quietly to a stop, a door swung open, and Kinnison emerged. He was neither unarmed nor unarmored now. Instead, he wore a full suit of G-P armor or a reasonable facsimile thereof, and carried a semiportable projector.

"You will excuse the seeming discourtesy, men," he announced, "when I tell you that a certain No. 1 has informed me that he will blast me out of the ether before I swap a necklace on this planet. Stand clear, please, until we see whether he meant business or was just warming up his jets. Now, No. 1, if you're around, come and get it!"

Apparently the challenged party was not present, for no overt move was made. Neither could Kinnison's sense of perception discover any sign of unfriendly activity within its range. Of mind reading there was none, for every man upon the floor was, as usual, both masked and screened.

Business was slack at first, for those present were not bold souls and the Lensman's overwhelmingly superior armament gave them very seriously to doubt his intentions. Many of them, in fact, had fled precipitately at the first sight of the armored truck, and of these more than a few—No. 1's thugs, no doubt—did not return. The others, however, came filtering back as they perceived that there was to be no warfare and as cupidity overcame their timorousness. And as it became evident to all that the stranger's armament was for defense only, that he was there to buy or to barter and not to kill and thus to steal, Cartiff trafficked ever more and more briskly, as the evening wore on, in the hottest gems of the planet.

Nor did he step out of character for a second. He was Cartiff the fence, all the time. He drove hard bargains, but not too hard. He knew jewels thoroughly by this time, he knew the code, and he followed it rigorously. He would give a thousand Patrol credits, in currency good upon any planet of Civilization or in bar platinum good anywhere, for an article worth five thousand, but which was so badly wanted by the law that its then possessor could not dispose of it at all. Or, in barter, he would swap for that article another item, worth fifteen hundred or so, but which was not hot—at least, not upon that planet. Fair enough—so fair that it was almost morning before the silently running truck slid into its storage inside the dead-black spaceship.

Then, in so far as No. 1, the Patrol, and Civilization were concerned, Cartiff and his outfit simply vanished. The zwilnik subchief hunted him viciously for a space, then bragged of how he had run him out of the region. The Patrol, as usual, bided its time, watching alertly. The general public forgot him completely in the next sensation to arise.

*

Fairly close although he then was to the rim of the Galaxy, Kinnison did not take any chances at all of detection in a line toward that rim. The spiral arm beyond Rift 85 was unexplored. It had been of so little interest to Civilization that even its various regions were nameless upon the charts, and the Lensman wanted it to remain that way, at least for the time being. Therefore he left the Galaxy in as nearly a straight nadir line as he could without coming within detection distance of any trade route. Then, making a prodigious loop, so as to enter the spiral arm from the nadir direction, he threw Nadreck's map into the pilot tank and began the computations which would enable him to place correctly in that three-dimensional chart the brilliant point of light which represented his ship.

In this work he was ably assisted by his chief pilot. He did not have Henderson now, but he did have Watson, who rated No. 2 only by the hair-splitting of the supreme Board of Examiners. Such hair-splitting was, of course, necessary: otherwise no difference at all could have been found within the ranks of the first fifty of the Patrol's master pilots, to say nothing of the first three or four. And the rest of the crew did whatever they could.

For it was only in the newscasts that Cartiff's crew was one of murderous and villainous pirates. They were, in fact, volunteers; and, since everyone is familiar with what that means in the Patrol, that statement is as efficient as a book would be.

The chart was sketchy and incomplete, of course; around the flying ship were hundreds, yes, thousands, of stars which were not in the chart at all; but Nadreck had furnished enough reference points so that the pilots could compute their orientation. No need to fear detectors now, in these wild, waste spaces; they set a right-line course for Lonabar and followed it.

As soon as Kinnison could make out the continental outlines of the planet upon the plates he took over control, as he alone of the crew was upon familiar ground. He knew everything about Lonabar that Illona had ever learned; and, although the girl was a total loss as an astronaut, she did know her geography.

Kinnison docked his ship boldly at the spaceport of Lonia, the planet's largest city and its capital. With equal boldness he registered as "Cartiff," filling in some of the blank spaces in the spaceport's routine registry form—not quite truthfully, perhaps—and blandly ignoring others. The armored truck was hoisted out of the hold and made its way to Lonia's largest bank, into which it disgorged a staggering total of bar platinum, as well as sundry coffers of hard, gray steel. These last items went directly into a private vault, under the watchful eyes and ready weapons of Kinnison's own guards.

The truck rolled swiftly back to the spaceport and Cartiff's ship took off—it did not need servicing at the time—ostensibly for another planet unknown to the Patrol, actually to go, inert, into a closed orbit around Lonabar and near enough to it to respond to a call in seconds.

Immense wealth can command speed of construction and service. Hence, in a matter of days, Cartiff was again in business. His salon was, upon a larger and grander scale, a repetition of his Tellurian shop. It was simple, and dignified, and blatantly expensive. Costly rugs covered the floor, impeccable works of art adorned the walls, and three precisely correct, flawlessly groomed clerks displayed, with the exactly right air of condescending humility, Cartiff's wares before those who wished to view them. Cartiff himself was visible, ensconced within a magnificent plate-glass-and-gold office in the rear, but he did not ordinarily have anything to do with customers. He waited; nor did he wait long before there happened that which he expected.

*

One of the superperfect clerks coughed slightly into a microphone.

"A gentleman insists upon seeing you personally, sir," he announced.

"Very well, I will see him now. Show him in, please," and the visitor was ceremoniously ushered into the Presence.

"This is a very nice place you have here, Mr. Cartiff, but did it ever occur to you that—"

"It never did and it never will," Kinnison snapped. He still lolled at ease in his chair, but his eyes were frosty and his voice carried an icy sting. "I quit paying protection to little shots a good many years ago. Or are you from Menjo Bleeko?"

The visitor's eyes widened. He gasped, as though even to utter that dread name were sheer sacrilege. "No, but No.—"

"Save it, slob!" The cold venom of that crisp but quiet order set the fellow back onto his heels. "I am thoroughly sick of this thing of every half-baked tinhorn zwilnik in space calling himself No. 1 as soon as he can steal enough small change to hire an ape to walk around behind him packing a couple of ray guns. If that louse of a boss of yours has a name, use it. If he hasn't, call him 'The Louse.' But cancel that No. 1 stuff. In my book there is no No. 1 in the whole damned Universe. Doesn't your mob know yet who and what Cartiff is?"

"What do we care?" The visitor gathered courage visibly. "A good big bomb—"

"Clam it, you squint-eyed slime-lizard!" The Lensman's voice was still low and level, but his tone bit deep and his words drilled in. "That stuff?" he waved inclusively at the magnificent hall. "Sucker bait, nothing more. The whole works cost only a hundred thousand. Chicken feed. It wouldn't even nick the edge of the roll if you blew up ten of them. Bomb it any time you feel the urge. But take notice that it would make me sore—plenty sore—and that I would do things about it; because I'm in a big game, not this petty-larceny racketeering and chiseling that your mob is doing, and when a toad gets in my way I step on it. So go back and tell that No. 1 of yours to case a job a lot more thoroughly than he did this one before he starts throwing his weight around. Now scram, before I feed your carcass to the other rats around here!"

Kinnison grinned inwardly as the completely deflated gangster slunk out. Good going. It wouldn't take long for *that* blast to get action. This little-shot No. 1 wouldn't dare to lift a hand, but Bleeko would have to. That was axiomatic, from the very nature of things. It was very definitely Bleeko's move next. The only moot point was as to which his nibs would do first—talk or act. He would talk, the Lensman thought. The prime reward of being a hot shot was to have people know it and bend the knee. Therefore, although Cartiff's salon was at all times in complete readiness for any form of violence, Kinnison was practically certain that Menjo Bleeko would send an emissary before he started the rough stuff.

He did, and shortly. A big, massive man was the messenger; a man wearing consciously an aura of superiority, of boundless power and force. He did not simply come into the shop—he made an entrance. All three of the clerks literally cringed before him, and at his casually matter-of-fact order they hazed the already uncomfortable customers out of the shop and locked the doors. Then one of them escorted the visitor, with a sickening servility he had never thought of showing toward his employer and with no thought of consulting Cartiff's wishes in the matter, into Cartiff's private sanctum. Kinnison knew at first glance that this was Ghundrith Khars, Bleeko's right-hand man. Khars, the notorious, who kneeled only to his supremacy, Menjo Bleeko himself; and to whom everyone else upon Lonabar and its subsidiary planets kneeled. The big shot waved a hand and the clerk fled in disorder.

*

"Stand up, worm, and give me that—" Khars began, loftily.

"Silence, fool! Attention!" Kinnison rasped, in such a drivingly domineering tone that the stupefied messenger obeyed involuntarily. The Lensman, psychologist par excellence that he was, knew that this man, with a background of twenty years of blind, dumb obedience to his every order, simply could not cope with a positive and self-confident opposition. "You will not be here long enough to sit down, even if I permitted it in my presence, which I very definitely do not. You came here to give me certain instructions and orders. Instead, you are going to listen merely; I will do all the talking.

"First. The only reason you did not die as you entered this place is that neither you nor Menjo Bleeko knows any better. The next one of you to approach me in this fashion dies in his tracks.

"Second. Knowing as I do the workings of that which your bloated leech of a Menjo Bleeko calls his brain, I know that he has a spy-ray on us now. I am not blocking it out, as I want him to receive ungarbled—and I know that you would not have the courage to transmit it accurately to his foulness—everything I have to say.

"Third. I have been searching for a long time for a planet that I like. This is it. I fully intend to stay here as long as I please. There is plenty of room here for both of us without crowding.

"Fourth. Being essentially a peaceable man, I came in peace and I prefer a peaceable arrangement. However, let it be distinctly understood that I truckle to no man or entity, dead, living, or yet to be born.

"Fifth. Tell Bleeko from me to consider very carefully and very thoroughly an iceberg; its every phase and aspect. That is all—you may go."

"Bub-bub-but," the big man stammered. "An *iceberg?*"

"An iceberg, yes—just that," Kinnison assured him. "Don't bother to try to think about it yourself, since you've got nothing to think with. But his putrescence, Bleeko, even though he is a mental, moral, and intellectual slime-lizard, can think—at least in a narrow, mean, small-souled sort of way—and I advise him in all seriousness to do so. Now get out of here, before I burn the seat of your pants off."

Khars got, gathering together visibly the shreds of his self-esteem as he did so, the clerks staring the while in dumfounded amazement. Then they huddled together, eying the owner of the establishment with a brand-new respect—a subservient respect, heavily laced with awe.

"Business as usual, boys," he counseled them, cheerfully enough. "They won't blow up the place until after dark."

The clerks resumed their places then and trade did go on, after a fashion; but Cartiff's force had not recovered its wonted blasé aplomb even at closing time.

"Just a moment." The proprietor called his employees together and, reaching into his pocket, distributed among them a sheaf of currency. "In case you don't find the shop here in the morning, you may consider yourselves on vacation at full pay until I call you."

They departed, and Kinnison went back to his office. His first care was to set up a spy-ray block—a block which had been purchased upon Lonabar and which was, therefore, certainly pervious to Bleeko's instruments. Then he prowled about, apparently in deep and anxious thought. But as he prowled, the eavesdroppers did not, could not know that his weight set into operation certain devices of his own highly secret installation, or that when he finally left the shop no really serious harm could be done to it except by an explosion sufficiently violent to demolish the neighborhood for blocks around. The front wall would go, of course. He wanted it to go; otherwise there would be neither reason nor excuse for doing that which for days he had been ready to do.

*

Since Cartiff lived rigorously to schedule and did not have a spy-ray block in his room, Bleeko's methodical and efficient observers always turned off their beams when the observee went to sleep. This night, however, Kinnison was not really asleep, and as soon as the ray went off he acted. He threw on his clothes and sought the street, where he took a taxi to a certain airport. There he climbed into a rocketplane which was already warmed up and waiting for him.

Hanging from her screaming props the fantastically powerful little plane bulleted upward in a vertical climb, and as she began to slow down from lack of air her projectors took over. A tractor reached out, seizing her gently. Her wings retracted and she was drawn into Cartiff's great spaceship; which, a few minutes later, hung poised above one of the largest, richest jewel mines of Lonabar.

This mine was, among others, Menjo Bleeko's personal property. Since overproduction would glut the market, it was being worked by only one shift of men—the day shift. It was now black night; the usual guards were the only men upon the premises. The big black ship hung there and waited.

"But suppose they don't, Kim?" Watson asked.

"Then we'll wait here every night until they do," Kinnison replied, grimly. "But they'll do it tonight, for all the tea in China. They'll have to, to save Bleeko's face."

And they did. In a couple of hours the observer at a high-powered plate reported that Cartiff's salon had just been blown to bits. Then the Patrolmen went into action.

Bleeko's mobsmen hadn't killed anybody at Cartiff's, therefore the Tellurians wouldn't kill anyone here. Hence, while ten immense beam-dirigible torpedoes were being piloted carefully down shafts and along tunnels into the deepest bowels of the workings, the guards were given warning that, if they got into their fliers fast enough, they could be fifty miles away and probably safe by zero time. They hurried.

At zero time the torpedoes let go as one. The entire planet quivered under the trip-hammer shock of detonating duodec. For those frightful, those appalling charges had been placed, by computations checked and rechecked, precisely where they would wreak the most havoc, the utmost possible measure of sheer destruction. Much of the rock, however hard, around each one of those incredible centers of demolition was simply blasted out of existence. That is the way duodec, in massive charges, works. Matter simply cannot get out of its way in the first instants of its detonation; matter's own inherent inertia forbids.

Most of the rock between the bombs was pulverized the merest fraction of a second later. Then, the distortedly spherical explosion fronts merging, the total incomprehensible pressure was exerted as almost pure lift. The field above the mine works lifted, then; practically as a mass at first. But it could not remain as such. It could not move fast enough as a whole; nor did it possess even a minute fraction of the tensile strength necessary to withstand the stresses being applied. Those stresses, the forces of the explosions, were to all intents and purposes irresistible. The crust disintegrated violently and almost instantaneously. Rock crushed grindingly against rock, practically the whole mass reducing in the twinkling of an eye to an impalpable powder.

Upward and outward, then, the ragingly compressed gases of detonation drove, hurling everything before them. Chunks blew out sidewise, flying for miles; the mind-staggeringly enormous volume of dust was hurled upward clear into the stratosphere.

Finally that awful dust cloud was wafted aside, revealing through its thinning haze a strangely and hideously altered terrain. No sign remained of the buildings or the mechanisms of Bleeko's richest mine. No vestige was left to show that anything built by or pertaining to man had ever existed there. Where those works had been, there now yawned an absolutely featureless crater; a crater whose sheer geometrical perfection of figure revealed with shocking clarity the magnitude of the cataclysmic forces which had wrought there.

Kinnison, looking blackly down at that crater, did not feel the glow of satisfaction which comes of a good deed well done. He detested it—it made him sick at the stomach.

But, since he had had it to do, he had done it. Why in all the nine hells of Valeria did he have to be a Lensman, anyway?

Back to Lonia, then, the Lensman made his resentful way, and back to bed.

And in the morning, early, workmen began the reconstruction of Cartiff's place of business.

X.

Since Kinnison's impenetrable shields of force had confined the damage to the store's front, it was not long before Cartiff's reopened. Business was and remained brisk; not only because of what had happened, but also because Cartiff's top-lofty and arrogant snobbishness had an irresistible appeal to the upper layers of Lonabar's peculiarly stratified humanity. The Lensman, however, paid little enough attention to business. Outwardly, seated at his ornate desk in haughty grandeur, he was calmness itself, but inwardly he was far from serene.

If he had figured things right, and he was pretty sure that he had, it was up to Bleeko to make the next move, and it would pretty nearly have to be a peaceable one. There was enough doubt about it, however, to make the Lensman a bit jittery inside. Also, from the fact that everybody having any weight at all wore thought-screens, it was almost a foregone conclusion that they had been warned against, and were on the lookout for, THE Lensman—that never-to-be-sufficiently-damned Tellurian Lensman who had already done so much hurt to the Boskonian cause. That they now thought that one to be a well-hidden, unknown director of Lensmen, and not an actual operative, was little protection. If he made one slip, they'd have him, cold.

He hadn't slipped yet, they didn't suspect him yet; he was sure of those points. With these people to suspect was to act, and his world-circling ship, equipped with every scanning, spying, and eavesdropping device known to science, would have informed him instantly of any untoward development anywhere upon or near the planet. And his fight with Bleeko was, after all, natural enough and very much in character. It was of the very essence of Boskonian culture that king snipes should do each other to death with whatever weapons came readiest to hand. The underdog was always trying to kill the upper, and if the latter was not strong enough to protect his loot, he deserved everything he got. A callous philosophy, it is true, but one truly characteristic of Civilization's inveterate foes.

The higher-ups never interfered. Their own skins were the only ones in which they were interested. They would, Kinnison reflected, probably check back on him, just to insure their own safety, but they would not take sides in this brawl if they were convinced that he was, as he appeared to be, a struggling young racketeer making his way up the ladder of fame and fortune as best he could. Let them check—Cartiff's past had been fabricated especially to stand up under precisely that investigation, no matter how rigid it were to be!

Hence Kinnison waited, as calmly as might be, for Bleeko to move. There was no particular hurry, especially since Chris was finding heavy going and thick ether at her end of the line, too. They had been in communication at least once every day, usually oftener;

and Clarrissa had reported seethingly, in near-masculine, almost deep-space verbiage, that that damned red-headed hussy of a Helen was a hard nut to crack.

Kinnison grinned sourly every time he thought of Lyrane II. Those matriarchs certainly were a rum lot. They were a pigheaded, self-centered, mulishly stubborn bunch of cockeyed knotheads, he decided. Non-galaxy minded; as shortsightedly antisocial as a flock of mad Radeligian cateagles. He'd better—no, he hadn't better, either—he'd have to lay off. If Chris, with all her potency and charm, with all her drive and force of will, with all her sheer power of mind and of Lens, couldn't pierce their armor, what chance did any other entity of Civilization have of doing it? Particularly any male creature? He'd like to half wring their beautiful necks, all of them; but that wouldn't get him to the first check station, either. He'd just have to wait until Chris broke through the matriarchs' crust—she'd do it, too, by Klono's prehensile tail!—and then they'd really ride the beam.

*

So Kinnison waited—and waited—and waited. When he got tired of waiting he gave a few more lessons in snobbishness and in the gentle art of self-preservation to the promising young Lonabarian thug whom he had selected to inherit the business, lock, stock, and barrel—including good will, if any—if, as, and when he was done with it. Then he waited some more; waited, in fact, until Bleeko was forced, by his silent pressure, to act.

It was not an overt act, nor an unfriendly—he simply called him up on the visiphone.

"What do you think you're trying to do?" Bleeko demanded, his darkly handsome face darker than ever with wrath.

"You." Kinnison made succinct answer. "You should have taken my advice about pondering the various aspects of an iceberg."

"Bah!" the other snorted. "That silliness?"

"Not as silly as you think. It was a warning, Bleeko, that that which appears above the surface is but a very small portion of my total resources. But you could not or would not learn by precept; you had to have it the hard way. Apparently, however, you have learned. That you have not been able to locate my forces I am certain. I am almost as sure that you do not want to try me again, at least until you have found out what you do not know. But I can give you no more time—you must decide now, Bleeko, whether it is to be peace or war between us. I still prefer a peaceful settlement, with an equitable division of the spoils; but if you want war, so be it."

"I have decided upon peace," the big shot said, and the effort of it almost choked him. "I, Menjo Bleeko the Supreme, will give you a place beside me. Come to me here, at once, so that we may discuss the terms of peace."

"We will discuss them now," Kinnison insisted.

"Impossible! Barred and shielded as this room is—"

"It would be," Kinnison interrupted with a nod, "for you to make such an admission as you have just made."

"—I do not trust unreservedly this communication line. If you join me now, you may do so in peace. If you do not come to me, here and now, it is war to the death."

"Fair enough, at that," the Lensman admitted. "After all, you've got to save your face, and I haven't—yet. And if I team up with you I can't very well stay out of your palace forever. But before I come there I want to give you three things—a reminder, a caution, and a warning. I remind you that our first exchange of amenities cost you a thousand times as much as it did me. I caution you to consider again, and more carefully this time, the iceberg. I warn you that if we again come into conflict you will lose not merely a mine, but everything you have, including your life. So see to it that you lay no traps for me. I come."

He went out into the shop. "Take over, Sport," he told his gangster protégé. "I'm going up to the palace to see Menjo Bleeko. If I'm not back in two hours, and if your grapevine reports that Bleeko is out of the picture, what I've left in the store here is yours until I come back and take it away from you."

"I'll take care of it, boss—thanks," and the Lensman knew that in true Lonabarian gratitude the youth was already, mentally, slipping a long, keen knife between his ribs.

*

Without a qualm, but with every sense stretched to the limit and in instant readiness for any eventuality, Kinnison took a cab to the palace and entered its heavily guarded portals. He was sure that they would not cut him down before he got to Bleeko's room—that room would surely be the one chosen for the execution. Nevertheless, he took no chances. He was supremely ready to slay instantly every guard within range of his sense of perception at the first sign of inimical activity. Long before he came to them, he made sure that the beams which were set to search him for concealed weapons were really search beams and not lethal vibrations.

And as he passed those beams each one of them reported him clean. Rings, of course; a stickpin, and various other items of adornment. But Cartiff, the great jeweler, would be expected to wear very large and exceedingly expensive gems. And the beam has never been projected which could penetrate those Worsel-designed, Thorndyke-built walls of force to show that any one of those flamboyant gems was not precisely what it appeared to be.

Searched, combed minutely, millimeter by cubic millimeter, Kinnison was escorted by a heavily armed quartet of Bleeko's personal guards into his supremacy's private study. All four bowed as he entered—but they strode in behind him, then shut and locked the door.

"You fool!" Bleeko gloated from behind his massive desk. His face flamed with sadistic joy and anticipation. "You trusting, greedy fool! I have you exactly where I want you now. How easy! How simple! This entire building is screened and shielded—by my screens and shields. Your friends and accomplices, whoever or wherever they are, can neither see you nor know what is to happen to you. If your ship attempts your rescue, it will be blasted out of the ether. I will, personally, gouge out your eyes, tear off your nails, strip your hide from your quivering carcass—" Bleeko was now, in his raging exaltation, fairly frothing at the mouth.

"That would be a good trick if you could do it," Kinnison remarked, coldly. "But the real fact is that you haven't even tried to use that pint of blue mush that you call a brain. Do you think that I am an utter idiot? I put on an act and you fell for it—"

"Seize him, guards! Silence his yammering—tear out his tongue!" His supremacy shrieked, leaping out of his chair as though possessed.

The guards tried manfully, but before they could touch him—before any one of them could take one full step—they dropped. Without being touched by material object or visible beam, without their proposed victim having moved a muscle, they died and fell. Died instantly, in their tracks; died completely, effortlessly, painlessly, with every molecule of the all-important compound without which life cannot even momentarily exist shattered instantaneously into its degradation products; died not knowing even that they died.

Bleeko was shaken, but he was not beaten. Needle-ray men, sharp-shooters all, were stationed behind those walls. Gone now the dictator's intent to torture his victim to death. Slaying him out of hand would have to suffice. He flashed a signal to the concealed marksmen, but that order, too, went unobeyed. For Kinnison had perceived the hidden gunmen long since, and before any of them could align his sights or press his firing stud each one of them ceased to live. The zwilnik then flipped on his communicator and gobbled orders. Uselessly; for death sped ahead. Before any mind at any switchboard could grasp the meaning of the signal, it could no longer think.

"You fiend!" Bleeko screamed, in mad panic now, and wrenched open a drawer in order to seize a weapon of his own. Too late. The Lensman had already leaped, and as he landed he struck—not gently. Lonabar's tyrant collapsed upon the thick-piled rug in a writhing, gasping heap; but he was not unconscious. To suit Kinnison's purpose he could not be unconscious; he had to be in full possession of his mind.

*

The Lensman crooked one brawny arm around the zwilnik's neck in an unbreakable strangle hold and flipped off his thought-screen. Physical struggles were of no avail: the attacker knew exactly what to do to certain nerves and ganglia to paralyze all such activity. Mental resistance was equally futile against the overwhelmingly superior power of the Tellurian's mind. Then, his subject quietly passive, Kinnison tuned in and began his search for information. Began it—and swore soulfully. This *couldn't* be so—it didn't make any kind of sense—but there it was.

The ape simply didn't know a thing about any ramification whatever of the vast culture to which Civilization was opposed. He knew all about Lonabar and the rest of the domain which he had ruled with such an iron hand. He knew much—altogether too much—about humanity and Civilization, and plainly to be read in his mind were the methods by which he had obtained those knowledges and the brutally efficient precautions he had taken to make sure that Civilization would not, in turn, learn of him.

Kinnison scowled blackly. His deductions simply *couldn't* be that far off—and besides, it wasn't reasonable that this guy was the top or that he had done all that work on his own account. He pondered deeply, staring unseeing at Bleeko's placid face; and as he pondered, some of the jig-saw blocks of the puzzle began to click into a pattern.

Then, ultracarefully, with the utmost nicety of which he was capable, he again fitted his mind to that of the dictator and began to trace, one at a time, the lines of memory. Searching, probing, coursing backward and forward along those deeply buried time tracks, until at last he found the breaks and the scars for which he was hunting. For, as he had told Illona, a radical mind operation cannot be performed without leaving scars. It is true that upon cold, unfriendly Jarnevon, after Worsel had so operated upon Kinnison's mind, Kinnison himself could not perceive that any work had been done. But that, be it remembered, was before any actual change had occurred; before the compulsion had been applied. The false memories supplied by Worsel were still latent, nonexistent; the true memory chains, complete and intact, were still in place.

This lug's brain had been operated upon, Kinnison now knew, and by an expert. What the compulsion was, what combination of thought stimuli it was that would restore those now nonexistent knowledges, Kinnison had utterly no means of finding out. Bleeko himself, even subconsciously, did not know. It was, it had to be, something external, a thought pattern impressed upon Bleeko's mind by the Boskonian higher-up whenever he wanted to use him; and to waste time in trying to solve *that* problem would be the sheerest folly. Nor could he discover how that compulsion had been or could be applied. If he got his orders from the Boskonian high command direct, there would have to be an intergalactic communicator; and it would in all probability be right here, in Bleeko's private rooms. No force-ball, or anything else that could take its place, was to be found. Therefore Bleeko was, probably, merely another Regional Director, and took orders from someone here in the First Galaxy.

Lyrane? The possibility jarred Kinnison. No real probability pointed that way yet, however; it was simply a possibility, born of his own anxiety. He couldn't worry about it—yet.

His study of the zwilnik's mind, unproductive although it was of the desired details of things Boskonian, had yielded one highly important fact. His supremacy of Lonabar had sent at least one expedition to Lyrane II; yet there was no present memory in his mind that he had ever done so. Kinnison had scanned those files with surpassing care, and knew positively that Bleeko did not now know even that such a planet as Lyrane II existed.

*

Could he, Kinnison, be wrong? Could somebody other than Menjo Bleeko have sent that ship? Or those ships, since it was not only possible, but highly probable, that that voyage was not an isolated instance? No, he decided instantly. Illona's knowledge was far too detailed and exact. Nothing of such importance would be or could be done without the knowledge and consent of Lonabar's dictator. And the fact that he did not now remember it was highly significant. It meant—it *must* mean—that the new Boskone or whoever was back of Boskone considered the solar system of Lyrane of such vital importance that knowledge of it must never, under any circumstances, get to Star A Star, the detested, hated, and feared Director of Lensmen of the Galactic Patrol! And Mac was on Lyrane II—ALONE! She had been safe enough so far, but—

"Chris!" he sent her an insistent thought.

"Yes, Kim?" came flashing answer.

"Thank Klono and Noshabkeming! You're QX, then?"

"Why, of course. Why shouldn't I be, the same as I was this morning?"

"Things have changed since then," he assured her, grimly. "I've finally cracked things open here, and I find that Lonabar is simply a dead end. It's a feeder for Lyrane, nothing else. It's not a certainty, of course, but there's a very distinct possibility that Lyrane is IT. If it is, I don't need to tell you that you're on a mighty hot spot. So I want you to quit whatever you're doing and run. Hide. Crawl into a hole and pull it in after you. Get into one of Helen's deepest crypts and have somebody sit on the lid. And do it right now—five minutes ago would have been better."

"Why, Kim!" she giggled. "Everything here is exactly as it has always been. And surely, you wouldn't have a Lensman hide, would you? Would you, yourself?"

That question was, they both knew, unanswerable. "That's different," he, of course, protested, but he knew that it was not. "Well, anyway, be careful," he insisted. "More careful than you ever were before in your life. Use everything you've got, every second, and if you notice anything, however small, the least bit out of the way, let me know, right then."

"I'll do that. You're coming, of course." It was a statement, not a question.

"I'll say I am—in force! 'By, Chris—BE CAREFUL!" and he snapped the line. He had a lot to do. He had to act fast, and had to be right—and he couldn't take all day in deciding, either.

*

Kinnison's mind flashed back over what he had done. Could he cover up? Should he cover up, even if he could? Yes and no. Better not even try to cover Cartiff up, he decided. Leave that trail just as it was; wide and plain—up to a certain point. This point, right here. Cartiff would disappear here, in Bleeko's palace.

He was done with Cartiff, anyway. They would smell a rat, of course—it stunk to high heaven. They might not—they probably would not—believe that he had died in the ruins of the palace, but they wouldn't *know* that he hadn't. And they would think that he hadn't found out a thing, and he would keep them thinking so as long as he could. The young thug in Cartiff's would help, too, all unconsciously. He would assume the name and station, of course, and fight with everything Kinnison had taught him. That *would* help—Kinnison grinned as he realized just how much it would help.

The real Cartiff would have to vanish as completely, as absolutely without a trace as was humanly possible. They would, of course, figure out in time that Cartiff had done whatever was done in the palace, but it was up to him to see to it that they could never find out how it was done. Wherefore he took from Menjo's mind every iota of knowledge which might conceivably be of use to him thereafter. Then Menjo Bleeko died. His corpse fell into a heap upon the floor and the Lensman strode along corridors and down stairways. And wherever he went, there Death went also.

This killing griped Kinnison to the core of his being, but it had to be. The fate of all Civilization might very well depend upon the completeness of his butchery this day; upon the sheer mercilessness of his extermination of every foe who might be able to cast any light, however dim, upon what he had just done.

Straight to the palace arsenal he went, where he labored briefly at the filling of a bin with bombs. A minute more to set a timer and he was done. Out of the building he ran.

775

No one stayed him; nor did any, later, say that they had seen him go. He dumped a dead man out of a car and drove it away at reckless speed. Even at that, however, he was almost too slow—hurtling stones from the dynamited palace showered down scarcely a hundred feet behind his screeching wheels.

He headed for the spaceport; then, changing his mind, braked savagely as he sent Lensed instructions to Watson. He felt no compunction about fracturing the rules and regulations made and provided for the landing of spaceships at spaceports everywhere by having his vessel make a hot blast, unauthorized, and quite possibly highly destructive landing to pick him up. Nor did he fear pursuit. The big shots were, for the most part, dead; the survivors and the middle-sized shots were too busy by far to waste time over an irregular incident at a spaceport. Hence nobody would give anybody any orders, and without explicit orders no Lonabarian officer would act. No, there would be no pursuit. But They—the Ones Kinnison was after—would interpret truly every such irregular incident; wherefore there must not be any.

Thus it came about that when the speeding ground car was upon an empty stretch of highway, with nothing in sight in any direction, a spaceship eased down upon muffled under jets directly above it. A tractor beam reached down; car and man were drawn upward and into the vessel's hold. Kinnison did not want the car, but he could not leave it there. Since many cars had been blown out of existence with Bleeko's palace, for this one to disappear would be natural enough; but for it to be found abandoned out in the open country would be a highly irregular and an all-too-revealing occurrence.

Upward through atmosphere and stratosphere the black cruiser climbed; out into interstellar space she flashed. Then, while Watson coaxed the sleek flier to do even better than her prodigious best, Kinnison seated himself at the ultrabeam communicator and drilled a beam to Prime Base and Port Admiral Haynes.

*

"Lens-to-Lens, chief, please," Kinnison cautioned, when the handsome old face, surmounted now by a shock of bushy gray hair, appeared upon his plate. "Didn't want to interrupt anything important, is why I called you through the office instead of direct."

"You always have the right of way, Kim, you know that—you're the most important thing in the Galaxy right now," Haynes said, soberly.

"Well, a minute or so wouldn't make any difference—not *that* much difference, anyway," Kinnison replied, uncomfortably. "I don't like to Lens you unless I have to," and he began his report.

Scarcely had he started, however, when he felt a call impinge upon his own Lens. Clarrissa was calling him from Lyrane II.

"Just a sec, admiral!" he thought, rapidly. "Come in, Chris—make it a three-way with Admiral Haynes!"

"You told me to report anything unusual, no matter what," the girl began. "Well, I finally managed to get almost chummy with Helen, and absolutely the only unusual thing I can find out about the whole planet or race is that the death rate from airplane crashes began to go up awhile ago and is still rising. I don't see how that fact can have any bearing, but am reporting it as per instructions."

"Hm-m-m. What kind of crashes?" Kinnison asked.

"That's the unusual feature of it. Nobody knows—they just disappear."

"WHAT?" Kinnison yelled the thought, so forcibly that both Clarrissa and Haynes winced under its impact.

"Why, yes," she replied, innocently. "But I don't see yet that it means—"

"It means that you *do*, right now, crawl into the deepest, most heavily thought-screened hole in Lyrane and stay there until I, personally, come and dig you out," he replied, grimly. "It means, admiral, that I want Worsel and Tregonsee as fast as I can get them—not orders, of course, but very, *very* urgent requests. And I want Van Buskirk and his gang of Valerians, and Grand Fleet, with all the trimmings, within easy striking distance of Dunstan's Region as fast as you can possibly get them there. And I want—"

"Why all the excitement, Kim?" and "What do you know, son?" The two interruptions came almost as one.

"I don't *know* anything." Kinnison emphasized the verb very strongly. "However, I suspect a lot. Everything, in fact, grading downward from the Eich."

"But they were all destroyed, weren't they?" the girl protested.

"Far from it." This from Haynes. "Would the destruction of Tellus do away with all mankind? I am beginning to think that the Eich are to Boskonia exactly what we are to Civilization."

"So am I," Kinnison agreed. "And, such being the case, will you please get hold of Nadreck of Palain VII for me? I don't know his pattern well enough to Lens him from here."

"Why?" Clarrissa asked, curiously.

"Because he's a frigid, poison-breathing second stage Gray Lensman," Kinnison explained. "As such he is much closer to the Eich, in every respect, than we are, and may very well have an angle that we haven't." And in a few minutes the Palainian Lensman became *en rapport* with the group.

"An interesting development, truly," his soft thought came in almost wistfully when the status quo had been made clear to him. "I fear greatly that I cannot be of any use, but I am not doing anything of importance at the moment and will be very glad indeed to give you whatever slight assistance may be possible to one of my small powers. I come at speed to Lyrane II."

XI.

Kinnison had not underestimated the power and capacity of his as yet unknown opposition. Well it was for him and for his Patrol that he was learning to think; for, as has already been made clear, this phase of the conflict was not essentially one of physical combat. Material encounters did occur, it is true, but they were comparatively unimportant. Basically, fundamentally, it was brain against brain; the preliminary but nevertheless prodigious skirmishing of two minds—or, more accurately, two teams of minds—each trying, even while covering up its own tracks and traces, to get at and to annihilate the other.

Each had certain advantages.

Boskonia—although we know now that Boskone was by no means the prime mover in that dark culture which opposed Civilization so bitterly, nevertheless, "Boskonia" it was and still is being called—for a long time had the initiative, forcing the Patrol to wage an almost purely defensive fight. Boskonia knew vastly more about Civilization than Civilization knew about Boskonia. The latter, almost completely unknown, had all the advantages of stealth and of surprise; her forces could and did operate from undeterminable points against precisely plotted objectives. Boskonia had the hyperspatial tube long before the Conference of Scientists solved its mysteries; and even after the Patrol could use it, it could do Civilization no good unless and until something could be found at which to aim it.

Upon the other hand, Civilization had the Lens. It had the backing of the Arisians; maddeningly incomplete and unsatisfactory though that backing seemed at times to be. It had a few entities, notably one Kimball Kinnison, who were learning to think really efficiently. Above all, it had a massed purpose, a loyalty, an *esprit de corps* backboning a morale which the whip-driven ranks of autocracy could never match and which the whip-wielding drivers could not even dimly understand.

Kinnison, then, with all the powers of his own mind and the minds of his friends and coworkers, sought to place and to identify the real key mentality at the destruction of which the mighty Boskonian Empire must begin to fall apart; that mentality, in turn, was trying with its every resource to find and to destroy the intellect which, pure reason showed, was the one factor which had enabled Civilization to throw the fast-conquering hordes of Boskonia back into their own galaxy.

Now, from our point of vantage in time and in space—through the vistas of years of time and of parsecs of space—we can study at leisure and in detail many things which Kimball Kinnison could only surmise and suspect and deduce. Thus, he knew definitely only the fact that the Boskonian organization did not collapse with the destruction of the planet Jarnevon.

We know now, however, all about the Thralian solar system and about Alcon of Thrale, its unlamented tyrant. The planet Thrale—planetographically speaking, Thrallis II—so much like Tellus that its natives, including the unspeakable Alcon, were human practically to the limit of classification; and about Onlo, or Thrallis IX, and its monstrous natives. We know now that the duties and the authorities of the Council of Boskone were taken over by Alcon of Thrale; we now know how, by reason of his absolute control over both the humanity of Thrale and the monstrosities of Onlo, he was able to carry on.

Unfortunately, like the Eich, the Onlonians simply cannot be described by or to man. This is, as is already more or less widely known, due to the fact that all such non-aqueous, subzero-blooded, nonoxygen-breathing peoples have of necessity a metabolic extension into the hyper-dimension; a fact which makes even their three-dimensional aspect subtly incomprehensible to any strictly three-dimensional mind.

Not all such races, it may be said here, belonged to Boskonia. Many essentially similar ones, such as the natives of Palain VII, adhered to our culture from the very first. Indeed, it is held that sexual equality is the most important criterion of that which we know as

Civilization. But, since this is not a biological treatise, this point is merely mentioned, not discussed.

The Onlonians, then, while not precisely describable to man, were very similar to the Eich—as similar, say, as a Posenian and a Tellurian are to each other in the perception of a Palainian. That is to say practically identical; for to the unknown and incomprehensible senses of those frigid beings the fact that the Posenian possesses four arms, eight hands, and no eyes at all, as compared with the Tellurian's simply paired members, constitutes a total difference so slight as to be negligible.

*

But to resume the thread of history, we are at liberty to know things that Kinnison did not. Specifically, we may observe and hear a conference which tireless research has reconstructed in toto. The place was upon chill, dark Onlo, in a searingly cold room whose normal condition of utter darkness was barely ameliorated now by a dim blue glow. The time was just after Kinnison had left Lonabar for Lyrane II. The conferees were Alcon of Thrale and his Onlonian cabinet officers. The armor-clad Tyrant, in whose honor the feeble illumination was, lay at ease in a reclining chair; the pseudoreptilian monstrosities were sitting or standing in some obscure and inexplicable fashion at a long, low bench of stone.

"The fact is," one of the Onlonians was radiating harshly, "that our minions in the other galaxy could not or would not or simply did not think. For years things went so smoothly that no one had to think. The Great Plan, so carefully worked out, gave every promise of complete success. It was inevitable, it seemed, that that entire galaxy would be brought under our domination, its Patrol destroyed, before any inkling of our purpose could be perceived by the weaklings of humanity.

"The Plan took cognizance of every known factor of any importance. When, however, an unknown, unforeseeable factor, the Lens of the Patrol, became of real importance, that Plan, of course, broke down. Instantly, upon the recognition of an unconsidered factor, the Plan should have been revised. All action should have ceased until that factor had been evaluated and guarded against. But no—no one of our commanders in that galaxy or handling its affairs ever thought of such a thing—"

"It is you who are not thinking now," the Tyrant of Thrale broke in. "If any underling had dared any such suggestion, you yourself would have been among the first to demand his elimination. The Plan should have been revised, it is true; but the fault does not lie with the underlings. Instead, it lies squarely with the Council of Boskone—by the way, I trust that those six of that council who escaped destruction upon Jarnevon by means of their hyperspatial tube have been dealt with?"

"They have been liquidated," another officer replied.

"It is well. They were supposed to think, and the fact that they neither coped with the situation nor called it to your attention until it was too late to mend matters, rather than any flaw inherent in the Plan, is what has brought about the present absolutely intolerable situation.

"Underlings are not supposed to think. They are supposed to report facts; and, if so requested, opinions and deductions. Our representatives there were well trained and

779

skillful. They reported accurately, and that was all that was required of them. Helmuth reported truly, even though Boskone discredited his reports. So did Prellin, and Crowninshield, and Jalte. The Eich, however, failed in their duties of supervision and correlation; which is why their leaders have been punished and their operators have been reduced in rank—why we have assumed a task which, it might have been supposed and was supposed, lesser minds could have and should have performed.

"Let me caution you now that to underestimate a foe is a fatal error. Lan of the Eich prated largely upon this very point, but in the eventuality he did, in fact, underestimate very seriously the resources and the qualities of the Patrol; with what disastrous consequences we are all familiar. Instead of thinking, he attempted to subject a purely philosophical concept, the Lens, to a mathematical analysis. Neither did the heads of our military branch think at all deeply, or they would not have tried to attack Tellus until after this new and enigmatic factor had been resolved. Its expeditionary forces vanished without sign or signal—in spite of its primaries, its negative-matter bombs, its supposedly irresistible planets—and accursed Tellus still circles untouched about Sol, its sun. The condition is admittedly not to be borne; but I have always said, and I now do and shall insist, that no further action be taken until the Great Plan shall have been so revised as reasonably to take into account the Lens. What of Arisia?" he demanded of a third cabineteer.

"It is feared that nothing can be done about Arisia at present," that entity replied. "Expeditions have been sent, but they were dealt with as simply and as efficiently as were Lan and Amp of the Eich. Planets have also been sent, but they were detected by the Patrol and were knocked out by far-ranging dirigible planets of the enemy. However, I have concluded that Arisia, of and by itself, is not of prime immediate importance. It is true that the Lens did in all probability originate with the Arisians. It is hence true that the destruction of Arisia and its people would be highly desirable, in that it would insure that no more Lenses would be produced. Such destruction would not do away, however, with the myriads of the instruments which are already in use and whose wearers are operating so powerfully against us. Our most pressing business, it seems to me, is to hunt down and exterminate all Lensmen; particularly the one whom Jalte called THE Lensman, who, Eichmil was informed by Lensman Morgan, was known to even other Lensmen only as Star A Star. In that connection, I am forced to wonder—is Star A Star in reality only one mind?"

"That question has been considered both by me and by your chief psychologist," Alcon made answer. "Frankly, we do not know. We have not enough reliable data upon which to base a finding of fact. Nor does it matter in the least. Whether one or two or a thousand, we must find and we must slay until it is feasible to resume our orderly conquest of the universe. We must also work unremittingly upon a plan to abate the nuisance which is Arisia. Above all, we must see to it with the utmost diligence that no iota of information concerning us ever reaches any member of the Galactic Patrol. I do not want either of our worlds to become as Jarnevon now is."

"Hear! Bravo! Nor I!" came a chorus of thoughts, interrupted by an emanation from one of the sparkling force-ball intergalactic communicators.

*

"Yes? Alcon acknowledging," the Tyrant took the call.

It was a zwilnik upon far Lonabar, reporting through Lyrane VIII everything that Cartiff had done. "I do not know—I have no idea—whether or not this matter is either unusual or important," the observer concluded. "I would, however, rather report ten unimportant things than miss one which might later prove to have had significance."

"Right. Report received," and discussion raged. Was this affair actually what it appeared upon the surface to be, or was it another subtle piece of the work of that never-to-be-sufficiently-damned Lensman?

The observer was recalled. Orders were given and were carried out. Then, after it had been learned that Bleeko's palace and every particle of its contents had been destroyed, that Cartiff had vanished utterly, and that nobody could be found upon the face of Lonabar who could throw any light whatever upon the manner or the time of his going; then, after it was too late to do anything about it, it was decided that this must have been the work of THE Lensman. And it was useless to storm or to rage. Such a happening could not have been reported sooner to so high an office. The routine events of a hundred million planets simply could not be reported, nor could they have been considered if they were. And since this Lensman never repeated—his acts were always different, alike only in that they were drably routine acts until their crashing finales—the Boskonian observers never had been and never would be able to report his activities in time.

"But he got nothing *this* time, I am certain of that," the chief psychologist exulted.

"How can you be so sure?" Alcon snapped.

"Because Menjo Bleeko of Lonabar knew nothing whatever of our activities or of our organization except at such times as one of my men was in charge of his mind," the scientist gloated. "I and my assistants know mental surgery as those crude hypnotists, the Eich, never will know it. Even our lowest agents are having those clumsy and untrustworthy false teeth removed as fast as my therapists can operate upon their minds."

"Nevertheless, you are even now guilty of underestimating," Alcon reproved him sharply, energizing a force-ball communicator. "It is quite eminently possible that he who wrought so upon Lonabar may have been enabled—by pure chance, perhaps—to establish a linkage between that planet and Lyrane—"

The cold, crisply incisive thought of an Eich answered the Tyrant's call.

"Have you of Lyrane perceived or encountered any unusual occurrences or indications?" Alcon demanded.

"We have not."

"Expect them, then," and the Thralian despot transmitted in detail all the new developments.

"We always expect new and untoward things," the Eich more than half sneered. "We are prepared momently for anything that can happen, from a visitation by Star A Star and any or all of his Lensmen up to an attack by the massed Grand Fleet of the Galactic Patrol. Is there anything else, your supremacy?"

THE LENSMAN

"No. I envy you your self-confidence and your assurance, but I mistrust exceedingly the soundness of your judgment. That is all." Alcon turned his attention to the chief psychologist. "Have you operated upon the minds of those Eich and those self-styled Overlords as you did upon that of Menjo Bleeko?"

"No!" the mind surgeon gasped. "Impossible! Not physically, perhaps, but would not such a procedure interfere so seriously with the work that it—"

"That is your problem—solve it," Alcon ordered, curtly. "See to it, however it is solved, that no traceable linkage exists between any of those minds and us. Any mind capable of thinking such thoughts as those which we have just received is not to be trusted."

*

As has been said, Kinnison-ex-Cartiff was en route for Lyrane II while the foregoing conference was taking place. Throughout the trip he kept in touch with Mac. At first he tried, with his every artifice of diplomacy, cajolery, and downright threats, to make her lay off; he finally invoked all his Unattached Lensman's transcendental authority and ordered her summarily to lay off.

No soap. How did he get that way, she wanted furiously to know, to be ordering her around as though she were an uncapped probe? She was a Lensman, too, by Klono's curly whiskers! She had a job to do and she was going to do it. She was on a definite assignment—his own assignment, too, remember—and she wasn't going to be called off of it just because he had found out all of a sudden that it might not be quite as safe as dunking doughnuts at a down-river picnic. What kind of a sun-baked, space-tempered crust did he have to pull a crack like that on *her*? Would he have the barefaced, unmitigated gall to spring a thing like that on any other Lensman in the whole cockeyed universe?

That stopped him—cold. Lensmen always went in; that was their code. For any Tellurian Lensman, anywhere, to duck or to dodge because of any possible personal danger was sheerly, starkly unthinkable. The fact that she was, to him, the sum total of all the femininity of the Galaxy could not be allowed any weight whatever; any more than the converse aspect had ever been permitted to sway him. Fair enough. Bitter, but inescapable. This was one—just one—of the consequences which Mentor had foreseen. He had foreseen it, too, in a dimly unreal sort of way, and now that it was here he'd simply have to take it. QX.

"But be careful, Chris, anyway," he surrendered. "Awfully careful—as careful as I would myself."

"I could be ever so much more careful than that and still be pretty reckless." Her low, entrancing chuckle came through as though she were present in person. "And by the way, Kim, did I ever tell you that I am fast getting to be a gray Lensman?"

"You always were, ace—you couldn't very well be anything else."

"No—I mean actually gray. Did you ever stop to consider what the laundry problem would be upon this heathenish planet?"

"Chris, I'm surprised at you—what do you need of a laundry?" he derided her, affectionately. "Here you've been blasting me to a cinder about not taking your

782

Lensmanship seriously enough, and yet you are violating one of the prime tenets—that of conformation to planetary customs. Shame on you!"

He felt her hot blush across all those parsecs of empty space. "I tried it at first, Kim, but it was just simply *terrible!*"

"You've got to learn how to be a Lensman or else quit throwing your weight around like you did a while back. No back chat, either, you insubordinate young jade, or I'll take that Lens away from you and heave you into the clink."

"You and what regiment of Valerians? Besides, it didn't make any difference," she explained, triumphantly. "These matriarchs don't like me one bit better, no matter what I wear or don't wear."

Time passed, and in spite of Kinnison's highly disquieting fears, nothing happened. Right on schedule the Patrol ship eased down to a landing at the edge of the Lyranian airport. Mac was waiting; dressed now, not in nurse's white, but in startlingly nondescript gray shirt and breeches.

"Not the gray leather of my station, but merely dirt color," she explained to Kinnison after the first fervent greetings. "These women are clean enough physically, but I simply haven't got a thing fit to wear. Is your laundry working?"

It was, and very shortly Sector Chief Nurse Clarrissa MacDougall appeared in her wonted immaculately white stiffly starched uniform. She did not, then or ever, wear the gray to which she was entitled; nor did she ever—except when defying Kinnison—lay claims to any of the rights or privileges which were so indubitably hers. She was not, never had been, and never would or could be a *real* Lensman, she always did insist. At best, she was only a synthetic—or an imitation—or a sort of an amateur—or maybe a "Red" Lensman—handy to have around, perhaps, for certain kinds of jobs, but absolutely and definitely not a regular Lensman. And it was this attitude which was to make the Red Lensman not merely tolerated, but loved as she was loved by Lensmen, Patrolmen, and civilians alike throughout the length, breadth, and thickness of Civilization's bounds.

*

The ship lifted from the airport and went north into the uninhabited temperate zone. The matriarchs did not have a thing which the Tellurians either needed or wanted; the Lyranians disliked the visitors so openly and so intensely that to move away from the populated belt was the only logical and considerate thing to do.

The *Dauntless* arrived a day later, bringing Worsel and Tregonsee; followed closely by Nadreck in his ultrarefrigerated speedster. Five Lensmen, then, studied intently a globular map of Lyrane II which Clarrissa had made. Four of them, the oxygen breathers, surrounded it in the flesh, while Nadreck was with them only in essence. Physically he was far out in the comfortably subzero reaches of the stratosphere, but his mind was *en rapport* with theirs; his sense of perception scanned the markings upon the globe as carefully and as accurately as did theirs.

"This belt which I have colored pink," Mac explained, "corresponding roughly to the torrid zone, is the inhabited area of Lyrane II. Nobody lives anywhere else. Upon it I have charted every unexplained disappearance that I have been able to find out about. Each of these black crosses is where one such person lived. The black circle—or circles, for frequently there are more than one—connected to each cross by a black line, marks the spot—or spots—where that person was seen for the last time or times. If the black circle is around the cross, it means that she was last seen at home. I'm sorry that I couldn't get any real information; that this jumble is all that I could discover for you."

The crosses were distributed fairly evenly all around the globe and throughout the populated zone. The circles, however, tended markedly to concentrate upon the northern edge of that zone; and practically all of the encircled crosses were very close to the northern edge of the populated belt. To four of the Lensmen present the full grisly meaning of the thing was starkly plain.

Nadreck was the first to speak. "Ah, very well done, Lensman MacDougall," he congratulated. "Your data are amply sufficient. A right scholarly and highly informative bit of work, eh, friend Worsel?"

"It is so—it is indeed so," the Velantian agreed, the while a shudder rippled along the thirty-foot length of his sinuous body. "I suspected many things, but not this—certainly not this, ever, away out here."

"Nor I." Tregonsee's four horn-lipped, toothless mouths snapped open and shut; his cabled arms writhed in detestation.

"Nor I," from Kinnison. "If I had, I'd've had a hundred Lyranians mob you, Chris, and tie you down. It would be just about here, I'd say, from the trend of the lines of vanishment." He placed a fingertip near the north pole of the globe. He thought for a moment, his jaw setting and his eyes growing hard, then spoke aloud to the girl. "Chris, the next time I tell you to hide and you don't do it I'm going to take that Lens away from you and flash it with a DeLameter—then you'll go back to Tellus and you'll stay there." His voice was grimmer than she had ever before heard it.

"You don't mean . . . why, it can't be . . . you're all thinking . . . Overlords!" she gasped. Her face turned white; both hands flew to her throat.

"Just that. Overlords. Nothing else but." He pictured in imagination his fiancée's body writhing in torment upon a Delgonian torture screen until his mind revolted; all unconscious that his thoughts were as clear as a telescreen picture to all the others. "If they had detected *you*—You know that they would do anything to get hold of a mind and a vital force like yours—But, thank all the gods of space, they didn't." He shook himself and drew a tremendously deep breath of relief. "Well, all I've got to say is that if we ever have any kids and they don't bawl when I tell them about this, I'll certainly give them something to bawl about!"

XII.

"But listen, Kim!" Clarissa protested. "What makes you all so sure that it's Overlords? There's nothing on my map there to prove—Why, it might be *anything*!"

"It might not, too," Kinnison stated. "Barring the contingency of the existence of a life form unknown to any one of the four of us and which operates exactly as the Overlords do operate, that hypothesis is the only one both necessary and sufficient to explain all the facts which you have plotted upon your chart. Think a minute—you know how they work. They tune in on some one mind, the stronger and more vital the better. The fact that the

Lyranians have such powerful minds is undoubtedly one big reason why the Overlords are here. In that connection, it's a mystery to me how Helen has lived so long—all the persons who disappeared had high-powered minds, didn't they?"

She thought for a space. "Now that you mention it, I believe that they did; as far as I know, anyway."

"Thought so. That clinches it, if it needed any clinching. But to go on, they tune in and blank out the victim's mind completely, filling it with an overwhelming urge to rush directly to the cavern. How else can you explain the number of these disappearances; and above all, the fact that the great majority of those lines of yours point directly to that one spot? For your information, I will add that the ones that do not so point are probably observational errors—the person was seen before she disappeared, instead of afterward."

"But that's so . . . so *evident*," she began. "Would they do anything—"

"It wasn't evident to you at first, was it?" he countered. "And, evident or not, they always have worked that way; and, as far as anyone has been able to find out, they never have worked any other way. Quite probably, therefore, they can't. The Eich undoubtedly told them to lay off, just as they did before; but apparently they can't do that, either—permanently. This torturing and life eating of theirs seems to be a racial vice—like a drug habit, only worse. They can quit it for a while, but after about so long they simply have to go on another bender. Convinced?"

"Wel-l-l, I suppose so," she admitted doubtfully, and Kinnison turned to the group at large.

"There is no doubt, I take it, as to what course of action we are to pursue in the matter of this cavern of Overlords?" he asked, superfluously.

There was none. The decision was unanimous and instant that it must be wiped out. The two great ships, the incomparable *Dauntless* and the camouflaged warship which had served Kinnison-Cartiff so well, lifted themselves into the stratosphere and headed north. The Lensmen did not want to advertise their presence and there was no great hurry, therefore both vessels had their thought-screens out and both rode upon baffled jets.

Practically all of the crewmen of the *Dauntless* had seen Overlords in the substance; so far as is known they were the only human beings who had ever seen an Overlord and had lived to tell of it. Twenty-two of their former fellows had seen Overlords and had died. Kinnison, Worsel and Van Buskirk had slain Overlords in unscreened hand-to-hand combat in the fantastically incredible environment of a hyperspatial tube—that uncanny medium in which man and monster could and did occupy the same space at the same time without being able to touch each other; in which the air or pseudoair is thick and viscous; in which the only substance common to both sets of dimensions and thus available for combat purposes is a synthetic material so treated and so saturated as to be of enormous mass and inertia.

*

It is easier to imagine, then, than to describe the emotion which seethed through the crew as the news flew around that the business next in order was the extirpation of a flock of Overlords.

"How about a couple or three nice duodec torpedoes, Kim, steered right down into the middle of that cavern and touched off—*powie!*—slick, don't you think?" Henderson insinuated.

"Aw, let's not, Kim!" protested Van Buskirk, who, as one of the three Overlord slayers, had been called into the control room. "This ain't going to be in a tube, Kim; it's in a cavern on a planet—made to order for ax work. Let me and the boys put on our screens and bash their ugly damn skulls in for 'em. How about it, huh?"

"Not duodec, Hen—not yet, anyway," Kinnison decided. "As for ax work, Bus—maybe, maybe not. Depends. We want to catch some of them alive, so as to get some information—but you and your boys will be good for that, too, so you might as well go and start getting them ready." He turned his thought to his snakish comrade in arms.

"What do you think, Worsel, is this hide-out of theirs heavily fortified, or just hidden?"

"Hidden, I would say from what I know of them—well-hidden," the Velantian replied promptly. "Unless they have changed markedly; and, like you, I do not believe that a race so old can change that much. I could tune them in, as I have done before, but it might very well do more harm than good."

"Certain to, I'm afraid." Kinnison knew as well as did Worsel that a Velantian was the tastiest dish which could be served up to any Overlord. Both knew also, however, the very real mental ability of the foe; knew that the Overlords would be sure to suspect that any Velantian so temptingly present upon Lyrane II must be there specifically for the detriment of the Delgonian race; knew that they would almost certainly refuse the proffered bait. And not only would they refuse to lead Worsel to their cavern, but in all probability they would cancel even their ordinary activities, thus making it impossible to find them at all, until they had learned definitely that the hook-bearing titbit and its accomplices had left the Lyranian solar system entirely. "No, what we need right now is a good, strong-willed Lyranian."

"Shall we go back and grab one? It would take only a few minutes," Henderson suggested, straightening up at his board.

"Uh-uh," Kinnison demurred. "That might smell a bit on the cheesy side, too, don't you think, fellows?" And Worsel and Tregonsee agreed that such a move would be ill-advised.

"Might I offer a barely tenable suggestion?" Nadreck asked diffidently.

"I'll say you can—come in."

"Judging by the rate at which Lyranians have been vanishing of late, it would seem that we would not have to wait too long before another one comes hither under her own power. Since the despised ones will have captured her themselves, and themselves will have forced her to come to them, no suspicion will be or can be aroused."

"That's a thought, Nadreck—that *is* a thought!" Kinnison applauded. "Shoot us up, will you, Hen? 'Way up, and hover over the center of the spread of intersections of those lines. Put observers on every plate you've got here—you, too, Captain Craig, please, all over the ship. Have half of them search the air all around as far as they can reach for an airplane in flight; have the rest comb the terrain below, both on the surface and underground, with spy-rays, for any sign of a natural or artificial cave."

"What kind of information do you think they may have, Kinnison?" asked Tregonsee the Rigellian.

"I don't know." Kinnison pondered for minutes. "Somebody—around here somewhere—has got some kind of a tie-up with some Boskonian entity or group that is fairly well up the ladder; I'm pretty sure of that. Bleeko sent ships here—one speedster, certainly, and there's no reason to suppose that it was an isolated case—"

"There is nothing to show, either, that it was not an isolated case," Tregonsee commented quietly, "and the speedster landed, not up here near the pole, but in the populated zone. Why? To secure some of the women?" The Rigellian was not arguing against Kinnison; he was, as they all knew, helping to subject every facet of the matter to scrutiny.

"Possibly—but this is a transfer point," Kinnison pointed out. "Illona was to start out from here, remember. And those two ships—coming to meet her, or perhaps each other, or—"

"Or perhaps called there by the speedster's crew, for aid," Tregonsee supplied the complete thought.

"One but quite possibly not both," Nadreck suggested. "We agreed, I think, that the probability of a Boskonian connection is sufficiently large to warrant the taking of these Overlords alive in order to read their minds?"

*

They were; hence the discussion then turned naturally to the question of how this none-too-easy feat was to be accomplished. The two Patrol ships had climbed and were cruising in great, slow circles; the spy-ray men and the other observers were hard at work. Before they had found anything upon the ground, however:

"Plane, ho!" came the report, and both vessels, with spy-ray blocks out now as well as thought-screens, plunged silently into a flatly slanting dive. Directly over the slow Lyranian craft, high above it, they turned as one to match its course and slowed down to match its pace.

"Come to life, Kim—don't let them have her!" Clarrissa exclaimed. Being *en rapport* with them all, she knew that both unhuman Worsel and monster Nadreck were perfectly willing to let the helpless Lyranian become a sacrifice; she knew that neither Kinnison nor Tregonsee had as yet given that angle of the affair a single thought. "Surely, Kim, you don't have to let them kill her, do you? Isn't showing you the gate or whatever it is, enough? Can't you rig up something to do something with when she gets almost inside?"

"Why . . . uh . . . I s'pose so." Kinnison wrenched his attention away from a plate. "Oh, sure, Chris. Hen! Drop us down a bit, and have the boys get ready to spear that crate with a couple of tractors when I give the word."

The plane held its course, directly toward a range of low, barren, precipitous hills. As it approached them it dropped, as though to attempt a landing upon a steep and rocky hillside.

"She can't land there," Kinnison breathed, "and Overlords would want her alive, not dead—suppose I've been wrong all the time? Get ready, fellows!" he snapped. "Take her at the very last possible instant—before—she—crashes—now!" As he yelled the command the powerful beams leaped out, seizing the disaster-bound vehicle in a gently unbreakable grip. Had they not done so, however, the Lyranian would not have crashed; for in that last split second a section of the rugged hillside fell inward. In the very mouth of that dread opening the little plane hung for an instant; then:

"Grab the woman, quick!" Kinnison ordered, for the Lyranian was going to jump.

And, such was the awful measure of the Overlords' compulsion, she did jump; without a parachute, without knowing or caring what, if anything, was to break her fall. But before she struck ground a tractor beam had seized her, and passive plane and wildly struggling pilot were both borne rapidly aloft.

"Why, Kim, it's *Helen!*" Clarrissa shrieked in surprise, then voice and manner became transformed. "The poor, poor thing," she crooned. "Bring her in at No. 6 Lock. I'll meet her there—you fellows keep clear. In the state she's in a shock—especially such a shock as seeing such a monstrous lot of males—would knock her off the beam, sure."

*

Helen of Lyrane ceased struggling in the instant of being drawn through the thought-screen surrounding the *Dauntless*. She had not been unconscious at any time. She had known exactly what she had been doing; she had wanted intensely—such was the insidiously devastating power of the Delgonian mind—to do just that and nothing else. The falseness of values, the indefensibility of motivation, simply could not register in her thoroughly suffused, completely blanketed mind. When the screen cut off the Overlords' control, however, thus restoring her own, the shock of realization of what she had done—what she had been forced to do—struck her like a physical blow. Worse than a physical blow, for ordinary physical violence she could understand.

This mischance, however, she could not even begin to understand. It was utterly incomprehensible. She knew what had happened; she knew that her mind had been taken over by some monstrously alien, incredibly powerful mentality, for some purpose so obscure as to be entirely beyond her ken. To her narrow philosophy of existence, to her one-planet insularity of viewpoint and outlook, the very existence, anywhere, of such a mind with such a purpose was in simple fact impossible. For it actually to exist upon her own planet, Lyrane II, was sheerly, starkly unthinkable.

She did not recognize the *Dauntless*, of course. To her all spaceships were alike. They were all invading warships, full of enemies. All things and all beings originating elsewhere than upon Lyrane II were, perforce, enemies. Those outrageous males, the Tellurian Lensman and his cohorts, had pretended not to be inimical, as had the peculiar, white-swathed Tellurian near-person who had been worming itself into her confidence in order to study the disappearances; but she did not trust even them.

She now knew the manner of, if not the reason for, the vanishment of her fellow Lyranians. The tractors of the spaceship had saved her from whatever fate it was that impended. She did not, however, feel any thrill of gratitude. One enemy or another, what difference did it make? Therefore, as she went through the blocking screen and recovered control of her mind, she set herself to fight; to fight with every iota of her mighty mind and with every fiber of her lithe, hard-schooled, tigress' body. The air-lock doors opened and closed—she faced, not an armed and armored male all set to slay, but the white-clad person whom she already knew better than she ever would know any other non-Lyranian.

"Oh, Helen!" the girl half sobbed, throwing both arms around the still-braced Chief Person. "I'm *so* glad that we got to you in time! And there will be no more disappearances, dear—the boys will see to that!"

Helen did not know, really, what disinterested friendship meant. Since the nurse had put her into a wide-open two-way, however, she knew beyond all possibility of doubt that these Tellurians wished her and all her kind well, not ill; and the shock of that knowledge, superimposed upon the other shocks which she had so recently undergone, was more than she could bear. For the first and only time in her hard, busy, purposeful life, Helen of Lyrane fainted; fainted dead away in the circle of the Earthgirl's arms.

The nurse knew that this was nothing serious; in fact, she was professionally quite in favor of it. Hence, instead of resuscitating the Lyranian, she swung the pliant body into a carry—as has been previously intimated, Clarrissa MacDougall was no more a weakling physically than she was mentally—and without waiting for orderlies and stretcher she bore it easily away to her own quarters. And there, instead of administering restoratives, she took out her ubiquitous hypodermic and made sure that her patient would rest quietly for many hours to come.

XIII.

In the meantime the more warlike forces of the *Dauntless* had not been idle. In the instant of the opening of the cavern's doors Captain Craig erupted orders, and as soon as the Lyranian was out of the line of fire, keen-eyed needle-ray men saw to it that those doors were in no mechanical condition to close. The *Dauntless* settled downward; landed in front of the entrance to the cavern. The rocky, broken terrain meant nothing to her; the hardest, jaggedest boulders crumbled instantly to dust as her enormous mass drove the file-hard, inflexible armor of her midzone deep into the ground. Then, while alert beamers watched the entrance and while spy-ray experts combed the interior for other openings which Kinnison and Worsel were already practically certain did not exist, the forces of Civilization formed for the attack.

Worsel was fairly shivering with eagerness for the fray. His was, and with plenty of reason, the bitterest by far of all the animosities there present against the Overlords. For Delgon and his own native planet, Velantia, were neighboring worlds, circling about the same sun. Since the beginning of Velantian space flights, the Overlords of Delgon had preyed upon the Velantians; in fact, the Overlords had probably caused the first Velantian spaceship to be built. They had called them, in a never-ending stream, across the empty gulf of space. They had pinned them against their torture screens, had flayed them and had tweaked them to bits, had done them to death in every one of the numberless slow and hideous fashions which had been developed by a race of sadists who had been specializing in the fine art of torture for thousands upon thousands of years. Then, in the last minutes of the long-drawn-out agony of death, the Overlords were wont to feed, with a passionate, greedy, ineradicably ingrained lust utterly inexplicable to any civilized mind, upon the life forces which the mangled bodies could no longer contain.

This horrible parasitism went on for ages. The Velantians fought vainly; their crude thought-screens were almost useless until after the coming of the Patrol. Then, with screens that were of real use, and with ships of power and with weapons of might, Worsel himself had taken the lead in the clean-up of Delgon. He was afraid, of course. Any Velantian was and is frightened to the very center of his being by the mere thought of an Overlord. He cannot help it; it is in his heredity, bred into the innermost chemistry of his body; the cold grue of a thousand thousand fiendishly tortured ancestors simply will not be denied or cast aside.

Many of the monsters had succeeded in fleeing Delgon, of course. Some departed in the ships which had ferried their victims to the planet, some were removed to other solar systems by the Eich. The rest were slain; and as the knowledge that a Velantian *could* kill an Overlord gained headway, the emotions toward the oppressors generated within minds such as the Velantians' became literally indescribable. Fear was there yet, and in abundance—it simply could not be eradicated. Horror and revulsion. Sheer, burning hatred; and, more powerful than all, amounting almost to an obsession, a clamoring, shrieking, driving urge for revenge which was almost tangible. All these, and more, Worsel felt as he waited, twitching.

*

The Valerians wanted to go in because it meant a hand-to-hand fight. Fighting was their business, their sport, and their pleasure; they loved it for its own sweet sake, with a simple, whole-hearted devotion. To die in combat was a Valerian soldier's natural and much-to-be-desired end; to die in any peaceful fashion was a disgrace and a calamity. They did and do go into battle with very much the same joyous abandon with which a sophomore goes to meet his date in Lovers' Lane. And now, to make physical combat all the nicer and juicier, they carried semiportable tractors and pressors, for the actual killing was not to take place until after the battle proper was over. Blasting the Overlords out of existence would have been simplicity itself; but they were not to die until after they had been forced to divulge whatever they might have of knowledge or of information.

Nadreck of Palain wanted to go in solely to increase his already vast store of knowledge. His thirst for facts was a purely scientific one; the fashion in which it was to be satisfied was the veriest, the most immaterial detail. Indeed, it is profoundly impossible to portray to any human intelligence the serene detachment, the utterly complete indifference to suffering exhibited by practically all of the frigid-blooded races, even those adherent to Civilization, especially when the suffering is being done by an enemy. Nadreck did know, academically and in a philological sense, from his reading, the approximate significance of such words as "compunction," "sympathy" and "squeamishness"; but he would have been astounded beyond measure at any suggestion that they would apply to any such matter-of-fact business as the extraction of data from the mind of an Overlord of Delgon, no matter what might have to be done to the unfortunate victim in the process.

Tregonsee went in simply because Kinnison did—to be there to help out in case the Tellurian should need him.

Kinnison went in because he felt that he had to. He knew full well that he was not going to get any kick at all out of what was going to happen. He was not going to like it, any part of it. Nor did he. In fact, he wanted to be sick—violently sick—before the business was well started. And Nadreck perceived his mental and physical distress.

"Why stay, Friend Kinnison, when your presence is not necessary?" he asked, with the slightly pleased, somewhat surprised, hellishly placid mental immobility which Kinnison was later to come to know so well. "Even though my powers are admittedly small, I feel eminently qualified to cope with such minor matters as the obtainment and the accurate transmittal of that which you wish to know. I cannot understand your emotions, but I realize fully that they are essential components of that which makes you what you fundamentally are. There can be no justification for your submitting yourself needlessly to such stresses, such psychic traumata."

And Kinnison and Tregonsee, realizing the common sense of the Palainian's statement and very glad indeed to have an excuse for leaving the outrageous scene, left it forthwith.

*

There is no need to go into detail as to what actually transpired within that cavern's dark and noisome depths. It took a long time, nor was any of it gentle. The battle itself, before the Overlords were downed, was bad enough in any Tellurian's eyes. Clad in armor of proof although they were, more than one of the Valerians died. Worsel's armor was shattered and rent, his almost steel-hard flesh was slashed, burned and mangled before the last of the monstrous forms was pinned down and helpless. Nadreck alone escaped unscathed—he did so, he explained quite truthfully, because he did not go in there to fight, but only to learn.

What followed the battle, however, was infinitely worse. The Delgonians, as has been said, were hard, cold, merciless, even among themselves; they were pitiless and unyielding and refractory in the extreme. It need scarcely be emphasized then, that they did not yield to persuasion either easily or graciously; that their own apparatus and equipment had to be put to its fullest grisly use before those stubborn minds gave up the secrets so grimly and so implacably sought. Worsel, the raging Velantian, used those torture tools with a vengeful savagery and a snarling ferocity which are at least partially understandable; but Nadreck employed them with a calm capability, a coldly, emotionlessly efficient callousness the mere contemplation of which made icy shivers chase each other up and down Kinnison's spine.

At long last the job was done. The battered Patrol forces returned to the *Dauntless*, bringing with them their spoils and their dead. The cavern and its every molecule of contents were bombed out of existence. The two ships took off; Cartiff's heavily armed "merchantman" to do the long flit back to Tellus, the *Dauntless* to drop Helen and her plane off at her airport and then to join her sister superdreadnoughts which were already beginning to assemble in Rift 94.

"Come down here, will you please, Kim?" came Clarrissa's thought. "I've been keeping her pretty well blocked out, but she wants to talk to you—in fact, she insists upon it—before she leaves the ship."

"Hm-m-m—now that *is* something!" the Lensman exclaimed, and hurried to the nurse's cabin.

There stood the Lyranian queen; a full five inches taller than Mac's five feet six, a good thirty-five pounds heavier than Mac's not inconsiderable one hundred and forty-five. Hard, fine, supple; erectly poised she stood there, an exquisitely beautiful statue of pale bronze, her flaming hair a gorgeous riot. Head held proudly high, she stared only slightly upward into the Earthman's quiet, understanding eyes.

"Thanks, Kinnison, for everything that you and yours have done for me and mine," she said simply, and held out her right hand in what she knew was the correct Tellurian gesture.

"Uh-uh, Helen," Kinnison denied, gently, making no motion to grasp the proffered hand—which was promptly and enthusiastically withdrawn. "Nice, and it's really big of you, but don't strain yourself." This was neither slang nor sarcasm; he meant precisely and only what he said. "Don't overdrive in trying to force yourself to like us men too much or too soon; you must get used to us gradually. We like you a lot, and we respect you even more, but we have been around and you haven't. You can't be feeling friendly enough yet to enjoy shaking hands with me—you certainly haven't got jets enough to swing *that* load—so this time we'll take the thought for the deed. Keep trying, though, Toots old girl, and you'll make it yet. In the meantime we're all pulling for you, and if you ever need any help, shoot us a beam on the communicator Chris is giving you. Clear ether, ace!"

"Clear ether, MacDougall and Kinnison!" Helen's eyes were softer than either of the Tellurians had ever seen them before. "There is, I think, something of wisdom, of efficiency, in what you have said. It may be . . . that is, there is a possibility . . . you of Civilization are, perhaps, persons—of a sort that is—after all. Thanks—*really* thanks, I mean, this time. Good-by."

Helen's plane had already been unloaded. She disembarked and stood beside it; watching, with a peculiarly untranslatable expression, the huge cruiser until it was out of sight.

"It was just like pulling teeth for her to be civil to me," Kinnison grinned at his fiancée, "but she finally made the lift. She's a grand girl, that Helen, in her peculiar, poisonous way."

"Why, Kim!" Mac protested. "She's nice, really, when you get to know her. And she's so stunningly, so ravishingly beautiful!"

"Uh-huh," Kinnison agreed, without a trace of enthusiasm. "Cast her in chilled stainless steel—she'd just about do as she is, without any casting—and she'd make a mighty fine statue."

"Kim! Shame on you!" the girl exclaimed. "Why, she's the most perfectly *beautiful* thing I ever saw in my whole life!" Her voice softened. "I wish that I looked like that," she added wistfully.

"She's beautiful enough—in her way—of course," the man admitted, entirely unimpressed. "But, then, so is a Radeligian cateagle, so is a spire of frozen helium, and so is a six-foot-long, armor-piercing punch. As for you wanting to look like her—I'm terrifically glad that you don't. That's sheer tripe, Chris, and you know it. If you want to look at something *really* beautiful, get a mirror—beside you, all the Helens that ever lived, with Cleopatra, Dessa Desplaines and Illona Potter thrown in, wouldn't make a baffled flare—"

That was, of course, what she wanted him to say; and what followed is of no particular importance here.

*

Shortly after the *Dauntless* cleared the stratosphere, Nadreck reported that he had finished assembling and arranging the data, and Kinnison called the Lensmen together in his con room for an ultraprivate conference. Worsel, it appeared, was still in the surgery.

"'Smatter, doc?" Kinnison asked, casually. He knew that there was nothing really serious the matter—Worsel had come out of the cavern under his own power, and a Velantian recovers with startling rapidity from any wound which does not kill him outright. "Having trouble with your stitching?"

"I'll say we are!" the surgeon grunted. "Have to bore holes with an electric drill and use linemen's pliers. Just about done now, though—he'll be with you in a couple of minutes," and in a very little more than the stipulated time the Velantian joined the other Lensmen.

He was bandaged and taped, and did not move at his customary headlong pace, but he fairly radiated self-satisfaction, bliss and contentment. He felt better, he declared, than he had at any time since he cleaned out the last cavern upon Delgon.

Kinnison stopped the interplay of thoughts by starting up his Lensman's projector. This mechanism was something like the ordinary three-dimensional color-and-sound machine, except instead of emitting sounds it radiated thoughts. Sometimes the thoughts of one or more Overlords, at other times the thoughts of the Eich or other beings as registered upon the minds of the Overlords, at still others the thoughts of Nadreck or of Worsel explaining or amplifying a preceding thought passage or some detail which was being shown at the moment. The spool of tape now being run, with others, formed the Lensmen's record of what they had done. This record would go to Prime Base under Lensman's Seal; that is, only a Lensman could handle it or see it. Later, after the emergency had passed, copies of it would go to various Central Libraries and thus become available to properly accredited students. Indeed, it is only from such records, made upon the scene and at the time by keen-thinking, logical, truth-seeking Lensmen, that such a factual, minutely detailed history as this can be compiled; and your historian is supremely proud that he was the first person other than a Lensman to be allowed to study a great deal of this priceless data.

Worsel knew the gist of the report, Nadreck the compiler knew it all; but to Kinnison, Mac and Tregonsee the unreeling of the tape brought shocking news. For, as a matter of fact, the Overlords had known more, and there was more in the Lyranian solar system to know than Kinnison's wildest imaginings had dared to suppose. That system was one of the main focal points for the zwilnik business of an immense volume of space; Lyrane II was the meeting place, the dispatcher's office, the nerve center from which thousands of invisible, immaterial lines reached out to thousands of planets peopled by warm-blooded oxygen breathers. Menjo Bleeko had sent to Lyrane II not one expedition, but hundreds of them; the affair of Illona and her escorts had been the veriest, the most trifling incident.

The Overlords, however, did not know of any Boskonian in the Second Galaxy. They had no superiors, anywhere. The idea of anyone or anything anywhere being superior to an Overlord was unthinkable. They did, however, co-operate with—here came the really stunning fact—certain of the Eich who lived upon eternally dark Lyrane VIII, and who managed things for the frigid-blooded, poison-breathing Boskonians of the region in much the same fashion as the Overlords did for the warm-blooded, light-loving races. To make the co-operation easier and more efficient, the two planets were connected by a hyperspatial tube.

"Just a sec!" Kinnison interrupted, as he stopped the machine for a moment. "The Overlords were kidding themselves a bit there, I think—they must have been. If they didn't report to or get orders from the Second Galaxy or some other higher-up office, the Eich must have; and since the records and plunder and stuff were not in the cavern, they must be upon Eight. Therefore, whether they realized it or not, the Overlords must have been inferior to the Eich and under their orders. Check?"

"Check," Nadreck agreed. "Worsel and I concluded that they knew the facts, but were covering up even in their own minds, to save face. Our conclusions, and the data from which they were derived, are in the introduction—another spool. Shall I get it?"

"By no means—just glad to have the point cleared up, is all. Thanks—" and the showing went on.

The principal reason why the Lyranian system had been chosen for that important headquarters was that it was one of the very few outlying solar systems, completely unknown to the scientists of the Patrol, in which both the Eich and the Overlords could live in their natural environments. Lyrane VIII was, of course, intensely, bitterly cold. This quality is not rare, since all No. 8 planets are; its uniqueness lay in the fact that its atmosphere was almost exactly like that of Jarnevon.

And Lyrane II suited the Overlords perfectly. Not only did it have the correct temperature, gravity and atmosphere, but also it offered that much rarer thing without which no cavern of Overlords would have been content for long—a native life form possessing strong and highly vital minds upon which they could prey.

There was more, much more; but the rest of it was not directly pertinent to the immediate question. The tape ran out, Kinnison snapped off the projector, and the Lensmen went into a five-way.

Why was not Lyrane II defended? Worsel and Kinnison had already answered that one. Secretiveness and power of mind, not armament, had always been the natural defenses of all Overlords. Why hadn't the Eich interfered? That was easy, too. The Eich looked after themselves—if the Overlords couldn't, that was just too bad. The two ships that had come to aid and had remained to revenge had certainly not come from Eight—their crews had been oxygen breathers. Probably a rendezvous—immaterial, anyway. Why wasn't the whole solar system ringed with outposts and screens? Too obvious. Why hadn't the *Dauntless* been detected? Because of her nullifiers; and if she had been spotted by any short-range stuff she had been mistaken for another zwilnik ship. They hadn't detected anything out of the way upon Eight because it had not occurred to anybody to swing an analyzer upon that particular planet. They would find that Eight was defended plenty. Had the Eich had time to build defenses? They must have had, or they wouldn't be there—they certainly were not taking that kind of chances. And, by the way, hadn't they better do a bit of snooping near Lyrane VIII before they went back to join the Z9M9Z and the Fleet? They had.

Thereupon the *Dauntless* faced about and retraced her path toward the now highly important system of Lyrane. In their previous approaches the Patrolmen had observed the usual precautions to avoid revealing themselves to any zwilnik vessel which might have been on the prowl. Those precautions were now intensified to the limit, since they knew that Lyrane VIII was the site of a base manned by the Eich themselves.

As the big cruiser crept toward her goal, nullifiers full out and every instrument of detection and reception as attentively outstretched as the whiskers of a tomcat slinking along a black alley at midnight, the Lensmen again pooled their brains in conference.

*

The Eich. This was going to be *no* push-over. Even the approach would have to be figured to a hair; because, since the Boskonians had decided that it would be poor strategy to screen in their whole solar system, it was a cold certainty that they would have their own planet guarded and protected by every device which their inhuman ingenuity could devise. The *Dauntless* would have to stop just outside the range of the electromagnetic detection, for the Boskonians would certainly have a five-hundred-percent overlap. Their nullifiers would hash up the electros somewhat, but there was no use in taking too many chances. Previously, on right-line courses to and from Lyrane II, that had not mattered, for two reasons—not only was the distance extreme for accurate electro work, but also it would have been assumed that their ship was a zwilnik. Laying a course for Eight, though, would be something else entirely. A zwilnik would take the tube, and they would not, even if they had known where it was.

That left the visuals. The cruiser was a mighty small target at interplanetary distances; but there were such things as electronic telescopes, and the occultation of even a single star might prove disastrous. Kinnison called the chief pilot.

"Stars must be thin in certain regions of the sky out here, Hen. Suppose you can pick us out a line of approach along which we will occult no stars and no bright nebulae?"

"I should think so, chief—just a sec; I'll see—Yes, easily. There is a lot of black background, especially to the nadir"—and the conference continued.

They would have to go through the screens of electros in Kinnison's inherently indetectable black speedster. QX, but she was nobody's fighter—she didn't have a beam hot enough to light a match. And besides, there were the thought-screens and the highly probable other stuff about which the Lensmen could know nothing.

Kinnison quite definitely did not relish the prospect. He remembered all too vividly what had happened when he had scouted the Eich's base upon Jarnevon; when it was only through Worsel's aid that he had barely—*just* barely—escaped with his life. And Jarnevon's defenders had probably been exerting only routine precautions, whereas these fellows were undoubtedly cocked and primed for *the* Lensman. He would go in, of course, but he'd probably come out feet first—he didn't know any more about their defenses than he had known before, and that was nothing, flat.

"Excuse the interruption, please," Nadreck's thought apologized, "but it would seem to appear more desirable, would it not, to induce the one of them possessing the most information to come out to us?"

"Huh?" Kinnison demanded. "It would, of course—but how in all your purple hells do you figure on swinging *that* load?"

"I am, as you know, a person of small ability," Nadreck replied in his usual circuitous fashion. "Also, I am of almost negligible mass and strength. Of what is known as bravery I have no trace—in fact, I have pondered long over that, to me, incomprehensible quality and have decided that it has no place in my scheme of existence. I have found it much more efficient to perform the necessary tasks in the easiest possible manner, which is usually by means of stealth, deceit, indirection and other cowardly artifices."

"Any of those, or all of them, would be QX with me," Kinnison assured him. "Anything goes, with gusto and glee, as far as the Eich are concerned. What I don't see is how we can put it across."

*

"Thought-screens interfered so seriously with my methods of procedure," the Palainian explained, "that I was forced to develop a means of puncturing them without upsetting their generators. The device is not generally known, as it is still in a very crude, experimental form; but it does function, in a meager, unsatisfactory way. Might I suggest that the four of you put on heated armor and come with me to my vessel in the hold? It will take some little time to transfer my apparatus and equipment to your speedster."

"Is it nonferrous—undetectable?" Kinnison asked.

"Of course," Nadreck replied in surprise. "I work, as I told you, by stealth. My vessel is, except for certain differences necessitated by racial considerations, a duplicate of your own."

"Why didn't you say so?" Kinnison wanted to know. "Why bother to move the gadget? Why not use your speedster?"

"Because I was not asked. We should not bother. The only reason for using your vessel is so that you will not suffer the discomfort of wearing armor," Nadreck replied, categorically.

"Cancel it, then," Kinnison directed. "You've been wearing armor all the time you were with us—turn about for a while will be QX. Better that way, anyway, as this is very definitely your party, not ours. Not?"

"As you say; and with your permission," Nadreck agreed. "Also it may very well be that you will be able to suggest improvements in my device whereby its efficiency may be increased."

"I doubt it." The Tellurian's already great respect for this retiring, soft-spoken, "cowardly" Lensman was increasing constantly. "But we would like to study it, and perhaps copy it, if you so allow."

"Gladly."

And so it was arranged.

The *Dauntless* crept among a black backgrounded pathway and stopped. Nadreck, Worsel and Kinnison—three were enough and neither Mac nor Tregonsee insisted upon going—boarded the Palainian speedster.

Away from the mother ship it sped upon muffled jets, and through the far-flung, heavily overlapped electromagnetic detector zones. Through the outer thought-screens. Then, ultra-slowly, as space speeds go, the speedster moved forward, feeling for whatever other blocking screens there might be.

All three of those Lensmen were in fact detectors themselves—their Arisian-imparted special senses made ethereal, even sub-ethereal, vibrations actually visible or tangible—but they did not depend only upon their bodily senses. That speedster carried instruments unknown to space pilotry, and the Lensmen used them unremittingly. When they came to a screen they opened it, so insidiously that its generating mechanisms gave no alarms. Even a meteorite screen, which was supposed to forbid the passage of any material object, yielded without protest to Nadreck's subtle manipulation.

Slowly, furtively, a perfectly absorptive black body sinking through blackness so intense as to be almost palpable, the Palainian speedster settled downward toward the Boskonian fortress of Lyrane VIII.

XIV.

This is perhaps as good a place as any to glance in passing at the fashion in which the planet Lonabar was brought under the aegis of Civilization. No attempt will or can be made to describe it in any detail, since any adequate treatment of it would fill a volume—indeed, many volumes have already been written concerning various phases of the matter—and since it is not strictly germane to the subject in hand. However, some knowledge of the modus operandi in such cases is highly desirable for the full understanding of this history, in view of the vast number of planets which Co-ordinator Kinnison and his associates did have to civilize before the Second Galaxy was made secure.

Scarcely had Cartiff-Kinnison moved out than the Patrol moved in. If Lonabar had been heavily fortified, a fleet of appropriate size and power would have cleared the way. As it was, the fleet which landed was one of transports, not of battleships, and all the fighting from then on was purely defensive.

Propagandists took the lead; psychologists; Lensmen skilled not only in languages but also in every art of human relationships. The case of Civilization was stated plainly and repeatedly, the errors and the fallacies of autocracy were pointed out. A nucleus of government was formed; not of Civilization's imports, but of solid Lonabarian citizens who had passed the Lensmen's tests of ability and trustworthiness.

Under this local government a pseudodemocracy began haltingly to function. At first its progress was painfully slow; but as more and more of the citizens perceived what the Patrol actually was doing, it grew apace. Not only did the invaders allow—yes, foster—free speech and statutory liberty; they suppressed ruthlessly any person or any faction seeking to build a new dictatorship, whatever its nature, upon the ruins of the old. *That* news traveled fast; and laboring always and mightily upon Civilization's side were the always-present, however deeply buried, urges of all intelligent entities toward self-expression.

There was opposition, of course. Practically all of those who had waxed fat upon the old order were very strongly in favor of its continuance. There were the hordes of the down-trodden who had so long and so dumbly endured oppression that they could not understand anything else; in whom the above-mentioned urges had been beaten and tortured almost out of existence. They themselves were not opposed to Civilization—for them it meant at worst only a change of masters—but those who sought by the same old wiles to re-enslave them were foes indeed.

Menjo Bleeko's sycophants and retainers were told to work or starve. The fat hogs could support the new order—or else. The thugs had to choose between honest co-operation with their fellow men and flitting to some zwilnik planet. Those who tried to prey upon and exploit the dumb masses were extirpated, one and all.

Little could be done, however, about the dumb themselves, for in them the spark was feeble indeed. The new government nursed that spark along, the while ruling them as definitely, although not as harshly, as had the old; the Lensmen backing the struggling young Civilization knowing full well that in the children or in the children's children of these unfortunates the spark would flame up into a great, white light.

It is seen that this government was not, and could not for many years become, a true democracy. It was in fact a benevolent semiautocracy; autonomous in a sense, yet controlled by the Galactic Council through its representatives, the Lensmen. It was, however, so infinitely more liberal than anything theretofore known by the Lonabarians as to be a political revelation, and since corruption, that cosmos-wide curse of democracy, was not allowed a first finger-hold, the principles of real democracy and of Civilization took deeper root year by year.

*

To get back into the beam of narrative, Nadreck's blackly indetectable speedster settled to ground far from the Boskonians' central dome; well beyond the far-flung screens. The Lensmen knew that no life existed outside that dome and they knew that no possible sense of perception could pierce those defenses. They did not know, however, what other resources of detection, of offense or of defense the foe might possess; hence the greatest possible distance at which they could work efficiently was the best distance.

"I realize that it is useless to caution any active mind not to think at all," Nadreck remarked as he began to manipulate various and sundry controls, "but you already know from the nature of our problem that any extraneous thought will wreak untold harm. For that reason I beg of you to keep your thought-screens up at all times, no matter what happens. It is, however, imperative that you be kept informed, since I may require aid or advice at any moment. To that end I ask you to hold these electrodes, which are connected to a receptor. Do not hesitate to speak freely to each other or to me; but please use only a spoken language, as I am averse even to Lensed thoughts at this juncture. Are we agreed? Are we ready?"

They were agreed and ready. Nadreck actuated his peculiar drill—a tube of force somewhat analogous to a Q-type helix except in that it operated within the frequency range of thought—and began to increase, by almost infinitesimal increments, its power. Nothing, apparently, happened; but finally the instruments upon the speedster's board registered the fact that it was through.

"This is none too safe, friends," the Palainian announced from one part of his multicompartmented brain, without distracting any part of his attention from the incredibly delicate operation he was performing. "Might I suggest, Kinnison, in my cowardly way, that you place yourself at the controls and be ready to take us away from this planet at speed and without notice?"

"I'll say you may!" and the Tellurian complied, with alacrity. "I'd a lot rather be a live coward than a dead hero!"

But through course after course of screen the hollow drill gnawed its cautious way without giving alarm; until at length there began to come through the interloping tunnel a vague impression of foreign thought. Nadreck stopped the helix, then advanced it by tiny steps until the thoughts came in coldly clear—the thoughts of the Eich going about their routine businesses. In the safety of their impregnably shielded dome the proudly self-confident monsters did not wear their personal thought-screens; which, for Civilization's sake, was just as well.

It had been decided previously that the mind they wanted would be that of a psychologist; hence the thought sent out by the Palainian was one which would appeal only to such a mind; in fact, one practically imperceptible to any other. It was extremely faint; wavering uncertainly upon the very threshold of perception. It was so vague, so formless, so inchoate that it required Kinnison's intensest concentration even to recognize it as a thought. Indeed, so starkly unhuman was Nadreck's mind and that of his proposed quarry that it was all the Tellurian Lensman could do to so recognize it. It dealt, fragmentarily and in the merest glimmerings, with the nature and the mechanisms of the First Cause; with the fundamental ego, its *raison d'être*, its causation, its motivation, its differentiation; with the stupendously awful concepts of the Prime Origin of all things ever to be.

Unhurried, monstrously patient, Nadreck neither raised the power of the thought nor hastened its slow tempo. Stolidly, for minute after long minute he held it, spraying it throughout the vast dome as mist is sprayed from an atomizer nozzle. And finally he got a bite. A mind seized upon that wistful, homeless, incipient thought; took it for its own. It strengthened it, enlarged upon it, built it up. And Nadreck followed it.

He did not force it; he did nothing whatever to cause any suspicion that the thought was or ever had been his. But as the mind of the Eich busied itself with that thought he all unknowingly let down the bars to Nadreck's invasion.

Then, perfectly in tune, the Palainian subtly insinuated into the mind of the Eich the mildly disturbing idea that he had forgotten something, or had neglected to do some trifling thing. This was the first really critical instant, for Nadreck had no idea whatever of what his victim's duties were or what he could have left undone. It had to be something which would take him out of the dome and toward the Patrolmen's concealed speedster, but what it was, the Eich would have to develop for himself: Nadreck could not dare to attempt even a partial control at this stage and at this distance.

THE LENSMAN

Kinnison clenched his teeth and held his breath, his big hands clutching fiercely the pilot's bars; Worsel unheedingly coiled his supple body into an ever smaller, ever harder and more compact bale.

"Ah!" Kinnison exhaled explosively. "It worked!" The psychologist, at Nadreck's impalpable suggestion, had finally thought of the thing. It was a thought-screen generator which had been giving a little trouble and which really should have been checked before this.

Calmly, with the mild self-satisfaction which comes of having successfully recalled to mind a highly elusive thought, the Eich opened one of the dome's unforcible doors and made his unconcerned way directly toward the waiting Lensmen; and as he approached, Nadreck stepped up by logarithmic increments the power of his hold.

"Get ready, please, to cut your screens and to synchronize with me in case anything slips and he tries to break away," Nadreck cautioned; but nothing slipped.

The Eich came up unseeing to the speedster's side and stopped. The drill disappeared. A thought-screen encompassed the group narrowly. Kinnison and Worsel released their screens and also tuned in to the creature's mind. And Kinnison swore briefly, for what they found was meager enough. It was well, however, that they got what they did when they did; for, as has been seen, even that little was very shortly thereafter to be removed.

He knew a great deal concerning the zwilnik doings of the First Galaxy; but so did the Lensmen; they were not interested in them. Neither were they interested, at the moment, in the files or in the records. Regarding the higher-ups, he knew of two, and only two, personalities. By means of an intergalactic communicator he received orders from, and reported to, a clearly defined, somewhat Eichlike entity known to him as Kandron; and vaguely, from occasional stray and unintentional thoughts of this Kandron, he had visualized as being somewhere in the background a human being named Alcon. He supposed that the planets upon which these persons lived were located in the Second Galaxy, but he was not certain, even of that. He had never seen either of them; he was pretty sure that none of his group ever would be allowed to see them. He had no means of tracing them and no desire whatsoever to do so. The only fact he really knew was that at irregular intervals Kandron got into communication with this base of the Eich.

That was all. Kinnison and Worsel let go and Nadreck, with a minute attention to detail which would be wearisome here, jockeyed the unsuspecting monster back into the dome. The native knew fully where he had been, and why. He had inspected the generator and had found it in good order. Every second of elapsed time was accounted for exactly. He had not the slightest inkling that anything out of the ordinary had happened to him or anywhere around him.

As carefully as the speedster had approached the planet, she departed from it. She rejoined the *Dauntless*, in whose control room Kinnison lined out a solid communicator beam to the Z9M9Z and to Port Admiral Haynes. He reported crisply, rapidly, everything that had transpired.

"So our best bet, chief, is for you and the Fleet to get out of here as fast as Klono will let you," he concluded. "Go straight out Rift 94, staying as far away as possible from both the spiral arm and the Galaxy proper. Unlimber every spotting screen you've got—put them to work along the line between Lyrane and the Second Galaxy. Plot all the punctures, extending the line as fast as you can. We'll join you at max and transfer to the Z9M9Z—her tank is just what the doctors ordered for the job we've got to do."

"Well, if you say so, I suppose that's the way it's got to be," Haynes grumbled. He had been growling and snorting under his breath ever since it had become evident what Kinnison's recommendation was to be. "I don't like this thing of standing by and letting zwilniks thumb their noses at us, like Prellin did on Bronseca. That once was once too damned often."

"Well, you got him, finally, you know," Kinnison reminded, quite cheerfully, "and you can have these Eich, too—sometime."

"I hope," Haynes acquiesced, something less than sweetly. "QX, then—but put out a few jets. The quicker you get out here the sooner we can get back and clean out this hooraw's nest."

Kinnison grinned as he cut his beam. He knew that it would be some time before the port admiral could hurl the metal of the Patrol against Lyrane VIII; but even he did not realize just how long a time it was to be.

What occasioned the delay was not the fact that the communicator was in operation only at intervals: so many screens were out, they were spaced so far apart, and the punctures were measured and aligned so accurately that the periods of non-operation caused little or no loss of time. Nor was it the vast distance involved; since, as has already been pointed out, the matter in the intergalactic void is so tenuous that spaceships are capable of enormously greater velocities than any attainable in the far denser medium filling interstellar space.

No; what gave the Boskonians of Lyrane VIII their greatly lengthened reprieve was simply the direction of the line established by the communicator-beam punctures. Reasoning from analogy, the Lensmen had supposed that it would lead them into a star cluster, fairly well away from the main body of the Galaxy in either the zenith or the nadir direction. Instead of that, however, when the Patrol surveyors got close enough to the Second Galaxy so that their cone of possible error was very small in comparison with the gigantic lens of the island universe which they were approaching, it became clear that their objective lay deep within the Galaxy itself. At least, the prolongation of their line led well into it, and that fact gave the Lensmen to pause.

*

"I don't like this line a bit, chief," Kinnison told the admiral then. "Maybe it runs into a cluster on this side, but we can't figure on it. It'd smell like Limburger to have a fleet of this size and power nosing into their home territory, along what must be one of the hottest lines of communication they've got."

"Check," Port Admiral Haynes agreed. "QX so far, but it would begin to stink pretty quick now. We've got to assume that they know about spotting screens, whether they really do or not. If they do, they'll have this line trapped from stem to gudgeon, and the minute they detect us they'll cut this line out entirely. Then where'll you be?"

"Right back where I started from—that's what I'm yapping about. And to make matters worse, it's a thousand to one that the ape we are looking for is not going to be anywhere near the end of this line."

"Huh? How do you dope that out?" Haynes demanded.

"Logic. We're getting up now to where these zwilniks can really think. You have already assumed that they know that we can trace their beam, and we know that they know about our detector nullifiers. Go further. Assume that they have deduced, from things we have already done, that we have ships—one or two, at least—that are inherently indetectable and almost perfectly absorptive. Where does that land you?"

"Hm-m-m. I see. Since they can't change the nature of the beam, they would run it through a series of relays, with each leg trapped with everything they could think of, and at the first sign of interference with any one of them they would switch to another, maybe halfway across the Galaxy. Also, they might very well move it around once in a while, anyway, just on general principles."

"Check. That's why you had better take the Fleet back home, leaving Nadreck and me to work the rest of this line with our speedsters."

"Don't be silly, son—I thought you could think"—and Haynes gazed quizzically at the younger man.

"What else? Where am I overlooking a bet?" Kinnison demanded.

"It is elementary tactics, young man," the admiral instructed, "to cover up any small, quiet operation with a large and noisy one. Thus, if I want to make an exploratory sortie in one sector I should always attack in force in another."

"But what would it get us?" Kinnison expostulated. "What's the advantage to be gained, to make up for the unavoidable losses?"

"Don't be dumb. Advantage? Listen!" Haynes' bushy gray hair fairly bristled in eagerness. "We've been on the defensive long enough. They must be weak, after their losses at Tellus; and now, before they can rebuild, is the time to strike. It's good tactics, as I said, to make a diversion to cover you up, but I want to do more than that. I think that we had better start an actual, serious invasion, right now. When you can swing it, the best possible defense—even in general—is a powerful offense, and we're all set to go. We will begin it with this fleet, and then, as soon as we are sure that they haven't got enough power to counter-invade, we will bring up everything we have except for some purely defensive stuff, such as sunbeams and so on, around Tellus and the other most important bases. We'll hit them so hard that they won't be able to worry about such a little thing as a communicator line."

"Hm-m-m. Never thought of it from that angle, but it'd be nice. We are coming over here sometime, anyway—why not now? I suppose that you'll start on the edge, or in a spiral arm, just as though you were going ahead with the conquest of the whole Galaxy?"

"Not 'just as though,'" Haynes declared. "We are going through with it. Find a planet on the outer edge of a spiral arm, as nearly like Tellus as possible—"

"Make it nearly enough like Tellus and maybe I can use it for our headquarters on this 'co-ordinator' thing." And Kinnison grinned.

"More truth than poetry in that, fellow. We find it and take it over. Comb out the zwilniks with a fine-tooth comb. Make it the biggest, toughest base the Universe ever saw—like Jarnevon, only more so. Bring in everything we've got and expand from that planet as a center, cleaning everything out as we go. We'll civilize 'em!"

And so, after considerable ultrarange communicator work, it was decided that the Galactic Patrol would forthwith assume the offensive.

*

Haynes assembled the Fleet. Then, while the two black speedsters kept unobtrusively on with the task of plotting the line, Civilization's mighty armada moved a few thousand parsecs aside and headed at normal touring blast for the nearest out-cropping of the Second Galaxy.

There was nothing of stealth in this maneuver, nothing of finesse, excepting in the arrangements of the units. First, far in the van, flew the prodigious, irregular cone of scout cruisers. They were comparatively small, not heavily armed or armored, but they were ultrafast and were provided with the most powerful detectors, spotters and locators known. They adhered to no rigid formation, but at the will of their individual commanders, under the direct supervision of Grand Fleet Operations in the Z9M9Z, flashed hither and thither ceaselessly—searching, investigating, mapping, reporting.

Backing them up came the light cruisers and the cruising bombers—a new type, this latter, designed primarily to bore in to close quarters and to hurl bombs of negative matter. Third in order were the heavy defensive cruisers. These ships had been developed specifically for hunting down Boskonian commerce raiders within the Galaxy. They wore practically an impenetrable screen, so that they could lock to and hold even a superdreadnought. They had never before been used in Grand Fleet formation; but since they were now equipped with tractor zones and bomb tubes, theoretical strategy found a good use for them in this particular place.

Next came the real war head—a solidly packed phalanx of maulers. All the ships up ahead had, although in varying degrees, freedom of motion and of action. The scouts had practically nothing else; fighting was not their business. They could fight, a little, if they had to; but they always ran away if they could, in whatever direction was most expedient at the time. The cruising bombers could either take their fighting or leave it alone, depending upon circumstances—in other words, they fought light cruisers, but ran away from big stuff, stinging as they ran. The heavy cruisers would fight anything short of a mauler, but never in formation: they always broke ranks and fought individual dog fights, ship-to-ship.

But that terrific spearhead of maulers had no freedom of motion whatever. It knew only one direction—straight ahead. It would swerve aside for an inert planet, but for nothing smaller; and when it swerved it did so as a whole, not by parts. Its function was to blast through—straight through—any possible opposition, if and when that opposition should have been successful in destroying or dispersing the screens of lesser vessels preceding it. A sunbeam was the only conceivable weapon with which that stolid, power-packed mass of metal could not cope; and, the Patrolmen devoutly hoped, the zwilniks didn't have any sunbeams—yet.

A similar formation of equally capable maulers, meeting it head-on, could break it up, of course. Theoretical results and war game solutions of this problem did not agree, either with each other or among themselves, and the thing had never been put to the trial of actual battle. Only one thing was certain—when and if that trial did come there was bound to be, as in the case of the fabled meeting of the irresistible force with the immovable object, a lot of very interesting by-products.

Flanking the maulers, streaming gracefully backward from their massed might in a parabolic cone, were arranged the heavy battleships and the superdreadnoughts; and directly behind the bulwark of flying fortresses, tucked away inside the protecting envelope of big battle wagons, floated the Z9M9Z—the brains of the whole outfit.

There were no free planets, no negaspheres of planetary antimass, no sunbeams. Such things were useful either in the defense of a Prime Base or for an all-out, ruthlessly destructive attack upon such a base. Those slow, cumbersome, supremely powerful weapons would come later, after the Patrol had selected the planet which they intended to hold against everything which the Boskonians could muster. This present expedition had as yet no planet to defend, it sought no planet to destroy. It was the vanguard of Civilization, seeking a suitable foothold in the Second Galaxy and thoroughly well equipped to argue with any force mobile enough to bar its way.

*

While it has been said that there was nothing of stealth in this approach to the Second Galaxy, it must not be thought that it was unduly blatant or obvious—any carelessness or ostentation would have been very poor tactics indeed. Civilization's Grand Fleet advanced in strict formation, with every routine military precaution. Its nullifiers were full on, every blocking screen was out, every plate upon every ship was hot and was being scanned by alert and keen-eyed observers.

But every staff officer from Port Admiral Haynes down, and practically every line officer as well, knew that the enemy would locate the invading fleet long before it reached even the outer fringes of the galaxy toward which it was speeding. That stupendous tonnage of ferrous metal could not be disguised; nor could it by any possible artifice be made to simulate any normal tenant of the space which it occupied.

The gigantic flares of the heavy stuff could not be baffled, and the combined grand flare of Grand Fleet made a celestial object which would certainly attract the electronic telescopes of plenty of observatories. And the nearest such 'scopes, instruments of incredible powers of resolution, would be able to pick them out, almost ship by ship, against the relatively brilliant background of their own flares.

The Patrolmen, however, did not care. This was, and was intended to be, an open, straightforward invasion; the first wave of an attack which would not cease until the Galactic Patrol had crushed Boskonia throughout the entire Second Galaxy.

Grand Fleet bored serenely on. Superbly confident in her awful might, grandly contemptuous of whatever she was to face, she stormed along; uncaring that at that very moment the foe was massing his every defensive arm to hurl her back or to blast her out of existence.

XV.

As Haynes and the Galactic Council had already surmised, Boskonia was now entirely upon the defensive. She had made her supreme bid in the effort which had failed so barely to overcome the defenses of hard-held Tellus. It was, as has been seen, a very near thing indeed, but the zwilnik chieftains did not and could not know that. Communication through the hyperspatial tube was impossible, no ordinary communicator beam could be driven through the Patrol's scramblers, no Boskonian observers could be stationed near enough to the scene of action to perceive or to record anything that had occurred, and no single zwilnik ship or entity survived to tell of how nearly Tellus had come to extinction.

And, in fine, it would have made no difference in the mind of Alcon of Thrale if he had known. A thing which was not a full success was a complete failure; to be almost a success meant nothing. The invasion of Tellus had failed. They had put everything they had into that gigantically climactic enterprise. They had shot the whole wad, and it had not been enough. They had, therefore, abandoned for the nonce humanity's galaxy entirely, to concentrate their every effort upon the rehabilitation of their own depleted forces and upon the design and construction of devices of hitherto unattempted capability and power.

But they simply had not had enough time to prepare properly to meet the invading Grand Fleet of Civilization. It takes time—lots of time—to build such heavy stuff as maulers and flying fortresses, and they had not been allowed to have it. They had plenty of lighter stuff, since the millions of Boskonian planets could furnish upon a few hours' notice more cruisers, and even more first-line battleships, than could possibly be used in Grand Fleet formation, but their backbone of brute force and firing power was woefully weak.

Since the destruction of a solid center of maulers was, theoretically, improbable to the point of virtual impossibility, neither Boskonia nor the Galactic Patrol had built up any large reserve of such structures. Both would now build up such a reserve as rapidly as possible, of course, but half-built structures could not fight.

The zwilniks had many dirigible planets, but they were *too* big. Planets, as has been seen, are too cumbersome and unwieldy for use against a highly mobile and adequately controlled fleet.

Conversely, humanity's Grand Fleet was up to its maximum strength and perfectly balanced. It had suffered staggering losses in the defense of Prime Base, it is true; but those losses were of comparatively light craft, which Civilization's inhabited worlds could replace as easily and as quickly as could Boskonia's. Very few maulers had been lost, and those empty places were filled by substitutes withdrawn from minor bases or other stations at which they were not imperatively necessary.

Hence, Boskonia's fleet was at a very serious disadvantage as it formed to defy humanity just outside the rim of its galaxy. At two disadvantages, really, for Boskonia then had neither Lensmen nor a Z9M9Z; and Haynes, canny old master strategist that he was, worked upon them both.

Grand Fleet so far had held to one right-line course, and upon this line the zwilnik defense had been built. Now Haynes swung aside, forcing the enemy to re-form—they had to engage him, he did not have to engage them. Then, as they shifted—raggedly, as he had supposed and had hoped that they would—he swung again. Again, and again; the formation of the enemy becoming more and more hopelessly confused with each shift.

The scouts had been reporting constantly; in the seven-hundred foot lenticular tank of the *Directrix* there was spread in exact detail the disposition of every unit of the foe. Four Rigellian Lensmen, now thoroughly trained and able to perform the task almost as routine, condensed the picture—summarized it—in Haynes' ten-foot tactical tank. And finally, so close that another swerve could not be made, and with the line of flight of his solid fighting core pointing straight through the loosely disorganized nucleus of the enemy, Haynes gave the word to engage.

The scouts, remaining free, flashed aside into their pre-arranged observing positions. Everything else went inert and bored ahead. The light cruisers and the cruising bombers clashed first, and a chill struck at Haynes' stout old heart as he learned that the enemy did have negative-matter bombs.

Upon that point there had been much discussion. One view was that the Boskonians would have them, since they had seen them in action and since their scientists were fully as capable as were those of Civilization. The other was that, since it had taken all the massed intellect of the Conference of Scientists to work out a method of handling and of propelling such bombs, and since the Boskonians were probably not as co-operative as were the civilized races, they could not have them.

Approximately half of the light cruisers of Grand Fleet were bombers. This was deliberate, for in the use of the new arm there were involved problems which theoretical strategy could not solve definitely. Theoretically, a bomber could defeat a conventional light cruiser of equal tonnage one hundred percent of the time, *provided*—here was the rub!—that the conventional cruiser did not blast her out of the ether before she could get her bombs into the vitals of the foe, in order to accommodate the new equipment, something of the old had to be decreased—something of power, of armament, of primary or secondary beams, or of defensive screen. Otherwise the size and mass must be so increased that the ship would no longer be a light cruiser, but a heavy one.

And the Patrol's psychologists had had ideas, based upon facts which they had gathered from Kinnison and from Illona and from various and sundry spools of tape—ideas by virtue of which it was eminently possible that the conventional light cruisers of Civilization, with their heavier screen and more and hotter beams, could vanquish the light cruisers of the foe, even though they should turn out to be negative-matter bombers.

Hence the fifty-fifty division of types; but, since Haynes was not thoroughly sold upon either the psychologists or their ideas, the commanders of his standard light cruisers had received very explicit and definite orders. If the Boskonians should have bombs and if the high-brows' ideas did not pan out, they were to turn tail and run, at maximum and without stopping to ask questions or to get additional instructions.

Haynes had not really believed that the enemy would have negabombs, they were so new and so atrociously difficult to handle. He wanted—but was unable—to believe implicitly in the psychologists' findings. Therefore, as soon as he saw what was happening, he abandoned his tank for a moment to seize a plate and get into full touch with the control room of one of the conventional light cruisers then going into action.

He watched it drive boldly toward a Boskonian vessel which was in the act of throwing bombs. He saw that the agile little vessel's tractor zone was out. He watched the bombs strike that zone and bounce. He watched the tractor men go to work and he saw the psychologists' idea bear splendid fruit. For what followed was a triumph, not of brute force and striking power, but of morale and manhood. The brain men had said, and it was now proved, that the Boskonian gunners, low class as they were and driven to their tasks like the slaves they were, would hesitate long enough before using tractor beams as pressors so that the Patrolmen could take their own bombs away from them!

For negative matter, it must be remembered, is the exact opposite of ordinary matter. It is built up of negative *mass*; in every equation of physics and mechanics where mass appears, a minus sign appears when negative matter is concerned. To it a pull is, or becomes, a push; the tractor beam which pulls ordinary matter toward its projector actually pushes negative matter away.

The "boys" of the Patrol knew that fact thoroughly. They knew all about what they were doing, and why. They were there because they wanted to be, as Illona had so astoundingly found out, and they worked with their officers, not because of them. With the Patrol's gun crews it was a race to see which crew could capture the first bomb and the most.

*

Aboard the Boskonian how different it was! There the dumb cattle had been told what to do, but not why. They did not know the fundamental mechanics of the bomb tubes they operated by rote, did not know that they were essentially tractor beam projectors. They did know, however, that tractor beams pulled things toward them; and when they were ordered to swing their ordinary tractors upon the bombs which the Patrolmen were so industriously taking away from them, they hesitated for seconds, even under the lash.

This hesitation was fatal. Haynes' gleeful gunners, staring through their special finders, were very much on their toes; seconds were enough. Their fierce-driven tractors seized the inimical bombs in midspace, and before the Boskonians could be made to act in the only possible opposition hurled them directly backward against the ship which had issued them. Ordinary defensive screen did not affect them; repulsor screen, meteorite and wall shields only sucked them inward the faster.

And ordinary matter and negative matter cannot exist in contact. In the instant of touching, one atom of negative matter and one of normal matter unite and disappear. One negabomb was enough to put any cruiser out of action, but here there were usually three or four at once. Sometimes as many as ten; enough, almost, to consume the total mass of a ship.

A bomb struck; ate in. Through solid armor it melted. Atmosphere rushed out, to disappear en route—for air is normal matter. Along beams and trusses the hellish hypersphere traveled freakishly, although usually in the direction of greatest mass. It clung, greedily. Down stanchions it flowed; leaving nothing in its wake, flooding all circumambient space with lethal emanations. Into and through converters. Into pressure tanks which blew up enthusiastically. Men's bodies it did not seem to favor—not massive enough, perhaps—but even them it did not refuse if offered. A Boskonian, gasping frantically for air which was no longer there and already half mad, went completely mad as he struck savagely at the thing and saw his hand and his arm to the shoulder vanish instantaneously, as though they had never been.

Satisfied, Haynes wrenched his attention back to his tank. Most of his light cruisers were through and in the clear; they were reporting by thousands. Losses were very small. The conventional-type cruisers had won either by using the enemies' own bombs, as he had seen them used, or by means of their heavier armor and armament. The bombers had won in almost every case; not by superior force, for in arms and equipment they were to all intents and purposes identical with their opponents, but because of their infinitely higher quality of personnel. To brief it, scarcely a handful of Boskonia's light cruisers were able to flee the fatal scene.

The heavy cruisers came up, broke formation, and went doggedly to work. They were the blockers. Each took one ship—a heavy cruiser or a battleship—out of the line, and held it out. It tried to demolish it with every weapon it could swing, but even if it could not vanquish its foe, it could and did hang on until some big bruiser of a battleship could come up and administer the *coup de grâce*.

And battleships and superdreadnoughts were coming up in the thousands and the myriads. All of them, in fact, but those enough to form a tight globe, packed screen to screen, around the Z9M9Z.

Slowly, ponderously, inert, the war head of maulers came crawling up. The maulers and fortresses of the Boskonians were hopelessly outnumbered and were badly scattered in position. Hence this meeting of the ultra-heavies was not really a battle at all, but a slaughter. Ten or more of Haynes' gigantic structures could concentrate their entire combined fire power upon any luckless one of the enemy; with what awful effect it would be superfluous to enlarge upon.

When the mighty fortresses had done their work they englobed the *Directrix*, enabling the guarding battleships to join their sister moppers-up; but there was very little left to do. Civilization had again triumphed; and, this time, at very little cost. Some of the pirates had escaped, of course; observers from afar might very well have had scanners and recorders upon the entire conflict; but, whatever of news was transmitted or how, Alcon of Thrale and Boskonia's other master minds would or could derive little indeed of comfort from the happenings of this important day.

"Well, that is that—for a while, at least, don't you think?" Haynes asked his Council of War.

It was decided that it was; that if Boskonia could not have mustered a heavier center for her defensive action here, she would be in no position to make any really important attack for months to come.

*

Grand Fleet, then, was reformed; this time into a purely defensive and exploratory formation. In the center, of course, was the Z9M9Z. Around her was a close-packed quadruple globe of maulers. Outside of them in order, came sphere after sphere of superdreadnoughts, of battleships, of heavy cruisers, and of light cruisers. Then, not in globe at all, but ranging far and wide, were the scouts. Into the edge of the nearest spiral arm of the Second Galaxy the stupendous formation advanced, and along it it proceeded at dead-slow blast—dead-slow, to enable the questing scouts to survey thoroughly each planet of every solar system as they came to it.

And finally an Earthlike planet was found. Several approximately Tellurian worlds had been previously discovered and listed as possibilities; but this one was so perfect that the search ended then and there. Apart from the shape of the continents and the fact that there was somewhat less land surface and a bit more salt water, it was practically identical with Tellus. As was to be expected, its people were human to the limit of classification. Entirely unexpectedly, however, the people of Klovia—which is as close as English can come to the native name—were not zwilniks. They had never heard of, nor had they ever been approached by, the Boskonians. Space travel was to them only a theoretical possibility, as was atomic energy.

They had no planetary organization, being still divided politically into sovereign states which were all too often at war with each other. In fact, a world war had just burned itself out, a war of such savagery that only a fraction of the world's population remained alive. There had been no victor, of course. All had lost everything—the survivors of each nation, ruined as they were and without either organization or equipment, were trying desperately to rebuild some semblance of what they had once had.

Upon learning these facts the psychologists of the Patrol breathed deep sighs of relief. This kind of thing was made to order; civilizing this planet would be simplicity itself. And it was. The Klovians did not have to be overawed by a show of superior force. Before this last, horribly internecine war, Klovia had been a heavily industrialized world, and as soon as the few remaining inhabitants realized what Civilization had to offer, that no one of their neighboring competitive states was to occupy a superior position, and that full, world-wide production was to be resumed as soon as was humanly possible, their relief and joy were immeasurable.

Thus the Patrol took over without difficulty. But they were, the Lensmen knew, working against time. As soon as the zwilniks could get enough heavy stuff built they would attack, grimly determined to blast Klovia and everything upon it out of space. Even though they had known nothing about the planet previously, it was idle to hope that they were still in ignorance either of its existence or of what was in general going on there.

Haynes' first care was to have the heaviest metalry of the Galactic Patrol—loose planets, sunbeams, fortresses, and the like—rushed across the void to Klovia at maximum. Then, as well as putting every employable of the new world to work, at higher wages than he had ever earned before, the Patrol imported millions upon millions of men, with their women and families, from hundreds of Earthlike planets in the First Galaxy.

They did not, however, come blindly. They came knowing that Klovia was to be primarily a military base, the most supremely powerful base that had ever been built.

They knew that it would bear the brunt of the most furious attacks that Boskone could possibly deliver; they knew full well that it might fall. Nevertheless, men and women, they came in their multitudes. They came with high courage and high determination, glorying in that which they were to do. People who could and did so glory were the only ones who came; which fact accounts in no small part for what Klovia is today.

People came, and worked, and stayed. Ships came, and trafficked. Trade and commerce increased tremendously. And further and further abroad, as there came into being upon that formerly almost derelict planet some seventy-odd gigantic defensive establishments, there crept out an ever-widening screen of scout ships, with all their high-powered feelers hotly outstretched.

*

Meanwhile Kinnison and frigid-blooded Nadreck had worked their line, leg by tortuous leg, to Onlo and thence to Thrale. A full spool should be devoted to that working alone; but, unfortunately, as space here must be limited to the barest essentials, it can scarcely be mentioned. As Kinnison and Haynes had foreseen, that line was heavily trapped. Luckily, however, it had not been moved so radically that the searchers could not rediscover it; the zwilniks were, as Haynes had promised, very busily engaged with other and more important matters. All of those traps were deadly, and many of them were ingenious indeed—so ingenious as to test to the utmost the "cowardly" Palainian's skill and mental scope. All, however, failed. The two Lensmen held to the line in spite of the pitfalls and followed it to the end. Nadreck stayed upon or near Onlo, to work in its frightful environment against the monsters to whom he was biologically so closely allied, while the Tellurian went on to Thrale, to try conclusions with that planet's physically human tyrant, Alcon.

Again he had to build up an unimpeachable identity and here there were no friendly thousands to help him do it. He had to get close—*really* close—to Alcon, without antagonizing him or in any way arousing his hair-trigger suspicions. Kinnison had studied that problem for days. Not one of his previously used artifices would work, even had he dared to repeat a procedure. Also, time was decidedly of the essence.

There was a way. It was not an easy way, but it was fast and, if it worked at all, it would work perfectly. Kinnison would not have risked it even a few months back, but now he was pretty sure that he had jets enough to swing it.

He needed a soldier of about his own size and shape—details were unimportant. The man should not be in Alcon's personal troops, but should be in a closely allied battalion, from which promotion into that select body would be logical. He should be relatively inconspicuous, yet with a record of accomplishment, or at least of initiative, which would square up with the rapid promotions which were to come.

The details of that man hunt are interesting, but not of any real importance here, since they did not vary in any essential from other searches which have been described at length. He found him—a lieutenant in the Royal Guard—and the ensuing mind study was as assiduous as it was insidious. In fact, the Lensman memorized practically every memory chain in the fellow's brain. Then the officer took his regular furlough and started for home—but he never got there.

Instead, it was Kimball Kinnison who wore the Thralian's gorgeous full-dress uniform and who greeted in exactly appropriate fashion the Thralian's acquaintances and lifelong friends. A few of these, who chanced to see the guardsman first, wondered briefly at his changed appearance or thought that he was a stranger. Very few, however, and very briefly; for the Lensman's sense of perception was tensely alert and his mind was strong. In moments, then, those chance few forgot that they had ever had the slightest doubt concerning this soldier's identity; they knew calmly and as a matter of fact that he was the Traska Gannel whom they had known so long.

Living minds presented no difficulty except for the fact that of course he could not get in touch with everyone who had ever known the real Gannel. However, he did his best. He covered plenty of ground and he got most of them—all that could really matter.

Written records, photographs, and tapes were something else again. He had called Worsel in on that problem long since, and the purely military records of the Royal Guards were QX before Gannel went on leave. Although somewhat tedious, that task had not proved particularly difficult. Upon a certain dark night a certain light circuit had gone dead, darkening many buildings. Only one or two sentries or guards had put their flashlights upon either Worsel or Kinnison, and they never afterward recalled having done so. And any record that has ever been made can be remade to order by the experts of the Secret Service of the Patrol!

*

And thus it was also with the earlier records. Gannel had been born in a hospital. QX—that hospital was visited, and thereafter Gannel's baby footprints were actually those of infant Kinnison. He had gone to certain schools—those schools' records also were made to conform to the new facts.

Little could be done, however, about pictures. No man can possibly remember how many times he has had his picture taken, or who has the negatives, or to whom he had given photographs, or in what papers, books, or other publications his likeness has appeared.

The older pictures, Kinnison decided, did not count. Even if the likenesses were good, he looked enough like Gannel so that the boy or the callow youth might just about as well have developed into something that would pass for Kinnison in a photograph as into the man which he actually did become. Where was the dividing line? The Lensman decided—or rather, the decision was forced upon him—that it was at his graduation from the military academy.

There had been an annual, in which volume appeared an individual picture, fairly large, of each member of the graduating class. About a thousand copies of the book had been issued, and now they were scattered all over space. Since it would be idle even to think of correcting them all, he could not correct any of them. Kinnison studied that picture for a long time. He didn't like it very well. The cub was just about grown up, and this photo looked considerably more like Gannel than it did like Kinnison. However, the expression was self-conscious, the pose strained—and, after all, people hardly ever looked at old annuals. He'd have to take a chance on that. Later poses—formal portraits, that is; snapshots could not be considered—would have to be fixed up.

Thus it came about that certain studios were raided very surreptitiously. Certain negatives were abstracted and were deftly re-retouched. Prints were made therefrom, and in several dozens of places in Gannel's home town, in albums and in frames, stealthy substitutions were made.

The furlough was about to expire. Kinnison had done everything that he could do. There were holes, of course—there couldn't help but be—but they were mighty small and, if he played his cards right, they would never show up. Just to be on the safe side, however, he'd have Worsel stick around for a couple of weeks or so, to watch developments and to patch up any weak spots that might develop. The Velantian's presence upon Thrale would not create any suspicion—there were lots of such folks flitting from planet to planet—and if anybody did get just a trifle suspicious of Worsel, it might be all the better.

So it was done, and Lieutenant Traska Gannel of the Royal Guard went back to duty.

XVI.

Nadreck, the furtive Palainian, had prepared as thoroughly in his own queerly underhanded fashion as had Kinnison in his bolder one. Nadreck was cowardly, in Earthly eyes, there can be no doubt of that; as cowardly as he was lazy—or at least, if not exactly lazy, highly averse to any unnecessary effort. To his race, however, those traits were eminently sensible; and those qualities did in fact underlie his prodigious record of accomplishment. Being so careful of his personal safety, he had lived long and would live longer; by doing everything in the easiest possible way he had conserved his resources. Why take chances with a highly valuable life? Why be so inefficient as to work hard in the performance of a task when it could always be done in some easy way?

Nadreck moved in upon Onlo, then, absolutely imperceptibly. His dark, cold, devious mind, so closely akin to those of the Onlonians, reached out, indetectably *en rapport* with theirs. He studied, dissected, analyzed and neutralized their defenses, one by one. Then, his ultra-black speedster securely hidden from their every prying mechanism and sense, although within easy working distance of the control dome itself, he snuggled down into his softly cushioned resting place and methodically, efficiently, he went to work.

Thus, when Alcon of Thrale next visited his monstrous henchmen, Nadreck flipped a switch and every thought of the zwilnik's conference went permanently on record.

"What have you done, Kandron, about the Lensman?" the Tyrant demanded in harsh tones. "What have you concluded?"

"We have done very little," the chief psychologist replied, coldly. "Beyond the liquidation of a few Lensmen—with nothing whatever to indicate that any of them had any leading part in our recent reverses—our agents have accomplished nothing.

"As to conclusions, I have been unable to draw any except the highly negative one that every Boskonian psychologist who has ever summed up the situation has, in some respect or other, been seriously in error."

"And only *you* are right!" Alcon sneered. "Why?"

"I am right only in that I admit my inability to draw any valid conclusions," Kandron replied, imperturbably. "The available data are too meager, too inconclusive, and above all, too contradictory to justify any positive statements. There is a possibility that there are two Lensmen who have been and are mainly responsible for what has happened. One of these, the lesser, may be—note well that I say 'may be,' not 'is'—a Tellurian or an Aldebaranian or some other definitely human being; the other and by far the more powerful one is apparently absolutely and entirely unknown, except by his works."

"Star A Star," Alcon declared.

"Call him so if you like," Kandron assented, flatly. "But this Star A Star is an operator. As the supposed Director of Lensmen he is merely a figment of the imagination."

"But this information came from the Lensman Morgan!" Alcon protested. "He was questioned under the drug of truth; he was tortured and all but slain; the Overlord of Delgon consumed all his life force except for the barest possible moiety!"

"How do you know all these things?" Kandron asked, unmoved. "Merely from the report of the Overlord and from the highly questionable testimony of one of the Eich, who was absent from the scene during all of the most important time?"

"You suspect, then, that—" Alcon broke off, shaken visibly.

"I do," the psychologist replied, dryly. "I suspect very strongly indeed that there is working against us a mind of a power and scope, but little inferior to my own. A mind able to overcome that of an Overlord; one able at least if unsuspected and hence unopposed, to deceive even the admittedly capable minds of the Eich. I suspect that the Lensman Morgan was, if he existed at all, merely a puppet. The Eich took him too easily by far. It is, therefore, eminently possible that he had no physical actuality of existence—"

"Oh, come, now! Don't be ridiculous!" Alcon snapped. "With all Boskone there as witnesses? Why, his hand and Lens remained!"

"Improbable, perhaps, I admit—but still eminently possible," Kandron insisted. "Admit for the moment that he was actual, and that he did lose a hand—but remember also that the hand and the Lens may very well have been brought along and left there as reassurances; we cannot be sure even that the Lens matched the hand. But admitting all this, I am still of the opinion that Lensman Morgan was not otherwise tortured, that he lost none of his vital force, that he and the unknown I have already referred to returned practically unharmed to their own galaxy. And not only did they return, they must have carried with them the information which was later used by the Patrol in the destruction of Jarnevon."

"Utterly preposterous!" Alcon snorted. "Tell me, if you can, upon what facts you have been able to base such fantastic opinions."

"Gladly," Kandron assented. "I have been able to come to no really valid conclusions, and it may very well be that your fresh viewpoint will enable us to succeed where I alone have failed. I will, therefore, summarize very briefly the data which seem to me most significant. Attend closely, please:

*

"For many years, as you know, everything progressed smoothly. Our first setback came when a Tellurian warship, manned by Tellurians and Valerians, succeeded in capturing almost intact one of the most modern and most powerful of our vessels. The Valerians may be excluded from consideration, in so far as mental ability is concerned. At least one

Tellurian escaped, in one of our own, supposedly derelict, vessels. This one, whom Helmuth thought of, and reported, as 'the' Lensman, eluding all pursuers, went to Velantia; upon which planet he so wrought as to steal bodily six of our ships sent there especially to hunt him down. In those ships he won his way back to Tellus in spite of everything Helmuth and his force could do.

"Then there were the two episodes of the Wheelmen of Aldebaran I. In the first one a Tellurian Lensman was defeated—possibly killed. In the second our base was destroyed—tracelessly. Note, however, that the base next above it in order was, so far as we know, not visited or harmed.

"There was the Boyssia affair, in which the human being Blakeslee did various unscheduled things. He was obviously under the control of some far more powerful mind; a mind which did not appear, then or ever.

"We jump then to this, our own galaxy—the sudden, inexplicable disappearance of the planet Medon.

"Back to theirs again—the disgraceful and closely connected debacles at Shingvors and Antigan. Traceless both, but again neither was followed up to any higher headquarters."

Nadreck grinned at that, if a Palainian can be said to grin. Those matters were purely his own. He had done what he had been requested to do—thoroughly—no following up had been either necessary or desirable.

"Then Radelix," Kandron's summary went concisely on. "The female agents, Bominger, the Kalonian observers—all wiped out. Was or was not some human Lensman to blame? Everyone, from Chester Q. Fordyce down to a certain laborer upon the docks, was suspected, but nothing definite could be learned.

"The senselessly mad crew of the 27L462P—Wynor—Grantlia. Again completely traceless. Reason obscure, and no known advantage gained, as this sequence also was dropped."

Nadreck pondered briefly over this material. He knew nothing of any such matters nor, he was pretty sure, did Kinnison. *The* Lensman apparently was getting credit for something that must have been accidental or wrought by some internal enemy. QX. He listened again:

"After the affair of Bronseca, in which so many Lensmen were engaged that particularization was impossible, and which again was not followed up, we jump to the Asteroid Euphrosyne, Miners' Nest, and Wild Bill Williams of Aldebaran II. If it was a coincidence that Bill Williams became William Williams and followed our line to Tressilia, it is a truly remarkable one—even though, supposedly, said Williams was so stupefied with drugs as to be incapable either of motion or perception.

"Jalte's headquarters was, apparently, missed. However, it must have been invaded—tracelessly—for it was the link between Tressilia and Jarnevon, and Jarnevon was found and was destroyed.

"Now, before we analyze the more recent events, what do you yourself deduce from the above facts?" Kandron asked.

While the Tyrant was cogitating, Nadreck indulged in a minor gloat. This psychologist, by means of impeccable logic and reasoning from definitely known facts, had arrived at *such* erroneous conclusions! However, Nadreck had to admit, his own performances and those in which Kinnison had acted indetectably, when added to those of some person or persons unknown, did make a really impressive total.

*

"You may be right," Alcon admitted finally. "At least two entirely different personalities and methods of operation. Two Lensmen are necessary to satisfy the above requirements—and, as far as we know, sufficient. One of the necessary two is a human being, the other an absolutely unknown. Cartiff was, of course, the human Lensman. A masterly piece of work, that—but, with the co-operation of the Patrol, both logical and fairly simple. This human being is always in evidence, yet is so cleverly concealed by his very obviousness that nobody ever considers him important enough to be worthy of a close scrutiny. Or—perhaps—"

"That is better," Kandron commented. "You are beginning to see why I was so careful in saying that the known Tellurian factor 'may be,' not 'is,' of any real importance."

"But he *must* be!" Alcon protested. "It was a human being who tried and executed our agent; Cartiff was a human being—to name only two."

"Of course," Kandron admitted half contemptuously. "But we have no proof whatever that any of those human beings actually did, of their own volition, any of the things for which they have been given credit. Thus, it is now almost certain that that widely advertised 'mind-ray machine' was simply a battery of spotlights—the man operating them may very well have done nothing else. Similarly, Cartiff may have been an ordinary gangster controlled by the Lensman—we may as well call him Star A Star as anything else—or a Lensman or some other member of the Patrol acting as a dummy to distract our attention from Star A Star, who himself did the real work, all unperceived."

"Proof?" the Tyrant snapped.

"No proof—merely a probability," the Onlonian stated flatly. "We *know*, however, definitely and for a fact—visiplates and long-range communicators cannot be hypnotized—that Blakeslee was one of Helmuth's own men. Also that he was the same man, both as a loyal Boskonian of very ordinary mental talents and as an enemy having a mental power which he as Blakeslee never did and never could possess."

"I see," Alcon thought deeply. "Very cogently put. Instead of there being two Lensmen, working sometimes together and sometimes separately, you think that there is only one really important mind and that this mind at times works with or through some Tellurian?"

"But not necessarily the same Tellurian—exactly. And there is nothing to give us any indication whatever as to Star A Star's real nature or race. We cannot even deduce whether or not he is an oxygen breather—and that is bad."

"Very bad," the Tyrant assented. "Star A Star, or Cartiff or both working together, found Lonabar. They learned of the Overlords, or at least of Lyrane II—"

"By sheer accident, if they learned it there at all, I am certain of that," Kandron insisted. "They did not get any information from Menjo Bleeko's mind; there was none there to get."

*

815

"Accident or not, what boots it?" Alcon impatiently brushed aside the psychologist's protests. "They found Bleeko and killed him. A raid upon the cavern of the Overlords upon Lyrane II followed immediately. From the reports sent by the Overlords to the Eich of Lyrane VIII we know that there were two Patrol ships involved. One, not definitely identified as Cartiff's, took no part in the real assault. The other, the superdreadnought *Dauntless*, did that alone. She was manned by Tellurians, Valerians, and at least one Velantian. Since they went to the trouble of taking the Overlords alive, we may take it for granted that they obtained from them all the information they possessed before they destroyed them and their cavern?"

"It is at least highly probable that they did so," Kandron admitted.

"We have, then, many questions and few answers," and the Tyrant strode up and down the dimly blue-lit room. "It would be idle, indeed, in view of the facts, to postulate that Lyrane II was left, as were some others, a dead end. Has Star A Star attempted Lyrane VIII? If not, why has he delayed? If so, did he succeed or fail in penetrating the defenses of the Eich? They swear that he did not, that he could not—"

"Of course," Kandron sneered. "But while asking questions, why not ask why the Patrol chose this particular time to invade our galaxy in such force as to wipe out our Grand Fleet? To establish themselves so strongly as to make it necessary for us of the High Command to devote our entire attention to the problem of dislodging them?"

"What!" Alcon exclaimed, then sobered quickly and thought for minutes. "You think, then, that—" His thoughts died away.

"I do so think," Kandron thought, glumly. "It is very decidedly possible—yes, perhaps even probable—that the Eich of Lyrane VIII were able to offer no more resistance to the penetration of Star A Star than was Jalte the Kalonian. That this massive thrust was timed to cover the insidious tracing of our lines of communication or whatever other leads the Lensman had been able to discover."

"But the traps—the alarms—the screens and zones!" Alcon exclaimed, manifestly jarred by this new and disquietingly keen thought.

"No alarm was tripped, as you know; no trap was sprung," Kandron replied, quietly. "The fact that we have not as yet been attacked here may or may not be significant. Not only is Onlo very strongly held, not only is it located in such a central position that their lines of communication would be untenable, but also—"

"Do you mean to admit *you* may have been invaded and searched—tracelessly?" Alcon fairly shrieked the thought.

"Certainly," the psychologist replied, coldly. "While I do not believe that it has been done, the possibility must be conceded. What we could do, we have done; but what science can do, science can circumvent. To finish my thought, it is a virtual certainty that it is not Onlo and I who are their prime objectives, but Thrale and you. Especially you."

"You may be right. You probably *are* right; but with no data whatever upon who or what Star A Star really is, with no tenable theory as to how he could have done what actually has been done, speculation is idle."

Upon this highly unsatisfactory note the interview closed. Alcon the Tyrant went back to Thrale; and as he entered his palace grounds he passed within forty inches of his

Nemesis. For Star A Star-Kinnison-Traska Gannel was, as Alcon himself so clearly said, rendered invisible and imperceptible by his own obviousness.

*

Although obvious, Kinnison was very busy indeed. As a lieutenant of Guardsmen, the officer in charge of a platoon whose duties were primarily upon the ground, he had very little choice of action. His immediate superior, the first lieutenant of the same company, was not much better off. The captain had more authority and scope, since he commanded aërial as well as ground forces. Then, disregarding side lines of comparative seniority, came the major, the colonel, and finally the general, who was in charge of all the regular armed forces of Thrale's capital city. Alcon's personal troops were, of course, a separate organization, but Kinnison was not interested in them—yet.

The major would be high enough, Kinnison decided. Big enough to have considerable authority and freedom of motion, and yet not important enough to attract undesirable attention.

The first lieutenant, a stodgy, strictly rule-of-thumb individual, did not count. He could step right over his head into the captaincy. The real Gannel had always, in true zwilnik fashion, hated his captain and had sought in devious ways to undermine him. The pseudo-Gannel despised the captain as well as hating him, and to the task of sapping he brought an ability enormously greater than any which the real Gannel had ever possessed.

Good Boskonian technique was to work upward by stealth and treachery, aided by a carefully built-up personal following of spies and agents. Gannel had already formed such a staff; had already selected the man who, in the natural course of events, would assassinate the first lieutenant. Kinnison retained Gannel's following, but changed subtly its methods of operation. He worked almost boldly. He himself criticized the captain severely, within the hearing of two men whom he knew to belong, body and soul, to his superior.

This brought quick results. He was summoned pre-emptorily to the captain's office; and, knowing that the company commander would not dare to have him assassinated there, he went. In that office there were a dozen people; it was evident that the captain intended this rebuke to be a warning to all upstarts, forever.

"Lieutenant Traska Gannel, I have had my eye upon you and your subversive activities for some time," the captain ordered. "Now, purely as a matter of form, and in accordance with Paragraph 5, Section 724 of General Regulations, you may offer whatever you have of explanation before I reduce you to the ranks for insubordination."

"I have a lot to say," Kinnison replied, coolly. "I don't know what your spies have reported, but to whatever it was I would like to add that having this meeting here as you are having it proves that you are as fat in the head as you are in the belly—"

"Silence! Seize him, men!" the captain commanded, fiercely. He was not really fat. He had only a scant inch of equatorial bulge; but that small surplusage was a sore point indeed. "Disarm him!"

"The first man to move dies in his tracks," Kinnison countered; his coldly venomous tone holding the troopers motionless. He wore two hand weapons more or less similar to

817

DeLameters, and now his hands rested lightly upon their butts. "I cannot be disarmed until after I have been disrated, as you know very well; and that will never happen. For, if you demote me, I will take an appeal, as is my right, to the colonel's court, and there I will prove that you are stupid, inefficient, cowardly, and unfit generally to command. You really are, and you know it. Your discipline is lax and full of favoritism; your rewards and punishments are assessed, not by logic, but by whim, passion, and personal bias. Any court that can be named would set you down into the ranks, where you belong, and would give me your place. If this is insubordination and if you want to make something out of it, you pussy-gutted, pusillanimous, brainless tub of lard, cut in your jets!"

The maligned officer half rose, white-knuckled hands gripping the arms of his chair, then sank back craftily. He realized now that he had blundered; he was in no position to face the rigorous investigation which Gannel's accusation would bring on. But there was a way out. This could now be made a purely personal matter, in which a duel would be *de rigueur*. And in Boskonian dueling the superior officer, not the challenged, had the choice of weapons. He was a master of the saber; he had outpointed Gannel regularly in the regimental games. Therefore he choked down his wrath and:

"These personal insults, gratuitous and false as they are, take the matter out of military channels," he declared smoothly. "Meet me, then, tomorrow, half an hour before sunset, in the Place of Swords. It will be with sabers."

"Accepted." Kinnison meticulously followed the ritual. "To first blood or to the death?" This question was superfluous—the stigma of the Lensman's epithets, delivered before such a large group, could not possibly be expunged by the mere letting of a little blood.

"To the death"—curtly.

"So be it, O Captain!" Kinnison saluted punctiliously, executed a snappy about-face, and marched stiffly out of the room.

QX. This was fine—strictly according to Hoyle. The captain was a swordsman, surely; but Kinnison was no slouch. He didn't think that he would have to use a thought beam to help him. He had had five years of intensive training. Quarterstaff, nightstick, club, knife, and dagger; foil, *épée*, rapier, saber, broadsword, scimitar, bayonet, what have you—with practically any nameable weapon any Lensman had to be as good as he was with fists and feet.

*

The Place of Swords was in fact a circular arena, surrounded by tiers of comfortably padded seats. It was thronged with uniforms, with civilian formal afternoon dress, and with modish gowns; for such duels as this were sporting events of the first magnitude.

To guard against such trickery as concealed armor, the contestants were almost naked. Each wore only silken trunks and a pair of low shoes, whose cross-ribbed, flexible composition soles could not be made to slip upon the corrugated surface of the corklike material of the arena's floor.

The colonel himself, as master of ceremonies, asked the usual perfunctory questions. No, reconciliation was impossible. No, the challenged would not apologize. No, the challenger's honor could not be satisfied with anything less than mortal combat. He then took two sabers from an orderly, measuring them to be sure that they were of precisely the same length. He tested each edge for keenness, from hilt to needle point, with an expert thumb. He pounded each hilt with a heavy testing club. Lastly, still in view of the spectators, he slipped a guard over each point and put his weight upon the blades. They bent alarmingly, but neither broke and both snapped back truly into shape. No spy or agent, everyone then knew, had tampered with either one of those beautiful weapons.

Removing the point guards, the colonel again inspected those slenderly lethal tips and handed one saber to each of the duelists. He held out a baton, horizontal and shoulder high. Gannel and the captain crossed their blades upon it. He snapped his stick away and the duel was on.

Kinnison fought in Gannel's fashion exactly; in his characteristic crouch and with his every mannerism. He was, however a trifle faster than Gannel had ever been—just enough faster so that by the exertion of everything he had of skill and finesse, he managed to make the zwilnik's blade meet steel instead of flesh during the first long five minutes of furious engagement. The guy was good, no doubt of that. His saber came writhing in, to disarm. Kinnison flicked his massive wrist. Steel slithered along steel; hilt clanged against heavy basket hilt. Two mighty right arms shot upward, straining to the limit. Breast to hard-ridged breast, left arms pressed against bulgingly corded backs, every taut muscle from floor-gripping feet up to powerful shoulders thrown into the effort, the battlers stood motionlessly *en tableau* for seconds.

The ape wasn't fat, at that, Kinnison realized then; he was as hard as cordwood underneath. Not fat enough, anyway, to be anybody's push-over; although he was probably not in good-enough shape to last very long—he could probably wear him down. He wondered fleetingly, if worse came to worst, whether he would use his mind or not. He didn't want to—but he might have to. Or would he, even then—*could* he? But he'd better snap out of it. He couldn't get anywhere with this body-check business; the zwilnik was fully as strong as he was.

They broke, and in the breaking Kinnison learned a brand-new cut. He sensed it coming, but he could not parry or avoid it entirely; and the crowd shrieked madly as the captain's point slashed into Gannel's trunks and a stream of crimson trickled down Gannel's left leg.

*

Stamp! Stamp! Cut, thrust, feint, slash and parry, the grim game went on. Again, in spite of all he could do, Kinnison was pinked; this time by a straight thrust aimed at his heart. He was falling away from it, though, so got only half an inch or so of the point in the fleshy part of his left shoulder. It bled spectacularly, however, and the throng yelled ragingly for the kill. Another—he never did know exactly how he got that one—in the calf of his right leg; and the bloodthirsty mob screamed still louder.

Then, the fine edge of the captain's terrific attack worn off, Kinnison was able to assume the offensive. He maneuvered his foe into an awkward position, swept his blade aside, and slashed viciously at the neck. But the Thralian was able partially to cover. He ducked frantically, even while his parrying blade was flashing up. Steel clanged, sparks flew; but the strength of the Lensman's arm could not be entirely denied. Instead of the whole head, however, Kinnison's razor-edged weapon snicked off only an ear and a lock of hair.

Again the spectators shrieked frenzied approval. They did not care whose blood was shed, so long as it *was* shed; and this duel, of two superb swordsmen so evenly matched, was the best they had seen for years. It was, and promised to keep on being, a splendidly gory show indeed.

Again and again the duelists engaged at their flashing top speed; once again each drew blood before the colonel's whistle shrilled.

Time out for repairs: to have either of the contestants bleed to death, or even to the point of weakness, was no part of the code. The captain had outpointed the lieutenant, four to two, just as he always did in the tournaments; but he now derived very little comfort from the score. He was weakening, and knew it, while Gannel's arm seemed as strong and as rock-steady as it had been at the bout's beginning. Kinnison also knew these facts.

Surgeons gave hasty but effective treatment, new and perfect sabers replaced the badly nicked weapons, the ghastly thing went on. The captain tired slowly but surely; Gannel took, more and more openly and more and more savagely, the offensive.

When it was over Kinnison flipped his saber dexterously, so that its point struck deep into the softly resilient floor beside that which had once been his captain. Then, while the hilt swung back and forth in slow arcs, he faced one segment of the now satiated throng and crisply saluted the colonel.

"Sir, I trust that I have won honorably the right to be examined for fitness to become the captain of my company?" he asked, formally; and:

"You have, sir," the colonel as formally replied.

XVII.

Kinnison's wounds, being superficial, healed rapidly. He passed the examination handily. He should have; since, although it was rigorous and comprehensive, Traska Gannel himself could have passed it and Kinnison, as well as knowing practically everything that the Thralian had ever learned, had his own vast store of knowledge upon which to draw. Also, if necessary, he could have read the answers from the minds of the examiners.

As a captain, the real Gannel would have been a hard and brilliant commander, noticeable even among the select group of tried and fire-polished veterans who officered the Guards. Hence Kinnison became so; in fact, considerably more so than most. He was harsh, he was relentless and inflexible; but he was absolutely fair. He did not punish a given breach of discipline with twenty lashes one time and with a mere reprimand the next; fifteen honest, scarring strokes it became for each and every time, whoever the offender. Whatever punishment a man deserved by the book he got, promptly and mercilessly; whatever reward was earned was bestowed with equal celerity, accompanied by a crisply accurate statement of the facts in each case, at the daily parade review.

His men hated him, of course. His noncoms and lieutenants, besides hating him, kept on trying to cut him down. All, however, respected him and obeyed him without delay and without question, which was all that any Boskonian officer could expect and which was far more than most of them ever got.

Having thus consolidated his position, Kinnison went blithely to work to undermine and to supplant the major. Since Alcon, like all dictators everywhere, was in constant fear of treachery and of revolution, war games were an almost constant form of drill. The general himself planned and various officers executed the mock attacks, by space, air, and land; the Royal Guards and Alcon's personal troops, heavily outnumbered, always constituted the defense. An elaborate system of scoring had been worked out long since, by means of which the staff officers could study in detail every weak point that could be demonstrated.

"Captain Gannel, you will have to hold Passes 25, 26, and 27," the obviously worried major told Kinnison, the evening before a particularly important sham battle was to take place.

The Lensman was not surprised. He himself had insinuated the idea into his superior's mind. Moreover, he already knew, from an intensive job of spying, that his major was to be in charge of the defense, and that the colonel, who was to direct the attacking forces, had decided to route his main column through Pass 27.

"Very well, sir," Kinnison acknowledged. "I wish to protest formally, however, against those orders. It is manifestly impossible, sir, to hold all three of those passes with two platoons of infantry and one squadron of speedsters. May I offer a suggestion—"

"You may not," the major snapped. "We have deduced that the real attack is coming from the north, and that any activity in your section will be merely a feint. Orders are orders, captain!"

"Yes, sir," Kinnison replied, meekly, and signed for the thick sheaf of orders which stated in detail exactly what he was to do.

*

The next evening, after Kinnison had won the battle by disregarding every order he had been given, he was summoned to the meeting of the staff. He had expected that, too, but he was not at all certain of how it was coming out. It was in some trepidation, therefore, that he entered the lair of the big brass hats.

"Har-rumph!" he was greeted by the adjutant. "You have been called—"

"I know why I was called," Kinnison interrupted, brusquely. "Before we go into that, however, I wish to prefer charges before the general against Major Delios of stupidity, incompetence, and inefficiency."

Sheer astonishment resounded throughout the room in a ringing silence, broken finally by the general.

"Those are serious charges indeed, Captain Gannel; but you may state your case."

"Thank you, sir. First, stupidity: He did not perceive, at even as late a time as noon, when he took all my air away from me to meet the feint from the north, that the attack was not to follow any orthodox pattern. Second, incompetence. The orders he gave me could not possibly have stopped any serious attack through any one of the passes I was supposed to defend. Third, inefficiency: No efficient commander refuses to listen to suggestions from his officers, as he refused to listen to me last night."

"Your side, major?" And the staff officers listened to a defense based upon blind, dumb obedience to orders.

"We will take this matter under advisement," the general announced then. "Now, captain, what made you suspect that the colonel was coming through Pass 27?"

"I didn't," Kinnison replied, mendaciously. "To reach any one of those passes, however, he would have to come down this valley"—tracing it with his forefinger upon the map. "Therefore I held my whole force back here at Hill 562, knowing that, warned by my air of his approach, I could reach any one of the passes before he could."

"Ah. Then, when your air was sent elsewhere?"

"I commandeered a flitter—my own, by the way, and sent it up so high as to be indetectable. I then ordered motorcycle scouts out, for the enemy to capture; to make the commander of any possible attacking or reconnaissance force think that I was blind."

"Ah—smart work. And then?"

"As soon as my scout reported troop movements in the valley, I got my men ready to roll. When it became certain that Pass 27 was the objective, I rushed everything I had into preselected positions commanding every foot of that pass. Then, when the colonel walked into the trap, I wiped out most of his main column. However, I had a theoretical loss of three-quarters of my men in doing it"—bitterly. "If I had been directing the defense, I would have wiped out the colonel's entire force, ground and air both, with a loss of less than two percent."

This was strong talk. "Do you realize, Captain Gannel, that this is sheer insubordination?" the general demanded. "That you are in effect accusing me also of stupidity in planning and in ordering such an attack?"

"Not at all, sir," Kinnison replied instantly. "It was quite evident, sir, that you did it deliberately, to show all of us junior officers the importance of thought. To show us that, while unorthodox attacks may possibly be made by unskilled tacticians, any such attack is of necessity fatally weak if it be opposed by good tactics. In other words, that orthodox strategy is the only really good strategy. Was not that it, sir?"

Whether it was or not, that viewpoint gave the general an out, and he was not slow in taking advantage of it. He decided then and there, and the always subservient staff agreed with him, that Major Delios had indeed been stupid, incompetent, and inefficient; and Captain Gannel forthwith became Major Gannel.

*

Then the Lensman took it easy. He wangled and phenagled various and sundry promotions and replacements, until he was once more surrounded by a thoroughly subsidized personal staff and in good position to go to work upon the colonel. Then, however, instead of doing so, he violated another Boskonian precedent by having a frank talk with the man whom normally he should have been trying to displace.

"You have found out that you can't kill me, colonel," he told his superior, after making sure that the room was really shielded. "Also that I can quite possibly kill you. You know that I know more than you do—that all my life, while you other fellows were helling around, I have been working and learning—and that I can, in a fairly short time, take your job away from you without killing you. However, I don't want it."

"You don't *want* it!" The colonel stared, narrow-eyed. "What *do* you want, then?" He knew, of course, that Gannel wanted something.

"Your help," Kinnison admitted, candidly. "I want to get onto Alcon's personal staff, as adviser. With my experience and training, I figure that there's more in it for me there than here in the Guards. Here's my proposition—if I help you, by showing you how to work out your field problems and in general building you up however I can instead of tearing you down, will you use your great influence with the general and Prime Minister Fossten to have me transferred to the Household?"

"Will I? I'll say I will!" the colonel agreed, with fervor. He did not add "if I cannot kill you first"—that was understood.

And Kinnison did build the colonel up. He taught him things about the military business which that staff officer had never even suspected; he sounded depths of strategy theretofore completely unknown to the zwilnik. And the more Kinnison taught him, the more eager the colonel became to get rid of him. He had been suspicious and only reluctantly co-operative at first; but as soon as he realized that he could not kill his tutor and that if the latter stayed in the Guards it would be only a matter of days—at most of weeks—until Gannel would force himself into the colonelcy by sheer force of merit, he pulled in earnest every wire that he could reach.

Before the actual transfer could be effected, however, Kinnison received a call from Nadreck.

"Excuse me, please, for troubling you," the Palainian apologized, "but there has been a development in which you may perhaps be interested. This Kandron has been given orders by Alcon to traverse a hyperspatial tube, the terminus of which will appear at co-ordinates 217-493-28 at hour eleven of the seventh Thralian day from the present."

"Fine business! And you want to chase him, huh?" Kinnison jumped at the conclusion. "Sure—go ahead. I'll meet you there. I'll fake up some kind of an excuse to get away from here and we'll run him ragged—"

"I do not," Nadreck interrupted, decisively. "If I leave my work here, it will all come undone. Besides, it would be dangerous—and foolhardy. Not knowing what lies at the other end of that tube, we could make no plans and could have no assurance of safety, or even of success. You should not go, either—that is unthinkable. I am reporting this matter in view of the possibility that you may think it significant enough to warrant the sending of some observer whose life is of little or no importance."

"Oh . . . uh-huh . . . I see. Thanks, Nadreck." Kinnison did not allow any trace of his real thought to go out before he broke the line. Then:

"Funny ape, Nadreck," he cogitated, as he called Haynes. "I don't get his angle at all—I simply can't figure him out. Haynes? Kinnison"—and he reported in full.

"The *Dauntless* has all the necessary generators and equipment, and the place is far enough out so that she can make the approach without any trouble," the Lensman concluded. "We'll burn whatever is at the other end of that tube clear out of the ether. Send along as many of the old gang as you can spare. Wish we had time to get Cardynge—he'll howl like a wolf at being left out—but we've got only a week—"

"Cardynge is here," Haynes broke in. "He has been working out some stuff for Thorndyke on the sunbeam. He is finished now, though, and will undoubtedly want to go along."

"Fine!"

And explicit arrangements for the rendezvous were made.

*

It was not unduly difficult for Kinnison to make his absence from duty logical, even necessary. Scouts and observers reported inexplicable interferences with certain communications lines. With thoughts of *the* Lensman suffusing the minds of the higher-ups, and because of Gannel's already demonstrated prowess and keenness, he scarcely had to signify a willingness to investigate the phenomena in order to be directed to do so.

Nor did he pick a crew of his own sycophants. Instead, he chose the five highest-ranking privates of the battalion to accompany him upon this supposedly extremely dangerous mission; apparently completely unaware two of them belonged to the colonel, two to the general, and one to the captain who had taken his place.

The colonel wished Major Gannel good luck, verbally, even while hoping fervently that *the* Lensman would make cold meat of him in a hurry; and Kinnison gravely gave his well-wisher thanks as he set out. He did not, however, go near any communications lines; although his spying crew did not realize the fact. They did not realize anything; they did not know even that they became unconscious within five minutes after leaving Thrale.

They remained unconscious while the speedster in which they were was drawn into the *Dauntless'* capacious hold. In the Patrol ship's sick bay, under expert care, they remained unconscious during the entire duration of their stay on board.

The Patrol pilots picked up Kandron's flying vessel with little difficulty; and, nullifiers full out, followed it easily. When the zwilnik ship slowed down to feel for the vortex, the *Dauntless* slowed also, and baffled her driving jets as she sneaked up to the very edge of electrodetector range. When the objective disappeared from three-dimensional space the point of vanishment was marked precisely, and up to that point the Patrol ship flashed in seconds.

The regular driving blasts were cut off, the special generators were cut in. Then, as the force fields of the ship reacted against those of the Boskonian "shore" station, the Patrolmen felt again in all their gruesome power the appallingly horrible sensation of interdimensional acceleration. For that sensation is, literally, indescribable. A man in good training can overcome seasickness, airsickness, and spacesickness. He can overcome the nausea and accustom himself to the queasily terrifying endless-fall sensation of weightlessness. He can, and does, become so inured to as to regard as perfectly normal the outrages to the sensibilities incident to inertialessness in its crudest forms. No man has, however, been able to get used to interdimensional acceleration.

It is best likened to a compression; not as a whole, but atom by atom. A man feels as though he were being twisted—cork-screwed in some monstrously obscure fashion which permits him neither to move from his place nor to remain where he is. It is a painless but utterly revolting transformation, progressing in a series of waves; a rearrangement, a writhing, crawling distortion, an incomprehensibly impossible extrusion of each ultimate particle of his substance in an unknowable, ordinarily nonexistent direction.

*

The period of acceleration over, the *Dauntless* traveled at uniform velocity along whatever course it was that the tube took and the men, although highly uncomfortable and uneasy, could once more move about and work. Sir Austin Cardynge in particular was actually happy and eager as he flitted from one to another of the automatic recording instruments upon his special panel. He resembled more closely than ever a lean, gray tomcat, Kinnison thought—he almost expected to see him begin to lick his whiskers and pur.

"You see, my ignorant young friend"—the scientist almost did pur as one of the recording pens swung widely across the ruled paper—"it is as I told you—the lack of exact data upon even one tiny factor of this extremely complex phenomenon is calamitous. While my notes were apparently complete and were certainly accurate, our experimental tubes did not function perfectly. The time factor was irreconcilable—completely so, in every aspect, even that of departure from and return to normal space—and it is unthinkable that time, one of the fundamental units, is or can be intrinsically variable—"

"You think so?" Kinnison broke in. "Look at that"—pointing to the ultimate of timepieces, Cardynge's own triplex chronometer. "No. 1 says that we have been in this tube for an hour, No. 2 says a little over nine minutes, and according to No. 3 we won't be starting for twenty minutes yet—it must be running backward—let's see you comb *that* out of your whiskers!"

"Oh-h . . . ah . . . a-hum." But only momentarily was Sir Austin taken aback. "Ah, I was right all the time!" he cackled gleefully. "I thought it practically impossible for me to commit an error or to overlook any possibilities, and I have now proved that I did not. Time, in this hyperspatial region or condition, *is* intrinsically variable, in major degree!"

"And what does that get you?" Kinnison asked, pointedly.

"Much, my impetuous youngster, much," Cardynge replied. "We observe, we note facts. From the observations and facts we theorize and we deduce; thus arriving very shortly at the true inwardness of time."

"You hope," the Lensman snorted, dubiously; and in his skepticism he was right and Sir Austin was wrong. For the actual nature and mechanism of time remained, and still constitute, a mystery, or at least an unsolved problem. The Arisians—perhaps—understand time; no other race does.

To some of the men, then, and to some of the clocks and other time-measuring devices, the time seemed—or actually was?—very long; to other and similar beings and mechanisms it seemed—or was—short. Short or long, however, the *Dauntless* did not reach the Boskonian end of the hyperspatial tube.

*

In midflight there came a crunching, twisting *cloonk!* and an abrupt reversal of the inexplicably horrible interdimensional acceleration—a deceleration as sickeningly disturbing, both physically and mentally, as the acceleration had been.

825

While within the confines of the hyperspatial tube every eye of the *Dauntless* had been blind. To every beam upon every frequency, visible or invisible, ether-borne or carried upon the infinitely faster waves of the sub-ether, the murk was impenetrable. Every plate showed the same mind-numbing blankness; a vague, eerily shifting, quasi-solid blanket of formless, textureless grayness. No lightness or darkness, no stars or constellations or nebulae, no friendly, deep-space blackness—nothing.

Deceleration ceased; the men felt again the wonted homeliness and comfort of normal pseudoinertia. Simultaneously the gray smear of the visiplates faded away into commonplace areas of jetty black, pierced the brilliantly dimensionless varicolored points of light which were the familiar stars of their own familiar space.

But were they familiar? Was that our galaxy, or anything like it? They were not. It was not. Kinnison stared into his plate, aghast.

He would not have been surprised to have emerged into three-dimensional space anywhere within the Second Galaxy. In that case, he would have seen a Milky Way; and from its shape, apparent size, and texture he could have oriented himself fairly closely in a few minutes. But the *Dauntless* was not within any lenticular galaxy—nowhere was there any sign of a Milky Way!

He would not have been really surprised to have found himself and his ship out in open intergalactic space. In that case he would have seen a great deal of dead-black emptiness, blotched with a hundred or so lenticular bodies which were in fact galaxies. Orientation would then have been more difficult; but, with the aid of the Patrol charts, it could have been accomplished. But here there were no galaxies—no nebulae of any kind!

XVIII.

Here, upon the background of a blackness so intense as to be obviously barren of nebular material, there lay a multitude of blazingly resplendent stars—and nothing except stars. A few hundred were of a visual magnitude of about minus three. Approximately the same number were of minus two or thereabouts, and so on down; but there did not seem to be a star or other celestial object in that starkly incredible sky of an apparent magnitude greater than about plus four.

"What do you make of this, Sir Austin?" Kinnison asked, quietly. "It's got me stopped like a traffic light."

The mathematician ran toward him and the Lensman stared. He had never known Cardynge to hurry—in fact, he was not really running now. He was walking, even though his legs were fairly twinkling in their rapidity of motion. As he approached Kinnison his mad pace gradually slowed to normal.

"Oh—time must be cockeyed here, too," the Lensman observed. "Look over there—see how fast those fellows are moving, and how slow those others over that way are?"

"Ah, yes. Interesting—intensely interesting. Truly, a most remarkable and intriguing phenomenon," the fascinated mathematician enthused.

"But that wasn't what I meant. Swing this plate—it's on visual—around outside, so as to get the star aspect and distribution. What do you think of it?"

"Peculiar—I might almost say unique," the scientist concluded, after his survey. "Not at all like any normal configuration or arrangement with which I am familiar. We could perhaps speculate, but would it not be preferable to secure data first? Say by approaching a solar system and conducting systematic investigations?"

"Uh-huh"—and again Kinnison stared at the wispy little physicist in surprise. Here was a *man*! "You're certainly something to tie to, ace, do you know it?" he asked, admiringly. Then, as Cardynge gazed at him questioningly, incomprehendingly:

"Skip it. Can you hear me, Henderson?"

"Yes—just barely."

"Shoot us across to one of those nearer stars, stop, and go inert."

"QX, chief." The pilot obeyed.

And in the instant of inerting, the visiplate into which the two men stared went blank. The thousands of stars studding the sky a moment before had disappeared as though they had never been.

"Why . . . . What . . . . How in all the yellow hells of space can *that* happen?" Kinnison blurted.

Without a word, Cardynge reached out and snapped the plate's receiver over from "visual" to "ultra," whereupon the stars reappeared as suddenly as they had vanished.

"Something's screwy somewhere!" the Lensman protested. "We *can't* have an inert velocity greater than that of light—it's impossible!"

"Few things, if any, can be said definitely to be impossible; and everything is relative, not absolute," the old scientist declared, pompously. "This space, for instance. You have not yet perceived, I see, even that you are not in the same three-dimensional space in which we have heretofore existed."

Kinnison gulped. He was going to protest about that, too, but in the face of Cardynge's unperturbed acceptance of the fact he did not quite dare to say what he had in mind.

"That is better," the old man declaimed. "Do not get excited—to do so dulls the mind. Take nothing for granted, do not jump at conclusions—to commit either of those errors will operate powerfully against success. Working hypotheses, young man, must be based upon accurately determined facts; not upon mere guesses, superstitions, or the figments of personal prejudices."

"Bub-bub-but . . . QX—skip it!" Nine-tenths of the *Dauntless'* crew would have gone out of control at the impact of the knowledge of what had happened; even Kinnison's powerful mind was shaken. Cardynge, however, was—not seemed to be, but actually was—as calm and as self-contained as though he were in his own quiet study. "Explain it to me, will you please, in words of as nearly one syllable as possible?"

"Our looser thinkers have for centuries speculated upon the possibility of an entire series of different spaces existing simultaneously, side by side in a hypothetical hypercontinuum. I have never indulged in such time-wasting; but now that actual corroborative data have become available, I regard it as a highly fruitful field of investigation. Two extremely significant facts have already become apparent; the variability of time and the non-applicability of our so-called 'laws' of motion. Different spaces, different laws, it would seem."

"But when we cut our generators in that other tube we emerged into our own space," Kinnison argued. "How do you account for that?"

"I do not as yet try to account for it!" Cardynge snapped. "Two very evident possibilities should already be apparent, even to your feeble brain. One, that at the moment of release your vessel happened to be situated within a fold of our own space. Two, that the collapse of the ship's force fields always returns it to its original space, while the collapse of those of the shore station always forces it into some other space. In the latter case, it would be reasonable to suppose that the persons or beings at the other end of the tube may have suspected that we were following Kandron, and, as soon as he landed, cut off their forces deliberately to throw us out of space. They may even have learned that persons of lesser ability, so treated, never return. Do not allow yourself to be at all impressed by any of these possibilities, however, as the truth may very well lie in something altogether different. Bear it in mind that we have as yet very little data upon which to formulate any theories, and that the truth can be revealed only by a very careful, accurate, and thorough investigation. Please note also that I would surely have discovered and evaluated all these unknowns during the course of my as yet incomplete study of our own hyperspatial tubes; that I am merely continuing here a research in which I have already made noteworthy progress."

Kinnison really gasped at that—the guy was certainly terrific! He called the chief pilot. "Go free, Hen, and start flitting for a planet—we've got to sit down somewhere before we can start back home. When you find one, land free. Stay free, and watch your Bergs—I don't have to tell you what will happen if they quit on us."

Then Thorndyke. "Verne? Break out some personal neutralizers. We've got a job of building to do—inertialess"—and he explained to both men in flashing thoughts what had happened and what they had to do.

"You grasp the basic idea, Kinnison," Cardynge approved, "that it is necessary to construct a station apart from the vessel in which we propose to return to our normal environment. You err grievously, however, in your insistence upon the necessity of discovering a planet, satellite, asteroid, or other similar celestial body upon which to build it."

"Huh?" Kinnison demanded.

"It is eminently possible—yes, even practicable—for us to use the *Dauntless* as an anchorage for the tube and for us to return in the lifeboats," Cardynge pointed out.

"What? Abandon this ship? Waste all that time rebuilding all the boats?"

"It is preferable, of course, and more expeditious, to find a planet, if possible," the scientist conceded. "However, it is plain that it is in no sense necessary. Your reasoning is fallacious, your phraseology is deplorable. I am correcting you in the admittedly faint hope of teaching you scientific accuracy of thought and of statement."

"Wow! Wottaman!" Kinnison breathed to himself, as, heroically, he "skipped it."

*

Somewhat to Kinnison's surprise—he had more than half expected that planets would be nonexistent in that space—the pilots did find a solid world upon which to land. It was a peculiar planet indeed. It did not move right, it did not look right, it did not feel right.

It was waterless, airless, desolate; a senseless jumble of jagged fragments, mostly metallic. It was neither hot nor cold—indeed, it seemed to have no temperature of its own at all. There was nothing whatever right about it, Kinnison declared.

"Oh, yes, there is!" Thorndyke contradicted. "Time is constant here, whatever its absolute rate may be, these metals are nice to work with, and some of this other stuff will make insulation. Or hadn't you thought of that? Which would be faster, cutting down an intrinsic velocity of fifteen lights to zero or building the projector out of native materials? And if you match intrinsics, what will happen when you hit our normal space again?"

"Plenty, probably . . . uh-huh, faster to use the stuff that belongs here. Careful, though, fella!"

And care was indeed necessary; extreme care that not a particle of matter from the ship was used in the construction and that not a particle of the planet's substance by any mischance got aboard the spaceship.

The actual work was simple enough. Cardynge knew exactly what had to be done. Thorndyke knew exactly how to do it, as he had built precisely similar generators for the experimental tubes upon Tellus. He had a staff of experts; the *Dauntless* carried a machine shop and equipment second to none. Raw material was abundant, and it was an easy matter to block out an inertialess room within which the projectors and motors were built. And, after they were built, they worked.

It was not the work, then, but the strain which wore Kinnison down. The constant, wearing strain of incessant vigilance to be sure that the Bergenholms and the small units of the personal neutralizers did not falter for a single instant. He did not lose a man, but again and again there flashed into his mind the ghastly picture of one of his boys colliding with the solid metal of the planet at a relative velocity fifteen times that of light! The strain of the endless checking and rechecking to make certain that there was no exchange of material, however slight, between the ship and the planet.

Above all, the strain of knowing a thing which, apparently, no one else suspected: that Cardynge, with all his mathematical knowledge, was not going to be able to find his way back! He had never spoken of this to the scientist. He did not have to. He knew that without a knowledge of the fundamental distinguishing characteristics of our normal space—a knowledge even less to be expected than that a fish should know the fundamental equations and structure of water—they never could, save by sheerest accident, return to their own space. And as Cardynge grew more and more tensely, unsocially immersed in his utterly insoluble problem, the more and more uneasy the Gray Lensman became. But this last difficulty was resolved first, and in a totally unexpected fashion.

*

"Ah, Kinnison of Tellus, here you are—I have been considering your case for some twenty-nine of your seconds," a deep, well-remembered voice resounded within his brain.

"Mentor!" he exclaimed, and at the sheer shock of his relief he came very near indeed to fainting. "Thank Klono and Noshabkeming you found us! How did you do it? How do we get ourselves out of here?"

"Finding you was elementary," the Arisian replied, calmly. "Since you were not in your own environment you must be elsewhere. If my mind had been really competent, I would have foreseen this event in detail. Even though I did not so foresee it, however, it required but little thought to perceive that it was a logical, in fact, an inevitable, development. Such being the case, it needed very little additional effort to determine what had happened, and how, and why; likewise precisely where you must now be. As for departure therefrom, your mechanical preparations are both correct and adequate. I could give you the necessary knowledge, but it is rather technically specialized and not negligible in amount; and since your brain is of very limited capacity, it is better not to fill any part of it with mathematics for which you will have no subsequent use. Put yourself *en rapport*, therefore, with Sir Austin Cardynge. I will follow."

He did so, and as mind met mind there ensued a conversation whose barest essentials Kinnison could not even dimly grasp. For Cardynge, as has been said, could think in the universal language of mathematics; in the esoteric symbology which very few minds have ever been able even partially to master. The Lensman did not get it, nor any part of it; he knew only that in that to him completely meaningless gibberish the Arisian was describing to the physicist, exactly and fully, the distinguishing characteristics of a vast number of parallel and simultaneously coexistent spaces.

If that was "rather" technical stuff, the awed Lensman wondered, what would really deep stuff be like? Not that he wanted to find out! No wonder these mathematical wizards were nuts—went off the beam—he'd be pure squirrel food if he had half that stuff in *his* skull!

But Sir Austin took to it like a cat lapping up cream or doing away with the canary. He brightened visibly; he swelled; and, when the Arisian had withdrawn from his mind, he preened himself and swaggered as he made meticulous adjustments of the delicate meters and controls which the technicians had already built.

Preparations complete, Cardynge threw in the switches and everything belonging to the *Dauntless* was rushed aboard. The neutralizers, worn so long and cherished so assiduously, were taken off with profound sighs of relief. The vessel was briefly, tentatively inerted. QX—no faster-than-light meteorites tore volatilizingly through her mass. So far, so good.

Then the ship's generators were energized and smoothly, effortlessly the big battle wagon took the interdimensional plunge. There came the expected, but nevertheless almost unendurable acceleration; the imperceptible, unloggable flight through the drably featureless grayness; the horrible deceleration. Stars flashed beautifully upon the plates.

"We made it!" Kinnison shouted in relief when he had assured himself that they had emerged into "real" space inside the Second Galaxy, only a few parsecs away from their point of departure. "By Klono's golden grin, Sir Austin, you figured it to a red whisker! And when the Society meets, Tuesday week, won't you just blast that ape Weingarde to a cinder! Hot dog!"

"Having the basic data, the solution and the application followed of necessity—automatically—uniquely," the scientist said, austerely. He was highly pleased with himself, he was tremendously flattered by the Lensman's ebullient praise; but not for anything conceivable would he have so admitted.

"Well, the first thing we had better do is to find out what time of what day it is," Kinnison went on, as he directed a beam to the Patrol headquarters upon Klovia.

"Better ask 'em the year, too," Henderson put in, pessimistically—he had missed Illona poignantly—but it was not that bad.

In fact, it was not bad at all; they had been gone only a little over a week of Thralian time. This finding pleased Kinnison immensely, as he had been more than half afraid that it had been a month. He could explain a week easily enough, but anything over two weeks would have been tough to handle.

The supplies of the Thralian speedster were adjusted to fit the actual elapsed time, and Worsel and Kinnison engraved upon the minds of the five unconscious Guardsmen completely detailed—even though equally completely fictitious—memories of what they and Major Gannel had done since leaving Thrale. Their memories were not exactly alike, of course—each man had had different duties and experiences, and no two observers see precisely the same things even while watching the same event—but they were very convincing. Also, and fortunately, not even the slightest scars were left by the operations, for in these cases no memory chain had to be broken at any point.

*

The *Dauntless* blasted off for Klovia; the speedster started for Thrale. Kinnison's crew woke up—without having any inkling that they had ever been unconscious or that their knowledge of recent events did not jibe exactly with the actual occurrences—and resumed work.

Immediately upon landing, Kinnison turned in a full official report of the mission, giving himself neither too much nor too little credit for what had been accomplished. They had found a Patrol sneak-boat near Line 11. They had chased it so many parsecs, upon such-and-such a course, before forcing it to engage. They had crippled it and boarded, bringing away material, described as follows, which had been turned over to Space Intelligence. And so on. It would hold, Kinnison knew; and it would be corroborated fully by the ultraprivate reports which his men would make to their real bosses.

The colonel made good; hence with due pomp and ceremony Major Traska Gannel was inducted into the Household. He was given one of the spy-ray-screened cigarette boxes in which Alcon's most trusted officers were allowed to carry their private, secret insignia. Kinnison was glad to get that—he could carry his Lens with him now, if the thing was really ray proof, instead of leaving it buried in a can outside the city limits.

The Lensman went to his first meeting of the Advisory Cabinet with his mind set on a hair trigger. He hadn't been around Alcon very much, but he knew that the Tyrant had a stronger mind shield than any untreated human being had any right to have. He'd have to play this mighty close to his chest—he didn't want any zwilnik reading his mind, yet he didn't want to create suspicion by revealing the fact that he, too, had an impenetrable block.

As he approached the cabinet chamber he walked into a zone of hypnosis, and practically bounced. He threw up his head: it was all he could do to keep his barriers down. It was general, he knew, not aimed specifically at him—to fight the hypnotist would be to call attention to himself as the only man able either to detect his work or to resist him; would give the whole show away. Therefore he let the thing take hold—with reservations—of his mind. He studied it. He analyzed it. Sight only, eh? QX—he'd let Alcon have superficial control, and he wouldn't put too much faith in anything he saw.

He entered the room; and, during the preliminaries, he reached out delicately, to touch imperceptibly mind after mind. All the ordinary officers were on the level; now he'd see about the prime minister. He'd heard a lot about this Fossten, but had never met him before—he'd see what the guy really had on the ball.

He did not find out, however. He did not even touch his mind, for that worthy also had an automatic block; a block as effective as Alcon's or as Kinnison's own.

Sight was unreliable; how about the sense of perception? He tried it, very daintily and gingerly, upon Alcon's feet, legs, arms, and torso. Alcon was real, and present in the flesh. Then the premier—and he yanked his sense back, canceled it, appalled. Perception was blocked, at exactly what his eyes told him was the fellow's skin!

That tore it—that busted it wide open. What in all the nine iridescent hells did that mean? He didn't know of anything except a thought-screen that could stop a sense of perception. He thought intensely. Alcon's mind was bad enough. It had been treated, certainly; mind shields like that didn't grow naturally on human or near-human beings. Maybe the Eich, or the race of super-Eich to which Kandron belonged, could give mental treatments of that kind. Fossten, though, was worse.

Alcon's boss! Probably not a man at all. It was he, it was clear, and not Alcon, who was putting out the zone of compulsion. An Eich, maybe? No, he was a warm-blooded oxygen breather; a frigid-blooded super-big-shot would make Alcon come to him. A monster, almost certainly, though; possibly of a type Kinnison had never seen before. Working by remote control? Possibly; but probably he was smaller than a man and was actually inside the dummy that everybody thought was the prime minister—that was it, for all the tea in China—

*

"And what do you think, Major Gannel?" the prime minister asked, smoothly, insinuating his mind into Kinnison's as he spoke.

Kinnison, who knew that they had been discussing an invasion of the First Galaxy, hesitated as though in thought. He was thinking, too, and ultracarefully. If that ape was out to do a job of digging he'd never dig again—QX, he was just checking Gannel's real thoughts against what he was going to say.

"Since I am such a newcomer to this Council I do not feel as though my opinions should be given too much weight," Kinnison said—and thought—slowly, with the exactly correct amount of obsequiousness. "However, I have a very decided opinion upon the matter. I believe very firmly that it would be better tactics to consolidate our position here in our own galaxy first."

"You advise, then, against any immediate action against Tellus?" the prime minister asked. "Why?"

"I do, definitely. It seems to me that shortsighted, half-prepared measures, based upon careless haste, were the underlying causes of our recent reverses. Time is not an important factor—the Great Plan was worked out, not in terms of days or of years, but of centuries and millennia—and it seems self-evident that we should make ourselves impregnably secure, then expand slowly; seeing to it that we can hold, against everything that the Patrol can bring to bear, every planet that we take."

"Do you realize that you are criticizing the chiefs of staff who are in complete charge of military operations?" Alcon asked, venomously.

"Fully," the Lensman replied coldly. "I ventured this opinion because I was asked specifically for it. The chiefs of staff failed, did they not? If they had succeeded, criticism would have been neither appropriate nor forthcoming. As it is, I do not believe that mere criticism of their conduct, abilities, and tactics is sufficient. They should be disciplined and demoted. New chiefs should be chosen; persons abler and more efficient than the present incumbents."

This was a bomb shell. Dissentions waxed rife and raucous, but amidst the turmoil the Lensman received from the prime minister a flash of coldly congratulatory approval.

And as Major Traska Gannel made his way back to his quarters two things were starkly plain:

First, he would have to cut Alcon down and himself become the Tyrant of Thrale. It was unthinkable to attack or to destroy this planet. It had too many too promising leads—there were too many things that didn't make sense—above all, there were the stupendous files of information which no one mind could scan in a lifetime.

Second, if he wanted to keep on living he would have to keep his detector shoved out to maximum—this prime minister was just about as touchy and just about as safe to play with as a hundred kilograms of dry nitrogen iodide!

XIX.

Nadreck, the Palainian Lensman, had not exaggerated in saying that he could not leave his job, that his work would come undone if he did.

As has been intimated, Nadreck was cowardly and lazy and characterized otherwise by traits not usually regarded by humankind as being noble. He was, however, efficient; and he was now engaged in one of the most colossal tasks ever attempted by any one Lensman. Characteristically, he had told no one, not even Haynes or Kinnison, what it was that he was trying to do—he never talked about a job until after it was done, and his talking then was usually limited to a taped, Lensman's-sealed, tersely factual report. He was "investigating" Onlo; that was all that anybody knew.

Onlo was at that time perhaps the most heavily fortified planet in the Universe. Compared to its massed might Jarnevon was weak; Tellus, except for its sunbeams and its other open-space safeguards, a joke. Onlo's defenses were all, or nearly all, planetary; Kandron's strategy, unlike Haynes', was to let any attacking force get almost down to the ground and then blast it out of existence.

THE LENSMAN

Thus Onlo was in effect one tremendously armed, titanically powered fortress; not one cubic foot of its poisonous atmosphere was out of range of projectors theoretically capable of puncturing any defensive screen possible of mounting upon a mobile base.

And Nadreck, the cowardly, the self-effacing, the apologetic, had tackled Onlo—alone!

Using the technique which has already been described in connection with his highly successful raid upon the Eich stronghold of Lyrane VIII, he made his way through the Onlonian defensive screens and settled down comfortably near one of the gigantic domes. Then, as though time were of no consequence whatever, he proceeded to get acquainted with the personnel. He learned the identifying symbol of each entity and analyzed every one psychologically, mentally, intellectually, and emotionally. He tabulated his results upon the Palainian equivalent of index cards, then very carefully arranged the cards into groups.

In the same fashion he visited and took the census of dome after dome. No one knew that he had been near, apparently he had done nothing; but in each dome as he left it there had been sown seeds of discord and of strife which, at a carefully calculated future time, would yield bitter fruit indeed.

For every mind has some weakness, each intellect some trait of which it does not care to boast, each Achilles his heel. That is true even of Gray Lensmen—and the Onlonians, with their heredity and environment of Boskonianism, were in no sense material from which Lensmen could be made.

Subtly, then, and coldly and callously, Nadreck worked upon the basest passions, the most ignoble traits of that far-from-noble race. Jealousy, suspicion, fear, greed, revenge—quality by quality he grouped them, and to each group he sent series after series of horridly stimulating thoughts.

Jealousy, always rife, assumed fantastic proportions. Molehills became mountains overnight. A passing word became a studied insult. No one aired his grievances, however, for always and everywhere there was fear—fear of discipline, fear of reprisal, fear of betrayal, fear of the double cross. Each monster brooded, sullenly intense. Each became bitterly, gallingly, hatingly aware of an unwarranted and intolerable persecution. Not much of a spark would be necessary to touch off such explosive material as that!

Nadreck left the headquarters dome until the last. In one sense it was the hardest of all; in another the easiest. It was hard in that the entities there had stronger minds than those of lower station; minds better disciplined, minds more accustomed to straight thinking and to logical reasoning. It was easy, however, in that those minds were practically all at war already—fighting either to tear down the one above or to resist the attacks of those below. On the whole, therefore, the headquarters dome was relatively easy, since every mind in it already hated, or feared, or distrusted, or was suspicious of or jealous of some other.

*

And while Nadreck labored thus deviously his wonders to perform, Kinnison went ahead in his much more conventional and straightforward fashion upon Thrale. His first care, of course, was to surround himself with the usual coterie of spies and courtiers.

The selection of this group gave Kinnison many minutes of serious thought. It was natural enough that he had not been able to place any of his own men in the secret service of Alcon or the prime minister, since they both had minds of power. It would not be natural, however, for either of them not to be able to get an agent into his. For to be too good would be to invite a mental investigation which he simply could not as yet permit. He would have to play dumb enough so that his hitherto unsuspected powers of mind would remain unsuspected.

He could, however, do much. Since he knew who the spies were, he was able quite frequently to have his more trusted henchmen discover evidence against them, branding them for what they were. Assassinations were then, of course, very much in order. And even a strong suspicion, even though it could not be documented, was grounds for a duel.

In this fashion, then, Kinnison built up his entourage and kept it reasonably free from subversive elements; and, peculiarly enough, those elements never happened to learn anything which the Lensman did not want them to know.

Building up a strong personal organization was now easy, for at last Kinnison was a real Boskonian big shot. As a major of the Household he was a power to be toadied to and fawned upon. As a personal adviser to Alcon the Tyrant he was one whose ill will should be avoided at all costs. As a tactician who had so boldly, and yet so altruistically, put the skids under the chiefs of staff, thereby becoming a favorite even of the dreaded prime minister, he was marked plainly as a climber to whose coat tails it would be wise to cling. In short, Kinnison made good in a big—it might almost be said in a stupendous—way.

With such powers at work the time of reckoning could not be delayed for long. Alcon knew that Gannel was working against him; learned very quickly, since he knew exactly the personnel of Kinnison's "private" secret service and could read at will any of their minds, that Gannel held most of the trumps. The Tyrant had tried many times to read the major's mind, but the latter, by some subterfuge or other, had always managed to elude his inquisitor without making an issue of the matter. Now, however, Alcon drove in a solid questing beam which, he was grimly determined, would produce results of one kind or another.

It did: but, unfortunately for the Thralian, they were nothing which he could use. For Kinnison, instead either of allowing the Tyrant to read his whole mind or of throwing up an all-too-revealing barricade, fell back upon the sheer native power of will which had made him unique in his generation. He concentrated upon an all-inclusive negation; which in effect was a rather satisfactory block and which was entirely natural.

"I don't know what you are trying to do, Alcon," he informed his superior, stiffly, "but whatever it is I do not like it. I think that you are trying to hypnotize me. If you are, know now that you cannot do it; that no possible hypnotic force can overcome my definitely and positively opposed will."

"Major Gannel, you will—" the Tyrant began, then stopped. He was not quite ready yet to come openly to grips with this would-be usurper. Besides, it was now plain that Gannel had only an ordinary mind. He had not even suspected all the prying that had occurred previously. He had not recognized even this last powerful thrust for what it really was; he had merely felt it vaguely and had supposed that it was an attempt at hypnotism!

A few more days and he would cut him down. Hence Alcon changed his tone and went on smoothly, "It is not hypnotism, Major Gannel, but a sort of telepathy which you cannot understand. It is, however, necessary; for in the case of a man occupying such a high position as yours, it is self-evident that we can permit no secrets whatever to be withheld from us—that we can allow no mental reservations of any kind. You see the justice and the necessity of that, do you not?"

Kinnison did. He saw as well that Alcon was being superhumanly forbearing. Moreover, he knew what the Tyrant was covering up so carefully—the real reason for this highly unusual tolerance.

"I suppose you are right; but I *still* don't like it," Gannel grumbled. Then, without either denying or acceding to Alcon's right of mental search, he went to his own quarters.

*

And there—or thereabouts—Kinnison wrought diligently at a thing which had been long in the making. He had known all along that his retinue would be useless against Alcon, hence he had built up an organization entirely separate from, and completely unknown to any member of, his visible following. Nor was this really secret outfit composed of spies or sycophants. Instead, its members were hard, able, thoroughly proven men, each one carefully selected for the ability and the desire to take the place of one of Alcon's present department heads. One at a time he put himself en *rapport* with them; gave them certain definite orders and instructions.

Then he put on a mechanical thought-screen. Its use could not make the prime minister any more suspicious than he already was, and it was the only way he could remain in character. This screen was, like those of Lonabar, decidedly pervious in that it had an open slit. Unlike Bleeko's, however, which had their slits set upon a fixed frequency, the open channel of this one could be varied, both in width and in wave length, to any setting which Kinnison desired.

Thus equipped, Kinnison attended the meeting of the Council of Advisers, and to say that he disrupted the meeting is no exaggeration. The other advisers perceived nothing out of the ordinary, of course, but both Alcon and the prime minister were so perturbed that the session was cut very short indeed. The other members were dismissed summarily, with no attempt at explanation. The Tyrant was raging, furious; the premier was alertly, watchfully intent.

"I did not expect any more physical privacy than I have been granted," Kinnison grated, after listening quietly to a minute or two of Alcon's unbridled language. "This thing of being spied upon continuously, both by men and by mechanisms, while it is insulting and revolting to any real man's self-respect, can—just barely—be borne. I find it impossible, however, to force myself to submit to such an ultimately degrading humiliation as the surrender of the only vestiges of privacy I have remaining; those of my mind. I will resign from the Council if you wish, I will resume my status as an officer of the line, but I cannot and will not tolerate your extinction of the last spark of my self-respect," he finished, stubbornly.

"Resign? Resume? Do you think that I will let you off *that* easily, fool?" Alcon sneered. "Don't you realize what I am going to do to you? That, were it not for the fact that I am going to watch you die slowly and hideously, I would have you blasted where you stand?"

"I do not, no, and neither do you," Gannel answered, as quietly as surprisingly. "If you were sure of your ability, you would be doing something instead of talking about it." He saluted, turned, and walked out.

Now the prime minister, as has been intimated, was considerably more than he appeared upon the surface to be. He was in fact the power behind the throne. His, not Alcon's, was the voice of authority, although he worked so subtly that the Tyrant himself never did realize that he was little better than a figurehead.

Therefore, as Gannel departed, the premier thought briefly but cogently. This major was smart—too smart. He was too able, he knew too much. His advancement had been just a trifle too rapid. That thought-screen was an entirely unexpected development. The mind behind it was not quite right, either—a glimpse through the slit had revealed a flash of something that might be taken to indicate that Major Gannel had an ability which ordinary Thralians did not have. This open defiance of the Tyrant of Thrale did not ring exactly true—it was not quite in character. If it had been a bluff, it was too good—much too good. If it had not been a bluff, where was his support? How could Gannel have grown so powerful without his, Fossten's, knowledge?

If Major Gannel were bona fide, all well and good. Boskonia needed the strongest possible leaders, and if any other man showed himself superior to Alcon, Alcon should and would die. However, there was a bare possibility that—Was Gannel bona fide? That point should be cleared up without delay. And the prime minister, after a quizzical, searching, more than half contemptuous inspection of the furiously discomfited Tyrant, followed the rebellious, the contumacious, the enigmatic Gannel to his rooms.

He knocked and was admitted. A preliminary and entirely meaningless conversation occurred. Then:

"Just when did you leave Eddore?" the visitor demanded.

"What do you want to know for?" Kinnison shot back. That question didn't mean a thing to him. Maybe it didn't to the big fellow, either—it could be just a catch—but he didn't intend to give any kind of an analyzable reply to any question that this ape asked him.

Nor did he, through thirty minutes of viciously skillful verbal fencing. That conversation was far from meaningless, but it was entirely unproductive of results; and it was a baffled, intensely thoughtful Fossten who at its conclusion left Gannel's quarters. From those quarters he went to the Hall of Records, where he requisitioned the major's dossier. Then to his own private laboratory, where he applied to those records every test known to the scientists of his ultrasuspicious race.

*

The photographs were right in every detail. The prints agreed exactly with those he himself had secured from the subject not twenty-four hours since. The typing was right. The ink was right. Everything checked. And why not? Ink, paper, fiber, and film were in fact exactly what they should have been. There had been no erasures, no alterations.

Everything had been aged to the precisely correct number of days. For Kinnison had known that this check-up was coming, and the experts of the Patrol would make no such crass errors as those.

Even though he had found exactly what he had expected to find, the suspicions of the prime minister were intensified rather than allayed. Besides his own, there were two unreadable minds upon Thrale, where there should have been only one. He knew how Alcon's had been treated—could Gannel's possibly be a natural phenomenon? If not, who had treated it, and why?

He left the palace then, ostensibly to attend a function at the military academy. There, too, everything checked. He visited the town in which Gannel had been born—finding no irregularities whatever in the records of the birth. He went to the city in which Gannel had lived for the greater part of his life; where he assured himself that school records, club records, even photographs and negatives, all dead-centered the beam.

He studied the minds of six different persons who had known Gannel from childhood. As one they agreed that the Traska Gannel who was now Traska Gannel was in fact the real Traska Gannel, and could not by any possibility be anyone else. He examined their memory tracks minutely for scars, breaks, or other evidences of surgery; finding none. In fact, none existed, for the therapists who had performed those operations had gone back clear to the very beginnings, to the earliest memories of the Gannel child.

In spite of the fact that all the data thus far investigated were so precisely what they should have been—or because of it—the prime minister was now morally certain that Gannel was, in some fashion or other, completely spurious. Should he go further, delve into unimportant but perhaps highly revealing side issues? It would be useless, he decided. The mind or minds who had falsified those records so flawlessly—if they had in fact been falsified—had done a beautiful piece of work: as masterly a job as he himself could have done. He himself would have left no traces; neither, in all probability, had they.

Who, then, and why? This was no ordinary plot, no part of any ordinary scheme to overthrow Alcon. It was bigger, deeper, far more sinister. Nothing so elaborate and efficient originating upon Thrale could possibly have been developed and executed without his knowledge and at least his tacit consent. Was there behind this thing someone who knew who and what he was and who was seeking his life and his place? Highly improbable. No—it must be—it *was*—the Patrol!

His mind flashed to Star A Star, reviewing everything that had been ascribed to that mysterious personage. Then something clicked—in fact, it stuck out.

BLAKESLEE!

This was much finer than the Blakeslee affair, of course; more subtle and more polished by far. It was not nearly as obvious, as blatant, but the basic similarity was nevertheless there. Could this similarity have been accidental? No—unthinkable. In this undertaking accidents could be ruled out—definitely. Whatever had been done had been done deliberately and after meticulous preparation.

But Star A Star *never* repeated. Therefore, this time, he *had* repeated; deliberately, to throw Alcon and his psychologists off the trail. But he, Fossten, was not to be deceived by even such clever tactics.

Gannel was, then, really Gannel, just as Blakeslee had really been Blakeslee. Blakeslee had obviously been under control. Here, however, there were two possibilities. First, Gannel might be under similar control. Second, Star A Star might have operated upon Gannel's mind so radically as to make an entirely different man of him. Either hypothesis would explain Gannel's extreme reticence in submitting to any except the most superficial mental examination. Each would account for Gannel's calm certainty that Alcon was afraid to attack him openly. Which of these hypotheses was the correct one could be determined later. It was unimportant, anyway, for in either case there was now accounted for the heretofore inexplicable power of Gannel's mind.

In either case it was not Gannel's mind at all, but that of THE Lensman, who was making Gannel act as he could not normally have acted. Somewhere hereabouts, in either case, there actually was lurking Boskonia's Nemesis; the mentality whom above all others Boskonia was raving to destroy; the one Lensman who had never been seen or heard or perceived; the feared and detested Lensman about whom nothing whatever had ever been learned.

That Lensman, whoever he might be, had at last met his match. Gannel, as Gannel, was of no importance whatever; the veriest pawn. But he who stood behind Gannel—Ah! He, Fossten himself, would wait and he would watch. Then, at precisely the correct instant, he would pounce!

*

And Kinnison, during the absence of the prime minister, worked swiftly and surely. Twelve men died, and as they ceased to live twelve others, grimly ready and thoroughly equipped for any emergency, took their places. And during that same minute of time Kinnison strode into Alcon's private sanctum.

The Tyrant hurled orders to his guards—orders which were not obeyed. He then went for his own weapons, and he was fast—but Kinnison was faster. Alcon's guns and hands disappeared and the sickened Tellurian slugged him into unconsciousness. Then grimly, relentlessly, he took every item of interest from the Thralian's mind, slew him, and assumed forthwith the title and the full authority of the Tyrant of Thrale.

Unlike most such revolutions, this one was accomplished with very little bloodshed and with scarcely any interference with the business of the realm. Indeed, if anything, there was an improvement in almost every respect, since the new men were more thoroughly trained and were more competent than the previous officers had been. Also, they had arranged matters beforehand so that their accessions could be made with a minimum of friction.

They were as yet loyal to Kinnison and to Boskonia; and in a rather faint hope of persuading them to stay that way, without developing any queer ideas anent in turn overthrowing him, the Lensman called them into conference.

"Men, you know how you got where you are," he began, coldly. "You are loyal to me at the moment. You know that real co-operation is the only way to achieve maximum productivity, and that true co-operation cannot exist in any regime in which the department heads, individually or en masse, are trying to do away with the dictator.

"Some of you will probably be tempted very shortly to begin to work against me instead of for me and with me. I am not pleading with you, nor even asking you out of gratitude for what I have done for you, to refrain from such activities. Instead, I am telling you as a simple matter of fact that any or all of you, at the first move toward any such disloyalty, will die. In that connection, I know that all of you have been exerting every resource to discover in what manner your predecessors came so conveniently to die, and that none of you have succeeded."

One by one they admitted that they had not.

"Nor will you, ever. Be advised that I know vastly more than Alcon did, and that I am far more powerful. Alcon, while in no sense a weakling, did not know how to command obedience. I do. Alcon's sources of information were meager and untrustworthy; mine are comprehensive and reliable. Alcon very often did not know that anything was being plotted against him until the thing was well along; I shall always know of the first seditious move. Alcon blustered, threatened, and warned; he tortured; he gave some offenders a second chance before he killed. I shall do none of those things. I do not threaten, I do not warn, I do not torture. Above all, I give no snake a second chance to strike at me. I execute traitors without bluster or fanfare. For your own good, gentlemen, I advise you in all seriousness to believe that I mean precisely every word that I have uttered."

They slunk out, but Boskonian habit was too strong. Thus, within three days, three of Kinnison's newly appointed headmen died. He called another cabinet meeting.

"The three new members have listened to the recording of our first meeting, hence there is no need to repeat what I said at that time," the Tyrant announced, in a voice so silkily venomous that his listeners cringed. "I will add to it merely that I will have full co-operation, and only co-operation, if I have to kill all of you and all of your successors to get it. You may go."

XX.

This killing made Kinnison ill; physically and mentally sick. It was ruthless, cowardly murder. It was worse than stabbing a man in the back; the poor devils didn't have even the faintest shadow of a chance. Nevertheless he did it.

When he had first invaded the stronghold of the Wheelmen of Aldebaran I, he had acted without thinking at all. Lensmen always went in, regardless of consequences. When he had scouted Jarnevon he had thought but little more. True—and fortunately—he took Worsel along; but he did not stop to consider whether or not there were minds in the Patrol better fitted to cope with the problem than was his own. It was his problem, he figured, and it was up to him to solve it.

Now, however, he knew bitterly that he could no longer act in that comparatively thoughtless fashion. At whatever loss of self-esteem, of personal stature, or of standing, he had to revise the Tellurian Lensmen's Code. It griped him to admit it, but Nadreck was right. It was not enough to give his life in an attempt to conquer a halfway station; he must remain alive in order to follow through to completion the job which was so uniquely his. He must *think*, assaying and evaluating every factor of his entire task. Then, without considering his own personal feelings, he must employ whatever forces and methods were best fitted to do the work at the irreducible minimum of cost and of risk.

Thus Kinnison sat unharmed upon the throne of the Tyrant of Thrale, and thus the prime minister returned to the palace to find a *fait accompli* awaiting him. That worthy studied with care every aspect of the situation then obtaining before he sought an audience with the new potentate.

"Allow me to congratulate you, Tyrant Gannel," he said, smoothly. "I cannot say that I am surprised, since I have been watching you and your activities for some little time—with distinct approval, I may add. You have fulfilled—more than fulfilled, perhaps—my expectations. Your regime is functioning superbly; you have established in this very short time a smoothness of operation and an *esprit de corps* among the rank and file which are decidedly unusual. There are, however, certain matters about which it is possible that you are not completely informed."

"It is possible," Kinnison agreed, with the merest trace of irony. "Such as?"

"In good time. You know, do you not, who is the real authority here upon Thrale?"

"I know who was," the Tellurian corrected, with the faintest perceptible accent upon the verb. "In part only, however, for if you had concerned yourself wholly, the late Alcon would not have made so many nor so serious mistakes."

"I thank you. That is, as of course you know, because I have only recently taken over. I want the Tyrant of Thrale to be the strongest man of Thrale, and I may say without flattery that I believe he now is. And I would suggest that you add 'sire' when you speak to me."

"I thank you in turn. I will so address you when you call me 'your supremacy'—not sooner."

"We will let it pass for the moment. To come to your question, you apparently do not know that the Tyrant of Thrale, whoever he may be, opens his mind to me."

*

"I have suspected that such a condition has existed in the past. However, please be informed that I trust fully only those who so trust me; and that thus far in my short life such persons have been few. You will observe that I am still respecting your privacy in that I am allowing your control of my sense of sight to continue. It is not because I trust you, but because your true appearance is to me a matter of complete indifference. For, frankly, I do not trust you at all. I will open my mind to you just exactly as wide as you will open yours to me—no wider."

"Ah—the bravery of ignorance. It is as I thought. You do not realize, Gannel, that I can slay you at any moment I choose, or that a very few more words of defiance from you will be enough." The prime minister did not raise his voice, but his tone was instinct with menace.

"I do not, and neither do you, as I remarked to the then Tyrant Alcon in this very room not long ago. I am sure that you will understand without elaboration the connotations and implications inherent in that remark." Kinnison's voice also was low and level, freighted in its every clipped syllable with the calm assurance of power. "Would you be interested in knowing why I am so certain that you will not accept my suggestion of a mutual opening of minds?"

"Very much so."

"Because I suspect that you are, or are in league with, Star A Star of the Galactic Patrol." Even at that astounding charge, Fossten gave no sign of surprise or of shock. "I have not been able as yet to obtain any evidence supporting that belief, but I tell you now that when I do so, you die. Not by power of thought, either, but in the beam of my personal ray gun."

"Ah—you interest me so strangely," and the premier's hand strayed almost imperceptibly toward an inconspicuous button.

"Don't touch that switch!" Kinnison snapped. He did not quite see why Fossten was letting him see the maneuver, but he would bite, anyway.

"Why not, may I ask? It is merely a—"

"I know what it is, and I do not like thought-screens. I prefer that my mind be left free to roam."

Fossten's thoughts raced in turn. Since the Tyrant was on guard, this was inconclusive. It might—or might not—indicate that Gannel was controlled by or in communication with Star A Star.

"Do not be childish," he chided. "You know as well as I do that your accusations are absurd. However, as I reconsider the matter, the fact that neither of us trusts unreservedly the other may not after all be an insuperable obstacle to our working together for the good of Boskonia. I think now more than ever that yours is the strongest Thralian mind, and as such, the logical one to wield the Tyrant's power. It would be a shame to destroy you unnecessarily, especially in view of the probability that you will come later of your own accord to see the reasonableness of that which I have suggested."

"It is possible," Kinnison admitted, "but not, I would say, probable." He thought that he knew why the lug had pulled in his horns, but he wasn't sure. "Now that we have clarified our attitudes toward each other, have decided upon an armed and suspicious truce, I see nothing to prevent us from working together in a completely harmonious mutual distrust for the good of all. The first thing to do, as I see it, is to devote our every effort to the destruction of the planet Klovia and all the Patrol forces based upon it."

"Right." If Fossten suspected that the Tyrant was somewhat less than frank, he did not show it, and the conversation became strictly technical.

"We must not strike until we are completely ready," was Kinnison's first statement, and he repeated it so often thereafter during the numerous conferences with the chiefs of staff that it came almost to be a slogan.

*

The prime minister did not know that Kinnison's main purpose was to give the Patrol plenty of time to make Klovia utterly impregnable. Fossten knew nothing of the Patrol's sunbeam, to which even the mightiest fortress possible for man to build could offer scarcely more resistance than could the lightest, the most fragile pleasure yacht.

Hence he grew more and more puzzled, more and more at a loss week by week, as Tyrant Gannel kept on insisting upon building up the strongest, the most logically perfect Grand Fleet which all the ability of their pooled brains could devise. Once or twice he offered criticisms and suggestions which, while defensible according to one theory, would actually have weakened Grand Fleet's striking power. These offerings Gannel rejected flatly; insisting, even to an out-and-out break with his co-administrator if necessary, upon the strongest possible armada.

The Tyrant wanted, and declared that he must and would have, more and bigger of everything. More and heavier flying fortresses, more and stronger battleships and superdreadnoughts, more and faster cruisers and scouts, more and deadlier weapons.

"We want more of everything than our operations officers can possibly handle in battle," he declared over and over; and he got them. Then:

"Now, you operations officers, learn how to handle them!" he commanded.

Even the prime minister protested at that, but it was finally accomplished. Fossten was a real thinker, as was Kinnison, and between them they worked out a system. It was crudeness and inefficiency incarnate in comparison with the Z9M9Z, but it was so much better than anything previously known to Boskonia's High Command that everyone was delighted. Even the suspicious and cynical Fossten began to entertain some doubts as to the infallibility of his own judgment.

And these doubts grew apace as the Tyrant drilled his Grand Fleet. He drove the personnel unmercifully, especially the operations officers; as relentlessly as he drove himself. He simply could not be satisfied, his ardor and lust for efficiency were insatiable. His reprimands were scathingly accurate; officer after officer he demoted bitingly during ever more complicated, ever more inhumanly difficult maneuvers; until finally he had what were unquestionably his best men in those supremely important positions. Then, one day:

"QX, Kim, come ahead—we're ready," Haynes Lensed him, briefly.

For Kinnison had been in touch with the port admiral every day. He had learned long since that the prime minister could not detect a Lensed thought, particularly when the Lensman was wearing a thought-screen, as he did practically constantly; wherefore the strategists of the Patrol were as well informed as was Kinnison himself of every move made by the Boskonians.

Then Kinnison called Fossten, and was staring glumly at nothing when the latter entered the room.

*

"Well, it would seem that we are about as nearly ready as we ever will be," the Tyrant brooded, pessimistically. "Have you any suggestions, criticisms, or other contributions to offer, of however minor a nature?"

"None whatever. You have done very well indeed."

"Unnhh," Gannel grunted, without enthusiasm. "You have observed, no doubt, that I have said little if anything as to the actual method of approach?"

The prime minister had indeed noticed that peculiar oversight, and said so. Here, undoubtedly, he thought, was the rub. Here was where Star A Star's minion would get in his dirty work.

"I have thought about it at length," Kinnison said, still in his brown study. "But I know enough to recognize and to admit my own limitations. I do know tactics and strategy, and thus far I have worked with only known implements toward known objectives. That condition, however, no longer exists. The simple fact is that I do not know enough about the possibilities, the techniques and the potentialities, the advantages and the disadvantages of the hyperspatial tube as an avenue of approach to enable me to come to a defensible decision one way or the other. I have decided, therefore, that if you have any preference in the matter I will give you full authority and let you handle the approach in any manner you please. I shall, of course, direct the actual battle, as in that I shall again be upon familiar ground."

The premier was flabbergasted. This was incredible. Gannel must really be working for Boskonia after all, to make such a decision as that. Still skeptical, unprepared for such a startling development as that one was, he temporized.

"The bad—the *very* bad—features of the approach via tube are two," he pondered aloud. "We have no means of knowing anything about what happens; and, since our previous such venture was a total failure, we must assume that, contrary to our plans and expectations, the enemy was not taken by surprise."

"Right," Kinnison concurred, tonelessly.

"Upon the other hand, an approach via open space, while conducive to the preservation of our two lives, would be seen from afar and would certainly be met by an appropriate formation."

"Check," came emotionlessly noncommittal agreement.

"Haven't you the slightest bias, one way or the other?" Fossten demanded, incredulously.

"None whatever," the Tyrant was coldly matter-of-fact. "If I had had any such, I would have ordered the approach made in the fashion I preferred. Having none, I delegated authority to you. When I delegate authority I do so without reservations."

This was a stopper.

"Let it be open space, then," the prime minister finally decided.

"So be it." And so it was.

*

Each of the component flotillas of Grand Fleet made a flying trip to some nearby base, where each unit was serviced. Every item of mechanism and of equipment was checked and rechecked. Stores were replenished, and munitions—especially munitions. Then the mighty armada, the most frightfully powerful aggregation ever to fly for Boskonia—the mightiest fleet ever assembled anywhere, according to the speeches of the politicians—remade its stupendous formation and set out for Klovia. And as it flew through space, shortly before contact was made with the Patrol's Grand Fleet, the premier called Kinnison into the control room.

"Gannel, I simply cannot make you out," he remarked, after studying him fixedly for five minutes. "You have offered no advice. You have not interfered with my handling of the Fleet in any way. Nevertheless, I still suspect you of treacherous intentions. I have been suspicious of you from the first—"

"With no grounds whatever for your suspicions," Kinnison reminded him, coldly.

"What? With all the reason possible!" Fossten declared. "Have you not steadily refused to bare your mind to me?"

"Certainly. Why not? Do we have to go over that again? Just how do you figure that I should so trust any being who refuses to reveal even his true shape to me?"

"That is for your own good," the prime minister stated. "I have not wanted to tell you this, but the truth is that no human being can perceive my true self and retain his sanity."

"I'll take a chance on that," Kinnison replied, skeptically. "I've seen a lot of monstrous entities in my time and I haven't conked out yet."

"There speaks the sheer folly of callow youth; the rashness of an ignorance so abysmal as to be possible only to one of your ephemeral race." The voice deepened, became more resonant. Kinnison, staring into those inscrutable eyes which he knew did not in fact exist, thrilled forebodingly; the timbre and the overtones of that voice reminded him very disquietingly of something which he could not at the moment recall to mind. "I forbear to discipline you, not from any doubt as to my ability to do so, as you suppose, but because of the sure knowledge that breaking you by force will destroy your usefulness. On the other hand, it is certain that if you co-operate with me willingly you will be the strongest, ablest leader that Boskonia has ever had. Think well upon these matters, O Tyrant."

"I will," the Lensman agreed, more seriously than he had intended. "But just what, if anything, has led you to believe that I am not working to the fullest and best of my ability for Boskonia?"

"Everything." Fossten summarized. "I have been able to find no flaw in your actions, but those actions do not fit in with your unexplained and apparently unexplainable reticence in letting me perceive for myself exactly what is in your mind. Furthermore, you have never even troubled to deny accusations that you are in fact playing a far deeper game than you appear upon the surface to be playing."

"That reticence I have explained over and over as an over-mastering repugnance—call it a phobia if you like," Kinnison rejoined, wearily. "I simply can't and won't. Since you cannot understand that, denials would have been entirely useless. Would you believe anything that I could possibly say—that I would swear to by everything I hold sacred—whether it was that I am whole-heartedly loyal to Boskonia or that I am in fact Star A Star himself?"

"Probably not," came the measured reply. "No, certainly not. Men—especially men such as you, bent ruthlessly upon the acquisition of power—are liars . . . ah, could it, by any chance, be that the reason for your intractability is that you have the effrontery to entertain some insane idea of supplanting ME?"

*

Kinnison jumped mentally. That tore it—that was a flare-lit tip-off. This man—this thing—being—entity—whatever he really was—instead of being just another Boskonian big shot, must be the clear quill—the real McCoy—BOSKONE HIMSELF! The end of the job must be right here! This was—*must* be—the real Brain for whom he had been searching so long; here within three feet of him sat the creature with whom he had been longing so fervently to come to grips!

"The reason is as I have said," the Tellurian stated, quietly. "I will attempt to make no secret, however, of a fact which you must already have deduced; that if and when it becomes apparent that you have any authority above or beyond that of the Tyrant of Thrale I shall take it away from you. Why not? Now that I have come so far, why should I not aspire to sit in the highest seat of all?"

"Hrrummphhh!" the monster—Kinnison could no longer think of him as Fossten, or as the prime minister, or as anything even remotely human—snorted with such utter, such searing contempt that even the Lensman's burly spirit quailed. "As well might you attempt to pit your vaunted physical strength against that of the heaviest forging ram ever built. Now, youth, have done. The time for temporizing is past. As I have said, I desire to spare you, as I wish you to rule this part of Boskonia as my viceroy. Know, however, that you are in no sense essential, and that if you do not yield your mind fully to mine, here and now, before this coming battle is joined, you most certainly die." At the grim finality, the calmly assured certainty of the pronouncement, a quick chill struck into the Gray Lensman's vitals.

This thing who called himself Fossten—who or what was he? What was it that he reminded him of? He thought and talked like . . . like . . . MENTOR! But it *couldn't* be an Arisian, possibly—that wouldn't make sense. But then, it didn't make any kind of sense, anyway, any way you looked at it. Whoever he was, he had plenty of jets—jets enough to lift a freighter off of the north pole of Valeria. And by the same token, his present line of talk didn't make sense, either—there must be some good reason why he hadn't made a real pass at him long before this, instead of arguing with him so patiently. What could it be? Oh, that was it, of course. He needed only a few minutes more, now; he could probably stall off the final showdown that long by crawling a bit—much as it griped him to let this zwilnik think that he was licking his boots.

"Your forbearance is appreciated, sire." At the apparently unconscious tribute to superiority and at the fact that the hitherto completely self-possessed Tyrant got up and began to pace nervously up and down the control room, the prime minister's austere mien softened appreciably. "It is, however, passing strange. It is not quite in character; it does not check quite satisfactorily with the facts thus far revealed. I may, perhaps, as you say, be stupid. I may be overestimating flagrantly my own abilities. To one of my temperament, however, to surrender in such a craven fashion as you demand comes hard—extremely, almost unbearably hard. It would be easier, I think, if your supremacy would condescend to reveal his true identity, thereby making plainly evident and manifest that which at present must be left to unsupported words, surmise, and not too much conviction."

"But I told you, and now tell you again, that for you to look upon my real form is to lose your reason!" the creature rasped.

"What do you care, really, whether or not I remain sane?" Kinnison shot his bolt at last, in what he hoped would be taken for a last resurgence of spirit. His time was about up. In less than one minute now the screens of scout cruisers would be in engagement, and either he or the prime minister or both would be expected to be devoting every cell of their brains to the all-important battle of giants. And in that very nick of time he would have to cripple the Bergenholms and thus inert the flagship. "Could it be that the real reason for your otherwise inexplicable forbearance is that you must know how my mind became as it now is, and that the breaking down of my barriers by mental force will destroy the knowledge which you, for your own security, must have?"

This was the blowoff. Kinnison still paced the room, but his pacings took him nearer and ever nearer to a certain control panel. Behind his thought-screen, which he could not now trust for a moment and which he knew starkly would be worse than useless in what was coming, he mustered every iota of his tremendous force of mind and of will. Only seconds now. His left hand, thrust into his breeches pocket, grasped the cigarette case within which reposed his Lens. His right arm and hand were tensely ready to draw and to fire his ray gun.

"Die, then! I should have known from the sheer perfection of your work that you were what you really are—Star A Star!"

*

The mental blast came ahead even of the first word, but the Gray Lensman, supremely ready, was already in action. One quick thrust of his chin flicked off the thought-screen. The shielded cigarette case flew open, his more-than-half-alive Lens blazed again upon his massive wrist. His weapon leaped out of its scabbard, flaming destruction as it came—a ravening tongue of incandescent fury which licked out of existence in the twinkling of an eye the Bergenholms' control panels and the operators clustered before it. The vessel went inert—much work would have to be done before the Boskonian flagship could again fly free!

These matters required only a fraction of a second. Well indeed it was that they did not take longer, for the ever-mounting fury of the prime minister's attack soon necessitated more—much more—than an automatic block, however capable. But Kimball Kinnison, Gray Lensman, Lensman of Lensmen, had more—ever so much more—than that!

He whirled, lips thinned over tight-set teeth in a savage fighting grin. Now he'd see what this zwilnik was and what he had. No fear, no doubt of the outcome, entered his mind. He had suffered such punishment as few minds have ever endured in learning to ward off everything that Mentor, one of the mightiest intellects of this or of any other universe, could send; but through that suffering he had learned. This unknown entity was an able operator, of course, but he certainly had a thick, hard crust to think that he could rub *him* out!

So thinking, the Lensman hurled a bolt of his own, a blast of power sufficient to have slain a dozen men—and, amazedly, saw it rebound harmlessly from the premier's hard-held block.

847

Which of the two combatants was the more surprised it would be hard to say; each had considered his own mind impregnable and invincible. Now, as the prime minister perceived how astoundingly capable a foe he faced, he sought to summon help by ordering the officers on duty to blast their Tyrant down. In vain. For, even so early in that ultimately lethal struggle, he could not spare enough of his mind to control effectively any outsider; and in a matter of seconds there were no minds left throughout that entire room in any condition to be controlled.

For the first reverberations, the ricochets, the spent forces of the monster's attack against Kinnison's shield had wrought grievously among the mentalities of the innocent bystanders. Those forces were deadly—deadly beyond telling—so inimical to and destructive of intelligence that even their transformation products affected tremendously the nervous systems of all within range.

Then, instants later, the spectacle of the detested and searingly feared Lens scintillating balefully upon the wrist of their own ruler was an utterly inexpressible shock. Some of the officers tried then to go for their guns, but it was already too late; their shaking, trembling, almost paralyzed muscles could not be forced to function.

*

An even worse shock followed almost instantly, for the prime minister, under the incredibly mounting intensity of the Lensman's poignant thrusts, found it necessary to concentrate his every iota of power upon his opponent. This revealed to all beholders, except Kinnison, what their prime minister actually was—and he had not been very much wrong in saying that that sight would drive any human being mad. Most of the Boskonians did go mad, then and there; but they did not rush about nor scream. They could not move purposefully, but only twitched and writhed horribly as they lay grotesquely asprawl. They could not scream or shriek, but only mouthed and mumbled meaningless burblings.

And ever higher, ever more brilliant flamed the Lens as Kinnison threw all of his prodigious will power, all of his tremendous, indomitable drive, through it and against the incredibly resistant thing to which he was opposed. This was the supreme, the climactic battle of his life thus far. Ether and sub-ether seethed and boiled invisibly under the frightful violence of the forces there unleashed. The men in the control room lay still; all life rived away. Now death spread throughout the confines of the vast spaceship.

Indomitably, relentlessly, the Gray Lensman held his offense upon that unimaginably high level; his Lens flooding the room with intensely coruscant polychromatic light. He did not know, then or ever, how he did it. It seemed as though his Lens, of its own volition in this time of ultimate need, reached out into unguessable continua and drew therefrom an added, an extra something. But, however it was done, Kinnison and his Lens managed to hold; and under the appalling, the never-ceasing concentration of force the monster's defenses began gradually to weaken and to go down.

Then sketchily, patchily, there was revealed to Kinnison's sight and sense of perception a . . . a . . . a BRAIN!

*

There was a body, of sorts, of course—a peculiarly neckless body designed solely to support that gigantic, thin-skulled head. There were certain appendages or limbs, and suchlike appurtenances and incidentalia to nourishment, locomotion, and the like; but to all intents and purposes the thing was simply and solely a brain.

Kinnison knew starkly that it was an Arisian—it looked enough like old Mentor to be his twin brother. He would have been stunned, except for the fact that he was far too intent upon victory to let any circumstance, however distracting, affect his purpose. His concentration upon the task in hand was so complete that nothing—literally nothing whatever—could sway him from it.

The monster's wall of illusion went down completely and then, step by short, hard, jerky step, Kinnison advanced. Close enough, he selected certain areas upon the sides of that enormous head and with big, hard, open hands he went viciously to work. Right, left, right, left, he slapped those bulging temples brutally, rocking monstrous head and repulsive body from side to side, pendulumlike, with every stunning blow.

His fist would have smashed that thin skull, would perhaps have buried itself deep within the soft tissues of that tremendous brain; and Kinnison did not want to kill his inexplicable opponent—yet. He had to find out first what this was all about.

He knew that he was due to black out as soon as he let go, and he intended to addle the thing's senses so thoroughly that he would be completely out of action for hours—long enough to give the Lensman plenty of time in which to recover his strength.

He did so.

Kinnison did not quite faint. He did, however, have to lie down flat upon the floor; as limp, almost, as the dead men so thickly strewn about.

And thus, while the two immense Grand Fleets met in battle, Boskonia's flagship hung inert and silent in space afar; manned by fifteen hundred corpses, one unconscious Brain, and one utterly exhausted Gray Lensman.

XXI.

Boskonia's Grand Fleet was, as has been said, enormous. It was not as large as the Patrol in total number of ships, since no ordinary brain nor any possible combination of such brains could have co-ordinated and directed the activities of so vast a number of units. Its center was, however, heavier; composed of a number and a tonnage of supermaulers which made it self-evidently irresistible.

In his training of his Grand Fleet operations staff, Kinnison had not overlooked a single bet, had not made a single move which by its falsity might have excited Premier Fossten's all-too-ready suspicions. They had handled Grand Fleet as a whole in vast, slow maneuvers; plainly the only kind possible to so tremendous a force. Kinnison and his officers had in turn harshly and thoroughly instructed the subfleet commanders in the various arts and maneuvers of conquering units equal to or smaller than their own.

That was all; and to the Boskonians, even to Fossten, that had been enough. That was obviously all that was possible. Not one of them realized that Tyrant Gannel very carefully avoided any suggestion that there might be any intermediate tactics, such as that of three or four hundred subfleets, too widely spread in space and too numerous to be handled by any ordinary mind or apparatus to inglobe and to wipe out simultaneously perhaps fifty subfleets whose commanders were not even in communication with each other. This technique was as yet the exclusive property of the Patrol and the Z9M9Z.

And in that exact operation, a closed book to the zwilniks, lay—supposedly and tactically—the Patrol's overwhelming advantage. For Haynes, through his four highly specialized Rigellian Lensmen and thence through the two hundred Rigellian operator-computers, could perform maneuvers upon any intermediate scale he pleased. He could handle his whole vast Grand Fleet and its every component part—he supposed—as effectively, as rapidly, and almost as easily as a skilled chess player handles his pieces and his pawns. Neither Kinnison nor Haynes can be blamed, however, for the fact that their suppositions were somewhat in error; it would have taken an Arisian to deduce that this battle was not to be fought exactly as they had planned it.

Haynes had another enormous advantage in knowing the exact number, rating, disposition, course, and velocity of every main unit of the aggregation to which he was opposed. And third, he had the sunbeam, concerning which the enemy knew nothing at all and which was now in good working order.

It is needless to say that the sunbeam generators were already set to hurl that shaft of irresistible destruction along the precisely correct line, or that Haynes' Grand Fleet formation had been made with that particular weapon in mind. It was not an orthodox formation; in any ordinary space battle it would have been sheerly suicidal. But the port admiral, knowing for the first time in his career every pertinent fact concerning his foe, knew exactly what he was doing.

His fleet, instead of driving ahead to meet the enemy, remained inert and practically motionless well within the limits of Klovia's solar system. His heavy stuff, instead of being massed at the center, was arranged in a vast ring. There was no center except for a concealing screen of heavy cruisers.

When the far-flung screens of scout cruisers came into engagement, then, the Patrol scouts near the central line did not fight, but sped lightly aside. So did the light and heavy cruisers and the battleships. The whole vast center of the Boskonians drove onward, unopposed, into—nothing.

*

Nevertheless they kept on driving. They could, without orders, do nothing else, and no orders were forthcoming from the flagship. Commanders tried to get in touch with Grand Fleet operations, but could not; and, in failing, kept on under their original instructions. They had, they could have, no suspicion that any minion of the Patrol was back of what had happened to their admirals. The flagship had been in the safest possible position and no attack had as yet been made. They probably wondered futilely as to what kind of a mechanical breakdown could have immobilized and completely silenced their High Command, but that was—strictly—none of their business. They had had orders, very definite orders, that no matter what happened they were to go on to Klovia and to destroy it. Thus, however wondering, they kept on. They were on the line. They would hold to it. They would blast out of existence anything and everything which might attempt to bar their way. They would reach Klovia and they would reduce it to its component atoms.

Unresisted, then, the Boskonian center bored ahead into nothing, until Haynes, through his Rigellians, perceived that it had come far enough. Then Klovia's brilliantly shining sun darkened almost to the point of going out entirely. Along the line of centers, through the space so peculiarly empty of Patrol ships, there came into being the sunbeam—a bar of quasi-solid lightning into which there had been compressed all the energy of well over four million tons *per second* of disintegrating matter.

Scouts and cruisers caught in that ravening beam flashed briefly, like sparks flying from a forge, and vanished. Battleships and superdreadnoughts the same. Even the solid war head of fortresses and maulers was utterly helpless. No screen has ever been designed capable of handling that hellish load; no possible or conceivable substance can withstand, save momentarily, the ardor of a sunbeam. For the energy liberated by the total annihilation of four million tons per second of matter is in fact as irresistible as it is incomprehensible.

The armed and armored planets did not disappear. They contained too much sheer mass for even that inconceivably powerful beam to volatilize in any small number of seconds. Their surfaces, however, melted and boiled. The controlling and powering mechanisms fused into useless pools of molten metal. Inert, then, inactive and powerless, they no longer constituted threats to Klovia's well-being.

The negaspheres also were rendered ineffective by the beam. Their antimasses were not decreased of course—in fact, they were probably increased a trifle by the fervor of the treatment—but, with the controlling super-structures volatilized away, they became more of menace to the Boskonian forces than to those of Civilization. Indeed, several of the terrible things were drawn into contact with ruined planets. Then negasphere and planet consumed each other, flooding all nearby space with intensely hard and horribly lethal radiation.

The beam winked out, Klovia's sun flashed on. The sunbeam was—and is—clumsy, unwieldy, quite definitely not rapidly maneuverable. But it had done its work; now the component parts of Civilization's Grand Fleet started in to do theirs.

*

Since the Battle of Klovia—it was and still is called that, as though it were the only battle which that warlike planet has ever seen—has been fought over in the classrooms of practically every civilized planet of two galaxies, it would be redundant to discuss it in detail here.

It was, of course, unique. No other battle like it has ever been fought, either before or since—and let us hope that no other such ever will be. It is studied by strategists, who have so far offered many thousands of widely variant profundities as to what Port Admiral Haynes should have done. Its profound emotional appeal, however, lies only and sheerly in its unorthodoxy. For in the technically proper space battle there is no hand-to-hand fighting, no purely personal heroism, no individual deeds of valor. It is a thing of logic and mathematics and of science, the massing of superior fire power against a well-chosen succession of weaker opponents. When the screens of a spaceship go down that ship is done, her personnel only memories.

But here how different! With the supposed breakdown of the lines of communication to the flagship, the subfleets carried on in formation. With the destruction of the entire center, however, all semblance of organization or of co-operation was lost. Every staff officer knew that no more orders would emanate from the flagship. Each knew chillingly that there could be neither escape nor succor. The captain of each vessel, thoroughly convinced that he knew vastly more than did his fleet commander, proceeded to run the war to suit himself. The outcome was fantastic, so utterly bizarre that the Z9M9Z and her trained co-ordinating officers were useless. Science and tactics and the million lines of communication could do nothing against a foe who insisted upon making it a ship-to-ship, yes, man-to-man affair!

The result was the most gigantic dog fight in the annals of military science. Ships—Civilization's perhaps as eagerly as Boskonia's—cut off their projectors, cut off their screens, the better to ram, to board, to come to grips personally with the enemy. Scout to scout, cruiser to cruiser, battleship to battleship, the insane contagion spread. Haynes and his staff men swore fulminantly, the Rigellians hurled out orders, but those orders simply could not be obeyed. The dog fight spread until it filled a good sixth of Klovia's entire solar system.

Board and storm! Armor—DeLameters—axes! The mad blood lust of hand-to-hand combat, the insensately horrible savagery of our pirate forebears, multiplied by millions and spread out to fill a million million cubic miles of space!

Haynes and his fellows wept unashamed as they stood by helpless, unable to avoid or to prevent the slaughter of so many splendid men, the gutting of so many magnificent ships. It was ghastly—it was appalling—it was WAR!

*

And far from this scene of turmoil and of butchery lay Boskonia's great flagship, and in her control room Kinnison began to recover his strength. He sat up groggily. He gave his throbbing head a couple of tentative shakes. Nothing rattled. Good—he was QX, he guessed, even if he did feel as limp as nine wet dish rags. Even his Lens felt weak; its usually refulgent radiance was sluggish, wan, and dim. This had taken plenty out of them, he reflected soberly; but he was mighty lucky to be alive. But he'd better get his batteries charged. He couldn't drive a thought across the room, the shape he was in now, and he knew of only one brain in the Universe capable of straightening out *this* mess.

After assuring himself that the highly inimical brain would not be able to function normally for a long time to come, the Lensman made his way to the galley. He could walk without staggering already—fine! There he fried himself a big, thick, rare steak—his never-failing remedy for all the ills to which flesh is heir—and brewed a pot of the coffeelike beverage affected by Thralians; making it viciously, almost corrosively strong. And as he ate and drank, his head cleared magically. Strength flowed back into him in waves. His Lens flamed into its normal splendor. He stretched prodigiously; inhaled gratefully a few deep breaths. He was QX.

Back in the control room, after again checking up on the still quiescent brain—he wouldn't trust this Fossten as far as he could spit—he hurled a thought to far-distant Arisia and to Mentor, its ancient sage.

"What's an Arisian doing in this Second Galaxy, working *against* the Patrol? Just what is somebody trying to pull off?" he demanded heatedly, and in a second of flashing thought reported what had happened.

"Truly, Kinnison of Tellus, my mind is far from capable," the deeply resonant, slow simulacrum of a voice resounded within the Lensman's brain. The Arisian never hurried; nothing whatever, apparently, not even such a cataclysmic upheaval as this, could fluster or excite him. "It does not seem to be in accord with the visualization of the Cosmic All which I hold at the moment that any one of my fellows is in fact either in the Second Galaxy or acting antagonistically to the Galactic Patrol. It is, however, a truism that hypotheses, theories, and visualizations must fit themselves to known or observed facts, and even your immature mind is eminently able to report truly upon actualities. But before I attempt to revise my Cosmos to conform to this admittedly peculiar circumstance, we must be very sure indeed of our facts. Are you certain, youth, that the being whom you have beaten into unconsciousness is actually an Arisian?"

"Certainly I'm certain!" Kinnison snapped. "Why, he's enough like you to have been hatched out of half of the same egg. Take a look!"—and he knew that the Arisian was studying every external and internal detail, part, and organ of the erstwhile prime minister of Thrale.

"Ah, it would appear to be an Arisian, at that, youth," Mentor finally agreed. "I do not know him, however, and I have been quite confident that I am acquainted with each member of my race. He is old, as you said—as old, perhaps, as I am. This will require some little thought—allow me therefore, please, a moment of contemplation." The Arisian fell silent, presently to resume:

"I have it now. Many millions of your years ago—so long ago that it was with some little difficulty that I recalled it to mind—when I was scarcely more than an infant, a youth but little older than myself disappeared from Arisia. It was determined then that he was aberrant—insane—and since only an unusually capable mind can predict truly the illogical workings of a diseased and disordered mind for even one year in advance, it is not surprising that in my visualization that unbalanced youth perished long ago. Nor is it surprising that I do not recognize him in the creature before you, for at the time of vanishment no permanent pattern had as yet been formed."

"Well, aren't you surprised that I could get the best of him?" Kinnison asked naïvely. He had really expected that Mentor would compliment him upon his prowess, he figured that he had earned a few pats on the back; but here the old fellow was mooning about his own mind and his own philosophy, and acting as though knocking off an Arisian were something to be taken in stride. And it wasn't, by half!

"No," came the flatly definite reply. "You have a force of will, a totalizable and concentratable power, a mental and psychological drive that no mind in the macrocosmic universe can break. I perceived those latent capabilities when I assembled your Lens, and developed them when I developed you. It was their presence which made it certain that you would return here for that development; they made you what you intrinsically are."

"QX, then—skip it. What shall I do with him? It's going to be a real job of work, any way you figure it, for us to keep him alive and harmless until we can get him back there to Arisia."

"We do not want him here," Mentor replied without emotion. "He has no present or future place within our society. Nor, however I consider the matter, can I perceive that he has any longer a permissible or condonable place in the all-inclusive Scheme of Things. He has served his purpose. Destroy him, therefore, forthwith, before he so much as recovers consciousness; lest much and grievous harm befall you."

"I believe you, chief. You chirped it then, if anybody ever did. Thanks"—and communication ceased.

*

The Lensman's ray gun flamed briefly and what was mortal of Fossten the prime minister became a smoking, shapeless heap.

Kinnison noticed then that a call light was shining brightly upon a communicator panel. This thing must have taken longer than he had supposed. The battle must be over, otherwise all space would still be filled with interference through which no long-range communicator beam could have been driven. Or—could Boskonia have—No, that was unthinkable. The Patrol *must* have won. This must be Haynes, calling him—

It was. The frightful Battle of Klovia was over. While many of the Patrol ships had yielded, either by choice or by necessity, to the Boskonians' challenge, most of them had not. And the majority of those who did so yield, came out victorious.

While fighting in any kind of recognized formation against such myriads of independently operating, widely spaced individual ships was, of course, out of the question, Haynes and his aids had been able to work out a technique of sorts. General orders were sent out to subfleet commanders, who in turn relayed them to the individual captains by means of visual beams. Single vessels, then, locked to equal or inferior craft—avoiding carefully anything larger than themselves—with tractor zones and held grimly on. If they could defeat the foe, QX. If not, they hung on; until shortly one of the Patrol's maulers—who had no opposition of their own class to face—would come lumbering up. And when the dreadful primary batteries of one of *those* things cut loose that was, very conclusively, that.

Thus Boskonia's mighty fleet vanished from the skies.

The all-pervading interference was cut off and Port Admiral Haynes, brushing aside a communications officer, sat down at his board and punched a call. Time after time he punched it. Finally he shoved it in and left it in; and as he stared, minute after minute, into the coldly unresponsive plate his face grew gray and old.

With a long, slightly tremulous sigh he was turning away from the plate when suddenly it lighted up to show the smiling, deeply space-tanned face of the one for whom he had just about given up hope.

"Thank God!" The commander in chief's exclamation was wholly reverent; his strained old face lost twenty years in half that many seconds. "Thank God you are safe. You did it, then?"

"I managed it, Pop, but just by the skin of my teeth—I didn't have half a jet to spare. It was Old Man Boskone himself, in person. And you?"

"Clean-up—one hundred point oh, oh, oh, oh percent."

"Fine business!" Kinnison exulted. "Everything's on the exact center of the green, then—come on!"

And Civilization's Grand Fleet went.

*

The Z9M9Z flashed up to visibility, inerted, and with furious driving blasts full ablaze, matched her intrinsic velocity to that of the Boskonian flagship—the only Boskonian vessel remaining in that whole vast volume of space. Tractors and pressors were locked on and balanced. Flexible—or, more accurately, not ultimately rigid—connecting tubes were pushed out and sealed. Hundreds, yes—thousands, of men—men in full Thralian uniform—strode through those tubes and into the Thralian ship. The *Directrix* unhooked and a battleship took her place. Time after time the maneuver was repeated, until it seemed as though Kinnison's vessel, huge as she was, could not possibly carry the numbers of men who marched aboard.

Those men were all human or approximately so—nearly enough human, at least, to pass as Thralians under a casual inspection. More peculiarly, that army contained an astounding number of Lensmen. So many Lensmen, it is certain, had never before been gathered together into so small a space. But the fact that they were Lensmen was not apparent; their Lenses were not upon their wrists, but were high upon their arms, concealed from even the most prying eyes within the heavy sleeves of their tunics.

Then the captured flagship, her Bergenholms again at work, the Z9M9Z, and the battleships which had already assumed the intrinsic velocity possessed originally by the Boskonians, spread out widely in space. Each surrounded itself with a globe of intensely vivid red light. Orders as to course and power flashed out. The word was given and spectacular fire flooded space as that vast host of ships, guided by those red beacons and by the ever-watchful observers of the *Directrix*, matched in one prodigious and beautiful maneuver its intrinsic velocity to theirs.

Finally, all the intrinsics in exact agreement, Grand Fleet formation was remade. The term "remade" is used advisedly, since this was not to be a battle formation. For Traska Gannel had long since sent a message to his capital; a terse and truthful message which was, nevertheless, utterly misleading. It was:

"My forces have won, my enemy has been wiped out to the last man. Prepare for a two-world broadcast, to cover both Thrale and Onlo, at hour ten today of my palace time."

The formation, then, was not one of warfare, but of boasting triumph. It was the consciously proud formation of a Grand Fleet which, secure in the knowledge that it has blasted out of the ether everything which can threaten it, returns victoriously to its Prime Base to receive as its just due the plaudits and the acclaim of the populace.

THE LENSMAN

Well in the van—alone in the van, in fact, and strutting—was the flagship. She, having originated upon Thrale and having been built specifically for a flagship, would be recognized at sight. Back of her came, in gigantic co-axial cones, the subfleets; arranged now not class by class of ships, but world by world of origin. One mauler, perhaps, or two; from four or five to a dozen or more battleships; an appropriate number of cruisers and of scouts; all flying along together in a tight little group.

But not all of the Patrol's armada was in that formation. It would have been very poor technique indeed to have had Boskonia's Grand Fleet come back to home ether forty percent larger than it had set out. Besides, the *Directrix* simply could not be allowed to come within detector range of any Boskonian lookout. She was utterly unlike any other vessel ever to fly: she would not, perhaps, be recognized for what she really was, but it would be evident to the most casual observer that she was not and could not be of Thrale or of Boskonia.

The Z9M9Z, then, hung back—far back—escorted and enveloped by the great number of warships which could not be made to fit into the roll call of the Tyrant's original Grand Fleet.

The subfleet which was originally from Thrale could land without any trouble; without arousing any suspicion. Boskonian and Patrol designs were not identical, of course; but the requirements of sound engineering dictated that externals should be essentially the same. The individual ships now bore the correct identifying symbols and insignia. The minor differences could not be perceived until after the vessels had actually landed, and that would be—for the Thralians—entirely too late.

*

Thralian hour ten arrived. Kinnison, after a long, minutely searching inspection of the entire room, became again in every millimeter Traska Gannel, the Tyrant of Thrale. He waved a hand. The scanner before him glowed: for a full minute he stared into it haughtily, to give his teeming millions of minions ample opportunity to gaze upon the inspiring countenance of His Supremacy the Feared.

He knew that the scanner revealed clearly every detail of the control room behind him, but everything there was QX. There was not even a chance that some person would fail to recognize a familiar face at any post, for not a single face except his own would be visible. Not a head back of him would turn, not even a rear quarter profile would show: it would be *lese majeste* of the most intolerable for any face, however inconspicuous, to share the limelight with that of the Tyrant of Thrale while his supremacy was addressing his subjects. Serenely and assuredly enough, then, Kinnison as Tyrant Gannel spoke:

"My people! As you have already been told, my forces have won the complete victory which my foresight and my leadership made inevitable. This milestone of progress is merely a repetition upon a grander scale of those which I have already accomplished upon a somewhat smaller; as extension and a continuation of the carefully considered procedure by virtue of which I shall see to it that My Great Plan succeeds.

"As one item in that scheduled procedure I removed the weakling Alcon, and in the stead of his rule of oppression, short-sightedness, corruption, favoritism, and greed, I substituted my beneficent regime of fair play, of mutual co-operation for the good of all.

856

"I have now accomplished the next major step in my program; the complete destruction of the armed forces which might be, which would be employed to hamper and to nullify the development and the fruition of My Plan.

"I shall take the next step immediately upon my return to my palace. There is no need to inform you now as to the details of what I have in mind. In broad, however, it pleases me to inform you that, having crushed all opposition, I am now able to institute and shall proceed at once to institute certain changes in policy, in administration, and in jurisdiction. I assure you that all of these changes will be, ultimately, for the best good of all, save the enemies of society.

"I caution you therefore to co-operate fully and willingly with my officers who may shortly come among you with instructions; some of these, perhaps, of a nature not hitherto promulgated upon Thrale. Those of you who do so co-operate will live and will prosper; you who do not will die in the slowest, most hideous fashions which hundreds of generations of Thralian torturers have been able to devise."

XXII.

Up to the present, Kinnison's revolution, his self-advancement into the dictatorship, had been perfectly normal; in perfect accordance with the best tenets of Boskonian etiquette. While it would be idle to contend that any of the others of the High Command really approved of it—each wanted intensely that high place for himself—none of them had been strong enough at the moment to challenge the usurper effectively and all of them knew that an ineffective challenge would mean certain death. Wherefore each perforce bided his time. Gannel would slip, Gannel would become lax or overconfident—and that would be the end of Gannel.

They were, however, loyal in their way to Boskonia. They were very much in favor of the rule of the strong and the ruthless. They believed implicitly that might made right. They themselves bowed the knee to anyone strong enough to command such servility from them; in turn they enforced brutally an even more degrading slavishness from those over whom they held in practice, if not at law, the power of life and death.

Thus Kinnison knew that he could handle his cabinet easily enough as long as he could make them believe that he was a Boskonian. There was, there could be, no real unity among them under those conditions; each would be fighting his fellows as well as working to overthrow His Supremacy the Tyrant. But they all hated the Patrol and all that it stood for with a whole-hearted fervor which no one adherent to Civilization can really appreciate. Hence at the first sign that Gannel might be in league with the Patrol they would combine forces instantly against him; automatically there would go into effect a tacit agreement to kill him first and then, later, to fight it out among themselves for the prize of the Tyrantcy.

And that combined opposition would be a formidable one indeed. Those men were really able. They were as clever and as shrewd and as smart and as subtle as they were hard. They were masters of intrigue; they simply could not be fooled. And if their united word went down the line that Traska Gannel was in fact a traitor to Boskonia, an upheaval would ensue which would throw into the shade the bloodiest revolutions of all history. Everything would be destroyed.

Nor could the Lensman hurl the metal of the Patrol against Thrale in direct frontal attack. Not only was it immensely strong, but also there were those priceless records, without which it might very well be the work of generations for the Patrol to secure the information which it must, for its own security, have.

No. Kinnison, having started near the bottom and worked up, must now begin all over again at the top and work down; and he must be very, *very* sure that no alarm was given until at too late a time for the alarmed ones to do anything of harm to the Lensman's cause. He didn't know whether he had jets enough to swing the load or not—a lot depended on whether or not he could civilize those twelve devils of his—but the scheme that the psychologists had worked out was a honey and he would certainly give it the good old college try.

*

Thus Grand Fleet slowed down, and, with the flagship just out of range of the capital's terrific offensive weapons, it stopped. Half a dozen maulers, towing a blackly indetectable, imperceptible object, came up and stopped. The Tyrant called, from the safety of his control room, a conference of his cabinet in the council chamber.

"While I have not been gone very long in point of days," he addressed them smoothly, via plate, "and while I, of course, trust each and every one of you, there are certain matters which must be made clear before I attempt to land. None of you has, by any possible chance, made any effort to lay a trap for me, or anything of the kind?" There may have been a trace of irony in the speaker's voice.

They assured him, one and all, that they had not had the slightest idea of even considering such a thing.

"It is well. None of you have discovered, then, that by changing locks and combinations, and by destroying or removing certain inconspicuous but essential mechanisms of an extremely complicated nature—and perhaps substituting others—I made it quite definitely impossible for any one or all of you to render this planet inertialess, I have brought back with me a negasphere of planetary antimass, which no power at your disposal can affect. It is here beside me in space; please study it attentively. It should not be necessary for me to inform you that there are countless other planets from which I can rule Boskonia quite as effectively as from Thrale; or that, while I do not relish the idea of destroying my home planet and everything upon it, I would not hesitate to do so if it became a matter of choice between that action and the loss of my life and my position."

They believed the statement. That was the eminently sensible thing to do. Any one of them would have done the same; hence they knew that Gannel would do exactly what he threatened—if he could. And as they studied Gannel's abysmally black ace of trumps they knew starkly that Gannel could. For they had found out, individually, that the Tyrant had so effectively sabotaged Thrale's Bergenholms that they could not possibly be made operative until after his return. Consequently repairs had not been started—any such activity, they knew, would be a fatal mistake.

By outguessing and outmaneuvering the members of his cabinet Gannel had once more shown his fitness to rule. They accepted that fact with a good enough grace; indeed, they admired him all the more for the ability thus shown. No one of them had given himself away by any overt moves; they could wait. Gannel would slip yet—quite possibly even before he got back into his palace. So they thought, not knowing that the Tyrant could read at will their most deeply hidden plans; and, so thinking, each one pledged anew in unreserved terms his fealty and his loyalty.

"I thank you, gentlemen." The boss did not, and the officers were pretty sure that he did not, believe a word of their protestations. "As loyal cabinet members, I will give you the honor of sitting in the front of those who welcome me home. You men and your guards will occupy the front boxes in the Royal Stand. With you and around you will be the entire palace personnel—I want no person, except the usual guards, inside the buildings or even within the grounds when I land. Back of these you will have arranged the Personal Troops and the Royal Guards. The remaining stands and all of the usual open ground will be for the common people—first come, first served.

"But one word of caution. You may wear your side arms, as usual. Bear in mind, however, that armor is neither usual nor a part of your full-dress uniform, and that any armored man or men in or near the concourse will be blasted by a needle ray before I land. Be advised also that I myself shall be wearing full armor. Furthermore, no vessel of the fleet will land until I, personally, from my private sanctum, order them to do so."

This situation was another poser; but it, too, they had to take. There was no way out of it, and it was still perfect Boskonian generalship. The welcoming arrangements were therefore made precisely as the Tyrant had directed.

*

The flagship settled toward ground, her under jets blasting unusually viciously because of her tremendous load; and as she descended Kinnison glanced briefly down at the familiar terrain. There was the immense space field, a dock-studded expanse of burned, scarred, pock-marked concrete and steel. Midway of its extreme northern end, that nearest the palace, was the berth of the flagship, Dock No. 1. An eighth of a mile straight north from the dock—the minimum distance possible because of the terrific fury of the under jets—was the entrance to the palace grounds. At the northern end of the western side of the field, a good three-quarters of a mile from Dock No. 1 and somewhat more than that distance from the palace gates, were the Stands of Ceremony. That made the Lensman completely the master of the situation.

The flagship landed, her madly blasting jets died out. A car of state rolled grandly up. Air locks opened. Kinnison and his bodyguards seated themselves in the car. Helicopters appeared above the stands and above the massed crowds thronging the western approaches to the field; hovering, flitting slowly and watchfully about.

Then from the flagship there emerged an incredible number of armed and armored soldiers. One small column of these marched behind the slowly moving car of state, but by far the greater number went directly to and through the imposing portals of the palace grounds. The people in general, gathered there to see a major spectacle, thought nothing of these circumstances—who were they to wonder at what the Tyrant of Thrale might choose to do?—but to Gannel's Council of Advisers they were extremely disquieting departures from the norm. There was, however, nothing that they could do about them, away out there in the grandstand; and they knew with a stark certainty what those helicopters had orders to do in case of any uprising or commotion anywhere in the crowd.

The car rolled slowly along before the fenced-back, wildly cheering multitudes, with blaring bands and the columns of armored spacemen marching crisply, swingingly behind it. There was nothing to indicate that those selected men were not Thralians; nothing whatever to hint that over a thousand of them were in fact Lensmen of the Galactic Patrol. And Kinnison, standing stiffly erect in his car, acknowledged gravely, with upraised right arm, the plaudits of his subjects.

The triumphal bus stopped in front of the most outthrust, the most ornate stand, and through loud-voiced amplifiers the Tyrant invited, as a signal honor, the twelve members of his Advisory Cabinet to ride with him in state to the palace. There were exactly twelve vacant seats in the great coach. The advisers would have to leave their bodyguards and ride alone with the Tyrant: even had there been room, it was unthinkable that any one else's personal killers could ride with the Presence. This was no honor, they knew chillingly, no matter what the mob might think—it looked much more like a death sentence. But what could they do? They glanced at their unarmored henchmen; then at the armor and the semiportables of Gannel's own heelers; then at the ranks of heavily armed and armored troopers; and finally at the 'copters now clustering thickly overhead, with the narrow snouts of needle-ray projectors very much in evidence.

They accepted.

*

It was in no quiet frame of mind, then, that they rode into the pretentious grounds of the palace. They felt no better when, as they entered the council chamber, they were seized and disarmed without a word having been spoken. And the world fairly dropped out from beneath them when Tyrant Gannel emerged from his armor with a Lens glowing upon his wrist.

"Yes, I am a Lensman," he gravely informed the stupefied but unshrinking Boskonians. "That is why I know that all twelve of you tried while I was gone to cut me down, in spite of all that I told you and all that you have seen me do. If it were still necessary for me to pose as Traska Gannel, I would have to kill you here and now for your treachery. That phase is, however, past.

"I am one of the Lensmen whose collective activities you have ascribed to 'the' Lensman or to Star A Star. All those others who came with me into the palace are Lensmen. All those outside are either Lensmen or tried and seasoned veterans of the Galactic Patrol. The Fleet surrounding this world is the Grand Fleet of that Patrol. The Boskonian force was destroyed *in toto*—every man and every ship except your flagship—before it reached Klovia. In short, the power of Boskonia is broken forever; Civilization is to rule henceforth throughout both galaxies.

"You are the twelve strongest, the twelve ablest men of the planet, perhaps of your whole dark culture. Will you help us to rule according to the principles of Civilization that which has been the Boskonian Empire, or will you die?"

The Thralians stiffened themselves rigidly against the expected blasts of death, but only one spoke. "We are fortunate at least, Lensman, in that you do not torture," he said coldly, his lips twisted into a hard, defiant sneer.

"Good!" and the Lensman actually smiled. "I expected no less. With that solid bottom, all that is necessary is to wipe away a few of your misconceptions and misunderstandings, correct your viewpoints, and—"

"Do you think for a second that your therapists can fit us into the pattern of your Civilization?" the Boskonian spokesman demanded bitingly.

"I don't have to think, Lanion—I know," Kinnison assured him. "Take them away, fellows, and lock them up—you know where. Everything will go ahead as scheduled."

And it did.

*

And while the mighty vessels of war landed upon the space-field and while the thronging Lensmen took over post after post in an ever-widening downward course, Kinnison led Worsel and Tregonsee to the cell in which the outspoken Thralian chieftain was confined.

"I do not know whether I can prevent you from operating upon me or not," Lanion of Thrale spoke harshly, "but I will certainly try. I have seen the pitiful, distorted wrecks left after such operations and I do not like them. Furthermore, I do not believe that any possible science can eradicate from my subconscious the fixed determination to kill myself the instant you release me. Therefore you had better kill me now, Lensman, and save your time and trouble."

"You are right, and wrong," Kinnison replied quietly. "It may very well be impossible to remove such a fixation." He knew that he could remove any such, but Lanion must not know it. Civilization needed those twelve hard, shrewd minds and he had no intention of allowing an inferiority complex to weaken their powers. "We do not, however, intend to operate, but only and simply to educate. You will not be unconscious at any time. You will be in full control of your own mind and you will know beyond peradventure that you are so in control. We shall engrave, in parallel with your own present knowledges of the culture of Boskonia, the equivalent or corresponding knowledges of Civilization."

They did so. It was not a short undertaking, nor an easy one; but it was thorough and it was finally done. Then Kinnison spoke.

"You now have completely detailed knowledge both of Boskonia and of Civilization, a combination possessed by but few intelligences indeed. You know that we did not alter, did not even touch, any track of your original mind. Being fully *en rapport* with us, you know that we gave you as unprejudiced a concept of Civilization as we possibly could. Also, you have assimilated completely the new knowledge."

"That is all true," Lanion conceded. "Remarkable, but true. I was, and remained throughout, myself; I checked constantly to be sure of that. I can still kill myself at any moment I choose."

"Right." Kinnison did not smile, even mentally, at the unconscious alteration of intent. "The whole proposition can now be boiled down into one clear-cut question, to which you can formulate an equally clear-cut reply. Would you, Lanion, personally, prefer to keep on as you have been, working for personal power, or would you rather team up with others to work for the good of all?"

The Thralian thought for moments, and as he pondered an expression of consternation spread over his hard hewn face. "You mean actually—personally—apart from all consideration of your so-called altruism and your other sissyish weaknesses?" he demanded resistantly.

"Exactly," Kinnison assured him. "Which would you *rather* do? Which would you, personally, get the most good—the most fun—out of?"

The bitter conflict was plainly visible in Lanion's bronzed face; so was the direction in which it was going.

"Well . . . I'll . . . be . . . damned! You win, Lensman!" and the ex-Boskonian big shot held out his hand. Those were not his words, of course; but as nearly as Tellurian English can come to it, that is the exact sense of his final decision. And the same, or approximately the same, was the decision of each of his eleven fellows, each in his turn.

*

Thus it was, then, that Civilization won over the twelve recruits who were so potently instrumental in the bloodless conquest of Thrale, and who were later to be of such signal service throughout the Second Galaxy. For they knew Boskonia with a sure knowledge, from top to bottom and from side to side, in every aspect and ramification; they knew precisely where and when and how to work to secure the desired ends. And they worked—*how* they worked!—but space is lacking to go into any of their labors here.

Specialists gathered, of a hundred different sorts; and when, after peace and security had been gained, they began to attack the stupendous files of the Hall of Records, Kinnison finally yielded to Haynes' insistences and moved out to the Z9M9Z.

"It's about time, young fellow!" the admiral snapped. "I've gnawed my fingernails off just about to the elbow and I still haven't figured out how to crack Onlo. Have you got any ideas?"

"Thrale first," Kinnison suggested. "Everything QX here, you sure?"

"Absolutely," Haynes grunted. "As strongly held as Tellus or Klovia. Primaries, helices, supertractors, Bergenholms, sunbeam—everything. They don't need us here any longer, any more than a hen needs teeth. Grand Fleet is all set to go, but we haven't been able to work out a feasible plan of campaign. The best way would be not to use the Fleet at all, but a sunbeam—but we can't move the Sun and Thorndyke has not as yet succeeded in making it hold together that far. I don't suppose that we could use a negasphere?"

"I don't see how," Kinnison pondered. "Ever since we used it first they've been ready for it. I'd be inclined to wait and see what Nadreck works out. He's a wise old owl, that bird—what does he tell you?"

"Nothing. Nothing, flat." Haynes' smile was grimly amused. "The fact that he is still 'investigating'—whatever that means—is all that he will tell me. Why don't you try him—you know him better than I do or ever will."

"It wouldn't do any harm," Kinnison agreed. "Nor good, either, probably. Funny egg, Nadreck. I'd tie fourteen of his arms into lover's knots if it'd make him give, but it wouldn't—he's a plenty tough number." Nevertheless he sent out a call, which was acknowledged instantly.

"Ah, Kinnison, greetings. I am even now on my way to Thrale and the *Directrix* to report upon the investigation."

"You are? Fine!" Kinnison exclaimed. "How did you come out?"

"I did not—exactly—fail, but the work was very incompletely and very poorly done," Nadreck submitted, the while the Tellurian's mind felt very strongly the Palainian equivalent of a painful blush of shame. "My report of the affair will be put and will forever remain under Lensman's Seal."

"But what did you *do?*" both Tellurians demanded as one.

"I scarcely know how to confess to such blundering," and Nadreck actually squirmed. "Will you not permit me to leave my shame to the spool of record?"

They would not, they informed him definitely.

"If you must have it, then, I yield. The plan was to make all of the armed forces upon Onlo destroy themselves. In theory it was sound and simple, but my execution was pitifully imperfect. My work was so poorly done that the commanding officer in each one of three of the domes remained alive, making it necessary for me to slay them personally, by the use of crude force. I regret exceedingly the lack of finish of this undertaking, and I apologize profoundly for it. I trust that you will not allow this information to become a matter of public knowledge"—and the apologetic, mentally sweating, really humiliated Palainian broke the connection.

*

Haynes and Kinnison stared at each other, for moments completely at a loss for words. The admiral first broke the silence.

"Hell's—jingling—bells!" he wrenched out, finally, and waved a hand at the points of light crowding so thickly his tactical tank. "A thing that the whole Grand Fleet couldn't do, and he does it alone, and then he *apologizes* for it as though he ought to be stood up in a corner or sent to bed without any supper!"

"Uh-huh, that's the way he is," Kinnison breathed, in awe. "What a brain!—what a man!"

Nadreck's black speedster arrived and a three-way conference was held. Both Haynes and Kinnison pressed him for the details of his really stupendous achievement, but he refused positively even to mention any phase of it.

"The matter is closed—finished," he declared, in a mood of anger and self-reproach which neither of the Tellurians had ever supposed that the gently scientific monster could assume. "I practically failed. It is the poorest piece of work of which I have been guilty since cubhood, and I desire and I insist that it shall not be mentioned again. If you wish to lay plans for the future, I will be very glad indeed to place at your disposal my

863

small ability—which has now been shown to be even smaller than I had supposed—but if you insist upon discussing my fiasco, I shall forthwith go home. I will *not* discuss it. The record of it will remain permanently under Lensman's Seal. That is my last word."

And it was. Neither of the two Tellurians mentioned the subject, of course, either then or ever, but many other persons—including your historian—have done so, with no trace whatever of success. It is a shame, it is positively outrageous, that no details are available of the actual fall of Onlo. No human mind can understand why Nadreck will not release his Seal, but the bitter fact of his refusal to do so has been made all too plain.

Thus, in all probability, it never will become publicly known how those monstrous Onlonians destroyed each other, nor how Nadreck penetrated the defensive screens of Onlo's embattled domes, nor in what fashion he warred upon the three surviving commanders. These matters, and many others of perhaps equal interest and value, must have been of such an epic nature that it is a cosmic crime that they cannot be recorded here; that this, one of the most important incidents of the campaign, must be mentioned merely and baldly as having happened. But, unless Nadreck relents—and he apparently never does—that is the starkly tragic fact.

*

Other Lensmen were called in then, and admirals and generals and other personages. It was decided to man the fortifications of Onlo immediately, from the several fleets of frigid-blooded poison breathers which made up a certain percentage of Civilization's forces. This decision was influenced markedly by Nadreck, who said in part:

"Onlo is a beautiful planet. Its atmosphere is perfect, its climate is ideal; not only for us of Palain VII, but also for the inhabitants of many other planets, such as—" and he mentioned some twenty names. "While I personally am not a fighter, there are many who are; and while those of a more warlike disposition man Onlo's defenses and weapons, my fellow researchers and I might very well be carrying on with the same type of work, which you fire-blooded oxygen breathers are doing upon Thrale and similar planets."

That was such an eminently sensible suggestion that it was adopted at once. The conference broke up. The selected subfleets sailed. Kinnison sought out the commander in chief.

"Well, sir, that's it—I hope. What do you think? Am I, or am I not, due for a spot of free time?" The Gray Lensman's face was drawn and grim.

"I wish I knew, son—but I don't." Eyes and voice were deeply troubled. "You ought to be . . . I hope you are . . . but you're the only judge of that, you know."

"Uh-huh . . . that is, I know how to find out . . . but I'm afraid to—afraid he'll say no. However, I'm going to see Chris first—talk it over with her. How about having a gig drop me down to the hospital?"

For he did not have to travel very far to find his fiancée. From the time of leaving Lyrane until the taking over of Thrale she had as a matter of course been chief nurse of the hospital ship *Pasteur*, and with the civilizing of that planet she had as automatically become chief nurse of the Patrol's Base Hospital there.

"Certainly, Kim—anything you want, whenever you please."

"Thanks, chief. Now that this fracas is finally over—if it is—I suppose that you'll have to take over as president of the Galactic Council?"

"I suppose so—after we clean Lyrane VIII, that you've been holding me away from so long—but I don't relish the thought. And you'll be Co-ordinator Kinnison."

"Uh-huh"—gloomily. "By Klono, I hate to put my Grays away! I'm not going to do it, either, until after we're married and really settled down onto the job."

"Of course not. You'll be wearing them for some time yet, I'm thinking." Haynes' tone was distinctly envious. "Getting *your* job settled down into a routine one will take a long, long time. It will take years even to find out what it is really going to be."

"That's so, too," Kinnison brightened visibly. "Well, clear ether, President Haynes!" and he turned away, whistling unmelodiously—in fact, somewhat raucously—through his teeth.

XXIII.

At Base Hospital it was midnight. The two largest of Thrale's four major moons were visible, close together in the zenith, almost at the full; shining brilliantly from a cloudless, star-besprinkled sky upon the magnificent grounds.

Fountains splashed and tinkled musically. Masses of flowering shrubs, bordering meandering walks, flooded the still air with a perfume almost cloying in its intensity. No one who has once smelled the fragrance of Thralian thorn flower at midnight will ever forget it—it is as though the poignant sweetness of the mountain syringa has been blended harmoniously with the heavy, entrancing scent of the jasmine and the appealing pungency of the lily of the valley. Statues of gleaming white stone and of glinting metal were spaced infrequently over acres and acres of springy, close-clipped turf. Trees, not overhigh but massive of bole and of tremendous spread and thickness of foliage, cast shadows of impenetrable black.

"QX, Chris?" Kinnison Lensed the thought as he arrived on the grounds. She had known that he was coming. "Kinda late, I know, but I wanted to see you, and I know that you don't have to punch the clock."

"Surely, Kim"—and her low, infectious chuckle welled out. "What's the use of being a Red Lensman, else? This is just right—you couldn't make it any sooner, and tomorrow would have been too late—much too late."

They met at the door and with each an arm around the other strolled wordless down a walk. Across the resilient sward they made their way and to a bench beneath one of the spreading trees.

Kinnison swept her into both arms, hers went eagerly around his neck. How long, how unutterably long it had been since they had stood thus, nurse's white crushed against Lensman's Gray!

"Chris . . . my Chris. How I love you!" he whispered, tense. "And now that I've got you again, by Klono's crimson claws, I'll never let you go!"

"Oh . . . oh, Kim, dear. I've missed you so terribly, Kim. If they separate us again, it will simply break my heart," she breathed, her low, rich voice pure music. Then womanlike, she faced the facts and made the man face them, too. "Let's sit down, Kim, and have this out. You know as well as I do that we can't go on if . . . if we can't . . . that's all."

They sat down upon the bench, arms still around each other. They had no need, these Lensmen, of sight. No need of language, either, although upon this page their thoughts must be put into words. They did, however, have need—a profound need—of physical contact.

"I do not," the man declared vigorously. "We've got a right to *some* happiness, Chris, you and I. They can't keep us apart forever, sweetheart—we're going straight through with it this time."

"Uh-uh, Kim," she denied gently, shaking her spectacular head. "What would have happened if we'd have gone ahead before, leaving these horrible Thralians free to ruin Civilization?"

"But Mentor stopped us then," Kinnison argued. Deep down, he knew that if the Arisian called he would have to answer, but he argued nevertheless. "If the job wasn't done, he would have stopped us before we got this far—I think."

"You hope, you mean," the girl contradicted. "What makes you think—if you really do—that he might not wait until the ceremony has actually begun?"

"Not a thing in the universe. He might, at that," Kinnison confessed, bleakly.

"You've been afraid to ask him, haven't you?" Clarrissa pursued.

*

"But the job must be done!" Kinnison insisted, avoiding the question. "The prime minister—that Fossten—*must* have been the top; you know very well that there couldn't possibly be anything bigger than an Arisian to be back of Boskone. It's unthinkable! They've got no military organization left—not a beam hot enough to light a cigarette or a screen that would stop a firecracker. We have all their records—everything. Why, it's just a matter of routine now for the boys to uproot them completely; system by system, planet by planet."

"Uh-huh." Chris eyed him shrewdly, there in the dark. "Cogent. Really pellucid. As clear as so much crystal—and twice as fragile. If you're so sure, why not call Mentor and ask him, right now? You're not afraid of just the calling part, like I am; you're afraid of what he will say."

"I'm going to marry you before I do another lick of work of any kind, anywhere," he insisted doggedly.

"I just love to hear you say that, even if I do know that you're just blasting off!" She giggled sunnily and snuggled deeper into the curve of his arm. "I feel that way, too, but both of us know very well that if Mentor stops us . . . even at the altar—" Her thought slowed, became intense, solemn. "We're Lensmen, Kim, you and I. We both realize to the full just what that means. We'll have to muster jets enough, some way or other, to swing the load. Let's call him now, Kim, together. I just simply can't stand this not knowing . . . I can't, Kim . . . I *can't!*" Tears come hard and seldom to such a woman as Clarrissa MacDougall; but they came then—and they hurt.

"QX, ace." Kinnison patted her back and her gorgeous head. "Let's go—but I tell you now that if he says 'no' I'll tell him to go hunt up an asteroid out on the Rim and take a swan dive off into intergalactic space."

She linked her mind with his, thinking in affectionate half reproach, "I'd like to, too, Kim, but that's pure baloney. You couldn't—" she broke off as he hurled their joint thought to Arisia the Old, going on frantically:

"You think at him, Kim, and I'll just listen. He scares me into a shrinking, quivering pulp!"

"QX, ace," he said again. Then: "Is it permissible that we do what we are about to do?" he asked crisply of Arisia's ancient sage.

"Ah, 'tis Kinnison and MacDougall; once of Tellus, henceforth of Klovia," the calmly unsurprised thought rolled in. "I was expecting you at this time. Any mind, however far from competent, could have visualized this event in its entirety. That which you contemplate is not merely permissible; it has now become necessary." And as usual, without tapering off or leave-taking, Mentor broke the line of thought.

The two clung together rapturously then for minutes, but something was obtruding itself disquietingly upon the nurse's mind.

"But his thought was 'necessary,' Kim?" she asked, rather than said. "Isn't there sort of a sinister connotation in that, somewhere? What did he mean?"

"Nothing—exactly nothing," Kinnison assured her, comfortably. "He's got a complete picture of the macrocosmic universe in his mind—his 'visualization of the Cosmic All,' he calls it—and in it we get married now, just as I've been telling you we are going to. Since it gripes him no end to have even the tiniest thing not to conform to his visualization, our marriage is NECESSARY, in capital letters. See?"

"Uh-huh . . . . Oh, I'm glad!" she exclaimed. "That shows you how scared of him I am." And thoughts and actions became such that, although they were no doubt of much personal pleasure and satisfaction, they do not require detailed treatment here.

*

Clarissa MacDougall resigned the next day, without formality or fanfare. That is, she thought that she did so then, and rather wondered at the frictionless ease with which it went through; it had simply not occurred to her that in the instant of being made an Unattached Lensman she had been freed automatically from every man-made restraint. That was one of the few lessons hard for her to learn; it was the only one which she refused consistently even to try to learn.

Nothing was said or done about the ten thousand credits which had been promised her upon the occasion of her fifteen-minutes-long separation from the Patrol following the fall of Jarnevon. She thought about it briefly, but with no real sense of loss. Some way or other, money did not seem important. Anyway, she had some—enough for a fairly nice, if limited, trousseau—in the bank upon Tellus. She could undoubtedly get it through the Disbursing Office here.

She took off her Lens and stuffed it into a pocket. That wasn't so good, she reflected. It bulged, and besides, it might fall out; and anyone who touched it would die. She didn't have a bag; in fact, she had with her no civilian clothes at all. Wherefore she put it back upon her wrist, pausing as she did so to admire the Manarkan star drop flashing pale fire from the third finger of her left hand. Of all his gems, Cartiff had retained only this one, the loveliest. It was a beauty.

It was not far to the Disbursing Office, so she walked; window-shopping as she went. It was a peculiar sensation, this being out of harness—it felt good, though, at that—and upon arriving at the bank she found to her surprise that she was both well known and expected. An officer whom she had never seen before greeted her cordially and led her into his private office.

"We have been wondering why you didn't pick up your kit, Lensman MacDougall," he went on, briskly. "Sign here, please, and press your right thumb in this box here, after peeling off this plastic strip, so." She wrote in her boldly flowing script, and peeled, and pressed; and watched fascinatedly as her thumbprint developed itself sharply black against the bluish off-white of the Patrol's stationery. "That transfers your balance upon Tellus to the Patrol's general fund. Now sign and print this, in quadruplicate. Thank you. Here's your kit. When this book of slips is gone you can get another one at any bank or Patrol station anywhere. It has been a real pleasure to have met you, Lensman MacDougall; come in again whenever you happen to be upon Thrale." And he escorted her to the street as briskly as he had ushered her in.

Clarrissa felt slightly dazed. She had gone in there to get the couple of hundred credits which represented her total wealth; but instead of getting it she had meekly surrendered her savings to the Patrol and had been given—what? She leafed through the little book. One hundred blue-white slips; small things, smaller than currency bills. A little printing, two lines for description, a blank for figures, a space for signature, and a plastic-covered oblong area for thumbprint. That was all—but what an all! Any one of those slips, she knew, would be honored without hesitation or question for any amount of cash money she pleased to draw; for any object or thing she chose to buy. Anything—absolutely *anything*—from a pair of half-credit stockings up to and beyond a hundred-million-credit spaceship. ANYTHING! The thought chilled her buoyant spirit, took away her zest for shopping.

"Kim, I can't!" she wailed through her Lens. "Why didn't they give me my own money and let me spend it the way I please?"

"Hold everything, ace—I'll be with you in a sec." He wasn't—quite—but it was not long. "You can get all the money you want, you know—just give them a chit."

"I know, but all I wanted was my own money. I didn't ask for this stuff!"

"None of that, Chris—when you get to be a Lensman, you've got to take what goes with it. Besides, if you spend money foolishly all the rest of your life, the Patrol knows that it will still owe you plenty for what you did on Lyrane II. Where do you want to begin?"

"Brenleer's," she decided, after she had been partially convinced. "They aren't the largest, but they give real quality at a fair price."

At the shop the two Lensmen were recognized at sight and Brenleer himself did the honors.

"Clothes," the girl said succinctly, with an all-inclusive wave of her hand. "All kinds of clothes, except nurse's uniforms."

They were ushered into a private room and Kinnison wriggled as mannequins began to appear before them in various degrees of enclothement.

"This is no place for me," he declared. "I'll see you later, Chris. How long—half an hour or so?"

"Half an hour!" The nurse giggled, and:

"She will be here all the rest of today, and most of the time for a week," the couturier informed him severely—and she was.

"Oh, Kim, I'm having the most *marvelous* time!" she told him excitedly, a few days later. "But it makes me feel sick to think of how much of the Patrol's money I'm spending."

"You may think that you're spending money, but you aren't," he informed her, cryptically.

"Huh? What do you mean?" she demanded, but he would not talk.

She found out, however, after the long-drawn-out business of selecting and matching and designing and fitting was over.

"You have seen me in civvies only a couple of times, and I got myself all prettied up in the beauty shop." She posed provocatively. "Do you like me, Kim?"

"*Like* you!" The man could scarcely speak. She had been a seven-sector call-out in faded moleskin breeches and a patched shirt. She had been a thionite dream in uniform. But now—radiantly, vibrantly beautiful, a symphony in her favorite dark green. "Words fail, ace. Thoughts, too. They fold up and quit. The universe's best, is all I can say—"

And—later—they sought out Brenleer.

"I would like to ask you to do me a tremendous favor," the merchant said hesitantly, without filling any of the blanks upon the credit slip the girl had proffered. "If, instead of paying for these things, you would write upon this voucher the date and 'my fall outfit and much of my trousseau were made by Brenleer of Thrale—'?" His voice expired upon a wistful note.

"Why . . . I never even thought of such a thing. Would it be quite ethical, do you think, Kim?"

"You said that he gives value for price, so I don't see why not. Lots of things they never let any of us pay for—" Then, to Brenleer, "Never thought of that angle, of what a terrific draw she would be. I suppose that this business of yours is worth fifty thousand credits more right now than it was before she cut loose here, and that it'll be worth twice that much when you have this chit unobtrusively displayed in a gold-and-platinum frame four feet square."

The man nodded. "Twice that already, but there isn't money enough upon Thrale to buy it."

"I'm not surprised," Kinnison grinned understandingly. "But you might as well give him a break, Chris. What tore it was your buying the stuff here, not admitting the fact over your signature and thumbprint."

She did so and they went out.

"Do you mean to tell me that I'm so . . . so—"

"Famous? Notorious?" he helped out.

"Uh-huh. Or words to that effect." A touch of fear darkened her glorious eyes.

"All of that, and then some," he declared. "I never thought of what your buying so much plunder in one store would do, but it'd have the pulling power of a planetary tractor. It's bad enough with us regulars—half the chits we sign are never cashed—but you are absolutely unique. The first Lady Lensman—the only Red Lensman—and *what* a Lensman! Wow! As I think it over one gets you a hundred if any chit you ever sign ever will get cashed. There have been collectors, you know, ever since Civilization began—maybe before."

"But I don't like it!" she stormed.

"That won't change the facts," he countered, philosophically. "Are you ready to flit? The *Dauntless* is hot, they tell me."

"Uh-huh, all my stuff is aboard." And soon they were en route to Klovia.

*

The trip was uneventful, and even before they reached that transformed planet it became evident that it was theirs from pole to pole. Their cruiser was met by a horde of spaceships of all types and sizes, which formed a turbulent and demonstrative escort of honor. The seething crowd at the spaceport could scarcely be kept out of range of the dreadnought's searing landing blasts. Half the brass bands of the world, it seemed, burst into "Our Patrol" as the Lensmen disembarked, and their ground car and the street along which it slowly rolled were decorated lavishly with deep-blue flowers.

"Thorn flowers!" Clarrissa choked. "Thralian thorn flowers, Kim—how could they?"

"They grow here as well as there, and when they found out that you liked them so well they imported them by the shipload"—and Kinnison himself swallowed a lump.

Their brief stay upon Klovia was a hectic one indeed. Parties and balls, informal and formal, and at least a dozen telenews poses every day. Receptions, at which there were presented the personages and the potentates of a thousand planets; at which the uniforms and robes and gowns put the solar spectrum to shame.

And from tens of thousands of planets came Lensmen, to make or to renew acquaintance with the Galactic Co-ordinator and to welcome into their ranks the Lensman-bride. From Tellus, of course, they came in greatest number and enthusiasm, but other planets were not too far behind. They came from Manark and Velantia and Chickladoria and Alsakan and Vandemar, from the worlds of Canopus and Vega and Antares, from all over the Galaxy. Human, near-human, nonhuman, monstrous; there even appeared briefly quite large numbers of frigid-blooded Lensmen, whose fiercely laboring refrigerators chilled the atmosphere for yards around their insulated and impervious suits. All those various beings came with a united purpose, with a common thought—to congratulate Kinnison of Tellus and to wish his Lensman-mate all the luck and all the happiness of the universe.

Kinnison was surprised at the sincerity with which they acclaimed him; he was amazed at the genuineness and the intensity of their adoption of his Chris as their own. He had been afraid that some of them would think that he was throwing his weight around when he violated precedent by making her a Lensman. He had been afraid of animosity and ill will. He had been afraid that outraged masculine pride would set up a sex antagonism.

But if any of these things existed, the keenest use of his every penetrant sense could not discover them.

Instead, the human Lensmen literally mobbed her as, en masse, they took her to their collective bosom. No party, wherever or for what reason held, was complete without her. If she ever had less than ten escorts at once, she was slighted. They ran her ragged, they danced her slippers off, they stuffed her to repletion, they would not let her sleep, they granted her the privacy of a goldfish—and she loved every tumultuous second of it.

She had wanted, as she had told Haynes and Lacy so long ago, a big wedding; but this one was already out of hand and was growing more so by the minute. The idea of holding it in a church had been abandoned long since; now it became clear that the biggest armory of Klovia would not hold even half of the Lensmen, to say nothing of the notables and dignitaries who had come so far. It would simply have to be the Stadium; a bowl so vast that no previous crowd had filled one tenth of its seats. Seeing and hearing there were excellent, however, as the spectators did not look at the scene itself, but into visiplates comfortably close.

Even the Stadium could not accommodate that throng, hence speakers and plates were run outside, clear up to the space-field fence. And, although neither of the principals knew it, this marriage had so fired public interest that Universal Telenews men had already arranged the hookup which was to carry it to every planet of Civilization. The number of entities who thus saw and heard that wedding has been estimated, but the figures are too fantastic to be repeated here.

But it was in no sense a circus. No ceremony ever held, in home or in church or in cathedral, was ever more solemn. For when half a million Lensmen concentrate upon solemnity, it prevails—no levity is possible within a radius of miles.

The whole vast bowl was gay with flowers—it seemed as though a state must have been stripped of blooms to furnish so many—and ferns and white ribbons were everywhere. There was a mighty organ, which pealed out triumphal melody as the bridal parties marched down the aisles, subsiding into a lilting accompaniment as the betrothed couple ascended the white-brocaded stairway and faced the Lensman-chaplain in the heavily garlanded little open-air chapel. The minister raised both hands. The massed Patrolmen and nurses stood at attention. A profound silence fell.

"Dearly beloved—" The grand old service—short and simple, but utterly impressive—was soon over. Then, as Kinnison kissed his wife, half a million Lensed members were thrust upward in silent salute.

Through a double lane of flowing Lenses the wedding party made its way up to the locked and guarded gate of the space-field, upon which lay the *Dauntless*—the superdreadnought "yacht" in which the Kinnisons were to take a honeymoon voyage to distant Tellus. The gate opened. The couple, accompanied by the port admiral and the surgeon general, stepped into the car, which sped out to the battleship; and as it did so the crowd loosed its pent-up feelings in a prolonged outburst of cheering.

And as the newlyweds walked up the gangplank, Kinnison turned his head and shouted to Haynes:

"You've been griping so long about Lyrane VIII, chief—I forgot to say that you can go mop up on it now!"

ACKNOWLEDGMENT

Your historian, not wishing to take credit which is not rightfully his, wishes to say here that without the fine co-operation of many persons and entities this history must have been of much less value and importance than it now is.

First, of course, there were the Lensmen. It is unfortunate that Nadreck of Palain VII could not be induced either to release his spool of the Fall of Onlo or to enlarge upon his other undertakings.

Co-ordinator Kinnison, Worsel of Velantia, and Tregonsee of Rigel IV, however, were splendidly co-operative, giving in personal conversations much highly useful material which is not heretofore of public record. The gracious and queenly Red Lensman also was of great assistance.

Dr. James R. Enright was both prolific and masterly in deducing that certain otherwise necessarily obscure events and sequences must have in fact occurred, and it is gratefully admitted here that the author has drawn heavily upon "Dr. Jim's" profound knowledge of the mind.

The Galactic Roamers, those intrepid spacemen, assisted no little: E. Everett Evans, their chief communications officer, Paul Leavy, Jr., Alfred Ashley, F. Edwin Counts; to name only a few who aided in the selection, arrangement, and presentation of material.

Verna Trestrail, the exquisite connoisseuse, was of help, not only by virtue of her knowledge of the jewels of Lonabar, but also in her interpretations of many things concerning Illona Potter of which Illona Henderson—characteristically—will not speak.

To all these, and to many others whose help was only slightly less, the writer extends his sincere thanks.

Edward E. Smith.

CHILDREN OF THE LENS

MESSAGE OF TRANSMITTAL

SUBJECT: The Conclusion of the Boskonian War; A Report:

BY: Christopher Kinnison, L3, of Klovia:

TO: The Entity Able to Obtain and to Read It.

To you, the third-level intellect who has been guided to this imperishable container and who is able to break the Seal and to read this tape, and to your fellows, greetings:

For reasons which will become obvious, this report will not be made available for an indefinite but very long time; perhaps ten million, perhaps ten million million Galactic-Standard years; my present visualization of the Cosmic All does not extend to the time at which such action will become necessary. Therefore it is desirable to review briefly the most pertinent facts of the earlier phases of Civilization's climatic conflict; information which, while widely known at present, will probably in that future time exist otherwise only in the memories of my descendants.

In early Civilization law enforcement lagged behind crime because the police were limited in their spheres of action, while criminals were not. Each technological advance made that condition worse until finally, when Bergenholm so perfected the crude inertialess space-drive of Rodebush and Cleveland that commerce throughout the Galaxy became an actuality, crime began to threaten Civilization's very existence.

Of course it was not then suspected that there was anything organized, coherent, or of large purpose about this crime. Centuries were to pass before my father, Kimball Kinnison of Tellus, now Galactic Co-ordinator, was to prove that Boskonia, an autocratic, dictatorial culture diametrically opposed to every ideal of Civilization—was, in fact, back of practically all of the pernicious activities of the First Galaxy. Even my father, however, has never had any inkling either of the existence and the doings of the Eddorians or of the fundamental *raison d'etre* of the Galactic Patrol—facts which can never be revealed to any mind not inherently stable at the third level of stress.

Virgil Samms, then Chief of the Secret Service of the Triplanetary League, perceived the general situation and foresaw the shape of the inevitable. He realized that unless and until his organization could secure an identifying symbol which could not be counterfeited, police work would remain relatively ineffectual. Tellurian science had done its best in the golden meteors of Triplanetary's Secret Service, and its best was not good enough.

Virgil Samms became the first wearer of Arisia's Lens, and during his life he began the rigid selection of those worthy of wearing it. For centuries the Patrol grew and spread. It became widely known that the Lens was a perfect telepath, that it glowed with colored light only when worn by the individual to whose ego it was attuned, that it killed any other living being who attempted to wear it. Whatever his race or shape, any wearer of the Lens was accepted as the embodiment of Civilization.

Kimball Kinnison was the first entity of Civilization to suspect that the Boskonian organization existed. He was the first Lensman to realize that the Lens was more than identification and a telepath. He was thus the first Lensman to return to Arisia to take the second stage of Lensmanship—their treatment which only an exceptional brain can withstand, but which gives the Second-Stage Lensman any mental power which he needs and which he can both visualize and control.

Aided by Lensman Worsel of Velantia and Tregonsee of Rigel IV—the former a winged reptile, the latter a four-legged, barrel-shaped creature with the sense of perception instead of sight—Kimball Kinnison traced and surveyed Boskone's military organization in the First Galaxy. He helped plan the attack upon Grand Base, the headquarters of Helmuth, who "spoke for Boskone." By flooding the control dome of Grand Base with thionite, that deadly drug native to the peculiar planet Trenco, he made it possible for Civilization's Grand Fleet, under the command of Port Admiral Haynes—now retired—to reduce that Base. He personally killed Helmuth in hand-to-hand combat.

He was instrumental in the almost-complete destruction of the Overlords; those sadistic, life-eating reptiles native to the planet Delgon of the Velantian solar system, who were the first to employ against humanity the hyperspatial tube.

He was wounded more than once; in one of his hospitalizations becoming acquainted with Surgeon General Lacy—now retired—and with Sector Chief Nurse Clarrissa MacDougall, who was later to become the widely-known "Red Lensman" and, still later, my mother.

In spite of the military defeat, however, Boskonia's real organization remained intact, and Kinnison's further search led into Lundmark's Nebula, thenceforth called the Second Galaxy. The planet Medon, being attacked by the Boskonians, was rescued from the enemy and was moved across intergalactic space to the First Galaxy. Medon made two notable contributions to Civilization: first, electrical insulation, conductors, and switches by whose means voltages and amperages theretofore undreamed-of could be handled; and, later, Phillips, a Posenian surgeon, was able there to complete the researches which made it possible for human bodies to grow anew any members or organs which had been lost.

Kinnison, deciding that the drug syndicate was the quickest and surest line to Boskone, became Wild Bill Williams the meteor miner, a hard-drinking, bentlam-eating, fast-shooting space-hellion. As Williams he traced the zwilnik line upward, step by step, to the planet Jarnevon in the Second Galaxy. Upon Jarnevon lived the Eich; frigid-blooded monsters more intelligent, more merciless, more truly Boskonian even than the Overlords of Delgon.

He and Worsel, Second-Stage Lensmen both, set out to investigate Jarnevon. He was captured, tortured, dismembered; but Worsel brought him back to Tellus with his mind and knowledge intact—the enormously important knowledge that Jarnevon was ruled by a Council of Nine of the Eich, a council named Boskone.

Kinnison was given a Phillips treatment, and again Clarrissa MacDougall nursed him back to health. They loved each other, but they could not marry until the Gray Lensman's job was done; until Civilization had triumphed over Boskonia.

The Galactic Patrol assembled its Grand Fleet, composed of millions of units, under the flagship Z9M9Z. It attacked. The planet of Jalte, Boskonia's Director of the First Galaxy, was consumed by a bomb of negative matter. Jarnevon was crushed between two colliding planets; positioned inertialess, then inerted especially for that crushing. Grand Fleet returned, triumphant.

But Boskonia struck back, sending an immense fleet against Tellus through a hyperspatial tube instead of through normal space. This method of approach was not, however, unexpected. Survey ships and detectors were out; the scientists of the Patrol had been for months hard at work upon the "sunbeam"—a device to concentrate all the energy of the sun into one frightful beam. With this weapon reinforcing the already vast powers of Grand Fleet, the invaders were wiped out.

Again Kinnison had to search for a high Boskonian; some authority higher than the Council of Boskone. Taking his personal superdreadnought, the *Dauntless*, which carried his indetectable, nonferrous speedster, he found a zwilnik trail and followed it to Dunstan's Region, an unexplored, virtually unknown, outlying spiral arm of the First Galaxy. It led to the planet Lyrane II, with its human matriarchy, ruled by Helen its queen.

There he found Illona Potter, the ex-Aldebaranian dancer; who, turning against her Boskonian kidnapers, told him all she knew of the Boskonian planet Lonabar, upon which she had spent most of her life. Lonabar was unknown to the Patrol and Illona knew nothing of its location in space. She did, however, know its unique jewelry—gems also completely unknown to Civilization.

Nadreck of Palain VII, a frigid-blooded Second-Stage Lensman, with one jewel as a clue, set out to find Lonabar; while Kinnison began to investigate Boskonian activities among the matriarchs.

The Lyranians, however, were fanatically nonco-operative. They hated all males; they despised and detested all nonhuman entities. Hence Kinnison, with the consent and assistance of Mentor of Arisia, made of Clarrissa MacDougall a Second-Stage Lensman and assigned to her the task of working Lyrane II.

Nadreck found and mapped Lonabar; and to build up an unimpeachable Boskonian identity Kinnison became Cartiff the jeweler; Cartiff the jewel thief and swindler; Cartiff the fence; Cartiff the murderer-outlaw; Cartiff the Boskonian Big Shot. He challenged and overthrew Menjo Bleeko, the dictator of Lonabar, and before killing him took from his mind everything he knew.

The Red Lensman secured information from which it was deduced that a cavern of the Overlords of Delgon existed upon Lyrane II. This cavern was raided and destroyed, the Patrolmen learning that the Eich themselves had a heavily-fortified base upon Lyrane III.

Nadreck, master psychologist, invaded that base tracelessly; learning that the Eich received orders from the Thrallian solar system in the Second Galaxy and that frigid-blooded Kandron of Onlo—Thrallis IX—was second in power only to human Alcon, the Tyrant of Thrale—Thrallis II.

Kinnison went to Thrale, Nadreck to Onlo; the operations of both being covered by the Patrol's invasion of the Second Galaxy. In that invasion Boskonia's Grand Fleet was defeated and the planet Klovia was taken and fortified.

Assuming the personality of Traska Gannel, a Thralian, Kinnison worked his way upward in Alcon's military organization. Trapped in a hyperspatial tube, ejected into an unknown one of the infinity of parallel, coexistent, three-dimensional spaces which comprise the Cosmic All, he was rescued by Mentor, working through the brain of Sir Austin Cardynge, the Tellurian mathematician.

Returning to Thrale, he fomented a revolution, in which he killed Alcon and took his place as the Tyrant of Thrale. He then discovered that his Prime Minister, Fossten, who concealed his true appearance by means of a zone of hypnosis, had been Alcon's superior instead of his adviser. Neither quite ready for an open break, but both supremely confident of victory when that break should come, subtle hostilities began.

Tyrant and Prime Minister planned and launched an attack upon Klovia, but just before engagement the hostilities between the two Boskonian leaders flared into an open fight for supremacy. After a terrific mental struggle, during the course of which the entire crew of the flagship died, leaving the Boskonian fleet at the mercy of the Patrol, Kinnison won. He did not know, of course, and never will know, either that Fossten was in fact an Eddorian or that it was Mentor who in fact overcame Fossten. Kinnison thought, and Mentor encouraged him to believe, that the Prime Minister was an Arisian who had been insane since youth, and that Kinnison himself killed Fossten without assistance. It is a mere formality to emphasize at this point that none of this information must ever become available to any mind below the third level; since to any entity able either to obtain or to read this report it will be obvious that such revealment would produce an inferiority complex which must inevitably destroy both the Galactic Patrol and the Civilization whose instrument it is.

With Fossten dead and with Kinnison already the Tyrant of Thrale, it was comparatively easy for the Patrol to take over. Nadreck drove the Onlonian garrisons insane, so that all fought to the death among themselves; thus rendering Onlo's mighty armament completely useless.

Then, thinking that the Boskonian War was over—encouraged, in fact, by Mentor so to think—Kinnison married Clarrissa MacDougall, established his headquarters upon Klovia and assumed his duties as Galactic Co-ordinator.

Kimball Kinnison, while not, strictly speaking, a mutant, was the penultimate product of a prodigiously long line of selective, controlled breeding. So was Clarrissa MacDougall. Just what course the science of Arisia took in making those two what they are I can deduce, but I do not as yet actually know. Nor, for the purpose of this record, does it matter. Port Admiral Haynes and Surgeon General Lacy thought that they brought them together and promoted their romance. Let them think so—as agents, they did. Whatever the method employed, the result was that the genes of those two uniquely complementary penultimates were precisely those necessary to produce the first, and at present the only Third-Stage Lensmen.

I was born upon Klovia, as were, three or four Galactic-Standard years later, my four sisters—two pairs of twins. I had little babyhood, no childhood. Fathered and mothered by Second-Stage Lensmen, accustomed from infancy to wide-open two-ways with such beings as Worsel of Velantia, Tregonsee of Rigel IV, and Nadreck of Palain VII, it would seem obvious that we did not go to school. We were not like other children of our age; but before I realized that it was anything unusual for a baby who could scarcely walk to be computing highly perturbed asteroidal orbits as "mental arithmetic," I knew that we would have to keep our abnormalities to ourselves, insofar as the bulk of mankind and of Civilization was concerned.

I traveled much; sometimes with my father or mother or both, sometimes alone. At least once each year I went to Arisia for treatment. I took the last two years of Lensmanship, for physical reasons only, at Wentworth Hall upon Tellus instead of upon my native Klovia—because upon Tellus the name Kinnison is not at all uncommon, while upon Klovia the fact that "Kit" Kinnison was the son of the Co-ordinator could not have been concealed.

I graduated, and with my formal enlensment this record properly begins. Much has been told elsewhere, notably in Smith's "History of Civilization"; but all such works are, and of necessity must be, pitifully incomplete.

I have recorded this material as impersonally as possible, realizing fully that my sisters and I did only the work for which we were specifically developed and trained; even as you who read this will do that for which you shall have been developed and are to be trained.

Respectfully submitted,
Christopher Kinnison, L3, Klovia.

I.

Galactic Co-ordinator Kimball Kinnison finished his second cup of Tellurian coffee, got up from the breakfast table, and prowled about in black abstraction. Twenty-odd years had changed him but little. He weighed the same, or a few pounds less; although a little of his mass had shifted downward from his mighty chest and shoulders. His hair was still brown, his stern face was only faintly lined. He was mature, with a conscious maturity which no young man can know.

"Since when, Kim, did you think that you could get away with blocking *me* out of your mind?" Clarrissa Kinnison directed the thought, quietly. The years had dealt as lightly with the Red Lensman as with the Gray. She had been gorgeous, she was now magnificent. "This room is shielded, you know, against even the girls."

"Sorry, Chris—I didn't mean it that way."

"I know," she laughed. "Automatic. But you've had that block up for two solid weeks, except when you force yourself to keep it down, and that means that you're 'way, '*way* off the beam."

"I've been thinking, incredible as it may seem."

"I know it. Let's have it—cold."

"QX—you asked for it. Queer things have been going on all over. Inexplicable things . . . no apparent reason."

"Such as?"

"Almost any kind of insidious deviltry you care to name. Disaffections, psychoses, mass hysterias, hallucinations; pointing toward a Civilization-wide epidemic of revolutions and uprisings for which there seems to be no basis or justification whatever."

"Why, Kim! How could there be? I haven't heard of anything like that!"

"It hasn't got around. Each solar system thinks that it's a purely local condition, but it isn't. As Galactic Co-ordinator, with a broad view of the entire picture, my office would, of course, see such a thing before anyone else could. We saw it, and set out to nip it in the bud . . . but—" He shrugged his shoulders and grinned wryly.

"But what?" Clarrissa persisted.

"It didn't nip. We sent Lensmen to investigate, but none of them got to the first check-station. Then I asked our Second-Stage Lensmen—Worsel, Nadreck, and Tregonsee—to drop whatever they were doing and solve it for me. They struck it and bounced. They followed, and are still following, leads and clues galore, but they haven't got a millo's worth of results so far."

"What? You mean to say it's a problem *they* can't solve?"

"That they haven't, to date," he corrected, absently. "And that 'gives me furiously to think'."

"It would," she conceded, "and it also would make you itch to join them. Think at me, and it'll help you correlate. You should have gone over the data with me right at first."

"I had reasons not to, as you'll see. But I'm stumped now, so here goes. We'll have to go away back, to before we were married. First: Mentor told me, quote, only your descendants will be ready for that which you now so dimly grope, unquote. Second: you were the only being ever able to read my thoughts without the aid of the Lens. Third: Mentor told us, when we asked him if it was QX for us to go ahead that our marriage was *necessary*, a choice of phraseology which bothered you somewhat at the time, but which I then explained as being in accord with his visualization of the Cosmic All. Fourth: the Patrol formula is to send the man best fitted for any job to do that job, and if he can't swing it, to send the Number One graduate of the current class of Lensmen. Fifth: a Lensman has got to use everything and everybody available, no matter what or who it is. I used even you, you remember, in that Lyrane affair and others. Sixth: Sir Austin Cardynge believed to the day of his death that we were thrown out of that hyperspatial tube, and out of space, deliberately."

"Well, go on. I don't see much, if any connection."

"You will, if you think of those six points in connection with our present predicament. Kit graduates next month, and he'll rank Number One of all Civilization, for all the tea in China."

"Of course. But after all, he's a Lensman. He will insist upon being assigned to some problem; why not to that one?"

"You don't yet see what that problem is. I've been adding two and two together for weeks, and can't get any other answer than four. And if two and two are four, Kit has got to tackle Boskone—the *real* Boskone; the one that I never did and very probably never can reach."

"No, Kim—no!" she almost shrieked. "Not Kit, Kim—he's just a boy!"

Kinnison waited, wordless.

She got up, crossed the room to him. He put his arm around her in the old but ever new gesture.

"Lensman's load, Chris," he said, quietly.

"Of course," she replied then, as quietly. "It was a shock at first, coming after all these years, but . . . if it has to be, it must. But he doesn't . . . surely we can help him, Kim?"

"Surely." The man's arm tightened. "When he hits space I go back to work. So do Nadreck and Worsel and Tregonsee. So do you, if your kind of a job turns up. And with us Gray Lensmen to do the blocking, and with Kit to carry the ball—" His thought died away.

"I'll say so," she breathed. Then: "But you won't call me, I know, unless you absolutely *have* to . . . and to give up you and Kit both . . . why did we have to be Lensmen, Kim?" she protested, rebelliously. "Why couldn't we have been ground-grippers? You used to growl that thought at me before I knew what a Lens really meant—"

"Vell, some of us has got be der first violiners in der orchestra," Kinnison misquoted, in an attempt at lightness. "Ve can't all push vind t'rough der trombone."

"I suppose that's true." The Red Lensman's somber air deepened. "Well, we were going to start for Tellus today, anyway, to see Kit graduate. This doesn't change that."

*

And in a distant room four tall, shapely, auburn-haired, startlingly identical girls stared at each other briefly, then went *en rapport*; for their mother had erred greatly in saying that the breakfast room was screened against their minds. Nothing was or could be screened against them: they could think above, below, or, by sufficient effort, straight through any thought-screen that had ever been designed. Nothing in which they were interested was safe from them, and they were interested in practically everything.

"Kay, we've got ourselves a job!" Kathryn, older by minutes than Karen, excluded pointedly the younger twins, Camilla and Constance—"Cam" and "Con".

"At last!" Karen exclaimed. "I've been wondering what we were born for, with nine-tenths of our minds so deep down that nobody except Kit even knows they're there and so heavily blocked that we can't let even each other in without a conscious effort. This is it. We'll go places now, Kat, and really do things."

"What do you mean *you'll* go places and do things?" Con demanded indignantly. "Do you think for a second that you've got jets enough to blast *us* out of all the fun?"

"Certainly," Kat said, equably. "You're too young."

"We'll let you know what we're doing, though," Kay conceded, magnanimously. "You might even conceivably contribute an idea that we could use."

"Ideas—phooey!" Con jeered. "A real idea would crack both of your skulls. You haven't any more plan than a—"

"Hush—shut up, everybody!" Kat commanded. "This is too new for any of us to have any worth-while ideas on, yet. Tell you what let's do—we'll all think this over until we're aboard the *Dauntless*, halfway to Tellus; then we'll compare notes and work out parts for all of us."

They left Klovia that afternoon. Kinnison's personal superdreadnought, the mighty *Dauntless*—the fourth to bear that name—bored through intergalactic space. Time passed. The four young redheads convened.

"I've got it all worked out!" Kat burst out enthusiastically, forestalling the other three. "There will be four Second-Stage Lensmen at work and there are four of us. We'll circulate—percolate, you might say—around and throughout the Universe. We'll pick up ideas and facts and feed 'em to our Gray Lensmen; surreptitiously, sort of, so they'll think they got them themselves. I'll take Dad for my partner. Kay can have—"

"You'll do no such thing!" A general clamor rose, Con's thought being the most insistent. "If we aren't going to work with all, indiscriminately, we'll draw lots or throw dice to see who gets him, so there!"

"Seal it, snake-hips, please," Kat requested, sweetly. "It is trite but true to say that infants should be seen, but not heard. This is serious business—"

"Snake-hips! Infant!" Con interrupted, venomously. "Listen, my steatopygous and senile friend!" Constance measured perhaps a quarter of an inch less in gluteal circumference than did her oldest sister; she tipped the beam at one scant pound below her weight. "You and Kay are a year older than Cam and me, of course; a year ago your minds were stronger than ours. That condition, however, no longer exists. We, too are grown up. And to put that statement to test, what can you do that I can't?"

"This." Kathryn extended a bare arm, narrowed her eyes in concentration. A Lens materialized about her wrist; not attached to it by a metallic bracelet, but a bracelet in itself, clinging sentiently to the smooth, bronzed skin. "I felt that in this work there would be a need. I learned to satisfy it. Can you match that?"

They could. In a matter of seconds the three others were similarly enlensed. They had not previously perceived the need, but after Kat had pointed it out to them by demonstrating the manner of its satisfaction, their acquisition of full knowledge had been virtually instantaneous.

"Or this, then." Kat's Lens disappeared.

So did the other three. Each knew that no hint of this knowledge or of this power should ever be revealed; each knew that in any moment of stress the Lens of Civilization could be and would be hers.

"Logic, then, and by reason, not by chance." Kat changed her tactics. "I still get Dad. Everybody knows who works best with whom. You, Con, have tagged around after Worsel all your life. You used to ride him instead of a horse—"

"She still does," Kay snickered. "He pretty nearly split her in two a while ago in a seven-gravity pull-out, and she almost broke a toe when she kicked him for it."

"Worsel is nice," Con defended herself vigorously. "He's more human than most people, and more fun, as well as having infinitely more brains. And you can't talk, Kay—what anyone can see in that Nadreck, so cold-blooded that he freezes you even through armor at twenty feet—you'll get as cold and hard as he is if you don't—"

"And every time Cam gets within five hundred parsecs of Tregonsee she goes into silences with him, contemplating raptly the whichnesses of the why," Kathryn interrupted, forestalling recriminations. "So you see, by the process of elimination, Dad has got to be mine."

*

Since they could not all have him it was finally agreed that Kathryn's claim would be allowed and, after a great deal of discussion and argument, a tentative plan of action was developed. In due course, the *Dauntless* landed upon Tellus. The Kinnisons went to

Wentworth Hall, the towering, chromium-and-glass home of the Tellurian cadets of the Galactic Patrol. They watched the impressive ceremonies of graduation. Then, as the new Lensmen marched out to the magnificent cadences of "Our Patrol," the Gray Lensman, leaving his wife and daughters to their own devices, made his way to his Tellurian office in Prime Base.

"Lensman Kinnison, sir, by appointment," his secretary announced, and as Kit strode in Kinnison stood up and came to attention.

"Christopher Kinnison of Klovia, sir, reporting for duty." Kit saluted crisply.

The Co-ordinator returned the salute punctiliously. Then: "At rest, Kit. I'm proud of you, mighty proud. We all are. The women want to heroize you, but I had to see you first, to clear up a few things. An explanation, an apology, and, in a sense, commiseration."

"An apology, sir?" Kit was dumbfounded. "Why, that's unthinkable—"

"For not graduating you in Gray. It has never been done, but that was not the reason. Your commandant, the Board of Examiners, and Port Admiral LaForge, all recommended it, agreeing that none of us is qualified to give you either orders or directions. I blocked it."

"Of course. For the son of the Co-ordinator to be the first Lensman to graduate Unattached would smell—especially since the fewer who know of my peculiar characteristics the better. That can wait, sir."

"Not too long, sir." Kinnison's smile was a trifle forced. "Here's your Release and your kit, and a request signed by the whole Galactic Council that you go to work on whatever it is is going on. We rather think that it heads up somewhere in the Second Galaxy, but that is little more than a guess."

"I can start out from Klovia, then? Good—I can go home with you."

"That's the idea, and on the way there you can study the situation. For your information we have made up a series of tapes, carrying not only all the available data, but also our attempts at analysis and interpretation. Complete and up to date, except for one item which came in this morning . . . . I can't figure out whether it means anything or not, but it should be inserted—" Kinnison paced the room, scowling.

"Might as well tell me. I'll insert it when I scan the tape."

"QX. I don't suppose that you have heard much about the unusual shipping trouble we have been having, particularly in the Second Galaxy?"

"Rumor—gossip only. I'd rather have it straight."

"It's all on the tapes, so I'll give you the barest possible background. Losses are twenty-five percent above normal. A few highly peculiar derelicts have been found—peculiar in that they seem to have been wrecked by madmen. Not only wrecked, but gutted, and with every mark of identification obliterated. We can't determine even origin or destination, since the normal disappearances outnumber the abnormal ones by four to one. On the tapes this is lumped in with the other psychoses you'll learn about. But this morning they found another derelict, in which the chief pilot had scrawled 'WARE HELL HOLE IN SP' across a plate. Connection with the other derelicts, if any, is obscure. If the pilot was sane when he wrote that message, it means something—but nobody knows what. If he wasn't, it doesn't, any more than the dozens of obviously senseless—excuse me, I should say apparently senseless—messages which we have already recorded."

"Hm-m-m. Interesting. I'll bear it in mind and tape it in its place. But speaking of peculiar things, I've got one I wanted to discuss with you—getting my Release was such a shock that I almost forgot it. Reported it, but nobody thought it was anything important. Maybe . . . probably . . . it isn't. Tune your mind up to the top of the range . . . there, did you ever hear of a race that thinks upon that band?"

"I never did—it's practically unreachable. Why—have you?"

"Yes and no. Only once, and that only a touch. Or, rather, a burst; as though a hard-held mind-block had exploded, or the creature had just died a violent, instantaneous death. Not enough of it to trace, and I never found any more of it."

"Any characteristics? Bursts can be quite revealing at times."

"A few. It was on my last break-in trip in the Second Galaxy, out beyond Thrale—about here." Kit marked the spot upon a mental chart. "Mentality very high—precisionist grade—possibly beyond social needs, as the planet was a bare desert. No thought of cities. Nor of water, although both may have existed without appearing in that burst of thought. The thing's bodily structure was RTSL, to four places. No gross digestive tract—atmosphere-nourished or an energy-converter, perhaps. The sun was a blue giant. No spectral data, of course, but at a rough guess I'd say somewhere around class B5 or A0. Although the temperature was normal for him, it was quite evident that the planet would be unbearably hot for us. That's all I could get."

"That's a lot to get from one burst. It doesn't mean a thing to me right now—but I'll watch for a chance to fit it in somewhere."

*

How casually they dismissed as unimportant that cryptic burst of thought! But if they both, right then, together, had been authoritatively informed that the description fitted exactly the physical form forced upon its denizens in its summer by the accurately-described, simply hellish climatic conditions obtaining during that season on noxious planet Ploor, the information would still not have seemed important to either of them—then.

"Anything else we ought to discuss before night?" The older Lensman went on without a break.

"Not that I know of."

"You said your Release was a shock. Ready for another one?"

"I can't think of a harder one. I'm braced—blast!"

"I have turned the office over to Vice Co-ordinator Maitland for the duration. I am authorized to tell you that Worsel, Nadreck, Tregonsee, and I have resumed our Unattached status and, while conducting our own various investigations, will be holding ourselves ready at all times for your call."

"That *is* a shock, sir. Thanks. I hadn't expected . . . it's really overwhelming. And you said something about *commiserating* me?" Kit lifted his red-thatched head—all of Clarissa's children had inherited her startling hair—and gray eyes stared level into eyes of gray.

"In a sense, yes. You'll understand later. Well, you'd better go hunt up Chris and the kids. After the festivities are over—"

"I'd better cut them, hadn't I?" Kit asked, eagerly. "Don't you think it'd be better for me to get started right away?"

"Not on your life!" Kinnison demurred, positively. "Do you think that I want that mob of strawberry blondes to snatch me bald-headed? You're in for a large day and evening of lionization, so take it like a man. As I was about to say, as soon as the brawl is over tonight we'll all board the *Dauntless* and do a flit for Klovia, where I'll fit you out with everything you want. Until then, son—" Two big hands gripped.

"But I'll be seeing you around the Hall!" Kit exclaimed. "You can't—"

"No, I can't dodge the lionizing, either," Kinnison grinned, "but we won't be in a sealed and shielded room. So, son . . . I'm proud of you."

"Right back at you, big fellow—and thanks a million." Kit strode out and, a few minutes later, the Co-ordinator did likewise.

*

The "brawl," which was the gala event of the Tellurian social year, was duly enjoyed by all the Kinnisons. The *Dauntless* made an uneventful flight to Klovia. Arrangements were made. Plans, necessarily sketchy and elastic, were laid.

Two big, gray-clad Lensmen stood upon the deserted spacefield, between two blackly indetectable speedsters. Kinnison was massive, sure, calm with the poised calmness of maturity, experience, and power. Kit, with the broad shoulders and narrow waist of his years and training, was taut and tense, fiery, eager to come to grips with Civilization's foes.

"Remember, son," Kinnison said as the two gripped hands. "There are four of us old-timers, who have been through the mill, on call every second. If you can use any one of us or all of us, don't wait to be too sure—snap out a call."

"I know, Dad . . . thanks. The four best, ablest Lensmen that ever lived. One of you may make a strike before I do. In fact, with the thousands of leads we have, and with no way of telling how many of them are false—deliberately or otherwise—and with your vastly greater experience and knowledge, you probably will. So remember that it cuts both ways. If any of you can use me at any time, I'll come at max."

"QX. We'll get in touch from time to time, anyway. Clear ether, Kit!"

"Clear ether, Dad!" What a wealth of meaning there was in that low-voiced, simple exchange of the standard bon voyage!

For minutes, as his speedster flashed through space, Kinnison thought only of the boy. He knew exactly how he felt; he relived in memory the supremely ecstatic moments of his own first launching into space as a Gray Lensman. But Kit had the stuff—stuff which he, Kinnison, knew that he could know nothing about—and he had his own job to do. Therefore, methodically, like the old campaigner he was, he set about it.

THE LENSMAN

II.

Worsel the Velantian, hard and durable and long-lived as Velantians are, had in twenty Tellurian years changed scarcely at all. As the first Lensman and the only Second-Stage Lensman of his race, the twenty years had been very fully occupied indeed.

He had solved the varied technological and administrative problems incident to the welding of Velantia into the structure of Civilization. He had worked at the many tasks which, in the opinion of the Galactic Council, fitted his peculiarly individual talents. In his "spare" time he had sought out in various parts of two galaxies, and had ruthlessly slain, widely-scattered groups of the Overlords of Delgon.

Continuously, however, he had taken an intense sort of godfatherly interest in the Kinnison children, particularly in Kit and in the youngest daughter, Constance; finding in the girl a mentality surprisingly akin to his own.

When Kinnison's call came he answered it. He was now out in space; not in the *Dauntless*, but in a ship of his own, under his own command. And what a ship! The *Velan* was manned entirely by beings of his own race. It carried Velantian air, at Velantian temperature and pressure. Above all, it was built and powered for inert maneuvering at the atrocious accelerations employed by the Velantians in their daily lives; and Worsel loved it with enthusiasm and elan.

He had worked conscientiously and well with Kinnison and with other entities of Civilization. He and they had all known, however, that he could work more efficiently alone or with others of his own kind. Hence, except in emergencies, he had done so; and hence, except in similar emergencies, he would so continue to do.

Out in deep space, Worsel entwined himself, in a Velantian's idea of comfort, in an intricate series of figures-of-eight around a couple of parallel bars and relaxed in thought. There were insidious deviltries afoot, Kinnison had said. There were disaffections, psychoses, mass hysterias, and—Oh happy thought!—hallucinations. There were also certain revolutions and sundry uprisings, which might or might not be connected or associated with the disappearances of a considerable number of persons of note. In these latter, however, Worsel of Velantia was not interested. He knew without being told that Kinnison would pounce upon such blatant manifestations as those. He himself would work upon something much more to his taste.

Hallucination was Worsel's dish. He had been born among hallucinations, had been reared in an atmosphere of them. What he did not know about hallucinations could have been printed in pica upon the smallest one of his scales.

Therefore, isolating one section of his multicompartmented mind from all of the others and from any control over his physical self, he sensitized it to receive whatever hallucinatory influences might be abroad. Simultaneously he set two other parts of his mind to watch over the one to be victimized; to study and to analyze whatever figments of obtrusive mentality might be received and entertained.

Then, using all of his naturally tremendous sensitivity and reach, all of his Arisian supertraining, and the full power of his Lens, he sent his mental receptors out into space. And then, although the thought is staggeringly incomprehensible to any Tellurian or near-human mind, he *relaxed*. For day after day, as the *Velan* hurtled randomly through the void, he hung blissfully slack upon his bars, most of his mind a welter of the indescribable thoughts in which it is a Velantian's joy to revel.

*

Suddenly, after an unknown interval of time, a thought impinged: a thought under the impact of which Worsel's body tightened so convulsively as to pull the bars a foot out of true. Overlords! The unmistakable, the body- and mind-paralyzing hunting call of the Overlords of Delgon!

His crew had not felt it yet, of course; nor would they feel it. If they should, they would be worse than useless in the conflict to come; for they could not withstand that baneful influence. Worsel could. Worsel was the only Velantian who could.

"Thought-screens all!" his commanding thought snapped out. Then, even before the order could be obeyed: "As you were!"

For the impenetrably shielded chambers of his mind told him immediately that this was no ordinary Delgonian hunting call; or rather, that it was more than that. Much more.

Mixed with, superimposed upon the overwhelming compulsion which generations of Velantians had come to know so bitterly and so well, were the very things for which he had been searching—hallucinations! To shield his crew or, except in the subtlest possible fashion himself, simply would not do. Overlords everywhere knew that there was at least one Velantian Lensman who was mentally their master; and, while they hated this Lensman tremendously, they feared him even more. Therefore, even though a Velantian was any Overlord's choicest prey, at the first indication of an ability to disobey their commands the monsters would cease entirely to radiate; would withdraw at once every strand of their far-flung mental nets into the fastnesses of their superbly hidden and indetectably shielded cavern.

Therefore Worsel allowed the inimical influence to take over, not only the total minds of his crew, but the unshielded portion of his own as well. And stealthily, so insidiously that no mind affected could discern the change, values gradually grew vague and reality began to alter.

Loyalty dimmed, and *esprit de corps*. Family ties and pride of race waned into meaninglessness. All concepts of Civilization, of the Galactic Patrol, degenerated into strengthless gossamer, into oblivion. And to replace those hitherto mighty motivations there crept in an overmastering need for, and the exact method of obtainment of, whatever it was that was each Velantian's deepest, most primal desire. Each crewman stared into an individual visiplate whose substance was to him as real and as solid as the metal of his ship had ever been; each saw upon that plate whatever it was that, consciously or unconsciously, he wanted to see. Noble or base, lofty or low, intellectual or physical, spiritual or carnal, it made no difference to the Overlords. Whatever each victim most wanted was there.

No figment was, however, even to the Velantians, actual or tangible. It was a picture upon a plate, transmitted from a well-defined point in space. There, upon that planet, was the actuality, eagerly awaited; toward and to that planet must the *Velan* go at maximum blast. Into that line and at that blast, then, the pilots set their vessel without

885

orders, and each of the crew saw upon his nonexistent plate that she had so been set. If she had not been, if the pilots had been able to offer any resistance, the crew would have slaughtered them out of hand. As it was, all was well.

And Worsel, watching the affected portion of his mind accept these hallucinations as truths and admiring unreservedly the consummate artistry with which the work was being done, was well content. He knew that only a hard, solidly-driven, individually probing beam could force him to reveal the fact that a portion of his mind and all of his bodily control were being withheld; he knew that unless he made a slip no such investigation was to be expected. He would not slip.

No human or near-human mind can really understand how the mind of a Velantian works. A Tellurian can, by dint of training, learn to do two or more unrelated things simultaneously. But neither is done very well and both must be more or less routine in nature. To perform any original or difficult operation successfully he must concentrate upon it, and he can concentrate upon only one thing at a time. A Velantian, however, can and does concentrate upon half-a-dozen totally unrelated things at once; and, with his multiplicity of arms, hands, and eyes, he can perform simultaneously an astonishing number of completely independent operations.

The Velantian is, however, in no sense such a multiple personality as would exist if six or eight human heads were mounted upon one body. There is no joint tenancy about it. There is only one ego permeating all those pseudoindependent compartments; no contradictory orders are, or ordinarily can be, sent along the bundled nerves of the spinal cord. While individual in thought and in the control of certain actions, the mind-compartments are basically, fundamentally, one mind.

Worsel had progressed beyond his fellows. He was different; unique. In fact, the perception of the need of the ability to isolate certain compartments of his mind, to separate them completely from his real ego, was one of the things which had enabled him to become the only Second-Stage Lensman of his race.

L2 Worsel, then, held himself aloof and observed appreciatively everything that went on. More, he did a little hallucinating of his own. Under the Overlords' compulsion he was supposed to remain motionless, staring raptly into an imaginary visiplate at an orgiastic saturnalia designed to make even his burly ego quail. Therefore, as far as the occupied portion of his mind and through it the Overlords were concerned, he did so. Actually, however, his body moved purposefully about, under the direction only of his own grim will; moved to make ready against the time of landing.

For Worsel knew that his opponents were not fools. He knew that they reduced their risks to the irreducible minimum. He knew that the mighty *Velan*, with her prodigious weaponry, would not be permitted to be within even extreme range of the cavern, if the Overlords could possibly prevent it, when that cavern's location was revealed. His was the task to see to it that she was not only within range, but was at the very portal.

*

The speeding spaceship approached the planet—went inert—matched the planetary intrinsic—landed. Her air locks opened. Her crew rushed out headlong, sprang into the air, and arrowed away *en masse*. Then Worsel, Grand Master of Hallucinations, went blithely but intensely to work.

Thus, although he stayed at the *Velan's* control board instead of joining the glamoured Velantians in their rush over the unfamiliar terrain, and although the huge spaceship lifted lightly into the air and followed them, neither the fiend-possessed part of Worsel's mind, nor any of his fellows, nor through them the many Overlords, knew that either of those two things was happening. To that part of his mind Worsel's body was, under full control, flying along upon tireless wings in the midst of the crowd; to it and to all of the other Velantians and hence to the Overlords the *Velan* lay motionless and deserted upon the rocks far below and behind them. They watched the vessel diminish in apparent size in the distance; they saw it vanish beyond the horizon!

This was eminently tricky work, necessitating as it did such nicety of synchronization with the Delgonian's own compulsions as to be indetectable even to the monsters themselves. Worsel was, however, an expert, one of the Universe's best; he went at the task not with any doubt whatever as to his ability to carry it through, but only with an uncontrollably shivering physical urge to come to grips with the hereditary enemies of his race.

The fliers shot downward, and as a boulder-camouflaged entrance yawned open in the mountain's side Worsel closed up and shot out a widely enveloping zone of thought-screen. The Overlords' control vanished. The Velantians, realizing instantaneously what had happened, flew madly back to their ship. They jammed through the air locks, flashed to their posts. The cavern's gates had closed by then, but the monsters had no screen fit to cope with the *Velan's* tremendous batteries. Down they went. Barriers, bastions, and a considerable portion of the mountain's face flamed away in fiery vapor or flowed away in molten streams. Through reeking atmosphere, over red-hot debris, the armored Velantians flew to the attack.

The Overlords had, however, learned. This cavern, as well as being hidden, was defended by physical, as well as mental, means. There were inner barriers of metal and of force, there were armed and armored defenders who, dominated completely by the monsters, fought with the callous fury of the robots which in effect they were. Nevertheless, against all opposition, the attackers bored relentlessly in. Heavy semiportables blazed, hand-to-hand combat raged in the narrow confines of that noisome tunnel. In the wavering, glaring light of the contending beams and screens, through the hot and rankly stinking steam billowing away from the reeking walls, the invaders fought their way. One by one and group by group the defenders died where they stood and the Velantians drove onward over their burned and dismembered bodies.

Into the cavern at last. To the Overlords. Overlords! They, who for ages had preyed upon generation after generation of helpless Velantians, torturing their bodies to the point of death and then devouring ghoulishly the life-forces which their mangled bodies could no longer retain!

Worsel and his crew threw away their DeLameters. Only when it is absolutely necessary does any Velantian use any artificial weapon against any Overlord of Delgon. He is too furious, too berserk, to do so. He is scared to the core of his being; the cold grue of a thousand fiendishly eaten ancestors has bred that fear into the innermost atoms of his chemistry. But against that fear, negating and surmounting it, is a hatred of such depth and violence as no human being has ever known; a starkly savage hatred which can be even partially assuaged only by the ultimate of violences—by rending his foe apart member by member; by actually feeling the Delgonian's life depart under gripping hands and tearing talons and constricting body and shearing tail.

It is best, then, not to go into too fine detail as to this conflict. Since there were almost a hundred of the Delgonians—insensately vicious fighters when cornered—and since their physical make-up was very similar to the Velantians' own, many of Worsel's troopers died. But since the *Velan* carried over fifteen hundred and since less than half of her personnel could even get into the cavern, there were plenty of them left to operate and to fight the spaceship.

*

Worsel took great care that the opposing commander was not killed with his minions. The fighting over, the Velantians chained this sole survivor into one of his own racks and stretched him out into immobility. Then, restraining by main strength the terrific urge to put the machine then and there to its fullest ghastly use, Worsel cut his screen, threw a couple of turns of tail around a convenient anchorage, and faced the Boskonian almost nose to nose. Eight weirdly stalked eyes curled out as he drove a probing thought-beam against the monster's shield.

"I could use this—or this—or this," Worsel gloated. As he touched various wheels and levers the chains hummed slightly, sparks flashed, the rigid body twitched. "I am not going to, however—yet. While you are still sane I want to take and I shall take your total knowledge."

And face to face, eye to eye, brain to brain, that silently and motionlessly cataclysmic battle was joined.

As has been said, Worsel had hunted down and had destroyed many Overlords. He had hunted them, however, like vermin. He had destroyed them with duodec bombs and with primary or secondary beams; or, at closest hand, with talons, teeth, and tail. He had not engaged an Overlord mind to mind for over twenty Tellurian years; not since he and Nadreck of Palain VII had captured alive the leaders of those who had been preying upon Helen's matriarchs and warring upon Civilization from their cavern upon Lyrane II. Nor had he ever dueled one mentally to death without powerful support; Kinnison or some other Lensman had always been near by.

But Worsel would need no help. He was not shivering in eagerness now. His body was as still as the solid rock upon which most of it lay; every chamber and every faculty of his mind was concentrated upon battering down or cutting through the Overlords' stubbornly-held shields.

Brighter and brighter glowed the Velantian's Lens, flooding the gloomy cave with pulsating polychromatic light. Alert for any possible trickery, guarding intently against any possibility of riposte or of counterthrust, Worsel leveled bolt after bolt of mental force. He surrounded the monster's mind with a searing, constricting field. He squeezed; relentlessly and with appalling power.

SUPER PACK

The Overlord was beaten. He, who had never before encountered a foreign mind or a vital force stronger than his own, knew that he was beaten. He knew that at long last he had met that half-fabulous Velantian Lensman with whom not one of his monstrous race could cope. He knew starkly, with the chilling, numbing terror possible only to such a being in such a position, that he was doomed to die the same hideous and long-drawn-out death which he had dealt out to so many others. He did not read into the mind of the bitterly vengeful, the implacably ferocious Velantian any more mercy or any more compunction than was actually there. He knew perfectly that of either there was no slightest trace. Knowing these things with the blackly appalling certainty that was his, he quailed.

There is an old but cogent saying that the brave man dies only once, the coward a thousand times. That Overlord, during that lethal combat, died more times than it is pleasant to contemplate. Nevertheless, he fought. A cornered rat will fight, and the Delgonian was not a rat—not exactly, that is, an ordinary rat. His mind was competent, keen, powerful, and utterly unscrupulous; and he brought to the defense of his beleaguered ego every resource of skill and of trickery and of sheer power at his command—in vain. Deeper and deeper, in spite of everything he could do, the relentless Lensman squeezed and smashed and cut and pried and bored; little by little the Overlord gave mental ground.

"This station is here . . . this staff is here . . . *I* am here, then . . . to wreak damage . . . all possible damage . . . to the commerce . . . and to the personnel of . . . the Galactic Patrol . . . and Civilization in every aspect—" the Overlord admitted haltingly as Worsel's pressure became intolerable; but such admissions, however unwillingly made or however revealing in substance, were not enough.

Worsel wanted, and would be satisfied with nothing less than, his enemy's total knowledge. Hence he maintained his assault until, unable longer to withstand the frightful battering, the Overlord's barriers went completely down; until every convolution of his brain and every track of his mind lay open, helplessly exposed to Worsel's poignant scrutiny. Then, scarcely taking time to gloat over his victim, Worsel did scrutinize.

Period.

*

Hurtling through space, toward a definite objective now, Worsel studied and analyzed some of the things which he had just learned. Worsel was not surprised that this Overlord had not known any of his superior officers in things or enterprises Boskonian; that he did not consciously know even that he had been obeying orders or that he had superiors. That technique, by this time, was familiar enough. The Boskonian psychologists were able operators; to attempt to unravel the unknowable complexities of their subconscious compulsions would be a sheer waste of time.

What the Overlords had been doing, however, was clear enough. That outpost had indeed been wreaking havoc with Civilization's commerce. Ship after ship had been lured from its course; had been compelled to land upon this barren planet. Some of those vessels had been destroyed; some of them had been stripped and rifled as though by pirates of old; some of them had been set upon new courses with hulls, mechanical equipment, and cargoes untouched. No crewman or passenger, however, escaped unscathed; even though only ten percent of them died in the Overlordish fashion which Worsel knew so well.

The Overlord himself had wondered why they had not been able to kill them all. He knew that such forbearance was unnatural, was against all instinct and training. He knew that they wanted, intensely enough, to kill every one of their victims; that their greedy lust for life-force simply could not be sated as long as life-force was to be had. He knew only that something, none of them knew what, limited their actual killing to ten percent of the bag.

Worsel grinned wolfishly at that thought, even while he was admiring the quality of the psychology which could impress such a compulsion as that upon such rapacious hellions as those. That was the work of the Boskonian higher-ups, who knew that ten percent was the limit above which the deaths would have been too revealing to the statisticians of the Galactic Patrol.

The other ninety percent, however, the Delgonians had "played with"—a procedure which, although less satisfying to the Overlords than the ultimate treatment, was not very different in so far as the victims' egos were concerned. For none of them emerged from the ordeal with any memory of what had happened, or of what or who he had ever been. They were not all completely mad; some were only partially so. All had, however, been—altered. Changed; shockingly transformed. No two were alike. Each Overlord, it appeared, had striven with all of his ultra-hellish ingenuity to excel his fellows in the manufacture of an outrageous something whose like had never been seen in or upon any land or sea or air or throughout any reach of space.

These and many other facts and items Worsel had studied carefully. He was now heading for the region in which the Patrol's computers had figured that the "Hell Hole in Space" must lie. The planet he had just left, the Overlords he had just slain, were not the original Hell Hole; could have had nothing to do with it. Too far apart—they were not in the same possible volume of space.

Worsel knew now, though, what the Hell Hole in Space really was. It was a cavern of Overlords. It simply couldn't be anything else. And, in himself and his crew and his mighty *Velan* he, Worsel of Velantia, Overlord-slayer par excellence of two galaxies, had in ample measure everything it took to extirpate any number of Overlords. With what he had just learned and with what he was so calmly certain he could do, the Hell Hole in Space would take no more toll. Wherefore Worsel, coiled loosely around his hard bars, relaxed in happily planful thought. And in a couple of hours a solid, clear-cut thought impinged upon his Lens.

"Worsel! Con calling. What goes on there, fellow old snake? You've stuck that sharp tail of yours into some of my business—I hope!"

III.

Each of the Second-Stage Lensmen had exactly the same facts, the same data, upon which to theorize and from which to draw conclusions. Each had shared his experiences, his findings, and his deductions and inductions with all of the others. They had discussed minutely, in wide-open four-ways, every phase of the Boskonian problem. Nevertheless the approach of each to that problem and the point of attack chosen by each was individual and characteristic.

Kimball Kinnison was by nature forthright; direct. As has been seen, he could use the approach circuitous if necessary, but he much preferred and upon every possible occasion employed the approach direct. He liked plain, unambiguous clues much better than obscure ones; the more obvious and factual the clue was, the better he liked it.

He was now, therefore, heading for Antigan IV, the scene of the latest and apparently the most outrageous of a long series of crimes of violence. He didn't know much about it; the request had come in through regular channels, not via Lens, that he visit Antigan and take personal charge of the investigation of the supposed murder of the Planetary President.

As his speedster flashed through space the Gray Lensman mulled over in his mind the broad aspects of this crime wave. It was spreading far and wide, and the wider it spread and the intenser it became the more vividly one salient fact stuck out. Selectivity—distribution. The solar systems of Thrale, Velantia, Tellus, Klovia, and Palain had not been affected. Thrale, Tellus, and Klovia were full of Lensmen. Velantia, Rigel, Palain, and a good part of the time Klovia, were the working headquarters of Second-Stage Lensmen. It seemed, then, that the trouble was roughly in inverse ratio to the numbers or the abilities of the Lensmen in the neighborhood. Something, therefore, that Lensmen—particularly Second-Stage Lensmen—were bad for. That was true, of course, for all crime. Nevertheless, this seemed to be a special case.

And when he reached his destination he found out that it was. The planet was seething. Its business and its everyday activities seemed to be almost paralyzed. Martial law had been declared; the streets were practically deserted except for thick-clustered groups of heavily-armed guards. What few people were abroad were furtive and sly; slinking hastily along with their fear-filled eyes trying to look in all directions at once.

"QX, Wainwright, go ahead," Kinnison directed brusquely when, alone with the escorting Patrol officers in a shielded car, he was being taken to the Capitol grounds. "There's been too much secrecy—pussyfooting—about the whole affair. Spill it, please."

"Very well, sir," and Wainwright told his tale. Things had been happening for months. Little things, but disturbing. Then murders and kidnapings and unexplained disappearances had begun to increase. The police forces had been falling farther and farther behind. The usual cries of incompetence and corruption had been raised, only further to confuse the issue. Circulars—dodgers—hand-bills appeared all over the planet; from where nobody knew. The keenest detectives could find no clue to papermakers, printers, or distributors. The usual inflammatory, subversive propaganda—"Down with the Patrol!" "Give us back our freedom!" and so on—but, because of the high tension already prevailing, the stuff had been unusually effective in breaking down the morale of the citizenry as a whole.

"Then this last thing. For two solid weeks the whole world was literally plastered with the announcement that at midnight on the thirty-fourth of Dreel—you're familiar with our calendar, I think?—President Renwood would disappear. Two weeks warning—daring us." Wainwright got that far and stopped.

"Well, go on. He disappeared, I know. How? What did you fellows do to prevent it? Why all the secrecy?"

"If you insist, I'll have to tell you, of course, but I'd rather not." Wainwright flushed uncomfortably. "You wouldn't believe it. Nobody could. I wouldn't believe it myself if I hadn't been there. I'd rather you'd wait, sir, and let the Vice President tell you, in the presence of the Treasurer and the others who were on duty that night."

"Um-m-m . . . I see . . . maybe." Kinnison's mind raced. "That's why nobody would give me details? Afraid I wouldn't believe it . . . that I'd think they'd been—" He stopped. "Hypnotized" would have been the next word, but that would have been jumping at conclusions. Even if true, there was no sense in airing that hypothesis—yet.

"Not afraid, sir. They *knew* that you wouldn't believe it."

*

After entering Government Reservation they went, not to the president's private quarters, but into the Treasury and down into the subbasement housing the most massive, the most utterly impregnable vault of the planet. There the nation's most responsible officers told Kinnison, with their entire minds as well as their tongues, what had happened.

Upon that black day business had been suspended. No visitors of any sort had been permitted to enter the Reservation. No one had been allowed to approach the president except old and trusted officers about whose loyalty there could be no question. Airships and spaceships had filled the sky. Troops, armed with semiportables or manning fixed-mount heavy stuff, had covered the grounds. At five minutes before midnight Renwood, accompanied by four secret service men, had entered the vault, which was thereupon locked by the treasurer. All the cabinet members saw them go in, as did the attendant corps of specially-selected guards. Nevertheless, when the treasurer opened the vault at five minutes after midnight, the five men were gone. No trace of any one of them had been found from that time on.

"And that—every word of it—is TRUE!" the assembled minds yelled as one, all unconsciously, into the mind of the Lensman.

During all this telling Kinnison had been searching mind after mind; inspecting each minutely for the telltale marks of mental surgery. He found none. No hypnosis. This thing had happened, exactly as they told it. Now, convinced of that fact, his eyes clouded with foreboding, he sent out his sense of perception and studied the vault itself. Millimeter by cubic millimeter he scanned the innermost details of its massive structure—the concrete, the neo-carballoy, the steel, the heat-conductors and the closely-spaced gas cells. He traced the intricate wiring of the networks of alarms. Everything was sound. Everything functioned. Nothing had been disturbed.

The sun of this system, although rather on the small side, was intensely hot; this planet, Four, was a long way out. Pretty close to Cardynge's limit . . . or the Boskonians had improved their technique—tightened up their controls. A tube, of course . . . for all the tea in China it had to be a tube. Kinnison sagged; for the first time in his life the indomitable Gray Lensman showed his years and more.

"I know that it happened." His voice was grim, quiet, as he spoke to the still protesting men. "I also know how it was done, but that's all."

"HOW?" they demanded, practically in one voice.

"A hyperspatial tube," and Kinnison went on to explain, as well as he could, the functioning of a thing which could not be grasped intrinsically by any nonmathematical three-dimensional mind.

"But what can we or you or anybody else do about it?" the treasurer asked, numbly.

"Nothing whatever." Kinnison's voice was flat. "When it's gone, it's gone. Where does the light go when a lamp goes out? No more trace. No more way—no way whatever—of tracing it. Hundreds of millions of planets in this galaxy, as many in the Second. Millions and millions of galaxies. All that in one Universe—our own universe. And there are an infinite number—too many to be expressed, let alone to be grasped—of universes, side by side, like pages in a book except thinner, in the hyperdimension. So you can figure out for yourselves the chances of ever finding either President Renwood or the Boskonians who took him—so close to zero as to be indistinguishable from zero absolute."

The treasurer was crushed. "Do you mean to say that there is no protection at all from this thing? That they can keep on doing away with us just as they please? The nation is going mad, sir, day by day—one more such occurrence and we will be a planet of maniacs."

"Oh, no—I didn't say that." The tension lightened. "Just that we can't do anything about the president and his aides. The tube can be detected while it is in place, and anyone coming through it can be shot as soon as he can be seen. What you need is a couple of Rigellian Lensmen, or Ordoviks. I'll see to it that you get them. I don't think, with them here, that they will even try to repeat." He did not add what he knew somberly to be a fact, that the enemy would go elsewhere, to some other planet not protected by a Lensman able to perceive the intangible structure of a sphere of pure force.

*

Frustrated, the Lensman again took to space. It was terrible, this thing of having everything happening where he wasn't, and when he got there having nothing left to work on. Hit-and-run—stab-in-the-back—how could a man fight something that he couldn't see or sense or feel or find? But this chewing his fingernails to the elbow wasn't getting him anywhere, either; he'd have to find something that he *could* stick a tooth into. What?

All former avenues of approach were blocked; he was sure of that. The Boskonians, who were now in charge of things, could really think. No underling would know anything about any one of them except at such times and places as the directors chose, and those conferences would be as nearly detection-proof as they could be made. What to do?

Easy. Catch a big operator in the act. He grinned wryly to himself. Easy to say, but not—However, it wasn't impossible. The Boskonians were not supermen—they didn't have any more jets than he did. Put himself in the other fellow's place—what would he do if he were a Boskonian big shot? He had had quite a lot of experience in the role. Were there any specific groups of crimes which revealed techniques similar to those which he himself would use in like case?

He, personally, preferred to work direct and to attack in force. At need, however, he had done a smooth job of boring from within. In the face of the Patrol's overwhelming superiority of armament, especially in the First Galaxy, they would have to bore from within. How? By what means? He was a Lensman; they were not. Jet back! Or were they, perhaps? How did he know that they weren't? Maybe they were, by this time. Fossten the renegade Arisian—No use kidding himself; Fossten might have known as much about the Lens as Mentor himself, and might have developed an organization that even Mentor didn't know anything about. Or Mentor might be figuring that it would be good for what ailed a certain fat-headed Gray Lensman to have to dope this out for himself. QX.

He shot a call to Vice Co-ordinator Maitland, who was now in complete charge of the office which Kinnison had temporarily abandoned.

"Cliff? Kim. Just gave birth to an idea." He explained rapidly what the idea was. "Maybe nothing to it, but we'd better get up on our toes and find out. You might suggest to the boys that they check up here and there, particularly around the rough spots. If any of them find any trace anywhere of off-color, sour, or even slightly rancid Lensmanship, with or without a Lens appearing in the picture, burn a hole in space getting it to me. QX? . . . Thanks."

Viewed in this new perspective, Renwood of Antigan IV might have been neither a patriot nor a victim, but a saboteur. The tube could have been a prop, used deliberately to cap the mysterious climax. The four honest and devoted guards were the real casualties. Renwood—or whoever he was—having accomplished his object of undermining and destroying the whole planet's morale, might simply have gone elsewhere to continue his nefarious activities. It was fiendishly clever. That spectacularly theatrical finale was certainly one for the book. The whole thing, though, was very much of a piece in quality of workmanship with what he had done in becoming the Tyrant of Thrale. Farfetched? No. He had already denied in his thoughts that the Boskonian operators were supermen. Conversely, he wasn't, either. He would have to admit that they might very well be as good as he was; to deny them the ability to do anything which he himself could do would be sheer stupidity.

Where did that put him? On Radelix, by Klono's golden gills! A good-sized planet. Important enough, but not too much so. People human. Comparatively little hell being raised there—yet. Very few Lensmen, and Gerrond the top. Hm-m-m. Gerrond. Not too bright, as Lensmen went, and inclined to be a bit brass-hattish. To Radelix, by all means, next.

*

He went to Radelix, but not in the *Dauntless* and not in gray. He was a passenger upon a luxury liner, a writer in search of local color for another saga of the spaceways. Sybly Whyte—one of the Patrol's most carefully-established figments—had a bulletproof past. His omnivorous interest and his uninhibited nosiness were the natural attributes of his profession—everything is grist which comes to an author's mill.

SUPER PACK

Sybly Whyte then prowled about Radelix. Industriously and, to some observers, pointlessly. He and his red-leather notebook were apt to be seen anywhere at any time, day or night. He visited spaceports, he climbed through freighters, he lost small sums in playing various games of so-called chance in spacemen's dives. Upon the other hand, he truckled assiduously to the social elite and attended all functions into which he could wangle or could force his way. He made a pest of himself in the offices of politicians, bankers, merchant princes, tycoons of business and manufacture, and all other sorts of greats.

He was stopped one day in the outer office of an industrial potentate. "Get out and stay out," a peg-legged guard told him. "The boss hasn't read any of your stuff, but I have, and neither of us wants to talk to you. Data, huh? What do you need of data on atomic cats and bulldozers to write them space operas of yours? Why don't you get a roustabout job on a freighter and learn something about what you're trying to write about? Get yourself a real space tan instead of that imitation you got under a lamp; work some of that lard off of your carcass!" Whyte was definitely fatter than Kinnison had been; and, somehow, softer; he peered owlishly through heavy lenses which, fortunately, did not interfere with his sense of perception. "Then maybe some of your tripe will be half-fit to read—beat it!"

"Yes, sir. Thank you, sir; very much, sir." Kinnison bobbed obsequiously and scurried out, writing industriously in his notebook the while. He had, however, found out what he wanted to know. The boss was nobody he was looking for.

Nor was an eminent statesman whom he buttonholed at a reception. "I fail to see, sir, entirely, any point in your interviewing *me*," that worthy informed him, frigidly. "I am not, I am . . . uh . . . sure, suitable material for any opus upon which you may be at work."

"Oh, you can't ever tell, sir," Kinnison said. "You see, I never know who or what is going to get into any of my stories until after I start to write it, and sometimes not even then." The statesman glared and Kinnison retreated in disorder.

To stay in character Kinnison actually wrote a story while upon Radelix; a story which was later acclaimed as one of Sybly Whyte's best.

"Qadgop the Mercotan slithered flatly around the after-bulge of the tranship. One claw dug into the meters-thick armor of pure neutronium, then another. Its terrible xmexlike snout locked on. Its zymolosely polydactile tongue crunched out, crashed down, rasped across. *Slurp! Slurp!* At each abrasive stroke the groove in the tranship's plating deepened and Qadgop leered more fiercely. Fools! Did they think that the airlessness of absolute space, the heatlessness of absolute zero, the yieldlessness of absolute neutronium, could stop QADGOP THE MERCOTAN? And the stowaway, that human wench Cynthia, cowering in helpless terror just beyond this thin and fragile wall—" Kinnison was tapping merrily and verbosely along, at a cento a word, when his first real clue developed.

*

A yellow "attention" light gleamed upon his visiphone panel, a subdued chime gave notice that a message of importance was about to be broadcast to the world. Kinnison-

Whyte flipped his switch and the stern face of the Provost Marshal appeared upon the screen.

"Attention, please," the image spoke. "Every citizen of Radelix is urged to be upon the lookout for the source of certain inflammatory and subversive literature which is beginning to appear in various cities of this planet. Our officers cannot be everywhere at once; you citizens are. It is hoped that by the aid of your vigilance this threat to our planetary peace and security can be removed before it becomes really serious; that we can avoid the imposition of martial law."

This message, while not of extreme or urgent import to most Radeligians, held for Kinnison a profound and unique meaning. He was right. He had deduced the thing one hundred percent. He knew what was going to happen next, and how; he knew that neither the law-enforcement officers of Radelix nor its massed citizenry could stop it. They could not even impede it. A force of Lensmen could stop it—but that would not get the Patrol anywhere unless they could capture or kill the beings really responsible for what was done. To alarm them would not do.

Whether or not he could do much of anything before the grand climax depended upon a lot of factors. Upon what that climax was; upon who was threatened with what; upon whether or not the threatened one was actually a Boskonian. A great deal of investigation was indicated.

If the enemy were going to repeat, as seemed probable, the president would be the victim. If he, Kinnison, could not get a line upon the higher-ups before the plot came to a head, he would have to let it develop right up to the point of disappearance; and for Whyte to appear upon the scene at that time would be to attract undesirable attention. No—by that time he must already have been kicking around underfoot long enough to have become an unnoticeable fixture.

Wherefore he moved into quarters as close to the Executive Offices as he could possibly get; and in those quarters he worked openly and wordily at the bringing of the affair of Qadgop and the beautiful-but-dumb Cynthia to a satisfactory conclusion.

IV.

In order to understand these and subsequent events it is necessary to cut back briefly some twenty-odd years, to the momentous interview upon chill, dark Onlo between monstrous Kandron and his superior in affairs Boskonian, the unspeakable Alcon, Tyrant of Thrale. At almost the end of that interview, when Kandron had suggested the possibility that his own base had perhaps been vulnerable to Star A Star's insidious manipulations:

"Do you mean to admit that *you* may have been invaded and searched—tracelessly?" Alcon fairly shrieked the thought.

"Certainly," Kandron replied, coldly. "While I do not believe that it has been done, the possibility must be conceded. What we could do we have done, but what science can do science can circumvent. It is a virtual certainty that it is not Onlo and I who are their prime objectives, but Thrale and you. Especially you."

"You may be right. With no data whatever upon who or what Star A Star really is, with no tenable theory as to how he could have done what actually has been done, speculation is idle." Thus Alcon ended the conversation and, almost immediately, went back to Thrale.

After the Tyrant's departure Kandron continued to think, and the more he thought the more uneasy he became. It was undoubtedly true that Alcon and Thrale were the Patrol's prime objectives. But, those objectives attained, was it reasonable to suppose that he and Onlo would be spared? It was not. Should he warn Alcon further? He should not. If the Tyrant, after all that had been said, could not see the danger he was in, he was not worth saving. If he preferred to stay and fight it out, that was his lookout. Kandron would take no chances with his own extremely valuable life.

Should he warn his own men? How could he? They were able and hardened fighters all; no possible warning could make them defend their fortresses and their lives any more efficiently than they were already prepared to do; nothing he could say would be of any use in preparing them for a threat whose basic nature, even, was completely unknown. Furthermore, this hypothetical invasion probably had not happened and very well might not happen at all, and to flee from an imaginary foe would not rebound to his credit.

No. As a personage of large affairs, not limited to Onlo, he would be called elsewhere. He would stay elsewhere until after whatever was going to happen had happened. If nothing happened during the ensuing few weeks, he would return from his official trip and all would be well.

He inspected Onlo thoroughly, he cautioned his officers repeatedly and insistently to keep alert against every conceivable emergency while he was so unavoidably absent. Then he departed, with a fleet of vessels manned by hand-picked crews, to a long-prepared and hitherto secret retreat.

From that safe place he watched, through the eyes and the instruments of his skilled observers, everything that occurred. Thrale fell, and Onlo. The Patrol triumphed. Then, knowing the full measure of the disaster and accepting it with the grim passivity so characteristic of his breed, Kandron broadcast certain signals and one of his—and Alcon's—superiors got in touch with him. He reported concisely. They conferred. He was given orders which were to keep him busy for over twenty Tellurian years.

He knew now that Onlo had been invaded, tracelessly, by some feat of mentality beyond comprehension and almost beyond belief. He knew that Onlo had fallen without any of its defenders having energized a single one of their gigantic engines of war. The fall of Thrale, and the manner of that fall's accomplishment, were plain enough. Human stuff. The work, undoubtedly, of human Lensmen; perhaps the work of the human Lensman who was so frequently associated with Star A Star.

But Onlo! Kandron himself had set those snares along those intricately zigzagged communications lines; he knew their capabilities. Kandron himself had installed Onlo's blocking and shielding screens; he knew their might. He knew, since no other path existed leading to Thrale, that those lines had been followed and those screens had been penetrated, and all without setting off a single alarm. Those things had actually happened. Hence Kandron set his stupendous mind to the task of envisaging what the being must be, mentally, who could do them; what the mind of this Star A Star—it could have been no one else—must in actuality be.

He succeeded. He deduced Nadreck of Palain VII, practically *in toto*; and for the Star A Star thus envisaged he set traps throughout both galaxies. They might or might not kill him. Killing him immediately, however, was not really of the essence; that matter could wait until he could give it his personal attention. The important thing was to see to it that Star A Star could never, by any possible chance, discover a true lead to any high Boskonian.

Sneeringly, gloatingly, Kandron issued orders; then flung himself with all his zeal and ability into the task of reorganizing the shattered fragments of the Boskonian Empire into a force capable of wrecking Civilization.

Thus it is not strange that for more than twenty years Nadreck of Palain VII made very little progress indeed. Time after time he grazed the hot edge of death. Indeed, it was only by the exertion of his every iota of skill, power, and callous efficiency that he managed to survive. He struck a few telling blows for Civilization, but most of the time he was strictly upon the defensive. Every clue that he followed, it seemed, led subtly into a trap; every course he pursued ended, always figuratively and all too often literally, in a cul-de-sac filled with semiportable projectors all agog to blast him out of the ether.

Year by year he became more conscious of some imperceptible, indetectable, but potent foe, an individual enemy obstructing his every move and determined to make an end of him. And year by year, as material accumulated, it became more and more certain that the inimical entity was in fact Kandron, once of Onlo.

When Kit went into space, then, and Kinnison called Nadreck into consultation the usually reticent and unloquacious Palainian was ready to talk. He told the Gray Lensman everything he knew, everything he deduced or suspected about the ex-Onlonian chieftain.

"Kandron of Onlo!" Kinnison exploded, so violently as to sear the subether through which the thought passed. "Holy Klono's brazen bowels! And you can sit there on your spiny tokus and tell me that Kandron got away from you back there? And that you knew it, and not only didn't do a thing about it yourself, but didn't even tell me or anybody else about it, so that we could take steps?"

"Certainly. Why take steps before they become necessary?" Nadreck was entirely unmoved by the Tellurian's passion. "My powers are admittedly small, my intellect feeble. However, even to me it was clear then and it is clear now that Kandron was then of no importance. My assignment was to reduce Onlo. I reduced it. Whether or not Kandron was there at the time did not then have and cannot now have anything to do with that task. Kandron, personally, is another, an entirely distinct problem."

Kinnison swore a blistering deep-space oath; then, by main strength, shut himself up. Nadreck wasn't human; there was no use even trying to judge him by human or near-human standards. He was fundamentally, incomprehensibly, and radically different. And it was just as well for humanity that he was. For if his hellishly able race had possessed the characteristically human abilities, in addition to their own, Civilization would of necessity have been basically Palainian instead of basically human, as it now is. "QX, ace," he growled, finally. "Skip it."

"But Kandron has been hampering my activities for years, and, now that you also have become interested in his operations against us, he has become a factor of which cognizance should be taken," Nadreck went imperturbably on. He could no more understand Kinnison's viewpoint than the Tellurian could understand his. "With your permission, therefore, I shall find—and slay—this Kandron."

"Go to it, little chum," Kinnison sighed, bitingly and uselessly. "Clear ether."

*

While this conference was taking place, Kandron reclined in a bitterly cold, completely unlighted room of his headquarters and indulged in a little gloating concerning the predicament in which he was keeping Nadreck of Palain VII, who was, in all probability, the once-dreaded Star A Star of the Galactic Patrol. It was true that THE Lensman was still alive. He would probably, Kandron mused quite pleasurably, remain alive until he himself could find the time to attend to him in person. He was an able operator, but one presenting no real menace, now that he was known and understood. There were other things more pressing, just as there had been ever since the fall of Thrale. The revised Plan was going nicely, and as soon as he had resolved that human thing—The Ploorans had suggested . . . could it be possible, after all, that Nadreck of Palain was not he who had been known so long only as Star A Star? That the human factor was actually—

Through the operation of some unknowable sense Kandron knew that it was time for his aide to be at hand to report upon those human affairs. He sent out a signal and another Onlonian scuttled in.

"That unknown human element," Kandron radiated harshly. "I assume that you are not reporting that it has been resolved?"

"Sorry, Supremacy, but your assumption is correct," the creature radiated back, in no very conciliatory fashion. "The trap at Antigan IV was set particularly for him; specifically to match the man whose mentality you computed and diagramed for us. Was it too obvious, think you, Supremacy? Or perhaps not quite obvious enough? Or, the Galaxy being large, is it perhaps that he simply did not learn of it in time? In the next attempt, what degree of obviousness should I employ and what degree of repetition is desirable?"

"The technique of the Antigan affair was flawless," Kandron decided. "He did not learn of it, as you suggest, or we should have caught him. He is a master workman, always concealed by his very obviousness until after he has done his work. Thus we can never, save by merest chance, catch him before the act; we must make him come to us. We must keep on trying until he does come to us. It is of no great moment, really, whether we catch him now or five years hence. This work must be done in any event—it is simply a fortunate coincidence that the necessary destruction of Civilization upon its own planets presents such a fine opportunity of trapping him.

"As to repeating the Antigan technique, we should not repeat it exactly . . . or, hold! It might be best to do just that. To repeat a process is, of course, the mark of an inferior mind; but if that human can be made to believe that our minds are inferior, so much the better. Keep on trying; report as instructed. Remember that he must be taken alive, so that we can take from his living brain the secrets we have not yet been able to learn.

Forget, in the instant of leaving this room, everything about me and about any connections between us until I force recollection upon you. Go."

The minion went, and Kandron set out to do more of the things which he could best do. He would have liked to take Nadreck's trail himself; he could catch and he could kill that evasive entity and the task would have been a pleasant one. He would have liked to supervise the trapping of that enigmatic human Lensman who might—or might not—be that frequently and copiously damned Star A Star. That, too, would be an eminently pleasant chore. There were, however, other matters more pressing by far. If the Great Plan were to succeed, and it absolutely must and would, every Boskonian must perform his assigned duties. Nadreck and his putative accomplice were side issues. Kandron's task was to set up and to direct certain psychoses and disorders; a ghastly train of mental ills of which he possessed such supreme mastery, and which were surely and safely helping to destroy the foundation upon which Galactic Civilization rested. That part was his, and he would do it to the best of his ability. The other things, the personal and nonessential matters, could wait.

Kandron set out then, and traveled fast and far; and wherever he went there spread still further abroad the already widespread blight. A disgusting, a horrible blight with which no human physician or psychiatrist, apparently, could cope; one of, perhaps the worst of, the corrosive blights which had been eating so long at Civilization's vitals.

*

And L2 Nadreck, having decided to find and slay the ex-ruler of Onlo, went about it in his usual unhurried but eminently thorough fashion. He made no effort to locate him or to trace him personally. That would be bad—foolish. Worse, it would be inefficient. Worst, it would probably be impossible. No, he would find out where Kandron would be at some suitable future time, and wait for him in that place.

To that end Nadreck collected a vast mass of data concerning the occurrences and phenomena which the Big Four had discussed so thoroughly. He analyzed each item, sorting out those which bore the characteristic stamp of the arch-foe whom by now he had come to know so well. The internal evidence of Kandron's craftsmanship was unmistakable; and, not now to his surprise, Nadreck discerned that the number of the Onlonian's dark deeds was legion.

There was the affair of the Prime Minister of DeSilva III, who at a cabinet meeting shot and killed his sovereign and eleven chiefs of state before committing suicide. The President of Viridon, who at his press conference, ran amuck with a scimitar snatched from a wall, hewed unsuspecting reporters to gory bits until he was overpowered, and then swallowed poison.

A variant of the theme, but still plainly Kandron's doing, was the interesting episode in which Galactic Counselor Edmundson, while upon an ocean voyage, threw fifteen women passengers overboard, then leaped after them dressed only in a life jacket stuffed with lead. Another out of the same whimsical mold was that of Dillway, the highly respected Operations Chief of Central Spaceways. That potentate called his secretaries one by one into his sixtieth floor office and unconcernedly tossed them, one by one, out of the window. He danced a jig upon a coping before diving after them to the street.

SUPER PACK

A particularly juicy and entertaining bit, Nadreck thought, was the case of Narkor Base Hospital, in which four of the planet's most eminent surgeons decapitated every other person in the place—patients, nurses, orderlies, and all, with a fine disregard of age, sex, or condition—arranged the several heads, each upright and each facing due north, upon the tiled floor to spell the word "Revenge," and then hacked each other to death with scalpels.

These, and a thousand or more other events of similar technique, Nadreck tabulated and subjected to statistical analysis. Scattered so widely throughout such a vast volume of space, they had created little or no general disturbance; indeed, they had scarcely been noticed by Civilization as a whole. Collected, they made a truly staggering, a revolting and appalling total. Nadreck, however, was inherently incapable of being staggered, revolted, or appalled. That repulsive summation, a thing which in its massed horror would have shaken to the core—shocked almost into paralysis—any being possessing any shred of sympathy or tenderness, was to Nadreck simply an interesting and not too difficult problem in psychology and mathematics.

He placed each episode in space and in time, correlating each with all of its fellows in a space-time matrix. He determined the locus of centers and derived the equations of its most probable motion. He extended it by extrapolation in accordance with that equation. Then, assuring himself that his margin of error was as small as he could make it, he set out for a planet which Kandron would most probably visit at a time far enough in the future to enable him to receive the Onlonian.

*

That planet, being inhabited by near-human beings, was warm, brightly sun-lit, and had an atmosphere rich in oxygen. Nadreck detested it, since his ideal of a planet was precisely the opposite. Fortunately, however, he would not have to land upon it until after Kandron's arrival—possibly not then—and the fact that his proposed quarry was, like himself, a frigid-blooded poison-breather, made the task of detection a simple one.

Nadreck set his indetectable speedster into a circular orbit around the planet, far enough out to be comfortable, and sent out course after course of delicate, extremely sensitive screen. Precision of pattern-analysis was, of course, needless. The probability was that all legitimate movement of personnel to and from the planet would be composed of warm-blooded oxygen-breathers; that any visitor not so classified would be Kandron. Any frigid-blooded visitor had at least to be investigated, hence his analytical screens had to be capable only of differentiating between two types of beings as far apart as the galactic poles in practically every respect. Nadreck knew that no supervision would be necessary to perform such an open-and-shut separation as that; he would have nothing more to do until his electronic announcers should warn him of Kandron's approach—or until the passage of time should inform him that the Onlonian was not coming to this particular planet.

Being a mathematician, Nadreck knew that any datum secured by extrapolation is of doubtful value. He thus knew that the actual probability of Kandron's coming was less, by some indeterminable amount, than the mathematical one. Nevertheless, having done all that he could do, he waited with the monstrous, unhuman patience known only to such races as his.

Day by day, week by week, the speedster circled the planet and its big, hot sun; and as it circled, the lone voyager studied. He analyzed more data more precisely; he drew deeper and deeper upon his store of knowledge to determine what steps next to take in the event that this attempt should end, as so many previous ones had ended, in failure.

V.

Kinnison, the author, toiled manfully at his epic of space whenever he was under any sort of observation, and enough at other times to avert any suspicion. Indeed, he worked as much as Sybly Whyte, an advertisedly temperamental writer, had ever worked. Besides interviewing the high and the low, and taking notes everywhere, he attended authors' teas, at which he cursed his characters fluently and bitterly for their failure to co-operate with him. With short-haired women and long-haired men he bemoaned the perversity of a public which compelled them to prostitute the real genius of which each was the unique possessor. He sympathized particularly with a fat woman writer of whodunits, whose extremely unrealistic yet amazingly popular Gray Lensman hero had lived through ten full-length novels and twenty million copies.

Even though her real field was the drama, she wasn't writing the kind of detective tripe that most of these crank-turners ground out, she confided to Kinnison. She had known lots of Gray Lensmen *very* intimately, and *her* stories were drawn from real life in every particular!

Thus Kinnison remained in character; and thus he was enabled to work completely unnoticed at his real job of finding out what was going on, how the Boskonians were operating to ruin Radelix as they had ruined Antigan IV.

His first care was to investigate the planet's president. That took doing, but he did it. He examined that mind line by line and channel by channel, with no results whatever. No scars, no sign of tampering. Calling in assistance, he searched the president's past even more rigidly than Fossten had searched that of Traska Gannel. Still no soap. Everything checked, even to widely distributed boyhood pictures. Boring from within, then, was out. His first hypothesis was wrong; this invasion and this sabotage were being done from without. How?

Those first leaflets were followed by others, each batch more vitriolic in tone than the preceding one. Apparently they came from empty stratosphere; at least, no ships were to be detected in the neighborhood after any shower of the hand-bills had appeared. But that was not surprising. With its inertialess drive any spaceship could have been parsecs away before the papers touched atmosphere. Or they could have been bombed in from almost any distance. Or, as Kinnison thought most reasonable, they could have been simply dumped out of the mouth of a hyperspatial tube. In any event the method was immaterial. The results only were important; and those results, the Lensman discovered, were entirely disproportionate to the ostensible causes. The subversive literature had some effect, of course, but essentially it must be a blind. No possible tonnage of anonymous printing could cause that much sheer demoralization.

SUPER PACK

Crackpot societies of all kinds sprang up everywhere, advocating everything from absolutism to anarchy. Queer cults arose, preaching free love, the imminent end of the world, and almost every other conceivable departure from the norm of thought. The Authors' League, of course, was affected more than any other organization of its size, because of its relatively large content of strong and intensely opinionated minds. Instead of becoming one radical group it split into a dozen.

*

Kinnison joined one of those "Down with Everything!" groups, not as a leader, but as a follower. Not too sheeplike a follower, but just inconspicuous enough to retain his invisibly average status; and from his place of concealment in the middle of the front rank he studied the minds of each of his fellow anarchists. He watched those minds change, he found out who was doing the changing. When Kinnison's turn came he was all set for trouble. He expected to battle a powerful mentality. He would not have been overly surprised to encounter another mad Arisian, hiding behind a zone of hypnotic compulsion. He expected anything, in fact, except what he found—which was a very ordinary Radeligian therapist. The guy was a clever enough operator, of course, but he could not work against even the feeblest opposition. Hence the Gray Lensman had no trouble at all, either in learning everything the fellow knew or, upon leaving him, in implanting within his mind the knowledge that he had made Sybly Whyte into exactly the type of anarchist desired.

The trouble was that the therapist didn't know a thing. This not entirely unexpected development posed Kinnison three questions. Did the higher-ups ever communicate with such small fry, or did they just give them one set of orders and cut them loose? Should he stay in this Radeligian's mind until he found out? If he was in control of the therapist when a big shot took over, did he have jets enough to keep from being found out? Risky business; better scout around first, anyway. He'd do a flit.

He drove his black speedster a million miles. He covered Radelix like a blanket, around the equator and from pole to pole. Everywhere he found the same state of things. The planet was literally riddled with the agitators; he found so many that he was forced to a black conclusion. There could be no connection or communication between such numbers of saboteurs and any higher authority. They must have been sent with one set of do-or-die instructions—whether they did or died was immaterial. Experimentally, Kinnison had a few of the ringleaders taken into custody. As each was arrested another took his place.

Martial law was finally declared, but this measure succeeded only in driving the conspirators underground. What the subversive societies lost in numbers they more than made up in desperation and violence. Crime raged unchecked and uncheckable, murder became an everyday commonplace, insanity waxed rife. And Kinnison, knowing now that no channel to important prey would be opened until the climax, watched grimly while the rape of the planet went on.

The president of Radelix and Lensman Gerrond sent message after message to Prime Base and to Klovia, imploring help. The replies to these pleas were all alike. The matter had been referred to the Galactic Council and to the Co-ordinator. Everything that could be done was being done. Neither office would say anything else, except that, with the galaxy in such a disturbed condition, each planet must do its best to solve its own problems.

*

The thing built up toward its atrocious finale. Gerrond invited the president to a conference in a downtown hotel room, and there, eyes glancing from moment to moment at the dials of a complete little test-kit held open upon his lap:

"I have just had some startling news, sir," Gerrond said, abruptly. "Kinnison has been here on Radelix for weeks."

"What? Kinnison? Where is he? Why didn't he—?"

"Yes, Kinnison. Kinnison of Klovia. The Co-ordinator himself. I don't know where he is, or was. I didn't ask him." The Lensman smiled fleetingly. "One doesn't, you know. He discussed the situation with me at length. I am still amazed—"

"Why doesn't he stop it, then?" the president demanded. "Or can't he stop it?"

"That's what I've got to explain to you. He can, but the time won't be ripe until the last act."

"Why not? I tell you, if this thing can be stopped it's *got* to be stopped, and no matter what has to be done it's *got* to be—"

"Just a minute!" Gerrond snapped. "I know that you're out of control—I don't like to see Radelix torn apart any better than you do—but you ought to know by this time that Galactic Co-ordinator Kimball Kinnison is in a better position to know what to do than any other man in the universe. Furthermore, his word is the last word. What he says, goes."

"Of course," the president apologized. "I am overwrought . . . but to see our entire world pulled down around us and upon us, our institutions, the work of centuries, destroyed, millions of lives lost . . . all needlessly—"

"It won't come to that, he says, if we all do our parts. And you, sir, are very much in the picture."

"I? How?"

"Are you familiar with exactly what happened upon Antigan IV?"

"Why, no. They had some trouble over there, I recall, but—"

"That's it. That's why this must go on. No planet cares particularly about what happens to any other planet, but the Co-ordinator cares about them all, as a whole. If this trouble is headed off now, it will simply spread to other planets; if it is allowed to come to a climax there is a good chance that we can put an end to the whole trouble, for good."

"But what has that to do with me? What can I, personally, do?"

"Much. The last act upon Antigan IV, the thing that made it a planet of maniacs, was the kidnaping of Planetary President Renwood. It is supposed that he was murdered, since no trace of him has ever been found."

"Oh." The older man's hands clenched, then loosened. "I am willing . . . provided—Is the Co-ordinator fairly certain that my death will enable him—"

"It won't get that far, sir. He intends to stop it just before that. He and his associates—I don't know who they are—have been listing every enemy agent they can find, and they will all be taken care of at once. He believes that Boskone will publish in advance a definite time at which they will take you away from us. That was the way it went at Antigan."

"Even from the Patrol?"

"From Base itself. Co-ordinator Kinnison is pretty sure that they can do it, except for something that he can bring into play only at the last moment. Incidentally, that is why we are having this meeting here, with this detector which he gave me. He is afraid that Base is porous."

"In that case . . . what can he—" The president fell silent.

"All that I know is that we are to dress you in a certain suit of armor and have you in my private office in Base a few minutes before the time they set. We and the guards leave the office at minus two minutes and walk down the corridor, just fast enough so that at minus one minute we are exactly in front of Room Twenty-four. We are to rehearse it until our timing is perfect. I have no idea what is going to happen then, but I know that something will. We are not to discuss this again, even via Lens, as he is pretty sure that you will very shortly be under surveillance every minute."

*

Time passed; the Boskonian infiltration progressed strictly according to plan. Upon the surface it appeared that Radelix was going in almost the same fashion in which Antigan IV had gone. Below the surface, however, there was one great difference. Every ship, whether liner or freighter or tramp, which docked at any spaceport of Radelix, brought at least one man who did not leave. Some of these visitors were tall and lithe, some were short and fat. Some were old, some were young. Some were pale, some were burned to the complexion of ancient leather by the fervent rays of space. They were alike only in the "look of eagles" in their steady, quiet eyes. Each landed and went about his ostensible business, interesting himself not at all in any of the others.

Again the Boskonians declared their contempt of the Patrol by setting the exact time at which the president was to be taken. Again the appointed hour was midnight.

Vice Admiral Lensman Gerrond was, as Kinnison had intimated frequently, somewhat of a brass hat. He did not, he simply could not believe that his Base was as pregnable as the Co-ordinator had assumed it to be. Kinnison, knowing that all ordinary defenses would be useless, had not even mentioned them. Gerrond, unable to believe that his hitherto invincible and invulnerable weapons and defenses were all of a sudden useless, mustered them of his own volition.

All leaves had been canceled. Every detector, every beam, every device of defense and of offense was fully manned. Every man was keyed up and alert. And Gerrond, while the least bit apprehensive that something was about to happen which was not in the book, was pretty sure in his stout old war-dog's soul that he and his men had stuff enough.

At two minutes before midnight the armored president and his escorts left Gerrond's private office. One minute later they were passing the door of the specified room. A bomb exploded shatteringly behind them, armored men rushed yelling out of a branch corridor in their rear. Everybody stopped and turned to look. So, the hidden Kinnison assured himself, did an unseen observer in an invisibly hovering, three-dimensional hypercircle.

Kinnison threw the door open, flashed an explanatory thought at the president, yanked him into the room and into the midst of a corps of Lensmen armed with devices not usually encountered even in Patrol bases. The door snapped shut and Kinnison stood where the president had stood an instant before, clad in armor identical with that which the president had worn. The exchange had required less than one second: it had been observed by no one.

"QX, Gerrond and you fellows!" Kinnison drove the thought. "The president is safe—I'm taking over. Double time straight ahead—hipe! Get into the clear—give us a chance to use our stuff!"

The unarmored men broke into a run, and as they did so the door of Room Twenty-four swung open and stayed open. Weapons snouted out, shoved by armored men. Armored men and heavy weapons erupted from other doors and from more branch corridors. The hypercircle, which was, in fact, the terminus of a hyperspatial tube, began to thicken toward visibility.

It did not, however, materialize. Only by the intensest effort of vision could it be discerned as the sheerest wisp, more tenuous than the thinnest fog. The men within the ship, if ship it was, were visible only as striations in air are visible, and no more to be made out in detail. Instead of a full materialization, the only thing that was or became solid or tangible was a dead-black thing which reached purposefully outward and downward toward Kinnison, a thing combined of tongs and coarse-meshed, heavy net.

Kinnison's DeLameters flamed at maximum intensity and minimum aperture. Useless. The stuff was dureum; that unbelievably dense and ultimately refractory synthetic which, saturated with pure force, is the only known substance which can exist as an actuality both in normal space and in that pseudospace which composes the hyperspatial tube. The Lensman flicked on his neutralizer and shot away inertialess; but that maneuver, too, had been foreseen. The Boskonian engineers matched every move he made, within a split second after he made it; the tong-net gripped and closed.

Semiportables flamed then—heavy stuff—but they might just as well have remained cold. Their beams could not cut the dureum linkages; they slid harmlessly *past*—not through—the wraithlike, figmental invaders at whom they were timed. Kinnison was hauled aboard the Boskonian vessel; its structure and its furnishings and its crew becoming ever firmer and more substantial to his senses as he went from normal into pseudospace.

As the pseudoworld became real, the reality of the base behind him thinned into unreality. In seconds it disappeared utterly, and Kinnison knew that to the senses of his fellow human beings he had vanished without leaving a trace. This ship, though, was real enough. So were his captors.

*

The net opened, dumping the Lensman ignominiously to the floor. Tractor beams wrenched his blazing DeLameters out of his grasp—whether or not hands and arms came with them was entirely his own lookout. Tractors and pressors jerked him upright, slammed him against the steel wall of the room, held him motionless against it.

Furiously he launched his ultimately lethal weapon, the Worsel-designed, Thorndyke-built, mind-controlled projector of thought-borne vibrations which decomposed the molecules without which thought and life itself could not exist. Nothing happened. He explored, finding that even his sense of perception was stopped a full foot away from every part of every one of those humanoid bodies. He settled down then and thought. A great light dawned; a shock struck sickeningly home.

No such elaborate and super-powered preparations would have been made for the capture of any civilian. Presidents were old men, physically weak and with no extraordinary powers of mind. No—this whole chain of events had been according to plan—a high Boskonian's plan. Ruining a planet was, of course, a highly desirable feature in itself, but it could not have been the main feature.

Somebody with a real brain was out after the four Second-Stage Lensmen and he wasn't fooling. And if Nadreck, Worsel, Tregonsee and himself were all to disappear, the Patrol would know that it had been nudged. But jet back—which of the four other than himself would have taken that particular bait? Not one of them. Weren't they out after them, too? Sure they were—they must be. Oh, if he could only warn them—but after all, what good would it do? They had all warned each other repeatedly to watch out for traps; all four had been constantly on guard. What possible foresight could have avoided a snare set so perfectly to match every detail of a man's physical and mental make-up?

But he wasn't licked yet. They had to know what he knew, how he had done what he had done, whether or not he had any superiors and who they were. Therefore they had had to take him alive, just as he had had to take various Boskonian chiefs. And they'd find out that as long as he was alive he'd be a dangerous buzzsaw to monkey with.

The captain, or whoever was in charge, would send for him; that was a foregone conclusion. He would have to find out what it was that he had caught; he would have to make a preliminary report of some kind. And somebody would slip. One hundred percent vigilance was impossible, and Kinnison would be on his toes to take advantage of that slip, whatever or however slight it might be.

But the captors did not take Kinnison to the captain. Instead, accompanied by half-a-dozen armored men, that worthy came to Kinnison.

"Start talking, fellow, and talk fast," the Boskonian directed crisply in the lingua franca of deep space as the armored soldiers strode out. "I want to know who you are, what you are, what you've done, and everything about you and the Patrol. So talk—or do you want me to pull you apart with these tractors, armor and all?"

Kinnison paid no attention, but drove at the commander with his every mental force and weapon. Blocked. This ape too had a full-body, full-coverage screen.

There was a switch, at the captain's hip, handy for finger-tip control. If he could only move! It would be so easy to flip that switch! Or if he could throw something, or make one of those other fellows brush against him just right, or if the guy happened to sit down a little too close to the arm of a chair, or if there were a pet animal of any kind around, or a spider or a worm or even a gnat—

THE LENSMAN

VI.

Second-Stage Lensman Tregonsee of Rigel IV did not rush madly out into space in quest of something or anything Boskonian in response to Kinnison's call. To hurry was not Tregonsee's way. He could move fast upon occasion, but before he would move at all he had to know exactly how, where, and why he should move.

He conferred with his three fellows, he furnished them with all the data he possessed, he helped integrate the totaled facts into one composite. That composite pleased the others well enough so that they went to work, each in his own fashion, but it did not please Tregonsee. He could not visualize any coherent whole from the available parts. Therefore, while Kinnison was investigating the fall of Antigan IV, Tregonsee was sitting—or rather, standing—still and thinking. He was still standing still and thinking when Kinnison went to Radelix.

Finally he called in an assistant to help him think. He had more respect for the opinions of Camilla Kinnison than for those of any other entity, outside of Arisia, of the two galaxies. He had helped train all five of the Kinnison children, and in Cam he had found a kindred soul. Possessing a truer sense of values than any of his fellows, he alone realized that the pupils had long since passed their tutors; and it is a measure of his quality that the realization brought into Tregonsee's tranquil soul no tinge of rancor, but only wonder. What those incredible Children of the Lens had he did not know, but he knew that they—particularly Camilla—had extraordinary gifts.

In the mind of this scarcely grown woman he perceived depths which he could not plumb, extensions and vistas the meanings of which he could not even vaguely grasp. He did not try either to plumb the abysses or to survey the expanses; he made no slightest effort, ever, to take from any of the children anything which the child did not first offer to reveal. In his own mind he tried to classify theirs; but, realizing in the end that that task was and always would be beyond his power, he accepted that fact as calmly as he accepted the numberless others of Nature's inexplicable facts. Tregonsee came the closest of any Second-Stage Lensman to the real truth, but even he never did suspect the existence of the Eddorians.

Camilla, as quiet as her twin sister Constance was boisterous, parked her speedster in one of the capacious holds of the Rigellian's spaceship and joined him in the control room.

"You believe, I take it, that Dad's logic is faulty, his deductions erroneous?" the girl thought; after a casual greeting. "I'm not surprised. So do I. He jumped at conclusions. But then, he does that, you know."

"Oh, I wouldn't say that, exactly. However, it seems to me," Tregonsee replied carefully, "that he did not have sufficient basis in fact to form any definite conclusion as to whether or not Renwood of Antigan was a Boskonian operative. It is that point which I wish to discuss with you first."

Cam concentrated. "I don't see that it makes any difference, fundamentally, whether he was or not," she decided, finally. "A difference in method only, not in motivation. Interesting, perhaps, but immaterial. It is virtually certain in either case that Kandron of Onlo or some other entity is the motive force and is the one who must be destroyed."

"Of course, my dear, but that is only the first differential. How about the second, and the third? Method governs. Nadreck, concerning himself only with Kandron, tabulated and studied only the Kandronesque manifestations. He may—probably will—eliminate Kandron. It is by no means assured, however, that that step will be enough. In fact, from my preliminary study, I would risk a small wager that the larger and worse aspects would remain untouched. I would, therefore, suggest that we ignore, for the time being, Nadreck's findings and examine anew all the data available."

"I wouldn't bet you a millo on that." Camilla caught her lower lip between white, even teeth. "Check. The probability is that Renwood was a loyal citizen. Let us consider every possible argument for and against that assumption—"

They went into a contact of minds so close that the separate thoughts simply could not be resolved into terms of speech. They remained that way, not for the period of a few minutes which would have exhausted any ordinary brain, but for four solid hours; and at the end of that conference they had arrived at a few tentative conclusions.

*

Kinnison had said that there was no possibility of tracing a hyperspatial tube after it had ceased to exist. There were millions of planets in the two galaxies. There was an indefinite, quite possibly an infinite number of coexistent parallel spaces, into any one of which the tube might have led. Knowing these things, Kinnison had decided that the probability was infinitesimally small that any successful investigation could be made along those lines.

Tregonsee and Camilla, starting with the same facts, arrived at entirely different results. There were many spaces, true, but the inhabitants of any one space belonged to that space and would not be interested in the conquest or the permanent taking over of any other. Foreign spaces, then, need not be considered. Civilization had only one significant enemy: Boskonia. Boskonia, then, captained possibly by Kandron of Onlo, was the attacker. The tube itself could not be traced and there were millions of planets, yes, but those facts were not pertinent.

Why not? Because "X," who might or might not be Kandron, was not operating from a fixed headquarters, receiving reports from subordinates who did the work. A rigid philosophical analysis, of which few other minds would have been capable, showed that "X" was doing the work himself, and was moving from solar system to solar system to do it. Those mass psychoses in which entire garrisons went mad all at once, those mass hysterias in which vast groups of civilians went reasonably out of control, could not have been brought about by any ordinary mind. Of all Civilization, only Nadreck of Palain VII had the requisite ability; was it reasonable to suppose that Boskonia had many such minds? No. "X" was either singular or a small integer.

Which? Could they decide the point? With some additional data, they could. Their linked minds went en rapport with Worsel, with Nadreck, with Kinnison, and with the principal statistician at Prime Base.

In addition to Nadreck's locus, they determined two more—one of all inimical manifestations, the other of those which Nadreck had not used in his computations. Their final exhaustive analysis showed that there were at least two, and very probably only two, prime intelligences directing those Boskonian activities. They made no attempt to identify either of them. They communicated to Nadreck their results and their conclusions.

"I am working on Kandron," the Palainian replied, flatly. "I made no assumptions as to whether or not there were other prime movers at work, since the point has no bearing. Your information is very interesting, and may perhaps prove valuable, and I thank you for it—but my present assignment is to find and to kill Kandron of Onlo."

*

Tregonsee and Camilla, then, set out to find "X"; not any definite actual or deduced entity, but the perpetrator of certain closely related and highly characteristic phenomena, viz., mass psychoses and mass hysterias. Nor did they extrapolate. They visited the last few planets which had been affected, in the order in which the attacks had occurred. They studied every phase of every situation. They worked slowly, but—they hoped and they believed—surely. Neither of them had any idea then that behind "X" lay Ploor, and beyond Ploor, Eddore.

Having examined the planet latest to be stricken, they made no effort to pick out definitely the one next to be attacked. It might be any one of ten worlds, or possibly even twelve. Hence, neglecting entirely the mathematical and logical probabilities involved, they watched them all, each taking six. Each flitted from world to world, with senses alert to perceive the first sign of subversive activity. Tregonsee was a retired magnate, spending his declining years in seeing the galaxy; Camilla was a Tellurian business girl on vacation.

Young, beautiful, innocent-looking girls who traveled alone were, then as ever, regarded as fair game by the Don Juan of any given human world. Scarcely had Camilla registered at the Hotel Grande when a well-groomed, self-satisfied man-about-town made an approach.

"Hel-lo, Beautiful! Remember me, don't you—old Tom Thomas? What say we split a bottle of fayalin, to renew old—" He broke off, for the red-headed eyeful's reaction was in no sense orthodox. She was not coldly unaware of his presence. She was neither coy nor angry, neither fearful nor scornful. She was only and vastly *amused.*

"You think, then, that I am human and desirable?" Her smile was devastating. "Did you ever hear of the Canthrips of Ollenole?" She had never heard of them either, before that instant, but this small implied mendacity did not bother her.

"No, I can't say that I have." The man, while very evidently taken aback by this new line of resistance, persevered. "What kind of a brush-off do you think you're trying to give me?"

"Brush-off? See me as I am, you beast, and thank whatever gods you recognize that I am not hungry, having eaten just last night." In his sight her green eyes darkened to a jetty black, the flecks of gold in them scintillated and began to emit sparks. Her hair turned into a mass of horribly clutching tentacles. Her teeth became fangs, her fingers talons, her strong, splendidly proportioned body a monstrosity out of Hell's grisliest depths.

After a moment she allowed the frightful picture to fade back into her charming self, keeping the Romeo from fainting by the power of her will.

"Call the manager if you like. He has been watching and has seen nothing except that you are pale and sweating. I, a friend of yours, have been giving you some bad news, perhaps. Tell your stupid police all about me, if you wish to spend the rest of your life in a padded cell. I'll see you again in a day or two, I hope. I'll be hungry again by that time." She walked away, serenely confident that the fellow would never willingly come within sight of her again.

She had not damaged his ego permanently—he was not a neurotic type—but she had given him a jolt which he never would forget. Camilla Kinnison nor any of her sisters had anything to fear from any male or males infesting any planet or roaming any depths of space.

*

The expected and awaited trouble developed. Tregonsee and Camilla landed and began their hunt. The League for Planetary Purity, it appeared, was the primary focal point; hence the two attended a meeting of that crusading body. That was a mistake; Tregonsee should have stayed out in deep space, concealed behind a solid thought-screen.

For Camilla was an unknown. Furthermore, her mind was inherently stable at the third level of stress; no lesser mind could penetrate her screens or, having failed to do so, could recognize the fact of failure. Tregonsee, however, was known throughout all civilized space. He was not wearing his Lens, of course, but his very shape made him suspect. Worse, he could not hide from any mind as powerful as that of "X" the fact that his mind was very decidedly not that of a retired Rigellian gentleman.

Thus Camilla had known that the procedure was a mistake. She intimated as much, but she could not sway the unswerving Tregonsee from his determined course without revealing things which must forever remain hidden from him. She acquiesced, therefore, but she knew what to expect.

Hence, when the invading intelligence blanketed the assemblage lightly, only to be withdrawn instantly upon detecting the emanations of a mind of real power, Cam had a bare moment of time in which to act. She synchronized with the intruding thought, began to analyze it and to trace it back to its source. She did not have time enough to succeed fully in either endeavor, but she did get a line. When the foreign influence vanished she shot a message to Tregonsee and they sped away.

Hurtling through space along the established line, Tregonsee's mind was a turmoil of thought; thoughts as plain as print to Camilla. She flushed uncomfortably—she could, of course, blush at will.

"I'm not half the superman whose picture you are painting," she said. That was true enough; no one this side of Arisia could have been. "You're so famous, you know, and I'm not—while he was examining you I had a fraction of a second to work in. You didn't."

"That may be true." Although Tregonsee had no eyes, the girl knew that he was staring at her; scanning, but not intruding, with his highly developed sense of perception. She lowered her barriers so far that he thought they were completely down. "You have, however, extraordinary and completely inexplicable powers . . . but, being the daughter of Kimball and Clarrissa Kinnison—"

"That's it, I think." She paused, then, in a burst of girlish confidence, went on: "I've got something, I really do think, but the trouble is that I don't know what it is or what to do with it. Maybe in fifty years or so I will."

This also was close enough to the truth, and it did serve to restore to Tregonsee his wonted poise. "Be that as it may, I will take your advice next time, if you will offer it."

"Try and stop me—I love to give advice." She laughed unaffectedly. "It might not have turned out any differently this time, though, and it may not be any better next time."

Then, further to quiet the shrewd Rigellian's suspicions, she strode over to the control panel and checked the course. Having done so, she fanned out detectors, centering upon that course, to the fullest range of their power. She swaggered a little when she speared with the CRX tracer a distant vessel in a highly satisfactory location. That act would cut her down to size in Tregonsee's mind.

"You think, then, that 'X' is in that ship?" he asked, quietly.

"Probably not." She could not afford to act too dumb—she could fool a Second-Stage Lensman a little, but nobody could fool one very much. "It may, however, give us a lead."

"It is practically certain that 'X' is not in that vessel," Tregonsee thought. "In fact, it may be a trap. We must, however, make the customary arrangements to take it into custody."

*

Cam nodded and the Rigellian communications officers energized their long-range beams. Far ahead of the fleeing vessel, centering upon its line of flight, fast cruisers of the Galactic Patrol began to form a gigantic cup. Hours passed, and—a not unexpected circumstance—Tregonsee's superdreadnought gained rapidly upon the supposed Boskonian.

The quarry did not swerve or dodge. Straight into the mouth of the cup it sped. Tractors and pressors reached out, locked on, and were neither repulsed nor cut. The strange ship did not go inert, did not put out a single course of screen, did not fire a beam. She did not reply to signals. Spy rays combed her from needle nose to driving jets, searching every compartment. There was no sign of life aboard.

Spots of pink appeared upon Camilla's deliciously smooth cheeks, her eyes flashed. "We've been had, Uncle Trig—how we've been had!" she exclaimed, and her chagrin was not all assumed. She had not quite anticipated such a complete fiasco as this.

"Score one for 'X,'" Tregonsee said. He not only seemed to be, but actually was, calm and unmoved. "We will now go back and pick up where we left off."

They did not discuss the thing at all, nor did they wonder how "X" had escaped them. After the fact, they both knew. There had been at least two vessels; at least one of them had been inherently indetectable and screened against thought. In one of these latter "X" had taken a course at some indeterminable angle to the one which they had followed.

"X" was now at a safe distance.

"X" was nobody's fool.

VII.

Kathryn Kinnison, trim and taut in black glamourette, strolled into the breakfast nook humming a lilting song. Pausing before a full-length mirror, she adjusted her cocky little black toque at an even more piquant angle over her left eye. She made a couple of passes at her riot of curls and gazed at her reflected self in high approval as, putting both hands upon her smoothly rounded hips, she—"wriggled" is the only possible term for it—in the sheer joy of being alive.

"Kathryn—" Clarrissa Kinnison chided gently, "don't be exhibitionistic, dear." Except in times of stress the Kinnison women used spoken language, "to keep in practice," as they said.

"Why not? It's fun." The tall girl bent over and kissed her mother upon the lobe of an ear. "You're sweet, Mums, you know that? You're the most *precious* thing—Ha! Bacon and eggs? Goody!"

The older woman watched half-enviously as her eldest daughter ate with the carefree abandon of one who has no cares whatever either for her digestion or for her figure. She had no more understood her children, ever, than a hen can understand the brood of ducklings she has so unwittingly hatched out, and that comparison was more strikingly apt than Clarrissa Kinnison ever would know. She now knew, more than a little ruefully, that she never would understand them.

She had not protested openly at the rigor of the regime to which her son Christopher had been subjected from birth. That, she knew, was necessary. It was inconceivable that Kit should not be a Lensman, and for a man to become a Lensman he had to be given everything which he could possibly take. She was deeply glad, however, that her four other babies had been girls. Her daughters were *not* going to be Lensmen. She, who had known so long and so heavily the weight of Lensman's load, would see to that. Herself a womanly, feminine woman, she had fought with every resource at her command to make her girl babies grow up into replicas of herself. She had failed.

They simply would not play with dolls, nor play house with other little girls. Instead, they insisted upon "intruding," as she considered it, upon Lensmen; preferably upon Second-Stage Lensmen, if any one of the four chanced to be anywhere within reach. Instead of with toys, they played with atomic engines and flitters; and, later, with speedsters and spaceships. Instead of primers, they read Galactic charts. One of them might be at home, as now, or all of them; or none. She never did know what to expect.

But they were in no sense disloyal. They loved their mother with a depth of affection which no other mother, anywhere, has ever known. They tried their very best to keep her from worrying about them. They kept in touch with her wherever they went—which might be at whim to Tellus or to Thrale or to Alsakan or to any unplumbed cranny of intergalactic space—and they informed her, apparently without reservation, as to everything they did. They loved their father and their brother and each other and themselves with the same whole-hearted fervor they bestowed upon her. They behaved always in exemplary fashion. None of them had ever shown or felt the slightest interest in any one of numerous boys and men; and this trait, if the truth is to be told, Clarrissa could understand least of all.

No. The only thing basically wrong with them was the fact, made abundantly clear since they first toddled, that they should not be and could not be subjected to any jot or tittle of any form of control, however applied.

Kathryn finished eating finally and gave her mother a bright, quick grin. "Sorry, Mums, you'll just have to give us up as hard cases, I guess." Her fine eyes, so like Clarrissa's except in color, clouded as she went on: "I *am* sorry, Mother, really, that we can't be what you so want us to be. We've tried so hard, but we just can't. It's something here, and here—" She tapped one temple and prodded her midsection with a pink forefinger. "Call it fatalism or anything you please, but I think that we're slated to do a job of some kind, some day, even though none of us has any idea what that job is going to be."

Clarrissa paled. "I have been thinking just that for years, dear . . . I have been afraid to say it, or even to think it. You are Kim's children, and mine. If there ever was a perfect, a predestined marriage, it is ours. And Mentor said that our marriage was necessary—" She paused, and in that instant she almost perceived the truth. She was closer to it than she had ever been before or ever would be again. But that truth was far too vast for her mind to grasp. She went on: "But I'd do it over again, Kathryn, knowing everything I know now. 'Vast rewards,' you know—"

"Of course you would," Kat interrupted. "Any girl would be a fool not to. The minute I meet a man like Dad I'm going to marry him, if I have to scratch Kay's eyes out and snatch Cam and Con bald-headed to get him. But speaking of Dad, just what do you think of l'affaire Radelix?"

Gone every trace of levity, both women stood up. Gold-flecked tawny eyes stared deeply into gold-flecked eyes of dark and velvety green.

"I don't know." Clarrissa spoke slowly, meaningfully. "Do you?"

"No. I wish that I did." Kathryn's was not the voice of a girl, but that of an avenging angel. "As Kit says, I'd give four front teeth and my right leg to the knee joint to know who or what is back of that, but I don't. I feel very much in the mood to do a flit out that way."

"Do you?" Clarrissa paused. "I'm glad. I'd go myself, in spite of everything he says, except that I know I couldn't do anything. If that should be the job you were talking about—Oh, do anything you can, dear; *anything* to make sure that he comes back to me!"

"Of course, Mums." Kathryn broke away almost by force from her mother's emotion. "I don't think it is; at least, I haven't got any cosmic hunch to that effect. And don't worry; it puts wrinkles in the girlish complexion. I'll do just a little look-see, stick around long enough to find out what's what, and let you know all about it. 'Bye."

*

At high velocity Kathryn drove her indetectable speedster to Radelix, and around and upon that planet she conducted invisible investigations. She learned a part of the true state of affairs, she deduced more of it, but she could not see, even dimly, the picture as a whole. This part, though, was clear enough.

An interdimensional expert, she did not have to be at the one apparent mouth of a hyperspatial tube in order to enter it; she knew that while communication was impossible either through such a tube from space to space or from the interior of the tube to either space, the quality of the tube was not the barrier. The interface was. Wherefore, knowing what to expect immediately and working diligently to solve the whole problem, she waited.

She watched Kinnison's abduction. There was nothing she could do about that. She could not interfere then without setting up repercussions which might very well shatter the entire structure of the Galactic Patrol. When the Boskonian ship had disappeared, however, she tapped the tube and followed it. Almost nose to tail she pressed it, tensely alert to do some helpful deed which could be ascribed to accident or to luck. For she knew starkly that Kinnison's present captors would not slip and that his every ability had been discounted in advance.

Thus she was ready, when Kinnison's attention concentrated upon the switch controlling the Boskonian captain's thought-screen generator. There were no pets or spiders or worms, or even gnats, but the captain could sit down. Around his screen, then, she drove a solid beam of thought, upon a channel which neither the pirate nor the Lensman knew existed. She took over in a trice the fellow's entire mind. He sat down, as Kinnison had so earnestly hoped that he would do, the merest fraction of an inch too close to the chair's arm. The switch-handle flipped over and Kathryn snatched her mind away. She was sure that her father would not suspect that that bit of luck was anything except purely fortuitous. She was equally sure that the thing was safe, for a time at least, in Kinnison's highly capable hands. She slowed down, allowed the distance between the two vessels to increase. But she kept within range, for it was more than probable that one or two more seemingly lucky accidents would have to happen before very long.

In the instant of the flicking of the switch the captain's mind became Kinnison's. He was going to issue orders, to take the ship over in an orderly way, but his first contact with the subjugated mind made him change his plans. Instead of uttering orders, the captain leaped out of the chair toward the beam-controllers.

And not an instant too soon. Others had seen what had happened, had heard that telltale click. All had been warned against that and many other contingencies. As the captain leaped, one of his fellows drew a bullet-projector and calmly shot him through the head.

The shock of that bullet, the death of the mind in his own mind's grasp, jarred the Gray Lensman to the core. It was almost the same as though he himself had been killed. Nevertheless, by sheer force of will he held on, by sheer power of will he made that dead body take those last three steps and forced those dead hands to cut the master circuit of the beams which were holding him helpless.

Freed, he leaped forward; but not alone. The others leaped, too, and for the same switch. Kinnison got there first—just barely first—and as he came he swung his armored fist.

What a dureum-inlaid glove, driven by all the brawn of Kimball Kinnison's mighty right arm and powerful torso backed by all the momentum of body- and armor-mass, will do to a human head met in direct central impact is nothing to dwell upon here. Simply, that head splashed. Pivoting nimbly, considering his encumbering armor, he swung a terrific leg. His massive steel boot sank calf-deep into the abdomen of the foe next in line.

915

THE LENSMAN

Two more utterly irresistible blows disposed of two more of the Boskonians; the last two turned and, frantically, ran. But the Lensman by that time had the juice back on; and when a man has been smacked against a solid armor-plate bulkhead by the full power of a D2P pressor, all that remains to be done must be accomplished with a scraper and a mop—or a sponge.

Kinnison picked up his DeLameters, reconnected them, and took stock. So far, so good. But there were other men aboard this heap—how many, he'd better find out—and at least some of them wore dureum-inlaid armor as capable as his own.

And in her speedster, concluding that this wasn't going to be so bad, after all, Kathryn glowed with pride in her father's prowess. She was no shrinking violet, this Third-Stage Lensman; she held no ruth whatever for Civilization's foes. She herself would have driven that beam as mercilessly as had the Gray Lensman. She could have told Kinnison what next to do; could even have inserted the knowledge stealthily into his mind; but, heroically, she refrained. She would let him handle this in his own fashion as long as he possibly could do so.

*

The Gray Lensman sent his sense of perception abroad. Twenty more of them—the ship wasn't very big. Ten aft, armored. Six forward, also armored. Four, unarmored, in the control room. That control room was poison; he'd go aft first. He searched around—surely they'd have dureum space-axes? Oh, yes, there they were. He hefted them, selected one of the correct weight and balance. He strode down the companionway to the wardroom. He flung the door open and stepped inside.

His first care was to blast the communicator panels with his DeLameters. That would delay the mustering of reinforcements. The control room couldn't guess, at least for a time, that one man was setting out to capture their ship single-handed. His second, ignoring the beams of hand-weapons splashing refulgently from his screens, was to weld the steel door solidly to the jamb. Then, sheathing his projectors, he swung up his ax and went grimly to work. He thought fleetingly of how nice it would be to have VanBuskirk, that dean of all ax-men, at his back; but he wasn't too old or too fat to swing a pretty mean ax himself. And, fortunately, these Boskonians, here in their quarters, didn't have axes. They were heavy, clumsy, and for emergency use only; they were not a part of the regular uniform, as upon Valeria.

The space-ax! Formerly that weapon had been forged from the hardest and toughest of alloy steels. For years, however, it had been made universally from dureum. A deceptive little thing, truly! A dainty-looking affair a little larger than a broad-hatchet. Unlike a hatchet, however, it had a mass of some twenty pounds and was equipped with a yard-long, double-gripped shaft. A sharply tapered spear-end for thrusting, gouging, and stabbing; a wickedly curved, needle-pointed beak for rending and tearing; a flatly rounded, razor-sharp blade capable of shearing through neo-carballoy as cleanly as a scalpel through butter.

The first foe swung up his DeLameter involuntarily as Kinnison's ax swept down. When the curved blade, driven as viciously as the Lensman's strength could drive it,

916

struck the ray-gun it did not even pause. Through it it sliced, the severed halves falling to the floor.

The dureum inlay of the glove held, and glove and ax smashed together against the helmet. The Boskonian went down with a crash; but, beyond a broken arm or some such trifle, he wasn't hurt much. And no armor that a man had to carry around could be made of solid dureum. Hence, Kinnison reversed his weapon and swung again, aiming carefully at a point between the inlay strips. The ax's wicked beak tore through steel and skull and brain, stopping only with the sharply ringing impact of dureum shaft against dureum stripping.

They were coming at him now, not only with DeLameters, but with whatever of steel bars and spanners and bludgeons they could find. QX—his armor could take oodles of that. They might dent it, but they couldn't possibly get through. Planting one boot solidly upon his victim's helmet, he wrenched his ax out through flesh and bone and metal—no fear of breakage; not even a Valerian's full savage strength could break that small, fragile-looking tool—and struck again. And struck—and struck.

He fought his way to the door—two of the survivors were trying to unseal it and to get away. They failed; and, in failing, died. A couple of the remaining enemies shrieked and ran in blind panic, and tried to hide; the others battled desperately on. But whether they ran or fought there was only one possible end, if the Patrolman were to survive. No enemy must or could be left alive behind him, to bring to bear upon his back some semiportable weapon with whose energies his armor's screens could not cope.

When the grisly business was over Kinnison, panting, rested briefly. This was the first real brawl he had been in for twenty years; and for a veteran—a white-collar man, a Co-ordinator to boot—he hadn't done so bad, he thought. That was hard work and, while he was maybe a hair short on wind, he hadn't weakened a particle. To here, QX.

*

And lovely Kathryn, far enough back but not too far and reading imperceptibly his every thought, agreed with him enthusiastically. She did not have a father complex, but in common with her sisters she knew exactly what her father was. With equal exactitude she knew what other men were. Knowing them, and knowing however imperfectly herself, each of the Kinnison girls knew that it would be a physical and psychological impossibility for her to become even mildly interested in any man not at least her father's equal. They each had dreamed of a man who would be her own equal, physically and mentally, but it had not yet occurred to any of them that one such man already existed.

Kinnison cut the door away and again sent out his sense of perception. With it fanning out ahead of him he retraced his previous path. The apes in the control room had done something; he didn't know just what. Two of them were tinkering with a communicator panel; probably the one to the ward room. They probably thought that the trouble was at their end. Or did they? Why hadn't they reconnoitered? He dismissed that problem as being of no pressing importance. The other two were doing something at another panel. What? He couldn't make head or tail of it—hang those full-coverage screens! And Nadreck's fancy drill, even if he had had one along, wouldn't work unless the screen were absolutely steady. Well, it didn't make much, if any, difference. They had called the men back from up forward, and here they came. He'd rather meet them in the corridor than in an open room, anyway, he could handle them a lot easier.

But tensely watching Kathryn gnawed her lip. Should she tell him, or control him, or not? No. She wouldn't—she couldn't—yet. Dad could figure out that pilot room trap without her help—and she herself, with all her power of brain, could not visualize with any degree of clarity the menace which was—which *must* be—at the tube's end or even now rushing along it to meet that Boskonian ship.

Kinnison met the oncoming six and vanquished them. By no means as easily as he had conquered the others, since they had been warned and since they also now bore space-axes, but just as finally. Kinnison did not consider it remarkable that he escaped practically unscathed—his armor was battered and dinged up, cut and torn, but he had only a couple of superficial wounds. He had met the enemy where they could come at him only one at a time; he was still the master of any weapon known to space warfare; it had been at no time evident that any outside influence was interfering with the normally rapid functioning of the Boskonians' minds.

He was full of confidence, full of fight, and far from spent when he faced about to consider what he should do about that control room. There was plenty of stuff in there—tougher stuff than he had met up with so far.

Kathryn in her speedster gritted her strong white teeth and clenched her shapely hands into hard little fists. This was bad—very, *very* bad—and it was going to get worse. Closing up fast, she uttered a bitter and exceedingly unladylike expletive.

Couldn't Dad *see*—couldn't the dumb darling *sense*—that he was apt to run out of time almost any minute now?

She fairly writhed in an agony of indecision; and indecision, in a Third-Stage Lensman, is a rare phenomenon indeed. She wanted intensely to take over, but if she did, was there any way this side of Palain's purple hells that she could cover up her tracks?

There was none—yet.

VIII.

But Kinnison's mind, while slower than his daughter's and in many respects less able, was sure. The four Boskonians in the control room were screened against his every mental force and it was idle even to hope for another such lucky break as he had just had. One was QX and to be received thankfully, but coincidences simply did not happen. They were armored by this time and they had both machine rifles and semiportable projectors. They were entrenched; evidently intending to fight a delaying and defensive battle, knowing that if they could keep the aggressor at bay until the pseudospace of the tube had been traversed, the Lensman would not have a chance. Armed with all they could use of the most powerful mobile weapons aboard and being four to one, they undoubtedly thought that they could win easily enough.

Kinnison thought otherwise. Since he could not use his mind against them he would use whatever he could find, and this ship, having come upon such a mission, would be carrying plenty of weapons—and those four men certainly hadn't had time to tamper with them all. He might even find some negative-matter bombs.

Setting up a spy-ray block, he proceeded to rummage. They couldn't see him, and, if any one of them had a sense of perception and cut his screen for even a fraction of a second to use it, the battle would end then and there. And, if they decided to rush him, so much the better. They remained, however, forted up, as he had thought that they would, and he rummaged in peace. Various death-dealing implements, invitingly set up, he ignored after one cursory glance into their interiors. He knew weapons—these had been fixed. He went on to the armory.

He did not find any negabombs, but he found plenty of untouched weapons like those now emplaced in the control room. The rifles were beauties, high-caliber, water-cooled things, each with a heavy dureum shield-plate and a single-ply screen. Each had also a beam, but machine-rifle beams weren't so hot. Conversely, the semiportables had lots of screen, but very little dureum. Kinnison lugged one rifle and two semiportables, by easy stages, into the room next to the control room; so placing them that the control panels would be well out of the line of fire.

What gave Kinnison his chance was the fact that the enemies' weapons were set to cover the door. Apparently they had not considered the possibility that the Lensman would attempt to flank them by blasting through an inch and a half of alloy. Kinnison did not know whether he could do it fast enough to mow them down from the side before they could reset their magnetic clamps, or not; but he'd give it the good old college try. It was bound to be a mighty near thing, and the Lensman grinned wolfishly behind the guard plates of his helmet as he arranged his weapons to save every possible fractional second of time.

Aiming one at a spot some three feet above the floor, the other a little lower, Kinnison cut in the full power of his semiportables and left them on. He energized the rifle's beam—every little bit helped—set the defensive screens at "full", and crouched down into the saddle behind the dureum shield. He had checked the feeds long since; he had plenty of rounds.

Two large spots and a small one smoked briefly, grew red. They turned bright red, then yellow, merged into one blinding spot. Metal melted, sluggishly at first, then thinly, then flaring, blowing out in raging coruscations of sparks as the fiercely-driven beams ate in. Through!

The first small opening appeared directly in line between the muzzle of Kinnison's rifle and one of the guns of the enemy, and in the moment of its appearance the Patrolman's weapon began its stuttering, shattering roar. The Boskonians had seen the hot spot upon the wall, had known instantly what it meant, and were working frantically to swing their gun mounts around so as to interpose their dureum shields and to bring their own rifles to bear. They had almost succeeded. Kinnison caught just the bulge of one suit of armor in his sights, but that was enough. The kinetic energy of the stream of metal tore him out of the saddle; he was literally riddled while still in air. Two savage bursts took care of the semiportables and their operators—as has been intimated, the shields of the semis were not designed to withstand the type of artillery Kinnison was using.

That made it cannon to cannon, one to one; and the Lensman knew that those two identical rifles could hammer at each other's defenses for an hour without doing any serious damage. He had, however, one big advantage. Being closer to the bulkhead he could depress his line of fire more than could the Boskonian. He did so, aiming at the clamps, which were not built to take very much of that sort of punishment. One front clamp let go, then the other, and the Lensman knew what to do about the rear pair, which he could not reach. He directed his fire against the upper edge of the dureum plate. Under the awful thrust of that terrific storm of steel the useless front clamps lifted from the floor. The gun mount, restrained from sliding by the unbreakable grip of the rear clamps, reared up. Over it went, straight backward, exposing the gunner to the full blast of Kinnison's fire. That, definitely, was that.

*

Kathryn heaved a sigh of relief; as far as she could "see", the tube was still empty. "That's my Pop!" she applauded inaudibly to herself. "Now," she breathed, "if the darling has just got jets enough to figure out what may be coming at him down this tube—and sense enough to run back home before it can catch him!"

Kinnison had no suspicion at all that any danger to himself might lie within the tube. He had no desire, however, to land alone in a strange and possibly half-crippled enemy ship in the exact center of an enemy base, and no intention whatever of doing so. Moreover, he had once come altogether too close to permanent immolation in a foreign space because of the discontinuance of a hyperspatial tube while he was in it, and once was once too many. Also, he had just got done leading with his chin, and once of that, too, was once too many. Therefore, his sole thought was to get back into his own space as fast as he could get there, so as soon as the opposition was silenced he hurried into the control room and reversed the vessel's drive.

Behind him, Kathryn flipped her speedster end for end and led the retreat. She left the tube before—"before" is an extremely loose and inaccurate word in this connection, but it conveys the idea better than any other ordinary term—she got back to Base. She caused an officer to broadcast an "evacuation" warning, then hung poised high above Base, watching intently. She knew that Kinnison could not leave the tube except at its terminus, hence would have to materialize inside Base itself. She had heard of what happened when two dense, hard solids attempted to occupy the same three-dimensional space at the same time; but to view that occurrence was not her purpose in lingering. She did not actually know whether there was anything in the tube or not; but she did know that if there were, and if it or they should follow her father out into normal space, even she would have need of every jet she could muster.

Kinnison, maneuvering his Boskonian cruiser to a halt just at the barest perceptible threshold of normal space, in the intermediate zone in which nothing except dureum was solid in either space or pseudospace, had already given a great deal of thought to the problem of disembarkation. The ship was small, as spaceships go, but even so it was a lot bigger than any corridor of Base. Those corridor walls and floors were thick and contained a lot of steel; the ship's walls were solid alloy. He had never seen metal materialize within metal and, frankly, he didn't want to be around, even inside D-armor, when it happened. Also, there were a lot of explosives aboard, and atomic power plants, and the chance of touching off a loose atomic vortex in the very middle of Base and within a few feet of himself was not one to be taken lightly.

He had already rigged a line to a master switch. Power off, with the ship's dureum catwalk as close to the floor of the corridor as the dimensions of the tube permitted, he reversed the controls and poised himself for the running headlong dive. He could not feel Radeligian gravitation, of course, but he was pretty sure that he could leap far enough to get through the interface. He took a short run, jerked the line, and hurled himself through the spaceship's immaterial wall. The ship disappeared.

Going through that interface was more of a shock than the Lensman had anticipated. Even taken very slowly, as it customarily is, interdimensional acceleration brings malaise to which no one has ever become accustomed, and taking it so rapidly fairly turned Kinnison inside out. He was going to land with the rolling impact which constitutes perfect technique in such armored maneuvering. As it was, he never did know how he landed, except that he made a boiler-shop racket and that he brought up against the far wall of the corridor with a climactic clang. Beyond the addition of a few more bruises and contusions to his already abundant collection, however, he was not harmed.

As soon as he could collect himself he leaped to his feet and rapped out orders. "Tractors—pressors—shears! Heavy stuff, to anchor, not to clamp! Hipe!" He knew what he was up against now, and, if they'd just come back, he'd yank them out of that tube so fast it'd break their neck!

*

And Kathryn, still watching intently, smiled. Her Dad was a pretty smart old duck, but he wasn't using his noggin now—he was cockeyed as Trenco's ether in thinking that they might come back. If anything at all erupted from that hypercircle, it would be something against which the stuff he was mustering would be precisely as effective as so much thin air. And she *still* had no concrete idea of what she so feared. It would not be essentially physical, she was pretty sure. It would almost have to be mental. But who or what could possibly put it across? And how? And above all, what could she do about it if they did?

Eyes narrowed, brow furrowed in concentration, she thought as she had never thought before; and the harder she thought the more clouded the picture became. For the first time in her triumphant life she felt small—weak—impotent. It was in that hour that Kathryn Kinnison really grew up.

The tube vanished; she heaved a tremendous sigh of relief. They, whoever they were, having failed to bring Kinnison to them—this time—were not coming after him—this time. Not an important enough game to play to the end? No, that wasn't it. Maybe they weren't ready. But the next time—

Mentor the Arisian had told her bluntly, the last time she had seen him, to come to him again when she had found out that she did not know everything there was to be known. Deep down, she had believed that that day would never come. Now, however, it had. This escape—if it had been an escape—had taught her much.

"Mother!" She shot a call to distant Klovia. "I'm on Radelix. Everything's on the green. Dad has just knocked a flock of Boskonians into an outside loop and come through QX. I've got to do a little flit, though, before I come home. 'Bye."

THE LENSMAN

*

Kinnison stood intermittent guard over Base for four days after the hyperspatial tube had disappeared before he gave up; before he did any very serious thinking upon what he should do next.

Could he and should he keep on as Sybly Whyte? He could and he should, he decided. He hadn't been gone long enough for Whyte's absence to have been noticed; nothing whatever connected Whyte with Kinnison. If he really knew what he was doing, a more specific alias might be better; but as long as he was merely smelling around, Whyte's was the best identity to use. He could go anywhere, do anything, ask anything of anybody, and all with a perfectly good excuse.

And as Sybly Whyte, then, for days that stretched into weeks, he roamed—finding, as he had been afraid that he would find, nothing whatever. It seemed as though all Boskonian activity of the type in which he was most interested had ceased with his return from the hyperspatial tube. Just what that meant he did not know. It was unthinkable that they had given up on him—much more probably they were hatching something brand new. And the frustration of inaction and the trying to figure out what was coming next was driving him not-so-slowly nuts.

Then, striking through the doldrums, came a call from Maitland.

"Kim? You told me to Lens you immediately about any off-color work. Don't know whether this is or not. The guy may be—probably is—crazy. Conklin, who reported him, couldn't decide—neither can I, from Conklin's report. Do you want to send somebody special, take over yourself, or what?"

"I'll take over," Kinnison decided instantly. If neither Conklin nor the Vice Co-ordinator, Gray Lensmen both, could decide, there was no point in sending anyone else. "Where and who?"

"Planet, Meneas II, not too far from where you are now. City, Meneateles; 116-3-29, 45-22-17. Place, Jack's Haven, a meteor miner's hangout at the corner of Gold and Sapphire Streets. Person, a man called 'Eddie'."

"Thanks. I'll check." Maitland did not send, and Kinnison did not want, any additional information. Both knew that since the Co-ordinator was going to investigate this thing himself, he should get his facts, and particularly his impressions, unprejudiced and at first hand.

To Meneas II, then, and to Jack's Haven, Sybly Whyte went, notebook very much in evidence. An ordinary enough space-dive Jack's turned out to be—higher-toned than that Radeligian space-dock saloon of Bominger's; much less flamboyant than notorious Miners' Rest on far Euphrosyne.

"I wish to interview a person named Eddie," he announced, as he bought a bottle of wine. "I have been informed that he has had deep-space adventures worthy of incorporation into one of my novels."

"Eddie? Haw!" The barkeeper laughed raucously. "That space-louse? Somebody's been kidding you, mister. He's nothing but a broken-down meteor miner—you know what a space-louse is, don't you?—that we let clean cuspidors and do such-like odd jobs for his

922

keep. We don't throw him out, like we do the others, because he's kind of funny in one way. Every hour or so he throws a fit, and that amuses people."

Whyte's eager-beaver attitude did not change; his face reflected nothing of what Kinnison thought of this callous speech. For Kinnison did know exactly what a space-louse was. More, he knew exactly what turned a man into one. Ex-meteor miner himself, he knew what the awesome depths of space, the ever-present dangers, the privations, the solitude, the frustrations, did to any mind not adequately integrated. He knew that only the strong survived; that the many weak succumbed. From sickening memory he knew just what pitiful wrecks those many became. Nevertheless, and despite the fact that the information was not necessary:

"Where is this Eddie now?"

"That's him, over there in the corner. By the way he's acting, he'll have another fit pretty quick now."

The shambling travesty of a man accepted avidly the invitation to table and downed at a gulp the proffered drink. Then, as though the mild potion had been a trigger, his wracked body tensed and his features began to writhe.

"Cateagles!" he screamed; eyes rolling, breath coming in hard, frantic gasps. "Gangs of cateagles! Thousands! They're clawing me to bits! And the Lensman! He's sicking them on! OW!! Yow!!!" He burst into unintelligible screams and threw himself to the floor. There, rolling convulsively over and over, he tried the impossible feat of covering simultaneously with his two clawlike hands his eyes, ears, nose, mouth, and throat.

Ignoring the crowding spectators, Kinnison invaded the helpless mind before him. He winced mentally as he photographed upon his own brain the whole atrocious enormity of what was there. Then, while Whyte busily scribbled notes, he shot a thought to distant Klovia.

*

"Cliff! I'm here in Jack's Haven, and I've got Eddie's data. What did you and Conklin make of it? You agree, of course, that the Lensman is the crux."

"Definitely. Everything else is hop-happy space-drift. The fact that there are not—there can't be—any such Lensman as Eddie imagined, makes him space-drift, too, in our opinion. We called you in on the millionth chance—sorry that we sent you out on a false alarm, but you said we had to be sure."

"You needn't be sorry." Kinnison's thought was the grimmest Clifford Maitland had ever felt. "Eddie isn't an ordinary space-louse. You see, I happen to know one thing that you and Conklin don't, since you've never been there. Did you happen to notice a woman in the picture? Very faint; decidedly in the background?"

"Now that you mention her—yes, there was one. So far in the background and so faint that it never occurred to either Conklin or me that she could be connected. How can she possibly have any bearing, Kim? Most every spaceman has a woman—or a lot of different ones—more or less on his mind all the time, you know. Definitely immaterial and not germane, I'd say."

"So would I, maybe, except for the fact that she isn't really a woman at all, but a Lyranian—"

923

"A LYRANIAN!" Maitland interrupted. Kinnison could feel the racing of his assistant's thoughts. "That complicates things. But how in Palain's purple hells, Kim, could Eddie ever have got to Lyrane—and if he did, how did he get away alive?"

"I don't know, Cliff." Kinnison's mind, too, was working fast. "But you haven't got all the dope yet. Not only is she a Lyranian, but I know her personally—she's that airport manager who tried her level best to kill me all the time I was on Lyrane II."

"Hm-m-m." Maitland tried to digest that undigestible bit. Tried, and failed. "That would seem to make the Lensman real, too, then—real enough, at least, to investigate—much as I hate to think of the possibility of a Lensman going that far off the beam." Maitland's convictions died hard. "Unless—could there be any possibility of coincidence?"

"Coincidence is out. Don't think it's a trap, either—hasn't got the right earmarks."

"You'll handle this yourself, then?"

"Check. At least, I'll help. There may be people better qualified than I am to do the heavy work. I'll get them at it. Thanks, Cliff—clear ether."

He lined a thought to his wife; and after a short, warmly intimate contact, he told her everything that had happened.

"So you see, Beautiful," he concluded, "your wish is coming true. I couldn't keep you out of this if I wanted to. So check with the girls, put on your Lens, take off your clothes, and go to work."

"I'll do that." Clarrissa laughed and her soaring spirit flooded his mind. "Thanks, my dear."

Then and only then did Kimball Kinnison, master therapist, pay any further attention to that which lay contorted upon the floor. But when Whyte folded up his notebook and left the place, the derelict was resting quietly; and in a space of time long enough so that the putative writer of space operas would not be connected with the cure, those fits would end. Moreover, Eddie would return, whole, to the void: he would become what he had never before been—a successful meteor miner.

Lensmen pay their debts; even to spiders and to worms.

IX.

Her adventure in the hyperspatial tube had taught Kathryn Kinnison much. Realizing her inadequacy and knowing what to do about it, she drove her speedster at high velocity to Arisia. Unlike the Second-Stage Lensmen, she did not even slow down as she approached the planet's barrier; but, as one sure of her welcome, merely threw out ahead of her an identifying thought.

"Ah, daughter Kathryn, again you are in time." Was there, or was there not, a trace of emotion—of welcome, even of affection?—in that usually utterly emotionless thought? "Land as usual."

She neutralized her controls as she felt the mighty beams of the landing engine take hold of her little ship. Upon previous visits she had questioned nothing—this time she was questioning everything. Was she landing, or not? Directing her every force inwardly, she probed her own mind to its profoundest depths. Definitely, she was her own mistress throughout—no conceivable mind could take *hers* over so tracelessly. As definitely, then, she was actually landing.

She landed. The ground upon which she stepped was real. So was the automatic flier—neither plane nor helicopter—which whisked her from the spaceport to her familiar destination, an unpretentious residence upon the grounds of an immense hospital. The graveled walk, the flowering shrubs, and the indescribably sweet and pungent perfume were real; as were the tiny pain and the drop of blood which resulted when a needle-sharp thorn pierced her incautious finger.

Through automatically opening doors she made her way into the familiar, comfortable, book-lined room which she knew was Mentor's study. And there, at his big desk, unchanged, sat Mentor. A lot like her father, but older—much older. About ninety, she had always thought, even though he didn't look over sixty. This time, however, she drove a probe—and got the shock of her life. Her thought was stopped—cold—not by superior mental force, which she could have taken unmoved, but by a seemingly ordinary thought-screen; and her fast-disintegrating morale began visibly to crack.

"Is all this . . . are you . . . real, or not?" she burst out, finally. "If it isn't, I'll go mad!"

"That which you have tested—and I—are real, for the moment and as you understand reality. Your mind in its present state of advancement cannot be deceived concerning such elementary matters."

"But it all wasn't, before? Or don't you want to answer that?"

"Since the sure knowledge will affect your growth, I will answer. It was not. This is the first time that your speedster has landed physically upon Arisia."

The girl shrank, appalled. "You told me to come to you again when I had learned that I did not know everything there was to know," she finally forced herself to say. "I learned that in the tube; but I did not realize until just now that I don't know *anything*. Do you really think, Mentor, that there is any use at all in going on with me?" she concluded, bitterly.

"Much," he assured her. "Your development has been eminently satisfactory, and your present mental condition is both necessary and sufficient."

"Well, I'll be a spr—" Kathryn bit off the expletive and frowned. "What were you doing to me before, then, when I thought I got everything?"

"Power of mind," he informed her. "Sheer power, and penetration, and control. Depth, and speed, and all the other factors with which you are already familiar."

"But what is left? I know there is—lots of it—but I can't imagine what."

"Scope," Mentor replied, gravely. "Each of those qualities and characteristics must be expanded to encompass the full sphere of thought. Neither words nor thoughts can give any adequate concept of what it means; a practically wide-open two-way will be necessary. This cannot be accomplished, daughter, in the adolescent confines of your present mind; therefore enter fully into mine."

She did so: and after less than a minute of that awful contact slumped to the floor.

*

The Arisian, unchanged, unmoved, unmoving, gazed at her until finally she began to stir.

"That . . . father Mentor, that was—" she blinked, shook her head savagely, fought her way back to full consciousness. "That was a shock."

"It was," he agreed. "More so than you think. Of all the entities of your Civilization, your brother and now you are the only ones it would not kill instantly. You now know what the word 'scope' means, and are ready for your last treatment, in the course of which I shall take your mind as far along the road of knowledge as mine is capable of going."

"But that would mean . . . you're implying—But my mind *can't* be superior to yours, Mentor! Nothing could be, *possibly*—it's sheerly, starkly unthinkable!"

"But true, daughter, nevertheless. While you are recovering your strength from that which was but the beginning of your education, I will explain certain matters previously obscure. You have long known, of course, that you five children are not like any others. You have always known many things without having learned them. You think upon all possible bands of thought. Your senses of perception, of sight, of hearing, of touch, are so perfectly merged into one sense that you perceive at will any possible manifestation upon any possible plane or dimension of vibration. Also, although this may not have occurred to you as extraordinary, since it is not obvious, you differ physically from your fellows in some important respects. You have never experienced the slightest symptom of physical illness; not even a headache or a decayed tooth. You do not really require sleep. Vaccinations and inoculations do not 'take'. No pathogenic organism, however virulent; no poison, however potent—"

"Stop, Mentor!" Kathryn gasped, turning white. "I can't take it . . . you really mean, then, that we aren't human at all?"

"Yes and no. A partial explanation, while long, may be in order. Many cycles of time ago it became apparent to our more advanced thinkers that the rise and fall of Civilizations was too rhythmic to be accidental. They studied this rhythm, but life was too short. They set out, then, deliberately to prolong their lives. Fewer and fewer in numbers, they lived longer and longer; and the longer each lived, the more he learned. Their visualizations of the Cosmic All became less tenuous, more complete. It became evident that there was some inimical force at work; a force implacably opposed to that which we know as Civilization. Like a mouse in the power of a torturing cat, any Civilization could go just so far, but no farther. For instance, that of Atlantis, upon your father's native planet, Tellus. I was personally concerned in that, and could not stop its fall." The Arisian *was* showing emotion now; his thought was bleak and bitter.

"Four of us were assigned to the problem of this opposing force. We learned that its final abatement would necessitate the development of a race superior to ours in every respect. We, therefore, selected blood lines in each of the four strongest races of the galaxy and began to eliminate as many as possible of their weaknesses and to concentrate all of their strengths. From your knowledge of genetics you realize the magnitude of the task; you know that it would take much time uselessly to go into the details of its accomplishment. Your father and your mother were the penultimates of long—*very* long—lines of matings; their procreative cells were such that in their fusion practically every gene carrying any trait of weakness was rejected. Conversely, you carry the genes of every trait of strength ever known to any member of your human race. Therefore, while in outward seeming you are human, in every factor of importance you are not; you are even less human than am I myself."

"And just how human is that?" Kathryn flared, and again her most penetrant probe of force flattened out against the Arisian's screen.

"Later, daughter, not now. That knowledge will come at the end of your education, not at its beginning."

"I was afraid so." She stared at the Arisian, her eyes wide and hopeless; brimming, in spite of her efforts at control, with tears. "You're a monster, and I am . . . or am going to be . . . a worse one. A monster . . . and I'll have to live a million years . . . alone . . . why? Why, Mentor, did you have to do this to me?"

"Calm yourself, daughter. The shock, while severe, will pass. You have lost nothing, have gained much."

"Gained? Bah!" The girl's thought was loaded with bitterness and scorn. "I've lost my parents—I'll still be a girl long after they have died. I've lost every possibility of ever really living. I want love . . . and a husband . . . and children . . . and I can't have any of them, ever. Even without this, I've never seen a man I wanted, and now I can't ever love anybody. I don't *want* to live a million years, Mentor—especially alone!" The thought was a veritable wail of despair.

*

"The time has come to stop this childish thinking." Mentor's thought, however, was only mildly reproving. "Such a reaction is only natural, but your conclusions are entirely erroneous. One single clear thought will show you that you have no present psychic, intellectual, emotional, or physical need of a complement."

"That's true—But other girls of my age—"

"Exactly," came Mentor's dry rejoinder. "Thinking of yourself as an adult Homo sapien, you were judging yourself by false standards. As a matter of fact, you are an adolescent, not an adult. In due time you will come to love a man, and he you, with a fervor and depth which you at present cannot even dimly understand."

"But that still leaves my parents," Kathryn felt much better. "I can apparently age, of course, as easily as I can put on a hat . . . but I really do love them, you know, and it will simply break mother's heart to have all her daughters turn out to be—as she thinks—spinsters."

"On that point, too, you may rest at ease. I am taking care of that. Kimball and Clarrissa both know, without knowing how they know it, that your life cycle is tremendously longer than theirs. They both know that they will not live to see their grandchildren. Be assured, daughter, that before they pass from this cycle of existence into the next—about which I know nothing—they shall know that all is to be supremely well with their line; even though, to Civilization at large, it shall apparently end with you Five."

"End with us? What do you mean?"

"You have a destiny, the nature of which your mind is not yet qualified to receive. In due time the knowledge shall be yours. Suffice it now to say that the next forty or fifty years will be but a fleeting moment in the span of life which is to be yours. But time, at the moment, presses. You are now fully recovered and we must get on with this, your last period of study with me, at the end of which you will be able to bear the fullest, closest impact of my mind as easily as you have heretofore borne full contact with your sisters'. Let us proceed with the work."

*

Work it was, and it went on for weeks. Kathryn took and survived those shattering treatments, one after another; emerging finally with a mind whose power and scope can no more be explained to any mind below the third level than can the general theory of relativity be explained to a chimpanzee.

"It was forced, not natural, yes," the Arisian said, gravely, as the girl was about to leave. "You are many millions of your years ahead of your natural time. You realize, however, the necessity of that forcing. You also realize that I can give you no more formal instruction. I will be with you or on call at all times; I will be of aid in crises; but in larger matters your further development is in your own hands."

Kathryn shivered. "I realize that, and it scares me clear through—especially this coming conflict, at which you hint so vaguely. I wish that you would tell me at least *something* about it, so that I could get ready for it!"

"Daughter, I can't." For the first time in Kathryn's experience, Mentor the Arisian was unsure. "It is certain that we have been on time; but since the Eddorians have minds of power little, if any, inferior to our own, there are many details which we cannot derive with certainty, and to advise you wrongly would be to do you irreparable harm. All I can say is that if my visualization in that respect is sound, and I am practically sure that it is, sufficient warning will be given by your learning, with no specific effort on your part and from some source other than myself, that there does in fact exist a planet named 'Ploor'—a name which to you is now only a meaningless symbol. Go now, daughter Kathryn, and work."

*

Kathryn went; knowing that the Arisian had said all that he would say. In truth, he had told her vastly more than she had expected him to divulge; and it chilled her to the marrow to think that she, who had always looked up to the Arisians as demigods of sorts, would from now on be expected to act as their equal—in some ways, perhaps, as their superior! As her speedster tore through space toward distant Klovia she wrestled with herself, trying to shake her new self down into a personality as well integrated as her old one had been. She had not quite succeeded when she felt a thought.

"Help! I am in difficulty with this, my ship. Will any entity receiving my call and possessing the tools of a mechanic please come to my assistance? Or, lacking such tools, possessing a vessel of power sufficient to tow mine to the place where I must immediately go?"

Kathryn was startled out of her introspective trance. That thought was on a terrifically high band; one so high that she knew of no race using it, so high that an ordinary human mind could not possibly have either sent or received it. Its phraseology, while peculiar, was utterly precise in definition—the mind behind it was certainly of precisionist grade.

928

She acknowledged upon the stranger's wave, and sent out a locator. Good—he wasn't far away. She flashed toward the derelict, matched intrinsics at a safe distance, and began scanning, only to encounter a screen around the whole vessel! To her it was porous enough—but if the creature thought that his screen was tight, let him keep on thinking so. It was his move.

"Well, what are you waiting for?" The thought fairly snapped. "Come closer, so that I may bring you in."

"Not yet," Kathryn snapped back. "Cut your screen so that I can see what you are like. I carry equipment for many environments, but I must know what yours is and equip for it before I can come aboard. You will note that my screens are down."

"Of course. Excuse me—I supposed that you were one of our own"—there came the thought of an unspellable and unpronounceable name—"since none of the lower orders can receive our thoughts direct. Can you equip yourself to come aboard with your tools?"

"Yes." The stranger's light was fierce stuff; ninety-eight percent of its energy being beyond the visible. His lamps were beam-held atomics, nothing less, but there was very little gamma and few neutrons. She could handle it easily enough, she decided, as she finished donning her heat-armor and a helmet of practically opaque, diamond-hard plastic.

As she was wafted gently across the intervening space upon a pencil of force, Kathryn took her first good look at the precisionist himself—or herself. She—it—looked something like a Dhilian, she thought at first. There was the squat, powerful, elephantine body with its four stocky legs; the tremendous double shoulders and enormous arms; the domed, almost immobile head. But there the resemblance ended. There was only the one head—the thinking head, and that one had no eyes and was not covered with bone. There was no feeding head—the thing could neither eat nor breathe. There was no trunk. And what a skin!

It was worse than a hide, really—worse even than a Martian's. The girl had never seen anything like it. It was incredibly thick, dry, pliable; filled minutely with cells of a liquid-gaseous something which she knew to be a more perfect insulator even than the fibers of the tegument itself.

"R-T-S-L-Q-P." She classified the creature readily enough to six places, then stopped and wrinkled her forehead. "Seventh place—that incredible skin—what? S? R? T? It would have to be R."

"You have the requisite tools, I perceive," the creature greeted Kathryn as she entered the central compartment of the strange speedster, no larger than her own. "I can tell you what to do, if—"

"I know what to do." She unbolted a cover, wrought briefly with pliers and splicer, and in ten minutes was done. "It doesn't seem to make sense to me that a person of your obvious intelligence, manifestly knowing enough to make such minor repairs yourself, would go so far from home, alone in such a small ship, without any tools. Burnouts and shorts are apt to happen any time, you know."

"Not in vessels of the—." Again Kathryn felt that unpronounceable symbol. She also felt the stranger stiffen in offended dignity. "We of the higher orders, you should know, do not perform labor. We think. We direct. Others work, and do their work well, or suffer accordingly. This is the first time in nine full four-cycle periods that such a thing has happened, and it will be the last. The punishment which I shall mete out to the guilty mechanic will insure that. I shall, at end, have his life."

"Oh, come, now!" Kathryn protested. "Surely it's no life-and-death mat—"

"Silence!" came curt command. "It is intolerable that one of the lower orders should attempt to—"

"Silence yourself!" At the fierce power of the riposte the creature winced, physically and mentally. "I did this bit of dirty work for you because you apparently couldn't do it for yourself. I did not object to the matter-of-course way you accepted it, because some races are made that way and can't help it. But if you insist on keeping yourself placed five rungs above me on any ladder you can think of, I'll stop being a lady—or even a good Girl Scout—and start doing things about it, and I'll start at any signal you care to call. Get ready, and say when!"

*

The stranger, taken fully aback, threw out a lightning tentacle of thought; a feeler which was stopped cold a full foot from the girl's radiant armor. This was a human female—or was it? It was not. No human being had ever had, nor ever would have, a mind like that. Therefore:

"I have made a grave error," the thing apologized handsomely, "in thinking that you are not at least my equal. Will you grant me pardon, please?"

"Certainly—if you don't repeat it. But I still don't like the idea of your having that mechanic skinned alive." She thought intensely, lip caught between strong white teeth. "Perhaps there is a way. Where are you going, and when do you want to get there?"

"To my home planet," pointing out, mentally, its location in the Galaxy. "I must be there in two hundred of your G-P hours."

"I see." Kathryn nodded her head. "You can—if you promise that you will do nothing whatever to punish your mechanic. And remember that I can tell whether you really mean it or not."

"As I promise, so I do. But suppose that I do not promise?"

"In that case you'll get there in about a hundred thousand G-P years, frozen stiff. For I shall fuse your Bergenholm down so that it can't ever be fixed; then, after welding your ports solidly to the outer shell, I'll attach to your plating the generator of a screen through which you cannot think. Since you have no tools, I'll leave the rest to your imagination. Decide, now, what you wish to do."

"I promise not to harm the mechanic in any way." He surrendered stiffly, and made no undue protest at Kathryn's entrance into his mind to make sure that the promise would be kept.

Flushed by her easy conquest of a mind which she would previously have been unable to touch, and engrossed in the problem of setting her own tremendously enlarged mind to rights, why should it have occurred to the girl that there was anything worthy of investigation concealed in the depths of that chance-met stranger's mentality?

Returning to her own speedster, she shed her armor and shot away; and it was just as well for her peace of mind that she was not aware of the tight-beamed thought even then speeding from the flitter so far behind her to dread and distant Ploor.

" . . . but it was very definitely not a human female. I could not touch it. It may very well have been one of the accursed Arisians themselves. But since I did nothing to arouse its suspicions, I got rid of it easily enough. Spread the warning!"

X.

While Kathryn Kinnison was working with her father in the hyperspatial tube and with Mentor of Arisia, and while Camilla and Tregonsee were sleuthing the inscrutable "X", Constance was also at work. Although she lay flat upon her back, not moving a muscle, she was working as she had never worked before. Long since she had put her indetectable speedster into the control of a director-by-chance. Now, knowing nothing and caring less of where she and her vessel might be or might go, physically completely relaxed, she drove her "sensories" out to the full limit of their prodigious range and held them there for hour after hour. Worsel-like, she was not consciously listening for any particular thing; she was merely increasing her already incredibly vast store of knowledge. One hundred percent receptive, attached to and concerned with only the brain of her physical body, her mind sped at large sampling, testing, analyzing, cataloguing every item with which its most tenuous fringe came in contact. Through thousands of solar systems that mind went; millions upon millions of entities either did or did not contribute something worth while.

Suddenly there came something that jarred her into physical movement—a burst of thought upon a band so high that it was practically always vacant. She shook herself, got up, lighted an Alsakanite cigarette, and made herself a pot of coffee.

"This is important, I think," she mused. "I'd better get to work on it while it's fresh."

She sent out a thought tuned to Worsel, and was surprised when it went unanswered. She investigated, finding that the Velantian's screens were full up and held hard—he was fighting Overlords so savagely that he had not felt her thought. Should she take a hand in this brawl? She should not, she decided, and grinned fleetingly. Her erstwhile tutor would need no help in that comparatively minor chore. She would wait, rest up a bit, and eat, before she called him.

"Worsel! Con calling. What goes on there, fellow old snake?" She finally launched her thought. "You've stuck that sharp tail of yours into some of my business—I hope."

"I hope so," Worsel sent back. "Been quite a while since I saw you close up—how about coming aboard?"

"Coming at max," and she did.

Before entering the *Velan*, however, she put on a personal gravity damper, set at nine hundred eighty centimeters. Strong, tough, and supple as she was she did not relish the thought of the atrocious accelerations used and enjoyed by Velantians everywhere.

"What did you make of that burst of thought?" she asked by way of greeting. "Or were you having so much fun that you missed it?"

"What burst?" Then, after Constance had explained, "I was busy—but *not* having fun."

931

"Somebody who didn't know you might believe that," the girl derided. "This thought was important, I think—much more so than dilly-dallying with Overlords, as you were doing. It was 'way up—on this band here." She illustrated.

"So?" Worsel came as near to whistling as one of his inarticulate race could come. "What were they like? Tell me all that you can."

"VWZY, to four places." Con concentrated. "Multilegged—not exactly carapaceous, but pretty nearly. Spiny, too, I believe. The world was cold, dismal, barren; but not frigid, but he . . . it . . . didn't seem exactly like an oxygen-breather—more like what a warm-blooded Palainian would perhaps look like, if you can imagine such a thing. Mentality very high—precisionist grade—no thought of cities as such. The sun was a typical yellow dwarf. Does any of this ring a bell in your mind?"

"No." Worsel thought intensely for minutes. So did Constance. Neither had any idea then that the girl was describing the form assumed in their autumn by the dread inhabitants of the planet Ploor!

"This may indeed be important," Worsel broke the mental silence. "Shall we explore together?"

"We shall." They tuned to the desired band. "Give it plenty of shove, too. Go!"

*

Out and out and out the twinned receptors sped; to encounter finally a tenuous, weak, and utterly cryptic vibration. One touch—the merest possible contact—and it disappeared. It vanished before even Con's electronics-fast reactions could get more than a hint of directional alignment; and neither of the observers could read any part of it.

Both of these developments were starkly incredible, and Worsel's long body tightened convulsively, rock-hard, in the violence of the mental force now driving his exploring mind. Finding nothing, he finally relaxed.

"Any Lensman, anywhere, can read and understand any thought, however garbled or scrambled, or however expressed," he thought at Constance. "Also, I have always been able to get an exact line on anything I could perceive, but all I know about this one is that it seemed to come mostly from somewhere over that way. Did you do any better?"

"Not much, if any." If the thing was surprising to Worsel, it was sheerly astounding to his companion. She, knowing the measure of her power, thought to herself—not to the Velantian: "Girl, file this one carefully away in the big black book!"

Slight as were the directional leads, the Velan tore along the indicated line at maximum blast. Day after day she sped, a wide-flung mental net out far ahead and out farther still on all sides. They did not find what they sought, but they did find—something.

"What is it?" Worsel demanded of the quivering telepath who had made the report.

"I don't know, sir. Not on that ultra-band, but well below it—there. Not an Overlord, certainly, but something perhaps equally unfriendly."

"An Eich!" Both Worsel and Con exclaimed the thought, and the girl went on, "It was practically certain that we couldn't get them all on Jarnevon, of course, but none have been reported before. Where are they, anyway? Get me a chart, somebody. It's Novena, and they're on the ninth planet out—Novena IX. Tune up your heavy artillery,

Worsel—it'd be nice if we could take the head man alive, but that much luck probably isn't in the cards."

The Velantian, even though he had issued instantaneously the order to drive at full blast toward the indicated planet, was momentarily at a loss. Kinnison's daughter entertained no doubts as to the outcome of the encounter she was proposing—but she had never seen an Eich close up. He had. So had her father. Kinnison had come out a very poor second in that affair, and Worsel knew that he could have done no better, if as well. However, that had been upon Jarnevon, actually inside one of its strongest citadels, and neither he nor Kinnison had been prepared.

"What's the plan, Worsel?" Con demanded, vibrantly. "How're you figuring on taking 'em?"

"Depends on how strong they are. If it's a long-established base, we'll simply have to report it to LaForge and go on about our business. If, as seems more probable from the fact that it hasn't been reported before, it is a new establishment of refugees from Jarnevon—or possibly only a grounded spaceship so far—we'll go to work on them ourselves. We'll soon be close enough to find out."

"QX," and a fleeting grin passed over Con's vivacious face. For a long time she had been working with Mentor the Arisian, specifically to develop the ability to "out-Worsel Worsel", and now was the best time she ever would have to put her hard schooling to test.

*

Hence, Master of Hallucination though he was, the Velantian had no hint of realization when his Klovian companion, working through a channel which he did not even know existed, took control of every compartment of his mind. Nor did the crew, in particular or en masse, suspect anything amiss when she performed the infinitely easier task of taking over theirs. Nor did the unlucky Eich, when the flying Velan had approached their planet closely enough to make it clear that their establishment was indeed a new one, being built around the nucleus of a crippled Boskonian battleship. Except for their commanding officer they died then and there—and Con was to regret bitterly, later, that she had made this engagement such a one-girl affair.

The battleship apparently was not in shape to meet the Velan in open space, since it did not; but it could have operated and to all seeming did operate as a formidable fortress indeed from its fixed position on the ground. Under the fierce impact of its offensive beams the Velantians saw their very wall shields flame violet. In return they saw their mighty secondary beams stopped cold by the Boskonian's inner screens, and had to bring into play the inconceivable energies of their primaries before the enemy's spaceship-fortress could be knocked out. And this much of the battle was real. Instrument- and recorder-tapes could be and were being doctored to fit; but spent primary shells could not be simulated. Nor was it thinkable that this tremendous ship and its incipient Base should be allowed to survive.

Hence, after the dreadful primaries had quieted the Eich's main batteries and had reduced the groundworks to flaming pools of lava, needle-beamers went to work on every minor and secondary control board. Then, the great vessel definitely helpless as a fighting unit, Worsel and his hard-bitten crew thought that they went—thought-screened, full-armored, armed with semiportables and DeLameters—joyously into the hand-to-hand combat which each so craved. Worsel and two of his strongest henchmen attacked the armed and armored Boskonian captain. After a satisfying terrific struggle, in the course of which all three of the Velantians—and some others—were appropriately burned and wounded, they overpowered him and carried him bodily into the control room of the *Velan*. This part of the episode, too, was real; as was the complete melting down of the Boskonian vessel which occurred while the transfer was being made.

*

Then, while Con was engaged in the exceedingly delicate task of withdrawing her mind from Worsel's without leaving any detectable trace that she had ever been in it, there happened the completely unexpected; the one thing for which she was utterly unprepared. The mind of the captive captain was wrenched from her control as palpably as a loosely-held stick is snatched from a physical hand; and at the same time there was hurled against her impenetrable barriers an attack which could not possibly have stemmed from any Eichian mind!

If her mind had been free, she could have coped with the situation, but it was not. She *had* to hold Worsel—she knew with cold certainty what would ensue if she did not. The crew? They could be blocked out temporarily—unlike the Velantian Lensman, no one of them could even suspect that he had been in a stasis unless it were long enough to be noticeable upon such timepieces as clocks. The procedure, however, occupied a millisecond or so of precious time; and a considerably longer interval was required to withdraw with the required tracelessness from Worsel's mind. Thus, before she could do anything except protect herself and the Velantian from that surprisingly powerful invading intelligence, all trace of it disappeared and all that remained of their captive was a dead body.

Worsel and Constance stared at each other, wordless, for seconds. The Velantian had a completely and accurately detailed memory of everything that had happened up to that instant, the only matter not quite clear being the fact that their hard-won captive was dead; the girl's mind was racing to fabricate a bulletproof explanation of that startling fact. Worsel saved her the trouble.

"It is, of course, true," he thought at her finally, "that any mind of sufficient power can destroy by force of will alone the entity of flesh in which it resides. I never thought about this matter before in connection with the Eich, but no detail of the experience your father and I had with them on Jarnevon would support any contention that they do not have minds of the requisite power, and today's battle, being purely physical, would not throw any light on the subject. I wonder if a thing like that could be stopped? That is, if we had been on time—?"

"That's it, I think." Con put on her most disarming, most engaging grin in preparation for the most outrageous series of lies of her long career. "And I don't think it can be stopped—at least I couldn't stop him. You see, I got into him a fraction of a second before you did, and in that instant, just like that," in spite of the fact that Worsel could not hear, she snapped her finger ringingly, "Faster even than that, he was gone. I didn't think of it until you brought it up, but you are as right as can be—he killed himself to keep us from finding out whatever it was that he knew about what is left of Boskonia."

Worsel stared at her with six eyes now instead of one, gimlet probes which glanced imperceptibly off her shield. He was not consciously trying to break down her barriers—to his fullest perception they were already down; no barriers were there. He was not consciously trying to integrate or reintegrate any detail or phase of the episode just past—no iota or trace of falsity had appeared at any point or instant. Nevertheless, deep down within those extra reaches that made Worsel of Velantia what he was, a vague disquiet refused to down. It was too . . . too—Worsel's consciousness could not supply the adjective.

Had it been too easy? Very decidedly it had not. His utterly worn-out, battered and wounded crew refuted that thought. So did his own body, slashed and burned, as well as did the litter of primary shells and the heaps of smoking slag which had once been an enemy stronghold.

Also, even though he had not theretofore thought that he and his crew possessed enough force to do what had just been done, it was starkly unthinkable that anyone, even an Arisian, could have helped him do anything without his knowledge. Particularly how could this girl, daughter of Kimball Kinnison although she was, possibly have stuff enough to play unperceived the part of guardian angel to him, Worsel of Velantia?

Least able of all the Second-Stage Lensmen to appreciate what the Children of the Lens really were, he did not, then or ever, have any inkling of the real truth. But Constance, far behind her cheerfully innocent mask, shivered as she read exactly his disturbed and disturbing thoughts. For, conversely, an unresolved enigma would affect him more than it would any of his fellow L2's. He would work on it until he did resolve it, one way or another. This thing had to be settled, *now*. And there was a way—a good way.

*

"But I *did* help you, you big lug!" she stormed, stamping her booted foot in emphasis. "I was in there every second, slugging away with everything I had. Didn't you even feel me, you dope?" She allowed a thought to become evident; widened her eyes in startled incredulity. "You *didn't!*" she accused, hotly. "You were reveling so repulsively in the thrill of body-to-body fighting, just like you were back there in that cavern of Overlords, that you couldn't have felt a thought if it was driven into you with a D2P pressor! And I'll bet credits to millos that I *did* help you, too—that if I hadn't been in there pitching, dulling their edges here and there at critical moments, you'd've had a time getting them at all! I'm going to flit right now, and I hope I *never* see you again as long as I live!"

This vicious counterattack, completely mendacious though it was, fitted the facts so exactly that Worsel's inchoate doubts vanished. Moreover, he was even less well equipped than are human men to cope with the peculiarly feminine weapons Constance was using so effectively. Wherefore the Velantian capitulated, almost abjectly, and the girl allowed herself to be coaxed down from her high horse and to become her usual sunny and impish self.

But when the *Velan* was once more on course and she had retired to her cabin, it was not to sleep. Instead, she thought. Was this intellect of the same race as the one whose burst of thought she had caught such a short time before, or not? She could not decide—not enough data. The first thought had been unconscious and quite revealing; this one simply a lethal weapon, driven with a power the very memory of which made her gasp again. They could, however, be the same—the mind with which she had been *en rapport* could very well be capable of generating the force she had felt. If they were the same, they were something that should be studied, intensively and at once; and she herself had kicked away her only chance to make that study. She had better tell somebody about this, even if it meant confessing her own bird-brained part, and get some competent advice. Who?

Kit? No. Not because he would smack her down—she *ought* to be smacked down!—but because his brain wasn't enough better than her own to do any good. In fact, it wasn't a bit better than hers.

Mentor? At the very thought she shuddered, mentally and physically. She would call him in, fast enough, regardless of consequences to herself, if it would do any good, but it wouldn't. She was starkly certain of that. He wouldn't smack her down, like Kit would, but he wouldn't help her, either. He'd just sit there and sneer at her while she stewed, hotter and hotter, in her own juice.

"In a childish, perverted, and grossly exaggerated way, Daughter Constance, you are right," the Arisian's thought rolled sonorously into her astounded mind. "You got yourself into this—get yourself out. One promising fact, however, I perceive—although seldom and late—you at last begin really to think."

In that hour Constance Kinnison grew up.

XI.

Any human or near-human Lensman would have been appalled by the sheer loneliness of Nadreck's long vigil. Almost any one of them would have cursed, fluently and bitterly, when the time came at which he was forced to concede that the being for whom he lay in wait was not going to visit that particular planet.

But utterly unhuman Nadreck was not lonely. In fact, there was no word in the vocabulary of his race even remotely resembling the term in definition, connotation, or implication. From his Galaxy-wide study he had a dim, imperfect idea of what such an emotion or feeling might be, but he could not begin to understand it. Nor was he in the least disturbed by the fact that Kandron did not appear. Instead, he held his orbit until the minute arrived at which the mathematical probability became point nine nine eight that his proposed quarry was not going to appear. Then, as matter-of-factly as though he had merely taken half an hour out for lunch, he abandoned his position and set out upon the course so carefully planned for exactly this event.

The search for further clues was long and uneventful; but monstrously, unhumanly patient Nadreck stuck to it until he found one. True, it was so slight as to be practically nonexistent—a mere fragment of a whisper of zwilnik instruction—but it bore Kandron's unmistakable imprint. The Palainian had expected no more. Kandron would not slip. Momentary leakages from faulty machines would have to occur from time to time, but Kandron's machines would not be at fault either often or long at a time.

Nadreck, however, had been ready. Course after course of the most delicate spotting screen ever devised had been out for weeks. So had tracers, radiation absorbers, and every other insidious locating device known to the science of the age. The standard detectors remained blank, of course—no more so than his own conveyance would that of the Onlonian be detectable by any ordinary instruments. And as the Palainian speedster shot away along the most probable course, some fifty delicate instruments in its bow began stabbing that entire region of space with a pattern of needles of force through which a Terrestrial barrel could not have floated untouched.

Thus the Boskonian craft—an inherently indetectable speedster—was located; and in that instant was speared by three modified CRX tracers. Nadreck then went inert and began to plot the other speedster's course. He soon learned that that course was unpredictable; that the vessel was being operated statistically, completely at random. This too, then, was a trap.

This knowledge disturbed Nadreck no more than had any more-or-less-similar event of the previous twenty-odd years. He had realized fully that the leakage could as well have been deliberate as accidental. He had at no time underestimated Kandron's ability; the future alone would reveal whether or not Kandron would at any time underestimate his. He would follow through—there might be a way in which this particular trap could be used against its setter.

Leg after leg of meaningless course Nadreck followed, until there came about that which the Palainian knew would happen in time—the speedster held a straight course for more parsecs than six-sigma limits of probability could ascribe to pure randomness. Nadreck knew what that meant. The speedster was returning to its base for servicing, which was precisely the event for which he had been waiting. It was the base he wanted, not the speedster; and that base would never, under any conceivable conditions, emit any detectable quantity of traceable radiation. To its base, then, Nadreck followed the little spaceship, and to say that he was on the alert as he approached that base is a gross understatement indeed. He expected to set off at least one, and probably many blasts of force. That would almost certainly be necessary in order to secure sufficient information concerning the enemy's defensive screens. It was unnecessary—but when those blasts arrived Nadreck was elsewhere, calmly analyzing the data secured by his instruments during the brief contact which had triggered the Boskonian projectors into action.

*

So light, so fleeting, and so unorthodox had been Nadreck's touch that the personnel of the now doomed base could not have known with any certainty that any visitor had actually been there. If there had been, the logical supposition would have been that he and his vessel had been resolved into their component atoms. Nevertheless Nadreck waited—as has been shown, he was good at waiting—until the burst of extra vigilance set up by the occurrence would have subsided into ordinary watchfulness. Then he began to act.

At first this action was in ultra-slow motion. One millimeter per hour his drill advanced. Drill was synchronized precisely with screen, and so guarded as to give an alarm at a level of interference far below that necessary to energize any probable detector at the generators of the screen being attacked.

Through defense after defense Nadreck made his cautious, indetectable way into the dome. It was a small base, as such things go; manned, as expected, by escapees from Onlo. Scum, too, for the most part; creatures of even baser and more violent passions than those upon whom he had worked in Kandron's Onlonian stronghold. To keep those intractable entities in line during their brutally long tours of duty, a psychological therapist had been given authority second only to that of the Base Commander. That knowledge, and the fact that there was only one populated dome, made the Palainian come as close to grinning as one of his unsmiling race can.

The psychologist wore a multiplex thought-screen, of course, as did everyone else; but that did not bother Nadreck. Kinnison had opened such screens many times; not only by means of his own hands, but also at various times by the use of a dog's jaws, a spider's legs and mandibles, and even a worm's sinuous body. Wherefore, through the agency of a quasi-fourth-dimensional life-form literally indescribable to three-dimensional man, Nadreck's ego was soon comfortably ensconced in the mind of the Onlonian.

That entity knew in detail every weakness of each of his personnel. It was his duty to watch those weaknesses, to keep them down, to condition each of his wards in such fashion that friction and strife would be minimized. Now, however, he proceeded to do exactly the opposite. One hated another. That hate became a searing obsession, requiring the concentration of every effort upon ways and means of destroying its object. One feared another. That fear ate in, searing as it went, destroying every normality of outlook and of reason. Many were jealous of their superiors. This emotion, requiring as it does nothing except its own substance upon which to feed, became a fantastically-spreading, caustically corrosive blight.

To name each ugly, noisome passion or trait resident in that dome is to call the complete roster of the vile; and calmly, mercilessly, unmovedly, ultra-efficiently, Nadreck worked upon them all. As though he were playing a Satanic organ he touched a nerve here, a synapse there, a channel somewhere else, bringing the whole group, with the lone exception of the commander, simultaneously to the point of explosion. Nor was any sign of this perfect work evident externally; for everyone there, having lived so long under the iron code of Boskonia, knew exactly the consequences of any infraction of that code.

The moment came when passion overmastered sense. One of the monsters stumbled, jostling another. That nudge became, in its recipient's seething mind, a lethal attack by his bitterest enemy. A forbidden projector flamed viciously—the offended one was sating his lust so insensately that he scarcely noticed the bolt that in turn rived away his own life. Detonated by this incident, the personnel of the Base exploded as one. Blasters raved briefly; knives and swords bit and slashed; improvised bludgeons crashed against pre-selected targets; hard-taloned appendages gouged and tore. And Nadreck, who had long since withdrawn from the mind of the psychologist, timed with a stop watch the duration of the whole grizzly affair, from the instant of the first stumble to the death of the last Onlonian outside the Commander's locked and armored sanctum. Ninety-eight and three tenths seconds. Good—a nice job.

SUPER PACK

*

The Base Commander, as soon as it was safe to do so, rushed out of his guarded room to investigate. Amazed, disgruntled, dismayed by the to him completely inexplicable phenomenon he had just witnessed, he fell an easy prey to the Palainian Lensman. Nadreck invaded his mind and explored it, channel by channel; finding—not entirely unexpectedly—that this Number One knew nothing whatever of interest.

Nadreck did not destroy the base. Instead, after setting up a small instrument in the Commander's office, he took that unfortunate wight aboard his speedster and drove off into space. He immobilized his captive, not by loading him with manacles, but by deftly severing a few essential nerve trunks. Then he really studied the Onlonian's mind—line by line, this time; almost cell by cell. A master—almost certainly Kandron himself—had operated here. There was not the slightest trace of tampering; no leads to or indications of what the activating stimulus would have to be; all that the fellow now knew was that it was his job to hold his Base inviolate against any and every form of intrusion and to keep that speedster flitting around all over space on a director-by-chance as much as possible of the time, leaking slightly a certain signal now and then.

Even under this microscopic re-examination, he knew nothing whatever of Kandron; nothing of Onlo or of Thrale; nothing of any Boskonian organization, activity, or thing; and Nadreck, although baffled still, remained undisturbed. This trap, he thought, could almost certainly be used against the trapper. Until a certain call came through his relay in the Base, he would investigate the planets of this system.

*

During the investigation a thought impinged upon his Lens from Karen Kinnison, one of the very few warm-blooded beings for whom he had any real liking or respect.

"Busy, Nadreck?" she asked, as casually as though she had seen him hours, instead of weeks before.

"In large, yes—in detail and at the moment, no. Is there any small problem in which I can be of assistance?"

"Not small—big. I just got the funniest distress call I ever heard or heard of. On a high band—'way, 'way up—there. Do you know of any race that thinks on that band?"

"I do not believe so." He thought for a moment. "Definitely, no."

"Neither do I. It wasn't broadcast, either, but was directed at any member of a special race or tribe—very special. Classification, straight Z's to ten or twelve places, she . . . or it . . . seemed to be trying to specify."

"A frigid race of extreme type, adapted to an environment having a temperature of only a few degrees absolute."

"Yes. Like you, only more so." Kay paused, trying to put into intelligible thought a picture inherently incapable of reception or recognition by her as yet strictly three-dimensional intelligence. "Something like the Eich, too, but not much. Their visible aspect was obscure, fluid . . . amorphous . . . indefinite? . . . skip it—I couldn't really perceive it, let alone describe it. I wish you had caught that thought."

"I wish so, too—it is extremely interesting. But tell me—if the thought was directed, not broadcast, how could you have received it?"

939

"That's the funniest part of the whole thing." Nadreck could feel the girl frown in concentration. "It came at me from all sides at once—never felt anything like it. Naturally I started feeling around for the source—particularly since it was a distress signal—but before I could get even a general direction of the origin it . . . it . . . well, it didn't really disappear or really weaken, but something happened to it. I couldn't read it any more—and *that* really did throw me for a loss." She paused, then went on. "It didn't so much go away as go *down*, some way or other. Then it vanished completely, without really going anywhere. I know that I'm not making myself clear—I simply can't—but have I given you enough leads so that you can make any sense at all out of any part of it?"

"I'm very sorry to say that I can not."

*

Nor could he, ever, for excellent reasons. That girl had a mind whose power, scope, depth, and range she herself did not, could not even dimly understand; a mind to be fully comprehended only by an adult of her own third level. That mind had in fact received in toto a purely fourth-dimensional thought. If Nadreck had received it, he would have understood it and recognized it for what it was only because of his advanced Arisian training—no other Palainian could have done so—and it would have been sheerly unthinkable to him that any warm-blooded and, therefore, strictly three-dimensional entity could by any possibility receive such a thought; or, having received it, could understand any figment of it. Nevertheless, if he had really concentrated the full powers of his mind upon the girl's attempted description, he might very well have recognized in it the clearest possible three-dimensional delineation of such a thought; and from that point he could have gone on to a full understanding of the Children of the Lens.

However, he did not so concentrate. It was constitutionally impossible for him to devote real mental effort to any matter not immediately pertaining to the particular task in hand. Therefore neither he nor Karen Kinnison were to know until much later that she had been *en rapport* with one of Civilization's bitterest, most implacable foes; that she had seen with clairvoyant and telepathic accuracy the intrinsically three-dimensionally-indescribable form assumed in their winter by the horrid, the monstrous inhabitants of that viciously hostile world, the unspeakable planet Ploor!

"I was afraid you couldn't." Kay's thought came clear. "That makes it all the more important—important enough for you to drop whatever it is that you're doing now and join me in getting to the bottom of it, if you could be made to see it, which, of course, you can't."

"I am about to take Kandron, and nothing in the Universe can be as important as that," Nadreck stated quietly, as a simple matter of fact. "You have observed this that lies here?"

"Yes." Karen, *en rapport* with Nadreck, was, of course, cognizant of the captive, but it had not occurred to her to mention the monster. When dealing with Nadreck she, against all the tenets of her sex, exhibited as little curiosity as did the coldly emotionless Lensman himself. "Since you bid so obviously for the question, why are you keeping it alive—or rather, not dead?"

"Because he is my sure link to Kandron." If Nadreck of Palain ever was known to gloat, it was then. "He is Kandron's creature, placed by Kandron personally as an agency of my destruction. Kandron's brain alone holds the key compulsion which will restore his memories. At some future time—perhaps a second from now, perhaps a cycle of years—Kandron will use that key to learn how his minion fares. Kandron's thought will energize my re-transmitter in the dome; the compulsion will be forwarded to this still-living brain. The brain, however, will be in my speedster, not in that undamaged fortress. You now understand why I cannot stray far from this being's base; you should see that you should join me instead of me joining you."

"No; not definite enough," Karen countered, decisively. "I can't see myself passing up a thing like this for the opportunity of spending the next ten years floating around in an orbit, doing nothing. However, I check you to a certain extent—when and if anything really happens, shoot me a thought and I'll rally 'round."

*

The linkage broke without formal adieus. Nadreck went his way, Karen went hers. She did not, however, go far along the way she had had in mind. She was still precisely nowhere in her quest when she felt a thought, of a type that only her brother or an Arisian could send. It was Kit.

"Hi, Kay!" A warm, brotherly contact. "How'r'ya doing, Sis? Are you growing up?"

"I'm grown up! What a question!"

"Don't get stiff, Kay, there's method in this. Got to be sure." All trace of levity gone, he probed her unmercifully. "Not too bad, at that, for a kid. As Dad would express it, if he could feel you this way, you're twenty-nine numbers Brinnell harder than a diamond drill. Plenty of jets for this job, and by the time the real one comes, you'll probably be ready."

"Cut the rigmarole, Kit!" she snapped, and hurled a vicious bolt of her own. If Kit did not counter it as easily as he had handled her earlier efforts, he did not reveal the fact. "What job? What d'you think you're talking about? I'm on a job now that I wouldn't drop for Nadreck, and I don't think that I'll drop it for you."

"You'll have to." Kit's thought was grim. "Mother is going to have to go to work on Lyrane II. The probability is pretty certain that there is or will be something there that she can't handle. Remote control is out, or I'd do it myself, but I can't work on Lyrane II in person. Here's the whole picture—look it over. You can see, Sis, that you're elected, so hop to it."

"I won't!" she stormed. "I can't—I'm too busy. How about asking Con, or Kat, or Cam?"

"They don't fit the picture," he explained patiently—for him. "In this case hardness is indicated, as you can see for yourself."

"Hardness, phooey!" she jeered. "To handle Ladora of Lyrane? She thinks she's a hard-boiled egg, I know, but—"

"Listen, you bird-brained knot-head!" Kit cut in, venomously. "You're fogging the issue deliberately—stop it! I spread you the whole picture—you know as well as I do that while there's nothing definite as yet, the thing needs covering and you're the one to cover it.

But no—just because I'm the one to suggest or ask anything of you, you've always got to go into that mulish act of yours."

"Be silent, children, and attend!" Both flushed violently as Mentor came between them. "Some of the weaker thinkers here are beginning to despair of you, but my visualization of your development is still clear. To mold such characters as yours sufficiently, and yet not too much, is a delicate task indeed; but one which must and shall be done. Christopher, come to me at once, in person. Karen, I would suggest that you go to Lyrane and do there whatever you find necessary to do."

"I won't—I've *still* got this job here to do!" Karen defied even the ancient Arisian sage.

"That, Daughter, can and should wait. I tell you solemnly, as a fact, that if you do not go to Lyrane you will never get the faintest clue to that which you now seek."

XII.

Christopher Kinnison drove toward Arisia, seething. Why couldn't those sisters of his have sense to match their brains—or why couldn't he have had some brothers? Especially—right now—Kay. If she had the sense of a Zabriskan fontema, she'd know that this job was *important* and would snap into it, instead of wild-goose-chasing all over space. If he were Mentor, he'd straighten her out. He had decided to straighten her out once himself, and he grinned wryly to himself at the memory of what had happened. What Mentor had done to him, before he even got started, was really rugged. What he would like to do, next time he got within reach of her, was to shake her until her teeth rattled.

Or would he? Uh-uh. By no stretch of the imagination could he picture himself hurting any one of them. They were swell kids—in fact, the finest people he had ever known. He had rough-housed and wrestled with them plenty of times, of course—he liked it, and so did they. He could handle any one of them—he surveyed without his usual complacence his two-hundred-plus pounds of meat, bone, and gristle—he ought to be able to, since he outweighed them by fifty or sixty pounds; but it wasn't easy. Worse than Valerians—just like taking on a combination of boa constrictor and cateagle—and when Kat and Con ganged up on him that time they mauled him to a pulp in nothing flat.

But jet back! Weight wasn't it, except maybe among themselves. He had never met a Valerian yet whose shoulders he couldn't pin flat to the mat in a hundred seconds, and the very smallest of them outweighed him two to one. Conversely, although he had never thought of it before, what his sisters had taken from him, without even a bruise, would have broken any ordinary woman up into a mess of compound fractures. They were—they must be—made of different stuff.

His thoughts took a new tack. The kids were special in another way, too, he had noticed lately, without paying it any particular attention. It might tie in. They didn't *feel* like other girls. After dancing with one of them, other girls felt like robots made out of putty. Their flesh *was* different. It was firmer, finer, infinitely more responsive. Each individual cell seemed to be endowed with a flashing, sparkling life; a life which, interlinking with that of one of his own cells, made their bodies as intimately one as were their perfectly synchronized minds.

But what did all this have to do with their lack of sense? QX, they were nice people. QX, he couldn't beat their brains out, either physically or mentally. But there ought to be *some* way of driving some ordinary common sense through their fine-grained, thick, hard, tough skulls!

Thus it was that Kit approached Arisia in a decidedly mixed frame of mind. He shot through the barrier without slowing down and without notification. Inerting his ship, he fought her into an orbit around the planet. The shape of the orbit was immaterial, as long as its every inch was well inside Arisia's innermost screen. For young Kinnison knew precisely what those screens were and exactly what they were for. He knew that distance of itself meant nothing—Mentor could give anyone either basic or advanced treatments just as well from a distance of a thousand million parsecs as at hand to hand. The reason for the screens and for the personal visits was the existence of the Eddorians, who had minds probably as capable as the Arisians' own. And throughout all the infinite reaches of the macrocosmic Universe, only within these highly special screens was there *certainty* of privacy from the spying senses of the ultimate foe.

*

"The time has come, Christopher, for the last treatment I am able to give you," Mentor announced without preamble, as soon as Kit had checked his orbit.

"Oh—so soon? I thought you were pulling me in to pin my ears back for fighting with Kay—the dim-wit!"

"That, while a minor matter, is worthy of passing mention, since it is illustrative of the difficulties inherent in the project of developing, without over-controlling, such minds as yours. En route here, you made a masterly summation of the situation, with one outstanding omission."

"Huh? What omission? I covered it like a blanket!"

"You assumed throughout, and still assume, as you always do in dealing with your sisters, that you are unassailably right; that your conclusion is the only tenable one; that they are always wrong."

"But they *are*! That's why you sent Kay to Lyrane!"

"In these conflicts with your sisters, you have been right in approximately half of the cases," Mentor informed him.

"But how about their fights with each other?"

"Do you know of any such?"

"Why . . . uh . . . can't say that I do." Kit's surprise was plain. "But since they fight with me so much, they must—"

"That does not follow, and for a very good reason. We may as well discuss that reason now, as it is a necessary part of the education which you are about to receive. You already know that your sisters are very different, each from the other. Know now, that each was specifically developed to be so completely different that there is no possible point which could be made an issue between any two of them."

It took some time for Kit to digest that news. "Then where do I come in that they *all* fight with me at the drop of a hat?"

943

"That, too, while regrettable, is inevitable. Each of your sisters, as you may have suspected, is to play a tremendous part in that which is to come. The Lensmen, we of Arisia, all will contribute, but upon you Children of the Lens—especially upon the girls—will fall the greater share of the load. Your individual task will be that of co-ordinating the whole; a duty which no Arisian is or ever can be qualified to perform. You will have to direct the efforts of your sisters; reinforcing every heavily-attacked point with your own incomparable force and drive; keeping them smoothly in mesh and in place. As a side issue, you will also have to co-ordinate the feebler efforts of us of Arisia, the Lensmen, the Patrol, and whatever other minor forces we may be able to employ."

"Holy . . . Klono's . . . claws!" Kit was gasping like a fish. "Just where, Mentor, do you figure I'm going to pick up the jets to swing *that* load? And as to co-ordinating the kids—that's out. I'd make just one suggestion to any one of them and she'd forget all about the battle and tear into me . . . no, I'll take that back. The stickier the going, the closer they rally 'round."

"Right. It will always be so. Now, youth, that you have these facts, explain these matters to me, as a sort of preliminary exercise."

"I think I see." Kit thought intensely. "The kids don't fight with each other because they don't overlap. They fight with me because my central field overlaps them all. They have no occasion to fight with anybody else, nor have I, because with anybody else our viewpoint is always right and the other fellow knows it—except for Palainians and such, who think along different lines than we do. Thus, Kay never fights with Nadreck. When he goes off the beam, she simply ignores him and goes on about her business. But with them and me—we'll have to learn to arbitrate, or something, I suppose—" his thought trailed off.

"Manifestations of adolescence; with adulthood, now coming fast, they will pass. Let us get on with the work."

"But wait a minute!" Kit protested. "About this co-ordinator thing. I can't do it. I'm too much of a kid. I won't be ready for a job like that for a thousand years!"

"You must be ready," Mentor's thought was inexorable. "And, when the time comes, you shall be. Now, come fully into my mind."

*

There is no use in repeating in detail the progress of an Arisian supereducation, especially since the most accurate possible description of the most important of those details would be intrinsically meaningless. When, after a few weeks of it, Kit was ready to leave Arisia, he looked much older and more mature than before; he felt immensely older than he looked. The concluding conversation of that visit, however, is worth recording.

"You now know, Kinnison," Mentor mused, "what you children are and how you came to be. You are the accomplishment of long lifetimes of work. It is with most profound satisfaction that I now perceive clearly that those lifetimes have not been spent in vain."

"Yours, you mean." Kit was embarrassed, but one point still bothered him. "Dad met and married mother, yes, but how about the others? Tregonsee, Worsel, and Nadreck? They and the corresponding females were also penultimates, of lines as long as ours. Your Council decided that the human stock was best, so none of the other Second-Stage

Lensmen ever met their female complements. Not that it could make any difference to them, of course, but I should think that three of your fellow students wouldn't feel so good."

"I am very glad indeed that you mention the point." The Arisian's thought was positively gleeful. "You have at no time, then, detected anything peculiar about this that you know as Mentor of Arisia?"

"Why, of course not. How could I? Or, rather, why should I?"

"Any lapse on our part, however slight, from practically perfect synchronization would have revealed to such a mentality as yours that I, whom you know as Mentor, am not an individual, but four. While we each worked as individuals upon all of the experimental lines, whenever we dealt with any one of the penultimates or ultimates we did so as a fusion. This was necessary, not only for your fullest possible development, but also to be sure that each of us had complete data upon every minute facet of the truth. While it was in no sense important to the work itself to keep you in ignorance of Mentor's plurality, the fact that we could keep you ignorant of it, particularly now that you have become adult, showed that our work was being done in a really workmanlike fashion."

Kit whistled; a long, low whistle which was tribute enough to those who knew what it meant. He knew what he meant, but there were not enough words or thoughts to express it.

"But you're going to keep on being Mentor, aren't you?" he asked.

"I am. The real task, as you know, lies ahead."

"QX. You say that I'm adult. I'm not. You imply that I'm more than several notches above you in qualifications. I could laugh myself silly about that one, if it wasn't so serious. Why, any one of you Arisians has forgotten more than I know, and could tie me up into bowknots!"

"There are elements of truth in your thought. That you can now be called adult, however, does not mean that you have attained your full power; only that you are able to use effectively the powers you have and are able to acquire other and larger powers."

"But what *are* those powers?" Kit demanded. "You've hinted on that same theme a thousand times, and I don't know what you mean any better than I did before!"

"You must develop your own powers." Mentor's thought was as final as fate. "Your mind is potentially far abler than mine. You will in time come to know my mind in full; I never will be able to know yours. For the lesser, but full mind to attempt to instruct in methodology the greater, although emptier one, is to set that greater mind in an under-sized mold and thus to do it irreparable harm. You have the abilities and the powers. You will have to develop them yourself, by the perfection of techniques concerning which I can give you no instructions whatever."

"But surely you can give me some kind of a hint!" Kit pleaded. "I'm just a kid, I tell you—I don't even know how or where to begin!"

Under Kit's startled mental gaze, Mentor split suddenly into four parts, laced together by a pattern of thoughts so intricate and so rapid as to be unrecognizable. The parts fused and again Mentor spoke.

"I can point the way in only the broadest, most general terms. It has been decided, however, that I can give you one hint—or, more properly, one illustration. The surest test of knowledge known to us is the visualization of the Cosmic All. All science is, as you know, one. The true key to power lies in the knowledge of the underlying reasons for the succession of events. If it is pure causation—that is, if any given state of things follows as an inevitable consequence because of the state existing an infinitesimal instant before—then the entire course of the macrocosmic universe was set for the duration of all eternity in the instant of its coming into being. This well-known concept, the stumbling block upon which many early thinkers came to grief, we now know to be false. On the other hand, if pure randomness were to govern, natural laws as we know them could not exist. Thus neither pure causation nor pure randomness alone can govern the succession of events.

"The truth, then, must lie somewhere in between. In the macro-cosmos, causation prevails; in the micro-, randomness; both in accord with the mathematical laws of probability. It is in the region between them—the intermediate zone, or the interface, so to speak—that the greatest problems lie. The test of validity of any theory, as you know, is the accuracy of the predictions which are made possible by its use, and our greatest thinkers have shown that the completeness and fidelity of any visualization of the Cosmic All are linear functions of the clarity of definition of the components of that interface. Full knowledge of that indeterminate zone would mean infinite power and a statistically perfect visualization. None of these things, however, will ever be realized; for the acquirement of that full knowledge would require infinite time.

"That is all I can tell you. It will, properly studied, be enough. I have built within you a solid foundation; yours alone is the task of erecting upon that foundation a structure strong enough to withstand the forces which will be thrown against it.

"It is perhaps natural, in view of what you have recently gone through, that you should regard the problem of the Eddorians as one of insuperable difficulty. Actually, however, it is not, as you will perceive when you have spent a few weeks in re-integrating yourself. You must not, you shall not, and in my clear visualization you do not, fail."

*

Communication ceased. Kit made his way groggily to his control board, went free, and lined out for Klovia. For a guy whose education was supposed to be complete, he felt remarkably like a total loss with no insurance. He had asked for advice and had got—what? A dissertation on philosophy, mathematics, and physics—good enough stuff, probably, if he could see what Mentor was driving at, but not of much immediate use. He did have a brainful of new stuff, though—didn't know yet what half of it was—he'd better be getting it licked into shape. He'd "sleep" on it.

He did so, and as he lay quiescent in his bunk the tiny pieces of an incredibly complex jig saw puzzle began to click into place. The ordinary zwilniks—all the small fry fitted in well enough. The Overlords of Delgon. The Kalonians . . . hm-m-m . . . he'd better check with Dad on that angle. The Eich—under control. Kandron of Onlo, ditto. "X" was in safe hands; Cam had already been alerted to watch her step. Some planet named Ploor—what in all the purple hells of Palain had Mentor meant by that crack? Anyway, that piece didn't fit anywhere—yet. That left Eddore—and at the thought a series of cold waves raced up and down the young Lensman's spine. Nevertheless, Eddore was his oyster—his, and nobody else's. Mentor had made that plain enough. Everything the Arisians had done for umpteen million years had been aimed at the Eddorians. They had picked him out to emcee the show—and how could a man co-ordinate an attack against something about which he knew nothing? And the only way to get acquainted with Eddore and its denizens was to go there. Should he call in the kids? He should not. Each of them had her hands full of her own job; that of developing her full self. He had his; and the more he studied the question, the clearer it became that the first number on the program of his self-development was—would *have* to be—a single-handed expedition against the key planet of Civilization's top-ranking foes.

He sprang out of his bunk, changed his vessel's course, and lined out a thought to his father.

"Dad? Kit. Been flitting around out Arisia way, and picked up an idea that I want to pass along to you. It's about Kalonians. What do you know about them?"

"They're blue—"

"I don't mean that."

"I know you don't. There were Helmuth, Jalte, Prellin, Crowninshield . . . all I can think of at the moment. Big operators, son, and smart hombres, if I do say so myself as shouldn't; but they're all ancient history . . . hold it! Maybe I know of a modern one, too—Eddie's Lensman. The only part of that picture that was sharp was the Lens, since Eddie was never analytically interested in any of the hundreds of types of people he met, but there was something about that Lensman . . . . I'll bring him back and focus him as sharply as I can—there." Both men studied the blurred statue posed in the Gray Lensman's mind. "Wouldn't you say he could be a Kalonian?"

"Check. I wouldn't want to say much more than that. But about that Lens—did you really examine it? It *is* sharp—under the circumstances, of course, it would be."

"Certainly! Wrong in every respect—rhythm, chroma, context, and aura. Definitely not Arisian; therefore Boskonian. That's the point—that's what I was afraid of, you know."

"Double-check. And that point ties in absolutely tight with the one that made me call you just now, that everybody, including you and me, seems to have missed. I've been searching my memory for five hours—you know what my memory is like—and I have heard of exactly two other Kalonians. They were big operators, too. I have never heard of the planet itself. To me it is a startling fact that the sum total of my information on Kalonia, reliable or otherwise, is that it produced seven big-shot zwilniks; six of them before I was born. Period."

Kit felt his father's jaw drop.

"No, I don't believe that I have ever heard anything about the planet, either," the older man finally replied. "But I'll bet that I can get you all the information you want in fifteen minutes."

"Credits to millos it'll be a lot nearer fifteen days. You can find it sometime, though, if anybody can—that's why I'm taking it up with you. While I don't want to seem to be giving a Gray Lensman orders"—that jocular introduction had come to be a sort of ritual in the Kinnison family—"I would very diffidently suggest that there might be some connection between that completely unnoticed planet and some of the things we don't know about Boskonia."

"Diffident! You?" The Gray Lensman laughed deeply. "Like an atomic bomb! I'll start a search on Kalonia right away. As to your credits-to-millos-fifteen-days thing, I'd be ashamed to take your money. You don't know our librarians or our system. Ten millos, even money, that we get full data in less than five G-P days from right now. Want it?"

"I'll say so. I'll wear that cento on my tunic as a medal of victory over the Gray Lensman. I *do* know the size of these here two galaxies!"

"QX—it's a bet. I'll let you know if we find anything. In the meantime, Kit, remember that you're my favorite son."

"Well, you're not so bad, yourself. Any time I want mother to divorce you so as to change fathers for me I'll let you know." What a terrific, what a tremendous meaning was heterodyned upon that seemingly light exchange! "Clear ether, Dad!"

"Clear ether, son!"

XIII.

Thousands of years were to pass before Christopher Kinnison could develop the ability to visualize, from the contemplation of one fact or artifact, the entire Universe to which it belonged. He could not even plan in detail his one-man invasion of Eddore until he could integrate all available data concerning the planet Kalonia into his visualization of the Boskonian Empire. One unknown, Ploor, blurred his picture badly enough; two such completely unknown factors made visualization, even in broad, impossible.

Anyway, he decided, he had one more job to do before he tackled the key planet of the enemy; and now, while he was waiting for the dope on Kalonia, would be the best time to do it. Wherefore he sent out a thought to his mother.

"Hi, First Lady of the Universe! 'Tis thy first-born who wouldst fain converse with thee. Art pressly engaged in matters of moment or import?"

"Art not, Kit." Clarrissa's characteristic chuckle was as infectious, as full of the joy of life, as ever. "Not that it would make any difference—but methinks I detect an undertone of seriosity beneath thy persiflage. Spill it."

"Let's make it a rendezvous, instead," he suggested. "We're fairly close, I think—closer than we've been for a long time. Where are you, exactly?"

"Oh! Can we? Wonderful!" She marked her location and velocity in his mind. She made no effort to conceal her joy at the idea of a personal meeting. She never had tried and she never would try to make him put first matters other than first. She had not expected to see him again, physically, until this war was over. But if she could—!

"QX. Hold your course and speed; I'll be seeing you in eighty-three minutes. In the meantime, it'll be just as well if we don't communicate, even by Lens."

"Why, son?"

"Nothing definite—just a hunch, is all. 'Bye, Gorgeous!"

The two speedsters approached each other—inerted—matched intrinsics—went free—flashed into contact—sped away together upon Clarrissa's original course.

948

"Hi, Mums!" Kit spoke into a visiphone. "I should, of course, come to you, but it might be better if you come in here—I've got some special rigs set up here that I don't want to leave. QX?" He snapped on one of the special rigs as he spoke—a device which he himself had built and installed; the generator of a screen which would detect upon every possible band and channel of thought or of intrusion.

"Why, of course!" She came, and was swept off her feet in the exuberance of her tall son's embrace; a greeting which she returned with a fervor at least the equal of his own.

"It's nice, Mother, seeing you again." Words, or thoughts even, were *so* inadequate! Kit's voice was a trifle rough: his eyes were not completely dry.

"Uh-huh. It *is* nice," she agreed, snuggling her spectacular head even more firmly into the curve of his shoulder. "Mental contact is better than nothing, of course, but *this* is perfect!"

"Just as much a menace to navigation as ever, aren't you?" He held her at arm's length and shook his head in mock disapproval. "Do you think it's quite right for one woman to have so much of everything when all the others have so little of anything?"

"Honestly, I don't." She and Kit had always been exceptionally close; now her love for and her pride in this splendid creature, her son and her first-born, simply would not be denied. "You're joking, I know, but that strikes too deep for comfort. I wake up in the night to wonder why, of all the women in existence, I should be so lucky, especially in my children. QX, skip it." Kit was shying away—she should have known better than to try in words even to skirt the profound depths of sentiment which both she and he knew so well were there.

*

"Get back onto the beam, Gorgeous, you know what I meant. Look at yourself in a mirror some day—or do you, perchance?"

"Once in a while—maybe twice." She giggled unaffectedly. "You don't think that all this charm and glamour comes without effort, do you? But maybe you'd better get back on the beam yourself—I know that you didn't come all these parsecs out of your way to say pretty things to your mother—even though I admit that they've built up my ego no end."

"On target, dead center." Kit had been grinning, but he sobered quickly. "I wanted to talk to you about Lyrane and the job you're figuring on doing out there."

"Why?" she demanded. "Do you know anything about it?"

"Unfortunately, I don't." Kit's black frown of concentration reminded her forcibly of his father's characteristic scowl. "Guesses—suspicions—theories—not even good hunches. But I thought . . . I wondered—" He paused, embarrassed as a schoolboy, then went on with a rush: "Would you mind it too much if I went into something pretty personal?"

"You know I wouldn't, son." In contrast to Kit's usual clarity and precision of thought, the question was highly ambiguous, but Clarrissa covered both angles. "I can conceive of no subject, event, action, or thing, in either my life or yours, too intimate or too personal to discuss with you in full. Can you?"

"No, I can't—but this is different. As a woman, you're tops—the finest and best that ever lived." This statement, made with all the matter-of-factness of stating that a triangle had three corners, thrilled Clarrissa through and through. "As a Gray Lensman you're over the rest of them like a cirrus cloud. But you should rate full Second Stage, and . . . well, you may run up against something too hot to handle, some day, and I . . . that is, you—"

"You mean that I don't measure up?" she asked, quietly. "I know very well that I don't, and admitting an evident fact should not hurt my feelings a bit. Don't interrupt, please," as Kit began to protest. "In fact, it is sheerest effrontery—it has always bothered me terribly, Kit—to be classed as a Lensman at all, considering what splendid men they all are and what each one of them had to go through to earn his Lens. You know as well as I do that I have never done a single thing to earn or to deserve it. It was handed to me on a silver platter. I'm not worthy of it, Kit, and all the real Lensmen know that I'm not. They *must* know it, Kit—they *must* feel that way!"

"Did you ever express yourself in exactly that way before, to anybody? You didn't, I know." Kit stopped sweating; this was going to be easier than he had feared.

"I couldn't, Kit, it was too deep; but as I said, I can talk *anything* over with you."

"QX. We can settle that fast enough if you will answer just one question. Do you honestly believe that you would have been given the Lens if you were not absolutely worthy of it? Perfectly—in every minute particular?"

"Why, I never thought of it that way . . . probably not . . . no, certainly not." Clarrissa's somber mien lightened markedly. "But I still don't see how or why—"

"Clear enough," Kit interrupted. "You were born with what the rest of them had to work so hard for—with stuff that no other woman, anywhere, ever had."

"Except the girls, of course," Clarrissa corrected, half-absently.

"Except the kids," he concurred. It could do no harm to agree with his mother's statement of a self-evident fact.

*

He crossed the room and adjusted a couple of dials. His vessel's screens would not now react to the thoughts of Mentor of Arisia, but would still announce the presence of any possible other. "You can take it from me, as one who *knows*, that the other Lensmen know that you've got plenty of jets. They all know also that the Arisians never did and never will make a Lens for anybody who hasn't got what it takes. And so, very neatly, we have stripped ship for the action I came over here to see you about. It isn't a case of you not measuring up, because you do, in every respect. It's simply that you're short a few jets that you ought by rights to have. You really are a Second-Stage Lensman—you know that, Mums—but you never went to Arisia for your real L2 work. I hate to see you blast off without full equipment into what may prove to be a big-time job; especially when you're so eminently able to take it. Mentor could give you the works in a couple of hours. Why don't you flit for Arisia right now, or let me take you there?"

"No—NO!" Clarrissa backed away, shaking her head emphatically. "Never! I couldn't, Kit, ever—not *possibly!*"

"Why not?" Kit was amazed. "Why, Mother, you're actually shaking!"

"I know I am—I can't help it. That's why. He's the only thing in the entire Universe that I'm really afraid of. I can talk *about* him without quite getting goosebumps all over me, but the mere thought of actually being with him simply scares me into shivering, quivering fits."

"I see . . . it might very well work that way, at that. Does Dad know it?"

"Yes . . . or, that is, he knows that I'm afraid of Mentor, but he doesn't know it the way you do . . . it simply doesn't register in true color. Kim can't even conceive of me being either a coward or a cry-baby. And I don't want him to, either, Kit, so please don't tell him, ever."

"I won't—he'd fry me to a cinder in my own grease if I did. Frankly, I can't see any part of your self-portrait, either. As a matter of cold fact, you are so obviously neither a coward nor a cry-baby that no refutation of that canard is either necessary or desirable. What you've really got, Mums, is a fixation, and if it can't be removed—"

"It can't," she declared flatly. "I've tried that, now and then, ever since before you were born. Whatever it is, it's a permanent installation and it's really deep. I have known all along that Kim didn't give me the whole business—he couldn't—and I've tried again and again to make myself go to Arisia, or at least to call Mentor about it, but I can't do it, Kit—I simply *can't!*"

"I understand." Kit nodded. He did understand, now. What she felt was not, in essence and at bottom, fear at all. It was worse than fear, and deeper. It was true revulsion; the basic, fundamental, subconscious, sex-based reaction of an intensely vital human female against a mental monstrosity who had not had a sexual thought for countless thousands of her years. She could neither analyze nor understand her feeling; but it was as immutable, as ineradicable, and as old as the surging tide of life itself.

"But there's another way, just as good—probably better, as far as you're concerned. You aren't afraid of me, are you?"

"What a *question!* Of course I'm not—Why, do you mean *you*—" Her expressive eyes widened. "You children—especially you—are far beyond us . . . as, of course, you should be . . . but *can* you, Kit? *Really?*"

*

Kit keyed a part of his mind to an ultra-high level. "I know the techniques, Mentor, but the first question is, should I do it?"

"You should. The time has come when it is necessary."

"Second—I've never done anything like this before, and she's my own mother. If I make one slip, I'll never forgive myself. Will you stand by and see that I don't slip?"

"I will stand by."

"I really can, Mums." Kit answered her question with no perceptible pause. "That is, if you are willing to put everything you've got into it. Just letting me into your mind isn't enough. You'll have to sweat blood—you'll think that you've been run through a hammer mill and spread out on a Delgonian torture screen to dry."

"No need for worry on that score, my son." All the passionate intensity of Clarrissa's being was in her vibrant voice. "If you just knew how utterly I have been longing for it—I'll work; and whatever you give me I can take."

"I'm sure of that. And, not to work under false pretenses, I'd better tell you how I know. Mentor showed me what to do and told me to do it."

"*Mentor!*"

"Mentor," Kit agreed. "He knew that it was a psychological impossibility for you to work with him, and that you could and would work with me. So he appointed me a committee of one." Clarrissa was reacting to this news as it was inevitable that she should react; and to give her time to steady down he went on:

"Mentor also knew, and so do you and I, that even though you are afraid of him, you know what he is and what he means to Civilization. It was necessary for me to tell you this so that you would know, without any tinge of doubt, that I am not a half-baked kid setting out to do a man's job of work."

"Jet back, Kit! I may have thought a lot of different things about you at times, but 'half-baked' was never one of them. That is your own thinking, not mine."

"I wouldn't wonder." Kit grinned wryly. "My ego could stand some stiffening right now. This isn't going to be funny. You're too fine a woman, and I think too much of you, to enjoy the prospect of mauling you around so unmercifully."

"Why, Kit!" Her mood was changing fast. Her old-time, impish smile came back in force. "You aren't weakening, surely? Shall I hold your hand?"

"Uh-huh—cold feet," he admitted. "It might be a smart idea, at that, holding hands. Physical linkage. Well, I'm as ready as I ever will be, I guess—whenever you are, say so. And you'd better sit down before you fall down."

"QX, Kit—come in."

*

Kit came; and at the first terrific surge of his mind within hers the Red Lensman caught her breath, stiffened in every muscle, and all but screamed in agony. Kit's fingers needed their strength as her hands clutched his and closed in a veritable spasm. She had thought that she knew what to expect; but the reality was different—much different. She had suffered before. On Lyrane II, although she had never told anyone of it, she had been burned and wounded and beaten. She had borne five children. This was as though every poignant experience of her past had been rolled into one, raised to the nth power, and stabbed deep into the tenderest, most sensitive centers of her entire being.

And Kit, boring in and in and in, knew exactly what to do; and now that he had started, he proceeded unflinchingly and with exact precision to do what had to be done. He opened up her mind as she had never dreamed it possible for a mind to open. He separated the tiny, jammed compartments, each completely from every other. He showed her how to make room for this tremendous expansion and watched her do it, against the shrieking protests of every cell and fiber of her body and of her brain. He drilled new channels everywhere, establishing an inconceivably complex system of communication lines of infinite conductivity. He knew just what he was doing to her, since the same thing had been done to him so recently, but he kept on relentlessly until the job was done. Completely done.

Then, working together, they sorted and labeled and classified and catalogued. They checked and double checked. Finally she knew, and Kit knew that she knew, every hitherto unplumbed recess of her mind and every individual cell of her brain. Every iota of every quality and characteristic, every scrap of knowledge she had ever acquired or ever would acquire, would be at her command instantaneously and effortlessly. Then, and only then, did Kit withdraw his mind from hers.

"Did you say that I was short just a *few* jets, Kit?" She got up groggily and mopped her face; upon which her few freckles stood out surprisingly dark upon a background of white. "I'm a wreck . . . I'd better go and—"

"As you were for just a sec—I'll break out a bottle of fayalin. This rates a celebration of sorts, don't you think?"

"Very much so." As she sipped the pungently aromatic red liquid her color began to come back. "No wonder I felt as though I were missing something all these years. Thanks, Kit. I really appreciate it. You're a—"

"Seal it, Mums." He picked her up and squeezed her, hard. He scarcely noticed her sweat-streaked face and disheveled hair, but she did.

"Good Heavens, Kit, I'm a perfect *hag*!" she exclaimed. "I've *got* to go and put on a new face!"

"QX. I don't feel quite so fresh, myself. What I need, though, is a good, thick steak. Join me?"

"Uh-uh. How can you even think of *eating*, at a time like this?"

"Same way you can think of war paint and feathers, I suppose. Different people, different reactions. QX, I'll be in there and see you in fifteen or twenty minutes. Flit!"

*

She left, and Kit heaved an almost explosive sigh of relief. Mighty good thing she hadn't asked too many questions—if she had become really curious, he would have had a horrible time keeping her away from the fact that that kind of work never had been done and never would be done outside of solid, multiply, Arisian screen. He ate, cleaned up, ran a comb through his hair, and, when his mother was ready, crossed over into her speedster.

"Whee . . . whee-yu!" Kit whistled descriptively. "*What* a seven-sector call-out! Just who do you think you're going to knock out of the ether on Lyrane II?"

"Nobody at all." Clarrissa laughed. "This is all for you, son—and maybe a little bit for me, too."

"I'm stunned. You're a blinding flash and a deafening report. But I've got to do a flit, Gorgeous. So clear—"

"Wait a minute—you *can't* go yet! I've got questions to ask you about these new networks and things. How do I handle them?"

"Sorry—you've got to develop your own techniques. You know that already."

"In a way. I thought maybe, though, I could wheedle you into helping me a little. I should have known better—but tell me, all Lensmen don't have minds like this, do they?"

"I'll say they don't. They're all like yours was before, but not as good. Except the other L2's, of course—Dad, Worsel, Tregonsee, and Nadreck. Theirs are more or less like yours is now; but you've got a lot of stuff that they haven't."

"Huh?" she demanded. "Such as?"

"'Way down—there." He showed her. "You worked all of that area yourself. I only showed you how, without getting in too close."

953

"Why? Oh, I see—you would. Life-force. I would have lots of that, of course." She did not blush, but Kit did.

"Life-force" was a pitifully inadequate term indeed for that which Civilization's only Lensman-mother had in such measure, but they both knew what it was. Kit ducked.

"You can always tell all about a Lensman by looking at his Lens; it's an absolute diagram of his whole mind. You've studied Dad's, of course."

"Yes. Three times as big as the ordinary ones—or mine—and much finer and brighter. But *mine* isn't, Kit?"

"It *wasn't*, you mean. Put it on and look at it now."

She opened a drawer, and even before she could snap the bracelet around her wrist, her eyes and mouth became three round O's of astonishment. She had never seen that Lens before, or anything like it. It was three times as big as hers, seven times as fine and as intricate, and ten times as bright.

"Why, this isn't mine!" she gasped. "But this is where I put—"

"Sneeze, Gorgeous," Kit advised. "Cobwebs. It lit up, didn't it? You aren't thinking a lick. Your mind changed, so your Lens had to. See?"

"I see." Clarrissa looked deep into her son's eyes, her face again paling under her make-up. "Now *I'm* going to get personal, Kit. Will you let me look at *your* Lens? You never seem to wear it—I haven't seen it since you graduated."

"Sure. Why not?" He reached into a pocket. "I take after you, that way; neither of us gets any kick out of throwing his weight around."

His Lens flamed upon his wrist. It was larger in diameter than Clarrissa's, and thicker. Its texture was finer; its colors were brighter, harsher, and seemed, somehow, more *solid*. Both studied both Lenses for a moment, then Kit seized his mother's hand, brought their wrists together, and stared.

"That's it," he breathed. "That's it—That's IT, just as sure as Klono has got teeth and claws."

"What's it? What do you see?" she demanded.

"I see how and why I got the way I am—and if the kids had Lenses theirs would be the same. Remember Dad's? Look at your dominants—notice that every one of them is duplicated in mine. Blank them out of mine, and see what you've got left—pure Kimball Kinnison, with just enough extras thrown in to make me an individual instead of a carbon copy. Hm-m-m credits to millos this is what comes of having Lensmen on both sides of the family. No wonder we're freaks! Don't know whether I'm in favor of it or not—I don't think that they should produce any more Lady Lensmen, do you? Maybe that's why they never did."

"Don't try to be funny," she reproved; but her dimples were again in evidence. "If it would result in more people like you and your sisters, I would be very much in favor of it; but, some way or other, I doubt it. I know that you're squirming to go, so I won't hold you any longer. What you just found out about Lenses is fascinating. For the rest of it . . . well . . . thanks, son, and clear ether."

"Clear ether, Mother. This is the worst part of being together, leaving so quick. I'll see you again, though, soon and often. If you get stuck, yell, and one of the kids or I—or all of us—will be with you in a split second."

He gave her a quick, hard hug; kissed her enthusiastically, and left. He did not tell her, and she never did find out, that his "discovery" of one of the secrets of the Lens was made to keep her from asking questions which he could not answer.

*

The Red Lensman was afraid that she would not have time to put her new mind in order before reaching Lyrane II; but, being naturally a good housekeeper, she did. More, so rapidly and easily did her mind now work, she had time to review and to analyze every phase of her previous activities upon that planet and to lay out in broad her first lines of action. She wouldn't put on the screws at first, she decided. She would let them think that she didn't have any more jets than before. Helen was nice, but a good many of the others, especially that airport manager, were simply quadruply-distilled vixens. She'd take it easy at first, but she'd be very sure that she didn't get into any such jams as last time.

She coasted down through Lyrane's stratosphere and poised high above the city she remembered so well.

"Helen of Lyrane!" she sent out a sharp, clear thought. "That is not your name, I know, but we did not learn any other—"

She broke off, every nerve taut. Was that, or was it not, Helen's thought; cut off, wiped out by a guardian block before it could take shape?

"Who are you, stranger, and what do you want?" the thought came, almost instantly, from a person seated at the desk of the Chief Executive of the planet.

Clarrissa glanced at the sender and thought that she recognized the face. Her new channels functioned instantaneously; she remembered every detail.

"Lensman Clarrissa, formerly of Sol III, Unattached. I remember you, Ladora, although you were only a child when I was here. Do you remember me?"

"Yes. I repeat, what do you want?" The memory did not decrease Ladora's hostility.

"I would like to speak to the former Elder Person, if I may."

"You may not. It is no longer with us. Leave at once, or we will shoot you down."

"Think again, Ladora." Clarrissa held her tone even and calm. "Surely your memory is not so short that you have forgotten the *Dauntless* and its capabilities."

"I remember. You may take up with me whatever it is that you wish to discuss with my predecessor Elder Person."

"You are familiar with the Boskonian Invasion of years ago. It is suspected that they are planning new and Galaxy-wide outrages, and that this planet is in some way involved. I have come here to investigate the situation."

"We will conduct our own investigations," Ladora declared, curtly. "We insist that you and all other foreigners stay away from this planet."

"*You* investigate a Galactic condition?" In spite of herself, Clarrissa almost let the connotations of that question become perceptible. "If you give me permission, I will land alone. If you do not, I shall call the *Dauntless* and we will land in force. Take your choice."

"Land alone, then, if you must land," Ladora yielded, seethingly. "Land at our City Airport."

"Under those guns? No, thanks; I am neither invulnerable nor immortal. I land where I please."

She landed. During her previous visit she had had a hard enough time getting any help from these pigheaded matriarchs, but this time she encountered a nonco-operation so utterly fanatical that it put her completely at a loss. None of them tried to harm her in any way; but not one of them would have anything to do with her. Every thought, even the friendliest, was stopped by a full-coverage block; no acknowledgment, even, was ever made.

"I can crack those blocks easily enough, if I want to," she declared, one bad evening, to her mirror, "And if they keep this up very much longer, by Klono's emerald-filled gizzard, I *will!*"

XIV.

When Kimball Kinnison received his son's call he was in Ultra Prime, the Patrol's stupendous Klovian base, about to enter his ship. He stopped for a moment; practically in mid-stride. While nothing was to be read in his expression or in his eyes, the lieutenant to whom he had been talking had been an interested, if completely uninformed, witness to many such Lensed conferences, and knew that they were usually important. He was, therefore, not surprised when the Lensman turned around and headed for an exit.

"Put her back, please. I won't be going out for a while, after all," Kinnison explained, briefly. "Don't know exactly how long."

A fast flitter took him to the hundred-story pile of stainless steel and glass which was the Co-ordinator's office. He strode along a corridor, through an unmarked door.

"Hi, Phyllis—the boss in?"

"Good morning, Chief. Yes, sir . . . no, I mean . . . ." His startled secretary touched a button and a door opened; the door of his private office.

"Hi, Kim—back so soon?" Vice Co-ordinator Maitland also showed surprise as he got up from the massive desk and shook hands cordially. "Good! Taking over?"

"Emphatically no. Hardly started yet. Just dropped in to use your plate, if you've got a free high-power wave. QX?"

"Certainly. If not, you can free one fast enough."

"Communications." Kinnison touched a stud. "Will you please get me Thrale? Library One; Principal Librarian Nadine Ernley. Plate-to-plate."

This request was surprising enough to the informed. Since the Co-ordinator practically never dealt personally with anyone except Lensmen, and usually Unattached Lensmen at that, it was a rare event indeed for him to use any ordinary channels of communication. And as the linkage was completed, subdued murmurs and sundry squeals gave evidence that intense excitement prevailed at the other end of the line.

"Mrs. Ernley will be on in one moment, sir." The operator's business was done. Her crisp, clear-cut voice ceased, but the background noise increased markedly.

"Sh . . . sh . . . sh! It's the Gray Lensman, himself!" Everywhere upon Klovia, Tellus, and Thrale, and in many localities of many other planets, the words "Gray Lensman", without surname, had only one meaning.

"Not the *Gray Lensman!*"

"It can't be!"

"It *is*, really . . . I know him . . . I actually *met* him once!"

"Let *me* look . . . just a peek!"

"Sh . . . sh! He'll *hear* you!"

"Switch on the vision. If we've got a moment, let's get acquainted," Kinnison suggested, and upon his plate there burst into view a bevy of excitedly embarrassed blondes, brunettes, and redheads. "Hi, Madge! Sorry that I don't know the rest of you, but I'll make it a point to get acquainted—before long, I think. Don't go away." The principal librarian was coming on the run. "You're all in on this. Hi, Nadine! Long time no see. Remember that bunch of squirrel food you rounded up for me?"

*

"I remember, sir." What a question! As though Nadine Ernley, nee Hostetter, could ever forget her share in that famous meeting of the fifty-three greatest—and least stable—scientific minds of all Civilization. "I'm sorry that I was out in the stacks when you called."

"QX—we all have to work sometimes, I suppose. What I'm calling about is that I've got a mighty big job for you and those smart girls of yours. Something like that other one, only a lot more so. I want all the information you can dig up about a planet named Kalonia, just as fast as you can possibly get it. What makes it extra tough is that I have never even heard of the planet itself and don't know of anyone who has. There may be a million other names for it, on a million other planets, but we don't know any of them. Here's all I know." He summarized; concluding: "If you can get it for me in less than four point nine five G-P days from now I'll bring you, Nadine, a Manarkan star-drop; and you can have each of your girls go down to Brenleer's and pick out a wrist watch or whatever she likes, and I'll have it engraved to her 'In appreciation, Kimball Kinnison'. This job is important—my son Kit has bet me ten millos that we can't do it that fast."

"Ten *millos!*" Four or five of the girls gasped as one.

"Fact," he assured them, gravely. "So whenever you get the dope, tell Communications . . . no, you listen while I tell them myself. Communications, all along the line, come in!" They came. "I expect one of these librarians to call me, plate-to-plate, within the next few days. When she does, no matter what time of the day or night it is, and no matter what I or anyone else happen to be doing, that call will have the right-of-way over any other business in the Universe. Cut!" The plates went dead and in Library One:

"But he was joking, surely!"

"Ten *millos*—one cento—and a star-drop—why, there aren't more than a dozen of them on all Thrale!"

"Wrist watches—or something—from the Gray Lensman!"

957

"Be quiet, everybody!" Madge exclaimed. "I see now. That's the way Nadine got *her* watch, that she always brags about so insufferably and that makes everybody's eyes turn green. But I don't understand that silly ten-millo bet . . . do you, Nadine?"

"I think so. He does the nicest things—things that nobody else would think of. You have seen Red Lensman's Chit, in Brenleer's." This was a statement, not a question. They all had, with what emotions they all knew. "How would you like to have that one-cento piece, in a thousand-credit frame, here in our main hall, with the legend 'won from Christopher Kinnison for Kimball Kinnison by . . .' and our names? He's got something like that in mind, I'm sure."

The ensuing clamor indicated that they liked the idea.

"He knew we would; and he knew that doing it this way would make us dig like we never dug before. He'll give us the watches and things anyway, of course, but we won't get that one-cento piece unless we win it. So let's get to work. Take everything out of the machines, finished or not. Madge, you might start by interviewing Lanion and the other—no, I'd better do that myself, since you are more familiar with the encyclopedia than I am. Run the whole English block, starting with K, and follow up any leads, however slight, that you can find. Betty, you can analyze for synonyms, starting with the Thralian equivalent of Kalonia and spreading out to the other Boskonian planets. Put half a dozen techs on it, with transformers. Frances, you can study Prellin and Bronseca. Joan, Leona, Edna—Jalte, Helmuth, and Crowninshield. Beth, as our best linguist, you can do us the most good by sensitizing a tech to the sound of Kalonia in each of all the languages you know or that the rest of us can find, and running and rerunning all the transcripts we have of Boskonian meetings. How many of us are left? Not enough—we'll have to spread ourselves thin on this list of Boskonian planets."

Thus Principal Librarian Ernley organized a search beside which the proverbial one of finding a needle in a haystack would have been as simple as locating a football in a bushel basket. And she and her girls worked. *How* they worked! And thus, in four days and three hours, Kinnison's top-priority person-to-person call came through. Kalonia was no longer a planet of mystery.

"Fine work, girls! Put it on a tape and I'll pick it up."

He then left Klovia—precipitately. Since Kit was not within rendezvous distance, he instructed his son—after giving him the high points of what he had learned—to forward one one-cento piece to Brenleer of Thrale, personal delivery. He told Brenleer what to do with it upon arrival. He landed. He bestowed the star-drop; one of Cartiff's collection of fine gems. He met the girls, and gave each one her self-chosen reward. He departed.

*

Out in open space, he ran the tape once—Second-Stage Lensmen do not forget any detail of anything they have ever learned—and sat still, scowling blackly. It was no wonder that Kalonia had remained unknown to Civilization for over twenty years. There was a lot of information on that tape—and all of it stunk—but it had been assembled, one unimportant bit at a time, from the more than eight hundred million cards of Thrale's Boskonian Archives; and all of the really significant items had been found on vocal transcriptions which had never before been played.

Civilization in general had assumed that Thrale had housed the top echelons of the Boskonian Empire, and that the continuing inimical activity had been due solely to momentum. Kinnison and his friends had had their doubts, but they had not been able to find any iota of evidence that any higher authority had ever issued any orders to Thrale. The Gray Lensman now knew, however, that Thrale had never been the top. Nor was Kalonia. The information on this tape, by its paucity, its brevity, its incidental and casual nature, made that fact startlingly clear. Thrale and Kalonia were *equals*. Neither gave the other any orders—in fact, they had surprisingly little to do with each other. While Thrale formerly directed the activities of a half-million or so planets—and Kalonia apparently still did much the same—their field of action had not overlapped at any point.

His conquest of Thrale, hailed so widely as such a triumph, had got him precisely nowhere in the solution of the real problem. It might be possible for him to conquer Kalonia in a similar fashion, but what would it get him? Nothing. There would be no more leads upward from Kalonia than there had been from Thrale. How in all of Noshabkeming's variegated and iridescent hells was he going to work this out?

A complete analysis revealed only one possible method of procedure. In one of the transcriptions—made twenty-one years ago and unsealed for the first time by Beth, the librarian-linguist—one of the speakers had mentioned casually that the new Kalonian Lensmen seemed to be doing a good job, and a couple of the others had agreed with him. That was all. It might, however, be enough; since it made it highly probable that Eddie's Lensman was in fact a Kalonian, and since even a Black Lensman would certainly know where he got his Lens. At the thought of trying to visit the Boskonian equivalent of Arisia he flinched, but only momentarily. Invasion, or even physical approach, would, of course, be impossible; but any planet, even Arisia itself, could be destroyed. If it could be found, that planet would be destroyed. He *had* to find it—that was probably what Mentor had been wanting him to do all the time! But how?

In his various previous enterprises against Boskonia he had been a gentleman of leisure, a dock-walloper, a meteor miner, and many other things. None of his already established aliases would fit on Kalonia; and besides, it was very poor technique to repeat himself, especially at this high level of opposition. To warrant appearance on Kalonia at all, he would have to be an operator of some kind—not too small, but not big enough so that an adequate background could not be synthesized in a hurry. A zwilnik—an actual drug-runner with a really worth-while cargo—would be the best bet.

His course of action decided, the Gray Lensman started making calls. He first called Kit, with whom he held a long conversation. He called the captain of his battleship-yacht, the *Dauntless*, and gave him many and explicit orders. He called Vice Co-ordinator Maitland, and various other Unattached Lensmen who had plenty of weight in Narcotics, Public Relations, Criminal Investigation, Navigation, Homicide, and many other apparently totally unrelated establishments of the Galactic Patrol. Finally, after ten solid hours of mind-wracking labor, he ate a tremendous meal and told Clarrissa—he called her last of all—that he was going to go to bed and sleep for one whole G-P week.

*

Thus it was that the name of Bradlow Thyron began to obtrude itself above the threshold of Galactic consciousness. For seven or eight years that name had been below the middle of the Patrol's long, black list of the wanted; now it was well up toward the top. That notorious zwilnik and his villainous crew had been chased from one side of the First Galaxy to the other. For a few months it had been supposed that they had been blown out of the ether. Now, however, it was known definitely that he was operating in the Second Galaxy, and he and every one of his cutthroat gang—fiends who had blasted thousands of lives with the noxious wares—were wanted for piracy, drug-mongering, and first-degree murder. From the Patrol's standpoint, the hunting was very poor. G-P planetographers have charted only a small percentage of the planets of the Second Galaxy; and only a few of those are peopled by the adherents of Civilization.

Therefore it required some time, but finally there came the message for which Kinnison was so impatiently waiting. A Boskonian pretty-big-shot drug-master named Harkleroy, on the planet Phlestyn II, city, Nelto, co-ordinates so-and-so, fitted his specifications to a "T"; a middle-sized operator neither too close to nor too far away from Kalonia. And Kinnison, having long since learned the lingua franca of the region from a local meteor miner, was ready to act.

First, he made sure that the mighty *Dauntless* would be where he wanted her when he needed her. Then, seated at his speedster's communicator, he put through regular channels a call to the Boskonian.

"Harkleroy? I've got a proposition you'll be interested in. Where and when do you want to see me?"

"What makes you think I want to see you at all?" a voice snarled, and the plate showed a gross, vicious face. "Who are you, scum?"

"Who I am is nobody's business—and if you don't clamp a baffle on that mouth of yours I'll come down there and shove a glop-skinner's glove so far down your throat you can sit on it."

At the first defiant word the zwilnik began visibly to swell; but in a matter of seconds he recognized Bradlow Thyron, and Kinnison knew that he did. That pirate could, and would be expected to, talk back to anybody.

"I didn't recognize you at first," Harkleroy almost apologized. "We might do some business, at that. What have you got?"

"Cocaine, heroin, bentlam, hashish, nitrolabe—most anything a warm-blooded oxygen-breather would want. The prize package, though, is two kilograms of clear-quill thionite."

"Thionite—two kilograms!" The Phlestan's eyes gleamed. "Where and how did you get it?"

"I asked the Lensman on Trenco to make it for me, special, and he did."

"So you won't talk, huh?" Kinnison could see Harkleroy's brain work. Thyron could be made to talk, later. "We can maybe do business at that. Come down here right away."

"I'll do that, but listen!" and the Lensman's eyes burned into the zwilnik's. "I know what you're figuring on, and I'm telling you right now not to try it if you want to keep on living. You know that this ain't the first planet I ever landed on, and if you've got a brain you know that a lot of guys smarter than you are have tried monkey business on me—and I'm still here. So watch your step!"

*

The Lensman landed, and made his way to Harkleroy's inner office in what seemed to be an ordinary enough, if somewhat oversize, suit of light space-armor. But it was no more ordinary than it was light. It was a powerhouse, built of dureum a quarter of an inch thick. Kinnison was not walking in it; he was merely the engineer of a battery of two-thousand-horsepower motors. Unaided, he could not have lifted one leg of that armor off the ground.

As he had expected, everyone he encountered wore a thought-screen; nor was he surprised at being halted by a blaring loud-speaker in the hall, since the zwilnik's search-beams were being stopped four feet away from his armor.

"Halt! Cut your screens or we'll blast you where you stand!"

"Yeah? Act your age, Harkleroy. I told you I had a lot of stuff up my sleeve besides my arm, and I meant it. Either I come as I am or I flit somewhere else, to do business with somebody who wants this stuff bad enough to act like half a man. 'Smatter—afraid you ain't got blasters enough in there to handle me?"

This taunt bit deep, and the visitor was allowed to proceed. As he entered the private office, however, he saw that Harkleroy's hand was poised near a switch, whose closing would signal a score or more of concealed gunners to burn him down. They supposed that the stuff was either on his person or in his speedster just outside. Time was short.

"I abase myself—that's the formula you insist on, ain't it?" Kinnison sneered, without bending his head a millimeter.

Harkleroy's finger touched the stud.

"*Dauntless!* Come down!" Kinnison snapped out the order.

Hand, stud, and a part of the desk disappeared in the flare of Kinnison's beam. Wall-ports opened; projectors and machine rifles erupted vibratory and solid destruction. Kinnison leaped toward the desk; the attack slowing down and stopping as he neared and seized the big shot. One fierce, short blast reduced the thought-screen generator to blobs of fused metal. Harkleroy screamed to his gunners to resume fire, but before bullet or beam took the zwilnik's life, Kinnison learned what he most wanted to know.

The ape did know something about Black Lensmen. He didn't know where the Lenses came from, but he did know how the men were chosen. More, he knew a Lensman personally—one Melasnikov, who had his office in Cadsil, on Kalonia III itself.

Kinnison turned and ran—the alarm had been given and they were bringing up stuff too heavy for even his armor to handle. But the *Dauntless* was landing already; smashing to rubble five city blocks in the process. She settled; and as the dureum-clad Gray Lensman began to fight his way out of Harkleroy's fortress, Major Peter VanBuskirk and a full battalion of Valerians, armed with space-axes and semiportables, began to hew and to blast their way in.

961

THE LENSMAN

XV.

Inch by inch, foot by foot, Kinnison fought his way back along the corpse-littered corridor. Under the ravening force of the attacker's beams his defensive screens flared into pyrotechnic splendor, but they did not go down. Fierce-driven metallic slugs spanged and whanged against the unyielding dureum of his armor, but that, too, held. Dureum is incredibly massive, unbelievably tough, unimaginably hard—against these qualities and against the thousands of horsepower driving that veritable tank and energizing its screens the zwilniks might just as well have been shining flashlights at him and throwing confetti. His immediate opponents could not touch him, but the Boskonians were bringing up reserves that he didn't like a little bit; mobile projectors with whose energies even his screens could not cope.

He had, however, one great advantage over his enemies. He had the sense of perception; they did not. He could see them, but they could not see him. All he had to do was to keep at least one opaque wall between them until he was securely behind the mobile screens, powered by the stupendous generators of the *Dauntless*, which VanBuskirk and his Valerians were so earnestly urging toward him. If a door was handy in the moment of need, he used it. If not, he went through a wall.

The Valerians were fighting furiously and were coming fast. Those two words, when applied to members of that race, mean something starkly incredible to anyone who has never seen Valerians in action. They average little less than seven feet in height; something over four hundred pounds in weight; and are muscled, boned, and sinewed against a normal gravitational force of almost three times that of Earth. VanBuskirk's weakest warrior could do, in full armor, a standing high jump of fourteen feet against one Tellurian gravity; he could handle himself and the thirty-pound monstrosity which was his space-ax with a blinding speed and a devastating efficiency literally appalling to contemplate. They are the deadliest hand-to-hand fighters ever known; and, unbelievable as it may seem to any really highly advanced intelligence, they did and still do fairly revel in that form of combat.

The Valerian tide reached the battling Gray Lensman—closed around him.

"Hi . . . you little . . . Tellurian . . . wart!" Major Peter VanBuskirk boomed this friendly thought, a yell of pure joy, in cadence with the blows of his utterly irresistible weapon. His rhythm broke—his frightful ax was stuck. Not even dureum-inlaid armor could bar the inward course of those furiously driven beaks; but sometimes it made it fairly difficult to get them out. The giant pulled, twisted—put one red-splashed boot on the battered breastplate—bent his mighty back—heaved viciously. The weapon came free with a snap that would have broken any ordinary man's arms, but the Valerian's thought rolled smoothly on: "Ain't we got fun?"

"Ho, Bus, you big Valerian baboon!" Kinnison thought back in kind. "Thought maybe we would need you and your gang—thanks for the ride. But back, now, and fast!"

Although the Valerians did not like to retreat, after even a successful operation, they knew how to do it. Hence in a matter of minutes all the survivors—and their losses had been surprisingly small—were back inside the *Dauntless*.

962

"You picked up my speedster, Frank." It was a statement, not a question, directed at the young Lensman standing beside the Chief Pilot's board.

"Of course, sir. They're massing fast, and without any hostile demonstration, as you said they would." He nodded unconcernedly at the plate, which showed the sky dotted with warlike shapes.

"No maulers?"

"None detectable as yet."

"QX. Original orders stand. At detection of one mauler, execute Operation Able without further instructions. Tell everybody that, while the announcement of Operation Able will put me out of control instantly and automatically, until such announcement I will give instructions. What they will be like I haven't the foggiest notion. It depends on what His Nibs upstairs decides to do—it's his move next."

*

As though the last phrase were a cue, a burst of noise rattled from the speaker—of which only the words "Bradlow Thyron" were intelligible to the un-Lensed members of the crew. That name, however, explained why they were not being attacked—yet. Kalonia had heard much of that intransigent and obdurate pirate and of the fabulous prowess of his ship; and Kinnison was pretty sure that they were much more interested in his ship than in him.

"I can't understand you!" The Gray Lensman barked, in the polyglot language he had so lately learned. "Talk pidgin!"

"Very well. I see that you are indeed Bradlow Thyron, as we were informed. What do you mean by this outrageous attack? Surrender! Disarm your men, take off their armor, and march them out of your vessel, or we will blast you as you lie there—Mendonai, vice admiral, speaking!"

"I abase myself." Kinnison-Thyron did not sneer—exactly—and he did incline his stubborn head perhaps one millimeter; but he made no move to comply with the orders so summarily issued. Instead:

"What kind of planet is this, anyway?" he demanded, hotly. "I come here to see this louse Harkleroy because a friend of mine tells me that he's a big shot and so interested in my line that we can do a lot of business with each other. I give the lug fair warning, too—tell him plain that I've been around plenty and that if he tries to give me the works I'll rub him out like a pencil mark. So what happens? In spite of what I just tell him he tries dirty work on me, and I go to work on him—which he certainly has got coming to him. Then you and your flock of little tin boats come barging in as though I'd busted a law or something. Who do you think you are, anyway? What license you got to be butting into a private business deal?"

"Ah, I had not heard that version." Vision came on; the face upon the plate was typically Kalonian—blue, cold, cruel, and keen. "Harkleroy was warned, you say? Definitely?"

"I warned him plenty definitely. Ask any of the zwilniks in that private office of his. Most of them are still alive, and they all must of heard it."

The plate fogged, the speaker again gave out gibberish. The Lensmen knew, however, that the commander of the cruisers above them was indeed questioning the dead zwilnik's guards. They knew that Kinnison's story was being corroborated in full.

"You interest me." The Boskonian's language again became intelligible to the group at large. "We will forget Harkleroy—stupidity brings its own reward and the property damage is of no present concern. From what I have been able to learn of you, you have never belonged to that so-called Civilization. I know for a fact that you are not, and never have been, one of us. How have you been able to survive? And why do you work alone?"

"'How' is easy enough—by keeping one jump ahead of the other guy, like I did with your pal here, and by being smart enough to have good engineers put into my ship everything that any other one ever had and everything they could dream up besides. As to 'why,' that's simple, too. I don't trust anybody except myself. If nobody except myself ever knows what I'm going to do, or when, nobody except myself is ever going to be able to stick a knife into me when I ain't looking—see? So far, it's paid off big. I'm still around, and still healthy, while them that trusted other guys ain't."

"I see. Crude, but graphic. The more I study you, the more convinced I become that you would be a worth-while addition to our force—"

"No deal, Mendonai," Kinnison interrupted, shaking his unkempt head positively. "I never yet took orders from no boss, and I ain't going to, never."

"You misunderstand me, Thyron." The zwilnik was queerly patient and much too forbearing. Kinnison's insulting omission of his title should have touched him off like a rocket. "I was not thinking of you in any minor capacity, but as an ally. An entirely independent ally, working with us in certain mutually advantageous undertakings."

"Such as?" Kinnison allowed himself to betray his first sign of interest. "You may be talking sense now, brother, but what's in it for me? Believe me, there's got to be plenty."

"There will be plenty. With the ability you have already shown, and with our vast resources back of you, you will take more every week than you have been taking in a year."

"Yeah? People like you just love to do things like that for people like me. What do *you* figure on getting out of it?" Kinnison wondered, and Lensed a sharp thought to his junior at the board.

"On your toes, Frank. He's stalling for something, and I'm betting it's maulers."

"None detectable yet, sir."

*

"We stand to gain, of course," the pirate admitted, smoothly. "For instance, there are certain features of your vessel which might—just possibly, you will observe, and speaking only to mention an example—be of some interest to our naval designers. Also, we have heard that you have an unusually hot battery of primary beams. You might tell me about some of those things now; or at least refocus your plate so that I can see something besides your not unattractive face."

"I might not, too. What I've got here is my own business, and stays mine."

"Is that what we are to expect from you in the way of co-operation?" The commander's voice was still low and level, but now bore a chill of deadly menace.

"Co-operation!" The cutthroat chief was unimpressed. "I'll maybe tell you a thing or two—eat out of your dish—after I get good and sold on your proposition, whatever it is, but not one second sooner!"

The commander glared. "I weary of this. You probably are not worth the trouble, after all. I might as well blast you out now as later. You know that I can, of course, as well as I do."

"Do I?" Kinnison did sneer, this time. "Act your age, pal. As I told that fool Harkleroy, this ain't the first planet I ever sat down on, and it won't be the last. And don't call no maulers," as the Boskonian officer's hand moved almost imperceptibly toward a row of buttons. "If you do, I start blasting as soon as we spot one on our plates—and they're full out right now."

"You would start blasting?" The zwilnik's surprise—almost amazement—was plain, but the hand stopped its motion.

"Yeah—me. Them heaps of scrap metal you got up there don't bother me a bit, but maulers I can't handle, and I ain't afraid to tell you so because you probably know it already. I can't stop you from calling 'em, if you want to, but bend both ears to this—I can outrun 'em, and I'll guarantee that you personally won't be alive to see me run. Why? Because your ship will be the first one I'll whiff on the way out. And if the rest of your heaps stick around long enough to try to stop me, I'll whiff twenty-five or thirty more of them before your maulers can get close enough so that I'll have to flit. Now, if your brains are made out of the same kind of thick, blue mud that Harkleroy's was, start something!"

This was an impasse. Kinnison knew what he wanted the other to do, but he could not give him a suggestion, or even a hint, without tipping his hand. The officer, quite evidently, was in a quandary. He did not want to open fire upon this tremendous, this fabulous ship. Even if he could destroy it, such a course would be unthinkable—unless, indeed, the very act of destruction would brand as false rumor the tales of invincibility and invulnerability which had heralded its coming, and thus would operate in his favor at the court-martial so sure to be called. He was very much afraid, however, that those rumors were not false—a view which was supported very strongly both by Thyron's undisguised contempt for the Boskonian warships threatening him and by his equally frank declaration of his intention to avoid engagement with craft of really superior force. Finally, however, the Boskonian perceived one thing that did not quite fit.

*

"If you are as good as you claim to be, why aren't you doing a flit right now?" Mendonai asked, smoothly. "If you could get away, I should think that you'd be doing it. We've got stuff, you know, that's both heavy and fast."

"Because I don't want to flit, that's why. Use your head, pal." This was better. Mendonai had shifted the conversation into a line upon which the Lensman could do a bit of steering. "I had to leave the First Galaxy because it got too hot for me, and I got no connections at all, yet, here in the Second. You folks need certain kinds of stuff that I've got, and I need other kinds, that you've got. So we could do a nice business, if you wanted to. That was what I had in mind with Harkleroy, but he got greedy. I don't mind saying that I'd like to do business with you, but I just got bit pretty bad, and I'll have to have some kind of solid guarantee that you mean business, and not monkey business, before I take a chance again. See?"

"I see. The idea is good, but its execution may prove difficult. I could give you my word, which I assure you has never been broken."

"Don't make me laugh." Kinnison snorted. "Would you take mine?"

"The case is different. I would not. Your point, however, is well taken. How about the protection of a high court of law? I will bring you an unalterable writ from any court you name."

"Uh-huh," the Gray Lensman dissented. "There never was no court yet that didn't take orders from the big shots who kept the fat cats fat, and lawyers are the crookedest crooks in the whole Universe. You'll have to do better than that, pal."

"Well, then, how about a Lensman? You know about Lensmen, don't you?"

"A Lensman!" Kinnison gasped. He shook his head violently. "Are you completely nuts, or do you think I am? I *do* know Lensmen—a Lensman chased me from Alsakan to Vandemar once, and if I hadn't had a dose of Hell's own luck, he'd have got me. Lensmen chased me out of the First Galaxy—why else do you think I'm here? Use your brain, mister, use your brain!"

"You're thinking of Civilization's Lensmen—particularly of Gray Lensmen." The officer was manifestly enjoying Thyron's passion. "Ours—the Black Lensmen—are different—entirely different. They have as much power, or more, but they use it as it should be used. They work with us right along. In fact, they have been bumping Gray Lensmen off right and left lately."

"You mean that he could open up, for instance, your mind and mine, so that we could see that the other guy wasn't figuring on running in no stacked decks? And that he'd stand by and sort of referee this business deal we got on the fire? And do you know one yourself—personally?"

"He could, and would, do all that. Yes, I know one personally. His name is Melasnikov, and his office is on Kalonia III, not an hour's flit from here. He may not be there at the moment, but he will come in if I call. How about it—shall I call him now?"

"Don't work up a sweat. Sounds like it might work, if we can figure out an approach. I don't suppose that you and him would come out to me in space?"

"Hardly. After the way you have acted, you wouldn't expect us to, would you?"

"It wouldn't be very bright of you. And since I want to do business, I guess I got to meet you part way. How would this be? You pull your ships away, out of range. My ship takes station right above this here Lensman's office. I go down in my speedster, like I did here, and go inside to meet him and you. I'll wear my armor—and when I say it's real armor I ain't just snapping my choppers, neither."

"I can see only one slight flaw." The Boskonian was really trying to work out a mutually satisfactory solution. "The Lensman will open our minds to you in proof, however, that we will have no intention of bringing up our maulers or other heavy stuff while we are in conference."

"Right then he'll show you that you hadn't better, too." Kinnison grinned, wolfishly.

"What do you mean?" The officer demanded.

"I mean that I've got enough good big superatomic bombs aboard to blow the planet apart, and that the boys'll drop 'em all if you start playing dirty. I've got to take a little chance, of course, to start doing business, but it's a small one. If you ain't smart enough to know that what would happen would be mighty poor business, your Lensman will be—especially when it won't get you any dope on what makes this ship of mine tick the way she does. And the clincher is that even if you bring up everything you've got, I never did figure on living forever, and going out in an atomic blast of that size, together with your fleet and half your planet and you and your Lensman and seven hundred million other people, is as good a way as I can think of."

"If the Lensman's examination bears that out, it will constitute an absolute guarantee," the officer agreed. Hard as he was, he could not conceal the fact that he had been shaken: "Everything, then, is satisfactory?"

"On the green. Are you ready to flit?"

"We are ready."

"Call your Lensman, then, and lead the way. Boys, take her upstairs!"

XVI.

Karen Kinnison was worried. She, who had always been so steady, so sure of herself, had for weeks been conscious of a gradually increasing . . . what was it, anyway? Not exactly a loss of control . . . a *change* . . . a something that manifested itself in increasingly numerous fits of senseless—sheerly idiotic—stubbornness. And always and only it was directed at—of all the people in the universe—her brother. She got along with her sisters perfectly; their tiny tiffs barely rippled the surface of any of their minds. But any time her path of action crossed Kit's, it seemed, the profoundest depths of her being flared into opposition like exploding duodec. Worse than senseless and idiotic, it was inexplicable, for the feeling which the Five had for each other was much deeper than that felt by ordinary brothers and sisters.

She didn't want to fight with Kit. She *liked* him! She liked to feel his mind *en rapport* with hers, just as she liked to dance with him; their bodies as completely in accord as were their minds. No change of step or motion, however suddenly conceived and executed or however bizarre, had ever succeeded in taking the other by surprise or in marring by a millimeter the effortless precision of their performance. She could do things with Kit that would tie any other man into knots and break half of his bones. All other men were lumps. Kit was so far ahead of any other man in existence that there was simply no comparison. If she were Kit she would give her a going-over that would . . . or could even he—

At the thought she turned cold inside. He could not. Even Kit, with all his tremendous power, would hit that solid wall and bounce. Well, there was one—not a man, but an entity—who could. He might kill her, but even that would be better than to allow the continued growth within her mind of this monstrosity which she could neither control nor understand. Where was she, and where was Lyrane, and where was Arisia? Good—not too far off line. She would stop off at Arisia en route.

She did so, and made her way to Mentor's quiet office on the hospital grounds. She told her story.

"Fighting with Kit was bad enough," she concluded, "but when I start defying *you*, Mentor, it's high time that something was done about it. Why didn't Kit ever knock me into a spiral? Why didn't you work me over? You called Kit in, with the distinct implication that he needed more education—why didn't you pull me in here, too, and pound some intelligence into me?"

"Concerning you, Christopher had definite instructions, which he obeyed. I did not touch you for the same reason that I did not ask you to come to me; neither course would have been of any use. Your mind, daughter Karen, is unique. One of its prime characteristics—the one, in fact, which is to make you an all-important player in the drama which is to come—is a yieldlessness very nearly absolute. Your mind might, just conceivably, be broken; but it cannot be bent by any imaginable external force, however applied. Thus it was inevitable from the first that nothing could be done about the untoward manifestations of this characteristic until you yourself should recognize the fact that your development was not complete. It would be idle for me to say that during adolescence you have not been more than a trifle trying. I was not speaking idly when I said that the development of you has been a tremendous task. It is with equal seriousness, however, that I now tell you that the reward is commensurate with the magnitude of the undertaking. It is impossible to express the satisfaction I feel—the fulfillment, the completion, the justification—as you children come, one by one, each in his proper time, for final instruction."

"Oh—you mean, then, that there's nothing really the matter with me?" Hard as Karen was, she trembled as her awful tension eased. "That I was *supposed* to act that way? And can I tell Kit, right away?"

"No need. Your brother now knows that it was a passing phase; he shall know very shortly that it has passed. It is not that you were 'supposed' to act as you acted. You could not help it. Nor could your brother, nor I. From now on, however, you shall be completely the mistress of your own mind. Come fully, daughter Karen, into mine."

She did so, and in a matter of time her "formal education" was complete.

*

"There is one thing that I don't quite understand—" she began, before she boarded her speedster.

"Consider it, and I am sure that you will," Mentor assured her. "Explain it, whatever it is, to me."

"QX—I'll try. It's about Fossten and Dad." Karen cogitated. "Fossten was, of course, an Eddorian—your making Dad believe him to be an insane Arisian was a masterpiece. I see, of course, how you did that—principally by making Fossten's 'real' shape exactly like the one he saw of you in Arisia. But his physical actions as Fossten—"

"Go on, daughter. I am sure that your visualization will be sound."

"While acting as Fossten he had to act as a Thralian would have acted," Kay decided with a rush. "He was watched everywhere he went, and knew it. To display his real power would have been disastrous. Just like you Arisians, they have to keep in the background to avoid setting up an inferiority complex that will ruin everything for them. Fossten's actions, then, were constrained. Just as they were when he was Gray Roger, so long ago—except that then he did make a point of unhuman longevity, deliberately to put an insoluble problem up to First-Lensman Samms and his men. Just as you—you *must* have . . . you *did* coach Virgil Samms, Mentor, and some of you Arisians were there, as men!"

"We were. We wrought briefly as men, and died as men. Up to the present moment, no one has ever been the wiser."

"But you weren't Virgil Samms, please!" Kay almost begged. "Not that it would break me if you were, but even I would much rather you hadn't been."

"No, none of us was Samms," Mentor assured her. "Nor Cleveland, nor Rodebush, nor Costigan, nor even Clio Marsden. We worked with—'coached,' as you express it—those persons and others from time to time in certain small matters, but we were at no time integral with any of them. One of us was, however, Dr. Bergenholm. The full inertialess space-drive became necessary at that time, and it would have been poor technique to have had either Rodebush or Cleveland develop so suddenly the ability to perfect the device as Bergenholm did perfect it."

"QX. Bergenholm isn't important—he was just an inventor. To get back onto the subject of Fossten: When he was there on the flagship with Dad, and in position to throw his full weight around, it was too late—you Arisians were on the job. You'll have to take it from there, though; I'm out beyond my depth."

"Because you lack data. Know, then, daughter, that the planet Eddore is screened as heavily as is our own Arisia; by screens which can be extended at will to any desired point in space. In those last minutes the Eddorian knew that Kimball Kinnison was neither alone nor unprotected. He called instantaneously for help, but help did not come. It could not. Eddore's screens were being attacked at every point by every force generable by the massed intellect of Arisia; they were compressed almost to the planet's surface. If the Eddorians had weakened those screens sufficiently to have sent through them a helping thought, every one of them would in that instant have perished. Nor could Fossten escape from the form of flesh he was then energizing. I myself saw to that." Karen had never before felt the Arisian display emotion, but his thought was grim and cold. "From that form, which your father never did perceive, he passed into the next plane of existence."

Karen shivered. "It served him right. That clears everything up, I think. But are you *sure*, Mentor, that you can't—or rather, shouldn't—teach me any more than you have? It's just about time for me to go, and I feel . . . well, 'incompetent' is putting it very mildly indeed."

"To a mind of such power and scope as yours, in its present state of development, such a feeling is inevitable. Nor can anyone except yourself do anything about it. Cold comfort, perhaps, but it is the stark truth that from now on your development is your own task. Yours alone. As I have already told Christopher and Kathryn, and will very shortly tell Camilla and Constance, you have had your last Arisian treatment. I will be on call to any of you at any instant of any day, to aid you or to guide you or to reinforce you at need; but of formal instruction there can be no more."

THE LENSMAN

Karen left Arisia and drove for Lyrane, her thoughts in a turmoil. The time was too short by far; she deliberately cut her vessel's speed and took a long detour so that the vast and chaotic library of her mind could be reduced to some semblance of order before she landed.

She reached Lyrane II, and there, again to all outward seeming a happy, carefree girl, she hugged her mother rapturously. Nor was this part of it acting in any sense—as has been said, those four girls loved each other and their mother and their father and their brother with a depth and fervor impossible to portray intelligibly in words.

"You're the most *wonderful* thing, Mums!" Karen exclaimed. "It's simply marvelous, seeing you again in the flesh."

"Now why bring *that* up?" Clarrissa had—just barely—become accustomed to working undraped, in the Lyranian fashion.

"I didn't mean it that way at all, and you know I didn't." Kay snickered. "Shame on you—fishing for compliments, and at your age, too!" Ignoring the older woman's attempt at protest she went on: "All kidding aside, Mums, you're a mighty smart-looking hunk of woman. I approve of you exceedingly much. In fact, we're a keen pair, and I like both of us. I've got one advantage over you, of course, in that I never did care a particle whether I ever had a stitch of clothes on or not, anywhere, and you still do, a little. But what I was going to ask, though, was how are you doing?"

"Not so well—of course, though, I haven't been here very long." Clarrissa, forgetting her undressedness, frowned. "I haven't found Helen, and I haven't found out yet why she retired. I can't quite decide whether to put pressure on now, or wait a while longer. Ladora, the new Elder Person, is . . . that is, I don't know—Oh, here she comes now. I'm glad—I want you to meet her."

If Ladora was glad to meet Karen, however, she did not show it. Instead, for an inappreciable instant of time which was nevertheless sufficient for the acquirement of full information, each studied the other. Like Helen—the former Queen of the matriarchy of Lyrane II—Ladora was tall, beautifully proportioned, flawless of skin and feature, hard and fine. But so, and in most respects even more so, to Ladora's astonishment and quickly-mounting wrath, was this pink-tanned stranger. Practically instantaneously, therefore, she hurled a vicious mental bolt—only to get the surprise of her life. She had not yet crossed wills in a serious enough way with this strange person, Clarrissa, to find out what she had in the way of equipment, but it certainly couldn't be much. She had never tried to do her harm, nor ever seemed to resent her studied and arrogant aloofness; and therefore her daughter, younger and less experienced, of course, would be easy enough prey.

But Ladora's bolt, the heaviest she could send, did not pierce even the outermost fringes of her intended victim's defenses, and so vicious was the almost simultaneous counterthrust that it went through the Lyranian's hard-held block in nothing flat. Inside her brain, it wrought such hellishly poignant punishment that the matriarch, forgetting everything, tried only and madly to scream. She could not. She could not move a muscle of her face or of her body. She could not even fall. And the one brief glimpse she had into the stranger's mind showed it to be such a blaze of incandescent fury that she, who had never feared in the slightest any living creature, knew now in full measure what fear was.

"I'd like to give that alleged brain of yours a real massage, just for fun." Karen forced her emotion to subside to a mere seething rage, and Ladora watched her do it. "But since this whole stinking planet is my mother's dish, not mine, she'd blast me to a cinder—she's done it before—if I dip in." She cooled further—visibly. "At that, I don't suppose you're too bad an egg, in your own poisonous way—you just don't know any better. So maybe I'd better warn you, you poor fool, since you haven't got sense enough to see it, that you're playing with a live fuse when you push my mother around like you've been doing. About one more millimeter of it and she'll get mad—like I did a second ago except more so—and you'll wish to Klono you had never been born. She'll never make a sign until she blows up, but I'm telling you that she's as much harder and tougher than I am as she is older, and what she always does to people who cross her I wouldn't want to watch happen again, even to a snake. Want to know what she'll do to you first? She'll pick you up, curl you into a perfect circle, pull off your arms, shove both your legs down your throat to the knees, and roll you down that chute there into the ocean. After that I don't know what she'll do—depends on how much pressure she develops before she blows up. One thing, though, she's always sorry afterward—why, she even attends the funeral, sometimes, and insists on paying the expenses!"

With which outrageous thought she kissed Clarrissa an enthusiastic good-by. "Told you I couldn't stay a minute. Got to do a flit—'see a man about a dog.' Came a million parsecs to squeeze you, Mums, but it was worth it. Clear ether!"

She was gone; and it was a dewy-eyed and rapt mother, not a Lensman, who turned to the still completely disorganized Lyranian. Clarrissa had perceived nothing whatever of what had happened—Karen had very carefully seen to that.

*

"My daughter," Clarrissa mused, as much to herself as to Ladora. "One of four. The four dearest, finest, sweetest girls that ever lived. I often wonder how a woman of my limitations, of my faults, could possibly have borne such children."

And Ladora of Lyrane, humorless and literal as all Lyranians are, took those thoughts at their face value and correlated their every connotation and implication with what she herself had perceived in that "dear, sweet" daughter's mind; with what that daughter had done and had said. The nature and quality of this hellish person's "limitations" and "faults" became eminently clear, and as she perceived what she thought was the truth, the Lyranian literally cringed.

"As you know, I have been in doubt as to whether or not to support you actively, as you wish," Ladora offered, as the two walked together across the field, toward the line of ground-cars. "On the one hand, the certainty that the safety, and perhaps the very existence, of my race will be at hazard; on the other the possibility that you are right in saying that the situation will continue to deteriorate if we do nothing. The decision has not been an easy one to make." Ladora was no longer aloof. She was just plain scared. She had been talking against time, and hoping that the help for which she had long since called would arrive in time. "I have touched only the outer surfaces of your mind. Will you allow me, without offense, to test its inner quality before deciding definitely?" she asked, and in the instant of asking sent out an exploratory tentacle of thought which was in actuality a full-driven probe.

"I will not." Ladora's beam struck a barrier which seemed to her exactly like the daughter's. None of her race had developed anything like it. She had never seen . . . yes, she had, too—years ago, when she was a child, that time in the assembly hall—that utterly hated male, Kinnison of Tellus! This visitor, then, was not a real person at all, but a *female*—Kinnison's female—the Red Lensman, of whom even Lyrane had heard—and that pers . . . that *thing* was their offspring! But behind that impenetrable block there might very well be—there probably was—exactly the kind of mind that the offspring had described. A creature who was physically a person, but mentally that inconceivable monstrosity, a *female*, might be anything and might do anything. Ladora temporized.

"Excuse me; I did not mean to intrude against your will," she apologized, smoothly enough. "Since your attitude makes it extremely difficult for me to co-operate with you, I can make no promises as yet. What is it that you wish to know first?"

"I wish to interview your predecessor Elder Person, the one we called Helen." Strangely refreshed, in a sense galvanized by the brief personal visit with her dynamic daughter, it was no longer Mrs. Kimball Kinnison who faced the Lyranian Queen. Instead, it was the Red Lensman; a full-powered Second-Stage Lensman who had finally decided that, since appeals to reason, logic, and common sense had no perceptible effect upon this stiff-necked near-woman, the time had come to bear down. "Furthermore, I intend to interview her now, and not at some such indefinite future time as your whim may see fit to allow."

*

Ladora sent out a final desperate call for help and mustered her every force against the interloper. Fast and strong as her mind was, however, the Red Lensman's was faster and stronger. The Lyranian's defensive structure was wrecked in the instant of its building, the frantically struggling mind was taken over *in toto*. Help arrived—uselessly; since, although Clarrissa's newly enlarged mind had not been put to warlike use, it was brilliantly keen and ultimately sure. Nor, in times of stress, did the softer side of her nature operate to stay mind or hand. While carrying Lensman's Load she contained no more of ruth for Civilization's foes than did abysmally frigid Nadreck himself.

Head thrown back, taut and tense, gold-flecked tawny eyes flashing, she stood there for a moment and took on her shield everything that those belligerent persons could send. More, she returned it in kind, plus; and under those withering blasts of force more than one of her attackers ceased to live. Then, still holding her block, she and her unwilling captive raced across the field toward the line of peculiar little fabric-and-wire machines which were still the last word in Lyranian air transport.

Clarrissa knew that the Lyranians had no modern offensive or defensive weapons. They did, however, have some fairly good artillery at that airport; and she hoped fervently as she ran that she could put out jets enough to spoil the aim and fusing—luckily, they hadn't developed proximity fuses yet!—of what ack-ack they could bring to bear on her crate during the few minutes she would have to use it. Fortunately, there was no artillery at the small, unimportant airport on which her speedster lay.

"Here we are. We'll take this tripe—it's the fastest thing here!"

Clarrissa could operate the triplane, of course—any knowledge or ability that Ladora had ever had was now and permanently the Lensman's. She started the queer engines; and as the powerful little plane screamed into the air, hanging from its props, she devoted what of her mind she could spare to the problem of antiaircraft fire. She could not handle all the guncrews; but she could and did command the most important members of most of them. Thus, nearly all of the shells either went wide or exploded too soon. Since she knew every point of aim of the few guns with whose operations she could not interfere, she avoided their missiles by not being at any one of those points at the predetermined instant of functioning.

Thus plane and passengers escaped unscathed and in a matter of minutes arrived at their destination. The Lyranians there had been alerted, of course; but they were few in number and they had not been informed that it would take physical force, not mental, to keep that red-headed pseudoperson from boarding her outlandish ship of space.

*

In a few more minutes, then, Clarrissa and her captive, safe in the speedster, were high in the stratosphere. Clarrissa sat Ladora down—hard—in a seat and fastened the safety straps.

"Stay in that seat and keep your thoughts to yourself," she directed, curtly. "If you don't, you'll never again either move or think in this life." She opened a sliding door, put on a couple of wisps of Manarkan glamourette, reached for a dress, and paused. Eyes glowing, she gazed hungrily at a suit of plain gray leather; a costume which she had not as yet so much as tried on. Should she wear it, or not?

She could work efficiently—at service maximum, really—in ordinary clothes. Ditto, although she didn't like to, unclothed. In Gray, though, she could hit absolute max if she had to. Nor had there ever been any question of right involved; the only barrier had been her own hypersensitivity.

For over twenty years she herself had been the only one to deny her right. What license, she was wont to ask, did an imitation or synthetic or amateur or "Red" Lensman have to wear the garb which meant so much to so many? Over those years, however, it had become increasingly widely known that hers was one of the five finest and most powerful minds in the entire Gray Legion; and when Co-ordinator Kinnison recalled her to active duty in Unattached status, that Legion passed by unanimous vote a resolution asking her to join them in Gray. Psychics all, they knew that nothing less would suffice; that if there was any trace of resentment or of antagonism or of feeling that she did not intrinsically belong, she would never don the uniform which every adherent of Civilization so revered and for which, deep down, she had always so intensely longed. The Legion had sent her these Grays. Kit had convinced her that she did actually deserve them.

She really should wear them. She would.

She put them on, thrilling to the core as she did so, and made the quick little gesture she had seen Kim make so many times. Lensman's Seal. No one, however accustomed, has ever donned or ever will don unmoved the plain gray leather of the Unattached Lensman of the Galactic Patrol.

Hands on hips, she studied herself minutely and approvingly, both in the mirror and by means of her vastly more efficient sense of perception. She wriggled a little, and giggled inwardly as she remembered deploring as "exhibitionistic" this same conduct in her oldest daughter.

The Grays fitted her perfectly. A bit revealing, perhaps, but her figure was still good—very good, as a matter of fact. Not a speck of dirt or tarnish. Her DeLameters were fully charged. Her tremendous Lens flamed brilliantly upon her wrist. She looked—and felt—ready. She could hit absolute max in a fraction of a microsecond. If she had to get really tough, she would. She sent out a call.

"Helen of Lyrane! I know they've got you around here somewhere, and, if any of your guards try to screen out *this* thought, I'll burn their brains out. Clarrissa of Sol III calling. Come in, Helen!"

"Clarrissa!" This time there was no interference. A world of welcome was in every nuance of the thought. "Where are you?"

"High up, at—" Clarrissa gave her position. "I'm in my speedster, so can get to anywhere on the planet in minutes. More important, where are you? And why?"

"In jail, in my own—the Elder Person's—office." Queens should have palaces, but Lyrane's ruler did not. Everything was strictly utilitarian. "The tower on the corner, remember? On the top floor. 'Why' is too long to discuss now—I'd better tell you as much as possible of what you should know, while there is time."

"Time? Are you in danger?"

"Yes. Ladora would have killed me long ago if it had dared. My following grows less daily, the Boskonians stronger. The guards have already summoned help. They are coming now, to take me."

"That's what *they* think!" Clarrissa had already reached the scene. She had exactly the velocity she wanted. She slanted downward in a screaming dive. "Can you tell whether they're limbering up any of that ack-ack around the office, or not?"

"I don't believe so—I don't feel any such thoughts."

"QX. Get away from the window." If they hadn't started already, they never would start, the Red Lensman was deadly sure of that.

*

She came within range—her range—of the guns. She was in time. Several gunners were running toward their stations. None of them arrived. The speedster leveled off and stuck its hard nose into and almost through the indicated room; reinforced concrete, steel bars, and glass showering abroad as it did so. The port snapped open. As Helen leaped in, Clarrissa practically threw Ladora out.

"Bring Ladora back!" Helen demanded. "I shall have its life!"

"Nix!" Clarrissa snapped. "I know everything that she does. We've other fish to fry, my dear."

The massive door clanged shut. The speedster darted forward, straight through the solid concrete wall. That small vessel, solidly built of beryllium alloys, had been designed to take brutal punishment. She took it.

Out in open space, Clarrissa went free, leaving the artificial gravity at normal. Helen stood up, took Clarrissa's hand, and shook it gravely and strongly; a gesture at which the Red Lensman almost choked.

Helen of Lyrane had changed even less than had the Earthwoman. She was still six feet tall; erect, taut, springy, and poised. She didn't weigh a pound more than the one-eighty she had scaled twenty-odd years ago. Her vivid auburn hair showed not one strand of gray. Her eyes were as clear and as proud; her skin almost as fine and firm.

"You are, then, alone?" In spite of her control, Helen's thought showed relief.

"Yes. My hus . . . Kimball Kinnison is very busy elsewhere." Clarrissa understood perfectly. Helen, after twenty years of thinking things over, really liked her; but she still simply couldn't stand a male, not even Kim; any more than Clarrissa could ever adapt herself to the Lyranian habit of using the neuter pronoun "it" when referring to one of themselves. She couldn't. Anybody who ever got a glimpse of Helen would have to think of her as "*she*"! But enough of this wool-gathering—which had taken perhaps one millisecond of time.

"There's nothing to keep us from working together perfectly," Clarrissa's thought flashed on. "Ladora didn't know much, and you do. So tell me all about things, so that we can decide where to begin!"

XVII.

When Kandron called his minion in that small and nameless base to learn whether or not he had succeeded in trapping the Palainian Lensman, Nadreck's relay station functioned so perfectly, and Nadreck was so completely in charge of his captive's mind, that the caller could feel nothing out of the ordinary. Ultra-suspicious though Kandron was, there was nothing whatever to indicate that anything had changed at, or pertaining to, that base since he had last called its commander. That individual's subconscious mind reacted properly to the key stimulus. The conscious mind took over, remembered, and answered properly a series of trick questions.

These things occurred because the Base Commander was still alive. His ego, the pattern and matrix of his personality, was still in existence and had not been changed. What Kandron did not and could not suspect was that that ego was no longer in control of the commander's mind, brain, or body; that it was utterly unable of its own volition, either to think any iota of independent thought or to stimulate any single physical cell. The Onlonian's ego was present—just barely present—but that was all. It was Nadreck who, using that ego as a guide and, in a sense, as a helplessly impotent transformer, received the call. Nadreck made those exactly correct replies. Nadreck was now ready to render a detailed and fully documented—and completely mendacious—report upon his own destruction!

Nadreck's special tracers were already out, determining line and intensity. Strippers and analyzers were busily at work on the fringes of the beam, dissecting out, isolating, and identifying each of the many scraps of extraneous thought accompanying the main beam. These side-thoughts, in fact, were Nadreck's prime concern. The Second-Stage Lensmen had learned that no being—except possibly an Arisian—could narrow a beam of thought down to one single, pure sequence. Only Nadreck, however, recognized in those side-bands a rich field; only he had designed and developed mechanisms with which to work that field.

The stronger and clearer the mind, the fewer and less complete were the extraneous fragments of thought; but Nadreck knew that even Kandron's brain would carry quite a few such nongermane accompaniments, and from each of those bits he could reconstruct an entire sequence as accurately as a competent paleontologist reconstructs a prehistoric animal from one fossilized piece of bone.

Thus Nadreck was completely ready when the harshly domineering Kandron asked his first real question.

"I do not suppose that you have succeeded in killing the Lensman?"

"Yes, Your Supremacy, I have." Nadreck could feel Kandron's start of surprise; could perceive without his instruments Kandron's fleeting thoughts of the hundreds of unsuccessful previous attempts upon his life. It was clear that the Onlonian was not at all credulous.

"Report in detail!" Kandron ordered.

*

Nadreck did so, adhering rigidly to the truth up to the moment in which his probes of force had touched off the Boskonian alarms. Then:

"Spy-ray photographs taken at the instant of alarm show an indetectable speedster, with one, and only one occupant, as Your Supremacy anticipated. A careful study of all the pictures taken of that occupant shows: first, that he was definitely alive at that time, and was neither a projection nor an artificial mechanism; and second, that his physical measurements agree in every particular with the specifications furnished by Your Supremacy as being those of Nadreck of Palain VII.

"Since Your Supremacy personally computed and supervised the placement of those projectors," Nadreck went smoothly on, "you know that the possibility is vanishingly small that any material thing, free or inert, could have escaped destruction. As a check, I caused to be taken seven hundred twenty-nine—three to the sixth power—samples of the circumambient space, statistically at random, for analysis. After appropriate allowances for the exactly-observed elapsed times of sampling, diffusion of droplets and molecular and atomic aggregates, temperatures, pressures, and all other factors known or assumed to be operating, I determined that there had been present in the center of action of our beams a mass of approximately four thousand six hundred seventy-eight point one metric tons. This value, Your Supremacy will note, is in close agreement with the most efficient mass of an indetectable speedster designed for long-distance work."

That figure was in fact closer than close. It was an almost exact statement of the actual mass of Nadreck's ship.

"Exact composition?" Kandron demanded.

Nadreck recited a rapid-fire string of elements and figures. They, too, were correct within the experimental error of a very good analyst. The Base Commander could not possibly have known them; but it was well within the bounds of possibility that the insidious Kandron would. He did. He was now practically certain that his ablest and bitterest enemy had been destroyed at last, but there were still a few lingering shreds of doubt.

"Let me look over your work," Kandron directed.

"Yes, Your Supremacy." Nadreck the Thorough was ready for even that extreme test. Through the eyes of the ultimately enslaved Base Commander Kandron checked and rechecked Nadreck's pictures, Nadreck's charts and diagrams, Nadreck's more than four hundred pages of mathematical, physical, and chemical notes and determinations; all without finding a single flaw.

In the end Kandron was ready to believe that Nadreck had in fact ceased to exist. However, he himself had not done the work. There was no corpse. If he himself had killed the Palainian, if he himself had actually felt the Lensman's life depart in the grasp of his own tentacles, then, and only then, would he have *known* that Nadreck was dead. As it was, even though the work had been done in exact accordance with his own instructions, there remained an infinitesimal uncertainty. Wherefore:

"Shift your field of operations to cover X-174, Y-240, Z-16. Do not relax your vigilance in the slightest because of what has happened." He considered briefly the idea of allowing his minion to call him, in case anything happened, but decided against it. "Are the men standing up?"

"Yes, Your Supremacy, they are in very good shape indeed."

And so on. "Yes, Your Supremacy, the psychologist is doing a very fine job. Yes, Your Supremacy . . . yes . . . yes . . . yes—"

*

Very shortly after the characteristically Kandronesque ending of that interview, Nadreck had learned everything he needed to know. He knew where Kandron was and what he was doing. He knew much of what Kandron had done during the preceding twenty years; and, since he himself figured prominently in many of those sequences, they constituted invaluable checks upon the validity of his other reconstructions. He knew the construction, the armament, and the various ingenious mechanisms, including the locks, of Kandron's vessel; he knew more than any other outsider had ever known of Kandron's private life. He knew where Kandron was going next, and what he was going to do there. He knew in broad what Kandron intended to do during the coming century.

Thus well informed, Nadreck set his speedster into a course toward the planet of Civilization which was Kandron's next objective. He did not hurry; it was no part of his plan to interfere in any way in the horrible program of planet-wide madness and slaughter which Kandron had in mind. It simply did not occur to him to try to save the planet as well as to kill the Onlonian; Nadreck, being Nadreck, took without doubt or question the safest and surest course.

Nadreck knew that Kandron would set his vessel into an orbit around the planet, and that he would take a small boat—a flitter—for the one personal visit necessary to establish

977

his lines of communication and control. Vessel and flitter would be alike indetectable, of course; but Nadreck found the one easily enough and knew when the other left its mother-ship. Then, using his lightest, stealthiest spy rays, the Palainian set about the exceedingly delicate business of boarding the Boskonian craft.

That undertaking could be made a story in its own right, for Kandron did not leave his ship unguarded. However, merely by thinking about his own safety, Kandron had all unwittingly given away the keys to his supposedly impregnable fortress. While Kandron was wondering whether or not the Lensman was really dead, and especially after he had been convinced that he most probably was, the Onlonian's thoughts had touched fleetingly upon a multitude of closely-related subjects. Would it be safe to abandon some of the more onerous precautions he had always taken, and which had served him so well for so many years? And as he thought of them, each one of his safeguards flashed at least partially into view; and for Nadreck, any significant part was practically as good as the whole. Kandron's protective devices, therefore, did not protect. Projectors, designed to flame out against intruders, remained cold. Ports opened; and as Nadreck touched sundry buttons, various invisible beams, whose breaking would have produced unpleasant results, ceased to exist. In short, Nadreck knew all the answers. If he had not been coldly certain that his information was complete, he would not have acted at all.

After entry, his first care was to send out spotting devices which would give ample warning in case the Onlonian should return unexpectedly soon. Then, working in the service-spaces behind instrument boards and panels, in junction boxes, and in various other out-of-the-way places, he cut into lead after lead, ran wire after wire, and installed item after item of apparatus and equipment upon which he had been at work for weeks. He finished his work undisturbed. He checked and rechecked the circuits, making absolutely certain that every major one of the vessel's controlling leads ran to or through at least one of the things he had just installed. With painstaking nicety he obliterated every visible sign of his visit. He departed as carefully as he had come; restoring to full efficiency as he went each one of Kandron's burglar alarms.

*

Kandron returned, entered his ship as usual, stored his flitter, and extended a tentacular member toward the row of switches on his panel.

"Don't touch anything, Kandron," he was advised by a thought as cold and as deadly as any one of his own; and upon the Onlonian equivalent of a visiplate there appeared the one likeness which he least expected and least desired to perceive.

"Nadreck of Palain VII—Star A Star—THE Lensman!" The Onlonian was physically and emotionally incapable of gasping, but the idea is appropriate. "You have, then, wired and mined this ship."

There was a subdued clicking of relays. The Bergenholm came up to speed, the speedster spun about and darted straight away from the planet under a couple of kilodynes of drive.

"I am Nadreck of Palain VII, yes. One of the group of Lensmen whose collective activities you have ascribed to Star A Star and *the* Lensman. Your ship is, as you have deduced, mined. The only reason you did not die as you entered it is that I wish to be absolutely certain; and not merely statistically so, that it is actually Kandron of Onlo, and not someone else, who dies."

"That unutterable fool!" Kandron quivered in helpless rage. "Oh, that I had taken the time and killed you myself!"

"If you had done your own work, the techniques I used here could not have been employed, and you might have been in no danger at the present moment," Nadreck admitted, equably enough. "My powers are small, my intellect feeble, and what might have been has no present bearing. I am inclined, however, to question the validity of your conclusions, due to the known fact that you have been directing a campaign against me for over twenty years without success; whereas I have succeeded against you in less than half a year. My analysis is now complete. You may now touch any control you please. By the way, you do not deny that you are Kandron of Onlo, do you?"

Neither of those monstrous beings asked, suggested, or even thought of mercy. In neither of their languages was there any word for or concept of such a thing.

"That would be idle. You have a record of my life pattern, of course, just as I have one of yours. But I cannot understand how you got through that—"

"It is not necessary that you should. Do you wish to close one of those switches or shall I?"

Kandron had been thinking for minutes, studying every aspect of his predicament. Knowing Nadreck, he knew just how desperate the situation was. However, there was one very small chance—just one. The way he had come was clear. He knew that that was the *only* clear way. Wherefore, to gain an extra instant of time, he reached out toward a switch; but even while he was reaching he put every ounce of his tremendous strength into a leap which hurled him across the room toward his flitter.

No luck. One of Nadreck's minor tentacles was already curled around a switch, tensed and ready. Kandron had not moved a foot when a relay snapped shut and four canisters of duodec detonated as one. Duodecaplylatomate, that frightful detonant whose violence is exceeded only by that of nuclear disintegration itself!

There was an appalling flash of viciously white light, which expanded in microseconds into an enormous globe of incandescent gas. Cooling and darkening as it expanded rapidly into the near-vacuum of interplanetary space, the gases and vapors soon became invisible. Through and throughout the entire volume of volatilization Nadreck drove analyzers and detectors, until it was a mathematical certainty that no particle of material substance larger in diameter than five microns remained of either Kandron or his spaceship. He then called the Gray Lensman.

*

"Kinnison. Nadreck of Palain VII calling, to report that my assignment has been completed. I have destroyed Kandron of Onlo."

"Good! Fine business, ace! What kind of a picture did you get? He must have known something about the higher echelons—or did he? Was he just another dead end?"

"I did not go into that."

"Huh? Why not?" Kinnison demanded, exasperation in every line of his thought.

"Because it was not included in the project," Nadreck explained, patiently. "You already know that one must concentrate in order to work efficiently. To secure the requisite minimum of information it was necessary to steer his thoughts into one, and only one, set of channels. There were some foreign side-bands, of course, and it may be that some of them touched upon this new subject which you have now, too late, introduced . . . no, there were no such."

"Damnation!" Kinnison exploded; then by main strength shut himself up. "QX, ace; skip it. But listen, my spiny and murderous friend. Get this—engrave it in big type right on the top-side inside of your thick skull—what we want is INFORMATION, not mere liquidation. Next time you get hold of such a big shot as Kandron must have been, don't kill him until either: first, you get some leads as to who or what the real head of the outfit is; or, second, you make sure that he doesn't know. Then kill him all you want to, but FIND OUT WHAT HE KNOWS FIRST. Have I made myself clear this time?"

"You have, and as Co-ordinator your instructions should and will govern. I point out, however, that the introduction of a multiplicity of objectives into a problem not only destroys its unity, but also increases markedly both the time necessary for, and the actual personal danger involved in, its solution."

"So what?" Kinnison countered, as evenly as he could. "That way, we may be able to get the answer some day. Your way, we never will. But the thing's done—there's no use yapping and yowling about it now. Have you any ideas as to what you should do next?"

"No. Whatever you wish, that I shall try to do."

"I'll check with the others." He did so, receiving no helpful ideas until he consulted his wife.

"Hi, Kim, my dear!" came Clarrissa's buoyant thought; and, after a brief but intense greeting: "Glad you called. Nothing definite enough yet to report to you officially, but there are indications that Lyrane IX may be an important—"

"Nine?" Kinnison interrupted. "Not Eight again?"

"Nine," she confirmed. "A new item. So I may be doing a flit over there one of these days."

"Uh-uh," he denied. "Lyrane IX would be none of your business. Stay away from it."

"Says who?" she demanded. "We went into this once before, Kim, about you telling me what I could and couldn't do."

"Yeah, and I came out second best." Kinnison grinned. "But now, as the Co-ordinator, I make suggestions to even Second-Stage Lensmen, and they follow them—or else. I, therefore, suggest officially that you stay away from Lyrane IX on the grounds that since it is colder than a Palainian's heart, it is definitely not your problem, but Nadreck's. And personally, I am adding that if you don't behave yourself I'll come over there and administer appropriate physical persuasion."

"Come on over—that would be fun!" Clarrissa giggled, then sobered quickly. "But seriously, you win, I guess—this time. You'll keep me informed?"

"I'll do that. Clear ether, Chris!" and he turned back to the Palainian.

" . . . so you see this is your problem. Go to it, little chum."

"I go, Kinnison."

XVIII.

For hours Camilla Kinnison and Tregonsee wrestled separately and fruitlessly with the problem of the elusive "X." Then, after she had studied the Rigellian's mind in a fashion which he could neither detect nor employ, Camilla broke the mental silence.

"Uncle Trig, my conclusions frighten me. Can you conceive of the possibility that it was contact with *my* mind, not yours, that made 'X' run away?"

"That is the only tenable conclusion. I know the limitations of my own mind, but I have never been able to guess at the capabilities of yours. I fear that I, at least, underestimated our opponent."

"I know that I did, and I was terribly wrong. I shouldn't have tried to fool you, either, even a little bit. There are some things about me that I just *can't* show to most people, but you are different—you're *such* a wonderful person!"

"Thanks, Camilla, for your trust." Understandingly, he did not go on to say that he would keep on being worthy of it. "I accept the fact that you Five, being children of two Second-Stage Lensmen, are basically beyond my comprehension. There are indications that you do not as yet thoroughly understand yourself. You have, however, decided upon a course of action."

"Oh—I'm *so* relieved! Yes, I have. But before we go into that, I haven't been able to solve the problem of 'X.' More, I have proved that I cannot solve it without more data. Therefore, you can't, either. Check?"

"I had not yet reached that conclusion, but I accept your statement as truth."

"One of those uncommon powers of mine, to which you referred a while ago, is a wide range of perception, from large masses down to extremely tiny components. Another, or perhaps a part of the same one, is that, after resolving and analyzing these fine details, I can build up a logical and coherent whole by processes of interpolation and extrapolation."

"I can believe that such things would be possible to such a mind as yours must be. Go on."

"Well, that is how I know that I underestimated Mr. 'X.' Whoever or whatever he is, I am completely unable to resolve the structure of his thought. I gave you all I got of it. Look at it again, please—hard. What can you make of it now?"

"It is exactly the same as it was before; a fragment of a simple and plain introductory thought to an audience. That is all."

"That's all I can see, too, and that's what surprises me so." The hitherto imperturbable and serene Camilla got up and began to pace the floor. "That thought is apparently absolutely solid; and since that is a definitely impossible condition, the truth is that its structure is so fine that I cannot resolve it into its component units. This fact shows that I am not nearly so competent as I thought I was. When you and Dad and the others reached that point, you each went to Arisia. I have decided to do the same thing."

"That decision seems eminently sound."

"Thanks, Uncle Trig—that was what I hoped you would say. I have never been there, you know, and the idea scared me a little. Clear ether!"

There is no need to go into detail as to Camilla's bout with Mentor. Her mind, like Karen's, had had to mature of itself before any treatment could be really effective; but once mature, she took as much in one session as Kathryn had taken in all her many. She had not suggested that the Rigellian accompany her to Arisia; they both knew that he had already received all that he could take. Upon her return she greeted him as casually as though she had been gone only a matter of hours.

"What Mentor did to me, Uncle Trig, shouldn't have been done to a Delgonian catlat. It doesn't show too much, though, I hope—does it?"

"Not at all." He scanned her narrowly, both physically and mentally. "I can perceive no change in detail. In general, however, you have changed. You have developed."

"Yes, more than I would have believed possible. I can't do much with my present very poor transcription of that thought, since the all-important fine detail is missing. We'll have to intercept another one. I'll get it *all*, this time, and it will tell us a lot."

"But you did something with this one, I am sure. There must have been some developable features—a sort of latent-image effect?"

"A little. Practically infinitesimal compared to what was really there. Physically, his classification to four places is TUUV; quite a bit like the Nevians, you notice. His home planet is big, and practically covered with liquid. No real cities, just groups of half-submerged, temporary structures. Mentality very high, but we knew that already. Normally, he thinks upon a very short wave, so short that he was then working at the very bottom of his range. His sun is a fairly hot main-sequence-star, of spectral class somewhere around F, and it's probably more or less variable, because there was quite a distinct implication of change. But that's normal enough, isn't it?"

Within the limits imposed by the amount and kind of data available, Camilla's observations and analyses had been perfect, her reconstruction flawless. She did not then have any idea, however, that "X" was in fact a spring-form Plooran. More, she did not even know that such a planet as Ploor existed, except for Mentor's one mention of it.

"Of course. Peoples of planets of variable suns think that such suns are the only kind fit to have planets. You cannot reconstruct the nature of the change?"

"No. Worse, I can't find even a hint of where his planet is in space—but then, I probably couldn't, anyway, even with a whole, fresh thought to study."

"Probably not. 'Rigel Four' would be an utterly meaningless thought to anyone ignorant of Rigel; and, except when making a conscious effort, as in directing strangers, I never think of its location in terms of galactic co-ordinates. I suppose that the location of a home planet is always taken for granted. That would seem to leave us just about where we were before in our search for 'X,' except for your implied ability to intercept another of his thoughts, almost at will. Explain, please."

"Not *my* ability—ours." Camilla smiled, confidently. "I couldn't do it alone, neither could you, but between us I don't believe that it will be too difficult. You, with your utterly calm, utterly unshakable certainty, can drive a thought to any corner of the universe. You can fix and hold it steady on any indicated atom. I can't do that, or anything like it, but with my present ability to detect and to analyze, I am not afraid of missing 'X' if we can come within parsecs of him. So my idea is a sort of piggy-back hunting trip; you to take me for a ride, mentally, very much as Worsel takes Con, physically. That would work, don't you think?"

"Perfectly, I am sure." The stolid Rigellian was immensely pleased. "Link your mind with mine, then, and we will set out. If you have no better plan of action mapped out, I would suggest starting at the point where we lost him and working outward, covering an expanding sphere."

"You know best. I will stick to you wherever you go. I am ready."

*

Tregonsee launched his thought; a thought which, at a velocity not to be measured even in multiples of that of light, generated the surface of a continuously enlarging sphere of space. And with that thought, a very part of it, sped Camilla's incomprehensibly delicate, instantaneously reactive detector web. The Rigellian, with his unhuman perseverance, would have surveyed total space had it been necessary; and the now adult Camilla would have stayed with him. However, the patient pair did not have to comb all of space. In a matter of hours the girl's almost infinitely tenuous detector touched, with infinitesimal power and for an inappreciable instant of time, the exact thought-structure to which it had been so carefully attuned.

"Halt!" she flashed, and Tregonsee's mighty superdreadnought shot away along the indicated line at maximum blast.

"You are not now thinking at him, of course, but how sure are you that he did not feel your detector?" Tregonsee asked.

"Positive," the girl replied. "I couldn't even feel it myself until after a million-fold amplification. It was just a web, you know, not nearly solid enough for an analyzer or a recorder. I didn't touch his mind at all. However, when we get close enough to work efficiently, which will be in about five days, we will have to touch him. Assuming that he is as sensitive as we are, he will feel us; hence we will have to work fast and according to some definite plan. What are your ideas as to technique?"

"I may offer a suggestion or two, later, but I resign leadership to you. You already have made plans, have you not?"

"Only a framework, I could not go into detail without consulting you. Since we agree that it was my mind that he did not like, you will have to make the first contact."

"Of course. But since the action of thought is so nearly instantaneous, are you sure that you will be able to protect yourself in case he overcomes me at that first contact?" If the Rigellian gave any thought at all to his own fate in such a case, no trace of it was evident.

"My screens are good. I am fairly certain that I could protect both of us, but it might slow me down a trifle; and even an instant's delay might keep me from getting the information we want. It would be better, I think, to call Kit in. Or, better yet, Kay. She can stop a superatomic bomb. With Kay covering us both, we will be free to put our full power into the offense."

"And that offense is to be—?"

"I have no idea. We will work that out together."

Again they went into a union of minds; considering, weighing, analyzing, rejecting, and—a few times—accepting. And finally, well within the five-day time limit, they had drawn up a completely detailed plan of battle.

How uselessly that time was spent! For that battle, instead of progressing according to their carefully worked-out plan, was ended almost in the instant of its beginning.

*

According to plan, Tregonsee tuned his mind to "X's" pattern as soon as they had come within working range. He reached out as delicately as he could; and his best was very fine work indeed. He might just as well have struck with all his power, for at the first touch of the fringe, extremely light and entirely innocuous though it was, the stranger's barriers flared into being and there came back instantly a mental bolt of such vicious intensity that it would have gone through Tregonsee's hardest-held block as though no barrier had been there. But that bolt did not strike Tregonsee's shield; he did not even know, until much later, that it had been sent. Instead, it struck Karen Kinnison's, which has already been described.

It did not exactly bounce, nor did it cling, nor did it linger, even for a microsecond, to do battle as expected. It simply vanished; as though that minute interval of time had been sufficient for the enemy to have recovered from the shock of encountering a completely unexpected resistance, to have analyzed the texture of the shield, to have deduced from that analysis the full capabilities of its owner and operator, to have decided that he did not care to have any dealings with the entity so deduced, and finally, as he no doubt supposed, to have begun to retreat in good order.

His retreat, however, was not in good order. He did not escape, this time. This time, as she had declared that she would be, Camilla was ready for anything—literally anything. Everything she had—and she had plenty—was on the trips; tense, taut, and poised. Knowing that Karen, the Ultimate of Defense, was on guard, she was wholly free to hurl her every force in the instant of perceiving the enemy's poignant thrust. Scarcely had the leading element of her attack touched the stranger's screens, however, when those screens, "X" himself, his vessel and any others that might have been accompanying it, and everything tangible in nearby space, all disappeared at once in the inconceivably violent, the ultimately cataclysmic detonation of a superatomic bomb.

It may not, perhaps, be generally known that the "completely liberating" or "superatomic" bomb liberates one hundred percent of the total component energy of two or more subcritical masses of an unstable isotope, in a space of time estimated to be sixty-nine hundredths of one microsecond. Its violence and destructiveness thus differ, both in degree and in kind, from those of the earlier type, which liberated only the energy of nuclear fission, very much as the radiation of S-Doradus differs from that of Earth's moon. Its mass attains, and holds for an appreciable length of time, a temperature to be measured only in millions of Centigrade degrees; which fact accounts in large part for its utterly incredible vehemence.

Nothing inert in its entire sphere of primary action can even begin to move out of the way before being reduced to its subatomic constituents and thus contributing in some measure to the cataclysm. Nothing is or becomes visible until the secondary stage begins;

until the frightful globe has expanded to a diameter of some hundreds of miles and by this expansion has cooled down to a point at which some of its radiation lies in the visible violet. And as for lethal radiation—there are radiations and they are lethal.

The battle with "X" had occupied approximately two milliseconds of actual time. The expansion had been progressing for a second or two when Karen lowered her shield.

"Well, that finishes that," she commented. "I'd better get back on the job. Did you find out what you want to know, Cam, or not?"

"I got a little in the moment before the explosion. Not much." Camilla was deep in study. "It is going to be quite a job of reconstruction. One thing of interest to you, though, is that this 'X' had quit sabotage temporarily and was on his way to Lyrane IX, where he had some kind of important—"

"Nine?" Karen asked, sharply. "Not Eight? I've been watching Eight, you know—I haven't even thought of Nine."

"Nine, definitely. The thought was clear. You might give it a scan once in a while. How is mother doing?"

"She's doing a grand job, and that Helen is quite an operator, too. I'm not doing much—just a touch here and there—I'll see what I can see on Nine. I'm not the scanner or detector that you are, though, you know—maybe you'd better come over here too, in person. Suppose?"

"I think so—don't you, Uncle Trig?" Tregonsee did. "We can do some exploring as we come, but since I have no definite patterns for web work, we may not be able to do much until we get close. Clear ether, Kay!"

*

"The fine structure is there, and I can resolve it and analyze it," Camilla informed Tregonsee, after a few hours of intense concentration. "There are quite a few clear extraneous sequences, instead of the blurred latent images we had before, but there is still no indication whatever of the location of his home planet. I can see his physical classification to ten places instead of four, more detail as to the sun's variation, the seasons, their habits, and so on. Things that seem mostly to be of very little importance, as far as we are concerned. I found one fact, though, that is new and important. According to my reconstruction, his business of Lyrane IX was the induction of Boskonian Lensmen—*Black* Lensmen, Tregonsee, just as father suspected!"

"In that case, he must have been the Boskonian counterpart of an Arisian, and hence one of the highest echelon. I am very glad indeed that you and Karen relieved me of the necessity of trying to handle him myself. Kinnison will be very glad to know that we have at last and in fact reached the top—"

Camilla was paying attention to the Rigellian's cogitations with only a fraction of her mind; most of it being engaged in a private conversation with her brother.

" . . . so you see, Kit, he was under a subconscious compulsion. He *had* to destroy himself, his ship, and everything in it, in the very instant of attack by any mind definitely superior to his own. Therefore he couldn't have been an Eddorian, possibly, but merely another intermediate, and I haven't been of much help."

"Sure you have, Cam! You got a lot of information, and some mighty good leads to Lyrane IX and what goes on there. I'm on my way to Eddore now; and by working down from there and up from Lyrane IX we can't go wrong. Clear ether, Sis!"

XIX.

Constance Kinnison did not waste much time in idle recriminations, even at herself. Realizing at last that she was still not fully competent, and being able to define exactly what she lacked, she went to Arisia for final treatment. She took that treatment and emerged from it, as her brother and sisters had emerged, a completely integrated personality.

She had something of everything the others had, of course, as did they all; but her dominants, the characteristics which had operated to make Worsel her favorite Second-Stage Lensman, were much like those of the Velantian. Her mind, like his, was quick and facile, yet of extraordinary power and range. She did not have much of her father's flat, driving urge or of his indomitable will to do; she was the least able of all the Five to exert long-sustained extreme effort. Her top, however, was vastly higher than theirs. Like Worsel's, her armament was almost entirely offensive—she was far and away the deadliest fighter of them all. She only of them all had more than a trace of pure killer instinct; and when roused to full fighting pitch her mental bolts were weapons of as starkly incomprehensible an effectiveness as the sphere of primary action of a superatomic bomb.

As soon as Constance had left the *Velan*, remarking that she was going to Arisia to take her medicine, Worsel called a staff meeting to discuss in detail the matter of the "Hell Hole in Space." That conference was neither long nor heated; it was unanimously agreed that that phenomenon was—*must* be—simply another undiscovered cavern of Overlords.

In view of the fact that Worsel and his crew had been hunting down and killing Overlords for more than twenty years, the only logical course of action was for them to deal similarly with one more, perhaps the only remaining large group of their hereditary foes. Nor did any doubt of their ability to do so enter any one of the Velantians' minds.

How wrong they were!

They did not have to search for the "Hell Hole." Long since, to stop its dreadful toll, a spherical cordon of robot guard ships had been posted to warn all traffic away from the outer fringes of its influence. Since they merely warned against, but could not physically prohibit, entry into the dangerous space, Worsel did not pay any attention to the guard ships or to their signals as the *Velan* went through the warning web. His plans were, he thought, well laid. His ship was free. Its speed, by Velantian standards, was very low. Each member of his crew wore a full-coverage thought-screen; a similar and vastly more powerful screen would surround the whole vessel if one of Worsel's minor members were either to tighten or to relax its grip upon a spring-mounted control. Worsel was, he thought, ready for anything.

But the "Hell Hole in Space" was not a cavern of Overlords. No sun, no planet, nothing material existed within that spherical volume of space. That *something* was there, however, there was no doubt. Slow as was the *Velan's* pace, it was still too fast by far; for in a matter of minutes, through the supposedly impervious thought-screens, there came an attack of utterly malignant ferocity; an assault which tore at Worsel's mind in a fashion he had never imagined possible; a poignant, rending, unbearably crescendo force whose violence seemed to double with every mile of advance.

The *Velan's* all-encompassing screen snapped on—uselessly. Its tremendous power was as unopposed as were the lesser powers of the personal shields—that highly inimical thought was coming past, not through, the barriers. An Arisian, or one of the Children of the Lens, would have been able to perceive and to block that band; no one of lesser mental stature could.

Strong and fast as Worsel was, mentally and physically, he got his vessel turned around just barely in time. All his resistance and all his strength had to be called into play to maintain his mind's control over his body; to enable him to spin his ship end for end and to kick her drive up to maximum blast. To his surprise, his agony decreased with distance as rapidly as it had built up; disappearing entirely well before the *Velan* reached the web she had crossed such a short time before.

Groggy, sick, and shaken, hanging slackly from his bars, the Velantian Lensman was roused to action by the mental and physical frenzy of his crew. Ten of them had died in the Hell Hole; six more were torn to bits before their commander could muster enough force to stop their insane rioting. Then Master Therapist Worsel went to work; and one by one he brought the survivors back. They remembered; but he made those memories bearable.

He then called Kinnison. " . . . but there didn't seem to be anything personal about it, as one would expect from an Overlord," he concluded his brief report. "It did not concentrate on us, reach for us, or follow us as we left. Its intensity seemed to vary only with distance . . . perhaps inversely as distance squared—it might very well have been radiated from a center. While it was nothing like anything I ever felt before, I still think that it must be an Overlord—maybe a sort of Second-Stage Overlord, just as you and I are Second-Stage Lensmen. He is too strong for me now, just as they used to be too strong for us before we met you. By the same reasoning, however, I am pretty sure that if you can come over here, you and I together could figure out a way of taking him. How about it?"

"Mighty interesting, and I'd like to, but I'm right in the middle of a job," Kinnison replied, and went on to explain rapidly what he, as Bradlow Thyron, had done and what he still had to do. "As soon as I can get away I'll come over. In the meantime, fellow old snake, keep away from there. Do a flit—find something else to keep you amused until I can join you."

*

Worsel set out, and after a few days . . . or weeks—idle time means practically nothing to a Velantian—a sharply-Lensed thought drove in.

"Help! A Lensman calling help! Line this thought and come at speed to System—" The message ended as sharply as it had begun; in a flare of agony which, Worsel knew, meant that that Lensman, whoever he was, had died.

Since the thought, although broadcast, had come in strong and clear, Worsel knew that its sender had been close by. While the time had been very short indeed, he had been able to get a line of sorts. Into that line he whirled the *Velan's* sharp prow and along it she hurtled at the literally inconceivable pace of her absolute-maximum drive. As the Gray Lensman had often remarked, the Velantian superdreadnought had more legs than a centipede, and now she was using them all. In minutes, then, the scene of battle grew large upon her plates.

The Patrol ship, hopelessly out-classed, could last only seconds longer. Her screens were down; her very wall shield was dead. Red pockmarks sprang into being along her sides as the Boskonian needle-beamers wiped out her few remaining controls. Then, as the helplessly raging Worsel looked on, his brain seething with unutterable Velantian profanity, the enemy prepared to board—a course of action which, Worsel could see, was changed abruptly by the fact—and perhaps as well by the terrific velocity—of his own unswerving approach. The conquered Patrol cruiser disappeared in a blaze of detonating duodec; the conqueror devoted his every jet to the task of running away; strewing his path as he did so with sundry items of solid and explosive destruction. Such things, however, whether dirigible or not, whether inert or free, were old and simple stuff to the *Velan's* war-wise crew. Their spotters and detectors were full out, as was also a practically solid forefan of annihilating and disintegrating beams.

Thus none of the Boskonian's missiles touched the *Velan*, nor, with all his speed, could he escape. Few indeed were the ships of space able to step it, parsec for parsec, with Worsel's mighty craft, and this luckless pirate vessel was not one of them. Up and up the pursuer rushed; second by second the intervening distance lessened. Tractors shot out, locked on, and pulled briefly with all the force of their stupendous generators.

Briefly, but long enough. As Worsel had anticipated, that savage yank had, in the fraction of a second required for the Boskonian commander to recognize and to cut the tractors, been enough to bring the two inertialess war craft practically screen to screen.

"Primaries! Blast!" Worsel hurled the thought even before his tractors snapped. He was in no mood for a long-drawn-out engagement. He *might* be able to win with his secondaries, his needles, his tremendously powerful short-range stuff and his other ordinary offensive weapons, but he was taking no chances. Besides, the Boskonians might very well have primaries of their own by this time, and if they did his only chance was to use them first. His men knew what to do and would do it without further orders. A dozen or so of those hellishly irresistible projectors of sheer destruction lashed out as one.

One! Two! Three! The three courses of Boskonian defensive screen scarcely winked as each, locally overloaded, flared through the visible into the black and went down.

Crash! The stubborn fabric of the wall shield offered little more resistance before it, too, went down, exposing the bare metal of the Boskonian's hull—and, as is well known, any conceivable material substance simply vanishes, tracelessly, at the merest touch of such fields of force as those.

Driving projectors carved away and main batteries silenced, Worsel's needle-beamers proceeded systematically to riddle every control panel and every lifeboat, to make of the immense space rover a completely helpless hulk.

"Hold!" An observer flashed the thought. "Number Eight slip is empty—Number Eight lifeboat got away!"

"Damnation!" Worsel, at the head of his armed and armored storming party, as furiously eager as they to come to grips with the enemy, paused briefly. "Trace it—or can you?"

"I did. My tracers can hold it for fifteen minutes, perhaps twenty. No longer than twenty."

Worsel thought intensely. Which had first call, ship or lifeboat? The ship, he decided almost instantly. Its resources were vastly greater; most of its personnel were probably practically unharmed. Given any time at all, they might very well be able to jury-rig a primary, and that would be bad—very bad. Besides, there were more people here; and even if, as was distinctly possible, the Boskonian big shot had abandoned his vessel and his crew in an attempt to save his own life, Worsel had plenty of time.

"Hold that lifeboat," he instructed the observer. "Ten minutes is all we need here."

*

And it was. The Boskonians—barrel-bodied, blocky-limbed monstrosities resembling human beings about as much as they did the Velantians—wore armor, possessed hand-weapons of power, and fought viciously. They had even managed to rig a few semiportable projectors, but none of these were allowed a single blast. Spy-ray observers were alert, and needle-beam operators; hence the fighting was all at hand to hand, with hand-weapons only. For, while the Velantians to a man lusted to kill, they had had it drilled into them for twenty years that the search for information came first; the pleasure of killing, second.

Worsel himself went straight for the Boskonian captain, his pre-selected prey. That wight had a couple of guards with him, but they did not matter—needle-ray men took care of them. He also had a pair of heavy beam guns, which he held steadily on the Velantian. Worsel paused momentarily; then, finding that his screens were adequate, he slammed the control room door shut with a flick of his tail and launched himself, straight and level at his foe, with an acceleration of seven gravities. The captain tried to dodge but could not. The frightful impact did not kill him, but it hurt him, badly. Worsel, on the other hand, was scarcely jarred. Hard, tough, and durable, Velantians are accustomed from birth to knockings-about which would pulverize human bones.

Worsel batted the Boskonian's guns away with two terrific blows of an armored paw, noting as he did so that violent contact with a steel wall did not do their interior mechanisms a bit of good. Then, after cutting off both his enemy's screens and his own, he batted the Boskonian's helmet; at first experimentally, then with all his power. Unfortunately, however, it held. So did the thought-screen, and there were no external controls. That armor was good stuff!

Leaping to the ceiling, he blasted his whole mass straight down upon the breastplate, striking it so hard this time that he hurt his head. Still no use. He wedged himself between two heavy braces, flipped a loop of tail around the Boskonian's feet, and heaved. The armored form flew across the room, struck the heavy steel wall, bounced, and dropped. The bulges of the armor were flattened by the force of the collision, the wall was dented—but the thought-screen still held!

Worsel was running out of time, fast. He couldn't treat the thing very much rougher without killing him, if he wasn't dead already. He couldn't take him aboard; he *had* to cut that screen here and now! He could see how the armor was put together; but, armored as he was, he could not take it apart. And, since the whole ship was empty of air, he could not open his own.

Or could he? He could. He could breathe space long enough to do what had to be done. He cut off his air, loosened a plate enough to release four or five gnarled hands, and, paying no attention to his involuntarily laboring lungs, set furiously to work. He tore open the Boskonian's armor, snapped off his thought-screen. The creature was not quite dead yet—good! He didn't know a thing, though, nor did any member of his crew, except . . . yes, one man—a big shot—had got away. Who or what, was he?

*

"Tell me!" Worsel demanded, with the full power of mind and Lens, even while he was exploring with all his skill and speed. "TELL ME!"

But the Boskonian was dying fast. The ungentle treatment, and now the lack of air, were taking toll. His patterns were disintegrating by the second, faster and faster. Meaningless blurs, which, under Worsel's vicious probing, condensed into something which seemed to be a Lens.

A *Lensman?* Impossible—starkly unthinkable! But jet back—hadn't Kim intimated a while back that there might be such things as Black Lensmen?

But Worsel himself wasn't feeling so good. He was only half conscious. Red, black, and purple spots were dancing in front of every one of his eyes. He sealed his suit, turned on his air, gasped, and staggered. Two of the nearest Velantians, all of whom had, of course, been *en rapport* with him throughout, came rushing to his aid; arriving just as he recovered full control.

"Back to the *Velan*, everybody!" he ordered. "No time for any more fun—we've got to get that lifeboat!" Then, as soon as he had been obeyed: "Bomb that hulk . . . good. Flit!"

Overtaking the lifeboat did not take long. Spearing it with a tractor and yanking it alongside required only seconds. For all his haste, Worsel found in it only something that looked as though it once might have been a Delgonian Lensman. It had blown itself apart with a grenade. Because of its reptilian tenacity of life, however, it was not quite dead; its Lens still showed an occasional flicker of light and its shattered mind was not yet entirely devoid of patterns. Worsel studied that mind until all trace of life had vanished, then again reported to the Co-ordinator.

" . . . so you see I guessed wrong. The Lens was too dim to read, but he must have been a Black Lensman. The only readable thought in his mind was an extremely fuzzy one of the planet Lyrane IX. I hate to have hashed the job up so—especially since I had one chance in two of guessing right."

"Well, no use in squawking now." Kinnison paused in thought. "Besides, he could have done it anyway, and would have. You haven't done so badly, at that. You found a Black Lensman who is not a Kalonian, and you've got confirmation of Boskonian interest in Lyrane IX. What more do you want? Stick around fairly close to the Hell Hole, Slim, and as soon as I can make it, I'll join you there."

XX.

"Boys, take her upstairs," Kinnison-Thyron ordered, and the tremendous raider—actually the *Dauntless* in disguise—floated serenely upward to a station immediately astern of the vice admiral's flagship. All three courses of multi-ply defensive screen were out, as were full-coverage spy-ray blocks and thought-screens.

As the fleet blasted in tight formation for Kalonia III, Vice Admiral Mendonai tested the *Dauntless'* defenses thoroughly, and found them bottle-tight. No intrusion was possible. The only open channel was that one plate-to-plate, the other end of which was so villainously fogged that nothing could be seen except Bradlow Thyron's face. Convinced at last of that fact, Mendonai sat back and seethed quietly, his pervasive Kalonian blueness pointing up his grim and vicious mood.

He had never, in all his long life, been insulted so outrageously. Was there anything—*anything!*—he could do about it? There was not. Thyron, personally, he could not touch—yet—and the fact that the outlaw had so brazenly and so nonchalantly placed his vessel in the exact center of the Boskonian fleet made it pellucidly clear to any Boskonian mind that he had nothing whatever to fear from that fleet.

Wherefore the Kalonian seethed, and his minions stepped ever more softly and followed with ever-increasing punctilio the rigid Boskonian code. For the grapevine carries news swiftly; by this time the whole fleet knew that His Nibs had been taking a God-awful kicking around, and that the first guy who gave him an excuse to blow off steam would be lucky if he only got boiled in oil.

As the fleet spread out for inert maneuvering above the Kalonian stratosphere, Kinnison turned again to the young Lensman.

"One last word, Frank. I am as sure as I can be that I am fully covered—a lot of smart people worked on this problem. Nevertheless, something may happen, so I will send you the data as fast as I get it. Remember what I told you before—if I get the dope we need, I'm expendable and it'll be your job to get it back to Base. No heroics. Is that clear?"

"Yes, sir." The young Lensman gulped. "I hope, though, that it doesn't—"

"So do I," Kinnison grinned as he climbed into his highly special dureum armor, "and the chances are a million to one that it won't. That's why I'm going down there."

In their respective speedsters Kinnison and Mendonai made the long drop to the ground, and side by side they went into the office of Black Lensman Melasnikov. That worthy, too, wore heavy armor; but he did not have a mechanical thought-screen. Arrogantly conscious of his tremendous power of mind, what did any Black Lensman need of mechanical shields? Thyron, of course, did; a fact of which Melasnikov became instantly aware.

"Release your screen," he directed, brusquely.

"Not yet, pal—don't be so hasty," Thyron advised. "There're some things about this here hookup that I don't exactly like. We got quite a bit of talking to do before I open up."

"No talk, worm. Talk, especially your talk, is entirely meaningless. From you I want, and will have, the truth, and not talk. CUT THOSE SCREENS!"

*

And lovely Kathryn, in her speedster not too far away, straightened up and sent out a call.

"Kit . . . Kay . . . Cam . . . Con—are you free?" They were, for the moment. "Stand by, please, all of you. I'm pretty sure something is going to happen. Dad can handle this Melasnikov easily enough, if none of the higher-ups step in, but they probably will. Their Lensmen are probably important enough to rate protection. Check?"

"Check."

"So, as soon as Dad begins to get the best of the argument, the protector will step in," Kathryn continued, "and whether I can handle him alone or not depends on how high a higher-up they send in. So I'd like to have you all stand by for a minute or two, just in case."

How different was Kathryn's attitude now than it had been in the hyperspatial tube! And how well for Civilization that it was!

"Hold it, kids. I've got a thought," Kit suggested. "We've never done any teamwork since you became able to handle heavy stuff, and we'll have to get in some practice before the big blow-off. What say we link up now, on this?"

"Oh, yes!" "Let's do!" "Take over, Kit!" Three approvals came as one, and:

"QX," came Kathryn's less enthusiastic concurrence, a moment later. Naturally enough, she would rather do it alone if she could; but she had to admit that her brother's plan was the better.

Kit laid out the matrix and the four girls came in. There was a brief moment of snuggling and fitting; then each of the Five caught his breath in awe. This was new—brand new. Each had thought himself complete and full; each had supposed that much practice and at least some give-and-take would be necessary before they could work efficiently as a group. But this! This was the supposedly unattainable—perfection itself! This was UNITY—full; round; complete. No practice was or ever would be necessary. Not one micro-microsecond of doubt or of uncertainty would or ever could exist. This was the UNIT, a thing for which there are no words in any written or spoken language; a thing theretofore undreamed-of save as a purely theoretical concept in an unthinkably ancient, four-ply Arisian brain.

"U.m.n.g.n.k," Kit swallowed a lump as big as his fist before he could think. "This, kids, is really some—"

"Ah, children, you have done it." Mentor's thought rolled smoothly in. "You now understand why I could not attempt to describe the Unit to any one of you. This is the culminating moment of my life—of our lives, we may now say. For the first time in more years than you can understand, we are at last sure that our lives have not been lived in vain. But attend—that for which you are waiting will soon be here."

"What is it?" "Who?" "Tell us how to—"

"We cannot." Four separate Arisians smiled as one—a wash of ineffable blessing and benediction suffused the Five. "We, who made the Unit possible, are almost completely ignorant of the details of its higher functions. But that it will need no help from our lesser minds is certain; it is the most powerful and the most nearly perfect creation this Universe has ever seen."

*

The Arisians vanished; and, even before Kimball Kinnison had released his screen, a cryptic, utterly untraceable and all-pervasive foreign thought came in.

To aid the Black Lensman? To study this disturbing new element? Or merely to observe? Or what? The only certainty was that that thought was coldly, clearly, and highly inimical to all Civilization.

Again everything happened at once. Karen's impenetrable block flared into being—not instantly, but instantaneously. Constance assembled and hurled, in the same lack of time, a mental bolt of whose size and power she had never dreamed herself capable. Camilla, the detector-scanner, synchronized herself with the attacking thought and steered. And Kathryn and Kit, with all the force, all the will, and all the drive of human heredity, got behind it and pushed.

Nor was this, any of it, conscious individual effort. The children of the Lens were not now five, but one. This was the Unit at work; doing its first job. It is literally impossible to describe what happened; but each of the Five knew that one would-be Protector, wherever he had been in space or whenever in time, would never think again. Seconds passed. The Unit held tense, awaiting the riposte. No riposte came.

"Fine work, kids!" Kit broke the linkage and each girl felt hard, brotherly pats on her back. "That's all there is to this one, I guess—must have been only one guard on duty. You're good eggs, and I like you. *How* we can operate now!"

"But it was too easy, Kit!" Kathryn protested. "Too easy by far for it to have been an Eddorian. We aren't that good. Why, I could have handled him alone . . . I think," she added, hastily, as she realized that she, although an essential part of the Unit, had as yet no real understanding of what that Unit really was.

"You *hope*, you mean!" Constance jeered. "If that bolt was as big and as hot as I'm afraid it was, anything it hit would have looked easy. Why didn't you slow us down, Kit? You're supposed to be the Big Brain, you know. As it was, we haven't the faintest idea of what happened. Who was he, anyway?"

"Didn't have time," Kit grinned. "Everything got out of hand. All of us were sort of inebriated by the exuberance of our own enthusiasm, I guess. Now that we know what our speed is, though, we can slow down next time—if we want to. As for your last question, Con, you're asking the wrong guy. Was it an Eddorian, Cam, or not?"

"What difference does it make?" Karen asked.

"On the practical side, none. For the completion of the picture, maybe a lot. Come in, Cam."

"It was not an Eddorian," Camilla decided. "It was not of Arisian, or even near-Arisian, grade. Sorry to say it, Kit, but it was another member of that high-thinking race that you've already got down on Page One of your little black book."

"I thought it might be. The missing link between Kalonia and Eddore. Credits to millos it's that dopey planet Ploor that Mentor was yowling about."

"Let's link up and let the Unit find it," Constance suggested, brightly. "That'd be fun."

"Act your age, baby," Kit advised. "Ploor is taboo—you know that as well as I do. Mentor told us all not to try to investigate it—that we'd learn of it in time, so we probably will. I told him a while back that I was going to hunt it up myself, and he told me that if I did he'd tie both my legs around my neck in a lovers' knot, or words to that effect. Sometimes I'd like to half-brain the old buzzard, but everything he has said so far has dead-centered the beam. We'll just have to take it, and try to like it."

*

Kinnison was eminently willing to cut his thought-screen, since he could not work through it to do what had to be done here. Nor was he over-confident. He knew that he could handle the Black Lensman—*any* Black Lensman—but he also knew enough of mental phenomena in general and of Lensmanship in particular to realize that Melasnikov might very well have within call reserves about whom he, Kinnison, could know nothing. He knew that he had lied outrageously to young Frank in regard to the odds applicable to this enterprise; that instead of a million to one, the actuality was one to one, or even less.

Nevertheless, he was well content. He had neither lied nor exaggerated in saying that he himself was expendable. That was why Frank and the *Dauntless* were upstairs now. Getting the dope and getting it back to Base were what mattered. Nothing else did.

He was coldly certain that he could get all the information that Melasnikov had, once he had engaged the Kalonian Lensman mind to mind. No Boskonian power or thing, he was convinced, could treat him rough enough to kill him fast enough to keep him from doing that. And he could and would shoot the stuff along to Frank as fast as he got it. And he stood an even—almost even, anyway—chance of getting away afterward. If he could, QX. If he couldn't . . . well, that would have to be QX, too.

Kinnison flipped his switch and there ensued a conflict of wills that made the subether boil. The Kalonian was one of the strongest, hardest, and ablest individuals of his hellishly capable race; and the fact that he believed implicitly in his own complete invulnerability operated to double and to quadruple his naturally tremendous strength.

On the other hand, Kimball Kinnison was a Second-Stage Lensman of the Galactic Patrol.

Back and back, then, inch by inch and foot by foot, the Black Lensman's defensive zone was forced; back to and down into his own mind. And there, appallingly enough, Kinnison found almost nothing of value.

No knowledge of the higher reaches of the Boskonian organization; no hint that any real organization of Black Lensmen existed; only the peculiarly disturbing fact that he had picked up his Lens on Lyrane IX. And "picked up" was literal. He had not seen, nor heard, nor had any dealings of any kind with anyone while he was there.

Since both armored figures stood motionless, no sign of the tremendous actuality of their mental battle was evident. Thus the Boskonians were not surprised to hear their Black Lensman speak.

"Very well, Thyron, you have passed this preliminary examination. I know all that I now need to know. I will accompany you to your vessel, to complete my investigation there. Lead the way."

Kinnison did so, and as the speedster came to rest inside the *Dauntless* the Black Lensman addressed Vice Admiral Mendonai via plate.

"I am taking Bradlow Thyron and his ship to the space yards on Four, where a really comprehensive study of it can be made. Return to and complete your original assignment."

"I abase myself, Your Supremacy, but . . . but I . . . I *discovered* that ship!" Mendonai protested.

"Granted," the Black Lensman sneered. "You will be given full credit in the report for what you have done. The fact of discovery, however, does not excuse your present conduct. Go—and consider yourself fortunate that, because of that service, I forbear from disciplining you for your intolerable insubordination."

"I abase myself, Your Supremacy. I go." He really did abase himself, this time, and the fleet disappeared.

*

Then, the mighty *Dauntless* safely away from Kalonia and on her course to rendezvous with the *Velan*, Kinnison again went over his captive's mind; line by line and almost cell by cell. It was still the same. It was still Lyrane IX and it still didn't make any kind of sense. Since Boskonians were certainly not supermen, and hence could not possibly have developed their own Lenses, it followed that they must have obtained them from the Boskonian counterpart of Arisia. Hence, Lyrane IX must be IT—a conclusion which was certainly fallacious—ridiculous—preposterous—utterly untenable. Lyrane IX never had been, was not, and never would be the home of any Boskonian super-race. Nevertheless, it was a definite fact that Melasnikov had got his Lens there. Also, if he had ever had any special training, such as any Lensman must have had, he didn't have any memory of it. Nor did he carry any scars of surgery. What a hash! How could *anybody* make any sense out of such a mess as that?

Ever-watchful Kathryn, eyes narrowed now in concentration, could have told him, but she did not. Her visualization was beginning to clear up. Lyrane was out. So was Ploor. The Lenses originated on Eddore; that was certain. The fact that their training was subconscious weakened the Black Lensmen in precisely the characteristics requisite for ultimate strength—although probably neither the Eddorians nor the Ploorans, with their warped, Boskonian sense of values, realized it. The Black Lensmen would never constitute a serious problem. QX.

The time of rendezvous approached. Kinnison, having attended to the unpleasant but necessary job of resolving Melasnikov into his component atoms, turned to his Lensman-aide.

"Hold everything, Frank, until I get back. This won't take long."

Nor did it, although the outcome was not at all what the Gray Lensman had expected.

Kinnison and Worsel, in an inert speedster, crossed the Hell Hole's barrier web at a speed of only miles per hour, and then slowed down. The ship was backing in on her brakes, with everything set to hurl her forward under full drive should either Lensman flick a finger. Kinnison could feel nothing, even though, being *en rapport* with Worsel, he knew that his friend was soon suffering intensely.

"Let's flit," the Gray Lensman suggested, and threw on the drive. "I probed my limit, and couldn't touch or feel a thing. Had enough, didn't you?"

"More than enough—I couldn't have taken much more."

Each boarded his ship; and as the *Dauntless* and the *Velan* tore through space toward far Lyrane, Kinnison paced his room, scowling in black abstraction. Nor would a mind reader have found his thoughts either cogent or informative.

"Lyrane IX . . . LYRANE IX . . . Lyrane IX . . . LYRANE IX . . . and something that I can't even feel or perceive, but that kills anybody and everybody else . . . KLONO'S tungsten TEETH and CURVING CARBALLOY CLAWS!!!"

*

XXI.

Helen's story was short and bitter. Human or near-human Boskonians came to Lyrane II and spread insidious propaganda all over the planet. Lyranian matriarchy should abandon its policy of isolationism. Matriarchs were the highest type of life. Matriarchy was the most perfect of all existing forms of government—why keep on confining it to one small planet, when it should by right be ruling the entire Galaxy? The way things were, there was only one Elder Person; all other Lyranians, even though better qualified than the then incumbent, were nothing—and so on. Whereas, if things were as they should be, each individual Lyranian person could be and would be the Elder Person of a planet at least, and perhaps of an entire solar system—and so on. And the visitors, who, they insisted, were no more males than the Lyranian persons were females, would teach them. They would be amazed at how easily, under Boskonian guidance, this program could be put into effect.

Helen fought the intruders with every jet she had. She despised the males of her own race; she detested those of all others. Believing that hers was the only existing matriarchal race, especially since neither Kinnison nor the Boskonians seemed to know of any other, she was sure that any prolonged contact with other cultures would result, not in the triumph of matriarchy, but in its fall. She not only voiced these beliefs as she held them—violently—but also acted upon them in the same fashion.

Because of the ingrained matriarchally conservative habit of Lyranian thought, particularly among the older persons, Helen found it comparatively easy to stamp out the visible manifestations; and, being in no sense a sophisticate, she thought that the whole matter was settled. Instead, she merely drove the movement underground, where it grew tremendously. The young, of course, rebellious as always against the hide-bound, mossbacked, and reactionary older generation, joined the subterranean New Deal in droves. Nor was the older generation solid. In fact, it was riddled by the defection of many thousands who could not expect to attain any outstanding place in the world as it was and who believed that the Boskonians' glittering forecasts would come true.

Disaffection spread, then, rapidly and unobserved; culminating in the carefully-planned uprising which made Helen an Ex-Chief Person and put her into the tower room to await a farcical trial and death.

"I see." Clarrissa caught her lower lip between her teeth. "Very unfunny. I noticed that you didn't mention or think of any of your persons as ringleaders . . . peculiar that you couldn't catch them, with your telepathy . . . no, natural enough, at that . . . but there's one I want very much to get hold of. Don't know whether she was really a leader, or not, but she was mixed up in some way with a Boskonian Lensman. I never did know her name. She was the wom . . . the person who managed your airport here when Kim and I were—"

"Cleonie? Why, I never thought . . . but it might have, at that . . . yes, as I look back—"

"Yes, hindsight is a lot more accurate than foresight," the Red Lensman grinned. "I've noticed that myself, lots of times."

"It did! It was a leader!" Helen declared, furiously. "I shall have its life, too, the jealous cat—the blood-sucking, back-biting louse!"

"She's all of that, in more ways than you know," Clarrissa agreed, grimly, and spread in the Lyranian's mind the story of Eddie the derelict. "So you see that Cleonie has got to be our starting-point. Have you any idea of where we can find her?"

"I haven't seen or heard anything of Cleonie lately." Helen paused in thought. "If, though, as I am now practically certain, it was one of the prime movers behind this brainless brat Ladora, it wouldn't dare leave the planet for very long at a time. As to how to find it, I don't quite know. Anybody would be apt to shoot me on sight. Would you dare fly this funny plane of yours down close to a few of our cities?"

"Certainly. I don't know of anything around here that my screens and fields can't stop. Why?"

"Because I know of several places where Cleonie might be, and if I can get fairly close to them, I can find it in spite of anything it can do to hide itself from me. But I don't want to get you into too much trouble, and I don't want to get killed myself, either, now that you have rescued me—at least, until after I have killed Cleonie and Ladora."

"QX. What are we waiting for? Which way, Helen?"

*

"Back to the city first, for several reasons. Cleonie probably is not there, but we must make sure. Also, I want my guns—"

"Guns? No. DeLameters are better. I have several spares." In one fleeting mental contact Clarrissa taught the Lyranian all there was to know about DeLameters. And that feat impressed Helen even more than did the nature and power of the weapon.

"What a mind!" she exclaimed. "You didn't have any such equipment as that, the last time I saw you. Or were you . . . no, you weren't hiding it."

"You're right; I have developed considerably since then. But about guns—what do you want of one?"

"To kill that nitwit Ladora on sight, and that snake Cleonie, too, as soon as you get done with it."

"But why guns? Why not the mental force you always used?"

"Except by surprise, I couldn't," Helen admitted, frankly. "All adult persons are of practically equal mental strength. But speaking of strength, I marvel that a craft as small as this should be able to ward off the attack of one of those tremendous Boskonian ships of space."

"But she *can't*! What made you think she could?"

"Your own statement—or were you thinking of purely Lyranian dangers, not realizing that Ladora, of course, called Cleonie as soon as you showed your teeth, and that Cleonie as surely called the Lensman or some other Boskonian? And that they must have ships of war not too far away?"

"Heavens, no! It never occurred to me!"

Clarrissa thought briefly. It wouldn't do any good to call Kim. Both the *Dauntless* and the *Velan* were coming, as fast as they could come, but it would be a day or so yet before they arrived. Besides, he would tell her to lay off, which was exactly what she was not going to do. She turned her thought back to the matriarch.

"Two of our best ships are coming, and I hope they get here first. In the meantime, we'll just have to work fast and keep our detectors full out. Anyway, Cleonie won't know that I'm looking for her—I haven't even mentioned her to anyone except you."

"No?" pessimistically. "Cleonie knows that *I* am looking for it, and since it knows by now that I am with you, it would think that both of us were hunting it even if we weren't. But we are nearly close enough now; I must concentrate. Fly around quite low over the city, please."

"QX. I'll tune in with you, too. 'Two heads,' you know." Clarrissa learned Cleonie's pattern, tuned to it, and combed the city while Helen was getting ready.

"She isn't here, unless she's behind one of those thought-screens," the Red Lensman remarked. "Can you tell?"

"Thought-screens! The Boskonians had a few of them, but none of us ever did. How can you find them? Where are they?"

"One there—two over there. They stick out like big black spots on a white screen. Can't you see them? I supposed that your scanners were the same as mine, but apparently they aren't. Take a quick peek at them with the spy—you work it like so. If they've got spy-ray blocks up, too, we'll have to go down there and blast."

"Politicians only," Helen reported, after a moment's manipulation of the suddenly familiar instrument. "They need killing, of course, on general principles, but perhaps we shouldn't take time for that now. The next place to look is a few degrees east of north of here."

*

Cleonie was not, however, in that city. Nor in the next, nor the next. But the speedster's detector screens remained blank and the two allies, so much alike physically, so different mentally, continued their hunt. There was opposition, of course—all that the planet afforded—but Clarrissa's second-stage mind took care of the few items of offense which her speedster's defenses could not handle.

Finally two things happened almost at once. Clarrissa found Cleonie, and Helen saw a dim and fuzzy white spot upon the lower left-hand corner of the detector plate.

"Can't be ours," the Red Lensman decided instantly. "Almost exactly the wrong direction. Boskonians. Ten minutes—twelve at most—before we have to flit. Time enough—I hope—if we work fast."

She shot downward, going inert and matching intrinsics at a lack of altitude which would have been suicidal for any ordinary pilot. She rammed her beryllium-bronze torpedo through the first-floor wall of a forbidding, almost windowless building—its many stories of massive construction, she knew, would help no end against the heavy stuff so sure to come. Then, while every hitherto-hidden offensive arm of the Boskone-coached Lyranians converged, screaming through the air and crashing and clanking along the city's streets, Clarrissa probed and probed and probed. Cleonie had locked herself into a veritable dungeon cell in the deepest subbasement of the structure. She was wearing a thought-screen, too, but she had been releasing it, for an instant at a time, to see what was going on. One of those instants was enough—that screen would never work again. She had been prepared to kill herself at need; but her full-charged weapons emptied themselves futilely against a massive lock and she threw her vial of poison across the corridor and into an empty cell.

So far, so good; but how to get her out of there? Physical approach was out of the question. There must be somebody around, somewhere, with keys, or hacksaws, or sledge-hammers, or something. Ha—oxyacetylene torches! Very much against their wills, two Lyranian mechanics trundled a dolly along a corridor, into an elevator. The elevator went down four levels. The artisans began to burn away a barrier of thick steel bars.

By this time the whole building was rocking to the detonation of high explosives. Much more of that kind of stuff and she would be trapped by the sheer mass of the rubble. She was handling six jackass-stubborn people already and that Boskonian warship was coming fast; she did not quite know whether she was going to get away with this or not.

But somehow, from the unplumbed and unplumbable depths which made her what she so uniquely was, the Red Lensman drew more and ever more power. Kinnison, who had once made heavy going of handling two-and-a-fraction Lensmen, guessed, but never did learn from her, what his beloved wife really did that day.

Even Helen, only a few feet away, could not understand what was happening. Left parsecs behind long since, the Lyranian could not help in any particular, but could only stand and wonder. She knew that this queerly powerful Lens-bearing Earth-person—white-faced, sweating, strung to the very snapping-point as she sat motionless at her board—was exerting some terrible, some tremendous force. She knew that the heaviest of the circling bombers sheered away and crashed. She knew that certain mobile projectors, a few blocks away, did not come any closer. She knew that Cleonie, against every iota of her mulish Lyranian will, was coming toward the speedster. She knew that many persons, who wished intensely to bar Cleonie's progress or to shoot her down, were physically unable to act. She had no faint idea, however, of how such work could possibly be done.

*

Cleonie came aboard and Clarrissa snapped out of her trance. The speedster nudged and blasted its way out of the wrecked stronghold, then tore a hole through protesting air into open space. Clarrissa shook her head, wiped her face, studied a tiny double dot in the corner of the plate opposite the one now showing clearly the Boskonian warship, and set her controls.

"We'll make it—I think," she announced. "Even though we're indetectable, they, of course, know our line, and they're so much faster that they'll be able to find us, even on their visuals, before long. On the other hand, they must be detecting our ships now, and my guess is that they won't dare follow us long enough to do us any harm. Keep an eye on things, Helen, while I find out what Cleonie really knows. And while I think of it, what's your real name? It isn't polite to keep on calling you by a name that you never even heard of until you met us."

"Helen," the Lyranian made surprising answer. "I liked it, so I adopted it—officially."

"Oh. That's a compliment, really, to both Kim and me. Thanks."

The Red Lensman then turned her attention to her captive, and as mind fitted itself precisely to mind her eyes began to gleam in gratified delight. Cleonie was a real find; this seemingly unimportant Lyranian knew a lot—an immense lot—about things that no adherent of the Patrol had ever heard before. And she, Clarrissa Kinnison, would be the first of all the Gray Lensmen to learn of them! Therefore, taking her time now, she allowed every detail of the queer but fascinating picture-story to imprint itself upon her mind.

*

And Karen and Camilla, together in Tregonsee's ship, glanced at each other and exchanged flashing thoughts. Should they interfere? They hadn't had to so far, but it began to look as though they would have to, now—it would wreck their mother's mind, if she could understand. She probably could not understand it, any more than Cleonie could—but even if she could, she had so much more inherent stability, even than Dad, that she might be able to take it, at that. Nor would she ever leak, even to Dad—and Dad, bless his tremendous boots, was not the type to pry. Maybe, though, just to be on the safe side, it would be better to screen the stuff, and to edit, if necessary, anything about Eddore. The two girls synchronized their minds all imperceptibly with their mother's and Helen's, and learned.

*

The time was in the unthinkably distant past; the location was unthinkably remote in space. A huge planet circled slowly about a cooling sun. Its atmosphere was not air; its liquid was not water. Both were noxious; composed in large part of compounds even yet unknown to man.

Yet life was there; a race which was even then ancient. Not sexual, this race. Not androgynous, nor hermaphroditic, but absolutely sexless. Except for the many who died by physical or by mental violence, its members lived endlessly. After many hundreds of thousands of years each being, having reached his capacity to live and to learn, divided into two individuals; each of which, although possessing in *toto* the parents' memories, knowledges, skills, and powers, had also a renewed and increased capacity.

And, since life was, there had been competition. Competition for power. Knowledge was desirable only insofar as it contributed to power. Power for the individual—the group—the city. Wars raged—*what* wars!—and internecine strifes which lasted while planets came into being, grew old, and died. And finally, to the few survivors, there came peace. Since they could not kill each other, they combined their powers and hurled them outward—together they would dominate and rule solar systems—regions—the Galaxy itself—the entire macrocosmic Universe.

Amorphous, amoeboid, each could assume at will any imaginable form, could call into being members to handle any possible tool. Nevertheless, as time went on they used their bodies less and less. More and more they used their minds, to bring across gulfs of space and to enslave other races, to labor under their direction. By nature and by choice they were bound to their own planet; few indeed were the planets upon which their race could possibly live. Also, it was easier to rejuvenate their own world, or to move it to a younger sun, than to enforce and to supervise the myriads of man-hours of slave labor necessary to rebuild any planet to their needs. Thus, then, they lived and ruled by proxy an ever-increasing number of worlds.

Although they had long since learned that their asexuality was practically unique, that bisexual life dominated the universe, this knowledge served only to stiffen their determination to rule, and finally to change to their own better standards, that universe. They were still seeking a better proxy race; the more nearly asexual a race, the better. One race, the denizens of a planet of a variable sun, approached that idea closely. So did the Kalonians, whose women had only one function in life—the production of men.

Now these creatures had learned of the matriarchs of Lyrane. That they were physically females meant nothing; to the Eddorians one sex was just as good—or as bad—as the other. The Lyranians were strong; not tainted by the weaknesses which seemed to characterize all races believing in even near-equality of the sexes. Lyranian science had been trying for centuries to do away with the necessity for males; in a few more generations, with some help, that goal could be achieved and the perfect proxy race would have been developed.

It is not to be supposed that this story was obtained in such straight-forward fashion as it is presented here. It was dim, murky, confused. Cleonie never had understood it. Clarrissa understood it better, but less accurately; for in the version the Red Lensman received, one minor change was made—in it the Ploorans and the Eddorians were one and the same race! She understood, however, that that actually unnamed and to her unknown race was the highest of Boskone, and the place of the Kalonians in the Boskonian scheme was plain enough.

"I am giving you this story," the Kalonian Lensman told Cleonie coldly, "not of my own free will but because I must. I hate you as much as you hate me. What I would like to do to you, you may imagine. Nevertheless, so that your race may have its chance, I am to take you on a trip and, if possible, make a Lensman out of you. Come with me." And, urged by her jealousy of Helen, her seething ambition, and probably, if the truth were to be known, by an Eddorian mind, Cleonie went.

There is no need to dwell at length upon the horrors, the atrocities, of that trip; of which the matter of Eddie the meteor miner was only a very minor episode. It will suffice to say that Cleonie was very good Boskonian material; that she learned fast and passed all tests successfully.

"That's all," the Black Lensman informed her then, "and I'm glad to see the last of you. You'll get a message when to hop over to Nine and pick up your Lens. Flit—and I hope that the first Gray Lensman you meet will ram his Lens down your throat and turn you inside out."

"The same to you, brother, and many of them," Cleonie sneered. "Or, better, when my race supplants yours as Proxies of Power, I shall give myself the pleasure of doing just that to you."

*

"Clarissa! Clarissa! Pay attention, please!" The Red Lensman came to herself with a start—Helen had been thinking at her, with increasing power, for seconds. The *Velan's* blunt nose filled half the plate.

In minutes, then Clarissa and her party were in Kinnison's private quarters in the *Dauntless*. There had been warm mental greetings; physical demonstrations would come later. Worsel broke in.

"Excuse it, Kim, but seconds count. Better we split, don't you think? You find out what the score around here is, from Clarissa, and take steps, and I'll chase that Boskonian. He's flitting—fast."

"QX, Slim," and the *Velan* disappeared.

"You remember Helen, of course, Kim." Kinnison bent his head, flipping a quick grin at his wife, who had spoken aloud. The Lyranian, trying to unbend, half-offered her hand, but when he did not take it she withdrew it as enthusiastically as she had twenty years before. "And this is Cleonie, the . . . the wench I've been telling you about. You knew her before."

"Yeah. She hasn't changed much—still as unbarbered a mess as ever. If you've got what you want, Chris, we'd better—"

"Kimball Kinnison, I demand Cleonie's life!" came Helen's vibrant thought. She had snatched one of Clarissa's DeLameters and was swinging it into line when she was caught and held as though in a vise.

"Sorry, Toots," the Gray Lensman's thought was more than a little grim. "Nice little girls don't play so rough. 'Scuse me, Chris, for dipping into your dish. Take over."

"Do you really mean that, Kim?"

"Yes. It's your meat—slice it as thick or as thin as you please."

"Even to letting her go?"

"Check. What else could you do? In a lifeboat—I'll even show the jade how to run it."

"Oh, Kim—"

"Quartermaster! Kinnison. Please check Number Twelve lifeboat and break it out. I am loaning it to Cleonie of Lyrane II."

XXII.

Kit had decided long since that it was his job to scout the planet Eddore. His alone. He had told several people that he was en route there, and in a sense he had been, but he was not hurrying. Once he started *that* job, he knew that he would have to see it through with absolutely undisturbed attention, and there had been altogether too many other

1002

things popping up. Now, however, his visualization showed a couple of weeks of free time, and that would be enough. He wasn't sure whether he was grown-up enough yet to do a man's job of work or not, and Mentor wouldn't tell him. This was the best way to find out. If so, QX. If not, he would back off, wait, and try again later.

The kids had wanted to go along, of course.

"Come on, Kit, don't be a pig!" Constance started what developed into the last violent argument of their long lives. "Let's gang up on it—think what a grand work-out that would be for the Unit!"

"Uh-uh, Con. Sorry, but it isn't in the cards, any more than it was the last time we discussed it," he began, reasonably enough.

"We didn't agree to it then," Kay cut in, stormily, "and I for one am not going to agree to it now. You don't have to do it today. In fact, later on would be better. Anyway, Kit, I'm telling you right now that if you go in, we all go, as individuals if not as the Unit."

"Act your age, Kay," he advised. "Get conscious. This is one of the two places in the Universe that can't be worked from a distance, and by the time you could get here I'll have the job done. So what difference does it make whether you agree or not? I'm going in now and I'm going in alone. Pick *that* one out of your pearly teeth!"

That stopped Karen, cold—they all knew that even she would not endanger the enterprise by staging a useless demonstration against Eddore's defensive screens—but there were other arguments. Later, he was to come to see that his sisters had some right upon their side, but he could not see it then. None of their ideas would hold air, he declared, and his temper wore thinner and thinner.

"No, Cam—NO! You know as well as I do that we can't all be spared at once, either now or at any time in the near-enough future. Kay's full of pickles, and you all know it. Right now is the best time I'll ever have."

"Seal it, Kat—you *can't* be that dumb! Taking the Unit in would blow things wide open. There isn't a chance that I can get in, even alone, without touching *something* off. I, alone, won't be giving too much away, but the Unit would be a flare-lit tip-off and all hell would be out for noon. Or are you actually nitwitted enough to think that, all Arisia to the contrary, we are ready for the grand showdown?

"Hold it, all of you! Pipe down!" he snorted, finally. "Have I got to bash in your skulls to make you understand that I can't co-ordinate an attack against something without even the foggiest idea of what its actual physical setup is? Use your brains, kids—*please* use your brains!"

He finally won them over, even Karen; and while his speedster covered the last leg of the flight he completed his analysis.

He had all the information he could get—in fact, all that was available—and it was pitifully meager and confusingly contradictory in detail. He knew the Arisians, each of them, personally; and had studied, jointly and severally, the Arisian visualizations of the ultimate foe. He knew the Lyranian impression of the Plooran version of the story of Eddore. Ploor! Merely a name. A symbol which Mentor had always kept rigorously apart from any Boskonian actuality. Ploor *must* be the missing link between Kalonia and Eddore. And he knew practically everything about it except the two really important facts—whether or not it really was that link, and where, within eleven thousand million parsecs, it was in space!

He and his sisters had done their best. So had many librarians; who had found, not at all to his surprise, that no scrap of information or conjecture concerning Eddore or the Eddorians was to be found in any library, however comprehensive or exclusive.

Thus he had guesses, hypotheses, theories, and visualizations galore; but none of them agreed and not one of them was convincing. He had no real facts whatever. Mentor had informed him, equally enough, that such a state of affairs was inevitable because of the known power of the Eddorian mind. That state, however, did not make Kit Kinnison any too happy as he approached dread and dreaded Eddore. He was in altogether too much of a dither as to what, actually, to expect.

As he neared the boundary of the star-cluster within which Eddore lay, he cut his velocity to a crawl. An outer screen, he knew, surrounded the whole cluster. How many intermediate protective layers existed, where they were, or what they were like, nobody knew. That information was only a small part of what he had to have.

His far-flung detector web, at practically zero power, touched the barrier without giving alarm and stopped. His speedster stopped. Everything stopped.

Christopher Kinnison, the matrix and the key element of the Unit, had tools and equipment about which even Mentor of Arisia knew nothing in detail; about which, it was hoped and believed, the Eddorians were completely in ignorance. He reached deep into the storehouse toolbox of his mind, arranged his selections in order, and went to work.

He built up his detector web, one infinitesimal increment at a time, until he could just perceive the structure of the barrier. He made no attempt to analyze it, knowing that any fabric or structure solid enough to perform such an operation would certainly touch off an alarm. Analysis could come later, after he had found out whether the generator of this outer screen was a machine or a living brain.

He felt his way along the barrier—slowly—carefully. He completely outlined one section, studying the fashion in which the joints were made and how it must be supported and operated. With the utmost nicety of which he was capable he synchronized a probe with the almost impossibly complex structure of the thing and slid it along a feeder beam into the generator station. A mechanism—they didn't waste live Eddorians, then, any more than the Arisians did, on outer defenses. QX.

A precisely-tuned blanket surrounded his speedster—a blanket which merged imperceptibly into, and in effect became an integral part of, the barrier itself. The blanket thinned over half of the speedster. The speedster crept forward. The barrier—unchanged, unaffected—was *behind* the speedster. Man and vessel were through!

Kit breathed deeply in relief and rested. This didn't prove much, of course. Nadreck had done practically the same thing in getting Kandron—except that the Palainian would never be able to analyze or to synthesize such screens as these. The real test would come later; but this had been mighty good practice.

*

The real test came with the fifth, the innermost screen. The others, while of ever-increasing sensitivity, complexity, and power, were all generated mechanically, and hence posed problems differing only in degree, and not in kind, from that of the first. The fifth problem, however, involving a living and highly capable brain, differed in both degree and kind from all the others. The Eddorian would be sensitive to form and to shape, as well as to interference. Bulges were out, unless he could do something about the Eddorian—and the speedster couldn't go through a screen without making a bulge.

Furthermore, this zone had visual and electromagnetic detectors, so spaced as not to let a microbe through. There were fortresses, maulers, battleships, and their attendant lesser craft. There were projectors, and mines, and automatic torpedoes with atomic warheads, and other such things. Were these things completely dependent upon the Eddorian guardian, or not?

They were not. The officers—Kalonians for the most part—would go into action at the guardian's signal, of course; but they would at need act without instructions. A nice setup—a mighty hard nut to crack! He would have to use zones of compulsion. Nothing else would do.

Picking out the biggest fortress in the neighborhood, with its correspondingly large field of coverage, he insinuated his mind into that of one observing officer after another. When he left, a few minutes later, he knew that none of those officers would initiate any action in response to the alarms which he would so soon set off. They were alive, fully conscious, alert, and would have resented bitterly any suggestion that they were not completely normal in every respect. Nevertheless, whatever colors the lights flashed, whatever pictures the plates revealed, whatever noises blared from the speakers, in their consciousnesses would be only blankness and silence. Nor would recorder tapes reveal later what had occurred. An instrument cannot register fluctuations when its movable member is controlled by a couple of steady fingers.

Then the Eddorian. To take over his whole mind was, Kit knew, beyond his present power. A partial zone, though, could be set up—and young Kinnison's mind had been developed specifically to perform the theretofore impossible. Thus the guardian, without suspecting it, suffered an attack of partial blindness which lasted for the fraction of a second necessary for the speedster to flash through the screen. And there was no recorder to worry about. Eddorians, never sleeping and never relaxing their vigilance, had no doubt whatever of their own capabilities and needed no checks upon their own performances.

Christopher Kinnison, Child of the Lens, was inside Eddore's innermost defensive sphere. For countless cycles of time the Arisians had been working toward and looking forward to the chain of events of which this was the first link. Nor would he have much time here: he would have known that even if Mentor had not so stressed the point. As long as he did nothing he was safe; but as soon as he started sniffing around he would be open to detection and some Eddorian would climb his frame in mighty short order. Then blast and lock on—he might get something, or a lot, or nothing at all. Then—win, lose, or draw—he had to get away. Strictly under his own power, against an unknown number of the most powerful and the most ruthless entities ever to live. The Arisian couldn't get in here to help him, and neither could the kids. Nobody could. It was strictly and solely up to him.

For more than a moment his spirit failed. The odds against him were far too long. The load was too heavy; he didn't have half enough jets to swing it. Just how did a guy as smart as Mentor figure it that he, a dumb, green kid, stood a chance against all Eddore?

He was scared; scared to the core of his being; scared as he had never been before and never would be again. His mouth felt dry, his tongue cottony. His fingers shook, even as he doubled them into fists to steady them. To the very end of his long life he remembered the fabric and the texture of that fear; remembered how it made him decide to turn back, before it was too late to retrace his way as unobserved as he had come.

Well, why not? Who would care, and what matter? The Arisians? Nuts! It was all their fault, sending him in half-ready. His parents? They wouldn't know what the score was and wouldn't care. They would be on his side, anyway, no matter what happened. The kids? The *kids*! Klono's Holy Claws!

They had tried to talk him out of coming in alone. They had fought like wildcats to make him take them along. He had refused. Now, if he sneaked back with his tail between his legs, how would they take it? What would they do? What would they *think*? Then, later, after he had loused up the big job and let the Arisians and the Patrol and all Civilization get knocked out—then what? The kids would know exactly how and why it had happened. He couldn't defend himself, even if he tried, and he wouldn't try. Did he have any idea how much sheer, vitriolic, corrosive contempt those four red-headed hellions could generate? Or, even if they didn't—or as a follow-up—their condescending, sisterly pity would be a thousand million times worse. And what would he think of himself? No soap. It was out. Definitely. The Eddorians could kill him only once. QX.

*

He drove straight downward, noting as he did so that his senses were clear, his hands steady, his tongue normally moist. He was still scared, but he was no longer paralyzed.

Low enough, he let his every perceptive sense roam abroad—and became instantly too busy to worry about anything. There was an immense amount of new stuff here—if he only could be granted time enough to get it all!

He wasn't. In a second or so, it seemed, his interference was detected and an Eddorian came in to investigate. Kit threw everything he had, and in the brief moment before the completely surprised denizen died, the young Klovian learned more of the real truth of Eddore and of the whole Boskonian Empire than all the Arisians had ever found out. In that one flash of ultimately intimate fusion, he *knew* Eddorian history, practically *in toto*. He knew the enemies' culture; he knew how they behaved, and why. He knew their ideals and their ideologies. He knew a great deal about their organization; their systems of offense and of defense. He knew their strengths and, more important, their weaknesses. He knew exactly how, if Civilization were to triumph at all, its victory must be achieved.

This seems—or rather, it is—incredible. It is, however, simple truth. Under such stresses as those, an Eddorian mind can yield, and the mind of such a one as Christopher Kinnison can absorb, an incredible amount of knowledge in an incredibly brief interval of time.

Kit, already seated at his controls, cut in his every course of thought-screen. They would help a little in what was coming, but not much—no mechanical screen then known to Civilization could block third-level thought. He kicked in full drive toward the one small area in which he and his speedster would not encounter either beams or bombs—the fortress whose observers would not perceive that anything was amiss. He did not fear physical pursuit, since his speedster was the fastest thing in space.

For a second or so it was not so bad. Another Eddorian came in, suspicious and on guard. Kit blasted him down—learning still more in the process—but he could not prevent him from radiating a frantic and highly revealing call for help. And although the other Eddorians could scarcely realize that such an astonishing thing as a physical invasion had actually happened, that fact neither slowed them down nor made their anger less violent.

When Kit flashed past his friendly fortress he was taking about all that he could handle, and more and more Eddorians were piling on. At the fourth screen it was worse; at the third he reached what he was sure was his absolute ceiling. Nevertheless, from some hitherto unsuspected profundity of his being, he managed to draw enough reserve force to endure that hellish punishment for a little while longer.

Hang on, Kit, hang on! Only two more screens to go. Maybe only one. Maybe less. Living Eddorian brains, and not mechanical generators, are now handling all the screens, of course; but if Mentor's visualization is worth a tinker's damn, he must have that first screen knocked down by this time and must be working on the second. Hang on, Kit, and keep on slugging!

And grimly—doggedly—toward the end sheerly desperately—Christopher Kinnison, eldest Child of the Lens, hung on and slugged.

XXIII.

If the historian has succeeded in his attempt to describe the characters and abilities concerned, it is not necessary to enlarge upon what Kit went through in escaping Eddore. If he has not succeeded, enlargement would be useless. Therefore, it is enough to say that the young Lensman, by dint of calling up and putting out everything he had, hung on long enough and slugged his way through.

Mentor's visualization had been sound. The Eddorian guardians had scarcely taken over the first screen when it was overwhelmed by a tremendous wave of Arisian thought. It is to be remembered, however, that this was the second time that the massed might of Arisia had been thrown against Eddore's defenses, and the Boskonians had learned much, during the intervening years, from their exhaustive analyses of the offensive and defensive techniques of that earlier conflict. Thus the Arisian drive was practically stopped at the second zone of defense as Kit approached it. The screen was wavering, shifting; yielding stubbornly wherever it must and springing back into place whenever it could.

Under a tremendous concentration of Arisian force the screen weakened in a limited area directly ahead of the hurtling speedster. A few beams lashed out aimlessly, uselessly—if the Eddorians could not hold their main screens proof against the power of the Arisian attack, how could they protect such minor things as gunners' minds? The little ship flashed through the weakened barrier and into the center of a sphere of impenetrable, impermeable Arisian thought.

At the shock of the sudden ending of his terrific battle—the instantaneous transition from supreme to zero effort—Kit fainted in his control chair. He lay slumped, inert, in a stupor which changed gradually into a deep and natural sleep. And as the sleeping man in his inertialess speedster traversed space at full touring blast, that peculiar sphere of force still enveloped and still protected him.

Kit finally began to come to. His first foggy thought was that he was hungry—then, wide awake and remembering, he grabbed his levers.

"Rest quietly and eat your fill," a grave resonant pseudovoice assured him. "Everything is exactly as it should be."

"Hi, Ment . . . well, well, if it isn't my old chum Eukonidor! Hi, young fellow! What's the good word? And what's the big idea of letting—or making—me sleep for a week when there's work to do?"

"Your part of the work, at least for the immediate present, is done; and, let me say, very well done."

"Thanks . . . but—" Kit broke off, flushing darkly.

"Do not reproach yourself, nor us. Consider, please, and recite, the manufacture of a fine tool of ultimate quality."

"The correct alloy. Hot working—perhaps cold, too. Forging—heating —quenching—drawing—"

"Enough. Think you that the steel, if sentient, would enjoy those treatments? While you did not enjoy them, you are able to appreciate their necessity. You are now a finished tool, forged and tempered."

"Oh, you may have something there, at that. But as to ultimate quality, don't make me laugh." There was no nuance of merriment in Kit's thought. "You can't square that with cowardice."

"Nor is there need. The term ultimate was used advisedly, and still stands. It does not mean or imply, however, a state of perfection, since that condition is unattainable. I am not advising you to try to forget; nor am I attempting to force forgetfulness upon you, since your mind cannot now be coerced by any force presently existing. Be assured that nothing that occurred should irk you; for the simple truth is, that although stressed as no other mind has ever before been stressed, you did not yield. Instead, you secured and retained information which we of Arisia have never been able to obtain; information which will in fact be the means of preserving your Civilization."

"I can't believe . . . that is, it doesn't seem—" Kit, knowing that he was thinking muddily and foolishly, paused and pulled himself together. Overwhelming, almost paralyzing as that information was, it must be true. It *was* true!

"Yes, it is the truth. While we of Arisia have at various times made ambiguous statements, to lead certain Lensmen and others to arrive at erroneous conclusions, you know that we do not lie."

"Yes, I know that." Kit plumbed the Arisian's mind. "It sort of knocks me out of my orbit—that's an awfully big bite to swallow at one gulp, you know."

"It is. That is one reason I am here, to convince you of the truth, which you would not otherwise believe fully. Also to see to it that your rest, without which you might have been hurt, was not disturbed, as well as to make sure that you were not permanently damaged by the Eddorians."

"I wasn't . . . at least, I don't think so . . . was I?"

"You were not."

"Good. I was wondering—Mentor will be tied up for quite a while, of course, so I'll ask you—they must have got a sort of pattern of me, in spite of all I could do, and they'll be camping on my trail from now on, so I suppose I'll have to keep a solid block up all the time?"

"They will not, Christopher, and you need not. Guided by those whom you knew as Mentor, I myself, as a Guardian, am to see to that. But time presses—I must rejoin my fellows."

"One more question first. You've been trying to sell me a bill of goods that I would like to buy. But, Eukonidor, the kids will know that I showed a streak of yellow a meter wide. What will *they think*?"

"Is *that* all?" Eukonidor's thought was almost a laugh. "They will make that eminently plain in a moment."

*

The Arisian's presence vanished, as did his sphere of force, and four clamoring thoughts came jamming in.

"Oh, Kit, we're *so* glad!" "We *tried* to help, but they wouldn't let us!" "They smacked us down!" "*Honestly*, Kit!" "Oh, if we had only been in there, too!"

"Hold it, everybody! Jet back!" This was Con, Kit knew, but an entirely new Con. "Scan him, Cam, as you never scanned anything before. If they burned out even one cell of his mind, I'm going over there right now and kick every one of Mentor's teeth out!"

"And listen, Kit!" This was an equally strange Kathryn blazing with fury and yet suffusing his mind with a more than sisterly tenderness, a surpassing richness. "If we had had the faintest idea of what they were doing to you, all the Arisians and all the Eddorians and all the devils in all the hells of the macrocosmic Universe couldn't have kept us away. You must believe that, Kit—or can you, quite?"

"Of course, Sis—you don't have to prove an axiom. Seal it, all of you. You're swell people—absolute tops. But I . . . you . . . that is—" He broke off and marshaled his thoughts.

He knew that they knew, in every minute particular, everything that had occurred. Yet to a girl they thought that he was wonderful. Their common thought was that they should have been in there, too—taking what he took—giving what he gave!

"What I don't get is that you are trying to blame yourselves for what happened to me, when you were on the dead center of the beam all the time. You *couldn't* have been in there, kids; it would have blown the whole works higher than up. You knew that then, and you know it even better now. You also know that I flew the yellow flag. Didn't that even *register*?"

"Oh, *that!*" Practically identical thoughts of complete dismissal came in unison, and Karen followed through:

"The only thing about that is that, since you knew what to expect, we marvel that you ever managed to go in at all—no one else could have, possibly. Or, once in, and seeing what was really there, that you didn't flit right out again. Believe me, brother of mine, you qualify!"

Kit choked. This was too much: but it made him feel good all over. These kids . . . the Universe's best—

As he thought, a partial block came unconsciously into being. For not one of those gorgeous, those utterly splendid creatures suspected, even now, that which he so surely knew—that each one of them was very shortly to be wrought and tempered as he himself had been. And, worse, he would have to stand aside and watch them, one by one, walk into it. Was there anything he could do to ward off, or even to soften, what was coming to them? There was not. With his present power, he could step in, of course—at what awful cost to Civilization only he, Christopher Kinnison, of all Civilization, really knew. No. That was out. Definitely. He could come in afterwards to ease their hurts, as each had come to him, but that was all—and there was a difference. They hadn't known about it in advance. It was tough.

Could he do *anything?*

He could not.

*

And on clammy, noisome Eddore, the Arisian attackers having been beaten off and normality restored, a meeting of the Highest Command was held. No two of those entities were alike in form; some were changing from one horrible shape into another; all were starkly, indescribably monstrous. All were concentrating upon the problem which had been so suddenly thrust upon them; each of them thought at and with each of the others. To do justice to the complexity or the cogency of that maze of intertwined thoughts is impossible; the best that can be done is to pick out a high point here and there.

"This explains the Star A Star whom the Ploorans and the Kalonians so fear."

"And the failure of our operator on Thrale, and its fall."

"Also our recent quite serious reverses."

"Those stupid—those utterly brainless underlings!"

"We should have been called in at the start!"

"Could you analyze, or even perceive, its pattern save in small part?"

"No."

"Nor could I—an astounding and highly revealing circumstance."

"An Arisian; or, rather, an Arisian development, certainly. No other entity of Civilization could possibly do what was done here. Nor could any Arisian as we know or deduce them."

"They have developed something very recently which we had not visualized."

"Kinnison's son? Bah! Think they to deceive us by the old device of energizing a form of ordinary flesh?"

"Kinnison—his son—Nadreck—Worsel—Tregonsee—what matters it?"

"Or, as we now know, the completely imaginary Star A Star."

"We must revise our thinking," an authoritatively composite mind decided. "We must revise our theory and our plan. It may be possible that this new development will necessitate immediate, instead of later, action. If we had had a competent race of proxies, none of this would have happened, as we would have been kept informed. To correct a situation which may become grave, as well as to acquire fullest and latest information, we must attend the conference which is now being held on Ploor."

*

They did so. With no perceptible lapse of time or mode of transit, the Eddorian mind was in an assembly room upon that now flooded world. Resembling Nevians as much as any other race with which man is familiar, the now amphibious Ploorans lolled upon padded benches and argued heatedly. They were discussing, upon a lower level, much of the same material which the Eddorians had been considering so shortly before.

Star A Star. Kinnison had been captured easily enough, but had, almost immediately, escaped from an escape-proof trap. Another trap was set, but would it take him? Would it hold him if it did? Kinnison was—must be—Star A Star. No, he could not be, there had been too many unrelated and simultaneous occurrences. Kinnison, Nadreck, Clarrissa, Worsel, Tregonsee, even Kinnison's young son, had all shown intermittent flashes of inexplicable power. Kinnison most of all. It was a fact worthy of note that the beginning of the long series of Boskonian setbacks coincided with Kinnison's appearance among the Lensmen.

The situation was bad. Not irreparable, by any means, but grave. The fault lay with the Eich, and perhaps with Kandron of Onlo. Such stupidity! Such incompetence! Those lower-echelon operators should have had brains enough to have reported the matter to Ploor before the situation got completely out of hand. But they didn't; hence this mess. None of them, however, expressed a thought that the present situation was already one with which they themselves could not cope; nor suggested that it be referred to Eddore before it should become too hot for even the Masters to handle.

"Fools! Imbeciles! We, the Masters, although through no foresight or design of yours, are already here. Know now that you have been and still are yourselves guilty of the same conduct which you are so violently condemning in others." Neither Eddorians nor Ploorans realized that that deficiency was inherent in the Boskonian scheme of things, or that it stemmed from the organization's very top. "Sheer stupidity! Gross overconfidence! Those are the reasons for our recent reverses!"

"But, Masters," a Plooran argued, "now that we have taken over, we are winning steadily. Civilization is rapidly going to pieces. In a few more years we will have smashed it flat."

"That is precisely what they wish you to think. They have been and are playing for time. Your bungling and mismanagement have already given them sufficient time to develop an object or an entity able to penetrate our screens, so that Eddore suffered the disgrace of an actual physical invasion. It was brief, to be sure, and unsuccessful, but it was an invasion, none the less—the first in our long history."

"But, Masters—"

"Silence! We are not here to indulge in recriminations, but to determine facts. Since you do not know Eddore's location in space, it is a certainty that you did not, either wittingly or otherwise, furnish that information. That in turn makes it clear who, basically, the invader was."

"Star A Star?" A wave of questions swept the group.

"One name serves as well as another for what is almost certainly an Arisian entity or device. It is enough for you to know that it is something with which your massed minds would be completely unable to deal. To the best of your knowledge, have you been invaded, either physically or mentally?"

"We have not, Masters; and it is unbelievable that—"

"Is it so?" The Masters sneered. "Neither our screens nor our Eddorian guardsmen gave any alarm. We learned of the Arisian's presence only when he attempted to probe our very minds, at Eddore's very surface. Are your screens and minds, then, so much better than ours?"

"We erred, Masters. We abase ourselves. What do you wish us to do?"

*

"That is better. You will be informed, as soon as a few last-minute details have been worked out. Although nothing is established by the fact that you know of no occurrences here on Ploor, the probability is that you are still unknown and unsuspected, since it is unthinkable that the enemies' minds are in any real sense as strong as ours. Nevertheless, one of us is now taking over control of the trap which you set for Kinnison, in the belief that he is Star A Star."

"Belief, Masters? It is certain that he is Star A Star!"

"In essence, yes. In exactness, no. Kinnison is, in all probability, merely a puppet through whom an Arisian works at times. If you take Kinnison in that trap, however, the entity you call Star A Star will assuredly kill you all."

"But, Masters—"

"Again, fools, silence!" The thought dripped vitriol. "Remember how easily Kinnison escaped from you? It was the supremely clever move of not following through and destroying you then that obscured the truth for years—that gave them all this additional time. As we have said, you are completely powerless against the one you call Star A Star. Against any lesser force, however—and the probability is exceedingly great that only such forces, if any, will be sent against you—you should be able to win. Are you ready?"

"We are ready, Masters." At last the Ploorans were upon familiar ground. "Since ordinary weapons will be useless against us, they will not attempt to use them—especially since they have developed three extraordinary and supposedly irresistible weapons of attack. First: projectiles composed of negative matter, particularly those of planetary antimass. Second: loose planets, driven inertialess, but inerted at the point at which their intrinsic velocities render collision unavoidable. Third, and worst: the sunbeam. These gave us some trouble, particularly the last, but the problems were solved and if any one of the three, or all of them, are used against us, disaster for the Galactic Patrol is assured.

"Nor did we stop there. Our psychologists, working with our engineers, after having analyzed exhaustively the capabilities of the so-called Second-Stage Lensmen, developed countermeasures against every super-weapon which they will be able to develop during the next century."

"Such as?" The Masters were unimpressed.

"The most probable one is an extension of the sunbeam principle, to operate from a distant sun; or, preferably, a nova. We are now installing fields and grids by the use of which we, not the Patrol, will direct that beam."

"Interesting—if true. Spread in our minds the details of all that you have foreseen and the fashions in which you have safeguarded yourselves."

*

It was a long operation, even at the speed of thought. At its end the Eddorians were unconvinced, skeptical, and pessimistic.

"We can visualize several other things which the forces of Civilization may be able to develop well within the century," the Master mind said, coldly. "We will assemble data concerning a few of them, for your study. In the meantime, hold yourselves in readiness to act, as we shall issue final orders very shortly."

"Yes, Masters," and the Eddorians went back to their home planet as effortlessly as they had left it. There they concluded their conference.

"It is clear that Kinnison will enter that trap. He cannot do otherwise. Kinnison's protector, whoever or whatever he or it may be, may or may not enter it with him. It may or may not be taken with him. Whether or not the new Arisian figment is taken, Kimball Kinnison must die. He is the very keystone of the Galactic Patrol. At his death, as we will advertise it to have come about, the Patrol will fall apart. The Arisians, themselves unknown, will be forced to try to rebuild it around another puppet; but neither his son nor any other man will ever be able to take Kinnison's place in the esteem of the hero-worshiping, undisciplined mob which is Civilization. Hence the importance of your project. You, personally, will supervise the operation of the trap. You, personally, will kill him."

"With one exception, I agree with everything said. I am not at all certain that death is the answer. One way or another, however, I shall deal effectively with Kinnison."

"Deal with? We said kill!"

"I heard you. I still say that mere death may not be adequate. I shall consider the matter at length, and shall submit in due course my conclusions and recommendations, for your consideration and approval."

*

Although none of the Eddorians knew it, their pessimism in regard to the ability of the Ploorans to defend their planet against the assaults of Second-Stage Lensmen was even then being justified. Kimball Kinnison, after pacing the floor for hours, called his son.

"Kit, I've been working on a thing for months, and I don't know whether I've got a workable solution at last, or not. It may depend entirely on you. Before I go into it, though, I take it that you check me in saying that when we find Boskonia's top planet we're going to have to blow it out of the ether, and that nothing that we have ever used before will work?"

"Check, on both." Kit thought soberly for minutes. "More, it will have to be practically instantaneous, as well as complete. Like the negabombs or the sunbeam, but a lot faster."

"My thought exactly. I've got something, I think, but nobody except old Cardynge and Mentor of Arisia—"

"Hold it, Dad, while I do a bit of spying and put out some coverage. QX, go ahead."

"Nobody except those two knew anything about the mathematics involved. Even Sir Austin knew only enough to be able to understand Mentor's directions—he didn't do any of the deep stuff himself. Nobody in the present Conference of Science could even begin to handle it. It's that foreign space, you know, that we called the nth space, where that hyperspatial tube dumped us that time. You've been doing a lot of work with some of the Arisians on that sort of stuff. Could you get them to help you compute a tube between Lyrane and there, so that Thorndyke and some of his boys and I could go there and get back?"

"Hm-m-m. Let me think a second. Yes, I can. When do you need it?"

"Today—or even yesterday."

"Too fast. It'll take a couple of days, but it'll be ready for you long before you can get your ship ready and get your gang and the stuff for your gadget aboard her."

"That won't take so long, son. Same ship we rode before. She's still in commission, you know—*Space Laboratory XII*, her name is now. Special generators, tools, instruments, everything. We'll be ready in two days."

They were, and Kit smiled as he greeted Vice Admiral LaVerne Thorndyke, Principal Technician, and the other surviving members of his father's original crew.

"*What* a tonnage of brass!" Kit said to Kim, later. "Heaviest load I ever saw on one ship. One sure thing, though, they earned it. You must have been able to pick *men*, too, in those days."

"What d'ya mean, 'those days,' you disrespectful young ape? I can still pick *men*, son!" Kim grinned back at Kit, but sobered quickly. "There's more to this than meets the eye. They went through the strain once, and know what it means. They can take it, and just about all of them will come back. With a crew of kids, twenty per cent would be a high estimate."

As soon as the vessel passed System Limits, Kit got another surprise. Even though those men were studded with brass and were, by a boy's standard, *old*, they were not passengers. In their old *Dauntless* and well away from port, they gleefully threw off their full-dress uniforms. Each donned the clothing of his status of twenty-odd years back and went to work. The members of the regular crew, young as all regular space crewmen are, did not know at first whether they liked the idea of working watch-and-watch with such heavy brass or not, but they soon found out that they did. Those men were men.

It is an ironclad rule of space, however, that operating pilots must be young. Master Pilot Henry Henderson cursed that ruling sulphurously, even while he watched with a proud, if somewhat jaundiced eye, the smooth performance of his son Henry at his own old board.

They approached their destination—cut the jets—felt for the vortex—found it—cut in the special generators. Then, as the fields of the ship reacted against those of the tube, every man aboard felt a malaise to which no being has ever become accustomed. Most men become immune rather quickly to seasickness, to airsickness, and even to space-sickness. Interdimensional acceleration, however, is something else. It is different—just how different cannot be explained to anyone who has never experienced it.

The almost unbearable acceleration ceased. They were in the tube. Every plate showed blank; everywhere there was the same drab and featureless gray. There was neither light nor darkness; there was simply and indescribably—nothing whatever, not even empty space.

Kit threw a switch. There was a wrenching, twisting shock, followed by a deceleration exactly as sickening as the acceleration had been. It ceased. They were in that enigmatic nth space which each of the older men remembered so well; in which so many of their "natural laws" did not hold. Time still raced, stopped, or ran backward, seemingly at whim; inert bodies had intrinsic velocities far above that of light—and so on. Each of those men, about to be marooned of his own choice in this utterly hostile environment, drew a deep breath and squared his shoulders as he prepared to disembark.

"That's computation, Kit!" Kinnison exclaimed after one glance into a plate. "That's the same planet we worked on before, right there. All our machines and stuff, untouched. If you'd figured it any closer, it'd have been a collision course. Are you dead sure, Kit, that everything's all set?"

"Dead sure, Dad, in full duplicate, and Thorndyke and Henderson both know the board."

"QX. Well, fellows, I'd like to stay here with you, and so would Kit, but we've got chores to do. I don't have to tell you to be careful, but I'm going to, anyway. BE CAREFUL! And as soon as you get done, come back home just as fast as Klono will let you. Clear ether, fellows!"

"Clear ether, Kim!"

Lensman father and Lensman son boarded their speedster and left. They traversed the tube and emerged into normal space, all without a word.

"Kit," the older man ground out, finally. "This gives me the colly wobblies, no less. Suppose some of them—or all of them—get killed out there? Is it worth it? I know it's my own idea, but will we need it badly enough to take the chance?"

"We will, Dad. Mentor says that we will."

And that was that.

XXIV.

Kit had had to get back to normal space as soon as possible, in order to be available in case of need. He wanted to get back in time to help his sisters pull themselves together. Think as he would, he could find no flaw in any one of them; but he knew that Mentor would find something or other the matter with each of them. Not a weakness in any ordinary sense, but a strength which was not the ultimate.

Kinnison had had to get back because his business was really pressing. He had called a conference of all the Second-Stage Lensmen and his children; a conference which, bizarrely enough, was to be held in person and not via Lens.

"Not strictly necessary, of course," the Gray Lensman half-apologized to his son as their speedster neared the point of rendezvous with the *Dauntless*. "I still think that it's a good idea, though, especially since we were all so close to Lyrane anyway."

"So do I. It's been a mighty long time since we were all together. Everybody's there now except Nadreck—he'll board about the same time we do."

They boarded. Spacehounds both, they saw to it that their speedster was dogged down solidly into her chocks before they went to the main saloon.

"Hi, Mums! Still stopping traffic at all intersections, I see!" Kit lowered his mother's feet to the floor and attempted the physically impossible feat of embracing all four of his sisters at once.

By common consent the Five used only their eyes. Nothing showed. Nevertheless, the girls blushed vividly and Kit's face twisted into a dry, wry grin.

"It was good for what ailed us, though, at that—I guess." Kit did not seem to be at all positive. "Mentor, the lug, told me no less than six times that I had arrived—or at least made statements which I interpreted as meaning that. And Eukonidor just told me that I was a 'finished tool,' whatever that means. Personally, I think that they were sitting back and wondering how long it was going to take us to realize that we never could be half as good as we used to think we were. Suppose?"

"Something like that, probably. We've shivered more than once, wondering whether we are really finished products yet or not."

"We've learned—I hope." Karen, hard as she was, did shiver, physically. "If we aren't it will be . . . *p-s-s-t*—Dad's starting the meeting!"

" . . . so settle down, all of you, and we'll get going."

What a group! Tregonsee of Rigel IV—stolid, solid, blocky, immobile; looking as little as possible like one of the profoundest thinkers Civilization had ever produced—did not move. Worsel, the ultrasensitive yet utterly implacable Velantian, curled out three or four eyes and looked on languidly while Constance kicked a few coils of his tail onto a comfortable chaise longue, reclined unconcernedly in the seat thus made, and lighted an Alsakanite cigarette. Clarrissa Kinnison, radiant in her Grays and looking scarcely older than her daughters, sat beside Kathryn, each with an arm around the other. Karen and Camilla, neither of whom could ordinarily be described by the adjective "cuddlesome," were on a davenport with Kit, snuggling as close to him as they could get. And in the farthest corner the heavily-armored, heavily-insulated spacesuit which contained Nadreck of Palain VII chilled the atmosphere for yards around.

"QX?" Kinnison began. "We'll take Nadreck first, since he isn't any too happy here, and let him flit—he'll keep in touch from outside after he leaves. Report, please, Nadreck."

*

"I have explored Lyrane IX *thoroughly*." Nadreck made the statement and paused. When he used such a thought at all, it meant much. When he emphasized it, which no one there had ever before known him to do, it meant that he had examined the planet practically atom by atom. "There was no life of the level of intelligence in which we are interested to be found on, beneath, or above its surface. I could find no evidence that such life has ever been there, either as permanent dwellers or as occasional visitors."

"When Nadreck settles anything as definitely as that, it stays settled," Kinnison remarked as soon as the Palainian had left. "I'll report next. You all know what I did about Kalonia, and so on. The only significant fact I have been able to find—the only lead to the Boskonian higher-ups—is that Black Lensman Melasnikov got his Lens on Lyrane IX. There were no traces of mental surgery. I can see two, and only two, alternatives. Either there was mental surgery which I could not detect, or there were visitors to Lyrane IX who left no traces of their visits. More reports may enable us to decide. Worsel?"

The Second-Stage Lensmen reported in turn. Each had uncovered leads to Lyrane IX, but Worsel and Tregonsee, who had also studied that planet with care, agreed with Nadreck that there was nothing to be found there.

"Kit?" Kinnison asked then. "How about you and the girls?"

"We believe that Lyrane IX was visited by beings having sufficient power of mind to leave no traces whatever as to who they were or where they came from. We also believe that there was no surgery, but an infinitely finer kind of work—an indetectable subconscious compulsion—done on the minds of the Black Lensmen and others who came into physical contact with the Boskonians. These opinions are based upon experiences which we five have had and upon deductions we have made. If we are right, Lyrane is actually, as well as apparently, a dead end and should be abandoned. Furthermore, we believe that the Black Lensmen have not been and cannot become important."

The Co-ordinator was surprised, but after Kit and his sisters had detailed their findings and their deductions, he turned to the Rigellian.

"What next, then, Tregonsee?"

"After Lyrane IX, it seems to me that the two most promising subjects are those entities who think upon such a high band, and the phenomenon which has been called 'The Hell Hole in Space.' Of the two, I preferred the first until Camilla's researches showed that the available data could not be reconciled with the postulate that the life-forms of her reconstruction were identical with those reported to you as Co-ordinator. This data, however, was scanty and casual. While we are here, therefore, I suggest that we review this matter much more carefully, in the hope that additional information will enable us to come to a definite conclusion, one way or the other. Since it was her research, Camilla will lead."

*

"First, a question," Camilla began. "Imagine a sun so variable that it periodically covers practically the entire possible range. It has a planet whose atmosphere, liquid, and distance are such that its surface temperature varies from approximately two hundred degrees Centigrade in midsummer to about five degrees absolute in midwinter. In the spring its surface is almost completely submerged. There are terrible winds and storms in the spring, summer, and fall; but the fall storms are the worst. Has anyone here ever heard of such a planet having an intelligent life-form able to maintain a continuing existence through such varied environments by radical changes in its physical body?"

A silence ensued, which Nadreck finally broke.

"I know of two such planets. Near Palain there is an extremely variable sun, two of whose planets support life. All of the higher life-forms, the highest of which are quite intelligent, undergo regular and radical changes, not only of form, but of organization."

"Thanks, Nadreck. That will perhaps make my story believable. From the thoughts of one of the entities in question, I reconstructed such a solar system. More, that entity himself belonged to just such a race. It was *such* a nice reconstruction," Camilla went on, plaintively, "and it fitted all those other life-forms so beautifully, especially Kat's 'four-cycle periods.' And to prove it, Kat—put up your block, now—you never told anybody the classification of your pet to more than seven places, did you, or even thought about it?"

"No." Kathryn's mind, since the moment of warning, had been unreadable.

"Take the seven. The next three were S-T-R. Check?"

"Check."

"But that makes it *solid*, Sis!" Kit exclaimed.

"That's what I thought, for a minute—that we had Boskone at last. However, when Tregonsee and I first felt 'X,' long before you met yours, Kat, his classification was TUUV. That would fit in well enough as a spring form, with Kat's as the summer form. What ruins it, though, is that when he killed himself, just a little while ago and long after a summer form could possibly exist—to say nothing of a spring form—his classification was *still* TUUV. To ten places it was TUUVWYXXWT."

"Well, go on," Kinnison suggested. "What do you make of it?"

"The obvious explanation is that one or all of those entities were planted or primed—not specifically for us, probably, since we are relatively unknown, but for any competent observer. If so, they don't mean a thing." Camilla was not now overestimating her own powers or underestimating those of Boskonia. "There are several others, less obvious, leading to the same conclusion. Tregonsee is not ready to believe any of them, however, and neither am I. Assuming that our data was not biased, we must also account for the fact that the locations in space were—"

"Just a minute, Cam, before you leave the classifications," Constance interrupted. "I'm guarded—what was my friend's, to ten places?"

"VWZYTXSYZY," Camilla replied, unhesitatingly.

"Right; and I don't believe that it was planted, either, so there—"

"Let me in a second!" Kit demanded. "I didn't know that you were on that band at all. I got that RTSL thing even before I graduated—"

"Huh? What RTSL?" Cam broke in, sharply.

"My fault," Kinnison put in then. "Skipped my mind entirely, when she asked me for the dope. None of us thought any of this stuff important until just now, you know. Tell her, Kit."

*

Kit repeated his story, concluding:

"Beyond four places was pretty dim, but Q P arms and legs—Dhilian, eh?—would fit, and so would an R-type hide. Both Kat's and mine, then, could very well have been summer forms, one of their years apart. The thing I felt was on its own planet, and it *died* there, and credits to millos the thought I got wasn't primed. And the location—"

"Brake down, Kit," Camilla instructed. "Let's settle this thing of timing first. I've got a theory, but I want some ideas from the rest of you."

"Maybe something like this?" Clarrissa asked, after a few minutes of silence. "In many forms which metamorphose completely the change depends upon temperature. No change takes place as long as the temperature remains the same. Your TUUV could have been flitting around in a spaceship at constant temperature. Could this apply here, Cam, do you think?"

"*Could* it?" Kinnison exclaimed. "That's it, Chris, sure!"

"That was my theory," Camilla said, still dubiously, "but there is no proof that it applies. Nadreck, do you know whether or not it applies to your neighbors?"

"Unfortunately, I do not; but I can find out—by experiment if necessary."

"It might be a good idea," Kinnison suggested. "Go on, Cam."

"Assuming its truth, there is still left the problem of location, which Kit has just made infinitely worse than it was before. Con's and mine were so indefinite that they might possibly have been reconciled with Kat's precisely-known co-ordinates; but yours, Kit, is almost as definite as Kat's, and cannot possibly be made to agree with it. After all, you know, there are many planets peopled by races humanoid to ten places. And if there are four different races, none of them can be the one we want."

"I don't believe it," Kit argued. "Not that I think on that peculiar band. I'm sure enough of my dope so that I want to cross-question Kat on hers. QX, Kat?"

"Surely, Kit. Any questions you like."

"Those minds both had plenty of jets—how do you know that he was telling you the truth? Did you drive in to see? Are you sure even that you saw his real shape?"

"Certainly I'm sure of his shape!" Kathryn snapped. "If there had been any zones of compulsion around, I would have known it and got suspicious right then."

"Maybe, and maybe not," Kit disagreed. "That might depend, you know, on how good the guy was who was putting out the zone."

"Nuts!" Kathryn snorted, inelegantly. "But as to his telling the truth about his home planet—I'm not sure of that, no. I didn't check his channels. I was thinking about other things then." The Five knew that she had just left Mentor. "But why should he want to lie about a thing like that—he would have, though, at that. Good Boskonian technique."

"Sure. In your official capacity of Co-ordinator, Dad, what do you think?"

"The probability is that all those four forms of life belong on one planet. Your location must be wrong, Kat—he gave you the wrong galaxy, even. Too close to Trenco, too—Tregonsee and I both know that region like a book and no such variable is anywhere near there. We've got to find out all about that planet as soon as possible. Worsel, will you please get the charts of Kit's region? Kit, will you check with the planetographers of Klovia as to the variable stars anywhere near where you want them, and how many planets they've got? I'll call Tellus."

THE LENSMAN

The charts were studied, and in due time the reports of the planetographers were received. The Klovian scientists reported that there were four long-period variables in the designated volume of space, gave the spatial co-ordinates and catalogue numbers of each, and all available data concerning their planets. The Tellurians reported only three, in considerably less detail; but they had named each sun and each planet.

"Which one did they leave out?" Kinnison wondered audibly as he fitted the two transparencies together. "This one they call Artonon, no planets. Dunlie, two planets, Abab and Dunster. Descriptions, and so on. Rontieff, one planet that they don't know anything about except the name they have given it. Silly-sounding names—suppose they assemble them by grabbing letters at random? Ploor—"

PLOOR: At last! Only their instantaneous speed of reaction enabled the Five to conceal from the linkage the shrieked thought of what Ploor really meant. After a flashing exchange of thought, Kit smoothly took charge of the conference.

"The planet Ploor should be investigated first, I think," he resumed communication with the group as though his attention had not wavered. "It is the planet nearest the most probable point of origin of that thought-burst. Also, the period of the variable and the planet's distance seem to fit our observations and deductions better than any of the others. Any arguments?"

No arguments. They all agreed. Kinnison, however, demanded action; direct and fast.

"We'll investigate it!" he exclaimed. "With the *Dauntless*, the Z9M9Z, and Grand Fleet; and with our very special knickknack as an ace up our sleeve!"

"Just a minute, Dad!" Kit protested. "If, as some of this material seems to indicate, the Ploorans actually are the top of the Boskonian culture, even that array may not be enough."

"You may be right—probably are. What, then? What do you say, Tregonsee?"

"Fleet action, yes," the Rigellian agreed. "Also, as you implied, but did not clearly state, independent but correlated action by us five Second-Stage Lensmen, with our various skills. I would suggest, however, that your children be put first—very definitely first—in command."

"We object—we haven't got jets enough to—"

"Overruled!" Kinnison did not have to think to make that decision. He knew. "Any other objections? . . . Approved. I'll call Cliff Maitland right now, then, and get things going."

*

That call, however, was never sent; for at that moment the mind of Mentor of Arisia flooded the group.

"Children, attend! This intrusion is necessary because a matter has come up which will permit of no delay. Boskonia is now launching the attack which has been in preparation for over twenty years. Arisia is to be the first point of attack. Kinnison, Tregonsee, Worsel, and Nadreck will take immediate steps to assemble the Grand Fleet of the Galactic Patrol in defense. I will confer at length with the younger Kinnisons.

1020

"The Eddorians, as you know," Mentor went on to the Children of the Lens, "believe primarily in the efficacy of physical, material force. While they possess minds of real power, they use them principally as tools in the development of more and ever more efficient mechanical devices. We of Arisia, on the other hand, believe in the superiority of the mind. A fully competent mind would have no need of material devices, since it could control all material substance directly. While we have made some progress toward that end, and you will make more in the cycles to come, Civilization is, and for some time will be, dependent upon physical things. Hence the Galactic Patrol and its Grand Fleet.

"The Eddorians, after ages of effort, have succeeded in inventing a mechanical generator able to block our most penetrant thoughts. They believe implicitly that their vessels, so protected, will be able to destroy our planet. They may believe that the destruction of our planet would so weaken us that they would be able to destroy us. It is assumed that you children have deduced that neither we nor the Eddorians can be slain by physical force?"

"Yes—the clincher being that no suggestion was made about giving Eddore a planet from nth space."

"We Arisians, during an equally long time, have been aiding Nature in the development of minds much abler than our own. While those minds will not attain their full powers until after many years of work and study, we believe that you will be able, immature as you are, to use the Patrol and its resources to defend Arisia and to destroy the Boskonian fleet. That we cannot do it ourselves is implicit in what I have said."

"But that means . . . this is the big show, then, that you have been hinting at so long?"

"Far from it. An important engagement, of course, but only preliminary to the real test, which will come when we invade Eddore. Do you agree with us that if Arisia were to be destroyed now, it would be difficult to repair the damage done to the morale of the Galactic Patrol?"

"Difficult? It would be impossible!"

"Not necessarily. We have considered the matter at length, however, and have decided that a Boskonian success at this time would not be for the good of Civilization."

"I'll say it wouldn't—that's a masterpiece of understatement if there ever was one! Also, a successful defense of Arisia would be about the best thing that the Patrol could possibly do for itself."

"Exactly so. Go, then, children, and work to that end."

"But how, Mentor—how?"

"Again I tell you that I do not know. You have powers—individually, collectively, and as the Unit—about which I know little or nothing. Use them!"

XXV.

The "Big Brass"—socially the *Directrix*, technically the Z9M9Z—floated through space at the center of a hollow sphere of maulers packed almost screen to screen. She carried the Brains. She had been built around the seventeen million cubic feet of unobstructed space which comprised her "tank"—the three-dimensional chart in which vari-colored lights, stationary and moving, represented the positions and motions of solar systems, ships, loose planets, negaspheres, and all other objects and items in which Grand Fleet Operations was, or might become, interested. Completely encircling the tank's more than two thousand feet of circumference was the Rigellian-manned, multimillion-plug board; a crew and a board capable of handling efficiently more than a million combat units.

In the "reducer," the comparatively tiny ten-foot tank set into an alcove, there were condensed the continuously-changing major features of the main chart, so that one man could comprehend and direct the broad strategy of the engagement.

Instead of Port Admiral Haynes, who had conned that reducer and issued general orders during the only previous experience of the Z9M9Z in serious warfare, Kimball Kinnison was now in supreme command. Instead of Kinnison and Worsel, who had formerly handled the big tank and the board, there were Clarrissa, Worsel, Tregonsee, and the Children of the Lens. There also, in a built-in, thoroughly competent refrigerator, was Nadreck. Port Admiral Raoul LaForge and Vice Co-ordinator Clifford Maitland were just coming aboard.

Might he need anybody else, Kinnison wondered. Couldn't think of anybody—he had just about the whole top echelon of Civilization. Cliff and Laf weren't L2's, of course, but they were mighty good men—besides, he *liked* them! Too bad that the fourth officer of their class couldn't be there, too—gallant Wiedel Holmberg, killed in action. At that, three out of four was a high average—mighty high.

"Hi, Cliff—Hi, Laf!"

"Hi, Kim!"

The three old friends shook hands cordially, then the two newcomers stared for minutes into the maze of lights flashing and winking in the tremendous space chart.

"Glad I don't have to try to make sense out of that," LaForge commented, finally. "Looks a lot different in battle harness than on practice cruises. You want me on that forward wall there, you said?"

"Yes. You can see it plainer down here in the reducer. The white star is Arisia. The yellows, all marked, are suns and other fixed points, such as the markers along the arbitrary rim of the Galaxy, running from there to there. Reds will be Boskonians when they get close enough to show. Greens are ours. Up in the big tank everything is identified, but down here there's no room for details—each green light marks the location of a whole operating fleet. That block of green circles, there, is your command. It's about eighty parsecs deep and covers everything within two hours—say a hundred and fifty parsecs—of the line between Arisia and the Second Galaxy. Pretty loose now, of course, but you can tighten it up and shift it as you please as soon as some reds show up. You'll have a Rigellian talker—here he is now—when you want anything done, think at him and he'll give it to the right panel on the board. QX?"

"I think so. I'll practice a bit."

"Now you, Cliff. These green crosses, halfway between the forward wall and Arisia, are yours. You won't have quite as much depth as Laf, but a wider coverage. The green tetrahedrons are mine. They blanket Arisia, you notice, and fill the space out to the second wall."

"Do you think that you and I will have anything to do?" Maitland asked, waving a hand at LaForge's tremendous barrier.

"I wish I could hope that we won't, but I can't. I have it from a usually reliable source that they're going to throw the book. That means hyperspatial tubes as well as open space—they'll probably strike everywhere at once."

*

Then for weeks Grand Fleet drilled, maneuvered, and practiced. All space within ten parsecs of Arisia was divided into minute cubes, each of which was given a reference number. Fleets were so placed that any point in that space could be reached by at least one fleet in thirty seconds or less of elapsed time.

Drill went on until, finally, it happened. Constance, on guard at the moment, perceived the slight "curdling" of space which presages the appearance of the terminus of a hyperspatial tube and gave the alarm. Kit, the girls, and all the Arisians responded instantly—all knew that this was to be a thing which not even the Five could handle unaided.

Not one, or a hundred, or a thousand, but at least two hundred thousand of those tubes erupted, practically at once. Kit could alert and instruct ten Rigellian operators every second, and so could each of his sisters; but since every tube within striking distance of Arisia had to be guarded or plugged within thirty seconds of its appearance, and since all of the work was done out in space and not in the tank, it is seen that the Arisians did practically all of the spotting and placing during those first literally incredible two or three minutes.

If the Boskonians could have emerged from a tube's terminus in the moment of its appearance, it is quite probable that nothing could have saved Arisia. As it was, however, the enemy required seconds, or sometimes even whole minutes, to traverse their tubes, which gave the defenders much valuable time.

One of the observers—an Arisian or a Third-Stage Lensman—at first perception of a terminus erupting, noted the number of the threatened space-cubicle, informed the Rigellian operator upon whose panel the number was, and flashed a message to all other observers that that number had been "handled." The observer flashed the number to the Communications board of the flagship of the fleet covering that space; a flash which was automatically relayed to every Communications and Navigations officer of that fleet, and which also automatically called upon Reserve for another fleet to take the place being vacated. Without further orders, the fleet drove toward its target cube. En route, tube-locators mapped the terminus and marked its exact location upon each vessel's tube plates.

Upon arriving, the fleet englobed the terminus and laced itself, by means of tractors and pressors, into a rigid although inertialess structure. Then, if there was time, and because the theory was that the pirates would probably send a negasphere through first, with an intrinsic velocity aimed at Arisia, a suitably equipped loose planet was tossed into "this end" of the tube. Since they might send a loose or an armed planet through first, however, the Fleet Admiral usually threw a negasphere in, too.

1023

THE LENSMAN

What happened when planet met negasphere, in the unknown medium which makes up the "interior" of a hyperspatial tube, is not and probably never will be surely known. Several highly abstruse mathematical treatises and many volumes of rather gruesome fiction have been written upon the subject—none of which, however, has any bearing here.

If the Patrol fleet did not get there first, the succession of events was different; the degree of difference depending upon how much time the enemy had had. If, as sometimes happened, a fleet was coming through it was met by superatomic bombs and by the concentrated fire of every primary projector that the englobing task force could bring to bear; with consequences upon which it is neither necessary or desirable to dwell. If a planet had emerged, it was met by a negasphere—

Have you ever seen a negasphere strike a planet?

The negasphere is built of negative matter. This material—or, rather, antimaterial—is in every respect the exact opposite of the everyday matter of normal space. Instead of electrons, its ultimate units are positrons—the "Dirac Holes" in an infinity of negative energy. To it a push, however violent, is a pull; a pull is a push. When negative matter strikes positive, then, there is no collision in the usual sense of the word. One electron and one positron neutralize each other and disappear; giving rise to two quanta of extremely hard radiation.

Thus, when the spherical hyper-plane which was the aspect of negasphere tended to occupy the same three-dimensional space in which the loose planet already was, there was no actual collision. Instead, the materials of both simply vanished, along the surface of what should have been a contact, in a gigantically crescendo burst of pure, raw energy. The atoms and the molecules of the planet's substance disappeared; the physically incomprehensible texture of the negasphere's antimass changed into that of normal space. And all circumambient space was flooded with inconceivably lethal radiation; so intensely lethal that any being not adequately shielded from it died before he had time to realize that he was being burned.

Gravitation, of course, was unaffected; and the rapid disappearance of the planet's mass set up unbalanced forces of tremendous magnitude. The hot, dense, pseudoliquid magma tended to erupt as the sphere of nothingness devoured so rapidly the planet's substance, but not a particle of it could move. Instead, it vanished. Mountains fell, crashingly. Oceans poured. Earth-cracks appeared; miles wide, tens of miles deep, hundreds of miles long. The world heaved—shuddered—disintegrated—vanished.

*

The shock attack upon Arisia itself, which in the Eddorian mind had been mathematically certain to succeed, was over in approximately six minutes. Kinnison, Maitland, and LaForge, fuming at their stations, had done nothing at all. The Boskonians had probably thrown everything they could; the probability was vanishingly small that that particular attack was to be or could be resumed. Nevertheless a host of Kinnison's task forces remained on guard and a detail of Arisians still scanned all nearby space.

"What shall I do next, Kit?" Camilla asked. "Help Connie crack that screen?"

Kit glanced at his youngest sister, who was stretched out flat, every muscle rigidly tense in an extremity of effort.

"No," he decided. "If she can't crack it alone, all four of us couldn't help her much. Besides, I don't believe that she can break through it. That's a mechanical screen, you know, powered by atomic-motored generators. My guess is that it'll have to be *solved*, not cracked, and the solution will take time. When she comes down off of that peak, Kay, you might tell her so, and both of you start solving it. The rest of us have another job. The moppers-up are coming in force, and there isn't a chance that either we or the Arisians can derive the counter-formula of that screen in less than a week. Therefore the rest of this battle will have to be fought out on conventional lines. We can do the most good, I think, by spotting the Boskonians into the big tank—our scouts aren't locating five per cent of them—for the L2's to pass on to Dad and the rest of the heavy brass so that they can run this battle the way it should be run. You'll do the spotting, Cam, of course; Kat and I will do the pushing. And if you thought that Tregonsee took you for a wild ride—It'll work, don't you think?"

"Of *course* it will work—and I like wild rides—the faster the better!"

Thus, apparently as though by magic, red lights winked into being throughout a third of the volume of the immense tank; and the three master strategists, informed of what was being done, heaved tremendous sighs of relief. They now had real control. They knew, not only the positions of their own task forces, but also, and exactly, the position of *every* task force of the enemy. More, by merely forming in his mind the desire for the information, any one of the three could know, with no appreciable lapse of time, the exact composition and the exact strength of any individual one of the horde of Boskonian fleets!

*

Kit and his two sisters stood close-grouped, motionless; heads bent and almost touching, arms interlocked. Kinnison perceived with surprise that Lenses, as big and as bright as Kit's own, flamed upon his daughters' wrists; a surprise which changed to awe as the very air around those three red-bronze-auburn heads began to thicken, to pulsate, and to glow with that indefinable, indescribable polychromatic effulgence which is so uniquely characteristic of the Lens of the Galactic Patrol. But there was work to do, and Kinnison did it.

Since the Z9M9Z was now working as not even the most optimistic of her planners and designers had dared to hope that she ever could work, the war could now be, and was now being fought strategically; that is, with the object of doing the enemy as much harm as possible with the irreducible minimum of risk. It was not sporting. It was not clubby. There was nothing whatever of chivalry. There was no thought whatever of giving the enemy a break. It was massacre—it was murder—it was war.

It was not ship to ship. No, nor fleet to fleet. Instead, ten or twenty Patrol task forces, under sure pilotage, dashed out to englobe at extreme range one fleet of the Boskonians. Then, before the opposing admiral could assemble a picture of what was going on, his entire command became the center of impact of hundreds or even thousands of detonating superatomic bombs, as well as the focus of an immensely greater number of scarcely less ravaging primary beams. Not a ship nor a scout nor a lifeboat of the englobed fleet escaped, ever. In fact, few indeed were the blobs, or even droplets, of hard alloy or of dureum which remained merely liquefied or which, later, were able to condense.

Fleet by fleet the Boskonians were blown out of the ether; one by one the red lights in the tank and in the reducer winked out. And finally the slaughter was done.

Kit and his two now Lensless sisters unlaced themselves. Karen and Constance came up for air, announcing that they knew how to work the problem Kit had handed them, but that they would need more time on it. Clarrissa, white and shaken by what she had driven herself to do, looked and felt sick. So did Kinnison; nor had either of the other two commanders derived any pleasure from the engagement. Tregonsee deplored it. Of all the Lensed personnel, only Worsel had enjoyed himself. He liked to kill enemies, at close range or far, and he could not understand or sympathize with squeamishness. Nadreck, of course, had neither liked nor disliked any part of the whole affair. To him his part had been merely another task, to be performed with the smallest outlay of physical and mental effort consistent with good workmanship.

"What next?" Kinnison asked then, of the group at large. "I say the Ploorans. They're not like these poor devils were—they probably sent them in. *They've* got it coming!"

"They certainly have!"

"Ploor!"

"By all means Ploor!"

"But how about Arisia here?" Maitland asked.

"Under control," Kinnison replied. "We'll leave a heavy guard and a spare tank—the Arisians will do the rest."

*

As soon as the tremendous fleet had shaken itself down into the course for Ploor, all seven of the Kinnisons retired to a small dining room and ate a festive meal. They drank after-dinner coffee. Most of them smoked. They discussed, for a long time and not very quietly, the matter of the Hell Hole in Space. Finally:

"I know it's a trap, as well as you do." Kinnison got up from the table, rammed his hands into his breeches pockets, and paced the floor. "It's got T-R-A-P painted all over it, in bill-poster letters seventeen meters high. So what? Since I'm the only one who can, I've got to go in, if it's still there after we knock Ploor off. And it'll still be there, for all the tea in China. All the Ploorans aren't on Ploor."

Four young Kinnisons flashed thoughts at Kathryn, who frowned and bit her lip. She had hit that hole with everything she had, and had simply bounced. She had been able to block the radiation, of course, but such solid barriers had been necessary that she had blinded herself by her own screens. That it was Eddorian there could be no doubt—warned by her own activities in the other tube—Plooran, of course—and Dad would be worth taking, in more ways than one.

"I can't say that I'm any keener about going in than any of you are about having me to do it," the big Lensman went on, "but unless some of you can figure out a reason for my *not* going in that isn't fuller of holes than a sponge-rubber cushion, I'm going to tackle it just as soon after we blow Ploor apart as I can possibly get there."

And Kathryn, his self-appointed guardian, knew that nothing could stop him. Nor did anyone there, even Clarrissa, try to stop him. Lensmen all, they knew that he had to go in; and why.

To the Five, the situation was not too serious. Kinnison would probably come through unhurt. The Eddorians could take him, of course. But whether or not they could do anything to him after they got him would depend no little on what the Kinnison kids would be doing in the meantime—and that would be plenty. They couldn't delay Dad's entry into the tube very much without making a smell, but they could and would hurry Arisia up. And even if, as seemed probable, Dad was already in the tube when Arisia was ready for the big business with Eddore, a lot could be done at the other end. Those amoeboid monstrosities would be fighting for their own precious lives, this time, not for the lives of slaves; and the Five promised each other grimly that the Eddorians would have too much else to worry about to waste any time on Kimball Kinnison.

*

Clarrissa Kinnison, however, fought the hardest and bitterest battle of her life. She loved Kim with a depth and a fervor which very few women, anywhere, have ever been able to feel. She knew with a sick, cold certainty, knew with every fiber of her mind and with every cell of her brain, that if he went into that trap he would die in it. Nevertheless, she would have to let him go in. More, and worse, she would have to send him in—to his death—with a smile. She could not ask him not to go in. She could not even suggest again that there was any possibility that he need not go in. He had to go in. He *had* to.

And if Lensman's Load was heavy on him, on her it was almost unbearable. His part was vastly the easier. He would only have to die; she would have to live. She would have to keep on living—without Kim—living a lifetime of deaths, one after another. And she would have to hold her block and smile, not only with her face, but with her whole mind. She could be scared, of course, apprehensive, as he himself was; she could wish with all her strength for his safe return: but if he suspected the thousandth part of what she really felt it would break his heart. Nor would it do a bit of good. However brokenhearted at her rebellion against the inflexible Code of the Lens, he would still go in. Being Kimball Kinnison, he could not do anything else.

As soon as she could, Clarrissa went to a distant room and turned on a full-coverage block. She lay down, buried her face in the pillow, clenched her fists, and fought.

Was there any way—any *possible* way—that she could die instead? None. It was not that simple.

She would have to let him go.

Not gladly, but proudly and willingly—for the good of the Patrol.

Clarrissa Kinnison gritted her teeth and writhed.

She would simply *have* to let him go into that ghastly trap—go to his absolutely sure and certain death—without showing one white feather, either to her husband or to her children. Her husband, her KIM, would have to die . . . and she—would—have—to—live.

She got up, smiled experimentally, and snapped off the block. Then, actually smiling and serenely confident, she strolled down the corridor.

Such is Lensman's Load.

THE LENSMAN

XXVI.

Twenty-odd years before, when the then *Dauntless* and her crew were thrown out of a hyperspatial tube and into that highly enigmatic nth space, LaVerne Thorndyke had been a Chief Technician. Mentor of Arisia found them, and put into the mind of Sir Austin Cardynge, mathematician extraordinary, the knowledge of how to find the way back to normal space. Thorndyke, working under nervebreaking difficulties, had been in charge of building the machines which were to enable the vessel to return to her home space. He built them. She returned.

He was now again in charge, and every man of his present crew had been a member of his former one. He did not command the spaceship or her regular crew, of course, but they did not count. Not one of these kids would be allowed to set foot on the fantastically dangerous planet to which the inertialess *Space Laboratory XII* was anchored with tractors and pressors.

Older, leaner, grayer, he was now, even more than then, Civilization's Past Master of Mechanism. If anything could be built, "Thorny" Thorndyke could build it. If it couldn't be built, he could build something that would do the work.

As soon as the Gray Lensman and his son left the vessel, Chief Technician Thorndyke—not the vice admiral of the same name—lined his crew up for inspection; men who, although many of them had as much rank and had had as many years of as much authority as their present boss, had been working for days to forget as completely as possible their executive positions and responsibilities. Each man wore not one, but three personal neutralizers, one inside and two outside of his spacesuit. Thorndyke, walking down the line, applied his test-kit to each individual neutralizer. He then tested his own. QX—all were at max.

"Fellows," he said then, "you all remember what it was like last time. This is going to be the same, except more so and for a longer time. How we did it before without any casualties I'll never know. If we can do it again, it'll be a major miracle—no less. Before, all we had to do was to build a couple of small generators and some controls out of stuff native to the planet, and we didn't find that any too easy a job. This time, for a starter, we've got to build a Bergenholm big enough to free the whole planet; after which we install the Bergs, tube generators, atomic blasts, and other stuff we brought along.

"But that native Berg is going to be a Class A Prime headache, and until we get it running it's going to be hell on wheels. The only way we can get away with it is to check and re-check every thing and every step. Check, check, double-check; then go back and double-check again.

"Remember that the fundamental characteristics of this nth space are such that inert matter can travel faster than light; and remember, every second of the time, that our intrinsic velocity is something like fifteen lights relative to anything solid in this space. I want every one of you to picture himself going inert accidentally. You *might* take a tangent course or higher—but you might not, too. And it wouldn't only kill the one who did it. It wouldn't only spoil our record. It could very easily kill us all and make a crater full of boiling metal out of our whole installation. So BE CAREFUL! Also bear in mind that one piece, however small, of this planet's material, accidentally brought aboard might wreck the *Dauntless*. Any questions?"

"If the fundamental characteristics—constants—of this space are so different, how do you know that the stuff will work here?"

"Well, the stuff we built here before worked. The Arisians told Kit Kinnison that two of the fundamentals, mass and length, are about normal. Time is a lot different, so that we can't compute power-to-mass ratios and so on, but we'll have enough power, anyway, to get any speed that we can use."

"I see. We miss the really fancy stuff?"

"Yes. Well, the quicker we get started the quicker we'll get done. Let's go."

*

The planet was airless, waterless, desolate; a chaotic jumble of huge and jagged fragments of various metals in a nonmetallic continuous phase. It was as though some playful child-giant of space had poured dipperfuls of silver, of iron, of copper, and of other granulated pure metals into a tank of something else—and then, tired of play, had thrown the whole mess away!

Neither the metals nor the nonmetallic substances were either hot or cold. They had no apparent temperature, to thermometers or to the "feelers" of the suits. The machines which these men had built so long before had not changed in any particular. They still functioned perfectly; no spot of rust or corrosion or erosion marred any part. This, at least, was good news.

Inertialess machines, extravagantly equipped with devices to keep them inertialess, were taken "ashore"; nor were any of these ever to be returned to the ship. Kinnison had ordered and reiterated that no unnecessary chances were to be taken of getting any particle of nth-space stuff aboard *Space Laboratory XII*, and none were taken.

Since men cannot work indefinitely in spacesuits, each man had periodically to be relieved; but each such relief amounted almost to an operation. Before he left the planet his suit was scrubbed, rinsed, and dried. In the vessel's air lock it was air-blasted again before the outer port was closed. He unshelled in the lock and left his suit there—everything which had come into contact with nth-space matter either would be left on the planet's surface or would be jettisoned before the vessel was again inerted. Unnecessary precautions? Perhaps—but Thorndyke and his crew returned unharmed to normal space in undamaged ships.

Finally the Bergenholm was done—by dint of what improvisation, substitution, and artifice only "Thorny" Thorndyke ever knew; at what strain and cost was evidenced by the gaunt bodies and haggard faces of his overworked and under-slept crew. To those experts, and particularly to Thorndyke, the thing was not a good job. It was not quiet, nor smooth. It was not in balance, statically, dynamically, or electrically. The chief technician, to whom a meter jump of one and a half thousandths had always been a matter of grave concern, swore feelingly in all the planetary languages he knew when he saw what those meters were doing.

He scowled morosely. There might have been poorer machines built sometime, somewhere, he supposed—but if so he had never seen any!

1029

But the improvised Berg ran, and kept on running. The planet became inertialess and remained that way. For hours, then, Thorndyke climbed over and around and through the Brobdingnagian fabrication, testing and checking the operation of every part. Finally he climbed down and reported to his waiting crew.

"QX, fellows, a nice job. A good job, in fact, considering—even though we all know that it isn't what any of us would call a good machine. Part of that meter jump, of course, is due to the fact that nothing about the heap is true or balanced, but most of it must be due to this cockeyed ether. Anyway, none of it is due to the usual causes—loose bars and faulty insulation. So my best guess is that she'll keep on doing her stuff while we do ours. One sure thing, she isn't going to fall apart, even under that ungodly knocking; and I don't *think* that she's going to shake herself off of the planet."

*

After Thorndyke's somewhat less than enthusiastic approval of his brain-child, the adventurers into that fantastic region attacked the second phase of their project. Two Patrol Bergenholms were landed and were installed. Their meters jumped, too, but the engineers were no longer worried about that. *Those* machines would run indefinitely; and a concerted sigh of relief arose when the improvised generator was shut down. Pits were dug. Atomic blasts and other engines were installed, as were many exceedingly complex instruments and mechanisms. A few tons of foreign matter on the planet's surface would now make no difference, but there was no relaxation of the extreme precautions against the transfer of any matter whatever from the planet to the spaceship.

When the job was done, but before the clean-up, Thorndyke called his crew into conference.

"Fellows, I know just what a beating you've been taking. We all feel as though we had been on a Delgonian clambake. Nevertheless, I've got to tell you something. Kinnison said that if we could get this one fixed up without too much trouble, it'd be a mighty good idea to have two of them. What do you say? Did we have too much trouble?"

He got exactly the reaction he had expected.

"Lead us to it!"

"Pick out the one you want!"

"Trouble? It's all over—we can tow this scrap heap on a space line, match intrinsics with clamp-on drivers, and plant it anywhere!"

Another metal-studded, barren, lifeless world was therefore found and prepared, and no real argument arose until Thorndyke broached the matter of selecting the two men who were to stay with him and Henderson in the two lifeboats which were to remain for a time near the two loose planets after *Space Laboratory XII* had returned to normal space. Everybody wanted to stay. Each one *was* going to stay, too, by all the gods of space, if he had to pull rank to do it!

"Hold it!" Thorndyke commanded. "We'll do the same as we did before, then, by drawing lots. Quartermaster Allerdyce—"

"No!" Uhlenhuth, formerly Atomic Technician 1/c, objected vigorously, and was supported by several others. "He's too clever with his fingers—look what he did to the original draw! We're not squawking about that one, you understand—a little fixing was QX back there—but we want this one to be honest."

"Now that you mention it, I do remember hearing that things were not left entirely to chance." Thorndyke grinned broadly. "So you hold the pot yourself, Uhly, and Hank and I will each pull out one name."

So it was. Henderson drew Uhlenhuth, to that burly admiral's loud delight, and Thorndyke drew Nelson, the erstwhile chief communications officer. The two lifeboats disembarked, each near one of the newly "loosened" planets. Two men would stay on or near each of those planets, to be sure that all the machinery functioned perfectly. They would stay there until the atomic blasts functioned perfectly. They would stay there until the atomic blasts went into action and it became clear that the Arisians would need no help in navigating those tremendous globes through nth space to the points at which two hyperspatial tubes were soon to appear.

*

Long before the advance scouts of the Grand Fleet were within surveying distance of Ploor, Kit and his sisters had spread a completely detailed chart of its defenses in the tactical tank. A white star represented Ploor's sun; a white sphere the planet itself; white Ryerson string lights marked a portion of the planetary orbit. Points of white light, practically all of which were connected to the white sphere by red string lights, marked the directions of neighboring stars and the existence of sunbeams, installed and ready. Pink globes were loose planets; purple ones negaspheres; red points of light were, as before, Boskonian task-force fleets. Blues were mobile fortresses; bands of canary yellow and amber luminescence showed the locations and emplacements of sunbeam grids and deflectors.

Layer after layer of pinks, purples, and blues almost hid the brilliant white sphere from sight. More layers of the same colors, not quite as dense, surrounded the entire solar system. Yellow and amber bands were everywhere.

Kinnison studied the thing briefly, whistling unmelodiously through his teeth. The picture was familiar enough, since it duplicated in practically every respect the chart of the neighborhood of the Patrol's own Ultra Prime, around Klovia. It did not require much study to make it clear that that defense could not be cracked by any concentration possible of any mobile devices theretofore employed in war.

"Just about what we expected," Kinnison thought to the group at large. "Some new stuff, but not much. What I want to know, Kit and the rest of you, is there anything there that looks as though it was supposed to handle our new baby? Don't see anything, myself."

"There is not," Kit stated definitely. "We looked. There couldn't be, anyway. It can't be handled. Looking backwards at it, they will probably be able to reconstruct how it was done, but in advance? No. Even Mentor couldn't—he had to call in a fellow who has studied ultra-high mathematics for Klono-only-knows-how-many-millions of years to compute the resultant vectors."

Kit's use of the word "they," which, of course, meant Ploorans to everyone except his sisters, concealed his knowledge of the fact that the Eddorians had taken over the defense of Ploor. Eddorians were handling those screens. Eddorians were directing and correlating those far-flung task forces, with a precision which Kinnison soon noticed.

"Much smoother work than I ever saw them do before," he commented. "Suppose they have developed a Z9M9Z?"

"Could be. They copied everything else you invented, why not that?" Again the highly ambiguous "they." "No sign of it around Arisia, though—but maybe they didn't think they'd need it there."

"Or, more likely, they didn't want to risk it so far from home. We can tell better after the mopping-up starts—if the widget performs as per specs. But if your dope is right, this is about close enough. You might tip the boys off, and I'll call Mentor." Kinnison could not reach nth space, but it was no secret that Kit could.

The terminus of one of the Patrol's hyperspatial tubes erupted into space close to Ploor. That such phenomena were expected was evident—a Boskonian fleet moved promptly and smoothly to englobe it. But this was an Arisian tube; computed, installed, and handled by Arisians. It would be in existence only three seconds; the nearest defending task force could not possibly get there in time.

To the observers in the Z9M9Z those three seconds stretched endlessly. What would happen when that utterly foreign planet, with its absolutely impossible intrinsic velocity of over fifteen times that of light, erupted into normal space and went inert? Nobody, not even the Arisians, knew.

Everybody there had seen pictures of what happened when the insignificant mass of a spaceship, traveling at only a hundredth of the velocity of light, collided with a planetoid. That was bad enough. This projectile, however, had a mass of about eight times ten to the twenty-first power—an eight followed by twenty-one zeros—metric tons; would tend to travel fifteen hundred times as fast; and kinetic energy equals mass times velocity squared.

There seemed to be a theoretical possibility, since the mass would instantaneously become some higher order of infinity, that all the matter in normal space would coalesce with it in zero time; but Mentor had assured Kit that operators would come into effect to prevent such an occurrence, and that untoward events would be limited to a radius of ten or fifteen parsecs. Mentor could solve the problem in detail, but since the solution would require some two hundred Klovian years and the event was due to occur in two weeks—

"How about the big computer at Ultra Prime?" Kinnison had asked, innocently. "You know how fast that works."

"Roughly two thousand years—if it could take that kind of math, which it can't," Kit had replied, and the subject had been dropped.

*

Finally it happened. What happened? Even after the fact none of the observers knew; nor did any except the L3's ever find out. The fuses of all the recorder and analyzer circuits blew at once. Needles jumped instantly to maximum and wrapped themselves around their stops. Charts and ultraphotographic films showed only straight or curved lines running from the origin to and through the limits in zero time. Ploor and everything around it disappeared in an utterly indescribable and completely incomprehensible blast of pure, wild, raw, uncontrolled and uncontrollable energy. The infinitesimal fraction of that energy which was visible, heterodyned upon the ultra as it was and screened as it was, blazed so savagely upon the plates that it seared the eyes.

And if the events caused by the planet aimed at Ploor were indescribable, what can be said of those initiated by the one directed against Ploor's sun?

When the heat generated in the interior of a sun becomes greater than its effective surface is able to radiate, that surface expands. If the expansion is not fast enough, a more or less insignificant amount of the sun's material explodes, thus enlarging by force the radiant surface to whatever extent is necessary to restore equilibrium. Thus come into being the ordinary novae; suns which may for a few days or for a few weeks radiate energy at a rate a few hundreds of thousands of times greater than normal. Since ordinary novae can be produced at will by the collision of a planet with a sun, the scientists of the Patrol had long since completed their studies of all the phenomena involved.

The mechanisms of supernovae, however, remained obscure. No adequate instrumentation had been developed to study conclusively the occasional supernova which occurred naturally. No supernova had ever been produced artificially—with all its resources of mass, atomic energy, cosmic energy, and sunbeams. Civilization could neither assemble nor concentrate enough power.

At the impact of the second loose planet, accompanied by the excess energy of its impossible and unattainable intrinsic velocity, Ploor's sun became a supernova. How deeply the intruding thing penetrated, how much of the sun's mass exploded, never was and perhaps never will be determined. The violence of the explosion was such, however, that Klovian astronomers reported—a few years later—that it was radiating energy at the rate of some five hundred and fifty million suns.

Thus no attempt will be made to describe what happened when the planet from nth space struck the Boskonians' sun.

It was indescribably cubed.

XXVII.

The Boskonian fleets defending Ploor were not all destroyed, of course. The vessels were inertialess. None of the phenomena accompanying the coming into being of the supernova were propagated at a velocity above that of light; a speed which to any spaceship is scarcely a crawl.

The survivors were, however, disorganized. They had lost their morale when Ploor was wiped out in such a spectacularly nerve-shattering fashion. Also, they had lost practically all of their High Command; for the Ploorans, instead of riding the ether as did Patrol commanders, remained in their supposedly secure headquarters and directed matters from afar. Mentor and his fellows had removed from this plane of existence the Eddorians who had been present in the flesh on Ploor. The Arisians had cut all communications between Eddore and the remnants of the Boskonian defensive force.

Grand Fleet, then, moved in for the kill; and for a time the action near Arisia was repeated. Following definite flight-and-course orders from the Z9M9Z, ten or more Patrol fleets would make short hops. At the end of those assigned courses they would discover that they had englobed a task force of the enemy. Bomb and beam!

Over and over—flit, bomb, and beam!

One Boskonian high officer, however, had both the time and the authority to act. A full thousand fleets massed together, their heaviest units outward, packed together screen to screen in a close-order globe of defense.

"According to Haynes, that was good strategy in the old days," Kinnison commented, "but it's no good against loose planets and negaspheres."

Six loose planets were so placed and so released that their inert masses would crash together at the center of the Boskonian globe; then, a few minutes later, ten negaspheres of high antimass were similarly launched. After those sixteen missiles had done their work and the resultant had attained an equilibrium of sorts, very little mopping-up was found necessary.

The Boskonian observers were competent. The Boskonian commanders now knew that they had no chance whatever of success; that to stay was to be annihilated; that the only possibility of life lay in flight. Therefore each remaining Boskonian vice admiral, after perhaps a moment of consultation with a few others, ordered his fleet to drive at maximum blast for his home planet.

"No use chasing them individually, is there, Kit?" Kinnison asked, when it became clear in the tank that the real battle was over; that all resistance had ended. "They can't do anything, and this kind of killing makes me sick at the stomach. Besides, I've got something else to do."

"No. Me, too. So have I." Kit agreed with his father in full.

As soon as the last Boskonian fleet was beyond detector range Grand Fleet broke up, its component fleets setting out for their respective worlds.

"The Hell Hole is still there, Kit," the Gray Lensman said, soberly. "If Ploor was the top—I'm beginning to think there *is* no top—it leads either to an automatic mechanism set up by the Ploorans or to Ploorans who are still alive somewhere. If Ploor was not the top, this seems to be the only lead we have toward that top. In either case I've got to take it. Check?"

"Well, I—" Kit tried to duck, but couldn't. "Yes, Dad, I'm afraid it's check."

Two big hands met and gripped; and Kinnison went to take leave of his wife.

There is no need to go into detail as to what those two strong souls said or did. He knew that he was going into danger; that he might not return. That is, he knew empirically or academically, as a nongermane sort of fact, that he might die. He did not, however, really believe that he would. No man who is not an arrant coward really believes, ever, that any given event will or can kill him. In his own mind he goes on living indefinitely.

Kinnison expected to be captured, imprisoned, questioned, and perhaps tortured. He could understand all of those things, and he did not like any one of them. That he was more than a trifle afraid and that he hated to leave her now more than he ever had before were both natural enough—he had nothing whatever to hide from her.

She, on the other hand, knew starkly that he would never come back. She knew that he would die in that trap. She knew that she would have to live a lifetime of emptiness, alone. Hence she had much to conceal from him. She must be just as scared and as apprehensive as he was, but no more; just as anxious for their continued happiness as he was, but no more; just as intensely loving, but no more and in exactly the same sense. Here lay the test. She must kiss him good-by as though he were going into mere danger. She *must not* give way to the almost irresistible urge to act in accordance with what she so starkly, chillingly knew to be the truth, that she would never—*never*—NEVER kiss her Kim again!

She succeeded. It is a measure of the Red Lensman's quality that she did not weaken, even when her husband approached the boundary of the Hell Hole and sent what she knew would be his last message.

"Here it is—about a second now. Don't worry—I'll be back very shortly. Clear ether, Chris!"

"Of *course* you will, dear. Clear ether, Kim!"

*

His speedster did not mount any special generators. He had not thought that they would be necessary. Nor were they. He and his ship were sucked into that trap as though it had been a maelstrom.

He felt again the commingled agonies of interdimensional acceleration. He perceived again the formless, textureless, spaceless void of blankly gray nothingness which was the three-dimensionally-impossible substance of the tube. A moment later, he felt a new and different acceleration—he was speeding up *inside the tube!* Then, very shortly, he felt nothing at all. Startled, he tried to jump up to investigate, and discovered that he could not move. Even by the utmost exertion of his will he could not stir a finger or an eyelid. He was completely immobilized. Nor could he feel. His body was as devoid of sensation as though it belonged to somebody else. Worse, for his heart was not beating. He was not breathing. He could not see. It was as though his every nerve, motor and sensory, voluntary and involuntary, had been separately anaesthetized. He could still think, but that was all. His sense of perception still worked.

He wondered whether he was still accelerating or not, and tried to find out. He could not. He could not determine whether he was moving or stationary. There were no reference points. Every infinitesimal volume of that enigmatic grayness was like each and every other.

Mathematically, perhaps, he was not moving at all; since he was in a continuum in which mass, length and time, and hence inertia and inertialessness, velocity and acceleration, are meaningless terms. He was outside of space and beyond time. Effectively, however, he was moving; moving with an acceleration which nothing material had ever before approached. He and his vessel were being driven along that tube by every watt of power generable by one entire Eddorian atomic power plant. His velocity, long since unthinkable, became incalculable.

All things end—even Eddorian atomic power was not infinite. At the very peak of power and pace, then, all the force, all the momentum, all the kinetic energy of the speedster's mass and velocity were concentrated in and applied to Kinnison's physical body. He sensed something, and tried to flinch, but could not. In a fleeting instant of what he thought was time he went *past*, not through, his clothing and his Lens; *past*, not

1035

through, his armor; and *past*, not through, the hard beryllium-alloy structure of his vessel. He even went past but not through the N-dimensional interface of the hyperspatial tube.

This, although Kinnison did not know it, was the Eddorian's climactic effort. He had taken his prisoner as far as he could possibly reach; then, assembling and concentrating all available power, he had given him a catapultic shove into the absolutely unknown and utterly unknowable. The Eddorian did not know any vector of the Lensman's naked flight; he did not care where he went. He did not know and could not compute or even guess at his victim's probable destination.

*

In what his spacehound's time sense told him was one second, Kinnison passed exactly two hundred million foreign spaces. He did not know how he knew the precise number, but he did. Hence, in the Patrol's measured cadence, he began to count groups of spaces of one hundred million each. After a few days, his velocity decreased to such a value that he could count groups of single millions. Then thousands—hundreds—tens—until finally he could perceive the salient features of each space before it was blotted out by the next.

How could this be? He wondered, but not foggily; his mind was as clear and as strong as it had ever been. Spaces were coexistent, not spread out like this. In the fourth dimension they were flat together, like pages in a book, except thinner. This was all wrong. It was impossible. Since it could not happen, it was not happening. He had not been and could not be drugged. Therefore some Plooran must have him in a zone of compulsion. *What* a zone! *What* an operator the ape must be!

It was, however, real—all of it. What Kinnison did not know, then or ever, was that he was actually outside the boundaries of space; actually beyond the confines of time. He was going past, not through, those spaces and those times.

He was now in each space long enough to study it in some detail. He was an immense distance above this one; at such a distance that he could perceive many globular super-universes; each of which in turn was composed of billions of lenticular galaxies.

Through it. Closer now. Galaxies only; the familiar random masses whose apparent lack of symmetrical grouping is due to the limitations of Civilization's observers. He was still going too fast to stop.

In the next space Kinnison found himself within the limits of a solar system and tried with all the force of his mind to get in touch with some intelligent entity upon one—any one—of its planets. Before he could succeed, the system vanished and he was dropping, from a height of a few thousand kilometers, toward the surface of a warm and verdant world, so much like Tellus that he thought for an instant that he must have circumnavigated total space. The aspect, the ice-caps, the cloud-effects, were identical. The oceans, however, while similar, were different; as were the continents. The mountains were larger and rougher and harder.

He was falling much too fast. A free fall from infinity wouldn't give him *this* much speed!

This whole affair was, as he had decided once before, absolutely impossible. It was simply preposterous to believe that a naked man, especially one without blood circulation or breath, could still be alive after spending as many weeks in open space as he had just spent. He *knew* that he was alive. Therefore none of this was happening; even though, as surely as he knew that he was alive, he knew that he was falling.

"Jet back, Lensman!" he thought viciously to himself; tried to shout it aloud.

For this could be deadly stuff, if he let himself believe it. If he believed that he was falling from any such height, he would die in the instant of landing. He would not actually crash; his body would not move from wherever it was that it was. Nevertheless the shock of that wholly imaginary crash would kill him just as dead and just as instantaneously as though all his flesh had been actually smashed into a crimson smear upon one of the neighboring mountain's huge, flat rocks.

"Pretty close, my bright young Plooran friend, but you didn't quite ring the bell," he thought savagely, trying with all the power of his mind to break through the zone of compulsion. "I admit that you're good, but I'm telling you that, if you want to kill me, you'll have to do it physically, and I don't believe that you carry jets enough to swing the job. You might as well cut your zone, because this kind of stuff has been pulled on me by experts, and it hasn't worked yet."

He was apparently falling, feet downward, toward an open, grassy mountain meadow, surrounded by forests, through which meandered a small stream. He was so close now that he could perceive the individual blades of grass in the meadow and the small fishes in the stream, and he was still apparently at terminal velocity.

Without his years of spacehound's training in inertialess maneuvering, he might have died even before he landed, but speed as speed did not affect him at all. He was used to instantaneous stops from light-speeds. The only thing that worried him was the matter of inertia. Was he inert or free?

He declared to himself that he was free. Or, rather, that he had been, was, and would continue to be motionless. It was physically, mathematically, intrinsically impossible that any of this stuff had actually occurred. It was all compulsion, pure and simple, and he—Kimball Kinnison, Gray Lensman—would not let it get him down. He clenched his mental teeth upon that belief and held it doggedly. One bare foot struck the tip of a blade of grass and his entire body came to a shockless halt. He grinned in relief—this was what he had wanted, but had not quite dared wholly to expect. There followed immediately, however, other events which he had not expected at all.

His halt was less than momentary; in the instant of its accomplishment he began to fall normally the remaining eight or ten inches to the ground. Automatically he sprung his space-trained knees, to take the otherwise disconcerting jar; automatically his left hand snapped up to the place where his controls should have been. *Legs and arms worked!*

He could see with his eyes. He could feel with his skin. He was drawing a breath, the first time he had breathed since leaving normal space. Nor was it an unduly deep breath—he felt no lack of oxygen. His heart was beating as normally as though it had never missed a beat. He was not unusually hungry or thirsty. But all that stuff could wait—where was that Plooran?

*

Kinnison had landed in complete readiness for strife. There were no rocks or clubs handy, but he had his fists, feet, and teeth; and they would do until he could find or make something better. But there was nothing to fight. Drive his sense of perception as he would, he could find nothing larger or more intelligent than a deer.

The farther this thing went along the less sense it made. A compulsion, to be any good at all, ought to be logical and coherent. It should fit into every corner and cranny of the subject's experience and knowledge. This one did not fit anything or anywhere. It didn't even come close. Yet, technically, it was a marvelous job. He couldn't detect a trace of it. This grass looked and felt real. The pebbles hurt his tender feet so much that he had to wince as he walked gingerly to the water's edge. He drank deeply. The water, real or not, was cold, clear, and eminently satisfying.

"Listen, you misguided what-is-it," he thought probingly, "you might as well open up now as later whatever you've got in mind. If this performance is supposed to be nonfiction, it's a flat bust. If it is supposed to be science-fiction, it isn't much better. If it's a space-opera, even, you're violating all the fundamentals. I've written better stuff myself—Qadgop and Cynthia were a lot more convincing." He waited a moment, then went on:

"Whoever heard of the intrepid hero of a space-opera as big as this one started out to be getting stranded on a completely Earth-like planet and then having nothing happen? No action at all? How about a couple of indescribable monsters of superhuman strength and agility, for me to tear apart with my steel-thewed fingers?"

He glanced around expectantly. No monster appeared.

"Well, then, how about a damsel in distress for me to rescue from a fate worse than death? Better make it two of them—safety in numbers, you know—a blonde and a brunette. No redheads. I'll play along with you part way on that oldie—up to the point of falling for either of them."

He waited again.

"QX, sport, no woman. Suits me perfectly. But I hope you haven't forgotten about the tasty viands. I can eat fish if I have to, but if you want to keep your hero happy, let's see you lay down here, on a platter, a one-kilogram steak, three centimeters thick, medium rare, fried in Tellurian butter and smothered in Venusian superla mushrooms."

No steak appeared, and the Gray Lensman recalled and studied intensively every detail of what had apparently happened. It *still* could not have occurred. He could not have imagined it. It could not have been compulsion or hypnosis. None of it made any kind of sense.

As a matter of plain fact, however, Kinnison's first and most positive conclusion was wrong. His memories were factual records of actual events and things. He would eat well during his stay upon that nameless planet, but he would have to procure his own food. Nothing would attack him, or even annoy him. For the Eddorian's *binding*—this is perhaps as good a word for it as any, since "geas" implies a curse—was such that the Gray Lensman could return to space and time only under such conditions and to such an environment as would not do him any iota of physical harm. He must continue alive and in good health for at least fifty more of his years.

*

And Clarrissa Kinnison, tense and strained, waited in her room for the instant of her husband's death. They two were one, with a oneness no other man and woman had ever known. If one died, from any cause whatever, the other would feel it.

She waited. Five minutes—ten—fifteen—half an hour—an hour. She began to relax. Her fists unclenched, her shallow breathing grew deeper.

Two hours. Kim was *still alive!* A wave of happy, buoyant relief swept through her; her eyes flashed and sparkled. If they hadn't been able to kill him in two hours, they never could. Her Kim had plenty of jets.

Even the top minds of Boskonia could not kill her Kim!

*

XXVIII.

The Arisians and the Children of the Lens had known that Eddore must be attacked as soon as possible after the fall of Ploor. They were fairly certain that the interspatial use of planets as projectiles was new; but they were completely certain that the Eddorians would be able to deduce in a short time the principles and the concepts, the fundamental equations, and the essential operators involved in the process. They would find nth space or one like it in one day; certainly not more than two. Their slaves would duplicate the weapon in approximately three weeks. Shortly thereafter both Ultra Prime and Prime Base, both Klovia and Tellus, would be blown out of the ether. So would Arisia—perhaps Arisia would go first. The Eddorians would probably not be able to aim such planets as accurately as the Arisians had, but they would keep on trying and they would learn fast.

This weapon was the sheer ultimate in destructiveness. No defense against it was possible. There was no theory which applied to it or which could be stretched to cover it. Even the Arisian Masters of Mathematics had not as yet been able to invent symbologies and techniques to handle the quantities and magnitudes involved when those interloping masses of foreign matter struck normal space.

Thus Kit did not have to follow up his announced intention of making the Arisians hurry up. They did not hurry, of course, but they did not lose or waste a minute. Each Arisian, from the youngest guardian up to the oldest philosopher, tuned a part of his mind to Mentor, another part to some one of the millions of Lensmen upon his list, and flashed a message.

"Lensman, attend—keep your mind sensitized to this, the pattern of Mentor of Arisia, who will speak to you as soon as all have been alerted."

That message went throughout the First Galaxy, throughout intergalactic space, and throughout what part of the Second Galaxy had felt the touch of Civilization. It went to Alsakan and Vandemar and Klovia, to Thrale and Tellus and Rigel IV, to Mars and Velantia and Palain VII, to Medon and Venus and Centralia. It went to flitters, battleships, and loose planets. It went to asteroids and moonlets, to planets large and small. It went to newly graduated Lensmen and to Lensmen long since retired; to Lensmen at work and at play. It went to every living wearer of the First-Stage Lens of the Galactic Patrol.

Wherever the message went, turmoil followed. Lensmen everywhere flashed questions at all the other Lensmen they knew or had ever met.

"What do you make of it, Fred?"

"Did you get the same thing I did?"

"*Mentor!* Grinning Noshabkeming, what's up?"

"Must be big for Mentor to be handling it."

"*Big!* It's immense! Whoever heard of Arisia stepping in before?"

"*Big!* Colossal! Mentor never talked to anybody except Kinnison before, did he?"

Millions of Lensed questions flooded every base and every office of the Patrol. Nobody, not even the vice co-ordinator, knew a thing.

"You might as well stop sending in questions as to what this is all about, because none of us knows any more about it than you do," Maitland finally sent out a general notice. "Apparently everybody with a Lens is getting the same message, no more and no less. All I can say is that it must be a Class A Prime emergency, and everyone who is not actually tied up in a life-and-death matter will please drop everything and stand by."

*

Mentor wanted, and had to have, high tension. He got it. Tension mounted higher and higher as eventless hours passed and as, for the first time in history, Patrol business slowed down almost to a stop.

And in a small cruiser, manned by four red-headed girls and one red-headed youth, tension was also building up. The problem of the mechanical screens had long since been solved. Atomic powered counter-generators were in place, ready at the touch of a button to neutralize the mechanically-generated screens of the enemy and thus to make the engagement a mind-to-mind combat. They were as close to Eddore's star-cluster as they could be without giving alarm. They had had nothing to do for hours except wait. They were probably keyed up higher than any other five Lensmen in all of space.

Kit, son of his father, was pacing the floor, chain-smoking. Constance was alternately getting up and sitting down—up—down—up. She, too, was smoking; or, rather, she was lighting cigarettes and throwing them away. Kathryn was sitting, stiffly still, manufacturing Lenses which, starting at her wrists, raced up both bare arms to her shoulders and disappeared. Karen was meticulously sticking holes in a piece of blank paper with a pin, making an intricate and meaningless design. Only Camilla made any pretense of calmness, and the others knew that she was bluffing. She was pretending to read a novel; but instead of absorbing its full content at the rate of one glance per page, she had read half of it word by word and still had no idea of what the story was about.

"Are you ready, Children?" Mentor's thought came in at last.

"Ready!" Without knowing how they got there, the Five found themselves standing in the middle of the room, packed tight.

"Oh Kit, I'm shaking like a fool!" Constance wailed. "I just *know* I'm going to louse up this whole war!"

"QX, baby, we're all in the same fix. Can't you hear my teeth chatter? Doesn't mean a thing. Good teams—champions—all feel the same way before a big game starts. And this is the capital IT.

"Steady down, kids. We'll be QX as soon as the whistle blows—I hope."

"*P-s-s-t!*" Kathryn hissed. "Listen!"

"Lensmen of the Galactic Patrol!" Mentor's resonant pseudovoice filled all space. "I, Mentor of Arisia, am calling upon you because of a crisis in which no lesser force can be of use. You have been informed upon the matter of Ploor. It is true that Ploor has been destroyed; that the Ploorans, physically, are no more. You of the Lens, however, already know dimly that the physical is not the all. Know now that there is a residuum of nonmaterial malignancy against which all the physical weapons of all the Universe would be completely impotent. That evil effluvium, intrinsically vicious, is implacably opposed to every basic concept and idea of your Patrol. It has been on the move ever since the destruction of the planet Ploor. Unaided, we of Arisia are not strong enough to handle it, but the massed and directed force of your collective mind will be able to destroy it completely. If you wish me to do so, I will supervise the work of so directing your mental force as to encompass the complete destruction of this menace, which I tell you most solemnly is the last weapon of power with which Boskonia will be able to threaten Civilization. Lensmen of the Galactic Patrol, met as one for the first time in Civilization's long history, what is your wish?"

A tremendous wave of thought, expressed in millions of variant phraseologies, made the wish of the Lensmen very clear indeed. They did not know how such a thing could be done, but they were supremely eager to have Mentor of Arisia lead them against the Boskonians, whoever and wherever they might be.

"Your verdict is unanimous, as I had hoped and believed that it would be. It is well. The part of each of you will be simple, but not easy. You will all of you, individually, think of two things, and of only two. First, of your love for and your pride in and your loyalty to your Patrol. Second, of the clear fact that Boskonia must not and shall not triumph over Civilization. Think these thoughts, each of you with all the strength that in him lies.

"You need not consciously direct those thoughts. Being attuned to my pattern, the force will flow at my direction. As it passes from you, you will replenish it, each according to his strength. You will find it the hardest labor you have ever performed, but it will be of permanent harm to none and it will not be of long duration. One hour will suffice. Are you ready?"

"WE ARE READY!" The crescendo roar of thought must have bulged the Galaxy to its poles.

"Children—strike!"

*

The Unit struck. The outermost Eddorian screen went down. It struck again, almost instantly. Down went the second. The third. The fourth.

It was that flawless Unit, not Camilla, who detected and analyzed and precisely located the Eddorian guardsman handling each of those far-flung screens. It was the Unit, not Kathryn and Kit, who drilled the pilot hole through each Eddorian's hard-held block and enlarged it into a working orifice. It was the Unit, not Karen, whose impenetrable shield held stubbornly every circular mil of advantage gained in making such ingress. It was the Unit, not Constance, who assembled and drove home the blasts of mental force in which the Eddorians died. No time whatever was lost in consultation or decision. Action was not only instantaneous, but simultaneous with perception. The Children of the Lens were not now five, but one. The UNIT.

"Come in, Mentor!" Kit snapped then. "All you Arisians and all the Lensmen. Nothing specialized—just a general slam at the whole screen. This fifth screen is the works—they've got twenty men on it instead of one, and they're top-notchers. Best strategy now is for us five to lay off for a second or two and show 'em what we've got in the line of defense, while the rest of you fellows give 'em hell!"

Arisia and the massed Lensmen struck, a tidal wave of such tremendous weight and power that under its impact the fifth screen sagged flat against the planet's surface. Any one Lensman's power was small, of course, in comparison with that of any Eddorian, but every First-Stage Lensman of the Galactic Patrol was giving, each according to his strength, and the output of one Lensman, multiplied by the countless millions which was the number of Lensmen then at work, made itself tellingly felt.

Countless? Yes. No one not of Arisia ever knew how many minds contributed to that stupendous flood of force. Bear in mind that in the First Galaxy alone there are over two thousand million suns: that each sun has, on the average, something over one and thirty-seven hundredths planets inhabited by intelligent life; that about one-half of these planets adhere to Civilization; and that Tellus, an average planet, graduates approximately one hundred Lensmen every year.

"So far, Kit, so good," Constance panted. Although she was no longer trembling, she was still highly excited. "But I don't know how many more shots like that I've . . . we've . . . got left in the locker."

"You're doing fine, Connie," Camilla soothed.

"Sure you are, baby. You've got plenty of jets," Kit agreed. Except in moments of supreme stress these personal, individual exchanges of by-thoughts did not interfere with the smooth functioning of the Unit. "Fine work, all of you, kids. I knew that we'd get over the shakes as soon as—"

"Watch it!" Camilla snapped. "Here comes the shock wave. Brace yourself, Kay. Hold us together, Kit!"

The wave came. Everything that the Eddorians could send. The Unit's barrier did not waver. After a full second of it—a time comparable to days of continuous atomic bombing in ordinary warfare—Karen, who had been standing stiff and still, began to relax.

"This is too, *too* easy," she declared. "Who is helping me? I can't feel anything, but I simply know that I haven't got this much stuff. You, Cam—or is it all of you?" Not one of the Five was as yet thoroughly familiar with the operating characteristics of the Unit.

"All of us, more or less, but mostly Kit," Camilla decided after a moment's thought. "He's got the weight of an inert planet."

"Not me," Kit denied, vigorously. "Must be you other kids. Feels to me like Kat, mostly. All I'm doing is just sort of leaning up against you a little—just in case. I haven't done a thing so far."

"Oh, no? Sure not!" Kathryn giggled, an infectious chuckle inherited or copied directly from her mother. "We know it, and that you're going to keep on loafing all the rest of the day. You wouldn't think of doing anything, even if you could. Just the same, we're all mighty glad that our big brother is here!"

"QX, kids, seal the chatter. We've had time to learn that they can't crack us—so have they, by the way—so let's get to work."

Since the Unit was now under continuous attack, its technique would have to be entirely different from that used previously. Its barrier must vanish for an infinitesimal period of time, during which it must simultaneously detect and blast. Or, rather, the blast would have to be directed in mid-flight, while the Unit's own block was open. Nor could that block be open for more than the barest possible instant before or after the passage of the bolt. It is true that the attack of the Eddorians compared with that of the Unit very much as the steady pressure of burning propellant powder compares with the disruptive force of detonating duodec; even so it would have wrought much damage to the minds of the Five had any of it been allowed to reach them.

Also, like parachute-jumping, this technique could not be practiced. Since the timing had to be so nearly absolute, the first two shots missed their targets completely; but the Unit learned fast. Eddorian after Eddorian died.

*

"Help, All-Highest, help!" a high Eddorian appealed, finally.

"What is it?" His Ultimate Supremacy, knowing that only utter desperation could be back of such intrusion, wasted no time.

"It is this new Arisian entity—"

"It is not an entity, fool, but a fusion," came curt reprimand. "We decided that point long ago."

"An entity, I say!" In his urgency the operator committed the unpardonable by omitting the titles of address. "No possible fusion can attain such perfection of timing, of synchronization. Our best fusions have attempted to match it, and have failed. Its screens are impenetrable. Its thrusts cannot be blocked. My message is this: Solve for us, and quickly, the problem of this entity. If you do not or cannot do so, we perish all of us, even to you of the Innermost Circle."

"Think you so?" The thought was a sneer. "If your fusions cannot match those of the Arisians you should die, and the loss will be small."

*

The fifth screen went down. For the first time in untold ages the planet of Eddore lay bare to the Arisian mind. There were inner defenses, of course, but Kit knew every one; their strengths and their weaknesses. He had long since spread in Mentor's mind an exact and completely detailed chart; they had long since drawn up a completely detailed plan of campaign. Nevertheless, Kit could not keep from advising Mentor:

"Pick off any who may try to get away. Start on Area B and work up. Be sure, though, to lay off of Area K or you'll get your beard singed off."

"The plan is being followed," Mentor assured him. "Children, you have done very well indeed. Rest now, and recuperate your powers against that which is yet to come."

"QX. Unlace yourselves, kids. Loosen up. Unlax. I'll break out a few beakers of fayalin, and all of us—you especially, Con—had better eat ten or fifteen of these candy bars."

1043

"*Eat!* Why, I *couldn't—*" Kit insisted, and Constance took an experimental bite. "But say, I *am* hungry, at that!"

"Of course you are. We've been putting out some stuff, and there's more and worse coming. Now rest, all of you."

*

They rested. Somewhat to their surprise, they were now seasoned enough campaigners so that they could rest; even Constance. But the respite was short. Area K, the headquarters and the citadel of His Ultimate Supremacy and the Innermost Circle of the Boskonian Empire, contained all that remained of Eddorian life.

"No tight linkage yet, kids," Kit the Organizer went smoothly to work. "Individual effort—a flash of fusion, perhaps, now and then, if any of us call for it, but no Unit until I give the word. Then give it everything you've got. Cam, analyze that screen and set us up a pattern for it—you'll find that it'll take some doing. See whether it's absolutely homogenous—hunt for weak spots, if any. Con, narrow down to the sharpest needle you can possibly make and start pecking. Not too hard—don't tire yourself—just to get acquainted with the texture of the thing and keep them awake. Kay, take over our guard so that Eukonidor can join the other Arisians. Kat, come along with me—you'll have to help with the Arisians until I call you into the Unit.

"You Arisians, except Mentor, blanket this dome. Thinner than that—solider, harder—there. A trifle off-balance yet—give me just a little more, here on this side. QX—hold it right there! SQUEEZE! Kat, watch 'em. Hold them right there and in balance until you're sure that the Eddorians aren't going to be able to put any bulges up through the blanket.

"Now, Mentor, you and the Lensmen. Tell them to give us, for the next five seconds, absolutely everything that they can deliver. When they're at absolute peak, hit us with it all. Hit us dead center, and don't pull your punch. We'll be ready.

"Con, get ready to stick that needle there—they'll think it's just another peck, I hope—and prepare to blast as you never blasted before. Kay, get ready to drop that screen and stiffen the needle—when those Lensmen hit us even you will know that you're not just being patted on the back. The rest of us will brace you and keep the shock from killing us all. Here it comes. Make Unit! GO!"

The Unit struck. The needle of pure force drove against the Eddorians' supposedly absolutely impenetrable shield. The Unit's thrust was, of itself, like nothing ever before known. The Lensmen's pile-driver blow—the integrated sum total of the top effort of every First-Stage Lensman of the entire Galactic Patrol—was of itself irresistible. Something had to give way.

For an instant it seemed as though nothing were happening or ever would happen. Strong young arms laced the straining Five into a group as motionless and as sculpturesque as statuary, while between their bodies and around them there came into being a gigantic Lens—a Lens whose splendor filled the entire room with radiance.

Under that awful concentration of force something *had* to give way. The Unit held. The Arisians held. The Lensmen held. The needle of force, superlatively braced, neither bent nor broke. Therefore the Eddorians' screen was punctured; and in the instant of its puncturing it disappeared as does a bubble when it breaks.

There was no mopping-up to do. Such was the torrent of force cascading into that citadel that within a moment after its shield went down all life within it was snuffed out.

The Boskonian War was over.

XXIX.

"Did you kids come through QX?" The frightful combat over, the dreadful tension a thing of the past, Kit's first thought was for his sisters.

They were unharmed. None of the Five had suffered anything except mental exhaustion. Recuperation was rapid.

"Better we hunt that tube up and get Dad out of it, don't you think?" Kit suggested.

"Have you got a story arranged that will hold together under examination?" Camilla asked.

"Everything except a few minor details, which we can polish up later."

Smoothly the four girls linked their minds with their brother's; effortlessly the Unit's thought surveyed all nearby space. No hyperspatial tube, nor any trace of one, was there. Tuned to Kinnison's pattern, the Unit then scanned not only normal space and the then present time, but also millions upon millions of other spaces and past and future times; all without finding the Gray Lensman.

Again and again the Unit reached out, farther and farther; out to the extreme limit of even its extraordinary range. Every space and every time was empty. The Children of the Lens broke their linkage and stared at each other, aghast.

They knew starkly what it must mean, but that conclusion was unthinkable. Kinnison—their Dad—the hub of the universe—the unshakable, immutable Rock of Civilization—he *couldn't* be dead. They simply could not accept the logical explanations as the true one.

And while they pondered, shaken, a call from their Red Lensman mother impinged upon their consciousness.

"You are together? Good! I have been *so* worried about Kim going into that trap. I have been trying to get in touch with him, but I cannot reach him. You children, with your greater power—"

She broke off as the dread import of the Five's surface thoughts became clear to her. At first she, too, was shaken, but she rallied magnificently.

"Nonsense!" she snapped; not in denial of an unwelcome fact, but in sure knowledge that the supposition was not and could not be a fact. "Kimball Kinnison is alive. He is lost, I know—I last heard from him just before he went into that hyperspatial tube—but I did not feel him die. And if he died, no matter where or when or how, I would most certainly have felt it. So don't be idiots, children, please. Think—*really* think! I am going to do something—somehow—but what? Mentor the Arisian? I've never called him and I'm terribly afraid that he might not be willing to do anything. I could go there and make him do something, but that would take so long—tell me, what shall I—what *can* I do?"

"Mentor, by all means," Kit decided. "The most logical, the only possible solution. I am sure that in this case he will act. It is neither necessary nor desirable to go to Arisia." Now that the Eddorians had ceased to exist, intergalactic space presented no barrier to Arisian thought, but Kit did not enlighten his mother upon that point. "Link your mind with ours." She did so.

"Mentor of Arisia!" the clear-cut thought flashed out. "Kimball Kinnison of Klovia is not present in this, his normal space and time, nor in any other continuum which we can reach. We ask assistance."

"Ah, 'tis Lensman Clarrissa and the Five." Imperturbably, Mentor's mind joined theirs on the instant. "I have given the matter no attention, nor have I scanned my visualization of the Cosmic All. It may be that Kimball Kinnison has passed on from this plane of exist—"

"He has NOT!" the Red Lensman interrupted violently, so violently that her thought had the impact of a physical blow. Mentor and the Five alike could see her eyes flash and sparkle; could hear her voice crackle as she spoke aloud, the better to drive home her passionate conviction. "Kim is ALIVE! I told the children so and I now tell you so. No matter where or when he might be, in whatever possible extra-dimensional nook or cranny of the entire macrocosmic universe or in any possible aisle of time between plus and minus eternity, he could not die—he could not possibly die—without my knowing it. So find him, please—*please* find him, Mentor—or, if you can't or won't, just give me the littlest, *tiniest* hint as to how to go about it and I will find him myself!"

The Five were appalled. Especially Kit, who knew, as the others did not, just how much afraid of Mentor his mother had always been. To direct such a thought as that to any Arisian was unthinkable; but Mentor's only reaction was one of pleased interest.

"There is much of truth, daughter, in your thought," he replied, slowly. "Human love, in its highest manifestation, can be a mighty, a really tremendous thing. The force, the power, the capability of such a love as yours is a sector of the truth which has not been fully examined. Allow me, please, a moment in which to consider the various aspects of this matter."

*

It took more than a moment. It took more than the twenty-nine seconds which the Arisian had needed to solve an earlier and supposedly similar Kinnison problem. In fact, a full half hour elapsed before Mentor resumed communication; and then he did so, not to the group as a whole, but only to the Five; using an ultrafrequency to which the Red Lensman's mind could not be attuned.

"I have not been able to reach him. Since you could not do so I knew that the problem would not be simple, but I have found that it is difficult indeed. As I have intimated previously, my visualization is not entirely clear upon any matter touching the Eddorians directly, since their minds were of great power. On the other hand, their visualizations of us were probably even more hazy. Therefore none of our analyses of each other were or could be much better than approximations.

"It is certain, however, that you were correct in assuming that it was the Ploorans who set up the hyperspatial tube as a trap for your father. The fact that the lower and middle operating echelons of Boskonia could not kill him established in the Ploorans' minds the necessity of taking him alive. The fact gave us no concern, for you, Kathryn, were on guard. Moreover, even if she alone should slip, it was manifestly impossible for them to accomplish anything against the combined powers of you Five. However, at some undetermined point in time the Eddorians took over, as is shown by the fact that you are all at a loss: it being scarcely necessary to point out to you that the Ploorans could neither transport your father to any location which you could not reach nor pose any problem, including his death, which you could not solve. It is thus certain that it was one or more of the Eddorians who either killed Kinnison or sent him where he was sent. It is also certain that, after the easy fashion in which he escaped from the Ploorans after they had captured him and had him all but in their hands, the Eddorians did not care to have the Ploorans come to grips with Kimball Kinnison; fearing, and rightly, that instead of gaining information, they would lose everything."

"Did they know that I was in that tube?" Kathryn asked. "Did they deduce us, or did they think that Dad was a superman?"

"That is one of the many points which are obscure. But it made no difference, before or after the event, to them or to us, as you should perceive."

"Of course. They knew that there was at least one third-level mind at work in the field. They must have deduced that it was Arisian work. Whether it was Dad himself, or whether it was coming to his aid at need, would make no difference. They knew very well that he was the keystone of Civilization, and that to do away with him would be the shrewdest move they could make. Therefore, we still do not understand why they didn't kill him out-right and be done with it—if they didn't."

"In exactness, neither do I—that point is the least clear of all. Nor is it at all certain that he still lives. It is sheerest folly to assume that the Eddorians either thought or acted illogically, even occasionally. Therefore, if Kinnison is not dead, whatever was done was calculated to be even more final than death itself. This premise, if adopted, forces the conclusion that they considered the possibility of our knowing enough about the next cycle of existence to be able to reach him there."

Kit frowned. "You still harp on the possibility of his death. Does not your visualization cover that?"

"Not since the Eddorians took control. I have not consciously emphasized the probability of your father's death; I have merely considered it—in the case of two mutually exclusive events, neither of which can be shown to have happened, both must be studied with care. Assume for the moment that your mother's theory is the truth, that your father is still alive. In that case, what was done and how it was done are eminently clear."

"Clear? Not to us!" the Five chorused.

"While they did not know at all exactly the power of our minds, they could establish limits beyond which neither they nor we could go. Being mechanically inclined, it is reasonable to assume that they had at their disposal sufficient energy to transport Kinnison and his vessel to some point well beyond those limits. They would have given control to a director-by-chance, so that his ultimate destination would be unknown and unknowable. He would of course land safely—"

"How? How could they, *possibly*—?"

"In time that knowledge will be yours. Not now. Whether or not the hypothesis just stated is true, the fact confronting us is that Kimball Kinnison is not now in any region which I am at present able to scan."

Gloom descended palpably upon the Five.

"I am not saying or implying that the problem is insoluble. Since Eddorian minds were involved, however, you already realize that its solution will require the evaluation of many millions of factors and will consume a not inconsiderable number of your years."

"You mean lifetimes!" an impetuous young thought broke in. "Why, long before that—"

"Contain yourself, daughter Constance," Mentor reproved, gently. "I realize quite fully all the connotations and implications involved. I was about to say that it may prove desirable to assist your mother in the application of powers which may very well transcend in some respects those of either Arisia or Eddore." He shifted the band of thought to include the Red Lensman and went on as though he were just emerging from contemplation:

"Children, it appears that the solution of this problem by ordinary processes will require more time than can conveniently be spared. Moreover, it affords a priceless and perhaps a unique opportunity of increasing our store of knowledge. Be informed, however, that the probability is exceedingly great that in this project you, Clarrissa, will lose your life."

"Better not, mother. When Mentor says anything like that, it means suicide. We don't want to lose you, too." Kit pleaded, and the four girls added their pleas to his.

Clarrissa knew that suicide was against the Code—but she also knew that, as long as there was any chance at all, Lensmen always went in.

"Exactly how great?" she demanded, vibrantly. "It isn't absolutely certain—it *can't* be!"

"No, daughter, it is not absolutely certain."

"QX, then, I'm going in. Nothing can stop me."

"Very well. Tighten your linkage, Clarrissa, with me. Yours will be the task of sending your thought to your husband, wherever and whenever in total space and in total time he may be. If it can be done, you can do it. You alone of all the entities in existence can do it. I can neither help you nor guide you in your quest; but by virtue of your relationship to him whom we are seeking, your oneness with him, you will require neither help nor guidance. My part will be to follow you and to construct the means of his return, but the real labor is and must be yours alone. Take a moment, therefore, to prepare yourself against the effort, for it will not be small. Gather your resources, daughter; assemble all your forces and your every power."

*

They watched Clarrissa, in her distant room, throw herself prone upon her bed. She closed her eyes, buried her nose in the counterpane, and gripped a side rail fiercely in each hand.

"Can't we help, too?" The Five implored, as one.

"I do not know." Mentor's thought was as passionless as the voice of Fate. "I know of no force at your disposal which can affect in any way that which is to happen. Since I do not know the full measure of your powers, however, it would be well for you to accompany us, keeping yourselves alert to take instant advantage of any opportunity to be of aid. Are you ready, daughter Clarrissa?"

"I am ready," and the Red Lensman launched her thought.

Clarrissa Kinnison did not know, then or ever, did not have even the faintest inkling of what she did or of how she did it. Nor, tied to her by bonds of heritage, love, and sympathy though they were and of immense powers of mind though they were, did any of the Five succeed, until after many years had passed, in elucidating the many complex phenomena involved. Even Mentor, the ancient Arisian sage, never did understand.

All that any of them knew was that an infinitely loving and intensely suffering woman, stretched rigidly upon a bed, hurled out through space and time a passionately questing thought—a thought behind which she put everything she had.

Clarrissa Kinnison, Red Lensman, had much—and every iota of that impressive sum total ached for, yearned for, and insistently *demanded* her Kim—her one and only Kim. Kim her husband; Kim the father of her children; Kim her lover; Kim her other half; Kim her all in all for so many perfect years.

"Kim! KIM! Wherever you are, Kim, or whenever, listen! Listen and answer! Hear me—you *must* hear me calling—I need you, Kim, from the bottom of my soul. Kim! My Kim! KIM!!"

Through countless spaces and through untellable times that poignant thought sped; driven by a woman's fears, a woman's hopes, a woman's all-surpassing love; urged ever onward and ever outward by the irresistible force of a magnificent woman's frankly bared soul.

Outward . . . farther . . . farther out . . . farther—

*

Clarrissa's body went limp upon her bed. Her heart slowed; her breathing almost stopped. Kit probed quickly, finding that those secret cells into which he had scarcely dared to glance were now empty and bare. Even the Red Lensman's tremendous reserves of vital force were exhausted.

"Mother, come back!"

"Come back to us!"

"Please, *please*, Mums, come back!"

"Know you, children, your mother so little?"

They knew her. They knew starkly that she would not come back. Regardless of any danger to herself, regardless of life itself, she would not return until she had found her Kim.

"But *do* something, Mentor—DO SOMETHING!"

"What? Nothing can be done. It was simply a question of which was the greater; the volume of the required hypersphere or her remarkable store of vitality."

"Shut up!" Kit blazed. "We'll do *something*! Come on, kids, and we'll try."

"The Unit!" Kathryn shrieked. "Link up, quick! Cam, make mother's pattern, all of it—hurry! Now, Unit, grab it—make her one of us, a six-ply Unit—*make* her come in, and snap it up! There! Now, Kit, drive us. DRIVE US!"

Kit drove. As the surging life-force of the Unit pushed a measure of vitality back into Clarrissa's inert body, she gained a little strength and did not grow weaker. The children, however, did; and Mentor, who had been entirely unmoved by the woman's imminent death, became highly concerned.

"Children, return!" He first ordered, then entreated. "You are throwing away not only your lives, but also long lifetimes of intensive labor and study!"

They paid no attention. He had known that they would not. No more than their mother would those children abandon such a mission unaccomplished. Seven Kinnisons would come back or none.

The Arisian pondered—and brightened. Now that a theretofore impossible linkage had been made, the outlook changed. The odds shifted. The Unit's delicacy of web, its driving force, had not been enough; or, rather, it would have taken too long. Adding the Red Lensman's affinity for her husband, however—Yes, definitely, this Unit of his should now succeed.

It did. Before any of the Five weakened to the danger point the Unit, again five-fold, snapped back. Clarrissa's life-force, which had tried so valiantly to fill all of space and all of time, was flowing back into her. A tight, hard beam ran, it seemed, to infinity and vanished. Mentor had been unable to follow the Unit, but he could and did follow that beam to Kimball Kinnison. Abruptly the trace was hidden by the walls of a hyperspatial tube.

"A right scholarly bit of work, children," Mentor approved. "I could not follow you, but I have arranged the means of his return."

"Thanks, children. Thanks, Mentor." Instead of fainting, Clarrissa sprang from her bed and stood erect. Flushed and panting, eyes flamingly alight, she was more intensely vital than any of her children had ever seen her. Reaction might—would—come later, but she was now all buoyantly vibrant woman. "Where will he come into our space, and when?"

"In your room before you. Now."

Kinnison materialized; and as the Red Lensman and the Gray went hungrily into each other's arms, Mentor and the Five turned their attention toward the future.

*

"First, the hyperspatial tube which was called the 'Hell Hole in Space,'" Kit began. "We must establish as fact in the minds of all Civilization that the Ploorans were actually at the top of Boskone. The story as we have arranged it is that Ploor was the top, and—which happens to be the truth—that it was destroyed through the efforts of the Second-Stage Lensmen. The 'Hell Hole' is to be explained as being operated by the Plooran 'residuum' which every Lensman knows all about and which he will never forget. The problem of Dad's whereabouts was different from the previous one in degree only, not in kind. To all except us, there never were any Eddorians. Any objections? Will that version hold?"

The consensus was that the story was sound and tight.

"The time has come, then," Karen thought, "to go into the very important matter of our reason for being and our purpose in life. You have intimated repeatedly that you Arisians are resigning your Guardianship of Civilization and that we are to take over; and I have just perceived the terribly shocking fact that you four are now alone, that all the other Arisians have already gone. We are not ready, Mentor; you know that we are not—this scares me through and through."

"You are ready, children, for everything that will have to be done. You have not come to your full maturity and power, of course; that stage will come only with time. It is best for you, however, that we leave you now. Your race is potentially vastly stronger and abler than ours. We reached some time ago the highest point attainable to us: we could no longer adapt ourselves to the ever-increasing complexity of life. You, a young new race amply equipped for any emergency within reckonable time, will be able to do so. In capability and in equipment you begin where we leave off."

"But we know—you've taught us—scarcely anything!" Constance protested.

"I have taught you exactly enough. That we do not know exactly what changes to anticipate is implicit in the fact that our race is out of date. Further Arisian teaching would tend to set you in the out-dated Arisian mold and thereby defeat our every purpose. As I have informed you repeatedly, we ourselves do not know what extra qualities you possess. Hence we are in no sense competent to instruct you in the natures or in the uses of them. It is certain, however, that you have those extra qualities. It is equally certain that you possess the abilities to develop them to the full. I have set your feet on the sure way to the full development of those abilities."

"But that will take much time, sir," Kit thought, "and if you leave us now we won't have it."

"You will have time enough and to spare."

"Oh—then we won't have to do it right away?" Constance broke in. "Good!"

"We are all glad of that," Camilla added. "We're too full of our own lives, too eager for experiences, to enjoy the prospect of living such lives as you Arisians have lived. I am right in assuming, am I not, that our own development will in time force us into the same or a similar existence?"

"Your muddy thinking has again distorted the truth," Mentor reproved her. "There will be no force involved. You will gain everything, lose nothing. You have no conception of the depth and breadth of the vistas now just beginning to open to you. Your lives will be immeasurably fuller, higher, greater than any heretofore known to this universe. As your capabilities increase, you will find that you will no longer care for the society of entities less able than your own kind."

*

"But I don't *want* to live forever!" Constance wailed.

"More muddy thinking." Mentor's thought was—for him—somewhat testy. "Perhaps, in the present instance, barely excusable. You know that you are not immortal. You should know that an infinity of time is necessary for the acquirement of infinite knowledge; and that your span of life will be just as short, in comparison with your capacity to live and to learn, as that of Homo sapiens. When the time comes you will want to—you will need to—change your manner of living."

"Tell us when?" Kat suggested. "It would be nice to know, so that we could get ready."

"I could tell you, since in that way my visualization is clear, but I will not. Fifty years—a hundred—a million—what matters it? Live your lives to the fullest, year by year, developing your every obvious, latent, and nascent capability; calmly assured that long before any need for your services shall arise, you shall have established yourselves upon some planet of your choice and shall be in every respect ready for whatever may come to pass."

"You are—you must be—right," Kit conceded. "In view of what has just happened, however, and the chaotic condition of both galaxies, it seems a poor time to vacate all Guardianship."

"All inimical activity is now completely disorganized. Kinnison and the Patrol can handle it easily enough. The real conflict is finished. Think nothing of a few years of vacancy. The Lensmakers, as you know, are fully automatic, requiring neither maintenance nor attention; what little time you may wish to devote to the special training of selected Lensmen can be taken at odd moments from your serious work of developing yourselves for Guardianship."

"We still feel incompetent," the Five insisted. "Are you sure that you have given us all the instruction we need?"

"I am sure. I perceive doubt in your minds as to my own competence, based upon the fact that in this supreme emergency my visualization was faulty and my actions almost too late. Observe, however, that my visualization was clear upon every essential factor and that we were not actually too late. The truth is that our timing was precisely right—no lesser stress could possibly have prepared you as you are now prepared.

"I am about to go. The time may come when your descendants will realize, as we did, their inadequacy for continued Guardianship. Their visualizations, as did ours, may become imperfect and incomplete. If so, they will then know that the time will have come for them to develop, from the highest race then existing, new and more competent Guardians. Then they, as my fellows have done and as I am about to do, will of their own accord pass on. But that is for the remote future. As to you children, doubtful now and hesitant as is only natural, you may believe implicitly what I now tell you is the truth, that even though we Arisians are no longer here, all shalt be well; with us, with you, and with all Civilization."

The deeply resonant pseudovoice ceased; the Kinnisons knew that Mentor, the last of the Arisians, was gone.

EPILOGUE

To you who have scanned this report, further greetings:

Since I, who compiled it, am only a youth, a Guardian only by title, and hence unable to visualize even approximately either the time of nor the necessity for the opening of this flask of force, I have no idea as to the bodily shape or the mental attainments of you, the entity to whom it has now been made available.

SUPER PACK

You already know that Civilization is again threatened seriously. You probably know something of the basic nature of that threat. While studying this tape you have become informed that the situation is sufficiently grave to have made it again necessary to force certain selected minds prematurely into the third-level of Lensmanship.

You have already learned that in ancient time Civilization after Civilization fell before it could rise much above the level of barbarism. You know that we and the previous race of Guardians saw to it that this, OUR Civilization, has not yet fallen. Know now that the task of your race, so soon to replace us, will be to see to it that it does not fall.

One of us will become en *rapport* with you as soon as you have assimilated the facts, the connotations, and the implications of this material. Prepare your mind for contact.

Kit Kinnison.

THE VORTEX BLASTER

To
Bob Heinlein
With Admiration and Esteem

CATASTROPHE

SAFETY DEVICES that do not protect.

"Unsinkable" ships that, before the days of Bergenholm and of atomic and cosmic energy, sank into the waters of Earth.

More particularly, safety devices which, while protecting against one agent of destruction, attract magnet-like another and worse. Such as the armored cable within the walls of a wooden house. It protects the electrical conductors within it against accidental external shorts; but, inadequately grounded, it may attract and upon occasion has attracted the stupendous force of lightning. Then, steel armor exploding into incandescence inside walls and ceilings, that house's existence thereafter is to be measured in minutes.

Specifically, four lightning rods. The lightning rods protecting the chromium, glass, and plastic home of Neal Cloud. Those rods were adequately grounded, with copper-silver cables the size of a big man's forefinger; for Neal Cloud, Doctor of Nucleonics, knew his lightning and was taking no chances whatever with the safety of his wife and children.

He did not know, did not even suspect, that under certain conditions of atmospheric potential and of ground-magnetic stress his perfectly-designed and perfectly-installed system would become a super-powerful attractor for flying vortices of atomic disintegration.

So now Neal Cloud, nucleonicist, sat at his desk in a strained, dull apathy. His face was a yellowish-gray white, his tendoned hands gripped rigidly the arms of his chair. His eyes, hard and lifeless, stared unseeingly past the small, three-dimensional block portrait of all that had made life worth living.

For his guardian against lightning had been a vortex-magnet at the moment when some luckless wight had tried to abate the nuisance of a "loose" atomic vortex. That wight dies, of course—they almost always did—and the vortex, instead of being destroyed, was simply broken up into a number of widely-scattered new vortices. And one of those bits of furious, uncontrolled energy, resembling a handful of substance torn from the depths of a sun, darted toward and shot downward to earth through Neal Cloud's new house.

That house did not burn; it exploded. Nothing of it, in it, or near it stood a chance, for in a few seconds the place where it had been was a crater of seething, boiling lava—a crater which filled the atmosphere with poisonous vapors; which flooded all nearby space with lethal radiations.

Cosmically, the whole thing was infinitesimal. Ever since man learned how to use atomic power the vortices of disintegration had been breaking out of control. Such

1054

accidents had been happening, and would continue to happen. More than one world, perhaps, had been or would be consumed to the last gram by such loose atomic vortices. What of that? Of what real importance are a few grains of sand to a pile five thousand miles long, a hundred miles wide, and ten miles deep?

Even to that individual grain of sand called "Earth"—or, in modern parlance, "Sol Three," or "Tellus of Sol," or simply "Tellus"—the affair was negligible. One man had died; but, in dying, he had added one more page to the thick bulk of negative results already on file. That Mrs. Cloud and her children had perished was merely unfortunate. The vortex itself was not yet a real threat to Tellus. It was a "new" one, and thus it would be a long time before it would become other than a local menace.

Nor, to any except a tiny fraction of Earth's inhabitants, was the question of loose atomic vortices a matter of concern. It was unthinkable that Tellus, the point of origin and the very center of Galactic Civilization, could cease to exist. Long before such vortices could eat away much of her mass, or poison much of her atmosphere, Earth's scientists would have solved the problem.

But to Neal Cloud the accident was ultimate catastrophe. His personal universe had crashed in ruins; what was left was not worth picking up. He and Jo had been married for more than fifteen years and the bonds between them had grown stronger, deeper, truer with every passing day. And the kids . . . it *couldn't* have happened . . . fate COULDN'T do this to him . . . but it had . . . it could. Gone . . . *gone* . . . GONE!

And to Neal Cloud, sitting there at his desk in black abstraction, with maggots of thought gnawing holes in his mind, the catastrophe was doubly galling because of its cruel irony. For he was second from the top in the Vortex Control Laboratory; his life's work had been a search for a means or method of extinguishing loose atomic vortices.

His eyes focused vaguely upon the portrait. Wavy brown hair . . . clear, honest gray eyes . . . lines of character, of strength and of humor . . . sweetly curved lips, ready to smile or to kiss. . . .

He wrenched his attention away and scribbled briefly upon a sheet of paper. Then, getting up stiffly, he took the portrait and moved woodenly across the room to a furnace. After the flaming arc had done its work he turned and handed the paper to a tall man, with a Lens glowing upon his wrist, who had been watching him with quiet, understanding eyes. Significant enough, to the initiate, of the importance of the laboratory is the fact that it was headed by a Lensman.

"As of now, Phil, if it's QX with you."

The Lensman took the document, glanced at it, and slowly, meticulously, tore it into sixteen equal pieces.

"Uh-uh, Storm," he denied, gently. "Not a resignation. Leave of absence, perhaps, but not severance."

"Why not?" It was scarcely a question; Cloud's voice was level, uninflected. "I wouldn't be worth the paper I'd waste."

"Now, no; but the future's another matter. I haven't said anything so far, because I knew you and Jo. Nothing could be said." Two hands gripped and held. "For the future, though, four words that were spoken long ago have never been improved upon. 'This, too, shall pass'."

"You think so?"

"I know so, Storm. I've been round a long time. You're too good a man to go down out of control. You've got a place in the world and a job to do. You'll be back—" a thought struck the Lensman and he went on, in a strangely altered tone: "But you wouldn't—of course you wouldn't—you couldn't."

"I don't think so. No." Suicide, tempting although it might be, was not the answer. "Good-bye, Phil."

"Not good-bye, Storm. Au revoir."

"Maybe." Cloud left the laboratory and took an elevator down to the garage. Into his big blue DeKhotinsky Special and away.

Through traffic so heavy that front-, rear-, and side-bumpers almost touched he drove with his wonted cool skill; even though he did not know, consciously, that the other cars were there. He slowed, turned, stopped, "shoveled on the coal," all correctly—and all purely automatically.

He did not know where he was going, nor care. His numbed brain was simply trying to run away from its own bitter imaginings—which, if he had thought at all, he would have known hopeless of accomplishment. But he did not think. He simply acted; dumbly, miserably.

Into a one-way skyway he rocketed; along it over the suburbs and into the trans-continental super-highway. Edging inward, lane after lane, he reached the "unlimited" way—unlimited, that is, except for being limited to cars of not less than seven hundred horsepower, in perfect mechanical condition, driven by registered, tested drivers at not less than one hundred twenty five miles per hour—flashed his number at the control station, and shoved his right foot down to the floor.

Everyone knows that an ordinary DeKhotinsky Sporter will do a hundred and forty honestly-measured miles in one honestly-timed hour; but very few drivers have ever found out how fast one of those brutal big souped-up Specials can wheel. Most people simply haven't got what it takes to open one up.

"Storm" Cloud found out that day. He held that six-thousand-pound Juggernaut onto the road, wide open, for mile after mile after mile. But it didn't help. Drive as he would, he could not out-run that which rode with him. Beside him and within him and behind him; for Jo was there.

Jo and the kids, but mostly Jo. It was Jo's car as much as it was his. "Babe, the big blue ox," was her pet name for it; because, like Paul Bunyan's fabulous beast, it was pretty nearly six feet between the eyes.

Jo was in the seat beside him. Every dear, every sweet, every luscious, lovely memory of her was there . . . and behind him, just beyond eye-corner visibility, were the three kids. And a whole lifetime of this loomed ahead—a vista of emptiness more vacuous by far than the emptiest reaches of inter-galactic space. Damnation! he couldn't stand much more of. . . .

High over the roadway, far ahead, a brilliant octagon flared red. That meant "STOP!" in any language. Cloud eased up on the accelerator; eased down on the brake-pedal; took his place in the line of almost-stalled traffic. There was a barrier and a trimly-uniformed policeman.

"Sorry, sir," the officer said, with a sweeping, turning gesture, "but you'll have to detour over to Twenty. There's a loose atomic vortex beside the road up ahead. . . . Oh, it's you, Doctor Cloud! You can go ahead, of course. Couple of miles yet before you'll need your armor. They didn't tell us they were sending for *you*. It's just a little new one, and the dope we got was that they were going to shove it over into the badlands with pressors."

"They didn't send for me." Cloud tried to smile. "I'm just driving around. No armor, even, so I might as well go back."

He turned the Special around. A loose vortex—new. There might be three or four of them, scattered over that many counties. Sisters of the one that had murdered his family—spawn of that damned Number Eleven that that bungling nitwit had tried to blow out. . . . Into his mind there leaped a picture, wire-sharp, of Number Eleven as he had last seen it, and simultaneously an idea hit him like the blow of a fist.

He thought. *Really* thought, now; intensely and clearly. If he could do it—could actually blow out the atomic flame of an atomic vortex . . . not exactly revenge, but . . . it *would* work . . . it would *have* to work—he'd *make* it work! And grimly, quietly, but alive now in every fiber, he drove back to the city almost as fast as he had come away.

If Philip Strong was surprised at Cloud's sudden reappearance in the laboratory he did not show it. Nor did he offer any comment as his erstwhile assistant went to various lockers and cupboards, assembling coils, tubes, armor, and other paraphernalia.

"Guess that's all I'll need, chief," Cloud remarked, finally. "Here's a blank check. If some of this stuff shouldn't happen to be in usable condition when I get done with it, fill it out to suit, will you?"

"No." The Lensman tore up the check just as he had torn up the resignation. "If you want the stuff for legitimate purposes, you're on Patrol business and it's the Patrol's risk. But if you're thinking of trying to snuff a vortex, the stuff stays here. That's out, Storm."

"But I'm going to *really* snuff 'em, starting with Number One and taking 'em in order. No suicide."

"Huh?" Skepticism incarnate. "It can't be done, except by an almost impossibly fortuitous accident, which is why you yourself have always been as opposed to such attempts as the rest of us. The charge of explosive must match, within very narrow limits, the activity of the vortex itself at the instant of detonation; and that activity varies so greatly and so unpredictably that all attempts at accurate extrapolation have failed. Even the Conference of Scientists couldn't develop a usable formula, any more than they could work out a tractor that could be used as a tow-line on one."

"Wait a minute!" Cloud protested. "They found that it could be forecast, for a length of time proportional to the length of the cycle in question, by an extension of the calculus of warped surfaces."

"Humph! I said a *usable* formula!" the Lensman snorted. "What good is a ten-second forecast when it takes a GOMEAC twice that long to solve. . . . Oh!" he broke off, staring.

"Oh," he repeated, slowly. "I forgot for a minute that you were born with a super-GOMEAC in your head. But there are other things."

"There were. Now there are none."

"No?"

"NO. I couldn't take such chances before, and I'd've tied myself up into knots if I did. Now nothing can throw me. I can compute all the elements of a sigma curve in nothing flat. A ten-second prediction gives me ten seconds of action. That's plenty."

"I see." Strong pondered, his fingers drumming softly upon his desk. Lensmen did not ordinarily use their Lenses on their Lensless friends, but this was no ordinary occasion. "You aren't afraid of death any more. But you won't invite it? And do you mind if I Lens you on that?"

"Come in. I'll not invite it, but that's as far as I'll go in promising. I won't make any superhuman effort to avoid it. I'll take all due precautions, for the sake of the job, but if one gets me, what the hell?"

"QX." The Lensman withdrew from Cloud's mind. "Not too good, but good enough. What's your plan? You won't have time for the usual method of attack."

"Like this." Cloud found a sheet of drafting paper and sketched rapidly. "There's the crater, with the vortex at the bottom—there. From the sigma curve I estimate the most probable value of the activity I'll have to shoot at. Then I select three duodec bombs from the hundred or so I'll have made up in advance—one on the mark, one each five percent over and under the mark. The bombs, of course, will be cased in neocarballoy thick enough for penetration. Then I take off in a shielded armored flying suit, say about here. . . ."

"If you take off at all, you and your suit will be inside a flitter," the Lensman interrupted. "Too many instruments for a suit, to say nothing of bombs, and you'll need heavier screen than a suit can put out. We can adapt a flitter for bomb-throwing easily enough."

"That'd be better, of course. QX, I set my flitter into a projectile trajectory toward the center of disturbance. Twelve seconds away, at about this point here, I take my instantaneous readings, solve the equations of that particular warped surface for some definite zero time. . . ."

"But s'pose the cycle won't give you a ten-second solution?"

"Then I'll swing around and try again until a long-enough cycle *does* show up."

"QX. It will, sometime."

"Sure. Then, having everything set for zero time, and assuming that the activity is somewhere near my assumed value. . . ."

"Assume it isn't—it probably won't be."

"I accelerate or decelerate. . . ."

"Solving new equations—differential equations at that—all the while?"

"Certainly. Don't interrupt so. I stick around until the sigma curve, extrapolated to zero time, matches one of my bombs. I build up the right velocity, cut that bomb loose, shoot myself off in a sharp curve, and Z-W-E-E-T–POWIE! She's out." With an expressive, sweeping gesture.

"You hope." Strong was frankly dubious. "And there you are, right in the middle of the damndest explosion you ever saw."

"Oh, no. I've gone free in the meantime, so nothing can touch me."

"*I* hope! But do you realize just how busy you are going to be during those ten or twelve seconds?"

"Yes." Cloud's face grew somber. "But I'll be in full control. I won't be afraid of anything that can happen—of *anything* that can happen. From my standpoint, that's the hell of it."

"QX," the Lensman decided, "You can go. We'll iron out the kinks as we go."

"We?"

"I'll be in the lookout shack with the boys, at least on the first ones. When do you want to start?"

"How long will it take to fix up the flitter?"

"Two days. Say we meet you there Saturday morning?"

"I'll be there," and again Neal Cloud and Babe, the big blue ox, hit the road; and as he rolled along the physicist mulled over in his mind the assignment to which he had set himself.

Like fire, only worse, atomic energy was a good servant, but a very bad master. Man had liberated it before he could really control it. In fact, control was not yet, and probably never would be, perfect. True, all except a minute fraction of one percent of the multitudes of small, tame, self-limiting vortices were perfect servants. But at long intervals, for some unknown reason—science knew so little, fundamentally, of nuclear reactions—one of them flared, nova-like, into a huge, wild, self-sustaining monster. It ceased being a servant, then, and became a master.

Such flare-ups occurred very infrequently; the trouble was that the loose vortices were so utterly, so damnably *permanent*. They never went out; and no data were ever obtained. Every living thing in the vicinity of a flare-up died; every instrument and every other solid thing within a radius of hundreds of feet melted down into the reeking, boiling slag of its crater.

Fortunately, the rate of growth was slow—as slow, almost, as it was persistent. But even so, unless something could be done about loose vortices before too many years, the situation would become extremely serious. That was why the Laboratory had been established in the first place.

Nothing much had been accomplished so far. Tractor beams would not hold. Nothing material was of any use. Pressors worked after a fashion—vortices *could* be moved from one place to another. One or two, through sheer luck, had been blown out by heavy charges of duodecaplylatomate. But duodec had taken many lives; and since it scattered a vortex as often as it fed it, duodec had caused vastly more damage than it had cured.

No end of fantastic schemes had been proposed, of course; of varying degrees of fantasy. Some of them sounded almost practical. Some of them had been tried; some were still being tried. Some, such as the perennially-appearing one of installing a free drive and flinging the whole neighborhood off into space, were perhaps feasible from an engineering standpoint. They were potentially so capable of making things worse, however, that they could not be used except as last-ditch measures. In short, the control of loose atomic vortices was very much an unsolved problem.

CLOUD BLASTS A VORTEX

NUMBER ONE, the oldest and worst vortex on Tellus, had been pushed out into the badlands, and there, at eight o'clock of the indicated morning, Cloud started to work on it.

The "lookout shack" was in fact a fully-equipped nucleonics laboratory. Its staff was not large—eight men worked in three staggered eight-hour shifts—but the development of its instrumentation had required hundreds of man-years of intensive research. Every factor of the vortex's activity was measured and recorded continuously, throughout every minute of every day of every year; and all of these measurements were summed up, integrated, into the "sigma" curve. This curve, which to the layman's eye was only a senselessly zig-zagging line, told the expert everything he wanted to know.

Cloud glanced at the chart and scowled, for one jagged peak, less than half an hour old, almost touched the top line of the paper.

"Bad, huh, Frank?"

"Bad, Storm, and getting worse. I wouldn't wonder if 'Calamity' were right—it certainly looks like she's getting ready to blow her top."

"No equation, I suppose," Strong said. The Lensman ignored as completely as did the observer, if not as flippantly, the distinct possibility that at any moment the observatory and all that it contained might be resolved into their sub-atomic components.

"None," Cloud stated. He did not need to spend hours at a calculating machine; at one glance he knew, without knowing how he knew, that no equation could fit that wildly-shifting sigma curve. "But most of these recent cycles cut ordinate seven fifty, so I'll take that for my value. That means nine point nine six zero kilograms of duodec for my basic, and nine four six two and ten point three five eight as alternates. On the wire?"

"It went out as you said it," the observer replied. "They'll be here in five minutes."

"QX. I'll get dressed, then."

The Lensman and one of the observers helped him into his cumbersome, heavily-padded armor; then all three men went out to the flitter. A tiny speedster, really; a slim torpedo with the stubby wings and the ludicrous tail-surfaces, the multifarious driving-, braking-, side-, top-, and under-jets so characteristic of the tricky, cranky, but ultra-maneuverable breed. Cloud checked the newly installed triplex launcher, made sure that he knew which bomb was in each tube, and climbed into the tiny operating compartment. The massive door—flitters are too small to have airlocks—rammed shut upon its teflon gaskets, the heavy toggles drove home. A heavily-padded form closed in upon the pilot, leaving only his left arm and his right leg free to move.

SUPER PACK

"Everybody in the clear?"

"All clear."

Cloud shot the flitter into the air and toward the seething inferno which was Loose Atomic Vortex Number One. The crater was a ragged, jagged hole perhaps two miles from lip to lip and a quarter of a mile in depth. The floor, being largely molten, was almost level except for a depression at the center, where the actual vortex lay. The walls of the pit were steeply, unstably irregular, varying in pitch and shape with the refractoriness of the strata composing them. Now a section would glare into an unbearably blinding white, puffing away in sparkling vapor. Again, cooled by an inrushing blast of air, it would subside into an angry scarlet, its surface crawling in a sluggish flow of lava. Occasionally a part of the wall might even go black, into pockmarked scoriae or brilliant planes of obsidian.

For always, at some point or other, there was a torrent of air rushing into that crater. It rushed in as ordinary air. It came out, however, in a ragingly uprushing pillar, as—as something else. No one knows exactly what a vortex does to air. Or, rather, the composition of the effluent gases varies as frequently and as unpredictably as does the activity of the vortex. Thus, the atmosphere emitted from a vortex-crater may be corrosive, it may be poisonous, it may be merely different; but it is no longer the air which we human beings are used to breathing. This conversion and corruption of Earth's atmosphere, if it could not be stopped, would end the possibility of life upon the planet's surface long before the world itself could be consumed.

As to the vortex itself . . . it is difficult indeed to describe such a phenomenon. Practically all of its frightful radiation lies in those octaves of the spectrum which are invisible to the human eye. Suffice it to say, then, that it was a continuously active atomic reactor, with an effective surface temperature of approximately twenty five thousand degrees Kelvin, and let it go at that.

Neal Cloud, driving his flitter through that murky, radiation-riddled atmosphere, extrapolating his sigma curve by the sheer power of his mathematical-prodigy's mind, sat appalled. For the activity level was, and even in its lowest dips remained, well above the figure he had chosen. Distant though he was from the rim of that hellish pit, his skin began to prickle and to burn. His eyes began to smart and to ache. He knew what those symptoms meant: even the flitter's powerful screens were leaking; even his suit-screens and his special goggles were not stopping the stuff. But he wouldn't quit yet: the activity might—probably would—take a nose-dive any second now. If it did, he'd have to be ready. On the other hand, it might blow up any second, too.

There were two schools of mathematical thought upon that point. One held that a vortex, without any essential change in its nature or behavior, would keep on growing bigger until, uniting with the other vortices of the planet, it had converted all the mass of the world into energy.

The second school, of which the forementioned "Calamity" Carlowitz was the loudest voice, taught that at a certain stage of development the internal energy of the vortex would become so great that generation-radiation equilibrium could not be maintained. This would of course result in an explosion, the nature and consequences of which this

Carlowitz was wont to dwell upon in ghoulishly mathematical glee. Neither school could prove its point, however—or, rather, each school proved its point with eminently plausible mathematics—and each hated and derided the other, with heat and at length.

Neal Cloud, as he studied through his almost opaque defenses that indescribably ravening fireball, that rapacious monstrosity which might very well have come from the very center of the hottest hell of mythology, felt strangely inclined to agree with Carlowitz. It didn't seem possible that it *could* get any worse without exploding.

The activity stayed high; 'way too high. The tiny control room grew hotter and hotter. His skin burned more and his eyes ached worse. He touched a stud and spoke.

"Phil? Better get me three more bombs. Like these, except up around. . . ."

"I don't check you. If you do that, it's apt to drop to a minimum and stay there. I'd suggest a wider interval."

"QX—that'd be better. Two, then, instead of three. Four point nine eight zero and thirteen point nine four zero. You might break out a jar of burn-dressing, too; some fairly warm stuff is leaking through."

"Will do. Come down, fast!"

Cloud landed. He stripped to the skin and his friends smeared him with the thick, gooey stuff that was not only added protection against radiation, but also a sovereign remedy for new burns. He exchanged his goggles for a heavier, darker pair. The two bombs arrived and were substituted for two of the original load.

"I thought of something while I was up there," Cloud said then. "Fourteen kilograms of duodec is nobody's firecracker, but it may be the least of what's going to go off. Have you got any idea of what's going to become of the intrinsic energy of the vortex when I snuff it?"

"Can't say I have." The Lensman frowned in thought. "No data."

"Neither have I. But I'd say you'd better go back to the new station—the one you were going to move to if it kept on getting worse. The clocks are ticking there, aren't they?"

"Yes. It might be the smart thing to do—just in case."

Again in air, Cloud found that the activity, while still very high, was not too high for his heaviest bomb, but that it was fluctuating too rapidly. He could not get even five seconds of trustworthy prediction, to say nothing of ten. So he waited, as close to the horrible center of disintegration as he dared.

The flitter hung poised in air, motionless, upon softly hissing under-jets. Cloud knew to a fraction his height above the ground. He knew to a fraction his distance from the vortex. He knew the density of the atmosphere and the velocity and direction of the wind. Hence, since he could also read, closely enough, the momentary variations in the cyclonic storms within the crater, he could compute very easily the course and velocity necessary to land the bomb in the exact center of the vortex at any given instant of time. The hard part—the thing that no one had as yet succeeded in doing—was to predict, for a time far enough ahead to be of any use, a usably close approximation to the vortex's quantitative activity.

Therefore Cloud concentrated upon the dials and gauges in front of him; concentrated with every fiber of his being and with every cell of his brain.

SUPER PACK

Suddenly, almost imperceptibly, the sigma curve gave signs of flattening out. Cloud's mind pounced. Simultaneous differential equations; nine of them. A quadruple integration in four dimensions. No matter—Cloud did not solve problems laboriously, one operation at a time. Without knowing how he had arrived at it, he knew the answer; just as the Posenian or the Rigellian can perceive every separate component particle of an opaque, three-dimensional solid, but without being able to explain to any Tellurian how his sense of perception works. It just *is*, that's all.

By virtue of whatever sense or ability it is which makes a mathematical prodigy what he is, Cloud knew that in exactly seven and three-tenths seconds from that observed instant the activity of the vortex would match precisely the rating of his heaviest bomb. Another flick of his mental switch and he knew exactly the velocity he would require. His hand swept over the studs, his right foot tramped down hard upon the firing pedal; and, even as the quivering flitter rammed forward under five Tellurian gravities of acceleration, he knew to the thousandth of a second how long he would have to hold that acceleration to attain that velocity. While not really long—in seconds—it was much too long for comfort. It would take him much closer to the vortex than he wanted to be; in fact, it would take him almost to the crater's rim.

But he stuck to the calculated course, and at the precisely correct instant he released his largest bomb and cut his dive. Then, in a continuation of the same motion, his hand slashed down through the beam of light whose cutting would activate the Bergenholm and make the vessel inertialess—safe from any form whatever of physical violence. For an instant nothing happened, and for that instant Cloud sat appalled. *Neutralization of inertia took time!* Not that he had ever been told that it was instantaneous—he had just assumed so. He had never noticed any time-lapse before, but now it seemed to be taking forever!

After that one instant of shocked inaction he went into ultra-speed action; kicking in the little vessel's all-out eight-G drive and whirling her around as only a flitter or a speedster can whirl; only to see in his plate the vortex opening up like a bell-flower, or like a sun going nova.

Cloud's forebodings were more than materialized then, for it was not only the bomb that was going off. The staggeringly immense energy of the vortex was merging with that of the detonating duodec to form an utterly indescribable explosion.

In part the flood of incandescent lava in the pit was beaten downward by the sheer, stupendous force of the blow; in part it was hurled abroad in masses, gouts, and streamers. And the raging blast of the explosion's front seized the fragments and tore and worried them to bits, hurling them still faster along their paths of violence. And air, so densely compressed as to act like a solid, smote the walls of the crater. Those walls crumbled, crushed outward through the hard-packed ground, broke up into jaggedly irregular blocks which hurtled screamingly in all directions.

The blast-wave or explosion front buffeted the flyer while she was still partially inert and while Cloud was almost blacked out and physically helpless from the frightful linear and angular accelerations. The impact broke his left arm and his right leg; the only parts of his body not pressure-packed. Then, milliseconds later, the debris began to arrive.

Chunks of solid or semi-molten rock slammed against the hull, knocking off wings and control-surfaces. Gobs of viscous slag slapped it liquidly, freezing into and clogging up jets and orifices. The little ship was knocked hither and thither by forces she could no more resist than can a floating leaf resist a cataract; Cloud's brain was addled as an egg by the vicious concussions which were hitting him so nearly simultaneously from so many different directions.

The concussions and the sluggings lightened . . . stopped . . . a vast peace descended, blanket-wise. The flitter was free—was riding effortlessly away on the outermost, most tenuous fringes of the storm!

Cloud wanted to faint, then, but he didn't—quite. With one arm and leg and what few cells of his brain were still in working order, he was still in the fight. It did not even occur to him, until long afterward, that he was not going to make any effort whatever to avoid death.

Foggily, he tried to look at the crater. Nine-tenths of his visiplates were dead, but he finally got a view. Good—it was out. He wasn't surprised—he knew it would be.

His next effort was to locate the secondary observatory, where he would have to land; and in that, too, he was successful. He had enough intelligence left to realize that, with practically all of his jets clogged and his wings and tail shot off, he couldn't land his flitter inert. He'd *have* to land her free.

Neal Cloud was not the world's best pilot. Nevertheless, by dint of light and somewhat unorthodox use of what few jets he had left, he did land her free. A very good landing, considering—he almost hit the observatory's field, which was only one mile square—and having landed her, he inerted her.

But, as has been intimated, his brain wasn't working quite so good; he had held his ship inertialess for quite a few seconds longer than he thought, and he did not even think of the terrific buffetings she had taken. As a result of these things, however, her intrinsic velocity did not match, anywhere nearly, that of the ground upon which she lay. Thus, when Cloud cut his Bergenholm, restoring thereby to the flitter the absolute velocity and the inertia she had before going free, there resulted a distinctly anticlimactic crash.

There was a last terrific bump as the motionless vessel collided with the equally motionless ground; and "Storm" Cloud, Vortex Blaster, went out like the proverbial light.

Help came, of course; on the double. Cloud was unconscious and the flitter's port could not be opened from the outside, but those were not insuperable obstacles. A plate, already loose, was torn away; the pilot was unclamped and rushed to Base Hospital in the "meat-crate" standing by.

Later, in a private office of that hospital, the head of the Vortex Control Laboratory sat and waited—not patiently.

"How is he, Lacy?" he demanded, as the surgeon-marshal entered the room. "He's going to live?"

"Oh, yes, Phil—definitely yes," Lacy replied, briskly. "A very good skeleton; very good indeed. His screens stopped all the really bad radiation, so the damage will yield quite readily to treatment. He doesn't really need the Phillips we gave him—for the replacement of damaged parts, you know—except for a few torn muscles and so on."

"But he was pretty badly smashed up—I helped take him out, you know—how about that arm and leg? He was a mess."

"Merely simple fractures—entirely negligible." Lacy waved aside with an airy gesture such minor ills as broken bones. "He'll be out in a couple of weeks."

"How soon can I see him? Business can wait, but there's a personal matter that can't."

"I know what you mean." Lacy pursed his lips. "Ordinarily I wouldn't allow it, but you see him now. Not too long, though, Phil; he's weak. Ten minutes at most."

"QX. Thanks." A nurse led the visiting Lensman to Cloud's bedside.

"Hi, stupe!" he boomed, cheerfully. " 'Stupe' being short for 'stupendous', this time."

"Ho, chief. Glad to see somebody. Sit down."

"You're the most-wanted man in the galaxy, not excepting Kimball Kinnison. Here's a spool of tape, which you can look at as soon as Lacy will let you have a scanner. It's only the first one. As soon as any planet finds out that we've got a sure-enough-vortex-blower-outer who can really call his shots—and *that* news gets around mighty fast—it sends in a double-urgent, Class A Prime demand for you.

"Sirius IV got in first by a whisker, but it was a photo finish with Aldebaran II and all channels have been jammed ever since. Canopus, Vega, Rigel, Spica. Everybody, from Alsakan to Zabriska. We announced right off that we wouldn't receive personal delegations—we had to almost throw a couple of pink-haired Chickladorians out bodily to make them believe we meant it—that our own evaluation of necessity, not priority of requisition, would govern. QX?"

"Absolutely," Cloud agreed. "That's the only way to handle it, I should think."

"So forget this psychic trauma. . . . No, I don't mean that," the Lensman corrected himself hastily. "You know what I mean. The will to live is the most important factor in any man's recovery, and too many worlds need you too badly to have you quit now. Check?"

"I suppose so," Cloud acquiesced, but somberly, "and I've got more will to live than I thought I had. I'll keep on pecking away as long as I last."

"Then you'll die of old age, Buster," the Lensman assured him. "We got full data. We know exactly how long it takes to go from fully inert to fully free. We know exactly what to do to your screens. Next time nothing will come through except light, and only as much of that as you like. You can wait as close to a vortex as you please, for as long as is necessary to get exactly the conditions you want. You'll be as safe as if you were in Klono's hip pocket."

"Sure of that?"

"Absolutely—or at least, as sure as we can be of anything that hasn't happened yet. But your guardian angel here is eyeing her clock a bit pointedly, so I'd better do a flit before she tosses me out on my ear. Clear ether, Storm!"

"Clear ether, chief!"

Thus "Storm" Cloud, nucleonicist, became the most narrowly-specialized specialist in the long annals of science; became "Storm" Cloud, the Vortex Blaster.

1065

And that night Lensman Philip Strong, instead of sleeping, thought and thought and thought. What could he do—what could *anybody* do—if Cloud should get himself killed? *Somebody* would have to do *something* . . . but who? And what? Could—or could not—another Vortex Blaster be found? Or trained?

And next morning, early, he Lensed a thought.

"Kinnison? Phil Strong. I've got a high-priority problem that will take a lot of work and a lot more weight than I carry. Are you free to listen for a few minutes?"

"I'm free. Go ahead."

CLOUD LOSES AN ARM

TELLURIAN PHARMACEUTICALS, INC., was Civilization's oldest and most conservative drug house. "Hide-bound" was the term most frequently used, not only by its younger employees, but also by its more progressive competitors. But, corporatively, Tellurian Pharmaceuticals, Inc., did not care. Its board of directors was limited by an iron-clad, if unwritten, law to men of seventy years more; and against the inertia of that ruling body the impetuosity of the younger generation was exactly as efficacious as the dashing of ocean waves against an adamantine cliff—and in very much the same fashion.

Ocean waves do in time cut into even the hardest rock; and, every century or two, TPI did take forward step—after a hundred years of testing by others had proved conclusively that the "new" idea conformed in every particular with the exalted standards of the Galactic Medical Association.

TPI's plant upon the planet Deka (Dekanore III, on the charts) filled the valley of Clear Creek and the steep, high hills on its sides, from the mountain spring which was the creek's source to its confluence with the Spokane River.

The valley floor was a riot of color, devoted as it was to the intensive cultivation of medicinal plants. Along both edges of the valley extended row after row of hydroponics sheds. Upon the mountains' sides there were snake dens, lizard pens, and enclosures for many other species of fauna.

Nor was the surface all that was in use. The hills were hollow: honeycombed into hundreds of rooms in which, under precisely controlled environments of temperature, atmosphere, and radiation, were grown hundreds of widely-variant forms of life.

At the confluence of creek and river, just inside the city limits of Newspoke—originally New Spokane—there reared and sprawled the Company's headquarters buildings; offices, processing and synthesizing plants, laboratories, and so on. In one of the laboratories, three levels below ground, two men faced each other. Works Manager Graves was tall and fat; Fenton V. Fairchild, M.D., Nu.D., F.C.R., Consultant in Radiation, was tall and thin.

"Everything set, Graves?"

"Yes. Twelve hours, you said."

"For the full cycle. Seven to the point of maximum yield."

"Go ahead."

"Here are the seeds. Treconian broadleaf. For the present you will have to take my word for it that they did not come from Trenco. These are standard hydroponics tanks, size one. The formula of the nutrient solution, while complex and highly critical, contains nothing either rare or unduly expensive. I plant the seed, thus, in each of the two tanks. I cover each tank with a plastic hood, transparent to the frequencies to be used. I cover both with a larger hood—so. I align the projectors—thus. We will now put on armor, as the radiation is severe and the atmosphere, of which there may be leakage when the pollenating blast is turned on, is more than slightly toxic. I then admit Trenconian atmosphere from this cylinder. . . ."

"Synthetic or imported?" Graves interrupted.

"Imported. Synthesis is possible, but prohibitively expensive and difficult. Importation in tankers is simple and comparatively cheap. I now energize the projectors. Growth has begun."

In the glare of blue-green radiance the atmosphere inside the hoods, the very ether, warped and writhed. In spite of the distortion of vision, however, it could be seen that growth was taking place, and at an astounding rate. In a few minutes the seeds had sprouted; in an hour the thick, broad, purplish-green leaves were inches long. In seven hours each tank was full of a lushly luxuriant tangle of foliage.

"This is the point of maximum yield," Fairchild remarked, as he shut off the projectors. "We will now process one tank, if you like."

"Certainly I like. How else could I know it's the clear quill?"

"By the looks," came the scientist's dry rejoinder. "Pick your tank."

One tank was removed. The leaves were processed. The full cycle of growth of the remaining tank was completed. Graves himself harvested the seeds, and himself carried them away.

Six days, six samples, six generations of seed, and the eminently skeptical Graves was convinced.

"You've got something there, Doc," he admitted then. "We can really go to town on that. Now, how about notes, or stuff from your old place, or people who may have smelled a rat?"

"I'm perfectly clean. None of my boys know anything important, and none ever will. I assemble all apparatus myself, from standard parts, and disassemble it myself. I've been around, Graves."

"Well, we can't be too sure." The fat man's eyes were piercing and cold. "Leakers don't live very long. We don't want you to die, at least not until we get in production here."

"Nor then, if you know when you're well off," the scientist countered, cynically. "I'm a fellow of the College of Radiation, and it took me five years to learn this technique. None of your hatchetmen could *ever* learn it. Remember that, my friend."

"So?"

"So don't get off on the wrong foot and don't get any funny ideas. I know how to run things like this and I've got the manpower and equipment to do it. If I come in I'm running it, not you. Take it or leave it."

The fat man pondered for minutes, then decided. "I'll take it. You're in, Doc. You can have a cave—two hundred seventeen is empty—and we'll go up and get things started right now."

THE LENSMAN

Less than a year later, the same two men sat in Graves' office. They waited while a red light upon a peculiarly complicated deskboard faded through pink into pure white.

"All clear. This way, Doc." Graves pushed a yellow button on his desk and a section of blank wall slid aside.

In the elevator thus revealed the two men went down to a sub-basement. Along a dimly-lit corridor, through an elaborately locked steel door, and into a steel-lined room. Four inert bodies lay upon the floor.

Graves thrust a key into an orifice and a plate swung open, revealing a chute into which the bodies were dumped. The two retraced their steps to the manager's office.

"Well, that's all we can feed to the disintegrator." Fairchild lit an Alsakanite cigarette and exhaled appreciatively.

"Why? Going soft on us?"

"No. The ice is getting too thin."

"Whaddya mean, 'thin'?" Graves demanded. "The Patrol inspectors are ours—all that count. Our records are fixed. Everything's on the green."

"That's what *you* think," the scientist sneered. "You're supposed to be smart. Are you? Our accident rate is up three hundredths; industrial hazard rate and employee turnover about three and a half; and the Narcotics Division alone knows how much we have upped total bootleg sales. Those figures are all in the Patrol's books. How can you give such facts the brush-off?"

"We don't have to." Graves laughed comfortably. "Even a half of one percent wouldn't excite suspicion. Our distribution is so uniform throughout the galaxy that they can't center it. They can't possibly trace anything back to us. Besides, with our lily-white reputation, other firms would get knocked off in time to give us plenty of warning. Lutzenschiffer's, for instance, is putting out Heroin by the ton."

"So what?" Fairchild remained entirely unconvinced. "Nobody else is putting out what comes out of cave two seventeen—demand and price prove that. What you don't seem to get, Graves, is that some of those damned Lensmen have *brains*. Suppose they decide to put a couple of Lensmen onto this job—then what? The minute anybody runs a rigid statistical analysis on us, we're done for."

"Um . . . m." This was a distinctly disquieting thought, in view of the impossibility of concealing anything from a Lensman who was really on the prowl. "That wouldn't be so good. What would you do?"

"I'd shut down two seventeen—and the whole hush-hush end—until we can get our records straight and our death-rate down to the old ten-year average. That's the only way we can be really safe."

"Shut down! The way they're pushing us for production? Don't be an idiot—the chief would toss us both down the chute."

"Oh, I don't mean without permission. Talk him into it. It'd be best for everybody, over the long pull, believe me."

"Not a chance. He'd blow his stack. If we can't dope out something better than that, we go on as is."

"The next-best thing would be to use some new form of death to clean up our books."

"Wonderful!" Graves snorted contemptuously. "What would we add to what we've got now—bubonic plague?"

"A loose atomic vortex."

"Wh-o-o-o-sh!" The fat man deflated, then came back up, gasping for air. "Man, you're completely *nuts*! There's only one on the planet, and it's . . . or do you mean . . . but *nobody* ever touched one of those things off deliberately . . . can it be done?"

"Yes. It isn't simple, but we of the College of Radiation know how—theoretically—the transformation can be made to occur. It has never been done because it has been impossible to extinguish the things; but now Neal Cloud is putting them out. The fact that the idea is new makes it all the better."

"I'll say so. Neat . . . very neat." Graves' agile and cunning brain figuratively licked its chops. "Certain of our employees will presumably have been upon an outing in the upper end of the valley when this terrible accident takes place?"

"Exactly—enough of them to straighten out our books. Then, later, we can dispose of undesirables as they appear. Vortices are absolutely unpredictable, you know. People can die of radiation or of any one of a mixture of various toxic gases and the vortex will take the blame."

"And later on, when it gets dangerous, Storm Cloud can blow it out for us," Graves gloated. "But we won't want him for a long, long time!"

"No, but we'll report it and ask for him the hour it happens . . . use your head, Graves!" He silenced the manager's anguished howl of protest. "Anybody who gets one wants it killed as soon as possible, but here's the joker. Cloud has enough Class-A-double-prime-urgent demands on file already to keep him busy from now on, so we won't be able to get him for a long, long time. See?"

"I see. Nice, Doc . . . very, *very* nice. But I'll have the boys keep an eye on Cloud just the same."

*

At about this same time two minor cogs of TPI's vast machine sat blissfully, arms around each other, on a rustic seat improvised from rocks, branches, and leaves. Below them, almost under their feet, was a den of highly venemous snakes, but neither man or girl saw them. Before them, also unperceived, was a magnificent view of valley and stream and mountain.

All they saw, however, was each other—until their attention was wrenched to a man who was climbing toward them with the aid of a thick club which he used as a staff.

"Oh . . . Bob!" The girl stared briefly; then, with a half-articulate moan, shrank even closer against her lover's side.

Ryder, left arm tightening around the girl's waist, felt with his right hand for a club of his own and tensed his muscles, for the climbing man was completely mad.

His breathing was . . . horrible. Mouth tight-clamped, despite his terrific exertion, he was *sniffing*—sniffing loathsomely, lustfully, each whistling inhalation filling his lungs to bursting. He exhaled explosively, as though begrudging the second of time required to empty himself of air. Wide-open eyes glaring fixedly ahead he blundered upward, paying no attention whatever to his path. He tore through clumps of thorny growth; he stumbled and fell over logs and stones; he caromed away from boulders; as careless of the needles which tore clothing and skin as of the rocks which bruised his flesh to the bone. He struck a great tree and bounced; felt his frenzied way around the obstacle and back into his original line.

He struck the gate of the pen immediately beneath the two appalled watchers and stopped. He moved to the right and paused, whimpering in anxious agony. Back to the gate and over to the left, where he stopped and howled. Whatever the frightful compulsion was, whatever he sought, he could not deviate enough from his line to go around the pen. He looked, then, and for the first time saw the gate and the fence and the ophidian inhabitants of the den. They did not matter. Nothing mattered. He fumbled at the lock, then furiously attacked it and the gate and the fence with his club—fruitlessly. He tried to climb the fence, but failed. He tore off his shoes and socks and, by dint of jamming toes and fingers ruthlessly into the meshes, he began to climb.

No more than he had minded the thorns and the rocks did he mind the eight strands of viciously-barbed wire surmounting that fence; he did not wince as the inch-long steel fangs bit into arms and legs and body. He did, however, watch the snakes. He took pains to drop into an area temporarily clear of them, and he pounded to death the half-dozen serpents bold enough to bar his path.

Then, dropping to the ground, he writhed and scuttled about; sniffing ever harder; nose plowing the ground. He halted; dug his bleeding fingers into the hard soil; thrust his nose into the hole; inhaled tremendously. His body writhed, trembled, shuddered uncontrollably, then stiffened convulsively into a supremely ecstatic rigidity utterly horrible to see.

The terribly labored breathing ceased. The body collapsed bonelessly, even before the snakes crawled up and struck and struck and struck.

Jacqueline Comstock saw very little of the outrageous performance. She screamed once, shut both eyes, and, twisting about within the man's encircling arm, burrowed her face into his left shoulder.

Ryder, however—white-faced, set-jawed, sweating—watched the thing to its ghastly end. When it was over he licked his lips and swallowed twice before he could speak.

"It's all over, dear—no danger now," he managed finally to say. "We'd better go. We ought to turn in an alarm . . . make a report or something."

"Oh, I can't, Bob—I can't!" she sobbed. "If I open my eyes I just know I'll look, and if I look I'll . . . I'll simply turn inside out!"

"Hold everything, Jackie! Keep your eyes shut. I'll pilot you and tell you when we're out of sight."

More than half carrying his companion, Ryder set off down the rocky trail. Out of sight of what had happened, the girl opened her eyes and they continued their descent in a more usual, more decorous fashion until they met a man hurrying upward.

"Oh, Dr. Fairchild! There was a. . . ." But the report which Ryder was about to make was unnecessary; the alarm had already been given.

"I know," the scientist puffed. "Stop! Stay exactly where you are!" He jabbed a finger emphatically downward to anchor the young couple in the spot they occupied. "Don't talk—don't say a word until I get back!"

Fairchild returned after a time, unhurried and completely at ease. He did not ask the shaken couple if they had seen what had happened. He knew.

"Bu . . . buh . . . but, doctor," Ryder began.

"Keep still—don't talk at all." Fairchild ordered, bruskly. Then, in an ordinary conversational tone, he went on: "Until we have investigated this extraordinary occurrence thoroughly—sifted it to the bottom—the possibility of sabotage and spying cannot be disregarded. As the only eye-witnesses, your reports will be exceedingly valuable; but you must not say a word until we are in a place which I *know* is proof against any and all spy-rays. Do you understand?"

"Oh! Yes, we understand."

"Pull yourselves together, then. Act unconcerned, casual; particularly when we get to the Administration Building. Talk about the weather—or, better yet, about the honeymoon you are going to take on Chickladoria."

Thus there was nothing visibly unusual about the group of three which strolled into the building and into Graves' private office. The fat man raised an eyebrow.

"I'm taking them to the private laboratory," Fairchild said, as he touched the yellow button and led the two toward the private elevator. "Frankly, young folks, I am a scared—yes, a badly scared man."

This statement, so true and yet so misleading, resolved the young couple's inchoate doubts. Entirely unsuspectingly, they followed the Senior Radiationist into the elevator and, after it had stopped, along, a corridor. They paused as he unlocked and opened a door; they stepped unquestioningly into the room at his gesture. He did not, however, follow them in. Instead, the heavy metal slab slammed shut, cutting off Jackie's piercing shriek of fear.

"You might as well cut out the racket," came from a speaker in the steel ceiling of the room. "Nobody can hear you but me."

"But Mr. Graves, I thought . . . Dr. Fairchild told us . . . we were going to tell him about. . . ."

"You're going to tell nobody nothing. You saw too much and know too much, that's all."

"Oh, *that's* it!" Ryder's mind reeled as some part of the actual significance of what he had seen struck home. "But listen! Jackie didn't see anything—she had her eyes shut all the time—and doesn't know anything. You don't want to have the murder of such a girl as *she* is on your mind, I know. Let her go and she'll never say a word—we'll both swear to it—or you could. . . ."

"Why? Just because she's got a face and a shape?" The fat man sneered. "No soap, Junior. She's not that much of a. . . ." He broke off as Fairchild entered his office.

"Well, how about it? How bad is it?" Graves demanded.

"Not bad at all. Everything's under control."

"Listen, doctor!" Ryder pleaded. "Surely you don't want to murder Jackie here in cold blood? I was just suggesting to Graves that he could get a therapist. . . ."

"Save your breath," Fairchild ordered. "We have important things to think about. You two die."

"But why?" Ryder cried. He could as yet perceive only a fraction of the tremendous truth. "I tell you, it's. . . ."

"We'll let you guess," said Fairchild.

Shock upon shock had been too much for the girl's overstrained nerves. She fainted quietly and Ryder eased her down to the cold steel floor.

"Can't you give her a better cell than this?" he protested then. "There's no . . . it isn't *decent*!"

"You'll find food and water, and that's enough." Graves laughed coarsely. "You won't live long, so don't worry about conveniences. But keep still. If you want to know what's going on, you can listen, but one more word out of you and I cut the circuit. Go ahead, Doc, with what you were going to say."

"There was a fault in the rock. Very small, but a little of the finest smoke seeped through. Barney must have been a sniffer before to be able to smell the trace of the stuff that was drifting down the hill. I'm having the whole cave tested with a leak-detector and sealed bottle-tight. The record can stand it that Barney—he was a snake-tender, you know—died of snake-bite. That's almost the truth, too, by the way."

"Fair enough. Now, how about these two?"

"Um . . . m. We've got to hold the risk at absolute minimum." Fairchild pondered briefly. "We can't disintegrate them this month, that's sure. They've got to be found dead, and our books are full. We'll have to keep them alive—where they are now is as good a place as any—for a week."

"Why alive? We've kept stiffs in cold storage before now."

"Too chancey. Dead tissues change too much. You weren't courting investigation then; now we are. We've got to keep our noses clean. How about this? They couldn't wait any longer and got married today. You, big-hearted philanthropist that you are, told them they could take their two weeks vacation now for a honeymoon—you'd square it with their department heads. They come back in about ten days, to get settled; go up the valley to see the vortex; and out. Anything in that set-up we can't fake a cover for?"

"It looks perfect to me. We'll let 'em enjoy life for ten days, right where they are now. Hear that, Ryder?"

"Yes, you pot-bellied. . . ."

The fat man snapped a switch.

It is not necessary to go into the details of the imprisonment. Doggedly and skillfully though he tried, Ryder could open up no avenue of escape or of communication; and Jacqueline, facing the inevitability of death, steadied down to meet it. She was a woman. In minor crises she had shrieked and had hidden her face and had fainted: but in this ultimate one she drew from the depths of her woman's soul not only the power to overcome her own weakness, but also an extra something with which to sustain and fortify her man.

SUPER PACK

"STORM" CLOUD ON DEKA

IN THE VORTEX CONTROL LABORATORY on Tellus, Cloud had just gone into Philip Strong's office.

"No trouble?" the Lensman asked, after greetings had been exchanged.

"Uh-huh. Simple as blowing out a match. You quit worrying about me long ago, didn't you?"

"Pretty much, except for the impossibility of training anybody else to do it. We're still working on that angle, though. You're looking fit."

He was. He carried no scars—the Phillips treatment had taken care of that. His face looked young and keen; his hard-schooled, resilient body was in surprisingly fine condition for that of a man crowding forty so nearly. He no longer wore his psychic trauma visibly; it no longer obtruded itself between him and those with whom he worked; but in his own mind he was *sure* that it still was, and always would be, there. But the Lensman, studying him narrowly—and, if the truth must be known, using his Lens as well—was *not* sure, and was well content.

"Not bad for an old man, Phil. I could whip a wildcat, and spot him one bite and two scratches. But what I came in here for, as you may have suspected, is—where do I go from here? Spica or Rigel or Canopus? They're the worst, aren't they?"

"Rigel's is probably the worst in property damage and urgency. Before we decide, though, I wish you'd take a good look at this data from Dekanore III. See if you see what I do."

"Huh? Dekanore III?" Cloud was surprised. "No trouble there, is there? They've only got one, and it's 'way down in Class Z somewhere."

"Two now. It's the new one I'm talking about. It's acting funny—*damned* funny."

Cloud went through the data, brow furrowed in concentration; then sketched three charts and frowned.

"I see what you mean. '*Damned* funny' is right. The toxicity is too steady, but at the same time the composition of the effluvium is too varied. Inconsistent. However, there's no real attempt at a gamma analysis—nowhere near enough data for one—this *could* be right; they're so utterly unpredictable. The observers were inexperienced, I take it, with medical and chemical bias?"

"Check. That's the way I read it."

"Well, I'll say this much—I never saw a gamma chart that would accept half of this stuff, and I can't even imagine what the sigma curve would look like. Boss, what say I skip over there and get us a full reading on that baby before she goes orthodox—or, should I say, orthodoxly unorthodox?"

"However you say it, that's my thought exactly; and we have a good excuse for giving it priority. It's killing more people than all three of the bad ones together."

"If I can't fix the toxicity with exciters I'll throw a solid cordon around it to keep people away. I won't blow it out, though, until I find out why it's acting so—if it is. Clear ether, chief, I'm practically there!"

It did not take long to load Cloud's flitter aboard a Dekanore-bound liner. Half-way there however, an alarm rang out and the dread word "Pirates!" resounded through the ship.

Consternation reigned, for organized piracy had disappeared with the fall of the Council of Boskone. Furthermore, this was not in any sense a treasure ship; she was an ordinary passenger liner.

She had had little enough warning—her communications officer had sent out only a part of his first distress call when the blanketing interference jammed his channels. The pirate—a first-class superdreadnought—flashed up and a visual beam drove in.

"Go inert," came the terse command. "We're coming aboard."

"Are you completely crazy?" The liner's captain was surprised and disgusted, rather than alarmed. "If not, you've got the wrong ship. Everything aboard—including any ransom you could get for our passenger list—wouldn't pay your expenses."

"You wouldn't know, of course, that you're carrying a package of Lonabarian jewelry, or would you?" The question was elaborately skeptical.

"I know damned well I'm *not*."

"We'll take the package you *haven't* got, then!" the pirate snapped. "Go inert and open up, or I'll do it for you—like this." A needle-beam lashed out and expired. "That was through one of your holds. The next one will be through your control room."

Resistance being out of the question, the liner went inert. While the intrinsic velocities of the two vessels were being matched, the pirate issued further instructions.

"All officers now in the control room, stay there. All other officers, round up all passengers and herd them into the main saloon. Anybody that acts up or doesn't do exactly what he's told will be blasted."

The pirates boarded. One squad went to the control room. Its leader, seeing that the communications officer was still trying to drive a call through the blanket of interference, beamed him down without a word. At this murder the captain and four or five other officers went for their guns and there was a brief but bloody battle. There were too many pirates.

A larger group invaded the main saloon. Most of them went through, only half a dozen or so posting themselves to guard the passengers. One of the guards, a hook-nosed individual wearing consciously an aura of authority, spoke.

"Take it easy, folks, and nobody'll get hurt. If any of you've got guns, don't go for 'em. That's a specialty that. . . ."

One of his DeLameters flamed briefly. Cloud's right arm, almost to the shoulder, vanished. The man behind him dropped—in two different places.

"Take it easy, I said," the pirate chief went calmly on. "You can tie that arm up, fella, if you want to. It was in line with that guy who was trying to pull a gun. You nurse over there—take him to sick-bay and fix up his wing. If anybody stops you tell 'em Number One said to. Now, the rest of you, watch your step. I'll cut down every damn one of you that so much as looks like he wanted to start something."

They obeyed.

In a few minutes the looting parties returned to the saloon.

"Did you get it, Six?"

"Yeah. In the mail, like you said."

"The safe?"

"Sure. Wasn't much in it, but not too bad, at that."

"QX. Control room! QX?"

"Ten dead," the intercom blatted in reply. "Otherwise QX."

"Fuse the panels?"

"Natch."

"Let's go!"

They went. Their vessel flashed away. The passengers rushed to their staterooms. Then:

"Doctor Cloud!" came from the speaker. "Doctor Neal Cloud! Control room calling Doctor Cloud!"

"Cloud speaking."

"Report to the control room, please."

"Oh—excuse me—I didn't know you were wounded," the officer apologized as he saw the bandaged stump and the white, sweating face. "You'd better go to bed."

"Doing nothing wouldn't help. What did you want me for?"

"Do you know anything about communicators?"

"A little—what a nucleonics man has to know."

"Good. They killed all our communications officers and blasted the panels, even in the lifeboats. You can't do much with your left hand, of course, but you may be able to boss the job of rigging up a spare."

"I can do more than you think—I'm left-handed. Give me a couple of technicians and I'll see what we can do."

They set to work, but before they could accomplish anything a cruiser drove up, flashing its identification as a warship of the Galactic Patrol.

"We picked up the partial call you got off," its young commander said, briskly. "With that and the plotted center of interference we didn't lose any time. Let's make this snappy." He was itching to be off after the marauder, but he could not leave until he had ascertained the facts and had been given clearance. "You aren't hurt much—don't need to call a tug, do you?"

"No," replied the liner's senior surviving officer.

"QX," and a quick investigation followed.

"Anybody who ships stuff like that open mail ought to lose it, but it's tough on innocent bystanders. Anything else I can do for you?"

"Not unless you can lend us some officers, particularly navigators and communications officers."

"Sorry, but we're short there ourselves—four of my best are in sick-bay. Sign this clearance, please, and I'll get on that fellow's tail. I'll send your copy of my report to your head office. Clear ether!"

The cruiser shot away. Temporary repairs were made and the liner, with Cloud and a couple of electronics technicians as communications officers, finished the voyage to Dekanore III without more interruption.

The Vortex Blaster was met at the dock by Works Manager Graves himself. The fat man was effusively sorry that Cloud had lost an arm, but assured him that the accident wouldn't lay him up very long. He, Graves, would get a Posenian surgeon over here so fast that. . . .

If the manager was taken aback to learn that Cloud had already had a Phillips treatment, he did not show it. He escorted the specialist to Deka's best hotel, where he introduced him largely and volubly. Graves took him to supper. Graves took him to a theater and showed him the town. Graves told the hotel management to give the scientist the best rooms and the best valet they had, and that Cloud was not to be allowed to spend any of his own money. All of his activities, whatever their nature, purpose, or extent, were to be charged to Tellurian Pharmaceuticals, Inc. Graves was a grand guy.

Cloud broke loose, finally, and went to the dock to see about getting his flitter.

It had not been unloaded. There would be a slight delay, he was informed, because of the insurance inspections necessitated by the damage—and Cloud had not known that there had been any! When he had learned what had been done to his little ship he swore bitterly and sought out the liner's senior officer.

"Why didn't you tell me we got holed?" he demanded.

"Why, I don't know . . . just that you didn't ask, is all, I guess. I don't suppose it occurred to anybody—I know it didn't to me—that you might be interested."

And that was, Cloud knew, strictly true. Passengers were not informed of such occurrences. He had been enough of an officer so that he could have learned anything he wished; but not enough of one to have been informed of such matters as routine. Nor was it surprising that it had not come up in conversation. Damage to cargo meant nothing whatever to the liner's overworked officers, standing double watches; a couple of easily-patched holes in the hull were not worth mentioning. From their standpoint the *only* damage was done to the communicators, and Cloud himself had set them to rights. This delay was his own fault as much as anybody else's. Yes, more.

"You won't lose anything, though," the officer said, helpfully. "Everything's covered, you know."

"It isn't the money I'm yowling about—it's the time. That apparatus can't be duplicated anywhere except on Tellus, and even there it's all special-order stuff. OH, DAMN!" and Cloud strode away toward his hotel.

During the following days TPI entertained him royally. Not insistently—Graves was an expert in such matters—but simply by giving him the keys to the planet. He could do anything he pleased. He could have all the company he wanted, male or female, to help him to do it. Thus he did—within limits—just about what Graves wanted him to do; and, in spite of the fact that he did not want to enjoy life, he liked it.

One evening, however, he refused to play a slot machine, explaining to his laughing companion that the laws of chance were pretty thoroughly shackled in such mechanisms—and the idle remark backfired. What was the mathematical probability that all the things that had happened to him could have happened by pure chance?

That night he analyzed his data. Six incidents; the probability was extremely small. Seven, if he counted his arm. If it had been his *left* arm—jet back! Since he wrote with his right hand, very few people knew that he was left-handed. Seven it was; and that made it virtually certain. Accident was out.

But if he *was* being delayed and hampered deliberately, who was doing it, and why? It didn't make sense. Nevertheless, the idea would not down.

He was a trained observer and an analyst second to none. Therefore he soon found out that he was being shadowed wherever he went, but he could not get any really significant leads. Wherefore:

"Graves, have you got a spy-ray detector?" he asked boldly—and watchfully.

The fat man did not turn a hair. "No, nobody would want to spy on me. Why?"

"I feel jumpy. I don't know why anybody would be spying on me, either, but—I'm neither a Lensman nor an esper, but I'd swear that somebody's peeking over my shoulder half the time. I think I'll go over to the Patrol station and borrow one."

"Nerves, my boy; nerves and shock," Graves diagnosed. "Losing an arm would shock hell out of anybody's nervous system, I'd say. Maybe the Phillips treatment—the new one growing on—sort of pulls you out of shape."

"Could be," Cloud assented, moodily. His act had been a flop. If Graves knew anything—and he'd be damned if he could see any grounds for such a suspicion—he hadn't given away a thing.

Nevertheless, Cloud went to the Patrol office, which was of course completely and permanently shielded. There he borrowed the detector and asked the lieutenant in charge to get a special report from the Patrol upon the alleged gems and what it knew about either the cruiser or the pirates. To justify his request he had to explain his suspicions.

After the messages had been sent the young officer drummed thoughtfully upon his desk. "I wish I could do something, Dr. Cloud, but I don't see how I can," he decided finally. "Without a shred of evidence, I *can't* act."

"I know. I'm not accusing anybody, yet. It may be anybody between here and Andromeda. Just call me, please, as soon as you get that report."

The report came, and the Patrolman was round-eyed as he imparted the information, that, as far as Prime Base could discover, there had been no Lonabarian gems and the rescuing vessel had not been a Patrol ship at all. Cloud was not surprised.

"I thought so," he said, flatly. "This is a hell of a thing to say, but it now becomes a virtual certainty—six sigmas out on the probability curve—that this whole fantastic procedure was designed solely to keep me from analyzing and blowing out that new vortex. As to where the vortex fits in, I haven't got even the dimmest possible idea, but one thing is clear. Graves represents TPI—on this planet he *is* TPI. Now what kind of monkey-business would TPI—or, more likely, somebody working under cover *in* TPI, because undoubtedly the head office doesn't know anything about it—be doing? I ask you."

"Dope, you mean? Cocaine—heroin—that kind of stuff?"

"Exactly; and here's what I'm going to do about it." Bending over the desk, even in that ultra-shielded office, Cloud whispered busily for minutes. "Pass this along to Prime Base immediately, have them alert Narcotics, and have your men ready in case I strike something hot."

"But listen, man!" the Patrolman protested. "Wait—let a Lensman do it. They'll almost certainly catch you at it, and if they're clean *nothing* can keep you from doing ninety days in the clink."

"But if we wait, the chances are it'll be too late; they'll have had time to cover up. What I'm asking you is, will you back my play if I catch them with the goods?"

"Yes. We'll be here, armored and ready. But I still think you're nuts."

"Maybe so, but even if my mathematics is wrong, it's still a fact that my arm will grow back on just as fast in the clink as anywhere else. Clear ether, lieutenant—until tonight!"

Cloud made an engagement with Graves for luncheon. Arriving a few minutes early, he was of course shown into the private office. Since the manager was busily signing papers, Cloud strolled to the side window and seemed to gaze appreciatively at the masses of gorgeous blooms just outside. What he really saw, however, was the detector upon his wrist.

Nobody knew that he had in his sleeve a couple of small, but highly efficient, tools. Nobody knew that he was left-handed. Nobody saw what he did, nor was any signal given that he did anything at all.

That night, however, that window opened alarmlessly to his deft touch. He climbed in, noiselessly. He might be walking straight into trouble, but he had to take that chance. One thing was in his favor; no matter how crooked they were, they couldn't keep armored troops on duty as night-watchmen, and the Patrolmen could get there as fast as their thugs could.

He had brought no weapons. If he was wrong, he would not need any and being armed would only aggravate his offense. If right, there would be plenty of weapons available. There were. A whole drawer full of DeLameters—fully charged—belts and everything. He leaped across the room to Graves' desk; turned on a spy-ray. The sub-basement—"private laboratories," Graves had said—was blocked. He threw switch after switch—no soap. Communicators—ah, he was getting somewhere now—a steel-lined room, a girl and a boy.

"Eureka! Good evening, folks."

"Eureka? I hope you rot in hell, Graves. . . ."

"This isn't Graves. Cloud. Storm Cloud, the Vortex Blaster, investigating. . . ."

"Oh, Bob, the Patrol!" the girl screamed.

"Quiet! This is a zwilnik outfit, isn't it?"

"I'll say it is!" Ryder gasped in relief. "Thionite. . . ."

"Thionite! How could it be? How could they bring it in here?"

"They don't. They're growing broadleaf and *making* the stuff. That's why they're going to kill us."

"Just a minute." Cloud threw in another switch. "Lieutenant? Worse than I thought. *Thionite!* Get over here fast with everything you got. Armor and semi-portables. Blast down the Mayner Street door. Stairway to right, two floors down, corridor to left, half-way along left side. Room B-Twelve. Snap it up, but keep your eyes peeled!"

"But wait, Cloud!" the lieutenant protested. "Wait 'til we get there—you can't do anything alone!"

"Can't wait—got to get these kids out—evidence!" Cloud broke the circuit and, as rapidly as he could, one-handed, buckled on gun-belts. Graves would *have* to kill these two youngsters, if he possibly could.

"For God's sake save Jackie, anyway!" Ryder prayed. He knew just how high the stakes were. "And watch out for gas, radiation, and traps—you must have sprung a dozen alarms already."

"What kind of traps?" Cloud demanded.

"Beams, deadfalls, sliding doors—I don't know what they haven't got. Graves said he could kill us in here with rays or gas or. . . ."

"Take Graves' private elevator, Dr. Cloud," the girl broke in.

"Where is it—which one?"

"It's in the blank wall—the yellow button on his desk opens it. Down as far as it will go."

Cloud jumped up listening with half an ear to the babblings from below as he searched for air-helmets. Radiations, in that metal-lined room, were out—except possibly for a few beam-projectors, which he could deal with easily enough. Gas, though, would be bad; but every drug-house had air-helmets. Ah! Here they were!

He put one on, made shift to hang two more around his neck—he had to keep his one hand free. He punched the yellow button; rode the elevator down until it stopped of itself. He ran along the corridor and drove the narrowest, hottest possible beam of a DeLamer into the lock of B-12. It took time to cut even that small semi-circle in that refractory and conductive alloy—altogether too much time—but the kids would know who it was. Zwilniks would open the cell with a key, not a torch.

They knew. When Cloud kicked the door open they fell upon him eagerly.

"A helmet and a DeLamer apiece. Get them on quick! Now help me buckle this. Thanks. Jackie, you stay back there, out of the way of our feet. Bob, you lie down here in the doorway. Keep your gun outside and stick your head out just far enough so you can see. No farther. I'll join you after I see what they've got in the line of radiation."

A spot of light appeared in a semi-concealed port, then another. Cloud's weapon flamed briefly.

"Projectors like those aren't much good when the prisoners have DeLamers," he commented, "but I imagine our air right now is pretty foul. It won't be long now. Do you hear anything?"

"Somebody's coming, but suppose it's the Patrol?"

"If so, a few blasts won't hurt 'em—they'll be in G P armor." Cloud did not add that Graves would probably rush his nearest thugs in just as they were; to kill the two witnesses before help could arrive.

The first detachment to round the corner was in fact unarmored. Cloud's weapon flamed white, followed quickly by Ryder's, and those zwilniks died. Against the next to arrive, however, the DeLamers raved in vain. But only for a second.

"Back!" Cloud ordered, and swung the heavy door shut as the attackers' beams swept past. It could not be locked, but it could be, and was, welded to the jamb with dispatch, if not with neatness. "We'll cut that trap-door off, and stick it onto the door, too—and any more loose metal we can find."

"I hope they come in time," the girl's low voice carried a prayer. Was this brief flare of hope false? Would not only she and her Bob, but also their would-be rescuer, die? "Oh! That noise—s'pose it's the Patrol?"

It was not really a noise—the cell was sound-proof—it was an occasional jarring of the whole immense structure.

"I wouldn't wonder. Heavy stuff—probably semi-portables. You might grab that bucket, Bob, and throw some of that water that's trickling in. Every little bit helps."

The heavy metal of the door was glowing bright-to-dull red over half its area and that area was spreading rapidly. The air of the room grew hot and hotter. Bursts of live steam billowed out and, condensing, fogged the helmets.

The glowing metal dulled, brightened, dulled. The prisoners could only guess at the intensity of the battle being waged. They could follow its progress only by the ever-shifting temperature of the barrier which the zwilniks were so suicidally determined to burn down. For hours, it seemed, the conflict raged. The thuddings and jarrings grew worse. The water, which had been a trickle, was now a stream and scalding hot.

Then a blast of bitterly cold air roared from the ventilator, clearing away the gas and steam, and the speaker came to life.

"Good work, Cloud and you other two," it said, chattily. "Glad to see you're all on deck. Get into this corner over here, so the Zwilniks won't hit you when they hole through. They won't have time to locate you—we've got a semi right at the corner now."

The door grew hotter, flamed fiercely white. A narrow pencil sizzled through, burning steel sparkling away in all directions—but only for a second. It expired. Through the hole there flared the reflection of a beam brilliant enough to pale the noon-day sun. The portal cooled; heavy streams of water hissed and steamed. Hot water began to spurt into the cell. An atomic-hydrogen cutting torch sliced away the upper two-thirds of the fused and battered door. The grotesquely-armored lieutenant peered in.

"They tell me all three of you are QX. Check?"

"Check."

"Good. We'll have to carry you out. Step up here where we can get hold of you."

"I'll walk and I'll carry Jackie myself," Ryder protested, while two of the armored warriors were draping Cloud tastefully around the helmet of a third.

"You'd get boiled to the hips—this water is deep and hot. Come on!"

The slowly rising water was steaming; the walls and ceiling of the corridor gave mute but eloquent testimony of the appalling forces that had been unleashed. Tile, concrete, plastic, metal—nothing was as it had been. Cavities yawned. Plates and pilasters were warped, crumbled, fused into hellish stalactites; bare girders hung awry. In places complete collapse had necessitated the blasting out of detours.

Through the wreckage of what had been a magnificent building the cavalcade made its way, but when the open air was reached the three rescued ones were not released. Instead, they were escorted by a full platoon of soldiery to an armored car, which was in turn escorted to the Patrol station.

"I'm afraid to take chances with you until we find out who's who and what's what around here," the young commander explained. "The Lensmen will be here in the morning, with half an army, so I think you'd better spend the rest of the night here, don't you?"

"Protective custody, eh?" Cloud grinned. "I've never been arrested in such a polite way before, but it's QX with me. You, too, I take it?"

"Us, too, decidedly," Ryder assented. "This is a very nice jail-house, especially in comparison with where we've. . . ."

"I'll say so!" Jackie broke in, giggling almost hysterically. "I never thought I'd be tickled to death at getting arrested, but I am!"

Lensmen came, and companies of Patrolmen equipped in various fashions, but it was several weeks before the situation was completely clarified. Then Ellington—Councillor Ellington, the Unattached Lensman in charge of all Narcotics—called the three into the office.

"How about Graves and Fairchild?" Cloud demanded before the councillor could speak.

"Both dead," Ellington said. "Graves was shot down just as he took off, but he blasted Fairchild first, just as he intimated he would. There wasn't enough of Fairchild left for positive identification, but it couldn't very well have been anyone else. Nobody left alive seems to know much of anything of the real scope of the thing, so we can release you three now. Thanks, from me as well as the Patrol. There is some talk that you two youngsters have been contemplating a honeymoon out Chickladoria way?"

"Oh, no, sir—that is. . . ." Both spoke at once. "That was just talk, sir."

"I realize that the report may have been exaggerated, or premature, or both. However, not as a reward, but simply in appreciation, the Patrol would be very glad to have you as its guests throughout such a trip—all expense—if you like."

They liked.

"Thank you. Lieutenant, please take Miss Cochran and Mr. Ryder to the disbursing office. Dr. Cloud, the Patrol will take cognizance of what you have done. In the meantime, however, I would like to say that in uncovering this thing you have been of immense assistance to us."

"Nothing much sir, I'm afraid. I shudder to think of what's coming. If zwilniks can grow Trenconian broadleaf anywhere. . . ."

"Not at all, not at all," Ellington interrupted. "If such an entirely unsuspected firm as Tellurian Pharmaceuticals, with all their elaborate preparations and precautions, could not do much more than start, it is highly improbable that any other attempt will be a success. You have given us a very potent weapon against zwilnik operations—not only thionite, but heroin, ladolian, nitrolabe, and the rest."

"What weapon?" Cloud was puzzled.

"Statistical analysis and correlation of apparently unrelated indices."

"But they've been used for years!"

"Not the way you used them, my friend. Thus, while we cannot count upon any more such extraordinary help as you gave us, we should not need any. Can I give you a lift back to Tellus?"

"I don't think so, thanks. My stuff is en route now. I'll have to blow out this vortex anyway. Not that I think there's anything unusual about it—those were undoubtedly murders, not vortex casualties at all—but for the record. Also, since I can't do any more extinguishing until my arm finishes itself up, I may as well stay here and keep on practising."

"Practising? Practising what?"

"Gun-slinging—the lightning draw. I intend to get at least a lunch while the next pirate who pulls a DeLameter on me is getting a square meal."

* * * * *

And Councillor Ellington conferred with another Gray Lensman; one who was not even vaguely humanoid.

"Did you take him apart?"

"Practically cell by cell."

"What do you think the chances are of finding and developing another like him?"

"With a quarter of a million Lensmen working on it now, and the number doubling every day, and with a hundred thousand million planets, with almost that many different cultures, it is my considered opinion that it is merely a matter of time."

THE BONEHEADS

SINCE BECOMING the Vortex Blaster, Neal Cloud lived alone. Whenever he decently could, he traveled alone and worked alone. He was alone now, hurtling through a barren region of space toward Rift Seventy One and the vortex next upon his list. In the interests of solitude, convenience, and efficiency he was now driving a scout-class ship which had been converted to one-man and automatic operation. In one hold was his vortex-blasting flitter; in the others his duodec bombs and other supplies.

During such periods of inaction as this, he was wont to think flagellantly of Jo and the three kids; especially of Jo. Now, however, and much to his surprise and chagrin, the pictures which had been so vividly clear were beginning to fade. Unless he concentrated consciously, his thoughts strayed elsewhere: to the last meeting of the Society; to the new speculations as to the why and how of supernovae; to food; to bowling—maybe he'd better start that again, to see if he couldn't make his hook roll smoothly into the one-two pocket instead of getting so many seven-ten splits. Back to food—for the first time in the Vortex Blaster's career he was really hungry.

Which buttons would he push for supper? Steak and Venerian mushrooms would be mighty good. So would fried ham and eggs, or high-pressured gameliope. . . .

An alarm bell jangled, rupturing the silence; a warm-blooded oxygen-breather's distress call, pitifully weak, was coming in. It would have to be weak, Cloud reflected, as he tuned it in as sharply as he could; he was a good eighty five parsecs—at least an hour at maximum blast—away from the nearest charted traffic lane. It was getting stronger. It hadn't just started, then; he had just gotten into its range. He acknowledged, swung his little ship's needle nose into the line and slammed on full drive. He had not gone far on the new course, however, when a tiny but brilliant flash of light showed on his plate and the distress-call stopped. Whatever had occurred was history.

Cloud had to investigate, of course. Both written and unwritten laws are adamant that every such call must be heeded by any warm-blooded oxygen-breather receiving it, of whatever race or class or tonnage or upon whatever mission bound. He broadcast call after call of his own. No reply. He was probably the only being in space who had been within range.

Still driving at max, he went to the rack and pulled down a chart. He had never been in on a space emergency before, but he knew the routine. No use to investigate the wreckage; the brilliance of the flare was evidence enough that the vessel and everything near it had ceased to exist. It was lifeboats he was after. They were supposed to stick around to be rescued, but out here they wouldn't. They'd have to head for the nearest planet, to be sure of air. Air was far more important than either food or water; and lifeboats, by the very nature of things, could not carry enough air.

Thus he steered more toward the nearest T-T (Tellus-Type) planet than toward the scene of disaster. He put his communicators, both sending and receiving, on automatic, then sat down at the detector panel. There might not be anything on the visuals or the audio. There had been many cases of boats, jammed with women and children, being launched into space with no one aboard able to operate even a communicator. If any lifeboats had gotten away from the catastrophe, his detectors would find them.

There was one; one only. It was close to the planet, almost into atmosphere. Cloud aimed a solid communicator beam. Still no answer. Either the boat's communicator was smashed or nobody aboard could run it. He'd have to follow them down to the ground.

But what was that? Another boat on the plate? Not a lifeboat—too big—but not big enough to be a ship. Coming out from the planet, apparently . . . to rescue? No—what the hell? The lug was *beaming* the lifeboat!

"Let's go, you sheet-iron lummox!" the Blaster yelled aloud, kicking in his every remaining dyne of drive. Then, very shortly, his plate came suddenly to life. To semi-life, rather, for the video was blurred and blotchy; the audio full of breaks and noise. The lifeboat's pilot was a Chickladorian; characteristically pink except for red-matted hair and red-streamed face. He was in bad shape.

"Whoever it is that's been trying to raise me, snap it up!" the pink man said in "Spaceal," the lingua franca of deep space. "I couldn't answer until I faked up this jury rig. The ape's aboard and he means business. I'm going to black out, I think, but I've undogged the locks. Take over, pal!"

The picture blurred, vanished. The voice stopped. Cloud swore, viciously.

* * * * *

The planet Dhil and its enormous satellite Lune are almost twin worlds, revolving around their common center of gravity and traversing as one the second orbit of their sun. In the third orbit revolves Nhal, a planet strikingly similar to Dhil in every respect of gravity, atmosphere, and climate. Thus Dhilians and Nhalians are, to intents and purposes, identical.

THE LENSMAN

The two races had been at war with each other, most of the time, for centuries; and practically all of that warfare had been waged upon luckless Lune. Each race was well advanced in science. Each had atomic power, offensive beams, and defensive screens. Neither had any degree of inertialessness. Neither had ever heard of Civilization or of Boskonia.

At this particular time peace existed, but only on the surface. Any discovery or development giving either side an advantage would rekindle the conflagration without hesitation or warning.

Such was the condition obtaining when Darjeeb of Nhal blasted his little space-ship upward from Lune. He was glowing with pride of accomplishment, suffused with self-esteem. Not only had he touched off an inextinguishable atomic flame exactly where it would do the most good, but also, as a crowning achievement, he had captured Luda of Dhil. Luda herself; the coldest, hardest, most efficient Minister of War that Dhil had ever had!

As soon as they could extract certain data from Luda's mind, they could take Lune in short order. With Lune solidly theirs, they could bomb Dhil into submission in two years. The goal of many generations would have been reached. He, Darjeeb of Nhal, would have wealth, fame, and—best of all—power!

Gazing gloatingly at his captive with every eye he could bring to bear, Darjeeb strolled over to inspect again her chains and manacles. Let her radiate! No mentality in existence could break *his* blocks. Physically, however, she had to be watched. The irons were strong; but so was Luda. If she could break free he'd probably have to shoot her, which would be a very bad thing indeed. She hadn't caved in yet, but she would. When he got her to Nhal, where proper measures could be taken, she'd give up every scrap of knowledge she had ever had!

The chains were holding, all eight of them, and Darjeeb kept on gloating as he backed toward his control station. To him Luda's shape was normal enough, since his own was the same, but in the sight of any Tellurian she would have been more than a little queer.

The lower part of her body was somewhat like that of a small elephant; one weighing perhaps four hundred pounds. The skin, however, was clear and fine and delicately tanned; there were no ears or tusks; the neck was longer. The trunk was shorter, divided at the tip to form a highly capable hand; and between the somewhat protuberant eyes of this "feeding" head there thrust out a boldly Roman, startlingly human nose. The brain in this head was very small, being concerned only with matters of food.

Above this not-too-unbelievable body, however, there was nothing familiar to us of Tellus. Instead of a back there were two pairs of mighty shoulders, from which sprang four tremendous arms, each like the trunk except longer and much stronger. Surmounting those massive shoulders there was an armored, slightly retractile neck which bore the heavily-armored "thinking" head. In this head there were no mouths, no nostrils. The four equally-spaced *pairs* of eyes were protected by heavy ridges and plates; the entire head, except for its junction with the neck, was solidly sheathed with bare, hard, thick, tough bone.

Darjeeb's amazing head shone a clean-scrubbed white. But Luda's—the eternal feminine!—was really something to look at. It had been sanded, buffed, and polished. It had been inlaid with bars and strips and scrolls of variously-colored metals; then decorated tastefully in red and green and blue and black enamel; then, to cap the climax, *lacquered!*

But that was old stuff to Darjeeb; all he cared about was the tightness of the chains immobilizing Luda's hands and feet. Seeing that they were all tight, he returned his attention to his visiplates; for he was not yet in the clear. Enemies might be blasting off after him any minute.

A light flashed upon his detector panel. Behind him everything was clear. Nothing was coming from Dhil. Ah, there it was, coming in from open space. But nothing *could* move that fast! A space-ship of some kind . . . Gods of the Ancients, *how* it was coming!

As a matter of fact the lifeboat was coming in at less than one light; the merest crawl, as space-speeds go. That velocity, however, was so utterly beyond anything known to his system that the usually phlematic Nhalian stood spellbound for a fraction of a second. Then he drove a hand toward a control. Too late—before the hand had covered half the distance the incomprehensibly fast ship struck his own without impact, jar, or shock.

Both vessels should have been blasted to atoms; but there the stranger was, poised motionless beside him. Then, under the urge of a ridiculously tiny jet of flame, she leaped away; covering miles in an instant. Then something equally fantastic happened. She drifted heavily *backward,* *against* the full force of her driving blasts!

Only one explanation was possible—inertialessness! What a weapon! With that and Luda—even without Luda—the solar system would be his. No longer was it a question of Nhal conquering Dhil. He himself would become the dictator, not only of Nhal and Dhil and Lune, but also of all other worlds within reach. That vessel and its secrets *must* be his!

He blasted, then, to match the inert velocity of the smaller craft, and as his ship approached the other he reached out both telepathically—he could neither speak nor hear—and with a spy-ray to determine the most feasible method of taking over this Godsend.

Bipeds! Peculiar little beasts—repulsive. Only two arms and eyes—only one head. Weak, no weapons—good! Couldn't *any* of them communicate? Ah yes, there was one—an unusually thin, reed-like creature, bundled up in layer upon layer of fabric. . . .

"I see that you are survivors of a catastrophe in outer space," Darjeeb began. He correlated instantly, if not sympathetically, the smashed panel and the pilot's bleeding head. If the creature had had a head worthy of the name, it could have wrecked a dozen such frailties with it, and without taking hurt. "Tell your pilot to let me in, so that I may guide you to safety. Hurry! Those will come at any moment who will destroy us all without warning or palaver."

"I am trying, sir, but I cannot get through to him direct. It will take a few moments." The strange telepathist began to make motions with her peculiar arms, hands, and fingers. Others of the outlanders brandished various repulsive members and gesticulated with ridiculous mouths. Finally:

"He says he would rather not," the interpreter reported. "He asks you to go ahead. He will follow you down."

"Impossible. We cannot land upon this world or its primary, Dhil," Darjeeb argued, reasonably. "These people are enemies—savages—I have just escaped from them. It is death to attempt to land anywhere in this system except on my own world Nhal—that bluish one over there."

"Very well, we'll see you there. We're just about out of air, but we can travel that far."

But that wouldn't do, either, of course. Argument took too much time. He'd have to use force, and he'd better call for help. He hurled mental orders to a henchman, threw out his magnetic grapples, and turned on a broad, low-powered beam.

"Open up or die," he ordered. "I do not want to blast you open, but time presses and I will if I must."

Pure heat is hard to take. The portal opened and Darjeeb, after donning armor and checking his ray-guns, picked Luda up and swung nonchalantly out into space. Luda was tough—a little vacuum wouldn't hurt her much. Inside the lifeboat, he tossed his captive into a corner and strode toward the pilot.

"I want to know right now what it is that makes this ship to be without inertia!" Darjeeb radiated, harshly. He had been probing vainly at the pink thing's mind-block. "Tell your pilot to tell me or I will squeeze it out of his brain."

As the order was being translated he slipped an arm out of his suit and clamped a huge hand around the pilot's head. But just as he made contact, before he put on any pressure at all, the weakling fainted.

Also, two of his senses registered disquieting tidings. He received, as plainly as though it was intended for him, a welcome which the swaddled-up biped was radiating in delight to an unexpected visitor rushing into the compartment. He saw that that visitor, while it was also a biped, was not at all like the frightened and harmless creatures already cluttering the room. It was armed and armored, in complete readiness for strife even with Darjeeb of Nhal.

The bonehead swung his ready weapon—with his build there was no need, ever to turn—and pressed a stud. A searing lance of flame stabbed out. Passengers screamed and fled into whatever places of security were available.

DRIVING JETS ARE WEAPONS

CLOUD'S SWEARING wasted no time; he could swear and act simultaneously. He flashed his vessel up near the lifeboat, went inert, and began to match its intrinsic velocity.

He'd have to board, no other way. Even if he had anything to blast it with, and he didn't—his vessel wasn't armed—he couldn't, without killing innocent people. What did he have?

He had two suits of armor; a G-P regulation and his vortex special, which was even stronger. He had his DeLameters. He had four semi-portables and two needle-beams, for excavating. He had thousands of duodec bombs, not one of which could be detonated by anything less violent than the furious heart of a loose atomic vortex.

What else? Well, there was his sampler. He grinned as he looked at it. About the size of a carpenter's hand-axe, with a savage beak on one side and a wickedly-curved, razor-sharp blade on the other. It had a double-grip handle, three feet long. A deceptive little thing, truly, for it was solid dureum. It weighed fifteen pounds, and its ultra-hard, ultra-tough blade could shear through neocarballoy as cleanly as a steel knife slices cheese. Considering what terrific damage a Valerian could do with a space-axe, he should be able to do quite a bit with this—it ought to qualify at least as a space-hatchet.

He put on his armor, set his DeLameters to maximum intensity at minimum aperture, and hung the sampler on a belt-hook. He eased off his blasts. There, the velocities matched. A minute's work with needle-beam, tractors, and pressor sufficed to cut the two smaller ships apart and to dispose of the Nhalian's magnets and cables. Another minute of careful manipulation and his scout was in place. He swung out, locked the port behind him, and entered the lifeboat.

He was met by a high-intensity beam. He had not expected instantaneous, undeclared war, but he was ready for it. Every screen he had was full out, his left hand held poised at hip a screened DeLameter. His return blast was, therefore, a reflection of Darjeeb's bolt, and it did vastly more damage. The hand in which Darjeeb held the projector was the one that had been manhandling the pilot, and it was not quite back inside the Nhalian's screens. In the fury of Cloud's riposte, then, gun and hand disappeared, as did also a square foot of panel behind them. But Darjeeb had other hands and other guns and for seconds blinding beams raved against unyielding screens.

Neither screen went down. The Tellurian bolstered his weapons. It wouldn't take much of this stuff to kill the passengers remaining in the saloon. He'd go in with his sampler.

He lugged it up and leaped straight at the flaming projector, with all of his mass and strength going into the swing of his "space-hatchet." The monster did not dodge, but merely threw up a hand to flick the toy aside with his gun-barrel. Cloud grinned fleetingly as he realized what the other must be thinking—that the man must be puny indeed to be making such ado about wielding such a trifle—for to anyone not familiar with dureum it is sheerly unbelievable that so much mass and momentum can possibly reside in a bulk so small.

Thus when fiercely-driven cutting edge met opposing ray-gun it did not waver or deflect. It scarcely even slowed. Through the metal of the gun that vicious blade sliced resistlessly, shearing flesh as it sped. On down, urged by everything Cloud's straining muscles could deliver. Through armor it slashed, through the bony plating covering that tremendous double shoulder, deep into the flesh and bone of the shoulder itself; being stopped only by the impact of the hatchet's haft against the armor.

Then, planting one steel boot on the helmet's dome, he got a momentary stance with the other between barrel body and flailing arm, bent his back, and heaved. The deeply-embedded blade tore out through bone and flesh and metal, and as it did so the two rear cabled arms dropped useless. That mighty rear shoulder and its appurtenances were out of action. The monster still had one good hand, however, and he was still full of fight.

That hand flashed out, to seize the weapon and to wield it against its owner. It came fast, too, but the man, strongly braced, yanked backward. Needle point and keen edge tore through flesh and snicked off fingers. Cloud swung his axe aloft and poised, making it limpidly clear that the next blow would be straight down into the top of the head.

That was enough. Darjeeb backed away, every eye glaring, and Cloud stepped warily over to Luda. A couple of strokes of his blade gave him a length of chain. Then, working carefully to keep his foe threatened at every instant, he worked the chain into a tight loop around the monster's front neck, pulled it unmercifully taut around a stanchion, and welded it there with his DeLameter. He did not trust the other monster unreservedly, either, bound as she was. In fact, he did not trust her at all. In spite of family rows, like sticks to like in emergencies and they'd gang up on him if they could. Since she wasn't wearing armor, however, she didn't stand a chance with a DeLameter, so he could take time now to look around.

The pilot, lying flat upon the floor, was beginning to come to. Not quite flat, either, for a shapely Chickladorian girl, wearing the forty one square inches of covering which were *de rigueur* in her eyes, had his bandaged head in her lap—or, rather, cushioned on one bare leg—and was sobbing gibberish over him. That wouldn't help. Cloud started for the first-aid locker, but stopped; a white-wrapped figure was already bending over the injured man with a black bottle in her hand. He knew what it was. Kedeselin. That was what he was after, himself; but he wouldn't have dared give a hippopotamus the terrific jolt she was pouring into him. She must be a nurse, or maybe a doctor; but Cloud shivered in sympathy, nevertheless.

The pilot stiffened convulsively, then relaxed. His eyes rolled; he gasped and shuddered; but he came to life and sat up groggily.

"What the hell goes on here?" Cloud demanded urgently, in spaceal.

"I don't know," the pink man replied. "All the ape said, as near as I could get it, was that I had to give him our free drive." He then spoke rapidly to the girl—his wife, Cloud guessed; if she wasn't, she ought to be—who was still holding him fervently.

The pink girl nodded. Then, catching Cloud's eye, she pointed at the two monstrosities, then at the nurse standing calmly near by. Startlingly slim, swathed to the eyes in billows of glamorette, she looked as fragile as a wisp of straw; but Cloud knew Manarkans. She, too, nodded at the Tellurian, then "talked" rapidly with her hands to a short, thick-set, tremendously muscled woman of some race entirely strange to the Blaster. She was used to going naked; that was very evident. She had been wearing a light "robe of convention," but it had been pretty well demolished in the melee and she did not realize that what was left of it was hanging in tatters down her broad back. The "squatty" eyed the gesticulating Manarkan and spoke, in a beautifully modulated deep bass voice, to a supple, lithe, pantherish girl with vertically-slitted yellow eyes, pointed ears, and a long and sinuous, meticulously-groomed tail. The Vegian—by no means the first of her race Cloud had seen—spoke to the Chickladorian eyeful, who in turn passed the message along to her husband.

"The bonehead you had the argument with says to hell with you," the pilot translated to Cloud in spaceal. "He says his mob will be out here after him directly, and if you don't cut him loose and give him the dope he wants they'll burn us all to cinders."

Luda was, meanwhile, trying to attract attention. She was bouncing up and down, rattling her chains, rolling her eyes, and in general demanding notice. More communication ensued, culminating in:

"The one with fancy-worked skull—she's a frail, but not the other bonehead's frail, I guess—says pay no attention to the ape. He's a murderer, a pirate, a bum, a louse, and so forth, she says. Says to take your axe—it's *some* cleaver, she says, and I check her to ten decimals on that—cut his goddam head clean off, chuck his stinking carcass out the port, and get the hell out of here as fast as you can blast."

That sounded to Cloud like good advice, but he didn't want to take such drastic action without more comprehensive data.

"Why?" he asked.

But this was too much for the communications relays to handle. Cloud did not know spaceal any too well, since he had not been out in deep space very long. Also, spaceal is a very simple language, not well adapted to the accurate expression of subtle nuances of thought; and all those intermediate translations were garbling things up terrifically. Hence Cloud was not surprised that nothing much was coming through, even though the prettied-up monster was, by this time, just about throwing a fit.

"She's quit trying to spin her yarn," the pilot said finally. "She says she's been trying to talk to you direct, but she can't get through. Says to unseal your ports—cut your screens—let down your guard—something like that, anyway. Don't know what she does mean, exactly. None of us does except maybe the Manarkan, and if she does she can't get it across on her fingers."

"Perhaps my thought-screen?" Cloud cut it.

"More yet," the Chickladorian went on, shortly. "She says there's another one, just as bad or worse. On your head, she says. . . . No, on your head-bone—what the hell! Skull? No, *inside* your skull, she says now. . . . Hell's bells! I don't know what she *is* trying to say!"

"Maybe I do—keep still a minute, all of you." A telepath undoubtedly, like the Manarkans—that was why she had to talk to her first. He'd never been around telepaths much—never tried it. He walked a few steps and stared directly into one pair of Luda's eyes—large, expressive eyes, now soft and gentle.

"That's it, chief! Now blast away . . . baffle your jets . . . relax, I guess she means. Open your locks and let her in."

Cloud did relax, but gingerly. He didn't like this mind-to-mind stuff at all, particularly when the other mind belonged to such a monster. He lowered his mental barriers skittishly, ready to revolt at any instant; but as soon as he began to understand the meaning of her thoughts he forgot completely that he was not talking man to man. And at that moment—such was the power of Luda's mind and the precision of her telepathy—every nuance of thought became sharp and clear.

"I demand Darjeeb's life!" Luda stormed. "Not because he is the enemy of all my race—that would not weigh with you—but because he has done what no one else, however base, has ever been so lost to shame as to do. In our city upon Lune he kindled an atomic flame which is killing us in multitudes. In case you do not know, such flames can never be extinguished."

"I know. We call them loose atomic vortices; but they can be extinguished. In fact, putting them out is my business."

"Oh—incredible but glorious news. . . ." Luda's thought seethed, became incomprehensible for a space. Then: "To win your help for my race I perceive that I must be completely frank. Observe my mind closely, please—see for yourself that I withhold nothing. Darjeeb wants at any cost the secret of your vessel's speed. With it, his race would destroy mine utterly. I want it too, of course—with it we would wipe out the Nhalians. However, since you are so much stronger than would be believed possible—since you defeated Darjeeb in single combat—I realize my helplessness. I tell you, therefore, that both Darjeeb and I have long since summoned help. Warships of both sides are approaching, to capture one or both of these vessels. The Nhalians are the nearer, and these secrets *must not*, under any conditions, go to Nhal. Dash out into space with both of these ships, so that we can plan at leisure. First, however, kill that unspeakable murderer—you have scarcely injured him the way it is—or give me that so-deceptive little axe and I'll be only too glad to do it myself."

A chain snapped ringingly; metal clanged against metal. Only two of Darjeeb's major arms had been incapacitated; his two others had lost only a few fingers apiece from their hands. His immense bodily strength was almost unimpaired. He could have broken free at any time, but he had waited; hoping to take Cloud by surprise or that some opportunity would arise for him to regain control of the lifeboat. But now, feeling sure that Luda's emminently sensible advice would be taken, he decided to let inertialessness go, for the moment, in the interest of saving his life.

"Kill him!" Luda shrieked the thought and Cloud swung his weapon aloft, but Darjeeb was not attacking. Instead, he was rushing into the airlock—escaping!

"Go free, pilot!" Cloud commanded, and leaped; but the inner valve swung shut before he could reach it.

As soon as he could operate the lock Cloud went through it. He knew that Darjeeb could not have boarded the scout, since her ports were locked. He hurried to his control room and scanned space. There the Nhalian was, falling like a plummet. There also were a dozen or so space-ships, too close for comfort, blasting upward.

Cloud cut in his Bergenholm, kicked on his driving blasts, cut off, and went back into the lifeboat.

"Safe enough now," he thought. "They'll never get out here inert. I'm surprised he jumped—didn't figure him as a suicidal type."

"He isn't. He didn't," Luda thought, dryly.

"Huh? He must have. That was a mighty long flit he took off on, and his suit wouldn't hold air."

"He would stuff something into the holes. If necessary he could have made it without air—or armor, either. He's tough. He still lives, curse him! But it is of no use for me to bewail that fact now. Let us make plans. You must put out the flame, and the leaders of our people will convince you. . . ."

"Just a second—some other things come first." He fell silent.

First of all, he had to report to the Patrol, so they could get some Lensmen and a task force out here to straighten up this mess. With ordinary communicators, that would take some doing—but wait, he had a double-ended tight beam to the laboratory. He could get through on that, probably, even from here. He'd have to mark the lifeboat as a derelict and get these people aboard his cruiser. No space-tube. The women could wear suits, but this Luda. . . .

"Don't worry about me!" that entity cut in. "You saw how I came aboard. I don't *enjoy* breathing vacuum, but I'm as tough as Darjeeb is. So *hurry!* During every moment you delay, more of my people are dying!"

"QX. While we're transferring, give me the dope."

Luda did so. Darjeeb's coup had been carefully planned and brilliantly executed. Drugged by one of her own staff, she had been taken without a struggle. She did not know how far-reaching the stroke had been, but she was pretty sure that most, if not all, of the Dhilian fortresses were now held by the enemy.

Nhal probably had the advantage in numbers and in firepower then upon Lune—Darjeeb would not have made his bid unless he had found a way to violate the treaty of strict equality. Dhil was, however, much the nearer of the two worlds. Hence, if this initial advantage could be overcome, Dhil's reenforcements could be brought up much sooner than the enemy's. If, in addition, the vortex could be extinguished before it had done irreparable damage, neither side would have any real advantage and the conflict would subside instead of flaring into another tri-world holocaust.

Cloud pondered. He would have to do something, but what? That vortex had to be snuffed; but, with the whole Nhalian army to cope with, how could he make the approach? His vortex-bombing flitter was screened against radiation, not war-beams. His cruiser was clothed to stop anything short of G-P primaries, but it would take a month at a Patrol base to adapt her for vortex work . . . and he'd have to analyze it, anyway, preferably from the ground. He had no beams, no ordinary bombs, no nega-bombs. How could he use what he had to clear a station?

"Draw me a map, will you, Luda?" he asked.

She did so. The cratered vortex, where an immense building had been. The ring of fortresses: two of which were unusually far apart, separated by a parkway and a shallow lagoon.

"Shallow? How deep?" Cloud interrupted. She indicated a depth of a couple of feet.

"That's enough map, then. Thanks." Cloud thought for minutes. "You seem to be quite an engineer. Can you give me exact details on your defensive screen? Power, radius, weave-form, generator type, phasing, interlocking, blow-off, and so on?"

She could. Complex mathematical equations and electrical formulae flashed through his mind, each leaving a residue of fact.

"Maybe we can do something," the Blaster said finally, turning to the Chickladorian. "Depends pretty much on our friend here. Are you a pilot, or just an emergency assignment?"

"Master pilot, Rating unlimited, tonnage or space."

"Good! Think you're in shape to take three thousand centimeters of acceleration?"

"Pretty sure of it. If I was right I could take three thousand standing on my head. I'm feeling better all the time. Let's hot 'er up and find out."

"Not until after we've unloaded these passengers somewhere," and Cloud went on to explain what he had in mind.

"Afraid it can't be done." The pilot shook his head glumly. "Your timing has got to be too ungodly fine. I can do the piloting, meter the blast, and so on. I can balance her down on her tail, steady to a hair, but piloting's only half what you got to have. Pilots never land on a constant blast, and your leeway here is damn near zero. To hit it as close as you want, your timing has got to be accurate to a tenth of a second. You don't know it, mister, but it'd take a master computer half a day to. . . ."

"I know all about that. I'm a master computer and I'll have everything figured. I'll give you a zero exact to plus-or-minus a hundredth."

"QX, then. Let's dump the non-combatants and flit."

"Luda, where shall we land them? And maybe you'd better call out your army and navy—we can't blow out that vortex until we control both air and ground."

"Land them there." Luda swung the plate and pointed. "The call was sent long since. They come."

They landed; but four of the women would not leave the vessel. The Manarkan *had* to stay aboard, she declared, or be disgraced for life. What would happen if the pilot passed out again, with only laymen around? She was right, Cloud conceded, and she could take it. She was a Manarkan, built of whalebone and rubber. She'd bend under 3 + G's, but she wouldn't break.

The squatty insisted upon staying. Since when had a woman of Tominga hidden from danger or run away from a fight? She could hold the pilot's head up through an acceleration that would put any damn-fragile Tellurian into a pack—or give her that funny axe and she'd show him how it *ought* to be swung!

The Chickladorian girl, too, stayed on. Her eyes—not pink, but a deep, cool green, brimming with unshed tears—flashed at the idea of leaving her man to die alone. She just knew they were all going to die. Even if she couldn't be of any use, what of it? If her Thlaskin died she was going to die too, right then, and that was all there was to it. If they made her go ashore she'd cut her own throat that very minute, so there! So that was that.

So did the Vegian. Tail-tip twitching slightly, eyes sparkling, she swore by three deities to claw the eyes out of, and then to strangle with her tail, anyone who tried to put her off ship. She had come on this trip to *see* things, and did Cloud think she was going to miss seeing *this*? Hardly!

Cloud studied her briefly. The short, thick, incredibly soft fur—like the fur on the upper lip of a week-old kitten, except more so—did not conceal the determined set of her lovely jaw; the tight shorts and the even tighter, purely conventional breastband did not conceal the tigerish strength and agility of her lovely body. It'd be better, the Blaster decided, not to argue the point.

A dozen armed Dhilians came aboard, as pre-arranged, and the cruiser blasted off. Then, while Thlaskin was maneuvering inert, to familiarize himself with the controls and to calibrate the blast, Cloud brought out the four semi-portable projectors. They were frightful weapons, designed for tripod mounting; so heavy that it took a very strong man to lift one on Earth. They carried no batteries or accumulators, but were powered by tight beams from the mother ship.

Luda was right; such weapons were unknown in that solar system. They had no beam transmission of power. The Dhilians radiated glee as they studied the things. They had stronger stuff, but it was fixed-mount and far too heavy to move. This was wonderful—these were magnificent weapons indeed!

High above the stratosphere, inert, the pilot found his spot and flipped the cruiser around, cross-hairs centering the objective. Then, using his forward, braking jets as drivers, he blasted her straight downward.

She struck atmosphere almost with a thud. Only her fiercely-driven meteorite-screens and wall-shields held her together.

"I hope to Klono you know what you're doing, chum," the Chickladorian remarked conversationally as the fortress below leaped upward with appalling speed. "I've made hot landings before, but I always had a hair or two of leeway. If you don't hit this to a couple of hundredths we'll splash when we strike. We won't bounce, brother."

"I can compute it to a thousandth and I can set the clicker to within five, but it's *you* that'll have to do the real hitting." Cloud grinned back at the iron-nerved pilot. "Sure a four-second call is enough to get your rhythm, allow for reaction time and lag, and blast right on the click?"

"Absolutely. If I can't get it in four I can't get it at all. Got your stuff ready?"

"Uh-huh." Cloud, staring into the radarscope, began to sway his shoulders. He knew the exact point in space and the exact instant of time at which the calculated deceleration must begin; by the aid of his millisecond timer—two full revolutions of the dial every second—he was about to set the clicker to announce that instant. His hand swayed back and forth—a finger snapped down—the sharp-toned instrument began to give out its crisp, precisely-spaced clicks.

"Got it!" Cloud snapped. "Right on the middle of the click! Get ready, Thlaskin—seconds! Four! Three! Two! One! Click!"

Exactly with the click the vessel's brakes cut off and her terrific driving blasts smashed on. There was a cruelly wrenching shock as everything aboard acquired suddenly a more-than-three-times-Earthly weight.

Luda and her fellows merely twitched. The Tomingan, standing behind the pilot, supporting and steadying his wounded head in its rest, settled almost imperceptibly, but her firmly gentle hands did not yield a millimeter. The Manarkan sank deeply into the cushioned bench upon which she was lying; her quick, bright eyes remaining fixed upon her patient.

The Chickladorian girl, in her hammock, fainted quietly.

The Vegian, who had flashed one hand up to an overhead bar at the pilot's first move, stood up—although she seemed to shorten a good two inches and her tight upper garment parted with a snap as back- and shoulder-muscles swelled to take the strain. *That* wouldn't worry her. Cloud knew—what *was* she stewing about? Oh—her tail! It was too heavy for its own strength, great as it was, to lift! Her left hand came down, around, and back; with its help the tail came up. To the bar above her head, around it, tip pointing stiffly straight upward. Then, smiling gleefully at both Thlaskin and the Blaster, she shouted something that neither could understand, but which was the war-cry of her race:

"Tails high, brothers!"

Downward the big ship hurtled, toward the now glowing screens of the fortress. Driving jets are not orthodox weapons, but properly applied, they can be deadly ones indeed: and these were being applied with micromatric exactitude.

Down! DOWN!! The threatened fortress and its neighbors hurled their every beam; Nhalian ships dived frantically at the invader and did their useless best to blast her down.

Down she drove, the fortress' screens flaming ever brighter under the terrific blast.

Closer! Hotter! Still closer! Hotter still! Nor did the furious flame waver—the Chickladorian was indeed a master pilot.

"Set up a plus ten, Thlaskin," Cloud directed. "Air density and temperature are changing. Their beams, too, you know."

"Check. Plus ten, sir—set up."

"Give it to her on the fourth click from . . . this."

"On, sir." The vessel seemed to pause momentarily, to stumble; but the added weight was almost imperceptible.

A bare hundred yards now, and the ship of space was still plunging downward at terrific speed. The screens were furiously incandescent, but were still holding.

A hundred feet, velocity appallingly high, the enemy's screens still up. Something *had* to give now! If that screen stood up the ship would vanish as she struck it, but Thlaskin the Chickladorian made no move and spoke no word. If the skipper was willing to bet his own life on his computations, who was he to squawk? But . . . he must have miscalculated!

No! While the vessel's driving projectors were still a few yards away the defending screens exploded into blackness; the awful streams of energy raved directly into the structures beneath. Metal and stone glared white, then flowed—sluggishly at first, but ever faster and more mobile—then boiled coruscantly into vapor.

The cruiser slowed—stopped—seemed to hang for an instant poised. Then she darted upward, her dreadful exhausts continuing and completing the utter devastation.

"That's computin', mister," the pilot breathed as he cut the fierce acceleration to a heavenly one thousand. "To figure a dive like that to three decimals and have the guts to hold to it cold—skipper, that's com-pu-*tation!*"

"All yours, pilot," Cloud demurred. "All I did was give you the dope. You're the guy that made it good. Hurt, anybody?"

Nobody was. "QX. We'll repeat, then, on the other side of the lagoon."

SUPER PACK

As the ship began to descend on the new course the vengeful Dhilian fleet arrived. Looping, diving, beaming, oftentimes crashing in suicidal collision, the two factions went maniacally to war. There were no attacks, however, against the plunging Tellurian ship. The Nhalians had learned that they could do nothing about that vessel.

The second fortress fell exactly as the first had fallen. The pilot landed the cruiser in the middle of the shallow lakelet. Cloud saw that the Dhilians, overwhelmingly superior in numbers now, had cleared the air of Nhalian craft.

"Can you fellows and your ships keep them off of my flitter while I take my readings?"

"We can," the natives radiated happily.

Four of the armored boneheads were *wearing* the semi-portable. They had them perched lightly atop their feeding heads, held immovably in place by two arms apiece. One hand sufficed to operate the controls, leaving two hands free to do whatever else might prove in order.

"Let us out!"

The lock opened, the Dhilian warriors sprang out and splashed away to meet the enemy, who were already dashing into the lagoon.

Cloud watched pure carnage. He hoped—yes, there they were! The loyalists, seeing that their cause was not lost, after all, had armed themselves and were smashing into the fray.

The Blaster broke out his flitter then, set it down near the vortex, and made his observations. Everything was normal. He selected three bombs from his vast stock, loaded them into the tubes, and lofted. He set his screens, adjusted his goggles, and waited; while far above him and wide around him his guardian Dhilian war-vessels toured watchfully, their drumming blasts a reassuring thunder.

He waited, eyeing the sigma curve as it flowed backward from the recording pen, until he got a ten-second prediction. He shot the flitter forward, solving instantaneously the problems of velocity and trajectory. At exactly the correct instant he released a bomb. He cut his drive and went free.

The bomb sped truly, striking the vortex dead center. It penetrated deeply enough. The carefully-weighed charge of duodec exploded; its energy and that of the vortex combining in a detonation whose like no inhabitant of that solar system had ever even dimly imagined.

The noxious gases and the pall of smoke and pulverized debris blew aside; the frightful waves of lava quieted down. The vortex was out and would remain out. The Blaster drove back to the cruiser and put his flitter away.

"Oh—you did it! Thanks! I didn't believe that you—that anybody—really could!" Luda was almost hysterical in her joyous relief.

"Nothing to it," Cloud deprecated. "How are you doing on the mopping up?"

"Practically clean," Luda answered, grimly. "We now know who is who. Those who fought against us or who did not fight for us are, or very soon will be, dead. But the Nhalian fleet comes. Does yours? Ours takes off in moments."

"Wait a minute!" Cloud sat down at his plate, made observations and measurements, calculated mentally. He turned on his communicator and conferred briefly.

"The Nhalian fleet will be here in seven hours and eighteen minutes. If your people go out to meet them it will mean a war that not even the Patrol can stop without destroying most of the ships and men both of you have in space. The Patrol task force will arrive in seven hours and thirty one minutes. Therefore, I suggest that you hold your fleet here, in formation but quiescent, under instructions not to move until you order them to, while you and I go out and see if we can't stop the Nhalians."

"*Stop* them!" Luda's thought was not at all ladylike. "What with, pray?"

"I don't know," Cloud confessed, "but it wouldn't do any harm to try, would it?"

"Probably not. We'll try."

All the way out Cloud pondered ways and means. As they neared the onrushing fleet he thought at Luda:

"Darjeeb is undoubtedly with that fleet. He knows that this is the only inertialess ship in this part of space. He wants it more than anything else in the universe. Now if we could only make him listen to reason . . . if we could make him see. . . ."

He broke off. No soap. You couldn't explain "green" to a man born blind. These folks didn't know and wouldn't believe what real firepower was. The weakest vessel in this oncoming task force could blast both of these boneheads' fleets into a radiant gas in fifteen seconds flat—and the superdreadnoughts' primaries would be starkly incredible to both Luda and Darjeeb. They simply *had* to be seen in action to be believed; and then it would be too late.

These people didn't stand the chance of a bug under a sledgehammer, but they'd have to be killed before they'd believe it. A damned shame, too. The joy, the satisfaction, the real advancement possible only through cooperation with each other and with the millions of races of Galactic Civilization—if there were only some means of *making* them believe. . . .

"We—and they—*do* believe." Luda broke into his somber musings.

"Huh? What? You do? You were listening?"

"Certainly. At your first thought I put myself en rapport with Darjeeb, and he and our peoples listened to your thoughts."

"But . . . you really believe me?"

"We all believe. Some will cooperate, however, only as far as it will serve their own ends to do so. Your Lensmen will undoubtedly have to kill that insect Darjeeb and others of his kind in the interest of lasting peace."

The insulted Nhalian drove in a protesting thought, but Luda ignored it and went on:

"You think, then, Tellurian, that your Lensmen can cope with even such as Darjeeb of Nhal?"

"I'll say they can!"

"It is well, then. Come aboard, Darjeeb—unarmed and unarmored, as I am—and we will together go to confer with these visiting Lensmen of Galactic Civilization. It is understood that there will be no warfare until our return."

"Holy Klono!" Cloud gasped. "He wouldn't do *that*, would he?"

"Certainly." Luda was surprised at the question. "Although he is an insect, and morally and ethically beneath contempt, he is, after all, a reasoning being."

"QX." Cloud was dumbfounded, but tried manfully not to show it.

Darjeeb came aboard. He was heavily bandaged and most of his hands were useless, but he seemed to bear no ill-will. Cloud gave orders; the ship flashed away to meet the Patrolmen.

The conference was held. The boneheads, after being taken through a superdreadnought and through a library by Lensmen as telepathic as themselves, capitulated to Civilization immediately and whole-heartedly.

"You won't need me any more, will you, admiral?" Cloud asked then.

"I don't think so—no. Nice job, Cloud."

"Thanks. I'll be on my way, then; the people I picked up must be off my ship by this time. Clear ether."

THE BLASTER ACQUIRES A CREW

CLOUD, RETURNING to his cruiser, found that most of his shipwrecked passengers had departed. Five of them, however—the two Chickladorians, the Manarkan, the squatty, and the Vegian—were still on board. Thlaskin, now back to normal, came to attention and saluted crisply; the women bowed or nodded and looked at him with varying degrees of interrogation.

"How come, Thlaskin? I thought all the passengers were going back with the task force."

"They are, boss. They've gone. We followed your orders, boss—chivied 'em off. I checked with the flagship about more crew besides us, and he says QX. Just tell me how many you want of what, and I'll get 'em."

"I don't want anybody!" Cloud snapped. "Not even you. Not *any* of you."

"Jet back, boss!" Spaceal was a simple language, and inherently slangy and profane, but there was no doubt as to the intensity of the pilot's feelings. "I don't know why you were running this heap alone, or how long, but I got a couple questions to ask. Do you know just how many million ways these goddam automatics can go haywire in? Do you know what to do about half of 'em when they do? Or are you just simply completely nuts?"

"No. Not too much. I don't think so." As he answered the three questions in order Cloud's mind flashed back to what Phil Strong and several other men had tried so heatedly to impress upon him—the stupidity, the lunacy, the sheer, stark idiocy of a man of *his* training trying to go it solo in deep space. How did one say "You have a point there, but before I make such a momentous decision we should explore the various possibilities of what is a completely unexpected development" in spaceal? One didn't! Instead:

"Maybe QX, maybe not. We'll talk it over. Tell the Manarkan to try to work me direct—maybe I can receive her now, after working the boneheads."

She could. Communication was not, perhaps, as clear as between two Manarkans or two Lensmen, but it was clear enough.

"You wish to know why I have included myself in your crew," the white-swathed girl began, as soon as communication was established. "It is the law. This vessel, the *Vortex Blaster I*, of Earth registry, belonging to the Galactic Patrol, is of a tonnage which obligates it to carry a medical doctor; or, in and for the duration of an emergency only, a registered graduate nurse. I am both R.N. and M.D. If you prefer to employ some other nursing doctor or doctor and nurse that is of course your right; but I can not and will not leave this ship until I am replaced by competent personnel. If I did such a thing I would be disgraced for life."

"But I haven't got a payroll—I never have had one!" Cloud protested.

"Don't quibble, please. It is also the law that any master or acting master of any ship of this tonnage is authorized to employ for his owner—in this case the Galactic Patrol—whatever personnel is necessary, whenever necessary, at his discretion. With or without pay, however, I stay on until replaced."

"But I don't *need* a doctor—or a nurse, either!"

"Personally, now, no," she conceded, equably enough. "I checked into that. As the chief of your great laboratory quoted to you, 'This too, shall pass.' It is passing. But you *must* have a crew; and any member of it, or you yourself, may require medical or surgical attention at any time. The only question, then, is whether or not you wish to replace me. Would you like to examine my credentials?"

"No. Having been en rapport with your mind, it is not necessary. But are you, after your position aboard the ship which was lost, interested in such a small job as this?"

"I would like it very much, I'm sure."

"Very well. If any of them stay, you can—at the same pay you were getting."

"Now, Thlaskin, the Vegian. No, hold it! We've got to have something better than spaceal, and a lot of Vegians go in for languages in a big way. She may know English or Spanish, since Vegia is one of Tellus' next-door neighbors. I'll try her myself."

Then, to the girl, "Do you speak English, miss?"

"No, eggzept in glimzzez only," came the startling reply. "Two Galactic Zdandard yearzz be pazz—come? Go?—'ere I mazzter zhe, zo perverze mood and tenze. Zhe izz zo difficult and abzdruze."

Switching to Galactic Spanish, which language was threatening to become the common tongue of Galactic Civilization, she went on:

"But I heard you say 'Zbanidge.' I know Galactic Spanish very well. I speak it well, too, except for the sounds of 'ezz' and 'zeta,' which all we Vegians must make much too hard—z-z-z, zo. One hears that nearly all educated Tellurians have the Spanish, and you are educated, of a certainty. You speak it, no?"

"Practically as well as I do English," Cloud made relieved reply. "You have very little accent, and that little is charming. My name is Neal Cloud. May I ask yours?"

"Neelcloud? I greet you. Mine is Vezzptkn . . . but no, you couldn't pronounce it. 'Vezzta,' it would have to be in your tongue."

"QX. We have a name very close to that—Vesta."

"That's exactly what I said—Vezz-ta."

"Oh—excuse me, please. You were talking to this lady—Tomingan, she said? What language were you using?"

"Fourth-continent Tomingan, Middle Plateau dialect. Hers. She was an engineer in a big power plant on Manarka, is how she came to learn their sign language. Tomingans don't go in for linguistics much."

"And you very evidently do. How many languages do you know, young lady?"

"Only fifty so far—plus their dialects, of course. I'm only half-way to my Master of Languages degree. Fifty more to learn yet, including your cursed *Englidge*. P-f-zt-k!" Vesta wrinkled her nose, bared her teeth, and emitted a noise very similar to that made by an alley cat upon meeting a strange dog. "I don't know whether spaceal will count for credit or not, but I'm going to learn it anyway."

"Nice going, Vesta. Now, why did *you* appoint yourself a member of this party?"

"I wanted to go, and since I can't pay fare. . . ."

"You wouldn't have had to!" Cloud interrupted. "If you lost your money aboard that ship, the Patrol would take you anywhere. . . ."

"Oh, I didn't mean *that*." She dipped into her belt-bag and held out for the man's inspection a book of Travelers' Cheques good for fifty thousand G-P credits! "I wanted to continue with you, and I knew this wasn't a passenger ship. I can be useful—who do you think lined up that translation relay?—and besides, I can work. I can cook—keep house—and I can learn any other job fast. You believe me?"

Cloud looked at her. She was as tall as he was, and heavier; stronger and faster. "Yes, you can work, if you want to, and I think you would. But you haven't said why you want to go along."

"Mostly because it's the best chance I'll ever have to learn English. I went to Tellus once before to learn it—but there are too many Vegians there. Young Vegians, like me, like to play too much. You know?"

"I've heard so. But teachers, courses. . . ?"

"I need neither teachers nor courses. What I need is what you have in your library—solid English."

"QX. I'll reserve judgment on you, too. Now let's hear what the Tomingan has to say. What's *her* name?"

"You'd be surprised!" Vesta giggled in glee. "Literally translated, it's 'Little flower of spring, dwelling bashfully by the brook's damply sweet brink.' And that's an *exact* transliteration, so help me—believe it or not!"

"I'll take your word for it. What shall we call her?"

"Um . . . m . . . 'Tommie' would be as good as anything, I guess."

"QX. Tommie of Tominga. Ask her why she thinks she has to be a member of our crew."

"Who else do you have who can repair one of your big atomic engines if it lets go?" came the answering question, in Vesta's flawlessly idiomatic Galactic Spanish.

Cloud was amazed at Tommie's changed appearance. She was powdered, perfumed, and painted: made up to the gills. Her heavy blonde hair was elaborately waved. If it wasn't for her diesel-truck build, Cloud thought—and for the long black Venerian cigar she was smoking with such evident relish—she'd be a knockout on anybody's tri-di screen!

"I can." The profoundly deep, but pleasantly and musically resonant voice went on; the fluent translation continued. "What I don't know about atomic engines hasn't been found out yet. I don't know much about Bergenholms and a couple of other things pertaining solely to flight, and I don't know *anything* about communicators or detectors, which aren't engineers' business. I've laid in a complete supply of atomic service manuals for class S-C ships, and I tell you this—if anything with a motor or an engine in it aboard this vessel ever has run, I can take it apart and put it back together so it'll run again. And by the way, you didn't have half enough spare parts aboard, but you have now. Besides, you might need somebody to really swing that axe of yours, some day."

Cloud studied the Tomingan narrowly. She *wasn't* bragging, he decided finally. She was simply voicing what to her were simple truths.

"Your arguments have weight. Why do you want the job?"

"Several reasons. I've never done anything like this before, and it'll be fun. Main reason, though, is that I think I'll be able to talk you into doing a job on Tominga that has needed doing for a long time. I was a passenger, not an officer, on my way to talk to a party about ways of getting it done. You changed my mind. You and I, with some others who'll be glad to help, will be able to do it better."

Tommie volunteered no more information, and Cloud asked no more questions. Explanation would probably take more time than could be spared.

"Now you, Thlaskin," the Blaster said in spaceal. "What have you got to say for yourself?"

"You've got me on a hell of a spot, boss," the pilot admitted, ruefully. "You've *got* to have a pilot, no question about that. You already know I'm one. I know automatics, and communicators, and detectors—the works. Ordinarily I'd say you'd *have* to have *me*. But this ain't a regular case. I wasn't a pilot on the heap that got knocked out of the ether, but a passenger. Maluleme—she's my . . . say, ain't there no word for. . . ."

He broke off and spoke rapidly to his wife, who relayed it to Vesta.

"They're newlyweds," the Vegian translated. "He was off duty and they were on their honeymoon. . . ."

Vesta's wonderfully expressive face softened, saddened. She appeared about to cry. "I wish *I* were old enough to be a newlywed," she said, plaintively.

"Huh? Aren't you?" the Blaster demanded. "You look old enough to me."

"Oh, I'm as big as I ever will be, and I won't change outside. It's inside. About half a year yet. But she's saying—

"We know that pilots on duty, in regular service, can't have their wives aboard. But this isn't a regular run, I know, so couldn't you—just this once—keep Thlaskin on as pilot and let me come too? *Please*, Mr. Neelcloud—she didn't know your name, but asked me to put it in—I can work my way. I'll do any of the jobs nobody else wants to do—I'll do *anything*, Mr. Neelcloud!"

The pink girl jumped up and took Cloud's left hand in both her own. Simultaneously Vesta took his right hand in her left, brought it up to her face, and laid the incredibly downy softness of her cheek against the five-hour bristles of his; sounding the while a soft, low-pitched but unmistakable *purr*!

"Just this once wouldn't do any harm, would it, Captain Neelcloud?" Vesta purred. "You zmell zo wonderful, and she zmells nice, too. *Pleeze* keep her on!"

"QX. You win!" The Blaster pulled himself loose from the two too-demonstrative females and addressed the group at large. "I think I ought to have my head examined, but I'm signing all of you on as crew. But *nobody else.* I'll get the book."

He got it. He signed them on. Chief Pilot Thlaskin. Chief Engineer Tommie. Linguist Vesta. Doctor . . . what? He tried to call her attention by thinking at her, but couldn't. Then, through Vesta: Manarkans didn't have names, but were known by their personality patterns. Didn't they sign something to documents? No, they used finger-prints only, without signatures.

"But we've got to have *something* we can put in the book!" Cloud protested. "Tell her to pick one."

"No preference," Vesta reported. "I'm to do it. I knew a lovely Tellurian named 'Nadinevandereckelberg' once. Let's call her that."

"Nadine van der Eckelberg? Better not. Not common enough—there might be repercussions. We can use part of it, though. 'Nadine,' bracketed with her prints . . . there. Now how about Maluleme?" He turned to the "Classification" listing and frowned. "What to class *her* as I'll never know. She's got just about as much business aboard this bucket as I would have in a sultan's harem."

"You might find quite a lot—and *that* I'd like to see!" Vesta snickered. "But look under 'Mizzelaneouz,' there."

Her stiff, sharp fingernail ran down the column almost to the end. " 'Zupercargo'? We have no cargo. 'Zupernumerary'? That's it! See? I read: 'Zupernumerary—Perzonnel beyond the nezezzary or uzhual; ezpedjially thoze employed not for regular zervize, but only to fill the plazez of otherz in caze of need.' Perfect!"

"Whose place could *she* fill?"

"The cook's—if the automatics break down," Vesta explained, gleefully. "She says she can really cook—so even if they didn't break down she can tape lots of nice things to eat that aren't in your kitchen banks."

"Could be. I can get away with that. 'Supernumerary (cook 1/c) Maluleme' and her prints . . . there. Now we're organized—let's flit. Ready, Thlaskin?"

"Ready, sir," and the good ship *Vortex Blaster I* took off.

"Now, Vesta, I s'pose you've all picked out your cabins and got located?"

"Yes, sir."

"QX. Tell 'em all, except Tommie, to go and do whatever they think they ought to be doing. Tell Tommie to sit down at the chart-table. We'll join her. I want to find out what she's got on her mind."

Pulling a chart and rolling it out flat on the table, Cloud went on: "We're in this unexplored region, here, about thirty two dash twenty five. We're headed for Nixson II, about sixty one dash forty six."

"Nixson? Why, that's only three thousand parsecs—a day and a half, say—from Tominga, where I want you to go!" Tommie exclaimed.

"Check. That's why I'm going to listen to what you have to say. We can pick Manarka up—sixty five dash thirty-five, here; they've got two really bad ones—on the way back. It's a long flit to Chickladoria—'way over there, one seventy seven dash thirty four—but I've got to go there pretty quick, anyway. It's way up on the A list. So, Tommie, start talking."

*

The run to Nixson II was uneventful, and Cloud rid that planet of its loose atomic vortices in a few hours. The cruiser then headed directly for Tominga, one man short, for Tommie was not aboard.

"Now remember, no matter what happens, you don't know any one of us," had been the Blaster's parting instructions to her. "After we've checked in at the hotel we'll meet in the lobby. Be sure you're sitting—or standing—some place where Vesta can pass a couple of words with you without anybody catching on. Check?"

"Check."

VESTA THE VEGIAN

IMMEDIATELY AFTER SUPPER Cloud called Vesta and Nadine into his cabin.

"You first, Nadine." He caught her eyes and stopped talking, but went on thinking. He was amazed at how easy it had been to learn the knack of telepathy with both Luda and the Manarkan. "How did you make out with Tommie? Can't she read you at all?"

"Not at all. I can read her easily enough, but she can neither send nor receive."

"How about Vesta, then? Any more progress?"

"No. Just like you. She learned very quickly to receive, but that is all. She cannot tune her mind; I have to do it all." It also amazed the Blaster that, after learning one half of telepathy so easily, he had been unable even to get a start on the other half. "We might try it again, though, all three of us together?"

They tried, but it was no use. Think as they would, of even the simplest things—squares, crosses, triangles, and circles—staring eye to eye and even holding hands, neither the Blaster nor the Vegian could touch the other's mind. Nor could the Manarkan tell them or show them what to do.

"Well, that's out, then." Cloud frowned in concentration, the fingers of his left hand drumming almost soundlessly on the table's plastic top. "Nadine, you can't send simultaneously to both Vesta and me, because we can't tune ourselves into resonance with you, as a real telepath could. However, could you read me and send my thoughts to Vesta, and do it fast enough to keep up? As fast as I talk, say?"

"Oh, easily. I don't have to tune sharply to receive—unless there's a lot of interference, of course—and even then, Vesta can read my shorthand. She learned it before we met you."

"Hm . . . m. Interesting. Let's try it out. I'll think at you, you put it down in shorthand. You, Vesta, tape it in Spanish. Get your notebook and recorder . . . ready? Let's go!"

There ensued a strange spectacle. Cloud, leaning back in his seat with his eyes closed, mumbled to himself in English, to slow his thoughts down to approximately two hundred words per minute. Nadine, paying no visible attention to the man, wrote unhurried, smoothly-flowing—most of the time—symbols. Vesta, throat-mike in place and yellow-eyed gaze nailed to the pencil's point, kept pace effortlessly—most of the time.

"That's all. Play it back, Vesta. If you girls got half of that, you're *good*."

SUPER PACK

The speaker came to life, giving voice to a completely detailed and extremely technical report on the extinction of an imaginary atomic vortex, and as the transcription proceeded Cloud's amazement deepened. It was evident, of course, that neither of the two translators knew anything at all about many of the scientific technicalities involved. Nevertheless the Manarkan had put down—and Vesta had recorded in good, idiomatic Galactic Spanish—an intelligent layman's idea of what it was that had been left out. That impromptu, completely unrehearsed report would have been fully informative to any expert of the Vortex Control Laboratory!

"Girls, you *are* good—*very* good." Cloud paid deserved tribute to ability. "First chance we get, I'll split a bottle of fayalin with you. Now we'd better hit the sack. We land early in the morning, and since we're going to stay here a while we'll have to go through quarantine and customs. So pack your bags and have 'em ready for inspection."

They landed at the spaceport of Tommie's home town, which Cloud, after hearing Vesta's literal translation of its native name, had entered in his log as "Mingia." They passed their physicals and healths easily enough—the requirements for leaving a planet of warm-blooded oxygen-breathers are so severe and so comprehensive that the matter of landing on a similar one is almost always a matter of simple routine.

"Manarkan doctors we know of old; you are welcome indeed. We see very few Tellurians or Vegians, but the standards of those worlds are very high and we are glad to welcome you. But Chickladoria? I never heard of it—we've had no one from that planet since I took charge of this port of entry. . . ."

The Tomingan official punched buttons, gabbled briefly, and listened.

"Oh, yes. Excellent! The health, sanitation, and exit requirements of Chickladoria are approved by the Galactic Medical Society. We welcome you. You all may pass."

They left the building and boarded a copter for their hotel.

". . . and part of its name is 'Forget-me-not'! Isn't that a dilly of a name for a hotel?" Vesta, who had been telepathing busily with Nadine, was giggling sunnily.

Suddenly, however, she stopped laughing and, eyes slitted, leaped for the door. Too late: the craft was already in the air.

"Do you know what that . . . that *clunker* back there *really* thought of us?" she flared. "That we're weak, skinny, insipid, under-developed little *runts*! By Zevz and Tlazz and Jadkptn, I'll show him—I'll take a tail-wrap around his neck and. . . ."

"Pipe down, Vesta—listen!" Cloud broke in, sharply. "You're smart enough to know better than to explode that way. For instance, you're stronger than I am, and faster—admitted. So what? I'm still your boss. And Tommie isn't, even though, as you ought to know by this time, she could pull your tail out by the roots and beat you to death with the butt end of it in thirty seconds flat."

"Huh?" Vesta's towering rage subsided miraculously into surprised curiosity. "But you're *admitting* it!" she marvelled. "Even that *I* am stronger and faster than *you* are!"

"Certainly. Why not? Servos are faster still, and ordinary derricks are stronger. It's *brains* that count. I'd much rather have your linguistic ability than the speed and strength of a Valerian."

"So would I, really," Vesta purred. "You're the *nicest* man!"

"So watch yourself, young lady," Cloud went on evenly, "and behave yourself. If you don't, important as you are to this project, I'll send you back to the ship in irons. That's a promise."

"P-f-z-t-k!" Vesta fairly spat the expletive. Her first thought was sheer defiance, but under the Blaster's level stare she changed her mind visibly. "I'll behave myself, Captain Neelcloud."

"Thanks, Vesta. You'll be worth a whole platoon of Tomingans if you do."

The copter landed on the flat roof of the hotel. The guests were registered and shown to their rooms. The Forget-Me-Not's air was hot and humid, and the visitors wore the only clothing to be seen. Nevertheless, Cloud was too squeamish to go all the way, so he still wore shorts and sandals, as well as the side-arm of his rank, when he went back up to the lobby to meet his crew.

Vesta, tail-tip waving gracefully a foot and a half above her head, was wearing only her sandals. Thlaskin wore shorts and space-boots. Maluleme had reduced her conventional forty one square inches of covering to a daring twenty five—two narrow ribbons and a couple of jewels. Nadine, alone of them all, had made no concession to that stickily sweltering climate. She'd be disgraced for life, Cloud supposed, if she cut down by even one the hundreds of feet of white glamorette in which she was swathed. But Manarkans didn't sweat like Tellurians, he guessed—if they did, she'd either peel or smother before this job was over!

Cloud scanned the lobby carefully. Were they attracting too much attention? They were not. They had had to pose for Telenews shots, of course—the Chickladorians in particular had been held in the spots for all of five minutes—but that was all. Like any other spaceport city, Mingia was used to outlandish forms of warm-blooded, oxygen-breathing life. Not counting his own group, he could see members of four different non-Tomingan races, two of which were completely strange to him. And Tommie, standing alone in front of one of the row of shop-windows comprising one wall of the lobby—and very close to a mirrored pillar—was intently studying a tobacconist's display of domestic and imported cigars.

"QX," the Blaster said then. "We aren't kicking up any fuss. Do your stuff, Vesta."

The girl sauntered over to the mirror, licked her forefinger, and began to smooth an imaginary roughness out of one perfect eyebrow. Thus, palm covering mouth—

"He still hangs out here, Tommie?"

"He still eats supper here every night, in the same private room." Tommie did not move or turn her head; her voice could not be heard three feet away.

"When he comes in, take one good look at him and think 'This is the one'—Nadine'll take over from there. Then sneak down to the chief's suite and join us."

Vesta, with a final approving pat at her sleek head, sauntered on; past a display of belt-pouches in which she was not interested, pausing before one of ultra-fancy candies in which she very definitely was, and back to her own group.

"On the green," she reported.

"Then I'll go on about my business of getting things lined up to blow out vortices. You, Thlaskin and Maluleme, just run around and play. Act innocent—you're just atmosphere for now. Nadine and Vesta, go down to my suite—here's a key—and get your recorder and stuff ready. I'll see you later."

Cloud came back, however, rather sooner than he had intended.

"I didn't get far—I'll have to take you along if I want to get any business done," he explained to Vesta. "Up to now, I've got along very nicely with English, Spanish, and spaceal, but not here. We're a long ways from either Tellus or Vegia."

"We are indeed. I don't know what they do use for an interstellar language here—I'll have to find out and see if I know it yet." Vesta then switched to English. "While we wait, do you mind if I zpeak at you in Englizh? And will you ztop me and correct, please, the errors I will make? My pronunziazion is getting better, but I ztill have much trouble with your irregular verbs and pronouns. I come, but I am not yet arrive."

"I'll say you're better!" Cloud knew that she had been studying hard; studying with an intensity of concentration comparable only to that of a cat on duty at a mouse-hole; but he had expected no such progress as this. "It's amazing—you have scarcely any more accent now in English than in Spanish. I'll be glad to coach you. What you just said was QX except for the last sentence. Idiomatically, you should have said 'I'm coming along, but I'm not there yet,' " and Cloud explained in detail. "Now, for practice, brief me on this job we've got here."

"Thankz a lot. Tommie's brother, whom we'll call Jim, runs a tobacco zhop here in town." Cloud had had to explain what "briefing" meant, and he corrected many slight errors which are not given here. "A man who called himself 'Number One' organized a Protective Azzoziazion. Anyone not joining, he zaid, would zuffer the conzequenzez of a looze atomic vortex in his power plant. When he zhowed he meant buzzinez by exploding one right where and when he zaid he would, many merchants joined and began to pay. Jim did not. Inztead, he . . . I forget the idiom?"

" 'Stalled.' That means delayed, played for time."

"Oh, yez. Jim ztalled, and Tommie went looking for help, knowing the government here thoroughly corrupt. Impozzible to alleviate intolerable zituazion."

"*What* a vocabulary!"

"Iz wrong?" Vesta demanded.

"No, is *right*," Cloud assured her. "I was complimenting you, young lady—you'll be teaching *me* English before this trip is over."

The class in English Conversation went on until the Manarkan warned its two participants to get ready; that Tommie, having identified the gangster, had left the lobby, had joined her brother, and was bringing him with her.

"Is that safe, do you think?" Vesta asked.

"For now, before anything starts, yes." Cloud replied. "After tonight, no."

The Tomingans arrived; Vesta let them in and introduced Jim to Nadine and Cloud. The brother was taller, heavier, craggier than the sister; his cigar was longer, thicker, and blacker than hers. Otherwise, they were very much alike. Cloud waved them both into comfortable chairs, for there was no time for conversation. Nadine began to write; Vesta to record.

The Big Shot—Nadine took an instant to flash into Cloud's mind a very good picture of the fellow—was in his private room, but if a dinner were to be on the program it would be later. There were two men in the room; Number One and another man, whom he thought of and spoke to as "Number Nine." At present the affair was strictly business. Number Nine was handing money to Number One, who was making notes in a book. Twenty credits from Number Seventeen; 50 from No. 20; 25 from No. 26; 175 from No. 29; 19 credits—all he could raise—from No. 30; 125 from No. 31, and so on. . . .

The gangsters thought that they were being very smart and cagey in using numbers instead of names, but neither had any idea of the power of a really good telepathic mind, or of that of a really good linguist. Each of those numbers meant something to either or to both of those men, and whatever it was—a name, a picture, a storefront or address, or a fleeting glimpse of personality pattern—Nadine seized and transmitted, either in shorthand or by force of mind, or both; and Vesta taped, in machine-gun-fast Spanish, every written word and every nuance of thought.

The list was long. At its end:

"Three more didn't pay up, huh? The same ones holding out as last time, and three more besides, huh?" This was Number One, thinking deeply. "I don't like it. . . . Ninety Two, huh? I don't like it a bit—or him, either. I'll have to do something about him."

"Yeah. Ninety Two. The others all give the same old tear-jerker that they didn't have it, that our assessments were too stiff for their take, and so on, but Ninety Two didn't, this time. He simply blew his top. He was hotter than the business end of a blow-torch." Not much to Cloud's surprise, Nadine at this point poured into his mind the picture of excessively angry Jim. "Not only he didn't fork over, he told me to tell you something."

There was a long pause.

"Well, spill it!" Number One barked. "What did he say?"

"Shall I give it to you straight boss, or maybe I better tone it down some?"

"Straight!"

"He said for you to go roast, for fourteen thousand years, in the hottest corner you can find of the hottest hell of Telemachia, and take your Srizonified association with you. Take your membership papers and stick 'em. Blow his place up and be damned to you, he says. If you kill him in the blast he's left stuff in a deposit box that'll blow all the Srizonified crooked politicians and lawmen in the Fourth Continent off of their perches and down onto their Srizonified butts. An' if you *don't* get him, he says, he'll come after you with blasters in both hands. Make it plain, he says, that it's *you* he'll be after—not me. That's exactly what he told me to tell you, boss."

"Me? ME?" Number One demanded. The towering rage, which he had been scarcely able to control, subsided into a warily intense speculation. "How did he find out about *me*? Somebody'll burn for this!"

"I dunno, boss, but it looks like you said a mouthful about having to do something about him. We got to make an example of *somebody*, boss—or else—in my book it'd better be 92. He's organizing, sure as hell, and if we don't knock him off it'll spread fast."

"Hm . . . m . . . m. Yes, but just him personally, not his place. I'm not afraid of any evidence he can leave, of itself, but in connection with the other thing it might be bad.

His place is too big; too centrally located. No matter what time of night it goes off it'll kill too many people and do too much damage. Yellow Castle might dump us instead of trying to ride out such a storm."

"Yeah, they might, at that. Prob'ly would. And the dogooders might get some of them Srizonified Lensmen in here besides. But an ordinary bomb would do the job."

"No. Got to be a vortex. We promised 'em an atomic flare, so that's what it's got to be. It doesn't have to be 92, though. We can get away easy enough with killing a few people, so I'd say somebody in the outskirts—53 would be as good as any. So tell 53 his place gets it at midnight tomorrow night, and the fewer people in it the more will stay alive."

"Check. And I'll take care of 92?"

"Of course. You don't have to be told *every* move to make."

"Just wanted to make sure, is all. What do I do in the big fireworks?" It was clear that the underling was intensely curious about the phenomenon, but his curiosity was not to be satisfied.

"Nothing," his chief informed him flatly. "That isn't your dish. Now we'll eat."

Number One stopped talking, but he did not stop thinking; and Nadine could read, and Vesta could transcribe, thoughts as well as words.

"Besides, it's about time for 31 to earn some of the credits we're paying him," was the grimly savage thought.

This thought was accompanied by a picture, which Nadine spread in full in Cloud's mind. A tall, lean, gray Tellurian was aiming a mechanism—the details of which were so vague that it could have been anything from a vest-pocket flash-pencil up to a half-track mobile projector—at a power-plant, which immediately and enthusiastically went out of control in a blindingly incandescent flare of raw energy.

Fairchild!

Cloud's mind raced. That vortex on Deka *hadn't* been accidental, then, even though there had been no evidence—no suspicion—even the Lensmen hadn't guessed that the radiationist had been anything other than a very minor cog in Graves' thionite-producing machine! Nobody except Fairchild knew what he did or how he did it—the mob must have tried to find out, too, but he wouldn't give—but this stuff was very definitely for the future; not for now.

"QX, girls. A nice job—thanks," he said. "Now, Vesta, please tape the actual facts and the actual words of the interview—none of the pictures or guesses—in Middle Plateau Tomingan. Wherever possible, bracket real names and addresses with the code numbers. Tommie and Jim can help you on that."

She did so.

When they came to that part of the transcription dealing with Number Ninety Two, Jim stiffened and swelled in rage.

"Ask him if that's an accurate report," Cloud directed.

"It's accurate enough as far as it goes," Jim boomed. His voice, deeper and louder than Tommie's, and not nearly as musical, almost shook the walls. "But he left out half of it. What I really told him would have burned all the tape off of that recorder."

"But they left in that . . . that awful one, three times." Tommie, tough as she was, was shocked. "You ought to be ashamed of yourself."

"Srizonified?" Cloud whispered to Vesta. "It sounded bad, but not *that* hot. Is it?"

"Yes, the hottest in the language. I never saw it in print, and heard it only once, and that was by accident. Like most such things, though, it doesn't translate–'descended from countless generations of dwellers in stinking, unflowering mud' is as close as I can come to it in Spanish."

"QX. Finish up the tape and make two copies of it."

When the copies were ready Cloud handed them to Tommie.

"Tell him to take one of these down to the Tomingan equivalent of the D. A.'s office the first thing in the morning," he instructed Vesta. "The other ought to go to a big law firm–an honest one, if she knows of any. Now ask Jim what he thinks he's going to do."

"I'm going to get a pair of blasters and. . . ."

"Yeah?" Cloud's biting monosyllable, so ably translated by the Vegian, stopped him in mid-sentence. "What chance do you think you stand of getting home tonight in one piece? Your copter is probably mined right now, and they've undoubtedly made arrangements to blast you if you leave here any other way, even on foot. If you want to stay alive, though, I've got a suggestion to make."

"You may be right, sir." Jim's bluster died away as he began really to think. "Do you see a way out?"

"Yes. Ordinary citizens don't wear armor here, any more than anywhere else, so ordinary gangsters don't use semi-portables. So, when you leave here, go to Tommie's room instead of out. They'll lay for you, of course, but while they're waiting Tommie will go out to our ship and bring back my G-P armor. You put it on, walk out openly, and take a ground-car–*not* a copter–to the ship. If they know armor they won't shoot at you, because you could shoot back. When you get to the ship go in, lock the port behind you, and stay there until I tell you to come out."

Jim, influenced visibly by the pleasant possibility of shooting back, accepted the plan joyously; and, after making sure that there were no spies or spy-rays on watch, the two Tomingans left the room.

A few minutes later, with the same precaution, Vesta and the Manarkan went to their own rooms; but they were on hand again after breakfast next morning.

"You know, of course, that you have no evidence admissible in even an honest court," Nadine began. "You knew it when you changed your mind about having a Tomingan voice, not Vesta's, on those tapes."

"Yes. Communicator-taps are out–violation of privacy."

"Exactly. And telepathy is worse. Any attempt to introduce telepathic testimony, on almost any non-telepathic world, does more harm than good. So, beyond establishing the fact of guilt in your own mind–a fact already self-evident, since such outrages can happen only when both courts and police are corrupt from top to bottom–I fail to see what you hope to gain."

"Wouldn't a Tomingan Lensman be interested?"

"There are none. There never have been any."

"Well, then, I'll take it up myself, with. . . ."

Cloud stopped in mid-thought. With whom? He could talk to Phil Strong, certainly, but he wouldn't get anywhere. He knew, as well as Nadine did, that the Galactic Patrol would not interfere with purely local politics unless something of inter-systemic scope was involved. The Galactic Council held, and probably rightly, that any people got the kind of local government they deserved. He certainly couldn't expect the Patrol to over-ride planetary sovereignty in regard to a thing that hadn't happened yet! He wrenched his mind away.

"Having any trouble following her, Nadine?" he asked.

"No. She's just leaving the fast-way now; going into his office."

Thus, through Nadine, Cloud accompanied Tommie into the office of the District Attorney, saw her tender the spool of tape, heard her explain in stormy language what it was.

"How did you get hold of it?" the D. A. demanded.

"How do you suppose?" Tommie shot back. "Do we have to come down to City Hall and take out a license to hang an ear onto such a stinking crumb, such a notorious mobster and general all-round heel as Number One is? Public Enemy Number One, it ought to be!"

"No, I wouldn't say that you would," the politician soothed. He had been thinking fast. "I'll run this tape as soon as I can take a minute alone in my chambers, and I promise you full and fast action. They've gone too far, this time. Just what, specifically, do you want me to do?"

"I'm no lawyer, so I don't know who does what, but I want this Protective Association junked and I want those murderers arrested. Today."

"Some of these matters lie outside the province of this office, but I can and will take initiatory steps. No one will be harmed, I assure you."

Apparently satisfied, Tommie left the D. A.'s office, but Nadine did not leave the D. A.'s mind. This was what the Blaster was after!

Sure enough, as soon as Tommie was out of sight, the official dashed into his private office and called Number One.

"One, they hung an ear on you last night!" he exclaimed, as soon as connection was made. "How come you didn't. . . ."

"Horsefeathers!" the gangster snarled. "Who d'ya think you're kidding?"

"But they did! I've got a copy of it right here."

"Play it!"

The tape was played, and it was very clear that it was in no Tomingan's voice.

"No, it wasn't an ear," the D. A. admitted.

"And I was blocked against spy-rays," said Number One, "so it must have been a snooper. A snooper with a voice. Manarkans are snoopers, but they can't talk. Most snoopers can't . . . except maybe Ordoviks. There were a couple of them around last night. Can Ordoviks talk? And Chickladorians—are they snoopers?"

"I don't know."

"I don't know either, but I'll find out, and when I do I'll go gunning."

Tommie came back to Cloud's room and her serenity, skin-deep at best, vanished completely as the new tape was played.

"Condemn and blast that lying, slimy, two-faced, double-crossing snake!" she roared. "I'll call out the. . . ."

"You won't either—pipe down!" Cloud ordered, sharply. "Mob rule never settled anything. That's what you expected, isn't it?"

"Well . . . more or less, I suppose . . . yes."

"QX. We got *something* to work on now, but we need more, and we've got only today to get it. Who's the crookedest judge in town—the one most apt to be in on this kind of a deal?"

"Trellis. High Judge Rose Trellis of the Enchanting. . . ."

"Skip the embellishments. Take both of these tapes to Judge Trellis and *insist* on seeing him at once."

"It isn't a him—she's a her."

"Her, then. Make it snappy. And don't blow up if she gives you the brush-off. We're after data. And on your way back, pick up that newspaper editor and bring him along."

TROUBLE ON TOMINGA

TOMMIE LEFT, accompanied mentally by Nadine, and reached the judge's antechamber; with Vesta taping in Middle-Plateau Tomingan everything that occurred. The approach was difficult, and Tommie's temper grew shorter and shorter.

"Get out of my way!" she bellowed finally at the sergeant-at-arms barring her way to the judicial Presence, in a voice that rattled the windows and was audible above four blocks of city traffic. "Or shoot, if you want to get yourself and this building and half of Mingia blown clear up into the stratosphere! Jump! Before I take that blaster and shove it so far down your throat it'll hit day-before-yesterday's breakfast!"

The guard did not have quite enough nerve to shoot, and Tommie almost wrenched the door of the judge's inner office off its hinges as she went in.

"What's this, pray? Get out! Sergeant-at. . . ."

"Shut up, Rose Trellis of the Enchanting Vistas of Exotic Blooms—you're listening, not talking. Here's two tapes of what Number One and his misbegotten scum have been doing. Play 'em! And then *do something* about 'em! And listen, you lying, double-crossing, back-biting slime-lizard!" Tommie's prettily-made-up face was in shocking contrast to the venomous fury in Tommie's eyes as she leaned over the judge's massive desk until nose was a scant ten inches from nose. "If that atomic blast goes off tonight you and your whole Srizonified crew will wish to all your devils you'd never been born!"

Whirling around, Tommie strode out; nor did anyone attempt to stop her. No one knew what would happen if they did; and no one cared to find out.

Judge Trellis did not play the tapes. In panic fashion she called the District Attorney, who promptly made it a three-way with Number One. The three talked busily for minutes, then met in person, together with several lesser lights, in a heavily-guarded room. This conference, the subject matter of which was so obvious as to require no detailing here, went on for a long time.

So long, in fact, that Tommie and the newspaper man got back to Cloud's hotel room while Vesta was still taping a word-by-word report of the proceedings. Tommie was subdued, almost apologetic.

"I know you told me not to blow up, Captain Cloud, but they made me so mad I couldn't help it."

"In this case just as well you did; maybe better. You scared her into calling a meeting, and they've spilled every bean in the pot. We've got exactly what we wanted—enough to stop that gang right in its tracks. Now, as soon as the girls get the last of it, we'll let your editor in on it."

It was soon over, and Cloud, after a quick run-down of the situation and a play-back of parts of the tapes for the newshawk's benefit, concluded:—

"So, over the long pull, the issue isn't—can't be—in doubt. Public opinion will be aroused. There are honest judges, there are a lot of honest cops. At the next election this corrupt regime will be thrown out of office. However, that election is a year away, the present powers-that-be are all in the syndicate, and we must do something *today* to stop the destruction scheduled for tonight. Little Flower-and-so-on tells me that you're a crusading type, fighting a losing battle against this mob—that they've got you just about whipped—so I thought you would be interested in taking a slug at 'em by getting out an extra—strong enough to stir up enough public sentiment so they wouldn't dare go ahead. Would you like to do that?"

"Would I?" The newsman grinned wolfishly. "I'll get out the extra, yes; but I'll do a lot more than that. I'll print a hundred thousand dodgers and drop 'em from copters. I'll have blimps dragging streamers all over the sky. I'll buy time on every radio and tri-di station in town—have the juiciest bits of these tapes broadcast, every hour on the hour. Mister, I'll tear this town wide open before sundown tonight!"

He left, breathing fire and sulphurous smoke, and Cloud made motions to attract the Manarkan's attention.

"Nadine? These Tomingans take things big, don't they? All to the good, with one exception—will any repercussions—flarebacks—hit you? Those characters are tough, and will be desperate, and I wouldn't want to put you in line with a blaster."

"No . . . almost certainly not," Nadine replied, after a minute of thought. "They are looking for a telepath with a voice, which they won't find on Tominga. They know Manarkans well—many of us live here permanently—and I'm quite sure that none of the gang would suspect such an unheard-of thing as Vesta and I have been doing. They are not imaginative, and such a thing never happened before—not here, at least."

"No? Why not? What's strange about it?"

"The whole situation is new—unique. This is probably the first time in history that these exact circumstances—especially in regard to personnel—have come together. Consider, please, the ingredients: a real and bitter grievance, victims willing and anxious to take drastic action, a sympathetic telepath who is also an expert in shorthand, a master linguist, and, above all, a director or programmer—you—both able and willing to fit the parts together so that they work."

"Um . . . m . . . m. Never thought of it in that way. Could be, I guess. Well, all we can do now is wait and see what happens."

They waited, and saw. The crusading editor did everything he had promised. The extra hit the streets, its headlines screaming "CORRUPTION!" in the biggest type possible to use. The taped conversations, with names, amounts, times, and places, were printed in full. The accompanying editorial should have been written with sulphuric acid on asbestos paper. The leaflets, gaily littering the city, were even more vitriolic. Every hour, on the hour, speakers gave out what sound-trucks were blaring continuously—irrefutable proof that the city of Mingia was being run by a corrupt, rotten, vicious machine.

Mingia's citizens responded, but not quite as enthusiastically as the Blaster, from his limited acquaintance with the breed, had expected. There was some organizing, some demonstrating; but there was also quite a lot of "So what? If they don't, some other gang of politicians will."

Cloud, however, when he went to his rooms after supper, was well pleased with what he had seen. They *couldn't* blast 53, not after the events of the afternoon. The Chickladorians and Vesta and Nadine, when they came in, agreed with him. The situation was under control. They were tired, they said. It had been a long, hard day, and they were going to hit the sack. They left.

Cloud intended to stay awake until midnight, just to see what would happen, but he didn't. He was tired, too, and within a couple of minutes after he relaxed, alone, he was sound asleep in his chair.

Thus he did not hear the vicious thunder-clap of the atomic explosion at midnight; did not see the reflected brilliance of its glare. Nor did he hear the hurrying footsteps in the hotel's corridors. What woke him up was the concussion that jarred the whole neighborhood when a half-ton bomb demolished the building which had been Number One's headquarters.

Cloud jumped up, then, and ran out into the hall and along it to Vesta's room. He pounded. No answer. The door was unlocked. He opened it. Vesta was not there!

Nadine was gone, too. So were the Chickladorians.

He rushed up to the lobby, only to encounter again the difficulty that had stopped him short before. *He could not make himself understood!* He didn't know three words of Upper Plateau, and nobody he could find knew even one word of English, Spanish, Spaceal, or any other language at his command.

He took an elevator down to the street level and flagged a cruising cab. He handed the driver the largest Tomingan bill he had; then, pointing straight ahead and making furious pushing motions, he made it plain that he knew where he wanted to go, and wanted to get there in a hurry. The hacker, stimulated by more cash than he had seen for a week, drove wherever Cloud pointed; and broke—or at least bent—most of Mingia's speed-laws in his eagerness to oblige.

Cloud's destination, of course, was the spaceport; but when he got to the *Vortex Blaster I*, Jim wasn't there any more. None of his crew was aboard, either. The lifeboats were all in place, but the flitter was gone. So were both suits of armor—and the semi-portables—and the spare DeLameters—and both needles—even his space-hatchet!

He went up to the control room and glanced over the board. Everything was on zero except one meter, which was grazing the red. All four semis and both needles were running wide open—pulling every watt they could possibly draw!

Angry as he was, Cloud did not think of cutting the circuit. If he had thought of it he wouldn't have done it. He didn't know exactly what his officers were doing, of course, but he could do a shrewd job of guessing. If he had known what they were up to he wouldn't have permitted it, but it was too late to do anything about it now. With those terrific weapons in operation they *might* get back alive—without them, they certainly would not. *What* a land-office business those semis were doing!

They were.

Tommie and her brother, wearing Cloud's two suits of armor, were each *carrying* a semi-portable; wielding it, if not as easily as an Earthly gunner wields a sub-machine-gun, much more effectively. They were burning down a thick steel door. Well behind them, the third semi was bathing the whole front of the building in a blinding glare of radiance. In back, the fourth was doing the same to the rear wall. On the sides, the two needle-beams were darting from window to window, burning to a crisp any gangster gunner daring to show his head to aim.

For the Tomingans had not been nearly as optimistic as had Cloud, and they had made complete preparation for reprisal in case Number One should make good his threat. The Manarkan had been willing to cooperate. Thlaskin, ditto. Vesta had been quiveringly eager. Maluleme had gone along. They had not mutinied—they simply did not tell Cloud a thing about what they were going to do.

Number One had not been in his headquarters, of course, when that thousand-pound bomb let go. He thought himself safe—but he wasn't. Nadine the telepath knew exactly where he was and exactly what he was doing. Vesta the linguist poured the information along, via the flitter's broadcaster, to the receivers of hundreds of ground-cars and copters far below. Thlaskin the Master Pilot kept the flitter close enough to the fleeing Number One so that Nadine could read him—fully, she thought—but far enough away to avoid detection. Thus, wherever he went, Number One was pursued relentlessly, and his merciless pursuers closed in faster and faster.

Number One's flight, however, was not aimless. He knew that a snooper was on him, and had enough power of mind to shield a few highly important thoughts. He wasn't really THE Big Shot. He had called Yellow Castle, though, and they had told him that he could come in in one hour—the army would be ready. But did he have an hour, or not?

He did; just barely. The saps were snapping at his heels when he switched to a jet job and took off in a screaming straight line for the Castle.

Vesta wanted to ram him to drop a lifeboat on him, to wreck him in any way possible; but Thlaskin refused. Captain Cloud would be mad enough at what they'd done already—any such rough stuff as *that* would be altogether too damn much! And, since the rebels' jets were still on the ground, Number One had reached sanctuary unharmed.

Yellow Castle, however, was not as impregnable as the gangsters had supposed. They had armor, true, but it was not at all like Cloud's. They had weapons, true, but nothing even faintly resembling the frightful semi-portable projectors of the Galactic Patrol—nothing even remotely approaching the Patrol's beam-fed needle beams.

Thus the Tomingans, Tommie and Jim, stood in armor of proof scarcely an arm's length from Yellow Castle's heavy steel door and burned it down into a brooklet of molten metal. Then on in; blasting down everything that resisted and, finally, everything that moved. Nor did any gangster escape. Those who managed to avoid the armored pair were blasted by one of the other semis or speared by one of the needles.

Yellow Castle, already furiously ablaze, was left to burn. Jim, after giving instructions as to how his lieutenants were to dispose of such small fry as might be left alive in the city proper, helped his sister load the Blaster's weapons and armor into a ground-car. They drove out into the middle of a great open field. The flitter landed; Cloud's borrowed equipment was hauled aboard. Tommie and Jim followed it.

"If you were really smart, I think you'd flit right now," Vesta said to Tommie. "Captain Cloud isn't going to like this a little bit."

"I know it. I'm not smart. This was worth anything he cares to do about it. Besides, I want to thank him myself and tell him good-bye in person."

The flitter took off and returned to her mother-ship. Tommie and Thlaskin put her away, then the peculiarly assorted six went up to the control room and faced the quietly seething Tellurian.

Not boldly—only Tommie and Nadine were really at ease. Jim was defiant. Thlaskin was nervous and apprehensive; Maluleme was just plain scared. So was Vesta—her tail drooped to the floor; she seemed to have shrunk to four-fifths her normal size; her usual free-swinging, buoyant gait had changed almost to a slink.

Cloud stared at Nadine—chill, stern, aloof; an up-to-date Joan of Arc or a veritable destroying angel—nodded at her to synchronize with his mind. She did so, and her mind bore out everything implied by her attitude and expression. She was outraged to her innermost fiber by the conditions she had just helped to correct.

"You were the prime operator in this thing," he thought, flatly. "With your knowledge of law and your supposed respect for it, how could you take it into your own hands? Become part of a law-breaking mob?"

"It was necessary. Law in Mingia was shackled—completely inoperative. We freed it."

"By murder?"

"It was not murder. The lives of all who were killed were already forfeit. The corrupt judges, officials, and police officers will be dealt with by Mingian law, now again operative. Of all your crew, only Tommie could by any chance have been taken or recognized. If our coup had failed, she and Jim would have been shot without trial. Since we succeeded, however, Tommie was not recognized, being in your armor, and Jim is now Mingia's hero. He is also the new Commissioner of Police. Hence, aside from breaking local laws—which, as I have explained, do not count—we are guilty only of unauthorized use of Patrol equipment."

"Huh? How about interfering in planetary affairs, the worst in the book? And revealing Stage Ten stuff to a Stage Eight planet?"

"You are wrong on both counts," Nadine informed him. "We were on shore leave—that fact is in the log. We volunteered, purely as individuals, for one day of service in the Underground. This procedure, while of course forbidden to armed personnel of the Patrol, is perfectly legal to its civilian employees. A special ruling would have to be made to cover this particular incident, and no *ex post facto* penalties could be imposed."

"That's quibbling if I ever heard any, but you're probably right—legally—at that. But how do you wiggle out of the 'revealing' charge?"

"In the specific meaning of the word, as defined by the highest courts, nothing was revealed. Weapons and armor were seen, of course; but they have been seen on Tominga before. Nothing new was learned; hence there was no revealment. And as for Jim's leaving the ship against your orders, you had no right to issue such orders in the first place."

Still seething, but on a considerably lower level, Cloud pondered. It *wasn't* murder—nobody would or could call it that. "Extermination" would be more like it—or "justifiable germicide." She was probably right on the rest of it, too. Even though he was, by virtue of being the captain of the *Vortex Blaster I*, an officer of the Patrol—strictly speaking a commander, not a captain—there wasn't a thing in the world he could do about it.

Nadine had been keeping Vesta posted; and the latter, recovering miraculously her wonted spirit and with tail again aloft, was passing the good news along to the others.

"Don't get *too* cocky, sister!" Tommie advised her sharply. "Not yet, anyway."

"Huh?" Vesta's tail dropped to half-mast. "Why not?"

"You just said she pleaded guilty for all of us to unauthorized use of Patrol equipment. For what we really did that's certainly a featherweight plea—if I ever get into a real jam I certainly want her for my lawyer—but he can make it plenty tough for us if he wants to."

"I got a question to ask, boss," Thlaskin put in, before Cloud said anything. "You got a license to be sore as hell, no argument about that, but I ask you—are you sore mostly because we took the stuff or because we didn't let you in on it? We *couldn't* do that, boss, and you know why."

Cloud did know why. The pilot had put his finger right on the sore spot, and the Blaster was honest enough to admit it.

"That's it, I guess." He grinned wryly.

Tommie, who had been whispering to Vesta, asked: "You got back here while we were still sucking juice, didn't you?"

"Yes, and as Nadine will undoubtedly point out if I don't, that fact makes me an accomplice for not pulling the switches on you. So, already being an accessory during and after the fact, I may as well go the route. If any of us gets hauled up, we all do."

"No fear of that," Tommie assured him. "One thing Tomingans are good at is keeping their mouths shut. Maluleme and Vesta will spill everything they know, and brag about it, sooner or later," the Vegian did not relish translating this passage, but she did so, and accurately, nevertheless, "but that won't do any harm. It's *you* that's in the driver's seat. You could've nailed us all to the cross if you liked, and I for one didn't expect to get off easy. Thanks. I'll remember this. So will everybody else who knows. You're washing me out, of course?"

"Not unless you want to stay here on Tominga. You're a good engineer, and I can't picture this as happening again, can you?"

"Hardly. I like this better than stationary work. Thanks again, chief. My brother wants to thank you, too."

After the sincerely grateful and appreciative Tomingan had gone, Cloud said:

"Vesta and Maluleme—if Tommie was right about you two having to talk, make a note of this. Don't do it as long as you're members of this crew. If you do, I'll fire you the second I find out about it. Now everybody—as far as I'm concerned none of this ever happened. We came here to blow out vortices and that's all we did. We'll go back to the hotel, get a few hours sleep, and. . . ."

The long-range communicator, silent for weeks, came suddenly to life in English.

"Calling space-ship *Vortex Blaster One*, Commander Neal Cloud. Acknowledge, please. Calling space-ship *Vortex Blaster One*. . . ."

"Space-ship *Vortex Blaster One* acknowledging." The detector-coupled projector had swung into exact alignment. "Commander Cloud speaking."

"Space-ship YB216P9, of First Continent, Tominga, relaying message from Philip Strong of Tellus. Will you accept message?"

"Will accept message. Ready."

"Begin message. Report in person as soon as convenient. Answer expected. End message. Signed Philip Strong. Repeat, please. We will relay reply."

Cloud repeated. Then: "Reply. To Philip Strong, Vortex Control Laboratory, Tellus. Begin message. Remess. Will leave Manarka fourteenth Sol for Tellus. End of message. Signed Neal Cloud. Repeat, please."

That done, he turned to his crew. "Now we'll *have* to go to work!"

With Vesta to translate, two days sufficed to rid Tominga of her loose atomic vortices; and no one so much as suspected that the Patrol ship or any of its crew had had anything to do with the upheaval in Mingia.

The trip to Manarka, a two-day flit, was uneventful. So was the extinguishment of Manarka's vortices.

When the job was done, Nadine's mind and Cloud's met briefly. No direct reference was made to the unpleasantness on Tominga, nor to their somewhat variant ideas concerning it. Nadine wanted to stay on. She liked the job and she liked Cloud. He was somewhat impractical and visionary, a bit too idealistic in his outlook at times; but a strong and able man and a top-bracket commander, nevertheless.

And the Manarkan, in Cloud's mind, was not only a top-bracket medico, but also a *very* handy hand to have around.

On the fourteenth of Sol, then, the good ship *Vortex Blaster I* took off for Tellus, with Cloud wondering more than a little as to what was in the wind. He wasn't the type to be unduly perturbed about being called up on the carpet *per se*; but Phil didn't go in for mystery much—he explained things . . . He couldn't possibly know anything about that Mingian business so soon . . . and he was going to tell him all about it anyway. . . .

There was plenty of Laboratory business that shouldn't be relayed all over space, and this was undoubtedly some of it. Whatever it was, it'd have to keep until he got to Tellus, anyway, so he'd forget it until then.

But he didn't.

JANOWICK

BACK ON TELLUS, Cloud took a fast copter to the Vortex Control Laboratory, still wondering what it was all about.

"Go right in, Dr. Cloud," Strong's secretary told him, even before he stopped at her desk. "He's been gnawing his nails ever since you landed."

Cloud went in. The Lensman was not alone; a woman who had been seated beside the desk was now standing, studying him eagerly.

"Hi, Phil," the Blaster said. "Why all the haste, and why so cryptic? I've been wondering if you found where I hid the body—and which body it was."

"Hi, Storm. Nothing like that!" Strong laughed. "Doctor Janowick, Doctor Cloud—or rather, Joan, this is Storm. You know all about him that anybody does."

They shook hands, Cloud wondering all the more, and as he wondered he studied the woman, just as she was studying him.

Janowick? *Janowick!* He'd never heard of any female Janowick, so she couldn't be anybody much in nucleonics. Not exactly fat, but definitely on the plump side. About a hundred and thirty-five pounds, he guessed; and about five feet two. About his own age—no, a bit younger, thirty-some, probably. Brown hair, with a few white ones showing; wide-spaced gray eyes—slightly myopic, by the looks of her pixeyish, you-be-damned spectacles. Smart and keen—all in all, a prime number.

"This is why I pulled you in, Storm," the Lensman went on. "As you know, we've been combing all Civilization, trying to find somebody—anybody—with enough of the right qualities. She's it. Head of the Department of Semantics at the Galactic Institute for Advanced Study. Doctor of Semantics, Ph.D. in cybernetics, D.Sc. in symbolic logic, and so on for half the alphabet. She is also a very good self-made telepath, and the only self-made perceiver I ever heard of. She's very good at that, too—she can outrange a Rigellian. And besides all that, she's a Past Grand Master at chess."

"*Past* Grand Master? Oh, I see—I don't suppose it *would* be quite *de rigueur* for a top-bracket telepath to win all the Grand Masters' championships. Also, in view of the perception business, I imagine all this is more than somewhat hush-hush?"

"Very much so. A few Lensmen and now you are all who are in on it. It'll have to stay top secret until we find out whether an ordinary mind can be developed into one like yours, or whether her brain, like yours, is something out of the ordinary."

"Yes, it'd be very bad to have billions of people screaming for a treatment that can't be given."

"Check. But to get back to Joan. She's done some almost unbelievable work and we think she'll do. You know what we're after, of course."

"All I'm afraid of is that you haven't looked far enough," the woman said, shaking her head dubiously. "You know, though, what an appalling job it was bound to be. I'll do whatever I can."

She did not state the problem, either. They all knew, too well, what it was. As matters then stood, the life of one man—Neal Cloud—was all that stood between Civilization and loose atomic vortices; and it was starkly unthinkable that the Galactic Patrol would leave, for a second longer than was absolutely necessary, that situation unremedied.

"I see." Cloud broke the short silence. "Assuming that you haven't been sitting still doing nothing while I've been gone, brief me."

"Smart boy!" Strong applauded. "The first thing Joan did was to figure out that a nine-second prediction was out of the question for any computer, digital or analogue, possible to build with today's knowledge. Asked us what we could do to cut the time and how far we could cut it. With your little bombing flitter you have to have about nine seconds because you have to build up your speed to the required initial velocity of the bomb. That could be done away with, of course, by firing the bomb out of a Q-gun or something. . . ."

"But you'd have to have a special ship, much bigger than a flitter!" Cloud protested. "And special guns . . . and the special pointers for those guns—or for the ship, if the guns were fixed-aligned—would be veree unsimple, believe me!"

"How right you are, Buster! Other things, too, that you haven't thought of yet, such as automatic compensation for air conditions and so on. Very much worth while, however, and all done—we've had a lot of people on this project. But to cut this short, the necessary ship turned out to be a scout cruiser; the minimum safe distance—assuming worst possible conditions and heaviest possible screening—is thirty two hundred meters. . . ."

"Wait a minute!" Cloud broke in. "I've worked closer than that!"

"You got badly burned once, too, remember; and, according to the medics, you've been taking some damage since. You won't from here on. But to resume; since the muzzle velocity we can use is limited, by the danger of prematuring on impact, to nine hundred sixteen meters per second, the time from circuit-closing to detonation is something over three and a half seconds—how much over depending on atmospheric conditions. That's absolutely the best we can do, so we gave Joan a minimum of three point six seconds of prediction to shoot at with her mechanical brains. She isn't quite there yet, but she's far enough along so that she has to work with you, on actual blasting, the rest of the way."

"Why?" Cloud argued. "If she stayed on the high side there'd be no danger of scattering; only of intensification, which wouldn't do any harm out in the badlands."

"Too chancy." The Lensman swept Cloud's argument aside with a wave of his hand. "So the quicker you get moved into your new ship, the *Vortex Blaster Two*, and get your practicing done, the sooner the two of you can be on your way to Chickladoria. Flit!"

"Just as you say, chief. Here's my report in full. Some of the stuff will jar you to the teeth; particularly Fairchild and the fact that every blow-up that has ever happened has been deliberate, not accidental."

"Huh? *Deliberate!* Have you blown your stack completely, Storm?"

"Uh-uh; but the proof is too long and involved to go into offhand. You'll have to get it from the tapes and it'll take you at least a week to check my math. Besides, you told us to flit. So come on, Joan—clear ether, Phil!"

The Blaster and his new assistant left the laboratory; and in the copter, en route to the field, Cloud wondered momentarily what it was about the Lensman's explanation that had not rung quite true. The first sight of his new vessel's control room, however, banished the unformed thought from his mind before it had taken any real root.

*

The transformed scout cruiser *Vortex Blaster II* hung poised and motionless over the badlands. The optical systems and beam-antennae and receptors of dozens of instruments, many of which were only months old, were focused sharply upon the loose atomic vortex a scant two miles distant.

A few of these instruments reported only to a small and comparatively simple integrator which, after classifying and combining the incoming signals, put out as end-product the thin, black, violently-fluctuating line which was the sigma curve. Some others reported only to a massive mechanism, too heavy for any smaller vessel to carry, upon whose electronic complexities there is no need to dwell. Most of the information-gathering instruments, however, reported to both integrator and computer.

Not strapped down into a shock-absorber, but sitting easily in an ordinary pilot's bucket, quietly but supremely intent, "Storm" Cloud concentrated upon his sigma curve; practically oblivious to everything else. Without knowing how he did it he was solving continuously the simultaneous differential equations of the calculus of warped surfaces; extrapolating the sigma curve to an ever-moving instant of time three and nine-tenths seconds—the flight-time of the bombs plus his own reaction time—ahead of the frantic pen-point of the chart.

In his flitter, where he had required a nine- or ten-second prediction, he had always seized the first acceptable match that appeared. Now, however, needing only to extrapolate to less than four seconds, his technique was entirely different. He was now matching, from instant to instant, the predicted value of the curve against one or another of the twelve bombs lying in the firing chambers of heavy guns whose muzzles ringed the cruiser's needle-sharp nose.

And, as he had been doing ever since beginning to work with Joan and her mechanical brains, he was passing up match after match, waiting to see whether or not the current brain could deliver the goods. There had been a long succession of them—Alice, Betty, Candace, Deirdre, and so on. This one was Lulu, and it didn't look as though she was any good, either. He waited a while longer, however; then fined down his figures and got ready to blast.

The flight-time of the bomb, under present atmospheric conditions, would be three point five nine eight seconds, plus or minus point zero zero one. His reaction time was point zero eight nine. . . .

"Storm!" Joan broke in sharply, "Can you hold up a minute."

"Sure."

"That reaction time. I never spotted that before. Why didn't I?"

"I don't know. Never thought of it. Lumped it in, you know. Separated it now, I suppose, because I'm working so slowly, to give Lulu more of a chance. Why?"

"Because I've *got* to know all the odd things about you, and that isn't merely odd; it's superhuman."

"Oh, I wouldn't say that. Chickladorians average about point zero eight, and Vegians are still faster, about point zero seven. I checked up on that because they always test me three times when I renew my driver's license and always pull a wise crack about me having a lot of cat blood in me. S'pose I could have?"

"Um . . . m . . . m. Probably not . . . I don't know for sure, but I don't believe that a Tellurian-Vegian cross would be possible; and even if possible, such a hybrid couldn't very well be fertile. But the more I find out about you, my friend, the more convinced I become that you're either a mutant or else have some ancestors who were most decidedly *not* Tellurians. But excuse this interruption, please—go ahead."

Cloud went. The flight time of the bomb, under present atmospheric conditions, would be three point five nine two seconds, plus or minus point zero zero two. His reaction time was point zero eight nine. In three point six eight one seconds the activity of the vortex would match bomb number eleven to within one-tenth of one percent.

His left hand flashed out, number eleven firing stud snapped down. The vessel shuddered as though struck by a trip-hammer as the precisely-weighed charge of propellant heptadetonite went off. The bomb sped truly, in both space and time. There was a detonation that jarred the planet to its core, a flare of light many times brighter than the sun at noon, a shock-wave that wrought havoc for miles.

But the scout cruiser and her occupants were unharmed. Completely inertialess, invulnerable, the vessel rode effortlessly away.

Neal Cloud glanced into his plate; turned his head.

"Out," he said, seemingly unnecessarily. "How'd Lulu work, Joan?"

"Better, but not good enough. She was on track all the way, but three point three was the best she could get . . . and I was *sure* we had it licked this time . . . oh, *damn!*" The voice broke, ending almost in a wail.

"Steady, Joan!" Cloud was surprised at his companion's funk. "Only three tenths of a second to get yet, is all."

"*Only* three tenths—what d'you mean, *only?*" the woman snapped. "Don't you know that those three tenths of a second are just about in the same class as the three thousandths of a degree just above zero absolute?"

"Sure I do, but I know you, too. You're really blasting, little chum. Both Jane and Katy, you remember, were just as apt to be off track as on. You'll get it, Joan. As Vesta says, 'Tail high sister!' "

"Thanks, Storm. I needed that. You see, to keep her on track we had to put in more internal memory banks and that slowed her down . . . we'll have to dream up some way of getting the information out of those banks faster. . . ."

"Can you tinker her—what'll the next version be? Margie?—up en route, or do you want to keep this ship near Sol while you work on it? Phil tells me I've got to flit for Chickladoria—and chop-chop, like quick."

"Oh . . . Thlaskin and Maluleme have been crying in his beer, too, as well as yours?"

"I guess so, but that wasn't it. It's next on the list, an urgent—they've been screaming bloody murder for months. So, with or without a brain, I've got to blast off."

"Start blasting as soon as you like, just as we are," she decided instantly. "Much more important, at this stage, to work with you than to have Earth's resources close by. Besides, I think everything we're apt to need is already aboard—machine shop, electronics labs, materials, and experts."

"QX." He gave orders. Then:

"As for me, I'm going to hit the sack. I'm just about pooped."

"I don't wonder. That kind of stuff takes a lot of doing. 'Night, Storm."

JOAN THE TELEPATH

THE FOLLOWING MORNING, en route to the planet of the pink humanoids, Cloud was studying a scratch-chart of the First Galaxy. He had been working on the thing for weeks; had placed several hundred crossed circles, each representing a loose atomic vortex. He was scrawling weird-looking symbols and drawing freehand connecting lines when Joan came swishing into the "office."

"Good morning, Effendi of Esoterica!" she greeted him gaily. "How's the massive intellect? Firing on all forty barrels, I hope and trust?"

"Missing on all forty is more like it. Ideas are avoiding me in droves." He looked her over amiably, in what he hoped she would think was a casual way.

He'd found himself doing quite a lot of that, lately . . . but she was *such* a swell egg! Why hadn't she ever married? What a waste *that* was! Face a bit on the strong side for vapid calendar-girl prettiness, but. . . .

"But kind of attractive, at that, in her own gruesome way, eh?" she finished the thought for him.

"Huh?" Cloud gulped, and, for the first time in years, blushed scarlet; flushed to the tips of his ears.

"I'm sorry, Storm, believe me. I don't think I was supposed to tell you—in fact, I know very well I wasn't—but I've simply got to. It isn't fair not to; besides, I've thought all along that Lensman Strong was wrong—that we'd go faster and farther if you knew than if you didn't."

"Oh—*that's* what Phil was holding out on me back there? I thought there was something fishy, but couldn't spot it."

"I was sure you did. So was Phil. You told me what the Tomingans call telepaths—snoopers? I *like* that word; it's so beautifully appropriate. Well, I'm snooping all the time. Not only while we're working, as you thought, but *all* the time, especially when you're relaxed and . . . and off-guard, so to speak. I've been doing it ever since I first met you."

Cloud blushed again. "So you knew exactly what I was thinking just then? You gave me a remarkably poor play-back."

"The portrait was much too flattering. But we'll skip that. Part of my job is to make a telepath out of you, so that you can show me with your mind—it can't be done in words or symbols—what it is that makes a mathematical prodigy tick."

"How are you figuring on going about it?"

"I don't know—yet."

"Phil tried, and so did a couple of Gray Lensmen, and I wasn't holding back a thing . . . oh, he emphasized that you're a *self-made* telepath. A different angle of approach? How did you operate on yourself?"

"I don't know that, either; but I hope to find out through you. I read, and studied, and tried, and all of a sudden—bang!—there it was. But words are useless; I'm coming into your mind. Now watch me closely, concentrate: *really* concentrate, as hard as you possibly can. Ready? It goes like this . . . did you get it?"

"No. I couldn't follow the details—it seemed like an instantaneous transition. Didn't you have more to begin with than I've got?"

"I don't think so . . . pretty sure I didn't. I could receive—I think it's impossible for anyone to become a telepath who can't—but I couldn't send a lick. My psi rating was a flat zero zero zero. Now try it again. Take a good, solid grip on a thought and *throw* it at me."

"QX. I'll try." Cloud's forehead furrowed, his muscles tensed in effort. "Since you already know I've been wondering why you never married—why? Standards too high?"

"You might call it that." It was the woman's turn to blush, but her thought was clear and steady. Cloud was working with her better than he had ever worked with either Luda or Nadine. "Since the days of my teen-age crushes on tri-di idols I simply haven't been able to develop any interest in a man who didn't have as much of a brain as I have, and the only such I met were either already married or didn't have anything *except* a brain—which wouldn't do, either, of course."

"Of course not." Cloud felt something stirring inside him that he thought completely dead, and tried, in near-panic fashion, to kill it again. He changed the subject abruptly. "No luck—I'm not getting through to you at all. We'd better start all over, at the bottom. What's the first thing I've got to do to learn to be a snooper?"

"You must learn how to concentrate—intensively and in a very special way. You're very good at ordinary concentration—especially mathematical stuff—now; but this kind is different—so much so as to be a difference in kind, not merely of degree."

"Check. Point one, a new kind of concentration. Next?"

"No next. That's all. When you get so you can concentrate correctly—I'll coach you mind to mind on that, of course—we'll concentrate together, first on one gateway, then another. Something will click into place, and there you'll be."

"I hope. But suppose it doesn't? Can't it be worked out? You're on record as saying that the mind is simply a machine."

"No, it can't. The mind *is* a machine; just as much a machine as one of your automatic pilots or one of my computers. The troubles are that it is almost infinitely more complex and that we do not understand its basic principles—the fundamental laws upon which it operates. We may *never* understand them . . . the mind may very well be so tied in with the life-principle—or soul; call it whatever you please—as to be knowable only to God."

"I'm glad you said that, Joan. I'm not formally religious, I suppose, but I do believe in a First Cause."

"One must, who knows as much about the Macrocosmic All as you do. But it's too early in the morning for very much of that sort of thing. What are you doing to that chart besides doodling all over it?"

"Those aren't doodles, woman!" he protested. "They're equations. In shorthand."

"Equations, I apologize. Doctor Cloud, elucidate."

"Doctor Janowick, I can't. This is where you came in. I had just pursued an elusive wisp of thought into what turned out to be a cul de sac. I whammed my head against a solid concrete wall." His light mood vanished as he went on:

"In spite of what everybody has always believed, I've *proved* that loose atomic vortices are not accidental. They're deliberate, every one of them, and. . . ."

"Yes, I heard you tell Phil so," she interrupted. "I wanted to start screaming about your hypothesis then, and it's taken superhuman self-control to keep me from screaming about it ever since. That kind of math, though, of course is 'way over my head. . . . For a long time I expected Phil to call up and blast you to a cinder, but he didn't . . . you may be—*must* be, I suppose—right."

"I am right," Cloud said, quietly. "Unless all the mathematics I know is basically, fundamentally fallacious, they've *got* to be deliberate; they simply *can't* be accidental. On the other hand, except for a few we know about which don't change the general picture in the least, I can't see any more than you can how they can possibly be deliberate, either."

"Are you trying to set up a paradox?"

"No. It's already set up. I'm trying to knock it down." Cloud's thought died away; his mind became a mathematical wilderness of such complexity that the woman, able mathematician that she was and scan as she would, was lost in seconds.

He finally shrugged himself out of it. "Another blind alley," he reported, sourly.

"With sufficient knowledge, any possible so-called paradox can be resolved," Joan mused, her mind harking back to the, to her, starkly unbelievable hypothesis Cloud had stated so baldly. "But I simply *can't* believe it, Storm!"

"I can't, either, hardly. However, it's easier for me to believe that than that all our basics are false. So that makes it another part of our job to find out what, or who, or why."

"Ouch! With a job of that magnitude on your mind, I'll make myself scarce. When you come up for air sometime give me a call on the squawk-box and we'll study concentration. 'Bye." She turned, started for the door.

"Wait a minute, Joan—why not start the ground-work now?"

"That's a thought—why not? But get away from that big table." She placed two chairs and they sat down knee to knee; almost eye to eye. "Now, Storm, come in. *Really* come in, this time; the first time you didn't really even half try."

"I did so!" he protested. "I tried then and I'm trying now. Just *how* do I go about it?"

"I can't tell you that, Storm; *nobody* can tell you that." She was thinking now, not talking. "There are no words, no symbology, even in the provinces of thought. And I can't do it for you: you *must* do it yourself. But if you can't—and you really can't be expected to, so soon—I'll come into your mind and try to *show* you what I mean."

She did so. There was a moment of fitting; of snuggling . . . there was a warmly intimate contact, much warmer and much more intimate than anything telepathic that either had ever experienced before; but it was not what they were after. Joan tried a different approach.

"Well, if that won't work, let's try this. Just imagine, Storm, that every cell of my brain—no, let's keep it on the immaterial level; every individual ultimate element of my mind—is a lock, but you can see exactly what the key must be like. You must make every corresponding unit of your mind into the appropriate key. . . . No? We'll try again. Imagine that each element of my mind is half of a jigsaw puzzle—make yours fill out each picture. . . ."

"I can't. Don't you know, Joan, how many thousands of millions of. . . ."

"What of it?" she flared. "You do things fully as complex every time you blast a vortex. . . . Oh, that's it! Treat it as though it were a problem in n-dimensional differential equations, but don't let your subconscious do it alone—get right down there and work with it—do that and you'll have it all!" She seized his hands, squeezed them hard, and spoke aloud, the better to drive home the intensity of her convictions. "Buckle down, Storm, and dig . . . you can do it, I know you can do it. I *know* you can . . . dig in, big fellow . . . you don't have to pay *too* much attention to detail; get a chain started, like a zipper, and it'll finish itself . . . dig, Storm, DIG!"

Storm dug. His jaw-muscles tightened into lumps. Sweat beaded his face and trickled down his chest under his shirt. And suddenly something happened. Not very much of anything, but something. Something more than mere contact, but not a penetration—more like a fusion—a fusion which, however instead of spreading rapidly to completion, as Joan had said it would, existed for the merest perceptible instant of time in an almost infinitesimal area and then vanished as instantaneously as it had come. But there was no doubt whatever that he had read, for an instant, a tiny portion of Joan's mind; there was no chance whatever that she had sent him *that* thought—in fact, she had been thinking at herself, not at him. And as he perceived the tenor of that thought he let go all his mental holds; tried frantically to bury the stolen thought so deeply that Joan would never, *never* find out what it had been. . . .

No, not bury it, either. Flesh, rock, metal—any material substance was perfectly transparent to thought. What wasn't? A thought-screen. He didn't have one, of course, but he knew the formula, and if he thought about that formula hard enough it might create interference enough. The catch would be whether he could talk at the same time . . . he probably could, if the subject matter didn't require concentration.

Joan, of course, knew instantly when Cloud pulled his mind away from hers; and, not waiting to ask why in words, drove in a probe to find out. Much to her surprise, however, her beam of mental force was stopped cold; she could not touch Cloud's mind at all!

"A block!" she exclaimed unbelievingly. "A real dilly, too—as hard and tight as a D7M29Z screen! What did you do, anyway, Storm, and how? I didn't feel you get in!"

He did not reply immediately. He was too busy; for, besides holding the screen-thought, he was also analyzing and studying the thought he had stolen from Joan: separating it out and arranging it into meaningful English words. It was amazing, how many words could be contained in one flashing, fleeting burst of thought.

"Joanie, my not-so-bright old friend," she had been thinking, "you've simply got to cut out this silly damn foolishness and act your age. You *must not* fall in love with him; there'd be nothing in it for either of you. You are thirty-four years old and he has had his Jo."

"Storm!" she snapped. "Answer me! Or did. . . ." Her tone changed remarkably: ". . . did something . . . happen to you?"

"No, Joanie." He shook his head and wrenched his attention back to reality. "But first, is whatever I'm doing really a mind-block, and is it really holding?"

"Yes—to both—curse it! And 'Joanie', eh? You *did* get in. How did it go?"

"Not so good. Barely a touch. It didn't spread after we got it started. Just one flash and it went out."

"Hm . . . m . . . m. That's funny. . . . Not the way it worked with me at all. However, I don't see that it makes any difference whether you get it by drips and driblets or all at once, just so you get the full ability eventually. What was it you picked up the first time, Storm?"

"That's one thing you'll never know, if I have to hold this block forever."

"Oh." Joan blushed, vividly. "I know what it was, then, I think. But don't you see. . . ?"

"No, I don't see," Cloud interrupted. "All I see is that it's worse than being a Peeping Tom in a girls' dormitory. I don't like it. I don't like any part of it."

"You wouldn't, of course—at first. Nevertheless, Storm, you and I have *got* to work together, whether either of us likes what happens or not. So let's get at it. Bring it out and look at it—let's see if it's so bad, really. It was just that I was afraid maybe I was going to fall in love with you and get burned to a crisp around the edges, wasn't it?"

"That was part of it. You were wrong in two things, though. No matter how much I loved Jo—and I really did love her, you know. . . ."

"I know, Storm." Her voice was very gentle. "Everybody knows you did. Not only did—you still do."

"Yes. So much so that I thought I'd never be able to talk about her without going off the deep end. But I can, now. I'm beginning to think that perhaps Phil Strong was right. Perhaps a man can love twice in his life, in exactly the same way."

The woman caught her breath and started to say something, then changed her mind. The man went on:

"The second point in error is that a woman at age thirty-four is not necessarily a doddering wreck with one foot in the grave and the other on a banana peel."

"Oh . . . I'm *so* glad, Storm!" she breathed; then changed mood with an almost audible snap. "There! It's done and your guard is down. It wasn't too bad, was it?"

"Not a bit." Cloud was surprised at how easily the thing had been ironed out. "You're a prime number, Joanie—a slick, smooth operator. As smooth as five feet and two inches of tan velvet."

"Uh-uh. Not me, so much; it's just that we're a very nicely-matched pair. But I think we'd better lay off a while before trying it again, don't you?"

"Check. Let our minds—mine, anyway—get over the jitters and collywobbles."

"Mine, too, brother; and I've got a sort of feeling that what that mind of yours is going to develop into, little by little, is something slightly different from ordinary telepathy. But in the meantime, you'd better get back to work."

"I don't know whether I can work up much enthusiasm for work right now or not."

"Sure you can, if you try. What were you doing to that chart when I came in? What have you got there, anyway?"

"Come on over and I'll show you." They bent over the work-table, heads almost touching. "The pink area is the explored part of the First Galaxy. The marks represent all the loose vortices I know of. I've been applying all the criteria I can think of to give me some kind of a toe-hold, but up to the present moment I'm completely baffled."

"Have you tried chronology yet? Peeling 'em off in layers—by centuries, say?"

"Not exactly, although I did run a correlation against time. Mostly been studying 'em either singly or en masse up to now. Might be worth a fling, though. Why? Got a hunch?"

"No. And no particular reason; just groping for more detailed data. Before you can solve any problem, you know, you must know exactly what the problem is—must be able to state it clearly. You can't do that yet, can you?"

"You know I can't. I've got some colored pins here somewhere . . . here they are. Read me the dates and I'll stick colors accordingly."

They soon ran out of colors; then continued with numbered-head thumb-tacks.

The job finished, they stood back and examined the results.

"See anything, Joan?"

"I see *something*, but before I mention it, give me a quick briefing on what you know already."

Cloud thought for a minute. "Well, the distribution in space is not random, but there is no significant correlation with location, age, size, power, load-factor, or actual number of power plants. Nor with nature, condition, or age of the civilization of any planet. Nor with anything else I've been able to dream up.

"They aren't random in time, either; but there again there's no correlation with the age of the power-plant affected, the age-status of atomic power of any particular planet, or any other thing except one—there is an extremely high correlation—practically unity—with time itself."

"I thought so," Joan nodded. "That was what I noticed. The older, the fewer."

"Exactly. But with your new classification, Joan, I think I see something else." Cloud's mathematical-prodigy's mind pounced. "And *how!* Until very recently, Joan, the data will plot exactly on the ideal-growth-of-population curve."

"Oh, they breed, some way or other. Nice—that gives us a. . . ."

"You said that, woman, I didn't. I stated a fact; if you wish to extrapolate it, that's your privilege—but it's also your responsibility."

"Huh! Don't go pedantic on me. Haven't you got any guesses?"

"Except for this recent jump, which we can probably ascribe to Fairchild and explosives, nary a guess. I can't see any possible point of application."

"Neither can I. But if that's the only positive correlation you can find, and it's just about unity, it must mean *something*."

"Check. It's *got* to mean something. All we have to do is find out what . . . I think maybe I see something else." Bending over, he sighted across the chart from various angles. "Too many pins. Let's clear a belt through here." They did so. "Will you read 'em to me in order, beginning with the oldest?"

"At your service, sir. Sol."

Cloud stuck a pin in Sol.

"G a l i e n — S a l v a d o r — D u P o n t — E a s t m a n — M e r c a t o r — C e n t r a l i a — Tressilia—Chickladoria—Crevenia—DeSilva—Wynor—Aldebaran. . . ."

"Hold it! Don't want Aldebaran—can't use it. Take a look at this!" For this first time Cloud's voice showed excitement.

She looked, and saw a gently curving line of pins running three-quarters of the way across the chart. "Why—that's a smooth curve—looks as though it could be the arc of a circle—clear across all explored space!" she exclaimed.

Cloud's mind pounced again. "It is a circle—pretty close, that is, according to these rough figures. Will you read me the exact coordinates—spatial—from the book?"

She did so, and through Cloud's mind there raced the appropriate equations of solid analytic geometry.

"Even closer. Now let's apply a final refinement. From their proper motions we can put each star back to where it was at the vortex date. It'll take a little time, but it may be worth it."

It was. Cloud's mien was solemn as he announced his final figures. "Those twelve suns all lay on the surface of a sphere. Radius, 53,327 parsecs, with a probable error of one point three zero parsecs—which, since the average density of the stars along that line is about point zero four five per cubic parsec, makes it as perfect a spherical surface as it is physically possible for it to be. The center of that sphere is almost exactly on the ecliptic; its coordinates are: Theta, 225°–12 –31.2647″; distance, 107.2259."

"Good heavens! It's *that* exact? And *that* far outside the Rim? That spoils my original idea of radiation from a center. But all of the twelve oldest vortices are on that surface, and *none* of them are anywhere else!"

"So they are. Which gets us where, lady?"

"Nowhere that I can see, with a stupendous velocity."

"You and me both. Another thing, why that particular time-space relationship in the first twelve? I can accept Tellus being first, because we had atomics first, but that logic doesn't follow through. Instead, the time order goes from Sol through Galien and so on to Eastman—to the very edge of unexplored territory along that arc—then, jumping back to the other side of Sol, goes straight on to the edge of Civilization in the opposite direction. Can you play *that* on any one of your brains, from Alice to Margie?"

"I don't see how."

"I don't, either. That relationship certainly means something, too, but I'm damned if I can make any sense out of it. And what sense is there in a spherical surface that big? And why so ungodly accurate? Alphacent, there, is less than one parsec outside the surface, but it didn't have a blow-up for over seven hundred years. How come? Anybody or anything capable of traveling that far could certainly travel half a parsec farther if he wanted to. And look at the time involved—over a thousand years! Assuming some purpose, what could it be? Human operations, or any other kind I know anything about, simply are not geared up to that kind of scope, either in space or in time. None of it makes any kind of sense."

"So you consider it purely fortuitous that this surface is as truly spherical as the texture of the medium will permit?" she asked, loftily.

"No, I don't, and you know I don't—and don't misquote me, woman! It's too fantastically accurate to be accidental. And that ties right in with the previous paradox—that vortices can't possibly be either accidental or deliberate."

"From a semantic viewpoint, your phraseology is deplorable. The term 'paradox' is inadmissible—meaningless. We simply haven't enough data. I simply *can't* believe, Storm, that those horrible things were set off on purpose."

"Deplorable phraseology or not, I've got enough data to put the probability out beyond the nine-sigma point—the same probability as that an automatic screw-machine running six-thirty-two brass hex nuts would accidentally turn out a thirty-six-inch jet-ring made of pure titanite, diamond-ground, finished, and fitted. We're getting nowhere faster and faster—with an acceleration of about 12 G's instead of any simple velocity."

He fell silent; remained silent so long that the woman spoke. "Well . . . what do you think we'd better do next?"

"All I can think of is to find out what's out there at the center of that sphere . . . and then to see if we can find any other leads in this mess on the chart. I'll call Phil."

VESTA PRACTICES SPACEAL

THE CONNECTION was made and he brought Lensman Strong up to date, concluding: "So will you please get hold of Planetography with a crash priority on anything they know about that point?"

"I'll do that, Storm. I'll call you back."

Since Lensmen are potent beings, the call came soon.

"There's one sun there," Strong reported, "but it doesn't amount to much. A red dwarf—it may or may not be a single. Unexplored. Astronomical data only."

"How close did I come to it?"

"Allowing for proper motion, you speared it. Less than two hundredths of a parsec off. And there's nothing else within twelve parsecs—stars are mighty thin out beyond the Rim, you know."

"I know. That nails it, Phil. They don't know, of course, whether it has any planets or not?"

"No . . . I see what you mean . . . shall I get a special on it for you?"

"I wish you would. It'd be worth while, I think."

"So do I. I'll call Haynes and ask him to rush a ship out there to get us a fine-tooth on it."

"Thanks, Phil."

"And there was something else. . . . Oh yes, your friend Fairchild. Narcotics wants him, badly."

"I'm not surprised. Alive? That might take some doing."

"Or dead. No difference, as long as they have his head for positive identification," and at Cloud's surprised expression Strong went on: "They don't want him planting any more Trenconian broadleaf, is all, which he'll keep on doing as long as he's alive and loose."

"I see. Wish I'd known sooner; we probably could have caught him on Tominga."

"I doubt it. They've been checking back on him, and he's a very, *very* sharp operator. He makes long flits, fast . . . in peculiar directions. But if you stumble across him again, grab him or blast. . . ."

"Just a minute, chief. You mean to say the *Patrol* can't *find* him?"

"Just that. He's in with a big, strong mob; probably heads it. They've been looking for him ever since you found out that he wasn't killed on Deka."

"I'm . . . I'm speechless. But Graves . . . but Graves was dead, of course . . . didn't *anybody* know Fairchild's personal pattern?"

"That's exactly it; nobody that they could get hold of knows his *real* pattern at all. All we've got that we can depend on are his retinals. That shows the kind of operator he is. So if you get a chance, blast him, but leave at least one eye whole and bring it in, in deep-freeze. Nothing else at the moment, is there?"

"Not that I know of. Clear ether, Phil!"

"Clear ether, Storm!"

The plate went black and Cloud turned soberly to Joan.

"Well, that clears Fairchild up, but doesn't help with the real mystery. So, unless we can dig some more dope out of this stuff on the chart, we can't do much until we get that finetooth."

Joan left the room, and Cloud, after racking his brain for an hour, got up, shook himself, and went down the corridor to his "private" office—which had long since ceased to be private, as far as his friends were concerned—where he found Vesta and Thlaskin talking busily in spaceal. Or, rather, the Vegian was talking; the pilot was listening attentively.

". . . think I'm built, you ought to've seen *this* tomato," Vesta was narrating blithely. "What I mean, she's a *dish!*" She went into a wrigglesome rhythm which, starting at the neck, flowed smoothly down her splendidly-modeled body to the ankles. "Stacked? She's stacked like Gilroy's Tower, Buster—an honest-to-god DISH, believe me, and raring to go. We were on one of those long-week-end jaunts around the system—you know, one of those deals where things are pretty apt to get just a hair off the green at times. . . ."

"But hey!" Thlaskin protested. "You said yourself a while back you wasn't old enough for that kind of monkey-business!"

"Oh, I wasn't," Vesta agreed, candidly enough. "I still ain't. I just went along for the ride."

1129

"And your folks *let* you?" Thlaskin was shocked.

"Natch." Vesta was surprised. "Why not? If a tomato don't learn the facts of life while she's young how's she going to decide what's good for her when she grows up?"

"With or without a license, I got to butt into this," Cloud announced, also in spaceal; seating himself on a couch and crossing his legs. He, too, was shocked; but he was also intensely curious. "Did you decide, Vesta?"

Before the girl could answer, however, Joan Janowick came strolling in.

"Is this a private brawl, or can anybody get in on it?" she asked, gaily.

"I invited myself in, so I'll invite you, too. Come in and sit down." He made room for her beside him and went on in English, speaking for her ear alone: "Just as well you don't know spaceal. This story Vesta is telling would curl your hair."

"Wake up, Junior." Joan did not speak, but poured the thought directly into his mind. "D'you think that cat-girl—that *kitten*—can block *me* out of her mind?"

"Oick! What a whiff! 'Scuse, please; my brain was out to lunch. But you'll get an earful, sister Janowick."

"It'll be interesting in a way you haven't thought of, too," Joan went on. "Vegians are essentially feline, you know, and cats as a race are both fastidious and promiscuous. Thus, conflict. Is that what this is about?"

"Could be—I haven't tried to read her." Then, aloud:

"Go ahead, Vesta. Did the experience help you decide?"

"Oh, yes. I'm too finicky to be a very good mixer. There's just too damn many people I simply can't stand the smell of."

"There's that *smell* thing again," Thlaskin said. "You've harped on it before. You mean to say you people's noses are *that* sensitive?"

"Absolutely. No two people smell alike, you know. Some smell nice and some just plain stink. F'rinstance, the boss here smells just wonderful—I could hug him all day and love it. Doctor Janowick, too, she smells almost like the skipper. You're nice, too, Thlaskin, and so is Maluleme, and Nadine. And Tommie ain't bad; but a lot of the others are just too srizonified much for my stomach."

"I see," Cloud said. "You *do* give some people a lot of room around here."

"Yeah, and that's what got this chick I was telling Thlaskin here about in such a jam. She's been bending her elbow pretty free, and taking a jab or so of this and that between drinks. But she ain't sozzled, y'understand, not by many a far piece; just lit up like Nyok spaceport. She's maybe been a bit on the friendly side with a few of her friends, so this big bruiser—not a Vegian; no tail, even; an Aldebaranian or some-such-like and a Class A-Triple-Prime stinker—gets interested in a big way. Well, he smells just like a Tellurian skunk, so she brushes him off, kind of private-like, a few times, but it don't take, so she finally has to give him the old heave-ho right out in front of everybody.

" 'You slimy stinker, I've told you a dozen times it's no dice—you stink!' she says, loud, clear, and plain. 'This ship ain't big enough to let me get far enough away from you to hold my breakfast down,' she says, and this burns the ape plenty.

" 'Lookit here, babe,' he says, coming to a boil, 'Bend an ear while I tell *you* something. No klevous Vegian chippie is going to play high and mighty with me, see? I'm fed up to the gozzle. So come down off your high horse right now, or I'll. . . .'

" 'You'll what?' she snarls, and puts a hand behind her back. She's seeing red now, and fit to be tied. 'Make just one pass at me, you kedonolating slime-lizard,' she says, 'and I'll bust your pfztikated skull wide open!'

"He goes for her then, but, being a Vegian, her footwork's a lot better than his. She ducks, sidesteps, pulls her sap, and lets him have it, but good, right behind the ear. It takes the ship's croaker an hour to bring him to, and the skipper's so scared he blasts right back to Vegia and the croaker calls the hospital and tells 'em to have a meat-wagon standing by when we sit down."

"A very interesting and touching tale, Vesta," Cloud said then, in English, "but pretty rough language for a perfect lady, don't you think?"

"How the hell else. . . ." Vesta started to reply in spaceal, then switched effortlessly to English: "How else can a lady, however ladylike she may be, talk in a language which, except for its highly technical aspects, is basically and completely profane, obscene, vulgar, lewd, coarse, and foul? Not that that bothers me, of course. . . ."

Nor did it, as Cloud well knew. When a Master of Languages studied a language he took it as a whole, no matter what that whole might be. Every nuance, every idiom, every possibility was mastered; and he used the language *as it was ordinarily used*, without prejudice or favor or motional bias.

". . . but it's so pitifully *inadequate*—there's so much that's completely missing! Thlaskin objected before, remember, that there wasn't any word in spaceal he could use—*would* use, I mean—to describe Maluleme as his wife. And my brother—Zambkptkn—I've mentioned him?"

"Once or twice," Cloud said, dryly. This was the understatement of the trip.

"He's a police officer. Not exactly like one of your Commissioners of Police, or Detective Inspector, but something like both. And in spaceal I can call him only one of four things, the English equivalents of which are 'cop,' 'lawman,' 'flatfoot,' and 'bull.' *What* a language! But I started to tell his story in spaceal and I'm going to finish it in spaceal. It'll be fun, in a way, to see how close I can come to saying what I want to say."

Then, switching back to the lingua franca of deep space;

"So that's how come my brother got into the act. The hospital called the cops, of course, so he was there with the meat-wagon and climbed aboard. He was all set to pinch the jane and throw her in the can, but when he got the whole story, and especially when she says she's changed her mind about circulating around so much—it ain't worth it, she says, she'd rather be an out-and-out hermit than have to have even one more fight with anybody who smelled like that—of course he let her go."

"Let her *go*!" Cloud exclaimed. "How *could* he?"

"Why, sure, boss." Vesta, wide-eyed, gazed innocently at her captain. "The ape didn't *die*, you know, and she wasn't going to do it again, and he wasn't a Vegian, so didn't have any relatives or friends to go to the mat for him, and besides, anybody with one-tenth of one percent of a brain would know better than to keep on making passes at a frail after she warned him how bad he stunk. What *else* could he do, chief?"

"What else, indeed?" Cloud said, in English. "I live; and—occasionally—I learn. Come on, Joan, let's go and devote the imponderable force of our massed intellects to the multifarious problems of loose atomic vortices."

On the way, Joan asked: "Our little Vesta surprised you, Storm?"

"Didn't she you? She had me gasping like a fish."

"Not so much. I know them pretty well and I used to breed cats. Scent: hearing—they can hear forty thousand cycles: the fact that they mature both mentally and physically long before they do sexually: some of their utterly barbarous customs: it's quite a shock to learn how—'queer,' shall I say?—some of the Vegian mores are to us of other worlds."

" 'Queer' is certainly the word—as queer as a nine-credit bill. But confound it, Joan, I *like* 'em!"

"So do I, Storm," she replied quietly. "They *aren't* human, you know, and by Galactic standards they qualify. And now we'll go and whack those vortices right on their center of impact."

"We'll do that, chum," he said. Then, in perfect silence he went on in thought: "Chum? Sweetheart, I meant. . . . My God, *what* a sweetheart you'd. . . ."

"Storm!" Joan half-shrieked, eyes wide in astonishment. "You're *sending!*"

"I'm not either!" he declared, blushing furiously. "I can't—you're *snooping!*"

"I'm not snooping—I haven't snooped a lick since I started talking. You *got* it back there, Storm!" She seized both his hands and squeezed. "You *did* it, and neither of us realized it 'til just this minute!"

GAMES WITHIN GAMES

THE METHODS of operation of the *Vortex Blaster II* had long since been worked out in detail. Approaching any planet Captain Ross, through channels, would ask permission of the various governments to fly in atmosphere, permission to use high explosive, permission to land and be serviced, and permission—after standard precautions—to grant planetary leave to his ship's personnel. All this asking was not, of course, strictly necessary in his case, since every world having even one loose atomic vortex had been demanding long and insistently that Neal Cloud visit it next, but it was strictly according to protocol.

Astrogators had long since plotted the course through planetary atmosphere; not by the demands of the governments concerned and not by any ascending or descending order of violence of the vortices to be extinguished, but by the simple criterion of minimum flight-time ending at the pre-selected point of entry to the planet.

Thus neither Joan nor Cloud had anything much to do with planetary affairs until the chief pilot notified Joan that he was relinquishing control to her—which never happened until the vessel lay motionless with respect to the planet's surface and with the tip of her nose three two zero zero point zero meters distant from the center of activity of the vortex.

Approaching Chickladoria, the routine was followed precisely up to the point where Joan's mechanical brain took over. This time, however, the brain was not working, since Joan was in the throes of rebuilding "Lulu" into "Margie." On Chickladoria, then, the chief pilot did the piloting and "Storm" Cloud did the blasting, and everything ran like clockwork. The ship landed at Malthester spaceport and everyone who could possibly be spared disembarked.

Ready to leave the ship, Cloud went to the computer room to make one last try. There, seated at desks, Joan and her four top experts were each completely surrounded by welters of reference books, pamphlets, wadded-up scratch-paper, tapes, and punched cards.

"Hi, Joan—Hi, fellows and gals—why don't you break down and come on out and get some fresh air?"

"Sorry, Storm, but the answer is still 'no'. We'll need all this week, and probably more. . . ." Joan looked up at him and broke off. Her eyes widened and she whistled expressively. "Myohmy, ain't he the *handsomest* thing, though? I wish I *could* go along, Storm, if only to see you lay 'em out in rows!"

For, since Chickladoria was a very warm planet—fully as hot as Tominga had been—Cloud was dressed even more lightly than he had been there; in sandals, breech-clout, and DeLameter harness, the shoulder-strap of the last-named bearing the three silver bars of a commander of the Galactic Patrol. He was not muscled like a gladiator, but his bearing was springily erect, his belly hard and flat, his shoulders were wide, his hips were narrow, and his skin was tanned to a smooth and even richness of brown.

"Wellwell! Not bad, Storm; not bad at all." One of the men got up and looked him over carefully. "If I looked like that, Joan, I'd play hookey for a couple of days myself. But I wouldn't dare to—in that kind of a get-up I'd look like something that had crawled out from under a rock and I'd get sunburned from here to there."

"That's your own fault, Joe," a tall, lissom, brunette lieutenant chipped in. "You *could* have the radiants on while you do your daily dozens, you know. Me, I'm mighty glad that *some* of the men, and not only us women, like to look nice."

"Wait a minute, Helen!" Cloud protested, blushing. "That's not it, and you know it. These fellows don't *have* to mix socially with people who run around naked, and I do."

"And how you hate it." The other man offered mock sympathy, with a wide and cheerful grin. "*How* you suffer—I don't think. But that holster-harness. It looks regulation enough, but isn't there somehing a little different about it?"

"Yes. Two things." Cloud grinned back. "Left-handed, and the holster's anchored so it can't flop around. Don't know as I ever told you, but ever since that alleged pirate burned my arm off I've been practising the gun-slick's draw."

"Did you get it?" Joan asked impishly. "How good are you?"

"Not bad—in fact, I'm getting plenty good," Cloud admitted. "Come on up to the range sometime with a stop-watch and I'll show you."

"I'll do that. Right now—shall we?"

"Uh-uh. Can't. I'm due at the High Mayor's Reception in twenty minutes, and besides, I want to breathe some air that hasn't been rehabilitated, rejuvenated, recirculated, reprocessed, repurified, and rebreathed until it's all worn out. Happy landings, gang—I'll be thinking of you while I'm absorbing all that nice new oxygen and stuff."

"Particularly the stuff—and especially the *liquid* stuff!" Joe called after him just before he shut the door on his way out to join Thlaskin and Maluleme.

Going through customs was of course the merest formality, and an aircab whisked them into the city proper. Cloud really did enjoy himself as he strode along the walkway from the cabpark toward the Mayor's . . . well, if not exactly a palace, it was close enough so as to make no difference. And he did attract plenty of attention. Not because of his dress or his build—most of the men on the street wore less than he did and many of them were just as trim and as fit—but because of the nature and variety of his bodily colors, which were literally astounding to these people, not one in twenty of whom had ever before seen a Tellurian in person.

For Chickladorians are pink; pink all over. Teeth, hair, skin, and nails; all pink. Not the pink of red blood showing through translucency, but that of opaque pigment. Most of their eyes, even—queerly triangular eyes with three lids instead of two—are of that same brick-reddish pink; although a few of the women have eyes of a dark and dusky green.

This visitor's skin, however, was of a color so monstrous it simply had to be seen to be believed. In fact, it wasn't the same color in any two places—it VARIED! His teeth were white; a horrible, dead-bone color. His lips, hair, and eyes—funny, round, flat-opening things—were of still other sheerly unbelievable colors—there wasn't a *bit* of natural, healthy pink about him anywhere!

Thus the crowds of Chickladorians studied him much more intensively than he studied them; and Maluleme, strutting along at his side, basked visibly in the limelight. And thus, except for the two Chickladorians at his side and except for the unobtrusive but efficient secret-service men who kept the crowding throng in hand, Cloud could very well have been mobbed.

The walk was very short, and at its end:

"How long we got to stay, boss?" Thlaskin asked, in spaceal. "As soon as we can get away we want to join our folks and grab a jet for home."

"As far as I'm concerned you don't need to stay at all, or even come. Why?"

"Just checking, is all. His Nibs sent us a special bid, so we got to at least show up. But he don't know us from nothing, so after we tell him hello and dance a couple of rounds and slurp a couple of slugs we can scram and nobody'll know it unless you spill."

"No spill," Cloud assured him. "You dance with Maluleme first. I'll take the second—that'll drive it in that she's here. After that, flit as soon as you like. For the record, you'll be here until the last gilot is picked clean."

"Thanks, boss," and the three, entering the extravagantly-decorated Grand Ballroom, were escorted ceremoniously up to the Presence and the Notables and their surrounding V. I. P.'s.

They were welcomed effusively, Cloud being informed through several different interpreters that he was the third-most-important human being who had ever lived. He made—through two interpreters, each checking the other's accuracy—his usual deprecatory speech concerning the extinguishment of loose atomic vortices. He led the Grand March with the president's wife, a lady whose name he did not quite catch and who, except for a pound or so of diamonds, rubies, emeralds, and other baubles, was just as bare as Maluleme was. So was the equally heavily bejeweled mayor's wife, with whom he had the first dance. She was neither young or slender, nor was she sexy. Then, as agreed, he danced with Maluleme, who was—but definitely!—all three.

However, as he circled the floor in time with the really excellent music, he thought, not of the attractive package of femininity in his arms—who was one of his crew and Thlaskin's wife—but of Joan. She'd been training down, he'd noticed, and wearing more makeup, since those other girls had come aboard. She was getting to be a regular seven-sector callout—he'd *like* to dance with Joan this way!

There were other dances; some with girls like Maluleme, some with women like Madam Mayor, most with in-betweens. There was food, which he enjoyed thoroughly. There were drinks; which, except for ceremonial beakers of fayalin with the president and the mayor, he did not touch. And, finally, there was the very comfortable bed in his special suite at the hotel. Instead of sleep, however, there came a thing he expected least of any—a sharp, carefully-narrowed Lensed thought.

"This is Tivor Nordquist of Tellus, Commander Cloud, on my Lens," the thought flowed smoothly in. "I have waited until now so as not to startle you, not to make you show any sign of anything unusual going on. There must be no suspicion whatever that you even know there's a Lensman on the planet."

"I can take care of my part of that. One thing, though; I've got exactly one week to work with you. One week from today any possible excuse for me staying on Chickladoria goes p-f-f-t."

"I know. One day should button it up, two at most. Here's the print. I'm a narcotics man, really but. . . ."

"Oh—Fairchild, eh?"

"Yes. Ellington told me you're quick on the uptake. Well, all leads to him via any drug channels fizzled out flat. So, since all these zwilnik mobs handle all kinds of corruption—racketeering, gambling, vice, and so on, as well as drugs—we decided to take the next-best line, which turned out to be gambling. After a lot of slow digging we found out that Fairchild's gang controls at least four planets; Tominga, Vegia, Chickladoria, and Palmer III."

"What? Why, those planets cover. . . ."

"Check. That's what made the digging so tough, and that's why they did it that way. And you're scheduled for Vegia next, is why I'm meeting you here. But to get back to the story, we haven't got dope enough to find Fairchild himself except by pure luck. So we decided to make Fairchild's mob tell us where he is."

"That'll be a slick trick if we can do it."

"Here's how. *Somebody* on this planet knows how to call Fairchild in emergencies, so we'll create an emergency and he'll do it."

"My mind is open, but I'm a bit skeptical. What kind of an emergency have you got in mind?"

"Some of the details you'll have to ad lib as you go along, but it'll be, basically, bold-faced robbery without a blaster and with them jittery as glaidos because they can't figure it. I was going to try to do it myself, but I can't work without my Lens and I can't come near the hot spots without their spy-rays catching the Lens and blowing the whole show. Doctor Janowick told Phil Strong that she could, without using her sense of perception and after only a short practise run, beat any crooked card game any gambler could dream up—something about random and nonrandom numbers. Can she?"

"Um-m . . . never thought of it . . . *random* numbers . . . Oh, I see. Yes, she can. Especially the most-played one, that over-and-under-seven thing. And with a little telepathy thrown in, I can do the same with any crooked game they've got except a magnetically-controlled wheel; and I could do a fair job on that."

"Better and better. You and Miss Janowick, then; and be sure and bring Vesta the Vegian along."

"Vesta? Um . . . Maybe, at that. Adolescent Vegians not only can be, but are, interested in everything that goes on, everywhere. They're born gamblers, and she's already got a reputation for throwing money around regardless—and she's rich enough to afford it. And in a winning streak she'll stir up so much excitement that nobody will pay any attention to anybody else. However, things being what they are, I'll have to be mighty careful about letting her go on a gambling spree."

"Not too much so. Just hint that you won't fire her if she takes a fling or two at the tables and she'll be so happy about it and love you so much that she won't even think of wondering why."

And so it proved. After a long discussion of details with the Lensman, Cloud went to sleep. The following afternoon he went back to the ship and sought out Vesta, whom he found slinking dejectedly about with her tail almost dragging on the floor. Scarcely had he begun his suggestion, however, when:

"*Really*, chief?" Vesta's tail snapped aloft, her pointed ears quivered with eagerness. She hugged him ecstatically, burying her face in the curve of his neck and inhaling deeply. "You zmell zo wonderful, chief—but a wonderful man like you would *have* to smell zo, wouldn't he? I thought you'd smack me bow-legged if I even hinted at wanting to lay a ten-cento chip on the line. But I *know* I can beat the games they've got on *this* planet . . . and besides, I've been gone half a year and haven't spent a hundred credits and I've learned nine languages including your cursed English. . . ."

She took out her book of Travelers' Cheques and stared at it thoughtfully. "Maybe, though, just to be on the safe side, I'd better tear one of these out and hide it in my room. It'd be *awful* to have to call my mother for jet fare home from the 'port. She and dad both'd yowl to high heaven—they'd claw me ragged."

"Huh? But listen!" Cloud was puzzled. "If you shoot such a terrific wad as that, what possible difference would it make whether you had plane fare for a few hundred miles left or not?"

"Oh, lots," she assured him. "They don't expect me to have much of any of my allowance left when I get home, and I never intended to, anyway. But *anybody* with half a brain is expected to be able to get home from a party—any kind of a party—without crying for help, and without walking, either; so I'll go hide one of these slips."

"If *that's* all that's bothering you, no matter," Cloud said quickly. "You've got another pay day coming before we get to Vegia, you know."

"Oh, I never thought of that—I've never been on a payroll before, you know, and can't get used to being paid for doing nothing. But can we go now, Captain Nealcloud, please? I can't wait!"

"If Joan's ready we can. We'll go see."

But Joan was not ready. "Did you actually think she would be?" Helen asked. "Don't you know that the less a woman puts on the longer it takes her to do it?"

"Nope—I s'posed Doctor Joan Janowick would be above such frippery."

"You'd be surprised. But say, how'd you talk her into this vacation? Your manly charm, no doubt."

"Could be, but I doubt it. All she wanted was half an excuse and the promise I wouldn't get sore if we have to kill a couple of days in space before starting shooting on Vegia . . . Hot Dog!—just *look* who's here!"

Joan came in, pausing in embarrassment, at the burst of applause and whistles that greeted her. She was richly, deeply tanned; taut, trim, and dainty—she had trained down to a hundred and fifteen pounds—her bra was a triumph of the couturier's art. She, too, was armed; her DeLameter harness sported the two-and-a-half silver bars of a lieutenant commander.

"Ouch—I'm bedazzled!" Cloud covered his eyes ostentatiously, then, gradually and equally ostentatiously recovering his sight: "Very nice, Joanie—you're a ver*ee* slick chick. With a dusting of powdered sugar and a dab of cream you'd make a right tasty snack. Just one thing—a bit overdressed, don't you think?"

"*Overdressed!*" she exclaimed. "Listen, you—I've never worn a bathing suit *half* as skimpy as this in my whole life, and if you think I'm going to wear any *less* than this you're completely out of your mind!"

"Oh, it isn't *me!*" Cloud protested. "Patrol Regs are strict that way—when in Rome you've got to be a Roman candle, you know."

"I know, but I'm Roman candle enough right now—in fact, I feel like a flaming skyrocket. Why, this thing I've got on is scarcely more than a G-string!"

"QX—we'll let it pass—this time. . . ."

"Hey, you know something?" Joe interrupted him before Joan did. "Vegia is a couple of degrees warmer than this, and they don't overdo the matter of clothes there, either. I *am* going to start basking under the radiants. If I get myself cooked to a nice, golden brown, Helen—like a slice of medium-done toast—will you do Vegiaton with me?"

"It's a date, brother!"

As Joe and Helen shook hands to seal the agreement, the two Patrol officers and Vesta strode out.

They took a copter to the Club Elysian, the plushiest and one of the biggest places on the planet. The resplendently decorated—in an undressed way, of course—doorman glanced at the DeLameters, but, knowing the side-arm to be the one indispensable item of the Patrol uniform wherever found, he greeted them cordially in impeccable Galactic Spanish and passed them along.

"The second floor, I presume, sir and mesdames?" The host, a very good rule-of-thumb psychologist, classified these visitors instantly and suggested the region where both class and stakes were high. Also, and as promptly, he decided to escort them personally. Two Patrol officers and a Vegian—especially the Vegian—rated special attention.

The second floor was really a place. The pile of the rug was over half an inch deep. The lighting was neither too garish nor too dim. The tastefully-placed paintings and tapestries adorning the walls were neither too large nor too small, each for its place; and each was a masterpiece.

"May we use Patrol currency, or would you rather we took chips?" Cloud asked.

"Either one, sir; just as you wish."

"We Tellurians are all set, then, but Miss Vesta here would like to cash a few Travelers' Cheques."

"Certainly, Miss Vesta. I'll be delighted to take care of it for you. How do you wish the money, please?"

"I'll want a little small stuff to get the feel of the house . . . say a thousand in tens and twenties. The rest of it in fifties and hundreds, please—mostly hundreds."

Vesta peeled off and thumb-printed ten two-thousand credit cheques and the host, bowing gracefully, hurried away.

"One thing, Vesta," Cloud cautioned. "Don't throw it away too fast. Save some for next time."

"Oh, I always do, chief. This'll last me the week, easily. I run wild only when I'm in a winning streak."

The host came up with her money; and as Vesta made a beeline for the nearest wheel:

"What do you like, Joan?" Cloud asked. "A wheel?"

"I don't think so; not at first, anyway. I've had better luck with the under-and-overs. They're over there, aren't they, sir?"

"Yes, madame. But is there anything I can do first? Refreshments of any kind—an appetizer, perhaps?"

"Not at the moment, thanks."

"If you wish anything, at any time, just send a boy. I'll look you up from time to time, to be sure you lack nothing. Thank you very much, sir and madame."

The host bowed himself away and the two officers strolled over to the bank of "under-and-over" tables, which were all filled. They stood at ease for a few minutes; chatting idly, enjoying their cigarettes, gazing with interest and appreciation around the huge, but wonderfully beautiful room. There was no indication whatever that either of the two Patrolmen was the least bit interested in the fall of the cards, or that two of the keenest mathematical minds in space knew exactly, before the man ahead of them got tired of losing fifty-credit chips, the denomination and the location of every card remaining in the rack.

Joan could, of course, have read either the cards, or the dealer's mind, or both; but she was not doing either—yet. This was a game—on the side, so to speak—between her and

Storm. Nor was it at all unequal, for Cloud's uncanny ability to solve complex mathematical problems was of very little assistance here. This was a matter of more-or-less simple sequences; of series; of arrangements; and her years of cybernetic training more than made up for his advantage in speed.

"Your pleasure, madame or sir? Or are you together?"

"We're together, thanks. We'll take the next, for an M." Cloud placed a one-thousand-credit note in the velvet-lined box.

Two thin stacks of cards lay on the table at the dealer's right; one pile face up, the other, face down. He took the top card from the rack, turned it over, and added it to the face-up stack. "The ten of clubs," he droned, sliding a one-thousand-credit bill across the table to Cloud. "What is your pleasure, sir and madame?"

"Let it ride. Two M's in the box," Cloud said, tossing the new bill on top of its mate. "Throw one."

"Discard one." The dealer removed the next card and, holding it so that neither he nor the players could see its face, added it to the face-down pile. "What is your pleasure, sir and madame?"

"Throw one."

"Discard one."

"We'll take this one," and there were four thousand credits in the box.

Throw one take one, and there were eight thousand.

The eight became sixteen; then thirty-two; and the dealer lost his urbanity completely. He looked just plain ugly.

"Maybe that's enough for now," Joan suggested. "After all, we don't want to take *all* the man's money."

"Tightwad's trick, huh? Quit while yer ahead?" the dealer sneered. "Why'n'cha let 'er ride just once more?"

"If you insist, we will," Cloud said, "but I'm warning you it'll cost you thirty two more M's."

"That's what *you* think, Buster—I think different. Call your play!"

"We'll take it!" Cloud snapped. "But listen, you clever-fingered jerk—I know just as well as you do that the top card is the king of clubs, and the one below it is the trey of diamonds. So, if you want to stay healthy, move slowly and be damned sure to lift just one card, not two, and take it off the top and not the bottom!"

Glaring in baffled fury, the dealer turned up the king of clubs and paid his loss.

At the next table the results were pretty much the same, and at the third. At the fourth table, however, instead of pyramiding, they played only single M-bills. They lost—won—lost—lost—won—lost—won—lost. In twenty plays they were only two thousand credits ahead.

"I think I've got it, Joan," Cloud said then. "Coming up—eight, six, jack, five, deuce?"

"Uh-uh. I don't think so. Eight, six, jack, three, one, I think. The trey of spades and the ace of hearts. A two-and-one shift with each full cycle."

"Um . . . m. Could be . . . but do you think the guy's that smart?"

"I'm pretty sure of it, Storm. He's the best dealer they have. He's been dealing a long time. He knows cards."

"Well, if you're done passing out compliments, how about calling a play?" the dealer suggested.

"QX. We'll take the eight for one M . . . and it *is* the eight, you notice . . . let it ride . . . throw the six—without looking, of course . . . we'll take the jack for two M's. . . ."

The host, accompanied by no less a personage than the manager himself, had come up. They stood quietly and listened as Cloud took three bills out of the box, leaving one, and went on:

"The next card is either a five or a trey. That M there is to find out which it is."

"Are you sure of that?" the manager asked.

"Not absolutely, of course," Cloud admitted. "There's one chance in approximately fourteen million that both my partner and I are wrong."

"Very good odds. But since you lose in either case, why bet?"

"Because if it's a trey, she solved your system first. If it's a five, I beat her to it."

"I see, but that isn't necessary." The manager took the remaining cards out of the rack, and, holding them carefully and firmly, wrapped the M-note tightly around them. Then, picking up the two small stacks of played cards, he handed the whole collection to Cloud, at the same time signalling the dealer to go ahead with his game. "We'll be smothered in a crowd very shortly, and I would like very much to play with you myself. Will you, sir and madame, be gracious enough to continue play in private?"

"Gladly, sir," Joan assented, at Cloud's questioning glance. "If it would not put you out too much."

"I am delighted," and, beckoning to a hovering waiter, he went on: "We will have refreshments, of course. In uniform, you might possibly prefer soft drinks? We have some very good Tellurian ginger ale."

"That'd be fine," Cloud said, even while he was thinking at the Lensman in contact with his mind: "Safe enough, don't you think? He couldn't be thinking of any rough stuff yet."

"Perfectly safe," Nordquist agreed. "He's just curious. Besides, he's in no shape to handle even the *Vortex Blaster* alone, to say nothing of the task force he knows would be here two hours after anything happened to either of you."

The four strolled in friendly fashion to the suggested private room. As soon as they were settled:

"You said the top card would be either a five or a trey," the manager said. "Shall we look?"

It was the trey of spades. "Congratulations, Joanie, a mighty swell job. You really clobbered me on that one." He shook her hand vigorously, then handed the bill to the manager. "Here's your M-note, sir."

"I couldn't think of it, sir. No tipping, you know. . . ."

"I know. Not a tip, but your winnings. I called the play, remember. Hence, I insist."

"Very well, if you insist. But don't you want to look at the next one?"

"No. It's the ace of hearts—can't be anything else."

"To satisfy my own curiosity, then." The manager flipped the top card delicately. It was the ace of hearts. "No compulsion, of course, but would you mind telling me how you can *possibly* do what you have just done?"

"I'll be glad to," and this was the simple truth. Cloud had to explain, before the zwilniks began to suspect that they were being taken by an organized force of Lensmen and snoopers. "We aren't even semi-habitual gamblers. The lieutenant-commander is Doctor Joan Janowick, the Patrol's ace designer of big, high-speed electronic computers, and I am Neal Cloud, a mathematical analyst."

"You are 'Storm' Cloud, the Vortex Blaster," the manager corrected him. "A super-computer yourself. I begin to see, I think . . . but go ahead, please."

"You undoubtedly know that random numbers, which underlie all games of chance, must be just that—purely random, with nothing whatever of system or of orderliness in their distribution. Also that a stacked deck, by definition, is most decidedly *not* random. We were kicking that idea around, one day, and decided to study stacked decks, to see how systematic such distributions actually were. Well—here's the new part—we learned that any dealer who stacks a deck of cards does so in some definite pattern; and that pattern, whether conscious or unconscious, is always characteristic of that one individual. The more skilled the dealer, the more complex, precise, complete, and definite the pattern. Any pattern, however complex, can be solved; and, once solved, the cards might just as well be lying face up and all in sight.

"On the other hand, while it is virtually impossible for any dealer to shuffle a deck into a really random condition, it can approach randomness so nearly that the patterns are short and hence very difficult to solve. Also, there are no likenesses or similarities to help. Worst of all, there is the house leverage—the sevens of hearts, diamonds, and clubs, you know—of approximately five point seven seven percent. So it is mathematically certain that she and I would lose, not win, against any dealer who was not stacking his decks."

"I . . . am . . . surprised. I'm *amazed*," the manager said. He was, too; and so was the host. "Heretofore it has always been the guest who loses by manipulation, not the house." It is noteworthy that neither the manager nor host had at any time denied, even by implication, that their games of "chance" were loaded. "Thanks, immensely, for telling me. . . . By the way, you haven't done this very often before have you?" the manager smiled ruefully.

"No." Cloud smiled back. "This is the first time. Why?"

"I thought I would have heard of it if you had. This of course changes my mind about wanting to deal to you myself. In fact, I'll go farther—any dealer you play with here will be doing his level best to give you a completely random distribution."

"Fair enough. But we proved our point, which was what we were primarily interested in, anyway. What'll we do with the rest of the day, Joan—go back to the ship?"

"Uh-uh. This is the most comfortable place I've found since we left Tellus, and if I don't see the ship again for a week it'll be at least a week too soon. Why don't you send a boy out with enough money to get us a chess kit? We can engage this room for the rest of the day and work on our game."

"No need for that—we have all such things here," the host said quickly. "I'll send for them at once."

"No no—no money, please," the manager said. "I am still in your debt, and as long as you will stay you are my guests. . . ." he paused, then went on in a strangely altered tone: "But chess . . . and Janowick . . . Joan Janowick, not at all a common name . . . surely not Past Grand Master Janowick? She—retired—would be a much older woman."

"The same—I retired for lack of time, but I still play as much as I can. I'm flattered that you have heard of me." Joan smiled as though she were making a new and charming acquaintance. "And you? I'm sorry we didn't introduce ourselves earlier."

"Permit me to introduce Host Althagar, assistant manager. I am called Thlasoval."

"Oh, I know of you, Master Thlasoval. I followed your game with Rengodon of Centralia. Your knight-and-bishop end game was a really beautiful thing."

"Thank you. I am *really* flattered that you have heard of *me*. But Commander Cloud. . . ?"

"No, you haven't heard of him. Perhaps you never will, but believe me, if he had time for tournament play he'd be high on the Grand Masters list. So far on this cruise he's won one game, I've won one, and we're on the eighty fourth move of the third."

The paraphernalia arrived and the Tellurians set the game up rapidly and unerringly, each knowing exactly where each piece and pawn belonged.

"You have each lost two pawns, one knight, and one bishop—in eighty three moves?" Thlasoval marveled.

"Right," Cloud said. "We're playing for blood. Across this board friendship ceases; and, when dealing with such a pure unadulterated tiger as she is, so does chivalry."

"If I'm a tiger, I'd hate to say what *he* is." Joan glanced up with a grin. "Just study the board, Master Thlasoval, and see for yourself who is doing what to whom. I'm just barely holding him: he's had me on the defensive for the last forty moves. Attacking him is just like trying to beat in the side of a battleship with your bare fist. Do you see his strategy? Perhaps not, on such short notice."

Joan was very willing to talk chess at length, because the fact that Fairchild's Chickladorian manager was a chess Master was an essential part of the Patrol's plan.

"No . . . I can't say that I do."

"You notice he's concentrating everything he can bring to bear on my left flank. Fifteen moves from now he'd've been focused on my King's Knight's Third. Three moves after that he was going to exchange his knight for my queen and then mate in four. But, finding out what he was up to, I've just derailed his train of operations and he has to revise his whole campaign."

"No wonder I didn't see . . . I'm simply not in your class. But would you mind if I stay and look on?"

"We'll be glad to have you, but it won't be fast. We're playing strict tournament rules and taking the full four minutes for each move."

"That's quite all right. I really *enjoy* watching Grand Masters at work."

Master though he was, Thlasoval had no idea at all of what a terrific game he watched. For Joan Janowick and Neal Cloud were not playing it; they merely moved the pieces.

The game had been played long since. Based upon the greatest games of the greatest masters of old, it had been worked out, move by move, by chess masters working with high-speed computers.

Thus, while Joan and Storm were really concentrating, it was not upon chess.

VESTA THE GAMBLER

JOAN WAS HANDLING the card games, Cloud the wheels. The suggestion that it would be smart to run honest games had been implanted in the zwilniks' minds, not because of the cards, but because of the wheels; for a loaded, braked, and magnetized wheel is a very tough device to beat.

Joan, then, would read a deck of cards, and a Lensman or a Rigellian would watch her do it. Then the observing telepath would, all imperceptibly, insert hunches into the mind of a player. And what gambler has ever questioned his hunches, especially when they pay off time after time after time? Thus more and more players began to win with greater or lesser regularity and the gambling fever—the most contagious and infectious disorder known to man—spread throughout the vast room like a conflagration in a box-factory.

And Storm Cloud was handling the wheels.

"Place your bets, ladies and gentlemen, before the ball enters Zone Green," the croupiers intoned. "The screens go up, no bets can be placed while the ball is in the Green."

If the wheels had not been rigged, Cloud could have computed with ease the exact number upon which each ball would come to rest. In such case the Patrol forces would not, of course, have given Vesta the Vegian complete or accurate information. With her temperament and her bank-roll, she would have put the place out of business in an hour; and such a single-handed killing was not at all what the Patrol desired.

But the wheels, of course, were rigged. Cloud was being informed, however, of every pertinent fact. He knew the exact point at which the ball crossed the green borderline. He knew its exact velocity. He knew precisely the strengths of the magnetic fields and the permeabilities, reluctances, and so on, of all the materials involved. He knew just about how much braking force could be applied without tipping off the players and transforming them instantly into a blood-thirsty mob. And finally, he was backed by Lensmen who could at need interfere with the physical processes of the croupiers without any knowledge on the part of the victims.

Hence Cloud did well enough—and when a house is paying thirty-five to one on odds that have been cut down to eight or ten to one, it is very, *very* bad for the house.

Vesta started playing conservatively enough. She went from wheel to wheel, tail high in air and purring happily to herself, slapping down ten-credit notes until she won.

"*This* is the wheel I like!" she exclaimed, and went to twenties. Still unperturbed, still gay, she watched nine of them move away under the croupier's rake. Then she won again.

Then fifties. Then hundreds. She wasn't gay now, nor purring. She wasn't exactly tense, yet, but she was warming up. As the tenth C-note disappeared, a Chickladorian beside her said:

"Why don't you play the colors, miss? Or combinations? You don't lose so much that way."

"No, and you don't win so much, either. When I'm gambling I *gamble*, brother . . . and wait just a minute . . ." the croupier paid her three M's and an L. . . . "See what I mean?"

The crowd was going not-so-slowly mad. Assistant Manager Althagar did what he could. He ordered all rigging and gimmicks off, and the house still lost. On again, off again; and losses still skyrocketed. Then, hurrying over to the door of a private room, he knocked lightly, opened the door, and beckoned to Thlasoval.

"All hell's out for noon!" he whispered intensely as the manager reached the doorway. "The crowd's winning like crazy—everybody's winning! D'you s'pose it's them damn Patrolmen there crossing us up—and how in *hell* could it be?"

"Have you tried cutting out the gimmicks?"

"Yes. No difference."

"It can't be them, then. It couldn't be anyway, for two reasons. The kind of brains it takes to work that kind of problems in your head can't happen once in a hundred million times, and you say everybody's doing it. They *can't* be, dammit! Two, they're Grand Masters playing chess. You play chess yourself."

"You know I do. I'm not a Master, but I'm pretty good."

"Good enough to tell by looking at 'em that they don't give a damn about what's going on out there. Come on in."

"We'll disturb 'em and they'll be sore as hell."

"You *couldn't* disturb these two, short of yelling in their ear or joggling the board." The two walked toward the table. "See what I mean?"

The two players, forearms on table, were sitting rigidly still, staring as though entranced at the board, neither moving so much as an eye. As the two Chickladorians watched, Cloud's left forearm, pivoting on the elbow, swung out and he moved his knight.

"Oh, no . . . no!" Shocked out of silence, Thlasoval muttered the words under his breath. "Your queen, man—your queen!"

But this opportunity, so evident to the observer, did not seem at all attractive to the woman, who sat motionless for minute after minute.

"But come on, boss, and look this mess over," the assistant urged. "You're on plus time now."

"I suppose so." They turned away from the enigma. "But *why* didn't she take his queen? I couldn't see a thing to keep her from doing it. I would have."

"So would I. However, almost all the pieces on that board are vulnerable, some way or other. Probably whichever one starts the shin-kicking will come out at the little end of the horn."

"Could be, but it won't be kicking shins. It'll be slaughter—and *how* I'd like to be there when the slaughter starts! And I *still* don't see why she didn't grab that queen. . . ."

"Well, you can ask her, maybe, when they leave. But right now you'd better forget chess and take a good, long gander at what that Vegian hell-cat is doing. She's wilder than a Radelgian cateagle and hotter than a DeLameter. She's gone just completely nuts."

Tense, strained, taut as a violin-string in every visible muscle, Vesta stood at a wheel; gripping the ledge of the table so fiercely that enamel was flaking off the metal and plastic under her stiff, sharp nails. Jaws hard set and eyes almost invisible slits, she growled deep in her throat at every bet she put down. And those bets were all alike—ten thousand credits each—and she was still playing the numbers straight. They watched her lose eighty thousand credits; then watched her collect three hundred and fifty thousand.

Thlasoval made the rounds, then; did everything he could to impede the outward flow of cash, finding that there wasn't much of anything he could do. He beckoned his assistant.

"This is bad, Althagar, believe me," he said. "And I simply can't figure any part of it . . . unless. . . ." His voice died away.

"You said it. I can't, either. Unless it's them two chess-players in there, and I'll buy it that it ain't, I haven't even got a guess . . . unless there could be some Lensmen mixed up in it somewhere. They could do just about anything."

"*Lensmen?* Rocket-juice! There aren't any—we spy-ray everybody that comes in."

"Outside, maybe, peeking in. Or some other snoopers, maybe, somewhere?"

"I can't see it. We've had Lensmen in here dozens of times, for one reason or another, business and social both, and they've always shot straight pool. Besides, all they're getting is money, and what in all eleven hells of Telemanchia would the Patrol want of our *money?* If they wanted us for anything they'd come and get us, but they wouldn't give a cockeyed tinker's damn for our *money.* They've already got all the money there is!"

"That's so, too. Money . . . hm, money in gobs and slathers. . . . Oh, you think . . . the Mob? D'ya s'pose it's got so big for its britches it thinks it can take *us* on?"

"I wouldn't think they could be *that* silly. It's a lot more reasonable, though, than that the Patrol would be horsing around this way."

"But how? Great Kalastho, *how?*"

"How do I know? Snoopers, as you said—or perceivers, or any other ringers they could ring in on us."

"Nuts!" the assistant retorted. "Just who do you figure as ringers? The Vegian isn't a snooper, she's just a gambling fool. No Chickladorian was ever a snooper, or a perceiver either, and these people are just about all regular customers. And *everybody's* winning. So just where does that put you?"

"Up the creek—I know. But dammit, there's *got* to be snoopery or some other funny stuff *somewhere* in this!"

"Uh-uh. Did you ever hear of a perceiver who could read a deck or spot a gimmick from half a block away?"

"No, but that doesn't mean there aren't any. But what stops me is what can we *do* about it? If the Mob *is* forted up in that hotel across the street or somewhere beside or behind us . . . there isn't a damn thing we can do. They'd have more gunnies than we could send in, even if we knew exactly where they were, and we can't send a young army barging around without anything but a flimsy suspicion to go on—the lawmen would throw us in the clink in nothing flat. . . . Besides, this Mob idea isn't exactly solid, either. How'd they get their cut from all these people? Especially the Vegian?"

"The Vegian, probably not; the rest, probably so. They could have passed the word around that this is the big day. Anybody'd split fifty-fifty on a cold sure thing."

"Uh-uh. I won't buy that, either. I'd've known about it—somebody would have leaked. No matter how you figure it, it doesn't add up."

"Well, then?"

"Only one thing we can do. Close down. While you're doing that I'll go shoot in a Class A Double Prime Urgent to top brass."

Hence Vesta's croupier soon announced to his clientele that all betting was off, at least until the following day. All guests would please leave the building as soon as possible.

For a couple of minutes Vesta simply could not take in the import of the announcement. She was stunned. Then:

"Whee . . . yow . . . ow . . . erow!" she yowled, at the top of her not inconsiderable voice. "I've won . . . I've *won* . . . I'VE WON!" She quieted down a little, still shell-shocked, then looked around and ran toward the nearest familiar face, which was that of the assistant manager. "Oh, senor Althagar, do you actually want me to quit while I'm *ahead*? Why, I never *heard* of such a thing—it certainly never happened to *me* before! And I'm going to stop gambling *entirely*—I'll *never* get such a thrill as this again if I live a million years!"

"You're *so* right, Miss Vesta—you never will." Althagar smiled—as though he had just eaten three lemons without sugar, to be sure, but it was still a smile. "It's not that we *want* you to quit, but simply that we can't pay any more losses. Right now I am most powerfully psychic, so take my advice, my dear, and stop."

"I'm going to—honestly, I am." Vesta straightened out the thick sheaf of bills she held in her right hand, noticing that they were all ten-thousands. She dug around in her bulging pouch; had to dig half-way to the bottom before she could find anything smaller. With a startled gasp she crammed the handful of bills in on top of the others and managed, just barely, to close and lock the pouch. "Oh, I've got to *fly*—I must find my boss and tell him all about this!"

"Would you like an armed escort to your hotel?"

"That won't be necessary, thanks. I'm going to take a copter direct to the ship."

And she did.

It was not until the crowd was almost all gone that either Thlasoval or Althagar even thought of the two chess-players. Then one signalled the other and they went together to the private room, into it, and up to the chess-table. To the casual eye, neither player had moved. The board, too, showed comparatively little change; at least, the carnage anticipated by Thlasoval had not materialized.

Althagar coughed discreetly; then again, a little louder. "Sir and madam, please. . . ." he began.

"I told you they'd be dead to the world," Thlasoval said; and, bending over, lifted one side of the board. Oh, very gently, and not nearly enough to dislodge any one of the pieces, but the tiny action produced disproportionately large results. Both players started as though a bomb had exploded beside them, and Joan uttered a half-stifled scream. With visible efforts, they brought themselves down from the heights to the there and the then. Cloud stretched prodigiously; and Joan, emulating him, had to bring one hand down to cover a jaw-cracking yawn.

"Excuse me, Grand Master Janowick and Commander Cloud, but the Club is being closed for repairs and we must ask you to leave the building."

"Closed?" Joan parroted, stupidly, and:

"For repairs?" Cloud added, with equal brilliance.

"Closed. For repairs." Thlasoval repeated, firmly. Then, seeing that his guests were coming back to life quite nicely, he offered Joan his arm and started for the door.

"Oh, yes, Grand Master Janowick," he said en route. "May I ask why you refused the Commander's queen?"

"He would have gained such an advantage in position as to mate in twelve moves."

"I see . . . thanks." He didn't, at all, but he had to say something. "I wonder . . . would it be possible for me to find out how this game comes out?"

"Why, I suppose so." Joan thought for a moment. "Certainly. If you'll give me your card I'll send you a tape of it after we finish."

*

The two Patrolmen boarded a copter. Joan looked subdued, almost forlorn. Cloud took her hand and squeezed it gently.

"Don't take it so hard, Joan," he thought. He found it remarkably easy to send to her now; in fact, telepathy was easier and simpler and more natural than talking. "We had it to do."

"I suppose so; but it was a dirty, slimy, stinking, *filthy* trick, Storm. I'm ashamed . . . I feel soiled."

"I know how you feel. I'm not so happy about the thing, either. But when you think of thionite, and what *that* stuff means. . . ?"

"That's true, of course . . . and they stole the money in the first place. . . . Not that two wrongs, or even three or four, make a right . . . but it does *help*."

She cheered up a little, but she was not yet her usual self when they boarded the *Vortex Blaster II*.

Vesta met them just inside the lock. "Oh, chief, I won—I won!" she shrieked, tail waving frantically in air. "Where'd you go after the club closed? I looked all *over* for you—do you know how much I won, Captain Nealcloud?"

"Haven't any idea. How much?"

"One million seven hundred sixty two thousand eight hundred and ten credits! Yow-wow-yow!"

"Whew!" Cloud whistled in amazement. "And you're figuring on giving it all back to 'em tomorrow?"

"I . . . I haven't quite decided." Vesta sobered instantly. "What do *you* think, chief?"

"Not being a gambler, I don't have hunches very often, but I've got one now. In fact, I know one thing for certain damn sure. There isn't one chance in seven thousand million of anything like this ever happening to you again. You'll lose your shirt—that is, if you had a shirt to lose," he added hastily.

"You know, I think you're right? I thought so myself, and you're the second smart man to tell me the same thing."

"Who was the first one?"

"That man at the club, Althagar, his name was. So, with three hunches on the same play, I'd be a fool not to play it that way. Besides, I'll *never* get another wallop like that . . . my uncle's been wanting me to be linguist in his bank, and with a million and three-quarters of my own I could buy half his bank and be a linguist and a cashier both. Then I couldn't *ever* gamble again."

"Huh? Why not?"

"Because Vegians, especially young Vegians, like me, haven't got any sense when it comes to gambling," Vesta explained, gravely. "They can't tell the difference between their own money and the bank's. So everybody who amounts to anything in a bank makes a no-gambling declaration and if one ever slips the insurance company boots him out on his ear and he takes a blaster and burns his head off. . . ."

Cloud flashed a thought at Joan. "Is this another of your strictly Vegian customs?"

"Not mine; I never heard of it before," she flashed back. "Very much in character, though, and it explains why Vegian bankers are regarded as being very much the upper crust."

". . . so I *am* going to buy half of that bank. Thanks, chief, for helping me make up my mind. Good night, you two lovely people; I'm going to bed. I'm just about bushed." Vesta, tail high and with a completely new dignity in her bearing, strode away.

"Me, too, Storm; on both counts," Joan thought at Cloud. "You ought to hit the hammock, too, instead of working half the night yet."

"Maybe so, but I want to know how things came out, and besides they may want some quick figuring done. Good night, little chum." His parting thought, while commonplace enough in phraseology, was in fact sheer caress; and Joan's mind, warmly intimate, accepted it as such and returned it in kind.

Cloud left the ship and rode a scooter across the field to a very ordinary-looking freighter. In that vessel's control room, however, there were three Lensmen and five Rigellians, all clustered around a tank-chart of a considerable fraction of the First Galaxy.

"Hi, Cloud!" Nordquist greeted him with a Lensed thought and introduced him to the others. "All our thanks for a really beautiful job of work. We'll thank Miss Janowick tomorrow, when she'll have a better perspective. Want to look?"

"I certainly do. Thanks." Cloud joined the group at the chart and Nordquist poured knowledge into his mind.

Thlasoval, the boss of Chickladoria, had been under full mental surveillance every minute of every day. The scheme had worked perfectly. As the club closed, Thlasoval had sent the expected message; not by ordinary communications channels, of course, but via long-distance beamer. It was beamed three ways; to Tominga, Vegia, and Palmer III. That proved that Fairchild wasn't on Chickladoria; if he had been, Thlasoval would have used a broadcaster, not a beamer.

Shows had been staged simultaneously on all four of Fairchild's planets, and only on Vegia had the planetary manager's message been broadcast. Fairchild was on Vegia, and he wouldn't leave it: a screen had been thrown around the planet that a microbe couldn't squirm through and it wouldn't be relaxed until Fairchild was caught.

"*Simultaneous shows?*" Cloud interrupted the flow of information. "On four planets? He won't connect the *Vortex Blaster* with it, at all, then."

"We think he will," the Lensman thought, narrowing down. "We're dealing with a *very* shrewd operator. We hope he does, anyway, because a snooper put on you or any one of your key people would be manna from heaven for us."

"But how *could* he suspect us?" Cloud demanded. "We couldn't have been on four planets at once."

"You will have been on three of them, though; and I can tell you now that routing was not exactly coincidence."

"Oh . . . and I wasn't informed?"

"No. Top Brass didn't want to disturb you too much, especially since we hoped to catch him before things got this far along. But you're in it now, clear to the neck. You and your people will be under surveillance every second, from here on in, and you'll be covered as no chief of state was ever covered in all history."

A few months later, Joan did send him the full game, which white of course won. Thlasoval studied it in secret for over five years; and then, deciding correctly that he never would be able to understand its terrifically complex strategy, he destroyed the tape. It is perhaps superfluous to all that this game was never published. E.E.S.

JOAN AND HER BRAINS

THE TRIP FROM Chickladoria to Vegia, while fairly long, was uneventful.

Joan spent her working hours, of course, at her regular job of rebuilding the giant computer. Cloud spent his at the galactic chart or in the control room staring into a tank; classifying, analyzing, building up and knocking down hypotheses and theories, wringing every possible drop of knowledge from all the data he could collect.

In their "spare" time, of which each had quite a great deal, they worked together at their telepathy; to such good purpose that, when so working, verbal communication between them became rarer and rarer. And, alone or in a crowd, within sight of each other or not, in any place or at any time, asleep or awake, each had only to think at the other and they were instantly in full mental rapport.

And oftener and oftener there came those instantaneously-fleeting touches of something infinitely more than mere telepathy; that fusion of minds which was so ultimately intimate that neither of the two could have said whether he longed for or dreaded its full coming the more. In fact, for several days before reaching Vegia, each knew that they could bring about that full fusion any time they chose to do so; but both shied away from its consummation, each as violently as the other.

Thus the trip did not seem nearly as long as it actually was.

The first order of business on Vegia, of course, was the extinguishment of its five loose atomic vortices—for which reason this was to be pretty much a planetary holiday, although that is of little concern here.

As the *Vortex Blaster II* began settling into position, the two scientists took their places. Cloud was apparently his usual self-controlled self, but Joan was white and strained—almost shaking. He sent her a steadying thought, but her block was up, solid.

"Don't take it so hard, Joanie," he said, soberly. "Margie'll take 'em, I hope—but even if she doesn't, there's a dozen things not tried yet."

"That's just the trouble—there *aren't*! We put just about everything we had into Lulu; Margie is only a few milliseconds better. *Perhaps* there are a dozen things not tried yet, but I haven't the faintest, foggiest smidgeon of an idea of what any of them could be. Margie is the last word, Storm—the best analogue computer it is possible to build with today's knowledge."

"And I haven't been a lick of help. I wish I could be, Joan."

"I don't see how you can be. . . . Oh, excuse me, Storm, I didn't mean that half the way it sounds. Do you want to check the circuitry? I'll send for the prints."

"No, I couldn't even carry your water-bottle on that part of the job. I've got just a sort of a dim, half-baked idea that there's a possibility that maybe I haven't been giving you and your brains a square deal. By studying the graphs of the next three or four tests maybe I can find out whether. . . ."

"Lieutenant-Commander Janowick, we are in position," a crisp voice came from the speaker. "You may take over when ready, madam."

"Thank you, sir." Joan flipped a switch and Margie took control of the ship and its armament—subject only to Cloud's overriding right to fire at will.

"Just a minute, Storm," Joan said then. "Unfinished business. Whether what?"

"Whether there's anything I can do—or fail to do—that might help; but I've got to have a lot more data."

Cloud turned to his chart, Joan to hers; and nothing happened until Cloud blew out the vortex himself.

The same lack of something happened in the case of the next vortex, and also the next. Then, as the instruments began working in earnest on the fourth, Cloud reviewed in his mind the figures of the three previous trials. On the first vortex, a big toughie, Margie had been two hundred fifty milliseconds short. On the second, a fairly small one, she had come up to seventy-five. On Number Three, middle-sized, the lag had been one twenty-five. That made sense. Lag was proportional to activity and it was just too bad for Margie. And just too *damn* bad for Joanie—the poor kid was just about to blow her stack. . . .

But wait a minute! What's this? This number four's a little bit of a new one, about as small as they ever come. Margie ought to be taking it, if she's ever going to take anything . . . but she isn't! She's running damn near three hundred mils behind! Why? Oh—amplitudes—frequencies extreme instability. . . . Lag isn't proportional *only* to activity, then, but jointly to activity and to instability.

That gives us a chance—but what in all nine of Palain's purple *hells* is that machine *doing* with that data?

He started to climb out of his bucket seat to go around to talk to Joan right then, but changed his mind at his first move. Even if Margie *could* handle this little one it wouldn't be a real test, and it'd be a crying shame to give Joan a success here and then kick her in the teeth with a flat failure next time. No, the next one, the only one left and Vegia's worst, would be the one. If Margie could handle *that*, she could snuff anything the galaxy had to offer.

Hence Cloud extinguished this one, too, himself. The *Vortex Blaster II* darted to its last Vegian objective and lined itself up for business. Joan put Margie to work as usual; but Storm, for the first time, did not take his own place. Instead, he came around and stood behind Joan's chair.

"How're we doing, little chum?" he asked.

"Rotten!" Joan's block was still up; her voice was choked with tears. "She's come so close half a dozen times today—why—*why* can't I get that last fraction of a second?"

"Maybe you can." As though it were the most natural thing in the world—which in fact it was—Cloud put his left arm around her shoulders and exerted a gentle pressure. "Bars down, chum—we can think a lot clearer than we can talk."

"That's better," as her guard went down. "Your differential 'scope looks like it's set at about one centimeter to the second. Can you give it enough vertical gain to make it about five?"

"Yes. Ten if you like, but the trace would keep jumping the screen on the down-swings."

"I wouldn't care about that—closest approach is all I want. Give it full gain."

"QX, but why?" Joan demanded, as she made the requested adjustment. "Did you find out something I can't dig deep enough in your mind to pry loose?"

"Don't know yet whether I did or not—I can tell you in a couple of minutes," and Cloud concentrated his full attention upon the chart and its adjacent oscilloscope screen.

One pen of the chart was drawing a thin, wildly-wavering red line. A few seconds behind it a second pen was tracing the red line in black; tracing it so exactly that not the tiniest touch of red was to be seen anywhere along the black. And on the screen of the differential oscilloscope the fine green saw-tooth wave-form of the electronic trace, which gave continuously the instantaneous value of the brain's shortage in time, flickered insanely and apparently reasonlessly up and down; occasionally falling clear off the bottom of the screen. If that needle-pointed trace should touch the zero line, however briefly, Margie the Brain would act; but it was not coming within one full centimeter of touching.

"The feeling that these failures have been partly, or even mostly, my fault is growing on me," Cloud thought, tightening his arm a little: and Joan, if anything, yielded to the pressure instead of fighting away from it. "Maybe I haven't been waiting long enough to give your brains the leeway they need. To check: I've been assuming all along that they work in pretty much the same way I do; that they handle all the data, out to the limit of validity of the equations, but aren't fast enough to work out a three-point-six-second prediction.

"But if I'm reading those curves right Margie simply isn't working that way. She doesn't seem to be extrapolating *anything* more than three and a half seconds ahead—'way short of the reliability limit—and sometimes a lot less than that. She isn't *accepting* data far enough ahead. She acts as though she can gulp down just so much information without choking on it—so much and no more."

"Exactly. An over-simplification, of course, since it isn't the kind of choking that giving her a bigger throat would cure, but very well put." Joan's right hand crept across her body, rested on Cloud's wrist, and helped his squeeze, while her face turned more directly toward the face so close to hers. "That's inherent in the design of all really fast machines . . . and we simply don't know any way of getting away from it. . . . Why? What has that to do with the case?"

"A lot—I hope. When I was working in a flitter I had to wait up to half an hour sometimes, for the sigma curve to stabilize enough so that the equations would hold valid will give a longer valid prediction."

"Stabilize? How? I've never seen a sigma curve flatten out. Or does 'stabilize' have a special meaning for you vortex experts?"

"Could be. It's what happens when a sigma becomes a little more regular than usual, so that a simpler equation will give a longer valid prediction."

"I see; and a difference in wave-form that would be imperceptible to me might mean a lot to you."

"Right. It just occurred to me that a similar line of reasoning may hold for this seemingly entirely different set of conditions. The less unstable the curve, the less complicated the equations and the smaller the volume of actual data. . . ."

"Oh!" Joan's thought soared high. "So Margie may work *yet*, if we wait a while?"

"Check. Browning can't take the ship away from you, can he?"

"No. Nobody can do anything until the job is done or I punch that red 'stop' button there. D'you suppose she *can* do it? Storm? How long can we wait?"

"Half an hour, I'd say. No, to settle the point definitely, let's wait until I can get a full ten-second prediction and see what Margie's doing about the situation then."

"Wonderful! But in that case, it might be a good idea for you to be looking at the chart, don't you think?" she asked, pointedly. His eyes, at the moment, were looking directly into hers, from a distance of approximately twelve inches.

"I'll look at it later, but right now I'm. . . ."

The ship quivered under the terrific, the unmistakable trip-hammer blow of propellant heptadetonite. Unobserved by either of the two scientists most concerned, the sigma curve had, momentarily, become a trifle less irregular. The point of the saw-tooth wave had touched the zero line. Margie had acted. The visiplate, from which the heavily-filtered glare of the vortex had blazed so long, went suddenly black.

"*She did it*, Storm!" Joan's thought was a mental shriek of pure joy. "*She really worked!*"

Whether, when the ship went free, Joan pulled Storm down to her merely to anchor him, or for some other reason; whether Cloud grabbed her merely in lieu of a safety-line or not; which of the two was first to put arms around the other; these are moot points impossible of decision at this date. The fact is, however, that the two scientists held a remarkably unscientific pose for a good two minutes before Joan thought that she ought to object a little, just on general principles. Even then, she did not object with her mind; instead she put up her block and used her voice.

"But, after all, Storm," she began, only to be silenced as beloved women have been silenced throughout the ages. She cut her screen then, and her mind, tender and unafraid, reached out to his.

"This might be the perfect time, dear, to merge our minds? I've been scared to death of it all along, but no more . . . let's?"

"Uh-huh," he demurred. "I'm *still* afraid of it. I've been thinking about it a lot, and doing some drilling, and the more I play with it the more scared I get. It's dangerous. It's like playing with duodec. I've just about decided that we'd better let it drop."

"Afraid? For yourself, or for me? Don't try to lie with your mind, Storm; you can't do it. You're afraid only for me, and you needn't be. I've been thinking, too, and digging deep, and I know I'm ready." She looked up at him then, her quick, bright, impish grin very much in evidence. "Let's go."

"QX, Joanie, and thanks. I've been wanting this more than I ever wanted anything before in my life. But not holding hands, this time. Heart to heart and cheek to cheek."

"Check—the closer the better."

They embraced, and again mind flowed into mind; this time with no thought of withholding or reserve on either side. Smoothly, effortlessly, the two essential beings merged, each fitting its tiniest, remotest members into the deepest, ordinarily most inaccessible recesses of the other; fusing as quickly and as delicately and as thoroughly as two drops of water coalescing into one.

In that supremely intimate fusion, that ultimate union of line and plane and cellule, each mind was revealed completely to the other; a revealment which no outsider should expect to share.

Finally, after neither ever knew how long, they released each other and each put up, automatically, a solid block.

"I don't know about you, Storm," Joan said then, "but I've had just about all I can take. I'm going to bed and sleep for one solid week."

"You and me both," Storm agreed, ungrammatically, but feelingly. "Good night, sweetheart . . . and this had all better be strictly hush-hush, don't you think?"

"I *do* think," she assured him. "Can't you just imagine the field-day the psychs would have, taking us apart?"

In view of the above, it might be assumed that the parting was immediate, positive, and undemonstrative; but such was not exactly the case. But they did finally separate, and each slept soundly and long.

And fairly early the next morning—before either of them got up, at least—Cloud sent Joan a thought.

"Awake, dear?"

"Uh-huh. Just. 'Morning, Storm."

"I've got some news for you, Joanie. My brain is firing on ten times as many barrels as I ever thought it had, and I don't know what half of 'em are doing. Among other things, you made what I think is probably a top-bracket perceiver out of me."

"So? Well, don't peek at me, please . . . but why should I say that, after having studied in Rigel Four for two years? Women are funny, I guess. But, for your information, I have just extracted the ninth root of an eighteen-digit number, in no time at all and to the last significant decimal place, and I *know* the answer is right. How do you like *them* potatoes, Buster?"

"Nice. We really absorbed each other's stuff, didn't we? But how about joining me in person for a soupcon of ham and eggs?"

"That's a thought, my thoughtful friend; a cogent and right knightly thought. I'll be with you in three jerks and a wiggle." And she was.

Just as they finished eating, Vesta breezed in. "Well, you two deep-sleepers finally crawled out of your sacks, did you? It is confusing, though, that ship's time never agrees with planetary time. But I live here, you know, in this city you call 'Vegiaton,' so I went to bed at noon yesterday and I've got over half a day's work done already. I saw my folks and bought half of my uncle's bank and made the no-gambling declaration and I want to ask you both something. After the Grand Uproar here at the 'port in your honor, will you two and Helen and Joe and Bob and Barbara come with me to a little dance some of my friends are having? You've been *zo* good to me, and I want to show you off a little."

"We'll be *glad* to, Vesta, and thanks a lot," Joan said, flashing a thought at Cloud to let her handle this thing her own way, "and I imagine the others would be, too, but . . . well, it's for *you*, you know, and we might be intruding. . . ."

"Why, not at all!" Vesta waved the objection away with an airy flirt of her tail. "You're friends of mine! And everybody's real friends are always welcome, you know, everywhere. And it'll be small and quiet; only six or eight hundred are being asked, they say. . . ." she paused for a moment: ". . . of course, after it gets around that we have *you* there, a couple of thousand or so strangers will come in too; but they'll all smell nice, so it'll be QX."

"How do you know what they'll smell like?" Cloud asked.

"Why, they'll smell like our crowd, of course. If they didn't they wouldn't *want* to come in. It's QX, then?"

"For us two, yes; but of course we can't speak for the others."

"Thanks, you wonderful people; I'll go ask them right now."

"Joan, have you blown your stack completely?" Cloud demanded. "Small—quiet—six or eight *hundred* invited—a couple of thousand or *so* gate-crashers—what do you want to go to a brawl like *that* for?"

"The chance is too good to miss—it's priceless. . . ." She paused, then added, obliquely: "Storm, have you any idea at all of what Vesta thinks of you? You haven't snooped, I'm sure."

"No, and I don't intend to."

"Maybe you ought to," Joan snickered a little, "except that it would inflate your ego too much. It's hard to describe. It's not exactly love—and not exactly worship, either god-worship or hero-worship. It isn't exactly adoration, but it's very much stronger than mere

1154

admiration. A mixture of all these, perhaps, and half a dozen others, coupled with a simply unbelievable amount of *pride* that you are her friend. It's a peculiarly Vegian thing, that Tellurians simply do not feel. But here's why I'm so enthused. It has been over twenty years since any non-Vegian has attended one of these uniquely Vegian parties except as an outsider, and a Vegian party with outsiders looking on isn't a Vegian party at all. But we Storm, will be going as insiders!"

"Are you sure of that?"

"Positive. Oh, I know it isn't *us* she wants, but *you*; but that won't make any difference. As Vesta's friend—'friend' in this case having a very special meaning—you're in the center of the inner circle. As friends of yours, the rest of us are in, too. Not in the inner circle, perhaps, but well inside the outside circle, at least. See?"

"Dimly. 'A friend of a friend of a friend of a very good friend of mine,' eh? I've heard that ditty, but I never thought it meant anything."

"It does here. We're going to have a time. See you in about an hour?"

"Just about. I've got to check with Nordquist."

"Here I am, Storm," the Lensman's thought came in. Then, as Cloud went toward his quarters, it went on: "Just want to tell you we won't have anything for you to do here. This is going to be a straight combing job."

"That won't be too tough, will it? A Tellurian, sixty, tall, thin, grave, distinguished-looking . . . or maybe. . . ."

"Exactly. You're getting the idea. Cosmeticians and plastic surgery. He could look like a Crevenian, or thirty years old and two hundred pounds and slouchy. He could look like anything. He undoubtedly has a background so perfectly established that fifteen thoroughly honest Vegians would swear by eleven of their gods that he hasn't left his home town for ten years. So every intelligent being on Vegia who hasn't got a live tail, with live blood circulating in it, is going under the Lens and through the wringer if we have to keep Vegia in quarantine for a solid year. He is *not* going to get away from us this time."

"I'm betting on you, Nordquist. Clear ether!"

The Lensman signed off and Cloud, at the end of the specified hour, undressed and redressed and went to the computer room. All the others except Joe were already there.

"Hi, peoples!" Cloud called; then did a double-take. "Wow! And likewise, Yipes! How come the tri-di outfits didn't all collapse, Joan, when those two spectaculars took up cybernetics?"

"I'll never know, Storm." Joan shook her head wonderingly, then went on via thought; and Cloud felt her pang of sheer jealousy. "Why is it that big girls are always so much more beautiful than little ones? And the more clothes they take off the better they look? It simply isn't *fair*!"

Cloud's mind reached out and meshed with hers. "Sure it is, sweetheart. They're beauties; you can't take that away from them. . . ."

And beauties they certainly were. Helen, as has been said, was lissom and dark. Her hair was black, her eyes a midnight blue, her skin a deep, golden brown. Barbara, not quite as tall—five feet seven, perhaps—was equally beautifully proportioned, and even more striking-looking. Her skin was tanned ivory, her eyes were gray, her hair was a shoulder-length, carefully-careless mass of gleaming, flowing, wavy silver.

". . . they've got a lot of stuff: but believe me, there are several grand lots of stuff they *haven't* got, too. I wouldn't trade half of you for either one of them—or both of them together."

"I believe that—at least, about *both* of them," Joan giggled mentally, "but how many men. . . ."

"Well, how many men do you want?" Cloud interrupted.

"Touché, Storm . . . but do you really. . . ."

What would have developed into a scene of purely mental lovemaking was put to an end by the arrival of Joe Mackay, who also paused and made appropriate noises of appreciation.

"But there's one thing I don't quite like about this deal," he said finally. "I'm not too easy in my mind about making love to a moll who is packing a Mark Twenty Eight DeLameter. The darn thing might go off."

"Keep your distance, then, Lieutenant Mackay!" Helen laughed. "Well, are we ready?"

They were. They left the ship and walked in a group through the throng of cheering Vegians toward the nearby, gaily-decorated stands in which the official greetings and thank-yous were to take place. Helen and Babs loved it; just as though they were parading as finalists in a beauty contest. Bob and Joe wished that they had stayed in the ship and kept their clothes on. Joan didn't quite know whether she liked this kind of thing or not. Of the six Tellurians, only Neal Cloud had had enough experience in public near-nudity so that it made no difference. And Vesta?

Vesta was fairly reveling—openly, unashamedly reveling—in the spotlight with her Tellurian friends. They reached the center stand, were ushered with many flourishes to a reserved section already partly filled by Captain Ross and the lesser officers and crewmen of the good-will-touring Patrol ship *Vortex Blaster II*. Not all of the officers, of course, since many had to stay aboard, and comparatively few of the crew; for many men insist on wearing Tellurian garmenture and refuse to tan their hides under ultra-violet radiation—and no untanned white Tellurian skin can take with impunity more than a few minutes of giant Vega's blue-white fury.

Of the ceremonies themselves, nothing need be said; such things being pretty much of a piece, wherever, whenever, or for whatever reason held. When they were over, Vesta gathered her six friends together and led them to the edge of the roped-off area. There she uttered a soundless (to Tellurian ears) whistle, whereupon a group of Vegian youths and girls formed a wedge around the seven and drove straight through the milling crowd to its edge. There, by an evidently pre-arranged miracle, they found enough copters to carry them all.

VEGIAN JUSTICE

THE NEARER THEY got to their destination the more fidgety Vesta became. "Oh, I *hope* Zambkptkn could get away and be there by now—I haven't seen him for over half a year!"

"Who?" Helen asked.

"My brother. Zamke, you'd better call him, you can pronounce that. The police officer, you know."

"I thought you saw him this morning?" Joan said.

"I saw my other brothers and sisters, but not him—he was tied up on a job. He wasn't sure just when he could get away tonight."

The copter dropped sharply. Vesta seized Cloud's arm and pointed. "That's where we're going; that big building with the landing-field on the roof. The Caravanzerie. Zee?" In moments of emotion or excitement, most of Vesta's sibilants reverted to Z's.

"I see. And this is your Great White Way?"

It was, but it was not white. Instead, it was a blaze of red, blue, green, yellow—all the colors of the spectrum. And crowds! On foot, on bicycles, on scooters, motorbikes, and motortricycles, in cars and in copters, it seemed impossible that *anything* could move in such a press as that. And as the aircab approached its destination Neal Cloud, space-hardened veteran and skillful flyer though he was, found himself twisting wheels, stepping on pedals, and cutting in braking jets, none of which were there.

How that jockey landed his heap and got it into the air again all in one piece without dismembering a single Vegian, Cloud never did quite understand. Blades were scant fractional inches from blades and rotors; people were actually shoved aside by the tapering bumpers of the cab as it hit the deck; but nothing happened. This, it seemed, was *normal!*

The group re-formed and in flying-wedge fashion as before, gained the elevators and finally the ground floor and the ballroom. Here Cloud drew his first full breath for what seemed like hours. The ballroom was tremendous—and it was less than three-quarters filled.

Just inside the doorway Vesta paused, sniffing delicately. "He *is* here—come on!" She beckoned the six to follow her and rushed ahead, to be met at the edge of the clear space in head-on collision. Brother and sister embraced fervently for about two seconds. Then, reaching down, the man broke his sister's grip and flipped her around sidewise, through half of a vertical circle, so that her feet pointed straight up. Then, with a sharp "*Blavzkt!*" he snapped into a back flip.

"*Blavzkt–Zemp!*" she shouted back, bending beautifully into such an arch that, as his feet left the floor, hers landed almost exactly where his had been an instant before. Then for a full minute and a half the joyous pair pinwheeled, without moving from the spot; while the dancers on the floor, standing still now, applauded enthusiastically with stamping, hand-clapping, whistles, cat-calls, and screams.

Vesta stopped the exhibition finally, and led her brother toward Cloud and Joan. The music resumed, but the dancers did not. Instead, they made a concerted rush for the visitors, surrounding them in circles a dozen deep. Vesta, with both arms wrapped tightly around Cloud and her tail around Joan, shrieked a highly consonantal sentence—which Cloud knew meant "Lay off these two for a couple of minutes, you howling hyenas, they're mine"—then, switching to English: "Go ahead, you four, and have fun!"

The first two men to lay hands on the two tall Tellurian beauties were, by common consent and without argument, their first partners. Two of the Vegian girls, however, were not so polite. Both had hold of Joe, one by each arm, and stood there spitting insults at each other past his face until a man standing near by snapped a few words at them and flipped a coin. The two girls, each still maintaining her grip, leaned over eagerly to see for themselves the result of the toss. The loser promptly relinquished her hold on Joe and the winner danced away with him.

"Oh, this is *wonderful*, Storm!" Joan thought. "We've been *accepted*—we're the first group I ever actually *knew* of to really break through the crust."

The Vegians moved away. Vesta released her captives and turned to her brother.

"Captain Cloud, Doctor Janowick, I present to you my brother Zamke," she said. Then, to her brother: "They have been very good to me, Zambktpkn, both of them, but especially the captain. You know what he did for me."

"Yes, I know." The brother spoke the English "S" with barely a trace of hardness. He shook Cloud's hand firmly, then bent over the hand, spreading it out so that the palm covered his face, and inhaled deeply. Then, straightening up: "For what you have done for my sister, sir, I thank you. As she has said, your scent is pleasing and will be remembered long, enshrined in the Place of Pleasant Odors of our house."

Turning to Joan, and omitting the handshake, he repeated the performance and bowed—and when an adult male Vegian sets out to make a production of bowing, it is a production well worth seeing.

Then, with the suddenest and most complete change of manner either Cloud or Joan had ever seen he said: "Well, now that the formalities have been taken care of, Joan, how about us hopping a couple of skips around the floor?"

Joan was taken slightly aback, but rallied quickly. "Why, I'd love it . . . but not knowing either the steps or the music, I'm afraid I couldn't follow you very well."

"Oh that won't make any. . . ." Zamke began, but Vesta drowned him out.

"Of *course* it won't make any difference, Joan!" she exclaimed. "Just go ahead and dance any way you want to. He'll match your steps—and if he so much as touches one of your slippers with his big, fat feet, I'll choke him to death with his own tail!"

"And I suppose it is irrefutable that you can and will dance with me with equal dexterity, aplomb, and insouciance?" Cloud asked Vesta, quizzically, after Joan and Zamke had glided smoothly out into the throng.

"You zaid it, little chum!" Vesta exclaimed, gleefully. "And I know what all those words mean, too, and if I ztep on either one of *your* feet I'll choke *my* zelf to death with my *own* tail, zo there!"

Snuggling up to him blissfully, Vesta let him lead her into the crowd. She of course was a superb dancer; so much so that she made him think himself a much better dancer than he really was. After a few minutes, when he was beginning to relax, he felt an itchy, tickling touch—something almost impalpable was creeping up his naked back—the fine, soft fur of the extreme tip of Vesta's ubiquitous tail!

He grabbed for it, but, fast as he was, Vesta was faster, and she shrieked with glee as he missed the snatch.

"See here, young lady," he said, with mock sternness, "if you don't keep your tail where it belongs I'm going to wrap it around your lovely neck and tie it into a bow-knot."

Vesta sobered instantly. "Oh . . . do you *really* think I'm lovely, Captain Nealcloud—my neck, I mean?"

"No doubt about it," Cloud declared. "Not only your neck—all of you. You are most certainly one of the most beautiful things I ever saw."

"Oh, thanks . . . I hadn't. . . ." she stared into his eyes for moments, as if trying to decide whether he really meant it or was merely being polite; then, deciding that he did mean it, she closed her eyes, let her head sink down onto his shoulder, and began to purr blissfully; still matching perfectly whatever motions he chose to make.

In a few minutes, however, they heard a partially-stifled shriek and a soprano voice, struggling with laughter, rang out.

"Vesta!"

"Yes, Babs?"

"What do you do about this tail-tickling business? I never had to cope with anything like *that* before!"

"Bite him!" Vesta called back, loudly enough for half the room to hear. "Bite him good and hard, on the end of the tail. If you can't catch the tail, bite his ear. Bite it good."

"*Bite* him? Why, I *couldn't*—not *possibly!*"

"Well, then give him the knee, or clout him a good, solid tunk on the nose. Or better yet; tell him you won't dance with him any more—he'll be good."

"*Now* you tell us what to do about tail-ticklers," Cloud said then. "S'pose I'd take a good bite at *your* ear?"

"I'd bite you right back," said Vesta, gleefully, "and I bet you'd taste just as nice as you smell."

The dance went on, and Cloud finally, by the aid of both Vesta and Zamke, did finally manage to get one dance with Joan. And, as he had known he would, he enjoyed it immensely. So did she.

"Having fun, chum? I never saw you looking so starry-eyed before."

"Oh, brother!" she breathed. "To say that I was never the belle of any ball in my schooldays is the understatement of the century, but here . . . can you imagine it, Storm, *me* actually outshining Barbara Benton and Helen Worthington both at once?"

"Sure I can. I told you. . . ."

"Of course it's probably because their own women are so big that I'm a sort of curiosity," she rushed on, "but whatever the reason, this dance is going down in my memory book in great big letters in the reddest ink I can find!"

"Good for you—hail the conquering heroine!" he applauded. "It'll do you good to have your ego inflated a little. But what do *you* do about this tail-tickling routine?"

"Oh, I grab their tails"—with her sense of perception, she could, of course—"and when they try to wiggle them free I wiggle back at them, like this," she demonstrated, "and we have a perfectly wonderful time."

"Wow! I'll bet you do—and when I get you home, you shameless. . . ."

"Sorry, Storm, my friend," the big Vegian who cut in wasn't sorry at all, and he and Cloud both knew it. "You can dance with Joan any time and we can't. So loosen all clamps, friend. Grab him, Vzelkt!"

Vzelkt grabbed. So, in about a minute, did another Vegian girl; and then after a few more minutes, it was Vesta's turn again. No other girl could dance with him more than once, but Vesta, by some prearranged priority, could have him once every ten minutes.

"Where's your brother, Vesta?" he asked once. "I haven't seen him for an hour."

"Oh, he had to go back to the police station. They're all excited and working all hours. They're chasing Public Enemy Number One—a Tellurian, they think he is, named Fairchild—why?" as Cloud started, involuntarily, in the circle of her arm. "Do you know him?"

"I know *of* him, and that's enough." Then, in thought: "Did you get that, Nordquist?"

"I got it." Cloud was, as the Lensman had said that he would be, under surveillance every second. "Of course, this one may not be Fairchild, since there are three or four other suspects in other places, but from the horrible time we and the Vegians both are having, trying to locate this bird, I'm coming to think he is."

The dance went on until, some hours later, there was an unusual tumult and confusion at the door.

"Oh, the police are calling Vesta—something has happened!" his companion exclaimed. "Let's rush over—oh, hurry!"

Cloud hurried; but, as well as hurrying, he sent his sense of perception on ahead, and meshed his mind imperceptibly with Vesta's as well.

Her mind was a queerly turbid, violently turbulent mixture of emotions: hot with a furiously passionate lust for personal, tooth-and-claw-revenge; at the same time icily cold with the implacable, unswervable resolve of the dedicated, remorseless, and merciless killer.

"Are you sure, beyond all doubt, that this is the garment of my brother's slayer?" Vesta was demanding.

"I am sure," the Vegian policeman replied. "Not only did Zambkptkn hold it pierced by the first and fourth fingers of his left hand—the sign positive, as you know—but an eyewitness verified the scent and furnished descriptions. The slayer was dressed as an Aldebaranian, which accounts for the size of the garment your brother could seize before he died; his four bodyguards as Tellurians, with leather belts and holsters for their blasters."

"QX." Vesta accepted a pair of offered shears and began to cut off tiny pieces of the cloth. As each piece began to fall it was seized in mid-air by a Vegian man or girl who immediately ran away with it. And in the meantime other Vegians, forming into a long line, ran past Vesta, each taking a quick sniff and running on, out into the street. Cloud, reaching outside the building with his perceptors, saw that all vehicular traffic had paused. A Vegian stood on the walkway, holding a bit of cloth pinched between thumb and fingernail. All passersby, on foot or in any kind of vehicle, would pause, sniff at the cloth, and—apparently—go on about their business.

But Cloud, after reading Vesta's mind and the policeman's, turned as white as his space-tan would permit. In less than an hour almost every Vegian in that city of over eight million would know the murderer by scent and would be sniffing eagerly for him; and when any one of them *did* find him. . . .

Except for the two Vegians and the six Tellurians, the vast hall was now empty. Vesta was holding a pose Cloud had never before seen—stiffly erect, with her tail wrapped tightly around her body.

"Can they get a scent—a *reliable* scent, I mean—that fast?" Cloud asked.

"Zertainly," Vesta's voice was cold, level, almost uninflected. "How long would it take you to learn that an egg you started to eat was rotten? The man who wore this shirt is a class A Triple Prime stinker—his odor is recognizable instantly and anywhere."

"But as to the rest of it—*don't* do this thing, Vesta! Let the law handle it."

"The law comes second. He killed my brother; it is my right and my privilege to kill him. . . ."

Cloud became conscious of the fact that Joan was in his mind. "You been here all along?" he flashed.

"In or near. You and I are one, you know," and Vesta's voice went on:

". . . and besides, the law is merciful. Its death is instant. Under my claws and teeth he will live for hours—for a full day, I hope."

"But officer, can't *you* do something?"

"Nothing. The law comes second. As she has said, it is her right and her privilege."

"But it's suicide, man—sheer *suicide*. You know that, don't you?"

"Not necessarily. She will not be working alone. Whether she lives or dies, however, it is still her right and her privilege."

Cloud switched to thought. "Nordquist, *you* can stop this if you want to. *Do* it."

"I can't, and you know I can't. The Patrol does not and cannot interfere in purely planetary affairs."

"You intend, then," Cloud demanded furiously, "to let this girl put her naked hands and teeth up against four trigger-happy gunnies with DeLameters?"

"Just that. There's nothing else I or any other Patrolman can do. To interfere in this one instance would alienate half the planets of Civilization and set the Patrol back five hundred years."

"Well, even though I'm a Patrolman—of sorts—I can do something about it!" Cloud blazed, "and by God, I will!"

"*We* will, you mean, and we *will*, too," Joan's thought came forcibly at first, then became dubious: "That is, if it doesn't mean getting *you* blasted, too."

"Just what?" Nordquist's thought was sharp. "Oh, I see . . . and, being a Vegian, as well as a Patrolman, and the acknowledged friend of both the dead man and his sister. . . ."

"Who's a Vegian?" Cloud demanded.

"You are, and so are the other five of your group, as you would have been informed if the party had not been broken up so violently. Honorary Vegians, for life."

"Why, I never *heard* of such a thing!" Joan exclaimed, "and I studied them for years!"

"No, you never did," Nordquist agreed. "There haven't been many honorary Vegians, and to my certain knowledge, not one of them has ever talked. Vegians are very strongly psychic in picking their off-world friends."

"You mean to tell me that that bleached blonde over there won't spill everything she knows fifteen minutes after we leave here?" Cloud demanded.

"Just that. You can't judge character by hair, even if it were bleached, which it isn't. You owe her an apology, Storm."

"If you say so, I do, and I hereby apologize, but. . . ."

"But to get back to the subject," the Lensman went on, narrowing his thought down so sharply as to exclude Joan. "You can do something. You're the *only* one who can. Such being the case, and since you are no longer indispensable. I withdraw all objections. Go ahead."

Cloud started a thought, but Joan blanked him out. "Lensman, has Storm been sending—*can* he send information to you that *I* can't dig out of his mind?"

"Very easily. He is an exceptionally fine tuner."

"I'm sorry, Joanie," Cloud thought, hastily, "but it sounded too much like bragging to let you in on. However, you're in from now on."

Then, aloud, "Vesta, I'm staying with you," he said, quietly.

"I was sure you would," she said, as quietly. "You are my friend and Zamke's. Although your customs are not exactly like ours, a man of your odor does not desert his friends."

Cloud turned then to the four lieutenants, who stood close-grouped. "Will you four kids please go back to the ship, and take Joan with you?"

"Not on Thursdays, Storm," Joe said, pointing to an inconspicuous bronze button set into a shoulder-strap. "We both rate Blaster Expert First. Count us in," and Bob added:

"Joan has been telling us an earful, and what she didn't tell us a couple of Vegian boys did. The Three Honorary Vegian Musketeers; that's us. Lead on, d'Artagnan!"

"Bob and Joe are staying, too, Vesta," Cloud said then.

"Of course. I'm sorry I didn't get to tell you myself about being adopted, but I knew somebody would. But you, Joan and Barbara and Helen, you three had better go back to the ship. You can be of no use here."

Two of them were willing enough to go, but:

"Where Neal Cloud goes, I go," Joan said, and there was no doubt whatever that she meant exactly that.

"Why?" Vesta demanded. "Commander Cloud, the fastest gunman in all space, is necessary for the success of this our mission. He can, from a cold, bell-tone start, at thirty yards, burn the centers out of six irregularly-spaced targets. . . ."

"Nordquist! Lay off! What in *hell* do you think you're doing?" Cloud thought, viciously.

"I don't think—I *know*," came instant reply. "Do you want her hanging on your left arm when the blasting starts? This is the only *possible* way Joan Janowick can be handled. Lay off yourself!" and Vesta's voice went calmly on:

". . . in exactly two hundred and forty nine mils. Lieutenant Mackay and Lieutenant Ingalls, although perhaps not absolutely necessary, are highly desirable. They are fast enough, and are of deadly accuracy. When either of them shoots a man in a crowd, however large, that one man dies, and not a dozen bystanders. Now just what good would *you* be, Lieutenant-Commander Janowick? Can you fire a blaster with any one of these men? Or bite a man's throat out with me?"

For probably the first time in her life, Joan Janowick stood mute.

"And suppose you *do* come along," Vesta continued relentlessly. "With *you* at his side, in the line of fire, do you suppose. . . ."

"Just a minute—shut up, Vesta!" Cloud ordered, roughly. "Listen, all of you. The Lensman is doing this, not Vesta, and I'll be damned if I'll let anybody, not even a Lensman, bedevil my Joan this way. So, Joan, wherever we go, you can come along. All I ask is, you'll keep a little ways back?"

"Of course I will, Storm," and Joan crept into the shelter of his arm.

"Ha—I thought you'd pop off at about this point," Nordquist's thought came chattily into Cloud's mind. "Good work, my boy; you've consolidated your position no end."

"Well, what do we do now?" Joe Mackay broke the somewhat sticky silence that followed.

"We wait," Vesta said, calmly. "We wait right here until we receive news."

They waited; and, as they waited the tension mounted and mounted. Before it became intolerable, however, the news came in, and Cloud, reading Vesta's mind as the ultra-sonic information was received, relayed it to other Tellurians. The murderer and his four bodyguards were at that moment entering a theater less than one city block away. . . .

"Why, they *couldn't* be!" Helen protested. "*Nobody* could be *that* stupid . . . or . . . I wonder. . . ?"

"I wonder, too." This from Joan. "Yes, it would be the supremely clever thing to do; the perfect place to hide for a few hours while the worst of the storm blows over and they can complete their planned getaway. Provided, of course, they're out-worlders and thus don't know what we Vegians can do with our wonderful sense of smell. Of course they aren't a Tellurian and four Aldebaranians any more, are they?"

"No, they are five Centralians now. Perfectly innocent. They think their blasters are completely hidden under those long over shirts, but now and again a bulge shows—they've still got blasters on their hips. The theater's crowded, but the five friends want to sit together. The manager thinks it could be arranged, by paying a small gratuity to a few seat-holders who would like to make a fast credit that way . . . he'll place them and it's almost time for us to go. 'Bye, Joanie—stay back, remember!" and she was in his arms.

"How about it, Helen?" Joe asked. "Surely you're going to kiss your Porthos good-bye, aren't you?"

"Of a surety, m'enfant!" she exclaimed, and did so with enthusiasm. "But it's more like Aramis, I think—he kissed everybody, you know—and since I'm not hooked like Joan is—yet—don't think that this is establishing a precedent."

"Well, Babs, that leaves you and me." Bob reached out—she was standing beside him—and pulled her close. "QX?"

"Why, I . . . I guess so." Barbara blushed furiously. "But Bob . . . is it really *dangerous?*" she whispered.

"I don't know. Not very, really, I don't think. At least I certainly *hope* not. But blasters are *not* cap-pistols, you know, and whenever one goes off it can raise pure hell. Why? Would you really miss me?"

"You *know* I would, Bob," and her kiss had more fervor than either she or he would have believed possible a few minutes before. And at its end she laughed, shakily, and blushed again as she said, "I've got sort of used to having you around, so be *sure* and come back."

They left the building and walked rapidly along a strangely quiet street to the theater. Without a word they were ushered up a short flight of stairs.

"Hold up, Vesta!" Cloud thought sharply. "We can't see a thing—wait a couple of minutes."

They waited five minutes, during which time they learned exactly where the enemy were and discussed every detail of the proposed attack.

"I *still* can't see well enough to shoot," Cloud said then. "Can they give us a little glow of light?"

They could. By almost imperceptible increments the thick, soft blackness was relieved.

"That's enough." The light, such as it was, steadied.

"Ready?" Vesta's voice was a savage growl, low, deep in her throat.

"Ready."

"No more noise, then."

They walked forward to the balcony's edge, leaned over it, looked down. Directly beneath Vesta's head was seated a man in Centralian garb; four others were behind, in front of, and at each side of, their chief.

"Now!" Vesta yelled, and flung herself over the low railing.

At her shout four Vegians ripped four Centralian shirts apart, seized four hip-holstered blasters, and shouted with glee—but they shouted too soon. For the real gun-slick, then as now, did not work from the hip, but out of his sleeve; and these were four of the coldest, fastest killers to be found throughout the far flung empire of Boskone. Thus, all four flashed into action even before they began rising to their feet.

But so did Storm Cloud; and his heavy weapon was already out and ready. He knew what those hands were doing, in the instant of their starting to do it, and his DeLameter flamed three times in what was practically one very short blast. He had to move a little before he could sight on the fourth guard—Vesta's furiously active body was in the way—so Joe and Bob each got a shot, too. Three bolts of lightning hit that luckless wight at once, literally cremating him in air as he half-crouched, bringing his blaster to bear on the catapulting thing attacking his boss.

When Vesta went over the rail she did not jump to the floor below. Instead, her hands locked on the edge; her feet dug into the latticework of the apron. She squatted. Her tail flashed down, wrapping itself twice around the zwilnik's neck. She heaved, then, and climbed with everything she had; and as she stood upright on the railing, eager hands reached down to help her tail lift its burden up into the balcony. The man struck the floor with a thud and Vesta jumped at him.

"Your fingers first—one at a time," she snarled; and, seizing a hand, she brought it toward her mouth.

She paused then as if thunderstruck; a dazed, incredulous expression spreading over her face. Bending over, she felt, curiously, tenderly, of his neck.

"Why, he . . . he's *dead!*" she gasped. "His neck . . . it's . . . it's *broken!* From such a little, tiny pull as *that?* Why, *anybody* ought to have a stronger neck than *that!*"

She straightened up; then, as a crowd of Vegians and the Tellurian women came up, she became instantly her old, gay self. "Well, shall we all go back and finish our dance?"

"What?" Cloud demanded. "After *this?*"

"Why certainly," Vesta said, brightly. "I'm sorry, of course, that I killed him so quickly, but it doesn't make any real difference. Zamke is avenged; he can now enjoy himself. We'll join him in a few years, more or less. Until then, what would you do? What you call 'mourn'?"

"I don't know . . . I simply don't know," Cloud said, slowly, his arm tightening around Joan's supple waist. "I thought I'd seen everything, but . . . I suppose you can have somebody take that body out to the ship, so they can check it for identity?"

"Oh, yes, I'll do that. Right away. You're sure you don't want to dance any more?"

"Very sure, my dear. *Very* sure. All *I* want to do is take Joan back to the ship."

"QX. I won't see you again this trip, then; your hours are so funny. I'll send for my things. And I won't say good-bye, Captain Nealcloud and you other wonderful people, because we'll see each other again, soon and often. Just so-long, and thanks tremendously for all you have done for me."

And Vesta the Vegian strode away, purring contentedly to herself—tail high.

THE CALL

THE LENSMEN and their Patrolmen, having made sure that the body of Zamke's murderer was in fact that of the long-sought Fairchild, went unostentatiously about their various businesses.

The six Tellurians, although shaken no little by their climactic experience on Vegia, returned soon to normal and resumed their accustomed routines of life—with certain outstanding variations. Thus, Helen and Joe flirted joyously and sparred dextrously, but neither was ever to be found tête-à-tête with anyone else. And thus, Bob and Barbara, neither flirting nor sparring, became quietly but enthusiastically inseparable. And thus, between Joan and Cloud, so close even before Vegia, the bonding became so tight that their two minds were, to all intents and purposes, one mind.

The week on Vegia was over. The *Vortex Blaster II* was loafing through the void at idling speed. Cloud was pacing the floor in his office. Joan, lounging in a deeply-cushioned chair with legs stuck out at an angle of forty-five degrees to each other, was smoking a cigarette and watching him, with her eyes agleam.

"Confound it, I wish they'd hurry up with that fine-tooth," he said, flipping his half-smoked cigarette at a receptacle and paying no attention to the fact that he missed it by over a foot. "How can I tell Captain Ross where to go when I don't know myself?"

"That's one thing I just *love* about you, my pet," Joan drawled. "You're so wonderfully, so superhumanly *patient*. You know as well as I do that the absolutely irreducible minimum of time is twenty-six minutes from now, and that they'll probably find something they'll want to study for a minute or so after they get there. So light somewhere, why don't you, and unseethe yourself?"

"Touché, Joan." He sat down with a thump. "Has Doctor Janowick a prescription specific for the ailment?"

"Nothing else but, chum. That tight-linkage snooping that we've been going to try, but never had time for. Let's start on Helen and Barbara. I've snooped them repeatedly, of course, but our fusion of minds, theoretically, should be able to pick their minds apart cell by cell; to tap their subconscious ancestral memories, even—if there are such things—for a thousand generations back."

He looked at her curiously. "You know, I think you must have some ghoul blood in you somewhere? I tell you again, those girls are *friends* of ours!"

"So what?" she grinned at him, entirely unabashed. "You'll have to get rid of that squeamishness some day; it's the biggest roadblock there is on the Way of Knowledge. If not them, how would Nadine suit you?"

"Worse yet. She's just as good at this business as we are, maybe better, and she probably wouldn't like it."

"You may have something there. We'll save her for last, and call on her formally, with announcements and everything. Vesta, then?"

"*Now* you're squeaking, little mouse. But no deep digging for a while. We'll take it easy and light—we don't want to do any damage we may not be able to undo. As I told you before, my brain is firing on altogether too damn many barrels that I simply don't know what are doing. Let's go."

They fused their minds—an effortless process now—and were at their objective instantaneously.

Vesta was primping; enjoying sensuously the physical feel of her physical body even as dozens of parts of speech of dozens of different languages went through her racing mind. And, one layer down, she was wishing she were old enough to be a newlywed; wishing she had a baby of her own . . . babies were so cute and soft and cuddlesome. . . .

Then Tommie. Cloud and Joan enjoyed with her the strong, rank, sense-satisfying flavor of a Venerian cigar and studied with her the intricate electronic equations of a proposed modification of the standard deep space drive. And, one layer down, the Tomingan engineer, too, was thinking of love and of babies. What was all this space hopping getting her, anyway? It didn't stop the ache, fill the void, satisfy the longing. As soon as this cruise was over, she was going back to Tominga, tell Hanko she was ready, and settle down. A husband and a family did tie a woman down something fierce—but what price freedom to wander when you wake up in the middle of the night from dreaming of a baby in your arms, only to find the baby isn't there?

Then Thlaskan and Maluleme. They were seated, arms around each other, on a davenport in their own home on Chickladoria. They were not talking, merely feeling. They were deeply, truly, tremendously in love. In the man's mind there was a background of his work, of pilotry, of orbits and charts and computations. There was a flash of sincere liking for Cloud, the best boss and the finest figure-man he had ever known; but practically all of his mind was full of love for the wonderful woman at his side. In hers, at the moment, there were only two things; love of her husband and longing for the child which she might already have succeeded in conceiving. . . .

Cloud wrenched their linked minds away.

"This is monstrous, Joan!"

"What's monstrous about it?" she asked, quietly. "Nothing. It isn't. Women *need* children, Storm. All women, everywhere. Now that I've found *you*, I can scarcely wait to have some myself. And listen, Storm, please. Before we visit Nadine, you *must* make up your mind to face facts—*any* kind of facts—without flinching and shying away and getting mental goose-bumps all over your psyche."

"I see what you mean. In a fully telepathic race there couldn't be any real privacy without a continuous block, and that probably wouldn't be very feasible."

"No, you *don't* see what I mean. You aren't even on the right road—your whole *concept* is wrong. There couldn't be any *thought*, even of privacy, no *conception* of such a thing. *Think* a minute! From birth—from the very birth of the whole race—full and open meetings of minds must have been the norm of thought. That kind of thing is—must be—what Nadine is accustomed to at home."

"Hm . . . I never thought . . . you go see her, Joan, and I'll stay home."

"What good would *that* do? Whatever you may be, my dear, I know darn well you're *not* stupid."

"Not exactly stupid, maybe, but I haven't thought this thing through the way you have . . . of course, if she's half as good as we know she is, she's read us both already, clear down to the footings of our foundations . . . but this thing of a *full* meeting of minds with anybody but you. . . ."

"You haven't a thing to hide, you know. At least, *I* know, whether you do or not."

"No? How do you figure that? Maybe *you* think so, but . . . I've tried, of course, but I've failed a lot oftener than I succeeded."

"Who hasn't? You're not unique, my dear. Shall we go?"

"We might as well, I guess . . . I'm as ready as I ever will be. . . . I'll try, but. . . ."

"Please do, Master," came Nadine's quiet, composed thought, in a vein completely foreign to her usual attitude of self-sufficient aloofness. "I have been observing; studying with awe and with wonder. If you will so deign, revered Master, come fully into my mind."

"Deign?" Cloud demanded. "What kind of a thought is that, Nadine, from you to me?"

"Deign." Nadine repeated, firmly. Deeply moved, she was feeling and sending a solemnity of respect Cloud had never before experienced. "My powers are ordinary, since I am of Type One. The two greatest Masters of Manarka are Fives, and have been the greatest Masters of the past. This is the first time I have ever encountered a mind of a type higher than Five. Come in, sir, I plead."

Cloud went in, and his first flash of comparison was that it was like diving into the pellucid depths of a clean, cool, utterly transparent mountain lake. This mind was *so* different from Joan's! Joan's was rich, warmly sympathetic, tender and emphatic, yet it was full of dark corners, secret nooks, recesses, and automatic blocks. . . . Huh? He had thought her mind as open as a book, but it wasn't. . . . On the other hand, Nadine's was wide open by nature. It was cool, poised—although at the moment uncomfortably worshipful—and utterly, *shockingly* open!

His second thought was that Joan was no longer with him. She was there, in a sense, but *outside*, some way; she wasn't in Nadine's mind the way he was.

"I'll say I'm not!" Joan agreed, fervently. "Thank God! I don't know what you did or how you did it, but when you went in you peeled me off like the skin of a banana, and I was clinging like a leech, too. I'm on the outside, looking in. Did you see how he did it, Nadine?"

"No, but since I am only a One, such insight would not be expected. I have called the Fives, and they come."

"We are here." Two close-linked minds linked themselves with the two already so closely linked. Each of the two visitors was grave, kindly, and old with an appalling weight of years; each mind bore an appalling freight of knowledge both mundane and esoteric. "We are here, fellow Master of Thought, to be of aid to you in the clarification of your newly-awakened mind, to the end that, in a future time, your superior powers will assist us along Paths of Truth which we could not otherwise traverse."

"Will you please tell me what this is all about?" Cloud asked. "Starting at the beginning and using words of as few syllables as possible?"

"Gladly. It has been known for some time that Janowick is Type Three. Self-developed, partially-developed, under-developed, struggling against she knew not what, but still a Three. Now Threes as such, while eminently noteworthy, are by no means phenomenal. There are some hundreds of Threes now alive. Being noteworthy, she has been watched. In time she would have completed her development and would have taken her rightful place in the School of Thought.

"You, however, have been a complete enigma to our most penetrant minds. Since no mind of lower type than Three can be an instantaneous calculator, it was clear that you were, basically, at least a Three. However, unlike other Threes, you did nothing whatever to develop the latent, potential abilities of whatever type you might be. Instead and excepting only the small and unimportant item of computation, you used the tremendous powers of your mind, not for any constructive purpose whatever, but only for the application of such rigid controls and suppressions that all the tremendous abilities you should have shown remained completely dormant and inert.

"Nor could we do anything about it. We tried, but you have blocks that not even the full power of two linked Fives can crack; which fact showed that you are of a type higher than Five. We were about to come to you in person, to plead with you, when you met Three Janowick and opened to her your hitherto impregnably-sealed inner mind. She does not know, and you do not know, what you jointly did; which was, in effect, to break and to dissolve the bindings which had been shackling both your minds. That brings us to the present. It has now become clear that you have been Called."

"Called?" Cloud winced, physically and mentally. No man likes to be reminded that he failed Lensman's Exam. "You're wrong. I didn't make even the first round."

"We did not mean the Call of the Lens. There are many Calls, of which that is only one. Nor is it the highest, as we have just discovered, in certain little-known aspects of that vast thing we call the mind. For, to the best of our knowledge, no Lensman of the present or of the past is or was of a type higher than Five. The exact nature of your Call is as yet obscure."

"I'd like to buy that, but I'm afraid it's. . . ." Cloud paused. Until he'd met Joan, he'd supposed his mind ordinary enough. Since then, however . . . all those extra barrels. . . .

"Exactly. We are specialists of the mind, young man. We perceive your mind, not as it is, but as it should be and will be. It should have and will have a penetrance, a range, a flexibility of directive force, and, above all, a scope of heights and depths we have never encountered before. It is eminently clear that you, and, very probably, Three Janowick as well, have been developed each for some specific Purpose in the Great Scheme of Things."

"A *Purpose?*" Cloud demanded. "*What* purpose? What could *I* do? What could both of us together do?"

"We can not surely know."

"Does that mean that you can make a well-informed guess? If so, let's have it."

"There is a very high probability that Three Janowick was developed specifically to develop you; to pierce and to dissolve those hampering barriers which were amenable to no other force. Concerning you, there are several possibilities, none of which have any very high degree of probability, since you are unique. The one we prefer at the moment is that you are to become the greatest living Master of Thought; the Prime Expounder of the Truth. But that is of no importance now, since in due time it will be revealed. Of present import is the fact that both your minds are confused, cloudy, and disorderly. We offer our services in reorienting and ordering them."

"We'd like that very much; but first, if I am going to develop into a mental giant of some kind—frankly, I have my doubts—why did it wait this long to show up?"

"The answer to that question is plain and simple. There is a time for everything, and everything that happens does so in its exact time. Let us to work."

They worked, and when it was done:

"We would like to dwell with you for long," the ancient Fives said, "but the time for such a boon will not come until you are much emptier of cares and much fuller of years."

The Fives split apart. "How do you type this new Master, brother? A full Six, I say."

"A full Six he is, brother, beyond doubt."

They fused. "In a time to come, Six Cloud, we will, with your help and under your guidance, explore many and many a Path of Truth which without you would remain closed. But we observe that there is about to arrive a message which is to you of some present concern. Until a day, then."

1169

The Fives disappeared as suddenly as they had come, and Cloud began to test and to exercise the new capabilities of his mind; in much the same fashion as that in which a good belly-dancer exercises and trains each individual muscle of her torso.

"But what. . . . I didn't. . . . How did they. . . ?" Joan shook her head violently and started all over again. "What did they *do* to us, Storm?"

"I don't know. It was over my head like a lunar dome. But it—whatever it was—was exactly what the doctor ordered. I can handle all those extra barrels now like van Buskirk handles a space-axe. How about you?"

"Me, too—I think." She hugged his arm. "It shocked me speechless for a minute, but it's all settling into place fast. . . . But that message? They could get it from your mind that you expected that fine-tooth pretty soon, but how could they know it's coming in right now? We don't—in fact, we know it *can't* get here for a good ten minutes yet."

"I wish I knew. I'd like to think they were bluffing, but I know they weren't."

"Hi Storm and Joan!" Philip Strong's face appeared upon a screen, his voice came from a speaker. "The Survey ship has just reported. Technical dope is still coming in. Communications is buzzing you a tape of the whole thing, but to save time I thought I'd call you and give you the gist. To make it short and unsweet, there's nothing there."

"*Nothing there!*"

"Nothing for you. They gave it the works, and all there is to that system, Cahuita, they call it, is one red dwarf with one red microdwarf circling it planetwise."

"Huh?" Cloud demanded. "Come again, chief."

"How could a micro-sun like that exist?" Strong laughed. "That had me bothered, too, but they've got a lot of cosmological double-talk to cover it. It's terrifically radioactive, they say. And even so, it's temporary. In the cosmological sense, that is; a hundred million years or so either way don't matter."

"No solid planets at all? Not even one?"

"Not one. Nothing really liquid, even. Incandescent, very highly radioactive gas. Nothing solid bigger than your thumb within twelve parsecs."

"And so it never has been solid, and won't be for millions of years. . . . Oh, *Damn!* Well, thanks, chief, a lot."

Then, as the Lensman signed off: "Joan, that puts us deeper in the dark than ever. We had twice too many unknowns and only half enough knowns before, and this really tears it. Well, it was a very nice theory while it lasted."

"It's *still* a very nice theory, Storm."

"Huh? How do you figure that?"

"I don't have to figure it. Listen! First, that point is significant, with a probability greater than point nine nine nine. Second, no other point in space has a probability as great as point zero zero one. Whoever or whatever was—is—there, the Survey ship missed. We've got to go there ourselves, Storm. We simply *must.*"

" 'Was' is probably right. Whatever used to be there is gone . . . but that doesn't make sense, either . . . that planet has *never* been solid, Joan. . . ." Cloud got up and began to pace the floor. "Dammit, Joan, *nothing* can live on a planet like that."

"Life as we know it, no."

"What do you mean by that?"

"Only that I am trying to keep an open mind. We simply haven't enough data."

"Do you think you and I have got jets enough to find data that the Patrol's best experts missed?"

"I don't know. All I am sure of, Doctor Neal Cloud, is this: If we *don't* go, we'll both wish we had, to the day we die."

"You're probably right . . . but I haven't got a glimmering of an idea as to what we're going to look for."

"I don't know whether I have or not, but we've simply *got* to go. Even if we don't find anything, we will at least have tried. Besides, your most pressing work is done, so you can take the time . . . and besides that . . . well, something those Fives said is bothering me terribly . . . the Purpose, you know . . . do you think. . . ?"

"That my Purpose in Life is to go solve the mystery of the Red Dwarf and its Enigmatic Microcompanion?" he gibed. "Hardly. Furthermore, the coincidence of the Fives getting here just one jump ahead of the fine-tooth is much—*very* much—too coincidental."

Joan caught her breath and, if possible, paled whiter than before. "You may *think* you're joking, Storm, but you aren't. Believe me, you aren't. That's one of the things that are scaring me witless. You see, if I learned anything at all in my quite-a-few years of semantics, philosophy, and logic, it was that coincidence has no more reality than paradox has. Both are completely meaningless terms. Neither does or can exist."

Cloud paled, then. "You believe that *is* my purpose in life?" he demanded.

"Now it's you who are extrapolating." Joan laughed, albeit shakily. "To quote you, 'I merely stated a fact,' et cetera."

"Facts hurt, when they hit as hard as that one did." Cloud paced about, immersed in thought, for minutes.

"I can't find any point of attack," he said, finally. "No foothold. No finger-hold, even. But what you just said rocked me to the foundations . . . you said, a while back, that you believe in God."

"I do. So do you, Storm."

"Yes . . . after a fashion . . . yes, I do. . . . Well, anyway, now I know what to tell Ross."

He called the captain and issued instructions. The *Vortex Blaster II* darted away at full touring blast.

"Now what?" Cloud asked.

"We practise."

"Practise what?"

"How should I know? Everything, I guess. Oh, no, the Fives emphasized 'scope,' whatever that means. 'Scope in heights and depths.' Does that ring any bells?"

"Not loud ones, if any. All it suggests to me is spectra of some kind or other."

"It could, at that." Joan caught her lower lip between her teeth. "But before we start playing scales, let's see if we can deduce anything helpful—examine our points of contact and so on. What have we got to go on?"

"We have one significant point in space. That's all."

"Oh no, it isn't. You're forgetting one other highly significant fact. The data fitted the growth-of-population curve *exactly*, remember."

"You mean to say you *still* think the things *breed?*"

"I can't get away from it, and it isn't because I'm a woman and obsessed with offspring, either. How else *could* your data fit that curve, and what else fits it so exactly?"

Cloud frowned in concentration, but made no reply. Joan went on: "Assume, as a working hypothesis, that the vortices are concerned, in that exact relationship, with the increase in some kind of life. Since the fewer assumptions we make, the better, we don't care at the moment what kind of life it is or whether it's intelligent or not. To fit the curve, just what would the vortices have to be? Not houses, certainly . . . nor bedrooms . . . nor eggs, since they don't hatch and the very oldest ones are still there, or would have been, except for you. . . . I'm about out of ideas. How about you?"

"Maybe. My best guess would be incubators . . . and one-shot incubators at that. But with this new angle of approach I've got to re-evaluate the data and see what it means now."

He went over to the work-table, studied charts and diagrams briefly, then thumbed rapidly through a book of tables. He whistled raucously through his teeth. "This gets screwier by the minute, but it still checks. Every vortex represents *twins*. Never singles or triplets, *always* twins. And the cycle is so long that the full span of our data isn't enough to even validate a wild guess at it. Now, Joan, you baby expert, just what kind of an infant would be just comfortably warm and cosy in the middle of a loose atomic vortex? Feed *that* one to Margie, chum, and let's see what she does with it."

"I don't have to; I can work it in my own little head. An exceedingly complex, exceedingly long-lived, exceedingly slow-growing baby of pure force. What else?"

"Ugh! And Ugh! again. That's twice you've slugged me right in the solar plexus." Cloud began again to pace the floor. "Up to now, I was just having fun. . . . I'm mighty glad we don't have to let anybody else in on this, the psychs would be on our tails in nothing flat . . . and the conclusion would be completely justifiable and we've both blown our stacks. . . . I've been trying to find holes in your theory . . . still am . . . but I can't even *kick* a hole in it. . . .

"When one theory, and only one, fits much observational data and does not conflict with any, nor with any known or proven law or fact," he said finally, aloud, "that theory, however bizarre, *must* be explored. The only thing is, just how are we going to explore it?"

"That's what we have to work out."

"Just like that, eh? But before we start, tell me the rest of it—that stuff you've been keeping behind a solid block down there in the south-east corner of your mind."

"QX. I was afraid to, before, but now that you're getting sold on the basic idea, I'll tell all. First, the planet. There are two possibilities about that. It could have been cold a long time ago and this race of—of beings, entities, call them whatever you please—with their peculiar processes of metabolism, or habits of life, or something, could have liquefied it and then volatilized it. Or perhaps it started out hot and the activities of this postulated race have kept it from cooling; perhaps made it get hotter and hotter. Either hypothesis is sufficient.

"Second, the Patrol couldn't find anything because it wasn't looking for the right category of objects; and besides, it didn't have the right equipment to find these particular objects even if it had known what to look for.

"Third, assuming that these beings once lived on that planet, or on or in its sun, perhaps, they simply *must* live there yet. Creatures of that type, with such a tremendously long life-span as you have just deduced and as methodical in thought as they must be, would not move away except for some very solid reason, and nothing in our data indicates any significant change in status. Tracking me so far?"

"On track to a micro, every millimeter."

"And you don't think I've got rooms for rent upstairs?"

"If you have, I have too. Now that I'm in, I'm going to follow this thing to its logical conclusion, wherever that may be. You've buttoned up the vortices themselves very nicely, but they were never the main point at issue, Joan. That spherical surface was, and still is. *Why* is it? And why such a terrifically long radius? Those have always been the stickers and they still are. If your theory can't explain them, and it hasn't, so far, it fails."

"I think you're wrong, Storm. I don't think they'll turn out to be important at all. They don't *conflict* with the theory in any way, you know, and as we get more data I'm pretty sure everything will fit. It fits too beautifully so far to fail the last test. Besides. . . ." her thought died away.

"Besides what? Unblock, chum. Give."

"I think those things fit in, already. You see, entities of pure energy can't be expected to think the way we do. When we meet them—if we can understand them at all—that surface, radius and all, will undoubtedly prove to be completely in accord with their mode of thought; system of logic; their semantics; or whatever they have along those lines."

"Could be." Cloud's attitude changed sharply. "You've settled one moot point. They're intelligent."

"Why, yes . . . of course they are! It's funny I didn't think of that myself. And you're really sold, Storm."

"I really am. Up to now I've just been receptive; but now I really believe the whole cockeyed theory. I suppose you've figured out an angle of approach?"

"You flatter me. I'm not that good. But perhaps . . . in a very broad and general way. . . . Heights and depths, remember? And superhuman scope therein or thereat? But *we* don't do it, Storm. *You* do."

"Uh-uh. Nix. You and I are one. Let's go!"

"I'll come along as far as I can, of course, but something tells me it won't be very far. Lead on, Six Cloud!"

"Where'll we start?"

"Now we're right back where we were before. Do you still favor spectra? Of vibration, say, for a start?"

"Nothing else but. So let's slide ourselves up and down the frequencies, seeing what we can see, hear, feel, or sense, and what we can do about 'em."

THE LENSMAN

CAHUITA

ON THE PLANET CAHUITA, unreckonable years before this story opens, an entity brooded.

This entity, Medury by symbol, was not even vaguely man-like; in fact, he—the third person singular pronoun, masculine, is used very loosely indeed; but since it is somewhat better than either "it" or "she" it will have to do—was not even vaguely corporeal or substantial.

Man's earliest ancestor, it is believed, came into being through the interaction of energy and matter in the waters of the infant seas of Earth. The first Cahuitans, however, originated in the unimaginably violent, raw, crude energy-flare of an atomic explosion.

This explosion did not take place on Tellus, nor in any time known to Tellurian history. The place of occurrence was a planet in the spiral arm of the galaxy across the tremendous gulf of empty space which we now call Rift Two Hundred Forty; the time, as has been said, was in the unthinkably remote past.

Cahuitans are not, strictly speaking, immortal; but as far as mankind is concerned, and except for exceedingly peculiar violences, they might as well be.

Medury brooded. His problem was old; it had probably been considered, academically, by every Cahuitan then alive. But only academically, and no Cahuitan had ever solved it, for the philosophy of the race had always been (and still is) the simple one of least action—no Cahuitan ever did any job until it became necessary; but, conversely, once any job was done it was done as nearly as possible for all time to come.

Medury was the first Cahuitan to be compelled, by one of the basic urges of life, to deal with the problem as a concrete, not an abstract, thing. The problem was, therefore, his. His alone.

His world, the only planet of its sun, was old, old. The last atoms of its fissionables had been fissioned; the last atoms of its fusibles had been fused; no more fires could be kindled.

The Cahuitans in general did not care. For the adolescents, the time of need for a source of high-level quanta had not yet come. For those already fulfilled$^{\triangle}$ it had passed. While entirely gaseous, the planet would stay comfortably warm for a long time. Its energies, with the outpourings of its parent sun, would feed billions of people instead of the mere hundreds of thousands comprising its present population. Jobs$^{\triangle}$, businesses$^{\triangle}$, commerce$^{\triangle}$, and industry$^{\triangle}$ went on as usual, unaffected.

But Medury was affected: basically, fundamentally affected. The time had come when he should progress into completion, and without a new fire the Change was impossible.

For a time which to a human race would have been fantastically long Medury brooded, considering every aspect of the problem; then stirred himself to action. Converting a tiny portion of his non-material being into three filaments of energy, he constructed a working platform by attaching the ends of these three filaments to the cores of three widely-separated suns. Thus assured of orientation, he launched into space a probing needle of pure force; a needle which, propagated in and through the sub-ether, covered parsecs of distances in microseconds of time. And thus for days, years, what might have been centuries and millennia as we of Tellus know time he searched; and finally, he found.

Pulling in all his extensions, he shot a tight beam to a fellow-being, Litosa by symbol, and tuned his mind precisely to hers. ("Hers" being perhaps a trifle better than either "his" or "its".)

"For some little time you too have felt the need of fulfillment," he informed his proposed complement in level, passionless thought. "You and I match well; there being no duplications, no incompatibles, no antagonistics in our twelve basics. Our fulfillment, Medosalitury, and our products, Midora and Letusy, would all three be super-primes."

"Yes." What a freight of rebellion against fate was carried by that monosyllable! "But why discuss it? Why reach for the unattainable? From now on we die—we *all* die—unfulfilled and without product. All life in this universe—in this galaxy, at least—ends with us now here."

"I hope not. I think not. There are many solar systems. . . ."

"To what end?" Litosa broke in, her thought a sneer. "Can you kindle utterly frigid fuel? Can you work in a sun's core? Or can you, perhaps, take a piece of star-core stuff through empty space to a cold planet and. . . ." The thought changed in tone, became what would have been on Earth a schoolgirl's squeal of rapture:

"You CAN! Or you wouldn't have brought up such a harrowing subject. You REALLY CAN!"

"Not that, exactly, but something just as good. I found sparks and kindling on a cold, solid planet."

"NO!" The thought was ecstasy. "You DIDN'T!"

"I did. Whenever you're ready, we'll go."

"I've been ready for CYCLES!"

The two beings linked themselves together in some fashion unknowable to man and shot away through the airless, heatless void. Heatless, but by no means devoid of energy; the travelers could draw sustenance enough for their ordinary needs from the cosmic radiation pervading all space.

Across Rift Two Hundred Forty they flew and on through interstellar space. They reached our solar system. On the third planet, our Earth, they found several atomic power plants. There were no loose atomic vortices—then.

"Hold on! Wait!" Litosa exclaimed, and the strangely-linked pair stopped just short of the glowing bit of warmth—the ragingly incandescent, furiously radiating reactor in the heart of one of Earth's largest generating stations—which was its goal. "There's something funny about this. How could there possibly be even one little spark like this, to say nothing of so many, on such an utterly frigid planet, unless some intelligent being started it and is maintaining it for some purpose? There MUST be intelligence on this planet and we must be intruding shamefully. Have you scanned? Scanned. CAREFULLY?"

"I have scanned. Carefully, completely. Not only on this planet's surface, but throughout its depths. I have scanned, area by area and volume by volume, this sun and its every planet, satellite, and asteroid. There is no intelligence here. More, there is no sign whatever of any kind of life, however rudimentary, latent, or nascent. I have been able to find nothing whatever to modify our conclusion of long and long ago that we are the only life, intelligent or otherwise, in existence. Scan for yourself."

Litosa scanned. She scanned the sun, the planets, the moons and moonlets, the asteroids down to grains of sand and particles of dust. Still unsatisfied, she scanned all neighboring solar systems, from Centralia to Salvador. Then, and only then, did she accept Medury's almost unacceptable conclusion that these providential sparks were in fact accidental and were in fact, by some process as yet unknown to Cahuitan science, self-balancing and self-sustaining.

Medury and Litosa, woven into a fantastically intricate and complex sphere of ultra-microscopic filaments, flashed into the heart of the reactor, which thereupon went instantaneously and enthusiastically out of control.

And from the pleasant warmth of the incubator-womb—to us of Earth the ravening fury of the first loose atomic vortex—there emerged the fulfillment Medosalitury. This entity, grave and complete and serene as an adult Cahuitan should be, wafted itself (there is no question as to which pronoun is to be used here) sedately back to its home planet.

And in the pleasant warmth of that same incubator-womb the two products, Midora and Letusy, began very slowly to gestate.

*   *   *   *   *

Joan and Storm, minds in fusion, set out to regions never before explored by man. Downward first. One cycle per second. One per minute. One per hour; per day; per year; per century. . . .

"Hold everything, Storm! You're getting out beyond my depth. Anyway, what *use* are they in what we're after?"

"None at all, that I can see; but it's *new knowledge*. Nobody ever dreamed—correction, please: nobody ever published—anything about it, or I'd've heard of it. Maybe the Fives know all about it, though; I'll check with them, first chance I get. QX, we'll jump up to the radio band."

"There wouldn't be any radio waves out here, and you couldn't understand the language if there were."

"How do you know? We'll go where there are some and find out. Maybe we can understand *any* kind of language now—maybe that's one of the natural abilities of a Type Three-Six fusion. Who knows?"

In an instant they were receiving a short-wave broadcast at the Heaviside Layer of a distant planet. They could receive it, could de-louse it, could separate signal from carrier wave, could read the information; but they could not understand it.

"Well, *that's* a relief," Joan sighed. "I was getting more than half afraid that a Type Six mind would be omniscient."

"If I'm a Six you needn't worry; there's altogether too much to know. Where do you want to go from here?"

"Let's look at the infra-red and the ultra-violet. I've often wondered what colors they would be."

The fusion looked, and saw things that made both participants gasp. That is, they did not really *see*, either. None of the six ordinary senses—of perception, sight, hearing, taste,

1176

smell, or touch—were involved. Or rather, perhaps, all of them were involved, or merged with or into some other, brand-new sense possessed only by high-type minds in full action.

"As a semanticist, Joan, can you write a paper on that? That would make any kind of sense, I mean?"

"I'll say I can't," Joan breathed. "*Especially* as a semanticist, I can't. No words, no symbology, in any language. But weren't they *beautiful*, Storm? And wonderful, and . . . and awful?"

"All of that. I'd like to write it up, or make a tri-di of it . . . or something . . . but of course we can't. What next? Shall we flirt a bit with the cosmics and ultras, or had we better jump right into the channels of thought?"

"Thought, by all means; the more practise we get, the better, and they'd be on a terrifically high band, don't you think?"

"Bound to be. The logical conclusion of this whole fantastically cockeyed set-up is that they've simply never even suspected that we exist; any more than we have that they do."

"Would the . . . the bodies, if I can call them that, radiate of themselves, or just thoughts?"

"Not of themselves, I don't think . . . no. An entity of pure energy would have to be held together by forces of magnitudes we can't even guess at; much too intense to permit bodily radiation. Something like the binding energies of particles, I imagine; but different and very probably even more so."

The fusion leaped then to the bands of thought. It sought out and seized the thoughts of various of the ship's personnel; gripping, molding, working, analyzing. Joan and Cloud were not reading minds now, at all; they were studying the fundamental mechanisms of the thoughts themselves. How they were generated; upon what, if anything, they were heterodyned; how they were transmitted; and, above all, exactly how they were received and exactly how they were converted from pure thought, couched at least in part in the symbols of language, into usefully assimilable information.

And, such was the power of that fusion, it succeeded.

Then up and up and up the scale of thought the fused minds went; seeking, finding, mastering. And up and up and up, into regions where no thoughts at all were to be found. And up and up, and up. . . .

"Stop it! Let me go! I'm burning out!" Joan shrieked aloud. "My God, Storm, is there no limit at all to your ceiling?"

Cloud stopped; loosed her mind. "I'm sorry, chick, but I was just getting nicely organized. We've got a long ways to go yet, I'm afraid."

"I'm sorry, too, Storm, sorrier than you'll ever know, but I simply can't take it. Three seconds more of that and I'd've gone stark, raving mad. And when we get to Cahuita I don't know what I'll do. I may blow up completely."

"You may think so, but you won't. You're not the type. And we aren't going to Cahuita—at least, not in the flesh. When we hit that band we'll be there automatically."

"Not quite automatically, of course, but we'll be there, yes. I want to stay with you, more than I ever wanted anything before in my whole life, and I want to help you . . .

couldn't we loosen the fusion just a little, so that I can pull away when the going gets too rough for me? Just enough to keep away from a burnout, but close enough to see and perhaps to help a little?"

"I don't know why not . . . sure, like this." He showed her.

Again the fusion went up and up and up, and this time it did not stop at Joan's ceiling. She pulled away a little, but not enough so that she could not sense and understand, in a way, what was going on.

Cloud, every muscle set and eyes closed tight, sat in a chair, his hands gripping fiercely its arms. Joan lay face down upon a davenport, her face buried in a pillow, her fists tight-clenched.

And the linked minds—linked now, not fused—went up . . . and up . . . and up. . . .

And, finally, they reached the band upon which a Cahuitan fulfillment was thinking.

It would probably be too much to say that the fulfillment was surprised. An adult, fulfilled Cahuitan is so serene, so sedate, so inherently stable at any possible level of stress, that it is probably impossible for it to feel any such sensation or emotion as surprise, even at the instantaneous unveiling of a whole new universe of thought. It was, however, in a calm, passionless, and scholarly way, interested. Not what could be called intensely interested, perhaps, but really interested, nevertheless.

As had been foreseen, the modes of thought of the Cahuitan and the linked Tellurians were different indeed. As has been shown, however, there were some points—the fulfillment could remember the emotions of its component products, even though it could no longer feel them—upon which even such divergent minds as those could find common ground. Also, it must be borne in mind that the Cahuitan was an able and seasoned thinker, trained for many millennia in the art, and that Neal Cloud was a Type Six mind; the only such mind then to be found in all Civilization. Hence, while it would serve no useful purpose here to go into detail as to how it was accomplished, a working understanding was at last attained.

Cloud came to understand, as well as any being of material substance ever could, the beings of pure energy. The Cahuitan learned, and broadcast, that intelligent life could and did exist in intimate association with ultimately frigid matter. While the probability was small that there would ever be any considerable amount of fruitful intercourse between the two kinds of life, some live-and-let-live arrangement should be and would be worked out. There were thousands, yes, millions, of planets absolutely useless to anybody or anything known to man; planets harboring no life of any kind. The Patrol would be glad to set up, on any desired number of these barren planets, as many atomic power plants as the Cahuitans wanted; with controls set either to let go in an hour or to maintain stability for twenty five thousand Galactic Standard years.

The Cahuitans would immediately extinguish all vortices not containing products, and would move all living products to the new planets as soon as the promised incubators were ready.

"*Products* indeed—they're *babies*!" Joan insisted, when Cloud stepped the information down to her level. "And how can they possibly move them?"

"Easily enough," the fulfillment told Cloud. "Blankets of force will retain the warmth necessary for such short trips, provided each new incubator is waiting, warm, and ready."

"I see. But there's one question I want to ask for myself," and Cloud went on to explain about the unbelievably huge sphere that crossed Civilization's vast expanse of space. "What's the *reason* for it?"

"To save time and effort. The product Medury devoted much of both to the evaluation of a sufficiently productive, esthetically satisfying, and mathematically correct construction. It would not be logical to waste time and labor in seeking a variant or an alternate, especially since Medury's work showed, almost conclusively, that his was in fact the most symmetrical construction possible. Now symmetry, to us, is what you might, perhaps, call a ruling passion in one of your own races."

"Symmetry? The first twelve vortices were symmetrical, of course, but from there on—nothing."

"Ah—that is due to the differences between our thinkings; particularly in our mathematical and philosophical thinkings. The circle, the sphere, the square, the cube—all such elementary forms—are common to both but the likenesses are few. The differences are many; so many that it will require several thousands of your Galactic Standard years for certain of my fellows and me to tabulate them and to make whatever may be possible of reconciliation."

"Well . . . thanks. One more question . . . maybe I shouldn't ask it, but . . . this that we have laid out is a wide-reaching and extremely important program. Are you sure that you are able to speak for all the Cahuitans who will be affected?"

"I am sure. Since we are a logical race we all think alike—logically. On the other hand, your race does not seem to me at the moment to be at all a logical one. Can you speak for it?"

"In this matter I can; and you, in my mind, will know that I can," and in this case Cloud could indeed speak for the Patrol. Philip Strong, after one glance in Cloud's mind, would issue the necessary orders himself and would explain later—to anyone capable of accepting the true explanation.

"Very well. We will destroy the empty incubators at once, and will go ahead with the rest of the project whenever you are ready."

The Cahuitan broke contact and vanished.

In the ship, Cloud got up. So did Joan. Without exchanging a word or a thought they went hungrily into each other's arms.

After a time, and still keeping one arm around his Joan, Cloud reached out and punched a button on his intercom.

"Captain Ross?"

"Ross speaking."

"Cloud. Mission accomplished. Return to Tellus, please, at full touring blast."

"Very well, sir."

And "Storm" Cloud, Vortex Blaster, was out of a job.

THE POSITRONIC SUPER PACK
E-BOOK SERIES

If you enjoyed this Super Pack you may wish to find the other books in this series. We endeavor to provide you with a quality product. But since many of these stories have been scanned typos do occasionally keep in. If you spot one please share it with us at positronicpress@yahoo.com so that we can fix it. We occasionally add additional stories to some of our Super Packs so make sure that you download fresh copies of your Super Packs from time to time to get the latest edition.

(PSP #1) Fantasy Super Pack #1: ISBN 978-1-63384-282-3
(PSP #2) Fantasy Super Pack #2: ISBN 978-1-5154-3932-5
(PSP #3) Conan the Barbarian Super Pack: ISBN 978-1-63384-292-2
(PSP #4) Science Fiction Super Pack #1: ISBN 978-1-63384-240-3
(PSP #5) Science Fiction Super Pack #2: ISBN 978-1-51540-477-4
(PSP #6) Lord Dunsany Super Pack: ISBN 978-1-63384-725-5
(PSP #7) Philip K. Dick Super Pack: ISBN 978-1-63384-799-6
(PSP #8) The Pirate Super Pack # 1: ISBN 978-1-51540-193-3
(PSP #9) The Pirate Super Pack # 2: ISBN 978-1-51540-196-4
(PSP #10) Harry Harrison Super Pack: ISBN 978-1-51540-217-6
(PSP #11) Andre Norton Super Pack: ISBN 978-1-51540-262-6
(PSP #12) Marion Zimmer Bradley Super Pack: ISBN 978-1-51540-287-9
(PSP #13) Frederik Pohl Super Pack: ISBN 978-1-51540-289-3
(PSP #14) King Arthur Super Pack: ISBN 978-1-51540-306-7
(PSP #15) Science Fiction Novel Super Pack #1: ISBN 978-1-51540-363-0
(PSP #16) Alan E. Nourse Super Pack: ISBN 978-1-51540-393-7
(PSP #17) Space Science Fiction Super Pack: ISBN 978-1-51540-440-8
(PSP #18) Wonder Stories Super Pack: ISBN 978-1-5154-454-5
(PSP #19) Galaxy Science Fiction Super Pack #1: ISBN 978-1-5154-0524-5
(PSP #20) Galaxy Science Fiction Super Pack #2: ISBN 978-1-51540-577-1
(PSP #21) Weird Tales Super Pack #1: ISBN 9-781-5154-0-548-1
(PSP #22) Weird Tales Super Pack #2: ISBN 978-1-5154-1-107-9
(PSP #23) Poul Anderson Super Pack: ISBN 978-1-5154-0-609-9
(PSP #24) Fantastic Universe Super Pack #1: ISBN 978-1-5154-0-981-6
(PSP #25) Fantastic Universe Super Pack #2: ISBN 978-1-5154-0-654-9
(PSP #26) Fantastic Universe Super Pack #3: ISBN 978-1-5154-0-655-6
(PSP #27) Imagination Super Pack: ISBN 978-1-5154-1-089-8
(PSP #28) Planet Stories Super Pack: ISBN 978-1-5154-1-125-3
(PSP #29) Worlds of If Super Pack #1: ISBN 978-1-5154-1-148-2
(PSP #30) Worlds of If Super Pack #2: ISBN 978-1-5154-1-182-6
(PSP #31) Worlds of If Super Pack #3: ISBN 978-1-5154-1-234-2
(PSP #32) The Dragon Super Pack: ISBN 978-1-5154-1-124-6
(PSP #33) Fritz Leiber Super Pack #1: ISBN 978-1-5154-1-847-4

SUPER PACK

(PSP #34) Wizard of Oz Super Pack: ISBN 978-1-5154-1-872-6
(PSP #35) The Vampire Super Pack: ISBN 978-1-5154-3-954-7
(PSP #36) The Doctor Dolittle Super Pack: ISBN 978-1-5154-4-296-7
(PSP #37) Charles Boardman Hawes Super Pack: ISBN 978-1-5154-4-384-1
(PSP #38) The Edgar Wallace Super Pack: ISBN 978-1-5154-4-387-2
(PSP #39) Inspector Gabriel Hanaud Super Pack: ISBN 978-1-5154-4-385-8
(PSP #40) Tarzan Super Pack: ISBN: 978-1-5154-4497-8
(PSP #41) Algis Budry Super Pack ISBN: 978-1-5154-4496-1
(PSP #42) Max Brand Western Super-Pack ISBN: 978-1-63384-841-2
(PSP #43) R. A. Lafferty Super Pack ISBN: 978-1-5154-4504-3
(PSP #44) Keith Laumer Super Pack ISBN: 978-1-5154-4511-1
(PSP #45) Robert F. Young Super Pack ISBN: 978-1-5154-4638-5
(PSP #46) Planet Stories Super Pack #2 ISBN: 978-1-5154-4672-9
(PSP #47) Leigh Brackett Super Pack ISBN: 978-1-5154-4707-8
(PSP #48) Ray Bradbury Super Pack ISBN 978-1-5154-4994-2
(PSP #49) Evelyn E. Smith Super Pack ISBN: 978-1-5154-5002-3
(PSP #50) Allen Steele Super Pack ISBN: 978-1-5154-5107-5
(PSP #51) Martian Super Pack ISBN: 978-1-5154-5110-5
(PSP #52) Argosy All-Story Weekly Super Pack ISBN: 978-1-5154-5125-9
(PSP #53) Science Fiction Super Pack #3 ISBN: 978-1-5154-6028-2
(PSP #54) The Lensman Super Pack ISBN:978-1-5154-6087-9

CPSIA information can be obtained
at www.ICGtesting.com
Printed in the USA
LVHW050845300523
748312LV00006B/79